The Angel Factory

ALADDIN PAPERBACKS
New York London Toronto Sydney Singapore

First Aladdin Paperbacks edition January 2004

Copyright © 2001 by Terence Blacker
First published in Great Britain by Macmillan
Children's Books

ALADDIN PAPERBACKS
An imprint of Simon & Schuster Children's
Publishing Division
1230 Avenue of the Americas New York, New York 10020

Also available in a Simon and Schuster Books for Young Readers
hardcover edition.
Designed by O'Lanso Gabbidon
The text of this book was set in Garamond.

Printed in the United States of America
2 4 6 8 10 9 7 5 3 1

The Library of Congress has cataloged the hardcover edition as
follows:
Blacker, Terence.
The angel factory / by Terence Blacker.—1st U.S. ed.
p. cm.
Originally published: Great Britain: Macmillan Children's Books,
© 2001.
Summary: Spurred on by his best friend, twelve-year-old Thomas
uncovers two major family secrets: that he was adopted, and that
his perfect-seeming family is part of an other-worldly
organization.
ISBN 0-689-85171-5 (hc)
[1. Adoption—Fiction. 2. Family life—London (England)—Fiction.
3. Angels—Fiction. 4. Extraterrestrial beings—Fiction. 5. London
(England)—Fiction.] I. Title.
PZ7.B53225 An 2002
[Fic]—dc21   2002001262

ISBN 0-689-86413-2 (Aladdin pbk.)

To Caroline Sheldon

1 · FAMILY

I CAN SEE US NOW, that morning, the sun shining through the kitchen window, lighting up our little family group at the breakfast table.

My father was reading a geography project on supermarkets that I had been working on for the last month. He had helped with some of the early research and the previous night I had printed out my final version on his computer.

A radio was playing, with some discussion over a big political meeting that was taking place in London the following month. Dad stirred slightly and, with that weird thought-reading process that my parents have, my mother stood up and switched it off.

Almost immediately, as if to fill the silence, there was a growling sound from under the table. Dougal, my white West Highland terrier, had found his toy woolen rabbit and was killing it once more.

"Oh, Dougal." My mum laughed, reached down to pick up the rabbit and put it on a sideboard. "What d'you think?" she asked my father as she washed her hands in the sink.

Dad sighed and closed my project, shaking his head as if it were the worst thing he had ever had to read. Then, joke over, he looked up at me and smiled. "Excellent," he said. "Absolutely excellent." He stood up and placed the folder in front of me, laying a hand on my shoulder. "I'm very proud of my son."

"Cheers, Dad," I said, my mouth full of cornflakes.

My mother glanced at her watch. "We're going to be a bit late tonight," she said. "Amy is gracing us with her presence for dinner."

"Oh, great," I muttered.

"No need to be rude about your big sister," said Dad automatically as he cleared the plates from the table.

It was time for them to go to work. They kissed me, each of them. Mum reminded me to lock up carefully and not to be late for school. I saw them to the front door. Shouting goodbyes, they made their way up the garden path, Dougal bouncing at their feet, in the morning sun.

I walked back to the kitchen and picked up my project. My father was right. It was excellent.

Everything was excellent.

2 · GIP

WE WERE ON THE SWINGS that afternoon, Gip
Sanchez and me.

There was nothing particularly unusual
about that. Gip was my best friend. On the
way back from school, we would often go to
the park and chat about things. Only, on
this occasion, we did something different.

We talked about my family. Now and
then an adult would walk by, glancing at us
as if to say we were too old to be in this part
of the playground, that we must be up to
something.

That's the way it is when Gip's around.
He gets glances. Before he says a word,
there's a sense of anger about him, with his
long, shaggy hair, his dodgy skin, his dark
eyes, his odd way of walking.

Life has never been kind to Gip. He was
born with one leg shorter than the other.
Before he was a year old, his dad left home.
The way he tells it, his mum is more interested in God, alcohol, and herself (not nec-

essarily in that order) than in her only son. He gets beatings in the playground like other people get school dinners.

There's something about Gip, a sort of pleasure in his own weirdness, that seems to annoy people within seconds of meeting him. It's not just that he shuffles about like a creature from another world but that he goes out of his way not to fit in. He actually likes to look disgusting. When some of the older kids at the school took to calling him "Gimpy" because he limps, and then "Gyppo" because there is something of the wild gypsy to him, he took the name "Gip" as if it were a special prize that had been awarded to him.

Which made them even more annoyed.

Which made Gip even more determined to be Gip.

In the end, people at school have learned to treat him with a sort of edgy respect. In spite of everything life has thrown at him, Gip's a winner. He knew about computers before anyone else. He was the first in school to have a mobile phone. Sometimes, when he talks about things, he seems ten years older than he is—in experience, in life.

No one quite understands why we are friends—Gip Sanchez, the well-known geek and neighborhood oddball, and Thomas Wisdom, a bright, normal kid from a bright, normal family. My parents, so easy about everything else, are not easy about this. Ever since they met Gip at a parents' evening, they wince when I mention his name.

Maybe that was why I liked him, why our friendship was so strong—it owed nothing to anyone but ourselves.

Maybe it was why, that afternoon in the park, I talked to him about my family.

"Sometimes I envy you," I said.

Gip swung backwards and forwards in silence, head down, his hair concealing his face.

"You can just be you," I said. "You've got no one to disappoint—no one to live up to."

"Yup," said Gip. "I've got to admit that it's all pretty great."

"I'm serious. You don't have to belong to this perfect family. You don't feel that, however well you do, it will never be quite as good as your parents expected."

Gip looked up, surprised. He had never been the biggest fan of my family but he knew it was unusual for me to talk about them like this.

"If I do anything well, I feel I've kind of borrowed my success from my family," I said. "And if I don't, the failure's all mine."

"That's families for you," said Gip. "I've never seen the point of them, myself."

"Sometimes I wish they would get drunk now and then." I laughed guiltily. "Or lose their tempers. Or shout at me when I do something wrong. Everything's so perfect in their lives. They even hold hands in public."

"Weird," said Gip.

"Everything has to be done together, as a family, this great Wisdom family team. They work together. We go to California for our holidays every year together. And you know what I've noticed recently? That they even go to the lavatory every morning at the same time. One after another. Everything they do is so orderly and . . . regular."

Gip was looking at me oddly.

"I don't make a habit of studying these things," I muttered. "I just notice stuff."

"Maybe it's not you that's out of step, but them," he said in the worryingly quiet voice which usually means that he has begun working on some strange, Gip-like theory. "What did you say they do for a job?"

"Food development. They don't tell me much about it."

"Of course they don't," said Gip thoughtfully. "They wouldn't, would they?"

"Why not?"

Gip jumped off the swing. "CIA," he said, almost to himself. "I've been reading how spies operate. Often they're the most ordinary people. In fact, the more ordinary they are, the more likely it is that they're some kind of spook." He turned and began walking towards the gate.

"Spook?" I was following Gip now, regretting that I had told him anything about my family.

"Are they at your place now?"

"They're working late."

"Perfect." He accelerated, with that odd swinging stride of his. "Let's go."

3 · SPOOKY

AS WE MADE OUR WAY to the house, I tried to explain to Gip that I wasn't exactly being serious. I had been in a bad mood all day because, although I knew my geography project would get an A, I felt the mark was not mine but my dad's. I said that it had all been a joke but, in Gip's upside-down world, anything serious is really a joke in disguise while what most people would see as a joke, he takes with deadly seriousness.

I realized that I had made a big mistake confiding in him about my parents. Then I made an even bigger one. I let Gip into my house.

As soon as we entered the hall, he asked to see my dad's computer. Still trying to play along with his little game, I showed him upstairs.

Moments later, he stood in the center of my father's small, super-tidy office, looking absurdly out of place, like some giant bit of litter that had been blown in from the street.

"My parents are kind of into neatness," I explained.

He took in the scene, the rows of folders on shelves, the filing-cabinet, the immaculately tidy desk. "It's plain unnatural," he muttered, sitting down in front of the computer. "It's spooky."

"Not everyone has to live like you," I said, suddenly resenting the way Gip mocked anyone whose life was not like his.

He switched on the computer. "Code-word," he said quietly. "We need a code-word to get in."

He tapped in my name, waited a few seconds then muttered, "Nope."

"Dougal?"

"Eh?"

"It's the name of my terrier."

Gip shook his head as he typed in the letters. "Your life, man," he muttered.

Nothing.

As if I weren't there, Gip opened the top drawer of my father's desk and took out an address book. He opened it at the first page. "What's the Seraph Organization?" he asked.

"Something to do with my parents' work. They're the food company that employs them."

Gip's fingers flew over the keys.

Nothing.

He returned to the address book, studying one page after another.

I glanced at my watch. "Gip, they'll be back soon. I'll be so dead if they find you here."

He ignored me. "Who are SO?" he asked suddenly.

"Search me."

"More to the point. Why does their telephone number have only five digits?" He tapped the numbers into the computer. Suddenly the screen came alive.

"Welcome," said a friendly cybernetic voice.

"Welcome to you," said Gip.

We were in.

Gip is one of those people who never feels more at home than when he's in front of a computer. Within seconds, he had called up my father's files. They read:

HOME

BILLS

SERAPH

TAX

"Gip, this is wrong," I said. "There's nothing here."

He opened "SERAPH."

It was full of letters from my dad about schedules, visits, advertising, deadlines—as dull and innocent as any business file could be.

Before I could stop him, he opened "HOME." It was stuff about insurance and rates.

"So much for the CIA theory," I said.

But Gip had double-clicked on "TAX." The screen suddenly filled with numbers—five pages of batched numbers, like a telephone directory without the names.

"Good thinking, guy," he muttered. "Nothing could look more boring and innocent than the old tax file. But you didn't fool old Gip." He closed the file. "OK," he said. "We print these out and then we leave."

"It's just some kind of tax thing," I said and I realized how absurd it all sounded. The truth was that, if my dad really did have some kind of secret life, I was suddenly not sure that I wanted to know about it.

"Knowledge is power," said Gip, pushing the "Print" key. "Now," he said, as the printer whined into life. "Where's this lavatory of yours?"

I told him and waited by the printer until it had finished spewing out pages full of numbers. When I had switched off the computer, I made my way downstairs to my room.

There are times when I forget just how weird my friend Gip is. After about five minutes, it occurred to me that he was spending more time than was entirely usual in my lavatory. I knocked on the door and asked if he was all right.

He said something but his voice sounded odd and echoey so that I couldn't catch the words. Then I noticed the door was not fully shut. I pushed it and nervously peered in.

Gip was on his knees in front of the lavatory. He looked like a headless man.

"What you doing, Gip?" I didn't know whether to leave him or to help.

His voice echoed weirdly from the depths of the lavatory bowl. "Uuggghh."

"Are you feeling sick?"

"I'm uunngghh," he said impatiently. Slowly, he emerged from the bowl. He stood up and shook his head. At the same time, both of us noticed that the ends of his hair were wet. Gip squeezed a few strands and wiped the palms of his hands down the sides of his jeans.

"Spies use lavatories to conceal information. I thought maybe there was some kind of secret hiding-place. That was why your parents are always slipping off to the bog—they're filing a report." He lifted the lid off the cistern.

"I was joking," I said desperately. "They were just going to the toilet like anyone else. Let's—"

"Yes." It was a low groan of triumph. Slowly he extricated his hand. He was holding a small, flat, black rubber plug.

"Well done, Gip," I said. "You just mashed up our plumbing."

"At the back of the cistern, there's a small metal plate."

He put his hand, still wet, on my shoulder and, with the other, pointed downwards into the water. There was, it was true, an oddly colored plaque behind the ball cock.

"It's called a bolt, Gip," I said. "It's what plumbers use."

"Yeah, right. And they use copper and cover it up with rubber. I don't think so." He opened the window that was just above the lavatory and, standing on the bowl, peered downwards.

When he came back into the room, he was smiling. "Transmitter," he said. "The bolt has a connection outside."

He returned the plug to where he had found it and put the lid back. This time he dried his hands by running them through his hair.

"You were right," he said. "Your parents are CIA. They're communicating to headquarters using the old lavatory trick. I was right. There's definitely something spooky going on here."

I sighed. At that moment, it seemed pointless to remind him that I had never ever claimed that my mum or dad were in the CIA, that all I had said, casually, was that I felt a bit out of place in my perfect family. It had been a joke and it had backfired and I wanted Gip to leave my house before he got any other crazy ideas about my family.

"They'll be back soon," I said. "You'd better go."

He picked up the sheaf of papers we had printed from my father's computer and waved them significantly in front of my face. "With the evidence, right?"

"Yeah, of course. With the evidence."

He glanced at me and winked—I may not be good at hiding my thoughts but luckily neither is Gip too good at reading them.

He limped his way to the front door. "It's good you brought ole Gippy in on this," he said. "We'll crack it together, right?"

"Sure," I said, eager to get shot of him. I glanced up and down the road. The coast was still clear but, at any moment now, my mum and dad would be rounding the corner from the station.

"All you got to do is check the precise times when your folks go to the john," he was saying. "Then, casual-like, try to listen outside the door, catch any noises in there that are kind of unusual, and leave the rest to me," he said.

"Right. I'll remember to do that."

I watched as he walked off with that swift scuttle, his right leg jerking outwards as if he were kicking out at some invisible thing with every stride. Then, suddenly I saw them. Walking towards him were Mum, Dad and, between them, my sister Amy with Dougal scuttling along ahead of them.

Briefly, I had this creepy sense that I was looking at two types of human—walking away from me, the frail, the strange, the sick and, walking towards me, the strong, the healthy, the normal.

My family turned into the short path leading to our front door. Dougal jumped up to greet me.

"Hi, Thomas," said my father. "What are you doing here?"

"I thought somebody rang the bell. Then I saw you."

My mum kissed me. "Amy's here to discuss the holiday," she said.

My sister kissed me too. "Hi, bruv," she said.

"Hi," I said.

I was glad that they were home. I glanced up the road to see Gip turning the bend, and began to relax.

We went inside for tea.

4 · NATURAL

ONCE, WHEN MUM, DAD, AMY, and I were returning from a walk in the park with Dougal, a neighbor, old Mr. Godwin from three doors down, was in his front garden. He looked up as we approached.

"What a lovely family you are," he said.

"Thank you, Mr. Godwin." My mother smiled politely but kept walking.

"You look like a band of angels," he called after us.

My father laughed, adding quietly, "If only he knew."

It was true, thinking about it later, that my mum and my dad look pretty good, considering their age. Most of my friends' fathers, for example, are a bit crumpled and battered—they've lost their hair, their waistline is history, whatever. But my dad, without making any particular fuss about it, looks like he's in shape. He's tall and has an open, smiling face, which people seem to trust. Not that he's vain about his appearance—he gets his light, sandy hair cut about once a month, goes to the same clothes shops, works out now and then at the gym. He's just one of those people whose looks don't change much as they get older.

If I told you that my mum has long blonde hair that comes down to the middle of her back, you might get the wrong idea. She's not some aging bimbo, or an old hippy who believes in astrology and feng shui and listens to Bob Dylan every night. She just likes her hair long. It suits her, makes her look natural. When she visits school on parents' day, I notice the way the male teachers (even nutty old Rendle, our math master) react to her. Normally they sit, slouched and grumpy, at their desks. As soon as Mum walks in, they straighten their backs, try (almost always unsuccessfully) to look like real men of the world. Yet, as soon as she starts talking in that quiet, reassuring voice of hers, they relax. She has the knack of making people feel better about themselves, more interesting and attractive than they really are.

Luckily, my sister Amy has not been back to school since she left three years ago. If she had, there might have been a riot. These days, even I have to admit that she looks good. Three years of success at university has given her a sort of glow of confidence. No way is she any kind of show-off but, when she enters a room, heads turn. "My daughter, the blonde bombshell," Dad calls her.

And me? Sometimes I wish I were like Gip and was able to go around, a walking mess of shabbiness, without caring, but the fact is, when Mum buys me nice clothes, I wear them. If I haven't had my hair cut for a few weeks, I begin to feel uncomfortable. I'm not a Nigel Neato—my room's as trashy as any of my friends' rooms (with the exception of Gip's which is literally a rubbish dump)—but, if you saw me out walking with my family, you would see the connection, all right, and I'm not ashamed of it. And yes, my hair is kind of blond too.

So Mr. Godwin, our wizened old neighbor, took one look at us and saw angels.

At the time, I thought his brain was out to lunch. These days, I'm not so sure.

5 · OXYMORON

A BLACKBIRD WAS HIGH in the poplar tree over-looking our garden, singing above the mur-muring sounds of the city, as the four of us sat at the garden table. There was some-thing in the air that evening. My father had opened a bottle of champagne. Amy was home. It was just like old times.

Dad raised a glass. "To Amy and her bril-liant degree," he said.

My sister smiled. "Maybe we should wait until we get the result," she said, but no one was fooled. Somehow, with Amy, the result has never exactly been a problem.

My mother held her glass in the air. "And to Thomas and his supermarket proj-ect. Another triumph," she said.

"Er, not," I mumbled.

They allowed me another half-glass of champagne. We chatted easily about school. Mum brought out pasta and Dad made one of his famous salads, over which we all cooed and clucked as if no one had ever made a salad before. The blackbird sang on as the sun went down. It was almost as if some trick of fate had created the perfect reply to Gip's crazy theories about my family.

We were well into the evening when my sister sprang a surprise on us.

"This holiday," she said, "would anyone object if I brought along a friend?"

We must have looked a little startled because Amy blushed. "All right," she said. "So I didn't tell you I've been seeing someone."

"Hold the front page," I muttered.

"Thomas." My mother gave me the look of mild warning—head tilted, eyebrows raised—that I knew so well.

"But it's not exactly big news," I said. "Jack. Rufus. Alex. The big news would be if she wasn't seeing someone."

"Ignore him, Amy," said my father. "Thomas will understand these things when he gets to university."

"Anyway, it's different this time," Amy said quietly.

Mum laid a hand on Amy's. "Tell us all about him," she said.

"He's a surfer—"

The three of us groaned in unison, then laughed.

"An intelligent surfer," said my sister.

"Intelligent surfer?" said Dad. "That sounds like an oxymoron to me."

"He's not a moron," said Amy. "He's very bright and good-looking and nice and I want him to come to Santa Barbara with us."

I was expecting objections from my parents. We have always done things together, as a family—not just the holiday in California but events at school or university. When one of us is playing in some team, or acting in a play, the other three will come along, show support. The rest of the world is beyond our little unit. As if only the best is suitable company for any member of the Wisdom family, Mum and Dad have always been wary and worried about who we pick as friends.

"He'll pay for himself," said Amy. "He's been saving up."

"He's just into that West Coast surf," I said.

"He says he's not going for the surfing." There was a new, wobbly smile on my sister's face. "He wants to be with me."

"Oh, puke," I said, just loud enough to be heard.

"Well, I think it's an excellent idea," said my mother decisively. "If he's brave enough to put up with us, I think we should take him."

"He can tackle twenty-foot waves, so I don't think the Wisdom family will be a problem," said my sister.

"You won't just hang out with him all the time, will you?" asked my father. "You'll be around for evening meals."

"Yes," said Amy. "But he's not exactly a conversationalist. He's sort of . . . quiet."

"The strong, silent type," said my father. "I like the sound of this man. What's his name?"

"Luke. Luke Ross."

"Tell us more," said Mum.

So we were treated to a little, damp-eyed version of the life and times of Luke the surfer-boy. How he had dropped out of university and traveled the world in search of the perfect wave. How any girl who had ever met him fell in love with him. How he worked in a hire-shop in Torquay when he wasn't riding surf. How, one day last summer, Amy had been down in the West Country with a couple of friends and had walked into Luke's shop and how it had first been a friendship thing, then became a bit more than a friendship thing, and now they met up every weekend.

It didn't take a genius to tell that my sister was more serious about this guy than she had been about any of her other boyfriends. When she had finished talking, we sat in silence for a moment, each of us thinking about how our little holiday group of four had just become five.

My father smiled at me. "Thomas, are you OK about Luke coming along?" he asked. "This is your holiday as well."

"No problem," I said. "He sounds . . . just great."

Every night, for as long as I can remember, my mother would sit on the edge of my bed before I went to sleep. She would read from a book, or tell me about things from her childhood in the country or just chat about little, everyday events. The words she said mattered less than the sound of her voice, soft and soothing and reassuring as sleep crept up on me.

There was a distraction that night. I heard my father going up to his office. He stayed there five, maybe ten minutes.

When he came downstairs, he looked into my room. Over my mother's shoulder, I saw him standing there at the door, looking at me, and in that moment I sensed not only that Dad knew about my visit to his office with Gip and that he knew that I knew, but that something—something I was unable to understand—was about to change forever.

Mum turned to see him and some kind of unspoken message seemed to pass between them because she squeezed my hand, kissed my forehead and turned out the bedside light.

I lay on my side and closed my eyes. Then, for some reason, I opened them again after a few seconds. My parents were standing together at the door, two shadows silhouetted by the light outside.

"What?" I raised my head. "What is it?"

"Night, old boy," said my father, and they left me there in the darkness.

6 · SPYBUSTER

THE END OF THE SUMMER term was approaching. I was looking forward to my holiday, even if the idea of Surfer-Boy tagging along with the family had cast a small, wave-shaped cloud over my thoughts. Both Dad and Mum seemed to be paying particular attention to me and, for a while, I wondered whether, having found out about about my inviting Gip back home, they were trying to guilt some kind of confession out of me.

Then I relaxed. Sometimes when my parents become more caring than usual, it can get on my nerves—their attention hangs on me like a weight—but now they seemed at ease, as if, without knowing it, I had passed some kind of test and was halfway to being treated like an adult.

I was OK. They were OK. Everything was going to be fine. I began to think that my worries about their being unusually ordered and perfect was my problem, not theirs. Maybe I had got depressed during the long summer term, or something at school had bothered me.

All would have been fine were it not for one Gip Sanchez, private detective and spybuster.

Some people take one look at Gip and take him to be some kind of loser. I know better. He likes to act chilled and laid-back but in reality he's as relaxed as a limpet. When he catches hold of something—an idea, a person—he hangs on until he is ready to let go.

I was that person. The idea was that my mother and father were fully paid-up members of the Central Intelligence Agency and were beaming messages back to America through our toilet. There was nothing I could say to shake this obsession from his head.

"It's an encryption thing," he called out to me as I made my way through the school gates one afternoon.

"What?" I may have allowed my irritation to show in my voice.

"Encryption." Gip loped along beside me, ignoring my pathetic attempt at disapproval. "It's a sort of code used in computers, logarithmic formulae to represent letters in the binary code or standard numerical form."

"Gimme a break, Gip. I'm not in the mood for a math lesson."

"Exactly," said Gip, who was clearly so excited that he was no longer receiving any messages from the outside world. "So all we need to do is, like, de-encrypt the encryption code and we'll find out what's in your father's secret file."

"Maybe we should forget it," I said. "It could be something just private and embarrassing."

Gip frowned as if this possibility had not occurred to him. "Yeah, what happens if it's some kind of creepy membership of the freemasons or something?"

I laughed. The idea of my dad belonging to a secret society was pretty wild, even by Gip's standards. "You don't know my father," I said coldly.

We walked on in silence for a few seconds. "So in the end," said Gip in a casual tone of voice that made me immediately suspicious. "I talked about it to Rendle."

I stopped in my tracks. I had always known that Mr. Rendle, the greasy-haired geek with stained trousers who taught math at school and whose nickname was "The Beast," was one of Gip's few other friends but not for a moment had I considered that he might actually share our silly little secret with him. "You did what?"

Gip shrugged. "Only the theory," he said. "I was chatting to him about encryption during break—"

"You are a sad person," I muttered.

"—and I brought the subject around to the way you break down codes. There are various degrees of difficulty. To put it simply, an encryptive logarithm working within conventional algebraic parameters can be resolved by—"

"Gip." I had stopped walking again. "Just put my mind at rest here. Have you or have you not shared a private personal document stolen from my father's computer with The Beast?"

Gip winced. "Only in so far as I lent it to him," he said.

"You what?"

"He promised to let me have it back. He doesn't even know where the pages came from. It's not a problem."

I had stopped walking. There was no point in being angry with Gip, or trying to explain why handing Dad's file over to a dorky math teacher felt like a betrayal. It was a family thing and Gip didn't do families. "Get it back." I spoke quietly.

"All right." Gip held up both hands in surrender. "I'll

get your precious numbers back."

"I want you to destroy everything we got from my father's computer."

"What about the CIA?"

"Gip."

He shrugged. "Suit yourself."

I walked away.

"Coming to the park?" he called after me.

I kept on walking.

Three days later, on the very evening after school had broken up for the summer, my big sister decided to introduce her darling surfer to the family.

They came to dinner—Amy smiling and blushing and casting adoring, proud glances in the direction of her boyfriend and Luke, tall, sandy-haired, blue-eyed, and mostly silent.

It was not an easy meal. My mind was too full of Gip's big mistake for me to want to talk much. Luke was one of those annoying, confident guys who seem to think that reasonable looks, floppy hair, a suntan and broad shoulders are enough to get him through life. He could leave it to lesser mortals to do the conversation thing.

He answered my mother's polite questions with answers so short that they were a hair's breadth from being openly rude.

Yeah, he was really into traveling.

Working in his shop was all right except when he had to deal with gonks who didn't understand the sea.

Sure, he surfed in winter. Like, a wetsuit? He'd caught some of his best waves in, like, January.

Nope, he hadn't thought about a long-term career. Like, carpe diem ("That's 'Seize the day,'" my sister added helpfully).

And, yeah, he was totally into the idea of coming to California. He had always wanted to hang out with the stars on Sunset Boulevard, you know?

Amy greeted this last remark as if it was the greatest wit-
ticism she had ever heard. My mother and father laughed
dutifully but, for some reason, I forgot to join in.

Surfer-Boy fixed me with his piercing blue eyes as if, in
his great worldly wisdom, he understood how I felt. I held
his look for a few seconds. He winked in that patronizing
way of adults, then gave a craggy smile to my sister who was
simpering away beside him.

Great. Suddenly, we had a total airhead in the family.

7 · CALIFORNIA

IT WAS A GOOD HOLIDAY. It was a fine holiday. It was always a fine holiday when we were in Santa Barbara. We swam and watched dolphins and toured a studio in Hollywood. We paid our annual visit to Donald, Mickey, and Goofy at Disneyland. Then we swam a bit more.

Luke was all right, too. Mum and Dad accepted his presence almost as if he had always been part of the family. Dad, who is not exactly a sports fan, tried to talk to him about waves and currents. Now and then I would catch Mum sneaking glances at the happy young couple in a way that suggested that, truly and honestly, she was pleased that her only daughter was now hanging out with a surfer.

As for me, I acted my normal, mellow self but, inside me, those old restless feelings were churning away once more. I began to wonder why it was all right for Amy to bring her boyfriend on a family holiday while, if I mentioned taking a friend—Gip, say—it would be nervous breakdowns all round. I started thinking about my family—how what was normal and good so often became confused with what was odd and suffocating. Sometimes, when I looked at Mum, Dad, Amy, and Luke together, the image of Gip in my house crept up on me. I heard his voice, "Your life, man."

I tried to concentrate on the holiday but there was no escaping these thoughts.

One afternoon, we were lying by the pool, just Luke and me. Amy and Mum were shopping for presents, Dad was working in his room.

"So what d'you think of the family then?" I asked.

Luke looked up slowly from one of the many surfer magazines that were the only thing he ever read. The question seemed to take some time to be processed through his brain. He gazed across the pool, working out an answer to this question.

"Cool," he said finally.

I waited for something a little more detailed but Luke turned back to his magazine. He frowned slightly, either because the description of a particular wave was kind of hard for him to grasp or maybe to discourage me from any more tricky questions.

"So you think my dad is cool," I said in an irritatingly chirpy voice.

Luke kept reading. "Yeah."

"What do you think is particularly cool about him? The way he lowers his glasses and says, 'Magic word?' His new knee-length Bermuda shorts?"

"Not that kind of cool." He spoke levelly as if there was another kind of cool that a kid of my age wouldn't be able to understand. "I just meant that your dad is one of the good guys."

"My mum and dad have never even had a row."

Surfer-Boy laid down his magazine and closed his eyes wearily.

"Never ever," I said. "Kind of unusual, isn't it? Not a cross word between them. Ever. And I can't even remember them ever raising their voice to me or Amy. It was all smiles or seriousness, family games or little outings. I guess I can be pretty annoying sometimes—"

"Too right."

"But, even when I leave my room in a mess or get into trouble at school or hang out with my friend Gip—who my parents hate—they never lose control. They just look at me, kind of puzzled and slightly disappointed."

"Let me get this right." Luke gazed at me through half-closed eyelids. "You're complaining because your parents don't bawl you out?"

"Yeah, right, exactly. That's what parents are for, isn't it?"

Luke gave a great sigh. "There was this dude," he said. "A rock star. Rich. Talented. Successful. Everybody loved him. One day he told the newspapers that he was going to see a shrink—some psychiatrist guy. What for? Because everything was just too goddam great in his life. It spooked him out. He called it 'the Paradise Syndrome.'"

It took me a moment to recover from the shock of hearing Surfer-Boy say something that was almost interesting. "You think that's what I've got?" I asked. "Paradise Syndrome? Like this . . . dude?"

"I do, Tom. Don't knock the good guys. If it ain't broke, don't fix it."

I smiled at him, hoping that maybe he would come out with one or two more choice items from the Bumper Book of Completely Pathetic Clichés. The grass is always greener, maybe. Or the one about every cloud having a silver lining.

"I guess that's very true," I said in my most serious voice.

Luke was all talked out. He held the magazine in front of his face.

"How about your folks?" I asked. "What are they like?"

"Cool," he said.

I lay there for a few moments, thinking about what a sad mess of a person I was to be living in Paradise, yet wanting to spoil it all, about how, even though I loved my parents, I seemed to want them to be different from the way they were.

"I'll be in my room," I said, standing up.

I walked into the hotel. When I picked up my key from the foyer, the guy behind the desk surprised me by giving me an envelope. "You seeing your father?" he asked.

"Sure." I took the envelope. "I'll give it to him."

In the lift, I glanced down. Above my father's name on the envelope in the top left-hand corner were printed, in smart, ornate letters, the words "The Seraph Organization."

Then I noticed something else. The envelope was not sealed.

On any other day, it would not even have occurred to me to open a private envelope, addressed to my dad. I would never have dreamed of reading the letter inside.

But this was not any other day. This was now and I was upset. When I reached my room, I opened the envelope and, after a moment's hesitation, unfolded it, and read the letter that would change my life.

Dear Mr. Wisdom,

We are glad to confirm that you will both be visiting the factory for your annual de-brief and reconfiguration service on Wednesday, August 13, at noon. Your direct transport to Seraph will leave at 10:30 A.M. You will be

free to leave at 5 P.M. Your visitation code this year is:
OOPSPIZ352TYO.
We look forward to seeing you.

S. di Luca
Head of Reconfiguration Services

It seemed kind of odd—not exactly the sort of letter the boss of a food development company would send to one of its employees.

Something else. At the head of the letter there was no postal or e-mail address, telephone or fax number, simply the word **SERAPH**, written in bold letters.

I shivered, wishing now that my nosiness had not got the better of me. I put the letter back in its envelope but then, thinking of what Gip would do, I took it out again and made a note on the pad by the telephone of the code-number mentioned by S. di Luca, Head of Reconfiguration Services.

Then I sealed up the envelope and took it along to my father's room.

The large dining-room at the Excelsior is about the most soulless place you could ever eat dinner at. At one end is the self-serve buffet. At the other is some kind of Latin American band, all banjos, maracas, and fake cheesy grins. Between them, guests eat their meals under the watchful eyes of waiters who swoop down to take away plates within seconds of your finishing. So you join in, grab your food, get it down you as quick as possible and scram. It is big and comfortable and efficient, the Excelsior, but it just doesn't do atmosphere.

Yet there was an atmosphere at our table that night. At

first I thought that my dad had somehow sensed that I had been reading his private mail, but as the meal went on, it became obvious—to my amazement—that it was not me that was in trouble but my sweet angelic sister Amy and Old Chatterbox, her boyfriend.

There were looks across the table, silences. Amy and Luke behaved as if they were feeling guilty about something. Once or twice Surfer-Boy did that narrow-eyed, gum-chewing thing that bad film actors do to show how tough they are deep down. Amy was all flustered. She made stupid small talk, now and then laughing unconvincingly at her own feeble jokes. Mum was unusually silent.

In fact, it was only when we reached the ice cream stage of the meal that I began to understand the problem.

"Thomas, Wednesday." My father spoke as if he had suddenly remembered some minor bit of information he had almost forgotten to tell me. "Mum and I have to take our little business trip, as usual."

I smiled innocently. "Oh yeah, right."

"We were worried about what you would do with yourself."

I glanced at Amy. "We'll go to the beach, hang out, do the usual stuff."

Unusually, it was Luke who replied.

"Thing is, Tom, I got an appointment with some waves up the coast. There's a surfing competition at Ventura Beach. A few of the guys are going to be there. No way can I miss out—it's a whole day thing."

"Of course, the answer would be for your sister to stay here," said my mother. "But she seems to have decided that being with Luke matters more than helping out her parents just for once."

Amy pursed her lips and looked down at her plate.

"Excuse me," I said. "You all seem to have forgotten something. I'm twelve years old. I don't actually need a nanny, thank you very much. I'll be fine all by myself. Was that what all this fuss was about?"

"You should be grateful that everyone's so concerned about your welfare," said Amy, once more back in big-sister mode.

"Yeah, right. I'm really grateful. Next time I need my nappies changed, I'll let you know."

"And there's absolutely no need to be vulgar," said my father.

Mum laid a hand on mine. "We'll catch the train soon after ten and we'll be back before dinner."

"I'll see you off if you like." The words had left my mouth before I had even thought of them. "I love stations."

I looked across at Amy. Normally she would have been the first to laugh at the idea of her little brother being some kind of sad trainspotter but, right now, she smiled as if my new enthusiasm for railway stations was the most natural thing in the world.

In fact, they all seemed more relaxed around the table—relieved that I had cleared up this big crisis by letting them all go to their meeting or surfing competitions without bursting into tears.

At the time, it all seemed so normal.

8 · STALKING

I HAD NEVER DONE ANYTHING like this before. I tried a cigarette once, bunked off school a couple of afternoons. When I was younger, I went through a phase of nicking sweets and packets of chewing-gum from shops but this was different. It was a plan, a calculated act of rebellion. For once in his life, Thomas Wisdom—the kind of boy that other parents would point out to their children and say, "Why can't you be more like that nice Thomas?"—was going to do something completely, wildly unpredictable. Something wrong.

Why did I want to follow my parents? I've asked myself that question almost every day since I took that fateful journey to Santa Barbara Train Station. The answer dated back to my conversation with Gip in the park earlier that summer. All logic, common sense and brains told me that Gip's spy theory was like the guy himself—strange, interesting, but basically out of whack.

Yet something else, an instinct, a feeling in my guts, niggled at me day and night. I sensed that, beneath the normality of everyday life, there was a secret at the heart of the Wisdom family.

Maybe it was crazy, paranoiac, but, one way or another, I had to lay the thing to rest.

So I became a spy.

It may have been my imagination but, as we took the fifteen-minute walk to the station that morning, my parents seemed unusually tense, less conversational than usual.

"I never knew you were interested in trains," my mother said at one point.

"Not trains, stations. I'm just interested in the way they look. And I've never been to an American station before."

My father, who had been walking ahead of us, turned and smiled vaguely. "Maybe you'll be an architect, old boy," he said.

"My son, the architect," said Mum, trying the idea on for size.

"Yeah," I said. "Yeah, right."

So when we reached the station, I suddenly had to be the architecture geek, gawping at the plain building with its really interesting platform, fascinating ticket office and unusual waiting-room as if I was being given this great treat.

In line with my new enthusiasm, I was even able to ask my dad which platform their train would be leaving from and where they were heading.

A brief flicker of alarm seemed to cross his face. "We're on the other side of the tracks," he said. "We had better say goodbye to you here, old boy."

My mother kissed me and told me to go straight back to the hotel. I walked through the bright station arches towards the car park, pausing once to wave at them. They stood together, waved, then turned back into the station and out of sight.

I made my way around the car park, then ducked back into the main waiting area. I took the underpass that led under the tracks to the platform on the far side. Cautiously, I climbed the stairs slowly and looked around me.

The platform was deserted except for a small, gray-haired man in an Amtrak uniform who stood looking down the tracks as if that was his only job.

I asked him when the next train to Seraph was due.

"Seraph City?" He shook his head. "Ain't no trains go direct to Seraph from here. You'd best go to LA and change there." He pointed across the tracks. "There'll be one coming along in a couple of minutes on Platform One."

"Is there another platform on this side?"

The man looked at me suspiciously. "Just the one you're standing on," he said.

I wandered towards the underpass, confused. Where had my parents disappeared to? And, if they had to change trains to reach Seraph, why had the note I read specifically mentioned "direct transport"?

I was about to give up on the spying game when I became aware that, trotting up the steps towards me, was a young businesswoman with a briefcase in her hand. She must have thought I was staring at her because, as she passed me, she held my eye briefly before making her way down the platform and pushing her way through a small swing-door.

On an impulse, I followed. The door led into another underpass, about 100 yards long, at the end of which stairs led upwards to another door. Without looking behind her, the businesswoman led me into the daylight beyond.

We seemed to have emerged in an area behind the station where there was a small, covered siding.

Ahead of us was the strangest train I had ever seen. A low, squat machine consisting of one gray carriage and with a long strip of darkened glass stretching the length of it, like a stain, it looked more like a missile or a submarine than any kind of land transport.

My watch showed 10:26. The woman stepped through an open door at the back of the carriage. I had seconds in which to decide whether this was the train my parents were catching. I knew that I had gone too far to turn back. With a confidence that I wasn't feeling, I walked quickly towards the heavy door and stepped up onto the train.

The interior of the carriage was brightly lit but strangely silent with all the passenger seats facing away from where I stood towards the front of the train. Although it was almost full now, no one chatted or busied themselves in the normal way of people at the beginning of a journey. They all sat there, silently, patiently.

There was a spare seat by a nearby window. I slunk into it, turning my face to the darkened pane, praying that I had made the right decision and that, somewhere in the train, were my parents.

Two minutes passed. Three. Four. A middle-aged man in a dark suit who had arrived with seconds to spare, slipped into the seat beside me without even glancing in my direction. The train gave a sort of sigh and began to glide forward soundlessly.

I gazed out of the window while the train gathered speed. Then, as the center of the town gave way to the suburbs, I dared to look around me at my fellow passengers.

There was something calm and orderly about these people, almost as if they knew each other so well that any kind of conversation was unnecessary. The man beside me smiled briefly in acknowledgment of my presence and then relaxed into the sort of trance I had seen on the face of commuters back in London. As I looked about, I noticed that there were no children in the carriage. It occurred to me that perhaps this was some kind of business train for employees of the Seraph Organization but, if that was the case, it seemed odd that no one seemed surprised or curious that I was on board.

I was peering forward, trying to catch a glimpse of Mum or Dad, when I saw something that made my stomach lurch. Two rows ahead of me, there was the cropped, sandy hair and broad shoulders that I knew well. Moving slightly to my left, I could see the back of the head of his companion. Medium-length blonde hair.

There was no mistaking it. I was within a few yards of Amy and her lover-boy, Luke.

Crazily, I thought for a moment that I had stepped onto the wrong train and that we were heading for Ventura Beach before realizing that none of the other passengers seemed the type to be going to the seaside.

More afraid than ever of discovery, I huddled down in my seat and stared out of the window. I thought of the row at dinner last night and realized that it must have been a little invented playlet in which Dad, Mum, Amy, and Luke had been acting out parts for their audience of one. Were they all spies? What was it with me that excluded me from this family outing? Suddenly I felt alone and scared and angry. Maybe I was doing the wrong thing, stalking my own parents, but what was that compared to their deception of me? If they lied about today, what else was invented? Nothing seemed secure anymore.

For an hour or so, the train traveled silently through the

baked, scrubby terrain of rock and sand and sagebrush and cactus, interrupted occasionally by little groups of houses standing like frontier settlements. Not once did any of the passengers look at the scenery outside as they sat in blank-eyed silence in the carriage. It was as if they were on their way to something so important, so momentous, that the normal, everyday business of talking and looking about them had mysteriously been suspended.

The train began to slow. Outside, there were giant bill-boards by the track, advertising beer and jeans. One showed a fat, bald man surrounded by gleaming cars. *We're Going Price-Crazy at Bargain Bob's, Seraph City's Premier Used-Car Dealer,* it read. Sure enough, we appeared to be approaching Seraph but, to my surprise, no one in the carriage made a move.

We glided past some passengers on the platform who stared at our strange gray ghost train, away from the station and out of the town into a wilder, more desolate desert. There were few buildings to be seen now. The only sign of life was the occasional truck or car making its way down a distant, single-track road across the desert.

We must have traveled another five miles or so before I became aware that the people around me were stirring, picking up their bags and briefcases, glancing at their watches. The train slowed almost to walking pace. With a sigh, it entered what seemed to be a kind of tunnel, then drew to a halt.

The passengers stood up and made their way, still in silence, towards the front of the carriage where there was another exit. Amy and Luke were among the first to move and, as I watched them making their way forward, I caught a glimpse of my father a few rows forward, then, beside him, my mother. The gang was all here.

I waited in my seat until the carriage was almost empty. I stood up and walked down the aisle, the last passenger on the train. I stepped down. I saw a group of people making their way down the kind of brightly lit tunnel you might find between terminals at an airport. Fifty yards ahead, daylight shone through an open door.

When I emerged into the dazzling desert landscape, the brightness hurt my eyes. I looked around me. There was no sign of human habitation—no road or building and certainly no factory. Ahead of me I saw the passengers were walking across some open scrubland, an orderly file of people, each carrying a briefcase. I was entirely exposed now, a figure standing alone in front of the tunnel, but no one looked back. They kept walking across the stony sand, staring straight ahead of them, almost as if they were in a dream.

Then I saw where the passengers were heading. A small concrete building, like some kind of defense bunker or an electricity generator, stood in isolation. No tracks led to it and there were no windows in its bright, nondescript walls, so that it seemed almost invisible, part of the scenery around it, almost as if it had grown out of the landscape itself.

As I watched, the group of people carrying briefcases seemed to be forming an orderly queue at the dark green door. Because the line stretched away from me, I was unable to see what was happening at the front of the queue but, over the next few minutes, the number of people outside the hut seemed to get fewer and fewer. At one point, I darted further down the track to get a better view.

My parents and Amy and Luke were gone. Slowly, one by one, the passengers were being let inside the building, absorbed into its tiny space as if some conjuring trick were being performed.

It was only when there were about ten figures left outside that I could see what was happening. As the next man reached the door, he extended his hand to some button or panel. A few seconds later, the green door rose vertically. The man stepped forward into the darkness. The door descended.

I felt scared. The third to last person, a youngish woman, disappeared into the building, then the second to last, leaving one man, a young guy in his late teens. He made precisely the same movements as the others, the door rose—and suddenly I was alone in a deserted, silent landscape.

Apart from the strangeness of a hut, miles away from anywhere, that could make 100 or so humans disappear, there had been something almost ghostly about what I had just seen—the way they all walked, staring fixedly ahead of them, unspeaking, the queue they formed as if standing in a row outside a tiny hut by a deserted railway line was the most natural thing in the world.

I stood up and made my way slowly across the wasteland. When I reached it, I found that the bunker was even smaller than I had imagined.

It had occurred to me that, if Gip had been right and this was some kind of CIA hideout, there would be a defense mechanism or spy camera in place but the only feature on the concrete block was its dark green front door.

As I had seen my parents and their fellow-passengers do, I stood before the door and held out my left hand towards the patch of wall to the side of it. I touched the rough surface. With the faintest of clicks, a small square in the wall slid across, revealing a square pad—numbers on one side, letters on the other—glowing phosphorescently.

A number. A key. It was like de-activating a burglar

alarm. I remembered the letter that had been sent to my father and reached into the back pocket of my jeans. There, on the hotel notepaper was what Seraph's S. di Luca had described as my parents' "visitation code."

I took a deep breath, then slowly entered the code: OOPSPIZ352TYO. As I touched the final letter, the door began to rise. I was staring into a small, white room.

I stepped through the door.

9 · HOME

I WAS IN A SMALL, brightly lit room. I looked around me and saw that there was no exit of any kind. Even the door behind me seemed to have mysteriously become a solid white wall. I was in a tiny, box-like prison.

The lights began to dim. Within seconds, I found myself in total darkness. I heard a faint click and suddenly the floor seemed to fall away from me. As the room descended into the earth at a terrifying speed, I crouched on the floor, eyes tight shut, groping for something—anything—to hold on to.

How long did I fall? Thirty seconds? A minute? Whatever it was, it felt like a lifetime before I felt the floor beneath pressing into my hands and knees as the tiny chamber soundlessly came to a halt.

It was several seconds before I dared to open my eyes. When I did, I was startled to see that the darkness around me seemed to have changed in quality and was now a strange, glowing purple color unlike anything I had seen before. The air had changed, becoming heavy and warm with a faint scent of sulfur. Beyond the sound of my own breath, I heard a ghostly chorus of sounds, a discordant, metallic music, which seemed almost like unearthly voices communicating with one another.

"Mum? Dad?" I spoke the words, I know I did, but all that came from me was a whisper that was lost in the clamor around me.

I could see nothing through the thick, purple murk. I reached out to touch the wall to my left but my hand found nothing. I edged my way forward and groped around me— that wall had gone too. The very room in which I had descended had faded into nothingness.

It was warm but I was trembling uncontrollably. After a minute or so, I stood up—slowly, unsteadily, like a one-year-old about to take his first step—and, at that moment, something passed in front of me brushing my cheek like a warm breeze.

The terror that had been gathering within me surged up like nausea. I screamed, again and again, until my throat burnt, my jaw ached from the effort. Yet it was as if I was trapped in a nightmare, alone, unheard, the sound that was coming from me no more than a helpless, strangled gasp.

I had to move. Both hands outstretched before me, I took a step forward, then another. My legs felt stronger now. The warmth was less oppressive. It seemed to me that, all around me, there were invisible presences in the haze but that, mysteriously, they were not hostile. They were talking to me, calming me, taking me forward. As I moved forward, it was almost as if, with every step, I was becoming not only closer to them, but part of them.

Ten paces, twenty. The purpleness seemed to stretch to

infinity yet I found that I was breathing more easily. My terror was ebbing away. The nagging voice of normality that, seconds ago, had questioned what was happening to me, where I was, how I was going to return to reality, was receding, becoming distant and irrelevant.

Forty paces, fifty. I felt more powerful now, more my true self. I knew that I was walking towards wisdom, maturity, understanding—towards salvation. I was among friends. I had returned home after a long journey—not to the normal kitchen-and-telly home but a real home, a place of utter safety, a home of the heart.

I walked onwards in the gloom, knowing that wherever I went, I would be taken care of. The outside world suddenly seemed trivial and pointless. This was the only reality that mattered. The past—the whole of my life until now—had been a sort of restless, frantic dream from which I had now awoken. If one of the strange presences I felt all around me had told me, in an easy, friendly whisper, that I could stay here forever, I would have smiled and agreed.

I lost all track of time and place but at some point I stopped, somehow knowing that I had reached my destination. I looked down. The ground beneath my feet had developed gentle lines and markings in a light green, glowing color, as if I were walking across some kind of illuminated map.

They drew me inwards, closer to them. Without quite knowing what I was doing, I slowly crouched, then knelt, my hands reaching out to the contours around me.

Now, with the perfect logic of a dream, I saw that the landscape of which I was a part was actually moving, breathing gently, part of one great, living organism. I closed my eyes for a moment. When I opened them, I knew that what I had taken to be lines and contours were alive too. They were human bodies, lying flat upon their backs, naked, palms upwards, eyes open, smiling, as far as the eye could see. They were men and woman of all ages and shapes and yet they seemed unified by the same tranquil, blonde beauty.

I was not afraid or embarrassed. I knew in my soul that these people were more at ease with themselves than I had ever been. In fact, I was only aware of one overpowering emotion. I wanted to be like them. I wanted to be one of them.

Surprised by this thought, I gazed at the figure who was nearest to me. It was a woman—light-haired, handsome, friendly—and, although her features were unclear, I knew who she was.

"Hi, Mum," I said.

The sound that came from me was just a sort of sigh. My mother smiled in a way that I had never seen her smile before. I looked beyond her to see my father whose eyes were turned towards me.

Neither of them spoke. Yet, in my head, I heard their voices speaking in unison with complete clarity.

"Well done, Thomas," they said. "Go home now. We shall follow later."

I closed my eyes and was surprised to feel tears rolling down my cheeks. I turned back from the landscape of naked beings and started walking back in the direction from which I had come.

After a minute or so, I saw before me about ten people, fully clothed, carrying briefcases in a line. I joined them, walking slowly. At the front of the queue, each of them stepped forward into the purple darkness. There was a gentle swish of a door and they disappeared.

When it was my turn, I stepped forward too. Soon I was

ascending. Doors opened behind me and I was dazzled by the light of the Californian sun.

I swayed, almost lost consciousness. My eyes ached from the brightness and I buried my face in my hands. At that moment, I wanted, more than anything in my life, to return to that underworld where everything was perfect, where love was in every breath and the sharp, scratchy reality of life above ground had no place.

Someone laid a hand upon my shoulder. I looked up to see the woman I had first followed on to the train, it seemed like a lifetime ago.

"It's all right, Thomas," she said softly. "It is time to re-enter the world."

"But I don't want to."

"I know. I understand." She smiled kindly and began to walk slowly towards the tunnel where the train was waiting for us.

Casting a single glance behind me at the small bunker that contained such secrets and joy, I followed her.

10 · SAGEBRUSH

I REMEMBER NOTHING of the journey back to the hotel. One moment, I was in the California wilderness, standing beside a track with a group of smiling strangers, the next I was back in my hotel room, lying, fully clothed, on my bed. There was a telephone ringing. Blearily, I picked it up.

"Where are you, Thomas?" It was the voice of my sister, sounding unusually bright and bouncy. "We're waiting for you in the dining-room."

I looked at my watch. It was past seven o'clock in the evening. The way I felt—heavy-limbed and spaced out—it might have been seven in the morning after a night without sleep. Within my head, I could hear muffled sounds that were both strange and yet oddly familiar to me.

"Thomas?" Amy's voice crashed into the foreground. "Are you all right?"

"Yeah." I sat up. "I fell asleep. I was feeling kind of bushed. I'll be right down."

I hung up and tottered into the bathroom. The sounds in my head were growing quieter now, becoming like waves on a distant shoreline. I stared in the mirror and, for the briefest of moments, I had the sensation that I was looking into the face of a stranger. The features were the same, if a little paler than normal, but there was something about my eyes that seemed different.

Seraph. The events of the day came back to me with crazy clarity, the upside-down logic of a dream. I was back in the hut, the lift, the lowering of light to a purple haze, the lines of glowing bodies, the faces of my parents staring up at me, welcoming and questioning as if they were expecting something of me.

If it had all been a dream, I wondered where it had started. I was certain that I had gone to the station with Mum and Dad. If I had returned to the hotel having seen them off, surely I would have remembered the journey back.

My head drooped and I closed my eyes for a few seconds. I needed to think logically. There was a reason for this fantasy, I told myself. I had become obsessed by the idea that my parents had some kind of secret life. My sleeping brain had done the rest. Now all I needed was a sign, the smallest hint of evidence, that would prove that I had been in the hotel room that afternoon.

I breathed in deeply several times, then opened my eyes. I was staring down at my trainers. Caught beneath the laces was a sprig of greenery. I picked it out and stared at it as the truth began to dawn on me. It was sagebrush—wild, scrubland sagebrush.

I groaned in despair. I had my sign.

I took the lift to the ground floor and walked to the dining-room where I stood at the door, looking for my family and Luke. Then I saw them. They were sitting at a table near the window, laughing and talking among themselves as if nothing had happened. Behind them, the sun was going down over a still, glassy sea and, for a few seconds, as I watched, it seemed as if the four of them emanated a sort of glow that set them apart from the rest of the room.

Then Dad spotted me and waved me over.

I took my seat. There were jokes about how much I slept these days. Mum asked me how my day had been.

I stared at her for a moment. She knew how my day had been. They all knew. Rage flared within me, then, for reasons I didn't understand, suddenly died. "It was good," I said. "Yours?"

"It was fine," said Mum.

"Pretty much the usual," said Dad.

There was a silence and they all looked at me, almost daring me to ask more questions.

"How was the surfing?" I asked Luke.

Surfer-Boy winked in that irritating way of his. "Cool," he said.

"So everything's cool," I said. There were smiles around the table. Each of them seemed strangely energized and bright that evening, making me feel like a pale outsider. We each knew what had happened that day yet none of us, I now realized, was going to speak about it. There was some kind of mysterious game going on and, for reasons that I was unable to understand, I was playing along with it.

Mum seemed to sense what was going through my mind. She leaned forward and laid a hand on my arm. The smile on her face reminded me distantly of the look she had given me in the purple underworld of Seraph. "We can all relax and enjoy the rest of the holiday," she said. "Together and happy."

"Yeah." I moved my arm away. "Just the five of us."

My father looked up from the wine-list. "Not quite," he said. "As it happens, Cy Gabriel, the guy who heads up our department at Seraph, may be joining us on the night before we return. He's in town for a meeting. If no one objects, I was going to ask him along for dinner."

"Fine," said Amy.

"Sounds cool to me," said Surfer-Boy.

My father had not taken his eyes off me. "How about you, old boy?" he asked quietly.

I shrugged. "Supercool," I said.

11 · CY

WE ATE. WE DRANK. We laughed. We talked.
We swam. We sat under parasols and stared
out to sea. It was Santa Barbara as usual.
Sometimes for minutes at a time, I managed to forget what I had seen that afternoon on the prairie.

In fact, from the way my parents
behaved, I might have believed that it was
all some kind of dream. They ignored my
silences, my regular hints that I knew something about their secret lives. If anything,
they seemed more at ease than usual.
Sometimes I would catch them gazing at
Amy and Luke, or at me, with a sort of
goofy, contented smile that I found plain
embarrassing.

Forget it, I would tell myself. You saw
nothing. The sun was playing tricks on your
imagination. Then, once or twice a day I
would open the drawer beside my bed and
take out the Gideon Bible. There, between
its crisp white pages was a sprig of sage-

brush. I knew that I had really seen what I had seen, that it may have been completely inexplicable but that it had happened. And I knew, for certain, that what had happened that afternoon had changed my life forever.

I was not afraid during these moments. In fact, when I remembered those voices and allowed myself to be transported back into that other-worldly purple haze, I felt more content than I had ever felt before. Once I had felt childish. I had believed that no one really listened to me. Now I had the strange, inexplicable conviction that I had it within my power to grow, to achieve my true potential.

Yet there was something about this holiday—the fact that Mum and Dad were lying to me, the way Amy seemed to have removed her brain whenever Luke was around—that had begun to make me restless. Although I was not entirely thrilled by the idea of my parents' boss crashing our last night at the Excelsior, I was not heartbroken either. At least he was a new face.

He was late. While we all waited for him in the bar, Dad regaled us with stories from the life and times of Cy Gabriel—how Cy's fourteen-year-old son had crashed his Chevrolet into a water-trough on his ranch, how Cy had been out sailing in the bay when his boat tipped up and he had to be rescued because there was a shark alert, the day Cy had accidentally spilled a glass of water all over his finance director during some kind of heavy meeting. To tell the truth, he was beginning to sound like a big-time loser to me.

But when he turned up, Cy Gabriel turned out to be very different from the way I had imagined. He was probably about Dad's age but there was something bouncy and enthusiastic about him which made him seem younger. His car had had a blow-out on the highway, he said, and, even though he had kept us waiting for forty-five minutes, we were made to feel as if this latest crazy adventure of his made it all worth it.

To tell the truth, Cy Gabriel brought that last evening alive. He shook us all up with his energy and curiosity. Soon even Luke was joining in, telling tales of life on the ocean wave and revealing that he wanted to create a Web site for international surfers.

"What about you, Thomas?" Cy turned to me. "Have you thought of a career yet?"

"Architect, maybe," I said, thinking quickly.

"Wow," Cy smiled. "Any particular area?"

"I'm quite interested in railway stations." As I said the words, I realized that they sounded a touch unconvincing. "But I'd probably start with smaller stuff—bus stations, houses. I'm interested in small buildings as well. I saw something out of town—a little concrete bunker in the middle of the desert. Do you have any idea what that might be for?"

He looked at me evenly. "Some kind of communications thing, I'd guess," he said. "We're cabled up to our eyes in this country. Ever thought of going into your parents' line?"

It was my turn to smile. "I would if I knew what they did. They never exactly talk about their work."

"That's good. Husbands and wives who work together need to build boundaries between their different lives."

"What is food development anyway?"

"It's a great profession, Thomas. Not badly paid, loads of travel, great prospects. One thing's for sure—the world's always going to eat. Food development is where the future is."

I was kind of surprised by the way this conversation was going. Instead of being secretive, like my parents, Cy Gabriel seemed to be making some kind of sales pitch. I must have looked startled because Mum interrupted our conversation at this point. "Don't let yourself get brainwashed by this man," she said to me. "He's a great salesman."

Cy held up both hands in surrender and, for the first time, I noticed a dark, red birthmark above his left wrist. "Only spreading the word," he said. "Just looking to save another soul."

"He's only twelve, Cy," said Amy and we all laughed, as if Cy had been a friend of the family for years.

The meal took its course and, explaining that he had a two-hour drive home, our guest said goodbye, shook hands with us all and, with many a promise that we would see each other next year, he made his way out of the door.

"What a great guy," said Amy, as soon as he had left. "That man is so nice."

"You seemed to be getting on well with him, Thomas," said my mother.

"He was all right," I said, suddenly anxious to be out of there and getting ready for bed. The truth was, I was suddenly wishing I had spoken to him longer. I wished—for reasons I was unable to understand—that, instead of driving to the airport the following morning, we were taking the freeway out to Cy's ranch.

"He comes over to England sometimes," said my father. "Maybe we'll fix up a Sunday lunch with him."

We made our way out of the dining-room. As we walked past the reception desk, the Spanish clerk called out, "Mr. Wisdom."

My father turned, but the clerk was holding out a piece of paper in my direction. "Other Mr. Wisdom," he smiled.

Puzzled, I took the paper. It was a message from the hotel receptionist.

It read, *Mr. Gip phoned. Please call tonight.*

"It's me."

There was a snuffling sound from the other end of the telephone and I imagined Gip in a tangle of whiffy bedclothes. It would be four or five in the morning where he was, yet I knew that Gip wouldn't mind being woken. Time means nothing to him. Now and then he would read right through the night and catch up on his sleep in class.

"Hope I didn't wake your mum," I said.

"Nah. Nah. Nah." Gip made one of his usual animal noises. "She isn't around right now. How's old Santa Barbara, then?"

"It's good but . . . things have been kind of strange around here."

"Yeah?"

I was about to talk about my afternoon in the underworld but suddenly I felt reluctant to let Gip share my secret. The experience had been so personal that even mentioning it felt like a betrayal—not so much of my parents but of myself. "I'll tell you about it when I get back."

"It was the CIA, right?"

"Gip, what did you need to talk about? This is costing, man."

"Yeah, yeah. I got news about your dad's secret file. Old Rendle has decoded it."

"Oh, great." I felt surprisingly annoyed that our geek of a math teacher had not given the file back, as I had asked, but had gone through my father's private documents. I imagined Dad's reaction—not so much angry as disappointed—and thought of how he might have to tell Cy that secret company documents had been lifted by his own son.

Aware that Gip had gone a bit quiet, I muttered, "And?"

"He's flipping out big-time."

"That's news?"

"Nah, it's worse than usual. He won't talk to me about this file thing. He says it's private stuff."

I shook my head. "Why did you give it to him, you bozo? A teacher, of all people."

"You wanted my help." Gip stifled a yawn. "Call me when you get back. I'll give you his number."

"Maybe he'll just give me the file back and forget about it."

"He says he can't do that."

I swore and Gip actually laughed, as if spreading some of my family's most personal secrets around the neighborhood was some kind of little joke.

He was muttering some Gip-like encouragement about hanging loose or getting real or mellowing out but I was no longer in the mood. I hung up.

12 · BEAST

I SLEPT BADLY on the flight back home.
Gazing out of the little circular window at
the clouds below, I kept turning over in my
mind the strange events that had occurred
in California and wondering what lay in
store for me back home. I cursed my own
curiosity. Why had I talked to Gip about my
family? What madness had led me to follow
Mum and Dad into their own underworld?
How was it that, of all people, Colin "The
Beast" Rendle had become involved in my
family crisis?

The Beast was not someone that you
could imagine having a life outside school.
It was rumored that he had once been a
genius but had some kind of serious brain-
box overload in his twenties and had
decided to do something nice and easy with
his life, a job that didn't require too much
thinking. So he became a teacher.

Some would say that he never did
recover from that crack-up. It was as if all

the energy and genes in his body had gravitated to his massive brain, leaving nothing left for looks, shape, teeth, breath, conversation, or bodily hygiene. With his long, greasy hair, fluffy sideburns and manky brown corduroy suit, blotched and caked with ancient stains, he looked like a joke figure out of some cartoon.

There were school legends about the things that had happened to him in the past. One class had locked him in a cupboard for a whole lesson. Someone had stuck a Post-It message reading WEIRDO on the back of his jacket, where it had stayed until he returned to the staffroom at lunchtime. In one lesson, everyone had pretended not to be able to understand him. There was no end to stories about the Beast and year after year children had discovered new ways of making his life a misery.

If our class was not the worst, it was for one reason only: Gip Sanchez. From the first day Rendle had taught us, Gip seemed to bond with him in a way which none of us could understand. He sat at the front, ignoring the pandemonium all around him, making notes, listening full-on to every saliva-filled word, even laughing at the occasional lame joke that the Beast made. Sometimes, the two of them could be seen in the Beast's classroom in break-time or after school, chatting away, happy as a couple of hairy monsters could ever be.

And now, thanks to Gip Sanchez, the Beast was in control of a small part of my life. Wondering what on earth could have been on Dad's file which had caused Rendle to freak out, I drifted off into a fitful sleep.

The flight passed too quickly. On the way from the airport, we called in at the kennels where my dog suffered his usual nervous breakdown on being released from his prison, running around me in small circles, yapping, before rolling on to his back, whining ecstatically. When we reached the house, I took him out for a walk in the park.

Then, lagged out of my brain, I went to my room and lay on my bed.

Rendle could wait.

I must have been more tired than I had thought. One moment it was two in the afternoon, the next it was almost midnight. Mysteriously, I was in my pajamas now and my bag, which I had slung on the floor, had been unpacked.

I reached into the back pocket of my jeans for the slip of paper on which I had written Rendle's number, then padded downstairs to the sitting-room. It was time to call the Beast.

He picked up on the second ring.

"It's Thomas Wisdom, Mr. Rendle. Sorry for calling a bit late."

"Ah, yes . . . hmm, hmm." Sometimes, when Rendle's feeling particularly stressed, he makes this odd nasal grunt, like the sound a boxer might make while hitting a punch-bag. "Thomas . . . hmm, hmm. Good, yes."

"Gip said I should call. Gary Sanchez, that is."

"Right, well, of course, yes. But the fact is, Thomas, I need to talk to your parents about this . . . hmm, hmm . . . document."

"My parents." It was an alarmed squawk. I hesitated, listening for any sign of activity from upstairs before adding more quietly, "That's no good, Mr. Rendle. Didn't Gip explain the problem?"

"He said that you'd been playing around with your dad's computer and that your . . . hmm . . . curiosity got the better of you."

"It was a bit more than that."

"So can I talk to your mother now?"

"I'm afraid Mum's away for a few days. So is Dad, unfortunately."

"Hmm? Hmm?"

"Mr. Rendle, I think we should talk about this face-to-face. There are things I need to explain."

The Beast seemed to be having difficulty finding any words at all, so I jumped in quickly. "If you give me your address, I'll be there tomorrow," I said.

"Hmm, 7 Penrith Terrace, off the High Street but, Thomas—"

"I'll be there at ten tomorrow. Bye, Mr. Rendle."

I suspected that I would need company when I visited Rendle the next day, so I took Dougal with me on a lead. We arrived fifteen minutes early.

Rendle opened the door, looking unrecognizably normal in jeans and a white shirt. I stuttered my apologies for being early. "Nice dog," he said and gave a smile that was almost normal.

"Is it all right if I bring him in?"

"Of course." He waved us into the house and led us down a corridor into a neat sitting-room. I suppose I had been expecting the Beast to live in a bed-sit strewn with old papers and exercise books and unwashed coffee mugs because, as I stood there, he gave a little laugh.

"Bit more tidy than my room at school, eh?" he said.

I mumbled something polite.

"My mother keeps me in order," he said.

"Mother? I never knew—" I hesitated but there was no going back now. "I mean, I never thought you had a mother."

"She would have liked to meet you but she likes to have a lie-in during the morning."

I glanced around the room. Patterned carpet. Neat little

old-fashioned china dogs on the mantelpiece. A few silver-framed photographs on the dark wooden bookshelf. A writing-desk in the corner, on which a few papers were neatly stacked. It was not exactly what I had been expecting. "Just you two, is it?" I asked.

"Yes." Rendle ran a hand through his hair. "I'm an only child."

An awkward silence descended on the room as I tried, unsuccessfully, to imagine a childhood version of Rendle. "I've got a sister," I said.

"I know." He stood up suddenly. "Tea," he said. "Milk?"

I'm not exactly a tea person but I nodded. "Sounds good."

"What about the beast?"

I started in surprise before realizing that Rendle was looking down at Dougal. "Your dog," he said. "Does he need some water?"

"He's fine."

Rendle went into the next room and I heard him humming as he clattered about. Seeing him in this neat, little house, looking after his old mother, made me feel guilty about some of the things people at school had done to him.

It was so curiously relaxing in this house that, when Rendle returned, carrying two mugs, I was on the point of chatting to him a bit more, when he raised the question of my dad's file.

"Quite a little code on that document of yours," he said casually, as if it were some kind of tricky crossword puzzle. "It was unlike anything I've come across before—took me two days to crack it. I'll show you how I did it some time."

"That would be great. Can I have it back now? I'll just chuck it and forget this all happened."

Rendle shook his head slowly. "I wish we could do that,"

he said. "But, as I told you last night, I have to speak to your parents."

"I could give it to them for you. Save you the trouble." A note of desperation had entered my voice. "You can trust me."

"I trust you and Gary more than anyone else in your class but you've stumbled upon something that is very private. I considered destroying it but I don't think I can."

I sipped at my tea, playing for time. "Does it happen to have anything to do with national security?" I asked casually.

Rendle looked puzzled.

"Spies?" I asked.

He laughed. "No," he said. "It's more a personal matter." He paused. "You know, Thomas, you're very lucky to have such a wonderful family around you."

Almost as if she could hear these words, Rendle's mother began to call for him in a trembly, ancient voice from upstairs.

"Won't be a moment, Mother," he shouted without moving from his place.

She ignored him, calling his name again and again, sounding increasingly agitated.

Rendle stood up and suddenly he was his normal, battered self. "I won't be a . . . hmm, hmm . . . moment," he said. "My mother needs her . . . hmm, hmm . . . breakfast."

He had been out of the room for about a minute when an idea occurred to me. I wandered over to the desk in the corner and glanced at the papers that were on it. Under a single blank sheet, I found the numbered document that we had printed out from my father's computer. Attached to it was another typed sheet. I took a quick glance at the words at the top of the page.

Time froze. I stood there, unable to read anymore, unable to move. In the distance, I heard the voice of Rendle, talking to his mother upstairs. I lay the document back on the desk. I began to turn back into the room, to take my seat as if nothing had happened. Then, without giving myself time to think of the enormity of what I was doing, I grabbed the papers, called Dougal and slipped out to the hall. I glanced up the stairs, then silently let us out of the house. The door closed behind us with a quiet click.

I walked quickly down the street. Across the main road, there was a park where I found a bench. I sat down, lifted Dougal on to the seat beside me. I turned over the numbered sheet to stare at the version that Rendle had decoded. I looked at the headline again.

Taking a deep breath, I began to read.

The Adoption Papers of Baby Michael
Reference number: 0372AC19
Name: "Michael"
Date of Birth: 10/5/89
Place of Birth: Norwich and Norfolk Hospital, Norwich
Ethnic Origin: Caucasian
Mother: Karen Garnham
Father: Unknown

Social Worker's Report: Karen is eighteen years old and currently works part-time in a pub. She has had one previous child (Ref. No. 0372YG27) who was also put up for adoption. There have been no reports of medical or social problems with this child.

Karen is a healthy, good-hearted girl, but her background is unstable. She has two brothers and two sisters, all older. One brother is currently in a youth detention center and the other has also been in trouble with the police. One sister is married and living near Ipswich and the other is thought to be living in London. The Garnham family has always lived in the Holt area and is known to the local social services. All four children were on the At-Risk Register between 1968 and 1976. Karen's first child, a son, was put up for adoption in May 1986. The identity of Michael's father is unknown.

The implications of adoption have been fully explained to Karen who appears to have no doubt that it is the right course.

I am convinced that adoption is in the best interests of Baby Michael.

Health: Michael weighed 8 lbs. 6 oz. at birth. He has had no medical problems.

Character: Michael is a placid, easy-going baby who sleeps well. He has shown early signs of anxiety in the absence of his mother but is anticipated to settle well in his new home.

Proposed Adoptive Parents: Mark and Mary Wisdom.

Signed
Sally Rookyard
Social Services Department

I read the words on the sheet several times. Sensing that something was wrong, Dougal whined.

I stood up, folded the papers and slid them into my back pocket.

In a sort of trance, I began to walk slowly in the direction of my home.

13 · LIES

No, *MY HEAD WAS NOT TEEMING* with thoughts as I walked. No, I was not working out what exactly I should say to the people I had, until now, thought were my parents. I was numb. I felt sleepy. I wished I had never been saved from my life with Karen Garnham. In fact, right then, I wished I had never been born at all.

I reached home and went straight to my room where I lay down on the bed, turned my face to the wall and closed my eyes. I didn't cry but my eyes were full and I noticed that the pillow was damp. I wanted the world to go away.

Behind me, the door opened. I heard my mother's voice. She called my name twice, then walked over and gently shook my shoulder.

I turned over and, staring into her eyes, forced myself to remember that this was no longer the face of my mother.

"Go away," I said.

She looked shocked—more surprised than angry. "Are you ill?"

"Yes," I said.

Later, she brought me soup and a cake. I refused to talk to her. When I finished it, I placed the tray outside the door.

I couldn't sleep. My mind churned over and over with what I knew. I cursed Gip for his pathetic spy-obsession. I writhed with rage that stupid, snaggle-toothed Rendle had interfered in my life. I tried to understand what I had done to Mark and Mary Wisdom to deserve what they had done to me.

The house was silent when, at some early hour in the morning, I rose from my bed. I walked slowly down the corridor to the room where my adoptive parents were sleeping. Without a moment's hesitation, I pushed open the door and switched on the light. They lay in bed, blinking, looking afraid and strangely old.

"I want to leave home," I said.

At first they thought I was sleepwalking. As I stood there at the end of their bed, eyes blazing, hands trembling, as if I had come to murder them in their bed, my former mother huddled close to my former father.

"I think he's having a dream," she said. "Don't wake him, Mark. Sleepwalkers have to come around gradually."

"I'm not sleepwalking." I heard my voice screaming these words. "This is me. This is real. You remember real, don't you? From like before you started lying to me? Or is that so long ago that you've forgotten about it?"

Normally, when I get stressed out or upset it's Mum who takes control but now her face was as pale as the sheets of her bed.

"Perhaps it would be a good idea if you went to your room before you say something you might regret." My former father spoke in his business voice. At any other time, that cool, grown-up, nothing-can-faze-me tone might have stopped me in my tracks, but not tonight.

"What about you? Isn't there anything you've said that you might regret? Over the last twelve years, for example—since the tenth of May 1989. Can you think of one little thing you might have forgotten to tell me?"

My ex-parents glanced at one another. They knew what my problem was now.

"Thomas." The woman formerly known as "Mum" made to get out of bed but the expression on her face, the gentle soothing voice—it was all just another lie.

I swore. I swore and swore and swore and swore. I said words that I never knew I knew, things that I had heard kids using at school. Once I had felt sorry for them with their pathetic need to shock but at least they belonged somewhere. At least their lives had not been one long, never-ending lie. At least they had families.

I was on my knees, swearing like a crazed madman, and the two people I had once trusted were each side of me, holding me, enveloping me in their arms, making soothing sounds, and I was fighting against them saying that I never wanted to see them again, that I wanted to go into a home where I belonged, asking why they hadn't left me where I belonged.

This weird, noisy wrestling-match must have continued for several minutes. Slowly, more out of exhaustion than anything else, I grew quiet. I was half-led, half-carried downstairs to the kitchen where I sat at the table between them. My former father placed a wine glass in front of me and told me to drink. The liquid burnt my throat and brought more tears to my eyes.

"Drink," he said. "You need it."

Feebly now, and with defeat in my voice, I swore once more. I took another gulp. My throat hurt but I welcomed the pain. So what if it made me ill? With a bit of luck, I would be sick all over their precious kitchen.

"We need to talk." My former father spoke gently and firmly. My former mother held my hand as if, at any moment, I might run from the kitchen, out of the house and into the darkness outside, never to be seen again.

There was silence for a moment. My head was swimming. The only sound I could hear was my own sobbing breaths.

"We were young and happy together. We had Amy. But we had been told that I couldn't have another baby." My former mother spoke quietly and deliberately, like someone who has been given a truth drug. "We talked about it, Dad and me. Amy was a lovely little thing but we had always dreamed of having a big family. Eventually, there seemed to be no choice. We weren't complete, the three of us. We were missing something in our lives. We put our names down at an agency. We were interviewed again and again. We were watched and studied for months. Everyone said that it was difficult to adopt a child. We had almost given up hope when we received word that something had gone wrong with a planned adoption, that there was a chance that our dreams might come true. A baby boy. Up in Norfolk."

"It was you, old boy," said my former father in a voice which I suppose he thought was full of love.

"You." My former mother squeezed my hand and gazed into my angry, wounded eyes. "We traveled up, the three of us. I can remember it as if it were yesterday. Amy had never been so excited. She chatted and laughed on the back seat of the car, asking every few minutes how much longer it would be. She was nine years old but the thought of having a baby brother was the best present she had ever been given. We were excited too, of course, but we were nervous—"

"Terrified," said my former father.

"What if you didn't like us? What if you looked up and screamed your little head off? Were we being fair on Amy? Would we be good enough parents for you? Thousands of couples wanted children. What made us think that we had the right to take over a life? But we got there. This woman met us, took us into an office and told us a bit about you— your mum, your background, how the couple who were to have adopted you had discovered something—not about you but about your would-be adoptive mother, a health thing—and all we could think of was what you were going to be like. All that drama you had caused in your short life. The woman led us into a room. There was a row of cots. A couple of the babies were crying. The room was all bright and colored and full of paintings and mobiles hanging from the ceiling but it was the saddest place I had ever been. We were led to the end cot and there you were, just lying there, a solemn little man staring up at us, more strangers there to cluck and chat over him. Amy leaned over the cot and touched your face. You took her finger with your left hand and you held on, your eyes looking into hers. She pretended to pull away but you held on. She laughed. You smiled. I cried. It was as if you had always belonged to us but had been waiting there all these months. It was the most perfect moment of my life. You were so beautiful."

"Yeah yeah," I muttered.

"They gave us your papers. We took you away in the carry-cot we had brought with us. They called you Michael but you somehow didn't look like a Michael. On the way back to London, we all decided on your name. Thomas. Thomas Wisdom."

I looked from one of them to the other. They both wore goofy, dazed half-smiles on their faces. I guess they expected me to burst into tears at this point, sob out words of gratitude that they had rescued me from the home, but my heart was stone.

"Year after year, we meant to tell you." My former father took up the story. "But we knew it would change everything. For the first five years, the agency kept in touch with me. They told us how important it was to explain to you where you came from. We would know the moment, they said. But the moment never came. When everything was good, we didn't want to spoil it. When it was more difficult, it seemed wrong to add to the difficulty."

"You know what?" I said. "I think you're still not telling me the truth."

My former father's head dropped, either from exhaustion or from shame. My former mother squeezed my hand more tightly.

"We're tired," she said. "We'll talk some more in the morning."

I went back to my room and lay on my bed. Although my limbs were aching as if I was coming down with a fever, my brain refused to close down for the night. It churned and turned and seethed with various hot, confused versions of what had happened to me over the previous hours. In a strange half-waking, half-dreaming state, I saw a procession of characters—my former parents, Rendle, Amy, my real mother, even Cy from California. They were caught up in some sort of game, a dance in which the person at the center of it all—little me—suddenly seemed utterly insignificant.

When I awoke, it was past nine. Briefly I had forgotten

what had happened, that I was no longer Thomas Wisdom from a neat street in suburbia, but Michael Garnham from wild and woolly Norfolk, but, within seconds, the truth came crashing in at me. I groaned, lay in bed for a moment, then sat up.

Normally at this time, Mr. and Mrs. Wisdom, my ex-parents, would have left for work but I heard them talking in low voices downstairs in the kitchen. As soon as I appeared, they would probably start at me again, giving me the new version of my life, telling me how I was more than a son to them because I was not actually their son, chucking in words like "belonging," "family," and "love"—above all, love—trying to rub away the past or make it into a pretty, fairy-tale picture.

I had had enough of it all. I needed to get some space between me and my former family's house. I crept to the bedroom and dialed the number of the one person in the world that I could trust.

Gip answered on the second ring.

"Meet me in the park," I said, and hung up.

14 · CHRISTMAS

GIP DOESN'T DO EMBARRASSMENT. Events—even big events like his mum moving out for a few weeks to live with some guy—seem to wash over him like a stream around a rock.

But that morning, when he arrived and found me sitting on our bench, he seemed almost worried. "You look rough," he said. "Tanned but rough." He offered me some chewing-gum.

As I took it, I noticed that my hand was shaking. He sat down beside me. Acting casual, he asked, "So how was Rendle?"

"He was OK."

"I rang him but he refused to tell me what happened. He kept saying you had run away from the house—that he needed to see you."

I looked across the park. Then, as casually I was able, I said, "He told me who I was." I stared Gip full in the face. "I'm adopted."

"Eh?" Gip gave an awkward, snickering

laugh as if I had made some kind of bad-taste joke. "You?"

"Me."

"But that's ridiculous. You look just like your parents. This must be some kind of mistake. Rendle's lost it."

I shook my head. Slowly, clearly, so that there could be no misunderstanding, I told him what had happened. Rendle. The file. Last night. The confession of my former parents. Now and then, Gip seemed about to ask a question but I needed to tell it all—every word that had been said, everything that I felt. I talked and talked and when I fell silent, Gip had nothing to say. He stared at me for a moment. His arm twitched as if he were about to reach out for me but he must have sensed that right now I didn't want to be touched. "Bummer," he said at last.

I smiled. Gip knew my secret—every foul, squalid, cheating little bit of it—but, now that it was out, nothing really changed. It was a bummer, but we were still Gip and Tom, sitting in the park, together. For the first time in twenty-four hours, it occurred to me that I might be strong enough to come through this thing without too many dents and scrapes and abrasions.

"Did you mean it about leaving home?" he asked.

I stared at the ground. "I've trusted them all my life," I said. "How can I go on living with them now that I know that everything was a lie? If they lied about that, what else were they lying about?" As I sat there, I remembered holidays, games in the garden, Christmases, parties, jokes, bedtime stories, breakfasts. Suddenly even my memories were a fraud.

"I could fix you up with a place to stay," Gip said suddenly. "Somewhere no one will find you."

I looked at him, surprised.

"I've got this room across town. It's a sort of hideaway I use when things get heavy at home."

I suppose I should have seen then how strange it was that Gip, at the age of twelve, had a second home but right then I could think of nothing but my own problem. "Thanks," I said. "But I've got to face this myself, head on."

"Colin Rendle wants to see you. He's panicking."

"Yeah." I laughed briefly. "What a heartbreaker that is."

"He might be able to help. He's the only person who knows about this."

"Help?" I shook my head. Was it really likely that a teacher so hopeless that he could be locked in a cupboard by his own class would be of any use whatsoever in a real crisis? But then I remembered the look on his face when I had seen him, the way he had called out to his mother.

"OK," I said, standing up. "Maybe it's worth a try."

Rendle was not exactly prepared for a visit. When he opened the door quickly and impatiently to see Gip and me standing there, it didn't take a genius to see that our timing had been kind of unfortunate. The sleeves of his shirt were rolled up. The V-necked patterned sweater that he liked to wear had little drops of water down the front. Flecks of soap were on his face and in his hair. He looked like the Mad Phantom of the Launderette.

"Thomas, Gary." He wiped his hands on the seat of his baggy brown corduroy trousers. "What a . . . hmm . . . surprise."

"Yeah, Colin, how you going?" Gip spoke to the teacher as if he were some kind of elder brother. "I found Thomas for you. We need some advice."

"Now?" Rendle winced. "Any chance of you coming back later?"

Gip gave a brief, shaggy nod in my direction. "It's kind of urgent."

"Hmm." The teacher turned, walked through the dark

hallway and into the sitting-room. "You'd better come in then."

We followed him inside, Gip first, then me, closing the front door behind us.

When we reached the sitting-room, we quickly became aware of the reason for Rendle's embarrassment. In an armchair, silhouetted against the net-curtained window, sat a gray, shriveled-up figure. As our eyes became accustomed to the light, we saw that she was a little old woman almost lost in a dark blue dressing-gown. Shining in the gloom were her two skinny legs, like white twigs. Her feet were in a plastic bowl, full of soapy water.

"These are my friends—Gary and Thomas." Rendle leaned over her and spoke in a loud, deliberate voice.

"Hi," said Gip.

"Hello," I said.

"Has Father Christmas been yet?" The old woman's voice was surprisingly clear.

We glanced at Rendle who smiled desperately.

Mrs. Rendle chuckled crazily. "You can tell me, boys," she said.

"Yeah." It was Gip who spoke first. "He has. Good old Santa. He was really generous too."

"He hasn't come to me. When you get old, he seems to forget all about you." Mrs. Rendle sighed and all the sorrows of the world seemed to be in her voice. She glanced contemptuously in the direction of her son. "He blocks the chimney, you know," she said.

"Mum, I don't think the boys should hear about that," said Rendle with a gentle despair in his voice that I had never heard before.

"He thinks I won't remember. Give the old bag a foot-wash and she'll forget all about Father Christmas—that's what he thinks." Mrs. Rendle made an odd clicking noise with her teeth then, without warning, said the worst swear word I've ever heard outside the school playground.

"Come on, Mother." Rendle smiled apologetically.

"I don't like Father Christmas anyway," said Gip quickly. "He always brings you exactly what you don't want. I wish he'd just give us all a break and . . . sugar off."

Rendle knelt down, lifted his mother's frail little feet, one by one, out of the bowl and dried them with neat, dabbing movements.

"He's a man; what can you expect?" said Rendle's mother. "Stop tickling me."

Rendle tenderly pulled down the old woman's nightdress and closed her dressing-gown. "Take a seat," he said. "I'll just take my mother upstairs."

Mrs. Rendle looked from Gip to me, then back again to Gip as if she had noticed that we were there for the first time. "Has Father Christmas been yet?" she asked.

"Mother." Rendle spoke more firmly. "Bedtime now." In one surprisingly graceful movement, he placed one arm beneath her legs, the other behind her back, and picked her up as easily as if she were a five-year-old child.

The old woman began to whimper. "Are you having a party?" she asked, looking up at her son. "Please, can I stay for the party? I promise to be good."

"We have to talk about something, Mother. Let's turn on the telly for you, upstairs. I think it's almost time for the weather-forecast." Murmuring quietly about areas of low-pressure, he left the room and made his way up the stairs, his mother in his arms.

"Lemme outta here," Gip muttered. We both laughed guiltily.

When Rendle reappeared, he had pulled down his

sleeves and wiped the soap off his face. He strode into the sitting-room with the fake authority he tried unsuccessfully to use at the beginning of a lesson at school.

"Sorry about that." He sat down but still seemed tense, as if ready to bound upstairs at any moment. "It's Christmas every day of the year in this house. Which is not as fun as you might think." Rendle sighed and stared ahead of him for a moment. Then he seemed to pull himself together. "And how is everything with Thomas?" He gave me a toothy smile.

"Fine," I replied automatically. Fact is, this little scene from the Beast's private life had made me forget my own problems for a moment. Now, with a lurch of the stomach, I remembered it all. "Actually, not fine at all," I said.

"You spoke to your parents."

"My ex-parents, yes. They told me where I came from. They said they had gone to this adoption agency, like it was some kind of pet shop for kids, and they picked me out and took me home. I think I'm meant to feel totally grateful to them, but I don't. I hate them."

"You're wrong, Thomas. I can see that—"

"I hate them and I'm moving out."

Rendle looked pale and unhappy. Somehow I could sense that he was not used to big family crises. His never-ending Christmas Day with his mother may have been difficult but at least it didn't require any decisions. He just had to wash her feet and keep her calm.

"I didn't know what to do," he said in a distant voice. "At first, all I could think of was solving the problem. I worked on the code for days. When I began to see how it worked, I laughed at the brilliance of it. I took some numbers in the middle of the file. It was a sentence about Karen Garnham. I thought it must be some kind of made-up story. Then I started from the beginning. It was a while before I began to understand what exactly it was that I was translating. By then it was too late to stop. When I got to the end, I agonized over whether I should pretend that the code had defeated me. But I thought you would take it to someone else. I tried to imagine how I would feel if I were you." His voice tapered off miserably.

"Thanks," I muttered. "I mean, really thanks. You were right. Twelve years of lies is enough."

"They're still your parents." Rendle spoke firmly. "I'm sure they love you as much as if they were your real mum and dad. Maybe more."

"Yeah, right."

"I've met them," said Rendle. "It's obvious that they care about you. They're good people—better than most of the parents I see."

I shook my head. "If you care for someone, you don't lie to them," I said.

"They thought it was for the best." There was a hint of desperation in Rendle's voice. "It was just one untruth. They probably thought that telling you about your real mother would upset the life they had made for you."

For some reason, a vision of my former parents lying naked in the haze of the sub-desert underworld entered my head. "It wasn't just one untruth," I said. "There are other lies—big lies—that they're not telling me about."

Gip and Rendle were looking at me but I was not in the mood to tell them more.

"What d'you think we should do, Colin?" Gip asked and, although I said nothing, I was grateful for that "we."

The teacher sighed. "Talk. Thomas has a lot of talking to do. He's got to try and understand the reasons for what happened."

"Yeah, right, understand. That's going to be easy," I said.

"The other question is what I should do." Rendle spoke more briskly now. "I have a professional problem in all this. For better or for worse, I have this knowledge about you—and you're a pupil. I really should talk to someone about it."

"Like who?" asked Gip.

"Like Mr. Dover—Mrs. Fredericks, maybe." He spoke the name of the headmaster and my class teacher with a sort of weariness.

"Won't they be on holiday?" Gip asked.

"There's an emergency number."

From upstairs could be heard the voice of his mother, calling his name. Rendle started like a child who has been caught doing something wrong. "Boys, I'd better see to my mother."

We stood up. "Mr. Rendle," I said. "I need to think about all this. Give me twenty-four hours. Promise you won't talk to anyone until we speak again."

He frowned, then nodded reluctantly. "So long as you don't do anything foolish. Stay at home. Talk to your . . . your folks. Try to understand." He laid a bony hand on my shoulder. "Right?"

"Right," I said.

"It's going to be OK."

"Somehow I don't think so," I said.

15 · EAST

THAT WAS THE DAY when I discovered that, whatever else was wrong in my life, I was lucky to have Gip Sanchez around—he was the best friend in the world.

He must have seen that I was kind of wasted by the time we left the weird, unhappy house of Mr. Rendle. In the past twenty-four hours, I had discovered that I was not who I'd always thought I was, I had faced up to the fact that my entire life had been a lie, I had spent a night of sleepless torment and then, just to round it all off, I had tiptoed through the wonky winter wonderland of the Beast's poor, Christmas-crazed mum.

I was in bad shape, and Gip took over.

"You've got to phone home," he said as we stood on the corner of the road where Rendle lived.

"Forget it," I muttered. "Home's not home anymore."

"OK, so you hate them right now but

there's no point in worrying them. Stay out too long and they'll go to the busies. Things are complicated enough, man."

My brain was working at half-speed and it took a few moments for me to realize that, when Gip referred to "the busies," he was talking about the police. "I don't care," I muttered.

"Call your folks," he said, taking a phone out of his pocket. He stopped beside it. "Either you do it, or I will."

There was something about Gip when he was in this mood that was so steely and strong that resistance was pointless. Somehow you knew that, whatever you were going through, he had survived worse. He had the power of a survivor.

He held the mobile phone out to me. "Your call, Tom," he said.

I dialed. Mum replied. She sounded kind of fraught. I told her not to worry about me. She asked me to come home. I said I had things to do. She started crying. I told her I would be back sometime. She asked me to promise I would return by nightfall. I hesitated. Suddenly everyone was asking me to make promises. I glanced at Gip, closed my eyes and sighed. I thought of my bed, my room. I nodded. She started talking again. "Yes, I said yes," I snapped. I hung up.

"Why am I always the person who has to behave?" I murmured.

Gip slung an arm round my shoulder and hugged me briefly. "Because you're Thomas Wisdom. That's the way you are. Now we're going to hit the town."

We took a bus, then another bus, then went by underground. We ended up in a part of town that I had never heard of, let alone visited. The streets were shadowy and litter-strewn and the windows of the shops were covered in wire mesh as if, at any moment, an invading army was going to swarm in, smashing and mugging and grabbing the few bits of manky food and tins that were on their shelves. About twenty yards above the road down which Gip led me was a giant motorway taking cars and lorries out of town. The rumble of engines and the swish of tires on tarmac seemed to come from another universe where there was color and money and hope, where people could escape from the gray, dingy world of city-dwellers.

We turned into a narrow street where a few wrecked cars seemed to have been dumped. The houses were big and solid and must have been elegant years ago but now the plaster was crumbling off them and most of their windows were boarded up.

"What is this place?" I asked, maybe a touch nervously.

"Home away from home." Gip smiled and it was true that he seemed more at ease than he usually was. His limp was almost a skip as he climbed the steps up to the last house on the right where all the windows were flung open and music could be heard from high up on the top floor. "This is where I come when things get heavy back at my place. It's a sort of refuge."

He took a key from his pocket and let himself into a hall where a big motorbike stood. Dark, gleaming bits of its engine lay on a greasy newspaper on the bare floorboards. Gip squeezed past it, kicking an empty beer can as he went, and made his way up the stairs.

"You rent a room here?" I asked in a low voice as I followed him.

He laughed. "Nobody rents here. The council's meant to be knocking the place down. In the meantime, it's a hangout for anyone who needs a roof over their heads."

"Like, a squat?"

"Something like that." Gip reached a bright open room on the first floor that had been painted in a wild, crazy, yellow color. A few cartoon-like pictures and graffiti had been scrawled on the walls but, although the spelling was dodgy—even the swear words looked wrong—there was nothing threatening about the place. In the far corner of the room, three people sprawled on the floor in front of a big, old-fashioned TV.

"Yo," said Gip, opening a fridge that was behind the door.

A girl with tangled dreadlocks and a lot of metalwork about her face glanced over her shoulder. "Gippy, where you been?" she said without any particular curiosity in her voice.

Gip was gazing into the moldy depths of the fridge. To my surprise, there was a six-pack of cola. He took two cans and handed one to me. He nodded in the direction of the door. "I'll show you my room," he said.

We went up another flight of stairs to a corridor with two closed doors on one side and one on the other. Gip walked to the last door, took out his keys, unlocked it and stood back to usher me in. "Welcome to the secret world of Gip Sanchez," he said.

The first thing I noticed when I stepped into the room was the noise. Within what seemed like a matter of yards from the low, small window, traffic was thundering by on the motorway flyover. Then I looked around me—it was like staring into Gip's soul. There were posters for computer games on one of the walls. In a corner lay a mattress with gray sheets and a few science fiction paperbacks scattered about on the floor. On a desk against the opposite wall was a laptop computer.

"Wow," I said quietly.

"Everything a guy could possibly need."

"But . . . how?"

"I was nine when I first stayed here. My mum had kicked me out for the weekend when she took up with some new guy. I met up with some kids in central London. This became the only place I could escape. I got a key cut. People come and go here but I kept my room."

"Where did the computer come from?"

Gip looked shifty. "That kind of fell off the back of a lorry. One of the other guys is good at hacking and stuff, so we can go on-line for free."

I walked over to the window and watched the stream of traffic—lorries and coaches and vans and cars with their drivers and passengers gazing ahead of them as if they were hypnotized. Now and then I caught sight of a child gazing blankly in our direction from a backseat. For them, I seemed to have become invisible. They belonged to a different universe—a place where people belonged together, where they knew where they were going.

"Quiet spot too," I said.

Gip laughed. "You should see it at rush hour."

"Where's the road heading?"

"Somewhere east, I guess."

There was an alcove underneath the window. I sat down and stared out at the traffic passing by. In spite of the roar and thump of the noise in the air, I felt at ease in this place. "Maybe I could stay for a while," I said.

Gip winced. "Not a good idea," he said. "We get a few hard cases hanging out now and then. It's not your sort of place."

"Thanks a bunch." I wasn't sure I liked this new Gip— all concerned and responsible and stopping me from doing things I wanted to do, almost as if he had become some kind of uncle or something.

Maybe he could tell the direction of my thoughts because he kicked my foot as if to tell me to snap out of it.

"So tell me what happened in the States," he said.

"I could use another Coke," I said.

An irritated look crossed Gip's face but he kept quiet. Then he shrugged and limped towards the door.

By the time he had returned with two more cans, I had made up my mind. It was true that Gip bore some responsibility for what had happened to me—in fact, it had been his crazy curiosity that set the whole thing in motion. The fact that he had kept this part of his life secret from me was none too thrilling, either. But, in the end, I had no one else to turn to.

Something within me resisted confiding any more in him but, at that moment, my defenses were down. I took a long swig of Coke.

"My parents went to a place called Seraph," I said. "And I followed them."

I told him everything. No matter how crazy and absurd, no matter how embarrassing, I spilled it all out. I told him I thought it might have all been a dream. I told him about the sprig of sagebrush. When I finished talking, I felt empty and desolate inside, like the biggest traitor who has ever lived.

Gip said nothing. He gave a long, disappointed sigh and stared out of the window.

"You don't believe me," I said. "I can tell. You think I've lost the plot." For reasons I couldn't understand, tears pricked my eyes. I found that my cheeks were wet.

"I believe you." He spoke sadly. "I believe every word you've spoken."

Our eyes locked for a long few seconds—not because it was some kind of gloopy buddy-moment, like in the movies, but because there was nothing left to say. He gave a shrug and a weird sort of grimace. "Here we go," he murmured under his breath.

It seemed a strange thing to say but then it was a strange moment. Later, I would remember that look and those words.

There was no turning back for either of us.

16 · WEST

I WENT HOME, BUT somehow it wasn't home anymore. As soon as I had said goodbye to Gip on the corner of my street and began walking towards the house where I had lived for all my life, I felt a lurch of anger in my stomach. In my mind, my home had been transformed into a prison with the people who had once been my parents as warders.

Twelve years ago they had collected me from where I really belonged, brought me back here as if I were some kind of thing, a family accessory, and had raised me, pretending for every second of every day and every night that I was theirs, not something that had been ripped from another place, other parents. I was not here because I belonged but because they needed a second child to make their precious lives complete. None of this was about me. I was just caught in the middle. In fact, I could have been another me, another spare child altogether, and it would have made no difference to Mr. and Mrs.Wisdom.

A prison, but one with a key. As I approached the house, I took the front-door key from my pocket. I slowed down as I reached the gate leading up our garden path, then walked on. The immaculate company car belonging to my former parents was parked, all smug and gleaming, on the other side of the road.

On an impulse, I crossed the road. I crouched down beyond the car and, without even bothering to check whether anyone was watching, drew the sharp edge of the key in my hand in great swooping strokes across the car's elegant, dark paintwork. The scratch sounded like a scream.

Feeling better, I stood up, walked across to the house and let myself in. I smiled when my former mother greeted me in the hall and, mistaking me for someone I used to be, she hugged me. I shook her off and told her I would be upstairs.

On the first floor, I hesitated. The door to my father's study was slightly open. I peered inside. The room was empty.

I sat down in his chair. Behind him was a rack filled with his precious classical music CDs. I glanced at them—Albinoni, Bach, Beethoven. They were, of course, in alphabetical order. I took the first on the rack and opened it. I took out my key again. Dad, dear Dad, would find a message where he least expected it.

I moved fast. I was like someone in a factory—grab, open, scratch, replace, again and again. I had reached Vivaldi by the time I heard footsteps on the stairs. I put back the last piece of my handiwork and, without even looking at my former mother, I went to my room and shut the door behind me.

I lay on my bed. I took the door-key out of my pocket. The end of it sparkled from the work it had done. I closed my eyes and remembered the magic, the power, I had felt as I made my mark.

I was me at last and no one was going to lie to me, pretend to me, patronize me ever again because I was a new person.

MG. I was MG. Michael Garnham. My mark was on the world and the world had better be ready for me.

I was expecting trouble. The two things in the world that were precious to my ex-father were his car and his music. But when I went down for supper that evening, I was in for a surprise. There was no sign of my former parents. Instead, casually reading a newspaper in the sitting-room, was Cy Gabriel.

"Thomas." He stood up as I walked in and shook my hand. "I've got a meeting tomorrow," he said. "Mark and Mary asked me over. I hope it's not inconvenient."

"Not really." I slumped into the chair opposite.

Cy laid down his paper. "So how you been doing?"

I tried for a smile but didn't make it. "I've been better as it happens."

There was silence in the room. At that moment, I wanted to confide in this man. Although he was virtually a stranger to me, he had the air of someone who had seen all kinds of stuff, who understood what it was like to be alone, confused, and lost.

As if he could read my mind, Cy said softly, "I know what happened, Thomas—I heard."

"I'm not Thomas."

Cy smiled. "Sure you are. You're the same smart guy you were when I met you in Santa Barbara. You've found out something about your past. That doesn't change who you are. Thomas Wisdom just got a bit more wisdom."

I looked out of the window. It was true that, however hard I tried, I was never going to be Michael Garnham.

"Your parents must have been crazy not to tell you before," Cy continued. "They know that now. They were afraid that it would spoil everything."

"You mean, our little game of happy families."

"No game, Thomas." Cy Gabriel looked serious. "Your happy family."

"Ex-family," I muttered.

"Tell me how you blew their cover."

I hesitated for a moment. It would be the first time I had spoken to someone not directly involved about the events which had changed my life. Instinctively, I wanted to hold on to my experience, keep it hidden, like my own private secret, but suddenly it occurred to me that there had been too many secrets in my shadowy little life. It was time for a bit of daylight.

"I've got this friend Gip," I said. "He's kind of a whiz with computers. He was here after school one day . . ."

It all came out—the file, Rendle, the coded adoption papers, even our weird visit to the Beast and his nutty mum. Cy was a good listener and talking to him was like losing this big sack of guilt that I had been lugging around with me all day.

"It was lucky you had someone to turn to," Cy said after I had finished speaking.

I sensed that Cy wanted me to tell him more but I was not about to blow the details of my friend's secret hide-away—not even to a stranger who would be flying back to America in a couple of days' time. "Yeah," I said. "He's all right is old Gip."

I heard my parents chatting upstairs. It seemed odd and

unlike them that they had left their guest unattended, particularly since the guest was meant to be their big boss-man.

"Sorry about the hosts," I said. "They seem to have gone walkabout."

"No problem. I arrived early." Cy paused as if something had just occurred to him. "You know what, Thomas? You need to get away from all this, take a break."

I was about to point out that I had only just returned from a holiday but he held up a hand. "Tomorrow I'm visiting our main depot over here. Limo, lunch, quick look around. Why not come along?"

Depot, limo, lunch? At any other time, the idea of spending the day at some lame workplace would have come a close second to a visit to the dentist as a way of spending my holiday time.

But to my surprise, I realized that the idea of a day away from home was what I wanted right now. It might even be interesting.

I heard the sound of voices as my ex-parents came down the stairs. If they became involved in any discussion about Cy's idea, I knew which way I would jump.

So I made a decision. "All right, then," I said.

"Deal," said Cy.

There was something unusual about this man. That night, over dinner, I began to get an idea of what it was. He had a simple, easy talent for making people feel good. At first, it bothered me. Who was this guy, this big-time American boss, who could just stroll into our lives and within seconds we were opening up like flowers in the sun? Was there some kind of trick involved, a creepy little technique they taught you at business school?

I fought against it and I lost. Cy was interested in other people. He seemed to want the best for them. His life had panned out pretty well and there was nothing he wanted more than to share his good fortune with the people he came into contact with. When strangers first met Gip, they would be suspicious of him. When they met the Beast, they would instinctively want to tease him. With Cy, they wanted to talk, to open up, to try to be as nice and easygoing as he was.

So, over dinner, I found myself joining in the conversation, sometimes even laughing, almost as if it was the old days and I was once more part of the family. At one point, late on in the meal, I caught my ex-mother's eye. She smiled at me and, before I could stop myself, I smiled back.

I was confused. It was as if the new me, Michael Garnham, was slipping away before I had even begun to understand him. Going to bed that night, I tried to feel within myself the burning anger that had become part of me over the past few days but somehow the friendliness and ease of that evening seemed to have doused the fire. I'm Michael, I whispered to myself, lying in bed but, as I drifted off to a dreamless sleep, I knew that Cy had been right. I was not Michael at all. I was Thomas Wisdom and there was no escaping from it.

Another thing. As hard as I tried to think of Mary and Mark Wisdom as fake family, former parents, I knew deep down that they were still my mum and my dad.

Late that night, when the house was dark and silent, I went downstairs and dialed Gip's number. "I need some help," I said.

"Shoot."

"I want to look for my real mother."

"All right, then. If you really want to."

"I do."

"Just don't pin your hopes, all right?"

"What d'you mean by that?"

"I know mothers," said Gip. "Doesn't do to put your trust in mothers."

Maybe it was because I just wanted to get out of the house but the next morning I woke early. Some time during the night Mum (she isn't my mum, and never has been, but I'm going to call her that from now on) had laid out some clothes for me on the chair near the bed but I took one glance at them and saw that they were the white-shirt-and-dark-trousers uniform that I'm forced into when weddings or Christmas come around. Sure, I wanted to please Cy Gabriel but there was a limit. I grabbed a T-shirt and jeans from my drawer. If the good folk of the Seraph Organization were shocked by that, it was their problem.

Cy rolled up in a flash, low-slung motor while my parents were still messing around upstairs getting ready for their day. It had worried me that we might all have to arrive at the office in one embarrassing gang but it turned out that the place Cy was taking me was some bigshot depot that Mr. and Mrs. Wisdom only visited once or twice a year themselves.

We drove. I'm never exactly talkative in the mornings and I was relieved that Cy was in relaxed, silent mode as well. He put on some classical music. The car whispered like a gray ghost through the town, and picked up speed when we hit a motorway. Surprisingly soon the scenery outside changed, rows of houses giving way to the golden stubble of summer cornfields. I watched the outside world as it raced by beyond the darkened windows and cool, air-conditioned comfort of the car.

At one point, I asked Cy where we were heading.

"West." He smiled at me. "The organization likes west."

"Right."

"You know why? Because west represents hope, the future. Man has always headed west. It's the next frontier. The east stands for lost hope, for erosion and age."

I looked at him to check whether he was taking the mickey out of me. He laughed again. "Go west, young man," he said.

I gazed out of the window, thinking all of a sudden of Gip and his hideaway out on the east of town. Then I pictured the neat suburban confidence of the west where we lived, which led as naturally as the course of a river into the opulent countryside I was looking at now.

Erosion. Hope. In a weird way, it all made sense.

We must have been driving for an hour or so when Cy swung off the motorway onto a small country road. We drove through one village, then another, before he stopped by an old-fashioned five-bar gate on the right of the road. Cy pressed something behind the lapel of his jacket and the gate swung open.

"The organization likes privacy," he said as we made our way down a narrow, high-banked road. After about a mile, we turned a bend. Without warning, the road opened out onto a big expanse of tarmac. A few hundred yards ahead of us, almost like a castle surrounded by a wide, solid moat, was a square white building.

Something of the look of it, the way it was designed, reminded me of the strange bunker I had visited that afternoon back in the desert beyond Seraph.

"Welcome to European HQ," he said, as we entered the car park where about fifty identical, executive-type motors were lined up as if for a race. Cy drew up in front of the building's main steps. He got out, stretched and, having taken his briefcase from the backseat, led me into the strangest office I had ever seen.

There was no receptionist. Doors opened before us as if somehow they could recognize that we belonged. We walked down a short corridor into a big, hall-like room. The bright screens of scores of computers gazed at us. In front of each of them was a man or a woman, gazing at the information in front of them as if their lives depended on it.

"This is where information comes through from all over the world." Cy spoke softly as if we were in a church or something. "Any tiny item of data that's relevant to our project is recorded, ordered, and deployed."

We walked between two of the rows of computers with their operators. Now and then he stopped by one of the workers, peered over a shoulder, at the screens, made a bit of small talk. When they became aware of his presence, each operative seemed to relax their concentration for a moment, more as if Cy was one of their best friends rather than the boss.

At the time I thought nothing odd of that, nor the fact that the information on the screens seemed to be in the form of numbers rather than words, but as we made our slow progress through the rooms I found it difficult to come up with the right kind of small talk.

"Wow," I said eventually. "All this for food."

"Yeah." The trace of a frown crossed Cy's face. "Food can be a complex business these days."

We took a lift to the first floor and he led me into his office, a big, bright room on the corner of the building with views over the rolling countryside.

"Want a drink?" Cy hung his jacket on the back of the door, wandered over to the corner and opened a fridge.

"Yeah. Yes, please," I said.

Cy took out two plastic bottles of sparkling water, handed one to me and opened his as he sat at his desk.

"Thomas, I've got a few calls to catch up on," he said casually. "Would you like to see a video about how this place works?"

A corporate video? Great, I thought gloomily. But I smiled and agreed.

For a moment, Cy stared at me as if considering whether to tell me something. Then he took a quick swig at the little bottle in his hand, stood up, and walked briskly to a small door on the far side of his office that I hadn't noticed before.

He opened it and, with a mock seriousness, ushered me in.

I stood on the threshold of the room. It was like a tiny cinema, with a couple of rows of comfortable seats in front of a large screen.

"I'm afraid we don't run to popcorn," said Cy as I sat down on one of the front-row seats. "Let me know if you need another drink."

I laid my bottle on the ledge of the chair.

"Enjoy." The voice of Cy was behind me but, when I turned to say something, he had closed the door behind him.

For a few seconds, I sat alone in the darkness. Then the screen flickered into life.

17 · PROJECT

HOW CAN I DESCRIBE WHAT happened next?

It was not like losing consciousness or being hypnotized or slipping into another reality. It was as if it was reality—more real than anything I had ever experienced but also more perfect and happy and peaceful. The everyday existence, which we all take for granted, suddenly seemed meaningless, full of futile argument and stress, like a restless dream.

The voices sounded, their music more beautiful than anything you have ever heard. A dark purple color, of a depth and warmth that no human painter or photographer has ever captured, filled the screen. I felt as if I was part of it, more serene and relaxed and content than I ever believed was possible. When the voice spoke, it was without sound—when I replied, it was by thought alone.

I was in the presence of the perfect parent, the perfect teacher, the perfect best friend. Together, we made the entire universe.

I was humble yet mighty, in control of all, yet as helpless as a new-born baby.

I had reached my destination.

YOU HAVE ARRIVED. IT HAS BEEN A LONG JOURNEY. YOU HAVE REQUIRED STRENGTH AND INTELLIGENCE TO REACH THIS PLACE. NOW YOU ARE HERE. THOMAS WISDOM, YOU ARE WELCOME.

Where am I?

YOU ARE BEYOND ALL LIMITS. NO HUMAN WORD EXISTS TO DESCRIBE THIS PLACE. IT IS FAR YET NEAR. BEYOND SPACE AND TIME YET WITHIN YOUR SOUL.

Am I on Earth?

YOU ARE CHOSEN. YOU ARE AMONG THE FEW, THE PRIVI-LEGED. IT IS YOU WHO WILL HELP US WITH OUR GREAT PROJ-ECT. ALL WILL BE DONE FOR THE GOOD OF THE EARTH, FOR THE SAVING OF HUMANKIND. THE PROJECT REQUIRES OF YOU ONLY TRUST.

What is the Project?

WE HAVE WATCHED YOUR WORLD. WE HAVE WATCHED AND WE HAVE DESPAIRED. YOU HAVE GROWN. YOU HAVE BEGUN TO UNDERSTAND THE PLANET WHERE YOU LIVE. YOU HAVE DEVELOPED THE MEANS TO BE STRONG AND TO SUR-VIVE. BUT WITH EVERY STEP FORWARD YOU MOVE NEARER THE ABYSS. WHAT YOU HAVE BEEN GIVEN FOR CREATION, YOU HAVE USED FOR DESTRUCTION. THE WISER YOU HAVE BECOME, THE MORE FOOLISHLY YOU HAVE BEHAVED. HUMAN-ITY IS STUMBLING AND FALLING. ITS LITTLE WORLD IS IN DANGER. IT NEEDS HELP.

AND YOU ARE HERE TO HELP US.

WE WATCHED FROM AFAR. WE DESPAIRED. THERE WERE THOSE WHO BELIEVED THAT EARTH SHOULD BE PERMITTED TO MEET ITS FATE. BUT WE ARE GOOD. WE BELIEVE YOU CAN

BE GOOD TOO. YOU NEED GUIDANCE TO BRING YOU OUT OF THE DARKNESS INTO THE LIGHT. WE HAVE SENT ANGELS TO SAVE YOU.

Angels?

ATTEND, THOMAS. ATTEND AND DO NOT FEAR. WE ARE GOOD. NOW THAT WE ARE HERE, YOU WILL BE SAFE. ANGELS ARE MOVING AMONG YOU. WE ARE GIVING YOU WHAT YOU LACKED, HEALING YOUR WOUNDS BEFORE YOU EVEN KNEW THAT YOU WERE SICK.

The Project.

THE PROJECT NEEDS YOU, YOU ARE AMONG THE CHOSEN. YOU SHALL BE GUIDED. YOU HAVE BEEN STRONG AND INTELLIGENT. NOW YOU ARE TO HELP US. ALL IS GOOD. ALL WILL BE RESOLVED.

ALL IS GOOD. ALL WILL BE RESOLVED.

YOU MUST TRUST US.

TRUST.

TRUST.

TRUST.

18 · ANGELS

I OPENED MY EYES and it took me several seconds to remember where I was. I had sunk down in the chair. The screen was blank in front of me. The air in the screening room seemed cool but, within me, there was a great warmth and sense of peace.

"Welcome back, Thomas."

The hand of Cy Gabriel was on my shoulder. Without thinking, I reached up and held on to it, eyes tightly shut. Then, gradually, I began to come round. I realized where I was, who I was. I released Cy's hand and looked at him.

He sat back in the seat beside me and smiled. A small leather-bound book was open in his lap.

"Did I sleep?" I asked.

"It wasn't exactly sleep."

"So it wasn't a dream."

Cy closed his book and sat forward in his seat. "It wasn't a dream, Thomas."

"What was it then?"

"You're going to have to forget everything you've ever assumed was true or logical." Cy spoke quietly. "You're about to believe the unbelievable."

Normally, I might have been frightened by what I was hearing but it was almost as if I had been slipped some kind of happiness pill. "Try me," I said quietly.

Cy Gabriel looked at the dark screen for a moment, then turned back to me. He seemed to tighten his grip on the book he was holding with both hands, almost as if it was the safety-bar on the roller-coaster that is edging forward at the start of a ride. When he spoke, it was in a quiet, deliberate voice.

"What you have just experienced is the Presence," he said. "The Presence is not a person or a thing or a voice. It is every person, every thing. Every voice you have heard comes from the Presence. It is in every thought. At the very center of your imagination, there is the Presence, day and night, from the moment you were born until the moment you die."

"Like God?" I asked warily. The happiness pill was beginning to wear off.

"No. Not like God at all. Nor like Buddha, Yahweh, Shiva, Allah. The Presence is beyond religion. It is not hope or faith. It is real."

There seemed no sensible reply to this. "Spooky," I said.

"Now, Thomas, I want you to imagine something." Cy hesitated and, for the first time, I realized that he was nervous. "Far away—further away than human mind can comprehend, there is a place like Earth, only different. It is occupied by a people that is similar to mankind but a mankind that has changed and developed. Time and space are no longer its masters, but its servants. It can live for as long as it wants. It has conquered the population problem.

It has discovered happiness. It can travel by thought. It can see beyond what you now understand as the universe into other universes, billions and billions of miles away. And one day—" Cy closed his eyes. "One day, this planet discovers it is not alone. There is life elsewhere, developing in its own strange, slow way. Its people—the people you are imagining—watch from afar."

"But how could they do that if—?"

"They watch, Thomas." For the first time, there was a hint of impatience in Cy's voice. "So we go forward another thousand years, more. And, guess what, the life on that distant planet is developing, but not in the way humankind had hoped. It fights. It kills. Its greed is ever-growing and seems as if it will never be satisfied. What should be done about this? Should the poor, distant, little planet be left to its fate? Should the watchers do nothing to help?"

I frowned, hearing an echo in Cy's words of what the voice behind the screen had been saying to me. "Not if it's good," I said softly.

"Not if it's good." His eyes were unblinking as they stared at me. I had been given the clues. It was for me to make the jump into the unknown.

"The poor, distant, little planet is us, isn't it? This . . . Presence thing has been watching us from out there in the universe."

"Beyond what you think of as the universe."

A chill of fear ran through me. "And now it's here."

"Yes." Cy smiled and I knew that I'd passed some sort of test. "Now we're here."

He took me back to his office where he gave me a glass of water. The midday sun shone through the darkened windows and, sipping slowly at the drink in my hand, I gazed at the field, the hedges, the trees, as if I were seeing them for the first time.

Gently, Cy guided me to the chair in front of his desk. I sat down. He slumped into his own chair and rubbed his eyes.

"There is a planet so far away from here that no human astronomer would ever dream of its existence," he said. "It has no name but it has its own highly advanced form of life. At first, when it discovered the existence of life on Earth, it was pleased. One day, when humanity was ready, it would visit. The two life forces in the universe would unite in friendship. It waited for hundreds of years. But something went wrong, not there but on Earth. Humankind seemed to take a wrong turning in its development. Those on that distant planet realized the life on Earth was so programmed to destructiveness that any contact was out of the question. Humankind would do what it always did when it was afraid. It would make war. Because it was so undeveloped, this would be like a two-year-old child attacking a tiger. It would be destroyed. So they left Earth alone."

Cy gazed out of the window for a moment, then started talking again. "But Earth did not leave itself alone. It used knowledge against itself. It developed the means to destroy itself. The distant power, the planet of the Presence, could not watch and do nothing as another life form snuffed itself out. So it developed the Project. It would join humankind. It would save Earth from within. It would send its own beings to guide humankind away from the path of death and destruction towards good. It would make angels on the surface of the Earth. The angels would work with humankind in a project of salvation."

"You're an angel," I whispered.

Cy nodded slowly.

"And my parents. They come from this distant planet too?"

"They were created here. But they're angels."

I thought of my mother and father for a moment. I saw Mum collecting me from school, Dad watching me as I played football in the park.

"But they're so normal," I said. "So ordinary."

"Angels are normal. They are essentially humans but . . . without the bad bits."

Cy Gabriel gazed at me across the desk, gently smiling. I became aware that my mouth was dry, my hands were clasped around the empty glass in my hand.

"I think I'd like to wake up now, please," I said faintly.

Leaning forward, Cy turned the monitor on his desk towards me. The screen, which had been full of numbers became a pixelated haze. When it cleared, I was staring at the face of a young, blonde woman.

"She's one of our people downstairs," said Cy. "As she works on the screen, I can watch her—or anyone else down there."

"Kind of like spying." My voice sounded more hostile than I had intended.

Cy smiled patiently. "We tend not to think like that," he said. "Her name's Hazel. She's working here for a while. She'll be leaving us within a few weeks."

"Yeah?"

"She's an angel."

"Yeah, she's not bad, I supp—" I blushed, realizing my mistake. "Oh, you mean, she's not from here."

"How old would you say she was, Thomas?"

"Twenty-five? Maybe thirty."

"She was born—she was made—two weeks ago."

I think I swore at that point. It seemed like the only logical reaction. "You don't expect me to believe all this," I said weakly.

He leaned forward and touched the screen. The blonde

woman's eyes refocused and she smiled. "Hi, Cy," she said as normal as you'd like.

"Hi, Hazel. Would you mind coming up for a moment? There's someone I'd like you to meet."

"Sure."

As the woman left her desk, the screen turned to the lists of numbers that had been there before.

I must have been looking kind of out of it because Cy said, "I realize this is a lot to take in, Thomas, but you'll get tuned in soon. Right now you're thinking that the Project is unnatural but it's not. It's just a different kind of nature."

Why me? That was the question which was suddenly the one I wanted to ask, which filled my entire being. Why? Me?

There was a knock on the office door and, without waiting for a reply, the blonde woman—the angel—who had been on Cy's screen a moment ago, entered the room.

"Hazel, this is Thomas Wisdom, a good friend of mine. Thomas, my colleague Hazel Webb."

The woman stepped forward. "Hi, Thomas," she said. Her hand when she shook mine was cool and smooth, but it was not the hand of a robot.

"Hi."

"Thomas knows about the Project," said Cy.

"Ah." Hazel Webb raised her eyebrows in that quick, clever way girls have of expressing mild surprise.

Hazel sat down and crossed her legs. "I'm twenty-six," she said. "I've been here a short time and have recently been accepted for a post in a head-hunting employment agency, which I shall be taking up next month." She smiled like someone at a job interview. Although she was neat and could talk easily and without hesitation, there was, to be honest, nothing weird about her. She was what they call the "girl next door" type.

Cy crossed his arms and frowned jokily. "And what about the personal stuff?"

To my surprise, Hazel seemed embarrassed. "I'm going out with a certain person," she said, her eyes on Cy. "We're engaged and hope to be married next year."

A thought occurred to me. "Is he—? I mean, where did you meet him?"

Hazel glanced at me and I sensed that I had gone too far. Angels had feelings too, it turned out.

"He's a colleague," she said coolly.

For a moment there was silence in the office. Then Cy leaned forward and said, in a mock confidential voice. "Why don't you show him your derm, Hazel?"

Derm? Derm? It seemed rude to ask what exactly he was talking about.

"You really want to see my derm?" Hazel asked, turning in her chair.

Now it was my turn to blush.

"Not . . . necessarily," I said.

She pulled her blouse back slightly. On her collar-bone was a dark, red patch of skin, like a small birthmark.

I looked at it politely and said, "Oh yeah" as if I really understood what this was all about.

"That little mark is more important to Hazel than her heart," said Cy. "It's a circuit that provides her with all the information and energy she needs from day to day. We all have one." He drew back the left sleeve of his jacket. There, showing through the silver hairs on his tanned forearm, was the red, circular mark I had noticed at dinner in Santa Barbara. It was identical to Hazel's.

"Give me your hand," he said, stretching his arm out to me.

Nervously, I reached out my hand. Like a policeman

taking a fingerprint, he took the index finger and placed it firmly on his arm.

"Sheesh!" I jumped back, startled. The flesh all around the derm was normal and warm but the spot itself radiated ice-cold.

They both laughed.

Cy smiled, first at Hazel, then at me. "We are built like human beings—except in that one tiny area."

"You've got that re-charging thing," I said. "You're like a mobile phone disguised as a human."

Cy held up two hands, less amused now. "Hey, easy," he said. "I didn't bring you here to get insulted."

I was about to tell him that I wanted to go home. Then I realized that home was no longer home. My mind was filled with a million questions but right now one mattered more than all the rest put together.

"So, why did you tell me all this?" I asked.

Cy gazed at me across the desk, and sighed.

"Go on then," I said. "Why me? Why am I here?"

He turned to Hazel with a boss-like smile. "Thanks, Hazel," he said. "Could you excuse us?"

The blonde angel stood up. "Good luck, Thomas," she said. Then she left, closing the door behind her.

"You want me to show you around the place before we grab some lunch?" Cy asked.

"Sure," I said. "When you've answered my question."

"You're tougher than you look, Thomas Wisdom," he said with a smile that somehow didn't convey much humor.

I sat back in my chair and folded my arms.

"Why me?"

The smile seemed to freeze on his face. He gazed at me unblinkingly for a moment or two.

"I'd like you to talk to your mom and dad about that.

Right now, let's just say that angels can't complete the Project alone. We need help from the next generation."

"Does Amy know about this?" I asked eventually.

"Sure."

"When did you tell her?"

Cy hesitated. "She didn't need to be told."

It took a second or two for me to understand what he was telling me. "You mean . . . she's an angel too?"

"Yup. And Luke."

I shook my head. "I don't believe this," I muttered. "I'm the only person in our house who was actually born on Earth in the normal way. Me and Dougal."

Cy winced and shook his head.

Now I'd heard it all. "You're not telling me that Dougal's an angel?"

"He's one of our better models."

"I always wondered why he was a bit crazy."

Cy remained straight-faced.

"Angels aren't crazy, Thomas," he said. "We are just minor variations on the standard human and animal model who happen to have arrived here by a different route."

"I should say." Somehow the idea of angel animals was more difficult to take on board than anything else. "So all over the world there are these pets who have been manu-factured by aliens—angel dogs, angel cats, angel hamsters, angel gerbils."

Cy frowned. "Not cats, as it happens," he murmured. "Dogs were a piece of cake to replicate but we couldn't do the cat thing. We're still working on that."

"Which is why cats always run away from my parents."

"Guess so." Cy seemed slightly irritated by the direction the conversation had taken. He glanced at his watch and stood up. "Let's go get some lunch," he said. "Then I'll show you around."

I followed him out of the office. We took the lift down to the first floor where we walked again past the rows of computers.

I looked more closely at their operators now. Most of them seemed to be in their twenties or thirties. The majority had light hair. Apart from that, there was nothing spooky or unusual about them. They worked. They answered telephones. They chatted. Some of them glanced up as we walked past.

Cy pushed through some swing doors ahead of me. We were in a light, high-ceilinged room. To our right, food was being served to a queue of angels with trays.

"Canteen," I said stupidly.

"Canteen." Cy handed me a tray. "Food. Drink. Lunch."

"I can't get used to how normal everything is."

As we queued, Cy lowered his voice. "You've got to shake off these prejudices of yours, Thomas," he said. "We don't just look the same as you. We feel the same as you. Heat, cold, fear, anger—" He hesitated. "Love."

I thought of my family of angels with their cute little angel dog.

As if he could read my mind, Cy said, "Mark and Mary love you like any parents would do—maybe more. It's not every son who gets to help with the Project."

A woman in a white coat was serving up shepherd's pie. She smiled at me confidentially as she served me as if she, like everyone else, knew why I was here. I realized that I had been so startled by the news Cy had given me about my family that I had forgotten to press him on where exactly I fitted into this famous Project of theirs.

"What help?" I asked when we had taken a table by the window. "What do you need me for?"

Cy shrugged. "Nothing too difficult," he said. "When you leave school, we'd like you to work in a certain area we'll tell you about later. You'll be a success at it—we'll make sure about that. Then you'll just go on and live your life in the way you see fit."

"Except I have to do the job you tell me to."

"We can discuss your career when the moment comes," Cy said smoothly. "I don't anticipate that we'll disagree."

"I dunno." I shook my head. "I was always kind of keen on the idea of making up my own mind about my life."

"You will. We'll just be there to offer advice."

"Angels to watch over me." As I said these words, half-joking, I experienced an odd sense of pride that I had been selected to play my part in the Project.

"We understand your concern about personal freedom. You probably hadn't figured on saving the world as a career option."

"Not exactly."

Cy smiled. "That's what we like about you. The world-savers are usually the dangerous ones."

So we chatted on. If you had caught sight of us through that big plate-glass window, you might have mistaken me for a guy telling his uncle what he had done on his holidays. In fact, we were talking about the Project, the Presence, and how angels were going to save humanity from itself.

But the events of that morning were beginning to have an effect on me. As soon as I finished my meal, I felt weary to my bones.

We stopped talking. Cy led me back to his car. Within minutes of his reaching the motorway, my head had slumped against the window and I was fast asleep.

19 · REBORN

NOW, WHEN I READ BACK over what I have written, I am amazed. A man, a virtual stranger, had taken me to an office. He had put me in front of a screen where I had had a sort of dream-conversation with a God-like voice in my head. The stranger had told me that my parents, my sister, and even my damn family dog were in fact from another planet. Oh yeah, and I had been chosen to help them all save the world from destruction.

I had believed it all because I knew that it was true.

Yet, rather than feeling terror and panic, a sort of mellowness crept over me. I was chosen. Everything in my life had an explanation. There was a plan and I was part of it. The mess and anger and confusion of the past were gone. I felt reborn.

Home was home once more. When Cy Gabriel brought me back that afternoon, I walked sleepily up the garden path. The door opened ahead of me. As if they had been waiting for me all day, Mum and Dad stood in the hall, with Amy just behind them and Dougal, wagging his stump of a tail, at her ankles. Mum opened her arms and I leaned against her for a few seconds, feeling her warmth against me.

"Well done, darling," she whispered through my hair.

I was no longer the outsider in the family. I belonged. I was loved.

Behind me, Cy said something about the day having gone perfectly. He had a meeting in town, he said. He laid a hand on my shoulder, squeezed slightly and told me he'd see me again soon. Still in my mother's arms, I thanked him and said goodbye. The front door closed.

We went to the sitting-room. On the table in front of the sofa, there was a silver bucket containing a bottle of champagne in it and four glasses. Dad unwrapped the gold foil, popped the cork, poured frothing champagne into each glass. Still standing, we raised our glasses. For a moment, I thought we would be toasting the Project or there would be some sort of extraterrestrial greeting but they all smiled and said after one another, all loving and solemn.

"To Thomas."

"To Thomas."

"To Thomas."

"Yeah, right," I said, embarrassed but pleased. "To me."

So it went on. The family together, the family repaired. For that evening and all the next day, Mum, Dad, Amy, and me talked and laughed about the adventure that was our lives.

They told me about being an angel.

"D'you feel different?" I asked, later that evening.

"Not at all," said my mother. "The danger is that you forget that you're not quite like other humans."

"Dare I ask in what way?"

"Configurations," said Amy, rolling her eyes, and all three of them laughed as if at some great private joke.

"What exactly are configurations?" I asked.

"We each have a derm." My father touched his shoulder, as if to reassure himself that his derm was still in place. "If possible, the information in the derm needs to be configured once a day. All we need is the presence of water and what we call a derm-node that receives messages from a transmitter. It's like a little metal plaque."

I remembered Gip's discovery on the wall of the house all those weeks ago. "The loo," I said. "You configure in the loo."

My mum smiled. "It only takes a few seconds."

"You know that new style of public toilet that has been appearing over the last few years?" My sister seemed particularly amused by this subject. "They were made for angels. Now we can configure anywhere we want."

"But what I don't get is why you don't just save the Earth yourselves? Why do you need the help of human beings? Where do I fit into all this?"

For the first time, I sensed awkwardness in my little family. After a few moments, Dad said, "It is important that humankind is involved in its own salvation."

"Otherwise, it could happen all over again," said my mother.

"Yeah?" There was more. I knew there was more. I could see it in their eyes.

It was Amy who cracked. "Mum? Dad?" she said. "That's not exactly the whole story, is it?"

My parents concentrated on eating their food. "Let's change the subject," Dad said eventually.

"So I'm part of the team except I'm not meant to know

what's really going on," I said. "That's just great."

"It's embarrassing," said my mother quietly. "It's not the sort of thing one should talk about."

I was beginning to get an uncomfortable idea of what the problem was when Amy turned to me with a sisterly smile. "Angels can't reproduce," she said.

"Ah."

My parents stared at the floor. "In every sense, we are human," Dad said eventually. "We feel emotion, we love, we hate, we laugh, we are vulnerable. But we don't . . . have babies. That is the one human function which is beyond our power."

"So you adopt," I whispered.

My mother covered my hand with hers and squeezed it tightly. "We adopt," she said.

I was not upset. I was calm. Through all this—this conversation and many more—I was aware of a serene sense of peace within me which I had never experienced before.

Nothing could hurt me. I was part of the Project.

Twice, as I talked to my family, the telephone rang, once in the morning and once in the evening. It was Gip Sanchez. He seemed kind of anxious about me.

A chill entered my heart. I no longer wished to speak to him. It was almost as if, overnight, he had become my enemy. I answered his questions briefly and coldly. I told him I would see him some time. No, he shouldn't call me. I would call him.

Why did I feel like this? Why was I so happy and warm within my family of angels? What had Gip done to set himself outside the walls I had built around myself?

I understood none of that then.

I do now.

There are some people who find it difficult to take a

hint. It's not that they don't want to be helpful or fit in with other people so much as a sort of deafness. It's as if they have been born without the gene that helps one human being understand another. The world hints and prods and nudges at them but they hear and feel nothing.

Rendle was like that—he never understood what was really going on in class until it was too late—and so was Luke the Surfer-Boy, although that might have been just good old-fashioned thickness. But nobody—that is, nobody—was better at hint-deafness than Gip Sanchez.

People laughed at him, bullied him, made jokes about his spots or his hair or his leg or his mum. A few even pitied him. It was all the same to Gip. It was not that he ignored them—he had never really seen them in the first place. Somewhere along the line, maybe early in his strange, rackety life, he had built this protective shell around him.

Now, for the first time in our friendship, I wished that just occasionally Gip could take a hint.

On my first morning alone since discovering the truth about my family, he telephoned in the middle of the morning.

"Yo," he said. "How you been?"

"Hello, Gip."

"We've really got to meet today. There are things going down, Colin-wise."

"Yeah?" I put as much lack of interest into the one word as I could manage. The truth was, ever since my day with Cy, I had been feeling woozy and tired, as if I was recovering from flu or something. "You know, Gip, I'm not feeling too clever right now. I fancy a day vegging out."

"Fine. I'll swing by in about half an hour then."

"Um, no."

"OK. So meet me at the flat."

I gave it a couple of seconds' thought before deciding that, right then, seeing Gip in his unofficial hangout would be preferable to him paying a visit to me in my house. Grumpily, I agreed to meet him at the squat in a couple of hours.

So I traveled across town—bus, train, walk. As I watched the townscape, it was as if I was seeing the world as it really was for the first time. The dead-eyed people on the bus, the mobile-phone twitchies, talking as they walked as if their lives depended on it, the traffic, the grimy pavements, the underground users descending into burrows beneath the city like zombie rabbits, the dossers slumped on pavements and platforms, hands out for money, their watching eyes expressing a flicker of hope before returning to despair as we pass. Spare change, mate? Spare change? Got any spare change, please?

And I knew that Cy was right. Humankind had lost the plot. The Project was good. They needed the help of the Presence. We needed it. I needed it.

When I reached the squat, Gip greeted me at the door.

"So?" he said as we climbed the stairs. "How was your day with good old Cy?"

"Fine," I muttered.

Gip glanced back at me.

"Interesting," I added.

"And?"

"That food development business is . . . kind of cool."

He waited until we reached the room on the top floor before speaking again and when he did it was with unusual seriousness. "Don't give me all this," he said suddenly. "Three days ago, we were together on this whole family, adoption thing. Now you're coming on like nothing happened. You even look different."

I heard the words in my head— "I am different"—but something stopped me from speaking them. "I'm kind of zonked."

To my surprise, Gip put a hand to my forehead, just like a mum. "Bull," he said briskly. "There's something going on and you're holding back on me."

"It's my life. For you, it may be just an adventure but this is my life, my family, my home." I wandered over to the window and was sitting on the floor, looking at the motorway when something occurred to me. "How did you know where I was?" I asked.

"Mmm?" Gip acted casual but I wasn't taken in.

"I never told you I was with Cy Gabriel but you asked me how my day with him went."

"Oh that. I was kind of worried about you so I called to see how you were. Your mum told me about your little outing."

For a moment, we stared at one another. Somehow the idea of Gip Sanchez as Mr. Concerned didn't quite cut it for me. "You mentioned Rendle," I said coldly.

"He started calling me. He seemed worried about you."

"Yeah yeah. The Beast with the heart."

"He's told the Head."

I stared at him for a moment. "You're kidding."

Gip shook his head. "He said that he had become more and more concerned. Because of him, you had got hold of this bit of life-shattering news about your life. He had decided he couldn't just leave it there. So he rang Daisy."

Daisy Dover, the head teacher, was a big favorite among the parents and the local councilors—they said that he had "turned the school around," whatever that meant—but, to me, he seemed to have as much warmth and sympathy as a dead fish on a slab. I hated the idea of him taking possession of my big news and adding it to the little folder under my name in his office.

"That's why I needed to see you." Gip spoke quietly. "I told him he could have talked to me but he started giving me this load of old rubbish about teachers' responsibilities—how, if anything should happen, it could destroy his career."

"Big tragedy that would be," I murmured. Although I understood that none of it was entirely Gip's fault, I didn't like the idea of him chatting away to the Beast about me and my life. I had thought we were in this together. "So what did Dover say?"

"He thanked Colin and said he would have to consider what to do."

"He'll call my parents."

"Maybe. He might just have a cozy chat with you next term."

I laughed briefly. Daisy Dover, a pale, neat man in his late thirties, was not exactly famous for his charm and sympathetic manner.

Gip wasn't smiling. "I've called Colin a few times since then. There's no answer."

"Maybe he went on holiday."

Gip shook his head and his long hair swayed like a dark curtain disturbed by the wind. "Colin doesn't do holidays."

"His mother probably got sick," I said, thinking more about how he betrayed me than any little problem he might now be having. "I wouldn't sweat about it, if I were you."

"I'm not sweating," said Gip quietly. "But I'm calling him tonight. If there's no reply, I'm going round there tomorrow."

"Suit yourself."

Gip gave me that long, wordless stare that I knew so well. I held out for about five seconds.

"All right. I'll come along with you."

"Thanks, Tom. You're all heart."

There was a chill between us that was new. It made me sad but there was nothing I could do about it.

I was in for another surprise that night. When I got home, Mum and Dad greeted me at the door and led me upstairs to my room. On my bed was a large cardboard box. I opened the top and saw what was inside.

"A computer! I don't believe this." I looked at the manual. Although I'm not exactly an expert on computers, I knew my parents well enough to know that it would be a good one.

I turned back to them. "But why?"

"You've had a tough time recently, old boy," said my father. "It was a thank-you from us."

I walked over and hugged my mother. Dad put his hand on my shoulder. We stood there for a moment, saying nothing, just holding on to each other.

"Thanks, Dad. Thanks, Mum," I said at last.

And I knew that those words, "Mum, Dad," were what they wanted to hear above all else.

20 · ACCIDENT

WHEN GIP TURNED UP on my doorstep the next morning, I told him about the computer. He has always been something of a techno-freak and I expected him at least to want to know stuff about its memory, make, and capacity.

But he gave me an odd look. "Yeah, the old computer," he said almost shiftily. "That figures."

I asked him what he meant, told him that my parents didn't need to buy themselves back into my favor, but he turned away and started walking down the garden path. "We'll talk about that later," he called back over his shoulder. "You coming?"

That was the way it was with Gip. Most of the time, he's Mr. Cruise Control, taking everything in his stride, but then, suddenly and without warning, he changes. The eyes narrow, the smile goes, and so do the words. He becomes cold and determined and focused on the target of the moment.

I walked beside him in silence.

We sat on the bus like an old married couple who had just had a row. We took the road to the Beast's house as grimly as gunslingers at high noon. By the time he rang the front doorbell, I had more or less decided that maybe Gip Sanchez was not my friend anymore.

A stranger opened the door—a plump, middle-aged woman with gray-blonde hair. She was wearing the blue uniform of a nurse.

"Is Mr. Rendle in, please?" Gip asked.

"Mr. Rendle?" The woman seemed strangely startled. "No, he's . . . he's not here."

"When will he be back?"

An uneasy look—part concerned, part irritated—crossed the woman's face. "Are you friends of his?" she asked.

"We go to his school," said Gip. "He teaches us math."

The woman extended her hand. "I'm Joan," she said. "I've been looking after Mrs. Rendle."

Something was going on here. As if she had suddenly reached a decision, the woman called Joan stepped back into the hall. "Come in, boys," she said.

Closing the door behind us, she turned and said, "There's been a bit of an accident."

"What kind of accident?" Gip's question was abrupt, almost rude.

"A motor accident," said Joan. "I'm afraid I have very sad news, boys. Colin Rendle has, very tragically, been involved in a fatal crash."

Gip shook his head. "But he doesn't drive."

That word "fatal" told me all I needed to know. "He's dead, isn't he?"

The woman lowered her head and nodded slowly. "He

stepped off a pavement while out for a walk last Monday. A car came out of nowhere." She spoke quietly, almost in a whisper. "He was gone by the time the ambulance arrived."

Gip and I stood there stupidly in silence for several seconds. "I don't believe it," I murmured. "He can't be dead."

"I'm very, very sorry." Joan spoke gently. "I never met the gentleman personally but I believe he was a very special man. I was called in by the council because our records showed there was a Mrs. Rendle."

Briefly, I thought that another shock was on the way, that suddenly a Mrs. Beast was about to be revealed. Then I remembered the old lady who was Rendle's mother. "How's she taking it?" I asked.

"She's confused, poor love."

"Maybe we should just say hello." I glanced across at Gip.

He said nothing but stared into Joan's face, his dark eyes sparkling against his deathly pale complexion. He seemed to be having trouble breathing.

"Gip?" I said.

Slowly he turned towards me. "They killed him." He shook his head. "How could they do that? They killed him. He had done nothing."

I laid a hand on his shoulder but he shrugged it off.

Joan seemed uneasy at the way Gip was reacting. "I'm sorry, I shouldn't have told you," she said. "I had no idea you were so . . . close. Maybe you should go home to your—"

"We'll see Mrs. Rendle," Gip interrupted, his voice hard now. He walked past her towards the sitting-room.

"She's under sedation." The nurse followed him. "She's not quite aware of what's happened."

When I entered the sitting-room, Gip was crouched in

front of the old woman. The room was darker than when we had last been here and Mrs. Rendle seemed to have shrunk over the past few days. She was just a gray wisp of a thing.

"All right, Mrs. Rendle?" Gip laid a hand on hers. "We just called by to see how you were doing."

"Hello, boys." The old woman's voice sounded like rustling leaves. "Have you been with that naughty Colin?"

"Er, no, we haven't," said Gip.

"I don't know." She shook her head slightly and clicked her teeth. "He said he had to see the headmaster but he's been ages now. Always late, that boy."

There seemed nothing that we could say.

"Matron's been looking for him." Slowly and with great effort, she looked up at Joan. "Haven't you, Matron?"

"I have, Mrs. Rendle." Joan smiled sadly.

Mrs. Rendle closed her eyes and, for a moment, I thought she had gone to sleep. But when she opened them, she was looking at me. "Are you in the same class as Colin?"

"Er, no," I said quickly. "We're in a different year."

"He's quite bright, you know." She sighed wearily. "More brains than sense, though. He was frightened of that head-master."

I noticed that Gip was trembling now. It occurred to me that he might say something that would upset the old woman.

"We'd better not stay too long," I muttered.

"Thanks for calling by, boys." Mrs. Rendle spoke almost cheerfully. "If you see Colin, tell him to hurry back." She shook her head sadly. "You know, he didn't even take his lunch with him. I made him sandwiches. Ham, it was, his favorite. Or was it egg?"

Joan stepped forward. She leaned over Mrs. Rendle, and

pulled the blanket up around the old woman's tiny wrinkled neck. For just the briefest moment, I saw something that made me draw in my breath in a sudden gasp.

Gip stood up slowly and walked past me to the door.

"Thank you for your visit, boys." Joan spoke, her back to us. "Could you let yourselves out?"

We nodded and said goodbye to Mrs. Rendle.

"He's such a naughty boy," she said, more to herself than to us.

We left, walking slowly down the street. After a few yards, we came to a low wall. Without a word, Gip dropped on to it and buried his face in his hands. He rocked backwards and forwards, making a low, rhythmic moan like some sort of animal in pain. I sat beside him, not knowing quite what to say. After a few seconds, I realized that the sound he was making were words, repeated again and again.

"It was me, it was me, it was me, it was me . . ."

"Come on, Gip," I said. "You know how absent-minded he was. It wasn't anything to do with the business of the file—it was an accident."

He looked up sharply, his eyes burning into mine with what almost seemed like hatred. "You know nothing," he said. "Nothing about anything."

I retreated into myself. Turning my back on him, I gazed at the house where Rendle had once lived.

I did know something and it filled my heart with dread and confusion.

Before me, in my mind's eye, I saw the figure of the nurse, Joan, as she crouched over Mrs. Rendle. She had extended an arm, lifting the blanket. At that moment, it was as clear as daylight. There could be no mistaking it. Where her neck joined her shoulder was a dark, circular mark.

It might have been a mole. It could have been a

birthmark. But I knew, with a cold, frightening certainty, that it was neither.

It was a derm.

We walked. We passed the bus stop. We reached the main road, not saying a word to one another.

Right now, silence suited me just fine. The nurse looking after Mrs. Rendle was an angel. I tried, again and again, to find an innocent, logical reason for it.

Angels were everywhere. What could be more natural than for one to be helping an old lady in her hour of need? Angels were here to help humanity. Joan seemed a kind, normal person. There was no need to be afraid. Angels were good. The idea that Rendle might be a victim of them was crazy. Why should they be worried about some math teacher? It was impossible. No, angels were good.

We walked until we reached my front gate. Gip stood there, hands in pockets, staring at the pavement, like someone being scolded by a voice in his head.

"Tomorrow?" I said.

"Yeah." Gip nodded, turned and limped off down the road.

My parents were back early from work. Hearing their voices in low discussion in the sitting-room, I went upstairs to my room and sat in front of the computer for a while, playing a game.

Mysteriously, it calmed me down. The terrible possibility that what Cy Gabriel had called the Project might involve killing and harming people was smoothed away by the sharp rhythms of the game. After a minute or two, I relaxed. Accidents happened. I could see that now. Gip would see it too in a couple of days' time. There was no need even to tell him about the Project or the Presence or Cy or my parents. Everything was good. Everything was going to be all right.

After some time, as I played, I felt the hand of my mother on my shoulder. She kissed the crown of my head.

"How's the computer?" she asked softly.

"It's good," I said.

"The games on it are OK?"

"They're fine." I zapped a guy with a machine-gun who was guarding the entrance to a cave. "Die, sucker," I muttered.

My mother sighed. "They're so violent, these games," she said.

"The bad guys get it, don't they?" I said, taking out a parachute descending on the right-hand side of the screen. "That's just the way it is."

I felt the hand on my shoulder tighten slightly and I sensed that she was about to say something, but then thought better of it. "Supper's in ten minutes," she said.

I played on, my mind calm and easy like that of a champion poker player.

21 · EVIL

THAT NIGHT I SLEPT HEAVILY but it was not a
dreamless sleep. I awoke the next morning,
knowing that during the night a message of
profound importance had reached me. It
was a warning, simple and impossible to
ignore.

SANCHEZ IS EVIL. HE SEEMS GOOD BUT
HE WILL DO YOU HARM. YOU MUST EXCLUDE
HIM FROM YOUR LIFE.

I lay in bed. My limbs were heavy, my
mind sluggish and numb. At some point, I
was aware that the front doorbell was ringing. Dougal barked downstairs. I got up
from my bed and stood on the landing. I
saw a shape through the glass of the front
door, heard someone call my name. It was
Gip.

That day, I needed to be alone. I went
back to bed.

It was one of those days when even
thinking seems too much like hard work.
I lay on the bed. I dozed. I played the

computer. Later that morning, Dougal scratched at the door. When I let him in, he whined and looked up at me as if to remind me that even angel-dogs have needs.

I slobbed into some clothes and out of the house, following Dougal in the direction of the park. Somewhere at the back of my mind was the niggling memory of yesterday's events—of hearing about Rendle's death, of the nurse and her derm—but, for reasons I was unable to understand, none of that seemed to touch my life anymore.

I was a boy walking his dog in the park. All would be good. All would be resolved.

I stood under a cherry tree and watched Dougal. Like me, he has his lazy days but right now he ranged about the place on his own little adventure, pretending to himself that he was a wild beast, a stranger to domestic life.

Then, beyond him, I saw a familiar figure enter the park through its big iron gate and limp determinedly towards me. Dougal was too far away for me to be able to escape.

"I've got news," Gip called out as he approached me. "We need to talk."

I looked away. "I'm not in the mood," I murmured.

Gip looked into my eyes. "You've been on that computer, haven't you?"

"How did you know that?"

"No big deal, it's what computers do to you." He spoke hurriedly, like someone who had more important things to discuss. "Rendle's death wasn't an accident," he said. "He was taken out by the Firm because he knew too much."

"This isn't a movie, Gip," I said wearily. "A klutzy teacher with stuff on his mind stepped into the road in front of a speeding car. It happens."

Gip reached into his back pocket and took out some papers. He passed me the top sheet. "Take a look at who was driving that speeding car."

It was a photocopy from a local paper. *Teacher Dies In Police Car Tragedy,* read the headline. "The cops," said Gip with a grim little smile. "He was killed by the cops."

I scanned the news-story quickly. Rendle had been hit while crossing the main road on his way to the shops one afternoon. A police car, answering an emergency call, had turned the corner at high speed and had no chance of avoiding him. There was to be "a full police enquiry".

I handed the photocopy back. "Those guys drive too fast," I said. "You read about this kind of thing all the time."

"With no siren? Down a busy street?"

I shrugged. "So why would the CIA want to murder a math teacher?" I asked.

Gip handed me the other two sheets of paper. "I checked him on the Net," he said. "It turns out that Colin was a bit more than your average teacher."

I looked at the photocopies. The first sheet, which seemed to be some kind of nerdy student essay, was headed Digital Modifications to the Rendle Circuit Inducer. For all I could understand, every word might have been in a foreign language.

"Now check out the other one," said Gip.

This was a shorter report, which seemed to have been taken from some kind of on-line science magazine.

Avionics community mourns
"black box" pioneer
Dr. Colin Rendle, whose work on circuit induction played a crucial part in the development of the modern "black box" flight recorder, has been killed in a motor accident in London. During his seven years at Marconi Instruments during the 1980s, Rendle pioneered the titration caliber system, a version of which is used in many passenger aircraft to this day. Rendle retired from

scientific research in 1991 following a spell of ill-health.
At the time of his death, he was a teacher of mathemat-
ics in a London Secondary School.

"So the rumors were true." I passed the photocopies back to Gip. "Old Rendle was a famous scientist."

"Maybe he knew something," said Gip. "He got out of research because he discovered that his work was being used for weapon guidance systems, OK? They've been tracking him ever since." Gip glanced towards the gate, as if expecting to see a squad of CIA hitmen, their jackets bulging with weaponry, entering the park.

"You've lost it," I said. "You've gone paranoiac on me again." I passed him back the papers.

Exhausted by his burst of exercise, Dougal had returned and sat at my feet with an expression suggesting that he had had enough of the wild prairies of the park and wanted to go home. "I've got to get back," I said and started walking away.

"Another thing," Gip called after me. "I put in a call to Daisy Dover."

I stopped. "What's it got to do with him?"

"Colin might have told him something. The Head was probably one of the last people he spoke to."

"So what did old Daisy have to say?"

Gip walked up to me slowly. "Tragic accident, talented teacher cut down in his prime, blah blah blah. I told him I knew that Colin had rung him about your adoption thing."

"My adoption thing. Thanks, Gip."

"He seemed to know all about it. He asked how you were taking it. I said you were kind of freaked. We chatted. Then he said, 'Goodbye, Gary,' and hung up."

"I told you he wouldn't help you."

"But he did." Gip smiled. "While we were talking about your adoption, he happened to tell me where your real mother comes from."

I stared at him for moment, not believing what I had just heard.

"It's a place called Cromer, in Norfolk," he said. "Fancy a little trip?"

I called Dougal but he refused to follow. Wearily, I turned and picked him up.

Gip shook his head. "Your dog, man. It's a total nutter."

I gave an angry little laugh. "That's good coming from you." With as much dignity as someone carrying a fat little dog in his arms can manage, I walked away.

"I could get us a lift up there," Gip called after me.

I made my way back home, wondering why, suddenly, I was so wary of Gip and his plans. Part of me, the old Thomas Wisdom, wanted to run down the street, to tell him about my parents, Cy Gabriel, the Project, the Presence, the derm on the nurse's neck, but the new, more powerful me was gripped by the certainty that confiding in Gip would be a terrible mistake.

I was part of a new and greater team.

When I returned to the house, I found Amy in the sitting-room watching TV. I sat down beside her, my mind still teeming with thoughts of my conversation with Gip.

"How's the old Project going these days?" I asked as casually as I could manage.

"Fine."

"Any hot news from the Presence?"

"It's not a joke, Thomas. There has been nothing more serious than this in the history of humankind."

We watched the TV in silence. Some sad game show was

on. As the latest member of the audience was brought on stage to giggle and gasp and blush as they competed for a holiday somewhere or other, it occurred to me that, for all humankind's faults, it was at least human.

I laughed loudly at some pathetic joke the show's host had made. My sister looked at me, surprised.

"What's the matter? Don't they do jokes where you come from?" I asked. "You'd think they would make humor part of the Project."

Amy turned to me. "You just don't get it, do you?" she said. "Mum and Dad and me have the same sort of emotions as you have. We feel what you feel."

"So why don't you want to talk about it?"

Amy returned to the screen. "Doesn't matter," she murmured.

Every fiber of my being seemed to be telling me to leave it there. All is good, all will be resolved. But the person I had once been could not be ignored. I thought of Rendle, of the nurse. If the Project was looking after Rendle's mother, who was to say the Project had not killed him? And, if angels could remove an innocent math teacher, who else was in danger? "What happens if something goes wrong?" I asked Amy.

"Wrong?"

"Yeah. Say someone found out about the Project and didn't fancy being saved."

Amy sighed a weary, big-sister sigh. "Won't happen," she said. "We're not stupid. It's all been worked out."

"But if it did. What would happen if a person found some kind of secret file, say, and put the Project in danger?"

"You're out of your depth, Tom." Amy looked at me and I noticed that blotches of color had appeared on her cheekbones, like when I had asked her about a boyfriend when she was younger. "Leave it, OK?"

I sat back. "I guess you'd just nix the guy, right?"

"Nix." Laughing unconvincingly, Amy shook her head. "You know, you can be just so childish sometimes."

"Sorry," I shrugged. "I'm only human. Unlike some people round here."

Amy took a deep breath as if to keep herself in check. "The Project comes first," she said quietly. She turned to look at me, and I could have sworn that there was warning, even threat in her eyes. "Just remember that. The Project comes first."

I sat back and watched the TV. Her answer had told me all I needed to know.

After supper that night, I called Gip.

"That stuff about my real mother," I said. "Were you serious about helping me find her?"

Gip laughed, a hard, unfriendly sound. "Good old Tom," he said. "I knew you'd come around."

"I'm just asking."

"We can get up to Norfolk tomorrow if you like."

"Gip, I'm not sure. Anyway, I haven't got any money."

"Don't worry about money. 8:30? After your parents have gone to work?"

"Can I think about it?"

"Nope. 8:30, it is. We're off to Cromer."

"My real mum."

"Yeah. Tom's going home. It's time."

22 · MIRACULO

WHEN GIP HAD A PROJECT, there was no shifting him. The next morning, at 8:30 precisely, he was there on my doorstep. I pleaded that I was feeling ill but he told me that he had paid his friend Manny to take us up to Norfolk. By the time he had led me down the street to where there sat a tall, black, dreadlocked guy, eyes closed and apparently asleep, in the driver's seat of his bright red, heavily dented Golf, there was no going back.

I climbed in the back. A few grunted introductions were made. At some point, Manny revealed that, since he had bought his car, he had been stopped by the police seventeen times. He had shaken his head as if he still couldn't believe that such a thing could happen. "It's racism, man," he muttered.

Right now, as we took the motorway out of London, I was praying for that eighteenth time. Manny's car seemed to have a

powerful engine but no exhaust so that, as we barreled up
the fast lane of a dual carriageway, we made a noise like an
angry chainsaw accompanied by the thump of the stereo. I
sat slumped gloomily in the back, feeling like a kidnap victim and wishing I had stayed in bed.

As we headed east, I gazed out of the window at the
parched gold-yellow stubble fields and wondered how all
this was happening to me. Where had Gip found the money
to pay Manny? How did these two know each other? What
were we going to do once we reached this Cromer place? I
felt guilty about my parents, about Cy. Apart from the small
matter of not telling me that I had been adopted, they had
been fair and open with me. Now, in return, I was on some
crazy hunt for my real mother. I hadn't even left them a
note.

It took us near on three hours to reach Cromer, which
turned out to be an old-fashioned seaside town full of fair-
grounds, ice cream vans and families wandering about in a
bored, happy, holiday kind of way. Manny found a car park
overlooking a pebbly beach and switched off the engine.
For a few moments, we sat there, our ears ringing from the
effects of rap and chainsaw.

"What a dump," Gip said eventually.

"Eh?" Manny looked across at him, surprised. "This is
great, here." He stepped out of the car, stretched his long
arms skyward and for the first time I realized just how tall
and broad-shouldered he was. As he gazed towards the
beach, the breeze catching his long hair, he looked like a
giant of the deep who had just emerged from the waves to
claim his kingdom. "Sea air," he said. "Just the ticket, man."

Gip and I got out of the car. "Manny used to work for
some debt collection agency," he said. "He knows how to
track people down, get them to talk."

"What, you were like a sort of private detective?" I asked.

"Yeah." Manny looked out to sea and seemed almost embarrassed. "Find the loser, remind him that he was behind with his payments, that sort of thing."

"And then, like, frighten him up a bit, right?" Gip laughed.

"Didn't like it." Manny shook his head. "They fired me when they discovered that I was pretending I couldn't find people. I felt sorry for them, man."

A middle-aged man, all dark glasses, Bermuda shorts and beer gut, was passing by.

"Excuse me," Manny spoke in a surprisingly genteel voice. "I was wondering if you could tell us where the post office was."

The man looked up nervously. "Post office?"

Manny smiled. "We've just arrived, you see."

Glancing suspiciously at Gip and me, the man pointed towards the town. "Tucker Street," he said. "Behind the church." He hurried on.

Manny, it was true, knew a bit about the person-finding business. At Cromer Post Office, we borrowed a telephone directory. There were about a hundred Garnhams in its pages but only about ten were listed with a local number. Of those, two had the initial "K."

Gip handed me his mobile phone.

I was about to make some excuse but Gip had turned away. "We're getting some ice cream," he said. "We'll catch you in ten."

I sat on a chair nearby, gazing at the phone in my hand. There was no way out. Gip had paid for this trip. Manny had spent a day of his life driving to this weird little town. Now it was my turn.

I dialed. The voice of an ancient woman answered. I explained that I was looking for Karen Garnham. She told me her name was Thea, then she started telling me about a million of her relatives, none of whom were called Karen. Before I got the full Garnham family history, I said goodbye and hung up.

The second number was the answering machine of a Ken Garnham. Relieved, I stood in the cubicle, looking around for Gip and Manny. I had done my best but, face it, the chance of finding my mum when every other person around here seemed to be called Garnham was pretty hopeless. Shame about that; let's go home.

But there was no sign of them. After a couple of minutes, I decided to take the telephone book back to the Post Office counter. I was just about to close the page when the name "NK Garnham" caught my eye. My heart beat faster. Some inexplicable instinct told me that this was the number that would lead to my mother.

I picked up the receiver and dialed.

A man answered. "Is Karen Garnham there, please?" I asked. My voice sounded odd and trembly as if I was suddenly a frightened little boy.

"Down the pier," said the man.

I closed my eyes and took a couple of deep breaths. When I spoke again, I had to force the words out. "Where would she be on the pier, please?" I asked.

"Usual place, on stage." The man sounded irritated. "Prancing about in a swimsuit in the end of the pier show." He hesitated. "Who is this?"

"My name's Thomas Wisdom. I need to see Karen Garnham on a matter of urgency."

The man grunted impatiently. "Now what's she been up to, then?"

"Nothing," I said quickly. "What time will Karen be . . . on stage?"

"Whenever that prat of a magician's on."

"Fine. Thanks."

"Oh, and she's not called Karen, by the way. Her professional stage name is Maria Procchutti." He chuckled. "Silly cow," he added almost to himself.

I thanked him and put the telephone down carefully. On stage. In a swimsuit. Maria Procchutti. What exactly had I let myself in for?

I stood there thinking for a moment. When I looked up, I realized that Gip and Manny had returned and were watching me. I closed the telephone book.

"We're in business," I said.

As we made our way down to the pier, people stared at us as if seeing a couple of small white blokes walking on either side of a Rastafarian twice their size was a rare sight in these parts.

"What's the matter with these people?" Gip muttered at one point.

"Racism, man," said Manny without any particular bitterness. After a while, he took to greeting passers-by.

"Good afternoon," he would say in a chipper, gentlemanly accent. "Lovely day, isn't it?" Children giggled at him but their parents hurried by as if even Manny's smiles were a danger to their little ones.

I had expected Cromer Pier to be a giant platform, jutting into the sea, full of sideshows and merry-go-rounds but it turned out to be little more than a hundred yards long with a single, ramshackle building at the end. Across the entrance, there hung a giant streamer reading *Fun for all the Family at Cromer's Famous SEASIDE SPECIAL!*

We joined the queue at the box-office. When we reached the front, the old woman selling tickets told us, with some satisfaction, that the matinée performance was sold out. A few tickets were left for the evening show. "We'll have three," said Gip, pulling £30 from his wallet as if he had money to burn.

"I'll pay you back," I said as he handed me my ticket.

"Course you will," said Gip.

The sun was shining, we were by the seaside, we had time on our hands but I wasn't in the mood for fun.

I went along with Gip and Manny, had a hot dog, watched them as they shared a bumper car, played a round of crazy golf. At some point, I rang home and left a message on the answering-machine, telling my parents not to worry, that I was safe with Gip, that I would be home tomorrow. As evening approached, we sat on the beach, staring out to sea, now and then chucking stones into the waves.

Nearby, parents were packing up their things, gathering their children after another tough day on the beach in Cromer. All day, it had been as if Cy Gabriel had never spoken to me, as if angels were nothing more scary than something you sang about at Christmastime.

I looked about me. Did these people—that bony, white-skinned dad in a floppy hat, that overweight mum wiping the ice cream off her little boy's mouth, those boys kicking a beach ball—really need saving? I thought of what had happened that day, of Gip setting up this trip, of Manny and his smile, even of the grumpy old girl in the box-office. Was all this so bad that it needed to be transformed by a great Project to make us all better people?

"All right then, Tom?" Gip lay on his back with his eyes closed. There was sand in his hair and a smear of chocolate ice cream had dried on his chin.

"Nervous," I said. "I'm not so sure this was such a great idea."

Gip sat up, drew his knees up to his chin and stared out to sea. "When Dover told me where your real mum lived, I thought about not telling you. Maybe things were stirred up enough in your life. Family stuff usually means trouble, as far as I can see."

"So what made you change your mind?"

"I put myself in your shoes. Would I want to meet my real mum? Of course I would. Knowing there was some stranger out there who had brought me into the world would be like a missing part of the jigsaw. I'd want to meet her, just so that I could get on with the rest of my life."

I nodded, knowing that Gip was right as usual. "Ever since I discovered that I was adopted, I've been wondering what she's like," I said. "I keep drifting into this fantasy—as if she's this perfect, older friend who understands me better than anyone else because we share the same blood. We'd meet and suddenly, by magic, I'd lose this feeling that I'm an outsider in the world. I'd belong at last."

Gip picked up a stone and threw it as far as he could. I watched it splash into the sea.

"Now I'm here, I realize how crazy that idea was," I said. "She's a stranger, leading her own life. She could be any woman on this beach and I wouldn't know any better. Just because I was once part of her won't make any difference at all."

"She'll be all right, mark my words," said Gip. "Face it, she can't be that bad—look at the way you've turned out."

"I wish I was on my own here."

Gip looked at me and smiled. "I know you do. But sometimes you need your friends—you can rely on your mates better than on any family."

Manny stood up. "It's showtime," he said and began trudging across the pebbles towards the pier.

I sat for a moment, reluctant to move. Meeting my real mum would be tough enough, but seeing her on stage in front of hundreds of people, including my own best friend, seemed a special kind of torture.

"Coming?" Gip asked.

"I want to go home," I murmured.

Gip nodded in the direction of Manny who was still striding across the beach. "Want to try and stop him?" he said.

Sighing, I stood up. Gip was right. It was too late to turn back.

We joined the people who were streaming into the theater on the pier, laughing and joking, ready for the show. Our seats were near the front and to the side which was kind of lucky since anyone sitting behind Manny would have seen nothing but his big dreadlocked head.

I remember little of the first half of the show. There were dancers who kicked up their legs and stared with fixed smiles beyond the back of the auditorium as if gazing at a brighter, better future than a Seaside Special in Cromer. The compère, a gray-haired guy with a Liverpool accent and a permanently startled expression on his face, introduced each act with a string of jokes. A dodgy-looking bloke with an Italian accent sang some old-fashioned songs. A family of jugglers threw stuff around the stage.

The audience loved it and, to tell the truth, I would have too were it not for the fact that I was just about to see my mother for the first time since I was a baby. Now and then I glanced to my left, where Gip was taking it all in with the cool lack of enthusiasm he showed in geography lessons. Manny, on my other side, was having the time of his life, guffawing so loudly at the jokes that nearby members of the audience soon began laughing at his laughter.

"Easy, Manny," I muttered after one particularly embarrassing and lengthy thunderclap. He looked across at me, eyes shining with pleasure. "This is so great, man," he said loudly.

And then it happened. The compère was introducing the Great Miraculo and his lovely assistant Maria. A couple of stage assistants brought a long table on to the stage. A man with a ridiculous top hat and a silly mustache wandered on to tumultuous applause. Behind him, wobbling on high heels, was a woman in a shiny blonde wig, wearing—or almost wearing—a swimsuit and fishnet tights.

"Oh no." I actually said these words out loud. "Please no."

Gip lay a hand on my arm. I recoiled, covering my face with both hands.

I saw little of the act. Every time I dared to look, the Miraculo guy seemed to be getting a laugh at my mother's expense. He dropped a handkerchief and leered at her as she picked it up. He followed her about and suddenly a white rabbit appeared out of his trouser pocket. He put her in a box on stage and set about sawing her in half but—big joke—he couldn't get the saw through her stomach.

I was never expecting this. The Great Miraculo was not so much a magician as a lame comic turn whose biggest joke was that his assistant—my poor, sad mother—was a bit too big to be wobbling about in a swimsuit.

Gip and I sat in silence as the audience, including Manny, rocked with laughter. Towards the end, I lowered my hands from my face, ignored the nightmare magician and stared into the face of my mother, the "lovely Maria."

Her smile, beneath the absurd blonde wig, never faltered. As the audience cheered and laughed, she gazed out at us with unseeing eyes like some overweight doll. When, after what seemed like an age, she tottered off the stage, followed by the Great Miraculo, who was still leering at her bottom, I found that I was damp with sweat.

"She was great, your mum." Chuckling, Manny shook his head. "Best act of the show, that was."

"Thanks a lot," I muttered.

"All right?" Gip smiled at me.

"Let's get out of here," I said.

But there were three or four more acts before the Seaside Special reached its climax. I sat there, numbed and silent, feeling like a freak among the happy families, a black hole of misery in the light and laughter. It seemed to me that my mood was reaching the people who were sitting close to me—not just Gip, or Manny, who was suddenly silent, but the family behind us. It was if they all could sense that in their midst was a boy who had just seen his mother for the first time for twelve years to discover that she was fat, with too much make-up, a joke bimbo in a seaside show.

She came on once again, for the final curtain-call. As she stepped forward to take her bow, she smiled up at the kinky-mustached magician, then at us, and, just for a split second, I thought I caught a glimpse of the real person behind the mask. Then the curtain fell and it was all over.

When we emerged onto the pier, it was almost dark. Frankly I wanted to forget what I had just seen. I began walking in the direction of the car.

"Hang on, Tom." Gip hobbled along, half a step behind me. "Is that it?"

"Yeah." I kept going. "I've seen all I need to see."

"You've seen your mum at work. You haven't even talked to her."

I laughed bitterly and shook my head. "Forget it," I muttered.

I felt a hand on my shoulder. It was Manny.

"We ain't traveled across half the country to watch you run away." He strengthened his grip alarmingly. "So you've got a bit of a crazy mama. Welcome to the club, man." He reached into his back pocket and pulled out a scrap of paper. "Besides, I want her autograph. I thought she was dead good."

Run away. It was those words that kept me from walking on. I knew that if I left it there, headed back to London, that image of my mother—pale, lit-up by the lights, spilling hopelessly out of her swimsuit—would be with me for the rest of my life. It made me sad—for me and for her.

I took the slip of paper. "Got a pen?" I asked Gip.

He reached into his jeans and passed me a ballpoint pen. "There you go, Tom." He smiled—one of those big Gip grins that are special because they are so rare. "We'll wait here for you."

I walked back to the gates of the theater and asked a man in a uniform where I might get the autographs of the stars of the Seaside Special. He looked at me suspiciously for a moment, then pointed to a dark passage down one side of the pier. "Towards the life-boat slip," he said. "They'll be coming out soon."

I made my way to the end of the passage. There I stood in the half-light, watching a small door with a green light over it, listening to the sound of the waves and the distant music, waiting for my mother.

23 · CHARMER

AFTER ABOUT FIVE MINUTES, the door opened. Against the lights from inside, I saw the outline of three figures. As they walked towards me, I recognized two of the dancers and the smoothie singer. The girls glanced at me, half-curious, but the guy stared ahead, chatting away. I guess that, since he was wearing dark glasses and it was almost dark, he didn't even see me.

The juggling family were next, all five of them. Then the compère who looked kind of old and lost now that he was back in the real world. Then three more dancers. "All right, love?" asked one.

"I'm waiting for Maria—Karen, that is."

"Yeah?" The dancer hesitated and I thought I saw a look of concern cross her face. "Friend of hers, are you?"

"I . . . I just want her autograph."

One of the other dancers muttered something in the ear of her friend. "Shut up, Steph," said the woman who had talked to me. "Would you like me to—?" The door opened again. "Well, talk of the devil," she said.

I turned. My mother stood in the doorway, her hand over the arm of the Great Miraculo. "Can I help you?" she said in a tone that was not exactly friendly.

"Could I have your autograph, please?"

"Sure." The magician stepped forward, reaching inside his jacket and taking out a pen.

"Not yours," I said quickly. "Karen's."

"Cheeky little devil." The man brushed past me. "Get on with it, love," he called over his shoulder. "I'm gasping for a pint."

My mother stood motionless. Something about my voice, my presence here, seemed to have alarmed her. "How did you know my real name?" she asked.

"I rang your home. The person who answered said you'd be here."

"That bloomin' bloke of yours." Miraculo stood about five yards away. "Never could keep his mouth shut."

"My home." My mother stepped forward and the lights from the pier caught her face. Without her blonde wig and wearing clothes, she looked more normal and younger than she had seemed on stage. "What's going on?"

"I'm a fan," I said, passing her the piece of paper and the ballpoint pen.

"Bit young for you, love." Miraculo laughed harshly behind me.

My mother signed and gave me the piece of paper. On it was written "Maria Procchutti" with three kisses and a heart. "Don't listen to him, love." She winked at me. "He's only jealous."

She was about to step past me and disappear out of my life forever. There was no time for second thoughts. I said the words in a low, firm voice that only she could hear.

"You're my mother. I'm your son."

The expression on her face changed, hardened, almost as if I had just insulted her. "What did you say?"

"Twelve years ago, you had me adopted. My name was Michael."

I had been imagining this moment. In my mind, I had seen my mother taking me in her arms, maybe crying a bit. But now, in real life, she stepped back. "Who put you up to this?" she asked, her eyes wide with alarm.

"I just wanted to see you."

Miraculo moved closer. "What's all this about? What you up to, sonny?"

"He's just having a bit of laugh, love." My mother glared at me, daring me to contradict her. "Nothing to worry about. He's got his autograph. Let's—"

"Please!" For the first time, there was a crack in my voice. "I've come all the way from London."

Miraculo stepped between me and my mother. Leaning forward towards me, his hands on his knees, "D'you know what they do to troublemakers round here? They pick them up and then they chuck them in the drink." He straightened up, took my mother by the arm and began to walk away. "Get lost, sonny," he said loudly. "Or I'll have to call Security."

"Security's here." It was the deep, unmistakable voice of Manny, who stood, arms crossed, blocking their exit. "That's my friend and he wants to talk to her," he said with polite menace. "And that's what he's going to do."

"You . . . you reckon, do ya?" Miraculo was unable to keep the fear out of his voice.

"I do."

"Are you threatening me?" Miraculo tried for a laugh but it sounded more like a wimper.

"Absolutely not." Manny looked shocked. "I'm just explaining. Making things clear."

My mother extricated her arm from Miraculo's. "Go to the pub, Brian," she said quietly. "I'll catch you later."

The magician hesitated. "I can't leave you here with this—" he glanced up at Manny, "this goon."

"Don't worry," said Manny in his most friendly manner. "We'll keep you company."

"Go on, love," said my mother. "I'll be all right."

I watched the Great Miraculo make his way down the pier, followed by Manny and Gip. My mother turned back to me and crossed her arms disapprovingly, looking for the first time like a real parent. "Nice friends you've got there," she said sarcastically.

"The best," I said.

"How about you telling me what this is all about?"

"That's all I want to do."

"Let's find somewhere where we can talk," she said, and began walking down the pier.

My mother and I sat on a bench looking out over the gray, dark sea. She lit a cigarette.

"What did you think of the act?" she asked after a few moments' uneasy silence.

"I thought it was good," I lied.

"We get some laughs, eh."

"Yeah." I thought of the blonde wig, the high heels, the tight, glittering swimsuit. "You certainly do."

"We've got a pantomime gig in Ipswich this year. There's talk of Blackpool next summer." She inhaled on her cigarette, then turned to look at me. "What about you?" she asked.

"I'm still at school."

"Tell me about yourself."

I told her. I spoke about my life with Mark and Mary Wisdom. I said we had a nice home in the suburbs. I was doing pretty well in my class, that I hoped to be in the football team for my year. I even mentioned Dougal. The more I spoke, the smaller and more predictable it all seemed.

Yet, by the way she gazed at me while I was talking, I might have been telling her how I was the youngest ever recipient of the Nobel Peace Prize. "My son," she said when I stopped talking. "I always knew you'd do well for yourself. Looks like I made the right choice, doesn't it?"

"Giving me away, you mean."

She chuckled to herself. "You've got to admit that you're better off where you are than tagging along after a magician's assistant."

"Maybe—"

"Oh, I know it might seem glamorous to you, the showbiz life, but it's no way to bring up a kid."

"It doesn't seem that—" I was about to say that her life had not struck me as being exactly glamorous but I thought better of it. "It doesn't seem too bad," I said.

She smiled. "You're very kind," she said. As if realizing that these words were a bit formal, considering the fact that she was my long-lost mother, she laid a cold hand on mine. I looked down at her long, curling fingernails. They looked like painted claws. I took my hand away.

"Why did you do it?" I asked.

She sat in silence for a while, then sighed. "I think I was always too selfish to be a mum. I never got on with kids, even when I was one myself. Anyway, I can hardly look after myself, let alone someone else."

I asked who my father was.

She winced like someone pretending to be embarrassed. "I was a bit of a tearaway when I was a teenager. I got into trouble at school and had a baby boy. The social took him away from me. After that I ran a bit wild. You came along when I was eighteen. I'd been seeing this bloke who ran a pub in North Walsham." She stared out to sea, lost in memory. "He was a bit married, so I had no choice but adoption. I didn't like it at the time but there wasn't much I could do—I weren't much more than a kid myself."

"A bloke who ran a pub," I murmured. "Great."

"He was nice—a real charmer, like you. I heard that his business went under and that he's gone down to the West country. Haven't heard from him for years."

"Are you married now?"

She shook her head. "I've lived with this bloke for a couple of years but, between you and me, it's not too clever between us right now. When Brian—that's Miraculo—gets his divorce, we'll probably get it together. We're all right, Brian and me."

And, quite suddenly, there didn't seem much more to say. There we were, mother and son, together at last. Yet, with every word we spoke to one another, the gulf between us seemed greater.

"Thank you for finding me." My mother took my hand again and this time I didn't move away. "Your dad was a weak man but I can tell that you're different. It's good that we've met at last."

I smiled. "It is," I said, and I meant it.

She looked at me for a moment. Then, without warning, she put her arms around me and pulled me close to her. The smell of tobacco and perfume on her coat was overpowering but I leaned against her without resisting. "Little Michael," she murmured. "You're a good kid."

She reached into the white leather bag that was on the bench beside her and took out a card. On it, in large, fancy letters, were written the words, The Great Miraculo (and his lovely assistant Maria Procchutti) Comedy and Magic! Underneath was written an address and a telephone number.

"Listen, I know I've been a bad mother and all that but, if you're ever in trouble, you can reach me here at any time," she said. "I'm not much good at relationships but I'd like to make it up to you somehow."

I stood up. "Thanks . . . Mum."

She laughed. "Don't," she said. "You make me feel so old. I think I'd better be Karen, don't you?"

I nodded. "And I'm not Michael. I'm Thomas—Thomas Wisdom."

We smiled at each other. Then she folded her arms and shivered. "Off you go then, Thomas Wisdom," she said softly.

I turned and walked towards the lights of Cromer. Gip and Manny were waiting for me by the car. We drove home in silence.

It was almost two in the morning by the time we reached London and Manny dropped us off at the squat and drove off to some private destination of his own. We made our way upstairs. As usual, the room next to the motorway was empty. We crashed out on a bed in the corner, huddling together under a thin blanket.

The roar of early-morning traffic awoke me. I lay on my side looking, beyond Gip's sleeping form, to the hazy brightness outside. My head ached, my body felt grimy. I longed to be able to get up, have a bath and clean my teeth in a neat, suburban bathroom and put on some fresh clothes. I realized that, unlike Gip, I was not one of life's natural squatters.

Something else. I thought of my mother, sitting there at the end of the bench, her hard, dark eyes staring out to sea, now and then putting a cigarette to her lips and drawing on it like it was a life-support machine. I remembered the smell on her coat. Then I thought of my other parents, Mark and Mary, and my sister Amy. I saw my home, my room, my crazy dog asleep on my bed.

Yesterday I had faced it all, my past and my present. I had stood up and walked away, no longer just somebody's son, a name on adoption papers, part of the Project, but me. No one was going to decide my future for me. I was free. I was strong. The time for secrets was over.

I prodded Gip. He swore at me. I sat up in bed, shook him by the shoulder. He turned over, blinking at the brightness.

"I've got something to tell you," I said.

"Eh?"

"It's called the Project . . ."

24 · CHAT

WITHIN HALF A NANO-SECOND of my entering my house the next morning, my parents were in the hall. They stood staring at me, as if unable quite to believe that I was there, and then my mother said "Thomas" in a voice that was gentle yet exasperated. She walked towards me and took me in her arms.

I glanced over her shoulder at my father. He seemed to have aged overnight.

"I think you owe us an explanation, old boy," he said.

"I told you. I went to look for my real mother. She turned out to be really nice."

My other mother, Mary Wisdom, released me and stood back. "You found her?"

"Of course. She's a brilliant magician. We're going to keep in touch. It's going to be great."

At that moment, voices could be heard coming from the sitting-room.

"There's a meeting going on," said my father.

At any other time, I might have noticed how strange this was but at that moment my only idea was to get away, to soak in a bath upstairs.

"We'd like you to join us," said my mother.

Now I was curious. I followed them into the sitting-room.

Three men were there, two of whom I knew. Sitting in front of the window was Cy Gabriel. Nearby on the sofa, in trim weekend clothes, was Daisy Dover, headmaster of my school. Beside him sat a tall man in his late thirties. He was wearing a police uniform.

"You know everyone except Chief Superintendent Wilson," said my mother as if we were at a neighborhood sherry party.

The policeman stood up, put the peaked cap that had been on his lap under his arm, and shook my hand.

"Glad to meet you at last, Thomas," he said in a gruff, leader-of-men voice.

"How do you do," I muttered.

"Take a seat, Thomas." My father smiled. I sat in the one remaining empty chair, feeling like the accused in a court of law.

"Things have kind of moved on since we discussed the Project at the office." It was Cy Gabriel who spoke.

I frowned. "I thought that was meant to be a big secret."

"It is."

I looked around the room, slowly coming to terms with what I was hearing. "You mean you're all—"

Cy smiled in a manner that he presumably meant to be reassuring. "We're angels, yes."

"Ah. Fine." I tried to keep the astonishment out of my voice but the fact was that, of all the people I knew, Daisy

Dover was the least angelic. He smiled at me now, thinly and insincerely, as if reading my thoughts.

"We're active pretty much everywhere," Cy was saying. "In schools. In the police force. In the media. In government. The Project is going very, very well."

"Great."

"We're now entering a new phase. What we call 'integration.' The next generation of indigenous humans is about to be introduced to the Project. All over the world children are being raised or educated by angels. Sometimes they are adopted. Sometimes we reach them at an early age with what we call 'mentors.'"

"What are—?"

"You remember when you were three or four. You had an imaginary friend, right?"

I shrugged, embarrassed by the memory. There was this guy, Ricky, who used to be there all day. He was the person I told everything to. Once or twice I had insisted that my mother laid a place at the table for Ricky. It was something of a family joke because, of course, Ricky belonged in my imagination. Or so I thought.

"He was a mentor," said Cy. "He was providing you with preparatory information about the Project."

I shook my head. "Are you telling me that all those imaginary friends children all over the world are talking to are not imaginary at all but little brainwashing mentors?"

"Brainwashing's the wrong word." Cy shook his head with the merest hint of irritation. "It's more like informal education. We're also getting through to other kids through certain computers. They don't know it but, every time they stare at that screen, they're learning about the path of goodness. One day, they will be the people to save the planet."

"So that was why I was given a computer—to give the Project a shortcut into my brain." I glanced at my parents. They were both staring at the floor.

"You guys, the adopted—you're the ones who matter right now," Cy continued. "You've got the knowledge. We have put our trust in you. All we need is for you is to put your trust in us in return."

The semi-circle of angels looked at me as if expecting me to say something, maybe to express my gratitude, but right then I was still annoyed about the computer. If Mum and Dad were prepared to let my mind be messed up by encouraging me to look at a screen, what else would they be prepared to do on behalf of the famous Project?

"You are prepared to put your trust in us, aren't you, Thomas?" Dad spoke and his words seemed more a statement than a question.

"I don't quite get it," I said. "If I hadn't hacked into your computer and then followed you and Mum in California, I'd still know nothing about all this."

My father glanced across at his boss and, in that moment, I sensed that more worrying news was on the way.

"Tom, those things weren't accidents," said Cy. "The Project was guiding you."

I frowned, at first unable to take in what I was being told. "I was set up," I whispered.

"We presented you with a few little tests. You passed them all—admittedly with the help of your friend Gary Sanchez. At that moment we knew you were worthy of our trust."

"Thanks." A sudden thought had occurred to me. "So where does that leave Gip?"

It was the headteacher Daisy Dover who sat forward at this point. "As you may know, Gary got in touch with me last week concerning the tragic accident that took Colin Rendle from us. He told me about your visit to his house, how you had certain suspicions concerning the nurse who is looking after Mrs. Rendle. He's a bright lad, Gary, but I rather fear that he's getting into something he doesn't understand. The first thing we need to know is if he has any knowledge of the Project."

"No." The lie tripped off my tongue with surprising ease. "If I told him, he'd think I had gone crazy."

"We'd like him on board." Cy spoke casually. "We need people of his caliber on our team."

"Gip was never exactly into teams."

"But first—" Cy smiled as if I were his greatest friend in the world. "First we need to find him."

The police guy, Wilson, stirred into life. "Our information is that Gary has not been living at home for the last week or two."

He looked at me expectantly. I said nothing.

"He must have some other hideout."

I shrugged. "He's always been a bit mysterious about that," I said.

This time no one believed me.

"I wish I could convey to you how important this is," said Cy in the voice of a teacher severely disappointed by your behavior. "Important for the Project, of course. But really important for Gary too."

There was something about that word "important" which worried me. It was like "good" and "helpful." When angels spoke, there was a hint of threat in the most innocent words. I realized that I had to say something to throw them off the track for a while, to give us some time.

"Maybe I could bring him here," I said. "We could tell him about the Project together."

I sensed relief in the room.

"That would be so great, Thomas," said Cy. "Could you do that for us?"

"No promises," I said. "But I could try."

I was bushed. After the meeting broke up, I lolled about in my room for a while. My parents went to work and I cooked myself a fry-up for lunch. I watched some TV. I did not look at my computer. Mum and Dad came home together at about six, almost as if nothing had happened. Over an early-evening dinner, my father casually asked me if I had spoken to Gary. I said Gip seemed not to be at home. After I had eaten, I went upstairs, fell into bed, and crashed out.

I awoke sharply, as if my unconscious mind had heard something. The house was dark and silent. It was half-past one. I got up, slipped into my clothes and silently let myself out of the house.

I made my way to the bus stop. There was a night bus route which seemed to be heading in the right direction for Gip's squat and I was in luck—a bus rumbled around the corner like some nocturnal beast and pulled up beside me.

The driver glanced at me like twelve-year-olds were always getting on his bus in the early hours of the morning. I asked him if he could tell me when we reached my stop. He shrugged his agreement.

On the backseat, a man with a heavy, matted beard lay stretched out, eyes closed, with a beer can in his hand. I sat near the front.

London was a different city at this time of night. People scurried like rats along the neon-lit streets. Now and then I would spot a figure huddled asleep in the entrance of a shop or a couple of people standing in the shadows, watching, waiting for someone or something. Beardo on the back-seat began singing a sort of football chant, again and again. Once he sat up and shouted something at me. I sat tight and ignored him. He swore at me and then seemed to go back to sleep.

After about half an hour, the driver mumbled something. I stepped off the bus.

I looked around me and realized that I was in luck—the street where I stood was the one Gip and I had walked down several times over the past few weeks. Head down, hands in pockets, I headed for the squat.

I turned into the row of condemned houses. It was dark here, unlit even by street lamps, and the buildings on each side of me seemed more bleak and threatening than they had in the daytime.

The house that was Gip's secret hideout showed no sign of life. I rang the bell, again and again. After about five minutes, a girl's voice could be heard on the other side of the door. "Who is it?" she called out.

"It's Thomas. Gip's friend."

The door opened slightly and, in the darkness, I saw the pale face of the girl I had seen in the kitchen the first time I had been here. With a wary look to check that I was alone, she stepped back to let me in. I saw now that she was carrying a candle.

"They cut off the power," she said, heading up the stairs. We reached the first floor. "You'll find him in his room," she said, nodding in the direction of the next flight of stairs before she disappeared into her room, leaving me in the pitch black of the corridor.

I groped my way upstairs and along the corridor until I reached the last door on the left. I knocked once. There was no reply. I opened the door.

Gip was awake. He was sitting on a stool, his back to the door, silhouetted by the glow of his laptop screen.

"Gip," I hissed.

He turned. Few things can startle Gip Sanchez and my appearing at his secret hideout in the middle of the night was not one of them. "How you doing?"

"We've got to talk," I said. I walked over to the window, the lights of cars on the motorway flashed by like meteors across the sky.

Gip switched off his laptop.

"I thought they cut the power," I said.

"Battery." There was a hint of chilly impatience in Gip's voice.

"I found out something about computers today. Angels sometimes use them to brainwash people about the Project."

"Not mine, mate." The voice came back through the semi-darkness. "No one knows I've got it. I'm as invisible on-line as I am in this room. Was that what you crossed London to tell me?"

"Daisy's an angel."

Now I had his attention. "You're kidding," he said.

"There was this meeting at my house today. Dover was there, and Cy Gabriel and some bloke from the police. They want you to join the Project. They've been looking all over for you. They asked me to bring you to them."

"Why me?"

"They seem to think you're their kind of guy. I guess they'd prefer you to be on their side."

"Did you tell them I knew about the Project?"

"Somehow that didn't seem a great idea."

"I'm in trouble," Gip murmured as if he were talking to himself. "First Rendle. Now me."

"What's Rendle got to do with this?"

"I've worked out why they killed him. Your parents were going to tell you about the Project at some stage, right?"

I nodded.

"But we kind of messed up their plans. We found your file on your dad's computer. They must have thought that would be no problem—after all, it was in this unbreakable code. But then we gave it to Colin Rendle. Big mistake. If he was just an ordinary math teacher, there was no way that he would have been able to do anything with it. But he wasn't. He happens to be this secret mathematical genius. He cracks the code and that's where everything starts going wrong. You find out you're adopted. Rendle speaks to Daisy. At that point, the angel guys must have thought that, if he had cracked that file, he must have access to all sorts of other stuff about the Project."

"Exit Rendle."

"Right. He knew too much for his own good."

"But they're always saying that the Project is meant to be the power of goodness on Earth."

"Yeah." Gip laughed bitterly. "Some angels."

We sat in silence for a moment. "So what are you going to do?" I asked.

"They want me to join the Project. That either means I get to help them save the world or some nasty little accident takes me out of the equation. To tell the truth, I'm not tempted either way."

"If you just stay here, they won't find you. You're safe while the holiday lasts. But what happens when term starts and you're not at school?"

"Maybe the Project will have moved on by then." Outside a car flashed by, lighting up Gip's face for an instant. I sensed that he was feeling less confident about his future than he was letting on. "I've been on-line today," he said suddenly.

"Yeah?"

"There are loads of chatrooms for kids, you know."

"And?"

"I've found one or two rooms and newsgroups that are particularly for adopted kids. So I've been doing a bit of research."

I hate it when Gip does this. He lets information out bit by bit, as if he's reluctant to let it go. "Research," I repeated wearily.

"Yeah. I've been asking adopted kids all over the world to look out for some tell-tale signs about their adoptive parents. Birthmarks on their necks and arms. Co-ordinated visits to the lavatory. Visits to California. Peculiar behavior, generally."

I couldn't believe what I was hearing. "What is it with you?" I said. "You've blown the whole thing."

"I was just curious." He turned back to the computer and pressed a button on the side console. "I wanted to know how serious this famous Project is."

"So what did you find out?" I went over and stood beside him in front of the screen.

Gip moved the mouse and double-clicked. A message appeared in the left-hand corner of the screen. It read, You have 437 messages.

"Looks like it's pretty serious," he said. He laughed briefly but his eyes, lit up by the glow of the computer screen, betrayed him.

Gip was scared.

I was back home before breakfast, my head throbbing with sleeplessness. Dumping my clothes in a heap on the floor, I tumbled into bed.

Although all I wanted to do was sleep, my mind was humming with the events of the last twelve hours. Gip was in danger. As if that was not bad enough, he was contacting people across the world who might be in the same situation as me. Until now I had managed to persuade myself that the events of the past few weeks were all about me. Now there was no escaping the fact that my little family crisis was part of a bigger, more frightening picture.

At some point, as I lay there thinking about all this, the door opened softly. My mother looked at me. Seeing that I was awake, she came over and sat on my bed.

"How did you sleep?" she asked softly.

"Good," I lied.

She laid a cool hand on my brow. "Don't worry about all this," she said. "We'll be back to normal soon."

"Yeah, right."

"Our own little family. Just like before."

I rolled on to my back and looked up at her. Was she serious, I wondered. What was more important for her—being an angel, part of the great universal Project to save poor little Planet Earth, or the fact that she was my mum?

"You know I love you very much," she said, as if she could read my thoughts.

I grunted, kind of embarrassed.

"An angel's love is the best." She smoothed the hair out of my face.

"Out of this world."

She nodded, smiling.

"What happens if Gip doesn't want to join the Project?" I asked.

"He will. I know I've never been too keen on Gip but I think he'll come through for us. You're not the sort of person who would be friends with someone who's evil."

"You don't have to be evil not to want to help the Project."

She took her hand away and sighed. "Those who aren't with us are against us," she said in a voice that was less motherly now. "If you are not prepared to help the power of goodness, you are . . . on the other side."

"Gip doesn't do sides. He's just Gip."

A flicker of concern crossed my mother's face. "Everyone does sides," she said quietly. "You must remember that. Everyone."

I was about to ask her what she meant, but she laid a finger on my lips. "Some of us have to work," she said. "We'll talk about this later." She kissed me gently on the forehead and left me in the semi-darkness.

25 · POWER

I WAS AWOKEN later that morning by something heavy jumping on to the bed. It was Dougal. He was in one of his cat moods. Sometimes, without warning, he would seem to decide that he was not a West Highland terrier at all and go all feline on me, refusing to go for a walk in the park, curling up on my lap, even now and then trying to climb the curtains.

As he lay on my stomach, I played along with his fantasy, stroking the side of his face as if he were a big, lazy tabby. Sleepily, I told him that if the Project was producing angeldogs like him, it must be in deep trouble. I asked him whether the Presence was trying to make a cat but somehow the recipe went wrong and the result was a Dougal-type mistake. He looked deeply into my eyes, as if to say that he was as confused by the way he carried on as I was. "You're a nutter, Doogie," I said, and he gave a little bark of embarrassment.

The door opened. I looked up to see Luke, the Surfer-Boy, standing there, a big, pearly-toothed smile on his face.

"Sorry to interrupt the conversation," he said. "I thought the dog was locked in here."

"I didn't know anyone was in the house."

Luke wandered over to my new computer and ran his hands over the keys. "Amy wanted to call by and pick up some stuff. We're taking off to Cornwall for a few days."

"Surf's up?"

I must have sounded more hostile than I intended because he looked up sharply.

"We're on the same side, Tom," he said in his most sincere voice.

"Oh yeah, of course." I smiled. "I keep forgetting that you're an angel—I can't think why."

"We're glad to have you with us."

"Who said I am?"

"I kind of assumed."

I pushed Dougal gently off my stomach and he lay on his back beside me, eyes closed, feet in the air. "I was told that the Project believed in free will."

"All is good. All will be resolved." Luke spoke these words with the unnerving inner conviction of someone who has found the way and the truth and just knows that you will be joining him soon.

"So it's my choice, right."

"Of course." He paused, then added casually, "You have a lot of power right now."

"I thought angels were meant to be the ones with the power."

"You have power over your own future." He strolled over the bed and began rubbing Dougal's stomach. "And power over your family's future."

"My family—in what way?"

He looked up at me with the perfect, Surfer-Boy smile and, at that moment, I sensed that this casual conversation was no accident. "Within the Project, we each have our own duties—our own little project, if you like," he said. "You are theirs."

"So you mean, if I fail to come through, they pay the price."

"Put it this way. There's a connection between what you decide and their future role in the Project."

"What has an angel got to worry about anyway?" I asked.

Lazily, Luke took his right hand out of his pocket. He flicked a tiny coin with his thumb, then passed it to me. "Take a look at that," he said. "We call it a kewl-disc."

"Yeah?"

"It's the key to the life of an angel—the life or the non-life."

"Are you saying angels can be killed?"

He moved his hand down Dougal's stomach and extended one of his stubby little hind legs. In the hollow between my dog's leg and his stomach, I caught sight of the tell-tale blemish. "Dougal's derm," said Luke. "Watch."

He lowered the disc on to the discolored flesh and held it there for a few seconds. Growling, Dougal opened his eyes. Then, after about five seconds, he gave a little whine, stiffened, and then relaxed as if the life was passing out of him. Luke placed a hand under his shoulder and raised him a few inches from the bed. The dog's head sagged, his tongue lolled out of his mouth.

"What have you done, you idiot?" I sat up in bed.

"The kewl-disc has closed down his circuits." Luke laid Dougal down gently on the bed. "The only way he can be re-activated is by placing the other side of the disc against his derm and that has to be done before brain death, which occurs within a few minutes."

"Do it." I looked at the unconscious form of our angel-dog. "Wake him up—now, Luke!"

"Sorry, Tom." Luke looked almost concerned. "I really didn't mean to upset you." He turned the disc over and held it against Dougal's derm. After a few seconds, the dog started breathing again.

"Don't let this worry you, Tom." Luke put his hand under Dougal's chin and seemed to be checking his eyes. "Although we each have one, kewl-discs are not used that often. I just wanted to give you a bit of guidance."

Amy appeared in the doorway. "What's going on in here?" she asked.

"Nothing much." Luke ruffled Dougal's head and winked at me. "Just three guys passing the time of day."

26 · ACTION

LATER THAT AFTERNOON, I called Gip on his mobile. I told him that Surfer-Boy had called by to tell me that angels could die too.

"How's that then?" Gip seemed distracted, almost uninterested.

"They've got a kind of disc thing that can close down an angel's circuit. Luke killed my dog and brought him back to life again. He said he was giving me guidance but his message was clear—this could happen to your mum and dad."

"Your former mum and dad," he murmured. "Don't forget that they come from a long, long way away."

"Not to me they don't." I was surprised by how angry Gip's words made me feel. "They're all right, my parents. They do their best for me and I know it's not because of some Project but because . . . because I'm me."

"Sure." Gip paused. "Of course, it's

possible that all those feelings are part of the deal—that there's a 'Love Thomas' circuit in their inner program."

"No." I didn't like Gip talking about my family like this. Just because he was unlucky enough to have had a dad who had scrammed while he was still in nappies and a mum who seemed to be some kind of psycho, it didn't mean that all families were a fraud. "They may be aliens but they're my aliens," I said weakly.

"So now they're telling you that it's your call. You're with the angels with their freaky little derms and their magic kewl-discs or you're a free spirit, a good old human being."

I paused, taking in what Gip had just said, every word of it. "Angels are not freaky. They're good," I said eventually. "Look outside your squat and tell me truthfully that we don't need the power of angels. We can use all the help we can get, right?"

"Maybe it's me." There was a sadness in Gip's voice. "I've never been one to worry too much about anyone else, let alone the human race."

"That's not true, Gip. You've been there for me when there was nothing in it for you."

"You reckon? Well—" Gip paused, almost as if he were considering telling me something but then changed his mind. "It's your decision," he said quietly. "But don't take too long. I've got a thousand responses from adopted kids on my computer. There's definitely an angelic pattern to their stories. Come over tomorrow and we can blow this story across the world."

"You can do that whatever I decide."

"No." He spoke quickly. "If you decide that the Project is good, that you're with the angels, I promise I'll do whatever you think best. I'll wipe the messages from my computer. I'll help in any way they want."

"You're saying it's down to me."

"I'm here by accident." Gip spoke quietly. "Remember the park at the end of last term? It was you who involved me in your parents and their weird games."

"I guess that's true."

"So you get to decide which way the old Gip-and-Tom combo is going to jump. Deal?"

I thought for a moment, then said, "Deal."

I sat on my bed and stared out of the window. On the pavement across the road, a mother was making her way to the shops, pushing a baby buggy in front of her. I could hear the sound of children in the playground nearby, a distant police siren, the ghostly scream of swifts as they cut across the sky. It was a dazzling, cloudless day, perfect for the holidays, but everything I saw and heard seemed different now. Poor old humankind. It had tried and it had failed. Even on a day like this, the mark of doom was on it.

I shook my head, as if to rid myself of these thoughts. I remembered how I had been before that fateful day when Gip and I had hacked into my father's computer. Since then, every step—the holiday in California, Rendle, the realization that angels were everywhere—had seemed to persuade me that, with the Project, all is good, all will be resolved, while humankind was lost and without hope.

In fact, looking back, my whole journey might have been planned. Every step had brought me closer to the decision I was about to make. It was almost as if I had been guided here.

In my mind, I went through it all—the things that had happened, the words that had been said—and suddenly, in spite of the heat, I found that I was shivering. I saw it all, the terrifying simplicity of it, the one part of the story that I had been blind to all this time.

I understood.

I returned to the house. I went upstairs, sat for a moment in front of my computer, and switched it on.

I was back. I knew that the Presence would reach me through the computer. What I hadn't realized was that I would be transported across the world to the place where I had first seen an angel.

Within seconds of my computer coming to life, the screen turned to an unearthly purple. I heard the voices of otherworldly music all around me and the reality of my room, my computer, me, faded as I seemed to become absorbed by the screen itself.

I was in the desert. I stood before the bunker. The door opened. I was descending in the lift. I stepped out.

There before me was the landscape made of a million naked human bodies, stretching as far as the eye could see.

I stood for a moment, uncertain as to what was expected of me. Then the Presence was there. When it spoke, no sound reached my ears because the voice was within me. It was as if my own soul was speaking.

YOU HAVE TRAVELED FAR, THOMAS, AND NOW YOU HAVE ARRIVED AT YOUR DESTINATION. YOU ARE HOME. YOU ARE PART OF OUR GREAT FAMILY.

I stared ahead of me. The bodies seemed to move gently as I watched, as if they formed a great, welcoming sea of humanity.

Where am I?

THIS IS THE ANGEL FACTORY. IT IS HERE THAT THE BEINGS WHICH WILL SAVE YOUR PLANET ARE CREATED.

What do you want from me now?

YOU WILL MAKE YOUR DECISION. YOU WILL PLACE YOUR TRUST IN THE PROJECT. NO SACRIFICE WILL BE REQUIRED OF YOU. YOU WILL KNOW WHAT TO DO.

I will know.

IT IS AN HONORABLE THING THAT YOU ARE DOING, THOMAS.

The music returned. I looked down and the angels that were there smiled their welcome. Although they were naked, I was free of any kind of embarrassment. I saw them as they were, as kind and innocent as babies. As I looked, I saw that, within a few strides of where I was standing, there was a space among the bodies and I knew that it was for me if I joined the Project. One last task awaited me back on Earth.

YOU WILL MAKE YOUR DECISION.

I WILL MAKE MY DECISION.

ALL IS GOOD. ALL WILL BE RESOLVED.

I turned and walked towards the bright, unearthly light of the lift. The door closed behind me and I felt a great feeling of loneliness and fear. The motion stopped and sunlight flooded the lift.

I shook my head, placed my thumb and forefinger over my eyes. The music faded.

I looked about me. I was back in my room. There on the screen before me was a single word against a deep purple background.

DECIDE.

I walked to my parents' bedroom. An hour or so remained before their return from work. I searched, methodically and without panic. And there, in my mother's jewelry box, I found what I was looking for.

I called Gip and told him that I knew what I had to do. We agreed to meet at the squat the following day. It was time for action.

27 · SEND

IT WAS SWELTERING the next day when I
headed east. As I waited in a queue at the
bus stop, a guy in a suit was talking to his
office on a cell phone, giving it full volume
for the benefit of the rest of us. From what
he said, I gathered that parts of Central
London were closed. There was, as he put
it, "traffic chaos big-time."

Chaos? Closed streets? My first thought
was that some kind of Project-related
weirdness was coming down but then the
mobile-shouter started complaining about
politicians messing everything up, as usual.
Apparently, there was a conference taking
place in the center of the city. Big-shot
leaders, including the American President,
had flown in from all over the world. There
were worries about demonstrations and the
rest of us, including Big-Mouth on his
mobile, were being made to suffer.

I reached the house an hour late but
Gip seemed not to have noticed. He looked

pale and ghost-like, as if he had been living off air and chewing-gum for the past few days. In the old days, when we met, we would slip into an easy kind of conversation, sometimes picking up where we left off hours or even days before. Now he glanced at me with a wary, dark-eyed look, said, "Hey, Tom," and turned into the house. Suddenly, for Gip, I represented all the trouble in his troubled life.

We went to his room. Because the window had to remain closed to keep out the noise and fumes of motorway traffic, it was steaming hot.

"It's like a sauna in here," I said.

"Yeah?" Gip flapped his big old denim shirt under which he was wearing his usual gray T-shirt. "Doesn't bother me."

I found a shady corner and sat on the floor. "I used my computer last night," I said.

He frowned and sat down slowly on the stool in front of his laptop. "I thought that was meant to be a dodgy, brainwashing thing."

"It is. I was taken back to Seraph."

Gip gave a sharp, humorless laugh. "They've got an airplane in there too?"

"I don't know how it's done. But I was there and it felt real. They call it the Angel Factory."

"An underground wonderworld—the same as before?"

"Sort of. Only this time, I had a guide. The Presence."

Gip glanced out of the window. He was acting casual but I wasn't taken in. "And what did old Presence have to say?" he asked.

"He told me the moment to decide had come. I would be with the Project. I was part of the family."

"Doesn't sound like much of a choice to me."

"The Presence told me what I should do but, even as it spoke, I knew one thing for sure. I am human, not an angel.

That means that I'm free to choose. It was why I risked turning on the computer. I needed to go through that. It gave me a sort of strength."

"Are you saying no to the Project?" Gip asked softly.

"I'm saying no to the Project."

Gip looked away. He gazed out of the window for a few seconds. The great traffic disaster had reached the motorway outside. A haze of smog and heat hung over the queues of cars and lorries. It was as if, at that moment, the whole world had stopped and was being baked under a pitiless sun.

A bead of sweat ran down the side of his face. He turned back to me and said in a voice that was almost a whisper, "Are you sure about this?"

I stood up and walked over to where he sat. "I'm sure. Turn on the computer." I looked down on his damp and matted hair. "And take off that stupid shirt, will you?" I said. "It's making me sweat just looking at you."

He wriggled out of the shirt, chucked it on the floor and switched on the laptop. When he went on-line, the message in the top left-hand corner read, You have 2,157 messages.

"Kids of the world unite," I said.

"Right," muttered Gip.

"So what we do is tell these people—every one of them—the facts about the Project. We say we're setting up a network for kids who are being recruited into it."

Gip opened up a blank e-mail. He typed in the words "AN IMPORTANT MESSAGE."

I began to dictate.

Here is some information of the greatest importance for you. There is an extraterrestrial force on earth. It is infiltrating mankind with human-like creatures it describes as "angels." Although its motives are said to be friendly, you should know that many children who have been adopted have been taken into families of angels. Your reply to my earlier message suggests that you may be one of them.

This means that each of you has a choice. You can either support what angels call the Project by remaining silent and agreeing to do what your adoptive parents tell you. Or you can resist.

I have decided to resist. I am offering a support group for those like me. I am not sure what our next step should be—only that, together, we are strong.

Remember, you may be adopted for all the usual, human reasons—if so, this message is not for you. But, if you know that you are among angels, then you need know only this.

You are not alone.
Signed
Thomas Wisdom

Gip sat back. "Seems kind of whacko," he said.

"Whacko, but true."

He looked over his shoulder at me, his hair falling to one side. "Once it's gone, there's no turning back," he said.

"I know that."

"The thing is—" Gip turned on his stool and faced me. He seemed smaller and more vulnerable than he had ever been before. "We can't send the messages out right now. We have to batch them."

"Batch?"

"There are rules about flaming on the Internet—that's sending out an e-mail to thousands of people. So, if we tried to send all the e-mails together, the server would close me down. Only ten or fifteen would make it. I'll batch them in fifties tonight." He shrugged his narrow shoulders. "It's a drag but at least we'll get through."

"I'll stay. We could do it together now."

"No." Gip's eyes held mine with an odd defiance. "I'll do it later."

"Why wait?"

"What's your problem? You think I'm bottling out, is that it?"

"Of course I don't." There was a hint of pleading in my voice. "Come on, Gip. How long would it take?"

I smiled at him, willing him with all my heart to be the Gip that I knew, that I understood, but he shook his head.

"I don't think so," he said. "The fact is, people around here are getting kind of iffy about your hanging out in the house. They've decided you're a security risk."

"They don't even know me."

"You look straight. You turn up in the middle of the night. If you had lived the kind of lives they lead, you'd understand."

"We've been in this together from the start. Now we've got—"

"What is this?" He leaned forward and for a moment I thought he was going to hit me. "Don't you trust me? After everything we've been through?"

For a full ten seconds we stared at each other. "The old Gip-and-Tom combo," I said quietly. "Of course I trust you."

Gip smiled with relief. "It'll be done by midnight."

I nodded in the direction of the laptop. "Hadn't you better save our message?"

He turned back to the screen and, as he crouched over the keyboard, the hair on his shoulders parted and I saw what I needed to see.

I got up and crossed the room. Standing behind him, I reached into my pocket and took out the kewl-disc. It radiated warmth into my fingers.

On the screen were the words "SEND" and "SAVE."

Gip was moving the cursor. With an unspoken prayer, I laid the disc gently on Gip, on his shoulder, on his derm. He froze for a few seconds. I held firm. Then he slumped forward, lifeless, and toppled sideways on to the floor.

I knelt over him, tears in my eyes. I felt his neck for a pulse. There was nothing.

I put the disc back into my pocket. I sat in front of the computer and double-clicked on "SAVE." For a few seconds, the screen seemed to freeze before a message appeared, reading, E-mail saved. I closed down the laptop, put it in its bag and, hooking it over my shoulder, walked to the door.

With one last look at the body of my best friend, I left the room and closed the door behind me. I walked down the stairs and let myself out of the house. The suffocatingly warm air hit me, startled me into life. Head down, I walked away quickly towards the bus stop.

28 · TRUTH

GIP WAS AN ANGEL.

The evidence had been there all the time, staring me in the face. His hideout, his computer, his mobile phone, the mysterious way that cash never seemed to be a problem for him. All could be explained by one terrifying truth.

Gip was an angel.

It was the unavoidable answer to questions that I had tried so hard to ignore. How had Dover known about my suspicions about Rendle's nurse when I had only talked to Gip after he had phoned the headteacher? What had he meant, after the teacher's death, that I "knew nothing about anything"? How was it that Dover had casually let slip to him the details of where my real mother could be found? Why was he so unsurprised by the effect my computer had on me?

Gip was an angel.

At first, I couldn't believe it. I wouldn't

believe it. But then, yesterday, the proof was there. He had let slip the words "that kewl-disc thing." The only problem was that I had said nothing about its name among angels—I had only mentioned that it was a disc.

Gip was an angel.

I had remembered Rendle, the subtle warnings I had been given by my mother, by Amy. "Those who aren't with us are against us." "The Project comes first." I understood that, in the deadly game of saving humanity from itself, a life here or there was expendable. Like Rendle, I knew too much. When Gip refused to send the message to the world, he left me no alternative.

Gip was an angel.

It was me or him. A world fit for humans or one run by the Project. I had no choice.

29 · KEY

FOR A WHILE I WALKED without thinking, holding the laptop against me, gazing ahead with unseeing eyes. Gip was my past, my present. Whatever had happened in my life, he had been there, unfazed by anything, my friend. I had become used to comparing my little misadventures with the bad things that had happened to him. If Gip could come through, I had believed, anyone could.

In my mind, I heard his voice. I tried to imagine a future without him. I saw my hand, pressed against his neck. I stopped walking, closed my eyes and the tears spilled over and ran down my cheeks.

I sat on a low wall, head down. Footsteps hurried by—in this part of town, people avoid trouble as if it's an infectious disease.

Gip was an angel, a dead angel. I thought back to the moment yesterday when Luke had shown me how the kewl-disc cut out the circuit of life in Dougal. He had brought Dougal back to life with the reverse side of the coin but he had said he had to act quickly.

I looked around. Across the road, which was clogged with traffic, there was a telephone box. I rang my father's work number.

"Thomas." He sounded eerily normal. "What a nice surprise."

"Gip." I managed the word with difficulty. "He's at 34 Chesterton Close."

"You've spoken to him? He's agreed?"

"Don't lie!" It was a bellow of agony. "You know what he is. Get there now. Please, save his life, Dad!"

I hung up.

As I stepped out into the blazing sun, my first instinct, without thinking, was to head back to the flat, to bring Gip round if it wasn't too late, to ask him what we should do next. But now I was on my own. Dead or alive, Gip was with the angels, on the other side. The laptop weighed heavy on my shoulder. In the electric circuits of that gray plastic box was a network of contacts with children about to be recruited for the Project. I understood why Gip had wanted to delay sending out the fateful e-mail that would blow the Project wide open, but why had he taken me to that point? Was he setting me up for some kind of sinister test or had he wanted to rebel against his angelic masters by helping me expose what they were doing? If so, why did he lose his nerve at that crucial last moment?

I thought back to how he looked at the flat. The Gip I had once known—so strong, so true to himself—was no longer there. He was a soul in torment, forced to act against his inner nature. But which was the true Gip—my friend or the servant of the angels? Maybe I would never know.

I remembered the laptop. It had been tempting to

dispatch the e-mails at the flat, to press "SEND" and leave the computer there, but I had sensed that Gip had been right about the batching business. At some point, that message to the 2,157 children who were waiting for it would have to be sent out systematically, but not now. I had to find somewhere to leave the laptop where no angel could find it.

At that moment, I noticed a bus edging towards me in the heavy traffic. The sign on the front read, Victoria Station. Travelers. Luggage. It was worth a try.

The doors drew back and I stepped on.

It took me almost two hours to get there. The traffic moved like sludge. Looking out the window, I noticed newspaper headlines—*PRESIDENT FOXX JETS IN*, they read, as if to remind me why, on this of all days, moving around town was almost impossible.

When I reached the station, I followed the signs to the Left-Luggage Office. At first, when I saw the wall of metal lockers, it seemed to me that there were none to spare but, as I stood in front of them, wondering what to do next, an American student type arrived, pulled a key out of his pocket, opened a locker and removed his suitcase.

I stepped forward, put the laptop into the locker, found a coin, and locked it.

Slowly, I walked through the milling crowds at the station, the small key held tightly in the palm of my hand. How many of these commuters were angels? Who could I trust with the key? I thought of Manny, who had seemed human enough, but then, as I had discovered, angels came in all shapes and sizes. Besides, I had no idea where to find him.

I slipped the key into my pocket and, as I did so, my fingers touched a card. I took it out and read the words, "The Great Miraculo (and his lovely assistant Maria Procchutti)

Comedy and Magic!" In my mind, I heard the voice of Karen, my real mother. "If you're ever in trouble . . . I'd like to make it up to you somehow."

There was a newsagent nearby. I bought some writing paper, a brown envelope, a ballpoint pen, and a stamp. Ignoring the stares of passers-by, I sat on the tarmac and, leaning against a wall, began to write a letter to the one person I knew who could not be an angel—the woman who had brought me into the world.

It was not a long letter and I knew that, when she read my hurried words, Karen Garnham would almost certainly conclude that I was some kind of nutter, but it was a risk I had to take.

I slipped the key into the envelope with the letter and posted it. Then, on an impulse, I walked to a phone-booth, took out the card and dialed the number of the mobile that was on it. She picked up on the third ring.

I hesitated, then spoke. "Er, Karen, it's Thomas Wisdom."

"Who?"

"Your son."

She laughed and I knew that she was pleased to hear my voice. "Oh hello, Thomas, love," she said.

"I can't talk for long. I just wanted to say that I've sent you a letter with a key. If anything happens to me, read the letter. It'll tell you where a computer is. You've got to send out an e-mail. I've explained it all."

I heard the voice of the Great Miraculo muttering in the background. "Listen, love." Karen sounded distracted. "It's not a good moment for a joke. We're on our way to an audition."

"This is not a joke. If I ever meant anything to you, please take it seriously."

"But I don't know anything about computers and all that."

"It's not difficult. Get someone to help you."

"Honestly, it's a bit of a—"

"Please. Remember what you said to me—about making it all up to me."

I heard that smoky chuckle of hers. "Me and my big mouth." She paused, as if she were thinking it over. "All right then."

"D'you promise?"

"Of course I promise," she said. "You're my son, aren't you?"

I thanked her and hung up.

It was time to go home.

30 · VIP

THEY WERE WAITING FOR ME. I knew they would be.

At the end of the street were two police motorbikes. Their riders stood chatting to one another, their helmets on the seats of the bikes. As I walked past, they glanced at me and one of them picked up the intercom from the side of his machine and muttered something into the mouthpiece.

A big black limo was outside the front door. As I approached, I recognized the man sitting at the driver's seat. It was Luke, wearing a dark suit. Surfer-Boy had gone straight. I raised a hand in greeting as I walked past. He stared back at me with a wary, guarded look and for the first time I realized that, to those involved in the Project, I now represented danger, the unpredictable.

As I let myself in, I heard my mother's voice. "Here he is," she said, and there was a warmth and relief in her voice that made the breath catch in my throat.

She came out of the kitchen, smiling. She held me in her arms for a moment. "Oh, Thomas," she murmured. My father stood at the sitting-room door. He looked as if he hadn't slept for a week. "Are you all right, old boy?" he asked.

"Did they get to Gip?"

"We haven't been told." My father gazed at me for a moment. "Why did you do it?" he asked quietly.

I shook my head. I was searching for words to explain what I had done when the voice of Cy Gabriel could be heard from the sitting-room. "We're on our way," he was saying. "We'll be there in fifteen."

He emerged from the room, slipping his mobile phone into his jacket pocket.

"Ready to roll, Wisdoms?" There was a new, boss-like coldness in his voice.

Mum looked at me. "Pop upstairs and wash your face," she said. "You look a mess."

"What's happening?" I asked.

Dad seemed about to answer but Cy cut in. "You'll find out, Thomas. Let's move it, OK?"

When I came back downstairs, the three of them were standing in silence. Cy and Dad made their way out of the front door. Mum put her arm around me and we followed.

The police motorbikes were in front of the car, their lights flashing. Cy stepped into the front seat. I sat between my parents in the back.

Suddenly we were in some kind of VIP motorcade. With the help of the robocops out front, we cut across traffic, through red lights, made our way out of London in the fast lane of the motorway.

I looked out of the darkened window but the world outside suddenly seemed far away, as if it belonged to a different planet. I had done something which had taken me beyond humanity and placed me, full of shame and self-hatred, among the angels. I had killed my best friend.

I turned to my mother. "What about Gip?" I said. "I must know what's happened to him."

She squeezed my hand. "All is good," she murmured. "All will be resolved."

After about ten minutes, we left the main road, heading towards some kind of air force base guarded by high-security wire. As we approached the gates, a barrier rose and we swept through without even slowing down.

We passed some buildings then took a sharp turn towards the open expanse of a runway.

"Where are we going?" I asked, alarmed now. "What's going on?"

No one answered. Ahead of us, on the runway, I saw a sleek private jet. "I haven't got my passport," I said.

I moved closer to my mother. "I don't want to be taken to the Angel Factory," I said. "Don't let them, Mum, please."

The limo drew up beside the long metal steps leading up to the plane. Cy, my mother, and my father got out of the car. I followed. A man in a trim dark suit was waiting at the top of the steps.

"We'll see you in a moment, Thomas," said Cy Gabriel.

I looked up the steps. "You're not coming?"

My mother smiled. "It's OK," she said. "We'll be here." She kissed me lightly on the cheek. "Remember your manners."

Slowly, I walked up the steps. At the top, the man smiled oddly. "Just a quick search now, son," he said in an American accent.

I held out my arms. He padded around my body for a while.

"Still got the disc?" he asked.

I had forgotten about that. I reached into my back pocket and handed the kewl-disc to him. "Follow me, please," he said, turning into the darkness of the plane.

He knocked on a door. A sing-song voice called out "Ya" from inside. The door opened into an office. Behind a big desk, wearing shirt-sleeves and smiling broadly, was the most powerful man in the world.

"So. Welcome, Thomas Wisdom," said the president of the United States.

31 · HUMAN

MY FIRST THOUGHT was that, through some angelic strangeness, I had been absorbed into a monitor screen once more, that all this—the journey, the plane, President Foxx—was not real but one of the living dreams that seem to be part of the Project. At the throw of a switch I would be back in my room, blinking in front of my computer.

But there was nothing virtual about President Jim Foxx. He stepped forward and, in one movement, grasped my right hand in that great paw of his while holding my left forearm. "At last we meet," he said, gazing at me with this big smile, as if his life had been empty until I walked into his plane. And, weirdly, I felt happy too at that moment—proud to be in the presence of this big, swaggering, blond-haired cowboy of a man.

He was gazing at me as if expecting some kind of response.

"Hi." The word emerged from the back

of my throat. It sounded like the distant cry of a seagull.

The President of the United States looked me straight in the eye as if what I had just said was the wisest thing he had ever heard. Reluctantly he let go of my hand. "Coke? Beer?" He walked over to a cocktail cabinet in the corner.

"Coke, please," I croaked.

He opened the cabinet and took out two cans. He gave me one, opened a can of beer for himself, then eased his big frame into the chair behind the desk. Taking a long, thirsty swig at the beer, he said, "Now don't you go telling the press that the President drinks on the job." He smiled at me as if we were best friends. "I got enough problems already."

"I don't understand." I spoke quietly. "What are you—? I mean, what am I doing here?"

The President chuckled, as if at the sheer craziness of the idea that good old Jim Foxx had ended up in Air Force One. "I didn't fly in to see Thomas Wisdom, if that's what you're thinking. There was a conference and my people mentioned that you and I might have a word about one or two problems we share." He picked up a sheet of typed paper that was lying on his desk and read it for a moment. "We need to talk, Thomas," he said, more serious now. "Man to man."

"Man to angel."

President Foxx smiled. "You ain't telling me you're surprised that the President is part of the Project?"

"Kind of."

"You seem to be in the habit of underestimating us."

I sat in silence. I suppose I should have felt alarmed at this point, maybe even afraid, but somehow the President exuded a warmth, almost a sense of companionship, that made me feel as if we were both in this together, that there was no problem in the world that could not be solved by a couple of guys, swigging their drinks and talking it over.

"Here's the thing," he said eventually. "You have a kinda privileged position in what we call the Project. You're the future, Thomas—the first generation of true humans that can change the course of history."

He looked at me significantly.

"Great," I said.

"See." He shifted his position as if he were about to tell a long story. "Our job is not to save humanity, but to empower it. You guys have to choose life yourselves. We're here to present the options. Then it's up to you."

I knew what I was meant to be doing. The President of the United States was talking to me about the future of the planet. My duty was to sit in respectful silence and listen. But the more this big, confident man treated me like his greatest buddy in the world, the less I was able to shift the image of my real friend, lying lifelessly on the floor of his room.

Mistaking my silence for nervousness, the President was about to start talking again, but it was me who spoke first.

"What happened to Gip?" I asked.

"Gip?" The President's eyes flickered uncertainly over the paper before him.

"Gary Sanchez," I said.

"Ah, Gary." The President sat back in his chair. "You mean the guy you killed."

"I thought angels were de-activated."

"Yeah, right, whatever. Gary's fine."

I was overcome by a great surge of relief. "He's not dead?"

"He's not dead—at least not in the important, Project sense of the word." The President smiled broadly like some dodgy preacher bringing news of the Promised Land. "When an angel is de-activated on Earth, his essence returns home. Believe me, Tom." He gazed at me with damp-eyed sincerity. "Your friend Gip is in a far better place."

I closed my eyes for a moment. I knew then that I hated the Project. The last doubt in my mind as to what I had to do had disappeared.

"You all right, Tom?"

"I'm fine," I said quietly. "You were telling me how it is down to me to decide my future."

"That's right. We prepared the ground. With our help, you discovered the truth about your adoption. You visited the Angel Factory. The Presence entered your life. You learned about the Project and its importance for mankind."

"All that was set up."

"We merely laid the path. You walked it."

"And Mr. Rendle? Was he part of the path?"

The President gave an easy, win-some-lose-some shrug. "Life's full of tough choices, Thomas. It was important for you to see that the Project is not just a bowl of candies. Sacrifices have to be made for the greater good."

"Are you saying that Mr. Rendle had to die just so that I understood how serious the Project was?"

"There was more to it than that. He knew stuff. Our people weren't happy about the way he had cracked our code. He might just have persuaded you to download more files from your dad's computer. It was all getting kinda messy."

"So you tidied up."

"That's right." The President spoke with a hint of impatience in his voice. "They say he wasn't the greatest teacher anyway."

"If everything was arranged for me, where did the choice come in?"

"OK." The President placed his big hands behind his head. "So you are guided by angels—Cy, your parents, your friend Gip."

"But Gip was always on my side."

"Precisely. His function was to offer you an alternative to joining the Project—the path of rebellion. To be a devil's advocate. We needed to see if an average guy like Thomas Wisdom—bright, kind, normal—would understand what we were doing. We would offer you everything but Gip would be there to tempt you with the other, less responsible way. He would show you how the Project sometimes came at a high human cost with the whole Rendle thing. He would take you to your real mother. He would even offer you the chance to destroy our work. Then it would be a true choice for you. We have one or two similar experiments going on in different parts of the world. Yours went critical before the rest."

"Except, when Gip contacted all those adopted kids across the world and I dictated that letter, that was where my freedom came to an end."

"We may be good, but we're not stupid. Gip was under instructions to delay sending your letter out, so that we could talk to you, show you the implications of what you were doing."

I thought of what had happened to Rendle. "Talk to me?"

"We were convinced you'd see sense. Until then you'd been a perfect subject."

"That's the thing about us humans," I said sharply. "Just when you think you understand us, we go and do the unpredictable thing."

"Yeah." The President frowned. "We're going to have to do something about that."

"I made a choice, didn't I? For the first time I left that precious path of yours. I found out Gip was an angel and I closed his circuits with my mother's kewl-disc."

For the first time, the President looked displeased. "You messed up our plans big-time."

"Sorry about that, Mr. President." I felt sad, thinking of Gip and how our friendship had been part of the Project.

"But, hey, let's be positive, Tom." The President leaned forward and rested his head on his big hands. "We know it's not too late. Our information is that there are no signs of inappropriate activity from our targeted children around the world. That e-mail hasn't been sent."

I said nothing.

"In which case—" He winked at me as if we were involved in some kind of private game. "There's absolutely no reason why we can't still do business."

"What kind of business?"

"All you need to do is let us know where to find the computer, agree to tell no one anything about this, and let us get back on track with the Project."

"What about the other kids around the world you've been taking down the path?"

"They're no longer your problem, Tom. You're free of all that."

There was silence in Air Force One. Through one of the small, circular windows, I could see two soldiers, both with serious-looking guns slung over the shoulders, chatting to one another.

"So." The President smiled. "Here's what we can do. You and I—together, now—can reach an agreement. You give us what we need and life goes back to normal. As far as you're concerned, none of this will have happened."

"Except my math teacher is dead, I've discovered that my parents come from outer space, and I've lost my best friend."

"Stuff happens, Tom. You'll learn that one day." He glanced at his watch and stood up. "So if you'd like to tell Cy Gabriel where to get hold of the computer, we can draw a line under the whole story."

He walked around to my side of the desk and stood over me, his hands sunk in his trouser pockets. "It's decision time, Tom," he said with quiet menace.

Suddenly, I felt small and alone. One by one, the people I loved or depended on had been revealed as angels. Now the President of the United States was giving me one, simple instruction. Yes. It was all I had to say in order to be given back my family, my life, for me to be free, for the events of the past weeks to start fading like a nightmare in the morning sun.

"Do yourself a favor, kid," said the President, jangling some loose change in his pocket.

I looked out of the window at the countryside beyond the tarmac of the airport. Out there, all over the world, men and women and children were going about their daily business. They were laughing and crying and loving and hurting and doing all the good and bad things, making all the right and wrong choices, that made them human. I saw Rendle crouched in front of his mum. I heard Manny's loud, innocent laugh in the darkness of the theater. I remembered my own, my real mother holding me in her arms. "You're a good kid," she had said.

Then I thought of the Presence, the Project, Cy Gabriel, and the President of the United States and the clean, trouble-free future they promised for us all.

"Well?" The President laid a hand on my shoulder.

I took a deep breath and tried to speak but my mouth was dry and all I could manage was a despairing croak. I swallowed, cleared my throat, closed my eyes—and said it loud and clear.

"No."

The President looked down at me, as if unable to believe what he had just heard. "What was that, Thomas?" he said.

"No."

He took his hand off my shoulder. "You're telling me you don't want to save humanity from self-destruction?"

"No." Feeling stronger now, I took a swig from my can of Coke. When I spoke again, my voice was flat and even, as if a machine were talking. I told him that it was all too late. The full story had been told to a human that no angel had reached. If anything happened to me, the computer would be found and the e-mail would be sent out to adopted children all over the world. I said that there was nothing anybody could do about this. "I am not going to change my mind," I said. "I've seen enough of the Project to know that, however noble its aims, all is not good."

The President turned his back on me and gazed down at the security guards outside.

"And all will not be resolved," I said. "Further down the line, there will be loads of people who'll feel like me. In the end, like it or not, you'd have to save us by force."

The President's shoulders gave a sort of shrug in reply.

"We might be a mess," I said. "But that's the way we like it. That's the way we are."

He turned and slumped back into his chair, looking tired and pale now, as if, at the throw of a switch, the warmth and color that had glowed from him moments ago had been closed down.

"Who the hell d'you think you are?" He spoke wearily. "Some geeky little kid who can throw all our plans for a loop because he can't see the big picture, because he's so—" An expression of disgust crossed his face "so human."

"That sounds about right," I said.

"Does it occur to you that, if the Project is deactivated, little Thomas Wisdom will be in the world without his parents, without his sister? You're not just letting me and the whole Project down, you're betraying your own family."

I thought for a moment of my life and how good it had been. I saw us in the garden, the sun shining, Dougal on the lawn engaged in a fight to the death with an old tennis ball. "I think I'm doing what they would want me to do," I said.

"They're angels, Tom."

"I know what they are."

He sighed wearily. "Let's go through this once more. Perhaps I can help you in some other areas—as a gesture of good faith."

"Mr. President, you're wasting your time."

"You don't know what you're turning down yet. I can make your life pretty good. Hey, how about making sure that your parents never have to work again?"

"I mean it," I said.

He glared at me for a moment, as if the sheer force of his will could make me change my mind, but I held his gaze. He swore quietly to himself, then pressed the button on his desk. The door behind me opened.

"I'll see Gabriel," he told the security guard as he scribbled something on the typed piece of paper on his desk. After a moment, he glanced up and seemed irritable that I was still in his presence. "Scram, kid," he said coldly.

"Thank you, Mr. President," I said.

I walked to the door.

"Go back to your family and don't leave home until we tell you," said the President.

The guard closed the door behind me. I made my way to the entrance of Air Force One and stepped out into the dazzling sun. My parents and Cy Gabriel were standing on the tarmac like a reception party.

I stood at the top of the steps, feeling suddenly tired, alone and frightened. I shook my head slowly and they understood. As I walked down, I noticed that the faces of my father and Cy Gabriel were not so much angry as blank and impassive. Only my mother smiled. She held out both arms as I approached and held me close.

The guard called Cy and my father over to him and they spoke for a few seconds. Cy climbed the steps for his meeting with the President.

Dad returned to us. He stood in front of me, hands in his pockets, an empty, desolate look on his face and I sensed that he was working on that stern-father act that he has never quite mastered. He shook his head slowly. "Another fine mess you've got us into," he said.

He walked on to the car where Luke was sitting in the driving-seat.

"Home," he said.

32 · HOPE

MAYBE, ALL OVER THE WORLD, there were people who were making the same decision as I had made, or were making the opposite decision, or had closed their eyes to the existence of angels altogether and were continuing their lives as if nothing had happened.

Right now, I didn't care. The future of Planet Earth was no longer what I was thinking about. As we drove back into town at a normal speed, unaccompanied by robocops on motorbikes, what was on my mind was the future of me.

I had told the President of the United States, the most powerful person—the most powerful angel—in the world, that I would be no part of the Project. He knew that I had betrayed it to humans.

What next? They had the power to destroy any little anti-angel movement. The President had rabbited on about my importance to their plans. Now that I stood in the way of the Project, what would happen to me? Some unfortunate little accident around the home, at school, on the street? Who could I trust? My mother's arm was around me now but it occurred to me that she might be comforting me or, on the other hand, restraining me from any crazy idea of escape. I was surrounded by angels. It would take one word for the little pocket of resistance that was Thomas Wisdom to be rubbed out.

We traveled home in silence. Luke dropped us off at the house and then swept away in his big black limousine. When we let ourselves in, Amy and Dougal greeted us in the hall. By the expression on my sister's face, I could tell that she had heard the news.

Muttering that I was tired, I went to my room and closed the door. In a moment of curiosity, I switched on the computer in the corner. It was dead, as if its circuits too had been closed down. I lay on my bed and closed my eyes.

It must have been several minutes later when I heard a soft knock on my door. Amy put her head round the door. "Got a moment?" she asked.

"Sure," I said.

She sat on the bed and gave me the that's-torn-it smile I knew so well. "Always the awkward one, eh, bro?" she murmured.

"I did what was right."

"Yeah. You did."

"So where do you stand on all this?"

"It doesn't matter what I think."

I sat up and asked the question that had been on my mind all day. "Could you have saved Gip?"

My sister looked out of the window for a moment. "No," she said. "We passed the information over. Apparently it was too late."

"They let him die."

Amy said nothing.

"And they are you," I said.

"Listen." Amy put an arm around my shoulders. "Mum's downstairs, crying. Dad's sitting like a stunned zombie in the kitchen. All I want to do is talk to my little brother. Even Dougal seems a bit more freaked than usual. D'you really have to ask? We love you. In fact—" she frowned as if she were surprised by what she was thinking. "We probably love you even more now than we did before. Our little Thomas, who told the President of the United States to get lost. Understand?"

I understood. "Thanks," I said.

And with that, weirdly, we returned to a sort of family routine. Mum cooked the meals I liked. We talked about the family and school and how I would miss Gip as if there was no great Project-shaped cloud hanging over the future of the Wisdom family. Only when one of the family went out, making sure that the other two stayed with me, was I reminded with a thump of anxiety in the solar plexus that I was under house arrest.

One day, two days, three. It is a strange fact that, locked away with my family, awaiting word of our fate, I felt closer to them than I had ever been. Before I had known that they came from another planet, I had been aware of a gulf of misunderstanding between us. Now I knew everything about the distance between us, there were no secrets, and we could all be ourselves, free of the secrets and lies of the past. Mum and Dad and Amy no longer went to work but spent their time with me.

Talking. Laughing. And waiting.

On the evening of the third day, Cy Gabriel appeared at our door without warning. He had the pale, crumpled look of a man who has done too much talking and not enough sleeping.

"Cy." When Dad uttered that word, it was as if an electric shock ran through the house. I had been in the kitchen with my mother, who moved closer to me, putting an arm around my shoulders as if that could protect me. When we followed Dad and Cy into the sitting-room, Amy was there, with Dougal.

I sat on the sofa between my mother and my father. Dougal looked up at me, as if he could sense that this was not a normal family gathering. I patted my lap and he jumped up.

Standing in the center of the room, Cy glanced at me, briefly and without affection.

My father noticed his look. "You say what you have to say to us all." He smiled coldly at his boss. "The four of us are in this together."

"Very touching." Cy smiled wearily and lowered himself into a chair like an old man. "But I guess you're right. The time for secrets is past."

He sat back and, as if reciting from a speech learned by heart, he told us our fate.

"Over the past few days, consultation has taken place over the future of the Project. This is our formal resolution. Some years ago, it was decided that a course of beneficent intervention was the best and most advisable way to prevent this planet from following a course of self-destruction. Angels were constructed in the form of humankind. Thanks to our co-operative network and intelligence assistance from the Presence, they reached positions of influence throughout the globe. Two years ago, the first phase of the Project was successfully completed with the election of James Foxx as President of the United States."

"Cut to the chase, Cy," Dad murmured.

"We are a force of peace. We represent goodness. It was always intended that we should enable humankind to save itself. Its future was, and is, in its children. The second phase of the Project would involve the recruitment of those who had been adopted nine, ten or eleven years ago by certain designated angels. They were guided towards the Project. They were introduced to its aims. They communicated with the Presence. Then they were asked to decide— as important a moment in our Project as the election of the President. The facts were laid before them. The path of goodness stretched into the future. All that was required of them was their co-operation with the force of angels."

Cy directed his gaze at me. "We now see that we underestimated the human desire for autonomy—what they like to call 'freedom.' During the second phase, a choice was made. We believe it was the wrong choice. The possibility of further persuasion, of selective elimination of problem areas, has been considered."

My mother moved closer to me and placed her hand on mine.

"We do not by nature abandon major projects of improvement before they are satisfactorily completed," Cy continued. "But, on this occasion, we will. The Project is over. The future of humankind will be left to humankind to resolve without our assistance. Within twelve hours, President Foxx will announce that he will not be seeking re-election for a second term."

"What about us?" Amy's voice was a whisper.

"Angels shall report to their factories for their annual reconfiguration in the normal manner but, on this occasion, a final circuit shall be installed in which the human genome, with all its faults and frailties, will be reproduced.

This will mean that angels will live as healthily or unhealthily, as happily or sadly, or as long or as short as any normal being. The randomness of life on Earth has been perfectly replicated. During their lives, angels will be part of humankind. When their circuit is closed—when they die, in human terms—they shall return to the Presence to be at peace. Within twelve months of this announcement, all traces of our involvement with humankind will have vanished."

As if he had suddenly realized what was being said affected him, Dougal looked up from my lap. "What about the animals?" I asked.

"The animals." Cy hesitated. "Angels will be provided with kewl-circuits to adapt them to a lifespan appropriate to Earth-life."

He turned to me. "Thomas, you are required to retrieve the computer from the hiding-place you chose for it. Its first contact with an electrical current will destroy the hard disk. Bring it home. Plug it in. Switch it on. It will then be good only for scrap."

I nodded my agreement.

He smiled coldly at me, then continued. "It is to be regretted that this great Project, perhaps one of the most ambitious policies in the history of the universe, has had to be terminated prematurely. Yet we are obliged to recognize that the desire of humankind for freedom, its need to decide its own fate for itself, has encouraged us. The future of the Earth, we always believed, rested in its children and its children have given us hope."

Cy Gabriel stood up. "On behalf of the Presence and the many guides and operatives behind our great Project, I bestow upon humankind our good wishes and prayers for the future."

He shook our hands, first Amy's, then my parents', finally—after a moment's hesitation—mine. "Good luck, Thomas," he said. "You're on your own now."

I smiled. "I guess."

We followed him from the room, let him out the front door. He walked away without a backward glance.

For a moment, after he was gone, the four of us stood wordlessly in the hall. Uneasy at this strange and unusual silence, Dougal looked up at us and barked.

"He needs a walk," my mother murmured.

"Life goes on," said Dad.

I picked up the key from the hall table, Dougal's lead from the hook behind the door.

"Yeah." I smiled and my smile took in all of them, all of my family. "Life goes on."

We were free. I was free. My family of angels was just the Wisdom family, now and for the future. After their next visit to the Angel Factory, Mum, Dad, and Amy would be on their own. Their lives would be as uncontrolled, mysterious, and surprising as any human's. It was going to take some getting used to but, through it all, we would be equal at last. That sense of not quite belonging to one another which first caused me to talk to Gip and set the events of the summer in motion was fading with every second.

Of course, life would never be quite the same. Mum and Dad would have to find a new job. Amy's relationship with Luke, the surfing chauffeur, would change.

I would be without Gip Sanchez. Every time I thought of him, I saw him lying at my feet, my right hand glowing with the kewl-disc, I felt a lurch of panic in my gut. No more chats on the phone, jokes, and meetings in the park. Right now, life seemed empty without him.

In kind of a daze, we each went about our business that

evening, chatting occasionally about what Cy Gabriel had said.

Later, I went upstairs and took out the card that was still in my trouser pocket. There was one more call to make. I walked to my parents' bedroom, closed the door, sat on their bed and dialed the number.

"Karen, it's Thomas."

"Hi, Thomas. What's cookin'?" The voice sounded slightly slurred.

"Did you get my letter and the key?"

"I did." She seemed uncertain as to what exactly she should say. "You are all right, aren't you, love? Your dad was a bit doolally sometimes. Maybe you should see someone."

"I'm not doolally, Karen. I'm fine."

"So what's all this stuff about angels?"

I hesitated. "It was nothing to worry about—it was a sort of game."

"A game? Thomas, love, I'm a busy woman. I've got a career to think of."

"I know. I'm sorry. Could you send me back the key?"

Grumbling, she took down my address.

"Will we be able to talk now and then?" I asked.

"Yeah. I'm coming down to London soon. Maybe we could go and have a meal."

"That'd be good."

"I'd better go now, love. I'm on stage soon."

"Say hi to the Great Miraculo for me."

She laughed. "Bloomin' kids," she said.

33 · FALLEN

IT WAS A TIME FOR NORMALITY, for starting again. Ten days remained before the start of the autumn term. The Wisdom family spent most of that time doing something the Wisdom family had never been particularly good at—it slobbed out.

Mum and Dad sat in the garden, chatting and drinking wine. Amy went out with Luke a couple more times, then told us kind of tearfully that she had broken up with him because she had decided that (hey, surprise!) he was a tad boring. I watched TV and read and enjoyed not having to worry about the future of mankind for a change.

I was, of course, missing Gip. Although I was no longer on a guilt trip about what I had done, I kept remembering times we had in the past, jokes I could make which only Gip really understood. I rang another friend, a guy called Matt, even went round his place to check out a new computer game he had been given for his birthday.

It was fine. It was good. Matt was a perfectly OK guy, his new game was great and his stories about meeting up with some girl he met on a camping holiday in France were kind of funny, if a little tame compared to what I had been doing that summer.

I listened and smiled and knew that I would be doing a lot of listening and smiling over the next few weeks. For the past few years, I had belonged to an exclusive club—with a membership of two. Now that club was closed and it was time for me to mix and match and make new friends. Like Mum, Dad, and Amy, I had to get human.

During that time, I avoided the corner of the park where Gip and I used to go. It was a place with too many memories. Then, on the day before school began, I decided that the only way to move into a new future was to face up to the past.

It was early evening, all gold and sad with a hint of chill in the air. I had slipped out of the house with Dougal, not telling anyone where I was going. I entered the park, sauntered past a group of kids playing football. I went to the bench behind the hut, our bench.

I looked around me, breathing heavily, my mind full of thoughts and echoes and regrets. I watched my dog as he scuttled about the undergrowth among the first leaves of autumn. I must have sat there for ten, maybe fifteen minutes.

It was getting cold. I called Dougal. Reluctantly, he made his way back to me. Then, suddenly, he stopped some five yards short of the bench where I sat. He growled, the hackles on his back rising.

"Hey, Doogie," I said. "Cut it out, what's your problem?"

I noticed that he was not looking at me but at a point

behind me. I was about to look over my shoulder when I heard a voice that I knew better than any other.

"I'm his problem."

Slowly, I turned. A figure was standing behind me, still and threatening. In one hand, glinting in the evening sun, was a knife.

"Gip," I said.

He stared at me in silence.

"How's it going then?" I asked.

He walked forward slowly, his eyes fixed on mine. As he reached the bench, he raised the knife to no more than a few inches from my throat. He sat down beside me.

"How d'you think it's going?" he asked huskily.

"You're alive," I said, ignoring the blade as best I could. "I'm . . . I'm so glad."

"The guys in the squat got to me," he said.

"They were angels too?"

"Yeah. The house was wall-to-wall angel. They saw you going and broke the rules by bringing me back. Two minutes later and I would have been a goner."

"I did ring my father. I told them where you were."

"You're all heart."

"I'm . . . I'm sorry about killing you and all that."

"No problem. You did what you had to do."

I looked beyond Gip. The park was emptying as the evening gloom began to descend. In the old days, Gip and I would be glad that no one checked that the place was empty before the iron gates were locked. Now I longed for some park-keeper to pass by.

"What's with the blade?" I asked gently.

Gip turned the knife slowly, showing me, as if I had any doubt, that it was no toy. "Kitchen jobby," he said. "Does the business, no problem."

I looked him in the eye. "What business?" I said.

"You think you're in such great shape." It was a whisper of despair. "You won. Everyone's going to be nice and normal from now on. You'll be with your perfect family" —he sneered in the general direction of Dougal— "with your sappy little Scottie dog."

"We can still be friends. I've been missing you."

"It's over, dead. I'm leaving the area. There won't be no Gip at school tomorrow."

"Why?"

"I had a job to do. That's why I was here. I was to be Thomas's friend, his mate, his guide. They fixed me up, gave me a life, slipped me money. So I did it. We were friends, right?"

I nodded. "The best."

"But I failed. All I had to do was bring you into the Project and I blew it."

"Maybe that was because our friendship was stronger than any instruction the Presence could give you."

"Yeah yeah." He shook his head dismissively.

"You mean you only liked me because that was your job, because it was part of the Project?"

"No!" Gip jabbed the knife towards me and I felt the tip of the blade pricking my throat. "It had nothing to do with me being an angel."

"I know it didn't."

"When they brought me back, you know what they did?" Suddenly Gip slipped away from me and did an athletic little twirl. "They fixed my leg. Gip is gimpy no more. The deal was that I was to tell people that I had this miracle operation during the summer. And, hey guys, Gip Sanchez is a normal, regular guy." He sat down, jiggling the knife in his right hand, its blade a few inches from my ribs. "So if you make a break for it, I'd catch you, no sweat. I'm lightning these days."

"I'm going nowhere."

"Joke is, I don't want to be normal. I want to be the way I was. And, if I can't be, I'll just have to prove that angels can be human too. They can be good, like your mummy and daddy, and—" He prodded me with the blade. "They can be bad."

I looked at him. He was even thinner than he used to be. There were dark rings under his eyes and smears of dirt across his face as if he had been sleeping in the open.

"I'm a fallen angel," he said. "I'm ready to do the one thing that will make me free." He smiled down at the knife. "And then I will disappear. I'll start again somewhere new."

There was silence between us broken only by the rasping sound of Gip's breath. I looked into his eyes. I wanted to say something, to make him feel better but I sensed that I had lost him. He was beyond me, gone.

"You were the best friend anyone could ever have," I said. "Without you, I never would have made it. You saved me. You gave me the strength to do what I did."

Gip's eyes glittered in the semi-darkness.

Slowly, gently, I laid my hand on the blade of the knife, then edged it forward to the hilt. With a sigh, Gip released it. I placed it on the ground and, with my right foot, kicked it out of reach. Scared, Dougal jumped back with a yelp. In spite of myself, I laughed.

Gip shook his head in a way that reminded me of the times we had spent together in the past. "Your life, man," he said.

We sat in silence for a minute or two. Then he sniffed and wiped his nose with the back of his hand. "Gotta go," he said.

"Gip. Stay. Please. You're not an angel anymore. It's all past. Now we're just a couple of humans. We can be friends—normal friends."

He stood up. "Gotta go," he repeated. He turned and walked away, with such a lithe and easy gait that I had to smile.

"Think about it," I called after him.

He looked over his shoulder, smiled that old Gip smile, and kept walking.

34 · SPARK

SOMETIMES, LATE AT NIGHT, I go into the garden and gaze up at the stars. I think of the Presence, the Project. I wonder if somewhere, millions of miles away, they're looking down at us and shaking their heads (or whatever they have in the place of heads) as they watch poor old humankind blundering onwards in that hopeless way of ours. Do they feel sorry for the angels they left down here—Mum, Dad, Amy, Luke, Gip, Cy, Daisy Dover, the President of the United States? Or are they secretly jealous of the human world with all its faults, its precious sense of freedom?

At home, the angels became normal, all right. Dad and Mum set up a computer consulting business. Amy went slightly crazy and decided at kind of a late stage that she wanted to be a doctor. Dougal still believes that, deep down, he's a cat.

Now and then, from friends at school, I hear rumors that Gip is at a school on the other side of town. They say he's wild and kind of crazy and that he's a rebel hero for the younger kids, so I guess he never changed that much. I met Manny on the street the other day and he gave me Gip's new number. One day soon, I'm going to pluck up the courage to make that call.

Something strange—it was Amy who pointed it out to me. After their final visit to the factory, angels changed slightly in the way they looked and they behaved. A sort of light, a spark of humor and humanity, entered their eyes. Slowly, their marks of distinction, the derm upon their necks or shoulders or arms, began to fade.

But it seems they never quite disappear. There will always be a faint trace of what was there.

Take a look at those around you—your friends, your teachers, maybe even your parents. Check them out for that tell-tale shadow of what once made them different from you and me.

For they are all around us, the humans who once were angels.

She's sharp.

She's smart.

She's confident.

She's unstoppable.

And she's on your trail.

Still sleuthing,

still solving crimes,

but she's got some new tricks up her sleeve!

NANCY DREW girl detective

Lonely planet

P9-DFZ-552

Cuba

Havana
p60

**Valle de Viñales &
Pinar del Río**
p174

**Artemisa &
Mayabeque**
p145

**Varadero &
Matanzas**
p198

Villa Clara
p252

Cienfuegos
p235

**Ciego de
Ávila**
p300

**Trinidad &
Sancti
Spíritus**
p273

**Isla de la Juventud
(Special Municipality)**
p159

Camagüey
p315

**Las
Tunas**
p334

Holguín
p344

Granma
p370

**Santiago
de Cuba**
p391

Guantánamo
p428

THIS EDITION WRITTEN AND RESEARCHED BY

Brendan Sainsbury

Luke Waterson

PLAN YOUR TRIP

Welcome to Cuba 6

Cuba Map 8

Cuba's Top 21 10

Need to Know 20

First Time Cuba 22

What's New 26

If You Like 27

Month by Month 30

Itineraries 34

Outdoor Activities 42

Travel with Children 51

Regions at a Glance 53

BIRD-WATCHING P496

CAVING P43

ON THE ROAD

HAVANA 60

Downtown Havana 61

Sights 64

Sleeping 96

Eating 104

Drinking & Nightlife 111

Entertainment 114

Shopping 118

Playa & Marianao 126

Parque Lenin Area 135

Santiago de las
Vegas Area 137

Regla 137

Guanabacoa 138

Cojímar Area 140

Casablanca 140

Playas del Este 141

**ARTEMISA &
MAYABEQUE
PROVINCES 145**

Artemisa Province 147

San Antonio de
los Baños 147

Artemisa 148

Soroa 149

Las Terrazas 151

Mayabeque Province . . .154

Playa Jibacoa Area 155

Jaruco 157

Surgidero de Batabanó . . .158

**ISLA DE LA JUVENTUD
(SPECIAL
MUNICIPALITY) . . . 159**

Isla de la Juventud 161

Nueva Gerona 161

East of Nueva Gerona . . . 167

South of Nueva Gerona . . 167

The Southern
Military Zone 168

Cayo Largo del Sur 169

**VALLE DE VIÑALES
& PINAR DEL RÍO
PROVINCE 174**

Valle de Viñales 175

Viñales 175

Parque Nacional Viñales . . . 183

West of Viñales 185

The Northern Coast . . . 185

Cayo Jutías 186

Puerto Esperanza 186

Cayo Levisa 186

Playa Mulata Area 187

**San Diego de los Baños
& Around 187**

San Diego de los Baños . . .187

Sierra la Güira 188

Pinar del Río Area 189

Pinar del Río 189

Southwest of Pinar
del Río 194

**Península de
Guanahacabibes 195**

Parque Nacional Península
de Guanahacabibes 195

**VARADERO &
MATANZAS
PROVINCE 198**

Northern Matanzas . . . 199

Varadero 199

Varadero to Matanzas . . . 215

Matanzas 216

Cárdenas 224

San Miguel de
los Baños & Around 226

Península de Zapata . . . 227

Central Australia
& Around 228

Boca de Guamá 228

Gran Parque Natural
Montemar 230

Playa Larga 231

Playa Girón 232

Contents

CIENFUEGOS PROVINCE........ 235

Cienfuegos 236

Rancho Luna........... 248

Castillo de Jagua 249

Laguna Guanaroca............. 250

Jardín Botánico de Cienfuegos.......... 250

El Nicho 250

Caribbean Coast........ 251

VILLA CLARA PROVINCE........ 252

Santa Clara 253

Remedios............. 264

Caibarién.............. 267

Cayerías del Norte 269

TRINIDAD & SANCTI SPÍRITUS PROVINCE........ 273

Trinidad 275

Playa Ancón & Around ... 286

Valle de los Ingenios 288

Topes de Collantes...... 289

Sancti Spíritus 291

Northern Sancti Spíritus Province............... 298

CIEGO DE ÁVILA PROVINCE........ 300

Ciego de Ávila.......... 302

Morón................. 307

Around Morón.......... 308

Florencia 310

Cayo Coco............. 310

Cayo Guillermo......... 313

CAMAGÜEY PROVINCE........ 315

Camagüey.............. 317

Florida 328

Sierra del Chorrillo...... 328

Guáimaro.............. 329

HAVANA P60

Nuevitas...............329	**HOLGUÍN**	**GRANMA**
Brasil & Around 330	**PROVINCE........344**	**PROVINCE......... 370**
Cayo Sabinal..........330	Holguín................345	Bayamo 372
Playa Santa Lucía 331	Gibara................357	Gran Parque Nacional
	Guardalavaca	Sierra Maestra 381
LAS TUNAS	& Around 360	Manzanillo............384
PROVINCE........334	Banes.................366	Media Luna 386
Las Tunas..............335	Birán..................367	Niquero 386
Monte Cabaniguan......341	Sierra del Cristal 367	Parque Nacional
Puerto Padre...........341	Cayo Saetía...........369	Desembarco del
Punta Covarrubias......342		Granma 386
Playas La Herradura,		Pilón.................388
La Llanita & Las Bocas...343		Marea del Portillo.......389

TRINIDAD P275

Contents

ARCHITECTURE P478

UNDERSTAND

Cuba Today 448

History 450

Food & Drink 463

The Cuban Way
of Life 467

Literature & the Arts . . . 473

Architecture 478

Music & Dance 486

Landscape & Wildlife . . . 492

SANTIAGO DE
CUBA PROVINCE . . 391

Santiago de Cuba 393

Siboney 418

La Gran Piedra 419

Parque Baconao 420

El Cobre 423

El Saltón 424

Chivirico 425

El Uvero 425

Pico Turquino Area 426

GUANTÁNAMO
PROVINCE 428

Guantánamo 430

Around Guantánamo
US Naval Base 435

South Coast 436

Punta de Maisí 436

Boca de Yumurí
& Around 436

Baracoa 437

Northwest of Baracoa . . . 444

Parque Nacional
Alejandro de
Humboldt 445

SURVIVAL
GUIDE

Directory A–Z 500

Transportation 511

Language 521

SPECIAL FEATURES

Guide to Getting
Off the Beaten Track . . . 40

Cuba's Best Diving
Sites 46

Old Havana
Walking Tour 72

Cuban Architecture
Feature 478

Welcome to Cuba

Timeworn but magnificent, dilapidated but dignified, fun yet maddeningly frustrating – Cuba is a country of indefinable magic.

Expect the Unexpected

Cuba is like a prince in a poor man's coat: behind the sometimes shabby facades, gold dust lingers. It's these rich dichotomies that make travel here the exciting, exhilarating roller-coaster ride it is. Trapped in a time warp and reeling from an economic embargo that has grated for more than half a century, this is a country where you can wave goodbye to Western certainties and expect the unexpected. If Cuba were a book, it would be James Joyce's *Ulysses*: layered, hard to grasp, serially misunderstood, but – above all – a classic.

Historical Heritage

Meticulously preserved, Cuba's colonial cities haven't changed much since musket-toting pirates stalked the Caribbean. The atmosphere and architecture is particularly stirring in the Unesco-listed cities – Havana, Trinidad, Cienfuegos and Camagüey – where grandiose squares and cobbled streets tell erstwhile tales of opulence and intrigue. Elsewhere many buildings lie ruined and tattered like aging dowagers waiting for a face lift. With more funds, these heirlooms may yet emulate the colonial treasures in Havana and Trinidad, further proof that the safeguarding of Cuba's historical legacy has been one of the revolution's greatest achievements.

Cultural Eclecticism

Cuba hemorrhages music, a dynamic mix of styles described by aficionados as a love affair between the African drum and the Spanish guitar. Allowed to marinate for over 500 years, these diverse sounds have given birth to an intricate culture, coloring it with echoes of Africa, flickers of colonial Spain, ghosts of Taíno tribes, and cultural idiosyncrasies imported from Haiti, Jamaica, France and even China. The beauty lies in its layers and nuances. It's an eclecticism that's mirrored in its dance, architecture, language, religion, and – most emphatically – its rainbow of people.

Beyond the Beaches

Although the attractive arcs of white sand that pepper its north coast are sublime, explore beyond Cuba's beaches and you're in a different domain, a land of fecund forests and crocodile-infested swamps, suburbia-free countryside and rugged mountains as famous for their revolutionary folklore as for their endemic species. Cuba, once observed German scientist Alexander von Humboldt, is a kind of Caribbean Galapagos where contradictory curiosities coexist.

Why I Love Cuba

By Brendan Sainsbury, Author

When I think of Cuba, I always think of my first night back in Havana after a break. I recall the busy atmospheric streets, the snapshots of lives lived out in the open, and the unmistakable aromas: tropical papaya mixed with tobacco leaf, petrol and musty carpets. Cuba is a forbidden fruit, a complex country of head-scratching contradictions, which, however many times you visit, will never adequately answer all your questions. Most of all I love Cuba's musicality, robust culture, wonderfully preserved history, and the fact that it can frustrate you one minute and unexpectedly inspire you the next.

For more about our authors, see page 544

Above: An iconic vintage car operates as a taxi in Havana

Cuba

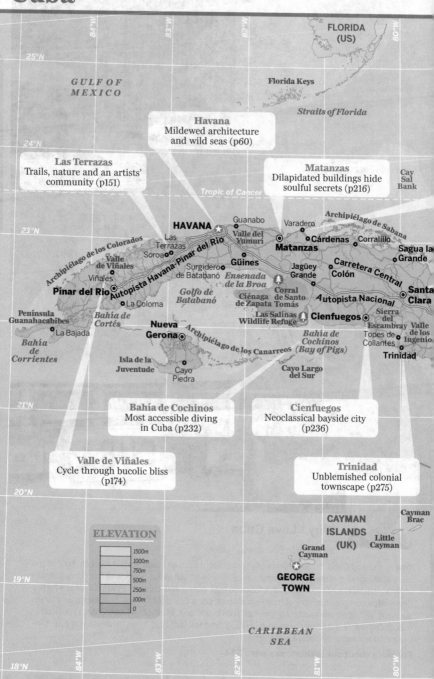

GULF OF MEXICO

FLORIDA (US)

Florida Keys

Straits of Florida

Havana
Mildewed architecture and wild seas (p60)

Las Terrazas
Trails, nature and an artists' community (p151)

Matanzas
Dilapidated buildings hide soulful secrets (p216)

Cay Sal Bank

Tropic of Cancer

Guanabo
HAVANA
Las Terrazas
Soroa
Valle de Viñales
Viñales
Pínar del Río
La Coloma
Península Guanahacabibes
La Bajada
Bahía de Cortés
Bahía de Corrientes

Archipiélago de los Colorados

Autopista Havana–Pinar del Río

Surgidero de Batabanó
Güines
Ensenada de la Broa
Golfo de Batabanó
Nueva Gerona
Archipiélago de los Canarreos

Valle del Yumurí
Matanzas
Varadero
Cárdenas
Corralillo
Archipiélago de Sabana

Jagüey Grande
Colón
Corral de Santo Tomás
Ciénaga de Zapata
Las Salinas Wildlife Refuge

Sagua la Grande

Carretera Central

Santa Clara

Cienfuegos
Autopista Nacional
Sierra del Escambray
Topes de Collantes
Bahía de Cochinos (Bay of Pigs)
Valle de los Ingenio
Trinidad

Isla de la Juventude
Cayo Piedra

Cayo Largo del Sur

Bahía de Cochinos
Most accessible diving in Cuba (p232)

Cienfuegos
Neoclassical bayside city (p236)

Valle de Viñales
Cycle through bucolic bliss (p174)

Trinidad
Unblemished colonial townscape (p275)

Cayman Brac

CAYMAN ISLANDS (UK)
Little Cayman
Grand Cayman
GEORGE TOWN

ELEVATION

	1500m
	1000m
	750m
	500m
	250m
	100m
	0

CARIBBEAN SEA

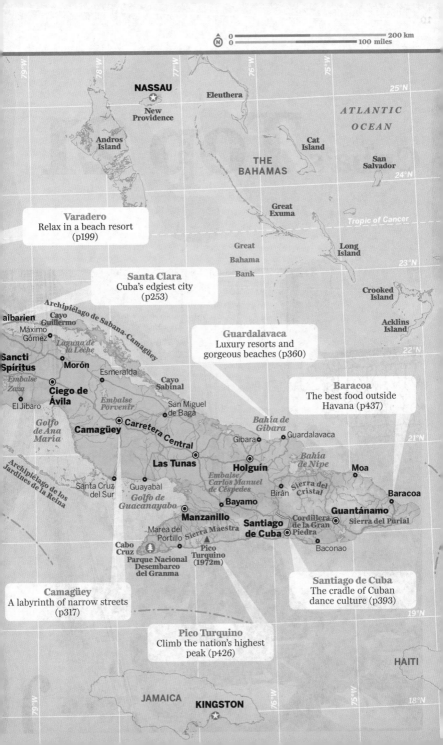

NASSAU

Eleuthera

25°N

New
Providence

ATLANTIC

OCEAN

Andros
Island

Cat
Island

San
Salvador

24°N

THE
BAHAMAS

Varadero
Relax in a beach resort
(p199)

Great
Exuma

Tropic of Cancer

Great
Bahama
Bank

Long
Island

23°N

Santa Clara
Cuba's edgiest city
(p253)

Crooked
Island

Archipiélago de Sabana-Camagüey

aibarién   Cayo
Guillermo
Máximo
Gómez

Acklins
Island

*Laguna de
la Leche*

22°N

**Sancti
Spíritus**

Morón

Esmeralda

Cayo
Sabinal

Guardalavaca
Luxury resorts and
gorgeous beaches (p360)

*Embalse
Zaza*

**Ciego de
Ávila**

*Embalse
Porvenir*

San Miguel
de Bagá

*Bahía de
Gibara*

Baracoa
The best food outside
Havana (p437)

El Jíbaro

Carretera Central

*Golfo
de Ana
María*

Camagüey

Gibara

Guardalavaca

21°N

Las Tunas

Holguín

*Bahía
de Nipe*

Moa

*Archipiélago de los
Jardines de la Reina*

Santa Cruz
del Sur

Guayabal

*Embalse
Carlos Manuel
de Céspedes*

*Sierra del
Cristal*

Baracoa

*Golfo de
Guacanayabo*

Manzanillo

Bayamo

Birán

Guantánamo

Marea del
Portillo

Sierra Maestra

**Santiago
de Cuba**

*Cordillera
de la Gran
Piedra*

Sierra del Purial

Cabo
Cruz

Pico
Turquino
(1972m)

Baconao

**Parque Nacional
Desembarco
del Granma**

Camagüey
A labyrinth of narrow streets
(p317)

Santiago de Cuba
The cradle of Cuban
dance culture (p393)

19°N

Pico Turquino
Climb the nation's highest
peak (p426)

HAITI

79°W

JAMAICA

KINGSTON

76°W

75°W

18°N

Cuba's Top 21

Live Music Scene

1 In Cuba piped music is considered a cop-out. Here in the land of *son*, salsa, rumba and *trova* everything is spontaneous, live and delivered with a melodic panache. There's the romantic bar-crawling troubadour, the gritty street-based rumba drummer, the bikini-and-feathers cabaret show and the late-night reggaetón party. Cuba's musical talent is legendary and rarely comes with the narcissistic 'star status' common in other parts of the world. Matanzas and Santiago have the deepest musical roots, Guantánamo is full of surprises, while Havana belts out pretty much everything. (p486) Musicians, Santiago de Cuba

Havana's Malecón

2 Only a fool comes to Havana and misses out on the Malecón (p92) sea drive, 8km of shabby magnificence that stretches the breadth of the city from Habana Vieja to Miramar and acts as a substitute living room for tens of thousands of cavorting, canoodling, romance-seeking *habaneros*. Traverse it during a storm when giant waves breach the wall, or tackle it at sunset with Benny Moré on your MP3 player, a bottle of Havana Club in your hand and the notion that anything is possible come 10pm.

BENJAMIN RONDEL / GETTY IMAGES ©

ARTMARIE / GETTY IMAGES ©

Cuba's Casas Particulares

3 Picture the scene: there are two rocking chairs creaking on a polished colonial porch, a half-finished bottle of rum being passed amiably between guest and host, and the sound of lilting music drifting ethereally through the humid tropical darkness. It could be any casa particular (private homestay; p501) in any street in any town – they're all the same. Shrugging off asphyxiating censorship and bleak Cold War–style totalitarianism, these private homes reveal Cuba at its most candid. Havana has the widest selection; Santa Clara's are the most palatial.

Eclectic Architecture

4 Cuba's architecture (p478), sometimes extreme yet rarely constant, mirrors its ethnic heritage. Take a muscular slice of Spanish baroque, then sprinkle in some French classicism, a generous portion of North American art deco and a hint of European art nouveau. Now add the sweat of Afro-Cuban slave labor and the odd spark of creative modernism, and there you have it. Visit the Unesco-listed cities of Havana, Trinidad, Cienfuegos and Camagüey to see for yourself. Colorful buildings line the street, Habana Vieja (p64)

Idyllic Beach Escapes

5 There's the big showy one in the resort; the wild, windswept one on the north coast; the sheltered palm-fringed one on a paradisical key; and the unashamedly nudist one on a secluded island. Search around long enough and you're sure to find your own slice of nirvana. Big resort areas such as Varadero have hijacked the best strips of sand, but isolated havens remain. Highlights include Playa Pilar (p314) on Cayo Guillermo, Playa Maguana (p445) near Baracoa and Playa Ancón (p286) near Trinidad.

Playa Ancón

Bird-Watching

6 Crocodiles aside, Cuba has little impressive fauna, but the paucity of animals is more than made up for by the abundance of birdlife. Approximately 350 species inhabit this distinct and ecologically weird tropical archipelago, a good two dozen of them endemic. Look out in particular for the colorful *tocororo,* the tiny bee hummingbird, the critically endangered ivory-billed woodpecker and the world's largest flamingo nesting site. The Península de Zapata and the Sierra del Rosario Biosphere Reserve are bird-watching highlights. (p496) *Zunzuncito* (bee hummingbird)

Revolutionary Heritage

7 An improbable escape from a shipwrecked yacht, bearded guerrillas meting out Robin Hood–style justice and a classic David-versus-Goliath struggle that was won convincingly by the (extreme) underdogs: Cuba's revolutionary war reads like the pages of a Steven Soderbergh movie script. Better than watching it on the big screen is visiting the revolutionary sites in person. Little changed in over 50 years are the disembarkation point of the Granma and Fidel's wartime HQ at mountaintop Comandancia de la Plata (p382). Guevara's mausoleum (p257)

Time-Warped Trinidad

8 Soporific Trinidad (p275) went to sleep in 1850 and never really woke up. This strange twist of fate is good news for modern travelers who can roam freely through the perfectly preserved mid-19th-century sugar town like voyeurs from another era. Though it's no secret these days, the time-warped streets still have the power to enchant with their grand colonial homestays, easily accessible countryside and exciting live-music scene. But this is also a real working town loaded with all the foibles and fun of 21st-century Cuba.

PAUL HARRIS / GETTY IMAGES ©

THOMAS COCKREM / ALAMY ©

Cienfuegos' Classical Architecture

9 There's a certain *je ne sais quoi* about bayside Cienfuegos (p236), Cuba's self-proclaimed 'Pearl of the South.' Through hell, high water and an economically debilitating Special Period, this is a city that has always retained its poise. The elegance is best seen in the architecture, a homogenous cityscape laid out in the early 19th century by settlers from France and the US. Dip into the cultural life around the city center and its adjacent garden suburb of Punta Gorda to absorb the Gallic refinement. Casa de la Cultura Benjamin Duarte (p238)

Ciénaga de Zapata's Wildlife

10 One of the few parts of Cuba that has never been truly tamed, the Zapata swamps (p227) are as close to pure wilderness as the country gets. This is the home of the endangered Cuban crocodile, various amphibians, the bee hummingbird and over a dozen different plant habitats. It also qualifies as the Caribbean's largest wetlands, protected in numerous ways, most importantly as a Unesco Biosphere Reserve and Ramsar Convention Site. Come here to fish, birdwatch, hike and see nature at its purest.

Folklórico Dance in Santiago de Cuba

11 Ahh...there's nothing quite as transcendental as the hypnotic beat of the Santería drums summoning up the spirits of the *orishas* (African deities). But, while most Afro-Cuban religious rites are only for initiates, the drumming and dances of Cuba's *folklórico* troupes are open to all. Formed in the 1960s to keep the ancient slave culture of Cuba alive, *folklórico* groups enjoy strong government patronage, and their energetic and colorful shows remain spontaneous, true to their roots and grittily authentic. (p412)

WOLFGANG POELZER / GETTY IMAGES ©

Diving & Snorkeling in the Caribbean

12 There will be protestations, no doubt, but let's say it anyway: Cuba is home to the best diving (p45) in the Caribbean. The reasons are unrivaled water clarity, virgin reefs and sheltered Caribbean waters that teem with millions of fish. Accessibility for divers varies from the swim-out walls of the Bahía de Cochinos (Bay of Pigs) to the hard-to-reach underwater nirvana of the Jardines de la Reina archipelago. For repeat visitors Punta Francés on Isla de la Juventud – host of an annual underwater photography competition – reigns supreme.

Cycling Valle de Viñales

13 With less traffic on the roads than 1940s Britain, Cuba is ideal for cycling and there's no better place to do it than the quintessentially rural Valle de Viñales (p175). The valley offers all the ingredients of a tropical Tour de France: craggy *mogotes* (flat-topped hills), impossibly green tobacco fields, bucolic *campesino* (country) huts and spirit-lifting viewpoints at every gear change. The terrain is relatively flat and, if you can procure a decent bike, your biggest dilemma will be where to stop for your sunset-toasting mojito.

Las Terrazas' Eco-Village

14 Back in 1968, when the fledgling environmental movement was a bolshie protest group for long-haired students in duffel coats, the prophetic Cubans – concerned about the ecological cost of island-wide deforestation – came up with rather a good idea. After saving hectares of denuded forest from an ecological disaster, a group of industrious workers built their own eco-village, Las Terrazas (p151), and set about colonizing it with artists, musicians, coffee growers and the architecturally unique Hotel Moka.

Santa Clara's Youthful Energy

15 Check your preconceived ideas about this country at the city limits. Santa Clara (p253) is everything you thought Cuba wasn't: erudite students, spontaneous nightlife, daring creativity and private homestays in abodes stuffed with more antiques than the local decorative-arts museum. Pop into the drag show at Club Mejunje or hang out for a while with the enthusiastic students in the bars around the main square. Dancer performs at Club Mejunje (p262)

Unlocking the Secrets of Matanzas

16 Matanzas (p216) was once the *Titanic* of Cuba, a sunken liner left to languish in the murky depths; but, more recently, flickers of its erstwhile beauty have started to reemerge. After manicured Varadero, the city hits you like a slap in the face but, with a little time, its gigantic historical legacy will teach you more about the real Cuba than 20 repeat visits to the resorts. Matanzas' refined culture congregates in the Teatro Sauto, while its African 'soul' manifests itself in energetic live rumba shows.

Baracoa

17 Over the hills and far away on the easternmost limb of Guantánamo province lies isolated Baracoa (p437), a small yet historically significant settlement, weird even by Cuban standards for its fickle Atlantic weather, eccentric local populace and unrelenting desire to be, well, different. Watch locals scale coconut palms, listen to bands play *kiribá* (the local take on *son*), and – above all – enjoy the infinitely spicier, richer and more inventive food, starting with the sweet treat *cucurucho*.

Ebullient Festivals

18 Through war, austerity, rationing and hardship, the Cubans have retained their infectious *joie de vivre*. Even during the darkest days of the Special Period, the feisty festivals never stopped, a testament to the country's capacity to put politics aside and get on with the important business of living. The best shows involve fireworks in Remedios, *folklórico* dancing in Santiago de Cuba, movies in Gibara and every conceivable genre of music in Havana. Arrive prepared to party. (p30)

Emerging Food Culture

19 Ever since new privatization laws lifted the lid off Cuba's creative pressure cooker in 2011, a culinary revolution has been in full swing. A country that once offered little more than rice and beans has rediscovered its gastronomic mojo with a profusion of new restaurants experimenting with spices, fusion and – perhaps best of all – a welcome re-evaluation of its own national cuisine. Havana leads the culinary field in the number and variety of eating establishments, Viñales offers the best traditional plates, while isolated Baracoa rules for regional originality. (p463)

Ropa vieja (shredded beef)

Labyrinthine Streets of Camagüey

20 Get lost! No, that's not an abrupt put-down; it's a savvy recommendation for any traveler passing through the city of *tinajones* (clay pots), churches and erstwhile pirates – aka Camagüey (p317). A perennial rule-breaker, Camagüey was founded on a street grid that deviated from almost every other Spanish colonial city in Latin America. Here the lanes are as labyrinthine as a Moroccan medina, hiding Catholic churches and triangular plazas, and revealing left-field artistic secrets at every turn.

Pico Turquino

21 The trek up Cuba's highest mountain, Pico Turquino (p426) (1972m), is a rare privilege. Guides are mandatory for this tough two- to three-day, 17km trek through the steep broccoli-green forests of the Sierra Maestra that act as a kind of history lesson, nature trail and bird-watching extravaganza all rolled into one. Revolutionary buffs should make a side trip to Fidel's wartime jungle HQ on the way up.

Need to Know

For more information, see Survival Guide (p499)

Currency
At the time of print, Cuba intended to unify its two currencies: Cuban convertibles (CUC$) and pesos (MN$).

Money
Cuba is primarily a cash economy. Credit cards are accepted in resort hotels and some city hotels. There are a growing number of ATMs.

Visas
A travel card valid for 30 days is usually included in your flight package.

Cell Phones
Check with your service provider to see if your phone will work (GSM or TDMA networks only). International calls are expensive. You can pre-buy services from the state-run phone company, Cubacel.

Time
Eastern Standard Time GMT/UTC minus five hours.

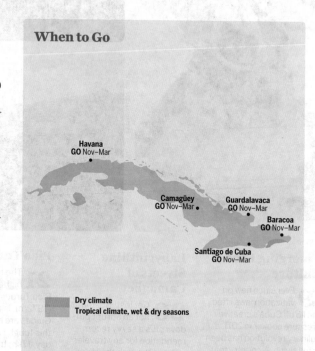

When to Go

Havana
GO Nov–Mar

Camagüey
GO Nov–Mar

Guardalavaca
GO Nov–Mar

Baracoa
GO Nov–Mar

Santiago de Cuba
GO Nov–Mar

Dry climate
Tropical climate, wet & dry seasons

High Season
(Nov–Mar & Jul–Aug)

➡ Prices are 30% higher and hotels may require advance bookings.

➡ Prices are at their highest around Christmas and New Year.

➡ Weather is cooler and drier November to March.

Shoulder
(Apr & Oct)

➡ Look out for special deals outside of peak season.

➡ Prices and crowds increase over Easter.

Low Season
(May, Jun & Sep)

➡ Some resort hotels offer fewer facilities or shut altogether.

➡ There's a hurricane risk between June and November and higher chance of rain.

Websites

AfroCuba Web (www.afro-cubaweb.com) Everything on Cuban culture.

BBC (www.bbc.co.uk) Interesting correspondent reports on Cuba.

Cuba Absolutely (www.cuba-absolutely.com) Art, culture, business and travel.

Cubacasas.net (www.cuba-casas.net) Information, photos and contact details for casas particulares.

Lonely Planet (www.lonely-planet.com/cuba) Destination information, articles, hotel bookings, traveler forum and more.

Exchange Rates

Argentina	ARS$1
Australia	A$1
Canada	C$1
Europe	€1
Japan	¥100
Mexico	MXN$1
New Zealand	NZ$1
UK	£1
US	US$1

For current exchange rates see www.xe.com.

Important Numbers

To call Cuba from abroad, dial your international access code, Cuba's country code (☏53), the city or area code (minus the '0,' which is used when dialing domestically between provinces), and the local number.

Emergency	☏106
Directory assistance	☏113
Police	☏106
Fire	☏105

Daily Costs

**Budget:
Less than CUC$60**

➜ Casas particulares: CUC$20–30

➜ Government-run restaurants: CUC$10–15

➜ Cheap museum entry: CUC$1–5

**Midrange:
CUC$60–120**

➜ Midrange hotels: CUC$35–60

➜ Meals in paladares (private restaurants): CUC$15–25

➜ Víazul bus travel: Havana–Trinidad CUC$25

**Top End:
More than CUC$120**

➜ Resort or historic hotel: CUC$150–200

➜ Car hire or taxis: CUC$60–70

➜ Evening cabaret: CUC$35–60

Arriving in Cuba

Aeropuerto Internacional José Martí (Havana) There are no regular buses or trains running direct from the airport into the city center. Taxis cost CUC$20 to CUC$25 and take 30 to 40 minutes to reach most of the city center hotels. You can change money at the bank in the arrivals hall.

Other International Airports Cuba has nine other international airports, but none of them has reliable public transport links; your best bet is always a taxi. Agree fares beforehand.

Getting Around

Buses are the most efficient and practical way of getting around.

Bus The state-run Víazul network links most places of interest to tourists on a regular daily schedule. Cubanacán runs a less comprehensive *conectando* service. Local buses are crowded and have no printed schedules.

Car Rental cars are quite expensive and driving can be a challenge due to the lack of signposts and ambiguous road rules.

Taxi Taxis are an option over longer distances if you are traveling in a small group. Rates are approximately CUC$0.50 per kilometer.

Train Despite its large train network, Cuban trains are slow, unreliable and lacking in comfort. For stoics only!

Opening Hours

Banks 9am to 3pm Monday to Friday

Cadeca Money Exchanges 9am to 7pm Monday to Saturday, 9am to noon Sunday. Many top-end city hotels offer money exchange late into the evening.

Pharmacies 8am to 8pm

Post Offices 8am to 5pm Monday to Saturday

Restaurants 10:30am to 11pm

Shops 9am to 5pm Monday to Saturday, 9am to noon Sunday

For much more on **getting around**, see p511

First Time Cuba

For more information, see Survival Guide (p499)

Checklist

➡ Preload credit card with funds in your home country, in case you run out of cash

➡ Print out copy of medical insurance to show at airport

➡ Check when booking air ticket that tourist card is included in your flight package

➡ Book some salsa dancing lessons and/or learn basic Spanish

What to Pack

➡ Latin American Spanish dictionary/phrasebook

➡ Plug adaptors for European and US sockets

➡ Good money belt that fits snugly around your waist

➡ Basic first aid kit, pain killers and any required medications

➡ Insect repellent, sunscreen and sunglasses

➡ Stash of cash in euros, Canadian dollars or sterling

➡ Energy bars for long road trips

Top Tips for Your Trip

➡ For a glimpse of the real Cuba and a chance to put your money directly into the pockets of individual Cubans, stay in a casa particular (private homestay).

➡ Carry toilet paper and antiseptic hand-wash, and drink bottled water.

➡ Roads can be rough and driving can be a challenge. It's cheaper to hire a taxi than a car over longer distances.

➡ Thanks to heavy bureaucracy, answers to simple requests aren't always straightforward. Probe politely and ask at least five different people before you make important decisions.

➡ Cuba is complex, and not always portrayed accurately in the international media. Travel with an open mind and be prepared to be regularly surprised, confused, confounded and astonished.

What to Wear

Cuba is a hot, humid country which, thankfully, has a casual approach to clothing. Locals generally opt for shorts, sandals and T-shirts; women favor tight-fitting lycra, men looser *guayabera* shirts (invented in Cuba). There are only two nude beaches in Cuba, frequented almost exclusively by foreigners. Cinemas and theaters usually have a 'no shorts' rule for men.

Sleeping

Reserve ahead for the more popular casas particulares, and for all-inclusive resorts to avoid expensive rack rates.

➡ **Casas particulares** Cuban homes that rent rooms to foreigners; an authentic and economic form of cultural immersion.

➡ **Campismos** Cheap, rustic accommodations in rural areas, usually in bungalows or cabins.

➡ **Hotels** All Cuban hotels are government-owned. Prices and quality range from cheap Soviet-era to high-flying colonial chic.

➡ **Resorts** Large international-standard hotels in resort areas that sell all-inclusive packages.

Money

Cuba has two currencies though the government is in the process of unifying them. At the time of writing, convertibles (CUC$) and pesos (*moneda nacional*; MN$) were both still in circulation. One convertible is worth 25 pesos. Non-Cubans deal almost exclusively in convertibles.

Cuba is a cash economy; credit cards aren't readily accepted outside international hotels.

ATMs are more widespread and usually accept debit and credit cards, though they are not as reliable as in Europe or North America. If in doubt, check inside the bank first (expect queues).

For more information, see p506.

Tipping

Tipping in Cuba is important. Since most Cubans earn their money in *moneda nacional* (MN$), leaving a small tip of CUC$1 (MN$25) or more can make a huge difference.

➡ **Resorts/Hotels** Tip for good service with bellboys, room maids and bar/restaurant staff.

➡ **Musicians** Carry small notes for the ubiquitous musicians in restaurants. Tip when the basket comes round.

➡ **Restaurants** Standard 10%, or up to 15% if service is excellent and/or you're feeling generous.

➡ **Taxis** 10% if you are on the meter, otherwise agree full fare beforehand.

Musicians perform on the street

Etiquette

➡ **Greetings** Shake hands with strangers; a kiss or double-cheek kiss is appropriate between people (men–women and women–women) who have already met.

➡ **Conversation** Although they can be surprisingly candid, Cubans aren't always keen to discuss politics, especially with strangers and if it involves being openly critical of the government.

➡ **Dancing** Cubans don't harbor any self-consciousness about dancing. Throw your reservations out of the window and let loose.

Eating

➡ **Private Restaurants & Casas Particulares** Private restaurants and homestays offer the best food and service in Cuba, and the portions are invariably huge.

➡ **Hotels & Resorts** The all-inclusives offer buffet food of an international standard but after a week it can get a bit bland.

➡ **State-run Restaurants** Varying food and service from top-notch places in Havana to unimaginative rations in the provinces. Prices often lower than private places.

Language

Cubans working in the tourist industry are usually proficient in English as well as other European languages. Elsewhere, Spanish predominates. Many casa particular owners speak limited or no English, and most museums print explanations in Spanish. Bring a phrasebook!

ROXANA GONZALEZ / GETTY IMAGES ©

1. Cuban cigars (p472)
Like coffee and rum, cigars are embedded in Cuban culture

2. Habana Vieja (p72)
Havana's Old Town is studded with architectural gems, and is the place to come for museums and street theater

3. National heroes
Havana street art immortalizes Cuban icons Che Guevara and Camilo Cienfuegos

4. Tobacco plantations (p174)
Cuba is arguably the world's premier place to grow tobacco

What's New

Culinary Revolution

Cuba's food culture has been stood on its head in the last five years. First inspired by the relaxation of laws governing private restaurants in January 2011, the culinary revolution continues unabated, especially in Havana, where the latest trend is for small bohemian cafes, slick arty cocktail bars, and ethnic restaurants specializing in Italian, Russian and even Iranian food. (p463)

Fábrica de Arte Cubano, Havana

A dynamic new cultural center in Havana that cleverly blends into the fabric of an old cooking oil factory. Come here for art, music, discussion and other 'happenings'. (p117)

The 500 Club

Three of Cuba's seven Spanish-founded 'villas' – Trinidad (p275), Sancti Spíritus (p291) and Camagüey (p317) – celebrated their quincentennials in 2014 and all have benefited from noticeable investment, with paint-jobs, new museums and new hotels.

Gay Nightlife, Havana

At last Havana's gay life is proudly displaying its flamboyance with the appearance of the city's first LGBT-specific bars and clubs, including the pioneering Humboldt 52. (p112)

Parque la Güira, Pinar del Río

A surreal and long-abandoned dream gets a reincarnation: La Güira has been brought to life with a surprise refurbishment and looks likely to become one of Cuba's finest landscaped parks. (p188)

Varadero Accommodations

Varadero's hotel zone has gone all hospitable: check the stunning new selection of casas particulares (private homestays) in the town, then let the new-look Marina Gaviota wash away your retail and restaurant cravings. (p205)

La Calle de los Cines, Camagüey

This street in the center of the city of Camagüey has been donned a movie theme by the City Historian and embellished with resurrected cinemas, bars and nightclubs. (p326)

Hotel Capri, Havana

After lying abandoned for 11 years, Havana's former Mafia hangout was reborn in 2014 as a slick four-star hotel part-run by the Spanish-based NH Hotel Group. (p103)

Remedios

Unsung colonial gem Remedios is no longer just eye candy: adding to its stand-out brigade of colonial casas particulares are two of Cuba's best boutique hotels, with four more on the cards. (p264)

Kiteboarding

Utilizing stiff winds off the north coast and taking advantage of new privatization laws, Cuba's first kiteboarders are hitting the waves in Cayo Guillermo and Guardalavaca. (p50)

Matanzas' Rejuvenation

Is the Athens of Cuba getting a dust-off? Gawk at the architectural pearls being polished off in central Matanzas. (p216)

For more recommendations and reviews, see lonelyplanet.com/cuba

If You Like...

Architecture

Habana Vieja Like an old attic full of dusty relics, Havana is a treasure chest of eclectic architecture. (p64)

Cienfuegos Cuba's most architecturally homogenous city is a love letter to French neoclassicism, full of elegant columns. (p236)

Camagüey An unusual street plan of labyrinthine lanes and baroque spires that hide a devout Catholic soul. (p317)

Trinidad One of the most beguiling and best-preserved towns in the Caribbean, tranquil Trinidad is a riot of colonial baroque. (p275)

Nightlife & Dancing

Santa Clara Where the 'next big thing' happens first; drag shows, rock 'n' roll music and everything in between. (p262)

Cabarets Cuba's flamboyant kitschy cabarets, like Havana's Tropicana, are something of opulent pre-revolutionary life that refused to die. (p134)

Casas de la Trova Cuba's old-fashioned spit-and-sawdust music houses are determined to keep the essence of traditional Cuban music alive. (p488)

Uneac Provincial free cultural centers full of latent artistic talent where everyone greets you like a long-lost friend. (p477)

Subcultures

Baseball Fanatics A national obsession; the hotspot for fans is Havana's *esquina caliente* in Parque Central. (p82)

Gay Culture GLBT life is beginning to flower in Cuba with new bars such as Humboldt 52 in Havana. (p112)

Roqueros Once frowned on by the authorities, rock 'n' rollers display their individuality in Havana's Submarino Amarillo. (p115)

Abakuá One of a handful of religions of African origin, the secrets of the Abakuá fraternity are best searched for in Matanzas. (p221)

Santería Discover live drumming and religious shrines at Havana's Afro-Cuban-tinged Callejón de Hamel. (p115)

Palo Monte Rare syncretized Afro-Cuba religion that worships dead spirits; evident in Matanzas and Santiago de Cuba. (p415)

Under the Radar

Gibara The home of the 'poor man's film festival' is rich in wild, ocean-side scenery and creeping Holguín magic. (p359)

Marea del Portillo Coastal resort close to magnificent mountains, untouched since the *Granma* yacht ran aground in 1956. (p390)

Matanzas Varadero's outcast sibling lacks sunlounges and stuff-yourself-silly buffets, but it has soul *asere*. (p216)

Las Tunas Cuba's least-visited provincial capital defies its 'boring' stereotype on Saturday night when there's a rodeo in town. (p335)

Holguín *Jinetero*-free streets, an underrated baseball team nicknamed 'the dogs' and a beer-drinking donkey named Pancho. (p345)

Wildlife-Watching

Ciénaga de Zapata Take a boat trip to see a microcosm of Cuban wildlife, including the critically endangered Cuban crocodile. (p231)

Parque Nacional Alejandro de Humboldt Sky-high levels of endemism make Humboldt, home to the world's smallest frog, an ecological rarity. (p445)

Sierra del Chorrillo Non-indigenous exotic animals, including zebra and deer, in a quintessentially Cuban grassland setting. (p328)

Río Máximo Behold the largest colony of nesting flamingos in the world on Camagüey's north coast. (p333)

Guanahacabibes Crabs and iguanas do battle with jeep traffic on the excursion to Cuba's western wilderness. (p196)

Diving & Snorkeling

Isla de la Juventud La Isla is famed for its clear water and hosts an underwater photography competition. (p161)

Jardines de la Reina Heavily protected archipelago with zero infrastructure boasts the most unspoiled reefs in the Caribbean. (p306)

María la Gorda Over 50 easily accessible dive sites off Cuba's western tip make this small resort 'diver's central'. (p196)

Bahía de los Cochinos Once infamous for another reason, the Bay of Pigs has rediscovered its raison d'être – damn good diving. (p232)

Playa Santa Lucía It's worth braving this rather tacky resort strip to experience the best diving on Cuba's north coast. (p332)

Relaxing at a Resort

Varadero The biggest resort in Cuba isn't to everyone's taste, but it's still insanely popular. (p199)

Cayo Coco An island getaway linked to the mainland by a causeway, Cayo Coco is low-rise and more subtle than Varadero. (p310)

Guardalavaca Three separate enclaves on Holguín's north coast offer three different price brackets from posh to bargain basement. (p360)

Cayerías del Norte The still-developing *cayos* of Villa Clara province retain a refreshingly tranquil feel. (p269)

Top: Beach, Guardalavaca (p360)
Bottom: Museo de la Revolución (p83), Havana

Cayo Largo del Sur Cuba's most isolated resort island isn't very Cuban, but its beaches are among the best in the nation. (p169)

Playa Santa Lucía Old and a little neglected, Camagüey's northern beach resort still offers the best bargains and excellent diving. (p331)

White-Sand Beaches

Playa Pilar Hemingway's favorite is much-decorated in travel mags and backed by big dunes but, as yet, no hotels. (p314)

Varadero Twenty kilometers of unbroken beach – there's a reason why Varadero is the largest resort in the Caribbean. (p199)

Playa Maguana Wind-whipped waves and bruised clouds all add to the ethereal ambience of Baracoa's finest beach. (p445)

Playa Pesquero Walk for 200m through clear bathwater-temperature ocean and still only be up to your waist.

Playa Sirena Huge football-field-sized beach on what is essentially a private tourist island where the dress code is 'bare all'. (p169)

Playa Los Pinos Just you, some driftwood, a good book and perhaps the odd local offering cooked lobster for lunch. (p331)

Revolutionary History

Santa Clara 'Che City' is the home of Guevara's mausoleum, myriad statues and a fascinating open-air museum. (p257)

Bayamo The understated capital of Granma province, where Cuba's first revolution was ignited in 1868. (p372)

Sierra Maestra Flecked with historical significance, including Castro's mountain ridge HQ during the revolutionary war. (p382)

Santiago de Cuba The self-proclaimed 'City of Revolutionaries' was where Castro staged his first insurrection at Moncada Barracks. (p402)

Museo de la Revolución Cuba's most comprehensive museum is a one-stop immersion in all things revolutionary. (p83)

Indigenous Culture

Chorro de Maita The most important archaeological site in Cuba; all pre-Columbian investigations should start here. (p360)

Museo Indocubano Bani Modest but enthusisatically curated museum in Cuba's archaeological 'capital' Banes. (p366)

El Guafe Short trail in western Granma province to a cave where a Taíno water deity is carved in bare rock. (p387)

Museo Arqueológico 'La Cueva del Paraíso' Innovative museum in a cave close to some of Cuba's oldest pre-Columbian remains. (p437)

Boca de Guamá Slightly kitschy attempt to recreate a Taíno village and pass it off as a tourist hotel. (p229)

Cueva de Punta del Este Large collection of cave paintings rightly dubbed the 'Sistine Chapel of the Caribbean'. (p169)

Pirates & Forts

Havana's Forts Four of the finest examples of 16th-century military architecture in the Americas. (p77)

Camagüey Moved twice to avoid the attentions of pirates, Camagüey redesigned its streets in a labyrinthine pattern to prevent repeat attacks. (p317)

La Roca Two hundred years in the making, Santiago's La Roca is today a Unesco World Heritage Site. (p404)

Baracoa Cuba's 'first city' has three stalwart forts that today serve as a museum, a hotel and a restaurant. (p437)

Matanzas Once breached by the British, Matanzas' little-visited Castillo de San Severino now harbors an interesting slave museum. (p220)

Live Music

La Casa de la Música Mixes live music with late-night dancing and pulls in big names like Los Van Van. (p115)

Casas de la Trova Son and boleros give an old-fashioned lilt to these cultural houses in every Cuban provincial town.

La Tumba Francesa Mysterious folklórico dance troupes in Guantánamo (p434) and Santiago de Cuba perform musical rites with a Haitian influence. (p412)

Street Rumba Salt-of-the-earth Havana and Matanzas (p222) specialize in mesmerizing drumming and dance rituals. (p115)

Jazz Cuba's best jazz venues are both in Havana's Vedado district: the Jazz Café (p114) and Jazz Club la Zorra y El Cuervo. (p115)

Month by Month

TOP EVENTS

Carnaval de Santiago de Cuba, July

Festival Internacional de Cine Pobre, April

Las Parrandas, December

Festival Internacional de Jazz, December

Festival Internacional de Ballet de la Habana, October

January

Tourist season hits full swing, and the whole country has added buoyancy. Cold fronts bring chilly evenings.

✨ Día de la Liberación

As well as seeing in the New Year with roast pork and a bottle of rum, Cubans celebrate January 1 as the triumph of the Revolution, the anniversary of Fidel Castro's 1959 victory.

✨ Incendio de Bayamo

Bayamo residents remember the 1869 burning of their city with music and theatrical performances in an *espectáculo* (show) culminating in explosive fireworks.

February

The peak tourist season continues and high demand can lead to overbooking, particularly in the rental-car market. Calm seas and less fickle weather promote better water clarity, making this an ideal time to enjoy diving and snorkeling.

✨ Feria Internacional del Libro

First held in 1930, the International Book Fair is headquartered in Havana's Fortaleza de San Carlos de la Cabaña, but it later goes on the road to other cities. Highlights include book presentations, special readings and the prestigious Casa de las Américas prize. (p77)

🏊 Diving with Clarity

Calm conditions promote clear water for diving, particularly on Cuba's south coast. The country's prime diving nexus, La Isla de la Juventud, consequently holds the annual Fotosub International Underwater Photography competition.

✨ Habanos Festival

Trade fairs, seminars, tastings and visits to tobacco plantations draw cigar aficionados to Havana for this annual cigar festival with prizes, rolling competitions and a gala dinner.

March

Spring offers Cuba's best wildlife-watching opportunities, particularly for migrant birds. With dryer conditions, it is also an ideal time to indulge in hiking, cycling or numerous other outdoor activities.

✨ Carnaval – Isla de la Juventud

Once famous for its citrus plantations, Isla de la Juventud still celebrates the annual grapefruit harvest with this animated excuse for a party in Nueva Gerona, even though the crop yield is now minimal.

✨ Festival Internacional de Trova

Held since 1962 in honor of *trova* pioneer Pepe Sánchez, this festival invades the parks, streets and music houses of Santiago de Cuba in a showcase of the popular verse/song genre.

🏃 Bird-Watching

March is a crossover period when migrant birds from both North and South America join Cuba's resident endemics en route for warmer or colder climes. There's no better time to polish off your binoculars.

April

Economy-seeking visitors should avoid the Easter holiday, which sees another spike in tourist numbers and prices. Otherwise April is a pleasant month with good fly-fishing potential off the south coast.

🎭 Semana de la Cultura

During the first week of April, Baracoa commemorates the landing of Antonio Maceo at Duaba on April 1, 1895, with a raucous carnival along the Malecón, expos of its indigenous music *nengon* and *kiribá,* and various culinary offerings.

🎭 Festival Internacional de Cine Pobre

Gibara's celebration of low- and no-budget cinema has been an annual event since 2003, when it was inaugurated by late Cuban film director Humberto Sales. Highlights include film-showing workshops and discussions on movie-making with limited resources.

🎭 Bienal Internacional del Humor

You can't be serious! Cuba's unique humor festival takes place in San Antonio de los Baños in out-of-the-way Artemisa province. Headquartered at the celebrated Museo del Humor, talented scribblers try to outdo each other by drawing ridiculous caricatures. Hilarious! (p147)

May

Possibly the cheapest month of all, May is the low point between the foreign crowds of winter and the domestic barrage of summer. Look out for special deals offered by resort hotels and significantly cheaper prices all round.

🎭 Romerías de Mayo

This religious festival takes place in the city of Holguín during the first week of May and culminates with a procession to the top of the city's emblematic Loma de la Cruz, a small shrine atop a 275m hill. (p350)

🎭 Cubadisco

An annual get-together of foreign and Cuban record producers and companies, Cubadisco hosts music concerts, a trade fair and a Grammy-style awards ceremony that encompasses every musical genre from chamber music to pop.

🎭 Cuban Campaign Against Homophobia

What passes for a pride parade in Havana has been held on May 17 since 2008. *Congas* (musical groups) wielding drums, trumpets and rainbow flags fan out along Calle 23, the climax of a three week LGBT campaign that includes workshops, discussion groups and art expos.

🎭 Festival Nacional de Changüí

Since 2003, Guantánamo has celebrated its indigenous music in this rootsy music festival held in late May. Look out for Elio Revé Jr and his orchestra.

June

The Caribbean hurricane season begins inauspiciously. A smattering of esoteric provincial festivals keeps June interesting. Prices are still low and, with the heat and humidity rising, travelers from Europe and Canada tend to stay away.

🎭 Jornada Cucalambeana

Cuba's celebration of country music, and the witty 10-line *décimas* (stanzas) that go with it, takes place about 3km outside unassuming Las Tunas at Motel el Cornito, the former home of erstwhile country-music king, Juan Fajardo 'El Cucalambé.' (p337)

🎭 Festival Internacional 'Boleros de Oro'

Organized by Uneac (Unión de Escritores y Artistas de Cuba; Union of Cuban Writers and Artists), the Boleros de Oro was created by Cuban composer and musicologist José Loyola Fernández in 1986 as a global celebration of this distinctive Cuban musical genre. Most events take place in Havana's Teatro Mella. (p116)

Fiestas Sanjuaneras

This feisty carnival in Trinidad on the last weekend in June is a showcase for the local *vaqueros* (cowboys), who gallop their horses through the narrow cobbled streets.

July

High summer is when Cubans vacation; expect the beaches, campismos and cheaper hotels to be mobbed. The July heat also inspires two of the nation's hottest events: Santiago's Carnaval and the annual polemics of July 26.

Festival del Caribe, Fiesta del Fuego

The so-called Festival of Caribbean Culture, Fire Celebration in early July kicks off an action-packed month for Santiago with exhibitions, song, dance, poetry and religious-tinged rituals from all around the Caribbean.

Día de la Rebeldía Nacional

On July 26 the Cubans 'celebrate' Fidel Castro's failed 1953 attack on Santiago's Moncada Barracks. The event is a national holiday and – in days when he enjoyed better health – Castro was famous for making five-hour speeches. Expect *un poco* (a little) politics and *mucho* (much) eating, drinking and being merry.

Carnaval de Santiago de Cuba

Arguably the biggest and most colorful carnival in the Caribbean, the famous Santiago shindig at the end of July is a riot of floats, dancers, rum, rumba and more. Come and join in the very *caliente* (hot) action.

August

While Santiago retires to sleep off its hangover, Havana gears up for its own annual celebration. Beaches and campismos still heave with holidaying Cubans while tourist hotels creak under a fresh influx of visitors from Mediterranean Europe.

Festival Internacional 'Habana Hip-Hop'

Organized by the Asociación Hermanos Saíz – a youth arm of Uneac – the annual Havana Hip-Hop Festival is a chance for the island's young musical creators to improvise and swap ideas.

Carnaval de la Habana

Parades, dancing, music, colorful costumes and striking effigies – Havana's annual summer shindig might not be as famous as its more rootsy Santiago de Cuba counterpart, but the celebrations and processions along the Malecón leave plenty of other city carnivals in the shade.

September

It's peak hurricane season. The outside threat of a 'big one' sends most Cubaphiles running for cover and tourist numbers hit a second trough. The storm-resistant take advantage of cheaper prices and near-empty beaches. But, beware – some facilities close down completely.

Festival Internacional de Música Benny Moré

The Barbarian of Rhythm is remembered in this biannual celebration (odd-numbered years) of his suave music, headquartered in the singer's small birth town of Santa Isabel de las Lajas in Cienfuegos province.

Fiesta de Nuestra Señora de la Caridad

Every September 8, religious devotees from around Cuba partake in a pilgrimage to the Basílica de Nuestra Señora del Cobre, near Santiago, to honor Cuba's venerated patron saint (and her alter ego, the Santería *orisha*, Ochún). (p423)

October

Continuing storm threats and persistent rain keep all but the most stalwart travelers away until the end of the month. While the solitude can be refreshing in Havana, life in the peripheral resorts can be deathly quiet and lacking in atmosphere.

Festival Internacional de Ballet de la Habana

Hosted by the Cuban National Ballet, this annual festival brings together dance companies, ballerinas and a mixed audience of foreigners and Cubans for a week of expositions, galas, and classical and contemporary ballet. It has been held in even-numbered years since its inception in 1960.

★ Festival del Bailador Rumbero

During the 10 days following October 10, Matanzas rediscovers its rumba roots with talented local musicians performing in the city's Teatro Sauto. (p222)

November

Get ready for the big invasion from the north – and an accompanying hike in hotel rates! Over a quarter of Cuba's tourists come from Canada; they start arriving in early November, as soon as the weather turns frigid in Vancouver and Toronto.

★ Fiesta de los Bandas Rojo y Azul

Considered one of the most important manifestations of Cuban *campesino* (country person) culture, this esoteric fiesta in the settlement of Majagua, in Ciego de Ávila province, splits the town into two teams (red and blue) that compete against each other in boisterous dancing and music contests.

🏃 Marabana

The popular Havana marathon draws between 2000

and 3000 competitors from around the globe. It's a two-lap course, though there is also a half-marathon and 5km and 10km races.

★ Ciudad Metal

Decidedly edgy when it was first established in Santa Clara in 1990, this celebration of hardcore punk and metal sees Cuban bands setting up in the local baseball stadium and quite literally rocking the rafters.

December

Christmas and the New Year see Cuba's busiest and most expensive tourist spike. Resorts nearly double their prices and rooms sell out fast. The nation goes firework-crazy in a handful of riotous festivals. Book ahead!

★ Festival Internacional del Nuevo Cine Latinoamericano

This internationally renowned film festival, held in cinemas across Havana, illustrates Cuba's growing influence in Latin American cinema around the world.

★ Festival Internacional de Jazz

The International Jazz Festival inaugurated in

1978 is staged in the Karl Marx (p134), Mella (p116) and Amadeo Roldán (p116) theaters in Havana and draws in top figures from around the world.

★ Procesión de San Lázaro

Every year on December 17, Cubans descend en masse on the venerated Santuario de San Lázaro in Santiago de las Vegas, on the outskirts of Havana. Some come on bloodied knees, others walk barefoot for kilometers to exorcize evil spirits and pay off debts for miracles granted. (p137)

★ Las Parrandas

A firework frenzy that takes place every Christmas Eve in Remedios in Villa Clara province, Las Parrandas sees the town divide into two teams that compete against each other to see who can come up with the most colorful floats and the loudest *bangs!*

★ Las Charangas de Bejucal

Didn't like Las Parrandas? Then try Bejucal's Las Charangas, Mayabeque province's cacophonous alternative to the firework fever further east. The town splits into the exotically named *Espino de Oro* (Golden Thorn) and *Ceiba de Plata* (Silver Silk-Cotton Tree).

Plan Your Trip
Itineraries

STRAITS OF FLORIDA

HAVANA

Viñales

Santa Clara

Cienfuegos

Trinidad

Camagüey

Bayamo

Baracoa

Santiago de Cuba

CARIBBEAN SEA

18 DAYS — The Classic

It's your first time in Cuba and you want to see as many eye-opening sights as possible countrywide. Even better, you don't mind a bit of road travel. This itinerary ferries you between the two rival cities of Havana and Santiago, bagging most of the nation's historical highlights on the way. Víazul buses link all of the following destinations.

Fall in love with classic Cuba in **Havana**, with its museums, forts, theaters and rum. Three days is the bare minimum here to get to grips with the main neighborhoods of Habana Vieja, Centro Habana and Vedado.

Head west next to the bucolic bliss of **Viñales** for a couple of days of hiking, caving and relaxing on a rocking chair on a sun-kissed colonial-era porch. Daily buses connect Viñales with French-flavored **Cienfuegos**, an architectural monument to 19th-century neoclassicism. After a night of Gallic style and Cuban music, travel a couple of hours down the road to colonial **Trinidad** with more museums per head than anywhere else in Cuba. The casas particulares (homestays) resemble

Valle de Viñales (p175)

historical monuments here, so stay three nights. On the second day you can break from the history and choose between the beach (Playa Ancón) or the natural world (Topes de Collantes).

Santa Clara is a rite of passage for Che Guevara pilgrims visiting his mausoleum but it's also a great place for luxurious private rooms and an upbeat nightlife. Check out Club Mejunje and have a drink in dive-bar La Marquesina. Further east, **Camagüey** invites further investigation with its maze of Catholic churches and giant *tinajones* (clay pots).

Laid-back **Bayamo** is where the Revolution was ignited, and it has an equally sparky street festival called Fiesta de la Cubanía, should you be lucky enough to be there on a Saturday. Allow plenty of time for the cultural nexus of **Santiago de Cuba**, where seditious plans for rebellion have been routinely hatched. The Cuartel Moncada, Cemeterio Ifigenia and Morro Castle will fill a busy two days. Save the best till last with a long, but by no means arduous, journey over the hills and far away to **Baracoa** for two days relaxing with the coconuts, chocolate and other tropical treats.

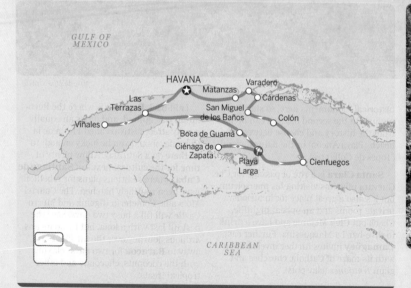

Escape from Varadero

Varadero has some cheap packages and is a popular gateway into Cuba, but once you've pacified your partner/kids and had your fill of the beach, what else is there for a curious Cuban adventurer to do? Plenty. Víazul or Conectando buses link the following places.

Take a bus west, stopping off for lunch in **Matanzas**, where Cuban reality will hit you like a sharp slap to the face. Investigate the Museo Farmacéutico, take a peep inside the Teatro Sauto and buy a unique handmade book in Ediciones Vigia. For a slow approach to Havana get on the Hershey train and watch as the lush fields of Mayabeque province glide by. Book a night in a fine colonial-era hotel in **Havana** and spend the next day admiring the copious sights of the old quarter, Habana Vieja. Essential stops include the cathedral, the Museo de la Revolución and a stroll along the Malecón.

The next day, head west to **Las Terrazas**, an eco-resort that seems a million miles from the clamorous capital (it's actually only 55km). You can bathe and bird-watch at the same time in the Baños del San Juan and recuperate with a night in the Hotel Moka. An optional two-day extension of this itinerary lies further west in **Viñales**, a stunningly picturesque Unesco World Heritage Site where you can decamp to a casa particular, eat some of the best roast pork in Cuba (the world?), go for a hike and then slump into a rocking chair on a rustic colonial porch.

Going back east, keep on the green theme in **Boca de Guamá**, a reconstructed Taíno village and crocodile farm with boat trips to and around a tranquil lake. Procure a night or two of accommodation at **Playa Larga**, where you can either dive or plan wildlife forays into the **Ciénaga de Zapata**. A couple of hours' drive east lies the city of **Cienfuegos**, an elegant last stopover with fine boutique hotels and sunset cruises on the bay.

On the leg back to Varadero you can uncover a more secretive Cuba in **Colón**, back in Matanzas province, and a dustier, time-warped Cuba in half-ruined **San Miguel de los Baños**, an erstwhile spa. Last stop before returning to your Varadero sunbed is **Cárdenas**, home to three superb museums.

Top: Plaza de la Catedral, Havana (p64)
Bottom: Cueva de los Peces (p232) near Playa Larga

Around the Oriente

12 DAYS

The Oriente is like another country; they do things differently here, or so they'll tell you in Havana. This circuit allows you to bypass the Cuban capital and focus exclusively on the culturally rich, fiercely independent eastern region. With poor transport links, a rental car is useful here.

Make your base in **Santiago de Cuba**, city of revolutionaries, culture and *folklórico* (Afro-Cuban folk dance) troupes. There's tons to do here pertaining to history (Morro Castle), music (Cuba's original Casa de la Trova) and religion (Basilica de Nuestra Señora del Cobre). On the second day reserve time to explore east into the Parque Bacanao and the ruined coffee farms around **Gran Piedra**.

Regular buses travel east into the mountains of Guantánamo province. Pass a night in **Guantánamo** to suss out the *changüí* music before climbing the spectacular road La Farola into **Baracoa**, where three days will bag you the highlights – beach time at Playa Maguana, a sortie into the Parque Nacional Alejandro de Humboldt and a day absorbing the psychedelic rhythms of the town itself.

Heading north via Moa is a tough jaunt, with taxis or rental cars required to get you to **Cayo Saetía**, a wonderful key with an on-site hotel where lonesome beaches embellish a former hunting reserve.

Pinares de Mayarí sits in the pine-clad mountains of the Sierra Crystal amid huge waterfalls and rare flora. Hiking married with some rural relaxation seal the deal at the region's eponymous hotel. If you have half a day to spare, consider a side trip to **Sitio Histórico de Birán** to see the surprisingly affluent farming community that spawned Fidel Castro.

Take a day off in hassle-free **Bayamo** with its smattering of small-town museums before tackling **Manzanillo**, where Saturday night in the main square can get feisty. More-adventurous transport options will lead you down to Niquero and within striking distance of the largely deserted **Parque Nacional Desembarco del Granma**, famous for uplifted marine terraces and aboriginal remains. Linger in one of **Marea del Portillo's** low-key resorts before attempting the spectacular but potholed coast road back to Santiago.

JANE SWEENEY / ROBERT HARDING ©

ESCUDERO PATRICK / HEMIS.FR / GETTY IMAGES ©

Top: Parque Céspedes (p395), Santiago de Cuba
Bottom left: *Bohío* (traditional Cuban hut) in
Parque Nacional Alejandro de Humboldt (p445)

STRAITS OF
FLORIDA

Sitio Histórico
de Birán

Pinares de
Mayarí

Cayo
Saetía

Bayamo

Manzanillo

Baracoa

Guantánamo

Gran
Piedra

Santiago
de Cuba

Parque Nacional
Desembarco del
Granma

Marea del
Portillo

CARIBBEAN
SEA

Cuba: Off the Beaten Track

GULF OF
MEXICO

FLORIDA
(USA)

SIERRA DE JATIBONICO

These little-explored hills in northern
Sancti Spíritus province are
accessible from the town of
Mayajigua. There are paths and
guided treks led by Ecotur among
rivers, semi-deciduous forest and
unusual karst topography. (p298)

CENTRAL MATANZAS

The towns of central Matanzas
province – most notably Colón and
Jovellanos – are known for their
strong Santería traditions and
penchant for rumba. Forget the
guidebook; this is a place for
independent sleuthing. (p216)

Straits
of Florida

HAVANA ✪

Matanzas

Sagua la
Grande

Artemisa○ Güines○

Colón

○ Pínar del Rio

Santa Clara

Bahía de
Cortés

Golfo de
Batabanó

Bahía de Cochinos
(Bay of Pigs)

○ Cienfuegos

Bahía de
Corrientes

Isla de la
Juventud

Trinidad ○

CARIBBEAN SEA

CAYMAN
ISLANDS
(UK)

✪ GEORGE TOWN

CAYOS DE SAN FELIPE

A small uninhabited archipelago and
national park that is home to birds,
turtles, a rare type of tree rat and 22
dive sites. (p172)

THE SOUTHERN ISLA

Cave paintings, wild monkeys,
deserted beaches and vast swamps
characterize the southern half of La
Isla de la Juventud, which is both a
military zone and a national park.
(p161)

0 — 200 km
0 — 100 miles

THE BAHAMAS

ATLANTIC OCEAN

GIBARA BEACH-BAGGING

Starting in colorful, off-the-radar Gibara, things only get more wild as you voyage via boat or bumpy track to desolate beaches with names such as Playa los Bajos or Playa Caletones, where there are also cave systems to explore. (p358)

SIERRA DEL CHORRILLO

Reconnoiter Camagüey province's surprise swath of serene upland with a stay in a sumptuous old hacienda, a ride on one of Cuba's finest steeds and an excursion to find rare birds or rarer-yet petrified trees. (p328)

Caibarién
Mayajigua
Morón
Sancti Spíritus
Ciego de Ávila
Nuevitas
Camagüey
Golfo de Ana María
Las Tunas
Bahía de Gibara
Gibara
Holguín
Moa
Baracoa
Santa Cruz del Sur
Golfo de Guacanayabo
Manzanillo
Bayamo
Guantánamo
Santiago de Cuba

SANTA CRUZ DEL SUR

Known mainly for disappearing off the map completely after a 1932 hurricane, this end-of-the-road fishing port, sporting fascinating monuments and a lovely casa, could kick-start a trip to the tranquil *cayos* of the Jardines de la Reina. (p306)

JAMAICA

BARACOA TO HOLGUÍN – THE BACK ROAD

Ever wondered what Cuba's most pristine and biodiverse protected area (Parque Nacional Alejandro de Humboldt) would look like were it juxtaposed with its ugliest industrial sight (Moa)? Hit this rarely traversed, pothole-ravaged back road to find out. (p445)

CARIBBEAN SEA

A tour boat on the underground river at Cueva del Indio (p18

Plan Your Trip

Outdoor Activities

Doubters of Cuba's outdoor potential need only look at the figures: six Unesco Biosphere Reserves, amazing water clarity, thousands of caves, three sprawling mountain ranges, copious bird species, the world's second-largest coral reef, barely touched tropical rainforest, and swaths of unspoiled suburb-free countryside.

Helpful Tips

Accessibility

Access to many parks and protected areas in Cuba is limited and can only be negotiated with a prearranged guide or on an organized excursion. If in doubt, consult Ecotur travel agency.

Private Guides

Since the loosening of economic restrictions in 2011, it has become legal for private individuals to set up as outdoor guides in Cuba, though, as yet, there are no full-blown nongovernment travel agencies. Most private guides operate out of casas particulares (private homestays) or hotels and many are very good. If you are unsure whether your guide is official, ask to see their government-issued license first.

Prebooking Tours

The following agencies organize outdoor tours from outside Cuba:

Scuba en Cuba (www.scuba-en-cuba.com) Diving trips.

Exodus (www.exodus.co.uk) Offers a 15-day walking trip.

WowCuba (www.wowcuba.com) Specializes in cycling trips.

Outdoor Opportunities

Travelers in search of adventure who've already warmed up on rum, cigars and all-night salsa dancing won't get bored in Cuba. Hit the highway on a bike, fish (as well as drink) like Hemingway, hike on guerrilla trails, jump out of an airplane or rediscover a sunken Spanish shipwreck off the shimmering south coast.

Thanks to the dearth of modern development, Cuba's outdoors is refreshingly green and free of the smog-filled highways and ugly suburban sprawl that infect many other countries.

While not on a par with North America or Europe in terms of leisure options, Cuba's facilities are well established and improving. Services and infrastructure vary depending on what activity you are looking for. The country's diving centers are generally excellent and instructors are of an international caliber. Naturalists and ornithologists in the various national parks and flora and fauna reserves are similarly conscientious and well qualified. Hiking has traditionally been limited and frustratingly rule-ridden, but opportunities have expanded in recent years, with companies such as Ecotur offering a wider variety of hikes in previously untrodden areas and even some multiday trekking. Cycling is refreshingly DIY, and all the better for it. Canyoning and climbing are new sports in Cuba that have a lot of local support but little official backing – as yet.

It's possible to hire reasonable outdoor gear in Cuba for most of the activities you will do (cycling excepted). But if you do bring your own supplies, any gear donated at the end of your trip to individuals you meet along the way (head lamps, snorkel masks, fins etc) will be greatly appreciated.

Boating & Kayaking

Boat rental is available on many of the island's lakes. Good options include the Laguna de la Leche and Laguna la Redonda, both in Ciego de Ávila province; Embalse Zaza in Sancti Spíritus province; and the Liberación de Florencia in Ciego de Ávila. You can also rent rowboats and head up the Río Canímar near Matanzas, oaring between the jungle-covered banks of this mini-Amazon.

Kayaking as a sport is pretty low-key in Cuba, treated more as a beach activity in the plusher resorts. Most of the tourist beaches will have *náutica* points that rent out simple kayaks, good for splashing around in but not a lot else.

Caving

Cuba is riddled with caves – more than 20,000 and counting – and cave exploration is available to both casual tourists and professional speleologists. The Gran Caverna

Divers at María la Gorda (p196)

de Santo Tomás, near Viñales, is Cuba's largest cavern, with over 46km of galleries; the Cueva de los Peces, near Playa Girón, is a flooded cenote (sinkhole) with colorful snorkeling; and the Cueva de Ambrosio and Cuevas de Bellamar, both in Matanzas, have tours daily.

Caving specialists have virtually unlimited caves from which to choose. With advance arrangements, you can explore deep into the Gran Caverna de Santo Tomás or visit the Cueva Martín Infierno, which has the world's largest stalagmite. Also ask about San Catalina, near Varadero, which has unique mushroom formations. Speleodiving is also possible, but only for those already highly trained. Interested experts should contact Angel Graña, secretary of the **Sociedad Espeleológica de Cuba** (☏7-209-2885; angel@fanj.cult.cu) in Havana.

Cycling

Riding a bike in Cuba is *the* best way to discover the island in close-up. Decent and quiet roads, wonderful scenery and the opportunity to get off the beaten track and meet Cubans make cycling here a pleasure, whichever route you take. For less dedicated pedalers, daily bike rental is sometimes available in hotels, resorts and cafes for about CUC$3 to CUC$7 per day, but don't bank on it. The bigger resorts in Varadero and Guardalavaca are more reliable and will often include bike use as part of the all-inclusive package, though it's unlikely the bikes will have gears. Alternatively, if you're staying in a casa particular, your host will generally be able to rig something together (sometimes quite literally) in order to get you from A to B.

The main problem with Cuban bikes is that they're usually substandard and, when combined with poor roads, you'll often feel like you're sitting atop an improvised coat hanger, not a well-oiled machine. Serious cyclists should bring boxed bikes with them on the airplane, along with plenty of spare parts. Since organized bike trips are common here, customs officials, taxi drivers and hotel staff are used to dealing with them.

Cycling highlights include the Valle de Viñales, the countryside around Trinidad, including the flat spin down to Playa Ancón, the quiet lanes that zigzag through Guardalavaca, and the roads out of Baracoa to Playa Maguana (northwest) and Boca de Yumurí (southeast). For a bigger challenge try La Farola between Cajobabo and Baracoa (21km of ascent), the bumpy but spectacular coast road between Santiago and Marea del Portillo – best spread over three days with overnights in Brisas Sierra Mar los Galeones and Campismo la Mula – or, for real wheel warriors, the insanely steep mountain road from Bartolomé Masó to Santo Domingo in Granma province. For good private cycling tours around Havana and its environs, try Cuba-Ruta Bikes (p96).

With a profusion of casas particulares offering cheap, readily available accommodations, cycle touring is a joy here as long as you keep off the Autopista and steer clear of Havana.

Off-road biking has not yet taken off in Cuba and is generally not permitted.

Diving

If Cuba has a blue ribbon activity, it is scuba diving. Even Fidel in his younger days liked to don a wetsuit and escape beneath the iridescent waters of the Atlantic or Caribbean (his favorite dive site was – apparently – the rarely visited Jardines de la Reina archipelago). Indeed, so famous was the Cuban leader's diving addiction that the CIA allegedly once considered an assassination plot that involved inserting an explosive device inside a conch and placing it on the seabed.

Excellent dive sites are numerous in Cuba. Focus on the area or areas where you want to dive rather than trying to cover multiple sites. The best areas – the Jardines de la Reina, María la Gorda and the Isla de la Juventud – are all fairly isolated, requiring travel time (and preplanning). The more sheltered south coast probably has the edge in terms of water clarity and dependable weather, though the north coast, offering easy access to one of the world's largest reefs, is no slouch.

What makes diving in Cuba special is its unpolluted seas, clear water conditions (average underwater visibility is 30m to 40m), warm seas (mean temperature is 24°C), abundant coral and fish, simple access (including a couple of excellent swim-out reefs) and fascinating shipwrecks (Cuba was a nexus for weighty galleons in the 17th and 18th centuries, and rough seas and skirmishes with pirates sunk many of them).

Diving Centers

In all, Cuba has 25 recognized diving centers spread over 17 different areas. The majority of the centers are managed by Marlin Náutica y Marinas (p50), though you'll also find representation from **Gaviota** (7-204-5708; gaviota@gaviota.cu; Av 47 No 2833, btwn Calles 28 & 34, Havana), **Cubanacán Náutica** (7-833-4090; www.cubanacan.cu) and **Cubamar** (7-833-2523; www.cubamarviajes.cu). Though equipment does vary between installations, you can generally expect safe, professional service with back-up medical support. Environmentally sensitive diving is where things can get wobbly, and individuals should educate themselves about responsible diving. As well as being Scuba Schools International (SSI), American Canadian Underwater Certification (ACUC) and Confédération Mondiale de Activités Subaquatiques (CMAS) certified, most dive instructors are multilingual, speaking a variety of Spanish, English, French, German and Italian. Because of US embargo laws, Professional Association of Diving Instructors (PADI) certification is generally not offered in Cuba.

SNORKELING

You don't have to go deep to enjoy Cuba's tropical aquarium: snorkelers will feel like divers, from Playa Larga to Caleta Buena, around Cienfuegos and along the Guardalavaca reef. In Varadero, daily snorkeling tours sail to Cayo Blanco promising abundant tropical fish and good visibility. If you're not into the group thing, you can don a mask at Playa Coral, 20km away.

Good boat dives for snorkeling happen around Isla de la Juventud and Cayo Largo especially, but also in Varadero and in the Cienfuegos and Guajimico areas. If you intend to do a lot of snorkeling, bring your own gear, as the rental stuff can be tattered and buying it in Cuba will mean you'll sacrifice both price and quality.

Cuba Diving

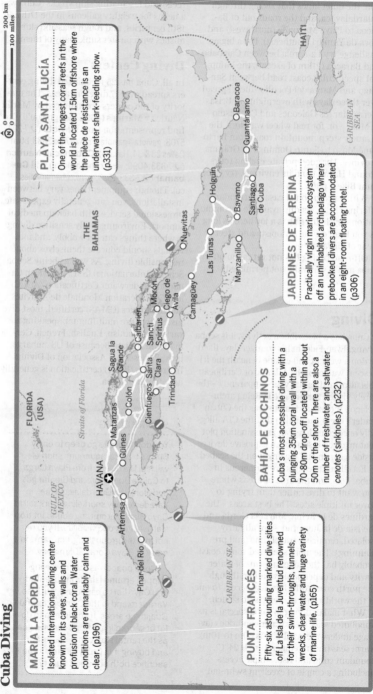

MARÍA LA GORDA

Isolated international diving center known for its caves, walls and profusion of black coral. Water conditions are remarkably calm and clear. (p196)

PLAYA SANTA LUCÍA

One of the longest coral reefs in the world is located 1.5km offshore where the piece de resistance is an underwater shark-feeding show. (p331)

JARDINES DE LA REINA

Practically virgin marine ecosystem off an uninhabited archipelago where prebooked divers are accommodated in an eight-room floating hotel. (p306)

BAHÍA DE COCHINOS

Cuba's most accessible diving with a plunging 35km coral wall with a 70-80m drop-off located within about 50m of the shore. There are also a number of freshwater and saltwater cenotes (sinkholes). (p232)

PUNTA FRANCÉS

Fifty-six astounding marked dive sites off La Isla de la Juventud renowned for their swim-throughs, tunnels, wrecks, clear water and huge variety of marine life. (p165)

FLORIDA (USA)

Straits of Florida

GULF OF MEXICO

Pinar del Río

Artemisa

Güines

Matanzas

Colón

HAVANA

Cienfuegos

Santa Clara

Trinidad

Sagua la Grande

Calbarién

Sancti Spíritus

Morón

Ciego de Ávila

Camagüey

Nuevitas

Las Tunas

Manzanillo

Bayamo

Holguín

Santiago de Cuba

Guantánamo

Baracoa

THE BAHAMAS

HAITI

CARIBBEAN SEA

CARIBBEAN SEA

200 km

100 miles

Dives and courses are comparably priced island-wide, from CUC$25 to CUC$50 per dive, with a discount after four or five dives. Full certification courses are CUC$310 to CUC$365, and 'resort' or introductory dives cost CUC$50 to CUC$60.

Fishing

Deep-Sea Fishing

Hemingway wasn't wrong. Cuba's fast-moving Gulf Stream along the north coast supports prime game fishing for sailfish, tuna, mackerel, swordfish, barracuda, marlin and shark pretty much year-round. Deep-sea fishing is a rite of passage for many and a great way to wind down, make friends, drink beer, watch sunsets and generally leave the troubles of the world behind. Not surprisingly, the country has great facilities for sport anglers, and every Cuban boat captain seems to look and talk as if he's walked straight from the pages of a Hemingway classic.

Cuba's best deep-sea fishing center is Cayo Guillermo, the small island (then uninhabited) that featured in Hemingway's *Islands in the Stream*. Papa may no longer be in residence, but there's still an abundance of fish. Another good bet is Havana, which has two marinas, one at Tarará and the other – better one – at Marina Hemingway to the west.

Elsewhere, all of Cuba's main resort areas offer deep-sea-fishing excursions for similar rates. Count on paying approximately CUC$280 per half-day and CUC$450 per full day for four people, including crew and open bar.

Fly-Fishing

Fly-fishing is undertaken mainly on shallow sand flats easily reached from the shoreline. Classic areas to throw a line are Las Salinas in the Ciénaga de Zapata, the protected waters surrounding Cayo Largo del Sur, parts of the Isla de la Juventud and – most notably – the uninhabited nirvana of the Jardines de la Reina archipelago. The archipelago is a national park and heavily protected. It is not unheard of to catch 25 different species of fish in the same day here.

A 'grand slam' for fly-fishers in Cuba is to bag tarpon, bonefish and permit in the

Fishing in crystal-clear waters

same day; bag a snook as well and they call it a 'superslam'. The best fishing season in this part of Cuba is February to June. The remoteness of the many islands, reefs and sand flats means fishing trips are usually organized on boats that offer on-board accommodations. They are coordinated through a company called Avalon (p306).

The north coast hides a couple of good fly-fishing havens. Most noted are the still-uninhabited keys of Cayo Romano and Cayo Cruz in the north of Camagüey province. Trips are coordinated by Ecotur (p50) and are based at an attractive lodge in the mainland town of Brasil.

Freshwater Fishing

Freshwater fishing in Cuba is lesser known than fly-fishing but equally rewarding, and many Americans and Canadians home in on the island's numerous lakes. Freshwater fly-fishing is superb in vast Ciénaga de Zapata in Matanzas, where enthusiasts can arrange multiday catch-and-release trips. *Trucha* (largemouth bass) was first introduced into Cuba in the early 20th century by Americans at King's Ranch and the United Fruit Company. Due to favorable environmental protection, the fish are now abundant in many Cuban lakes. Good places to cast a line are the Laguna del Tesoro in Matanzas, the Laguna de la Leche and Laguna la Redonda in Ciego de Ávila province, Embalse Zaza in Sancti Spíritus and Embalse Hanabanilla in Villa Clara – 7.6kg specimens have been caught here!

Hiking & Trekking

European hikers and North American wilderness freaks take note: while Cuba's trekking potential is enormous, the traveler's right to roam is restricted by badly maintained trails, poor signage, a lack of maps and rather draconian restrictions about where you can and cannot go without a guide. Cubans aren't as enthusiastic about hiking for enjoyment as Canadians or Germans. Instead, many park authorities tend to assume that all hikers want to be led by hand along short, relatively tame trails that are rarely more than 5km or 6km in length. You'll frequently be told that hiking alone is a reckless and dangerous activity, despite the fact that Cuba harbors no big fauna and no poisonous snakes. The best time of year for hiking is outside the rainy season and before it gets too hot (December to April).

The dearth of available hikes isn't always the result of nitpicking restrictions. Much of Cuba's trekkable terrain is in ecologically sensitive areas, meaning access is carefully managed and controlled.

Multiday hiking in Cuba has improved in the last couple of years and, though information is still hard to get, you can piece together workable options in the Sierra Maestra and the Escambray Mountains. The most popular by far is the three-day trek to the summit of Pico Turquino, followed by the overnight San Claudio trail in the Reserva Sierra del Rosario.

More challenging day hikes include El Yunque, a mountain near Baracoa; the Balcón de Iberia circuit in Parque Nacional Alejandro de Humboldt; and some of the hikes around Las Terrazas and Viñales.

Topes de Collantes probably has the largest concentration of hiking trails in its protected zone (a natural park). Indeed, some overseas groups organize four- to five-day treks here, starting near Lago Hanabanilla and finishing in Parque el Cubano. Inquire in advance at the Carpeta Central information office in Topes de Collantes if you are keen to organize something on behalf of a group.

Other, tamer hikes include Cueva las Perlas and Del Bosque al Mar in the Península de Guanahacabibes, the guided trail in Parque Natural el Bagá, El Guafe trail in Parque Nacional Desembarco del Granma and the short circuit in Reserva Ecológica Varahicacos in Varadero. Some of these hikes are guided and all require the payment of an entry fee.

If you want to hike independently, you'll need patience, resolve and an excellent sense of direction. It's also useful to ask the locals in your casa particular. Try experimenting first with Salto del Caburní or Sendero la Batata in Topes de Collantes or the various hikes around Viñales. There's a beautiful, little-used DIY hike on a good trail near Marea del Portillo and some gorgeous options around Baracoa – ask the locals.

Horseback Riding

Cuba has a long-standing cowboy culture, and horseback riding is available countrywide in both official and unofficial capacities. If you arrange it privately, make sure you check the state of the horses and equipment first. Riding poorly kept horses is both cruel and potentially dangerous.

The state-owned catering company Palmares owns numerous rustic ranchos across Cuba that are supposed to give tourists a feel for traditional country life. All of these places offer guided horseback riding, usually for around CUC$5 per hour. You'll find good ranchos in Florencia in Ciego de Ávila province and Hacienda la Belén in Camagüey province.

La Guabina is a horse-breeding center near the city of Pinar del Río that offers both horse shows and horseback-riding adventures.

Rock Climbing

The Valle de Viñales has been described as having the best rock climbing in the Western hemisphere. There are more than 150 routes now open (at all levels of difficulty,

Top: Rock climbing in Valle de Viñales (p175)

Bottom: Hiking in Topes de Collantes (p289)

FLAVIO VALLENARI / GETTY IMAGES ©

USEFUL AGENCIES

Ecotur (www.ecoturcuba.co.cu) Runs organized hiking, trekking, fishing and bird-watching trips to some of the country's otherwise inaccessible corners. It has offices in every province and a main HQ in Havana.

Cubamar Viajes (www.cubamarviajes.cu) Runs Cuba's 80-plus campismos (rural chalets). It has Reservaciones de Campismo offices in every provincial capital and a helpful head office in Havana.

Marlin Náutica y Marinas (www.nauticamarlin.com) State-run company that oversees many of Cuba's marinas. They also offer fishing, diving, boating and other water-based excursions.

Viñales is still not technically legal, though it is rumored the government is considering giving it official sanction. Check on the ground for updates. You're unlikely to get arrested or even warned, but take extreme care and do not under any circumstances do anything that damages the delicate Parque Nacional Viñales ecosystem.

Wind- & Kiteboarding

With stiff east-northeast winds fanning its jagged northern coastline, it was only a matter of time before the Cubans (and visiting tourists) woke up to the country's excellent wind- and kiteboarding potential. The sport is still relatively new in Cuba, especially to equipment-strapped locals, although an increasing number of foreigners are now flying in with their boards and kite rigs in tow before decamping to the main kite-surfing hubs, Varadero, Cayo Guillermo and Guardalavaca. Varadero has even sprouted a couple of private kite-surfing businesses offering board rental and courses. Look out for **Caribbean Riders Kite School** (http://varaderokiteschool.com) located between the Laguna Azul and Memories Varadero hotels, or **Cuba Kiters** (www.cubakiters.com) between Solymar and Hotel Internacional. Four-hour basic courses cost CUC$140–160 while one hour/day rental will set you back CUC$25/47. Further east, Cayo Guillermo offers rentals and courses at three resort hotels, although many DIY-ers bring their own gear. You'll also find enthusiastic surfers in Guardalavaca in Holguín province.

with several rated as YDS Class 5.14) and the word is out among the international climbing crowd, who are creating their own scene in one of Cuba's prettiest settings. Independent travelers will appreciate the free rein that climbers enjoy here.

Though you can climb year-round, the heat can be oppressive, and locals stick to an October-to-April season, with December to January being the optimum months. For more information, visit **Cuba Climbing** (www.cubaclimbing.com) or head straight to Viñales.

It is important to note that, though widely practiced and normally without consequence, climbing in the Valle de

Plan Your Trip

Travel with Children

Cubans love kids and kids invariably love Cuba. Welcome to a culture where children still play freely in the street and wait staff unconsciously ruffle your toddler's hair as they glide past your table on their way back to the kitchen. There's something wonderfully old-fashioned about kids' entertainment here, which is less about sophisticated computer games and more about messing around in the plaza with an improvised baseball bat and a rolled-up ball of plastic.

Cuba for Kids

There are certain dichotomies regarding child facilities in Cuba. On the one hand Cuban society is innately family-friendly, child-loving and tactile; on the other, economic challenges have meant that common 'Western' provisions such as pushchair ramps, changing tables and basic safety measures are often thin on the ground. The one place where you'll find generic international standards of service is in the modern resorts, most of which have dedicated and professionally run 'kids clubs'.

Children's Highlights

Forts & Castles

➡ **Fortaleza de San Carlos de la Cabaña** (p77) Havana's huge fort has museums, battlements and a nightly cannon ceremony with soldiers in period costume.

➡ **Castillo de San Pedro de la Roca del Morro** (p404) Santiago's Unesco-listed fort is best known for its exciting pirate museum.

➡ **Castillo de la Real Fuerza** (p67) This centrally located Havana fort has a moat, lookouts and scale models of Spanish galleons.

Best Regions for Children

Havana

The streets of Habana Vieja can't have changed much since the days of *Pirates of the Caribbean*, so your kids' imaginations will be allowed to run wild in forts, squares, museums and narrow streets. Havana also has Cuba's largest amusement park (Isla del Coco), and its best aquarium.

Varadero

Cuba's biggest resort has the largest – if most predictable – stash of specifically tailored kids' activities, including nighttime shows, organized sports, beach games and boat trips.

Trinidad

The south coast's southern gem is awash with economic casas particulares (private homestays), an ideal opportunity for your kids to mix and mingle with Cuban families. Throw in an excellent beach (Playa Ancón), easily accessible snorkeling waters and a profusion of pleasant pastoral activities (horseback riding is popular) and you've got the perfect nonresort family option.

Playgrounds

➡ **Parque Maestranza** (p64) Bouncy castles, fairground rides and sweet snacks overlooking Havana Harbor.

➡ **Isla del Coco** (p127) Huge, newish, Chinese-funded amusement park in Havana's Playa neighborhood.

➡ **Parque Lenin** (p136) More 'rustic' playground rides, boats, a minitrain and horses for rent in Havana.

Animal Encounters

➡ **Acuario Nacional** (p126) Various reproductions of Cuba's coastal ecosystems including a marine cave and a mangrove forest at the nation's main aquarium in Havana's Miramar district.

➡ **Criaderos de Cocodrilos** (Map p420; admission CUC$1; ⊘8am-5pm) Of the half-dozen croc farms spread across the country, the best is in Guamá, Matanzas province.

➡ **Horseback riding** Possible all over Cuba and usually run out of rustic *fincas* (farms) in rural areas such as Pinar del Río and Trinidad.

Festivals

➡ **Las Parrandas** Fireworks, smoke and huge animated floats: Remedios' Christmas Eve party is a blast for kids *and* adults.

➡ **Carnaval de Santiago de Cuba** A colorful celebration of Caribbean culture with floats and dancing that takes place every July.

➡ **Carnaval de la Habana** More music, dancing and effigies, this time along Havana's Malecón in August.

Planning

Travelers with kids are not unusual in Cuba and the trend has proliferated in recent years with more Cuban-Americans visiting their families with offspring in tow; these will be your best sources for on-the-ground information. Be forewarned that physical contact and human warmth are so typically Cuban: strangers will effusively welcome your kids, give them kisses or take their hands with regularity. Chill, it's all part of the Cuban way.

Local children run around freely in Cuba and, with strong local community organizations, the safety of your child shouldn't be a problem as long as you take normal precautions. Be careful with the unforgiving motorized traffic, watch for unprotected roadworks and be aware of the general lack of modern safety equipment.

Your kids shouldn't need any specific pre-trip inoculations for Cuba, though you may want to check with your doctor about individual requirements before departing. Medicines are in short supply in Cuba, so take all you think you might need. Useful stuff to have is acetaminophen, ibuprofen, antinausea medicines and cough drops. Insect repellent is also helpful in lowland areas. Diapers (nappies) and baby formula can be hard to find; bring your own. A copy of your child's birth certificate containing the names of both parents could also prove useful, especially if you have different surnames.

Car seats are not mandatory in Cuba, and taxi and rental-car firms don't carry them. Bring your own if you're planning on renting a car. High chairs in restaurants are also almost nonexistent, though waiters will try to improvise. The same goes for travel cribs. Cuba's pavements weren't designed with pushchairs in mind. If your child is small enough, carry him/her in a body harness.

Casas particulares are nearly always happy to accommodate families and are exceptionally child-friendly. Resort hotels are family-friendly too.

Eating with Kids

With a dearth of exotic spices and an emphasis on good, plain, nonfancy food, kids in Cuba are often surprisingly well accommodated. The family-oriented nature of life on the island certainly helps. Few eating establishments turn away children, and waiters and waitresses in most cafes and restaurants will, more often than not, dote on your boisterous young offspring and go out of their way to try to accommodate unadventurous or childish tastes. Rice and beans are good staples, and chicken and fish are relatively reliable sources of protein. The main absent food group – though your kid probably won't think so – is a regular supply of fresh vegetables.

Regions at a Glance

Cuba's provinces are splayed end to end across the main island, with the oft-forgotten comma of La Isla de la Juventud hanging off the bottom. All of them have coast access and are embellished with beautiful beaches, the best hugging the north coast. Equally ubiquitous are the vivid snippets of history, impressive colonial architecture and potent reminders of the 1959 Revolution. The country's highest mountain range, the Sierra Maestra, rises in the east with another significant range, the Sierra del Escambray, positioned south-central. Cuba's main wilderness areas are the Ciénaga de Zapata (Zapata Swamp), the marine terraces of Granma, the tropical forests of Guantánamo and the uninhabited (for now) northern keys. Urban highlights include Havana, Santiago de Cuba, Camagüey and colonial Trinidad.

Havana

Museums
Architecture
Nightlife

Museos Históricos

The capital's 4-sq-km historic center has history wherever you look and museums dedicated to everything from silverware to Simón Bolívar. Kick off with the Museo de la Revolución, garner more cultural immersion in the Museo de la Ciudad and schedule at least half a day for the fine Museo Nacional de Bellas Artes.

Eclectic Architecture

Havana's architecture is not unlike its flora and fauna: hard to categorize and sometimes a little – well – weird. Stroll the streets of Habana Vieja and Centro Habana and choose your own highlights.

Life's a Cabaret

Every Cuban music style is represented in Havana, from street rumba to glitzy cabaret, making it the best place in the country for live concerts, spontaneous busking and racy nightlife.

p60

Artemisa & Mayabeque Provinces

Beaches
Ecotourism
Coffee Ruins

Secret Beaches

Rather surprisingly, considering it's stuck on the main highway between Havana and Varadero, Mayabeque province has its own unheralded and delightful beaches, spearheaded by Playa Jibacoa. Get there quick before the (planned) golf courses start springing up.

Small Footprints

The stark white eco-village of Las Terrazas was practicing environmentally friendly living long before the urgencies of the Special Period or the adoption of eco-practices in the world outside. Today it carries on much as it has always done: quietly, confidently and – above all – sustainably.

Plantation Past

Las Terrazas has dozens of plantations, half-covered by jungle, while Artemisa has its own Antiguo Cafetal Angerona, a larger, more refined, but no-less-weathered ruin that once functioned as a coffee plantation employing 500 slaves.

p145

Isla de la Juventud (Special Municipality)

Diving
Wildlife
History

Into the Blue

Outside the hard-to-access Jardines de la Reina archipelago, La Isla offers the best diving in Cuba and is the main reason many people come here. Ultra-clear water, abundant sea life and a protected marine park at Punta Francés are the high points.

Rejuvenated Fauna

If you missed it in the Ciénaga de Zapata, La Isla is the only other place in the world where you can view the Cuban crocodile in its natural state. It has been successfully reintroduced into the Lanier Swamp.

Cuba's Alcatraz

Not one but two of Cuba's verbose spokesmen were once imprisoned on the archipelago's largest outlying island that also doubled up as a big jail: José Martí and Fidel Castro. Their former incarceration sites are riddled with historical significance.

p159

Valle de Viñales & Pinar del Río Province

Diving
Food
Flora & Fauna

Divers' Dream

Isolated at the westernmost tip of the main island, María la Gorda has long lured travelers for its spectacular diving, enhanced by electrically colored coral, huge sponges and gorgonians, and a knowledgeable but laid-back dive community.

Roast Pork

There's nothing like a true Cuban pork roast and there's no place better to try it than among the *guajiros* (country folk) of Viñales who offer up humongous portions of the national dish with trimmings of rice, beans and root vegetables.

Parks of Pinar

With more protected land than any other province, Pinar is a green paradise. Go hiking in Parque Nacional Viñales, spot a sea turtle in Parque Nacional Península de Guanahacabibes or train your binoculars on the feathered action around Cueva de los Portales.

p174

Matanzas Province

Diving
Flora & Fauna
Beaches

Accessible Aquatics

Bahía de Cochinos (Bay of Pigs) might not have Cuba's best diving, but it certainly has its most accessible. You can glide off from the shore here and be gawping at coral-encrusted drop-off walls within a few strokes.

Swamp Life

In contrast to the resort frenzy on the north coast, Matanzas' southern underbelly is one of Cuba's last true wildernesses and an important refuge for wildlife, including Cuban crocodiles, manatees, bee hummingbirds and tree rats.

Sands of Varadero

Even if you hate resorts, there's still one reason to go to Varadero – an unbroken 20km ribbon of golden sand that stretches the whole length of the Península de Hicacos. It's arguably the longest and finest beach in Cuba.

p198

Cienfuegos Province

Architecture
Music
Diving

French Classicism

Despite its position as one of Cuba's newer cities, founded in 1819, Cienfuegos retains a remarkably homogenous urban core full of classical facades and slender columns that carry the essence of 19th-century France, where it drew its inspiration.

Benny Moré Trail

Benny Moré, Cuba's most adaptable and diverse musician, who ruled the clubs and dance halls in the 1940s and '50s, once called Cienfuegos the city he liked best. Come see if you agree and, on the way, visit the village where he was born.

Secrets of Guajimico

Welcome to one of Cuba's least-discovered diving spots, run out of a comfortable campismo on the warm, calm south coast and renowned for its coral gardens, sponges and scattered wrecks.

p235

Villa Clara Province

Beaches
History
Nightlife

Spectacular Keys

Cuba's newest resorts on the keys off the coast of Villa Clara hide some stunning and still relatively uncrowded beaches, including the publicly accessible Las Salinas on Cayo las Brujas and the more-refined Playa El Mégano and Playa Ensenachos on Cayo Ensenachos.

Che Guevara

Love him or hate him, his legacy won't go away, so you might as well visit Santa Clara to at least try to understand what made the great *guerrillero* (warrior) tick. The city hosts Che's mausoleum, a museum cataloguing his life and the historic site where he ambushed an armored train in 1958.

Student Scene

The city of Santa Clara has the edgiest and most contemporary nightlife scene in Cuba, where local innovators are constantly probing for the next big thing.

p252

Sancti Spíritus Province

Museums
Hiking
Music

Revolution to Romance

Trinidad has more museums per square meter than anywhere outside Havana, and they're not token gestures either. Themes include history, furniture, counterrevolutionary wars, ceramics, contemporary art and romance.

Trails & Topography

Topes de Collantes has the most comprehensive trail system in Cuba and showcases some of the best scenery in the archipelago, with waterfalls, natural swimming pools, precious wildlife and working coffee plantations. Further trails can be found in the less-heralded Alturas de Banao and Jobo Rosado reserves.

Spontaneous Sounds

In Trinidad – and to a lesser extent Sancti Spíritus – music seems to emanate out of every nook and cranny, much of it spontaneous and unrehearsed. Trinidad, in particular, has the most varied and condensed music scene outside Havana.

p273

Ciego de Ávila Province

Fishing
Beaches
Festivals

Hemingway's Haunts

Cayo Guillermo has all the makings of a fishing trip extraordinaire: a warm tropical setting; large, abundant fish; and the ghost of Ernest Hemingway to follow you from port to rippling sea and back. Pack a box of beer and follow the Gulf Stream.

Pilar Paradise

Colorados, Prohibida, Flamingo and Pilar – the beaches of the northern keys lure you with their names as much as their reputations and, when you get there, there's plenty of room for everyone.

Fiestas & Fireworks

No other province has such a varied and – frankly – weird stash of festivals. Ciego is home to an annual cricket tournament, rustic country dancing, strange voodoo rites and explosive fireworks.

p300

Camagüey Province

Diving
Architecture
Beaches

Feeding Sharks

OK, the resorts aren't exactly refined luxury, but who cares when the diving's this good? Playa Santa Lucía sits astride one of the largest coral reefs in the world and is famous for its shark-feeding show.

Urban Maze

Camagüey doesn't conform to the normal Spanish colonial building manual when it comes to urban layout, but that's part of the attraction. Lose yourself in Cuba's third-largest city that, since 2008, has been a Unesco World Heritage Site.

Limitless Sand

The beaches on the province's north coast are phenomenal. There's 20km-long Playa Santa Lucía, the Robinson Crusoe–like Playa los Pinos on Cayo Sabinel, and the shapely curve of Playa los Cocos at the mouth of the Bahía de Nuevitas.

p315

Las Tunas Province

Beaches
Art
Festivals

Eco-Beaches

Hardly anyone knows about them, but they're still there. Las Tunas' northern eco-beaches are currently the preserve of local Cubans, seabirds and the odd in-the-know outsider. Come and enjoy them before the resort-building bulldozers wreck the tranquility.

City of Sculptures

Scout around the congenial streets of the provincial capital Las Tunas and you'll uncover an esoteric collection of revolutionary leaders, two-headed Taíno chiefs and oversize pencils crafted in stone.

Country Music

The bastion of country music in Cuba, Las Tunas hosts the annual Jornada Cucalambeana festival, where songwriters from across the country come to recite their quick-witted satirical *décimas* (10-line stanzas).

p334

Holguín Province

Beaches
Ecotourism
Archaeology

Little-Known Beaches

Most tourists gravitate to the well-known beaches of Playa Pesquero and Guardalavaca that are backed by big resorts. Less touted, but equally *linda* (pretty), are Playa Caleta near Gibara and Las Morales near Banes.

Mountains & Keys

Strangely, for a province that hosts Cuba's largest and dirtiest industry (the Moa nickel mines), Holguín has a profusion of green escapes tucked away in pine-clad mountain retreats or hidden on exotic keys. Discover Cayo Saetía and Pinares de Mayarí.

Pre-Columbian Culture

Holguín preserves Cuba's best stash of archaeological finds. The region's long-lost pre-Columbian culture is showcased at the Museo Chorro de Maita and its adjacent reconstructed Taíno village. There are more artifacts on display at the Museo Indocubano Bani in nearby Banes.

p344

Granma Province

History
Hiking
Festivals

Revolutionary Sites

History is never as real as it is in Cuba's most revolutionary province. Here you can hike up to Castro's 1950s mountaintop HQ, visit the sugar mill where Céspedes first freed his slaves or ponder the poignant spot where José Martí fell in battle.

Bagging a Peak

With the Sierra Maestra overlaying two national parks, Granma has tremendous hiking potential, including the trek up to the top of the nation's highest peak, Pico Turquino.

Street Parties

Granma is famous for its street parties. Towns such as Bayamo and Manzanillo have long celebrated weekly alfresco shindigs with whole roast pork, chess tournaments and music provided by old-fashioned street organs.

p370

Santiago de Cuba Province

Dance
History
Festivals

Folklórico Groups

As magical as they are mysterious, Santiago's *folklórico* (Afro-Cuban folkdance) troupes are a throwback to another era when slaves hid their traditions behind a complex veneer of singing, dancing and syncretized religion.

Revolutionary Legacy

Cuba's hotbed of sedition has inspired multiple rebellions and many key sites can still be visited. Start at Cuartel Moncada (Moncada Barracks) and head south through the birth houses of local heroes Frank País and Antonio Maceo, to the eerily named Museo de la Lucha Clandestina (Clandestine War Museum).

Caribbean Culture

Santiago has a wider variety of annual festivals than any other Cuban city. July is the top month, with the annual Carnaval preceded by the Festival del Caribe, celebrating the city's rich Caribbean culture.

p391

Guantánamo Province

Flora & Fauna
Hiking
Food

Endemic Eden

Guantánamo's historical isolation and complex soil structure has led to high levels of endemism, meaning you're likely to see plant and animal species here that you'll see nowhere else in the archipelago. Aspiring botanists should gravitate towards Parque Nacional Alejandro de Humboldt.

Unsung Trails

As Baracoa grows as an ecological center, hiking possibilities are opening up. Try the long-standing treks up El Yunque or into Parque Nacional Alejandro de Humboldt, or tackle newer trails around the Río Duaba or to the beaches near Boca de Yumurí.

Coconut & Cocoa

What do you mean you didn't come to Cuba for the food? Baracoa is waiting to blow away your culinary preconceptions with a sweet-and-spicy mélange of dishes concocted from the ubiquitous cocoa, coffee, coconuts and bananas.

p428

On the Road

Havana
p60

Varadero & Matanzas
p198

Artemisa & Mayabeque
p145

Villa Clara
p252

Ciego de Ávila
p300

Valle de Viñales & Pinar del Río
p174

Cienfuegos
p235

Trinidad & Sancti Spíritus
p273

Camagüey
p315

Las Tunas
p334

Holguín
p344

Isla de la Juventud (Special Municipality)
p159

Granma
p370

Guantánamo
p428

Santiago de Cuba
p391

Havana

☑ 7 / POP 2,130,431

Includes ➜

Downtown Havana....61
Playa & Marianao....126
Parque Lenin Area...135
Santiago de las
Vegas Área.........137
Regla..............137
Guanabacoa........138
Cojímar Area........140
Casablanca.........140
Playas del Este......141

Best Places to Eat

➡ Doña Eutimia (p104)

➡ Café Laurent (p109)

➡ San Cristóbal (p108)

➡ Paladar Los Mercaderes (p106)

➡ Espacios (p131)

Best Places to Stay

➡ Hotel Los Frailes (p97)

➡ Hotel Iberostar Parque Central (p101)

➡ Hostal Peregrino Consulado (p99)

➡ Casa 1932 (p99)

➡ Hostal Conde de Villanueva (p97)

Why Go?

Close your eyes for a moment and imagine you are there. Waves crashing against a mildewed sea wall; a young couple cavorting in a dark, dilapidated alley; guitars and voices harmonizing over a syncopated drum rhythm; sunlight slanting across rotten peeling paintwork; a handsome youth in a *guayabera* shirt leaning against a Lada; the smell of diesel fumes and cheap aftershave; tourists with Hemingway beards; Che Guevara on a billboard, a banknote, a keyring, a t-shirt...

No one could have invented Havana. It's too audacious, too contradictory, and – despite 50 years of withering neglect – too damned beautiful. How it does it, is anyone's guess. Maybe it's the swashbuckling history, the survivalist spirit, or the indefatigable salsa energy that ricochets off walls and emanates most emphatically from the people. Don't come here looking for answers. Just arrive with an open mind and prepare yourself for a long, slow seduction.

When to Go

➡ February is peak season meaning there's extra life in the city and plenty of extracurricular activities, including a cigar festival and an international book fair.

➡ Havana's summer heat can be stifling. To avoid it, come in October, a wonderfully quiet month when there's still plenty to do – such as enjoy the annual Festival Internacional de Ballet.

➡ Busier (for a reason) is December, when people line up for the Festival Internacional del Nuevo Cine Latinamericano, Cuba's premiere movie shindig.

➡ August is hot, but fun, if you time your visit to coincide with Havana's ostentatious Carnaval.

History

In 1514 San Cristóbal de La Habana was founded on the south coast of Cuba near the mouth of the Río Mayabeque by Spanish conquistador Pánfilo de Narváez. Named after the daughter of a famous Taíno chief, the city was moved twice during its first five years due to mosquito infestations and wasn't permanently established on its present site until December 17, 1519. According to local legend, the first Mass was said beneath a ceiba tree in present-day Plaza de Armas.

Havana was the most westerly and isolated of Diego Velázquez' original villas, and life was hard in the early days. Things didn't get any better in 1538 when French pirates and local slaves razed the city.

It took the Spanish conquest of Mexico and Peru to swing the pendulum in Havana's favor. The town's strategic location, at the mouth of the Gulf of Mexico, made it a perfect nexus for the annual treasure fleets to regroup in its sheltered harbor before heading east. Thus endowed, its ascension was quick and decisive, and in 1607 Havana replaced Santiago as the capital of Cuba.

The city was sacked again by French pirates led by Jacques de Sores in 1555. The Spanish replied by building La Punta and El Morro forts between 1558 and 1630 to reinforce an already formidable protective ring. From 1674 to 1740, a strong wall around the city was added. These defenses kept the pirates at bay but proved ineffective when Spain became embroiled in the Seven Years' War with Britain.

On June 6, 1762, a British army under the Earl of Albemarle attacked Havana, landing at Cojímar and striking inland to Guanabacoa. From there they drove west along the northeastern side of the harbor, and on July 30 they attacked El Morro from the rear. Other troops landed at La Chorrera, west of the city, and, by August 13, the Spanish were surrounded and forced to surrender. The British held Havana for 11 months.

When the Spanish regained the city a year later in exchange for Florida, they began a building program to upgrade the city's defenses in order to avoid another debilitating siege. A new fortress, La Cabaña, was built along the ridge from which the British had shelled El Morro, and by the time the work was finished in 1774 Havana had become the most heavily fortified city in the New World, the 'bulwark of the Indies.'

The British occupation resulted in Spain opening Havana to freer trade. In 1765 the city was granted the right to trade with seven Spanish cities instead of only Cádiz, and from 1818 Havana was allowed to ship its sugar, rum, tobacco and coffee directly to any part of the world. The 19th century was an era of steady progress: first came the railway in 1837, followed by public gas lighting (1848), the telegraph (1851), an urban transport system (1862), telephones (1888) and electric lighting (1890).

By 1902 the city, which had been physically untouched by the devastating wars of independence, had a quarter of a million inhabitants. It had expanded rapidly west along the Malecón and into the wooded glades of formerly off-limits Vedado. A large influx of rich Americans arrived at the start of the Prohibition era, and the 'good times' began to roll with abandon. By the 1950s Havana was a decadent gambling city frolicking amid the all-night parties of American mobsters and scooping fortunes into the pockets of various disreputable hoods such as Meyer Lansky.

For Fidel Castro, it was an aberration. On taking power in 1959, the new revolutionary government promptly closed down all the casinos and sent Lansky and his henchmen back to Miami. The once-glittering hotels were divided up to provide homes for the rural poor. Havana's long decline had begun.

Today the city's restoration is ongoing and a stoic fight against the odds in a country where shortages are part of everyday life and money for raw materials is scarce. Since 1982 City Historian Eusebio Leal Spengler has been piecing Habana Vieja back together street by street and square by square with the aid of Unesco and a variety of foreign investors. Slowly but surely, the old starlet is starting to reclaim her former greatness.

DOWNTOWN HAVANA

For simplicity's sake downtown Havana can be split into three main areas: Habana Vieja, Centro Habana and Vedado. Between them they contain the bulk of the tourist sights. Centrally located Habana Vieja is the city's atmospheric historic masterpiece; dense Centro Habana, to the west, provides an eye-opening look at the real-life Cuba in close-up; and the more majestic spread-out Vedado is the once-notorious Mafia-run district replete with hotels, restaurants and a pulsating nightlife.

Straits of Florida

Architecture

**Museo Nacional de
Bellas Artes**

**Fortaleza de
San Carlos de la
Cabaña**

COJÍMAR

See Parque Histórico Militar
Morro-Cabaña Map (p78)

Malecón

Malecón (Av Maceo)

Habana Vieja

C 23

Callejón de
Hamel

See Habana
Vieja Map (p66)

Vía Blanca

**Necrópolis
Cristóbal
Colón**

Plaza de la
Revolución

See Centro
Habana
Map (p80)

Parque
Martí

REGLA

GUANABACOA

See Vedado Map (p88)

Bahía de La
Habana

CERRO

Havana

AV 5

Marina
Hemingway

See Playa & Marianao Map (p128)

C 51   C 100

Av de la Independencia

Carretera
Central

SAN
FRANCISCO
DE PAULA

C23

Av San Francisco

Parque
Zoológico
Nacional

ARROYO
NARANJO

Parque
Lenin

Embalse
Ejército
Rebelde

Embalse
Paso Sequito

Calzada de Bejucal

Río Pancho Simón

Autopista Habana

Doble Vía

Aeropuerto
Internacional
José Martí

RANCHO
BOYEROS

Jardín
Botánico
Nacional

SANTIAGO
DE LAS
VEGAS

Havana Highlights

❶ Strolling through Havana's
mosaic of art deco, colonial
baroque and neoclassical
architecture (p75).

❷ Taking in the dramatic
sweep of the **Malecón** (p92)
at sunset.

❸ Seeing how tourist money
has helped to rehabilitate
Habana Vieja (p64).

❹ Investigating street art,
rumba drumming and Santería
in the **Callejón de Hamel**
(p115).

❺ Storming the gates of the
**Fortaleza de San Carlos de la
Cabaña** (p77) and staying for
the *cañonazo* (shooting of the
cannons) ceremony.

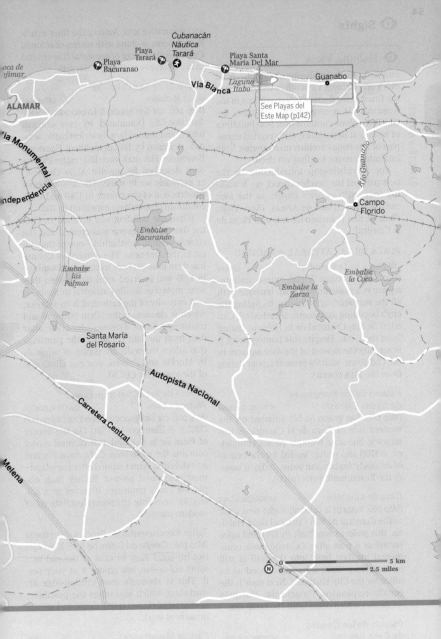

Playa Bacuranao

Playa Tarará

Cubanacán Náutica Tarará

Playa Santa María Del Mar

Guanabo

Vía Blanca

Laguna Itabo

See Playas del Este Map (p142)

oca de ojímar

ALAMAR

ia Monumental

Independencia

Embalse Bacuranao

Embalse las Palmas

Río Guanabo

Campo Florido

Embalse la Coca

Embalse la Zarza

Santa María del Rosario

Autopista Nacional

Carretera Central

Melena

0   5 km
0   2.5 miles

N

6 Tracing the history of Cuban painting in the **Museo Nacional de Bellas Artes** (p83).

7 Trying not to get spooked in the strangely beautiful **Necrópolis Cristóbal Colón** (p92).

◉ Sights

◉ Habana Vieja

Studded with architectural jewels from every era, Habana Vieja offers visitors one of the finest collections of urban edifices in the Americas. At a conservative estimate, the Old Town alone contains over 900 buildings of historical importance, with myriad examples of illustrious architecture ranging from intricate baroque to glitzy art deco.

For a whistle-stop introduction to the best parts of the neighborhood, try a walking tour (p72) or stick closely to the four main squares: Plaza de Armas, Plaza Vieja, Plaza de San Francisco de Asís and Plaza de la Catedral.

PLAZA DE LA CATEDRAL & AROUND

★ **Plaza de la Catedral**   SQUARE
(Map p66) Habana Vieja's most uniform square is a museum to Cuban baroque with all the surrounding buildings, including the city's beguiling asymmetrical cathedral, Catedral de San Cristóbal de la Habana, dating from the 1700s. Despite this homogeneity, it is actually the newest of the four squares in the Old Town, with its present layout dating from the 18th century.

Palacio de los Marqueses de Aguas Claras   HISTORIC BUILDING
(Map p66; San Ignacio No 54) Situated on the western side of Plaza de la Catedral is this majestic one-time baroque palace completed in 1760 and widely lauded for the beauty of its shady Andalucian patio. Today it houses the Restaurante Paris (p106).

Casa de Lombillo   HISTORIC BUILDING
(Map p66; Plaza de la Catedral) Right next door to the Catedral de San Cristóbal de la Habana, this *palacio* was built in 1741 and once served as a post office (a stone-mask ornamental mailbox built into the wall is still in use). Since 2000 it has functioned as an office for the City Historian. Next door is the equally resplendent **Palacio del Marqués de Arcos**, which dates from the same era.

Palacio de los Condes de Casa Bayona   HISTORIC BUILDING
(Map p66; San Ignacio No 61) The square's southern aspect is taken up by its oldest building, constructed in 1720. Today it functions as the **Museo de Arte Colonial** (Map p66; San Ignacio No 61; admission CUC$2; ☉9:30am-4:45pm), a small museum displaying colonial furniture

and decorative arts. Among the finer exhibits are pieces of china with scenes of colonial Cuba, a collection of ornamental flowers and many colonial-era dining-room sets.

Catedral de San Cristóbal de la Habana   CATHEDRAL
(Map p66; cnr San Ignacio & Empedrado; ☉9am-4pm Mon-Sat) Dominated by two unequal towers and framed by a theatrical baroque facade designed by Italian architect Francesco Borromini, Havana's incredible cathedral was once described by novelist Alejo Carpentier as 'music set in stone.' The Jesuits began construction of the church in 1748 and work continued despite their expulsion in 1767.

When the building was finished in 1787, the diocese of Havana was created and the church became a cathedral – one of the oldest in the Americas. The remains of Columbus were brought here from Santo Domingo in 1795 and interred until 1898, when they were moved to Seville Cathedral in Spain.

A curiosity of the cathedral is its interior, which is classical rather than baroque and relatively austere. Frescoes above the altar date from the late 1700s and the paintings that adorn the walls are copies of originals by Murillo and Rubens. You can climb one of the towers for CUC$1.

Centro de Arte Contemporáneo Wilfredo Lam   CULTURAL CENTER
(Map p66; cnr San Ignacio & Empedrado; admission CUC$3; ☉10am-5pm Mon-Sat) On the corner of Plaza de la Catedral, this cultural center contains the melodious **Cafe Amarillo** and an exhibition center named after the island's most celebrated painter. Rather than displaying Lam's paintings, it serves as a gallery for revolving temporary exhibitions of modern painters.

Taller Experimental de Gráfica   ARTS CENTER
(Map p66; Callejón del Chorro No 6; ☉10am-4pm Mon-Fri) **FREE** Easy to miss at the end of a short cul-de-sac, but ignore it at your peril. This is Havana's most cutting-edge art workshop, which also offers the possibility of engraving classes (p95). Come and see the masters at work.

Parque Maestranza   PARK
(Map p66; Av Carlos Manuel de Céspedes; admission CUC$1) Small-scale but fun kids playground (children under four years only) with inflatable castles and other games overlooking the harbor.

PLAZA DE ARMAS & AROUND

Plaza de Armas
SQUARE

(Map p66) Havana's oldest square was laid out in the early 1520s, soon after the city's foundation, and was originally known as Plaza de Iglesia after a church – the Parroquial Mayor – that once stood on the site of the present-day Palacio de los Capitanes Generales.

The name Plaza de Armas (Square of Arms) wasn't adopted until the late 16th century, when the colonial governor, then housed in the Castillo de la Real Fuerza, used the site to conduct military exercises. Today's plaza, along with most of the buildings around it, dates from the late 1700s.

In the center of the square, which is lined with royal palms and hosts a daily (except Sundays) secondhand book market, is a marble statue of Carlos Manuel de Céspedes (Map p66), the man who set Cuba on the road to independence in 1868. The statue replaced one of unpopular Spanish king, Ferdinand VII, in 1955.

Also of note on the square's eastern aspect is the late-18th-century Palacio de los Condes de Santovenia (Map p66; Calle Baratillo No 9), today the five-star, 27-room Hotel Santa Isabel (p98).

Museo el Templete
MUSEUM

(Map p66; Plaza de Armas; admission CUC$2; ⊙8:30am-6pm) This museum is housed in the tiny neoclassical Doric chapel on the east side of Plaza de Armas, which was erected in 1828 at the point where Havana's first Mass was held beneath a ceiba tree in November 1519. A similar ceiba tree has now replaced the original. Inside the chapel are three large paintings of the event by the French painter Jean Baptiste Vermay (1786–1833).

Museo de la Ciudad
MUSEUM

(Map p66; Tacón No 1; admission CUC$3; ⊙ 9:30am-6pm) Filling the whole west side of Plaza de Armas, this museum is housed in the Palacio de los Capitanes Generales (Map p66), dating from the 1770s. Built on the site of Havana's original church, it's a textbook example of Cuban baroque architecture hewn out of rock from the nearby San Lázaro quarries. Since 1968 the building has been home to the City Museum, one of Havana's most comprehensive and interesting, but has served many purposes over the years.

From 1791 until 1898 it was the residence of the Spanish captains general. From 1899 until 1902, the US military governors were based here, and during the first two decades of the 20th century the building briefly became the presidential palace. These days, the museum wraps its way regally around a splendid central courtyard adorned with a white marble statue of Christopher Columbus (1862). Artifacts include period furniture, military uniforms and old-fashioned 19th-century horse carriages, while old photos vividly recreate events from Havana's roller-coaster history, such as the 1898 sinking of

HAVANA IN...

Two Days

Explore Habana Vieja by strolling the streets between the four main colonial squares. There is a plethora of museums, so you'll want to weed out the good ones. The **Museo de la Ciudad** (p65) is a highlight in the colonial core, while in Centro Habana don't miss the **Museo de la Revolución** (p83) and the dual-site **Museo Nacional de Bellas Artes** (p83). You can cover a lot of ground on Havana's **open-topped bus tour** (p125), although the **Malecón** (p92) sea drive is best plied on foot. For nightlife, soak up the nocturnal essence of Habana Vieja, dipping into bars on Calle Obispo and Plaza Vieja.

Four Days

With two extra days, make sure you check out the 1950s-era kitsch of the Vedado neighborhood. Essential stops are the **Hotel Nacional** (p86) for a mojito on the alfresco terrace and **Plaza de la Revolución** (p91) for a look at the Che mural and the **Memorial a José Martí** (p92). Stick around in the evening for some excellent nightlife in jazz clubs, lounge bars and cabarets.

One Week

Three more days gives you time to get out to suburban sights such as the **Museo Hemingway** (p139), the historic colonial forts on the east side of the harbor and **Fusterlandia** (p132) in Playa.

Habana Vieja

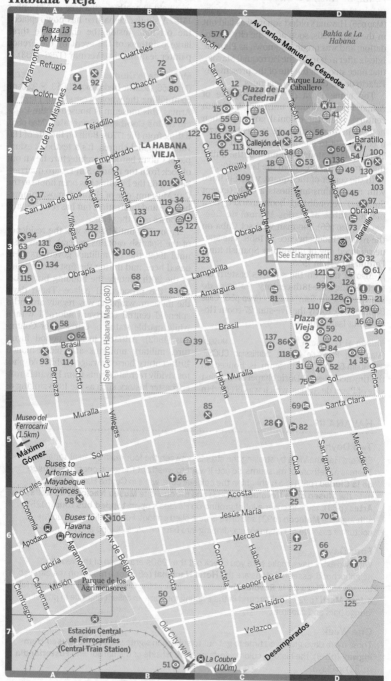

US battleship Maine in the harbor. It's better to body-swerve the pushy attendants and wander around at your own pace.

Palacio del Segundo Cabo HISTORIC BUILDING
(Map p66; O'Reilly No 4; ☺9am-6pm Mon-Sat) Wedged into the square's northwest corner, this building was constructed in 1772 as the headquarters of the Spanish vice-governor. After several reincarnations as a post office, the palace of the Senate, the Supreme Court, the National Academy of Arts and Letters, and the seat of the Cuban Geographical Society, the building is today a well-stocked bookstore.

Pop-art fans should take a look at the palace's **Sala Galería Raúl Martínez**. The building was being renovated at the time of writing.

Gabinete de Arqueologia MUSEUM
(Map p66; Tacón No 12; ☺9am-5pm Tue-Sat, 9am-2:30pm Sun) **FREE** See the rainbow of influences on Cuba's colonial culture from everyday artifacts dug up nearby. Of particular interest are the ceramics that demonstrate a 17th- and 18th-century penchant for English china, Chinese porcelain and Mexican ceramics among the Spanish-Cuban aristocracy. Upstairs rooms are dedicated to older pre-Columbian finds.

Castillo de la Real Fuerza FORT
(Map p66) On the seaward side of Plaza de Armas is one of the oldest existing forts in the Americas, built between 1558 and 1577 on the site of an earlier fort destroyed by French privateers in 1555. The west tower is crowned by a copy of a famous bronze weather vane called **La Giraldilla**.

The original was cast in Havana in 1632 by Jerónimo Martínez Pinzón and is popularly believed to be of Doña Inés de Bobadilla, the wife of gold explorer Hernando de Soto. The original is now kept in the Museo de la Ciudad, and the figure also appears on the Havana Club rum label. Imposing and indomitable, the castle is ringed by an impressive moat and today shelters the **Museo de Navegación** (Map p66; Castillo de la Real Fuerza; admission CUC$3; ☺9am-5pm), which displays interesting exposés on the history of the fort and Old Town, and its connections with the erstwhile Spanish Empire. Look out for the huge scale model of the *Santíssima Trinidad* galleon.

Habana Vieja

◉ **Top Sights**
1	Plaza de la Catedral	C2
2	Plaza Vieja	D4

◉ **Sights**
3	Armería 9 de Abril	F7
4	Cámara Oscura	D4
5	Casa de África	E7
6	Casa de Asia	F6
7	Casa de la Obra Pía	E6
8	Casa de Lombillo	C2
9	Casa de México Benito Juárez	F6
10	Casa Oswaldo Guayasamín	F6
11	Castillo de la Real Fuerza	D1
12	Catedral de San Cristóbal de la Habana	C1
13	Catedral Ortodoxa Nuestra Señora de Kazán	E4
14	Centro Cultural Pablo de la Torriente Brau	D4
15	Centro de Arte Contemporáneo Wifredo Lam	C2
16	Coche Mambí	D4
17	Edificio Bacardí	A3
18	Edificio Santo Domingo	C2
19	El Caballero de París	D3
20	Fototeca de Cuba	D4
21	Fuente de los Leones	D3
22	Gabinete de Arqueología	D2
23	Iglesia de San Francisco de Paula	D6
24	Iglesia del Santo Ángel Custodio	A1
25	Iglesia Parroquial del Espíritu Santo	D6
26	Iglesia y Convento de Nuestra Señora de Belén	B5
27	Iglesia y Convento de Nuestra Señora de la Merced	D6
28	Iglesia y Convento de Santa Clara	C5
29	Iglesia y Monasterio de San Francisco de Asís	D4
30	Il Genio di Leonardo da Vinci	D4
31	La Casona Centro de Arte	D4
32	Lonja del Comercio	D3
33	Maqueta de La Habana Vieja	E6
34	Museo 28 Septiembre de los CDR	B3
35	Museo Alejandro Humboldt	D4
36	Museo de Arte Colonial	C2
	Museo de Arte Religioso	(see 29)
37	Museo de Bomberos	F7
38	Museo de la Ciudad	D2
39	Museo de la Farmacia Habanera	B4
40	Museo de Naipes	D4
41	Museo de Navegación	D2
42	Museo de Numismático	B3
43	Museo de Pintura Mural	F6
44	Museo de Simón Bolívar	F7
45	Museo de Transporte Automotor	D2
46	Museo del Ron	E4
47	Museo del Tabaco	F6
48	Museo el Templete	D2
49	Museo Nacional de Historia Natural	D2
50	Museo-Casa Natal de José Martí	B7
51	Old City Wall	B7
52	Palacio Cueto	D4
53	Palacio de los Capitanes Generales	D2
	Palacio de los Condes de Casa Bayona	(see 36)
54	Palacio de Los Condes de Santovenia	D2
55	Palacio de los Marqueses de Aguas Claras	C2
56	Palacio del Segundo Cabo	D2
57	Parque Maestranza	C1
58	Parroquial del Santo Cristo del Buen Viaje	A4
59	Planetario	D4
60	Plaza de Armas	D2
61	Plaza de San Francisco de Asís	D3
62	Plaza del Cristo & Around	A4
	Statue of Carlos Manuel de Céspedes	(see 60)
63	Statue of Francisco de Albear	A3
64	Statue of Simón Bolívar	F6
65	Taller Experimental de Gráfica	C2

◉ **Activities, Courses & Tours**
66	Gimnasio de Boxeo Rafael Trejo	D6
67	La Casa del Son	A2
	Taller Experimental de Gráfica	(see 65)

◉ **Sleeping**
68	Casa Colonial del 1715	B3
69	Casa de Pepe & Rafaela	D5

Museo de Transporte Automotor MUSEUM
(Map p66; Oficios No 13; admission CUC$1.50;
⊙9am-5pm Tue-Sat, 9am-1pm Sun) Few miss
the irony of this vaguely surreal museum
stuffed with ancient Thunderbirds, Pontiacs
and Ford Model Ts, most of which appear to
be in better shape than the dinosaurs that
ply the streets outside.

★**Calle Mercaderes** STREET
Cobbled, car-free Calle Mercaderes (Merchant's Street) has been extensively restored by the City Historian's Office and is

an almost complete replica of its splendid
18th-century high-water mark. Interspersed
with the museums, shops and restaurants
are some real-life working social projects,
such as a maternity home and a needlecraft
cooperative.

Most of the myriad museums are free, including the **Casa de Asia** (Map p66; Mercaderes
No 111; ⊙10am-6pm Tue-Sat, 9am-1pm Sun) FREE,
with paintings and sculpture from China
and Japan; the **Armería 9 de Abril** (Map p66;
Mercaderes No 157; ⊙10am-6pm Mon-Sat) FREE,

70 Greenhouse	D6
71 Hostal Conde de Villanueva	F7
72 Hostal Peregrino El Encinar	B1
73 Hostal Valencia	D3
74 Hotel Ambos Mundos	E6
75 Hotel Beltrán de la Santa Cruz	D4
76 Hotel Florida	C2
77 Hotel Habana 612	C4
78 Hotel Los Fraile	D4
79 Hotel Palacio del Marqués de San Felipe y Santiago de Bejucal	D3
80 Hotel Palacio O'Farrill	B1
81 Hotel Raquel	C3
Hotel Santa Isabel	(see 54)
82 Noemi Moreno	D5
83 Palacio de Pascua	B3
84 Penthouse Plaza Vieja	D4

✪ Eating

85 Agropecuario Belén	C5
86 Café Bohemia	D4
87 Café del Oriente	D3
88 Café Lamparilla	F7
89 Café Santo Domingo	E6
90 Casa del Queso La Marriage	C3
91 Doña Eutimia	C2
El Mercurio	(see 32)
92 Fumero Jacqueline	A1
93 Hanoi	A4
94 Harris Brothers	A3
95 La Imprenta	F7
96 La Mina	F5
97 Mama Inés	D3
98 Mercado Agropecuario Egido	A6
99 Mesón de la Flota	D3
100 Nao Bar Paladar	D2
101 O'Reilly 304	B2
102 Paladar Los Mercaderes	F7
103 Restaurante el Templete	D2
104 Restaurante la Dominica	C2
Restaurante Paris	(see 55)
105 Restaurante Puerto de Sagua	B6
106 Sandwichería La Bien Paga	B3
107 Tres Monedas Creative Lounge	B2

◉ Drinking & Nightlife

108 Bar Dos Hermanos	E4
Café el Escorial	(see 84)
109 Café París	C2
110 Café Taberna	D4
111 Cervecería Antiguo Almacén de la Madera y Tabaco	E6
112 Dulcería Bianchini I	E4
113 Dulcería Bianchini II	C2
114 El Chanchullero	A4
115 El Floridita	A3
116 La Bodeguita del Medio	C2
117 La Dichosa	B3
118 La Factoria Plaza Vieja	D4
119 La Lluvia de Oro	B3
120 Monserrate Bar	A4
121 Museo del Chocolate	D3

◉ Entertainment

Basílica Menor de San Francisco de Asís	(see 21)
122 Fundación Alejo Carpentier	C2
123 Oratorio de San Felipe Neri	C3

◉ Shopping

124 Casa de Carmen Montilla	D3
125 Centro Cultural Antiguos Almacenes de Deposito San José	D7
126 Estudio Galería los Oficios	D4
127 Fayad Jamás	B3
128 Fundación Havana Club Shop	E4
129 Habana 1791	F6
Hostal Condes de Villanueva	(see 71)
130 La Casa del Café	D2
131 Librería la Internacional	A3
132 Librería Venecia	A3
133 Longina Música	B3
134 Moderna Poesía	A3
135 Palacio de la Artesanía	B1
136 Plaza de Armas Secondhand Book Market	D2
137 Taller de Serigrafía René Portocarrero	C4

an old gun shop (now museum) stormed by revolutionaries on the said date in 1958; and the **Museo de Bomberos** (Map p66; cnr Mercaderes & Lamparilla; ⊗10am-6pm Mon-Sat) **FREE**, which has antediluvian fire equipment dedicated to 19 Havana firefighters who lost their lives in an 1890 railway fire.

Just off Mercaderes down Obrapía, it's worth slinking into the gratis **Casa de África** (Map p66; Obrapía No 157; ⊗9:30am-5pm Tue-Sat, 9:30am-1pm Sun) **FREE**, which houses sacred objects relating to Santería and the secret Abakuá fraternity collected by ethnographer Fernando Ortíz.

The corner of Mercaderes and Obrapía has an international flavor, with a bronze **statue of Simón Bolívar** (Map p66), the Latin America liberator, and across the street you'll find the **Museo de Simón Bolívar** (Map p66; Mercaderes No 160; donations accepted; ⊗9am-5pm Tue-Sun) dedicated to Bolívar's life. The **Casa de México Benito Juárez** (Map p66; Obrapía No 116; admission CUC$1; ⊗10:15am-5:45pm Tue-Sat, 9am-1pm Sun) exhibits Mexican folk art and plenty of books, but not a lot on Señor Juárez (Mexico's first indigenous president) himself. Just east is the Casa Oswaldo Guayasamín (Map p66; Obrapía No 111; donations accepted; ⊙9am-2:30pm Tue-Sun), now a museum, but once the studio of the great Ecuadorian artist who painted Fidel in numerous poses.

Mercaderes is also characterized by its restored shops, including a perfume store and a spice shop. Wander at will.

Maqueta de La Habana Vieja MUSEUM

(Map p66; Mercaderes No 114; admission CUC$1.50; ⊙9am-6:30pm; ⊕) Herein lies a 1:500 scale model of Habana Vieja complete with an authentic soundtrack meant to replicate a day in the life of the city. It's incredibly detailed and provides an excellent way of geographically acquainting yourself with the city's historical core.

The on-site Cinematógrafo Lumière (Maqueta de La Habana Vieja, Mercaderes No 114; admission CUC$2) is a small cinema that shows nostalgia movies for senior citizens, and educational documentaries about the restoration for visitors.

Casa de la Obra Pía HISTORIC BUILDING

(Map p66; Obrapía No 158; admission CUC$1.50; ⊙9:30am-5:30pm Tue-Sat, to 12:30pm Sun) One of the more muscular sights on Calle Mercaderes is this typical Havana aristocratic residence originally built in 1665 and rebuilt in 1780. Baroque decoration – including an intricate portico made in Cádiz, Spain – covers the exterior facade. There are some colonial artifacts displayed inside.

PLAZA DE SAN FRANCISCO DE ASÍS & AROUND

Plaza de San Francisco de Asís SQUARE

(Map p66) Facing Havana harbor, the breezy Plaza de San Francisco de Asís first grew up in the 16th century when Spanish galleons stopped by at the quayside on their passage

---

HAVANA STREET NAMES

Havana's streets have two names: the official new name that you'll see on street signs, and the colloquial old name still used by the locals. The following table will help sort out some of the confusion.

OLD NAME	NEW NAME
Av de los Presidentes	Calle G
Av de Maceo	Malecón
Av del Puerto	Av Carlos Manuel de Céspedes
Av de Rancho	Av de la Independencia Boyeros (Boyeros)
Belascoaín	Padre Varela
Cárcel	Capdevila
Carlos III (Tercera)	Av Salvador Allende
Cristina	Av de México
Egido	Av de Bélgica
Estrella	Enrique Barnet
Galiano	Av de Italia
La Rampa	Calle 23
Monserrate	Av de las Misiones
Monte	Máximo Gómez
Paseo del Prado	Paseo de Martí
Paula	Leonor Pérez
Reina	Av Simón Bolívar
San José	San Martín
Someruelos	Aponte
Teniente Rey	Brasil
Vives	Av de España
Zulueta	Agramonte

through the Indies to Spain. A market took root in the 1500s, followed by a church in 1608, though when the pious monks complained of too much noise, the market was moved a few blocks south to Plaza Vieja.

The Plaza de San Francisco underwent a full restoration in the late 1990s and is most notable for its uneven cobblestones and the white marble **Fuente de los Leones** (Fountain of Lions; Map p66) carved by the Italian sculptor Giuseppe Gaggini in 1836. A more modern statue outside the square's famous church depicts **El Caballero de París** (Map p66), a well-known street person who roamed Havana during the 1950s, engaging passers-by with his philosophies on life, religion, politics and current events. On the eastern side of the plaza stands the Terminal Sierra Maestra cruise terminal, which dispatches shiploads of weekly tourists, while nearby the domed **Lonja del Comercio** (Map p66; Plaza de San Francisco de Asís) is a former commodities market erected in 1909 and restored in 1996 to provide office space for foreign companies with joint ventures in Cuba. You can enter the Lonja to admire its central atrium and futuristic interior.

Iglesia y Monasterio de San Francisco de Asís
MUSEUM

(Map p66; Oficios, btwn Amargura & Brasil; ⊙ concert hall from 5pm or 6pm) Originally constructed in 1608 and rebuilt in baroque style from 1719 to 1738, this church/convent ceased to have a religious function in the 1840s. In the late 1980s crypts and religious objects were excavated, and many were later incorporated into the **Museo de Arte Religioso** (Map p66; ⌨ 7-862-3467; unguided/guided tour CUC$2/3; ⊙ 9am-6pm) which opened on the site in 1994. Since 2005, part of the old monastery has functioned as a children's theater for the neighborhood's young residents. Some of Havana's best classical concerts are hosted here.

For information on upcoming events check the listings in the *Bienvenidos* booklet, available in hotels and Infotur offices.

Il Genio di Leonardo da Vinci
MUSEUM

(Map p66; Churruca, btwn Oficios & Av Carlos Manuel de Céspedes; admission CUC$2; ⊙ 9:30am-4pm Tue-Sat) A permanent exposition in the Convento de San Francisco de Asís' Salón Blanco (use separate entrance on the church's south side behind the Coche Mambí) that has cleverly built mock-ups of many of Leonardo's famous drawings –

gliders, odometers, bikes, parachutes and tanks – the antecedents to pretty much half the inventions in the modern world. It's beautifully laid out with explanations in six languages, including Russian.

Museo Alejandro Humboldt
MUSEUM

(Map p66; cnr Oficios & Muralla; ⊙ 9am-5pm Tue-Sat) **FREE** Often referred to as the 'second discoverer' of Cuba, German scientist, Alexander von Humboldt's huge Cuban legacy goes largely unnoticed by outsiders. This small museum displays a historical trajectory of his work collecting scientific and botanical data across the island in the early 1800s. Nearby is the **Coche Mambí** (Map p66; ⊙ 9am-2pm Tue-Sat) **FREE**, an elaborate train carriage built in the US in 1900 and brought to Cuba in 1912. A palace on wheels, it once served as the Presidential Car.

Museo del Ron
MUSEUM

(Map p66; San Pedro No 262; admission incl guide CUC$7; ⊙ 9am-5:30pm Mon-Thu, to 4:30pm Fri-Sun) You don't have to be an Añejo Reserva quaffer to enjoy the Museo del Ron in the Fundación Havana Club, but it probably helps. The museum, with its trilingual guided tour, shows rum-making antiquities and the complex brewing process, but lacks detail or passion. A not overgenerous measure of rum is included in the price.

There's a bar and shop on site, but the savvy reconvene to Bar Dos Hermanos (p112) next door. The museum sits opposite Havana harbor.

PLAZA VIEJA & AROUND

★ Plaza Vieja
SQUARE

(Map p66) Laid out in 1559, Plaza Vieja (Old Square) is Havana's most architecturally eclectic square, where Cuban baroque nestles seamlessly next to Gaudí-inspired art nouveau. Originally called Plaza Nueva (New Square), it was initially used for military exercises and later served as an open-air marketplace.

During the Batista regime an ugly underground parking lot was constructed here, but this monstrosity was demolished in 1996 to make way for a massive renovation project. Sprinkled liberally with bars, restaurants and cafes, Plaza Vieja today has its own microbrewery, the Angela Landa primary school, a beautiful fenced-in fountain and, on its west side, some of Havana's finest *vitrales* (stained-glass windows).

Habana Vieja

WALKING TOUR OF OLD HAVANA

This easy 'four plaza' walking tour, though less than 2km in length, could fill a day with its museums, shops, bars and street theater. It highlights Havana's unique historical district, built up around four main squares. Start at **Catedral de San Cristóbal de la Habana** ❶ which anchors the Plaza de la Catedral. This compact square has bags of atmosphere and is always awash with interesting characters. Then take Calle Empedrado followed by Calle Mercaderes to Plaza de Armas, once used for military exercises and still guarded by the **Castillo de la Real Fuerza** ❷. The fort's museum is worth a quick look. Worth more time is the Museo de la Ciudad in the **Palacio de los Capitanes Generales** ❸; eschew the on-site guides and wander alone. Walk up **Calle Obispo** ❹ next, Havana's busy main drag, before turning left into **Calle Mercaderes** ❺, where old shops and several museums make ambling a pleasure. Turn left on Calle Amargura and dive into Plaza de San Francisco de Asís, dominated by **Iglesia y Monasterio de San Francisco de Asís** ❻. Make a note of upcoming classical concerts (great acoustics!) and try to take in one of the church's two museums (Il Genio di Leonardo da Vinci is best). Turn right on Calle Brasil and you'll enter **Plaza Vieja** ❼, home to a planetarium and several museum-galleries. And when you're museumed-out, crash at Factoria Plaza Vieja for a smooth microbrewed beer.

MUSEUMS

Dip into some of the museums you will pass on the way (in order):

» **Museo de Arte Colonial** Colonial furniture

» **Museo de Navegación** Maritime history

» **Museo de la Ciudad** City history

» **Museo de Pintura Mural** Frescos

» **Maqueta de la Habana Vieja** Scale model of Havana

» **Museo de Naipes** Playing cards

Catedral de San Cristóbal de la Habana

The cathedral's interior was originally baroque, like its main facade. However, in the early 19th century, a renovation project redecorated the church's inner sanctum in a more sober classical tone.

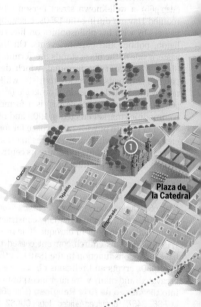

Plaza de la Catedral

Calle Obispo

The lower section of Obispo is an architectural crossroads. The row of buildings on the south are the oldest townhouses in Havana, dating from the 1570s. Opposite is the Hotel Ambos Mundos, Hemingway's 1930s hangout.

Castillo de la Real Fuerza

The highlight of this fort's onsite maritime museum is a 4m-long model of the *Santissima Trinidad*, a ship built in Havana in the 1760s that fought at the Battle of Trafalgar in 1805.

MARK LEWIS/GETTY IMAGES©

Palacio de los Capitanes Generales

An interesting feature of this sturdy building is the marine fossils embedded in its limestone walls. The street outside is lined with wooden bricks designed to deaden the sound of horses' hooves.

BRENT WINEBRENNER/GETTY IMAGES©

DANITA DELIMONT/GETTY IMAGES©

Iglesia y Monasterio de San Francisco de Asís

Once Havana's tallest building, the bell tower of this former church/monastery was originally topped by a statue of St Francis of Assisi; the figurine fell off during an 1846 hurricane.

Plaza de Armas

Barillo

Cuba tacón

Oficios

Baratillo

Plaza de San Francisco de Asís ⑥

Obispo

Mercaderes

O'Reilly

San Ignacio

Lamparilla

Amargura

Cuba

Brasil

Muralla

Sol

Calle Mercaderes

Pedestrian-friendly 'Market Street' is notable for its esoteric shops. On the corner of Calle Obrapía sits the Casa de la Obra Pía, one of the first renovation projects of city historian Eusebio Leal in 1968.

RICK RUDNICKI/GETTY IMAGES©

Plaza Vieja

Plaza Vieja's buildings were constructed as private residences rather than municipal buildings. They housed some of Havana's richest families, who would gather to watch the plaza's gory public spectacles, including executions.

WALTER BIBIKOW/GETTY IMAGES©

Cámara Oscura
LANDMARK

(Map p66; Plaza Vieja; admission CUC$2; ⊙9am-5pm Tue-Sat, 9am-1pm Sun) On the northeastern corner of Plaza Vieja is this clever optical device providing live, 360-degree views of the city from atop a 35m-tall tower. Explanations are in Spanish and English.

Fototeca de Cuba
GALLERY

(Map p66; Mercaderes No 307; ⊙10am-5pm Tue-Fri, 9am-noon Sat) FREE A photographic archive of Old Havana since the early 20th century that was started by former City Historian, Emilio Roig de Leuchsenring in 1937. There are an estimated 14,000 photos inside, and they have been instrumental in providing the graphic pointers for the current restoration.

Museo de Naipes
MUSEUM

(Map p66; Muralla No 101; ⊙9am-6pm Tue-Sun) FREE Encased in Plaza Vieja's oldest building is this quirky playing-card museum with a 2000-strong collection that includes rock stars, rum drinks and round cards.

La Casona Centro de Arte
GALLERY

(Map p66; Muralla No 107; ⊙10am-5pm Mon-Fri, to 2pm Sat) FREE Housed in one of Plaza Vieja's most striking buildings (note the sturdy colonial overtones), this gallery/shop has great solo and group shows by up-and-coming Cuban artists.

Palacio Cueto
HISTORIC BUILDING

(Map p66; cnr Muralla & Mercaderes) Kissing the southeast corner of Plaza Vieja is this distinctive Gaudí-esque building, which remains Havana's finest example of art nouveau. Its outrageously ornate facade once housed a warehouse and a hat factory before it was rented by José Cueto in the 1920s as the Palacio Vienna hotel. Habaguanex, the commercial arm of the City Historian's Office, is in the process of restoring the building, which was constructed in 1906 and has lain empty and unused since the early 1990s.

Planetario
OBSERVATORY

(Map p66; Mercaderes No 311; admission CUC$10; ⊙10am-3:30pm Wed-Sun) Havana's planetarium includes a scale reproduction of the solar system inside a giant orb, a simulation of the Big Bang, and a theater that allows viewing of over 6000 stars. All pretty exciting stuff. It's only accessible by guided tours booked in advance. Tours take place Wednesday to Sunday and can be booked (in person) on Monday and Tuesday. There are four tours daily and two on Sunday.

Centro Cultural Pablo de la Torriente Brau
CULTURAL CENTER

(Map p66; www.centropablo.cult.cu; Muralla No 63; ⊙9am-5:30pm Tue-Sat) FREE Tucked away behind Plaza Vieja, the 'Brau' is a leading cultural institution that was formed under the auspices of the Unión de Escritores y Artistas de Cuba (Uneac; Union of Cuban Writers and Artists) in 1996. The center hosts expositions, poetry readings and live acoustic music. Its Salón de Arte Digital is renowned for its groundbreaking digital art.

CALLE OBISPO & AROUND

Calle Obispo
STREET

Narrow, car-free Calle Obispo (Bishop's Street), Habana Vieja's main interconnecting artery, is packed with art galleries, shops, music bars and people. Four- and five-story buildings block out most of the sunlight, and the swaying throng of people seems to move in time to the all-pervading live music.

Museo de Numismático
MUSEUM

(Map p66; Obispo, btwn Aguiar & Habana; admission CUC$1.50; ⊙9am-5pm Tue-Sat, 9:30am-12:45pm Sun) This numismatist's heaven brings together various collections of medals, coins and banknotes from around the world, including a stash of 1000 mainly American gold coins (1869–1928) and a full chronology of Cuban banknotes from the 19th century to the present.

Museo 28 Septiembre de los CDR
MUSEUM

(Map p66; Obispo, btwn Aguiar & Habana; admission CUC$2; ⊙9am-5:30pm) A venerable building on Obispo that dedicates two floors to a rather one-sided dissection of the nationwide Comites de la Defensa de la Revolución (CDR; Committees for the Defense of the Revolution). Commendable neighborhood-watch schemes, or grassroots spying agencies? Sift through the propaganda and decide.

Museo de Pintura Mural
MUSEUM

(Map p66; Obispo, btwn Mercaderes & Oficios; ⊙10am-6pm) FREE A simple museum that exhibits some beautifully restored original frescoes in the Casa del Mayorazgo de Recio, popularly considered to be Havana's oldest surviving house.

HISTORICAL JIGSAW

Never in the field of architectural preservation has so much been achieved by so many with so few resources. You hear plenty about the sterling performance of the Cuban education and healthcare systems in the international press, but relatively little about the remarkable work that has gone into preserving the country's valuable but seriously endangered historical legacy, most notably in Havana Vieja.

A work-in-progress since the late 1970s, the piecing back together of Havana's 'old town' after decades of neglect has been a foresighted and startlingly miraculous process considering the economic odds stacked against it. The genius behind the project is Eusebio Leal Spengler, Havana's celebrated City Historian who, unperturbed by the tightening of the financial screws during Cuba's Special Period, set up Habaguanex in 1994, a holding company that earns hard currency through tourism and re-invests it in a mix of historical preservation and city-wide urban regeneration. The process has reaped multiple benefits since its inception. By safeguarding Havana's historical heritage, Leal and his cohorts have attracted more tourists to the city and earned a bigger slice of revenue for Habaguanex to plough back into further restoration work and much-needed social projects.

Eschewing the temptation to turn Havana's old quarter into a historical theme-park, Leal has sought to rebuild the city's urban jigsaw as an authentic 'living' center that provides tangible benefits for the neighborhood's 91,000-plus inhabitants. As a result, schools, neighborhood committees, care-homes for seniors, and centers for children with disabilities sit seamlessly alongside the cleaned-up colonial edifices. This local/tourist juxtaposition is both commendable and unique. Sip an alfresco mojito in gorgeous Plaza Vieja and you will be sharing the space with children from the Angela Landa School that abuts the square. Stroll around the 17th-century Convento Belén and you will be rubbing shoulders with Havana's senior citizens in a convalescent home. In essence, every time you put your money into a Habaguanex hotel, museum or restaurant, you are contributing, not just to the quarter's continued restoration, but to a whole raft of social projects that directly benefit the local population.

Today, Habaguanex (www.habaguanex.ohc.cu) splits its annual tourist income (reported to be in excess of US$160 million) between further restoration (45%) and social projects in the city (55%), of which there are now over 400. The company is renowned for its meticulous attention to detail using old texts, drawings, history books and – where available – photos archived in the Fototeca museum (p74) in its restoration projects. So far, one quarter of Havana Vieja has been returned to the height of its colonial-era splendor with ample tourist attractions including 20 Habaguanex-run hotels, four classic forts and over 30 museums.

Edificio Santo Domingo   MUSEUM
(Map p66; Mercaderes, btwn Obispo & O'Reilly) **FREE** On Obispo is the site of Havana's original university, which stood here between 1728 and 1902. It was originally part of a convent; the contemporary modern office block was built by Habaguanex in 2006 over the skeleton of an uglier 1950s office, the roof of which was used as a helicopter landing pad. It has been ingeniously refitted with the convent's original bell tower and baroque doorway – an interesting juxtaposition of old and new.

Many of the university's arts faculties have now moved back here, and a small museum/art gallery displays a scale model of the original convent and various artifacts that were rescued from it.

Plaza del Cristo & Around   SQUARE
(Map p66) Habana Vieja's fifth (and most overlooked) square lies at the west end of the neighborhood, a little apart from the historical core. The presence of temporary fences suggest a lengthy City Historian makeover is underway. It's worth a look for the **Parroquial del Santo Cristo del Buen Viaje** (Map p66), a church dating from 1732, although there has been a Franciscan hermitage on this site since 1640.

In the throes of a renovation project, the building is most notable for its intricate stained-glass windows and brightly painted wooden ceiling. The Plaza del Cristo also hosts a primary school (hence the noise) and a microcosmic slice of everyday Cuban life without tourists.

Museo de la Farmacia Habanera MUSEUM
(Map p66; cnr Brasil & Compostela; ◎9am-5pm)
FREE A few blocks east from Plaza del Cristo, this museum-store founded in 1886 by Catalan José Sarrá still acts as a working pharmacy for Cubans. The small museum section displays an elegant mock-up of an old drugstore with some interesting historical explanations.

SOUTHERN HABANA VIEJA

Iglesia y Convento de Santa Clara CONVENT
(Map p66; Cuba No 610) South of Plaza Vieja is Havana's largest and oldest convent built between 1638 and 1643, though since 1920 it has served no religious purpose. For a while it housed the Ministry of Public Works, and today part of the Habana Vieja restoration team is based here. It was being renovated at the time of research.

Iglesia y Convento de Nuestra Señora de Belén CONVENT
(Map p66; Compostela, btwn Luz & Acosta; ◎by appointment) This huge 1718 building first functioned as a convalescent home and later as a Jesuit convent. Abandoned in 1925, it fell into disrepair, exacerbated in 1991 by a damaging fire. The City Historian reversed the decline in the late 1990s using tourist coffers to transform it into an active community center; guided tours of the splendidly restored building are available through San Cristóbal Agencia de Viajes (p123).

It's now a community hub for families, young people, the physically and mentally impaired, and the elderly (there are 18 permanent apartments for senior citizens here).

Iglesia y Convento de Nuestra Señora de la Merced CHURCH
(Map p66; Cuba No 806; ◎8am-noon & 3-5:30pm)
Built in 1755, this hemmed-in church was reconstructed in the 19th century. Beautiful gilded altars, frescoed vaults and a number of old paintings create a sacrosanct mood; there's a quiet cloister adjacent. Two blocks away is the rather neglected **Iglesia Parroquial del Espíritu Santo** (Map p66; Acosta 161; ◎8am-noon & 3-6pm), Havana's oldest surviving church, built in 1640 and rebuilt in 1674.

Iglesia de San Francisco de Paula CHURCH
(Map p66; cnr Leonor Pérez & Desamparados) One of Havana's most attractive churches, this building was fully restored in 2000. It is all that remains of the San Francisco de Paula women's hospital from the mid-1700s. Lit up at night for classical music concerts, the stained glass, heavy cupola and baroque facade are romantic and inviting.

Catedral Ortodoxa Nuestra Señora de Kazán CHURCH
(Map p66; Av Carlos Manuel de Céspedes, btwn Sol & Santa Clara) One of Havana's newest buildings, this beautiful gold-domed Russian Orthodox church was built in the early 2000s and consecrated at a ceremony attended by Raúl Castro in October 2008. The church was part of an attempt to reignite Russian-Cuban relations after they went sour in 1991.

Museo-Casa Natal de José Martí MUSEUM
(Map p66; Leonor Pérez No 314; admission CUC$1.50, camera CUC$2; ◎9am-5pm Tue-Sat)
Opened in 1925, this tiny museum, set in the house where the apostle of Cuban independence was born on January 28, 1853, is considered to be the oldest in Havana. The City Historian's Office took the house over in 1994, and its succinct stash of exhibits devoted to Cuba's national hero continues to impress.

Old City Wall HISTORIC SITE
(Map p66) In the 17th century, anxious to defend the city from attacks by pirates and overzealous foreign armies, Cuba's paranoid colonial authorities drew up plans for the construction of a 5km-long city wall. Built between 1674 and 1740, the wall on completion was 1.5m thick and 10m high, running along a line now occupied by Av de las Misiones and Av de Bélgica.

Among the wall's myriad defenses were nine bastions and 180 big guns aimed toward the sea. The only way in and out of the city was through 11 heavily guarded gates that closed every night and opened every morning to the sound of a solitary gunshot. The walls were demolished starting in 1863, but a few segments remain, the largest of which stands on Av de Bélgica close to the train station.

Museo del Ferrocarril MUSEUM
(cnr Av de México & Arroyo; admission CUC$2; ◎9am-5pm) A peripheral museum housed in the old Cristina train station built in 1859. There's a big collection of signaling and communication gear here plus old locos and an overview of Cuba's pioneering railway history. Train rides are possible by prior appointment.

AVENIDA DE LAS MISIONES

Edificio Bacardí
LANDMARK

(Bacardí Building; Map p66; Av de las Misiones, btwn Empedrado & San Juan de Dios; ⊙ hours vary) Finished in 1929, the magnificent Edificio Bacardí is a triumph of art deco architecture with a whole host of lavish finishings that somehow manage to make kitsch look cool. Hemmed in by other buildings, it's hard to get a full kaleidoscopic view of the structure from street level, though the opulent bell tower can be glimpsed from all over Havana.

There's a bar in the lobby, and for CUC$1 you can travel up to the tower for an eagle's-eye view.

Iglesia del Santo Ángel Custodio
CHURCH

(Map p66; Compostela No 2; ⊙ during Mass 7:15am Tue, Wed & Fri, 6pm Thu, Sat & Sun) Originally constructed in 1695, this church was pounded by a ferocious hurricane in 1846, after which it was entirely rebuilt in neo-Gothic style. Among the notable historical and literary figures that have passed through its handsome doors are 19th-century Cuban novelist Cirilo Villaverde, who set the main scene of his novel *Cecilia Valdés* here, and Félix Varela and José Martí, who were baptized in the church in 1788 and 1853 respectively.

The church has been renovated, as has the tiny colonial square, the **Plazuela de Santo Ángel**, now embellished with a statue, a private restaurant and an artist's studio.

◉ Parque Histórico Militar Morro-Cabaña

The sweeping views of Havana from the other side of the bay are spectacular, and a trip to the two old forts of the Parque Histórico Militar Morro-Cabaña is a must. Despite their location on the opposite side of the harbor, both forts are included in the Habana Vieja Unesco World Heritage Site. Sunset is a good time to visit when you can stay over for the emblematic *cañonazo* ceremony.

To get to the forts, use the P-15, P-8 or P-11 metro buses (get off at the first stop after the tunnel), but make sure you're near an exit as very few other people get out there. Otherwise, a metered tourist taxi from Habana Vieja should cost around CUC$4. Another alternative is via the Casablanca ferry, which departs from Av Carlos Manuel de Céspedes in Habana Vieja. From the Casablanca landing follow the road up to the huge Estatua de Cristo (Christ Statue), where you bear left and traverse another road past the Área Ex-

positiva Crisis de Octubre. The entrance to La Cabaña is on your left.

★ Castillo de los Tres Santos Reyes Magnos del Morro
FORT

(Map p78; El Morro; admission CUC$6; ⊙ 8am-8:30pm) This imposing fort was erected between 1589 and 1630 to protect the entrance to Havana harbor from pirates and foreign invaders (French corsair Jacques de Sores had sacked the city in 1555). Perched high on a rocky bluff above the Atlantic, the fort's irregular polygonal shape, 3m-thick walls and deep protective moat offer a classic example of Renaissance military architecture.

For more than a century the fort withstood numerous attacks by French, Dutch and English privateers, but in 1762, after a 44-day siege, a 14,000-strong British force captured El Morro by attacking from the landward side. The Castillo's famous lighthouse was added in 1844.

Aside from the fantastic views over the sea and the city, El Morro also hosts a **maritime museum** (Map p78) that includes a riveting account of the fort's siege and eventual surrender to the British in 1762 using words (in English and Spanish) and paintings. To climb to the top of the **lighthouse** (Map p78; admission CUC$2; ⊙ 8am-8pm) is an additional CUC$2.

★ Fortaleza de San Carlos de la Cabaña
FORT

(Map p78; admission day/night CUC$6/8; ⊙ 8am-11pm) This 18th-century colossus was built between 1763 and 1774 on a long, exposed ridge on the east side of Havana harbor to fill a weakness in the city's defenses. In 1762 the British had taken Havana by gaining control of this strategically important ridge, and it was from here that they shelled the city mercilessly into submission.

In order to prevent a repeat performance, the Spanish King Carlos III ordered the construction of a massive fort that would repel future invaders. Measuring 700m from end to end and covering a whopping 10 hectares, it is the largest Spanish colonial fortress in the Americas.

The impregnability of the fort meant that no invader ever attacked it, though during the 19th century Cuban patriots faced firing squads here. Dictators Machado and Batista used the fortress as a military prison, and immediately after the Revolution Che Guevara set up his headquarters inside the ramparts

HAVANA SIGHTS

Parque Histórico Militar Morro-Cabaña

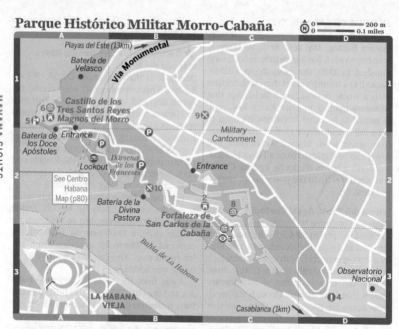

N 0 ——— 200 m
0 ——— 0.1 miles

Parque Histórico Militar Morro-Cabaña

◎ Top Sights
1 Castillo de los Tres Santos Reyes
   Magnos del Morro..............................A1
2 Fortaleza de San Carlos de la
   Cabaña...C2

◎ Sights
3 Cañonazo Ceremony..........................C3
4 Estatua de Cristo D3
5 Lighthouse..A1
6 Maritime Museum A1
7 Museo de Comandancia del Che.......C3
8 Museo de Fortificaciones y
   Armas..C2

⊗ Eating
9 Paladar Doña Carmela.......................C1
10 Restaurante la Divina Pastora B2

to preside over another catalog of grisly executions (this time of Batista's officers).

These days the fort has been restored for visitors, and you can spend at least half a day checking out its wealth of attractions. As well as bars, restaurants, souvenir stalls and a cigar shop (containing the world's longest cigar), La Cabaña hosts the Museo de Fortificaciones y Armas (Map p78) and the engrossing Museo de Comandancia del Che (Map p78). The nightly 9pm cañonazo ceremony (Map p78) is a popular evening excursion in which actors dressed in full 18th-century military regalia reenact the firing of a cannon over the harbor. You can visit the ceremony independently or as part of an organized excursion.

◎ Centro Habana

A key tied to a piece of string is lowered from a 3rd-story window. Two kids in mustard-colored school uniforms play improvised baseball with an old stick and a rolled up ball of plastic. Old ladies in curlers step over a headless chicken lying abandoned on a street corner, a macabre offering to the *orishas* (Santería gods). Life in Centro Habana goes on irrespective of tourism, inclement weather or the distractions of the internet age. During the day, this crowded, ebullient but spectacularly dilapidated neighborhood is a microcosm of Cuban life at the sharp end, the city's most densely populated region with 170,000 people squeezed into an area measuring just 3 sq km. At night it resembles an old-fashioned movie set from a black-and-white film noir.

★ **Capitolio Nacional**   LANDMARK
(Map p80; cnr Dragones & Paseo de Martí;
unguided/guided tour CUC\$3/4; ◷9am-8pm)
The incomparable Capitolio Nacional is Havana's most ambitious and grandiose building, constructed after the post-WWI sugar boom ('Dance of the Millions') gifted the Cuban government a seemingly bottomless treasure box of sugar money. Similar to the Washington, DC Capitol Building, but (marginally) taller and much richer in detail, the work was initiated by Cuba's US-backed dictator Gerardo Machado in 1926 and took 5000 workers three years, two months and 20 days to build at a cost of US\$17 million.

Formerly it was the seat of the Cuban Congress, but since 1959 it has housed the Cuban Academy of Sciences and the National Library of Science and Technology.

Constructed with white Capellanía limestone and block granite, the entrance is guarded by six rounded Doric columns atop a staircase that leads up from Paseo de Martí (Prado). Looking out over the Havana skyline is a 62m stone cupola topped with a replica of 16th-century Florentine sculptor Giambologna's bronze statue of Mercury in the Palazzo de Bargello. Set in the floor directly below the dome is a copy of a 24-carat diamond. Highway distances between Havana and all sites in Cuba are calculated from this point.

The entryway opens up into the **Salón de los Pasos Perdidos** (Room of the Lost Steps; so named because of its unusual acoustics), at the center of which is the statue of the republic, an enormous bronze woman standing 11m tall and symbolizing the mythic Guardian of Virtue and Work.

The Capitolio has been undergoing lengthy renovations, so check with Infotur (p122) for the latest updates and admission prices.

**Real Fábrica de Tabacos
Partagás**   HISTORIC BUILDING
(Map p80; Industria No 520, btwn Barcelona & Dragones; tours CUC\$10; ◷tours every 15min from 9-10:15am & noon-1:30pm) One of Havana's oldest and most famous cigar factories, the landmark neoclassical Real Fábrica de Tabacos Partagás was founded in 1845 by Spaniard Jaime Partagás. Today some 400 workers toil for up to 12 hours a day rolling such famous cigars as Montecristos and Cohibas. As far as tours go, Partagás is the most popular and reliable factory to visit, though many people find its tours rushed, robotic and a tad contrived.

The factory was being renovated at the time of writing, but you can visit it at its temporary location on the corner of Calles San Carlos and Penalver in Centro Habana. Tickets must be booked in advance in the lobby of the Hotel Saratoga (p101).

La Manzana de Gómez   BUILDING
(Map p80; cnr Agramonte & San Rafael) This once-elegant European-style covered shopping mall was built in 1910 and was once the pride of polite Havana society. By the 1990s it had degenerated into a haunted version of Gotham City full of empty-shelved shops. It has subsequently been taken over by a Swiss hotel group which is in the process of returning it to its former glory complete with shops and a five-star hotel.

Parque de la Fraternidad   PARK
(Map p80) Leafy Parque de la Fraternidad was established in 1892 to commemorate the fourth centenary of the Spanish landing in the Americas. A few decades later it was remodeled and renamed to mark the 1927 Pan-American Conference. The name is meant to signify American brotherhood, hence the many busts of Latin and North American leaders that embellish the green areas, including one of US president Abraham Lincoln.

Today the park is the terminus of numerous metro bus routes, and is sometimes referred to as 'Jurassic Park' because of the plethora of photogenic old American cars now used as *colectivos* (collective taxis) that congregate here.

The **Fuente de la India** (Map p80; Paseo de Martí), on a traffic island across from the park, is a white Carrara marble fountain, carved by Giuseppe Gaggini in 1837 for the Count of Villanueva. It portrays a regal Indian woman adorned with a crown of eagle's feathers and seated on a throne surrounded by four gargoyle-like dolphins. In one hand she holds a horn-shaped basket filled with fruit, in the other a shield bearing the city's coat of arms.

**Asociación Cultural Yoruba
de Cuba**   MUSEUM
(Map p80; Paseo de Martí No 615; admission CUC\$10; ◷9am-4:30pm Tue-Sun) A museum that provides a worthwhile overview of the Santería religion, the saints and their powers, although some travelers have complained that the exhibits don't justify the price. There are *tambores* (Santería drum ceremonies) on alternate Fridays at 4:30pm.

Centro Habana

See Vedado Map (p88)

Malecón (Av de Maceo)

Humboldt

49 65

Príncipe

CAYO HUESO

Vapor

Jovellar

San Lázaro

Calz de la Infanta

Callejón de Hamel

68

Concordia

6

Neptuno

69

San Francisco

Espada

Hospital

Aramburu

Soledad

San Miguel

San Rafael

San Martín

Zanja

Salud

Oquendo

Marqués Gonzáz

Lucena

Padre Varela

Virtues

Santiago

29

14

San Lázaro

Lagunas

Ánimas

Gervasio

Escobar

Lealtad

47

52

58

34

56

Pocito

Av Salvador Allende

Retiro

77

Enrique Barnet

San Carlos

11

Padre Varela

Escobar

Lealtad

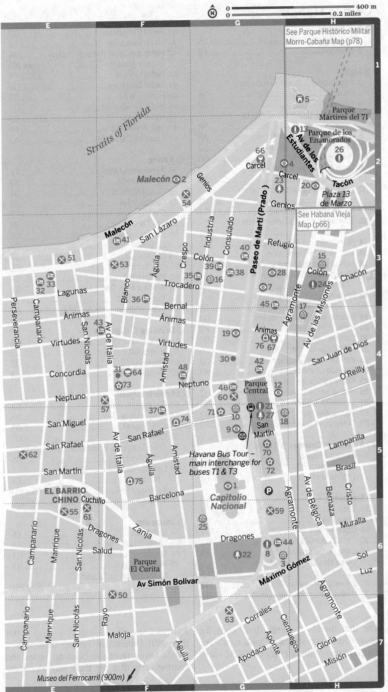

N

0 — 400 m
0 — 0.2 miles

Straits of Florida

See Parque Histórico Militar
Morro-Cabaña Map (p78)

Parque
Mártires del 71

Av de los Estudiantes

Parque de los
Enamorados

13

26

Malecón 2

54

66
Carcel

4

Carcel

Tacón

23

20

Plaza 13
de Marzo

Genios

Genios

See Habana Vieja
Map (p66)

Malecón

San Lázaro

Paseo de Martí (Prado)

41

Industria

Consulado

Refugio

40

15

Colón

Chacón

51

53

Águila

Crespo

Colón

39

28

24

35

16

38

7

Trocadero

45

17

33

32

Lagunas

Blanco

36

Bernal

Ánimas

Ánimas

Virtudes

19

Ánimas

76

67

San Juan de Dios

Perseverancia

Campanario

San Nicolás

Av de Italia

43

Virtudes

Virtudes

30

42

O'Reilly

Concordia

31

64

Amistad

Neptuno

48

46

Parque
Central

12

Neptuno

73

57

60

Av de Italia

San Miguel

37

74

71

10

21

27

18

9

San
Martín

Lamparilla

San Rafael

San Rafael

62

Águila

Amistad

Havana Bus Tour –
main interchange for
buses T1 & T3

70

Brasil

San Rafael

San Martín

72

Av de Bélgica

EL BARRIO
CHINO

Cuchillo

75

Barcelona

Capitolio
Nacional

1

59

Cristo

55

61

Campanario

Manrique

San Nicolás

Dragones

Zanja

25

Muralla

Bernaza

Agramonte

P

Salud

Parque
El Curita

Dragones

44

22

8

3

Sol

Luz

Av Simón Bolívar

Máximo Gómez

50

Campanario

Manrique

San Nicolás

Rayo

Maloja

63

Corrales

Aponte

Apodaca

Cienfuegos

Agramonte

Gloria

Misión

Museo del Ferrocarril (900m)

Centro Habana

◉ **Top Sights**

1	Capitolio Nacional	G5
2	Malecón	F2

◉ **Sights**

3	Asociación Cultural Yoruba de Cuba	G6
4	Cárcel	G2
5	Castillo de San Salvador de la Punta	H1
6	Convento & Iglesia del Carmen	A5
7	Escuela Nacional de Ballet	G3
8	Fuente de la India	G6
9	Gran Teatro de la Habana	G5
10	Hotel Inglaterra	G5
11	Iglesia del Sagrado Corazón de Jesús	D7
12	La Manzana de Gómez	G4
13	Memorial a los Estudiantes de Medicina	H2
14	Monumento a Antonio Maceo	B3
15	Museo de la Revolución	H3
16	Museo Lezama Lima	G3
17	Museo Nacional de Bellas Artes (Arte Cubano)	H4
18	Museo Nacional de Bellas Artes (Arte Universal)	G5
19	Palacio de los Matrimonios	G4
20	Palacio Velasco	H2
21	Parque Central	G5
22	Parque de la Fraternidad	G6
23	Parque de los Enamorados	G2
24	Pavillón Granma	H3
25	Real Fábrica de Tabacos Partagás	G6
26	Statue of General Máximo Gómez	H2
27	Statue of José Martí	G5
28	Teatro Fausto	G3
29	Torreón de San Lázaro	B3

◉ **Activities, Courses & Tours**

30	Centro Andaluz	G4
	Havana Super Tour	(see 32)
31	Teatro América	F4

◉ **Sleeping**

32	Casa 1932	E3
33	Casa 1940	E3
34	Casa Amada	D4
35	Casa Colonial Joel & Yadilis	G3
36	Casa de Lourdes & José	F3
37	Dulce Hostal – Dulce María González	F5
38	Eumelia & Aurelio	G3
39	Hostal Peregrino Consulado	G3

40	Hotel Caribbean	G3
41	Hotel Deauville	F3
42	Hotel Iberostar Parque Central	G4
	Hotel Inglaterra	(see 10)
43	Hotel Lincoln	F4
44	Hotel Saratoga	G6
45	Hotel Sevilla	G3
46	Hotel Telégrafo	G4
47	Hotel Terral	D3
48	Loly & Alejandro	F4
49	Lourdes Cervantes	A3

◉ **Eating**

50	Almacenes Ultra	F6
51	Café Neruda	E3
52	Casa Miglis	D4
53	Castas y Tal	F3
54	Castropol	F2
55	Chi Tack Tong	E6
56	Flor de Loto	D6
57	La Época	F4
58	La Guarida	D4
59	Los Nardos	G6
60	Pastelería Francesa	G4
61	Restaurante Tien-Tan	E6
62	San Cristóbal	E5
63	Supermercado Isla de Cuba	G7

◉ **Drinking & Nightlife**

64	Café Archangel	F4
65	Humboldt 52	A3
66	Prado No 12	G2
67	Sloppy Joe's	G4

◉ **Entertainment**

68	Callejón de Hamel	B4
69	Cine Infanta	A5
70	Cine Payret	G5
71	Cinecito	G5
	Gran Teatro de la Habana	(see 9)
72	Kid Chocolate	G5
73	La Casa de la Música Centro Habana	F4
	Teatro América	(see 31)
	Teatro Fausto	(see 28)

◉ **Shopping**

74	El Bulevar	F5
75	Librería Luis Rogelio Nogueras	F5
76	Memorias Librería	G4
77	Plaza Carlos III	B7
	Real Fábrica de Tabacos Partagás	(see 25)

Note that there's a church dress code for the *tambores* (no shorts or tank tops). For groups of two or more entry is CUC$6 each.

Parque Central PARK

(Map p80) Diminutive Parque Central is a scenic haven from the belching buses and roaring taxis that ply their way along the

Paseo de Martí (Prado). The park, long a microcosm of daily Havana life, was expanded to its present size in the late 19th century after the city walls were knocked down. The 1905 marble statue of José Martí (Map p80) at its center was the first of thousands to be erected in Cuba.

Raised on the 10th anniversary of the poet's death, the monument is ringed by 28 palm trees planted to signify Martí's birth date: January 28. Hard to miss over to one side is the group of baseball fans who linger 24/7 at the famous Esquina Caliente, discussing form, tactics and the Havana teams' prospects in the play-offs.

Gran Teatro de la Habana   THEATER

(Map p80; Paseo de Martí No 458) 'A style without style that in the long run, by symbiosis, by amalgamation, becomes baroquism.' So wrote Cuban novelist and sometime architectural dabbler, Alejo Carpentier, of the ornate neobaroque Centro Gallego erected as a Galician social club between 1907 and 1914. Standing the test of time, the theater was renovated in 2013–14 and now sparkles afresh from its perch in Parque Central. Ask about guided tours at the box office.

The original Centro Gallego was built around the existing Teatro Tacón, which opened in 1838 with five masked Carnaval dances. This connection is the basis of claims by the present 2000-seat theater that it's the oldest operating theater in the Western hemisphere. History notwithstanding, the architecture is brilliant, as are many of the weekend performances.

Hotel Inglaterra   HISTORIC BUILDING

(Map p80; Paseo de Martí No 416) Havana's oldest hotel first opened its doors in 1856 on the site of a popular bar called El Louvre (the hotel's alfresco bar still bears the name). Facing leafy Parque Central, the building exhibits the neoclassical design features in vogue at the time, although the interior decor is distinctly Moorish. At a banquet here in 1879, José Martí made a speech advocating Cuban independence, and much later US journalists covering the Spanish-Cuban-American War stayed at the hotel.

Just behind lies Calle San Rafael, a riot of peso stalls, 1950s department stores and local cinemas, which gives an immediate insight into everyday life in economically challenged Cuba.

★ Museo Nacional de Bellas Artes   MUSEUM

(www.bellasartes.cult.cu; admission to both sites CUC$8) Cuba has a huge art culture, and at this dual-site art museum you can spend a whole day viewing everything from Greek ceramics to Cuban pop art.

Arranged inside the fabulously eclectic Centro Asturianas – a work of art in its own right – the Museo Nacional de Bellas Artes – Arte Universal (Map p80; San Rafael, btwn Av de las Misiones & Agramonte; admission CUC$5, under 14yr free; ⊗9am-5pm Tue-Sat, 10am-2pm Sun) exhibits international art from 500 BC to the present day on three separate floors. Highlights include an extensive Spanish collection (with a canvas by El Greco), some 2000-year-old Roman mosaics, Greek pots from the 5th century BC and a suitably refined Gainsborough canvas (in the British room).

Two blocks away, the Museo Nacional de Bellas Artes – Arte Cubano (Map p80; Trocadero, btwn Agramonte & Av de las Misiones; admission CUC$5, under 14yr free; ⊗9am-5pm Tue-Sat, 10am-2pm Sun) displays purely Cuban art and, if you're pressed for time, is the better of the duo. Works are displayed in chronological order starting on the 3rd floor and are surprisingly varied. Artists to look out for are Guillermo Collazo, considered to be the first truly great Cuban artist; Rafael Blanco with his cartoonlike paintings and sketches; Raúl Martínez, a master of 1960s Cuban pop art; and the Picasso-like Wilfredo Lam.

Museo de la Revolución   MUSEUM

(Map p80; Refugio No 1; adult/child CUC$8/4, camera CUC$2; ⊗9am-5pm) This museum resides in the former Presidential Palace, constructed between 1913 and 1920 and used by a string of cash-embezzling Cuban presidents, culminating in Fulgencio Batista. The world-famous Tiffany's of New York decorated the interior, and the shimmering Salón de los Espejos (Room of Mirrors) was designed to resemble the eponymous room at the Palace of Versailles.

The museum itself descends chronologically from the top floor starting with Cuba's pre-Columbian culture and extending to the present-day socialist regime (with mucho propaganda). The downstairs rooms have some interesting exhibits on the 1953 Moncada attack and the life of Che Guevara, and highlight a Cuban penchant for displaying blood-stained military uniforms. Most of the labels are in English and Spanish.

In front of the building is a fragment of the former city wall, as well as an SAU-100 tank used by Castro during the 1961 battle of the Bay of Pigs.

In the space behind the museum you'll find the **Pavillón Granma** (Map p80), a memorial to the 18m yacht that carried Fidel Castro and 81 other revolutionaries from Tuxpán, Mexico, to Cuba in December 1956. It's encased in glass and guarded 24 hours a day, presumably to stop anyone from breaking in and making off for Florida in it. The pavilion is surrounded by other vehicles associated with the Revolution and is accessible from the Museo de la Revolución.

Paseo de Martí (Prado)   STREET

Construction of this stately European-style boulevard – the first street outside the old city walls – began in 1770, and the work was completed in the mid-1830s during the term of Captain General Miguel Tacón (1834–38). The original idea was to create a boulevard as splendid as any found in Paris or Barcelona (Prado owes more than a passing nod to Las Ramblas). The famous bronze lions that guard the central promenade at either end were added in 1928.

Notable Prado buildings include the neo-Renaissance **Palacio de los Matrimonios** (Map p80; Paseo de Martí No 302), the streamline-modern **Teatro Fausto** (Map p80; cnr Paseo de Martí & Colón) and the neoclassical **Escuela Nacional de Ballet** (Map p80; cnr Paseo de Martí & Trocadero), Alicia Alonso's famous ballet school.

These days, the Prado hosts a respected alfresco art market at weekends and countless impromptu soccer matches during the week.

Although officially known as Paseo de Martí, the street is almost universally referred to by its old name: 'Prado'.

Statue of General Máximo Gómez   MONUMENT

(Map p80; cnr Malecón & Paseo de Martí) On a large traffic island overlooking the mouth of the harbor is a rather grand statue on the right-hand side. Gómez was a war hero from the Dominican Republic who fought tirelessly for Cuban independence in both the 1868 and 1895 conflicts against the Spanish. The impressive statue of him sitting atop a horse was created by Italian artist Aldo Gamba in 1935 and faces heroically out to sea.

Museo Lezama Lima   MUSEUM

(Map p80; Trocadero No 162, cnr Industria; unguided/guided tours CUC$1/2; ⊙9am-5pm Tue-Sat, 9am-1pm Sun) The modest book-filled house of the late Cuban man of letters, José Lezama Lima, is an obligatory pit stop for anyone attempting to understand Cuban literature beyond Hemingway. Lima's magnus opus was the rambling classic, *Paradiso,* and he wrote most of it here.

Parque de los Enamorados   PARK

(Map p80) Preserved in Parque de los Enamorados (Lovers' Park), surrounded by streams of speeding traffic, lies a surviving section of the colonial **Cárcel** (Map p80) or Tacón Prison, built in 1838, where many Cuban patriots including José Martí were imprisoned.

A brutal place that sent unfortunate prisoners off to perform hard labor in the nearby San Lázaro quarry, the prison was finally demolished in 1939 with this park dedicated to the memory of those who had suffered so horribly within its walls. Two tiny cells and an equally minute chapel are all that remain. The beautiful wedding-cake-like building (art nouveau with a dash of eclecticism) behind the park, flying the Spanish flag, is the old **Palacio Velasco** (Map p80) (1912), now the Spanish embassy.

Beyond that, on a traffic island, is the **Memorial a los Estudiantes de Medicina** (Map p80), a fragment of wall encased in marble marking the spot where eight Cuban medical students were shot by the Spanish in 1871 as a reprisal for allegedly desecrating the tomb of a Spanish journalist.

Castillo de San Salvador de la Punta   FORT

(Map p80; museum admission CUC$6; ⊙museum 10am-6pm Wed-Sun) One in a quartet of forts defending Havana harbor, La Punta was designed by the Italian military engineer Giovanni Bautista Antonelli and built between 1589 and 1600. During the colonial era a chain was stretched 250m to the castle of El Morro every night to close the harbor mouth to shipping.

The castle's **museum** displays artifacts from sunken Spanish treasure fleets, a collection of model ships and information on the slave trade.

El Barrio Chino   NEIGHBORHOOD

One of the world's more surreal Chinatowns, Havana's Barrio Chino is notable for its gaping lack of Chinese people, most of whom left as soon as a newly inaugurated Fidel Castro uttered the word *'socialismo.'* Nevertheless, it's worth a wander on the basis of its novelty and handful of decent restaurants.

The first Chinese arrived as contract laborers on the island in the late 1840s to fill in the gaps left by the decline of the transatlantic slave trade. By the 1920s Havana's Chinatown had burgeoned into the biggest Asian neighborhood in Latin America, a bustling hub of human industry that spawned its own laundries, pharmacies, theaters and grocery stores. The slide began in the early 1960s when thousands of business-minded Chinese relocated to the US. Recognizing the tourist potential of the area in the 1990s, the Cuban government invested money and resources into rejuvenating the district's distinct historical character with bilingual street signs, a large pagoda-shaped arch at the entrance to Calle Dragones, and incentives given to local Chinese business people to promote restaurants. Today most of the action centers on Calle Cuchillo and its surrounding streets.

Iglesia del Sagrado Corazón de Jesús
CHURCH

(Map p80; Av Simón Bolívar, btwn Gervasio & Padre Varela; ⊙ hours vary) A little out on a limb but well worth the walk is this inspiring marble creation with a distinctive white steeple – it's one of Cuba's few Gothic buildings. The church is rightly famous for its magnificent

stained-glass windows, and the light that penetrates through the eaves first thing in the morning (when the church is deserted) gives the place an ethereal quality.

Convento & Iglesia del Carmen
CHURCH

(Map p80; Calzada de la Infanta, cnr Neptuno; ⊙ 7:30am-noon & 3-7pm Tue-Sun) Could this be the finest church in Cuba? If so, count your blessing so few know about it. The church's craning bell tower dominates the Centro Havana skyline and is topped by a huge statue of Nuestra Señora del Carmen, but the real prizes lie inside: rich Seville-style tiles, a gilded altarpiece, ornate woodcarving and swirling frescoes. Surprisingly, the church was only built in 1923 to house the Carmelite order. The building is considered 'eclectic'.

Monumento a Antonio Maceo
MONUMENT

(Map p80) Lying in the shadow of Hospital Nacional Hermanos Ameijeiras, a Soviet-era 24-story hospital built in 1980, is this bronze representation of the *mulato* general who cut a blazing trail across the entire length of Cuba during the First War of Independence. The nearby 18th-century Torreón de San Lázaro (Map p80; cnr Malecón & Vapor) is a watchtower that quickly fell to the British during the invasion of 1762.

HAVANA SIGHTS

A BRITISH INTERLUDE

In 1762 Spain, hedging its bets in one of Europe's great colonial conflicts, joined on the side of France against the British in what became known as the Seven Years' War. For their important colony of Cuba it turned out to be a fatal omen. The mighty British Navy, sensing an opportunity to disrupt trade in Spain's economically lucrative Caribbean empire, promptly turned up uninvited off the coast of Havana on June 6, 1762 with over 50 ships and 20,000 men (the largest cross-Atlantic fleet ever amassed), intending to breach the supposedly impregnable El Morro castle and hence make both the city and Cuba a cricket-playing, Yorkshire-pudding-eating colony of Britain.

Under the command of the 3rd Earl of Albemarle, the British caught the Spanish off-guard, landing 12,000 men near the village of Cojímar without the loss of a single British life and marching on nearby Guanabacoa where they established an important base and food supply. After a seaborne attack of El Morro failed (the castle was too high for the British cannons), Albemarle decided to attack the castle from the rear and had his army build bastions on the woefully unprotected Cabaña hill on the harbor's eastern side. From here the British fired relentlessly on the thick castle walls until, 44 days into the siege, the plucky but demoralized Spanish raised a white flag. With El Morro gone, it was only a matter of time before the walled city of Havana fell. From the captured castle, the British lobbed cannonballs across the harbor at La Punta fort until the city finally signaled it was ready to surrender, on August 13, 1762. Victory couldn't have come soon enough. Although Britain's military casualties were light, they had lost over 4000 men to tropical disease, mainly yellow fever.

The British occupation turned out to be brief but incisive. Within 11 months, with the Seven Years' War brought to an end by the Treaty of Paris, the British elected to swap Cuba for the Spanish colony of Florida, which would act as an important buffer for their American colonies to the north. Oh, how history could have been so different.

◉ Vedado

Vedado (known officially as the municipality of 'Plaza de la Revolución') is Havana's commercial hub and archetypal residential district, older than Playa but newer than Centro Habana. The first houses penetrated this formerly protected forest reserve in the 1860s, with the real growth spurt beginning in the 1920s and continuing until the 1950s.

Laid out in a near-perfect grid, Vedado has more of a North American feel than other parts of the Cuban capital, and its small clutch of *rascacielos* (skyscrapers) – which draw their inspiration from the art deco giants of Miami and New York – are largely a product of Cuba's 50-year dance with the US.

During the 1940s and 1950s, Vedado was a louche and tawdry place where Havana's prerevolutionary gambling party reached its heady climax. The Hotel Nacional once boasted a Las Vegas–style casino, the ritzy Hotel Riviera was the former stomping ground of influential mobster Meyer Lansky, while the Hotel Capri was masterfully managed by Hollywood actor (and sometime mob associate) George Raft. Everything changed in January 1959 when Fidel Castro rolled into town with his army of bearded rebels in tow and set up shop on the 24th floor of the spanking-new Havana Hilton hotel (promptly renamed Hotel Habana Libre).

Today, Vedado has a population of approximately 175,000, and its leafy residential pockets are interspersed with myriad theaters, nightspots and restaurants. Bisected by two wide Parisian-style boulevards, Calle G and Paseo, its geometric grid is embellished by a liberal sprinkling of pleasant parks and the gargantuan Plaza de la Revolución laid out during the Batista era in the 1950s.

Hotel Nacional   HISTORIC BUILDING

(Map p88; cnr Calles O & 21; ⊙free tours 10am & 3pm Mon-Sat) Built in 1930 as a copy of the Breakers Hotel in Palm Beach, Florida, the eclectic art deco/neoclassical Hotel Nacional is a national monument and one of Havana's architectural emblems.

The hotel's notoriety was cemented in October 1933 when, following a sergeant's coup by Fulgencio Batista that toppled the regime of Gerardo Machado, 300 aggrieved army officers took refuge in the building hoping to curry favor with resident US ambassador, Sumner Wells, who was staying there. Much to the officers' chagrin, Wells promptly left,

allowing Batista's troops to open fire on the hotel, killing 14 of them and injuring seven. More were executed later, after they had surrendered.

In December 1946 the hotel gained notoriety of a different kind when US mobsters Meyer Lansky and Lucky Luciano used it to host the largest ever get-together of the North American Mafia, who gathered here under the guise of a Frank Sinatra concert.

These days the hotel maintains a more reputable face and the once famous casino is long gone, though the kitschy Parisian cabaret is still a popular draw. Nonguests can admire the Moorish lobby, stroll the breezy grounds overlooking the Malecón or partake in a free guided hotel tour that runs at 10am and 3pm every day except Sunday.

Hotel Habana Libre   BUILDING

(Map p88; Calle L, btwn Calles 23 & 25) This classic modernist hotel – the former Havana Hilton – was commandeered by Castro's revolutionaries in 1959 just nine months after it had opened, and promptly renamed the Habana Libre. During the first few months of the Revolution, Fidel ruled the country from a luxurious suite on the 24th floor.

A 670-sq-meter Venetian tile mural by Amelia Peláez is splashed across the front of the building, while upstairs Alfredo Sosa Bravo's *Carro de la Revolución* utilizes 525 ceramic pieces. There are some good shops here and an interesting photo gallery inside, displaying snaps of the all-conquering *barbudas* (literally 'bearded ones') lolling around with their guns in the hotel's lobby in January 1959.

Edificio Focsa   LANDMARK

(Focsa Building; Map p88; cnr Calles 17 & M) Unmissable on the Havana skyline, the modernist Edificio Focsa was built between 1954 and 1956 in a record 28 months using pioneering computer technology. In 1999 it was listed as one of the seven modern engineering wonders of Cuba. With 39 floors housing 373 apartments, it was, on its completion in June 1956, the second-largest concrete structure of its type in the world, constructed entirely without the use of cranes.

Falling on hard times in the early 1990s, the upper floors of the Focsa became nests for vultures, and in 2000 an elevator cable snapped, killing one person. Rejuvenated once more after a restoration project, this skyline-dominating Havana giant nowadays

UNDERSTANDING JOSÉ MARTÍ

'Two fatherlands, have I; Cuba and the Night', wrote poet, journalist, philosopher and all-round Renaissance man, José Martí in 1882, perfectly summing up the dichotomies of late-19th-century Cuba, his words still as relevant today as they were 130 years ago.

Ironically, Martí – the brains behind Cuba's Second Independence War – remains the one figure who binds Cubans worldwide, a potent unifying force in a country fractiously divided by politics, economics and 90 miles of shark-infested ocean.

Born in Havana in 1851, Martí spent well over half his life outside the country he professed to love in sporadic exile, shunting between Spain, Guatemala, Venezuela and the United States. But his absence hardly mattered. Martí's importance was in his words and ideas. An accomplished political commentator and master of aphorisms, he was responsible, in many ways, for forming the modern Cuban identity and its dream of self-determination. It's difficult to meet a Cuban today who can't eloquently quote stanzas of his poetry. Similarly, there is barely a town or village across the country that doesn't have a statue or plaza named in his honor. The homage extends to the exile community in the US where the Cubans have named a radio station after him. Indeed, Martí is venerated all across the American continent where he is often viewed as the ideological successor to Simón Bolívar.

A basic understanding of Martí and his far-reaching influence is crucial in understanding contemporary Cuba. Havana, the city of his birth, is dotted with poignant monuments, but there are important sites elsewhere. The following are the bare essentials.

Memorial a José Martí (p92) This giant tower (the tallest in Havana) has a massive statue of el Maestro at its foot and a comprehensive museum inside.

Museo-Casa Natal de José Martí (p76) Modest but lovingly curated birth house of Cuba's national hero.

Museo Finca el Abra (p163) Small poignant house on Isla de la Juventud where Martí was briefly imprisoned in 1870.

Cementerio Santa Ifigenia (p404) The apostle's beautiful mausoleum in Santiago de Cuba has a grand guard changing ceremony every half hour.

Dos Ríos Obelisk (p381) Simple but appropriate monument marking where Martí died in battle in 1895 near Bayamo.

contains residential apartments and – in the shape of top-floor restaurant La Torre (p110) – one of the city's most celebrated eating establishments.

Universidad de la Habana UNIVERSITY
(Map p88; cnr Calle L & San Lázaro) Founded by Dominican monks in 1728 and secularized in 1842, Havana University began life in Habana Vieja before moving to its present site in 1902. The existing neoclassical complex dates from the second quarter of the 20th century, and today some 30,000 students follow courses in social sciences, humanities, natural sciences, mathematics and economics here.

Perched on a Vedado hill at the top of the famous *escalinata* (stairway), near the **Alma Mater statue**, the university's central quadrangle, the Plaza Ignacio Agramonte, displays a tank captured by Castro's rebels in 1958. Directly in front is the **Librería Alma Mater** (library) and, to the left, the **Museo de Historia Natural Felipe Poey** (Map p88; admission CUC$1; 9am-noon & 1-4pm Mon-Fri Sep-Jul), the oldest museum in Cuba, founded in 1874 by the Royal Academy of Medical, Physical and Natural Sciences. Many of the stuffed specimens of Cuban flora and fauna date from the 19th century. Upstairs is the **Museo Antropológico Montané** (Map p88; admission CUC$1; 9am-noon & 1-4pm Mon-Fri Sep-Jul), established in 1903, with a rich collection of pre-Columbian Indian artifacts including the wooden 10th-century Ídolo del Tabaco.

Monumento a Julio Antonio Mella MONUMENT
(Map p88; cnr Neptuno & San Lázaro) At the bottom of the university steps there is a monument to the student leader who founded the first Cuban Communist Party in 1925. In 1929 the dictator Machado had Mella

Vedado

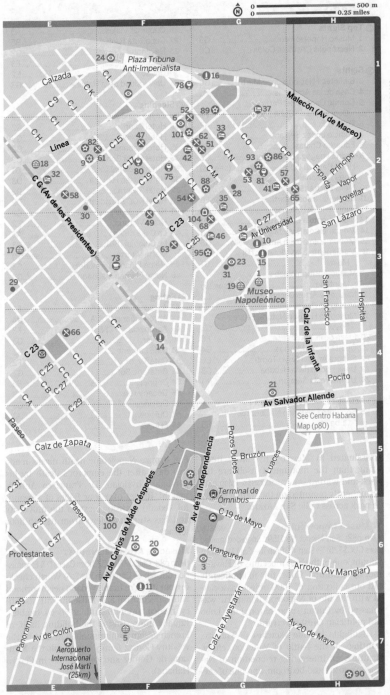

Vedado

◎ **Top Sights**
1 Museo Napoleónico.................................G3
2 Necrópolis Cristóbal Colón C6

◎ **Sights**
3 Biblioteca Nacional José Martí G6
4 Casa de las Américas............................D1
5 Comité Central del Partido
   Comunista de Cuba............................F7
6 Edificio Focsa F2
7 Edificio López Serrano F1
8 Eduardo Chibás......................................C6
9 Gran Synagoga Bet Shalom.................E2
   Hotel Habana Libre.......................(see 35)
   Hotel Nacional................................(see 37)
10 Mella Portraits......................................G3
11 Memorial a José Martí............................F6
12 Ministerio del Interior............................F6
13 Monumento a Calixto García.................D1
14 Monumento a José Miguel Gómez.......F4
15 Monumento a Julio Antonio Mella........G3
16 Monumento a las Víctimas del
   Maine...G1
   Museo Antropológico
   Montané ....(see 19)
17 Museo de Artes Decorativas.................E3
18 Museo de Danza E2
19 Museo de Historia Natural Felipe
   Poey..G3
20 Plaza de la Revolución...........................F6
21 Quinta de los Molinos G4
22 Señora Amelia Goyri Tomb C6
23 Universidad de la Habana.....................G3
24 US Interests Section F1

◎ **Activities, Courses & Tours**
25 Conjunto Folklórico Nacional de
   Cuba C3

26 Cubamar Viajes A3
27 CubaRuta Bikes.....................................B5
28 Havanatur..G2
29 Paradiso...E3
30 Uneac..E2
31 Universidad de la Habana G3

◎ **Sleeping**
32 Casavana Cuba......................................E2
33 Hotel Capri..G2
34 Hotel Colina...G3
35 Hotel Habana Libre...............................G2
36 Hotel Meliá Cohiba C2
37 Hotel Nacional G1
38 Hotel Paseo Habana D3
39 Hotel Riviera..B2
40 Hotel ROC Presidente...........................D2
41 Hotel Vedado G2
42 Hotel Victoria F2
43 La Casa de Ana A6
44 La Colonial 1861....................................B3
   Marta Vitorte...............................(see 32)
45 Melba Piñada Bermudez.......................C3
46 Nelsy Alemán Machado.........................G3

◎ **Eating**
47 Agropecuario 17 & K F2
48 Agropecuario 19 & A D4
49 Agropecuario 21 & J F3
50 Atelier..C3
51 Café Laurent G2
52 Café TV F2
53 Cafetería Sofía......................................G2
54 Coppelia...F2
55 Decameron...C3
56 Dulcinea...C3
57 Dulcinea...G2
58 El Idilio...E2

assassinated in Mexico City. More interesting than the monument itself are the black-and-white **Mella portraits** (Map p88) permanently mounted on the wall in the little park across Calle San Lázaro.

★ **Museo Napoleónico**   MUSEUM
(Map p88; San Miguel No 1159; unguided/guided tours CUC$3/5; ⏰ 9am-4:30pm Tue-Sat) Without a doubt, one of the best museums in Havana and, by definition, Cuba, this magnificently laid out collection of 7000 objects associated with the life of Napoleon Bonaparte was amassed by Cuban sugar baron Julio Lobo and politician Orestes Ferrara.

Highlights include sketches of Voltaire, paintings of the battle of Waterloo, china, furniture, an interesting re-creation of Napoleon's study and bedroom, and one of several bronze Napoleonic death masks made two days after the emperor's death by his personal physician, Dr Francisco Antommarchi. It's set over four floors of a beautiful Vedado mansion next to the university and has stunning views from its 4th-floor terrace.

Museo de Artes Decorativas   MUSEUM
(Map p88; Calle 17 No 502, btwn Calles D & E; admission CUC$3; ⏰ 11am-7pm Tue-Sat) Worth checking out if you're in the Vedado neighborhood is this decorative arts museum with its fancy rococo, oriental and art deco baubles. Equally interesting is the building itself, of French design, commissioned in 1924 by the wealthy Gómez family (who built the Manzana de Gómez shopping center in Centro Habana).

59	La Catedral	B3
60	La Chucheria	C2
	La Torre	(see 6)
61	Le Chansonnier	F2
62	Paladar los Amigos	G2
63	Paladar Mesón Sancho Panza	F3
64	Restaurant Bar Razones	D1
	Supermercado Meridiano	(see 103)
65	Toke Infanta y 25	H2
66	Topoly	E4
67	VIP Havana	D2
68	Waoo Snack Bar	G3

⊜ Drinking & Nightlife

69	3D Café	C2
70	Bar-Club Imágenes	C2
71	Bar-Restaurante 1830	A4
	Cabaret Las Vegas	(see 65)
	Café Cantante	(see 100)
72	Café Fresa y Chocolate	C5
73	Café Literario del 'G'	F3
74	Café Madrigal	D4
75	Club la Red	F2
76	Club Tropical	D2
77	Cuba Libro	B6
78	Discoteca Amanecer	F1
79	Gabanna Café	C2
80	Karachi Club	F2
	Piano Bar Delirio Habanero	(see 100)
81	Pico Blanco	G2

✪ Entertainment

	Cabaret Parisién	(see 37)
	Cabaret Turquino	(see 35)
82	Café Teatro Brecht	E2
	Casa de las Américas	(see 4)
83	Casa del ALBA Cultural	D2

	Centro Cultural El Gran Palenque	(see 25)
84	Cine 23 & 12	C5
85	Cine Charles Chaplín	C5
86	Cine la Rampa	G2
87	Cine Trianón	C3
88	Cine Yara	G2
89	El Gato Tuerto	G1
	El Hurón Azul	(see 30)
90	Estadio Latinoamericano	H7
91	Fábrica de Arte Cubano	A5
	Habana Café	(see 36)
92	Instituto Cubano de Amistad con los Pueblos	D4
	Jazz Café	(see 103)
93	Jazz Club la Zorra y El Cuervo	G2
94	Sala Polivalente Ramón Fonst	F5
95	Sala Teatro el Sótano	G3
96	Sala Teatro Hubert de Blanck	C3
97	Submarino Amarillo	C4
98	Teatro Amadeo Roldán	D2
99	Teatro Mella	D3
100	Teatro Nacional de Cuba	F6
101	Teatro Nacional de Guiñol	F2

⊜ Shopping

	Andare – Bazar de Arte	(see 88)
102	Feria de la Artesanía	D2
	Galería de Arte Latinoamericano	(see 4)
103	Galerías de Paseo	C2
	Instituto Cubano del Arte e Industria Cinematográficos	(see 72)
104	La Habana Sí	G3
	Librería Centenario del Apóstol	(see 57)
	Librería Rayuela	(see 4)

Museo de Danza MUSEUM
(Map p88; Línea No 365; admission CUC$2; ☉10am-5pm Mon-Sat) A dance museum in Cuba – well, there's no surprise there. This well laid out exhibition space in an eclectic Vedado mansion collects objects from Cuba's rich dance history, with many artifacts drawn from the collection of ex-ballerina, Alicia Alonso.

Plaza de la Revolución SQUARE
(Map p88) Conceived by French urbanist Jean Claude Forestier in the 1920s, the gigantic Plaza de la Revolución (known as Plaza Cívica until 1959) was part of Havana's 'new city,' which grew up between 1920 and 1959. As the nexus of Forestier's ambitious plan, the square was built on a small hill (the Loma de los Catalanes) in the manner of Paris' Place de l'Étoile, with various avenues fanning out toward the Río Almendares, Vedado and the Parque de la Fraternidad in Centro Habana.

Surrounded by gray, utilitarian buildings constructed in the late 1950s, the square today is the base of the Cuban government and a place where large-scale political rallies are held. In January 1998, one million people (nearly one-tenth of the Cuban population) crammed into the square to hear Pope Jean Paul II say Mass.

The ugly concrete block on the northern side of the plaza is the **Ministerio del Interior** (Map p88; Plaza de la Revolución), well known for its huge mural of Che Guevara (a copy of Alberto Korda's famous photograph taken in 1960) with the words *Hasta la Victoria Siempre* (Always Toward Victory) emblazoned underneath. In 2009 a similarly designed image of Cuba's other heroic *guerrillero,* Camilo

Cienfuegos, was added on the adjacent telecommunications building. Its wording reads: *Vas Bien Fidel* (You're going well, Fidel).

On the eastern side is the 1957 **Biblioteca Nacional José Martí** (Map p88; admission free; ⊘ 8am-9:45pm Mon-Sat), which has a photo exhibit in the lobby, while on the west is the Teatro Nacional de Cuba (p116).

Tucked behind the Martí Memorial are the governmental offices housed in the heavily guarded **Comité Central del Partido Comunista de Cuba** (Map p88; Plaza de la Revolución).

Memorial a José Martí MONUMENT
(Map p88; Plaza de la Revolución; admission CUC$5; ⊘ 9:30am-5pm Mon-Sat) Center-stage in Plaza de la Revolución is this monument, which at 138.5m is Havana's tallest structure. Fronted by an impressive 17m marble statue of a seated Martí in a pensive *Thinker* pose, the memorial houses a **museum** – the definite word on Martí in Cuba – and a 129m lookout reached via a small CUC$2 lift (broken at last visit) with fantastic city views.

Quinta de los Molinos LANDMARK
(Map p88; cnr Av Salvador Allende & Luaces) The former stately residence of General Máximo Gómez, the Quinta sits amid lush botanical gardens on land that once belonged to Havana University. The residence and grounds seem to be stuck in a perennial renovation project, with promises of a new museum and touched-up botanical gardens in the everdistant future. The laid-back guards may let you wander around the gardens.

★ Necrópolis Cristóbal Colón CEMETERY
(Map p88; admission CUC$5; ⊘ 8am-5pm) Once described as an 'exercise in pious excesses,' this cemetery (a national monument), one of the largest in the Americas, is renowned for its striking religious iconography and elaborate marble statues. Far from being eerie, a walk through these 56 hallowed hectares can be an educational and emotional stroll through the annals of Cuban history. A guidebook with a detailed map (CUC$5) is for sale at the entrance.

After entering the neo-Romanesque **northern gateway** (1870), there's the tomb of independence leader **General Máximo Gómez** (1905) on the right (look for the bronze face in a circular medallion). Further along past the first circle, and also on the right, are the **monument to the firefighters** (1890) and

the neo-Romanesque **Capilla Central** (1886) in the center of the cemetery.

Just northeast of this chapel is the graveyard's most celebrated (and visited) tomb, that of **Señora Amelia Goyri** (Map p88; cnr Calles 1 & F), better known as La Milagrosa (the miraculous one), who died while giving birth on May 3, 1901. The marble figure of a woman with a large cross and a baby in her arms is easy to find due to the many flowers piled on the tomb and the local devotees in attendance. For many years after her death, her heartbroken husband visited the grave several times a day. He always knocked with one of four iron rings on the burial vault and walked away backwards so he could see her for as long as possible.

When the bodies were exhumed some years later, Amelia's body was uncorrupted (a sign of sanctity in the Catholic faith) and the baby, who had been buried at its mother's feet, was allegedly found in her arms. As a result, La Milagrosa became the focus of a huge spiritual cult in Cuba, and thousands of people come here annually with gifts in the hope of fulfilling dreams or solving problems. In keeping with tradition, pilgrims knock with the iron ring on the vault and walk away backwards when they leave.

Also worth seeking out is the tomb of Orthodox Party leader **Eduardo Chibás** (Map p88; Calle 8, btwn Calles E & F). During the 1940s and early 1950s Chibás was a relentless crusader against political corruption, and as a personal protest he committed suicide during a radio broadcast in 1951. At his burial ceremony a young Orthodox Party activist named Fidel Castro jumped atop Chibás' grave and made a fiery speech denouncing the old establishment – the political debut of the most influential Cuban of the 20th century.

Also worth looking out for are the graves of novelist Alejo Carpentier (1904–80), scientist Carlos Finlay (1833–1915), the Martyrs of Granma and the Veterans of the Independence Wars.

★ Malecón STREET
(Map p80) The Malecón, Havana's evocative 8km-long sea drive, is one of the city's most soulful and quintessentially Cuban thoroughfares. Long a favored meeting place for assorted lovers, philosophers, poets, traveling minstrels, fisherfolk and wistful Florida-gazers, the Malecón's atmosphere is most potent at sunset when the weak yellow light from creamy Vedado filters like a dim

torch onto the buildings of Centro Habana, lending their dilapidated facades a distinctly ethereal quality.

Laid out in the early 1900s as a salubrious ocean-side boulevard for Havana's pleasure-seeking middle classes, the Malecón expanded rapidly eastward in the century's first decade with a mishmash of eclectic architecture that mixed sturdy neoclassicism with whimsical art nouveau. By the 1920s the road had reached the outer limits of burgeoning Vedado, and by the early 1950s it had metamorphosed into a busy six-lane highway that carried streams of wave-dodging Buicks and Chevrolets from the gray hulk of the Castillo de San Salvador de la Punta to the borders of Miramar. Today the Malecón remains Havana's most authentic open-air theater, a real-life 'cabaret of the poor' where the whole city comes to meet, greet, date and debate.

Fighting an ongoing battle with the corrosive effects of the ocean, many of the thoroughfare's magnificent buildings now face decrepitude, demolition or irrevocable damage. To combat the problem, 14 blocks of the Malecón have been given special status by the City Historian's Office in an attempt to stop the rot.

The Malecón is particularly evocative when a cold front blows in and massive waves crash thunderously over the sea wall. The road is often closed to cars at these times, meaning you can walk right down the middle of the empty thoroughfare and get very wet.

Monumento a las Víctimas del Maine
MONUMENT

(Map p88; Malecón) West beyond Hotel Nacional is a monument to the victims of USS *Maine*, the battleship that blew up mysteriously in Havana harbor in 1898. Once crowned by an American eagle, the monument (first raised during the American-dominated period in 1926) was decapitated during the 1959 Revolution.

US Interests Section
LANDMARK

(Map p88; Calzada, btwn Calles L & M) The modern seven-story building with the high security fencing at the western end of this open space is the US Interests Section, set up by the Carter administration in the late 1970s.

Facing the office front is Plaza Tribuna Anti-Imperialista (also known as Plaza de la Dignidad), built during the Elián González saga in 2000 to host major protests under the nose of the Americans. The mass of flag-poles were put up by the Cubans to block out an electronic message board mounted on the Interests Section that flashed up messages, or propaganda, depending on which side you're on.

With Cuba and the US due to restore diplomatic relations, it is likely that the building will have become a full-blown US embassy by the time you read this.

Edificio López Serrano
LANDMARK

(Map p88; Calle L, btwn Calles 11 & 13) Tucked away behind the US Interests Section is this art deco tower, which looks like the Empire State with the bottom 70 floors chopped off. One of Havana's first *rascacielos* when it was built in 1932, the López Serrano building now houses apartments.

Av de los Presidentes
STREET

Statues of illustrious Latin American leaders line the Las Ramblas–style Calle G (officially known as Av de los Presidentes), including Salvador Allende (Chile), Benito Juárez (Mexico) and Simón Bolívar. At the top of the avenue is a huge marble Monumento a José Miguel Gómez (Map p88), Cuba's second president. At the other end, the monument to his predecessor – Cuba's first president – Tomás Estrada Palma (long considered a US puppet) has been toppled, with just his shoes remaining on the original plinth.

Guarding the entrance to Calle G on the Malecón is the equestrian Monumento a Calixto García (Map p88; cnr Malecón & Calle G), paying homage to the valiant Cuban general who was prevented by US military leaders in Santiago de Cuba from attending the Spanish surrender in 1898. Twenty-four bronze plaques around the statue provide a history of García's 30-year struggle for Cuban independence.

Casa de las Américas
BUILDING

(Map p88; www.casa.cult.cu; cnr Calles 3 & G; ⊙10am-4:40pm Tue-Sat, 9am-1pm Sun) FREE Just off the Malecón at the ocean end of Calle G, this cultural institution was set up by Moncada survivor Haydee Santamaría in 1959 and awards one of Latin America's oldest and most prestigious literary prizes. Inside there's an art gallery, a bookstore and an atmosphere of erudite intellectualism.

Gran Synagoga Bet Shalom
SYNAGOGUE

(Map p88; Calle I No 251, btwn Calles 13 & 15) Cuba has three synagogues servicing a Jewish

HAVANA'S GREAT AQUEDUCT

Thousands of people pass by his image every day, but few spare a glance for the marble **statue of Francisco de Albear** (Map p66) in a small square at the junction of Calle Obispo and Av de los Misones in Havana Vieja. Yet Albear is a Havana hero, the man responsible for what City Historian Eusebio Leal Spengler has called the most important engineering work in Havana's history, the Acueducto de Albear, constructed between 1861 and 1893 to provide safe drinking water for the city's exploding population.

The Albear aqueduct was a marvel of 19th-century engineering incorporating attractive neoclassical architecture into a modern-for-its-time industrial power complex that still works today. Capturing and treating high-quality drinking water from the de Vento springs and employing gravity to bring it cheaply down to the city, it also helped rid Havana of its killer curse: cholera. The aqueduct won many contemporary plaudits and reaped a gold medal at the 1878 Paris Exposition before it was even operational.

The main aqueduct buildings are located at the **Nudo de Palatino** in Havana's Cerro neighborhood. Consisting of a handsome entrance building and a series of water installations covered by an attractive neoclassical arcade, the aqueduct was named a national monument in 2010 and has been partially restored. The Nudo, which lies 2km southeast of Plaza de la Revolución, is further beautified by an adjacent park, the **Parque de las Estaciones**, which contains four Italianate statues dedicated to the four seasons.

population of approximately 1500. The main community center and library are located here, where the friendly staff would be happy to tell interested visitors about the fascinating and little-reported history of the Jews in Cuba.

Activities

Havana's two marinas, Marina Tarará (east) and Marina Hemingway (west), lie in its outer suburbs. They offer numerous fishing, diving and boating opportunities.

Havana, with its spectacular Malecón sea drive, possesses one of the world's most scenic municipal jogging routes. The path from the Castillo de San Salvador de la Punta to the outer borders of Miramar measures 8km, though you can add on a few extra meters for holes in the pavement, splashing waves, veering *jineteros* (touts) and old men with fishing lines. The recent upsurge in fume-belching traffic has meant that the air along the Malecón has become increasingly polluted. If you can handle it, run first thing in the morning.

Boxing is hugely popular in Cuba and the country has a long list of Olympic gold medals to demonstrate its skills. Boxing enthusiasts should check out **Gimnasio de Boxeo Rafael Trejo** (Map p66; ☑ 7-862-0266; Cuba No 815, btwn Merced & Leonor Pérez, Habana Vieja). At this boxing gym you can see fights on Friday at 7pm (CUC$1), or drop by any day after 4pm to watch the training. Travelers inter-

ested in boxing can find a trainer here. Inquire within; they're very friendly.

Festivals & Events

Havana has a packed program of annual events. As well as those listed here, you can check out February's **Habanos Festival**, a nexus for cigar-puffing aficionados; May's **Cubadisco** musical trade fair/awards ceremony; and the **Cuban Campaign against Homophobia** with its accompanying pride parade, also held in May. Super-hot August hosts the **Carnaval de la Habana** with parade floats and good-natured mayhem. Cooler November allows breathing space for the **Marabana**, Havana's exhausting marathon.

Feria Internacional del Libro LITERATURE
(http://feriadellibro.cubaliteraria.cu; ☉ Feb) Headquartered in La Cabaña fort, the annual book fair kicks off in Havana in February before going on tour around the country.

Festival Internacional de Ballet de la Habana DANCE
(www.festivalballethabana.cult.cu; ☉ Oct) Cuba demonstrates its ballet prowess at this annual festival with energetic leaps and graceful pirouettes starting in late October.

Festival Internacional del Nuevo Cine Latinoamericano FILM
(☉ Dec) Widely lauded celebration of Cuba's massive film culture with plenty of nods to other Latin American countries. Held at various cinemas and theaters across the city.

Courses

Aside from Spanish-language courses, Havana offers a large number of learning activities for aspiring students. Private lessons can be arranged by asking around locally – try your casa particular. Casa owners can also probably point you in the direction of dance classes. If the owner says they can't dance, they're either lying or not endowed with sufficient Cuban blood!

Universidad de la Habana LANGUAGE
(Map p88; ☎ 7-831-3751, 7-832-4245; www.uh.cu; Calle J No 556, Edificio Varona, 2nd fl, Vedado) Offers Spanish courses 12 months a year, beginning on the first Monday of each month. Costs start at CUC$100 for 20 hours (one week), including textbooks, and cover all levels from beginners to advanced. You must first sit a placement test to determine your level. Aspiring candidates can sign up at the university or reserve beforehand via email or phone.

La Casa del Son DANCE, LANGUAGE
(Map p66; ☎ 7-861-6179; www.bailarencuba.com; Empedrado No 411, btwn Compostela & Aguacate; per hour from CUC$10) Relatively new operator with a HQ in Havana Vieja where you can arrange lessons in Spanish, dance or percussion. Very flexible with times.

Uneac LANGUAGE
(Map p88; ☎ 7-832-4551; cnr Calles 17 & H, Vedado) The pulse of the Cuban arts scene, this place is the first point of call for anyone with more than a passing interest in poetry, literature, art and music.

Cubamar Viajes DANCE, LANGUAGE
(Map p88; ☎ 7-830-1220; www.cubamarviajes.cu; Calle 3, btwn Calle 12 & Malecón, Vedado; ⏰8:30am-5pm Mon-Sat) Cuban travel agency that offers language and dance classes. Inquire through its website.

Teatro América DANCE
(Map p80; ☎ 7-862-5416; www.teatroamerica.cult.cu; Av de Italia No 253, btwn Concordia & Neptuno, Centro Habana) Next to the Casa de la Música, this place can fix you up with both a class and a partner for approximately CUC$8 per hour.

Conjunto Folklórico Nacional de Cuba DANCE
(Map p88; ☎ 7-830-3060; www.folkcuba.cult.cu; Calle 4 No 103, btwn Calzada & Calle 5, Vedado) Teaches highly recommended classes

in *son,* salsa, rumba, mambo and more. It also teaches percussion. Classes start on the third Monday in January and the first Monday in July, and cost CUC$500 for a 15-day course. An admission test places students in classes of four different levels.

Paradiso CULTURE
(Map p88; ☎ 7-832-9538; www.paradiso.cu; Calle 19 No 560, Vedado) A cultural agency that offers an astounding array of courses between four and 12 weeks on everything from Afro-Cuban dance to ceramics workshops. Check the website for a full list of options.

Centro Andaluz DANCE, MUSIC
(Map p80; ☎ 7-863-6745; Paseo de Martí, btwn Virtudes & Neptuno, Centro Habana) Typically, Cubans perform flamenco as well as the Spanish, and you can take dance classes or even inquire about the possibility of taking guitar lessons here.

Taller Experimental de Gráfica ART
(Map p66; ☎ 7-862-0979; Callejón del Chorro No 6, Habana Vieja) Offers classes in the art of engraving. Individualized instruction lasts one month, during which the student creates an engraving with 15 copies; longer classes can be arranged. It costs around CUC$250.

Tours

Most general agencies offer the same tours, with some exceptions noted below. The regular tour diet includes a four-hour city tour (CUC$19), a specialized Hemingway tour (from CUC$20), a *cañonazo* ceremony (the shooting of the cannons at the Fortaleza de San Carlos de la Cabaña; without/with dinner CUC$15/25), a Varadero day trip (from CUC$35) and, of course, excursions to Tropicana Nightclub (starting at CUC$65).

Other options include tours to Boca de Guamá crocodile farm (CUC$79), Playas del Este (CUC$20 including lunch), Viñales (CUC$59), Cayo Largo del Sur (CUC$199) and a Trinidad-Cienfuegos overnight (CUC$129). Children usually pay a fraction of the price for adults, and solo travelers get socked with a CUC$15 supplement. Note that if the minimum number of people don't sign up, the trip will be canceled. Any of the listed agencies can arrange these tours and more.

Infotur (p122) is Cuba's state-run information agency with offices at the airport and in Habana Vieja. It can furnish you with further details about these and other tours.

HAVANA'S BEST CITY TOURS

For the best tours in the city, sign up with San Cristóbal Agencia de Viajes (p123), the official travel agency of the City Historian's office, Habaguanex. The agency's unique excursions encourage small groups (there is no minimum), offer decent prices, and provide well-versed, interested guides who are true experts in their field. Trips can be booked in any Habaguanex Hotel. Listed prices are per person traveling in a group of two.

Conservation (from CUC$10) A tour of Havana Vieja's pioneering social projects, including a convalescent home and a needlecraft cooperative, that have been financed through tourist money.

The Magic of Art Deco (from CUC$24) Part walking tour, part driving tour through Havana's amazing assemblage of art deco architecture.

Art & Color (CUC$12) Take in art galleries, learn about Cuban painters and visit the dual-site Museo Nacional de Bellas Artes.

Religion (from CUC$22) A look at some of Havana's restored churches, and a peep into the mysterious rites of Santería, including a visit to the suburb of Regla.

★ **CubaRuta Bikes** CYCLING
(Map p88; ☑52-47-66-33; www.cubarutabikes.com; Calle 16 No 152; city tour CUC$29) 🚲 At last! Havana had long lacked a decent bicycle-hire place, let alone a business offering guided cycling tours, but here they are, the guys with the bikes, who'll lead you on a three-hour city tour from the verdant Bosque de la Habana to the ferry across the harbor. Helmets, bike hire and a bottle of water are included in the price.

Ask about their other tours in Playas del Este and beyond.

Havana Super Tour GUIDED TOUR
(Map p80; ☑52-65-71-01; www.campanario63.com; Campanario No 63, btwn San Lázaro & Lagunas; tours CUC$35) Private three-hour architectural tours around the city in a classic American car focusing on Havana's massive art deco heritage. The company also offers similarly priced Mafia Tours that track the pre-revolutionary antics of Meyer Lansky et al.

Havanatur GUIDED TOUR
(Map p88; ☑7-835-3720; www.havanatur.cu; Calle 23, cnr Calle M, Vedado) All of Habana's main travel agencies offer a Hemingway tour, and the packages are much the same. The itinerary (CUC$24) includes a visit to the author's house, La Finca Vigía, a side trip to the fishing village of Cojímar (where Papa moored his boat), plus an opportunity to down copious cocktails in Hemingway's favorite watering holes, the overhyped Bodeguita del Medio and El Floridita.

Paradiso CULTURAL TOUR
(Map p88; ☑7-832-9538; Calle 19 No 560, Vedado) Offers tours with an emphasis on art. Tours depart from many cities and are in several languages. Check out 'Aché Cuba', a trip through Cuba's Santería sites.

🛏 Sleeping

With literally thousands of private houses letting out rooms, you'll never struggle to find accommodation in Havana. Casas particulares go for anywhere between CUC$20 and CUC$50 per room, with Centro Habana offering the best bargains. Rock-bottom budget hotels can match casas for price, but not comfort. There's a dearth of decent hotels in the midrange price bracket, while Havana's top-end hotels are plentiful and offer oodles of atmosphere, even if the overall standards can't always match facilities elsewhere in the Caribbean.

Many of Havana's hotels are historic monuments in their own right. Worth a look, even if you're not staying over, are Hotel Sevilla and Hotel Saratoga (in Centro Habana), the Raquel, Hostal Condes de Villanueva and Hotel Florida (all in Habana Vieja), and the iconic Hotel Nacional (in Vedado).

🛏 Habana Vieja

★ **Greenhouse** CASA PARTICULAR $
(Map p66; ☑7-862-9877; San Ignacio No 656, btwn Merced & Jesús María; r CUC$30-40; ❉) Fabulous Old Town casa run by Eugenio and Fabio, who have added superb design features to their huge colonial home (check out

the terrace fountain and the backlit model of Havana on the stairway). There are five rooms in this virtual hotel all with modern private bathrooms.

Hostal Peregrino El Encinar CASA PARTICULAR $
(Map p66; ☑7-860-1257; www.hostalperegrino. com; Chacón No 60 (Altos), btwn Cuba & Aguiar; s/d/tr CUC$30/35/40; ☀) This outpost of Centro Habana's Hostal Peregrino is probably the closest Cuba has yet to come to a private hotel. Eight rooms all with private bathrooms are approaching boutique standard with classy tilework, hairdryers, TVs and mini-bars. The delightful roof terrace overlooks the bay with views toward La Cabaña fort.

Casa Colonial del 1715 CASA PARTICULAR $
(Map p66; ☑7-864-1914; rozzo99@gmail.com; Lamparilla No 324, btwn Aguacate & Compostela; r CUC$30; ☀) This lovely mint-green colonial house stands out amid the superficial scruffiness of Calle Lamparilla. The bright tone is continued inside with a wonderful patio set off by a collection of a dozen or more international flags, a welcome that is matched by the congenial owners. There are three clean rooms and fine breakfasts.

Penthouse Plaza Vieja CASA PARTICULAR $
(Map p66; ☑7-861-0084; Mercaderes No 315-317; r CUC$40-50; ☀) A private penthouse in a historic central square. It would cost thousands anywhere else, but in Havana you can still bag it for CUC$40. Fidel and Bertha's two rooms high above Plaza Vieja share a leafy terrace guarded by a Santería shrine.

Casa de Pepe & Rafaela CASA PARTICULAR $
(Map p66; ☑7-862-9877; San Ignacio No 454, btwn Sol & Santa Clara; r CUC$30; ☀) One of Havana's better casas: antiques and Moorish tiles throughout, two rooms with balconies and gorgeous bathrooms, excellent location and great hosts.

Noemi Moreno CASA PARTICULAR $
(Map p66; ☑7-862-3809; Cuba No 611 apt 2, btwn Luz & Santa Clara; r CUC$25-30; ☀) Offering two nicely renovated, clean rooms sharing a bathroom, Noemi has a great location behind the Santa Clara convent. If full, there are five more apartments in the same building that also rent.

Palacio de Pascua CASA PARTICULAR $$
(Map p66; ☑7-867-9412; www.palaciodepascuahabana.com; Habana No 506, btwn Amargura & Lamparilla; r all-incl CUC$111; ☀) A huge colonial house that reeks of faded colonial grandeur

and is topped with a phenomenal roof terrace. High-ceilinged rooms (six at last count) retain a dusty elegance though some share bathrooms. Service is spot on, local info is given out generously and all-inclusive rates (with meals provided) make it a rare mid-range option.

★Hotel Los Frailes HISTORIC HOTEL $$$
(Map p66; ☑7-862 9383; www.habaguanexhotels. com; Brasil No 8, btwn Oficios & Mercaderes; s/d CUC$100/170; ☀@) There's nothing austere about Los Frailes (The Friars), despite the monastic theme (staff wear hooded robes) inspired by the nearby San Francisco de Asís convent. Instead, this is the kind of hotel you'll look forward to coming back to after a long day, to recline in large, historical rooms in your monkish dressing gown with candlelight flickering on the walls.

An added perk is the resident woodwind quartet in the lobby; the musicians are so good that they regularly lure passing tour groups for impromptu concerts.

★Hostal Conde de Villanueva HOTEL $$$
(Map p66; ☑7-862-9293; www.habaguanexhotels.com; Mercaderes No 202; s/d CUC$120/200; ☀@) If you want to splash out on one night of luxury in Havana, check out this highly lauded colonial hotel. Restored under the watchful eye of the City Historian in the late 1990s, the Villanueva has been converted from a grandiose city mansion into a thoughtfully decorated hotel with nine bedrooms spread around an attractive inner courtyard (complete with resident peacock).

Upstairs suites contain stained-glass windows, chandeliers, arty sculptures and – in one – a fully workable whirlpool bathtub.

Hotel Palacio del Marqués de San Felipe y Santiago de Bejucal HOTEL $$$
(Map p66; ☑7-864-9191; www.habaguanexhotels. com; cnr Oficios & Amargura; s/d CUC$170/280; ☀@☎) Cuban baroque meets modern minimalist in one of Habaguanex more expensive offerings, and the results are something to behold. Spreading 27 rooms over six floors in the blustery Plaza de San Francisco de Asís, this place is living proof that Habaguanex delicate restoration work is getting better and better.

Hotel Raquel HOTEL $$$
(Map p66; ☑7-860-8280; www.habaguanexhotels. com; cnr Amargura & San Ignacio; s/d CUC$120/200; ☀@) Encased in a dazzling 1908 palace (that was once a bank), the Hotel Raquel takes

your breath away with its grandiose columns, sleek marble statues and intricate stained-glass ceiling. Behind its impressive architecture, the Raquel offers well-presented if noisy rooms, a small gym/sauna, friendly staff and a great central location.

Painstakingly restored, the reception area in this marvelous eclectic building is a tourist sight in its own right – it's replete with priceless antiques and intricate art nouveau flourishes.

Hotel Santa Isabel   HOTEL $$$

(Map p66; ☑7-860-8201; www.habaguanex-hotels.com; Baratillo No 9; s/d incl breakfast CUC$170/280; ❋@) Considered one of Havana's finest hotels, as well as one of its oldest (operations began in 1867), Hotel Santa Isabel is housed in the Palacio de los Condes de Santovenia, the former crash pad of a decadent Spanish count. This three-story, five-star baroque beauty has 17 regular rooms full of historic charm with attractive Spanish-colonial furniture and paintings by contemporary Cuban artists.

No small wonder ex-US president Jimmy Carter stayed here during his historic 2002 visit.

Hotel Florida   HOTEL $$$

(Map p66; ☑7-862-4127; www.habaguanex-hotels.com; Obispo No 252; s/d incl breakfast CUC$120/200; ❋@) They don't make them like this anymore. The Florida is an architectural extravaganza built in the purest colonial style, with arches and pillars clustered around an atmospheric central courtyard. Habaguanex has restored the 1836 building with loving attention to detail: the amply furnished rooms retain their original high ceilings and wonderfully luxurious finishes.

Anyone with even a passing interest in Cuba's architectural heritage will want to check out this colonial palace, complemented with an elegant cafe and a popular bar-nightspot (from 8pm).

Hostal Valencia   HOTEL $$$

(Map p66; ☑7-867-1037; www.habaguanexhotels.com; Oficios No 53; s/d incl breakfast CUC$120/200; ❋@) Slap-bang in the historic core, Valencia is decked out like a Spanish *posada* (inn), with hanging vines, doorways big enough to ride a horse through and a popular on-site paella restaurant. One of the cheapest Habaguanex offerings, it's an excellent old-world choice, with good service and atmosphere aplenty. You can almost see the ghosts of Don Quixote and Sancho Panza floating by.

Hotel Palacio O'Farrill   HOTEL $$$

(Map p66; ☑7-860-5080; www.habaguanexhotels.com; Cuba No 102-108, btwn Chacón & Tejadillo; s/d CUC$120/200; ❋@) Not an Irish joke, but one of Havana's most impressive period hotels, the Hotel Palacio O'Farrill is a staggeringly beautiful colonial palace that once belonged to Don Ricardo O'Farrill, a Cuban sugar entrepreneur who was descended from a family of Irish nobility. Compared to the lavish communal areas, the bedrooms are plainer and more modest.

Taking the Emerald Isle as its theme, there's plenty of greenery in the plant-filled 18th-century courtyard. The 2nd floor, which was added in the 19th century, provides grandiose neoclassical touches, while the 20th-century top floor merges seamlessly with the magnificent architecture below.

Hotel Beltrán de la Santa Cruz   HOTEL $$$

(Map p66; ☑7-860-8330; www.habaguanexhotels.com; San Ignacio No 411, btwn Muralla & Sol; s/d incl breakfast CUC$88/145; ❋@) Excellent location, friendly staff and plenty of old-world authenticity make this compact inn just off Plaza Vieja a winning combination. Housed in a sturdy 18th-century building and offering just 11 spacious rooms, intimacy is assured and the standard of service has been regularly lauded by both travelers and reviewers.

Hotel Ambos Mundos   HOTEL $$$

(Map p66; ☑7-860-9529; www.habaguanexhotels.com; Obispo No 153; s/d CUC$120/200; ❋@) This pastel-pink Havana institution was Hemingway's hideout and where he's said to have penned his seminal guerrilla classic *For Whom the Bell Tolls* (Castro's bedtime reading during the war in the mountains). Small, sometimes windowless rooms suggest overpricing, but the lobby bar is classic enough (follow the romantic piano melody) and drinks in the rooftop restaurant one of Havana's finest treats.

It's an obligatory pit stop for anyone on a world tour of 'Hemingway-once-fell-over-in-here' bars.

Hotel Habana 612   HISTORIC HOTEL $$$

(Map p66; ☑7-867-1039; www.habaguanexhotels.com; Habana No 612; s/d CUC$100/170; ❋@) Habaguanex newest hotel opened in November 2014 and parades 11 rooms that skilfully mix modern furnishings with old world elegance, just two blocks from Plaza Vieja.

🛏 Centro Habana

★ Hostal Peregrino

Consulado   CASA PARTICULAR $

(Map p80; ☑7-861-8027; www.hostalperegrino. com; Consulado No 152, btwn Colón & Trocadero; s/d/tr CUC$30/35/40; ❄) Julio Roque is a pediatrician who, along with his wife Elsa, has expanded his former two-room casa particular into a growing web of accommodations. His HQ, Hostal Peregrino, offers three rooms just a block from Paseo de Martí (Prado) and is one of the most professionally run private houses in Cuba. Super-helpful Julio and Elsa are fluent in English and a mine of local information.

Extra services include airport pickup, internet, laundry and cocktail bar. The family offers three more places: one in Havana Vieja, one in Calle Lealtad and a cheaper house a few doors away. They're all bookable through the same number.

★ Casa 1932   CASA PARTICULAR $

(Map p80; ☑7-863-6203, cell 52-64-38-58; www. casahabana.net; Campanario 63, btwn San Lázaro & Lagunas; r CUC$20-40; ❄) The charismatic Luis Miguel is an art deco fanatic who offers his house as both boutique private homestay and museum to the 1930s, when his preferred architectural style was in vogue. Collectibles, including old signs, mirrors, toys, furniture and stained glass, will make you feel like you've walked into a Clark Gable movie. The three rooms and services are excellent.

Check the pancakes and peanut butter on the breakfast table, or ask Luis Miguel to take you on an art deco architectural tour of the city.

Casa Colonial Yadilis & Yoel   CASA PARTICULAR $

(Map p80; ☑7-863-0565; www.casacolonialyadilisyyoel.com; Industiria No 120 (Altos), btwn Trocadero & Colón; r CUC$25-30; ❄) A magic formula. Take a solid-pink colonial house in the thick of Centro Havana's street life; throw in four well-maintained, spacious rooms, an ample terrace and lavish breakfasts; then add charming English-speaking hosts Yoel and Yadilis, who go above and beyond with tips and local information. The result: a casa that's highly professional and refreshingly down-to-earth.

The couple also owns a second house nearby with a sea-view roof terrace.

Casa Amada   CASA PARTICULAR $

(Map p80; ☑7-862-3924; www.casaamada.net; Lealtad No 262 (Altos), btwn Neptuno & Concordia; r CUC$25-30; ❄) A huge house with gracious hosts that offers four rooms (all with private bathrooms) and a communal roof terrace. An enclosed balcony out front overlooks the gritty cinematic street life that is Centro Habana.

Casa de Lourdes & José   CASA PARTICULAR $

(Map p80; ☑7-863-9879; Águila 168B, btwn Ánimas & Trocadero; r CUC$25; ❄) These wonderful hosts have a house in the midst of Centro with en suite rooms and set-you-up-for-the-day breakfasts. If you like good old-fashioned hospitality and the feeling that you're staying with a tight-knit Cuban family, look no further.

Loly & Alejandro   CASA PARTICULAR $

(Map p80; ☑7-861-4293; cantero@informed.sld. cu; Industria 270, 10th fl, btwn Neptuno & Virtudes; r without bathroom CUC$25; ❄) Loly is a doctor who lets out two rooms on the 10th floor of an apartment building in Centro Havana. Rooms are on the small side but the views from the shared balcony are spectacular.

Casa 1940   CASA PARTICULAR $

(Map p80; ☑7-863-6203; San Lázaro No 409; r CUC$25-30; ❄) Run by the owners of atmospheric Casa 1932, near neighbor Casa 1940 jumps forward eight years with furnishings coming from the era when art deco gave way to modernism. Bookings are made through Casa 1932.

Lourdes Cervantes   CASA PARTICULAR $

(Map p80; ☑7-879-2243; lourdescervantesparades@yahoo.es; Calzada de la Infanta No 17, btwn Calle 23 & Humboldt; r CUC$25-30; ❄) On the border of Vedado and Centro Habana, just a stone's throw from the Hotel Nacional, this 1st-floor apartment offers two large rooms with balconies. The bathroom is large but shared. Lourdes, the host, is fluent in English and French.

Dulce Hostal – Dulce María González   CASA PARTICULAR $

(Map p80; ☑7-863-2506; Amistad No 220, btwn Neptuno & San Miguel; r CUC$20; ❄) The good old Dulce (Sweet) Hostal on Amistad (Friendship) St makes an appropriately sweet and friendly combination. The nostalgic colonial house has tile floors and soaring ceilings. Even better, Dulce is a gregarious and helpful host. One room only.

MEET THE LOCALS

Havana's streets might be grubby, noisy and full of unconventional obstacles (decapitated chickens, fruit carts, uncovered holes in the pavement and pop-up barber chairs), but they are refreshingly full of life. This is a city where people congregate outside to talk, work, play dominoes or spontaneously strum guitars.

Here are some of Havana's most popular gathering spots and their raison d'être:

Parque Central (p82) Follow the shouts emanating from the omnipresent group of Cuban men who stand arguing boisterously near the José Martí statue in Parque Central. The topic of conversation is generally baseball and the melee is popularly known as the *esquina caliente* or hot corner, after the corner of Calles 23 and 12 in Vedado where it originally convened.

Callejón de Hamel (p115) That cauldron full of old sticks is called a *nganga* (a Palo Monte altar) and those people dressed all in white are *Iyabós* (Santería initiates). Welcome to Callejón de Hamel, the paint-splattered back alley that acts as a center for Havana's Afro-Cuban culture and is rightly famous for its free outdoor rumba drummers.

Paseo de Martí (Prado; p84) At weekends the tree-covered European-style walkway that cuts through the center of El Prado is filled with Cuban artists producing, displaying and selling their work. The rest of the week, you can practice your side-stepping skills with kids playing soccer and school teachers holding PE classes.

Coppelia (p110) During the day, the Coppelia park is characterized by its snaking lines of people. The fuss? Ice cream. Love affairs have been forged in these patient queues and the plot of Oscar-nominated film *Fresa y chocolate* hinged on a spontaneous Coppelia meeting in its alfresco ice-cream parlor. Park yourself at a communal table and it's pretty much guaranteed that you'll meet some interesting Cubans.

Malecón & Rampa The Malecón (p92) is the favored meeting place for half of Havana on sultry weekend evenings, but the area of the sea wall at the intersection with (La Rampa) Calle 23 in front of Vedado's Hotel Nacional (Map p88) has long been the nexus of Havana's gay life. Come here to find out about upcoming gay parties, karaoke nights and drag shows.

Calles 23 & G A lack of decent rock-music venues in the 1990s meant that denizens of Havana's *roquero* (rock music) subculture were forced to hang around on street corners – more specifically the corner of Calles 23 and G in Vedado (Map p88) – to discuss AC/DC guitar riffs and Led Zeppelin song meanings. Plenty still linger.

Eumelia & Aurelio CASA PARTICULAR **$**

(Map p80; ☑ 7-867-6738; eumelialonchan@gmail.com; Consulado No 157, btwn Colón & Trocadero; r CUC$25-30; ❄) New bathrooms, minibars and digitally controlled air-con feature in this pleasant house close to Paseo de Martí (Prado) with two rooms and a couple more in the offing.

Hotel Lincoln HOTEL **$**

(Map p80; ☑ 7-862-8061; Av de Italia, btwn Virtudes & Ánimas; s/d CUC$34/45; ❄) This peeling nine-story giant on busy Av de Italia (Galiano) was the second-tallest building in Havana when it was built in 1926. Overshadowed by taller opposition these days, it still offers 135 air-con rooms with bathroom and TV in an atmosphere that is more 1950s than 2010s.

Notoriety hit in 1958 when Castro's 26th of July Movement kidnapped motor-racing world champion Juan Manuel Fangio from the lobby on the eve of the Cuban Grand Prix. A small 'museum' on the 8th floor records the event for posterity. Otherwise, the facilities are best described as timeworn.

Hotel Deauville HOTEL **$$**

(Map p80; ☑ 7-866-8812; Av de Italia No 1, cnr Malecón; s/d/tr CUC$42/50/71; P ❄ @ ☒) A long-term fixture on the Malecón, this former Mafia gambling den doesn't quite match up to the stellar views. Currently reborn in sea-blue and already showing the effects of the corrosive sea water, the Deauville's handy facilities (money exchange and car rental) and reasonably priced restaurant are ever popular with the mid-priced tour-circuit crowd. Savvy independents hit the casas particulares.

Hotel Caribbean HOTEL $$

(Map p80; ☑ 7-860-8233; Paseo de Martí No 164, btwn Colón & Refugio; s/d CUC$31/50; ✳) Cheap but not always cheerful, the Caribbean offers aspiring Cuban renovators a lesson in how not to decorate. Rooms are a tad dark and poky, but it's one of the few midrange options.

★ Hotel Iberostar Parque Central HOTEL $$$

(Map p80; ☑ 7-860-6627; www.iberostar.com; Neptuno, btwn Agramonte & Paseo de Martí; s/d CUC$240/320; ✳✳@⛱✳) If you have a penchant for hanging out in expensive five-star hotel lobbies sipping mojitos, the Parque Central will suit you just fine. Reserving a room is another (more expensive) matter. With the exception of perhaps the Saratoga, the Iberostar is, without a doubt, Havana's best international-standard hotel, with service and business facilities on par with top-ranking five-star facilities elsewhere in the Caribbean.

Although the fancy lobby and classily furnished rooms may lack the historical riches of the Habaguanex establishments, the ambience here is far from antiseptic. Bonus facilities include a full-service business center, a rooftop swimming pool/fitness center/Jacuzzi, an elegant lobby bar, the celebrated El Paseo restaurant, plus excellent international telephone and internet links. Two of the bedrooms are wheelchair-accessible. There's also an even swankier newer wing across Calle Virtudes, connected to the rest of the hotel by means of an underground tunnel. As well as state-of-the-art rooms, the addition includes its own luxurious restaurant, cafe and reception area.

Hotel Terral BOUTIQUE HOTEL $$$

(Map p80; ☑ 7-860-2100; www.habaguanex-hotels.com; Malecón, cnr Lealtad; s/d CUC$108/175; ✳@) At last, Havana's semi-ruined sea drive gets a boutique hotel that can look out across the water at Florida and compare notes. Despite being built (and run) by the City Historian's Office, Terral is not historic. On the contrary, the 14 ocean-facing rooms are chic, clean-lined and minimalist. A sinuous glass-fronted cafe-bar downstairs offers inviting sofas and great coffee.

Hotel Saratoga HOTEL $$$

(Map p80; ☑ 7-868-1000; www.saratogahotel-cuba.com; Paseo de Martí No 603; s/d CUC$253/352; ✳✳@⛱✳) The glittering Saratoga is an architectural work of art that stands imposingly at the intersection of Paseo de Martí (Prado) and Dragones with fantastic views over toward the Capitolio. Sharp, if officious, service is a feature here, as are the extra-comfortable beds, power showers and a truly decadent rooftop swimming pool. The Saratoga is Havana's most expensive hotel, but also one of its most internationally lauded.

Hotel Sevilla HOTEL $$$

(Map p80; ☑ 7-860-8560; www.hotelsevilla-cuba.com; Trocadero No 55, btwn Paseo de Martí & Agramonte; s/d incl breakfast CUC$105/160; ✳✳@⛱✳) Al Capone once hired out the whole 6th floor, Graham Greene used room 501 as a setting for his novel Our Man in Havana and the Mafia requisitioned it as operations center for its prerevolutionary North American drugs racket. Nowadays the Moorish Sevilla boasts an ostentatious lobby that could have been ripped straight out of the Alhambra and spacious, comfortable rooms.The hotel still drips with history as countless old black-and-white photos of past celebrity guests testify.

Hotel Telégrafo HOTEL $$$

(Map p80; ☑ 7-861-4741, 7-861-1010; www.hotel-telegrafo-cuba.com; Paseo de Martí No 408; s/d CUC$120/200; ✳@) This bold royal-blue Habaguanex beauty on the northwest corner of Parque Central juxtaposes old-style architectural features (the original building hails from 1888) with futuristic design flourishes; these include large luxurious sofas, a huge winding central staircase and an intricate tile mosaic emblazoned on the wall of the downstairs bar. The rooms are equally spiffy.

Hotel Inglaterra HOTEL $$$

(Map p80; ☑ 7-860-8595; www.hotelinglaterra-cuba.com; Paseo de Martí No 416; s/d CUC$96/154; ✳@) It was José Martí's one-time Havana hotel of choice and it's still playing on the fact. Despite a renovation, the Inglaterra remains a better place to hang out in than stay in, with its exquisite Moorish lobby and crusty colonial interior easily outshining the lackluster and often viewless rooms.

The rooftop bar is a popular watering hole, and the downstairs foyer is a hive of activity where there's always live music blaring. Beware the streets outside, which are full of hustlers waiting to pounce.

🛏 Vedado

★ Casavana Cuba CASA PARTICULAR $

(Map p88; ☎58-04-92-58; www.casavanacuba.com; Calle G No 301, 5th & 11th fl, btwn Calles 13 & 15; r CUC$40-50; ✱) When casas particulares start to look like four-star hotels, you know you're onto something. Encased in a *rascacielo* in Vedado, Casavana's huge rooms are positively luxurious with precious furniture and floors so polished you can virtually see your face in them. Behold the carved wooden beds and then drink in the wondrous views from your personal balcony.

The accommodations are spread over two floors (floors 5 and 11) in a 20-story apartment building on Av de los Presidentes. It's a little pricier than your average casa, but well worth it.

Marta Vitorte CASA PARTICULAR $

(Map p88; ☎7-832-6475; www.casamartainhavana.com; Calle G No 301 apt 14, btwn Calles 13 & 15; r CUC$35-45; ℗✱) Marta has lived in this craning apartment block on Av de los Presidentes since the 1960s. One look at the view and you'll see why – the glass-fronted wraparound terrace that soaks up 270 degrees of Havana's stunning panorama makes it seem as if you're standing atop the Martí monument. Not surprisingly, her four rooms are deluxe with lovely furnishings, minibars and safes.

Then there are the breakfasts, the laundry, the parking space, the lift attendant… Get the drift? Marta also rents a self-contained apartment with garage nearby (CUC$70 to CUC$80).

La Casa de Ana CASA PARTICULAR $

(Map p88; ☎7-833-5128; www.anahavana.com; Calle 17 1422, btwn Calles 26 & 28; r CUC$30-35; ✱@) Don't be put off by the out-of-the-way location (western Vedado); there's plenty going on in this neck of the woods and the highly professional Casa de Ana will put you straight on everything from cheap transport to where to find the best mojitos. Rooms are modern and clean, and service goes well beyond the call of duty. Book well in advance.

La Colonial 1861 CASA PARTICULAR $

(Map p88; ☎7-830-1861; www.lacolonail1861.com; Calle 10 No 60, btwn Av 3 & 5; r CUC$30-35; ✱) It's unusual to find a house this old in western Vedado, so make the most of the 1861, whose four private rooms are a riot of wrought-iron, stained glass and mosaic floor tiles. The house is self-contained with its own patio, common areas and antique furniture.

Nelsy Alemán Machado CASA PARTICULAR $

(Map p88; ☎7-832-8467; Calle 25 No 361 apt 1, btwn Calles K & L; r CUC$25; ✱) Nelsy is one of two renters in this house up by the university and a stone's throw from the Hotel Habana Libre. It's a no-frills, low-key place unfazed by the recent surge of new private businesses, meaning it's quiet and hospitable.

Melba Piñada Bermudez CASA PARTICULAR $

(Map p88; ☎7-832-5929; lienafp@yahoo.com; Calle 11 No 802, btwn Calles 2 & 4; r CUC$30; ✱) This 100-year-old villa in a shady tree-lined Vedado street would be a millionaire's pad anywhere else. Here in Havana, it's an unpretentious casa particular with two large rooms and affable hosts.

Hotel Colina HOTEL $

(Map p88; ☎7-836-4071; cnr Calles L & 27; s/d CUC$34/42; ✱@) The friendliest and least fussy of Vedado's cheaper options, the 80-room Colina is situated directly outside the university and is an OK choice if you're here for a Spanish course.

Hotel Victoria HOTEL $$

(Map p88; ☎7-833-3510; www.hotelvictoriacuba.com; Calle 19 No 101; s/d incl breakfast CUC$70/90; ✱@✱) A well-heeled and oft-overlooked Vedado option, the diminutive five-story Victoria is a venerable establishment housed in an attractive neoclassical building dating from 1928. It contains a swimming pool, a bar and a small shop. A sturdy (and rare) midrange choice.

Hotel Paseo Habana HOTEL $$

(Map p88; ☎7-836-0808; cnr Calles 17 & A; s/d CUC$55/70; ✱) First things first. The Hotel Paseo Habana is not actually in Paseo, rather it's one block east on the corner of Calle A. If you can overlook this and a couple of other small foibles (dodgy water pressure, missing light fittings), this is a veritable Havana bargain. Relax on one of the terrace rocking chairs and count your savings.

Hotel Vedado HOTEL $$

(Map p88; ☎7-836-4072; www.hotelvedadocuba.com; Calle O No 244, btwn Calles 23 & 25; s/d CUC$46/73; ✱@✱) Ever popular with the tour-bus crowd, the Hotel Vedado's regular refurbishments never quite break the three-star barrier despite an OK pool (rare in Havana), passable restaurant and not unpleasant rooms.

Elsewhere the patchy service, perennially noisy lobby and almost total lack of character will leave you wondering if you wouldn't have been better off staying in a local casa particular – for half the price.

★ Hotel Nacional   HOTEL $$$

(Map p88; ☑ 7-836-3564; www.hotelnacionalde-cuba.com; cnr Calles O & 21; s/d CUC$132/187; P ✳ @ 🛜 ☎) The cherry on the cake of Cuban hotels and a flagship of the government-run Gran Caribe chain, the neoclassical/neocolonial/art deco (let's call it eclectic) Hotel Nacional is as much a city monument as it is an international accommodations option. Even if you haven't got the money to stay here, find time to sip at least one minty mojito in its exquisite ocean-side bar.

Steeped in history and furnished with rooms with plaques that advertise details of illustrious past occupants, the towering Havana landmark sports two swimming pools, a sweeping manicured lawn, a couple of lavish restaurants and its own top-class nighttime cabaret, the Parisién. While the rooms might lack some of the fancy gadgets of deluxe Varadero, the ostentatious communal areas and the erstwhile ghosts of Winston Churchill, Frank Sinatra, Lucky Luciano and Errol Flynn that haunt the Moorish lobby make for a fascinating and unforgettable experience.

Hotel Capri   HOTEL $$$

(Map p88; ☑ 7-839 7200; cnr Calles 21 & N; s/d CUC$135/180; P ✳ @ 🛜 ☎) It's back! After 11 years as a rotting ruin, one of Havana's most famous hotels has been reborn as a quieter, less notorious version of its former self. And, rather like *The Godfather*, the sequel is better. The 19-story Capri has a sharp minimalist lobby (with good wi-fi) and a rooftop pool. The rooms are slick and modern but not ostentatious. The views from the higher ones are stunning.

Built in modernist style with Mafia money in 1957, the hotel in its (brief) heyday was owned by mobster Santo Trafficante who used American actor George Raft as his debonair front-man. When Castro's guerrillas came knocking in January 1959, Raft allegedly told them where to stick it and slammed the door in their faces.

The hotel has also featured in two movies: Carol Reed's *Our Man in Havana* and Mikhail Kalatozov's *Soy Cuba* (in an astounding 'tracking shot'). It was also the setting for Michael Corleone's meeting with Hyman Roth in *The Godfather: Part II*, though, due to the embargo, Coppola shot the scenes in the Dominican Republic.

Hotel Meliá Cohiba   HOTEL $$$

(Map p88; ☑ 7-833-3636; www.meliacuba.com; Paseo, btwn Calles 1 & 3; s/d CUC$235/285; P ✳ @ 🛜 ☎) Cuba's most business-like city hotel is an ocean-side concrete giant built in 1994 (it's the only building from this era on the Malecón) that will satisfy the highest of international expectations with its knowledgeable, consistent staff and modern, well-polished facilities. After a few weeks in the Cuban outback, you'll feel like you're on a different planet here.

For workaholics there are special 'business-traveler rooms' and 59 units have Jacuzzis. On the lower levels gold-star facilities include a shopping arcade, one of Havana's plushest gyms and the ever-popular Habana Café.

Hotel Habana Libre   HOTEL $$$

(Map p88; ☑ 7-834-6100; www.meliacuba.com; Calle L, btwn Calles 23 & 25; d/ste incl breakfast CUC$205/240; P ✳ @ 🛜 ☎) Havana's biggest and boldest hotel opened in March 1958 on the eve of Batista's last waltz. Originally Havana Hilton, it was commandeered by Castro's rebels in January 1959, who turned it into their temporary HQ. Now managed by Spain's Meliá chain as an urban Tryp Hotel, this skyline-hogging giant has all 574 rooms kitted out to international standard, though the furnishings are somewhat lackluster.

The tour desks in the lobby are helpful for out-of-town excursions and the 25th-floor Cabaret Turquino is a city institution.

Hotel Riviera   HOTEL $$$

(Map p88; ☑ 7-836-4051; www.hotelhavanarivi-era.com; cnr Paseo & Malecón; s/d CUC$84/138; P ✳ @ ☎) Meyer Lansky's magnificent Vegas-style palace has leapt back into fashion with its gloriously retro lobby almost unchanged since 1957. Though luxurious 50 years ago, the 354 rooms are now looking a little rough around the edges and struggle to justify their price tag, but you can readily dampen the dreariness in the fabulous '50s-style pool, gambling-era bar and good smattering of restaurants.

The location on a wild and wave-lashed section of the Malecón is spectacular, although a good bus or taxi ride from the Old Town.

Hotel ROC Presidente   HOTEL $$$

(Map p88; ☑ 7-838-1801; www.roc-hotels.com/en; cnr Calzada & Calle G; s/d CUC$105/150; P ✳ @ 🛜 ☎) This art deco influenced hotel on Av de los Presidentes wouldn't be out of place on a street just off Times Sq in New York. Built the same year as nearby Hotel Victoria (1928), the Presidente is similar but larger, with more officious staff. Unless you're a walker or fancy getting some elbow exercise on Havana's crowded bus system, the location can be awkward.

Eating

Habana Vieja

Havana's Old Town has the most consistent stash of government-run restaurants in Cuba, most of them competently operated by the City Historian's agency, Habaguanex. Experimenting beyond the usual *comida criolla* (Creole food), you'll find decent ethnic places here (eg Italian, Arabic and Chinese), albeit run primarily by Cubans.

Habana Vieja's private restaurants are some of the city's most ambitious and are often housed in plush colonial digs.

★ Café Bohemia   TAPAS, CAFE $
(Map p66; ☎7-836-6567; www.havanabohemia. com; San Ignacio No 364; tapas CUC$3-7; ☺10am-10pm) Inhabiting a beautifully curated space in a mansion on Plaza Vieja, Café Bohemia manages to feel appropriately bohemian, but also serves great cocktails, tapas, and extremely addictive cakes.

There's also a boutique apartment (CUC$80) and en-suite bedroom (CUC$45) available for rent.

Fumero Jacqueline   CAFE $
(Map p66; ☎7-862-6562; Compostela No 1, cnr Cuarteles; breakfast CUC$4; ☺8am-11pm) Guarding the heavenly small square behind the Santo Ángel Custodio church (the result of a foresighted community project), the highly minimalist Fumero is part cocktail bar, part ladies clothing boutique, and part the best breakfast spot in Havana Vieja. Pull up a trendy plastic chair for eggs, pancakes and super hot coffee.

Café Lamparilla   INTERNATIONAL $
(Map p66; Lamparilla, btwn Mercaderes & San Ignacio; snacks CUC$3-5; ☺noon-midnight) Crowding out the cobbled street with its alfresco tables, the Lamparilla is perennially popular – your best bet for a seat is in the air-conditioned refinement of the sinuous art deco bar. Most people drop by for a beer or a cocktail, but the food is surprisingly good and plentiful, and the prices economical.

Casa del Queso La Marriage   CHEESE & WINE $
(Map p66; ☎7-866-7142; San Ignacio, cnr Amargura; cheese board CUC$1-3; ☺10am-10pm) In a country which, until recently, produced just one rubbery tasteless cheese, a multifarious cheese shop is a big deal. You can extinguish bad memories of peso pizza and the 'Special Period' over plates of gouda, blue and cheddar washed down with a fruity Chilean red wine.

Sandwichería La Bien Paga   SANDWICHES $
(Map p66; Aguacate No 259; sandwiches CUC$1-2; ☺9am-6pm) Jumping into a niche that has yet to be properly filled in Havana, this casual sandwich shop, beloved by locals as much as tourists, makes up savory snacks as you wait in a space barely big enough to swing a small kitten. A classic 'Cuban' (ham, cheese, pork and pickles) goes for a giveaway CUC$1.50.

Café Santo Domingo   CAFE $
(Map p66; Obispo No 159, btwn San Ignacio & Mercaderes; snacks CUC$2-4; ☺8am-7pm) Tucked away above Habana Vieja's best bakery – and encased in one of its oldest buildings – this laid-back cafe is aromatic and light on the wallet. Check out the delicious fruit shakes, huge *sandwich especial,* or smuggle some cakes upstairs to enjoy over a steaming cup of *café con leche* (coffee with warm milk).

Hanoi   INTERNATIONAL $
(Map p66; cnr Brasil & Bernaza; meals CUC$3-5; ☺noon-midnight) The name might suggest solidarity with 'communist' Vietnam, but don't get too excited – you won't find any Saigon-flavored spring rolls here. Instead, what you get is straight-up Creole cuisine, with a couple of fried-rice dishes thrown in to justify the (rather misleading) name.

One of the only fully restored buildings in untouristy Plaza del Cristo, the Hanoi is a backpacker favorite, where the foreign clientele usually has its communal nose in a guidebook.

Restaurante Puerto de Sagua   SEAFOOD $
(Map p66; Av de Bélgica No 603; meals CUC$5-8; ☺noon-midnight) This nautically themed eating joint in Habana Vieja's grittier southern quarter is characterized by its small porthole-style windows. It serves mostly seafood at reasonable prices.

★ Doña Eutimia   CUBAN $$
(Map p66; Callejón del Chorro 60C; meals CUC$7-9; ☺noon-midnight) Keep it simple. The secret

at Doña Eutimia is there *is* no secret. Just serve decent-sized portions of incredibly tasty Cuban food (the *ropa vieja* – shredded beef – and minced beef *picadillo* both deserve mentions) from a pretty spot next to the cathedral and charge highly reasonable prices. The rest is history.

O'Reilly 304
INTERNATIONAL $$

(Map p66; 52-64-47-25; O'Reilly No 304; meals CUC$8-13; noon-midnight) Thinking up the name (the restaurant's address) can't have taken much imagination, so it is perhaps a little ironic that O'Reilly 304 serves up some of the most imaginative cuisine in Havana. Exquisite seafood with crispy veg is presented on metal pans set into wooden trays, while the cocktails and tacos are fast becoming legendary.

This new place's small interior is cleverly laid out making the most of a mezzanine floor, while the walls are adorned with bold, edgy art – think nudes, screen prints and studies of fallen matadors.

Mama Inés
CUBAN $$

(Map p66; 7-862-2669; Obrapía No 62; meals CUC$8-11; noon-10:30pm Tue-Sun) Fidel Castro, Jane Fonda, Jack Nicholson, Jimmy Carter, Hugo Chávez: executive chef, Erasmo, has cooked for a who's who of celebrity 'lefties.' Joining the culinary revolution, he's recently chucked his hat in the paladar (private restaurant) ring, opening a restaurant in gorgeous colonial digs just off Calle Oficios, serving fine renditions of Cuban classics: *ropa vieja*, breaded prawns and roast pork, at decidedly uncelebrity prices.

Tres Monedas Creative Lounge
INTERNATIONAL $$

(Map p66; 7-862-7206; www.tresmonedascafe.com; Aguiar No 209, btwn Empedrado & Tejadillo; snacks CUC$2-5, mains CUC$8-15; noon-midnight) Behind Habana Vieja's grubby facades lie havens of arty magnificence, no more so than in Tres Monedas, a 'creative lounge' cum cafe-restaurant where the decor designed by artist/owner Kadir López flaunts images of gaudy 1950s Havana – old Coke adverts, Esso signs and bottletop-shaped bar stools. Tuck into snacks and more substantial dishes, plus liquid refreshment and at the hipster-cool bar.

Nao Bar Paladar
SEAFOOD $$

(Map p66; 7-867-3463; Obispo No 1; meals CUC$6-12; noon-midnight) No 1 in Havana's main drag and not far behind in its food

BEST BOHEMIAN CAFES

Intriguing new one-of-a-kind cafes have proliferated in Havana in the last couple of years taking advantage of the freer business climate. You'll find good coffee, creative decor and a buzzing atmosphere in all of the following places.

➡ El Chanchullero (p111)

➡ Café Archangel (p112)

➡ Café Madrigal (p113)

➡ Café Bohemia (p104)

➡ Dulcería Bianchini (p111)

ranking, Nao occupies a 200-year-old building near the docks that plays on its seafaring theme. The small upstairs space is good for main courses (seafood dominates); the downstairs bar and outdoor seating excels in snacks including possibly the best warm baguettes in Cuba (try the *jamón-serrano* one).

Mesón de la Flota
TAPAS $$

(Map p66; Mercaderes No 257, btwn Amargura & Brasil; tapas CUC$3-6; noon-midnight) This nautically themed tapas bar-restaurant might have been transported from Cádiz' Barrio de Santa María, so potent is the atmosphere. Old-world tapas include *garbanzos con chorizo* (chickpeas with sausage), calamari and tortilla, but there are also more substantial seafood-biased *platos principales* (main meals).

For music lovers the real drawcard is the nightly *tablaos* (flamenco shows), the quality of which could rival anything in Andalucia. Sit back and soak up the intangible spirit of *duende* (the climactic moment in a flamenco concert inspired by the fusion of music and dance).

El Mercurio
INTERNATIONAL $$

(Map p66; Plaza de San Francisco de Asís; meals CUC$5-10; 7am-11pm) An elegant indoor-outdoor cafe-restaurant, with cappuccino machines, intimate booths and waiters in black ties, that serves cheap lunches (Cuban sandwich) and more substantial dinners (lobster and steak tartare).

Restaurante la Dominica
ITALIAN $$

(Map p66; O'Reilly No 108; meals CUC$7-10; noon-midnight) Despite a tendency to be a little overgenerous with the olive oil, La

Dominica – with its wood-fired pizza oven and al dente pasta – delivers the Mediterranean goods in an elegantly restored dining room with alfresco seating on Calle O'Reilly. Professional house bands serenade diners with a slightly more eclectic set than the obligatory Buena Vista Social Club staples.

La Mina
CARIBBEAN **$$**

(Map p66; Obispo No 109, btwn Oficios & Mercaderes; meals CUC$6-10; ⊙24hr) With a mediocre menu, but top-class location, La Mina graces a scenic corner of Plaza de Armas, meaning every tourist in Havana walks past it at some point. Food options – displayed on a streetside stand and backed up by an army of verbose waiters – include chicken, pork and prawns cooked in a variety of ways, but lacking culinary panache.

There's a tempting *heladería* (ice-cream parlor) around the corner in Calle Oficios.

★ Paladar Los Mercaderes
CUBAN **$$$**

(Map p66; ☑7-861-2437; Mercaderes No 207; meals CUC$12-19; ⊙11am-11pm) This private restaurant in a historic building has to be one of Cuba's most refined paladares for ambience, service *and* food, both Cuban and international. Follow a staircase strewn with flower petals to a luxurious 1st floor dining room where musicians play violins and fine international dishes combine meat with exotic sauces. *Muy romántico!*

Restaurante el Templete
SEAFOOD **$$$**

(Map p66; Av Carlos Manuel de Céspedes No 12; meals CUC$15-30; ⊙noon-11pm) Welcome to a rare Cuban breed: a restaurant that could compete with anything in Miami – and a government-run one at that! The Templete's specialty is fish, and special it is: fresh, succulent and cooked simply without the pretensions of celebrity-chef-obsessed America. Sure, it's a little *caro* (expensive), but it's worth every last *centivo*.

Café del Oriente
CARIBBEAN, FRENCH **$$$**

(Map p66; Oficios 112; meals CUC$20-30; ⊙noon-11pm) Havana suddenly becomes posh when you walk through the door at this longstanding state-run establishment in Plaza de San Francisco de Asís. Smoked salmon, caviar (yes, caviar!), goose-liver pâté, lobster thermidor, steak au poivre, cheese plate and a glass of port. Plus service in a tux, no less. There's just one small problem: the price. But what the hell?

Restaurante Paris
CARIBBEAN **$$$**

(Map p66; San Ignacio No 54; meals CUC$15-20; ⊙noon-midnight) Recently renamed, this place is all about location – slap-bang in the Plaza de la Catedral, one of the most romantic settings on the planet when the hustlers stay away, the mojitos (briefly) sharpen your senses and the band breaks spontaneously into your favorite tune. The food has improved since the rebranding and does its best to appeal – visually, at least.

La Imprenta
INTERNATIONAL **$$$**

(Map p66; Mercaderes No 208; meals CUC$10-17; ⊙noon-midnight) This Habaguanex restaurant has a resplendent interior filled with memorabilia from the building's previous incarnation as a printing works. The food isn't quite as spectacular although service is thorough and the menu offers previously unheard-of Cuban innovations such as al dente pasta, creative seafood medleys and a stash of decent wines.

Self-Catering

Harris Brothers
SUPERMARKET

(Map p66; O'Reilly No 526; ⊙9am-9pm Mon-Sat) The best-stocked grocery store in Habana Vieja sells everything from fresh pastries to baby's nappies. It's just off Parque Central and is open until late.

Agropecuario Belén
MARKET

(Map p66; Sol, btwn Habana & Compostela) Vieja's modest local farmers market.

✕ Parque Histórico Militar Morro-Cabaña

★ Restaurante la Divina Pastora
INTERNATIONAL **$$$**

(Map p78; Parque Histórico Militar Morro-Cabaña; meals CUC$10-18; ⊙noon-11pm) Near Dársena de los Franceses and a battery of 18th-century cannons lies one of the more progressive outlets of Cuban cooking. Eschewing the iron rations of yore, La Divina Pastora offers creamy soups, grilled octopus, pesto-doused vegetables and excellent seafood. Formerly state-run, it is now managed privately, but the *savoir faire* of the waitstaff and the wine-list credibility remain undiminished.

Paladar Doña Carmela
CUBAN **$$$**

(Map p78; ☑7-867-7472; Calle B No 10; meals CUC$15-35; ⊙noon-11pm) A private eating option near Havana's forts that offers quality dishes such as octopus in garlic and whole roast pork cooked in a wood oven. Tables are arranged in a very pleasant garden. Makes for a good dinner before or after the fort's *cañonazo* ceremony.

🍴 Centro Habana

Centro offers scanter fare than Habana Vieja, though a handful of outstanding private restaurants punctuate its dense grid. Look out for Spanish clubs run by the Centro Asturiano and dip into the restaurant strip on Calle Cuchillo in the Barrio Chino (Chinatown).

Café Neruda   INTERNATIONAL $
(Map p80; Malecón No 203, btwn Manrique & San Nicolás; snacks CUC$2-5; ☺11am-11pm) Barbecued Chilean ox, Nerudian skewer, Chilean turnover? Poor old Pablo Neruda would be turning in his grave if this weren't such a romantically disheveled place on the Malecón. Spend a poetic afternoon writing your own verse as the waves splash over the sea wall.

Pastelería Francesa   CAFE $
(Map p80; Parque Central No 411; snacks CUC$1-2; ☺8am-midnight) This cafe has all the ingredients of a Champs-Élysées classic: a great location in Parque Central, waiters in waistcoats, and delicate pastries displayed in glass cases. But the authentic French flavor is diminished by grumpy staff and the swarming *jineteras* (female touts) who roll in with Hans from Hamburg or Marco from Milano for cigarettes and strong coffee.

Restaurante Tien-Tan   CHINESE $
(Map p80; Cuchillo No 17, btwn Rayo & San Nicolás; meals from CUC$3; ☺11am-midnight) One of the Barrio Chino's best authentic Chinese restaurants, Tien-Tan (the 'Temple of Heaven') is run by a Chinese-Cuban couple and serves up an incredible 130 different dishes.

Try chop suey with vegetables, or chicken with cashew nuts and sit outside in action-packed Cuchillo, one of Havana's most colorful and fast-growing 'food streets.'

Casa Miglis   SWEDISH $$
(Map p80; ☎7-864-1486; www.casamiglis.com; Lealtad No 120, btwn Ánimas & Lagunas; meals CUC$6-12; ☺noon-1am) There's a place for everything in Havana these days, even Swedish-Cuban fusion food. Emerging improbably from a kitchen in the battle-scarred tenements of Centro Habana comes toast *skagen* (shrimp on toast), seviche, couscous, and the *crème de la crème:* melt-in-your-mouth meatballs with mashed potato.

The owner's Swedish (no surprise) and the decor (empty picture frames, and chairs attached to the wall) has a touch of Ikea minimalism about it.

Castropol   SPANISH $$
(Map p80; ☎7-861-4864; Malecón 107, btwn Genios & Crespo; meals CUC$6-12; ☺6pm-midnight) Run by the local Spanish Asturianas society, Castropol's reputation has expanded in line with its fleshed out restaurant space over the last few years. Word is now out that the venerable two-story establishment with its upstairs balcony overlooking Havana's dreamy 8km sea drive serves some of the most economical Spanish and Caribbean food in Havana.

Go for the paella, *garbanzos fritos* (fried chickpeas), prawns in a tangy sauce and generous portions of lobster pan-fried in butter.

Los Nardos   SPANISH $$
(Map p80; Paseo de Martí No 563; meals from CUC$4-10; ☺noon-midnight) An open secret opposite the Capitolio, but easy to miss (look out for the queue), Los Nardos is a semiprivate restaurant operated by the Spanish Asturianas society. Touted in some quarters as one of the best eateries in the city, the dilapidated exterior promises little, but the leather/mahogany decor and astoundingly delicious dishes inside suggest otherwise.

The menu includes lobster in a Catalan sauce, garlic prawns with sautéed vegetables and an authentic Spanish paella. Portions are huge, service is attentive and the prices, for what you get, are mind-bogglingly cheap.

Flor de Loto   CHINESE $$
(Map p80; Salud No 303, btwn Gervasio & Escobar; meals CUC$6-8; ☺noon-midnight) Popularly considered to be Havana's best Chinese restaurant, as the queues outside will testify. Camouflaged beneath Centro Habana's decaying facades, it serves up extra-large portions of lobster, fried rice and sweet-and-sour sauce in a frigidly air-conditioned interior.

Castas y Tal   CUBAN $$
(Map p80; ☎7-864-2177; Av de Italia No 51, cnr San Lázaro; meals CUC$5-8; ☺noon-midnight) Recently relocated from Vedado to Centro Habana, C & T has gone from old-school private restaurant (ensconced in someone's 11th floor apartment) to trendy bistro-style restaurant. What hasn't changed is the quality of the food, which adds nouveau touches to a traditional Cuban base. Try the chicken in orange sauce, prawn and fruit *brochetas* with peanut dip, and creamy carrot soup.

HAVANA EATING

Chi Tack Tong
CHINESE $$

(Map p80; Dragones No 356, btwn San Nicolás & Manrique; meals CUC$6-9; ⊙noon-midnight) Upstairs in Calle Dragones, this place is famous for being one of the few cheap restaurants in Havana where you won't hear the words 'No hay' (we don't have it) when you place your order. The menu is a little limited, but portion sizes are huge. Box up your leftovers.

★ San Cristóbal
CUBAN $$$

(Map p80; ☑7-867-9109; San Rafael, btwn Campanario & Lealtad; meals CUC$9-18; ⊙noon-midnight) At San Cristóbal you can sit down in front of a Catholic/Santería altar flanked by pictures of Maceo and Martí and give thanks for extraordinarily good food. Located in the thick of Centro Habana, the menu and decor share Cuban, African and Spanish influences. Admire the Hemingway-esque animal skins while enjoying a generous starter plate of *jamón serrano* and six different cheeses.

La Guarida
INTERNATIONAL $$$

(Map p80; ☑7-866-9047; www.laguarida.com; Concordia No 418, btwn Gervasio & Escobar; meals CUC$12-20; ⊙noon-3pm & 7pm-midnight) On the top floor of a spectacularly dilapidated Havana tenement, La Guarida's lofty reputation rests on its movie-location setting (*Fresa y chocolate* was filmed in this building) and a clutch of swashbuckling international newspaper reviews. The food is up there with Havana's best, shoehorning its pioneering brand of Nueva Cocina Cubana into dishes such as tuna with a sugarcane glaze. Reservations recommended.

Self-Catering

Supermercado Isla de Cuba SUPERMARKET

(Map p80; cnr Máximo Gómez & Factoría; ⊙10am-6pm Mon-Sat, 9am-1pm Sun) On the southern side of Parque de la Fraternidad, this supermarket stocks yogurt, cereals, pasta etc. You have to check your bag outside, to the right of the entrance.

Almacenes Ultra SUPERMARKET

(Map p80; Av Simón Bolívar No 109, cnr Rayo; ⊙9am-6pm Mon-Sat, to 1pm Sun) A decent supermarket in Centro Habana.

La Época SUPERMARKET

(Map p80; cnr Av de Italia & Neptuno; ⊙9am-9pm Mon-Sat, to noon Sun) A hard-currency department store with a supermarket in the basement. Check your bags outside before entering this epic Havana emporium.

Mercado Agropecuario Egido MARKET

(Map p66; Av de Bélgica, btwn Corrales & Apodaca) For fresh produce hit this free-enterprise market.

🍴 Vedado

Vedado's culinary scene has continued to grow and adapt inside Cuba's new economic reality with more adventurous private restaurants opening all the time.

Topoly
IRANIAN $

(Map p88; ☑7-832-3224; www.topoly.fr; Calle 23 No 669, cnr Calle D; small plates CUC$4-6; ⊙10am-midnight) Cuba finds solidarity with Iran in Havana's first Iranian restaurant corralled in a lovely colonnaded mansion on arterial Calle 23. Sit on the wraparound porch beneath iconic prints of Gandhi, José Martí and Che Guevara and enjoy pureed aubergine, lamb *brochetas*, fantastic coffee, and tea in ornate silver pots.

Belly dancers entertain on Wednesday, Friday and Saturday nights at 9pm.

La Catedral
INTERNATIONAL $

(Map p88; ☑7-830-0793; Calle 8 No 106, btwn Calzada & Calle 5; meals CUC$4-6; ⊙noon-midnight) Welcome to what is possibly the first Cuban restaurant to have adopted the American custom of the 'doggy bag', necessary when the enormous portions of food have defeated you. Popular with Cubans more than tourists, the reasonably priced Catedral tackles a number of culinary genres – including pizza, pasta and tapas – and in big portions too.

Restaurant Bar Razones
CUBAN, INDIAN $

(Map p88; ☑7-832-8732; Calle F No 63, btwn Avs 3 & 5; meals CUC$3-6; ⊙noon-midnight; ⊞) With the closing of Cuba's first Indian restaurant 'Bollywood', it's left for Razones to pick up the spicy pieces. Take note: this is not an Indian restaurant, just one that bravely attempts a couple of curry dishes on its multifarious menu. It also does interesting things with lobster (flavored with pineapple sauce and even coffee extract).

The clientele is a good mix of Cubans and tourists.

La Chucheria
SNACKS $

(Map p88; Calle 1, btwn Calles C & D; snacks CUC$2-7; ⊙7am-midnight) Clinging to its perch close to the Malecón, this sleek sports bar owned by a Cuban comedian looks as if it floated mockingly across the straits from Florida like a returning exile. But you can forget about politics momentarily as you contemplate pizza toppings and ice-cream milkshakes so thick you can stand your straw up in them.

The restaurant's diminutive interior, with its clear plastic chairs and flat-screen TVs replaying Messi's latest match-winner, demonstrates how the line between *socialismo* and *capitalismo* is becoming ever more blurred.

Waoo Snack Bar SNACK BAR $
(Map p88; Calle L No 414, cnr Calle 25; snacks CUC$2-6; ⊗ noon-midnight) Wow! The Waoo snack bar truly impresses with its wooden wraparound bar, happening locale close to 23 and L and quick dishes you might want to savor – think carpaccio, cheese plates and coffee with accompanying desserts.

Toke Infanta y 25 SNACK BAR $
(Map p88; cnr Calzada de la Infanta & Calle 25; snacks CUC$2-4; ⊗ 7am-midnight) Plush, slick, minimalist, economical and above all tasty, Toke helps fill the huge gap between insipid state-run joints and more formal private restaurants. It sits pretty amid the bruised edifices of Calzada de la Infanta on the cusp of Vedado and Centro Habana luring enamored *habaneros* (and tourists) with cool neon, smart color accents and excellent *hamburguesas* (hamburgers) and chocolate brownies.

Dulcinea BAKERY $
(Map p88; Calle 25 No 164, btwn Calzada de la Infanta & Calle O; snacks CUC $0.50-2; ⊗ 8am-midnight) Formerly part of the small but precious Pain de París chain, this cake shop cum bakery can still cut it with good pastries, coffee and space to sit down. There's a **24-hour branch** (Map p88) on Línea, adjacent to the Trianón cinema.

Café TV FAST FOOD $
(Map p88; cnr Calles N & 19; snacks CUC$2-5; ⊗ 10am-9pm) Hidden in the bowels of Edificio Focsa, this TV-themed cafe is a funky dinner/performance venue lauded by those in the know for its cheap food and hilarious comedy nights. If you're willing to brave the frigid air-con and rather foreboding underground entry tunnel, head here for fresh burgers, healthy salads, pasta and chicken cordon bleu.

Cafetería Sofía FAST FOOD $
(Map p88; Calle 23 No 202; snacks CUC$1-3; ⊗ 24hr) Late-night hair-of-the-dog seekers meet annoyingly chirpy early risers at this

24-hour institution on La Rampa (Calle 23), where you can pick up coffee, and unadorned cheese-and-ham sandwiches.

★ Café Laurent INTERNATIONAL $$
(Map p88; ☑ 7-832-6890; Calle M No 257, 5th fl, btwn 19 & 21; meals CUC$10-14; ⊗ noon-midnight) Talk about a hidden gem. The unsigned Café Laurent is a sophisticated fine-dining restaurant encased, incongruously, in a glaringly ugly 1950s apartment block next to the Focsa building. Starched white tablecloths, polished glasses and fancy drapes furnish the bright modernist interior, while sautéed pork with dry fruit and red wine, and seafood risotto headline the menu. Viva the culinary revolution!

Paladar Mesón Sancho Panza MEDITERRANEAN $$
(Map p88; ☑ 7-831-2862; Calle J No 508, btwn Calles 23 & 25; meals CUC$4-10; ⊗ noon-11pm) Appropriately situated next to Parque Don Quijote, Paladar Mesón Sancho Panza doesn't let down its loyal literary *compañero*. Fine Spanish-influenced food is served in a lovely semi-alfresco restaurant adorned with ponds and plant-covered trellises, and there's a cake case that could make skipping dessert difficult. Set yourself up with paella (CUC$12 to CUC$16), lasagna or *brochetas* first.

Bonus: there's live flamenco on Saturday nights.

El Idilio CUBAN $$
(Map p88; ☑ 7-830-7921; Av de los Presidentes, cnr Calle 15; meals CUC$5-9; ⊗ noon-midnight) New, bold, adventurous – Idilio epitomises the Cuban culinary scene as it spreads its wings and flies. Anything goes here: pasta, seviche and Cuban standards, or opt for the seafood medley peeled freshly off the barbecue before your very eyes.

Paladar los Amigos CUBAN $$
(Map p88; Calle M No 253; meals CUC$8-11; ⊗ noon-midnight) Anthony Bourdain's private restaurant of choice while making his 2011 episode of *No Reservations,* Los Amigos sticks to the basics, offering traditional Cuban fare with lashings of rice and beans. The snarky one was suitably impressed, so they must be doing something right.

Atelier CUBAN $$$
(Map p88; ☑ 7-836-2025; Calle 5 No 511 (Altos), btwn Paseo & Calle 2; meals CUC$12-25; ⊗ noon-midnight) The first thing that hits you at Atelier is the stupendous wall art – huge,

COPPELIA ICE CREAM

The **Coppelia** (Map p88; cnr Calles 23 & L, Vedado; ⊙10am-9:30pm Tue-Sat), Havana's celebrated ice-cream parlor housed in a flying-saucer-like structure in a park in Vedado, is as celebrated for its massive queues as much as it is for its ice cream. Insanely popular since opening in 1966 (through some very rough economic times), this state-run institution is about far more than mere ice cream. Relationships have been forged here, fledgling novels drafted, birthday parties celebrated and Miami-bound escape plots hatched. The ultimate accolade came in 1993 when the Coppelia served as a location and major plot device in the Oscar-nominated Cuban movie *Fresa y chocolate* (the film's title alludes to two flavors of Coppelia ice cream: strawberry and chocolate).

As a tourist visiting the Coppelia, you'll probably be directed by a security guard into a smaller convertible-paying outdoor section of the park, but dodge the directives. Queueing is an integral part of Coppelia folklore, as traditional as the table-sharing, the cheap ice cream (you'll pay in Cuban pesos) and the uncensored people-watching opportunities that abound inside.

thought-provoking, religious-tinged paintings. The second is the antique wooden ceiling, terrace and general old-school elegance. At some point you'll get around to the food – Cuban with a French influence – and it doesn't falter. Try the duck (the specialty) or the exotic (for Cuba) salmon and eggplant.

Le Chansonnier   FRENCH $$$
(Map p88; ☎7-832-1576; www.lechansonnierhabana.com; Calle J No 257, btwn Calles 13 & 15; meals CUC$12-20; ⊙7pm-2am Mon-Sat) A great place to dine if you can find it (there's no sign) hidden in a faded mansion-turned-private-restaurant whose revamped interior is dramatically more modern than the front facade. French wine and French flavors shine in house specialties such as rabbit in red-wine sauce, eggplant caviar, and octopus with garlic and onions. Opening times vary and it's often busy; phone ahead.

VIP Havana   INTERNATIONAL $$$
(Map p88; ☎7-832-0178; Calle 9 No 454, btwn Calles E & F; meals CUC$15-21; ⊙noon-3am) You don't have to be a very important person to eat at VIP Havana, but it probably helps. This is one of Havana's newest and poshest restaurants with a suave veneer and equally suave food (the seafood is good). The atmosphere manages to be refined and quiet, but not at all snobby.

Decameron   ITALIAN $$$
(Map p88; ☎7-832-2444; Línea No 753, btwn Paseo & Calle 2; meals CUC$12-18; ⊙noon-midnight; ✐) Ugly from the outside, but far prettier within, the Decameron is an intimate Italian-

influenced restaurant where you can order from the varied menu with abandon. Veggie pizza, lasagna bolognese, steak au poivre and a divine *calabaza* (pumpkin) soup – it's all good. On top of that, there's a decent wine selection and the kitchen is sympathetic to vegetarians.

La Torre   FRENCH, CARIBBEAN $$$
(Map p88; ☎7-838-3088; Edificio Focsa, cnr Calles 17 & M; mains from CUC$15; ⊙11:30am-12:30am) One of Havana's tallest and best state-run restaurants is perched high above downtown Vedado atop the skyline-hogging Focsa building. A colossus of both modernist architecture and French/Cuban haute cuisine, this lofty fine-dining extravaganza combines sweeping city views with a progressive French-inspired menu that serves everything from artichokes to foie gras to *tarte amandine* (almond tart).

The prices are as distinctly non-Cuban as the ingredients, but with this level of service, it might be worth it.

Self-Catering

Supermercado Meridiano   SUPERMARKET
(Map p88; Galerías de Paseo, cnr Calle 1 & Paseo; ⊙10am-5pm Mon-Fri, to 2pm Sun) Across the street from the Hotel Meliá Cohiba, this supermarket has a good wine and liquor selection, lots of yogurt, cheese and crisps.

Agropecuario 17 & K   MARKET
(Map p88; cnr Calles 17 & K; ⊙8am-4:40pm Mon-Sat, 8am-noon Sun) A 'capped' market with cheap prices, but limited selection.

Agropecuario 19 & A MARKET
(Map p88; Calle 19, btwn Calles A & B; ⊘8am-4:40pm Mon-Sat, 8am-noon Sun) Havana's 'gourmet' market, with cauliflower, fresh herbs and rarer produce during shoulder seasons.

Agropecuario 21 & J MARKET
(Map p88; cnr Calles 21 & J; ⊘8am-4:40pm Mon-Sat, 8am-noon Sun) Good selection of cheap fruit and veg.

🍷 Drinking & Nightlife

Havana's cafe scene has entered an interesting stage. Bland international franchises have yet to gain a foothold but, with more freedom to engage in private business, local entrepreneurs are directing their artistic creativity into a growing number of bohemian bars and cafes.

🍷 Habana Vieja

★El Chanchullero BAR
(Map p66; www.el-chanchullero.com; Brasil, btwn Bernaza & Christo; ⊘1pm-midnight) *Aqui jamás estuvo Hemingway* (Hemingway was never here) reads the sign outside roguish Chanchullero, expressing more than a hint of irony. It had to happen. While rich tourists toast Hemingway in the Bodeguita del Medio, Cubans and backpackers pay peanuts (CUC$2) for cocktails in their own boho alternative.

It's a small, clamorous, graffiti-ridden dive-bar where the music rocks in 4/4 time rather than 6/8. Stuff that in your cigar and smoke it, Ernesto!

La Factoria Plaza Vieja BAR
(Map p66; cnr San Ignacio & Muralla; ⊘11am-midnight) Havana's original microbrewery occupies a boisterous corner of Plaza Vieja and sells smooth, cold homemade beer at sturdy wooden benches set up outside on the cobbles or indoors in an atmospheric beer hall. Gather a group together and you'll get the amber nectar in a tall plastic tube drawn from a tap at the bottom. There's also an outside grill.

Dulcería Bianchini II CAFE
(Map p66; www.dulceria-bianchini.com; San Ignacio No 68; ⊘9am-9pm) Cubans seemed to have long forgotten about the Spanish *merienda* – that lovely afternoon pause for hot drinks and cake. Then along came Bianchini, with its sweet snacks and excellent coffee, to remind everyone why tea time matters. This tiny bohemian abode abuts Plaza de la

Catedral; another branch, **Dulcería Bianchini I** (Map p66; Calle Sol No 12; ⊘9am-8.30pm Mon-Fri, 10am-9pm Sat & Sun), is next to Museo del Ron.

Sloppy Joe's BAR
(Map p80; Agramonte, cnr Ánimas; ⊘noon-3am) This bar, opened by young Spanish immigrant José García (aka 'Joe') in 1919, earned its name due to 1) its dodgy sanitation and 2) a soggy *ropa vieja* (shredded-beef) sandwich. Legendary among expats pre-revolution, it closed in the '60s after a fire, but was reincarnated in 2013 beneath the same noble neoclassical facade. And it's still serving decent cocktails and the soggy sandwich.

Granted, it's tourist-ville these days, but the interior is equally true to its predecessor as old black-and-white photos (most of which feature Sinatra with a glass in his hand) on the wall testify.

Museo del Chocolate CAFE
(Map p66; cnr Amargura & Mercaderes; ⊘9am-10pm) Chocolate addicts beware: this unmissable place in Habana Vieja's heart is a lethal dose of chocolate, truffles and yet more chocolate (all made on the premises). Situated – with no irony intended – in Calle Amargura (literally, Bitterness Street), it's more a cafe than a museum, with a small cluster of marble tables set amid a sugary mélange of chocolate paraphernalia.

Not surprisingly, everything on the menu contains one all-pervading ingredient: have it hot, cold, white, dark, rich or smooth – the stuff is divine, whichever way you choose.

Cervecería Antiguo Almacén de la Madera y Tabaco PUB
(Map p66; cnr Desamparados & San Ignacio; ⊘noon-midnight) Down on the docks lies Havana's newest brewpub. which makes and serves three Austrian-style beers in an old lumber and tobacco warehouse. The interior is huge, recalling the ambience of an Oktoberfest beer tent, but without the thick crowds – yet.

There's barbecued food on offer and a central stage for live music, but this place is best for its beer – CUC$2 for a half liter, or CUC$12 for a 3L theatrical beer tower.

La Bodeguita del Medio BAR
(Map p66; Empedrado No 207; ⊘11am-midnight) Made famous thanks to the rum-swilling exploits of Ernest Hemingway (who by association instantly sends the prices soaring), this is Havana's most celebrated bar. A

visit here has become *de rigueur* for tourists who haven't yet cottoned on to the fact that the mojitos are better and (far) cheaper elsewhere.

Past visitors have included Salvador Allende, Fidel Castro, Nicolás Guillén, Harry Belafonte and Nat King Cole, all of whom have left their autographs on La Bodeguita's wall – along with thousands of others (save for the big names, the walls are repainted every few months). These days the clientele is less luminous, with package tourists from Varadero outnumbering beatnik bohemians. Purists claim the CUC$4 mojitos have lost their Hemingway-esque shine in recent years. Only one way to find out...

Café el Escorial
CAFE

(Map p66; Mercaderes No 317, cnr Muralla; ⊙9am-9pm) Opening onto Plaza Vieja and encased in a finely restored colonial mansion, there's something definitively European about El Escorial. Among some of the best caffeine infusions in the city served here are *café cubano, café con leche,* frappé, coffee liquor and even *daiquirí de café.* There's also a sweet selection of delicate cakes and pastries.

Bar Dos Hermanos
BAR

(Map p66; San Pedro No 304; ⊙24hr) This once seedy, now polished bar down by the docks broadcasts a boastful list of former celebrity rum-sluggers on a plaque by the door, Federico Lorca, Marlon Brando, Errol Flynn and, of course, Hemingway among them. With its long wooden bar and salty seafaring atmosphere, it still spins a little magic.

El Floridita
BAR

(Map p66; Obispo No 557; ⊙11am-midnight) Promoting itself as the 'cradle of the daiquirí,' El Floridita was a favorite of expat Americans long before Hemingway dropped by in the 1930s, hence the name (which means 'Little Florida'). Bartender Constante Ribalaigua invented the daiquirí soon after WWI, but it was Hemingway who popularized it and ultimately the bar christened a drink in his honor: the Papa Hemingway Special (a grapefruit-flavored daiquirí).

His record – legend has it – was 13 doubles in one sitting. Any attempt to equal it at the current prices (CUC$6 for a shot) will cost you a small fortune – and a huge hangover.

La Lluvia de Oro
BAR

(Map p66; Obispo No 316; ⊙9am-1am) It's on Obispo and there's always live music belting through the doorway, so it's always crowded. But with a higher-than-average *jinetero/jinetera* (tout) to tourist ratio, it might not be your most intimate introduction to Havana. Small snacks are available and the musician's 'hat' comes round every three songs.

La Dichosa
BAR

(Map p66; cnr Obispo & Compostela; ⊙10am-midnight) It's hard to miss rowdy La Dichosa on busy Calle Obispo. Small and cramped with at least half the space given over to the resident band, this is a good place to sink a quick mojito.

Café Taberna
BAR

(Map p66; cnr Brasil & Mercaderes; ⊙noon-midnight) Founded in 1772 and still glowing after a 21st-century makeover, this drinking and eating establishment is a great place to prop up the (impressive) bar and sink a few cocktails before dinner. The music, which gets swinging around 8pm, doffs its cap, more often than not, to one-time resident mambo king Benny Moré. Skip the food.

Café París
BAR

(Map p66; Obispo No 202; ⊙24hr) Things never stand still at this rough-hewn Habana Vieja dive-bar, known for its live music and gregarious tourist-heavy atmosphere. On good nights, the rum flows and spontaneous dancing erupts.

Monserrate Bar
BAR

(Map p66; Obrapía No 410; ⊙noon-midnight) A couple of doors down from the famous Hemingway haunt of El Floridita, Monserrate is a Hemingway-free zone, meaning the daiquirís are half the price.

🍸 Centro Habana

★Café Archangel
CAFE

(Map p80; ☎7-867-7495; Concordia No 57; ⊙8:30am-8:30pm) Excellent coffee, fine *tortas* (cakes), suave non-reggaetón music and Charlie Chaplin movies projected on the wall – what more could you want?

Humboldt 52
BAR

(Map p80; ☎53-30-29-89; Humboldt 52; ⊙10pm-4am) Havana's first bona fide gay bar was a long time coming (Santa Clara had one years ago), but was worth the wait. Drag shows, dexterous dancing and kitschy karaoke entertain the open-minded in a cool, luminously lit interior where people of all persuasions will feel welcome. It's small and usually packed.

Prado No 12 BAR

(Map p80; Paseo de Martí No 12; ◎noon-11pm) A slim flat-iron building on the corner of Paseo de Martí (Prado) and San Lázaro that serves drinks and simple snacks, Prado No 12 still resembles Havana in a 1950s timewarp. Soak up the atmosphere of this amazing city here after a sunset stroll along the Malecón.

Vedado

★Café Madrigal BAR

(Map p88; Calle 17 No 302, btwn Calles 2 & 4; ◎6pm-2am Tue-Sun) Vedado flirts with bohemia in this dimly lit romantic bar that might have materialized serendipitously from Paris' Latin Quarter in the days of Joyce and Hemingway. Order a *tapita* (small tapa) and a cocktail, and retire to the atmospheric art nouveau terrace where the buzz of nighttime conversation competes with the racket of vintage American cars rattling past below.

Gabanna Café BAR

(Map p88; Calle 3, cnr Calle C; ◎5pm-3am) Sleek, new, trendy and embellished with black-and-white overtones, this à la mode cocktail bar is what the modern Havana scene is all about. Beautiful people sip equally attractive cocktails in its small super-cool interior.

Bar-Club Imágenes BAR

(Map p88; Calzada No 602; ◎9pm-5am) This upscale piano bar attracts something of an older crowd with its regular diet of *boleros* (ballads) and *trova* (traditional music), though there are sometimes comedy shows; check the schedule posted outside. Affordable meals are available (minimum CUC$5).

Cuba Libro CAFE

(Map p88; ☑7-830-5205; cnr Calles 24 & 19; ◎10am-8pm Mon-Sat; 🖶) 🖉 Cafe, book-lending library, socially responsible community resource, and great place for Cubans and non-Cubans to interact: Cuba Libro wears many different hats. Although it's a bit of a walk from the main sights, it's a good place to find out more about Havana below the radar. Grab a juice or coffee and join the discussion.

Aside from lending books, the cafe displays emerging Cuban art, gives out free condoms, provides toys for kids and follows sustainable practices.

3D Café BAR

(Map p88; ☑7-863-0733; www.3dcafecuba.com; Calle 1 No 107, btwn Calles C & D; ◎noon-3am) An ice-cool place to see and be seen, this tiny but super slick bar-club close to the Malecón is full of dry ice and beautiful people enjoying nightly humor and live-music shows. Food comes in small tapas and cocktails are *de rigueur*. Drop by or phone ahead as it has a reservation policy.

Café Fresa y Chocolate CAFE

(Map p88; Calle 23, btwn Calles 10 & 12; ◎9am-11pm) No ice cream here, just movie memorabilia. This is the HQ of the Cuban Film Institute and a nexus for coffee-quaffing students and art-house movie addicts. You can debate the merits of Almodóvar over Scorsese on the pleasant patio before disappearing next door for a film preview.

Café Literario del 'G' CAFE

(Map p88; Calle 23, btwn Calles G & H, Vedado; ◎noon-11pm) An unkempt student hangout full of arty wall scribblings and coffee-quaffing intellectuals discussing the merits of Guillén over Lorca. Relax on the streetside front patio and keep an ear out for one of the regular *trova*, jazz and poetry presentations.

Café Cantante CLUB

(Map p88; ☑7-879-0710; cnr Paseo & Calle 39; cover CUC$10; ◎9pm-5am Tue-Sat) Below the Teatro Nacional de Cuba (side entrance), this is a hip disco that offers live salsa music and dancing, as well as bar snacks and food. The clientele is mainly 'yummies' (young urban Marxist managers) and ageing male tourists with their youthful Cuban girlfriends. The Café tends to get feistier than the adjacent Piano Bar Delirio Habanero. Musically, there are regular appearances from big-name singers such as Haila María Mompie. No shorts, T-shirts or hats may be worn, and no under-18s are allowed.

Piano Bar Delirio Habanero CLUB

(Map p88; cnr Paseo & Calle 39; cover CUC$10; ◎from 6pm Tue-Sun) This suave lounge upstairs in the Teatro Nacional de Cuba hosts everything from young *trovadores* to smooth, improvised jazz. The deep red couches abut a wall of glass overlooking the Plaza de la Revolución – it's stunning at night with the Martí Memorial alluringly backlit. Come up for air here when the adjoining Café Cantante nightclub gets too hot.

Bar-Restaurante 1830 DANCE

(Map p88; cnr Malecón & Calle 20; ◎noon-1:45am) If you want to salsa dance, this is *the* place to go. After the Sunday night show literally everyone takes to the floor. Touristy but fun. Skip the food.

GAY HAVANA

The Revolution had a hostile attitude toward homosexuality in its early days. While the Stonewall riots were engulfing New York City, Cuban homosexuals were still being sent to re-education camps by a government that was dominated by macho, bearded ex-guerrillas dressed in military fatigues.

But since the 1990s, the tide has been turning, spearheaded somewhat ironically by Mariela Castro, daughter of current president, Raúl Castro and the director of the Cuban National Center for Sex Education in Havana. In 2013, Mariela was granted a visa by the American government to travel to the US in order to accept an award from Equality Forum for her gay rights advocacy.

An important landmark for the LGBT community was reached in June 2008 when the Cuban government passed a law permitting free sex-change operations to qualifying citizens courtesy of the country's famously far-sighted health system. In November 2012, Cuba elected its first transgender person to public office when Adela Hernández (a woman) won a municipal seat in Villa Clara province.

Havana's LGBT scene has taken off in the last couple of years. The focus of gay life is on the cusp of Centro Havana and Vedado in the 'triangle' that stretches between Calzada de la Infanta, Calle L and Calle 23 (La Rampa). Calle 23 at its intersection with the Malecón has long been a favored meeting spot for gay people, while Cine Yara and the Coppelia park opposite are well-known cruising spots. Nightlife centers on Havana's first real gay bar, Humboldt 52 (p112). Other good spots nearby are the Pico Blanco disco in Hotel St John's and Cabaret Las Vegas, both known for their drag shows.

In more discriminatory days, Havana's only gay beach was Mi Cayito, a quiet secluded stretch of Playa Boca Ciega in Playas del Este. The beach remains popular. You can now also enjoy gay film nights at the Icaic headquarters on the corner of Calles 23 and 12 in Vedado and, since 2009, an annual gay parade along Calle 23 in mid-May. Legally, lesbians enjoy the same rights as gay men, though there is a less evident lesbian 'scene'.

Cabaret Las Vegas CLUB
(Map p88; Calzada de la Infanta No 104, btwn Calles 25 & 27; admission CUC$5; ☺10pm-4am) Rough and slightly seedy local music dive (with a midnight show) where a little rum and a lot of *No moleste, por favor* will help you withstand the overzealous entreaties of the hordes of haranguing *jineteras* (female touts). Vegas is also known for its drag shows.

Pico Blanco CLUB
(Map p88; Calle O, btwn Calles 23 & 25; admission CUC$5-10; ☺from 9pm) An insanely popular nightclub, the Pico Blanco is on the 14th floor of the mediocre Hotel St John's in Vedado and kicks off nightly at 9pm. The program can be hit or miss. Some nights it's karaoke and cheesy *boleros;* others it's drag queens and boys in tight T-shirts.

Club la Red CLUB
(Map p88; cnr Calles 19 & L; admission CUC$3-5) Local neighborhood disco with the occasional bemused foreigner thrown in.

Karachi Club CLUB
(Map p88; cnr Calles 17 & K; admission CUC$3-5; ☺10pm-5am) Ferociously *caliente* (hot).

Discoteca Amanecer CLUB
(Map p88; Calle 15 No 12, btwn Calles N & O; admission CUC$3-5; ☺10pm-4am) Fun if your budget is blown.

Club Tropical CLUB
(Map p88; cnr Línea & Calle F; ☺4pm-2am) Relaxed evening cafe that turns into a hot local club after 10pm. Friday and Saturday nights are best.

☆ Entertainment

Nightlife exists in the Old Town, but it's more of the live-music-in-a-bar variety and fizzles out early. Don't forget the excellent flamenco shows in Mesón de la Flota (p105) and – occasionally – Hostal Valencia (p98). Although it may have lost its prerevolutionary reputation as a ritzy casino quarter, Vedado is still the place for nightlife in Havana while Centro's nightlife is edgier and more local.

Live Music

Jazz Café LIVE MUSIC
(Map p88; top fl, Galerías de Paseo, cnr Calle 1 & Paseo, Vedado; cover after 8pm CUC$10; ☺noon-late) This upscale joint, located improbably in a

shopping mall overlooking the Malecón, is a kind of jazz supper club, with dinner tables and a decent menu. At night, the club swings into action with live jazz, *timba* and, occasionally, straight-up salsa. It attracts plenty of big-name acts.

Basílica Menor de San Francisco de Asís
CLASSICAL MUSIC

(Map p66; Plaza de San Francisco de Asís, Habana Vieja; tickets CUC$3-8; ☺from 6pm Thu-Sat) Plaza de San Francisco de Asís' glorious church, which dates from 1738, has been reincarnated as a 21st-century museum and concert hall. The old nave hosts choral and chamber music two to three times a week (check the schedule at the door) and the acoustics inside are excellent. It's best to bag your ticket at least a day in advance.

Submarino Amarillo
LIVE MUSIC

(Map p88; cnr Calles 17 & 6; ☺2-7:30pm, 9pm-2am Tue-Sat, 2-10pm Sun, 9pm-2am Mon) You can't escape The Beatles in Cuba, their iconic status epitomized in clubs such as this one which abuts Parque Lennon and hosts all types of live music as long as it's in 4/4 time and a subgenre of 'rock'. Look out for top Cuban band, Los Kents. Afternoons are more laidback, when you can nibble tapas while watching surreal '60s videos.

Oratorio de San Felipe Neri
LIVE MUSIC

(Map p66; cnr Aguiar & Obrapía, Habana Vieja; CUC$2; ☺performances at 7pm) The Neri has had many incarnations since its founding in 1693; first as a church under various religious orders (Oratorianas, Capuchinos, Carmelitas), then as a bank, and, since 2004, as one of Havana's top venues for classical music (mainly choral).

Callejón de Hamel
LIVE MUSIC

(Map p80; ☺from noon Sun) Aside from its funky street murals and psychedelic art shops, the main reason to come to Havana's high temple of Afro-Cuban culture in Centro Habana is the frenetic rumba music that kicks off every Sunday at around noon.

For aficionados, this is about as raw and hypnotic as it gets, with interlocking drum patterns and lengthy rhythmic chants powerful enough to summon up the spirit of the orishas (Santería deities).

Due to a liberal sprinkling of tourists these days, some argue that the Callejón has lost much of its basic charm. Don't believe them. This place can still deliver.

Jazz Club la Zorra y El Cuervo
LIVE MUSIC

(Map p88; cnr Calles 23 & O, Vedado; admission CUC$5-10; ☺from 10pm daily) Havana's most famous jazz club (The Vixen and the Crow) opens its doors nightly at 10pm to long lines of committed music fiends. Enter through a red English phonebox and descend into a cramped, dark basement. The freestyle jazz here is second to none, and in the past the club has hosted such big names as Chucho Valdés and George Benson.

La Casa de la Música Centro Habana
LIVE MUSIC

(Map p80; Av de Italia, btwn Concordia & Neptuno, Centro Habana; admission CUC$5-25; ☺5pm-3am) One of Cuba's best and most popular nightclubs and live-music venues. All the big names play here, from Bamboleo to Los Van Van – and you'll pay peanuts to see them. Of the city's two Casas de la Música, this Centro Habana version is a little edgier than its Miramar counterpart (some say it's too edgy), with big salsa bands and little space. Price varies depending on the band.

El Hurón Azul
LIVE MUSIC

(Map p88; cnr Calles 17 & H, Vedado; ☺hours vary) If you want to rub shoulders with some socialist celebrities, hang out at Hurón Azul, the social club of Uneac. Replete with priceless snippets of Cuba's under-the-radar cultural life, most performances take place outside in the garden. Wednesday is the Afro-Cuban rumba, Saturday is authentic Cuban *boleros*, and alternate Thursdays there's jazz and *trova*. You'll never pay more than CUC$5.

El Gato Tuerto
LIVE MUSIC

(Map p88; Calle O No 14, btwn Calles 17 & 19, Vedado; drink minimum CUC$5; ☺noon-6am) Once the HQ of Havana's alternative artistic and sexual scene, the 'one-eyed cat' is now a nexus for karaoke-crazy baby-boomers who come here to knock out rum-fuelled renditions of traditional Cuban *boleros*. It's hidden just off the Malecón in a quirky two-story house with turtles swimming in a front pool.

The upper floor is taken up by a restaurant, while down below late-night revelers raise the roof in a chic nightclub.

Centro Cultural El Gran Palenque
DANCE

(Map p88; Calle 4 No 103, btwn Calzada & Calle 5, Vedado; admission CUC$5; ☺3-6pm Sat) Founded in 1962, the high-energy Conjunto Folklórico Nacional de Cuba specializes in Afro-Cuban dancing (all of the drummers are Santería priests). See them perform, and dance along during the regular Sábado de Rumba – three full hours of mesmerizing drumming and dancing. This group also performs at Teatro Mella.

A major festival called **FolkCuba** unfolds here biannually during the second half of January.

Casa del ALBA Cultural LIVE MUSIC
(Map p88; Línea, btwn Calles C & D, Vedado) This venue was designed to strengthen cultural solidarity between the ALBA nations (Cuba, Venezuela, Bolivia, Ecuador, Nicaragua), but in reality it hosts a variety of artistic and music-based shows and expos. It was opened in December 2009 with Raúl Castro, Daniel Ortega and Hugo Chávez in attendance.

Theater

⭐ **Gran Teatro de la Habana** THEATER
(Map p80; ☑ 7-861-3077; cnr Paseo de Martí & San Rafael, Centro Habana; per person CUC$20; ⊙ box office 9am-6pm Mon-Sat, to 3pm Sun) A theater since 1838, the amazing neobaroque Gran Teatro across from Parque Central is the seat of the acclaimed Ballet Nacional de Cuba, founded in 1948 by Alicia Alonso. It is also the home of the Cuban National Opera. For upcoming events inquire at the ticket office.

The building also contains the grandiose Teatro García Lorca, along with two smaller concert halls: the Sala Alejo Carpentier and the Sala Ernesto Lecuono – where art films are sometimes shown.

Teatro Nacional de Cuba THEATER
(Map p88; ☑ 7-879-6011; cnr Paseo & Calle 39, Vedado; per person CUC$10; ⊙ box office 9am-5pm & before performances) One of the twin pillars of Havana's cultural life, the Teatro Nacional de Cuba on Plaza de la Revolución is the modern rival to the Gran Teatro in Centro Habana. Built in the 1950s as part of Jean Forestier's grand city expansion, the complex hosts landmark concerts, foreign theater troupes and La Colmenita children's company.

The main hall, Sala Avellaneda, stages big events such as musical concerts or plays by Shakespeare, while the smaller Sala Covarrubias along the back puts on a more daring program (the seating capacity of the two halls combined is 3300). The 9th floor is a rehearsal and performance space where the newest, most experimental stuff happens. The ticket office is at the far end of a separate single-story building beside the main theater.

Teatro Amadeo Roldán THEATER
(Map p88; ☑ 7-832-1168; cnr Calzada & Calle D, Vedado; per person CUC$10) Constructed in 1922 and burnt down by an arsonist in 1977, this wonderfully decorative neoclassical theater was rebuilt in 1999 in the exact style of the original. Named after the famous Cuban composer and the man responsible for bringing Afro-Cuban influences into modern classical music, the theater is one of Havana's grandest with two different auditoriums.

The Orquesta Sinfónica Nacional plays in the 886-seat Sala Amadeo Roldán, while soloists and small groups are showcased in the 276-seat Sala García Caturla.

Teatro Mella THEATER
(Map p88; Línea No 657, btwn Calles A & B, Vedado) Occupying the site of the old Rodi Cinema on Línea, the Teatro Mella offers one of Havana's most comprehensive programs, including an international ballet festival, comedy shows, theater, dance and intermittent performances from the famous Conjunto Folklórico Nacional. If you have kids, come to the children's show Sunday at 11am.

The adjacent **Jardines del Mella** is a good place to chill with a drink before or after a performance.

Teatro América THEATER
(Map p80; Av de Italia No 253, btwn Concordia & Neptuno, Centro Habana) Housed in a classic art deco *rascacielo* on Av de Italia (Galiano), the América seems to have changed little since its theatrical heyday in the 1930s and 1940s. It plays host to vaudeville variety, comedy, dance, jazz and salsa; shows are normally staged on Saturdays at 8:30pm and Sundays at 5pm. You can also inquire about dance lessons here.

Teatro Fausto THEATER
(Map p80; Paseo de Martí No 201, Centro Habana) Rightly renowned for its side-splitting comedy shows, Fausto is a streamlined art deco theater on Prado (Paseo de Martí).

Sala Teatro Hubert de Blanck THEATER
(Map p88; Calzada No 657, btwn Calles A & B, Vedado) This theater is named for the founder of Havana's first conservatory of music (1885). The Teatro Estudio based here is Cuba's leading theater company. You can usually see plays in Spanish on Saturday at 8:30pm and on Sunday at 7pm. Tickets are sold just prior to the performance.

Sala Teatro el Sótano
THEATER

(Map p88; Calle K No 514, btwn Calles 25 & 27, Vedado; ☉5-8:30pm Fri & Sat, 3-5pm Sun) If you understand Spanish, it's well worth attending some of the cutting-edge contemporary theater that's a staple of Grupo Teatro Rita Montaner at this venue near the Hotel Habana Libre.

Café Teatro Brecht
THEATER

(Map p88; cnr Calles 13 & I, Vedado) Varied performances take place. Your best bet is 10:30pm on a Saturday (tickets go on sale one hour before the performance).

Teatro Nacional de Guiñol
THEATER

(Map p88; Calle M, btwn Calles 17 & 19, Vedado; ☝) This venue has quality puppet shows and children's theater.

Cabaret

★Cabaret Parisién
CABARET

(Map p88; ☎7-836-3564; Hotel Nacional, cnr Calles 21 & O, Vedado; admission CUC$30; ☉9pm) One rung down from Marianao's world-famous Tropicana, but cheaper and closer to the city center, the nightly Cabaret Parisién in the Hotel Nacional is well worth a look, especially if you're staying in or around Vedado. It's the usual mix of frills, feathers and semi-naked women, but the choreography is first class and the whole spectacle has excellent kitsch value.

Habana Café
CABARET

(Map p88; Paseo, btwn Calles 1 & 3, Vedado; admission CUC$15; ☉from 9:30pm) A hip and trendy nightclub cum cabaret show at the Hotel Meliá Cohiba laid out in 1950s American style. After 1am the tables are cleared and the place rocks to 'international music' until the cock crows. Excellent value.

Cabaret Turquino
CABARET

(Map p88; Hotel Habana Libre, Calle L, btwn Calles 23 & 25, Vedado; admission CUC$10; ☉from 10:30pm) Spectacular shows in a spectacular setting on the 25th floor of the Hotel Habana Libre.

Cultural Centers

★Fábrica de Arte Cubano
CULTURAL CENTER

(Map p88; www.fabricadeartecubano.com; cnr Calles 26 & 11, Vedado; admission CUC$2; ☉8pm-4am Thu-Sat, to 2am Sun) The brainchild of Afro-Cuban fusion musician X-Alfonso, this is one Havana's finest new art projects. An intellectual nexus for live music, art expos, fashion shows and invigorating debate over coffee and cocktails, there's no pecking order or surly bouncers in this converted cooking-oil factory in Vedado.

Instead you can mingle with the artists, musicians and mainly Cuban clientele for events that kick off at 8pm Thursday to Sunday in the Bauhaus-like interior. Check their Facebook page for upcoming acts.

Fundación Alejo Carpentier
CULTURAL CENTER

(Map p66; www.fundacioncarpentier.cult.cu; Empedrado No 215, Habana Vieja; ☉8am-4pm Mon-Fri) Near the Plaza de la Catedral. Check for cultural events at this baroque former palace of the Condesa de la Reunión (1820s) where Carpentier set his famous novel *El Siglo de las Luces*.

Instituto Cubano de Amistad con los Pueblos
CULTURAL CENTER

(ICAP; Map p88; ☎7-830-3114; Paseo No 416, btwn Calles 17 & 19, Vedado; ☉11am-11pm) Rocking cultural and musical events in a 1926 elegant mansion; there's also a restaurant, bar and cigar shop.

Casa de las Américas
CULTURAL CENTER

(Map p88; ☎7-838-2706; www.fundacioncarpentier.cult.cu; cnr Calles 3 & G, Vedado) Powerhouse of Cuban and Latin American culture, with conferences, exhibitions, a gallery, book launches and concerts. The Casa's annual literary award is one of the Spanish-speaking world's most prestigious. Pick up a schedule of weekly events in the library. See the website for the schedule of upcoming events.

Cinemas

There are about 200 cinemas in Havana. Most have several screenings daily, and every theater posts the *Cartelera Icaic*, which lists show times for the entire city. Tickets are usually CUC$2; queue early. Hundreds of movies are screened throughout Havana during the Festival Internacional del Nuevo Cine Latinamericano in late November/early December. Schedules are published daily in the *Diario del Festival*, available in the morning at big theaters and the Hotel Nacional. A lot of films are obviously in Spanish, but you'll find some in English (with Spanish subtitles) including Hollywood blockbusters.

Cine Infanta
CINEMA

(Map p80; Calzada de la Infanta No 357, Centro Habana) Possibly Havana's plushest cinema. It's an important venue during the international film festival.

Cine 23 & 12
CINEMA

(Map p88; ☎ 7-833-6906; Calle 23, btwn Calles 12 & 14, Vedado) One of a clutch of well-maintained cinemas on Icaic's Vedado movie strip, this is also one of the HQs of Havana's film festival.

Cine Charles Chaplín
CINEMA

(Map p88; Calle 23 No 1157, btwn Calles 10 & 12, Vedado) An art-house cinema adjacent to the Icaic HQ. Don't miss the poster gallery of great Cuban classic films next door or the movie grapevine that is the Café Fresa y Chocolate opposite.

Cine Yara
CINEMA

(Map p88; cnr Calles 23 & L, Vedado) One big screen and two video *salas* (cinemas) here at Havana's most famous cinema. The venue for many a hot date.

Cine la Rampa
CINEMA

(Map p88; Calle 23 No 111, Vedado) Ken Loach movies, French classics, film festivals – catch them all at this Vedado staple, which houses the Cuban film archive.

Cine Payret
CINEMA

(Map p80; Paseo de Martí No 505, Centro Habana) Opposite the Capitolio, this is Centro Habana's largest and most luxurious cinema, erected in 1878. Plenty of American movies play here.

Sports

Sala Polivalente Ramón Fonst
SPORTS

(Map p88; Av de la Independencia, Vedado; admission 1 peso) Basketball and volleyball games are held at this tatty-looking stadium opposite the main bus station.

Kid Chocolate
SPORTS

(Map p80; Paseo de Martí, Centro Habana) A boxing club directly opposite the Capitolio, which usually hosts matches on Friday at 7pm.

🔒 Shopping

Shopping isn't Havana's big draw – this, after all, is a city where disposable income is something of an oxymoron. That said, there are some decent outlets for travelers and tourists, particularly if you're after the standard Cuban shopping triumvirate of

WATCHING SPORT

As economic standards nosedived during the early 1990s, the nation's sporting prowess moved in the other direction, peaking at the 1992 Barcelona Olympics when Cuba (the world's 106th largest nation) came fifth in the overall medals table with 14 golds. The Cubans continue to excel in baseball, boxing, the high jump (Javier Sotomayor has held the World Record since 1993) and volleyball. Soccer is a growing sport attracting an ever-expanding fan-base, particularly since the 2014 FIFA World Cup. Havana's main sporting stadiums are located in the peripheral municipalities of Playa, Cerro and Habana del Este. Going to a game is an 'experience'. No bookings required; just turn up, pay the nominal ticket price and find a (hard) seat.

Estadio Latinoamericano (Map p88; Zequiera No 312, Vedado; tickets CUC$2) The largest stadium in the country holds 55,000 and was built before the revolution in 1946. It's the home of Havana's widely revered (or reviled – depending on where you're from) baseball team, Los Industriales. Entrance to games costs small change. The season runs late October to April with play-offs running until May.

Estadio Pedro Marrero (cnr Av 41 & Calle 46, Kohly) The slightly down-at-heel Estadio Pedro Marrero in Playa holds 28,000 spectators and is home to FC Ciudad de La Habana, the capital's main soccer team who have won the Campeonato Nacional de Fútbol six times, the last one in 2001.

Estadio Panamericano Built for the 1991 Panamerican Games, this shabby stadium was fitted with a new athletics track in 2008 though it still looks neglected and unloved. It's supposed to hold 50,000 although 34,000 is quoted as the current capacity. It's used mainly for athletics and soccer.

Coliseo de la Ciudad Deportiva (cnr Av de la Independencia & Vía Blanca, Vedado; admission 5 pesos) A multi-use 15,000-capacity indoor sports arena that opened in 1958 and is the HQ of Cuba's men's volleyball team. It also hosts big boxing tournaments.

rum, cigars and coffee. Art is another lucrative field. Havana's art scene is cutting edge and ever changing, and collectors, browsers and admirers will find many galleries in which to while away hours. There are at least a dozen private studios in Calle Obispo alone. For gallery events, look for the free *Arte en La Habana,* a triquarterly listings flyer (the San Cristóbal agency on Plaza de San Francisco de Asís usually has them).

🏛 Habana Vieja

★ Centro Cultural Antiguos Almacenes de Deposito San José   ARTS & CRAFTS
(Map p66; cnr Av Desamparados & San Ignacio; ⊙ 10am-6pm Mon-Sat) Havana's open-air handicraft market sits under the cover of an old shipping warehouse in Desamparados. Check your socialist ideals at the door. Herein lies a hive of free enterprise and (unusually for Cuba) haggling. Possible souvenirs include paintings, *guayabera* shirts, woodwork, leather items, jewelry and numerous apparitions of the highly marketable El Che.

There are also snacks, clean-ish toilets and a tourist information representative from the San Cristóbal agency. It's as popular with Cubans as it is with tourists.

Librería Venecia   BOOKS
(Map p66; Obispo No 504; ⊙ 9am-9pm) Nice little private secondhand bookshop in Obispo where you might uncover all number of mysteries. It's particularly good for its old Cuban posters, which steer clear of the standard Che Guevara shots.

Palacio de la Artesanía   SOUVENIRS
(Map p66; Cuba No 64; ⊙ 9am-7pm) A former 18th-century colonial palace turned into a shopping mall! Gathered around a shaded central patio is this one-stop shopping spot for souvenirs, cigars, crafts, musical instruments, CDs, clothing and jewelry at fixed prices. Join the gaggles of tour-bus escapees and fill your bag.

Longina Música   MUSIC
(Map p66; Obispo No 360, btwn Habana & Compostela; ⊙ 10am-7pm Mon-Sat, to 1pm Sun) This place on the pedestrian mall has a good selection of CDs, plus musical instruments such as bongos, guitars, maracas, *guiros* (gourds) and *tumbadoras* (conga drums). It often places loudspeakers in the street outside to grab the attention of passing tourists.

Casa de Carmen Montilla   ARTS
(Map p66; Oficios No 164; ⊙ 10:30am-5:30pm Tue-Sat, 9am-1pm Sun) An important art gallery named after a celebrated Venezuelan painter who maintained a studio here until her death in 2004. Spread across three floors, the house exhibits the work of Montilla and other popular Cuban and Venezuelan artists. The rear courtyard features a huge ceramic mural by Alfredo Sosabravo.

Plaza de Armas Secondhand Book Market   BOOKS
(Map p66; cnr Obispo & Tacón; ⊙ 9am-7pm Tue-Sun) A book market stocking old, new and rare books, including Hemingway, some weighty poetry and plenty of written pontifications from Fidel. It's all here under the leafy boughs in Plaza de Armas. Browse to your heart's content.

Habana 1791   PERFUME
(Map p66; Mercaderes No 156, btwn Obrapía & Lamparilla; ⊙ 9:30am-6pm) A specialist shop that sells perfume made from tropical flowers, Habana 1791 retains the air of a working museum. Floral fragrances are mixed by hand – you can see the petals drying in a laboratory out the back.

Fayad Jamás   BOOKS
(Map p66; Obispo, btwn Habana & Aguiar; ⊙ 9am-7pm Mon-Sat, to 1pm Sun) This bookstore, a throwback to the 1920s, was refurbished by Habaguanex to fit in with its Old Town surroundings. Editions are mainly in Spanish, but there are some interesting cultural magazines including *Temas.*

Librería la Internacional   BOOKS
(Map p66; Obispo No 526; ⊙ 9am-7pm Mon-Sat, to 3pm Sun) Good selection of guides, photography books and Cuban literature in English; next door is Librería Cervantes, an antiquarian bookseller.

Estudio Galería los Oficios   ARTS
(Map p66; Oficios No 166; ⊙ 10am-5:30pm Mon-Sat) Pop into this gallery to see the large, hectic but intriguing canvases by Nelson Domínguez, whose workshop is upstairs.

Taller de Serigrafía René Portocarrero   ARTS
(Map p66; Cuba No 513, btwn Brasil & Muralla; ⊙ 9am-4pm Mon-Fri) Paintings and prints by young Cuban artists are exhibited and sold here (from CUC$30 to CUC$150). You can also see the artists at work.

WHERE TO BUY RUM, CIGARS & COFFEE

Shops selling Cuba's top three homegrown products are relatively common in Havana. All are government-run. As a rule of thumb, never buy cigars off the street, as they will almost always be damaged and/or substandard. Havana's prime factory-outlet cigar shop is at the **Real Fábrica de Tabacos Partagás** (Map p80; Industria No 520, btwn Barcelona & Dragones; ⊙9am-7pm) and is always well stocked (check in Hotel Saratoga as to current status due to renovations). Another excellent option is La Casa del Habano (p134) in Miramar, which has an air-conditioned smoking room and a reputable bar-restaurant. While many top hotels stock cigars, the best shop is in the **Hostal Condes de Villanueva** (Map p66; Mercaderes No 202, Habana Vieja; ⊙10am-6pm) which has an on-site roller and smoking room and expert sales staff. There's another good option just down the street in the **Museo del Tabaco** (Map p66; Mercaderes No 120, Habana Vieja; ⊙10am-5pm Mon-Sat).

For rum, look no further than the **Fundación Havana Club shop** (Map p66; San Pedro No 262, Habana Vieja; ⊙9am-9pm) at the Museo de Ron in Habana Vieja.

Coffee is sold at all of the above places, but for a bit more choice and a decent taster cup, pop into **La Casa del Café** (Map p66; Baratillo, cnr Obispo; ⊙9am-5pm) just off Plaza de Armas in Habana Vieja.

Moderna Poesía　　　BOOKS
(Map p66; Obispo 525; ⊙10am-8pm) Perhaps Havana's best spot for Spanish-language books is this classic art deco building at the western end of Calle Obispo.

Centro Habana

★**Memorias Librería**　　　BOOKS
(Map p80; ☑7-862-3153; Ánimas No 57, btwn Paseo de Martí & Agramonte; ⊙9am-5pm) A new shop for beautiful old artifacts, the recently opened Memorias Librería is Havana's first genuine antique bookstore. Delve into its gathered piles and you'll find wonderful rare collectibles including old coins, postcards, posters, magazines and art deco signs from the 1930s. Priceless!

El Bulevar　　　MARKET
(Map p80; San Rafael, btwn Paseo de Martí & Av de Italia) This is the pedestrianized part of Calle San Rafael near the Hotel Inglaterra. Come here for peso snacks and surprises, and 1950s shopping nostalgia.

Plaza Carlos III　　　SHOPPING CENTER
(Map p80; Av Salvador Allende, btwn Arbol Seco & Retiro; ⊙10am-6pm Mon-Sat) After Plaza América in Varadero, this is probably Cuba's flashiest shopping mall – and there's barely a tourist in sight. Go on a Saturday and see the double economy working at a feverish pitch.

Librería Luis Rogelio Nogueras　　　BOOKS
(Map p80; Av de Italia No 467, btwn Barcelona & San Martín; ⊙10am-5pm Mon-Sat) Literary magazines and Cuban literature in Spanish at one of Centro's best bookstores.

Vedado

Galería de Arte Latinoamericano　　　ARTS
(Map p88; cnr Calles 3 & G; admission CUC$2; ⊙10am-4:30pm Tue-Sat, 9am-1pm Sun) Situated inside the Casa de las Américas and featuring art from all over Latin America.

Instituto Cubano del Arte e Industria Cinematográficos　　　SOUVENIRS
(Map p88; Calle 23, btwn Calles 10 & 12; ⊙10am-5pm) The best place in Havana for rare Cuban movie posters and DVDs. The shop is inside the Icaic (Cuban Film Institute) building and accessed through the Café Fresa y Chocolate.

Feria de la Artesanía　　　SOUVENIRS
(Map p88; Malecón, btwn Calles D & E; ⊙from 10:30am, closed Wed) This artisan market is a pale imitation of Habana Vieja's Antiguos Almacenes, with a few handmade shoes and sandals, and some old stamps and coins thrown in for good measure.

Andare – Bazar de Arte　　　SOUVENIRS
(Map p88; cnr Calles 23 & L; ⊙10am-6pm Mon-Fri, to 2pm Sat) A fabulous selection of old movie posters, antique postcards, T-shirts and, of course, all the greatest Cuban films on videotape are sold at this shop inside the Cine Yara.

Galerías de Paseo　　　SHOPPING CENTER
(Map p88; cnr Calle 1 & Paseo; ⊙9am-6pm Mon-Sat, to 1pm Sun) Across the street from the Hotel Meliá Cohiba, this place is an upscale

(for Cuba) shopping center with some designer labels and even a car dealership. It sells well-made clothes and other consumer items to tourists and affluent Cubans.

Librería Centenario del Apóstol BOOKS
(Map p88; Calle 25 No 164; ⊙10am-5pm Mon-Sat, 9am-1pm Sun) Great assortment of used books with a José Martí bias in downtown Vedado.

Librería Rayuela BOOKS
(Map p88; cnr Calles 3 & G; ⊙9am-4:30pm Mon-Fri) This small but respected store in the bookish Casa de las Américas building is great for contemporary literature, compact discs and some guidebooks.

La Habana Sí SOUVENIRS
(Map p88; cnr Calles 23 & L; ⊙10am-10pm Mon-Sat, to 7pm Sun) This shop opposite the Hotel Habana Libre has a good selection of CDs, cassettes, books, crafts and postcards.

ℹ Information

EMERGENCY

Asistur (☑7-866-4499, emergency 7-866-8527; www.asistur.cu; Paseo de Martí No 208, Centro Habana; ⊙8:30am-5:30pm Mon-Fri, 8am-2pm Sat) Emergency help for tourists. Someone on staff should speak English; the emergency center here is open 24 hours.
Fire Service (☑105)
Police (☑106)

INTERNET ACCESS

Havana doesn't have any private internet cafes. Your best bet outside the Etecsa Telepuntos is the posher hotels. Most Habaguanex hotels in Habana Vieja have internet terminals and sell scratch cards (CUC$6 per hour) that work throughout the chain. You don't have to be a guest to use them.

You could also try the Hotel Business Centers at **Hotel Habana Libre** (Calle L, btwn Calles 23 & 25, Vedado), **Hotel Inglaterra** (Paseo de Martí No 416, Centro Habana), **Hotel Nacional** (cnr Calles O & 21, Vedado) and **Hotel Iberostar Parque Central** (Neptuno, btwn Agramonte & Paseo de Martí). Costs vary at these places.

Wi-fi is increasing but still very limited and it's never free. You can purchase cards to use in the public areas of the following hotels: Hotel Iberostar Parque Central, Hotel Saratoga, Hotel ROC Presidente, Hotel Meliá Cohiba, Hotel Habana Libre and Hotel Sevilla.
Etecsa Telepunto (Habana 406, cnr Obispo; ⊙9am-7pm) has six terminals in a back room. Cost is CUC$4.50 per hour.

MEDICAL SERVICES

Most of Cuba's specialist hospitals offering services to visitors are based in Havana; see www.cubanacan.cu for details. The Playa and Marianao areas also have international clinics and pharmacies.

There are pharmacies at **Hotel Habana Libre** (☑7-831-9538; Calle L, btwn Calles 23 & 25, Vedado), where products are sold in convertibles,

---

HAVANA SCAMS

Tourist scams are the bane of travelers in many countries, and Cuba is no exception, although places like Havana rate more favorably than plenty of other Latin American cities. Some Cuban con tricks are familiar to anyone who has traveled internationally. Agree on taxi fares before getting in a cab, don't change money on the street, and always check your bill and change in restaurants. Cuba's professional tricksters are called *jineteros* (literally, jockeys). They are particularly proficient in Havana where their favorite pastime is selling knock-off cigars to unsuspecting tourists.

Cuba's dual currency invites scammers. Although the two sets of banknotes look very similar, there are actually 25 *moneda nacional* (MN$; sometimes called Cuban pesos) to every Cuban convertible (CUC$). Familiarize yourself with the banknotes early on (most banks have pictorial charts) and double-check all money transactions to avoid being left seriously out of pocket.

Casas particulares (private homestays) attract *jineteros* who prey on both travelers and casa owners. An increasingly common trick is for a *jinetero* to pose falsely as a reputed casa particular owner who a traveler has booked in advance (often ones listed in this book), and then proceed to lead you to a different house where they will extract CUC$5 to CUC$10 commission (added to your room bill). On some occasions, travelers are not aware they have been led to the wrong home. There have even been reports of people writing bad reviews online.

If you've prebooked a casa, or are using this book to find one, make sure you turn up without a commission-seeking *jinetero*.

and **Hotel Sevilla** (☎ 7-861-5703; cnr Paseo de Martí & Trocadero, Central Habana).

Centro Oftalmológico Camilo Cienfuegos (☎ 7-832-5554; Calle L No 151, cnr Calle 13, Vedado) Head straight here with eye problems; also has an excellent pharmacy.

Farmacia Taquechel (☎ 7-862-9286; Obispo No 155, Habana Vieja; ☺ 9am-6pm) Next to the Hotel Ambos Mundos. Cuban wonder drugs such as anticholesterol medication PPG sold in pesos here.

Hospital Nacional Hermanos Ameijeiras (☎ 7-877-6053; San Lázaro No 701, Centro Habana) Special hard-currency services, general consultations and hospitalization. Enter via the lower level below the parking lot off Padre Varela (ask for CEDA in Section N).

MONEY

Banco de Crédito y Comercio Vedado (cnr Línea & Paseo, Vedado; ☺ 9am-3pm Mon-Fri); **Vedado** (☎ 7-870-2684; Airline Bldg, Calle 23, Vedado; ☺ 9am-3pm Mon-Fri) Expect lines.

Banco Financiero Internacional Habana Vieja (☎ 7-860-9369; cnr Oficios & Brasil, Habana Vieja; ☺ 9am-3pm Mon-Fri); **Vedado** (Hotel Habana Libre, Calle L, btwn Calles 23 & 25, Vedado; ☺ 9am-3pm Mon-Fri)

Banco Metropolitano Centro Habana (☎ 7-862-6523; Av de Italia No 452, cnr San Martín; ☺ 9am-3pm Mon-Fri); **Vedado** (☎ 7-832-2006; cnr Línea & Calle M, Vedado; ☺ 9am-3pm Mon-Fri)

Cadeca Centro Habana (cnr Neptuno & Agramonte, Centro Habana; ☺ 8am-12:30pm, 1-3pm, 4-6:30pm & 7-10pm); **Habana Vieja** (cnr Oficios & Lamparilla, Habana Vieja; ☺ 8am-7pm Mon-Sat, to 1pm Sun); **Vedado** (Calle 23, btwn Calles K & L, Vedado; ☺ 7am-2:30pm & 3:30-10pm); **Vedado** (Mercado Agropecuario, Calle 19, btwn Calles A & B, Vedado; ☺ 7am-6pm Mon-Sat, 8am-1pm Sun); **Vedado** (Hotel Meliá Cohiba, Paseo, btwn Calles 1 & 3; ☺ 8am-8pm) Cadecas are best for speedy service and more flexible hours.

Cambio (Obispo No 257, Habana Vieja; ☺ 8am-10pm) The best opening hours in town and has ATMs.

POST

For important mail, you're better off using DHL, which can be found at two locations in **Vedado** (☎ 7-832-2112; Calzada No 818, btwn Calles 2 & 4, Vedado; ☺ 8am-5pm Mon-Fri) and **Vedado.** (☎ 7-836-3564; Hotel Nacional, cnr Calles O & 21, Vedado)

Post offices include those in **Centro Habana** (Map p80; Gran Teatro, cnr San Martín & Paseo de Martí); **Habana Vieja** (Map p66; Plaza de San Francisco de Asís, Oficios No 102); **Habana Vieja** (Map p66; Obispo No 518, Unidad de Filatelía; ☺ 9am-7pm); **Vedado** (Map p88; cnr Línea & Paseo; ☺ 8am-8pm Mon-Sat); **Vedado** (Map p88; cnr Calles 23 & C; ☺ 8am-6pm Mon-Fri, to noon Sat); **Vedado** (Map p88; Av de la Independencia, btwn Plaza de la Revolución & Terminal de Ómnibus; ☺ stamp sales 24hr). The Independencia branch one has many services, including photo developing, a bank and a Cadeca. The **Museo Postal Cubano** (☎ 7-870-5581; admission CUC$1; ☺ 10am-5pm Sat & Sun) here has a philatelic shop. The post office at Obispo, Habana Vieja, also has stamps for collectors.

TELEPHONE

National phone company Etecsa runs two telepuntos (internet-cafes-cum-call-centers) in Habana: **Centro Habana** (Aguilar No 565; ☺ 8am-9:30pm) and one in **Habana Vieja** (Habana 406; ☺ 8:30am-7pm). Buy a one-hour user card (CUC$4.50) with a scratch-off user code and *contraseña* (password), and help yourself to a free computer. The Centro Habana center has a **Museo de las Telecomunicaciones** (☺ 9am-6pm Tue-Sat) if you get bored waiting.

TOURIST INFORMATION

State-run Infotur is based at the **airport** (☎ 7-642-6101; Terminal 3 Aeropuerto Internacional José Martí; ☺ 24hr) and has two branches in Habana Vieja. It books tours and sells maps and phone cards.

Infotur (☎ 7-863-6884; cnr Obispo & San Ignacio, Habana Vieja; ☺ 9:30am-noon & 12:30-5pm).

Infotur (Map p66; ☎ 7-866-4153; Obispo No 524, btwn Bernaza & Villegas, Habana Vieja)

TRAVEL AGENCIES

Many of the following agencies also have offices at the airport, in the international arrivals lounge of Terminal 3.

Cubamar Viajes (☎ 7-833-2523, 7-833-2524; www.cubamarviajes.cu; Calle 3, btwn Calle 12 & Malecón, Vedado; ☺ 8:30am-5pm Mon-Sat) Travel agency for Campismo Popular cabins countrywide.

Cubanacán (☎ 7-873-2686; www.cubanacan.cu; Hotel Nacional, cnr Calles O & 21, Vedado; ☺ 8am-7pm) Very helpful; head here if you want to arrange fishing or diving at Marina Hemingway; also in Hotel Iberostar Parque Central, Hotel Inglaterra and Hotel Habana Libre.

Cubatur (☎ 7-835-4155; cnr Calles 23 & M, Vedado; ☺ 8am-8pm) Below Hotel Habana Libre. This agency pulls a lot of weight and finds rooms where others can't, which goes a long way toward explaining its slacker attitude. It has desks in most of the main hotels.

Ecotur (☎ 7-649-1055; www.ecoturcuba.co.cu; Av Independencia No 116, cnr Santa Catalina, Cerro) Sells all kinds of naturalistic excursions.

San Cristóbal Agencia de Viajes (☎7-861-9171, 7-861-9172; www.viajessancristobal.cu; Oficios No 110, btwn Lamparilla & Amargura, Habana Vieja; ⊙8:30am-5:30pm Mon-Fri, to 12:30pm Sat) Habaguanex agency operating Habana Vieja's classic hotels; income helps finance restoration. It offers the best tours in Havana.

❶ Getting There & Away

AIR

Aeropuerto Internacional José Martí is at Rancho Boyeros, 25km southwest of Havana via Av de la Independencia. There are four terminals here. Terminal 1, on the southeastern side of the runway, handles only domestic Cubana flights. Three kilometers away, via Av de la Independencia, is Terminal 2, which receives flights and charters from Miami and New York and to and from the Cayman Islands. All other international flights use Terminal 3, a well-ordered, modern facility at Wajay, 2.5km west of Terminal 2. Charter flights on Aerocaribbean, Aerogaviota, Aerotaxi etc to Cayo Largo del Sur and elsewhere use the Caribbean Terminal (also known as Terminal 5) at the northwestern end of the runway, 2.5km west of Terminal 3 (Terminal 4 hasn't been built yet). Check carefully which terminal you'll be using.

Cubana Airlines (p166) has its head office at the Malecón end of the Airline Building on Calle 23. You can buy international or domestic tickets here. Beware, it's often packed.

Aerocaribbean (☎7-832-7584; Airline Bldg, Calle 23 No 64, cnr Calzada de la Infanta, Vedado) is another airline with domestic services.

BOAT

Buses connecting with the hydrofoil service to Isla de la Juventud leave at 9am from the **Terminal de Ómnibus** (Map p88; ☎7-878-1841; cnr Av de la Independencia & 19 de Mayo, Vedado), near the Plaza de la Revolución, but they're often late. You'll be told to arrive at least an hour before the bus to buy your ticket, and it's best to heed this advice. Bus/boat combo tickets are sold at the kiosk marked 'NCC' between gates 9 and 10. Tickets cost CUC$50 for the boat and CUC$5 for the bus. Bring your passport.

BUS

Víazul (☎7-881-5652, 7-881-1413; www.viazul. com; cnr Calle 26 & Zoológico, Nuevo Vedado) covers most destinations of interest to travelers, in safe, air-conditioned coaches. All buses are direct except those to Guantánamo and Baracoa; for these destinations you must change in Santiago de Cuba. You board all Víazul buses at the inconveniently located terminal 3km southwest of Plaza de la Revolución. This is where you'll also have to come to buy tickets from the **Venta de Boletines** (⊙7am-9:30pm) office,

preferably a day or two in advance. You can get full schedules on the website or at Infotur. Some casa particular owners may offer help with pre-arranging bus tickets.

Havana-bound, you *might* be able to get off the Víazul bus from Varadero/Matanzas in Centro Habana right after the tunnel (check with the driver beforehand), but if you arrive from most other points you'll be let out at the Nuevo Vedado terminal. Buses from the Nuevo Vedado terminal to the city are unreliable unless you want to do a bit of walking. Taxis will charge around CUC$10 for the ride to central Havana.

A newer alternative to the increasingly crowded Víazul buses is Conectando run by Cubanacán, which offers six itineraries linking Havana with Viñales, Trinidad, Varadero and Santiago de Cuba. The smaller buses, which run daily, pick up from various hotels and charge similar prices to Víazul. Tickets can be reserved at Infotur or with any Cubanacán hotel rep.

Buses to points in the Artemisa and Mayabeque provinces leave from Apodaca No 53, off Agramonte, near the main train station in Habana Vieja. They go to Güines, Jaruco, Madruga, Nueva Paz, San José, San Nicolás and Santa Cruz del Norte, but expect large crowds and come early to get a peso ticket.

TAXI

Small Lada taxis, operated by Cubataxi, park on Calle 19 de Mayo beside the Terminal de Ómnibus in Vedado. They charge approximately CUC$0.50 per kilometer. This translates as CUC$70 to Varadero, CUC$80 to Pinar del Río, CUC$140 to Santa Clara, CUC$125 to Cienfuegos and CUC$165 to Trinidad. Up to four people can go for the price. It's worth considering in a pinch and is perfectly legal.

TRAIN

Trains to most parts of Cuba depart from **Estación Central de Ferrocarriles** (Central Train Station; ☎7-861-8540, 7-862-1920; cnr Av de Bélgica & Arsenal, Habana Vieja), on the southwestern side of Habana Vieja. Foreigners must buy tickets in convertibles at **La Coubre station** (☎7-862-1006; cnr Av del Puerto & Desamparados, Habana Vieja; ⊙9am-3pm Mon-Fri). To get to La Coubre from the main station, head down Calle Egido toward the harbor and turn right. The ticket office is located 100m down the road on the right-hand side. If it's closed, try the Lista de Espera office adjacent, which sells tickets for trains leaving immediately. Kids under 12 travel half price.

Cuba's best train, the *Tren Francés* (an old French SNCF train), runs every third day between Havana and Santiago stopping in Santa Clara (CUC$21) and Camagüey (CUC$40). It leaves Havana at 6:27pm and arrives in Santiago the following morning at 9am. There are no

VÍAZUL BUS DEPARTURES FROM HAVANA

Check for the most up-to-date departure times on www.viazul.com.

DESTINATION	COST (CUC$)	DURATION (HR)	DEPARTURE TIMES
Bayamo	44	13	6:30am, 3pm, 10pm
Camagüey	33	9	6:30am, 9:30am, 3pm, 7:45pm, 10pm, 12:30am
Ciego de Ávila	27	7	6:30am, 3pm, 7:45pm, 10pm
Cienfuegos	20	4	7am, 10:45am, 10:55am
Holguín	44	12	9:30am, 3pm, 7:45pm
Las Tunas	39	11½	6:30am, 3pm, 7:45pm, 10pm
Matanzas	7	2	6am, 8am, 1pm, 5:30pm
Pinar del Río	11	3	8:40am, 2pm
Sancti Spíritus	23	5¾	6:30am, 3pm, 7:45pm, 10pm
Santa Clara	18	3¾	6:30am, 3pm, 9:30pm, 10pm
Santiago de Cuba	51	15	6:30am, 3pm, 10pm, 12:30am
Trinidad	25	5-6	7am, 10:45am, 10:55am
Varadero	10	3	6am, 8am, 1pm, 5:30pm
Viñales	12	4	8:40am, 2pm

sleeper cars, but carriages are comfortable and air-conditioned, and there's a snack service. Tickets cost CUC$62 for 1st class and CUC$50 for 2nd class.

Slower *coche motor* (cross-island train) services run to Santiago, stopping in smaller stations such as Matanzas (CUC$4), Sancti Spíritus (CUC$13), Ciego de Ávila (CUC$16), Las Tunas (CUC$23), Bayamo (CUC$26), Manzanillo (CUC$28) and Holguín (CUC$27). One train goes as far as Guantánamo (CUC$32). There are separate branch lines to Cienfuegos (CUC$11) and Pinar del Río (CUC$6.50).

The above information is only a rough approximation; services are routinely delayed or canceled (including the *Tren Francés*, which was temporarily out of service at the time of writing). Always double-check scheduling and which terminal your train will leave from.

ⓘ Getting Around

TO/FROM THE AIRPORT

Public transportation from the airport into central Havana is practically nonexistent. A standard taxi will cost you approximately CUC$20 to CUC$25 (40 minutes). You can change money at the bank in the arrivals hall.

True adventurers with light luggage and a tight budget can chance their arm on the P-12 metro bus from the Capitolio or the P-15 from the Hospital Hermanos Ameijeiras on the Malecón, both of which go to Santiago de las Vegas, stopping close to the airport (about 1.5km away) on Av Boyeros. This is a lot easier for departing travelers, who will have better knowledge of local geography.

BICI-TAXI

Two-seater bici-taxis will take you anywhere around Centro Habana for CUC$1/2 for a short/long trip, after bargaining. It's a lot more than a Cuban would pay, but cheaper and more fun than a tourist taxi.

BOAT

Passenger **ferries** (☎ 7-867-3726) shuttle across the harbor to Regla and Casablanca, leaving every 10 or 15 minutes from Muelle Luz, at the corner of San Pedro and Santa Clara, on the southeast side of Habana Vieja. The fare is a flat 10 centavos, but foreigners are often charged CUC$1. Since the ferries were hijacked to Florida in 1994 and again in 2003 (the hijackers never made it outside Cuban waters), security has been tightened. Expect bag searches and airport-style screening.

CAR

There are lots of car-rental offices in Havana, so if you're told there are no cars or there isn't one in your price range, just try another office or agency. All agencies have offices at Terminal 3 at Aeropuerto Internacional José Martí. Otherwise, there's a car-rental desk in any three-star (or higher) hotel. Prices for equivalent models are nearly always the same between the companies; it's called *socialismo*.

Cubacar (☑ 7-835-0000) has desks at most of the big hotels, including Meliá Cohiba, Meliá Habana, Iberostar Parque Central, Habana Libre and Sevilla.

Rex Rent a Car (☑ 7-836-7788; www.rex.cu; cnr Línea & Malecón, Vedado) rents fancy cars for extortionate prices.

Servi-Cupet gas stations are in Vedado at Calles L and 17; Malecón and Calle 15; Malecón and Paseo, near the Riviera and Meliá Cohiba Hotels; and on Av de la Independencia (northbound lane) south of Plaza de la Revolución. All are open 24 hours a day.

Guarded parking is available for approximately CUC$1 all over Havana, including in front of the Hotel Sevilla, Hotel Inglaterra and Hotel Nacional.

PUBLIC TRANSPORTATION

The handy hop-on/hop-off **Havana Bus Tour** (Map p80) runs on two routes, numbers T1 and T3 (route T2 had been suspended at the time of research). The main stop is in Parque Central opposite the Hotel Inglaterra. This is the pickup point for bus T1, which runs from Habana Vieja via Centro Habana, the Malecón, Calle 23 and Plaza de la Revolución to La Cecilia at the west end of Playa; and bus T3, which runs from Centro Habana to Playas del Este (via Parque Histórico Militar Morro-Cabaña). Bus T1 is an open-top double-decker. Bus T3 is an enclosed single-decker. All-day tickets are CUC$5. Services run from 9am to 9pm and routes and stops are clearly marked on all bus stops. Beware: these bus routes and times have been known to change. Check latest route maps at the bus stop in Parque Central.

Havana's metro bus service calls on a relatively modern fleet of Chinese-made 'bendy' buses and is far less dilapidated than it used to be. These buses run regularly along 17 different routes, connecting most parts of the city with the suburbs. Fares are 40 centavos (five centavos if you're using convertibles), which you deposit into a small slot in front of the driver when you enter.

Cuban buses are crowded and little used by tourists. Beware of pickpockets and guard your valuables closely.

All bus routes have the prefix P before their number:

P-1 La Rosita – Playa (via Virgen del Camino, Vedado, Línea, Av 3)

P-2 Alberro – Línea y G (via Vibora and Ciudad Deportiva)

P-3 Alamar – Túnel de Línea (via Virgen del Camino and Vibora)

P-4 San Agustín – Terminal de Trenes (via Playa, Calle 23, La Rampa)

P-5 San Agustín – Terminal de Trenes (via Lisa, Av 31, Línea, Av de Puerto)

P-6 Reparto Eléctrico – La Rampa (via Vibora)

P-7 Alberro – Capitolio (via Virgen del Camino)

P-8 Reparto Eléctrico – Villa Panamericano (via Vibora, Capitolio and harbor tunnel)

P-9 Vibora – Hospital Militar (via Cuatro Caminos, La Rampa, Calle 23, Av 41)

P-10 Vibora – Playa (via Altahabana and Calle 100)

P-11 Alamar – Vedado (via harbor tunnel)

P-12 Santiago de las Vegas – Capitolio (via Av Boyeros)

P-13 Santiago de las Vegas – Vibora (via Calabazar)

P-14 San Agustín – Capitolio (via Lisa and Av 51)

P-15 Alamar/Guanabacoa – Capitolio (via Av Boyeros and Calle G)

P-16 Santiago de las Vegas – Vedado (via Calle 100 and Lisa)

PC – Hospital Naval – Playa (via Parque Lenin)

Infotur offices now publish a free map of Havana metro bus routes entitled *Por La Habana en P*.

TAXI

Metered tourist taxis are readily available at all of the upscale hotels, with the air-conditioned Nissan taxis charging higher tariffs than the non-air-con Ladas. The cheapest official taxis are operated by **Panataxi** (☑ 7-55-55-55), with a CUC$1 starting fare, then CUC$0.50 per kilometer. Tourist taxis, under the umbrella name 'Cubataxi' charge CUC$1 per kilometer and can be found waiting outside all the major hotels. Drivers are government employees who work for a peso salary. They'll usually find you before you find them.

Since 2011, legal private taxis have become more common, though they're often older yellow-and-black Ladas. You've got more chance haggling here, but agree on the fare before getting into the car. If you're non-Cuban, you'll be expected to pay in convertibles.

There are usually classic-car taxis parked around Parque Central.

WALKING

Yes, walking! It's what the gas-starved *habaneros* have been doing for decades. Most parts of Habana Vieja, Centro Habana and Vedado can be easily navigated on foot if you're energetic and up for some exercise. You'll see a lot more of the local street life in the process.

OUTER HAVANA

Splaying out on three sides from the downtown district, Havana's suburbs are full of quirky and easy-to-reach sights and activities that can make interesting trips from the city center. Playa boasts a decent aquarium, top-class conference facilities and Cuba's best restaurants; Guanabacoa and Regla are famous for their Afro-Cuban religious culture.

Playa & Marianao

The municipality of Playa, west of Vedado across the Río Almendares, is a paradoxical mix of prestigious residential streets and tough proletarian housing schemes.

Gracious Miramar is a leafy neighborhood of broad avenues and weeping laurel trees, where the traffic moves more sedately and diplomats' wives – clad in sun visors and Lycra leggings – go for gentle afternoon jogs along Av Quinta (Fifth Ave). Many of Havana's foreign embassies are housed here in old pre-Revolution mansions, and business travelers and conference attendees flock in from around the globe to make use of some of Cuba's grandest and most luxurious facilities. If you're interested primarily in sightseeing and entertainment, commuting to Vedado or Habana Vieja is a nuisance and an expense. However, some of the best salsa clubs, discos and restaurants are out this way and the casas particulares are positively luxurious.

Despite the austerity of the *período especial* (Special Period), vast resources have been plowed into biotechnological and pharmaceutical research institutes in this area. Yachties, anglers and scuba divers will find themselves using the Marina Hemingway at Playa's west end.

Marianao is world-famous for the Tropicana Nightclub, but locally it's known as a tough, in parts rough, neighborhood with a powerful Santería community and a long history of social commitment.

⊙ Sights

⊙ Miramar

★**Fundación Naturaleza y El Hombre** MUSEUM
(🕾7-204-0438; www.fanj.org; Av 5B No 6611, btwn Calles 66 & 70; admission CUC$2; ⊙8:30am-3pm Mon-Fri) This fascinating museum displays artifacts from the 17,422km canoe trip from the Amazon source to the sea, led by Cuban intellectual and anthropologist Antonio Núñez Jiménez in 1987. Other exhibits in an astounding collection include one of Cuba's largest photography collections, books written by the prolific Núñez Jiménez, and the famous Fidel portrait by Guayasamín.

'The glass house' displays glass cases containing all kinds of intriguing ephemera from the founder's life. The museum is a foundation and one of Havana's most rewarding.

La Maqueta de la Capital MUSEUM
(Calle 28 No 113, btwn Avs 1 & 3; admission CUC$3; ⊙8am-4:30pm Mon-Fri) Havana itself is somewhat dilapidated in parts and so, ironically, is this huge 1:1000 scale model of the city that looks like it could do with a good dusting. The model was originally created for urban-planning purposes, but is now a tourist attraction.

Nearby, the two **parks** on Av 5, between Calles 24 and 26, with their immense banyan trees and dark lanes, are an atmospheric pocket.

Acuario Nacional AQUARIUM
(cnr Av 3 & Calle 62; adult/child CUC$10/7; ⊙10am-6pm Tue-Sun) Founded in 1960, the national aquarium is a Havana institution that gets legions of annual visitors, particularly since its 2002 revamp. Despite its rather scruffy appearance, this place leaves most other Cuban *acuarios* (aquatic centers) in the shade (which isn't saying much), though Miami it certainly isn't. Saltwater fish are the specialty, but there are also sea lions and dolphins.

Dolphin performances are almost hourly from 11am, with the final show at 9pm; admission price includes the show. However, these performances have received criticism by animal welfare groups who claim the captivity of marine life is debilitating and stressful for the animals, and that this is exacerbated by human interaction.

Russian Embassy LANDMARK
(Av 5 No 6402, btwn Calles 62 & 66) In case you were wondering, that huge Stalinist obelisk that dominates the skyline halfway down Av Quinta is the Russian (formerly Soviet) embassy, testament to the days when Castro was best mates with Brezhnev et al.

Iglesia Jesús de Miramar CHURCH
(cnr Av 5 & Calle 82) Despite its modernity, Playa cradles Cuba's second-largest church. The Jesús is an aesthetically pleasing

neo-Romanesque structure topped by a giant dome. Built in 1948, it protects Cuba's largest pipe-organ and unusual murals depicting the Stations of the Cross.

Parque Almendares　　　　　PARK
Running along the banks of the city's Río Almendares, below the bridge on Calle 23, is this welcome oasis of greenery and fresh air in the heart of chaotic Havana. The park has been undergoing a slow restoration (and cleaning up) since the mid-1990s; benches now line the river promenade and plants grow profusely, though the river water is far from crystal clear.

The park has a stash of so-so facilities, including an antiquated **miniature golf course**, the **Anfiteatro Parque Almendares** (a small outdoor performance space), a playground and a **dinosaur park** containing stone reproductions of the monstrous reptiles. There are several OK places to eat.

◉ Marianao

Museo de la Alfabetización　　MUSEUM
(cnr Av 29E & Calle 76; ☺ 8am-noon & 1-4:30pm Mon-Fri, 8am-noon Sat) **FREE** The former Cuartel Colombia military airfield at Marianao is now a school complex called **Ciudad Libertad**. Pass through the gate to visit this inspiring museum, which describes the 1961 literacy campaign, when 100,000 youths aged 12 to 18 spread out across Cuba to teach reading and writing to farmers, workers and the aged.

In the center of the traffic circle, opposite the entrance to the complex, is a tower in the form of a syringe in memory of Carlos Juan Finlay, who discovered the cause of yellow fever in 1881.

◉ Cubanacán

Palacio de las Convenciones　NOTABLE BUILDING
(Calle 146, btwn Avs 11 & 13) Also known as the Havana Convention Center, this is one of Cuba's most dramatic modern buildings. Built for the Nonaligned Conference in 1979, the four interconnecting halls contain a state-of-the-art auditorium with 2101 seats and 11 smaller halls. The 589-member National Assembly meets here twice a year, and the complex hosts more than 50,000 conference attendees annually.

Not far from here is **Pabexpo** (cnr Av 17 & Calle 180), 20,000 sq meters of exhibition space in four interconnecting pavilions that hosts about 15 trade shows a year.

Isla del Coco　　　AMUSEMENT PARK
(cnr Av 5 & Calle 112, Playa; admission CUC$2; ☺ noon-8pm Fri-Sun) A huge Chinese-built amusement park in Playa with big wheels, bumper cars, roller coasters, the works.

◉ Marina Hemingway

Marina Hemingway　　　　MARINA
(cnr Av 5 & Calle 248) Havana's premier marina was constructed in 1953 in the small coastal community of Santa Fe. After the Revolution it was nationalized and named after Castro's favorite *Yanqui*. The marina has four 800m-long channels, a dive center, motley shops and restaurants, and two hotels (one currently disused), so is only worth visiting if you're docking your boat or utilizing the water sports facilities.

Like much of Cuba's infrastructure, the place retains a strangely abandoned air and is crying out for a renovation.

🏃 Activities

Marlin Náutica　　　　WATER SPORTS
(www.nauticamarlin.com; cnr Av 5 & Calle 248, Marina Hemingway, Barlovento) There are many water activities available at Marina Hemingway in Barlovento, 20km west of central Havana. Marlin Náutica runs fishing trips for four anglers and four hours of bottom fishing/deep-sea fishing for CUC$150/CUC$280, including an open bar and tackle; Marlin season is June to October. Scuba packages (CUC$35 per dive) and catamaran tours of Havana's littoral (CUC$60) are also available.

La Aguja Marlin Diving Center　　DIVING
(☏ 7-204-5088; cnr Av 5 & Calle 248, Marina Hemingway, Barlovento) Between Marlin Náutica and the shopping center at Marina Hemingway, this center offers scuba diving for CUC$30 per dive, plus CUC$5 for gear. It has one morning and one afternoon departure. A diving excursion to Varadero or Playa Girón can also be arranged. Reader reviews have been favorable.

🛏 Sleeping

Playa's hotels are the preserve of diplomats, the convention crowd and people whose flights have been bumped. There are a couple of good 'uns amongst the dross, but the general location is detached from Havana's main sights and you'll need taxis or strong legs to get around.

Playa & Marianao

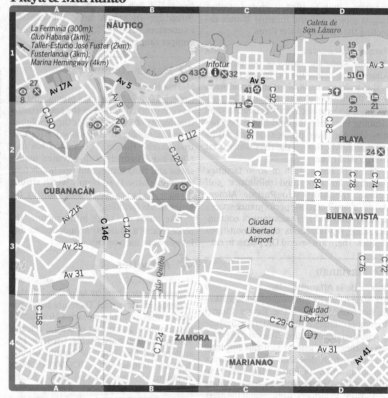

La Ferminia (300m);
Club Habana (1km);
Taller-Estudio José Fuster (2km);
Fusterlandia (3km);
Marina Hemingway (4km)

NÁUTICO

Caleta de
San Lázaro

Infotur

Av 5

PLAYA

CUBANACÁN

Ciudad
Libertad
Airport

BUENA VISTA

Río Quibú

Ciudad
Libertad

ZAMORA

MARIANAO

🛏 Miramar & Around

Casa Guevara Alba   CASA PARTICULAR $
(📞7-202-6515; Av 5F No 9611, btwn Calles 96 & 98;
r/apt CUC$25/35; P❄) A welcome homestay
in Playa's main hotel zone that outsmarts
most of the hotels when it comes to price,
service and comfort. On offer are an apartment and a separate room upstairs. It's modern for Cuba, but still has plenty of character.

Complejo Cultural La Vitrola   HOTEL $
(📞7-202-7922; Calle 18 No 103, btwn Avs 1 & 3; r
CUC$30; ❄) Imagine staying at London's Ab-
bey Road recording studios. Well, this is the
Cuban equivalent. The Egrem studios – working space for Cuba's top musical artists – now
has a lovely on-site hotel whose five rooms
have bright interiors with song lyrics painted
on the walls. Hang around in the downstairs
Bar Bilongo and you might even bump into
Silvio Rodríguez.

Hotel el Bosque   HOTEL $
(📞7-204-9232; www.hotelelbosquehabana.com;
Calle 28A, btwn Calles 49A & 49C, Kohly; s/d
CUC$36/48; ❄@) Economical and often
underrated, El Bosque is the better and less
costly arm of the Gaviota-run Kohly-Bosque
complejo (complex). Clean and friendly, the
hotel lies on the banks of the Río Almendares surrounded by the Bosque de La Habana – the city's green lungs – and is a quiet
choice in this neck of the woods.

Memories Montehabana   HOTEL $$
(📞7-206-9595; Calle 70, btwn Avs 5A & 7, Playa;
s/d/tr CUC$75/85/120; P❄@🛜🏊) This Gavi-
ota giant opened in 2005 with the promise
of something a little different. Of the rooms
here, 101 are apartments with living rooms
and fully equipped kitchens – a great oppor-
tunity to hit the Havana markets and find
out how Cubans cook. In the kitchens there
are microwaves, refrigerators, toasters and
coffee machines – even your own cutlery.

If you're not up to cooking, the restaurant does a CUC$10 breakfast and a CUC$15 dinner buffet. Elsewhere the facilities are comprehensive but, after a decade in operation, need an upgrade. Guests share the gym, pool and tennis courts with the Memories Miramar next door.

Hotel Kohly HOTEL $$
(☎ 7-204-0240; cnr Calles 49A & 36, Kohly; s/d CUC$47/63; P ✿ @ ☎) The Kohly makes up for its utilitarian exterior with a few handy extras including a swimming pool, bowling alley and gym.

Hotel Copacabana HOTEL $$
(☎ 7-204-1037; Av 1, btwn Calles 44 & 46; s/d CUC$72/104; P ✿ @ ☎) Slightly better than some of its tired competitors thanks to a 2010 refurbishment, though there's still an inherent dankness about the Copacabana, despite its fine ocean-side location.

Boutique Chateau Miramar HOTEL $$
(☎ 7-204-0224; Av 1, btwn Calles 60 & 70, Playa; s/d CUC$67/84; P ✿ @ ☎) It's marketed as a 'boutique hotel,' but seriously – this *château* ain't no Loire Valley retreat. Still, techno addicts will appreciate the free internet, flat-screen TV and direct international phone service that come with the otherwise mediocre rooms.

★**Hotel Meliá Habana** HOTEL $$$
(☎ 7-204-8500; www.meliacuba.com; Av 3, btwn Calles 76 & 80; s/d CUC$215/260; P ✿ @ 🛜 ☎) Ugly outside but beautiful within, Miramar's gorgeous Hotel Meliá Habana is one of the city's best-run and best-equipped accommodation options. The 409 rooms (four of which are wheelchair-accessible) are positioned around a salubrious lobby with abundant hanging vines, marble statues and gushing water features. Outside, Cuba's

Playa & Marianao

◎ Top Sights
1 Fundación Naturaleza y El Hombre E2

◎ Sights
2 Acuario Nacional.................................. E1
3 Iglesia Jesús de Miramar D1
4 Instituto Superior de Arte...................B2
5 Isla del Coco B1
6 La Maqueta de la Capital G1
7 Museo de la Alfabetización..................D4
8 Pabexpo A1
9 Palacio de las Convenciones.............. A2
10 Parque Almendares.............................G3
11 Russian Embassy.................................E1

⑤ Sleeping
12 Boutique Chateau Miramar.................. E1
13 Casa Guevara Alba C2
14 Complejo Cultural La Vitrola................G1
15 H10 Habana Panorama E1
16 Hotel Copacabana............................... E1
17 Hotel el Bosque...................................G3
18 Hotel Kohly..G3
19 Hotel Meliá Habana D1
20 Hotel Palco... B2
21 Memories Miramar...............................D1
22 Memories Montehabana.......................E2
23 Quinta Avenida Habana D1

⊗ Eating
24 Bom Apetite... D2
Casa Española............................(see 25)
Doctor Café ....(see 6)
25 Dos Gardenias......................................F2
26 El Aljibe...G2

27 El Palenque.. A1
28 El Tocororo...G1
29 Espacios G2
30 La Carboncita.......................................F1
31 La Casa del Habano G2
32 La Cecilia C1
33 La Cocina de Lilliam.............................E2
34 La Esperanza G1
35 La Fontana..E1
Le Garage ....(see 2)
36 Paladar Vista Mar................................G1
37 Pan.com..F2
38 Supermercado 70 ....E1
39 Tabarish..G2

◎ Drinking & Nightlife
40 Café Fortuna F1

◎ Entertainment
41 Café Jazz Miramar C1
42 Casa de la Música.................................G2
43 Circo Trompoloco C1
44 Don Cangrejo G1
45 Estadio Pedro Marrero F3
46 Salón Rosado Benny Moré....................F3
47 Teatro Karl Marx..................................H1
48 Tropicana Nightclub E4

◎ Shopping
Casa de la Música........................(see 42)
Egrem Tienda de Música................(see 14)
La Casa del Habano ....(see 31)
49 La Maison G2
50 La Puntilla..H1
51 Miramar Trade Center..........................D1

largest and most beautiful swimming pool stands next to a desolate, rocky shore.

Throw in polite service, an excellent buffet restaurant and the occasional room discount, and you could be swayed.

Quinta Avenida Habana   HOTEL $$$
(☎ 7-214-1470; www.hotelquintaavenidahabana.com; Av 5, btwn Calles 76 & 80; s/d CUC$110/130; ▣✳@☎☀) One of Playa's newer hotels, Quinta Avenida completes a trio of plush accommodations behind the Miramar Trade Center. While the facilities claim a high star-rating with expansive rooms (all with separate showers and bathtubs) and a good on-site restaurant, the place suffers from the usual foibles of humongous chain-run establishments: a cold, generic feel and a weirdly un-Cuban lack of personality.

H10 Habana Panorama   HOTEL $$$
(☎ 7-204-0100; www.h10hotels.com/en/havana-hotels/h10-habana-panorama; cnr Av 3 & Calle 70; s/d CUC$100/135; ▣✳@☀) This flashy 'glass cathedral' on Playa's rapidly developing hotel strip opened in 2003. The rather strange aesthetics – acres of blue-tinted glass – improve once you step inside the monumental lobby where space-age elevators whisk you promptly up to one of 317 airy rooms, offering great views over Miramar and beyond.

Extra facilities include a business center, a photo shop, numerous restaurants and a spacious and shapely swimming pool. But the Panorama is almost too big: its scale makes you feel small and gives the place a rather deserted and antiseptic feel.

Memories Miramar   HOTEL $$$
(☎ 7-204-3583, 7-204-3584; www.memoriesresorts.com; cnr Av 5 & Calle 74; s/d CUC$100/130; ▣✳☎☀) Now onto its third name change, the facilities in this 427-room giant built in 2000 haven't kept abreast with its re-branding. The staff are friendly and the business

facilities serviceable, but the nitty-gritty (ie the rooms) need some care and attention.

There are plenty of sporty extras if the isolated location starts to grate, including tennis courts, swimming pool, sauna, gym and games room.

Marina Hemingway

Hotel Club Acuario HOTEL $$
(☑7-204-6336; cnr Aviota & Calle 248; s/d CUC$79/108; P❄) Don't come to Marina Hemingway for the hotels. With El Viejo y el Mar perennially on hiatus, the only real option is the strung-out Acuario, Havana's only all-inclusive (outside Playas del Este), splayed between two harbor channels and infested with cheap out-of-date furnishings. If you're booked for an early morning dive, it might just qualify; otherwise stay in Havana and commute.

✗ Eating

Playa has been a bastion of some of Cuba's best private restaurants since the 1990s and many of the old stalwarts continue to impress despite an abundance of new competition. There are also some surprisingly good state-run restaurants. It's worth the CUC$5 to CUC$10 taxi fare from the city center to eat out here.

✗ Miramar

Le Garage FAST FOOD $
(cnr Av 3 & Calle 60; snacks CUC$2-4; ⊙noon-2am, till 6am Fri-Sun) Not actually a garage but a small private fast-food joint with some indoor booths and an outdoor patio where you can stop for milkshakes, burgers and onion rings – all rare pickings in Cuba until recently. Note the generous opening hours.

Pan.com FAST FOOD $
(☑7-204-4232; cnr Av 7 & Calle 26; snacks CUC$1-4; ⊙10am-2am) Not an internet cafe but a haven of Havana comfort food with hearty sandwiches, fantastic burgers and ice-cream milkshakes to die for. Join the diplomats under the airy front canopy.

★Espacios TAPAS, INTERNATIONAL $$
(☑7-202-2921; Calle 10 No 513, btwn Avs 5 & 7; tapas CUC$3-6; ⊙noon-6am) Hipsters don't really populate Havana as yet, but if they did they'd probably seek solace in Espacios, a fabulously chilled and arty tapas bar and restaurant that occupies an unsignposted house in Miramar.

Select from an internationally inpired menu while mingling with Havana's brainy and beautiful, split between a mix of in-the-know expats and Cubans with artistic sensibilities.

Spread around several interior rooms and a back patio, the interior is as beautiful as the clientele with fabulous wall art.

El Aljibe CARIBBEAN $$
(☑7-204-1584, 7-204-1583; Av 7, btwn Calles 24 & 26; meals CUC$12; ⊙noon-midnight) On paper a humble Palmares restaurant, but in reality a rip-roaring culinary extravaganza, El Aljibe has been delighting both Cuban and foreign diplomats' taste buds for years. The furore surrounds the gastronomic mysteries of just one dish: the obligatory *pollo asado* (roast chicken), which is served up with as-much-as-you-can-eat helpings of white rice, black beans, fried plantain, French fries and salad.

The accompanying bitter orange sauce is said to be a state secret.

La Carboncita ITALIAN $$
(Av 3 No 3804, btwn Calles 38 & 40; pasta & pizza CUC$7-8; ⊙noon-midnight) The food appears mysteriously from the garage of this Miramar house-turned-Italian-restaurant with both indoor and outdoor front porch seating, but there's nothing mechanical about the flavors. On the contrary, the pasta is homemade by the Italian owner and you can

CLUB HABANA

The fabulously eclectic **Club Habana** (☑7-204-5700; Av 5, btwn Calles 188 & 192; day pass CUC$20) in Flores once housed the Havana Biltmore Yacht & Country Club. These days the history of the 1928 mansion seems to have swung full circle and it is again a popular hangout for foreign correspondents and diplomats. The club has its own beach, swimming pool, tennis courts, bar, boutiques and health club. Annual membership is CUC$1500, but should you wish to hobnob spontaneously with the high and mighty, you can get a daily pass for CUC$20.

In the 1950s the establishment gained brief notoriety when it famously denied entry to Cuban president Fulgencio Batista on the grounds that he was 'black.' Castro had better luck when he dropped by for dinner some 30 years later and the club remains one of the few places where he dined in public.

FUSTERLANDIA

Where does art go after Gaudí and Picasso? For a hint, head west from central Havana through Miramar and Playa to the seemingly low-key district of Jaimanitas where Cuban artist José Fuster (b 1946) has turned his home neighborhood into a masterpiece of tiles, turrets and extraordinary Barcelona-worthy beauty.

The result is what is unofficially known as Fusterlandia, an ongoing project first hatched 20 years ago that has covered several suburban blocks with whimsical but highly stylized public art. The centerpiece is Fuster's own studio, a sizeable residence decorated from roof to foundations by art, sculpture and – above all – mosaic tiles of every color and description. The overall impression defies written description (just go!); it's a fantastical mishmash of spiraling walkways, rippling pools and sunburst fountains that make Gaudí's Park Güell look positively staid. The work mixes homages to Picasso and Gaudí with snippets of Gauguin and Wilfredo Lam, elements of magic realism, strong maritime influences, a cap doffed to Santería, the curvaceous lines of *modernisme*, plus a large dose of Fuster's own Cuban-ness, which runs through almost everything (look for the Cuban flags, a mural of the *Granma* yacht, and the words *Viva Cuba* emblazoned across eight chimney pots).

Fusterlandia stretches way beyond Fuster's own residence. Over half the neighborhood has been given similar artistic treatment from street signs to bus stops to the local doctor's house. Wandering around its quiet streets is a surreal and psychedelic experience.

Jaimanitas is located just off Quinta Avenida in the far west of Playa sandwiched between Club Havana and Marina Hemingway. Its nexus is the **Taller-Estudio José Fuster** (Calle 226, cnr Av 3; ☉9am-4pm Wed-Sun) **FREE**, where you can view the artist's paintings and ceramics, and, if you're lucky, see him at work. A taxi here from downtown costs CUC$10 to CUC$12.

choose from a multitude of authentic sauces including pesto. The thin-crust pizzas are good too.

Tabarish   RUSSIAN **$$**
(☑7-202-9188; Calle 20 No 503, btwn Avs 5 & 7; meals CUC$7-12; ☉noon-11pm) From Russia with love comes Tabarish, Havana's first post–Cold War Russian restaurant and an agreeably friendly one at that. You can relive the Castro-Khruschev years (or toast their passing) over borscht, blintze, beef stroganoff and chicken kiev. There's Russian dancing on Sundays.

Paladar Vista Mar   SEAFOOD **$$**
(☑7-203-8328; Av 1, btwn Calles 22 & 24; meals CUC$8-15; ☉noon-midnight) The Paladar Vista Mar in Miramar is in the 2nd-floor family-room-turned-restaurant of a private residence, which faces the sea. The oceanside ambience is embellished by a beautiful swimming pool that spills its water into the ocean. If enjoying delicious seafood dishes overlooking crashing waves sounds enticing, this could be your bag.

Bom Apetite   INTERNATIONAL **$$**
(Calle 11 No 7210, btwn Calles 72 & 74; meals CUC$5-10; ☉noon-midnight) Way out in eastern Playa, Bom Apetite is all about the setting, which is refined and upscale in a quiet private house with its own separate bar. The food mixes Cuban favorites with North American staples such as filet mignon, and throws in some strong Italian inflections with pasta and pizza.

Casa Española   SPANISH **$$**
(☑7-206-9644; cnr Calle 26 & Av 7; meals CUC$7-12; ☉noon-midnight) A medieval parody built in the Batista-era by the silly-rich Gustavo Gutiérrez y Sánchez, this crenellated castle in Miramar has found new life as a Spanish-themed restaurant cashing in on the Don Quixote legend. The ambience is rather fine, if you don't mind suits of armor watching you as you tuck into paella, Spanish omelet or *lanja cerdo al Jerez* (pork fillet).

Dos Gardenias   CARIBBEAN **$$**
(cnr Av 7 & Calle 28; meals CUC$7-10; ☉noon-11pm) You can choose from a grill or a pasta restaurant in this complex, which is famous as a *bolero* hot spot. Stick around to hear the singers belting out ballads later on.

La Casa del Habano   CUBAN $$
(cnr Av 5 & Calle 16; meals CUC$8-15) Most head here for its reputation as Havana's best cigar store, but repeat visitors come back for the food in the adjoining restaurant – classic Cuban with some rather good lobster dishes.

★**La Fontana**   BARBECUE $$$
(✆7-202-8337; www.lafontanahavana.info; Av 3A No 305; meals CUC$12-20; ⊘noon-midnight) Fontana exhibits the barbecue or, more to the point, the full-on charcoal grill. Huge portions of meat and fish are served up in this villa-cum-private restaurant established in 1995, so go easy on the starters, which include lobster seviche, tuna tartar and beef carpaccio with rocket. The delightful decor includes ponds, ferns and fountains.

Favorable reviews in the international press testify to a long-standing legend.

La Esperanza   INTERNATIONAL $$$
(✆7-202-4361; Calle 16 No 105, btwn Avs 1 & 3; meals CUC$8-17; ⊘7-11pm Mon-Sat) The unassuming Esperanza was being gastronomically creative long before the 2011 reforms made life for chefs a lot easier. The interior of this vine-covered house is a riot of quirky antiques, old portraits and refined 1940s furnishings, while the food from the family kitchen includes such exquisite dishes as *pollo luna de miel* (chicken flambéed in rum) and lamb brochette.

La Cocina de Lilliam   FUSION $$$
(✆7-209-6514; www.lacocinadelilliam.com; Calle 48 No 1311, btwn Avs 13 & 15; meals CUC$15-25; ⊘noon-midnight) Slick service, secluded ambience and freshly cooked food to die for: La Cocina de Lilliam has all the ingredients of a prize-winning restaurant. Set in an illustrious villa in Miramar and surrounded by a garden with trickling fountains and lush tropical plants, diners can tuck into such Cuban rarities as salmon soufflé and tuna bruschetta in an atmosphere more European than Caribbean. Not a cheese-and-ham sandwich in sight!

Doctor Café   CUBAN $$$
(✆7-203-4718; Calle 28, btwn Avs 1 & 3; meals CUC$10-18) Exotic dishes such as seviche, red snapper and grilled octopus are served in either a fern-filled patio or cooler indoor dining area; this doctor is obviously getting the treatment spot on. The menu is from all over the globe, and there are numerous rarities you'll find at few other places in Cuba. Bypass the (endangered) turtle, if offered.

El Tocororo   CARIBBEAN $$$
(✆7-202-4530; Calle 18 No 302; meals CUC$12-35; ⊘noon-11:45pm) Once considered (along with El Aljibe) to be one of Havana's finest government-run restaurants, El Tocororo has lost ground to its competitors in recent years and is often criticized for being overpriced. Nonetheless, the candlelit tables and grandiose interior are still worth a visit, while the menu, with such luxuries as lobster's tail and (occasionally) ostrich, still has the ability to surprise.

Supermercado 70   SUPERMARKET
(cnr Av 3 & Calle 70; ⊘9am-6pm Mon-Sat, to 1pm Sun) Still known as the 'Diplomercado' from the days when only diplomats came here, this place is large by Cuban standards and has a decent selection of groceries.

✗ Cubanacán & Around

El Palenque   INTERNATIONAL $
(✆7-208-8167; cnr Av 17A & Calle 190, Siboney; meals CUC$3-10; ⊘10am-10pm) A huge place, next to the Pabexpo exhibition center, that sprawls beneath a series of open-sided thatched *bohíos* (traditional Cuban huts), the Palenque offers an extensive menu at prices cheap enough to attract both Cubans and visitors. The cuisine is Cuban/Italian, with pizzas, steak and fries, and lobster *mariposa*.

La Cecilia   CARIBBEAN $$$
(✆7-204-1562; Av 5 No 11010, btwn Calles 110 & 112; meals CUC$12-20; ⊘noon-midnight) This place presents food good enough to attract the diplomatic crowd (check out the *ropa vieja*), but trumps all-comers with its big-band music, which blasts out on weekend nights inside its large but atmospheric courtyard.

La Ferminia   CARIBBEAN $$$
(✆7-273-6786; Av 5 No 18207, Flores; meals from CUC$15; ⊘noon-midnight) Havana gets swanky at this memorable restaurant set in an elegant converted colonial mansion in the leafy neighborhood of Flores. Dine inside in one of a handful of beautifully furnished rooms, or outside on a glorious garden patio – it doesn't matter. The point is the food. Try the mixed grill, pulled straight from the fire, or lobster tails panfried in breadcrumbs.

There's a strict dress code here: no shorts or sleeveless T-shirts (guys). It's one of the few places where Fidel Castro has dined in public.

✖ Marina Hemingway

Restaurante la Cova
ITALIAN $$
(cnr Av 5 & Calle 248; meals CUC$8; ☺ noon-midnight) Part of the Pizza Nova chain, this place, like much of the marina, has seen better days. OK if you're short on options (which you will be).

Papa's Complejo Turístico
CARIBBEAN, CHINESE $$
(cnr Av 5 & Calle 248; meals CUC$5-10; ☺ noon-3am) There's all sorts of stuff going on here, from beer-swilling boatmen to warbling *American Idol* wannabes hogging the karaoke machine. The eating options are equally varied, with a posh Chinese place (with dress code) and an outdoor *ranchón* (rural restaurant). Good fun if there's enough people.

🍷 Drinking & Entertainment

★ Café Fortuna
CAFE, BAR
(cnr Av 3 & Calle 28, Miramar; ☺ 8am-10pm) Most of Miramar's best social joints are half-hidden, semisecret places like Casa Fortuna, which lies in the bowels of an average state restaurant on Av 3. The interior is like an old curiousity shop filled with antediluvian cameras, accordians, typewriters, half a car and various Chaplin prints but the tapa-like snacks are good and there are 20 different coffees.

Casa de la Música
LIVE MUSIC
(☎ 7-202-6147; Calle 20 No 3308, cnr Av 35, Miramar; admission CUC$5-20; ☺ from 10pm Tue-Sat) Launched with a concert by renowned jazz pianist Chucho Valdés in 1994, this Miramar favorite is run by national Cuban recording company Egrem, and the programs are generally a lot more authentic than the cabaret entertainment you see at the hotels.

Platinum players such as NG la Banda, Los Van Van and Aldaberto Álvarez y Su Son play here regularly; you'll rarely pay more than CUC$20. It has a more relaxed atmosphere than its Centro Habana namesake.

Café Jazz Miramar
LIVE MUSIC
(Av 5 No 9401, cnr Calle 94, Playa; cover CUC$2) Havana's newest jazz club wouldn't cut ice with bebop-era jazz greats who would smirk at the sanitized airs and no smoking rule, but it doesn't seem to bother today's young innovators. The club is encased in the Cine Teatro Miramar and belongs to government agency ARTex. Things usually get jamming at 10pm-ish and there's cheap food.

Teatro Karl Marx
LIVE MUSIC
(☎ 7-209-1991; cnr Av 1 & Calle 10, Miramar) Sizewise the Karl Marx puts other Havana theaters in the shade with a seating capacity of 5500 in a single auditorium. The very biggest events happen here, such as the closing galas for the jazz and film festivals and rare concerts by *trovadores* like Silvio Rodríguez.

Tropicana Nightclub
CABARET
(☎ 7-267-1871; Calle 72 No 4504, Marianao; tickets from CUC$75; ☺ from 10pm) A city institution since its 1939 opening, the world-famous Tropicana was one of the few bastions of Havana's Las Vegas–style nightlife to survive the Revolution. Immortalized in Graham Greene's 1958 classic *Our Man in Havana*, this open-air cabaret show is little changed since its 1950s heyday, with scantily clad senoritas descending from palm trees to dance Latin salsa amid bright lights.

Don Cangrejo
LIVE MUSIC
(Av 1 No 1606, btwn Calles 16 & 18, Miramar; cover CUC$5; ☺ 11pm-3am) We kid you not. The daytime restaurant of the Cuban fisheries becomes party central particularly on Friday night with alfresco live music (big-name acts) and an atmosphere akin to an undergraduate freshers' ball.

Salón Rosado Benny Moré
LIVE MUSIC
(El Tropical; ☎ 7-206-1281; cnr Av 41 & Calle 46, Kohly; admission 10 pesos-CUC$10; ☺ 9pm-late) For something completely different, experienced travelers, preferably accompanied by Cuban friends, can check out the very *caliente* action at this outdoor venue. The Rosado (aka El Tropical) packs in hot, sexy Cuban youths dancing madly to Pupy y Los que Son Son, Habana Abierta et al. It's a fierce scene and female travelers can expect aggressive come-ons. Friday to Sunday is best.

Some travelers pay pesos, others dollars – more of that Cuban randomness for you.

Circo Trompoloco
CIRCUS
(www.circonacionaldecuba.cu; cnr Av 5 & Calle 112, Playa; admission CUC$5-10; ☺ 7pm Fri, 4pm & 7pm Sat & Sun;) Havana's permanent 'Big Top' with a weekend matinee featuring strongmen, contortionists and acrobats.

🛍 Shopping

La Casa del Habano
CIGARS
(cnr Av 5 & Calle 16, Miramar; ☺ 10am-6pm Mon-Sat, to 1pm Sun) Smokers and souvenir seekers will like La Casa, arguably Havana's top

cigar store. You'll find a comfy smoking lounge and a decent restaurant here as well.

La Maison
CLOTHING

(Calle 16 No 701, Miramar; ⊙9am-5pm) The Cuban fashion fascination is in high gear at this place, with a large boutique selling designer clothing, shoes, handbags, jewelry, cosmetics and souvenirs. It also holds regular fashion shows.

Egrem Tienda de Música
MUSIC

(Calle 18 No 103, Miramar; ⊙9am-6pm Mon-Sat) There's a small CD outlet here hidden in leafy Miramar at the site of Havana's most celebrated recording studios.

Casa de la Música
MUSIC

(Calle 20 No 3308, cnr Av 35, Miramar; ⊙10am-10pm) A small musical outlet graces Miramar's famous music venue.

Miramar Trade Center
SHOPPING CENTER

(Av 3, btwn Calles 76 & 80, Miramar) Cuba's largest and most modern shopping and business center houses myriad stores, airline offices and embassies.

La Puntilla
SHOPPING CENTER

(cnr Calle A & Av 1, Miramar; ⊙8am-8pm) Decade-old shopping center spread over four floors at the Vedado end of Miramar; fairly comprehensive by Cuban standards.

ℹ Information

INTERNET ACCESS

Hotel Business Center (Hotel Meliá Habana, Av 3, btwn Calles 76 & 80, Miramar) Meliá Habana charges CUC$7 an hour for wi-fi. Most other hotels have terminals for similar prices.

MEDICAL SERVICES

Clínica Central Cira García (☑7-204-2811; Calle 20 No 4101, cnr Av 41, Playa; ⊙9am-4pm Mon-Fri, emergencies 24hr) Emergency, dental and medical consultations for foreigners.

Farmacia Internacional Miramar (☑7-204-4350; cnr Calles 20 & 43, Playa; ⊙9am-5:45pm) Across the road from Clínica Central Cira García.

Pharmacy (☑7-204-2880; Calle 20 No 4104, cnr Calle 43, Playa; ⊙24hr) In Clínica Central Cira García; one of the city's best.

MONEY

There are Banco Financiero Internacional branches in **Miramar** (Sierra Maestra Bldg, cnr Av 1 & Calle 0) and **Playa** (cnr Av 5 & Calle 92).

Cadeca is also located in **Miramar** (Av 5A, btwn Calles 40 & 42) and **Playa** (☑7-204-9087; cnr Av 3 & Calle 70).

POST

DHL (cnr Av 1 & Calle 26, Miramar; ⊙8am-8pm) For important mail, you're better off using DHL.

Post Office (Calle 42 No 112, btwn Avs 1 & 3, Miramar; ⊙8am-11:30am & 2-6pm Mon-Fri, 8am-11:30am Sat)

TOURIST INFORMATION

Infotur (cnr Av 5 & Calle 112, Playa; ⊙8:30am-noon & 12:30-5pm Mon-Sat) Oddly located but highly informative office.

TRAVEL AGENCIES

The following agencies also sell organized tours.

Cubanacán (☑7-204-8500; www.cubanacan.cu; Hotel Meliá Habana, Av 3, btwn Calles 76 & 80) Desk in Hotel Meliá Habana.

Gaviota (☑7-204-4411; www.gaviota-grupo.com) Represented in all Gaviota hotels including the H10 Habana Panorama.

ℹ Getting There & Away

The best way to get to Playa from Havana is on the Havana Bus Tour, which plies most of the neighborhoods' highlights all the way to La Cecilia on Av 5, cnr Calle 110, in Cubanacán (CUC$5 for all-day ticket). Plenty of metro buses also make the trip, though they often detour around the residential neighborhoods; P-1 and P-10 buses are the most useful.

ℹ Getting Around

Cubacar (☑7-204-1707) has offices at the Chateau Miramar and the Meliá Habana hotels. Rental depends on the type of car and duration of rent. Take CUC$70 per day as an average.

Vía Rent a Car (☑7-204-3606; cnr Avs 47 & 36, Kohly) has an office opposite the Hotel el Bosque.

There are Servi-Cupet gas stations at Av 31 between Calles 18 and 20 in Miramar, on the corner of Calle 72 and Av 41 in Marianao (near the Tropicana), as well as on the traffic circle at Av 5 and Calle 112 in Cubanacán. The Oro Negro gas station is at Av 5 and Calle 120 in Cubanacán. All are open 24 hours.

Parque Lenin Area

Parque Lenin, off the Calzada de Bejucal in Arroyo Naranjo, 20km south of central Havana, is the city's largest recreational area. Constructed between 1969 and 1972 on the orders of Celia Sánchez, a long-time associate of Fidel Castro, it is one of the few developments in Havana from this era. The 670 hectares of green parkland and beautiful old trees surround an artificial lake, the

Embalse Paso Sequito, just west of the much larger Embalse Ejército Rebelde, which was formed by damming the Río Almendares.

Although the park itself is attractive enough, its mishmash of facilities has fallen on hard times since the 1990s. Taxi drivers complain it's *muy abandonado* and wax nostalgic about when 'Lenin' was an idyllic weekend getaway for scores of pleasure-seeking Havana families. These days the place retains a neglected and surreal air. Help has long been promised, though the words tend to be louder than the actions. To date, some Chinese investment has filtered through, but it's a big job that's still a long way from completion.

◎ Sights

Parque Lenin   PARK
The main things to see in the park are south of the lake, including the **Galería de Arte Amelia Peláez** (admission CUC$1). Up the hill there's a dramatic white marble **monument to Lenin** (1984) by the Soviet sculptor LE Kerbel, and west along the lake is an overgrown **amphitheater** and a lackluster aquarium with freshwater fish and crocodiles. The 1985 bronze **monument to Celia Sánchez**, who was instrumental in having Parque Lenin built, is rather hidden beyond the aquarium.

Most of these attractions are open 9am to 5pm Tuesday to Sunday, and admission to the park itself is free. You can sometimes rent a **rowboat** on the Embalse Paso Sequito from a dock behind the **Rodeo Nacional**, an arena where some of Cuba's best rodeos take place (the annual **Cattlemen's Fair** is also held here). A 9km **narrow-gauge railway** with four stops operates inside the park from 10am to 3pm Wednesday to Sunday.

ExpoCuba   EXHIBITION HALL
(admission CUC$1; ◎ 9am-5pm Wed-Sun) A visit to Parque Lenin can be combined with a trip to ExpoCuba at Calabazar on the Carretera del Rocío in Arroyo Naranjo, 3km south of Las Ruinas restaurant. Opened in 1989, this large permanent exhibition showcases Cuba's economic and scientific achievements in 25 pavilions based on themes such as sugar, farming, apiculture, animal science, fishing, construction, food, geology, sports and defense.

Jardín Botánico Nacional   GARDENS
(admission CUC$3; ◎ 10am-4pm Wed-Sun) Across the highway from ExpoCuba is this 600-hectare botanical garden. The **Pabellones de Exposición** (1987), near the entry gate, is a series of greenhouses with cacti and tropicals, while 2km beyond is the garden's highlight, the tranquil **Japanese Garden** (1992). Nearby is the celebrated Restaurante el Bambú, where a vegetarian buffet is served (a rare treat in Cuba).

The **tractor train ride** around the park departs four times a day and costs CUC$3, gardens admission included. Parking costs CUC$2.

🏃 Activities

Centro Ecuestre   HORSE RIDING
(Parque Lenin; ◎ 9am-5pm) The stables in the northwestern corner of Parque Lenin are run by environmental agency, Flora y Fauna. At the time of writing they were offering horseback riding for CUC$12 per hour from their equestrian center.

Horse Riding   HORSE RIDING
(Parque Lenin) Legalized under Raúl Castro's reforms, the *chicos* who gallop around Parque Lenin's northeast entrance on horseback offer their mounts for more relaxed excursions ($4/8 half/full hour). Check the state of your horse before mounting (and the official license of your hirer).

Club de Golf la Habana   GOLF
(Carretera de Venta, Km 8, Reparto Capdevila, Boyeros; 9-hole green fees excl gear from CUC$20; ◎ 8am-8pm, bowling alley noon-11pm) A curiosity as much as a place to swing a nine-iron, this golf club lies between Vedado and the airport and is one of only two in Cuba. There are nine holes on the rough-and-rutted par-35 course. Green fees are CUC$20 for nine holes with extra for clubs, cart and caddie. The club also has tennis courts and a bowling alley.

Originally titled the Rover's Athletic Club, it was established by a group of British diplomats in the 1920s, and the diplomatic corps is largely the clientele today. Fidel and Che Guevara played a round here once as a publicity stunt soon after the Cuban missile crisis in 1962. The photos of the event are still popular. Che – an ex-caddy – won, apparently.

Poor signposting makes the club hard to find and most taxi drivers get lost looking: ask locals for directions to the *golfito* or Dilpo Golf Club.

🍴 Eating

Restaurante el Bambú   VEGETARIAN $
(Jardín Botánico Nacional; meals CUC$1; ◎ noon-5pm, closed Mon; 🍴) This was once the only example of vegetarian dining in Havana, and has long been a leading advocate for the

benefits of a meatless diet (a tough call in the challenging economy of Cuba). The all-you-can-eat lunch buffet is served alfresco, deep in the botanical gardens, with the natural setting paralleling the wholesome tastiness of the food.

Gorge on soups and salads, root vegetables, tamales and eggplant caviar.

Las Ruinas   CARIBBEAN $

(Parque Lenin, Cortina de la Presa; meals CUC$6; ⊘ 11am-midnight Tue-Sun) Once celebrated for its architecture (a modernist structure incorporating the ruins of a sugar mill), Las Ruinas is now, like much else in Parque Lenin, a ruin itself, although it still tries to pass itself off as a restaurant. While the eye-catching stained glass by Cuban artist René Portocarrero impresses, the food, ambience and service don't, though alternatives are scant.

ⓘ Getting There & Away

Your public transport choices to Parque Lenin are bus, car or taxi. The bus isn't easy. The P-13 will get you close, but to catch it you have to first get to Víbora. The best way to do this is to get on the P-9 at Calles 23 and L. Havana taxi drivers are used to this run and it should be easy to negotiate a rate with stops for CUC$25 and up.

ⓘ Getting Around

There's a Servi-Cupet gas station on the corner of Av de la Independencia and Calle 271 in Boyeros, north of the airport. It's accessible only from the northbound lane and is open 24 hours a day.

Santiago de las Vegas Area

While not exactly brimming with tourist potential, downbeat and dusty Santiago de las Vegas offers a fleeting glimpse of Cuba that isn't featured in coffee-table photo spreads. Visitors, if they come here at all, usually encounter this settlement – a curious amalgamation of small town and sleepy city suburb – in December during the annual 5000-strong devotional crawl to the Santuario de San Lázaro (named after a Christian saint known for his ministrations to lepers and the poor) in the nearby village of El Rincón.

◉ Sights

Mausoleo de Antonio Maceo   MONUMENT

On a hilltop at El Cacahual, 8km south of Aeropuerto Internacional José Martí via Santiago de las Vegas, is the little-visited mausoleum of the hero of Cuban independence, General Antonio Maceo, who was killed in the Battle of San Pedro near Bauta on December 7, 1896. An open-air pavilion next to the mausoleum shelters a historical exhibit.

Santuario de San Lázaro   CHURCH

(Carretera San Antonio de los Baños) The focus of Cuba's biggest annual pilgrimage lacks ostentation and is tucked away in the rustic village of El Rincón. The saint inside the church is San Lázaro (represented by the *orisha* Babalú Ayé in the Santería religion), the patron saint of healing and the sick. Hundreds come to light candles and lay flowers daily.

There's a small **museum** displaying a raft of previous offerings to San Lázaro in a chapel next door.

ⓘ Getting There & Away

To get here, take bus P-12 from the Capitolio or bus P-16 from outside Hospital Hermanos Ameijeiras just off the Malecón in Centro Habana.

Regla

The old town of Regla, just across the harbor from Habana Vieja, is an industrial port town known as a center of Afro-Cuban religions, including Santería, Palo Monte and the all-male secret society Abakuá. Long before the triumph of the 1959 Revolution, Regla was known as the Sierra Chiquita (Little Sierra, after the Sierra Maestra) for its bolshie revolutionary spirit. A largely working-class neighborhood, it is also notable for a large thermoelectric power plant and shipyard. Regla is almost free of tourist trappings, and makes an easily reachable afternoon trip away from the city; the skyline views from this side of the harbor offer a different perspective.

◉ Sights

★ **Iglesia de Nuestra Señora de Regla**   CHURCH

(⊘ 7:30am-6pm) As important as it is diminutive, Iglesia de Nuestra Señora de Regla, which sits close to the boat dock in the municipality of Regla, has a long and colorful history. Inside on the main altar you'll find La Santísima Virgen de Regla.

The virgin, represented by a black Madonna, is venerated in the Catholic faith and associated in the Santería religion with Yemayá, the *orisha* of the ocean and the patron of sailors (always represented in blue). Legend claims that this image was carved by St Augustine 'The African' in the 5th century, and that in AD 453 a disciple brought the statue to Spain to safeguard it from barbarians. The small vessel in which the image was traveling survived a storm in the Strait of Gibraltar, so the figure was recognized as the patron of sailors. These days rafters attempting to reach the US also evoke the protection of the Black Virgin.

To shelter a copy of the image, a hut was first built on this site in 1687 by a pilgrim named Manuel Antonio. But this structure was destroyed during a hurricane in 1692. A few years later a Spaniard named Juan de Conyedo built a stronger chapel, and in 1714 Nuestra Señora de Regla was proclaimed patron of the Bahía de la Habana. In 1957 the image was crowned by the Cuban Cardinal in Havana cathedral. Every year on September 8 thousands of pilgrims descend on Regla to celebrate the saint's day, and the image is taken out for a procession through the streets.

The current church dates from the early 19th century and is always busy with devotees from both religions stooping in silent prayer before the images of the saints that fill the alcoves. In Havana, there is probably no better (public) place to see the layering and transference between Catholic beliefs and African traditions.

Museo Municipal de Regla   MUSEUM
(Martí No 158; admission CUC$2; ⊙ 9am-5pm Mon-Sat, to 1pm Sun) If you've come across to see Regla's church, you should also check out this important museum. Spread over two sites, one adjacent to the church and the other (better half) a few blocks up the main street from the ferry, it records Regla's history and Afro-Cuban religions. Don't miss the Palo Monte *ngangas* (cauldrons) and the masked Abakuá dancing figurines.

There's also an interesting, small exhibit on Remigio Herrero, first *babalawo* (priest) of Regla, and a bizarre statue of Napoleon with his nose missing. Price of admission includes both museum outposts and the Colina Lenin exhibit.

Colina Lenin   MONUMENT
From the museum, head straight (south) on Martí past Parque Guaicanamar, and turn left on Albuquerque and right on 24 de Febrero, the road to Guanabacoa. About 1.5km from the ferry you'll see a high metal stairway that gives access to Colina Lenin, one of two monuments in Havana to Vladimir Ilyich Ulyanov (better known to his friends and enemies as Lenin).

The monument was conceived in 1924 by the socialist mayor of Regla, Antonio Bosch, to honor Lenin's death (in the same year). Above a monolithic image of the man is an olive tree planted by Bosch, surrounded by seven lithe figures. There are fine harbor views from the hilltop.

❶ Getting There & Away

Regla is easily accessible on the passenger ferry that departs every 15 minutes (CUC$0.25) from Muelle Luz at the intersection of San Pedro and Santa Clara, in Habana Vieja. Bicycles are readily accepted via a separate line that boards first.
Bus P-15 runs from the Capitolio to Guanabacoa via Regla.

Guanabacoa

Guanabacoa is the little village that got swallowed up by the big city. In spite of this, the settlement's main thoroughfare, diminutive Parque Martí, still retains a faintly bucolic small-town air. Locals call it *el pueblo embrujado* (the bewitched town) for its strong Santería traditions, though there are indigenous associations too. In the 1540s the Spanish conquerors concentrated the few surviving Taínos at Guanabacoa, 5km east of central Havana, making it one of Cuba's first official *pueblos Indios* (Indian towns). A formal settlement was founded in 1607, and this later became a center of the slave trade. In 1762 the British occupied Guanabacoa, but not without a fight from its mayor, José Antonio Gómez Bulones (better known as Pepe Antonio), who attained almost legendary status by conducting a guerrilla campaign behind the lines of the victorious British. José Martí supposedly gave his first public speech here, and it was also the birthplace of the versatile Cuba singer Rita Montaner (1900–58), after whom the Casa de la Cultura is named.

Today, Guanabacoa is a sleepy yet colorful place that can be tied in with an excursion to nearby Regla (easily accessible by ferry).

◎ Sights

Iglesia de Guanabacoa   CHURCH
(cnr Pepe Antonio & Adolfo del Castillo Cadenas; ⊙ parochial office 8-11am & 2-5pm Mon-Fri) This church, on Parque Martí in the center of

WORTH A TRIP

MUSEO HEMINGWAY

There's only one reason to visit the mundane if tranquil Havana suburb of San Francisco de Paula – the **Museo Hemingway** (admission CUC$5, guide CUC$5; ⊙10am-5pm Mon-Sat, to 1pm Sun). In 1939 US novelist Ernest Hemingway rented the Finca la Vigía villa on a hill here, 15km southeast of central Havana. A year later he bought the 1888 house and property and lived there continuously until 1960, when he moved back to the US.

The villa's interior has remained unchanged since the day Hemingway left (there are lots of stuffed trophies), and the wooded estate is now a museum. Hemingway left his house and its contents to the 'Cuban people,' and his house has been the stimulus for some rare shows of US–Cuban cooperation. In 2002 Cuba agreed to a US-funded project to digitalize the documents stored in the basement of Finca la Vigía, and in May 2006 sent 11,000 of Hemingway's private documents to the JFK Presidential Library in America for digitalization. This literary treasure trove (including a previously unseen epilogue for *For Whom the Bell Tolls*) was finally made available online in January 2009.

To prevent the pilfering of objects, visitors are not allowed inside the house, but there are enough open doors and windows to allow a proper glimpse into Papa's universe. There are books everywhere (including beside the toilet), a large Victrola and record collection, and an astounding number of knickknacks. Don't come when it's raining as the house itself will be closed. A stroll through the garden is worthwhile to see the surprisingly sentimental dog cemetery, Hemingway's fishing boat *El Pilar* and the pool where actor Ava Gardner once swam naked. You can chill out here on a chaise longue below whispering palms and bamboo.

To reach San Francisco de Paula, take metro bus P-7 (Alberro) from the Capitolio in Centro Habana. Tell the driver you're going to the museum. You get off in San Miguel del Padrón; the house entrance is on Calle Vigia, 200m east of the main road, Calzada de Guines.

town, is also known as the Iglesia de Nuestra Señora de la Asunción, and was designed by Lorenzo Camacho and built between 1721 and 1748 with a Moorish-influenced wooden ceiling.

The gilded main altar and nine lateral altars are worth a look, and there is a painting of the *Assumption of the Virgin* at the back. In typical Cuban fashion, the main doors are usually locked; knock at the parochial office out back if you're keen.

Museo Municipal de Guanabacoa MUSEUM (Martí No 108; admission CUC$2; ⊙10am-6pm Mon & Wed-Sat, 9am-1pm Sun) The town's main sight is the renovated museum two blocks west of Parque Martí. Founded in 1964, it tracks the development of the neighborhood throughout the 18th and 19th centuries and is famous for its rooms on Afro-Cuban culture, slavery and the Santería religion, with a particular focus on the *orisha* Elegguá.

The museum has another arm further west along Calle Martí in the **Museo de Mártires** (Martí No 320; admission free; ⊙10am-6pm Tue-Sat, 9am-1pm Sun), which displays material relevant to the Cuban Revolution.

✖ Eating

Centro Cultural Recreativo los Orishas CARIBBEAN **$$** (☎7-794-7878; Martí No 175, btwn Lamas & Cruz Verde; mains CUC$6-10; ⊙noon-midnight) Situated in the hotbed of Havana's Santería community, this funky bar-restaurant hosts live rumba music at weekends, including regular visits from the Conjunto Folklórico Nacional, and serves up a good selection of food, from a CUC$1 pizza to CUC$20 lobster, to go with the beats. The pleasant garden bar is surrounded by colorful Afro-Cuban sculptures of various Santería deities.

Well off the beaten track and hard to get to at night, there are nonetheless excellent Afro-Cuban shows (admission CUC$3) at 9pm on Fridays. It also offers dance classes.

❶ Getting There & Away

Bus P-15 from the Capitolio in Centro Habana goes to Guanabacoa via Av del Puerto. Alternatively, you can walk uphill from Regla where the Havana ferry docks, to Guanabacoa (or vice versa) in about 45 minutes, passing the Colina Lenin monument on the way.

Cojímar Area

Situated 10km east of Havana is the little port town of Cojímar, famous for harboring Ernest Hemingway's fishing boat *El Pilar* in the 1940s and 1950s. This picturesque, if slightly run-down, harbor community served as the prototype for the fishing village in Hemingway's novel *The Old Man and the Sea,* which won him the Nobel Prize for Literature in 1954. It was founded in the 17th century at the mouth of the Río Cojímar. In 1762 an invading British army landed here on its way through to take Havana; in 1994 thousands of 'rafters' split from the sheltered but rocky bay, lured to Florida by US radio broadcasts and promises of political asylum.

To the southwest of Cojímar just off the Vía Blanca is the rather ugly sporting complex and athletes' village **Estadio Panamericano,** built when Cuba staged the 1991 Pan-American Games.

Sights

Torreón de Cojímar   FORT

Overlooking the harbor is an old Spanish fort (1649) presently occupied by the Cuban Coast Guard. It was the first fortification taken by the British when they attacked Havana from the rear in 1762. Next to this tower and framed by a neoclassical archway is a gilded **bust of Ernest Hemingway,** erected by the residents of Cojímar in 1962.

Alamar   NEIGHBORHOOD

East across the river from Cojímar is a large housing estate of prefabricated apartment blocks built by *micro brigadas* (small armies of workers responsible for building much of the post-Revolution housing, beginning in 1971. This is the birthplace of Cuban rap and the annual hip-hop festival is still centered here.

Sleeping

Hostal Marlin   CASA PARTICULAR **$**

(☎ 7-766-6154; Real No 128, btwn Santo Domingo & Chacón; r CUC$30; ✳) Chilled apartment with a sea view and a terrace on the roof that offers a potential escape from the tumult of Havana. There's a kitchenette, a separate entrance and plenty of privacy.

Eating

Just down from the Hotel Panamericano is a **bakery** (Paseo Panamericano; ☺8am-8pm). Across the Paseo Panamericano is a grocery store, the **Mini-Super Caracol** (Paseo Panamericano; ☺9am-8pm), and a clean and reasonably priced Italian restaurant, **Allegro** (Paseo Panamericano; meals CUC$3-4; ☺noon-11pm), which offers lasagna, risotto, spaghetti and pizza.

Restaurante la Terraza   SEAFOOD **$$**

(Calle 152 No 161; meals CUC$7-15; ☺noon-11pm) Another photo-adorned shrine to the ghost of Hemingway, La Terraza specializes in seafood and does a roaring trade from the hordes of Papa fans who pour in daily. The terrace dining room overlooking the bay is pleasant. More atmospheric, however, is the old bar out front, where mojitos haven't yet reached El Floridita rates. The food is surprisingly mediocre.

🛈 Information

Bandec (Paseo Panamericano; ☺8:30am-3pm Mon-Fri, to 11am Sat), on Paseo Panamericano, changes traveler's checks and gives cash advances.

🛈 Getting There & Away

Metro bus P-8 goes to the Hotel Panamericano on Paseo Panamericano from the Capitolio in Centro Habana. From the hotel it's around 2km downhill through the village to the Hemingway bust on the harbor.

Casablanca

Casablanca, just across the harbor from Habana Vieja and in the shadow of La Cabaña fort, is a small village surrounded by urbanization. It's dominated by a white marble statue of Christ **Estatua de Cristo** (Map p78), created in 1958 by Jilma Madera. It was promised to President Batista by his wife after the US-backed dictator survived an attempt on his life in the Presidential Palace in March 1957, but was (ironically) unveiled on Christmas Day 1958 one week before the dictator fled the country. As you disembark the Casablanca ferry, follow the road uphill for about 10 minutes until you reach the statue. The views from up here are stupendous and it is a favorite nighttime hangout for locals. Behind the statue is the **Observatorio Nacional** (closed to tourists).

🛈 Getting There & Away

Passenger ferries to Casablanca depart Muelle Luz, on the corner of San Pedro and Santa Clara in Habana Vieja, about every 15 minutes (CUC$0.25). Bicycles are welcome.

The Casablanca train station, next to the ferry wharf, is the western terminus of the only electric railway in Cuba. In 1917 the Hershey Chocolate Company of the US state of Pennsylvania built this line to Matanzas. Trains still depart for Matanzas three times a day, ostensibly at 4:45am, 12:21pm and 4:35pm (though, be warned, they're notoriously fickle). You'll travel via Guanabo (CUC$0.75, 25km), Hershey (CUC$1.40, 46km), Jibacoa (CUC$1.65, 54km) and Canasí (CUC$1.95, 65km) to Matanzas (CUC$2.80, 90km) and dozens of smaller stations. No one on a tight schedule should use this train; it usually leaves Casablanca on time but often arrives an hour late. Bikes aren't officially allowed. It's a scenic four-hour trip (on a good day), and tickets are easily obtainable at the station.

Playas del Este

In Cuba you're never far from an idyllic beach. Havana's very own pine-fringed Riviera, Playas del Este, begins just 18km to the east of the capital at the small resort of Bacuranao, before continuing east through Tarará, El Mégano, Santa María del Mar and Boca Ciega to the town of Guanabo. Although none of these places has so far witnessed the kind of megadevelopment redolent of Cancún or Varadero, Playas del Este is still a popular tourist drawcard. During the summer months of July and August, all of Havana comes to play and relax on the soft white sands and clear aquamarine waters of the beautiful Atlantic coastline.

While the beaches might be suitably sublime, Playas del Este can't yet claim the all-round tourist facilities of other Cuban resorts such as Varadero and Cayo Coco, much less the all-out luxury of celebrated Caribbean getaways. Come here in the winter and the place often has a timeworn and slightly abandoned air, and even in the summer, seasoned beach bums might find the tatty restaurants and ugly Soviet-style hotel piles more than a little incongruous.

Each of the six beaches that dot this 9km stretch of attractive coastline has its own distinctive flavor. Tarará is a yacht and diving haven, Santa María del Mar is where the largest concentration of resorts (and foreigners) can be found, Boca Ciega is popular with gay couples, while Guanabo is the rustic Cuban end of the strip, with shops, a nightclub and plenty of cheap casas particulares.

🏃 Activities

Yacht charters, deep-sea fishing and scuba diving are offered by **Cubanacán Náutica Tarará** (☑ 7-796-0240; VHF channels 16 & 77; cnr Av 8 & Calle 17, Tarará), at the marina 22km east of Havana, but only 3km west of Santa María del Mar. Details can be procured at the hotel tour desks.

There are a number of **Club Náutica** points spaced along the beaches. The most central is outside Club Atlántico in the middle of Playa Santa María del Mar. Here you can rent pedal boats (CUC$6 per hour; four to six people), banana boats (CUC$5 per five minutes; maximum five people), one-/two-person kayaks (CUC$2/4 per hour), snorkel gear (CUC$4) and catamarans (CUC$12 per hour; maximum four people plus lifeguard). A paddle around the coast exploring the mangrove-choked canals is a pleasure.

Beach toys such as sailboards, water bikes and badminton gear may also be available: ask. Many people rent similar equipment all along the beach to Guanabo, but check any water vessels and gear carefully, as we've received complaints about faulty equipment. Consider leaving a deposit instead of prepaying in full, should anything go awry.

🛏 Sleeping

🛏 Guanabo

Guanabo has dozens of casas particulares and one passable hotel.

Elena Morina   CASA PARTICULAR **$**
(☑ 7-796-7975; Calle 472 No 7B11, btwn Avs 7B & 9; r CUC$25-30; P 🌢) *Hay Perro* reads the sign, but don't worry, the pit bull that lives here is friendly (really), as is the host Elena, who once lived in Italy. This house makes great coffee and rents five decent rooms with a leafy patio a few blocks back from the beach.

La Gallega y Teresa   CASA PARTICULAR **$**
(☑ 7-796-6860; Calle 472 No 7B07, btwn Avs 7B & 9; apt CUC$20-30; P 🌢) The four rooms here are realistically mini-apartments with their own kitchens and eating areas. Teresa has put a lot of work into renovating her house and the grey stone brickwork lends the spacious rooms a handsome glow.

Neida y Glenda   CASA PARTICULAR **$**
(☑ 7-796-5862; pineda.lerena@informed.sld.cu; Av 7B No 47007, btwn Calles 470 & 472; r CUC$25-30; P 🌢) Four rooms with en-suite bathrooms

Playas del Este

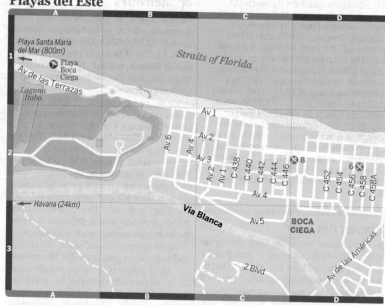

Playas del Este

🛏 Sleeping

1 Elena Morina	F3
2 La Gallega y Teresa	F3
3 Neida y Glenda	E2
4 Villa Playa Hermosa	F2

🍴 Eating

5 Chicken Little	H2
6 El Cubano	D2
7 El Piccolo	H1
8 Minisuper la Barca	D2
9 Pan.com	F2

🎭 Entertainment

10 Cabaret Guanimar	E2
11 Cine Guanabo	F2
12 Teatro Avenida	F2

that can be split into two substantial apartments if required, each with their own kitchen, eating area and terrace.

Villa Playa Hermosa   HOTEL **$**
(📞7-796-2774; Av 5D, btwn Calles 472 & 474; s/d with shared bathroom CUC$13/20; P ✴ @ 🏊) The rooms are ultra-cheap, but you'll have to put up with some ear-splitting recorded music at this Islazul pile with 47 rooms set in small bungalows with shared bathrooms and TV. Playa Hermosa is 300m away.

🛏 Santa María del Mar

None of Santa María's hotels is a knockout and some are downright ugly.

**Complejo Atlántico –
Las Terrazas**   APARTMENT, HOTEL **$$**
(📞7-797-1494; Av de las Terrazas, btwn Calles 11 & 12; s/d all-incl CUC$95/150; P ✴ @ 🏊) An amalgamation of a beach hotel and an old *aparthotel,* this place offers 60 or so apartments (with kitchenettes) along with the low- to midrange Atlántico hotel, one of only three all-inclusives in the city of Havana. Rooms are clean and the beach is lovely, but, take note: this isn't high-end Varadero. Manage your expectations.

Hotel Tropicoco   RESORT **$$**
(📞7-797-1371; cnr Av de las Terrazas & Av de las Banderas; all-incl s/d/tr CUC$57/92/133; P ✴ @ 🏊) Picked up by Cubanacán from the cheaper Horizontes chain, this big blue monster is an architectural disaster both inside and out. Pity the poor travelers who book this online without looking at the photos first. The main (only) benefit for the terribly unfussy is the price (cheap) and the location (you could hit a big home run onto the beach from here).

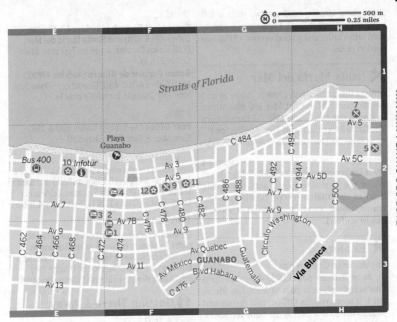

0 — 500 m
0 — 0.25 miles

Straits of Florida

Playa Guanabo

Bus 400 10 Infotur

Av 3
Av 5 9 11

Av 5 12

Av 7

4

3 2

Av 7B

1

Av 462 Av 464 Av 466 Av 468 Av 7 Av 9 C 472 C 474 Av 9 C 476 C 478 C 480 C 482 C 486 C 488 C 492 C 494 C 494A C 500

C 484

7 Av 5

5 Av 5C

Av 5D

Av 7

Av 9

Circulo Washington

Av Quebec

Av 11 Av México GUANABO Guatemala

Blvd Habana

C 476

Av 13

Via Blanca

Villa Los Pinos APARTMENT, HOTEL **$$$**

(☎ 7-797-1085; Av de las Terrazas, btwn Calles 11 & 12; all-incl 2/3/4-bed house CUC$145/185/225; P❄@≋) Hands down Playas del Este's best resort, Los Pinos is a collection of little houses (two to four bedrooms) with kitchens and TVs that were holiday homes before the Revolution. Big bonus: some of them come with their own private swimming pool.

There's a small supermarket nearby if you're playing chef, or an on-site restaurant if you're not. El Mégano beach is under 100m away.

🛏 Bacuranao

Villa Bacuranao HOTEL **$**

(☎ 7-763-9241; s/d CUC$38/44; P❄≋) On the Vía Blanca, 18km east of Havana, this is the closest beach resort to Havana. There's a long sandy beach between the resort and mouth of the Río Bacuranao, across which is the old Torreón de Bacuranao (inside the inaccessible military academy compound). The hotel is a standard Cuban midrange, a little dated but OK if you're not seeking luxury.

✕ Eating

Surprise! Playas del Este does some good pizza.

✕ Guanabo

Pan.com FAST FOOD **$**

(Av 5 No 47802; snacks CUC$1-2; ⊙24hr) Lackluster outlet of the sometimes good local snack chain. Try the milkshakes.

★ El Piccolo ITALIAN **$$**

(☎ 7-796-4300; cnr Av 5 & Calle 502; meals CUC$7-9; ⊙noon-11pm) This private restaurant is a bit of an open secret among *habaneros,* some of whom consider it to be the best pizza restaurant in Cuba. Out of the way and a little more expensive than Playas del Este's other numerous pizza joints, it's well worth the walk.

Chicken Little INTERNATIONAL **$$**

(☎ 7-796-2351; Calle 504 No 5815, btwn Calles 5B & 5C; mains CUC$5-8; ⊙noon-11pm) Forgive the kitschy name: Chicken Little could yet make it big. Defying Guanabo's ramshackle image, this deluxe restaurant is staffed with polite waiters in bow ties who'll talk you through a menu of pesto chicken, chicken in orange and honey, and some decent fish.

✕ Boca Ciega

El Cubano CUBAN **$$**

(☎ 7-796-4061; Av 5, btwn Calles 456 & 458; meals CUC$6-9; ⊙11am-midnight) This is a spick-and-span place almost in Guanabo, with a full wine rack (French and Californian), checkered tablecloths and a good version of chicken cordon bleu.

✖ Santa María del Mar

Among the many small grocery stores in and around Santa María del Mar are **Minisuper la Barca** (cnr Av 5 & Calle 446; ☉ 9:15am-6:45pm Mon-Sat, to 2:45pm Sun) and **Tienda Villa los Pinos** (Av del Sur, btwn Calles 5 & 7; ☉ 9am-6:45pm).

Don Pepe   SEAFOOD $
(Av de las Terrazas; meals CUC$5-7; ☉ 10am-11pm) When the Guanabo pizza gets too much, head to this thatched-roof, beach-style restaurant about 50m from the sand. It specializes in seafood.

✖ El Mégano

Restaurante Costarenas   CUBAN $
(Av de las Terrazas; pizza CUC$2-4; ☉ 9am-11pm) This scruffy place is part of Villa Los Pinos, but it'll serve you its OK-ish fish dishes and pizzas either on a breezy 1st-floor terrace or under thatched umbrellas right on the beach.

Pizzería Mi Rinconcito   ITALIAN $
(cnr Av de las Terrazas & Calle 4; pizza CUC$2-3; ☉ noon-9:45pm) Located near Villa Los Pinos, this place contains a surprisingly good pizzafest, plus cannelloni, lasagna, salads and spaghetti.

☆ Entertainment

Playas del Este's gay scene revolves around a couple of beach bars on Playa Boca Ciega near the north end of Laguna Itabo, at the east end of Santa María del Mar.

Cabaret Guanimar   CABARET
(cnr Av 5 & Calle 468, Guanabo; per couple CUC$10; ☉ 9pm-3am Tue-Sat) An outdoor club with a cabaret show at 11pm and a heavy assemblage of *jinetero/as* (touts).

Teatro Avenida   THEATER
(Av 5 No 47612, btwn Calles 476 & 478, Guanabo) General theater with children's matinees at 3pm Saturday and Sunday.

❶ Information

MEDICAL SERVICES

Farmacia (cnr Av 5 & Calle 466, Guanabo; ☉ 9am-6pm Mon-Fri) Basics only.

MONEY

Cadeca is at **Guanabo** (Av 5 No 47612, btwn Calles 476 & 478) and **Santa María del Mar.** (Edificio los Corales, Av de las Terrazas, btwn Calles 10 & 1).

Banco Popular de Ahorro (Av 5 No 47810, btwn Calles 478 & 480, Guanabo; ☉ 9am-3pm Mon-Fri) Changes traveler's checks.

POST

Post Office (Av 5, btwn Calles 490 & 492, Guanabo; ☉ 9am-5pm Mon-Sat)

TOURIST INFORMATION

Infotur has helpful offices in **Guanabo** (Av 5, btwn Calles 468 & 470; ☉ 8:15am-4:15pm) and **Santa María del Mar** (Av de las Terrazas, Edificio los Corales, btwn Calles 10 & 11; ☉ 8:15am-4:15pm).

TRAVEL AGENCIES

Cubatur and Cubanacán both have desks at Hotel Tropicoco, between Av del Sur and Av de las Terrazas in Santa María del Mar. Their main business is booking bus tours, though they might be willing to help with hotel reservations.

❶ Getting There & Away

BUS & TAXI

The Havana Bus Tour runs a regular (hourly) service from Parque Central out to Playa Santa María, stopping at Villa Bacuranao, Tarará, Club Mégano, Hotel Tropicoco and Club Atlántico. It doesn't go as far as Guanabo. All-day tickets cost CUC$5.

Bus 400 stops at various points along Av 5 in Guanabo before heading into Havana where it terminates near the central train station in Havana Vieja. It's usually crowded but costs a mere CUC$0.05 and runs every 20 minutes.

Taxis from Playas del Este to Havana will cost from CUC$15 (Lada) to CUC$20 (tourist taxi).

TRAIN

One of the most novel ways to get to Guanabo is on the Hershey Train, which leaves three to four times a day from either Casablanca train station or Matanzas. The train will drop you at Guanabo station, approximately 2km from the far eastern end of Guanabo. It's a pleasant walk along a quiet road to the town and beaches.

❶ Getting Around

A large guarded parking area is off Calle 7, between Av de las Terrazas and Av del Sur, near Hotel Tropicoco (CUC$1 a day from 8am to 7pm). Several other paid parking areas are along Playa Santa María del Mar. You can find Cubacar branches at Complejo Atlántico (p142) and in **Guanabo** (☎ 7-796-6997; cnr Calle 478 & Av 9). Rents average-sized cars for far from average prices – bank on CUC$70 a day with insurance.

Artemisa & Mayabeque Provinces

☎ 47 / POP 885,545

Includes ➡

Artemisa Province . . . 147

San Antonio de
los Baños 147

Artemisa 148

Soroa 149

Las Terrazas 151

Mayabeque Province . . 154

Playa Jibacoa Area . . . 155

Jaruco 157

Surgidero de
Batabanó 158

Best Hiking

➡ La Rosita (p149)

➡ Sendero la Serafina (p152)

➡ El Contento (p152)

➡ Parque Escaleras de Jaruco (p157)

Best Places To Stay

➡ Memories Jibacoa Beach (p157)

➡ Campismo los Cocos (p156)

➡ Don Agapito (p150)

➡ Hotel Moka (p153)

Why Go?

Leap-frogged by almost all international visitors, Cuba's two smallest provinces, created by dividing Havana province in half in 2010, are the reserve of more everyday concerns – like growing half of the crops that feed the nation, for example. But in amongst the patchwork of citrus and pineapple fields lie a smattering of small towns that will satisfy the curious and the brave.

The most interesting corner is Las Terrazas and Soroa, Cuba's most successful eco-project and an increasingly important nexus for trekking and bird-watching. East of Havana, Jibacoa's beaches are the domain of a trickle of Varadero-avoiding tourists who guard their secret tightly. Wander elsewhere and you'll be in mainly Cuban company (or none at all), contemplating sugar-plantation ruins, weird one-of-a-kind museums and improbably riotous festivals. For a kaleidoscope of the whole region, take the ridiculously slow Hershey train through the nation's proverbial backyard and admire the view.

When to Go

➡ The provinces' attractions vary considerably climate-wise. Because of their unique geographical situation, Soroa and Las Terrazas have a microclimate: more rain and minimum monthly temperatures 2°C to 3°C colder than Havana.

➡ The big parties around here are December for the carnival-esque frivolity of Bejucal's Las Charangas and April for the International Humor Festival in San Antonio de los Baños.

➡ December through April is best for the beaches at Playa Jibacoa.

Artemisa & Mayabeque Provinces Highlights

1 Roaming the ruins of the region's once-mighty coffee plantations at **Antiguo Cafetal Angerona** (p149) and in **Las Terrazas** (p151).

2 Hiking the hills above verdant **Soroa** (p149).

3 Going green at Cuba's primary eco-village in **Las Terrazas** (p151).

4 Refreshing yourself at squeaky-clean, green **Hotel Moka** (p153), the country's first and best eco-hotel.

5 Trying to suppress giggles at San Antonio de los Baños' **Museo del Humor** (p147).

6 Escaping the tourist trails on the historic **Hershey Electric Railway** (p156).

7 Bagging a beach retreat beside Playa Jibacoa at elegant **Superclub Breezes** (p157).

8 Feasting with a view and weekending Havana folk at scenic **Parque Escaleras de Jaruco** (p157).

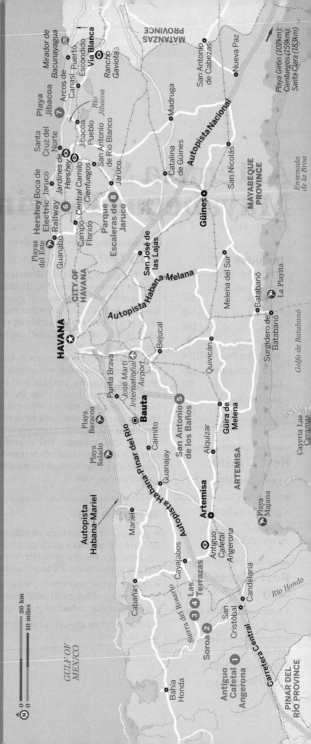

History

Havana was originally founded on the site of modern-day Surgidero de Batabanó in 1515 but rapidly relocated; the region's role in shaping Cuba was to become an almost exclusively agricultural one. Coffee and sugar were the key crops cultivated. Western Artemisa was the center of the country's short-lived coffee boom from 1820 until 1840, when sugar took over as the main industry. Large numbers of slaves were recruited to work on the plantations during the second half of the 19th century when Cuba became the center of the Caribbean slave trade and, as such, the area became a focus for the events leading up to the abolition of slavery in the 1880s.

The success of the sugar industry swept over into the 20th century: sweets mogul Milton S Hershey turned to Mayabeque as a dependable source for providing sugar for his milk chocolate in 1914. This lucrative industry would later suffer under Fidel Castro, once the Americans and then the Russians ceased to buy Cuba's sugar at over-the-odds prices. The region was hard-hit economically, and this deprivation was perhaps best epitomized by the 1980 Mariel Boatlift, when a port on the coast west of Havana became the stage for a Castro-sanctioned (and Jimmy Carter–endorsed) mass exodus of Cubans to Florida.

A major step against the area's downturn was taken in 1968. Neglected land in Western Artemisa province, around the very coffee plantations that had once sustained it, was reforested and transformed into a pioneering eco-village – now one of the region's economic mainstays through the tourism it has generated.

ARTEMISA PROVINCE

In many ways a giant vegetable patch for Havana, Artemisa province's fertile delights include the eco-village of Las Terrazas and the outdoor action on offer among the scenic forested slopes of the Sierra del Rosario mountain range. Then there are myriad mystery-clad coffee-plantation ruins and the ever-inventive town of San Antonio de los Baños, which has spawned an internationally renowned film school as well as some of Cuba's top artists. On the north coast, good beaches and great back roads entice the adventurous.

San Antonio de los Baños

POP 35,980

Full of surprises, artsy San Antonio de los Baños, 35km southwest of central Havana, is Cuba on the flip side, a hard-working municipal town where the local college churns out wannabe cinematographers and the museums are more about laughs than crafts.

Founded in 1986 with the help of Nobel Prize–winning Colombian novelist Gabriel García Márquez, San Antonio's Escuela Internacional de Cine y TV invites film students from around the world to partake in its excellent on-site facilities, including an Olympic-sized swimming pool for practicing underwater shooting techniques. Meanwhile, in the center of town, an unusual humor museum makes a ha-ha-happy break from the usual stuffed animal/revolutionary artifact double act.

San Antonio is also the birthplace of *nueva trova* music giant Silvio Rodríguez, born here in 1946. Rodríguez went on to write the musical soundtrack to the Cuban Revolution almost single-handedly. His best-known songs include *Ojalá*, *La Maza* and *El Necio*.

⊙ Sights

San Antonio de los Baños has several attractive squares, the most resplendent of which is the square at the intersection of Calles 66 and 41, which boasts a stately church.

**Iglesia de San Antonio
de los Baños** CHURCH
(cnr Calles 66 & 41) This impressive early-19th-century church has twin towers and porthole windows and is the largest, grandest religious building in Artemisa and Mayabeque.

Museo del Humor MUSEUM
(cnr Calle 60 & Av 45; admission CUC$2; ⊙10am-6pm Tue-Sat, 9am-1pm Sun) Unique in Cuba is this fun selection of cartoons, caricatures and other entertaining ephemera. Among the drawings exhibited in a neoclassical colonial house are saucy cartoons, satirical scribblings and the first known Cuban caricature, dating from 1848. Visit in April for extra laughs at the International Humor Festival (entries remain on display for several weeks during this period).

The museum houses the work of Cuba's foremost caricaturist, Carlos Julio Villar Alemán, a member of Unión de Escritores y Artistas de Cuba (Uneac) and one-time judge at the festival. A few times monthly music and ballet are also staged here.

Galería Provincial Eduardo Abela GALLERY
(Calle 58 No 3708 cnr Calle 37; ☺noon-8pm Mon-Fri, 8am-8pm Sat, 8am-noon Sun) **FREE** This bold and groundbreaking art gallery is anything but provincial. The first room focuses on painting while others showcase poignant black-and-white photography. The gallery is named after city son Eduardo Abela, a Cuban artist perhaps most famous for creating El Bobo (The Fool), a cartoon character who poked fun at the Gerardo Machado dictatorship of the 1920s and '30s.

Activities

Boat trips on the Río Ariguanabo take off from a boat dock at the Hotel Las Yagrumas. A motor boat will take you on an 8km spin for CUC\$3. Rowing boats go for CUC\$1 an hour.

☰ Sleeping & Eating

The main shopping strip is Av 41, and there are numerous places to snack on peso treats along this street.

Hotel Las Yagrumas HOTEL \$
(☏47-38-44-60; Calle 40 y Final Autopista; s/d from CUC\$21/28; **P❄❄❄**) A hotel of untapped potential, Las Yagrumas, 3km north of San Antonio de los Baños, overlooks the picturesque but polluted Río Ariguanabo. Its 120 rooms with balcony and terrace (some river facing) are popular with peso-paying Cubans as opposed to foreign tourists, but many fixtures are falling apart. Sports facilities are better; there's table tennis and a gigantic pool (nonguests fee CUC\$6).

Boat trips take off on the nearby river.

Don Oliva CUBAN \$
(Calle 62 No 3512, btwn Calles 33 & 35; mains CUC\$3-5; ☺noon-11pm Tue-Sun) Quite possibly the cheapest lobster in Cuba is served on Don Oliva's secluded covered patio; the price coming in at less than CUC\$5, and it's not bad either. Not surprisingly this is a refreshingly untouristed new private restaurant with prices displayed in *moneda nacional*. Opt for the seafood.

☳ Drinking & Nightlife

Taberna del Tío Cabrera CLUB
(Calle 56 No 3910, btwn Calles 39 & 41; ☺2-5pm Mon-Fri, 2pm-1am Sat & Sun) An attractive garden nightclub that puts on occasional humor shows (organized in conjunction with the Museo del Humor). The clientele is a mix of townies, folk from surrounding villages and film-school students.

❶ Getting There & Away

Hard to get to without a car, San Antonio is supposedly connected to Havana's Estación 19 de Noviembre (four trains a day), but check well ahead. Otherwise, a taxi should cost CUC\$35 one way from central Havana.

Artemisa
☑ POP 57,160

Becoming the capital of Artemisa province is unlikely to ever transform Artemisa into a tourist mecca: this farming town's days of affluence and appeal lie firmly embedded in the past. Having once attracted notables such as Ernest Hemingway and the Cuban poet Nicolás Guillén, and having grown wealthy on the back of 19th-century sugar and coffee booms, Artemisa's importance declined when the bottom fell out of the sugar and coffee industries. It's known today as the Villa Roja (Red Town) for the famous fertility of its soil, which still yields a rich annual harvest of tobacco, bananas and sugarcane.

Artemisa has no accommodations for tourists: Soroa is the nearest option. As if in compensation, several stalls at the town end of the road to Antiguo Cafetal Angerona do mean peso pizza.

◉ Sights

If you're passing, Artemisa contains two national monuments, along with a restored section of the **Trocha Mariel-Majana**, a defensive wall erected by the Spanish during the Wars of Independence.

Mausoleo a los Mártires de Artemisa MAUSOLEUM
(☏47-36-32-76; Av 28 de Enero; admission CUC\$1; ☺9am-5pm Tue-Sun) Revolution buffs may want to doff a cap to the Mausoleo a los Mártires de Artemisa. Of the 119 revolutionaries who accompanied Fidel Castro in the 1953 assault on the Moncada Barracks, 28 were from Artemisa or this region. Fourteen of the men buried below the cube-shaped bronze mausoleum died in the assault or were killed soon after by Batista's troops. The other Moncada veterans buried here died later in the Sierra Maestra. A small subterranean museum contains combatants' photos and personal effects.

NORTH COAST BEACHES

The coastline along the north of Artemisa is occasionally visited for its little-used back road from Havana through to Bahía Honda and on to Pinar del Río Province (mostly by cyclists). The monstrous, and highly polluted, main settlement here, Mariel, is best known for the 125,000 Cubans who left here for Florida in the 1980 Mariel Boatlift. But east of Mariel are a couple of decent (and unpolluted) beaches. **Playa Salado** is a largely deserted beach with some 15 dive sites lying offshore, mostly accessed via excursion groups from Havana. **Playa Baracoa**, a few kilometers further east, is more developed. Near the shoreline big dudes lean on old American cars sipping beer while fishers throw lines from the rocky shore. A couple of basic beach shacks sell food, but there are no notable accommodations in the area.

Antiguo Cafetal Angerona HISTORIC SITE

FREE The Antiguo Cafetal Angerona, 5km west of Artemisa on the road to the Autopista Habana–Pinar del Río (A4), was one of Cuba's earliest *cafetales* (coffee farms). It's now a national monument. Erected between 1813 and 1820 by Cornelio Sauchay, Angerona once employed 450 slaves tending 750,000 coffee plants. Behind the ruined mansion lie the slave barracks, an old watchtower from which the slaves were monitored and multiple storage cellars. There's also a small museum with a reconstructed model of the *cafetal* buildings.

The estate is mentioned in novels by Cirilo Villaverde and Alejo Carpentier, and James A Michener devotes several pages to it in *Six Days in Havana*. It's a quiet and atmospheric place that has the feel of a latter-day Roman ruin. Look for the stone-pillared gateway and sign on the right after you leave Artemisa.

ℹ️ Getting There & Away

The bus station is on the Carretera Central in the center of town.

The **Artemisa train station** (Av Héroes del Moncada) is four blocks east of the bus station. There are supposed to be two trains a day from Havana at noon and midnight, but don't bank on it.

Soroa

📞48

Known appropriately as the 'rainbow of Cuba,' Soroa, a gorgeous natural area and tiny settlement 95km southwest of Havana, is the closest mountain resort to the capital. Located 8km north of Candelaria in the Sierra del Rosario, the easternmost and highest section of the Cordillera de Guaniguanico, the region's heavy rainfall (more than 1300mm

annually) promotes the growth of tall trees and orchids. The area gets its name from Jean-Pierre Soroa, a Frenchman who owned a 19th-century coffee plantation in these hills. One of his descendants, Ignacio Soroa, created the park as a personal retreat in the 1920s, and only since the Revolution has this luxuriant region been developed for tourism. This is a great area to explore by bike.

👁️ Sights & Activities

All Soroa's sights are conveniently near Hotel & Villas Soroa (p150), where you can organize horseback riding and a couple of hikes (guided for around CUC$6 hourly) into the surrounding forest. Other trails lead to a rock formation known as **Labyrinth de la Sierra Derrumbada** and an idyllic bathing pool, the **Poza del Amor** (Pond of Love). Ask at the hotel; it's the main information point for the area.

Orquideario Soroa GARDENS

(admission CUC$3, camera CUC$2; ⊗8:30am-4:30pm) Tumbling down a landscaped hillside garden next door to Hotel & Villas Soroa is a labor of love built by Spanish lawyer Tomás Felipe Camacho in the late 1940s in memory of his wife and daughter. Camacho traveled round the world to amass his collection of 700 orchid species (the largest in Cuba), including many endemic plants. Though he died in the 1960s, the Orquideario, connected to the University of Pinar del Río, lives on with guided tours in Spanish or English.

⭐ La Rosita VILLAGE

🐾 For some great bird-watching, head out on this, one of the most adventurous trails in Soroa, to the former eco-village of La Rosita (itself sadly destroyed by a recent hurricane), perched in the hills beyond the Hotel

> **ⓘ CODE WATCH**
> ....
> Whilst the rest of recently created Artemisa & Mayabeque got given area telephone code ☏ 47, Soroa and Las Terrazas fixed lines still use Pinar del Río's code (☏ 48).

& Villas Soroa. Nevertheless, this is one of the all-too-rare, hands-on opportunities to experience rural life as Cubans do – without the 'acting up' to tourists. Organize guides at Hotel & Villas Soroa.

La Rosita is accessed via the El Brujito path; the route is 5km or 17km, depending on your preference.

Castillo de las Nubes   CASTLE

A romantic castle with a circular tower on a hilltop 1.5km up a rough road beyond the Orquideario Soroa, the Castillo de las Nubes (Castle of the Clouds) makes for a good leg stretch. There are stunning views of the Valle de Soroa and the coastal plain from the ridge beyond the bar, but the interior – formerly a restaurant – is currently undergoing a refurbishment and will soon re-emerge as a boutique hotel.

Salto del Arco Iris   WATERFALL

(admission CUC$3; ⊙ 9am-6pm) This is a 22m waterfall on the Arroyo Manantiales. The entrance to the park encompassing it is to the right just before the Hotel & Villas Soroa. A path corkscrews to two viewpoints above and below the falls, at their most impressive in the May-to-October rainy season and at other times a trickle. You can swim here.

Baños Romanos   SWIMMING

(per hour CUC$5) On the opposite side of the stream from the Salto del Arco Iris car park is a stone bathhouse with a pool of cold sulfurous water. Ask at Hotel & Villas Soroa about the baths and massage treatments.

El Mirador   HIKING

Starting at the Baños Romanos, take the signposted well-trodden path 2km uphill to the Mirador, a rocky crag with an incredible sweeping panorama of all Soroa and the coastal flats beyond. Hungry turkey vultures circle below you.

Bird-Watching

This part of the Sierra del Rosario is one of the best bird-watching sites in western Cuba after the Ciénaga de Zapata. You don't have to ven-

ture far from Hotel & Villas Soroa to see species such as the Cuban trogon and the entertaining Cuban tody. Guided tours, arranged through the hotel, are CUC$6 per hour.

⊨ Sleeping & Eating

Several signposted houses on the road from Candelaria to Soroa, 3km below the Hotel & Villas Soroa, rent rooms and concoct meals. These are also worth considering as bases for visiting Las Terrazas.

★ Don Agapito   CASA PARTICULAR $

(☏ 58-12-17-91; Carretera a Soroa Km 8; r CUC$20-25; P ❈) Two fantastic, well-lit, super-clean rooms and some professional touches, including a personalized giant map of the province, make a stopover at this Soroa casa particular right next to the Orquideario a real pleasure. The food is equally marvelous. Check the garden with its own plant-festooned mini-cave!

Maité Delgado   CASA PARTICULAR $

(☏ 52-27-00-69; Carretera a Soroa Km 7; r CUC$20-25; P ❈ ❈) This bright three-room casa is within easy walking distance of the Soroa sights, the family is pleasant and there are kitchen privileges. If it's full, the owners will point you down the road in the direction of a few other houses.

Hotel & Villas Soroa   RESORT $$

(☏ 48-52-35-34; s/d all-incl CUC$51/72; P ❈ ❈) You can't knock the setting of this place nestled in a narrow valley amid stately trees and verdant hills (though you might wonder about the juxtaposition of these scattered blocklike cabins against such a breathtaking natural backdrop). Isolated and tranquil, there are 80 rooms in a spacious complex just shouting distance from the forest, along with an inviting pool, a small shop and an ordinary restaurant.

Restaurante el Salto   CARIBBEAN $

(CUC$5-12; ⊙ 9am-7pm) This simple place next to the Baños Romanos is your only eating option outside the hotel.

ⓘ Getting There & Away

The Havana–Viñales Víazul bus stops in Las Terrazas, but not Soroa; you can cover the last 16km in a taxi for CUC$15. If staying at a casa particular, ask about lifts. Transfer buses (not to be depended upon) sometimes pass through Soroa between Viñales and Havana. Inquire at Hotel & Villas Soroa, or at Havanatur in Viñales or Havana.

The only other access to Soroa and the surrounding area is with your own wheels: car, bicycle or moped. The Servi-Cupet gas station is on the Autopista at the turn-off to Candelaria, 8km below Soroa.

Las Terrazas

🎵 48 / POP 1200

The pioneering eco-village of Las Terrazas dates back to a reforestation project in 1968. Today it's a Unesco Biosphere Reserve, a burgeoning activity center (with Cuba's only canopy tour) and the site of the earliest surviving coffee plantations in Cuba. Not surprisingly, it attracts day-trippers from Havana by the busload.

Overnighters can stay in the community's sole hotel, the mold-breaking Hotel Moka, an upmarket eco-resort built between 1992 and 1994 by workers drawn from Las Terrazas to attract foreign tourists. Close by, in the picturesque whitewashed village that overlooks a small lake, there's a vibrant art community with open studios, woodwork and pottery workshops. But the region's biggest attraction is its verdant natural surroundings, which are ideal for hiking, relaxing and bird-watching.

◉ Sights

Aside from the coffee-estate ruins sequestered away in the fecund forest around Las Terrazas, the community has a good museum and an even better art gallery.

Peña de Polo Montañez   MUSEUM
(◷ Tue-Sun) FREE The former lakeside house of local *guajiro* (country folk) musician Polo Montañez, regarded as one of Cuba's finest-ever folk singers, is now a small museum containing various gold records and assorted memorabilia. It's right in the village overlooking the lake.

Polo's most famous songs included 'Guajiro Natural' and 'Un Monton de Estrellas'; they captured the heart of the nation between 2000 and 2002 with simple lyrics about love and nature. His stardom was short-lived, however: he died in a car accident in 2002.

Galleria de Lester Campa   GALLERY
(◷ daily, hours vary) FREE Several well-known Cuban artists are based at Las Terrazas, including Lester Campa, whose work has been exhibited internationally. Pop into his lakeside studio-gallery, on the right-hand side a few houses after Peña de Polo Montañez.

ARTEMISA & MAYABEQUE PROVINCES LAS TERRAZAS

LAS TERRAZAS: NEW MODEL VILLAGE

Back in 1968, when Al Gore was still cramming at Harvard and the nascent environmental movement was a prickly protest group for renegades with names like 'Swampy', the forward-thinking Cubans – concerned about the ecological cost of island-wide deforestation – came up with an idea.

The plan involved taking a 50-sq-km tract of degraded land in Cuba's mountainous west around the remains of some old French *cafetales* (coffee farms) and reforesting it on terraced, erosion-resistant slopes. In 1971, with the first phase of the plan completed, the workers on the project created a reservoir and on its shores constructed a groundbreaking model village to provide much-needed housing for the area's disparate inhabitants.

The result was Las Terrazas, Cuba's first eco-village, a thriving community of 1200 inhabitants whose self-supporting, sustainable settlement includes a hotel, myriad artisan shops, a vegetarian restaurant and small-scale organic farming techniques. The project was so successful that, in 1985, the land around Las Terrazas was incorporated into Cuba's first Unesco Biosphere Reserve, the Sierra del Rosario.

In 1994, as the tourist industry was expanded to counteract the economic effects of the Special Period (p460), Las Terrazas opened Hotel Moka (p153), an environmentally congruous hotel designed by minister of tourism and green architect Osmani Cienfuegos, brother of the late revolutionary hero Camilo.

Now established as Cuba's most authentic eco-resort, Las Terrazas operates on guiding principles that include energy efficiency, sustainable agriculture, environmental education and a sense of harmony between buildings and landscape. The area is also home to an important ecological research center.

La Plaza
PLAZA

(⊙24hr) In the village, the area just above Hotel Moka encompasses a cinema, a library and an ecological museum. All are generally open throughout the day, or can become so if you ask.

🏃 Activities

Hiking

The Sierra del Rosario has some of the best hikes in Cuba. However, they're all guided, so you can't officially do any of them on your own (nonexistent signposting deters all but the hardiest from trying). On the upside, most of the area's guides are highly trained, which means you'll emerge from the experience both fitter and wiser. The cost of hikes varies depending on the number of people and the length of the walk. Bank on anything between CUC$15 and CUC$25 per person. Book at the Oficinas del Complejo (p154) or Hotel Moka.

San Claudio
HIKING

The biosphere's toughest hike is a 20km trail traversing the hills to the northwest of the community, and culminating in the 20m-high San Claudio waterfall. It was once offered as an overnighter (with opportunities to camp out in the forest), but hurricane damage had curtailed the time of writing.

El Contento
HIKING

This 7.6km ramble takes you through the reserve's foothills between the Campismo el Taburete (rustic accommodation for Cubans only) and the Baños del San Juan, taking in two coffee-estate ruins: San Ildelfonso and El Contento.

El Taburete
HIKING

This 5.6km hike has the same start/finish point as El Contento, but follows a more direct route over the 452m Loma el Taburete, where a poignant monument is dedicated to the 38 Cuban guerrillas who trained in these hills for Che Guevara's ill-fated Bolivian adventure.

Sendero la Serafina
HIKING

The easy 6.4km La Serafina loop starts and finishes near the Rancho Curujey. It's a well-known paradise for bird-watchers (there are more than 70 bird species on show). Halfway through the walk you will pass the ruins of the Cafetal Santa Serafina, one of the first coffee farms in the Caribbean.

Sendero las Delicias
HIKING

This 3km route runs from Rancho Curujey to the Cafetal Buenavista, incorporating some fantastic views.

Bajo del Corte del Tocororo
HIKING

A 6km hike that ventures out from the village, traverses the skirts of Loma El Salón, and finishes at Hacienda Unión. It is ideal for spotting Cuba's national bird, the *tocororo* (Cuban trogon).

Swimming

Baños del San Juan
SWIMMING

(admission with lunch CUC$10) It's hard to envisage more idyllic natural swimming pools than those situated 3km to the south of Hotel Moka down an undulating paved road. These *baños* (baths) are surrounded by naturally terraced rocks, where the clean, bracing waters cascade into a series of pools.

Riverside, there are a handful of open-air eating places, along with changing rooms, showers and overnight cabins, though the spot still manages to retain a sense of rustic isolation.

Baños del Bayate
SWIMMING

(admission CUC$3) Natural baths.

Cycling

A 30km guided cycling tour takes in most of the area's highlights for CUC$22. Inquire at Hotel Moka, which hires bicycles out for CUC$2 per hour.

Ziplining

Cuba's only canopy tour (per person CUC$35) maintains three zip lines that catapult you over Las Terrazas village and the Lago del San Juan like an eagle in flight. The total 'flying' distance is 800m. Professional instructors maintain high safety standards. To book the ziplining, get in touch with the Oficinas del Complejo (p154) near Rancho Curujey.

🛏 Sleeping & Eating

Through Hotel Moka you can also book five rustic cabins 3km away in Río San Juan (single/double CUC$15/25) or arrange tent camping (CUC$12). There are also three villas (single/double CUC$60/85) available for rent in the village.

You'll find other *ranchónes* (rural farms) at Cafetal Buenavista, Baños del Bayate and Baños del San Juan.

COFFEE REPUBLIC

The Las Terrazas area once supported 54 *cafetales* (coffee estates) at the height of the Cuban coffee boom in the 1820s and '30s. Today, coffee is barely grown at all here, but you can discover the jungle-immersed ruins of at least half-a-dozen old *cafetales*. In addition to the below, the ruins of **San Ildefonso** and **El Contento** *cafetales* can be seen on the El Contento hike; you can explore what's left of **Santa Sefarina** *cafetal* on the Sendero la Sefarina hike.

Cafetal Buenavista The most moving ruins are about 1.5km up the hill from the Puerta las Delicias (eastern) gate, and accessible by road. Cafetal Buenavista is Cuba's oldest (now partially restored) coffee plantation, built in 1801 by French refugees from Haiti. The huge *tajona* (grindstone) out the back once extracted coffee beans from their shells. Next, the beans were sun-dried on huge platforms. Ruins of the quarters of some of the 126 slaves held here can be seen alongside the driers.

The attic of the master's house (now a restaurant) was used to store the beans until they could be carried down to the port of Mariel by mule. There are decent views from here, best appreciated on the Sendero las Delicias hike which incorporates the *cafetal*.

San Pedro & Santa Catalina These 19th-century coffee-estate ruins are down a branch road at **La Cañada del Infierno** (Trail to Hell), midway between the Hotel Moka access road and the Soroa side entrance gate. A kilometer off the main road, just before the ruins of the San Pedro coffee estate, a bar overlooks a popular swimming spot. After this it's another kilometer to Santa Catalina. A trail leads on from here to Soroa.

Hacienda Unión About 3.5km west of the Hotel Moka access road, the Hacienda Unión is another partially reconstructed coffee-estate ruin that features a country-style restaurant, a small flower garden known as the **Jardín Unión** and horseback riding (CUC$6 per hour).

Villa Duque CASA PARTICULAR $
(☑ 52-32-68-71, 53-22-14-31; Carretera a Caya-jabos Km 2, Finca San Andres; r CUC$20; P ❄) Eco-tourism doesn't have to come at a cost. Those on a budget might wish to check out this farmhouse 2km before the eastern entrance of Las Terrazas, which has two spick-and-span rooms, a fridge full of beer, a wrap-around balcony and breakfast included in the price. The fresh country smells come free of charge too.

★**Hotel Moka** RESORT $$
(☑ 48-57-86-00; Las Terrazas; s/d all-incl CUC$105/120; P ❄ ☀) ✔ Cuba's only *real* eco-hotel might not qualify for the four stars it advertises, but who's arguing? With its trickling fountains, blooming flower garden and resident tree growing through the lobby, Moka would be a catch in any country. The 26 bright, spacious rooms have fridges, satellite TV and bathtubs with a stupendous view (there are blinds for the shy).

Equipped with a bar, restaurant, shop, pool and tennis court, the hotel also acts as an information center for the reserve and can organize everything from hiking to fishing.

★**El Romero** VEGETARIAN $
(Las Terrazas; ☺ noon-9pm; ☑) ✔ The most interesting place to grab a bite, this full-blown eco-restaurant specializes in vegetarian fare. El Romero uses solar energy and home-grown organic vegetables and herbs, and keeps its own bees. You'll think you've woken up in San Francisco when you browse the menu replete with hummus, bean pancake, pumpkin and onion soup, and extra-virgin olive oil.

Patio de María CAFE $
(Las Terrazas; snacks CUC$0.50-2; ☺ 9am-10pm) ✔ Patio de María is a small, brightly painted coffee bar that might just qualify for the best brew in Cuba. The secret comes in the expert confection (María lives upstairs) and the fact that the beans are grown about 20m away from your cup in front of the flowery terrace.

Rancho Curujey CARIBBEAN $
(Las Terrazas; ☺ 9am-6pm) This *ranchón*-style set-up offers beer and snacks under a small thatched canopy overlooking Lago Palmar.

Casa del Campesino CARIBBEAN $
(Las Terrazas; ☺ 9am-9pm) Of the *ranchón*-style restaurants dotted around, this one adjacent to the Hacienda Unión about 3.5km west of the Hotel Moka access road, is a visitor favorite.

ℹ️ Information

Las Terrazas is 20km northeast of Hotel & Villas Soroa and 13km west of the Havana–Pinar del Río Autopista at Cayajabos. There are toll gates at both entrances to the reserve (CUC$3 per person). The eastern toll gate, Puerta las Delicias, is a good source of information on the park, while the best place to get information and arrange excursions is at the **Oficinas del Complejo** (☑️ 48-57-87-00, 48-57-85-55), adjacent to Rancho Curujey, or on the other side of the road at Hotel Moka (p153); both places act as nexus points for the reserve. None of these information points should be confused with the Centro de Investigaciones Ecológicas, a research station approached via a separate driveway east of Rancho Curujey.

ℹ️ Getting There & Away

Two Víazul buses a day currently stop at the Rancho Curujey next door to Las Terrazas; one

at around 10am from Havana to Pinar del Río and Viñales, the other around 4pm heading in the opposite direction. Occasional transfer buses pass through bound for Havana or Viñales. Inquire at Hotel Moka or contact the Viñales office of Infotur (p182).

ℹ️ Getting Around

The Esso station is 1.5km west of the Hotel Moka access road. Fill up here before heading east to Havana or west to Pinar del Río. Most excursions organize transport. Otherwise, you'll have to rely on hire car, taxi or your own two feet to get around.

MAYABEQUE PROVINCE

Tiny Mayabeque, now the country's smallest province, is a productive little place, cultivating citrus fruit, tobacco, grapes for wine and the sugarcane for Havana Club rum, the main distillery of which is also here. Tour-

TRAINS & FLOATS & GAMES: BEJUCAL'S ATTRACTIONS

The provincial town of Bejucal in Mayabeque province is a workaday sort of place, with two notable exceptions: its foundational role in Cuba's fascinating rail history; and its riotous end-of-year street party, Las Charangas.

Bejucal was the destination of Cuba's first pioneering train, which chugged into action in November 1837, long before any other country in Latin America had a rail network and, ironically, 11 years before colonial overlord Spain. The inaugural line ran for 27.5km, connecting Havana with Bejucal. This success was followed up by an 80km line from Camagüey to the port of Nuevitas on Cuba's north coast, and by 1848 tramways were crisscrossing the streets of Havana, before any European city outside of Paris.

Until the beginning of the 20th century, 80% of Cuban railways were associated with the sugar industry. It wasn't until 1902 that the west–east passenger network was joined for the first time by US-Canadian railway magnate William Van Horne (builder of the first Canadian transcontinental railway), creating a line that stretched 1100km from Guane in Pinar del Río province to Guantánamo in the east.

After the Revolution and the US trade embargo that ensued, Cuba's once ground-breaking rail network struggled to find new rolling stock and fuel. Artemisa and Mayabeque Provinces remain the best turf in the country for spotting the locomotives still out there trundling, being the network nexus, but the outlook for trainspotters is increasingly lean outside of the museums.

Bejucal's station – the nation's first – is a gaily painted affair, although the railway museum here no longer operates; there are others in Havana (p76) and at the Museo de Agroindustria Azucarero Marcelo Salado (p268) near Caibarién in Villa Clara province. But a couple of daily trains pass through from Havana's Estación Central, so you can still run (read: chug) that inaugural rail route.

There is one other overwhelming reason to visit Bejucal – if you happen to be in Havana around Christmas – and that is for one of Cuba's brightest, most riotous street parties, **Las Charangas**. The town splits into two competing groups – the Ceiba de Plata (Silver Ceiba), and the Espina de Oro (Golden Thorn) – who hit the streets dancing and singing among outrageously large, dazzling floats and the famous Bejucal *tambores* (drums) in a tradition harking back to the early 1800s.

There's no real accommodation in town for travelers, but at 40km from Havana, Bejucal is within easy day-tripping reach. The only option for reaching Bejucal other than train is by taxi/private car (for around CUC$40 one-way).

ists, predominantly Cubans, come here principally for the sandy coast in the northeast, drawn by the good-value resorts that back onto beautiful beaches for a fraction of the price of a Varadero vacation. Inland amid the workaday agricultural atmosphere lie some luxuriant scenic treats: landscaped gardens, the picturesque protected area of Jaruco, Cuba's best bridge and *the* classic Cuban train journey transecting the lot.

Playa Jibacoa Area

Playa Jibacoa is the Varadero that never was, or the Varadero yet to come – depending on your hunch. For the time being it's a mainly Cuban getaway with a coastal branch road from the main Vía Blanca highway winding by an all-inclusive resort, a hotel-standard campismo (cheap rustic accommodation in bungalows) and several other scenic sleeping options thrown in for good measure. Punctuated by a series of small but splendid beaches and blessed with good offshore snorkeling, Jibacoa is backed by a lofty limestone terrace overlooking the ocean. The terrace offers excellent views and some short DIY hikes.

Travelers with children will find interesting things to do in the surrounding area, and the popularity of the region with Cuban families means fast friends are made wherever you go. The Vía Blanca, running between Havana and Matanzas, is the main transport artery in the area, although few buses make scheduled stops here, making Playa Jibacoa a more challenging pit stop than it should be. Just inland are picturesque farming communities and tiny time-warped hamlets linked by the Hershey Electric Railway.

◉ Sights

Puente de Bacunayagua   BRIDGE
Marking the border between Havana and Matanzas provinces, this is Cuba's longest (314m) and highest (103m) bridge. Begun in 1957 and finally opened by Fidel Castro in September 1959, it carries the busy Vía Blanca across a densely wooded canyon that separates the Valle de Yumurí from the sea. There's a snack bar and observation deck (8am to 10pm) on the Havana side of the bridge where you can sink some drinks in front of one of Cuba's most awe-inspiring views.

HAVANA CLUB'S HUB

Some 30km west of the province-spanning bridge, Santa Cruz del Norte is a quiet town that's home to a famous rum factory: the Ronera Santa Cruz, producer of Havana Club rum and one of the biggest plants of its kind in Cuba. Havana Club, founded in 1878 by the Arechabala family of Cárdenas, opened its first distillery at Santa Cruz del Norte in 1919, and in 1973 a new factory was built with the capacity to produce 30 million liters of rum annually. No tours are currently run, but Havana Club is widely available throughout the country.

Imagine hundreds of royal palm trees standing like ghostly sentries down the sheering valley slopes and in the distance dark, bulbous hills, splashes of blue ocean. The bridge restaurant is a favorite stopping-off point for tour buses and taxis, and aside from hire car, these are your only means of visiting.

Central Camilo Cienfuegos   LANDMARK
Standing disused on a hilltop like a huge rusting iron skeleton, this former sugar mill, 5km south of Santa Cruz del Norte, was one of Cuba's largest and a testimony to the country's previous production clout. Opened in 1916, it once belonged to the Philadelphia-based Hershey Chocolate Company, which used the sugar to sweeten its world-famous chocolate. The Hershey Electric Railway used to transport produce and workers between Havana, Matanzas and the small town that grew up around the mill.

While the train still runs three times a day (and stops in the town center), the mill was closed in July 2002.

Jardines de Hershey   GARDENS
These gardens, formerly owned by the famous American chocolate tycoon Milton Hershey who ran the nearby sugar mill, are charmingly wild these days, with attractive paths, abundant green foliage and a beautiful river, plus a couple of thatched-roof restaurants. It's a serene spot for lunch and a stroll. The gardens are approximately 1km north of Camilo Cienfuegos train station on the Hershey train line. From Playa Jibacoa, it's a pleasantly walkable 4km south of Santa Cruz del Norte.

WORTH A TRIP

THE HERSHEY TRAIN

'Cow on the line,' drawls the bored-looking ticket seller. 'Train shut for cleaning' reads a scruffy hand-scrawled notice. To *habaneros* (people from Havana), the catalog of daily transport delays is tediously familiar. While the name of the antique Hershey Electric Railway might suggest a sweet treat to most visitors, in Cuba it signifies a more bitter mix of bumpy journeys, hard seats and interminable waits.

Built in 1921 by US chocolate 'czar' Milton S Hershey (1857–1945), the electric-powered railway line was originally designed to link the American mogul's humungous sugar mill in eastern Havana province with stations in Matanzas and the capital. Running along a trailblazing rural route, it soon became a lifeline for isolated communities cut off from the provincial transport network.

In 1959 the Hershey factory was nationalized and renamed Central Camilo Cienfuegos after Cuba's celebrated rebel commander. But the train continued to operate, clinging unofficially to its chocolate-inspired nickname. In the true tradition of the postrevolutionary 'waste not, want not' economy, it also clung to the same tracks, locomotives, carriages, signals and stations.

While a long way from *Orient Express*–style luxury, an excursion on today's Hershey train is a captivating journey back in time to the days when cars were for rich people and sugar was king. For outsiders, this is Cuba as the Cubans see it. It's a microcosm of rural life with all its daily frustrations, conversations, foibles and – er – fun.

The train seemingly stops at every house, hut, horse stable and hillock between Havana and Matanzas. Getting off is something of a toss-up. Beach bums can disembark at Guanabo and wander 2km north for a taste of Havana's rustic eastern resorts. History buffs can get off at Central Camilo Cienfuegos and stroll around the old Hershey sugar-mill ruins. You can also alight at Jibacoa for Playa Jibacoa's tucked-away beach paradise and at indeterminate stops through the beautiful Valle de Yumurí.

Activities

There is good snorkeling from the beach facing Campismo los Cocos; heading westward along the coast you'll find unpopulated pockets where you can don a mask or relax under a palm.

Finca Campensino
Rancho Gaviota   HORSEBACK RIDING, KAYAKING
(☏ 47-61-47-02; admission incl meal CUC$8; ☺9am-5pm) This activities center, 12km inland from Puerto Escondido via the pretty, palm-sprinkled Valle de Yumurí, is usually incorporated into day trips from Matanzas and Varadero. The hilltop ranch overlooks a reservoir and offers horseback riding, kayaking and cycling, plus a massive feast of local Cuban fare. Huts showcase various elements of Cuban agriculture, such as coffee and sugarcane – with tastings.

This is normally offered as a day tour. To get to the *ranchón*, take the inland road for 2km to Arcos de Canasí and turn left at the fork for another 10km to the signpost.

Sleeping & Eating

Casas particulares are coming to Playa Jibacoa; they're currently only for Cuban guests (although you can sometimes sneak a night at them) and line the Matanzas end of the coast road after the last of the hotels. Eating is a grim prospect over this way unless you're in a hotel. You could try the Puente de Bacunayagua restaurant; otherwise there are a couple of bars around selling microwave pizza.

Campismo los Cocos   CAMPISMO $
(☏ 47-29-52-31; s/d CUC$19/28; P❄☀♿) The newest and nicest of Cubamar's 80 or more campismo sites, Los Cocos has facilities to match a midrange hotel and a beachside setting that emulates the big shots in Varadero. Ninety self-contained cabins are clustered around a pool set in the crook of the province's low steplike cliffs.

Facilities include a small library, a medical post, an à la carte restaurant, a games room, rooms for travelers with disabilities and walking trails (up to a mirador on the limestone terrace backing the site). Note that amenities are showing their age and there's often blaring poolside music to contend with.

Cameleón Villas Jibacoa RESORT $$

(☏47-29-52-05; s/d all-incl CUC$70/100; P❄@☲) This friendly, well-landscaped resort has great snorkeling and large spick-and-span rooms (including new ones in a pink block set further back from the coast). It's pretty good bang for your buck. It's marketed as a three-star resort and is popular with package tourists from Canada.

★ Memories Jibacoa Beach RESORT $$$

(☏47-29-51-22; www.memoriesresorts.com; s/d all-incl CUC$106/170; P❄@☲) Who knew? One of Cuba's best all-inclusive resorts isn't in Varadero (or any other resort strip for that matter), but in the more tranquil confines of Jibacoa. The secret? This 250-room resort doesn't try too hard. The trickling fountains, 24-hour pool and narrow but idyllic beach are elegantly unpretentious.

Then there's the joy of the surf and turf surroundings – boat trips from the shore and trekking into the uplifted terraces just inland. Formerly SuperClub Breezes, the resort has a 100-room expansion planned. Coming from Matanzas, the turn-off is 13km west of the Puente de Bacunayagua.

❶ Getting There & Away

The best – some would say the *only* – way to get to Playa Jibacoa is on the Hershey Electric Railway from Casablanca train station in Havana to Jibacoa Pueblo. There's no bus to the beach from the station and traffic is sporadic, so bank on hiking the last 5km – a not unpleasant walk if you don't have too much gear.

One other option is to take crowded thrice-daily bus 669 from outside La Coubre Station (p123), just south of Havana's Estación Central, to Santa Cruz del Norte, still 9km from Jibacoa. Another alternative is to go to the Havana bus station and take any bus headed for Matanzas along the Vía Blanca. Talk to the driver to arrange a drop-off at Playa Jibacoa, just across a long bridge from Villa Loma de Jibacoa.

Jaruco

POP 18,107

Jaruco, set back from the coast between Havana and Matanzas, is a good day trip for travelers with a car, moped or bike who want to give the beaches a miss and instead sample quintessential rural Cuba.

Jaruco village is a wash of pastel-hued houses bunched along steeply pitching streets that wouldn't look amiss in the Peruvian Andes. The **Parque Escaleras de Jaruco**, 6km west via hushed unmarked lanes, is a protected area featuring forests, caves and strangely shaped limestone cliffs similar to the *mogotes* of the Viñales valley. *Habaneros* (people from Havana) come here for bucolic weekend breaks Thursday through Sunday, the park's only official opening days, but with a minor road bisecting the park between Tapaste (off the Autopista Nacional) and Jaruco, you can slip in any time. This forgotten oasis has outstanding *miradors* (viewpoints) over Mayabeque province. A handful of restaurants open up from Thursday to Sunday and blare out cheesy music, which can disrupt the serenity. The best of these is the pleasant *ranchón*-style **El Criollo** (◷11:30am-5pm Thu-Sun), where you'll pay in pesos for various pork- and fish-focused offerings.

It's 32km to Jaruco from Guanabo in a southeasterly direction via Campo Florido, and you can make it a loop by returning through Santa Cruz del Norte, 18km northeast of Jaruco via Central Camilo Cienfuegos. A taxi from Havana costs CUC$35 one way.

UN BOCADITO, POR FAVOR

One part of bussing it around by Víazul that you'll get accustomed to pretty quickly is the overly lengthy stop at a government restaurant in the middle of nowhere. There's a couple of classic stopovers in Mayabeque province (Havana–Varadero buses always stop here) and if you're hungry (or bored) in the 30 minutes you'll be waiting you'll also get acquainted intimately with the *bocadito*, as often as not the only available item on the menu. A *bocadito* is a savory snack in many Latin American countries but in Cuba it translates onto the plate as a sandwich. Almost always, the filling is ham and cheese. A pungent cheese similar to the Alsace region's Munster is used, but the notable bit is the ham. In a tried-and-tested money-saving throwback to the Special Period (p460), the ham will look from the front of the sandwich like it's several layers thick. Open the bread, however, and you'll see the ham folded multiple times at the front to give a mere appearance of an ample portion: at the back, it will be just the one lonesome layer of meat.

Surgidero de Batabanó

POP 22,313

Spanish colonizers founded the original settlement of Havana on the site of Surgidero de Batabanó on August 25, 1515, but quickly abandoned it in favor of the north coast. Looking around the decrepit town today, with its ugly apartment blocks and grubby beachless seafront, it's not difficult to see why. The only reason you're likely to end up in this fly-blown port is during the purgatorial bus-boat trip to the Isla de la Juventud. Should there be unforeseen delays, either staying within the port confines or cabbing it back to Havana, however depressing, are preferable to spending any time in the town itself.

Fidel Castro and the other Moncada prisoners disembarked here on May 15, 1955, after Fulgencio Batista granted them amnesty.

🛈 Getting There & Away

The ferry from Surgidero de Batabanó to Isla de la Juventud is supposed to leave daily at 1pm with an additional sailing at 4pm on Friday and Sunday (two hours). It is highly advisable to buy your bus-boat combo ticket (CUC$55) in Havana from the office at the main Astro bus station rather than turning up and doing it here. More often than not convertible tickets are sold out to bus passengers.

There's a **Servi-Cupet gas station** (Calle 64 No 7110, btwn Calles 71 & 73) in Batabanó town. The next Servi-Cupet station east is in Güines.

Isla de la Juventud (Special Municipality)

POP 86,420

Includes ➡

Isla de la Juventud...161

Nueva Gerona.......161

East of Nueva
Gerona.............167

South of Nueva
Gerona.............167

The Southern
Military Zone........168

Cayo Largo del Sur ..169

Best Beaches

➡ Playa Sirena (p169)

➡ Cayo Rico (p170)

➡ Playa Larga (p169)

➡ Punta Francés (p165)

Best Places to Stay

➡ Sol Cayo Largo (p171)

➡ Villa Choli – Ramberto Pena Silva (p164)

➡ Hotel Colony (p167)

➡ Villa Marinera (p171)

Why Go?

Historic refuge from the law for everyone from 16th-century pirates to 20th-century gangsters, La Isla is perhaps the quirkiest castaway destination you ever will see. Dumped like a crumpled apostrophe 100km off mainland Cuba, this pine-tree-clad island is the Caribbean's sixth largest. But the Cayman Islands this isn't. Other tourists? Uh-uh. And if you thought other Cuban towns were time-warped, try blowing the dust off island capital Nueva Gerona, where the main street doubles as a baseball diamond and the food 'scene' is stuck in the Special Period. Yet, if you make it here, you're in for a true adventure. The main lure is diving some of the Caribbean's most pristine reefs but otherwise, get used to being becalmed – as locals have – with the coral, the odd crocodile and a colorful history that reads like an excerpt from *Treasure Island*.

Further east, Cayo Largo del Sur is La Isla's polar opposite, a manufactured tourist enclave renowned for its wide, white-sand beaches.

When to Go

➡ The beach life, diving and snorkeling are highlights of La Isla, Cayo Largo or any of the other mini-paradises in the Archipiélago de los Canarreos. The hottest times are the best: July to August along with the cooler-but-balmy high season in December to April.

➡ Always-spirited Nueva Gerona ups the ante for its biggest party, Carnaval, in March.

Isla de la Juventud Highlights

1 Getting the lowdown on local life in petite, sleepy **Nueva Gerona** (p161).

2 Lolling away the scorching afternoons at the tranquil reservoir of **Presa El Abra** (p163).

3 Exploring the ominous prison where Fidel Castro was once incarcerated at **Presidio Modelo** (p167).

4 Gawking at ancient cave paintings at **Cueva de Punta del Este** (p169).

5 Diving amid wrecks, walls, coral gardens and caves at **Punta Francés** (p165), *the* best place to dive in Cuba.

6 Watching turtles nesting on the moonlit beaches of **Cayo Largo del Sur** (p169).

7 Trekking along the wide, white (sometimes nudist) beaches to Cayo Largo del Sur's **Playa Sirena** (p169).

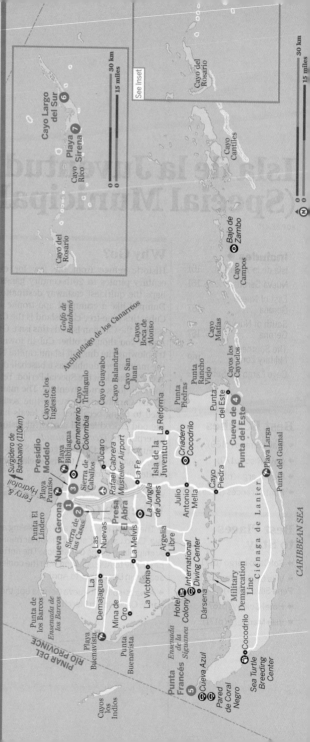

History

La Isla's star-studded history starts with its first settlers, the Siboney, a pre-ceramic civilization who came to the island around 1000 BC via the Lesser Antilles. They named their new homeland Siguanea and created a fascinating set of cave paintings, which still survive in Cueva de Punta del Este.

Columbus arrived in June 1494 and promptly renamed the island Juan el Evangelista, claiming it for the Spanish crown. But the Spanish did little to develop their new possession, which was knotted with mangroves and surrounded by shallow reefs.

Instead La Isla became a hideout for pirates, including Francis Drake and Henry Morgan. They called it Parrot Island, and their exploits are said to have inspired Robert Louis Stevenson's novel *Treasure Island*.

In December 1830 the Colonia Reina Amalia (now Nueva Gerona) was founded, and throughout the 19th century the island served as a place of imposed exile for independence advocates and rebels, including José Martí. Twentieth-century dictators Gerardo Machado and Fulgencio Batista followed this Spanish example by sending political prisoners – Fidel Castro included – to the island, which had by then been renamed a fourth time as Isla de Pinos (Isle of Pines).

As the infamous 1901 Platt amendment placed Isla de Pinos outside the boundaries of the 'mainland' part of the archipelago, some 300 US colonists also settled here, working the citrus plantations and building the efficient infrastructure that survives today (albeit a tad more dilapidated). By the 1950s La Isla had become a favored vacation spot for rich Americans, who flew in daily from Miami. Fidel Castro abruptly ended the decadent party in 1959.

In the 1960s and 1970s, thousands of young people from across the developing world volunteered to study here at specially built 'secondary schools' (although their presence is almost non-existent today). In 1978 their role in developing the island was officially recognized when the name was changed for the fifth time to Isla de la Juventud (Isle of Youth).

ISLA DE LA JUVENTUD

♪ 46

Large, very detached and set to a slow metronome, La Isla is both historically and culturally different to the rest of the Cuban archipelago. Mass sugar and tobacco production never existed here and, until the Castro revolution, the island yielded to a greater American influence. Eclectic expat communities, which call on Cayman Island, American and Japanese ancestry, have even thrown up their own musical style, a sub-genre of Cuban *son* known as *sucu sucu*. Today the island, bereft of the foreign students that once populated its famous schools, is sleepy but extravagantly esoteric: where else do prisons masquerade as museums and scuppered ships await for you to dive down to – or to party in? The opportunities for getting (way) off the beaten track will appeal to divers, escape artists, adventurers and committed contrarians.

Nueva Gerona

Flanked by the Sierra de las Casas to the west and the Sierra de Caballos to the east, Nueva Gerona is a small, unhurried town that hugs the left bank of the Río las Casas, the island's only large river. Its museums and vivacious entertainment scene will detain, entertain and drain you for a day or two before you trundle out to explore the swashbuckling south, and it has almost 100% of the island's somewhat scant services.

◉ Sights

Museo Casa Natal Jesus Montané MUSEUM
(cnr Calles 24 & 45; ⊘9:30am-5pm Tue-Sat, 8:30am-noon Sun) **FREE** This museum documents the life of revolutionary Jesús Montané, who was born here, took part in the Moncada Barracks attack in 1953, fought alongside Fidel Castro in the Sierra Maestra, and served in the post-1959 government. It's a small but fascinating place and well worth 30 minutes of your time.

Museo Municipal MUSEUM
(Calle 30, btwn Calles 37 & 39; admission CUC$1; ⊘8am-1pm & 2-5pm Mon-Fri, to 4pm Sat, to noon Sun) In the former Casa de Gobierno (1853), the Museo Municipal houses a small historical collection that romps through the best of the island's past. It begins with a huge wall-mounted map of La Isla and continues through themed *salas* (rooms) relating to aboriginals, pirates, US occupiers (most interestingly including gangster Charles 'Lucky' Luciano) and some local art.

Nueva Gerona

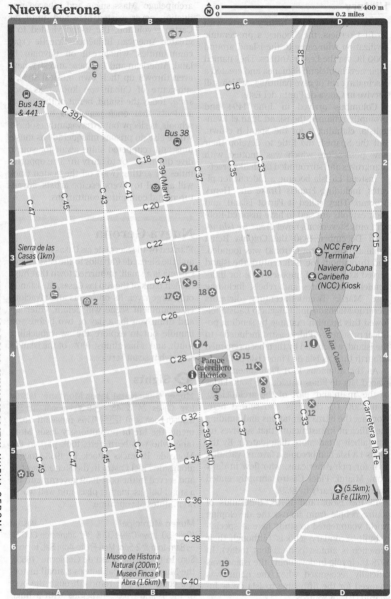

El Pinero MONUMENT

(Calle 28, btwn Calle 33 & river) Two blocks east of Parque Guerrillero Heroico, you'll see a huge black-and-white ferry set up as a tatty memorial next to the river. This is *El Pinero*, the original boat used to transport passengers between La Isla and the main island. On May 15, 1955, Fidel and Raúl Castro, along with the other prisoners released from Moncada, returned to the main island on this vessel. These days it's a meeting point for young reggaetón fanatics (read: very loud music).

Nueva Gerona

◎ Sights
1 El Pinero D4
2 Museo Casa Natal Jesus
   Montané A3
3 Museo Municipal C4
4 Nuestra Señora de los Dolores B4

⊜ Sleeping
5 Tu Isla A3
6 Villa Mas – Jorge Luis Mas
   Peña A1
7 Villa Peña B1

⊗ Eating
8 Cubalse Supermarket C4
9 El Cochinito B3
10 Mercado Agropecuario C3
11 Pizzería la Góndola C4
12 Restaurante Río D5
   Restaurante Tu Isla .... (see 5)

◎ Drinking & Nightlife
13 Disco la Movida D2
   El Pinero ....(see 1)
14 La Rumba B3

⊕ Entertainment
15 Cine Caribe C4
16 Estadio Cristóbal Labra A5
17 Sucu Suco B3
18 Uneac C3

⊕ Shopping
19 Centro Experimental de Artes
   Aplicadas C6

Nuestra Señora de los Dolores   CHURCH
(cnr Calles 28 & 39) On the northwest side of Parque Guerrillero Heroico, this dinky, Mexican colonial-style church was built in 1926, after the original was destroyed by a hurricane. In 1957 the parish priest, Guillermo Sardiñas, left Nueva Gerona to join Fidel Castro in the Sierra Maestra, the only Cuban priest to do so.

Museo de Historia Natural   MUSEUM
(cnr Calles 41 & 52; admission CUC$1; ⊙8am-5pm Tue-Sat, to noon Sun) Realistically, this is a dusty heap of stuffed animals crying out for government investment. It's worth visiting only if you are passing en route to Museo Finca El Abra. It's just before the distinctive tower of the Archivo Histórico on Calle 41, the Hotel Colony road.

Museo Finca el Abra   MUSEUM
(Carretera Siguanea Km 2; admission CUC$1; ⊙9am-5pm Tue-Sat, to noon Sun) On October 17,

1870, the teenage José Martí spent nine weeks of exile at this farm before his deportation to Spain. Legend has it that the revolutionary's mother forged the shackles he wore here into a ring, which Martí wore to his death. Set below the Sierra de las Casas, the old hacienda's surroundings are as much of an attraction as the museum. It's signed off the main road to Hotel Colony (a continuation of Calle 41), 3km southwest of Nueva Gerona.

The house is still occupied by descendants of Giuseppe Girondella, who hosted Martí here. A dirt road just before the museum leads north to the island's former marble quarry, clearly visible in the distance. The quarry is moderately interesting (if you like big holes in the ground), but the real attraction is the climb up the hill, from where there are lovely views. After descending, continue north between a garbage dump and several rows of pig pens to Calle 54 on the right. This street will bring you back into town via the Museo de Historia Natural, six blocks to the east.

🏃 Activities

★**Presa El Abra**   WATER SPORTS
(Carretera Siguanea; ⊙noon-5:30pm) Where have all the folk from Nueva Gerona gone? Gone to cool off in Presa El Abra, every one. On a scalding La Isla afternoon, you'd best join them. With verdant shores (perfect for picnics), this wide *presa* (reservoir) has Nueva Gerona's best restaurant (p164), plus various craft for aquatic shenanigans, including kayaks (CUC$1.50 per hour) and aquatic bicycles (CUC$3 per hour).

Sierra de las Casas   HIKING
Behold the view from the northernmost face of the craggy Sierra de las Casas! From the west end of Calle 22, a few hundred meters along a dirt track, a sinuous trail on the left heads toward the hills, at the foot of which is a deep cave and local swimming hole.

ℹ ON YOUR BIKE

The area around Nueva Gerona is a good area to discover on bicycle, with beaches, and the big three attractions of the Presa El Abra reservoir, Museo Finca el Abra and the Presidio Modelo all only a few kilometers from the town centre. The folk at Villa Choli (p164) in Nueva Gerona organize bike rental.

ISLA DE LOS CASINOS?

Oh, what could have been. Charles 'Lucky' Luciano (the 'Boss of Bosses' of the mafia world of the 1940s and 1950s) having sized up the Isla de los Pinos (as Isla de la Juventud was then known), decided in about 1946 that the isle was ripe for conversion into a gambling destination to rival Monte Carlo. American narcotics agents tracked down Luciano, who consequently had to flee Cuba, but his partner-in-crime Meyer Lansky did proceed with the scheme. In 1958 a Hilton Hotel with a casino was duly opened (now the Hotel Colony, p167). But the days of decadence were short-lived. The coming of Fidel Castro a year later put a stop to gambling in Cuba for good. At least, that is the official line. However, merchandise produced to celebrate the opening of La Isla to high-stakes gaming can still be found in Cuban shops today.

Beyond here a trail ascends steeply to the mountaintop.

The view from the summit is amazing, taking in half the island, though the final stretch of the ascent is a bit closer to rock scrambling than hiking.

Tours

Ecotur TOUR
(46-32-71-01; Calle 39 btwn Calles 28 & 30; 8am-4pm Mon-Fri) Organizes trips into the militarized zone (where the Cueva de Punta del Este cave paintings and Cocodrilo are located) and to Punta Francés; also offers four-day packages to Cayo Largo del Sur. Passes to the Southern Military Zone are available here (CUC$8 for Ecotur-run excursions, CUC$15 if you go with your own vehicle).

Festivals & Events

Carnaval CARNIVAL
(Mar) This is the big one. Get over here for a knees-up involving parades characterized by giant puppet-like heads, rodeo, sports competitions and perhaps just a little drinking.

Sleeping

Casas particulares are your only town centre options and will provide meals; the owners will invariably meet arriving ferries. Nueva

Gerona's two run-down state-run hotels are south of town.

★**Villa Choli –
Ramberto Pena Silva** CASA PARTICULAR $
(46-32-31-47, 52-48-79-16; Calle C No 4001A, btwn Calles 6 & 8; r CUC$20-25; P ❄ @) Three large, modern 1st-floor rooms with TV, internet access, secure parking space, delicious food and – possibly the highlight – a great terrace with a hammock. A second terrace opens for alfresco grill-ups on occasion. There are bicycles for rent, and port pick-up/tickets can be arranged. Otherwise, turn right (north) on Calle 39 after Hospital General Héroes de Baire, then ask.

Tu Isla CASA PARTICULAR $
(46-50-91-28; Calle 24, btwn Calles 45 & 47; r CUC$20-25; ❄ ❄) This fabulous new casa close to the center is the building with the big anchor motif just past Museo Casa Natal Jesus Montané. Currently with six rooms (three have private balconies), with plans to extend to eight, it touts spacious terraces, a plunge pool, internal murals and a 3r-floor rooftop restaurant.

Villa Peña CASA PARTICULAR $
(46-32-23-45; cnr Calles 10 & 37; r CUC$15-20; ❄) A comfortable, secure option in a pretty bungalow near the hospital with two clean rooms (and plans for three more) and meals.

**Villa Mas –
Jorge Luis Mas Peña** CASA PARTICULAR $
(46-32-35-44; Calle 41 No 4108 apt 7, btwn Calles 8 & 10; r CUC$20; ❄) Forget the rather ugly apartment-block setting; there are two above-average rooms here with refurbished marble bathrooms. Good meals are served on a rooftop terrace. It's in the northern part of town behind the hospital.

Eating

As far as food goes, La Isla is still living in the 1990s. After one night of fruitless searching most travelers sensibly elect to dine in their casa particular. Small sandwich and churros vendors set up on Martí (Calle 39) and peso ice-cream sellers appear spontaneously in various windows.

Restaurante El Abra CUBAN $
(Carretera Siguanea Km 4; meals CUC$1-4; noon-5:30pm) If you value your palate you'll consider a trip to this open-air place on delightful Presa El Abra, 4km southwest of the center, worthwhile. The cuisine is

comida criolla (Creole food), but *muy rico* (very rich). Pork (would you believe it?) is a favorite for the grill-ups but there' are good fish options too. Or simply sip a cold beer and salute the view.

Restaurante Tu Isla CUBAN $
(Calle 24, btwn Calles 45 & 47; mains CUC$4-8; ☻7pm-midnight Sun-Thu, to 2am Fri & Sat) This rooftop restaurant above the casa particular of the same name serves good Cuban classics with an Italian twist. The decor is nautical and traditional live music gets going most nights.

Pizzería la Góndola ITALIAN $
(cnr Calles 30 & 35; MN$20-50; ☻noon-10pm) The pleasant mural of an Italian piazza may temporarily conjure taste-bud-tingling memories but they'll be banished when the pizza arrives (although it's roughly a twelfth of the price of what you'd pay in Venice). But if you're sick of the pork offerings elsewhere…

Restaurante Río SEAFOOD $
(Calle 32, btwn Calle 33 & river; MN$20-50; ☻noon-10pm) A dog-eared establishment by the river which, on a good day, serves fresh river- and sea-fish (one of the few places in Cuba where you can eat both) priced in *moneda nacional*. It has an outside terrace with a stereo blasting out the latest Cuban pop and an air-conditioned interior.

El Cochinito CARIBBEAN $
(cnr Calles 39 & 24; ☻noon-10pm Thu-Tue) The ominously named 'little pig' offers *desperados* pork concoctions in a smart but disturbing interior decorated with pigs' heads (some appear to be squealing).

Self-Catering

Mercado Agropecuario MARKET
(cnr Calles 24 & 35; ☻dawn-dusk) Market with fresh vegetables and meat.

Cubalse Supermarket SUPERMARKET
(Calle 35, btwn Calles 30 & 32; ☻9:30am-6pm Mon-Sat) Sells life-saving Pringles and biscuits.

Drinking & Nightlife
Call it pent-up boredom, but Nueva Gerona likes a party.

La Rumba CLUB
(Calle 24, btwn Calles 37 & 39; ☻10pm-2am) Buy your drinks in the cage-like bar next door then head to the courtyard and hectic disco round the corner. If you don't dance hard, you'll stand out here.

El Pinero CLUB
(Calle 28, btwn Calle 33 & river) Extremely loud music along with most of the town's teenagers and 20-somethings converge by the historic boat for alfresco dancing. Drink and snack stalls also set up shop. Fridays and Saturdays are liveliest.

ISLA DE LA JUVENTUD (SPECIAL MUNICIPALITY) NUEVA GERONA

INTO THE BLUE

Protected from sea currents off the Gulf of Mexico and blessed with remarkable coral and marine life, Isla de la Juventud offers some of the Caribbean's best diving: 56 buoyed and little-visited dive sites here will make you truly feel like a castaway. The dive sites here are an underwater adventure park of everything from caves and passages to vertical walls and coral hillocks, whilst further east, in an area known as **Bajo de Zambo**, you can dive to the remains of some 70-odd shipwrecks.

International Diving Center (☎46-39-82-82, ext 166), run from the Marina Siguanea just south of Hotel Colony on the island's west coast, is the center of diving operations. The establishment has a modern on-site recompression chamber along with the services of a dive doctor. It's from here that you can be transported out to the National Maritime Park at **Punta Francés**.

Boat transfers to Punta Francés take an hour and deliver you to a gorgeous stretch of white-sand beach, from which most main dive sites are easily accessible. The cream of the crop is **Cueva Azul** (advanced), a trench of cerulean blue with a small *cueva* (cave) about 40m down, followed by **Pared de Coral Negro** (intermediate), a wall of black coral. You'll see lots of fish, including tarpon, barracuda, groupers, snooks and angelfish, along with sea turtles.

Diving costs start at CUC$43 for one immersion. Inquire at Hotel Colony (p167) about diving and other nautical activities on offer first.

Disco la Movida   CLUB

(Calle 18; ⊙ from 11pm) For a little atmospheric booty shaking, join the throngs of locals dancing in an open-air locale hidden among the trees near the river.

☆ Entertainment

Live music is sometimes staged outside the Cine Caribe.

Uneac   CULTURAL CENTER

(Calle 37, btwn Calles 24 & 26) Your best bet for a non-reggaetón night out is this nicely renovated colonial house with patio, bar and suave live music.

Sucu Suco   LIVE MUSIC

(Calle 39, btwn Calles 24 & 26; ⊙ 11am-late) A joint with live music and theater: there's a board out front with upcoming events. When nothing else is on, it serves as an intimate drinking spot.

Cine Caribe   CINEMA

(cnr Calles 37 & 28) Surprisingly colorful and happening cinema right on Parque Guerrillero Heroico.

Estadio Cristóbal Labra   SPORTS

(cnr Calles 32 & 53) Nueva Gerona's baseball stadium, Estadio Cristóbal Labra is seven blocks west of Calle 39. Ask at your local casa particular for details of upcoming games (staged from October to April).

Shopping

Calle 39, also known as Calle Martí, is a pleasant pedestrian mall interspersed with small parks.

Centro Experimental de
Artes Aplicadas   ARTS & CRAFTS

(Calle 40, btwn 39 & 37; ⊙ 8am-4pm Mon-Fri, to noon Sat) Near the Museo de Historia Natural. Makes artistic ceramics.

ⓘ Information

Banco Popular y Ahorro (cnr Calles 39 & 26; ⊙ 8am-7pm Mon-Fri) Has an ATM.

Cadeca (Calle 39 No 2022; ⊙ 8:30am-6pm Mon-Sat, to 1pm Sun) ATM.

Etecsa Telepunto (Calle 41 No 2802, btwn Calles 28 & 30; per hour CUC$4.50; ⊙ 8:30am-7:30pm) Internet.

Hospital General Héroes de Baire (✆ 46-32-30-12; Calle 39A) Has a recompression chamber.

Post office (Calle 39 No 1810, btwn Calles 18 & 20; ⊙ 8am-6pm Mon-Sat)

Radio Caribe Broadcasts varied music programs on 1270AM.

ⓘ Getting There & Away

AIR

The most hassle-free and (often) cheapest way to get to La Isla is to fly. Unfortunately, most people have cottoned onto this, so flights are usually booked out days in advance.

Rafael Cabrera Mustelier Airport (airport code GER) is 5km southeast of Nueva Gerona.

Cubana Airlines Havana (✆ 7-834-4446; www.cubana.cu; Airling Bldg, Calle 23 No 64, cnr Calzada de la Infanta, Vedado; ⊙ 8:30am-4pm Mon-Fri, to noon Sat; **Nueva Gerona** (✆ 46-32-25-31, 46-32-42-59; www.cubana.cu; Calle 39 No 1415, btwn Calles 16 & 18) flies here from Havana twice daily from as little as CUC$35 one way. There are no international flights.

There are no regular flights from Isla de la Juventud to Cayo Largo del Sur.

ⓘ Getting Around

TO/FROM THE AIRPORT

From the airport, look for the bus marked 'Servicio Aéreo,' which will take you into town for one peso. To get to the airport, catch this bus in front of Cine Caribe, on the corner of Calles 37 and 28. A taxi to town will cost about CUC$5, or CUC$30 to CUC$35 to the Hotel Colony.

BUS

Ecotur (p164) can organize trips/transfers from Nueva Gerona to the diving areas and into the militarized zone. A taxi (easily arranged through your casa or hotel) from Nueva Gerona to Hotel Colony should cost approximately CUC$30 to CUC$35.

There are less reliable local buses: buses 431 to La Fe (26km) and 441 to the Hotel Colony (45km) leave from a stop opposite the cemetery on Calle 39A, just northwest of the hospital. Bus 38 leaves from the corner of Calles 18 and 37, departing for Chacón (Presidio Modelo), Playa Paraíso and Playa Bibijagua, about four times a day.

CAR

Cubacar (✆ 46-32-44-32; cnr Calles 32 & 39; ⊙ 7am-7pm) rents cars from CUC$65 with insurance and, as you'll need your own vehicle to enter the military zone (unless on an organized tour), is the best bet for arranging transport here.

The **Oro Negro gas station** (cnr Calles 39 & 34) is in the center of town.

HORSE CART

Horse *coches* (carts) often park next to the Cubalse supermarket on Calle 35. You can easily rent one at CUC$10 per day for excursions to the Presidio Modelo, Museo Finca el Abra, Playa Bibijagua and other nearby destinations. If you've got the time, you can be sure the driver will.

East of Nueva Gerona

◉ Sights

★ Presidio Modelo
NOTABLE BUILDING

(admission CUC$1; ⊘8:30am-4:30pm Tue-Sat, 9am-1pm Sun) Welcome to the island's most impressive yet depressing sight. Located near Reparto Chacón, 5km east of Nueva Gerona, this striking prison was built between 1926 and 1931, during the repressive regime of Gerardo Machado. The four rather scary-looking, six-story, yellow circular blocks were modeled after those of a notorious penitentiary in Joliet, Illinois, and could hold 5000 prisoners at a time.

During WWII, assorted enemy nationals who happened to find themselves in Cuba (including 350 Japanese, 50 Germans and 25 Italians) were interned in the two rectangular blocks at the north end of the complex.

The Presidio's most famous inmates, however, were Fidel Castro and the other Moncada rebels, who were imprisoned here from October 1953 to May 1955. They were held separately from the other prisoners, in the hospital building at the south end of the complex.

In 1967 the prison was closed and the section where Castro stayed was converted into a museum. There is one room dedicated to the history of the prison and another focusing on the lives of the Moncada prisoners. Admission includes a tour, but cameras/videos are CUC$3/25 extra. Bring exact change. Admission to the circular blocks (the most moving part of the experience) is free.

Cementerio Colombia
CEMETERY

The cemetery here contains the graves of Americans who lived and died on the island during the 1920s and 1930s. It's about 7km east of Nueva Gerona and 2km east of Presidio Modelo. Bus 38 passes by.

Playa Paraíso
BEACH

About 2km north of Chacón (about 6km northeast of Nueva Gerona), Playa Paraíso is a dirty brown beach with good currents for water sports. The wharf was originally used to unload prisoners heading to the Presidio Modelo.

Playa Bibijagua
BEACH

One of the better beaches on the Isla's northern coast, Playa Bibijagua lies 4km to the east of Chacón. Here there are pine trees, a peso restaurant and plenty of low-key Cuban ambience. Nondrivers can catch bus 38 from Nueva Gerona.

South of Nueva Gerona

◉ Sights & Activities

The main reason to come here is for the diving at Punta Francés, but there are a couple of other diversions for those who have time.

La Jungla de Jones
GARDENS

(admission CUC$3; ⊘24hr) Situated 6km west of La Fe in the direction of Hotel Colony, this is a botanical garden containing more than 80 tree varieties, established by two American botanists, Helen and Harris Jones, in 1902. The highlight is the aptly named Bamboo Cathedral, an enclosed space surrounded by huge clumps of craning bamboo that only a few strands of sunlight manage to penetrate, although it's all pretty overgrown these days.

Criadero Cocodrilo
CROCODILE FARM

(admission CUC$3; ⊘7am-5pm) ✐ This farm has played an important part in crocodile conservation in Cuba over the last few years and the results are interesting to see. Harboring more than 500 crocodiles of all shapes and sizes, the *criadero* (hatchery) acts as a breeding center, raising and then releasing groups of crocs back into the wild when they reach a length of about 1m.

To get to the *criadero* turn left 12km south of La Fe just past Julio Antonio Mella.

The center is similar to the one in Guamá in Matanzas, although the setting here is infinitely wilder.

⌂ Sleeping & Eating

★ Hotel Colony
HOTEL $$

(☎46-39-81-81; s/d all-incl CUC$38/59; P ❄ ≋ ☸) The Colony, 46km southwest of Nueva Gerona, originated in 1958 as part of the Hilton chain, but was confiscated by the revolutionary government. Today the main building is a bit run-down, but the newer bungalows are clean, bright and airy. You might save a few cents by taking a package that includes meals and scuba diving.

The water off the hotel's white-sand beach is shallow, with sea urchins littering the bottom. Take care if you decide to swim. A safer bet is the Colony's convivial pool. A long wharf (with a bar perfect for sunset mojitos) stretches out over the bay, but the snorkeling in the immediate vicinity of the hotel is mediocre. The diving (p165), however, is to die for.

❶ Getting There & Away

Transport is tough on La Isla, and bus schedules make even the rest of Cuba seem efficient. Try bus 441 from Nueva Gerona. Otherwise, your best bet to get to Hotel Colony is by taxi (approximately CUC$35 from the airport), moped or rental car.

The Southern Military Zone

The entire area south of Cayo Piedra is a military zone, and to enter you must first procure a one-day pass (per person CUC$8/15)

from Ecotur (p164) in Nueva Gerona. For CUC$8 you get an Ecotur-run excursion taking in Cueva de Punta del Este, Playa Larga, Cocodrilo and the Sea Turtle Breeding Center; CUC$15 is the fee for entering with your own vehicle. Either way, the company will provide you with a Spanish-/English-/German-/French-/Italian-speaking guide (obligatory). Hiring your own vehicle can be organized with Cubacar (p166) in Nueva Gerona. Traveling in the military zone is not possible without a guide or an official pass, so don't arrive at the Cayo Piedra checkpoint

GETTING TO THE ISLA BY BOAT: A BEGINNER'S GUIDE

The overbureaucratic, typically Cuban experience of getting to La Isla by boat isn't as simple as it ought to be. To do it you'll need eight hours (if you're lucky), decent supplies of food (breakfast and lunch at least) and saintly amounts of patience. A reasonable command of Spanish, though not a prerequisite, will minimize confusion.

It is advisable to reserve and pay for your ticket ($5 in *moneda nacional* if your Spanish and appearance is enough to pass as Cuban, CUC$5 otherwise) at least a day in advance at the **Naviera Cubana Caribeña (NCC) kiosk** (☎ 7-878-1841; ⊙ 7am-noon) in Havana's main Terminal de Ómnibus (p123), not the Víazul terminal. The best time to do this is between 9am and noon. You'll need your passport and an additional CUC$50 for the boat, which you pay for here too. Plump for the earlier ferry as the later one (supposedly running Friday and Sunday) is less reliable.

On the day of departure you'll need to turn up no later than 7:30am (earlier if you still haven't bought your ticket). The bus leaves from bay 9 of Havana's Terminal de Ómnibus between 9am and 9:30am (although airport-style check-in starts at 8am) and trundles slowly to the disheveled port in Surgidero de Batabanó, where you'll have to join the lengthy, disorderly queues to reconfirm your boat ticket to Nueva Gerona. You'll then be ushered through airport-style security into a waiting room for a likely period of one to two hours before the boat finally departs (officially at 1pm).

The crossing by catamaran takes about 2½ hours; there are no printed schedules. If you take the early bus/boat and all goes well you'll be on La Isla at 4pm (total journey time eight hours, total ticket cost CUC$50.25 to CUC$55).

Refreshments on this trip are either basic (a can of Coke) or not available as it's mostly Cubans traveling. Furthermore, the air-con on the catamarans is arctic and the unrelenting 'action' films deafening. Unfortunately, there's no escape. Access above deck is barred.

Do not show up independently in Batabanó with the intention of buying a ferry ticket direct from the dock. Travelers are usually told that tickets have been sold out through the NCC kiosk in Havana. Furthermore, bedding down overnight in Batabanó holds little appeal for travelers.

The return leg is equally problematic. Procure your ticket the day before you wish to travel in Nueva Gerona's **NCC ferry terminal** (☎ 46-32-49-77, 46-32-44-15; cnr Calles 31 & 24), beside the Río las Casas. The **ticket office** (⊙ Mon-Fri) is across the road. The ferry leaves for Surgidero de Batabanó daily at 8am (CUC$50), but you'll need to get there at least two hours beforehand to tackle the infamous queues. The Havana bus will be waiting for you when you get off the boat, and the transfer process is smoother going this way. A second boat is supposed to leave at 1pm on Fridays and Sundays (for this one, get here by 11am).

Don't take anything as a given until you have booked your ticket. Isla boat crossings, rather like Cuban trains, have a tendency to be late, break down or get cancelled altogether.

Traveling in either direction, you'll need to show your passport.

A glint of light: a new, faster ferry is supposed to be arriving in the near future. Let's wait and see.

without either. As the whole excursion can wind up being rather expensive, it helps to split the transport costs with other travelers. For more up-to-date advice on the region inquire at Hotel Colony (p167) or Ecotur in Nueva Gerona.

The southern Isla is replete with unusual wildlife. Look out for monkeys, deer, crocodiles (three types), lizards and turtles.

Cueva de Punta del Este

The Cueva de Punta del Este, a national monument 59km southeast of Nueva Gerona, has been called the 'Sistine Chapel' of Caribbean Indian art. Long before the Spanish conquest (experts estimate around AD 800), Indians painted some 235 pictographs on the walls and ceiling of the cave. The largest has 28 concentric circles of red and black, and the paintings have been interpreted as a solar calendar. Discovered in 1910, they're considered the most important of their kind in the Caribbean. There's a small visitor center and meteorological station. The long, shadeless white beach nearby is another draw (for you and the mosquitoes – bring repellent).

Cocodrilo

A potholed road runs south from Cayo Piedra to the gorgeous white-sand beach of Playa Larga, then west 50km to the friendly village of Cocodrilo. Barely touched by tourism, and with a population of just 750, Cocodrilo was formerly known as Jacksonville, and was colonized in the 19th century by families from the Cayman Islands. You still occasionally meet people here who can converse in English. Through the lush vegetation beside the potholed road you can catch glimpses of cattle, birds, lizards and beehives. The rocky coastline, sporadically gouged by small, white sandy beaches lapped by crystal blue water, is magnificent

One kilometer west of Cocodrilo, the Sea Turtle Breeding Center (admission CUC$1; ☺8am-6pm) ✎does an excellent job in conserving one of Cuba's rarest and most endangered species. Rows of green-stained glass tanks teem with all sizes of turtles. The turtles are then released back into the wild again.

CAYO LARGO DEL SUR

🗷45

If you came to Cuba to witness historic colonial cities, exotic dancers, asthmatic Plymouths and peeling images of Che Guevara, then 38-sq-km Cayo Largo del Sur, 114km east of Isla de la Juventud, will hugely disappoint. If, instead, you booked tickets while dreaming of glittering white sandy expanses, coral reefs teeming with fish, fabulous all-inclusive resorts and lots of fleshy Canadians and Italians wandering around naked, then this small mangrove-covered tropical paradise is undeniably the place for you.

No permanent Cuban settlement has ever existed on the Cayo. Instead, the island was developed in the early 1980s purely as a tourism enterprise. Cayo Largo del Sur (Cayo Largo for short) is largely frequented by Italian tourists – several resorts here cater exclusively for them. The other all-inclusives are less picky. The heavenly beaches (26km of them) surpass most visitors' expectations of Caribbean paradise and are renowned for their size, emptiness and – during summer – nesting turtles. There's also a profusion of iguanas and birdlife, including cranes, *zunzuncitos* (bee hummingbirds) and flamingos.

The island can be visited as an expensive day trip from Havana, but most people come here on prebooked packages for a week or two.

In 2001, Hurricane Michelle (category 4) caused a storm surge that inundated the whole of Cayo Largo del Sur. It took the island years to recover. But of all the Cuban cayos with resort infrastructure, the beaches here are still the loveliest.

◎ Sights

★Playa Sirena   BEACH

Cayo Largo's (and, perhaps, Cuba's) finest beach is the broad westward-facing Playa Sirena, where 2km of powdery white sand is wide enough to accommodate several football pitches. Tourists on day trips from Havana and Varadero are often brought here, and the usual nautical activities (kayaks, catamarans) are available. Set back from the beach there's a *ranchón*-style bar and restaurant, along with showers and toilets.

Just southeast is Playa Paraíso, a narrower and less shady but nonetheless wonderful strip of sand, serviced by a small bar.

ISLA DE LA JUVENTUD (SPECIAL MUNICIPALITY) CAYO LARGO DEL SUR

Cayo Largo del Sur

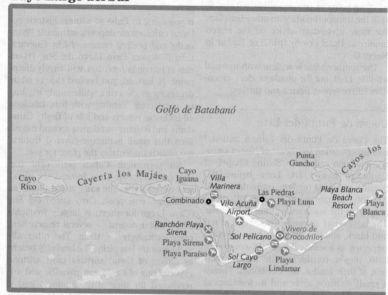

Golfo de Batabanó

Granja de las Tortugas   TURTLE FARM

(Combinado; admission CUC$1; ⊙8am-noon & 1-5:45pm) A small, often-closed complex on the northwest end of the island beyond the airstrip in the settlement of Combinado. From May to September guides here can organize nighttime **turtle watching** on the Cayo's beaches.

★ Vivero de Crocodrilos   WILDLIFE RESERVE

(⊙dawn-dusk) **FREE** A beautiful, old building on Cayo Largo? You'd better believe it. Just past the turn-offs to the Sol resorts, the stone tower marking the Vivero de Crocodrilos dates from 1951 – the island's first construction. Here, you can even meet real Cubans who will show you the few animals that reside in and around the small lagoon – Kimbo the croc, Lola the Iguana and a couple of turtles. A fleeting glimpse of how Cuba actually looks.

You can also climb the rickety ladder for decent views. This is also where the plants that decorate your hotel grounds are grown.

Playa los Cocos   BEACH

You can head up the island's east coast via this beach, where there is good snorkeling (the paved road gives out after Playa Blanca).

Playa Tortuga   BEACH

Beyond Playa los Cocos at the far end of the island is this beach, where sea turtles lay their eggs in the sand in the summer.

Cayo del Rosario & Cayo Rico   ISLANDS

The other big day-trip destinations are these islands between Cayo Largo and Isla de la Juventud. Boat excursions to these islands leave from the hotels (for around CUC$56 per person) and also from Marina Internacional Cayo Largo (where you'll pay less).

Cayo Iguana   ISLAND

Off the northwest tip of Cayo Largo, Cayo Iguana is home to, that's right, hundreds of iguanas. A yacht trip with **snorkeling** will cost you CUC$44.

🏃 Activities

The island's best (and only) hike is from Playa Sirena round to Sol Cayo Largo along the beach (7km) or vice versa. A broken path follows the dune ridge for much of the way if the tide is high. You can also procure a bicycle if you're staying in one of the resorts and head east beyond the Playa Blanca Beach Resort to some of the island's remoter beaches.

0 5 km
0 3 miles

Punta
del Este

Punta
Iguanita

Punta
Mangle
Prieto

Playa Tortuga

Pájaros

Playa los Cocos

*CARIBBEAN
SEA*

Other activities available on the island include snorkeling (from CUC$19), windsurfing, sailing and tennis. There is a boat adventure in the mangroves (CUC$29; you drive the boat) and swimming with a couple of dolphins (CUC$90) near Playa Sirena. You can also organize day trips to Havana and Trinidad (approximately CUC$150). Ask to book any of the above at the hotels.

**Marina Internacional
Cayo Largo** DIVING, FISHING
(☑ 45-24-81-33; Combinado) Just beyond the turtle farm in Combinado, this is the departure point for deep-sea fishing trips (CUC$349 to CUC$369 for four hours for a minimum of four people) and diving (CUC$40 for one immersion including hotel transfer). Prices are more expensive here because you can't shop around. Transfers from here to Playa Sirena are free for island guests and depart during the morning.

🛏 Sleeping

All of Cayo Largo del Sur's hotels face the 4km beach on the south side of the island. Though largely shadeless, the beach here is gorgeous and rarely crowded (as no one lives here). If you're on a day trip, day passes to the Sol resorts are CUC$35 including lunch. Whilst new construction beavers

away at the eastern end of the hotel strip, to date the only other resorts in addition to the following belong to the vast Hotel Isla del Sur & Eden Village Complex, including Villas Coral, Soledad and Lindamar (all catering for Italians only and bookable through Italian travel agencies).

★**Villa Marinera** RESORT **$$**
(☑ 45-24-80-80; Combinado; s/d all-incl CUC$60/100; 🅿 ❄ ☎) We like this peaceful, unassuming hotel right in the center of Combinado. Whilst all-inclusive here doesn't have the caché of the bigger resorts, there's the advantage of being alongside Combinado's 'facilities' (snack bar, bank, marina etc). And these log cabins are really quite nice (there's 20 altogether) and bigger than many resort rooms elsewhere.

It even comes with a bit of resort-style sparkle: rows of sun loungers lining the stretch of beach. 'Beach' means rocky ledge, but the Playa Sirena transfer is next door. Book through the Playa Blanca Beach Resort: bargain!

★**Sol Cayo Largo** RESORT **$$$**
(☑ 45-24-82-60; www.meliacuba.com; s/d all-incl from CUC$165/220; 🅿 ❄ @ ☎) Sol Meliá's best property is four-star Sol Cayo Largo, with its Greek-temple-like lobby and trickling Italianate fountains. The beach out here is fantastic (and nudist) and the brightly painted (but not luxurious) rooms all have terraces with sea views. To date, it's Cayo Largo's most exclusive resort and great if you want to escape the families and poolside bingo further east.

Check out the on-site spa and gym.

Playa Blanca Beach Resort RESORT **$$$**
(☑ 45-24-80-80; s/d all-incl CUC$84/135; 🅿 ❄ @ ☎ ♨) Cayo Largo's newest resort is set apart from the rest on an expansive stretch of Playa Blanca. Rather drab architecture is augmented by three different dining options, an array of sporting activities and some of the only poolside music in Cuba which opts for classical over maxvolume reggaetón.

There's an individual touch, too. Artworks by leading Cuban artist Carlos Guzmán decorate the public areas, and the suites in the upper echelons with their mezzanine sleeping areas could hold their own in Greenwich Village. Well, nearly. Some shade wouldn't go amiss, though.

OFF THE BEATEN TRACK

CAYOS DE SAN FELIPE

Technically, they're in Pinar del Río province, but, as yet, the only way to get to the almost virgin Cayos de San Felipe is with an organized excursion arranged through Hotel Colony on La Isla de la Juventud or the Marina Internacional Cayo Largo on Cayo Largo del Sur. One of Cuba's 14 national parks, this small necklace of keys approximately 30km south of Pinar del Río and 30km northwest of La Isla are uninhabited save for the odd environmental researcher. The Cayos were home to a rare subspecies of the tree rat called the Little Earth Jutia, but the rodent hasn't been seen since 1978 when black rats were introduced to the archipelago. The flat mangrove-infested isles also support turtles and numerous bird species.

Fauna aside, the main reason to come here is to dive in 22 Columbus-era-quality dive sites that see little or no dive traffic. The trip starts in Pinar del Río before transferring by bus to the fishing village of La Coloma, where a boat takes you out to the Cayos for diving. After lunch on board, you will be spirited over the sea to Hotel Colony on La Isla without having to suffer the purgatory of the crowded regular ferry.

There is also the option to make this into one (or two) multi-day multi-dive odysseys: the Ruta de los Indios (the Cayos between La Coloma and Isla de la Juventud) and the Ruta Los Galeones (those between La Isla and Cayo Largo del Sur).

Inquire at Hotel Colony (p167) or Marina Internacional Cayo Largo (p171) for rates and availability.

Sol Pelícano   RESORT $$$

(☑ 45-24-82-33; www.meliacuba.com; s/d all-incl CUC$235/335; P ❄ @ ≋ 🐾) This Spanish-style resort, flush on the beach 5km southeast of the airport, has 203 rooms in a series of three-story buildings and two-story duplex *cabañas* (cabins) built in 1993. This is the island's largest resort but it's open only in high season. Facilities include a nightclub and many family-friendly concessions. Low-season prices drop to almost half: book online for the best deals.

🍴 Eating & Drinking

Of the all-inclusives, the Sol Cayo Largo serves the best food.

Discoteca el Torreón   CARIBBEAN $$

(Combinado; ⊙ noon-midnight) Good food is served, and drinking and dancing goes on at this fortlike building by the marina, although these days it always seems to be closed.

★ Ranchón Playa Sirena   SEAFOOD $$$

(⊙ 9am-5pm) A rather fetching beach bar amid the Playa Sirena palm trees, with Latino Tom Cruises tossing around the cocktail glasses. Good food is also served here and a buffet (CUC$20) happens if enough tourists are around. It offers no-nonsense, salt-of-the-earth *comida criolla* (Creole food) and good grilled *pargo* (red snapper) for CUC$12.

Taberna el Pirata   CAFE, CLUB

(Combinado; ⊙ 24hr) Taberna el Pirata, alongside Marina Internacional Cayo Largo is primarily a haunt for boat-hands, resort workers and the odd escaped tourist. Icy beer, throat-burningly strong coffee, sandwiches and chips in pleasant environs.

❶ Information

There's a **Cubatur** (☑ 45-24-82-58) in the Sol Pelícano and further information offices in the Sol Cayo Largo and Playa Blanca resorts. You can change money at the hotels; otherwise Combinado houses the island's main bank, **Bandec** (⊙ 8:30am-3pm Mon-Sat, 8am-noon Sun). Combinado also offers a **Casa de Habano** (☑ 45-24-82-11; ⊙ 8am-8pm) cigar shop, a **Clínica Internacional** (☑ 45-24-82-38; ⊙ 24hr) medical clinic, the Marina Internacional Cayo Largo (p171), the snack-bar-disco duo of Discoteca el Torreón, a usually closed Bolera bowling alley and a couple of souvenir stands. Euros are accepted at tourist installations here.

Due to dangerous currents, swimming is occasionally forbidden. This will be indicated by red flags on the beach. Mosquitoes can be a nuisance too.

❶ Getting There & Away

Vilo Acuña International Airport is a bright-enough place with a big snack bar and a souvenir stand. Several charter flights arrive directly from Canada weekly, and Cubana has weekly flights from Montreal and Milan.

For pop-by visitors, daily flights from Havana to Cayo Largo del Sur with **Aerogaviota** (☑ 7-203-8686; Av 47 No 2814, btwn Calles 28 & 34, Kohly, Havana) or Cubana (p166) cost CUC$129 for a return trip. Included will be airport transfer at both ends and a boat trip from Cayo Largo's marina (but you don't have to go). The island makes a viable day trip from Havana, although you'll have to get up early for the airport transfer (all Cayo Largo flights depart between 7am and 8am from the drab airport at Playa Baracoa, a few miles west of Marina Hemingway).

Organized day trips from Havana or Varadero to Cayo Largo del Sur cost about CUC$150, including airport transfers and lunch, plus trips to Playa Sirena and Cayo Iguana. The Havana airport transfer starts its rounds of the hotels about 5am; check to make sure it's stopping at your hotel. All the Havana travel agencies offer this.

ℹ Getting Around

Getting around Cayo Largo shouldn't present too many challenges.

A taxi or transfer bus can transport you the 5km from the airport to the hotel strip (included in your flight price). From here a complementary mini bus-train (the *trencito*) carts tourists out to Playa Paraíso (6km) and Playa Sirena (7km). The train returns in the afternoon, or you can hike back along the beach.

The tiny settlement of Combinado is 1km north of the airport and 6km from the nearest resort.

For taxis hang around outside the hotels, airport and Combinado. Rides cost between CUC$5 and CUC$10. The hotels have moped and car rental too; Playa Blanca Beach Resort is best stocked because it's furthest from the 'action'.

In the mornings, there are a couple of boat departures from the marina to Playa Sirena (the boat returns to Combinado in the afternoon).

ISLA DE LA JUVENTUD (SPECIAL MUNICIPALITY) CAYO LARGO DEL SUR

Valle de Viñales & Pinar del Río Province

🗺 48 / POP 595,000

Includes ➡

Viñales 175
Parque Nacional
Viñales 183
Cayo Jutías 186
Cayo Levisa 186
San Diego de los
Baños 187
Pinar del Río 189
Parque Nacional
Península de
Guanahacabibes 195

Best Tobacco Tours

➡ Alejandro Robaina Tobacco Plantation (p194)

➡ Fábrica de Tabacos Francisco Donatien (p189)

➡ La Casa del Veguero (p178)

➡ Finca Raúl Reyes (p178)

Best Water-Based Fun

➡ Centro Internacional de Buceo (p196)

➡ La Cueva de Palmarito (p184)

➡ Cayo Jutías (p186)

➡ Cayo Levisa (p186)

Why Go?

The fragrant aroma of a fine cigar is an unmistakable scent and within Cuba, its smoky drift can be traced back to Pinar del Río province, the world's premier place to grow tobacco. The region is a rolling rustic canvas of fertile, rust-red oxen-furrowed fields, thatched tobacco-drying houses and sombrero-clad *guajiros* (country folk).

Jewels in the crown of this emerald land are the Valle de Viñales, a Unesco World Heritage Site studded with the alluring and distinctive *mogotes* (limestone monoliths) that nigh-on beseech you to get hiking, and Península de Guanahacabibes, a remote Unesco Biosphere Reserve abutting María la Gorda's swath of 50-plus dive sites.

Your obvious base is serene Viñales, a hassle-free village ringed by craggy hills and Van Gogh–like rural beauty, which beckons you to forge into some of the Caribbean's best caves, explore tobacco plantations and secluded swimming holes, lounge on idyllic sandy beaches and lose yourself in a laid-back land where every horizon harbors a host of quintessential 'come to the Cuban countryside' images. So come.

When to Go

➡ May through August to see prized wildlife, such as the Guanahacabibes turtles.

➡ October through March is best for bird-watching.

➡ December through March is ideal beach weather.

History

The pre-Columbian history of western Cuba is synonymous with the Guanahatabeys, a group of nomadic people who lived in caves and procured their livelihood largely from the sea. Less advanced than the other indigenous peoples who lived on the island, the peaceful, passive Guanahatabeys developed more or less independently of the Taíno and Siboney cultures further east. These people were extinct by the time the Spanish arrived in 1492.

Post-Columbus the Spanish left rugged Pinar del Río largely to its own devices, and the area developed lackadaisically only after Canary Islanders began arriving in the late 1500s. Originally called Nueva Filipina (New Philippines) for the large number of Filipinos who came to the area to work the burgeoning tobacco plantations, the region was renamed Pinar del Río in 1778, supposedly for the pine forests crowded along the Río Guamá. By this time the western end of Cuba was renowned for its tobacco and already home to what is now the world's oldest tobacco company, Tabacalera, dating from 1636. Cattle ranching also propped up the economy. The farmers who made a living from the delicate and well-tended crops here became colloquially christened *guajiros*, a native word that means – literally – 'one of us.' By the mid-1800s, Europeans were hooked on tobacco and the region flourished. Sea routes opened up and the railway was extended to facilitate the shipping of the fragrant weed.

These days tobacco, along with tourism, keeps Pinar del Río both profitable and popular, with Viñales now the third-most visited tourist destination in Cuba after Havana and Varadero.

VALLE DE VIÑALES

Embellished by soaring pine trees and bulbous limestone cliffs that teeter like top-heavy haystacks above placid tobacco plantations, Parque Nacional Viñales is one of Cuba's most magnificent natural settings. Wedged spectacularly into the Sierra de los Órganos mountain range, this 11km-by-5km valley was recognised as a national monument in 1979, with Unesco World Heritage status following in 1999 for its dramatic steep-sided limestone outcrops (known as *mogotes*), coupled with the vernacular architecture of its traditional farms and villages.

Once upon a time the whole region was several hundred meters higher. Then, during the Cretaceous period 100 million years ago, underground rivers ate away at the limestone bedrock, creating vast caverns. Eventually the roofs collapsed, leaving only the eroded walls we see today. It is the finest example of a limestone karst valley in Cuba and contains the Gran Caverna de Santo Tomás, the island's largest cave system.

Viñales also offers opportunities for fine hiking, rock climbing and horseback trekking. On the accommodations front it boasts first-class hotels and some of the best casas particulares in Cuba. Despite drawing in day-trippers by the busload, the area's well-protected and spread-out natural attractions have somehow managed to escape the frenzied tourist circus of other less well-managed places, while the atmosphere in and around the town remains refreshingly hassle-free.

Viñales

When you spy a cigar-chewing *guajiro* driving his oxen and plough through a rust-colored tobacco field, you know that you must be within striking distance of Viñales. Despite its longstanding love affair with tourism, this slow, relaxed, wonderfully traditional settlement is a place that steadfastly refuses to put on a show. What you see here is what you get – a tiny agricultural town that just happens to occupy one of Cuba's most beautiful natural corners. Grab a *sillon* (rocking chair), sit back on a rustic porch and enjoy a slice of real rural Cuba.

⊙ Sights

Founded in 1875, Viñales is more about setting than sights with most of its activities of a lung-stretching outdoor nature. Nevertheless the town has some engaging architecture and a lively main square backed by the sturdy colonial **Casa de la Cultura** (Map p179), one of the oldest structures in the valley. Next door is a tiny **art gallery** (Map p179) while nearby is an equally diminutive (and recently restored) **church** (Map p179).

Museo Municipal   MUSEUM
(Map p179; Salvador Cisneros No 115; admission CUC$1; ⊙9am-8pm Tue-Sat, to 9pm Sun) Positioned halfway down Cisneros, Viñales' pine-lined main street, the Museo Municipal occupies the former home of independence

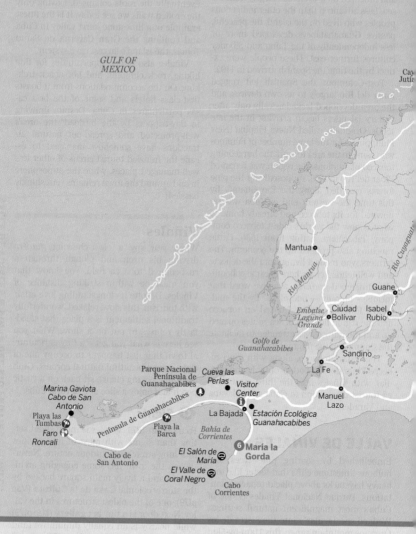

GULF OF
MEXICO

Cay
Jutí

Mantua

Guane

Río Mantua

Embalse
Laguna
Grande

Ciudad
Bolívar

Isabel
Rubio

Río Chaguani

Golfo de
Guanahacabibes

Sandino

Parque Nacional
Península de
Guanahacabibes

Cueva las
Perlas

La Fe

Marina Gaviota
Cabo de San
Antonio

Península de Guanahacabibes

Visitor
Center

Manuel
Lazo

Playa las
Tumbas

La Bajada

Estación Ecológica
Guanahacabibes

Faro
Roncali

Playa la
Barca

Bahía de
Corrientes

Cabo de
San Antonio

El Salón de
María

6 María la
Gorda

El Valle de
Coral Negro

Cabo
Corrientes

Valle de Viñales & Pinar del Río Province Highlights

❶ See, smell and taste the
beauty of **Parque Nacional
Viñales** (p183).

❷ Ride a horse or hike up
with the *guajiros* into the **Valle
de Palmarito** (p183).

❸ Get gobsmacked by the
grottos of **Gran Caverna de
Santo Tomás** (p185), one
of Latin America's largest
subterranean cave systems.

❹ Recharge your batteries
on dreamy **Cayo Levisa**
(p186).

❺ See where Che Guevara
played chess during the Cuban

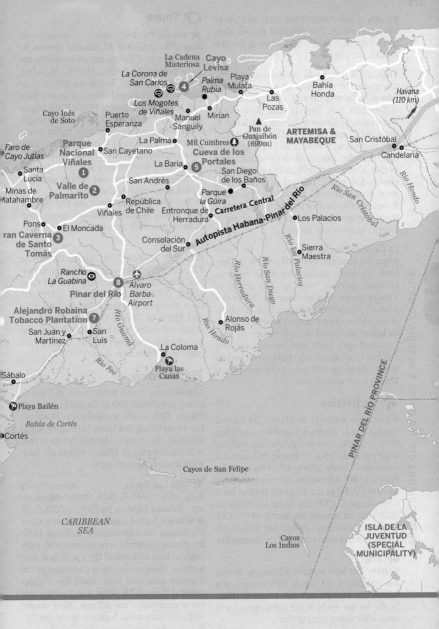

La Cadena Misteriosa

Cayo Levisa

La Corona de San Carlos ④

Palma Rubia

Playa Mulata

Las Pozas

Bahía Honda

Havana (110 km)

Cayo Inés de Soto

Puerto Esperanza

Los Mogotes de Viñales

Manuel Sanguily

Mirian

Pan de Guajaibón (699m)

ARTEMISA & MAYABEQUE

San Cristóbal

Faro de Cayo Jutías

Parque Nacional Viñales ①

San Cayetano

La Palma

Santa Lucía

La Baria

Cueva de los Portales ⑤

San Diego de los Baños

Candelaria

Minas de Matahambre

Valle de Palmarito ②

San Andrés

Río Hondo

Río San Cristóbal

Pons

República de Chile

Parque la Güira

Carretera Central

El Moncada

Viñales

Entronque de Herradura

ran Caverna de Santo Tomás ③

Consolación del Sur

Los Palacios

Autopista Habana-Pinar del Río

Sierra Maestra

Río los Palacios

Río San Diego

Río Herradura

Rancho La Guabina ⑧

Álvaro Barba Airport

Pinar del Río

Río Guamá

Alejandro Robaina Tobacco Plantation ⑦

San Juan y Martínez

San Luis

Alonso de Rojas

Río Hondo

La Coloma

Sábalo

Río Feo

Playa las Canas

Playa Bailén

Bahía de Cortés

Cortés

Cayos de San Felipe

PINAR DEL RÍO PROVINCE

CARIBBEAN SEA

Cayos Los Indios

ISLA DE LA JUVENTUD (SPECIAL MUNICIPALITY)

Missile Crisis in **Cueva de los Portales** (p188).

⑥ Dip down under the azure waters with a scuba dive at **María la Gorda** (p196).

⑦ Take what must be the world's best tobacco-plantation tour at **Alejandro Robaina Tobacco Plantation** (p194).

⑧ Relish the outlandishly opulent old facades and museums of **Pinar del Río** (p189).

heroine Adela Azcuy (1861–1914) and tracks the local history. Five different guided hikes leave from here daily; check times at the museum a day ahead.

El Jardín Botanico de las Hermanas Caridad y Carmen Miranda GARDENS

(Map p179; Salvador Cisneros; donations accepted; ◷8am-5pm) Just opposite the Servi-Cupet gas station as Cisneros swings north out of town, you'll spot an outlandish, vine-choked gate beckoning you in. This is the entrance to a sprawling garden, work on which began in 1918. Cascades of orchids bloom alongside plastic doll heads, thickets of orange lilies grow in soft groves and turkeys run amok. Knock on the door of the Little Red Riding Hood cottage and someone will probably emerge to show you around.

La Casa del Veguero FARM

(Map p180; Carretera a Pinar del Río Km 24; ◷10am-5pm) To learn about the local tobacco-growing process, stop by just south of Viñales on the way to Pinar del Río at this tobacco plantation and see a fully functional *secadero* (drying house) in which tobacco leaves are cured from February to May. The staff give brief explanations and you can buy loose cigars (the unbranded variety most Cubans smoke) here at discount prices. There's a restaurant too.

🏃 Activities

While most activities in Viñales are located outside town, there's a handful – including some climbing routes – within easy walking distance. Even if you're staying in a casa, it's worth strolling the 2km uphill to the lovely La Ermita (p181) where you can **swim** (including bar cover CUC$7) in the gorgeous pool or book a **massage** (CUC$20-35). Hotel los Jazmines (p180) has an equally amazing pool (CUC$7, including bar cover) though the ubiquitous tour buses can sometimes kill the tranquility.

Cycling

Despite the hilly terrain, Viñales is one of the best places in Cuba to cycle (most roads follow the valleys and are relatively flat). Traffic on the roads is still light. Agencies in town offer valley cycling tours.

Bike Rental Point CYCLING

(Map p179; bike hire 1/8hr CUC$1/6) There is a Bike Rental Point offering modern Chinese-made bikes with gears in Viñales' main plaza. Some casa particular owners also rent bikes.

Tours

★ Yoan & Yarelis Reyes HIKING, CYCLING

(Map p179; ☏52-74-17-34; Salvador Cisneros No 206C) Yoan and Yarelis are undoubtedly the go-to people for local activities, including walks, cycling tours, horseback riding, massage, salsa lessons and visits to a nearby farm and tobacco plantation **Finca Raúl Reyes** (Map p179), run by Yoan's father 1km outside town. Here you can enjoy fruit, coffee, puros (cigars)and a dose of throat-warming rum, plus a stunning hike to **Cueva de la Vaca**.

The cave itself carves a tunnel through the *mogotes*: from the cave mouth, unforgettable valley vistas roll before you.

The two highlight trips are the 'Sunrise tour' to Los Aquaticos and the 'Sunset tour' to the wonderfully peaceful Valle del Silencio.

Cubanacán TOUR

(Map p179; ☏48-79-63-93; Salvador Cisneros No 63C; ◷9am-7pm Mon-Sat) Cubanacán organizes perennially popular day trips to Cayo Levisa (CUC$29), Cayo Jutías (CUC$20), Gran Caverna de Santo Tomás (CUC$20) and María la Gorda (CUC$35). There's an organized valley bike tour for CUC$20 and horseback riding from CUC$5. Official park hikes leave from here daily (CUC$8).

🛏 Sleeping

Almost every house rents rooms in Viñales, giving you almost 300 to choose from (you'll always find space somewhere). Most are fair to middling, but those listed here stand out from the crowd. The two hotels within walking distance of Viñales village are both spectacularly located gems.

★ Villa Los Reyes CASA PARTICULAR $

(Map p179; ☏48-79-33-17; http://villalosreyes. com; Salvador Cisneros No 206C; r CUC$20-25; P❄@⌂) A great modern house with three big rooms, all amenities, a secluded patio for dining on some scrumptious and truly original food and one of the town's best roof terraces. Hostess, Yarelis, is a biologist at the national park and host, Yoan, has Viñales running through his veins. A taxi service and other excursions are offered. More rooms and a restaurant out back are in the works.

Villa Pitín & Juana CASA PARTICULAR $

(Map p179; ☏48-79-33-38; emilitin2009@yahoo. es; Carretera a Pinar del Río No 2 Km 25; r CUC$25; P❄) By the long-standing top-notch hospitality alone, Pitín and Juana's place would grace any self-respecting list of top Cuba

Viñales

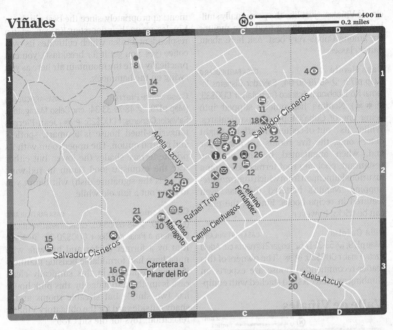

N 0 ——— 400 m
0 ——— 0.2 miles

Viñales

◎ Sights
1 Art Gallery.......................................C2
2 Casa de la Cultura.........................C2
3 Church...C2
4 El Jardín Botanico de las Hermanas
  Caridad y Carmen Miranda.........D1
5 Museo Municipal............................B2

✚ Activities, Courses & Tours
6 Bike Rental Point...........................C2
7 Cubanacán......................................C2
8 Finca Raúl Reyes...........................B1
  Yoan & Yarelis Reyes..................(see 15)

🛏 Sleeping
9 Casa Daniela...................................B3
10 Casa Jean-Pierre.............................B2
11 Casa Nenita.....................................C1
12 El Balcón...C2
13 Hostal Doña Hilda...........................B3
14 Villa Cafetal....................................B1

15 Villa Los Reyes...............................A3
16 Villa Pitín & Juana..........................B3

🍴 Eating
17 Cocinita del Medio..........................B2
18 El Barrio...C1
19 El Olivo..C2
20 Restaurant Fernan-2.......................D3
21 Restaurante la Casa de Don
   Tomás..B2

🍷 Drinking & Nightlife
22 JP Bar & Tapas................................C2

🎭 Entertainment
23 Centro Cultural Polo Montañez.......C2
24 Patio del Decimista.........................B2

🛍 Shopping
25 ARTex...B2
26 La Vega...C2

casas. But the owners have an insatiable work ethic too. There's now four wonderful rooms on separate floors, with the upper three connected by a terrace on which delicious meals are served.

Soon to come: a street-front coffee-and-cake shop, jointly run with Hostal Doña Hilda next door.

Hostal Doña Hilda CASA PARTICULAR $
(Map p179; ☑ 48-79-60-53; flavia@correodecuba.cu; Carretera a Pinar del Río No 4 Km 25; r CUC$25; ❄)
One of the first houses in town on the road from Pinar del Río, Hilda's (Chichi to her friends) house should have morphed from one to three rooms by the time you read this. More importantly, this unpretentious place is

classic Viñales – just like the perennially smiling hostess – with divine food. The mojitos are among Cuba's very best. Ask here about dance classes.

Casa Nenita
CASA PARTICULAR $

(Map p179; ☑ 48-79-60-04; Salvador Cisneros Internal No 1, behind policlinico (hospital); r CUC$35; P ✱ ☀) Nenita's has quietly slipped into being one of Cuba's top casas particulares. While its out-of-center location might deter some, the five rooms are above par and, when augmented by the amazing restaurant, pool and roof terrace, give you a luxurious launchpad from which to go *mogote*-hopping. Nenita's battered fish has even featured in recipe books. Finding the place can be tricky, however.

Villa Cafetal
CASA PARTICULAR $

(Map p179; ☑ 53-31-17-52; edgar21@nauta.cu; Adela Azcuy Final; r CUC$20; P ✱) The owners of this reader-recommended house are experts on climbing and have a shed stacked with equip-ment: appropriately, since the best climbs in Viñales are on their doorstep. Ensconced in a resplendent garden which cultivates its own coffee (yes, you get it for breakfast), you can practically taste the mountain air here as you swing on the hammock.

Casa Jean-Pierre
CASA PARTICULAR $

(Map p179; ☑ 48-79-33-34; cnr Celso Maragoto & Salvador Cisneros; r CUC$25; P ✱) Jean-Pierre's tangerine-hued house is a smart, spotless and central option. The upper room with its private terrace shades the lower, but either way the exquisite food (lamb in red-wine sauce is the signature dish) will tempt you to hang out a fair old while.

Casa Daniela
CASA PARTICULAR $

(Map p179; ☑ 48-69-55-01; casadaniela@nauta.cu; Carretera a Pinar del Rio; r CUC$20-25; P ✱ 🖶) Run by a former doctor and his wife who must have had formidable bedside manners if their hospitality in this surgically clean casa is anything to judge by, this pink house has two simple but sizeable rooms and a shady outside yard for the obligatory Viñales relaxation. Toys for the kids, too.

El Balcón
CASA PARTICULAR $

(Map p179; ☑ 48-69-67-25; elbalcon2005@yahoo.es; Rafael Trejo No 48, altas; r CUC$20-30; ✱ ☀) Situated a block south of the plaza, El Balcón has four modern 1st-floor private rooms (there is another house for rent below), a street-facing balcony (of course), and a huge roof terrace where fine food is served. Friendly owners Mignelys and Juanito speak English.

★ Hotel los Jazmines
HOTEL $$

(Map p180; ☑ 48-79-64-11; Carretera a Pinar del Río; s/d from CUC$52/86, ste from CUC$54/88; P ✱ ☀ 🖶) Prepare yourself: the vista from this pastel-pink colonial-style hotel is one of the best in Cuba. Open the shutters of your classic valley-facing room and drink in the shimmering sight of magnificent *mogotes*, oxen-ploughed red fields and palm-frond-covered tobacco drying houses. While no five-star palace, Los Jazmines benefits from its unrivaled location and a gloriously inviting swimming pool.

Handy extras include an international clinic, massage room and small shop/market. The setting comes at a cost: bus tours stop off here almost hourly, thus eroding some of the ethereal ambience. The hotel is walkable from Viñales: 4km south on the Pinar del Río road. The Viñales tour bus stops here; so may Víazul drivers if you ask nicely.

Valle de Viñales

N 0 ——— 2 km
0 ——— 1 miles

La Carreta (1.5km);
Puerto Esperanza (18km)

Hotel Rancho San Vicente

Cueva del Indio

Valle de San Vicente

Underground Trail

Sierra la Guasasa

Cueva de San Miguel

Mogote la Esmeralda

Mogote

Valle del Silencio

Underground River

Valle de la Guasasa

Valle de Palmarito

Mogote Dos Hermanas (400m)

Mogote del Valle (402m)

Mogote Coco Solo

Campismo Dos Hermanas

See Viñales Map (p179)

VIÑALES

Mural de la Prehistoria

La Ermita

Los Aquáticos (3km)

Valle de Viñales

La Casa del Veguero

Balcón del Valle

Parque Nacional Viñales Visitors Center

Hotel los Jazmines

Pinar del Río (26km)

La Ermita
HOTEL **$$**

(Map p180; 📞48-79-64-11, 48-79-62-50; Carretera de La Ermita Km 1.5; s/d incl breakfast CUC$61/92; P🅿❄🏊) La Ermita takes Viñales' top honors for architecture, interior furnishings and all-round services and quality. Notably peaceful for its absence of tour buses, the rooms with views here are housed in handsome two-story colonial edifices and the restaurant is an ideal breakfast perch. Extracurricular attractions include an excellent pool, skillfully mixed cocktails, tennis courts, a shop, horseback riding and massage.

You can walk the 2km downhill to the village or take the Viñales tour bus.

Eating & Drinking

As with many tourist towns, there is now a very good and ever-evolving array of innovative private restaurants too.

El Olivo
MEDITERRANEAN **$**

(Map p179; Salvador Cisneros No 89; pasta CUC$3-4; ☺noon-11pm) Tremendous lasagna and pasta dishes are backed up by other Med classics such as duck *à l'orange*. The joker in the pack is rabbit with herbs in a dark chocolate sauce.

★Balcón del Valle
CUBAN **$$**

(Map p180; Carretera a Pinar del Río; meals CUC$6-8; ☺noon-midnight) With three deftly constructed wooden decks overhanging a panorama of tobacco fields, drying houses and craggy *mogotes*, this aptly named restaurant (translation: Balcony of the Valley) has food that stands up to its sensational views. The unwritten menu gives a four-way choice between chicken, pork, fish and lobster, all prepared country-style with copious trimmings. It's 3km outside Viñales towards Hotel los Jazmines.

★Cocinita del Medio
CUBAN **$$**

(Map p179; Salvador Cisneros, btwn Celso Maragoto & Adela Azcuy; platters CUC$10; ☺noon-11pm) Sometimes simple is best. Generous platters of grilled meat and fish – in size and in seasoning. Eat here at least once.

El Barrio
MEDITERRANEAN **$$**

(Map p179; Salvador Cisneros 58A; meals CUC$2.50-12.50; ☺9am-late) This grungily cool joint is cornering a new market in Viñales: the right-round-the-clock market. Breakfast here, lunch here, knock back cocktails here. The tapas and the pizza are good; the pasta less so. An animated clientele of travelers keeps the terrace buzzing.

VALLE DEL SILENCIO

When you've had your fill of the big city therapist, decamp to Viñales and book a vacation in the Valle del Silencio for an alternative cure. This is the park's gentlest, least explored and – arguably – most picturesque valley, where the lion's share of the municipality's tobacco is grown. It gets its name from...well, sit on a rocking chair on a rustic porch at sunset at one of the valley's beautiful rustic *fincas* (farms) and you'll soon deduce how it got its name. Golden silence.

You can go it alone in the valley or hitch up with an organized excursion. Yoan & Yarelis Reyes (p178) in Viñales arrange a sublime sunset trip that ends at a beautiful eco-farm where you can banter with local farmers and share life-changing views of the sun's orb slipping behind the *mogotes* (limestone monoliths).

Restaurant Fernan-2
INTERNATIONAL **$$**

(Map p179; Carretera a la Ermita Km 1; mains CUC$6-9; ☺10am-midnight) Perched like a tree house below Hotel Ermita, Fernan-2 (it's a pun on the Cuban way of saying two – 'do'), run by the ever-obliging Fernan-do, is a collection of fine details: check the water features made with old bottles, and the terraced gardens and ponds. The food is plentiful, with an emphasis on rustic flavors.

Restaurante la Casa de Don Tomás
CUBAN, INTERNATIONAL **$$**

(Map p179; Salvador Cisneros No 140; mains around CUC$10; ☺10am-11pm) The oldest house in Viñales was once its best restaurant, but no more. Nonetheless, with its terracotta roof, terrace and flowering vines, it remains a salubrious place to try *las delicias de Don Tomás*: an egg-topped rice, lobster and meat fest (CUC$10).

JP Bar & Tapas
BAR

(Map p179; Salvador Cisneros No 45; ☺24hr) Is Viñales' nightlife about to unleash itself into an unprecedented 24-hour dimension? JP's aspires to be the joint that ushers in that possibility. The town's first privately owned bar slickly serves up tapas with the expected gargantuan array of Cuban spirits, plus breakfasts to soak up nights of excess.

☆ Entertainment

Centro Cultural Polo Montañez LIVE MUSIC
(Map p179; cnr Salvador Cisneros & Joaquin Pérez; admission after 9pm CUC$1; ☺music 9pm-2am) Named for the late Pinar del Río resident-turned-*guajiro* hero and legendary folk singer, Polo Montañez, this open-to-the-elements patio off the main plaza is a bar-restaurant with a full-blown stage that comes alive after 9pm.

Patio del Decimista LIVE MUSIC
(Map p179; Salvador Cisneros No 102; ☺music from 9pm) The ebullient and long-standing Patio del Decimista serves up live music, cold beers, snacks and great cocktails.

🛍 Shopping

ARTex SOUVENIRS
(Map p179; Salvador Cisneros No 102; ☺10am-5pm) You can get postcards, T-shirts and CDs here. It's attached to the Patio del Decimista.

La Vega CIGARS, RUM
(Map p179; ☑48-79-60-80; Salvador Cisneros No 57; ☺9am-9pm) A hot selection of cigars – many made right on-site – and rum too.

La Casa del Veguero CIGARS, SOUVENIRS
(Carretera a Pinar del Río Km 24; ☺10am-5pm) Cigars straight from the fields plus a good selection of books and souvenirs.

❶ Information

INTERNET ACCESS & TELEPHONE

Etecsa Telepunto (Ceferino Fernández No 3; internet per hour CUC$4.50; ☺8:30am-7pm Mon-Sat, to 5pm Sun) A few terminals in a tiny office; for phone calls you get the card but will need to use a call box elsewhere.

MEDICAL SERVICES

Clinica (☑48-79-33-48; Salvador Cisneros interior s/n)

Farmacia Internacional (☑48-79-64-11; Hotel los Jazmines, Carretera a Pinar del Río) Pharmacy in Hotel los Jazmines.

MONEY

Banco de Crédito y Comercio (Salvador Cisneros No 58; ☺8am-noon & 1:30-3pm Mon-Fri, 8-11am Sat)

Cadeca (cnr Salvador Cisneros & Adela Azcuy; ☺8:30am-4pm Mon-Sat) Gives cash advances and changes traveler's checks at higher commissions than banks.

POST

Post office (Map p179; Ceferino Fernández 14, cnr Salvador Cisneros; ☺9am-6pm Mon-Sat)

TOURIST INFORMATION

Infotur (Map p179; Salvador Cisneros No 63B; ☺9:30am-5:30pm)

TRAVEL AGENCIES

Cubanacán (p178) arranges tours, excursions and transfer buses.

❶ Getting There & Around

BUS

The well-ordered **Víazul ticket office** (Map p179; Salvador Cisneros No 63A; ☺8am-noon & 1-3pm) is opposite the main square in the same building as Cubataxi. The daily Víazul bus departs from here for Havana via Pinar del Río at 6:45am and 9:10am (CUC$12). The early bus continues to Cienfuegos (CUC$32, eight hours) and Trinidad (CUC$37, 9½ hours). Only the later bus stops in Las Terrazas.

Conectando buses run by Cubanacán (p178) (and departing from outside the Cubanacán office) have daily transfers to Havana (CUC$15), as well as Trinidad (CUC$37) via Cienfuegos. Book a day ahead. You may also be able to pick up transfers to Soroa and Las Terrazas. To get to Cayo Levisa or Cayo Jutías take the day-trip buses. A bus runs to María la Gorda (one-way/return CUC$30/41; six-person minimum). It leaves Viñales at 7am and María La Gorda at 5pm.

CAR & MOPED

To reach Viñales from the south, take the long and winding road from Pinar del Río; the roads from the north coast are not as sinuous, but due to their condition, way more time-consuming. The remote mountain road from the Península de Guanahacabibes through Guane and Pons is one of Cuba's most spectacular routes. Allow a lot of travel time.

Car hire can be arranged at **Cubacar** (☑48-79-60-60; Salvador Cisneros No 63C; ☺9am-7pm) in the Cubanacán office and **Havanautos** (☑48-76-63-30; Salvador Cisneros final) opposite the Servi-Cupet gas station at the northeast end of Viñales town.

Mopeds can be rented for CUC$24 a day at Restaurante la Casa de Don Tomás (p181).

TAXI

Cubataxi (☑48-79-31-95; Salvador Cisneros No 63A) shares an office with Víazul. Drivers hanging around outside will take you to Pinar del Río for approximately CUC$15, Palma Rubia (for the boat to Cayo Levisa) for CUC$28 or Gran Caverna de Santo Tomás for CUC$13. Good value at around CUC$70 are the cabs to José

Martí International Airport: the ride from Havana to the airport alone costs CUC$25.

For cheaper travel to Pinar, head to the intersection of the Carretera a Pinar del Río and Salvador Cisneros, just down from Restaurante la Casa de Don Tomás: old 1950s *colectivo* taxis splutter along the route for CUC$1 per seat.

VIÑALES BUS TOUR

The Viñales Bus Tour is a hop-on/hop-off minibus that runs nine times a day between the valley's spread-out sites. Starting and finishing in the town plaza, the whole circuit takes an hour and five minutes with the first bus leaving at 9am and the last at 4:50pm. There are 18 stops along the route, which runs from Hotel los Jazmines to Hotel Rancho San Vicente, and all are clearly marked with route maps and timetables. All-day tickets cost CUC$5 and can be purchased on the bus.

Parque Nacional Viñales

Parque Nacional Viñales' extraordinary cultural landscape covers 150 sq km and supports a population of 25,000 people. A mosaic of *mogote*-studded settlements grow coffee, tobacco, sugarcane, oranges, avocados and bananas on some of the oldest, most tradition-steeped landscapes in Cuba.

⊙ Sights

Mural de la Prehistoria   PUBLIC ART
(Map p180; admission incl drink CUC$3; ⊙9am-6pm) Four kilometers west of Viñales village on the side of Mogote Pita is a 120m-long painting designed in 1961 by Leovigildo González Morillo, a follower of Mexican artist Diego Rivera (the idea was hatched by Celia Sánchez, Alicia Alonso and Antonio Núñez Jiménez). On a cliff at the foot of the 617m-high Sierra de Viñales, the highest portion of the Sierra de los Órganos, this massive mural took 18 people four years to complete.

The huge snail, dinosaurs, sea monsters and humans on the cliff symbolize the theory of evolution and are either impressively psychedelic or monumentally horrific, depending on your viewpoint. You don't really have to get up close to appreciate the artwork, but the admission fee is waived if you take the delicious, if a little overpriced, CUC$15 lunch at the site restaurant (p185). Horses are usually available here (CUC$5 per hour) for various excursions.

Los Aquáticos   VILLAGE
🏊 A kilometer beyond the turn-off to Dos Hermanas and the Mural de la Prehistoria, a dirt road twists up to the mountain community of Los Aquáticos, founded in 1943 by followers of visionary Antoñica Izquierdo, who discovered the healing power of water when the *campesinos* (country people) of this area had no access to conventional medicine. They colonized the mountain slopes and two families still live there. Los Aquáticos is accessible only by horse or on foot. Guided tours (p178) can be organized in Viñales.

You can also go it alone. Although no signs mark the path, there are plenty of homesteads en route where you can ask the way. From the main road follow a dirt road for approximately 400m before branching left and heading cross-country. You should be able to pick out a blue house halfway up the mountain ahead of you. This is your goal. Once there, you can admire the view, procure grown-on-site coffee and chat to the amiable owners about the water cure. After your visit, you can make a loop by returning via Campismo Dos Hermanas and the Mural de la Prehistoria cliff paintings; it's a wonderfully scenic route (the complete Los Aquáticos–Dos Hermanas circuit totals 6km from the main highway).

Cueva de San Miguel   CAVE
(Map p180; admission incl drink CUC$3; ⊙9am-5:30pm) This is a small cave at the jaws of the Valle de San Vicente, the entrance of which is a bar-nightspot. Your entrance fee gets you into a gaping cave that engulfs you for a brief, kind of absorbing 10-minute tour before dumping you a tad cynically in El Palenque de los Cimarrones restaurant on the other side.

Cueva del Indio   CAVE
(Map p180; admission CUC$5; ⊙9am-5:30pm) In a pretty nook 5.5km north of Viñales village, this cave is very popular with tourists. An ancient indigenous dwelling, it was rediscovered in 1920. Motor boats now ply the underground river through the electrically lit cave.

🏃 Activities
Hiking

The Parque Nacional Viñales has an ever-changing number of official hikes: even the visitor center here doesn't seem able to keep track. The current count is 15 – although don't bank on always being able to get a guide (which you will officially need for any hike). All hikes can be arranged directly at the Parque Nacional Viñales Visitor Center, at the Museo Municipal or the town's tour agencies. The cost is about CUC$8 per person.

Below are just a selection of the official hikes. There are many more unofficial treks available and asking around at your casa particular will elicit further suggestions: try the hike to Los Aquáticos (p183) with its incredible vistas or the **Valle de Palmarito**, infamous among in-the-know locals for its high-stakes cockfights, and with a great swimming hole (Cueva de Palmarito).

Coco Solo & Palmarito Mogotes HIKING
This walk starts on a spur road just before La Ermita hotel and progresses for 8km taking in the Valle del Silencio, the Coco Solo and Palmarito *mogotes* and the Mural de la Prehistoria. There are good views and ample opportunities to discover the local flora and fauna including a visit to a tobacco *finca* (farmhouse; ask about lunch with one of the families there). It returns you to the main road back to Viñales.

Maravillas de Viñales HIKING
A 5km loop beginning 1km before El Moncada and 13km from the Dos Hermanas turnoff, this hike takes in endemic plants,

orchids and the biggest leaf-cutter ant hive in Cuba (so they say).

San Vicente/Ancón HIKING
The trail around the more remote Valle Ancón enables you to check out still-functioning coffee communities in a valley surrounded by *mogotes:* it's an 8km loop.

Cueva El Cable HIKING
A 3.5km hike into a local cave typical of Viñales' karst topography.

Mirador del Cuajaní HIKING
Starting at Hotel los Jazmines, this bucolic 5.5km loop ushers you up through woods to a hilltop *mirador* (viewpoint) and returns you via typically delightful tobacco-plantation scenery.

Horseback Riding
The lush hills and valleys (and the *guajiros,* indeed) around town lend themselves to horseback riding, particularly the Valle de Palmarito and the route to Los Aquáticos. Ask at Villa los Reyes (p178) or the Mural de la Prehistoria (p183).

Swimming
It is possible to swim in a natural pool at La Cueva de Palmarito in the Valle de Palmarito. This place is a doable hike/horseback ride from Viñales. Ask the locals for directions or take a tour through Yoan & Yarelis Reyes (p178) in Viñales.

CLIMBING IN VIÑALES

You don't need to be Reinhold Messner to recognize the unique climbing potential of Viñales, Cuba's mini-Yosemite. Sprinkled with steep-sided *mogotes* (limestone monoliths) and blessed with whole photo-albums' worth of stunning natural vistas, climbers from around the world have been coming here for over a decade to indulge in a sport that has yet to be officially sanctioned by the Cuban government.

Viñales' climbing remains very much a word-of-mouth affair. There are no printed route maps and no official on-the-ground information (indeed, most state-employed tourist reps will deny all knowledge of it). If you are keen to get up onto the rock face, your first points of reference should be the comprehensive website of **Cuba Climbing** (www.cubaclimbing.com) along with the book *Cuba Climbing* by Anibal Fernandez and Armando Menocal (2009). Once on the ground, the best nexus for climbers are the casas of Oscar Jaime Rodríguez and Villa Cafetal (p180) in Viñales. Ask any local for directions to either.

Viñales has numerous well-known climbing routes, including the infamous 'Wasp Factory,' and a handful of skillful Cuban guides, but there's no official equipment hire (bring your own) and there are no adequate safety procedures in place. Everything you do is at your own risk, and this includes any sticky situations you may encounter with the authorities, who don't currently sanction climbing (although they generally turn a blind eye). Climbing in Viñales is expected to become an official activity in the near future, so check the latest situation on the ground. Also consider that in the meantime, unregulated climbing in a national park area has the potential to damage endangered flora and ecosystems, so proceed with caution and care.

🛏 Sleeping

Campismo Dos Hermanas   CAMPISMO $
(Cubamar; Map p180; ☑48-79-32-23; Mogote Dos
Hermanas; s/d CUC$9.50/13) Trapped between
the sheer-sided jaws of two *mogotes* (it takes
its name from the Mogote Dos Hermanas
which lies about 1km to the west) and in
view of the Mural de la Prehistoria is one
of Cubamar's best international campismos. Bonuses include a restaurant, pool and
horseback riding, a geological museum and
nearby hiking trails. The only incongruity is
the loud music that spoils the tranquil ambience of this beautiful valley.

Hotel Rancho San Vicente   HOTEL $$
(Map p180; ☑48-79-62-01; Carretera a Esperanza
Km 33; s/d CUC$45/70; P ❋ ☎) After Viñales'
two spectacularly located hotels, you prob-
ably thought it couldn't get any better, but
Rancho San Vicente does a good job trying.
Situated 7km north of the village, this highly
attractive hotel, nestled in a grove with two
dozen or more wooden cabins, is lush and –
for once – the interior furnishings match the
magnificent setting.

There's a restaurant, pool and massage
facility on-site.

🍴 Eating & Drinking

La Carreta   MEDITERRANEAN $$
(Carretera a Esperanza Km 36; meals CUC$10-15;
⊙10am-5pm) A *carreta* might be a simple
oxen-drawn cart but there's nothing basic
about how this restaurant transports you up
its steep steps and into the privileged pan-
theons of wonderful Cuban food laced with
Mediterranean influences. The classic dish?
Lamb with red-wine sauce. It's 2km north of
Hotel Rancho San Vincente.

Restaurante Mural
de la Prehistoria   CUBAN, INTERNATIONAL $$
(set lunch CUC$15; ⊙8am-7pm) Steep but al-
most worth it, the Mural's humongous set
lunch – tasty pork roasted and smoked over
natural charcoal – ought to keep you fueled
at least until tomorrow's breakfast.

ℹ Information

The park is administered through the highly
informative **Parque Nacional Viñales Visitors
Center** (Map p180; ☑48-79-61-44; Carretera
a Pinar del Río Km 22; ⊙8am-6pm) on the hill
just before you reach Hotel los Jazmines. Inside,
colorful displays (in Spanish and English) map
out the park's main features. Hiking information
and guides are also on hand.

ℹ Getting Around

Bike (p178), car, moped or the Viñales Bus Tour
(p183); take your pick.

West of Viñales

El Moncada, a pioneering post-revolution-
ary workers' settlement lies 14km west of
Dos Hermanas and 1.5km off the road to Mi-
nas de Matahambre and Cayo Jutías. Here
you'll find the greatest of Cuba's caves and
the 'Los Malagones' memorial.

Gran Caverna de Santo Tomás   CAVE
(admission CUC$10; ⊙9am-3pm) Welcome to
Cuba's largest cave system and the second-
largest on the American continent. There
are over 46km of galleries on eight levels,
with a 1km section accessible to visitors.
There's no artificial lighting, but headlamps
are provided for the 90-minute guided tour.
Highlights include bats, stalagmites and sta-
lactites, underground pools, interesting rock
formations and a replica of an ancient na-
tive Indian mural.

Wear suitable shoes and be aware that the
cave requires some steep climbs and scram-
bling over slippery rocks. Most people visit
the cave on an organized trip from Viñales
(CUC$20).

El Memorial 'Los Malagones'   MONUMENT
(admission CUC$1) Los Malagones, from the
community of El Moncada, comprised the
first rural militia in Cuba formed from 12
men who rooted out a counterrevolutionary
band from the nearby mountains in 1959. A
mausoleum and memorial fountain inaugu-
rated in 1999 contains niches dedicated to
the 12 militia (all but two are now dead).

It is crowned by a stone re-creation of their
leader, Leandro Rodríguez Malagón. The wa-
ter features are designed to replicate (with
unerring accuracy) the sound of machine-
gun fire. A tiny museum is on site.

THE NORTHERN COAST

Considering their relative proximity to Ha-
vana, Pinar del Río province's northern
shores are largely unexplored. Facilities are
sparse and roads are rutted, though visitors
who take the time to make the journey out
have reported memorable DIY adventures,
famously hospitable locals...and, of course,
those fantastic beaches.

Cayo Jutías

Pinar del Río's most discovered 'undiscovered' beach is the 3km-long blanket of sand that adorns the northern coast of Cayo Jutías, a mangrove-covered key situated approximately 65km northwest of Viñales and attached to the mainland by a short *pedraplén* (causeway). Jutías – named for its indigenous tree rats – vies with Cayo Levisa to the east for the title of the province's most picturesque beach and, while the latter might be prettier, the former has less crowds and more tranquility.

The Cayo's access road starts about 4km west of Santa Lucía. Four kilometers further on you'll come to the beginning of the causeway and ten minutes later the **Faro de Cayo Jutías** appears; this metal lighthouse was built by the US in 1902 and makes for an interesting walk along the abutting mangrove-studded sands. The road kinks sharp left to culminate at the main Jutías beach, caressed by crystal-clear water, at 12.5km from the coastal highway.

The serenity here is thanks to the lack of any permanent accommodations (unlike Levisa). The only facilities on the island are the thatched oceanside **Restaurante Cayo Jutías** (Cayo Jutías; ☉10am-5:30pm), specializing in local seafood, and a small **dive center** that rents out kayaks for CUC$1 per hour, runs snorkeling trips for CUC$12, other boat trips for CUC$10 to CUC$25 and organizes diving from CUC$37 for one immersion (there are seven dive sites nearby). Beyond the initial arc of sand the beach continues for 3km; you can hike barefoot through the mangroves.

Tours from Viñales (just transport and a snack lunch) cost CUC$20 and will give you six hours' beach time. Otherwise you will have to make your own transport arrangements. The fastest, and by far the prettiest, route is via Minas de Matahambre, through rolling pine-clad hills.

Puerto Esperanza

Becalmed at the end of a long, bumpy road, the fishing village of Puerto Esperanza (Port of Hope), 6km north of San Cayetano and 25km north of Viñales, isn't sleepy so much as veritably slumbering. The clocks haven't worked here since...oh...1951. According to town lore, the giant mango trees lining the entry road were planted by slaves in the 1800s. A long pier pointing out into the bay, a favored perch for catatonic fisherfolk, is decent for a jump in the ocean.

⊙ Sights & Activities

Itineraries? Forget them. Relax. Read. Eat lobster. Discover some transcendental Santería ritual, chat to the old timers with the fishing rods or take a spontaneous tour around your neighbor's tobacco plantation in search of pungent peso cigars. Eat more lobster. Clue: check Centro Cultural Esperanza by the dock for after-dark shenanigans.

🛏 Sleeping & Eating

Teresa Hernández Martínez CASA PARTICULAR **$**
(☎48-79-37-03; Calle 4 No 7; r CUC$15-20) The charismatic Teresa is as colorful as her three bright and clean rooms furnished unsubtly in lurid pink, blue and green. She also runs a private restaurant in a jungle-like garden out back where fish (seafood plate CUC$10) headlines the menu.

❶ Getting There & Away

You'll need your own wheels to get to Puerto Esperanza. There's a handy Servi-Cupet gas station at San Cayetano. The road on to Cayo Jutías deteriorates to dirt outside of San Cayetano: expect a throbbing backside if you're on a bike or moped.

Cayo Levisa

More frequented than Cayo Jutías and perhaps still more splendid, Cayo Levisa sports a beach-bungalow-style hotel, basic restaurant and fully equipped diving center, yet still manages to feel relatively isolated. Separation from the mainland obviously helps. Unlike other Cuban keys, there's no causeway here, and visitors must make the 35-minute journey by boat from Palma Rubia. It's a worthwhile trip: 3km of sugar-white sand and sapphire waters earmark Cayo Levisa as Pinar del Río's best beach. American writer Ernest Hemingway first 'discovered' the area, part of the Archipiélago de los Colorados, in the early 1940s after he set up a fishing camp on Cayo Paraíso, a smaller coral island 10km to the east. These days Levisa attracts up to 100 visitors daily as well as the 50-plus hotel guests. While you won't feel like an errant Robinson Crusoe here, you should find time (and space) for plenty of rest and relaxation.

◉ Sights & Activities

Levisa has a small marina offering scuba diving for CUC$40 per immersion, including gear and transport to the dive site. Fourteen dive sites are peppered off the coast. These include the popular La Corona de San Carlos (San Carlos' Crown), the formation of which allows divers to get close to marine life unobserved, and Mogotes de Viñales, so called for their towering coral formations said to bear a likeness to *mogotes*: precipitous limestone hills outside Viñales. La Cadena Misteriosa (Mysterios Chain) is a shallow reef where some of the most colorful fish hereabouts – including barracudas and rays – can be seen. Snorkeling plus gear costs CUC$12 and a sunset cruise goes for the same price. Kayaking and aqua biking are also possible.

🛏 Sleeping & Eating

Hotel Cayo Levisa — HOTEL $$$

(☑48-75-65-01; www.hotelcayolevisa-cuba.com; s/d CUC$93/142; ❄) With an idyllic tropical beach just outside your front door, you won't worry about the slightly outdated *cabañas* (cabins) and dull food choices here. Expanded to a 40-room capacity in 2006, the Levisa's newer wooden cabins (all with bathroom) are an improvement on the old concrete blocks. Service has pulled its socks up too. Book ahead as this place is understandably popular.

ⓘ Getting There & Away

The landing for Cayo Levisa is around 21km northeast of La Palma or 40km west of Bahía Honda. Take the turnoff to Mirian and proceed 4km through a large banana plantation to reach the coast-guard station at Palma Rubia, where there is a snack bar (10am to 6pm) and the departure dock for the island. The Cayo Levisa boat leaves at 10am and returns at 5pm, and costs CUC$25 per person round-trip (CUC$15 one way if you have a hotel reservation) including lunch. From the Cayo Levisa dock you cross the mangroves on a wooden walkway to the resort and gorgeous beach along the island's north side. If you are without a car, the easiest way to get here is via a day excursion from Viñales, great value at CUC$29 including the boat and lunch.

Playa Mulata Area

Squeezed into the edge of the province on the road to Bahía Honda, the countryside around Playa Mulata is the domain of *guajiros*, meditative cattle and the occasional fisher. Away beyond the roughshod beaches rears the ridge of the Pan de Guajaibón, one of western Cuba's highest peaks. There is a bust of independence leader Antonio Maceo and an abandoned radar station at the summit.

By the turnoff to Playa Mulata, Villa José Otaño Pimentel (☑52-54-98-10; r CUC$15; ℗) is the only accommodation around, in a serene fruit-tree-festooned garden (with a dinky restaurant). José can organize horseback rides (per hour CUC$5) up Pan de Guajaibón.

The nearest public transport terminates 16km west at the Cayo Levisa turn-off. If terrible tarmac isn't an issue, you can continue along this secluded coast road to Bahía Honda, Soroa and even Havana. This route is popular with cyclists.

SAN DIEGO DE LOS BAÑOS & AROUND

Halfway between Viñales and Soroa, San Diego de los Baños is a famous spa town but there's more to this area than mud baths and massages. Stop by for some memorable wildlife-watching and to discover one of Che Guevara's old hideaways.

San Diego de los Baños

Sitting 130km southwest of Havana, this nondescript town just north of the Carretera Central is popularly considered the country's best spa location. As with other Cuban spas, its medicinal waters were supposedly 'discovered' in the early colonial period when a sick slave stumbled upon a sulfurous spring, took a revitalizing bath and was miraculously cured. Thanks to its proximity to Havana, San Diego's fame spread quickly and a permanent spa was established here in 1891. During the early 20th century American tourists flocked here, leading to the development of the current hotel-bathhouse complex in the early 1950s.

Sitting beside the Río San Diego, the town enjoys an attractive natural setting, with the Sierra del Rosario to the east and the Sierra de Güira to the west, an area replete with pine, mahogany and cedar forests. It's a favorite spot for bird-watchers. Despite numerous possibilities for tourism, San Diego has been long due an overhaul by the authorities.

◉ Sights & Activities

Balneario San Diego — THERMAL BATHS

(☺8am-5pm) Finally due to reopen to the public in 2015 after a protracted refurbishment, the Balneario bathing complex's thermal waters of 30°C to 40°C are used to treat all manner of muscular and skin afflictions. The sulfurous waters are potent and immersions of only 20 minutes per day are allowed. Mud from the Río San Diego is also used here for revitalizing mud baths.

Other health services include massage and a 15-day course of acupuncture. Don't expect fluffy towels and complimentary cups of coffee, the Balneario San Diego is more like a Moroccan hammam than a five-star hotel facility, though it's perennially popular with Cubans undergoing courses of medical treatment, plus the odd curious tourist.

If you're looking for cold water, you can swim at the Hotel Mirador **pool** (admission CUC$1; ⊙9am-6pm).

Bird-Watching & Trekking

Bird-watching and trekking trips into Parque la Güira can be organized at Hotel Mirador with qualified guide Julio César Hernández (📞52-48-66-31;carpeta@mirador.sandiego.co.cu). You'll need your own wheels.

🍽 Sleeping & Eating

Hotel Mirador HOTEL $
(📞48-77-83-38, 48-54-88-66; s/d CUC$27/36, grill meals from CUC$3; 🅿❄🐾) The Mirador is a low-key stop-off. Predating the Revolution by five years, the hotel was built in 1954 to accommodate spa-seekers headed for the adjacent Balneario San Diego. Well-tended terraced gardens slope up to rooms which match the pretty exterior: crisp, cozy and looking for the most part onto balconies with garden and *balneario* (spa) views. Downstairs there's a pleasant swimming pool and an outdoor grill that does whole roast pig on a spit. There's also a proper restaurant *con una vista* (with a view) inside, serving Cuban cuisine.

Villa Julio & Cary CASA PARTICULAR $
(📞48-54-80-37; Calle 29 No 4009; r CUC$20-25) The town's only casa is an agreeable hole with a garden, colorful mural and porches (with rockers) guarding clean, tidy rooms.

Sierra la Güira

The Sierra la Güira kicks off just west of San Diego de los Baños with the surreal Hacienda Cortina, the grounds of which splay out into a 219-sq-km tract of protected parkland, **Parque la Güira**, an untrameled karst and forest landscape. Little trodden it may be,

but this did not prevent the region from being a retreat for some of the Revolution's most renowned figures in the past, and to this day it's a haven for birdlife.

👁 Sights

Hacienda Cortina HISTORIC ESTATE
(⊙dawn-dusk) A grand crenellated entry gate a few kilometers west of San Diego de los Baños announces the surreal, long-abandoned grounds of Hacienda Cortina. The brainchild of wealthy lawyer José Manuel Cortina, this rich-man's-fantasy-made-reality was built as a giant park during the 1920s and 1930s, with Cortina plonking a stately home in its midst. After nigh-on a century of neglect, in 2014 refurbishment money arrived out of the blue and the Hacienda is being restored to its former glory.

The grandiose entrance buildings are back up and running as a **restaurant** (basic food but eyecatchingly designed with rainbow-colored glass) and next-door is a **swimming pool**. You can climb the crumbling water tower outside for some good views of the wild bamboo-splashed grounds, whilst down below a **boating lake** like Cortina used to have is being prepared. Some rambling gardens have been replanted, with statues, fountains and the signature cartwheel-shaped flower border redone. New chalet-style accommodation was also being constructed at the time of research.

The Hacienda grounds fan out into Parque la Güira and, beyond, the Sierra de Güira.

Cueva de los Portales CAVE
(admission CUC$1) During the October 1962 Cuban Missile Crisis, Ernesto 'Che' Guevara transferred the headquarters of the Western Army to this vast and spectacular cave, 11km west of Parque la Güira and 16km north of Entronque de Herradura on the Carretera Central. The cave is set in a beautiful remote area among steep-sided vine-covered *mogotes* and was declared a national monument in the 1980s.

Within the cave-mouth, a small outdoor museum exhibits Che's roughshod artifacts including his bed and the table where he played chess (while the rest of the world stood at the brink of nuclear Armageddon). Three other caves called El Espejo, El Salvador and Cueva Oscura are further up the hillside. This area is brilliant **bird-watching** turf: birding tours can be arranged at San Diego de los Baños' Hotel Mirador, or you can ask staff at the cave entrance. There's a good campismo

VALLE DE VIÑALES & PINAR DEL RÍO PROVINCE SIERRA LA GÜIRA

(which may or may not accept foreign guests) and a small restaurant outside the cave. You'll need your own wheels to get here.

ℹ Getting Around

To reach the Cueva de los Portales by bus, ask the Havana–Pinar del Río Víazul drivers nicely and they may stop at the Carretera Central turnoff 10km from town. The walk isn't too bad.

By car, the road across the mountains from San Diego de los Baños to Che Guevara's cave is beautiful, but narrow and full of potholes. But it is driveable: just. The approach from Entronque de Herradura is an easier drive. There's a Servi-Cupet gas station at the entrance to San Diego de los Baños from Havana.

PINAR DEL RÍO AREA

Pinar del Río

POP 191,660

Surrounded by beautiful verdant countryside and given an economic boost by its proximity to the world's best tobacco-growing terrain, the city of Pinar del Río emits a strange energy, exacerbated by its famous *jineteros* (hustlers) who can abrade the most thick-skinned traveler. As a result, the place probably has more detractors than fans, especially since the bucolic *jinetero*-free paradise of Viñales is so close by. But a stopover here needn't be purgatorial. There's a good tobacco factory to visit, some weirdly interesting architecture, and a hot, frenetic after-dark scene if you're up for it.

Pinar del Río was one of the last provincial capitals on the island to take root, and still seems stuck in the slow lane. Overlooked by successive central governments who preferred sugarcane to tobacco, the city became an urban backwater and the butt of countless jokes about the supposedly easy-to-fool *guajiros* who were popularly portrayed as simple-minded rural hicks. But the city fought back. It's overcome neglect, derision and several furious hurricanes and is busily trying to overturn its negative connotations.

History

Pinar del Río was founded in its current form in 1774 by a Spanish army captain. In 1896 General Antonio Maceo brought the Spanish-Cuban-American War to Pinar del Río in an ambitious attempt to split the island in two, and the town rallied to his wake-up call.

Following the 1959 Revolution, Pinar del Río's economic fortunes improved exponentially; this was facilitated further by the building of the Autopista Nacional from Havana and the development of tourism in the 1980s. The city baseball team has also historically reared some of the best players in the country after the big boys from Havana and Santiago: many, such as Alexi Ramírez and José Contreras, have defected to the USA.

◎ Sights

Try beginning at Plaza de la Independencia, then working your way down Martí.

⭐ **Fábrica de Tabacos Francisco Donatien**   CIGAR FACTORY
(Antonio Maceo Oeste No 157; admission CUC$5; ⊙9am-noon & 1-4pm Mon-Fri) You can observe people busily rolling some of Pinar's (read: the world's) finest cigars in this factory, which is now tobacco central on the tourist circuit.

Smaller than the Partagás factory in Havana, you get a more intimate insight here, though the foibles are the same – robotic guides, rushed tours and the nagging notion that it's all a bit voyeuristic. There's an excellent cigar shop opposite.

⭐ **Casa Taller**   GALLERY
(Martí 160; ⊙hours variable) FREE The Plaza de la Independencia is the hub of the art scene. First and foremost, on the northwest side, is the workshop-gallery of renowned Cuban artist Pedro Pablo Oliva. The key point of the gallery is to promote and encourage artistic talent in Pinar del Río; several local artists have work displayed. Stop by most days for a browse.

Centro Provincial de Artes Plásticas Galería   GALLERY
(Antonio Guiteras; ⊙8am-9pm Mon-Sat) FREE This top-notch Pinar gallery on Plaza de la Independencia houses many local works.

⭐ **Palacio de los Matrimonios**   HISTORIC BUILDING
(Martí, btwn Rafael Morales & Plaza de la Independencia) FREE Wow! West on Martí, the grand neoclassical facades give way to the gushingly opulent in the shape of this building dating from 1924, now primarily a wedding venue. That said, the amiable guards will let you look around the lavish interior, which includes a plethora of artwork, much of it Chinese in origin.

Pinar del Río

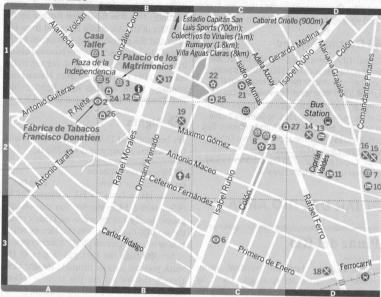

Pinar del Río

◎ **Top Sights**
1 Casa Taller A1
2 Fábrica de Tabacos Francisco
   Donatien... A2
3 Palacio de los Matrimonios B1

◎ **Sights**
4 Catedral de San Rosendo...................... B2
5 Centro Provincial de Artes
   Plásticas Galería B1
6 Fábrica de Bebidas Casa Garay............ C3
7 Museo de Ciencias Naturales
   Sandalio de Noda................................. D2
8 Museo Provincial de Historia C2
9 Teatro José Jacinto Milanés................. C2

◎ **Sleeping**
10 Gladys Cruz Hernández........................ D2
11 Hostal Sr Handy Santalla..................... D2
12 Hotel Vueltabajo B1
13 Pensión El Moro D2

◎ **Eating**
14 Café Ortuzar.. D2
15 El Gallardo D2
16 El Mesón D2
17 Heladería B1
18 Mercado Agropecuario.......................... D3
19 Panadería Doña Neli.............................. B2

◎ **Drinking & Nightlife**
20 Disco Azul E2

◎ **Entertainment**
21 Café Pinar.. C1
22 Casa de la Música.................................. C1
23 La Piscuala C2

◎ **Shopping**
24 Casa del Habano.................................... B1
25 Fondo Cubano de Bienes
   Cultural C1
26 La Casa del Ron.................................... B2
27 Todo Libro Internacional....................... C2

Teatro José Jacinto Milanés HISTORIC BUILDING
(☑48-75-38-71; Martí No 160, btwn Colón & Isabel
Rubio) Often included in a set of seven classic
19th-century Cuban provincial theaters, the
540-seat Milanés dates from 1845 – making it
one of Cuba's oldest. It reopened in 2006 after
lengthy renovations and, with its three-tiered

auditorium, antique seats, and Spanish-style
patio and cafe, is well worth a look.

Museo de Ciencias Naturales
Sandalio de Noda   MUSEUM
(Martí Este No 202; admission CUC$1, camera
CUC$1; ◷9am-5pm Mon-Fri, to 1pm Sun) A
mad but magnificent neo-Gothic-meets-

Moorish-meets-Hindu-meets-Byzantium mansion built by local doctor and world traveler Francisco Guasch in 1914. Once you've got over the shock of the whimsical exterior (gargoyles, turrets and sculpted seahorses), the decrepit exhibits inside will slow your pulse right down again. The giant stone T-Rex in the garden is fun though.

Museo Provincial de Historia　　MUSEUM
(Martí Este No 58, btwn Colón & Isabel Rubio; admission CUC$1; ⏱ 8:30am-6:30pm Mon-Fri, 9am-1pm Sat) A museum collecting the history of the province from pre-Columbian times to the present, including Enrique Jorrín ephemera (Jorrín was the creator of the *chachachá*). It was closed for renovation at the time of research.

Catedral de San Rosendo　　CHURCH
(Maceo Este No 3) The city's understated cathedral is four blocks southeast of the cigar factory. It dates from 1883 and its pastel-yellow exterior seems to get a more regular paint job than the rest of the city's buildings. As with most Cuban churches, the interior is often closed. Get a peek during Sunday-morning service.

Fábrica de Bebidas
Casa Garay　　BRANDY FACTORY
(Isabel Rubio Sur No 189, btwn Ceferino Fernández & Frank País; admission CUC$1; ⏱ 9am-3:30pm Mon-Fri, to 12:30pm Sat) Workers here use a secret recipe to distill sweet and dry versions of the city's signature liquor, Guayabita del Pinar guava brandy. Whistle-stop 15-minute multilingual factory tours are topped off with a taste of the brew in the sampling room. There's a shop adjacent.

⭐ Festivals & Events

Carnaval　　CARNIVAL
(⏱ Jul) Carnaval in early July features a procession of *carrozas* (carriages) through the streets with couples dancing between the floats. It's a big, drunken dance party.

🛏 Sleeping

⭐ Gladys Cruz Hernández　CASA PARTICULAR **$**
(☎ 48-77-96-98; casadegladys@gmail.com; Av Comandante Pinares Sur No 15, btwn Martí & Máximo Gómez; r CUC$20; ❄) Gladys' place is the most dependable place in Pinar del Río, if top-notch colonial rooms and sunny service are what you like for the night. There are two rooms with recently redone tiled bathrooms and fridges, a TV and an attractive rear patio. It's near the train station.

Villa Aguas Claras　　CAMPISMO **$**
(☎ 48-77-84-27; s/d incl breakfast CUC$34/38; P ❄) This campismo lies 8km north of town on the Carretera a Viñales (off Rafael Morales). The 50 bungalows with hot showers sleep two (10 have air-con). Rooms are ailing but landscaping is lush. Besides an OK restaurant, Aguas Claras also offers horseback riding and day trips. You're out of the way a bit here though, and insect repellent is essential. The campismo is accessible from Pinar del Río by bus several times daily.

Pensión El Moro　　CASA PARTICULAR **$**
(☎ 48-77-43-35; Adela Azcuy No 46, btwn Colón & Ciprián Valdés; r CUC$20-25; ❄) Two bright little apartments; one down, one up. The inviting kitchen with its breakfast bar is currently shared between both. The upper room is ultimately best: right alongside a roof terrace.

Hostal Sr Handy Santalla　CASA PARTICULAR **$**
(☎ 48-72-12-22; Máximo Gómez No 169A, btwn Ciprián Valdés & Comandante Pinares; r CUC$20-25; P ❄) Keen young owner giving it a shot in the new economy with two small 2nd-floor

rooms with sparkling new bathroom fittings, and a patio and garage downstairs.

Hotel Vueltabajo
HOTEL $$
(📞 48-75-93-81; cnr Martí & Rafael Morales; s/d CUC$35/55; 🅿) Stylishly colonial with high ceilings and striped Parisian window awnings, the rooms at this fabulous hotel are so spacious you almost think they must have run out of furniture. Old-fashioned shutters open onto the street and downstairs there's an OK bar-restaurant; a reasonable breakfast is included in the price.

✗ Eating

El Mesón
CUBAN $
(Martí Este 205; meals CUC$4-6; ⊙11am-11pm) This rather good private restaurant serves up liberal helpings of simple *comida criolla* (Creole food) heavy on the rice and beans, with plenty of Cuban company.

El Gallardo
CUBAN $
(Martí Este 207; MN$40-125; ⊙11am-11pm) A rather lavish entrance leads back to a more typical *ranchón*-style main eating area. Great food, particularly the fish, but why the rather grotesque gnomes? Pay in pesos.

Heladería
ICE CREAM $
(cnr Martí & Rafael Morales; ⊙9am-9pm) A substantial *tres gracias* (three scoops) at this clean, cheerful place is the price of half a teaspoon's worth of Häagen Dazs.

★ Café Ortuzar
CUBAN, INTERNATIONAL $$
(Martí 127; 3-course meal CUC$15; ⊙11:30am-midnight) Slurp a coffee in the street-side cafe or gravitate into the elegant air-conditioned, two-floor interior for the city's best eating experience, where abstract pictures of the province's famous *guajiros* watch on while you eat the CUC$15 three-course meals – a proud part of the new wave of rich, refined Cuban cuisine.

Rumayor
CUBAN $$
(Carretera a Viñales Km 1; mains CUC$10; ⊙noon-midnight) Some of Pinar's best food can be found at Rumayor, 2km north of the town center off the Carretera a Viñales. Justly famous for its succulent *pollo ahumado* (smoked chicken), you'll pay a little extra here, but it is definitely worth it. It's also one of Pinar's premier cabaret spots in the evening.

Self-Catering

Mercado Agropecuario
MARKET
(Rafael Ferro; ⊙8am-6pm Mon-Sat, to 1pm Sun) Pinar del Río's colorful open-air market is almost on top of the tracks near the train station. You'll see the odd tour group tramping through here getting a grip on Special Period economics.

Panadería Doña Neli
BAKERY
(cnr Gerardo Medina Sur & Máximo Gómez; ⊙7am-7pm) Gives you each day your daily bread.

🍷 Drinking & Entertainment

Disco Azul
CLUB
(cnr Gonzales Alcorta & Autopista; admission CUC$5; ⊙from 10pm Tue-Sun) A drab hotel, but a kicking disco – this glittery nightclub in Hotel Pinar del Río, on the edge of town coming from the Autopista, is the city's most popular.

Rumayor
CABARET
(📞 48-76-30-51; Carretera a Viñales Km 1; cover charge CUC$5; ⊙noon-midnight) Besides serving very good food, this place undergoes a metamorphosis at night from Tuesday through Sunday to a kitschy cabaret with a fantastic floor show that starts at 11pm. At weekends there's daytime shows too.

PINAR DEL RÍO STREET NAMES

Locals stick to the old street names; this chart should help.

OLD NAME	NEW NAME
Calzada de la Coloma	Rafael Ferro
Caubada	Comandante Pinares
Recreo	Isabel Rubio
Rosario	Ormani Arenado
San Juan	Rafael Morales
Vélez Caviedes	Gerardo Medina
Virtudes	Ceferino Fernández

VALLE DE VIÑALES & PINAR DEL RÍO PROVINCE PINAR DEL RÍO

Café Pinar
LIVE MUSIC

(Gerardo Medina Norte No 34; admission CUC$3; ⊘10am-2am) This spot gets the local youth vote and is also the best place to meet other travelers (if there are any around). Situated on a lively stretch of Calle Gerardo Medina, there are bands playing at night on the open patio, and light menu items such as pasta, chicken and sandwiches available during the day. Mondays and Saturdays are the best nights.

La Piscuala
CULTURAL CENTER

(cnr Martí & Colón) Peaceful patio alongside the Teatro José Jacinto Milanés. Check the schedule posted outside for nightly cultural activities.

Cabaret Criollo
CABARET

(Carretera Central Km 1, btwn Av Aeropuerto & Carretera a Viñales; ⊘9pm-2am Mon-Sat) The musical half of an eponymous restaurant, locals rate this nightly cabaret in an enormous open-air patio highly.

Casa de la Música
LIVE MUSIC

(Gerardo Medina Norte No 21; admission CUC$1; ⊘concerts start nightly at 9pm) After warming up at nearby Café Pinar, many revelers cross the street for more live music here.

Estadio Capitán San Luis Sports
SPORTS

(☑48-75-38-95; admission MN$1; ⊘matches 7pm Tue-Thu & Sat, 4pm Sun) From October to April, exciting baseball games happen at this stadium on the north side of town. Pinar del Río is one of Cuba's best teams, often challenging the Havana–Santiago monopoly (and national champions in 2011 and 2014). Pop by evenings to see the players going through a training session.

🛍 Shopping

Fondo Cubano de Bienes Cultural
ARTS & CRAFTS

(cnr Martí & Gerardo Medina; ⊘9am-4:30pm Mon-Fri, 8:30am-3:30pm Sat) The most interesting selection of regional handicrafts, although revenue goes almost exclusively to the government rather than the makers themselves.

Casa del Habano
CIGARS

(Antonio Maceo Oeste No 162; ⊘9am-5pm Mon-Sat) Opposite the Fábrica de Tabacos Francisco Donatien tobacco factory, this store is one of the better outlets of this popular government cigar chain, with a patio bar, air-conditioned shop and smoking room.

La Casa del Ron
ARTS & CRAFTS, RUM

(Antonio Maceo Oeste No 151; ⊘9am-4:30pm Mon-Fri, to 1pm Sat & Sun) Near the Fábrica de Tabacos Francisco Donatien, sells souvenirs, CDs and T-shirts, plus plenty of the strong stuff.

Todo Libro Internacional
BOOKS

(cnr Martí & Colón; ⊘8am-noon & 1:30-6pm Mon-Fri, 8am-noon & 1-4pm Sat) Selection of maps, books and office supplies in same building as the Cubanacán office.

ℹ Information

DANGERS & ANNOYANCES
For a relatively untouristed city Pinar del Río has plenty of unsolicited touts or *jineteros*. The majority are young men who hang around Calle Martí, offering everything from paladar meals to 'guided tours' of tobacco plantations. Most will back off at your first or second *'no me moleste, por favor'* but bolder ones have been known to mount bicycles and accost tourist cars (identifiable by their purple/brown number plates) when they stop at traffic lights. Although they're generally nonaggressive, it's best to be firmly polite from the outset and not invite further attention.

INTERNET ACCESS & TELEPHONE
Etecsa Telepunto (cnr Gerardo Medina & Juan Gómez; per hour CUC$4.50; ⊘8:30am-7:30pm) Telephone and internet access.

MEDIA
Guerrillero is published on Friday. Radio Guamá airs on 1080AM or 90.2FM.

MEDICAL SERVICES
Farmacia Martí (Martí Este No 50; ⊘8am-11pm)
Hospital Provincial León Cuervo Rubio (☑78-75-44-43; Carretera Central) Two kilometers north of town.

MONEY
Banco Financiero Internacional (Gerardo Medina Norte No 46; ⊘8:30am-3:30pm Mon-Fri) Opposite Casa de la Música.
Cadeca (Martí No 46; ⊘8:30am-5:30pm Mon-Sat)

POST
Post office (Martí Este No 49; ⊘8am-8pm Mon-Sat)

TOURIST INFORMATION
Infotur (☑48-72-86-16; Hotel Vueltabajo, cnr Martí & Rafael Morales; ⊘9am-5.30pm Mon-Fri) At the Hotel Vueltabajo, and one of the city's most helpful sources of information.

TRAVEL AGENCIES

Cubanacán (☑ 48-75-01-78, 48-77-01-04; Martí No 109, cnr Colón) Has moped rental.

❶ Getting There & Away

BUS

The city's **bus station** (Adela Azcuy, btwn Colón & Comandante Pinares) is conveniently close to the center. Pinar del Río is on the Víazul network, with all services to Havana and destinations east originating in Viñales. There are departures to Havana at 7:45am and 10:10am (CUC$11, 2½ hours). The later Havana bus also stops in Las Terrazas while the earlier one continues to Cienfuegos and Trinidad. Buses to Viñales leave at 12:05pm and 5:10pm (CUC$6, 45 minutes).

Conectando buses running most days offer services to Havana and a direct service to Viñales bypassing Havana. You'll need to book ahead with Cubanacán. Ask here about other transfers to Cayo Levisa, Cayo Jutías and María la Gorda.

TAXI

Private taxis hanging around outside the bus station will offer prices all the way to Havana. Sometimes these are worth considering. A fare to José Martí International Airport, for example, could cost around CUC$60 compared to the standard CUC$25 just from Havana.

Colectivos (collective taxis) congregate at the start of the Carretera a Viñales outside the hospital north of town, offering the scenic Viñales jaunt Cuban-style for CUC$1 per passenger (four-person minimum).

TRAIN

Before planning any train travel, check the station blackboards for canceled/suspended/rescheduled services. From the **train station** (cnr Ferrocarril & Comandante Pinares Sur; ☉ ticket window 6:30am-noon & 1-6:30pm) there's a painfully slow train to Havana (CUC$6.50, 5½ hours) every other day. You can buy your ticket for this train the day of departure; be at the station a good hour before departure. Local trains go southwest to Guane via Sábalo (CUC$2, two hours). This is the closest you can get by train to the Península de Guanahacabibes.

❶ Getting Around

Cubacar (☑ 48-75-93-81) has an office at Hotel Vueltabajo and **Havanautos** (☑ 48-77-80-15) has one at Hotel Pinar del Río. Mopeds can be rented from Cubanacán.

Servicentro Oro Negro is two blocks north of the Hospital Provincial on the Carretera Central.

The Servi-Cupet gas station is 1.5km further north on the Carretera Central toward Havana; another is on Rafael Morales Sur at the south entrance to town.

Horse carts (MN$1) on Isabel Rubio near Adela Azcuy go to the Hospital Provincial and out onto the Carretera Central. Bici-taxis cost MN$5 around town.

Southwest of Pinar del Río

If Cuba is the world's greatest tobacco producer and Pinar del Río its proverbial jewel box, then the verdant San Luis region southwest of the provincial capital is the diamond in the stash. Few deny that the pancake-flat farming terrain around the smart town of San Juan y Martínez churns out the *crème de la crème* of the world's tobacco and the agricultural scenery is picturesque. Further southwest, there are a couple of little-visited southern beaches and the freshwater Embalse Laguna Grande, stocked with largemouth bass.

◉ Sights

Alejandro Robaina Tobacco
Plantation   FARM
(☑ 48-79-74-70; admission CUC$2; ☉ 9am-5pm) This is the only real opportunity in Cuba to tour a working tobacco plantation – take it! The famous Robaina *vegas* (fields), in the rich Vuelta Abajo region southwest of Pinar del Río, have been growing quality tobacco since 1845, but it wasn't until 1997 that a brand of cigars known as Vegas Robaina was first launched to wide international acclaim.

Despite the death of former owner Alejandro Robaina, who made the brand so famous, in April 2010, the show must go on, and it does at the plantation today: it's been open to outside visitors for some years. With some deft navigational skills, you can roll up at the farm and get the lowdown on the tobacco-making process from delicate plant to aromatic wrapper: tours are 25 minutes long. There's a small on-site cafe and all guests receive a souvenir *puro* (cigar).

To get there, take the Carretera Central southwest out of Pinar del Río for 12km, turn left toward San Luis and left again after approximately 3km at the Robaina sign. This rougher track continues for 1.5km to the farm. Do not hire a *jinetero* (hustler) to lead you, as they often take you to the wrong farm. Tours are available every day. The tobacco-growing season runs from October to February and this is obviously the best time to visit. Plants only reach an impressive height from December.

Rancho La Guabina RANCH
(☑48-75-76-16; Carretera de Luis Lazo Km 9.5; ☉horse shows at 10am & 4pm Mon, Wed & Fri) A former Spanish farm spread over 1000 hectares of pasture, forest and wetlands, the Rancho La Guabina is a jack of all trades and a master of at least one. You can partake in horseback riding here, go boating on a lake, enjoy a scrumptious Cuban barbecue, or even see a cockfight. The big drawcard for most, though, is the fantastic horse shows.

The *rancho* is a long-standing horse-breeding center that raises fine Pinto Cubano and Appaloosa horses, and minirodeo-style shows run on Monday, Wednesday and Friday from 10am to noon and from 4pm to 6pm. Agencies in Viñales and Pinar del Río run excursions here starting at CUC$29, or you can arrive on your own. It's a great place to enjoy the peaceful *guajiro* life. Limited accommodations are available.

Playa Bailén BEACH
The beach life here can't match the alluring north coast; still, this makes a pleasant, sandy deviation on the way out west.

🛏 Sleeping & Eating

San Juan y Martínez and Sandino (25km from Laguna Grande via Ciudad Bolivar) are the best hunting grounds for casas particulares. Playa Bailén has rough cabins for rent.

Rancho La Guabina HOSTEL $$
(☑48-75-76-16; Carretera de Luis Lazo Km 9.5; r per person CUC$39; P☀🐴) Just outside Pinar del Río, this expansive farm offers eight rooms, five in a cottage-style house and three in separate cabins. A few have TVs and fridges. It's a charming and unhurried place with excellent food and friendly staff.

⊙ Getting There & Away

Theoretically two trains a day travel between Pinar del Río and Guane stopping at San Luis, San Juan y Martínez, Sábalo and Isabel Rubio (two hours). Passenger trucks run periodically between Guane and Sandino but, southwest of there, public transport is sparse, apart from the sporadic Havanatur transfer. Fill your tank in Sandino if you intend to drive to Cabo de San Antonio, as this is the last (official) gasp for gas.

PENÍNSULA DE GUANAHACABIBES

As the island narrows at its western end, you fall upon the low-lying and ecologically rich Península de Guanahacabibes. One of Cuba's most isolated enclaves, it once provided shelter for its earliest inhabitants, the Guanahatabeys. A two-hour drive from Pinar del Río, this region lacks major tourist infrastructure, meaning it feels far more isolated than it is. There are two reasons to come here: a national park (also a Unesco Biosphere Reserve) and the international-standard diving center at María la Gorda.

Parque Nacional Península de Guanahacabibes

Flat and deceptively narrow, the elongated Península de Guanahacabibes begins at the straggled-out village of La Fe, itself 94km southwest of Pinar del Río or 29km southwest of the western terminus of Cuba's railway in Guane. In 1987, 1015 sq km of this uninhabited sliver of idyllic coastline was declared a Biosphere Reserve by Unesco – one of only six in Cuba. The reasons for the protection measures were manifold. First, the reserve's submerged coastline features a wide variety of different landscapes including broad mangrove swamps, low-scrub-thicket vegetation and an uplifted shelf of alternating white sand and coral rock. Second, the area's distinctive limestone karst formations are home to a plethora of unique flora and fauna including 172 species of bird, 700 species of plant, 18 types of mammal, 35 types of reptile, 19 types of amphibian, 86 types of butterfly and 16 orchid species. Sea turtles, including loggerhead and green turtles, come ashore at night in summer to lay their eggs – the park is the only part of mainland Cuba where this happens. Another curiosity is the swarms of *cangrejos colorados* (red and yellow crabs) that crawl across the peninsula's rough central road only to be unceremoniously crushed under the tires of passing cars. The stench of the smashed shells is memorable.

The area is thought to shelter at least 100 important archaeological sites relating to the Guanahatabey people.

Activities

Península de Guanahacabibes is a paradise for divers, eco-travelers, conservationists and bird-watchers – or, at least, it ought to be. With no official settlements, the peninsula is one of Cuba's most untouched. However, thanks to strict park rules (you can't go anywhere without a guide), some travelers have complained that the experience is too limiting.

Centro Internacional de Buceo DIVING
(☑48-77-13-06; María la Gorda; 1-immersion dive CUC$35, diving gear CUC$7.50) Diving is María la Gorda's raison d'être and the prime reason people come to Cuba's western tip. The nerve center is this well-run base next to the eponymous hotel at the Marina Gaviota. Good visibility and sheltered offshore reefs are highlights, plus the proximity of the 32 dive sites to the shore. Couple this with the largest formation of black coral in the archipelago and you've got a recipe for arguably Cuba's best diving reefs outside the Isla de la Juventud.

A dive here costs CUC$35 (night dive CUC$40), plus CUC$7.50 for equipment. The center offers a full CMAS scuba certification course (CUC$365, four days) and snorkelers can hop on the dive boat for CUC$12. The dive center also offers four hours of deep-sea fishing for CUC$200 for up to four people and line fishing/trolling at CUC$30 per person, four maximum.

Among the 50 identified dive sites in the vicinity, divers are shown El Valle de Coral Negro, a 100m-long black-coral wall, and El Salón de María, a cave 20m deep containing feather corals and brilliantly colored corals. The concentrations of migratory fish can be incredible. The furthest entry is only 30 minutes by boat from shore.

Marina Gaviota Cabo de San Antonio DIVING
(☑48-75-01-18) Cuba's most westerly located boat dock is on Playa las Tumbas at the end of the Península Guanahacabibes. The marina has fuel, boat mooring, a small restaurant, shop and easy access to 27 diving sites. The Villa Cabo San Antonio is nearby.

Cueva las Perlas HIKING
(admission CUC$8) The three-hour, 3km trek to the 'pearl cave' traverses deciduous woodland replete with a wide variety of birds, including *tocororos, zunzuncitos* and woodpeckers. You'll clock evidence of indigenous occupants from former centuries en route. After 1.5km you come to the cave itself, where you can spy (and hear) screech owls: it's a multi-gallery cavern with a lake of which 300m is accessible to hikers.

Del Bosque al Mar HIKING
(admission CUC$6) Leaving from near the Estación Ecológica Guanahacabibes, this 1.5km trail passes a lagoon where you can view resident birdlife, and takes in some interesting flora as well as a cenote (a kind of water-submerged cave) for swimming.

At 90 minutes it's rather short for such an immense park, but the guides are highly trained and informed, and tours can be conducted in Spanish, English or Italian.

Tours

Cabo de San Antonio Excursion WILDLIFE TOUR
(tour CUC$10) The visitor center can arrange guides, specialized visits and a five-hour tour to the park's (and Cuba's) western tip at Cabo de San Antonio. The responsibility is yours to supply transport, sufficient gas, water, sunscreen, insect repellent and food, which makes the task a little more difficult for travelers without their own wheels.

During most of the 120km round-trip you'll have dark, rough *diente de perro* (dog's teeth) rock on one side and the brilliant blue sea on the other. Iguanas will lumber for cover as you approach and you might see small deer, *jutías* (tree rats) and lots of birds. Beyond the lighthouse is deserted Playa las Tumbas where you'll be given 30 minutes for a swim. Thanks to the upgraded road surface, any hire car can make this trip. The five-hour excursion costs CUC$10 per person, plus the CUC$80 or so you'll need to hire a car (there's car rental at Hotel María la Gorda). Besides the diving, the beaches and the chance to see turtles, the wealth of lesser-known activities (such as exploring caves and viewing rare wildlife at Cabo San Antonio makes staying out here worthwhile.

Sleeping & Eating

The crescent of scruffy beach at La Bajada has very basic rooms for rent.

Hotel María la Gorda HOTEL $$
(☑48-77-81-31; www.hotelmarialagorda-cuba.com; s/d/tr incl breakfast CUC$42/60/86; Ⓟ❋⊛) This is among Cuba's remotest hotels, and the isolation has its advantages. The adjoining palm-fringed beach is pretty (if a little rocky), but 90% of people come here to

TURTLE-WATCHING

Guanahacabibes is still a park in tentative development, but it has recently introduced turtle-monitoring opportunities to its limited stash of organized excursions. The turtle program has been running since 1998 under the direction of environmental researchers and with involvement from the local population (primarily schoolchildren), but now outsiders are allowed to participate. Approximately 1500 nesting green turtles lay their eggs on half a dozen of the peninsula's south-facing beaches between June and August, and willing participants are invited to observe, monitor and aid in the process. In 2013, a record 900 turtle nests were recorded. To take part, inquire in advance at the park office at La Bajada. Tours take place nightly between 10pm and 2am in season, and there are observation shelters at Playa La Barca, the main turtle-watching beach. The release of baby turtles begins in mid-September.

dive; reefs and vertical drop-offs beckon just 200m from the hotel. María la Gorda (literally 'Maria the Fatso') is on the Bahía de Corrientes, 150km southwest of Pinar del Río.

Room-wise you get a choice of three beach-hugging pink-concrete, motel-type buildings or, further back, either attractive white two-floor apartment blocks or rustic wooden cabins connected by walkways. Far from being a posh resort, María la Gorda is an easygoing place where hammocks are strung between palm trees, cold beers are sipped at sunset and dive talk continues into the small hours.

Buffet meals cost CUC$15 for lunch or dinner; reports on the food vary. There are two restaurants and a beach bar. A small shop sells water and basic provisions. There's a rip-off CUC$10 (including a sandwich) charge to visit Hotel María la Gorda and its adjoining 5km beach for nonguests, although sneaking down for free beach time would hardly be hard if you can bear to forgo the sandwich.

Villa Cabo San Antonio   CABINS **$$**
(☑ 48-75-76-55; Playa las Tumbas; s/d incl breakfast CUC$55/70; P ❄) A 16-villa complex on the almost-virgin Península de Guanahacabibes behind idyllic Playa las Tumbas, set 3km beyond the Faro Roncali (Roncali Lighthouse) and 4km shy of the Gaviota Marina. It's a friendly and surprisingly well-appointed place which has satellite TV, car rental, bike/quadbike hire and a small restaurant.

Ask about its lavish Casa Leñador, a CUC$160-per-night house sleeping nine and with a private pool, by Faro Roncali.

ℹ Information

Although the park border straddles the tiny community of La Fe, the reserve entrance is at La Bajada. Some 25km before the reserve proper, Manuel Lazo has the last accommodations for budget-conscious travelers.

It's advisable to phone the **visitor center** (☑ 48-75-03-66; ⊙ 8:30am-3pm) at La Bajada to arrange park activities before showing up at the park entrance, as with limited resources there are often not the staff to arrange impromptu guided tours.

The visitor center, adjacent to the Estación Ecológica Guanahacabibes, has interpretive displays on the local flora and fauna. French, English and Italian are spoken. You can arrange to meet guides here for all activities except the diving, which is organized from Hotel María la Gorda. Just beyond the center the road splits with the left-hand branch going south to María la Gorda (14km along a deteriorating coastal road) and the right fork heading west toward the end of the peninsula.

It's a 120km round-trip to Cuba's westernmost point from here. The lonesome Cabo de San Antonio is populated by a solitary lighthouse, the Faro Roncali, inaugurated by the Spanish in 1849, the Gaviota Marina and Villa Cabo San Antonio. Four kilometers northwest is Playa las Tumbas, an idyllic beach where visitors to the park are permitted to swim.

ℹ Getting There & Away

A transfer bus (return CUC$35) operates between Viñales and María la Gorda most days, but check and book ahead. It is scheduled to leave Viñales at 7am and arrive at the peninsula at 9:30am. The return leg leaves María la Gorda at 5pm and arrives in Viñales at 7pm. Reserve at Cubanacán (p178) in Viñales or Infotur (p193) in Pinar del Río.

Via Gaviota (☑ 48-77-81-31) has an office at Hotel María la Gorda, offering car hire from around CUC$75 per day for a small car.

Varadero & Matanzas Province

📞 45 / POP 692,536

Includes ➔

Varadero 199
Matanzas 216
Cárdenas 224
San Miguel de los
Baños & Around 226
Península de Zapata . . 227
Central Australia
& Around 228
Boca de Guamá 228
Gran Parque Natural
Montemar 230
Playa Larga 231
Playa Girón 232

Best Outdoor Adventures

➔ Wildlife-watching, Río Hatiguanico (p231)

➔ Diving, Bahía de Cochinos (p232)

➔ Boat trip, Río Canímar (p215)

➔ Skydiving, Varadero (p201)

Best Casas Particulares

➔ Hostal Azul (p220)

➔ Villa Mar (p221)

➔ Casa Mary y Angel (p205)

➔ El Caribeño (p231)

Why Go?

With a name translating as 'massacres,' Matanzas province conceals an appropriately tumultuous past beneath its modern-day reputation for glam all-inclusive holidays. In the 17th century pillaging pirates ravaged the region's prized north coast, while three centuries later, more invaders grappled ashore in the Bahía de Cochinos (Bay of Pigs) under the dreamy notion that they were about to liberate the nation.

The Bahía de Cochinos attracts more divers than mercenaries these days, while sunbathers rather than pirates invade the northern beaches of Varadero, the vast Caribbean resort and lucrative economic 'cash cow' that stretches 20km along the sandy Península de Hicacos.

Providing a weird juxtaposition is the scruffy city of Matanzas, the music-rich provincial capital that has gifted the world with rumba, *danzón,* countless grand neoclassical buildings and Santería (the province is the veritable cradle of Afro-Cuban religion). Tourists may be scant here outside of Varadero, but soulful, only-in-Cuba experiences are surprisingly abundant.

When to Go

➔ December through April the all-inclusive hotels in the tourist set-piece, Varadero, hike prices for the *temporada alta* (high season), the best time for beach-basking.

➔ Hit Matanzas city around October 10 for the annual rumba festival, Festival del Bailador Rumbero.

➔ November to April are the best months for bird-watching in the Ciénaga de Zapata.

NORTHERN MATANZAS

Home to Cuba's largest resort area (Varadero) and one of its biggest ports (Matanzas), the northern coastline is also the province's main population center and a hub for industry and commerce. Despite this, the overriding feel is distinctly green, and most of the region is undulating farmland – think a cross between North American prairie and the UK's Norfolk Broads – occasionally rupturing into lush, dramatic valleys like the Valle de Yumurí, or sinking into enigmatic caves outside Matanzas.

Varadero

POP 27,630

Varadero, located on the sinuous 20km-long Hicacos peninsula, stands at the vanguard of Cuba's most important industry – tourism. As the largest resort in the Caribbean, it guards a huge, unsubtle and constantly evolving stash of hotels (over 50), shops, water activities and poolside entertainment; though its trump card is its beach, an uninterrupted 20km stretch of blond sand that is undoubtedly one of the Caribbean's best. But, while this large, tourist-friendly mega-resort may be essential to the Cuban economy, it offers little in the way of unique Cuban experiences. For these you'll need to escape the wristband wearing crowds from Canada and Europe and dip into the readily accessible hinterland for nearby 'reality checks' in Matanzas, Cárdenas or Bahía de Cochinos.

Most Varadero tourists buy their vacation packages overseas (you need to book in advance to get the best rates) and are content to idle for a week or two enjoying the all-inclusiveness of their resort (and why not?). However, if you're touring Cuba independently, and want to alternate your esoteric rambles with some less stressful beach life, Varadero can provide a few nights of well-earned sloth after a dusty spell on the road. For spur-of-the-moment stop-offs there are plenty of economical hotels and casas particulares in Varadero town at the western end of the peninsula that are baggable on the spot.

◉ Sights

For art and history, you're in the wrong place; nevertheless, there are a few sights worth checking out if the beach life starts to bore you. Varadero town's two central squares, **Parque de las 8000 Taquillas** (sporting a small subterranean shopping center) and **Parque Central** are disappointingly bland, save for a somewhat out-of-place colonial-style church, **Iglesia de Santa Elvira** (Map p204; cnr Av 1 & Calle 47), one block east.

Parque Josone   PARK
(Map p204; cnr Av 1 & Calle 58; ⊙9am-midnight) If you're set on sightseeing in the town, ensconce yourself in this pretty green oasis. These landscaped gardens date back to 1940 and take their name from the former owners, José Fermín Iturrioz y Llaguno and his wife Onelia, who owned the Arechabala rum distillery in nearby Cárdenas and built a neoclassical mansion here: the Retiro Josone.

Expropriated after the Revolution, the mansion became a guesthouse for visiting foreign dignitaries. The park is now a public space for the enjoyment of all – you may see Cuban girls celebrate their *quinciñeras* (15th-birthday celebrations) here. Josone's expansive, shady grounds feature a lake with rowboats (CUC$0.50 per person per hour) and water-bikes (CUC$5 per hour), atmospheric eateries, resident geese, myriad tree species and a minitrain (CUC$1 for a ride). There's a public swimming pool (admission CUC$2) in the south of the park and the odd ostrich lurking nearby. Good music can be heard nightly.

Museo Municipal de Varadero   MUSEUM
(Map p204; Calle 57; admission CUC$1; ⊙10am-7pm) Walking up Calle 57 from Av 1, you'll see many typical wooden beach houses with elegant wraparound porches. The most attractive of the bunch, Varadero's Museo Municipal, has been turned into a balconied chalet displaying period furniture and a snapshot of the resort's history. It's more interesting than you'd think.

Mansión Xanadú   NOTABLE BUILDING
(Map p206; cnr Av las Américas & Autopista Sur) Everything east of the small stone water tower (it looks like an old Spanish fort, but was built in the 1930s), next to the Restaurant Mesón del Quijote, once belonged to the Du Pont family. Here the millionaire American entrepreneur, Irénée, built the three-story Mansión Xanadú. It's now an upscale hotel atop Varadero's 18-hole golf course with a top-floor bar conducive to sipping sunset cocktails.

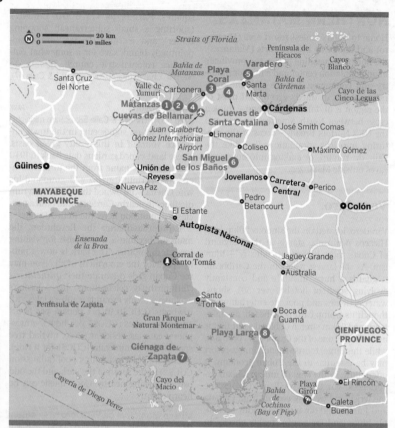

Varadero & Matanzas Province Highlights

❶ Unlocking the buried secrets of dusty **Matanzas** (p216), the 'Athens of Cuba'.

❷ Catching a performance at Matanzas' splendid new **Sala de Conciertos José White** (p219).

❸ Immersing yourself in the crystalline waters of

Playa Coral (p215) for a spot of snorkeling.

❹ Delving deep into the cave systems of **Cuevas de Bellamar** (p215) or **Cuevas de Santa Catalina** (p215).

❺ Going tandem skydiving over diamond-dusted **Varadero** (p201).

❻ Admiring forgotten

grandeur in **San Miguel de los Baños** (p226).

❼ Exploring the vast, varied vegetation zones of the **Ciénaga de Zapata** (p230).

❽ Discovering the plunging drop-offs and colorful coral walls while diving off **Playa Larga** (p232).

Cueva de Ambrosio   CAVE
(Map p206; admission CUC$3; ◷9am-4:30pm)
Beyond Marina Chapelín, Varadero sprawls east like a displaced North American suburb with scrubby mangroves interspersed with megahotel complexes, the odd iron crane and a dolphin show. Past all this and 500m beyond the Club Amigo Varadero on the Autopista Sur, you'll find this cave, interesting

for its 47 pre-Columbian drawings, discovered in a 300m recess in 1961.

The black-and-red drawings feature the same concentric circles seen in similar paintings on the Isla de la Juventud, perhaps a form of solar calendar. The cave was also used as a refuge by escaped slaves.

Reserva Ecológica Varahicacos   PARK

(Map p206; www.varahicacos.cu; 45min hiking trails CUC$3; ☉9am-5pm) A few hundred meters beyond Cueva de Ambrosio is the entrance to Varadero's nominal green space and a wildlife reserve that's about as 'wild' as New York's Central Park. Bulldozers have been chomping away at its edges for years. There are three underwhelming trails. Highlights are the **Cueva de Musalmanes** with its 2500-year-old human remains, followed by the giant cactus called **El Patriarca**, accessed from a different road several hundred meters further on again towards the peninsula tip.

Marina Gaviota   MARINA

At the peninsula's eastern tip, Marina Gaviota's impressive expansion now encompasses a wide *malecón* (waterside promenade) alongside the marina joining new hotel Meliá Marina Varadero with designer shops and restaurants, and the popular Sala de la Musica music venue. Cubans come from miles around to marvel: it's a little bit more of Florida that's found its way across the water.

Cayo Piedras del Norte   MARINE PARK

Five kilometers north of Playa las Calaveras (one hour by boat), Cayo Piedras del Norte has been made into a 'marine park' through the deliberate sinking of an assortment of vessels and aircraft in 15m to 30m of water during the late 1990s.

Scuttled for the benefit of divers and glass-bottom boat passengers are a towboat, a missile-launching gunboat (with missiles intact), an AN-24 airplane and the yacht *Coral Negro*.

🏃 Activities

Diving & Snorkeling

Varadero has several excellent dive centers, although, this being tourist-ville, the prices are double those in the Bahía de Cochinos on the province's south coast. All of the 21 dive sites around the Península de Hicacos require a boat transfer of approximately one hour. Highlights include reefs, caverns, pitchers and a Russian patrol boat sunk for diving purposes in 1997. The nearest shore diving is 20km west at Playa Coral (p215). The centers also offer day excursions to superior sites at the Bahía de Cochinos (p232) (one/two immersions CUC$50/70, with transfer) – or you could bus it there yourself and dive unrushed with local instructors, including an overnight stay at a local casa for just a fraction more.

Barracuda Scuba Diving Center   DIVING

(Map p202; ☑45-61-34-81; Av Kawama, btwn Calles 2 & 3; ☉8am-5pm) Varadero's top scuba facility is the mega-friendly, multilingual Barracuda Scuba Diving Center. Diving costs CUC$50 per dive with equipment, cave diving is CUC$60 and night diving costs CUC$55. Packages of multiple dives work out cheaper. Barracuda conducts introductory resort courses for CUC$70, and ACUC (American Canadian Underwater Certifications) courses starting at CUC$220, plus many advanced courses. Snorkeling with a guide is CUC$30.

When a north wind is blowing and diving isn't possible in the Atlantic, you can be transferred to the Caribbean coast in a minibus (90-minute drive); this costs a total of CUC$55/75 for one/two dives. Other popular trips include Cueva Saturno for cave diving and Playa Coral for snorkeling.

Marina Gaviota   DIVING

(Map p206; ☑45-66-47-22, 45-66-77-55; Autopista Sur y Final) A professional outfit at the eastern end of Autopista Sur, the fancy new-look Marina Gaviota runs scuba diving/snorkeling excursions both locally (in Cayo Piedras del Norte) and at the Bahía de Cochinos, for slightly cheaper prices than the competition.

Marlin Marina Chapelín
(Aquaworld) Diving Center   DIVING

(☑45-66-88-71; Autopista Sur Km 12) Organizes diving/snorkeling trips.

Fishing

Varadero has three marinas, all of which offer a similar variety of nautical activities and facilities.

Marlin Marina Chapelín
(Aquaworld)   FISHING

(Map p206; ☑45-66-75-50; Autopista Sur Km 12) Situated close to the entrance to Hotel Riu Turquesa, five hours of deep-sea fishing here costs CUC$290 for four people (price includes hotel transfers, open bar and licenses; nonfishing companions pay CUC$30).

Marina Gaviota   FISHING

(☑45-66-47-22; Autopista Sur y Final) At the eastern end of Autopista Sur. Deep-sea fishing is among the available activities.

Skydiving

Centro Internacional de
Paracaidismo   SKYDIVING

(☑45-66-28-28; http://skydivingvaradero.com; Carretera Vía Blanca Km 1.5; skydive per person

VARADERO & MATANZAS PROVINCE VARADERO

Varadero Town – West

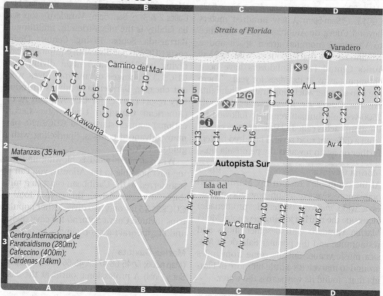

Straits of Florida

Varadero Town – West

Activities, Courses & Tours
1	Barracuda Scuba Diving Center	A1
2	Gaviota	C2

Sleeping
3	Casa Betty y Jorge	F2
4	Hotel Kawama	A1
5	Villa Sunset	C1

Eating
6	Caracol	E1
7	Grocery Store	C2
8	La Vaca Rosada	D1
9	Lai-Lai	D1
10	Salsa Suárez	F2

Shopping
11	Casa del Habano	F1
12	Gran Parque de la Artesanía	C1

CUC$180) For those with a head for heights, Varadero's greatest thrill has to be skydiving at this base at the old airport just west of Varadero. The terminal is 1km up a dirt road, opposite Marina Acua. Skydivers take off in an Antonov AN-2 biplane of WWII design (don't worry, it's a replica) and jump from 3000m using a two-harness parachute with an instructor strapped in tandem on their back.

After 35 seconds of free fall the parachute opens and you float tranquilly for 10 minutes down onto Varadero's white sandy beach. The center also offers less spectacular (but equally thrilling) ultralight flights at various points on the beach. Prices for skydiving are CUC$180 per person with an extra CUC$45 for photos and CUC$60 for video. Ultralight flights start at CUC$30 and go up to CUC$300 depending on the length of time. If you are already a qualified skydiver, solo jumps are also available on production of the relevant certification.

A day's notice is usually required for skydiving (which many hotels can book on your behalf), and jumps are (obviously) weather dependent. Since opening in 1993 the center has reported no fatalities. Find out more at the Cubatur (p213) office.

Golf

Varadero Golf Club GOLF

(Map p206; ☎ 45-66-77-88; www.varaderogolfclub.com; Mansión Xanadú; green fees 18 holes CUC$95; ☺ 7am-7pm) While it's no Pebble Beach, golfers can have a swinging session at this uncrowded and well-landscaped club: Cuba's first and only fully fledged 18-hole course (par 72). The original nine holes created by the Du Ponts are between Hotel Bella Costa and Du Pont's Mansión Xanadú; another

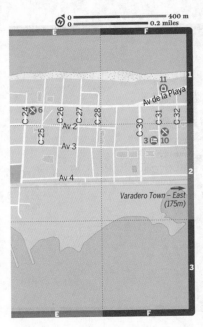

🎓 Courses

Many of Varadero's all-inclusive hotels lay on free Spanish lessons for guests. If you're staying in cheaper digs, ask at the reception of one of these larger hotels and see if you can find your way onto an in-house language course by offering to pay a small fee.

Agencia Turismo Central   DANCING
(Map p204; ☎ 45-61-26-43; cnr Av 1 & Calle 36; ⏲ 9am-7pm) Like several of the casas particulares, this agency offers dancing lessons (CUC$15), as well as numerous other activities.

☞ Tours

Tour desks at the main hotels book most of the nautical or sporting activities and arrange organized sightseeing excursions from Varadero.

Among the many off-peninsula tours offered are a half-day trip to the Cuevas de Bellamar near Matanzas, a bus tour to the Bahía de Cochinos and a whole range of other bus tours to places as far away as Santa Clara, Trinidad, Viñales and, of course, Havana.

Gaviota   HELICOPTER TOUR
(Map p202; ☎ 45-66-78-64, 45-61-24-75; Calle 13, btwn Avs 2 & 3) This operator features a variety of helicopter tours in Russian M1-8 choppers; the Trinidad trip (CUC$199) is popular. The Tour de Azúcar (sugarcane tour) visits a disused sugar mill and takes a steam-train ride to Cárdenas station. Prices are CUC$39/30 per adult/child. It also organizes 4WD safaris to the scenic Valle de Yumurí.

The excursion (adult/child CUC$45/34) includes a visit to a *campesino* family and a huge, delicious meal at Ranchón Gaviota.

**Marlin Marina Chapelín
(Aquaworld)**   BOAT TOUR, WATER SPORTS
(Map p206; ☎ 45-66-75-50; Autopista Sur Km 12) Aquaworld Marina Chapelín organizes Varadero's nautical highlight in the popularity stakes: the **Seafari Cayo Blanco**, a seven-hour sojourn (CUC$95) from Marina Chapelín to nearby Cayo Blanco and its idyllic beach. The trip includes an open bar, lobster lunch, two snorkeling stops, live music and hotel transfers.

There's also a shorter CUC$45 catamaran tour with snorkeling, open bar and a chicken lunch.

nine holes added in 1998 flank the southern side of the three Meliá resorts.

Bookings for the course are made through the pro shop next to the Mansión Xanadú (now a cozy hotel with free, unlimited tee time). Bizarrely, golf carts (CUC$30 per person) are mandatory.

El Golfito   MINIGOLF
(Map p204; cnr Av 1 & Calle 42; per person CUC$0.50; ⏲ 24hr) Golf neophytes can play the miniature version of the game here.

Other Activities

There are **sailboards** available for rent at various points along the public beach (CUC$10 per hour), as are small catamarans, banana boats, sea kayaks etc. The upmarket resorts usually include these water toys in the all-inclusive price.

Centro Todo En Uno   BOWLING
(Map p204; cnr Calle 54 & Autopista Sur; per game CUC$2.50; ⏲ 24hr) Bowling alleys are popular in Cuba and the *bolera* here, including a small shopping/games complex on Autopista Sur, is usually full of Cuban families who also come to enjoy the adjacent kids' playground and fast-food joints.

Varadero Town – East

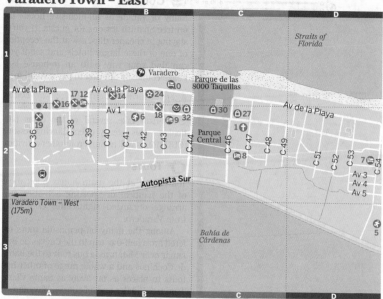

Varadero Town – East

◉ Sights
1 Iglesia de Santa Elvira C2
2 Museo Municipal de Varadero E2
3 Parque Josone E2

✪ Activities, Courses & Tours
4 Agencia Turismo Central A2
5 Centro Todo En Uno D3
6 El Golfito B2

🛏 Sleeping
7 Beny's House D2
8 Casa Marlén y Javier C2
9 Casa Mary y Angel B2
10 Dormiendo en las Olas B1
11 Hotel Cuatro Palmas F2
12 Hotel los Delfines A1

✕ Eating
13 Dante E2
14 La Bodeguita del Medio B1
15 La Fondue F2
16 La Vicaria A2
17 Paladar Nonna Tina A1
18 Panadería Doña Neli B2

19 Restaurante Esquina Cuba A2
20 Restaurante La Barbacoa F2
   Restaurante Mallorca .... (see 15)
21 Varadero 60 .... F3
22 Waco's Club E3

🍷 Drinking & Nightlife
   Calle 62 .... (see 15)
23 Discoteca Havana Club F2

✪ Entertainment
24 Casa de la Música B1
25 Centro Cultural Comparsita F2
26 The Beatles Bar-Restaurant E2

🛍 Shopping
27 ARTex C2
   Casa de las Américas .... (see 31)
28 Casa del Habano F2
29 Casa del Ron F2
30 Centro Comercial Hicacos C2
   Centro Todo En Uno .... (see 5)
31 Galería de Arte Varadero F2
32 Librería Hanoi B2
   Taller de Cerámica Artística .... (see 31)

Boat Adventure BOAT TOUR
(Map p206; ☎45-66-84-40; per person CUC$41; ⊙9am-4pm) This two-hour guided trip, leaving from the Marlin Marina Chapelín, is a speedy sortie through the adjacent man-groves on two-person jet skis or motorboats to view myriad wildlife including friendly crocs. Bookings for all these watery excursions can also be made at most of the big hotels.

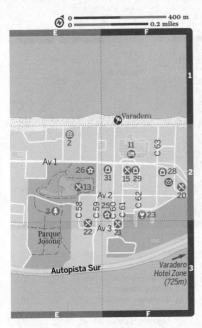

Festivals & Events

Golf tournaments are held at the Varadero Golf Club in June and October. Varadero also hosts the annual tourism convention in the first week in May when accommodations are tight and some places are reserved solely for conference participants.

Varadero Regatta SPORTS
(May) Held in May, this historic regatta dates back to 1910 and features many different types of boat races.

Sleeping

Varadero is huge – there are easily 50 hotels and 20-plus casas particulares. Want to hunt down that bargain room? Book ahead or concentrate your efforts on the peninsula's southwest end where all the casas particulares lie, where hotels are cheaper and where the town retains a semblance of Cuban life.

All-inclusive hotel packages booked through travel agents in your home country may have differing (cheaper) rates to those given here.

Varadero Town

The best choices in the town, covering the southwest end of the peninsula, are undoubtedly the new wave of casas particulares, most of which trounce the dated, lackluster hotels in this zone in class. Staying here also means good access to the town's facilities.

★**Casa Mary y Angel** CASA PARTICULAR $
(Map p204; ☎45-61-23-83; cnr Calle 43 & Av 1; r CUC$35; ❄) The array of shady terraces at this leading private accommodation option will have hotels hereabouts looking enviously over their shoulders – as will the three gleaming, well-appointed rooms. Breakfast will run to several courses, and to several hours if the rich, strong coffee has anything to do with it. Good salsa lessons are available here.

Beny's House CASA PARTICULAR $
(Map p204; ☎45-61-17-00; www.benyhouse.com; Calle 55, btwn Avs 1 & 2; r CUC$35; P❄) Reminiscent of an upmarket English guesthouse surrounded by better weather, you approach Beny's through a landscaped garden and patio that puts the rooms (smart, with new queen-size beds and flat-screen TVs) way back from any noise. The very good restaurant specializes in fish.

Villa Sunset CASA PARTICULAR $
(Map p202; ☎52-39-45-42; Calle 13, btwn Avs 1 & Camino del Mar; r CUC$35; ❄🍴) The sedate three-room Villa Sunset comes with a large well-appointed kitchen and the absence of on-site *dueños* (owners), meaning the house ushers in a new concept for Varadero, which sits somewhere between fancy boutique hostel and self-catering apartment. A good option for families, with a garden at the rear. It's owned by the same people that brought you the excellent casa particular, Beny's House.

Dormiendo en las Olas CASA PARTICULAR $
(Map p204; ☎45-61-23-63, 52-68-81-95; cnr Av de la Playa & Calle 43; r CUC$35-40; P❄) 'Sleeping in the waves' is how the name of this beach-fronting house translates and you almost are – at least, you're far closer to them than you would be at most all-inclusives. The rooms themselves are clean, but unexceptional: the real beauty is that the back terrace here leads straight out onto a prime stretch of sandy strand.

Varadero Hotel Zone

Varadero Hotel Zone

◎ Sights
1 Cueva de Ambrosio F1
2 Cueva de Muselmanes F1
3 El Patriarca G1
4 Mansión Xanadú B1
5 Marina Gaviota H2
6 Reserva Ecológica Varahicacos F1

◎ Activities, Courses & Tours
Boat Adventure ....(see 7)
Marina Gaviota ....(see 5)
7 Marlin Marina Chapelín
   (Aquaworld) D1
   Marlin Marina Chapelín
   (Aquaworld) Diving
   Center ....(see 7)
8 Varadero Golf Club B1

◎ Sleeping
9 Blau Marina Palace H2
10 Blau Varadero E1
11 Hotel Tuxpán B1
    Mansión Xanadú ....(see 4)
12 Meliá Las Américas B1

13 Meliá Península Varadero G1
14 Meliá Varadero.. C1
15 Memories Varadero G1
16 Planta Real H2
17 Royalton Hicacos Resort....................... F1
18 Villa Cuba.. A1

◎ Eating
La Isabelica Casa del Cafe .... (see 5)
19 Restaurante Mesón del Quijote............ A1

◎ Drinking & Nightlife
Bar Mirador Casa Blanca ....(see 4)
Discoteca la Bamba ....(see 11)
20 Palacio de la Rumba............................... B1

◎ Entertainment
21 Cabaret Continental............................... A1
22 Cabaret Cueva del Pirata D1
23 Club Mambo...E1
    Sala de la Musica ....(see 5)

◎ Shopping
24 Plaza América.. C1

Casa Marlén y Javier CASA PARTICULAR $
(Map p204; ☑45-61-32-86; Av 2, btwn Calles 46 & 47; r CUC$30-35; ❄) A superb house with three rooms on a quiet back street, with hosts that are amongst Varadero's favorites with travelers. There is a *ranchón*-style rooftop terrace where meals are served. English spoken.

Casa Betty y Jorge CASA PARTICULAR $
(Map p202; ☑45-61-25-53; Calle 31 No 108A; r CUC$30-35; ❄) Two rooms, one with its own neat little breakfast bar, front a peaceful private courtyard below, whilst up and round the corner, Betty will cook for you (inside or on the upper terrace) and Jorge will chinwag with you (in English if you like) about the peaks and pitfalls of the Varadero hospitality trade.

Hotel Kawama RESORT $$
(Map p202; ☑45-61-44-16; cnr Av 1 & Calle 1; s/d all-incl from CUC$74/120; ℗❄@☀) A venerable old 1930s hacienda-style building, the huge Kawama was the first of the 50-plus hotels to inhabit this once-deserted pen-

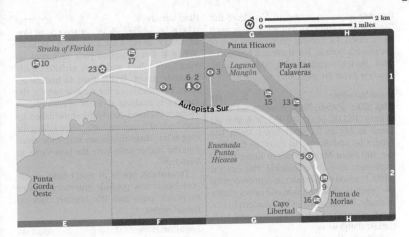

insula more than 70 years ago. The service is dire and facilities are a tad haggard, but optimists will still detect some silver linings in the 235 colorful rooms, which blend artfully into the sliver of beach that's Varadero's western extremity.

All-inclusive prices include everything from tennis to aquabike usage.

Hotel los Delfines
RESORT **$$**

(Map p204; ☑ 45-66-77-20; cnr Av de la Playa & Calle 39; s/d all-incl from CUC$80/120; ❀ ☎) Hotel chain Islazul goes (almost) all-inclusive in this friendlier, cozier copy of the big resorts further northeast. The 100 rooms come packed with additional extras such as satellite TV, minibar and safe deposit box, and there's a lovely scoop of wide protected beach.

Hotel Cuatro Palmas
RESORT **$$$**

(Map p204; ☑ 45-66-70-40; Av 1, btwn Calles 60 & 62; s/d all-incl CUC$106/170; ℗ ❀ @ ☎) One wonders if this former personal residence of dictator Fulgencio Batista would still appeal to his opulent taste. The first of what could be termed the big all-inclusive resorts as you head east has succumbed to tourist kitsch in recent years, though it's still close enough to town for getting around on foot. The beach is adjacent, though you may need earmuffs.

⌖ Varadero Hotel Zone

The Hotel Zone kicks off properly near the start of Av las Américas, at the site of the Hotel Varadero Internacional, currently in the throes of reconstruction. Remember that the further east you stay, the more reliant you will be on resort entertainment:

end-of-the-peninsula hotels are over 10km from the town. In most cases, isolation equals cheesy poolside shows, not desert island tranquillity.

★ Mansión Xanadú
RESORT **$$$**

(Map p206; ☑ 45-66-73-88; www.varaderogolf-club.com; cnr Av las Americas & Autopista Sur; s/d all-incl CUC$184/286; ℗ ❀ @) Varadero's most intriguing, intimate lodging is in the grand former residence of US chemical-entrepreneur Irénée Du Pont, where eight lavish rooms tempt guests. The first large-scale building on the peninsula's eastern end and an outstanding jewel in a bland architectural desert, Mansión Xanadú still boasts the millions of dollars' worth of Cuban marble and furnishings commissioned by Du Pont in the 1930s.

Rates here include unlimited tee time at the adjoining golf club (Cuba's first).

Villa Cuba
RESORT **$$$**

(Map p206; ☑ 45-66-82-80; Av las Américas Km 2; all-incl 2-/3-/4-/5-/6-bed villas CUC$176/249/314/395/447; ℗ ❀ @ ☎ ⚐) Imagine a multistory car park crossed with a tacky 1970s holiday camp and you'll get an inkling of the look at Villa Cuba. It offers a multitude of room sizes and prices for those on a budget and a color scheme that might have been thrown together by a hyperactive five-year-old let loose with Lego bricks.

Hotel Tuxpán
RESORT **$$$**

(Map p206; ☑ 45-66-75-60; Av las Américas Km 2; s/d all-incl from CUC$87/140; ℗ ❀ @ ☎) Concrete-block architecture and palm-fringed beaches make jarring bedfellows that are all too common in Varadero. But the Tuxpán is famous for other reasons, such as its disco, La Bamba, purportedly one of the resort's hottest. For those not enamored with Soviet architectonics, the beautiful beach is never far away.

Meliá Varadero
RESORT $$$

(Map p206; ☎45-66-70-13; Autopista Sur Km 7; all-incl s CUC$180-240, d 340-400; P❋🖥❄✈🚲) Twice as big as its sister hotel Meliá Las Américas, and happy to cater to families, the 490-room Meliá Varadero immediately impresses with its cylindrical vine-draped lobby. Perched on a small rocky promontory, the beach is set to one side and offers plenty of shade. Unlike many of its Varadero brethren it offers guests free bike hire and wi-fi that (usually) works.

And psst: the restaurants here are superior to its supposedly more illustrious sister; the Japanese restaurant Sakura is first-class.

Meliá Las Américas
RESORT $$$

(Map p206; ☎45-66-76-00; Autopista Sur Km 7; all-incl s CUC$210-260, d CUC$465-520; P❋@✈) The smaller, more grown-up alternative to the Meliá Varadero next door, Las Américas has a no-kids policy, a nice slice of palm-tree-embellished beach and fancy chandeliers. With 225 rooms, it's too large to be intimate, though there's a more refined ambience here than in the other resort giants nearby.

Blau Varadero
RESORT $$$

(Map p206; ☎45-66-75-45; Carretera de las Morlas Km 15; all-incl s CUC$150-221, d CUC$230-322; P❋@✈) Suspend your judgment on Varadero's tallest and most architecturally unsubtle resort. Trying hard to imitate an Aztec pyramid from the outside (why?), the interior is nothing short of spectacular: a 14-story enclosed courtyard embellished by hundreds of hanging plants, some falling for over 80m. Huge rooms are surgically clean and the higher ones have the best views in Varadero.

Downstairs, you're in resort land, so expect loquacious poolside entertainers, beer in plastic cups and iffy Michael Jackson theme nights.

Royalton Hicacos Resort
RESORT $$$

(Map p206; ☎45-66-88-44, 45-66-88-51; www.royalhicacosresort.com; Punta Hicacos; s/d all-incl CUC$172/264; P❋@✈) Having a more understated look (and more personable service) than many of its neighbors has made Royalton Hicacos Resort one of the most appealing resorts on the end-point of the peninsula, with vast *ranchón*-style public areas and babbling water features lending a mellifluous air. Bedrooms, done up in sunny yellows and oranges, have their own reception areas and huge bathrooms.

VARADERO'S HOTELS IN A NUTSHELL

Varadero's confusingly large hotel zone can, for simplicity's sake, be broken into four broad segments.

The accommodations in the spread-out Cuban town at the west end of the peninsula consist of older budget hotels wedged in among the shops, banks, bars and vintage beach-houses. Since 2011, town residents have been able to legally rent out rooms to foreigners and over 20 casas particulares have now taken root.

The section from Calle 64 northeast to the golf course is punctuated by a thin strip of hodgepodge architecture, from kitschy Holiday Camp to bloc-style Sovietesque. Selling cheap packages to mainly foreign tourists, many of these hotels are already looking dated after only three or four decades in operation.

East of the Mansión Xanadú is a cluster of large single structure hotels with impressive lobbies and multiple stories built mostly in the early 1990s. The tallest is the spectacular 14-story Blau Varadero, designed to resemble an Aztec pyramid.

The nearer you get to the end of the peninsula, the more it starts to look like a Florida suburb. Contemporary Cuban all-inclusive resorts favor detached one-to-three story blocks that are laid out like mini-towns and spread over multiple acres. Most of these sprawling resorts have been built since 2000 and it is here that you'll find Varadero's largest (the 1025-room Memories Varadero) and most exclusive (Blau Marina Palace's Planta Real) accommodations, although every year brings tidings of new resorts opening with new never-seen-before attributes.

Memories Varadero RESORT $$$
(Map p206; ✆45-66-70-09; www.memoriesresorts.com; Autopista Sur Km 8; all-incl standard s/d CUC$195/242; ᴾ❋@☀) By the time you reach the end of the peninsula all of the strung-out resorts appear to merge into one – this one. The Memories (opened 2008, changed its name 2012) is a kind of identikit of a modern beach hotel: 1025 rooms, international cuisine, wall-to-wall entertainment, and lots of sunburned Europeans whizzing around on golf carts.

Meliá Península Varadero RESORT $$$
(Map p206; ✆45-66-88-00; www.meliacuba.com; Reserva Ecológica Varahicacos; r all-incl from CUC$180; ᴾ❋@☀) Some may revel in this Meliá's (until recently Tryp's) five-star luxuries. A lavish plant-draped lobby leads to 490 rooms, with the recently added set of digs on 'The Level' raising the stakes with their own private concierge service. The hotel grows its own mint for the mojitos it serves, and facilities here are admittedly plush, but there's not much cross-fertilizing with the real Cuba.

Meliá Marina Varadero RESORT $$$
(✆45-66-73-30; www.meliacuba.com; Autopista Sur Final; s/d all-incl from CUC$175/250) No, that's not a beached cruise liner, but a brand-new Meliá! Part of the plushly redeveloped Marina Gaviota, this has several key advantages over its competitors up at this end of the peninsula: gleaming marina views and access to a host of eateries and shops within the marina complex that makes the stay that little bit more varied than at the other all-inclusives.

There's no beach here (a walkway over the road connects you to one, however) and reports on the rooms vary, but everything is still gleaming with that all-pervading sheen only new mega-resorts can give you. The hotel also offers some non-all-inclusive apartments.

Blau Marina Palace RESORT $$$
(Map p206; ✆45-66-99-66; Autopista Sur Final; all-incl s/d CUC$235/366, Planta Real s/d/ste CUC$279/448/848; ᴾ❋@☀) The last stop on the peninsula before Florida and looking a lot like it, Blau Marina follows the modern Varadero resort trend, ie spread-out low-rise units, lush spacious grounds and exemplary service. There's an imitation lighthouse, acres of swimming pools and a fine adjacent beach.

For added luxury (and irony) you can plump for the 'royal' upgrade on the **Planta Real** part of the complex on a small adjoining island, Cayo Libertad, connected by a bridge where butlers cater for your every need. Ahh....*socialismo!*

✖ Eating

You can eat well for under CUC$10 in Varadero in a variety of state restaurants and a new stash of private ones, legalized in 2011. As 95% of the hotels on the eastern end of the peninsula are all-inclusive, you'll find the bulk of the independent eating joints west of Calle 64.

✖ Varadero Town

Paladar Nonna Tina ITALIAN $
(Map p204; www.paladar-nonnatina.it; Calle 38, btwn Av 1 & Av de la Playa; pizza & pasta CUC$6-10; ⊗noon-11pm) Veteran Cuba visitors will remember an era when the word 'pasta' was a euphemism for 'mush.' But, times have changed and, thanks to inspired new restaurants such as Italian-owned Nonna Tina, the word 'al dente' is no longer an untranslatable foreign term. You'll find proof in this restaurant's pretty front garden where traveling Italio-philes enjoy wood-fired thin-crust pizza, pesto linguine and proper cappuccinos.

La Bodeguita del Medio CUBAN $
(Map p204; Av de la Playa, btwn Calles 40 & 41; mains CUC$5-8; ⊗10:30am-11:30pm) Hooray! Varadero has one too. La Bodeguita del Medio is a grittily cool place: musicians strum in the outside courtyard and you can admire the graffiti inside whilst you chow down on Cuban classics or sip afternoon mojitos.

La Vicaria CUBAN $
(Map p204; Av 1, btwn Calles 37 & 38; mains from CUC$4; ⊗noon-10:30pm; ✎) Inexplicably, this *ranchón*-style but unspectacular government-run restaurant remains popular in the new era and it's surely something to do with the generosity of the portions: in particular the whopping house special, lobster with chicken and pork (CUC$12.95).

Salsa Suárez INTERNATIONAL $$
(Map p202; ✆45-61-41-94; Calle 31 No 103, btwn Avs 1 & 3; mains CUC$8-12; ⊗10:30am-11pm; ✎) With possibly the most all-encompassing menu of Varadero's new private restaurants, Salsa Suárez impresses with its salubrious greenery-covered patio and menu items written artistically on a large blackboard.

Food influences are all over the map (tapas, quesadillas, risotto, sushi and good old Cuban fare), but it's consistently good, right down to the details of complimentary bread baskets and excellent Italian-style coffee.

Dante
ITALIAN $$

(Map p204; Parque Josone; pizza CUC$7.50; ☺noon-10:45pm) Going strong since 1993, Dante takes its name from its entrepreneurial chef who has been rustling up delectable Italian fare to complement the lakeside setting since the place started up. Antipasto starts at CUC$6; Varadero's most impressive wine stash also awaits. Spoil your taste buds in Cuba while you have the chance.

La Fondue
FRENCH $$

(Map p204; cnr Av 1 & Calle 62; mains CUC$10; ☺noon-midnight) Locals rate this fondue-focused restaurant next to Restaurante Mallorca as the best state-run joint in town and it's a welcome change for the palate, too. Beef-fillet fondue is the signature dish.

Restaurante Esquina Cuba
CUBAN $$

(Map p204; cnr Av 1 & Calle 36; mains CUC$8-13; ☺noon-11pm) This place was one-time favorite of Buena Vista Social Club luminary Compay Segundo, and the man obviously had taste. Salivate over the pork special (CUC$13) with lashings of beans, rice and plantain chips under the gaze of the great Cuban ephemera that line the walls – and the resident American car.

Restaurante Mallorca
SPANISH $$

(Map p204; Av 1, btwn Calles 61 & 62; mains CUC$10; ☺noon-midnight) This is a fine, intimate venue renowned for its paella. It's surprisingly spacious inside, with a well-stocked bar (with a good South American wine selection) and generous servings and service.

La Vaca Rosada
SEAFOOD $$

(Map p202; Calle 21, btwn Avs 1 & 2; mains CUC$7.50-23; ☺6:30-11:30pm) Surf and turf on an atmospheric rooftop terrace.

Restaurante La Barbacoa
STEAKHOUSE $$

(Map p204; cnr Calle 64 & Av 1; steaks CUC$11-15; ☺noon-11pm) An old-world decor (stags' heads, horsey paraphernalia) and great steak served by very straight-faced waiters.

Lai-Lai
CHINESE $$

(Map p202; cnr Av 1 & Calle 18; meals CUC$6-10; ☺noon-11pm) An old stalwart set in a two-story mansion on the beach, Lai Lai has traditional Chinese set menus. Food gets mixed reports but, well, if you've been craving that wonton soup...

★Varadero 60
INTERNATIONAL $$$

(Map p204; ✏45-61-39-86; cnr Calle 60 & Av 3; mains CUC$9-19; ☺noon-midnight) Upping the ante considerably in Varadero's new private-restaurant scene is this fine-dining establishment that exudes an aura of refinement not seen since Benny Moré last cleared his throat and shouted 'dilo!'. Lobster and solomillo (steak) are the house specialties, best washed down with some excellent Chilean and Spanish wine and rounded off with one of the quality cigars or rums on offer.

In almost a decade of repeat visits to Cuba, we've rarely seen such impeccable service. There's double meaning in the name – it's on Calle 60 and its theme is 1960s advertisements, which adorn the walls of the elegant interior.

Waco's Club
INTERNATIONAL $$$

(Map p204; ✏45-61-21-26; Av 3, btwn Calles 58 & 59; mains CUC$12-28; ☺noon-11pm; 🏠) Travelers rate this sequestered-away spot, which was once Varadero's Club Nautico. The restaurant is clearly aiming high with its impressive international menu (nothing as wacko as you might think with a name like this, but all well-presented and flavorsome) and refined upstairs dining terrace. Families are made to feel very welcome, although prices are still steep.

✖ Varadero Hotel Zone

La Isabelica Casa del Cafe
CAFE $

(Marina Gaviota, Autopista Sur Final; snacks/sweets from CUC$2; ☺9am-11pm) Cuba announces a new breed of cafe, which looks...totally un-Cuban! This vast, neatly finished just-opened place at Marina Gaviota looks like it's just been shipped in from Seattle or Austin, with coffee-growing scenes on the walls, sofas, Cuban coffee beans for sale and a wide range of caffeinated drinks and tempting cakes, plus a few savory snacks.

Restaurante Mesón del Quijote
SPANISH $$$

(Map p206; Reparto la Torre; mains CUC$8-16.50; ☺noon-midnight; 🏠) Next to a statue of Cervantes' famous Don who seems to be making off rather keenly toward the all-inclusive resorts, this restaurant is one of the eastern peninsula's only nonresort options. Perched on a grassy knoll above Av las Américas next to an old tower good to let the kids loose at, its Spanish-tinged menu (delicious paella) makes a refreshing change from the all-you-can-eat buffet.

Self-Catering
There's a handy **grocery store** (Map p202; Calle 15; ⊘9am-7pm) beside Aparthotel Varazul, and also a **Caracol** (Map p202; cnr Av 1 & Calle 24; ⊘9am-7:45pm) supermarket at the western end of town.

Panadería Doña Neli BAKERY
(Map p204; cnr Av 1 & Calle 43; ⊘24hr) Bread and pastries. Stock up and head for the beach.

🍷 Drinking & Nightlife
Remember a fair few of the restaurants are also fine places for drinks.

Palacio de la Rumba CLUB
(Map p206; Av las Américas Km 2; admission CUC$10; ⊘10pm-3am) Overall, the most banging night out on the peninsula. There's live salsa music at weekends and a good mix of Cubans and tourists. Admission includes your drinks. It's located by the Hotel Bella Costa.

Cafeccino CAFE
(Circuito Norte, btwn Calles J & I, Santa Marta; ⊘24hr) Time to venture outside of the tourist zone to down a delicious coffee or cake with the off-duty resort workers in Santa Marta, the real Cuban town clustering around the base of the peninsula. This goes in at number one in our list of Varadero caffeine fixes; the cakes are delicious and no matter when you finish partying, this place will be open.

Bar Mirador Casa Blanca BAR
(Map p206; Mansión Xanadú, Av las Américas; admission CUC$2; ⊘11am-midnight) On the top floor of Mansión Xanadú, Bar Mirador Casa Blanca is Varadero's ultimate romantic hangout where happy hour conveniently coincides with sunset cocktails.

Calle 62 CAFE, BAR
(Map p204; cnr Av 1 & Calle 62; ⊘8am-2am) Set in the transition zone between old and new Varadero, this simple snack bar attracts clientele from both ends. It's good for a cheese sandwich during the day, and the ambience becomes feistier after dark with live music going on until midnight.

Discoteca Havana Club CLUB
(Map p204; cnr Av 3 & Calle 62; admission CUC$5; ⊘10pm-3am) Near the Centro Comercial Copey. Expect big, boisterous crowds and plenty of male posturing.

Discoteca la Bamba CLUB
(Map p206; Hotel Tuxpán, Av las Américas Km 2; guests/nonguests free/CUC$10; ⊘10pm-4am) Varadero's most modern video disco is at Hotel Tuxpán, in eastern Varadero. It plays mostly Latin music and is considered 'hot.'

☆ Entertainment
While Varadero's nightlife might look enticing on paper, there's no real entertainment 'scene' as such, and the concept of bar-hopping à la Cancún or Miami Beach is almost nonexistent, unless you're prepared to incorporate some long-distance hiking into your drinking schedule. Many happening spots – the good and, more often than not, the bad – are attached to the hotels.

★ Beatles Bar-Restaurant LIVE MUSIC
(Map p204; cnr Av 1 & Calle 59) A *roquero's* delight on the edge of Parque Josone honoring the previously banned Beatles in a bar that evokes the swinging spirit of the decidedly un-Cuban 1960s. Simple food and beer are served but the real draw is the live rock 'n' roll kicking off alfresco at 10pm Monday, Wednesday and Friday.

Count on energetic covers of Led Zep, the Stones, Pink Floyd and you-know-who.

Cabaret Continental CABARET
(Map p206; Hotel Internacional, Av las Américas; admission incl drink CUC$25; ⊘show 10pm Tue-Sun) The Hotel Internacional stages a shamelessly over-the-top, Tropicana-style floor show (Tuesday to Sunday), which is, arguably, second only to 'the one' in Havana. Book dinner at 8pm (booking through your hotel is best) and stay after midnight for the tie-loosening disco. The hotel is being rebuilt in a new location across the road; doubtless the show will go on.

Casa de la Música LIVE MUSIC
(Map p204; cnr Av de la Playa & Calle 42; admission CUC$10; ⊘10:30pm-3am Wed-Sun) Aping its two popular Havana namesakes, this place has some quality live acts and a definitive Cuban feel. It's in town and attracts a local crowd who pay in pesos.

Club Mambo LIVE MUSIC
(Map p206; Av las Américas; admission CUC$10; ⊘11pm-2am Mon-Fri, to 5am Sat & Sun) Cuba's 1950s mambo craze lives on at this quality live-music venue – arguably one of Varadero's hippest and best. Situated next to Club Amigo Varadero in the eastern part of town, the CUC$10 entry includes all your drinks.

A DJ spins when the band takes a break, but this place is all about live music.

There's a pool table if you don't feel like dancing.

Cabaret Cueva del Pirata
CABARET

(Map p206; ☑ 45-66-77-51; Autopista Sur; CUC$10; ☺ 10pm-3am Mon-Sat) A kilometer east of the Hotel Sol Elite Palmeras, Cabaret Cueva del Pirata presents scantily clad dancers in a Cuban-style floor show with a buccaneer twist (eye patches, swashbuckling moves). This cabaret is inside a natural cave and once the show is over, the disco begins. It's a popular place, attracting a young crowd. Monday's the best night. Book through your hotel. Admission includes drinks.

Centro Cultural Comparsita
CULTURAL CENTER

(Map p204; Calle 60, btwn Avs 2 & 3; admission CUC$1-5; ☺ 10pm-3am) An ARTex cultural center on the edge of Varadero town with concerts, shows, dancing, karaoke and plenty of local flavor. Check the current schedule taped on the door.

Sala de la Musica
LIVE MUSIC

(Marina Gaviota, Autopista Sur Final; admission CUC$10-15; ☺ 10pm-late) This place at the new Marina Gaviota complex is pencilled in to be Varadero's next massive night out and was *the* talked-about spot (but had only just opened) on our last visit. The waterfront venue impresses; live music happens a couple of times weekly. Check what's on here at the place you're staying in advance of turning up.

🛍 Shopping

Caracol shops in the main hotels sell souvenirs, postcards, T-shirts, clothes, alcohol and snack foods. See the new private sector at play in nebulous **Mercado Alegría**, an umbrella term for the private vendors who set up stalls on Av 1 between Calles 42 and 48.

Centro Comercial Hicacos
SHOPPING CENTER

(Map p204; Parque de las 8000 Taquillas; ☺ 10am-10pm) Varadero town's modern subterranean mall in Parque de las 8000 Taquillas is small by American standards, but serves the basics including souvenirs, cigars, a spa/gym and an Infotur office.

Casa del Ron
RUM

(Map p204; cnr Av 1 & Calle 62; ☺ 9am-9pm) The best selection of rum in Varadero as well as tasting opportunities. It's in a venerable old building with a through-the-ages look at Cuba's spirited relationship with the drink, including a scale model of Matanzas' Santa Elena distillery to admire as you sup.

Casa de las Américas
BOOKS, MUSIC

(Map p204; cnr Av 1 & Calle 59; ☺ 9am-7pm) A retail outlet of the famous Havana cultural institution, this place sells CDs, books and art.

Casa del Habano
CIGARS

The place for cigars: it has top-quality merchandise from humidors to perfume and helpful service. There's one Av de la Playa **branch** (Map p202; btwn Calles 31 & 32; ☺ 9am-6pm); another on **Av 1** (Map p204; ☑ 45-66-78-43; cnr Av 1 & Calle 63; ☺ 9am-9pm), which serves a wicked cup of coffee in the upstairs cafe.

Galería de Arte Varadero
ARTS

(Map p204; Av 1, btwn Calles 59 & 60; ☺ 9am-7pm) Antique jewelry, museum-quality silver and glass, paintings and other heirlooms from Varadero's bygone bourgeois days are sold here. As most items are of patrimonial importance, everything is already conveniently tagged with export permission.

Plaza América
SHOPPING CENTER

(Map p206; Autopista Sur Km 7; ☺ 10am-8:30pm) Built in 1997, but already looking dated, Cuba's first bona fide shopping mall is one of Varadero's less inspired architectural creations, though it serves its purpose. Useful outlets include a pharmacy, bank, an Egrem music store, Benetton, restaurants and various souvenir shops.

Taller de Cerámica Artística
ARTS & CRAFTS

(Map p204; Av 1, btwn Calles 59 & 60; ☺ 9am-7pm) Next door to Galería de Arte Varadero and Casa de las Américas, you can buy fine artistic pottery that's made on the premises. Most items are in the CUC$200 to CUC$250 range.

Gran Parque de la Artesanía
MARKET

(Map p202; Av 1, btwn Calles 15 & 16; ☺ 9am-7pm) Open-air artisans' market.

Librería Hanoi
BOOKS

(Map p204; cnr Av 1 & Calle 44; ☺ 9am-9pm) Books in English, from poetry to politics.

ARTex
SOUVENIRS

(Map p204; Av 1, btwn Calles 46 & 47; ☺ 9am-8pm) Showcases CDs, T-shirts, musical instruments and more.

ⓘ Information

DANGERS & ANNOYANCES

Crime-wise, Varadero's dangers are minimal. Aside from getting drunk at the all-inclusive bar and tripping over your bath mat on the way to the toilet, you haven't got too much to worry about. Watch out for mismatched electrical outlets in hotels. In some rooms, a 110V socket might sit right next to a 220V one. They should be labeled, but aren't always.

Out on the beach, a red flag means no swimming allowed due to the undertow or some other danger. A blue jellyfish known as the Portuguese man-of-war, most common in summer, can produce a bad reaction if you come in contact with its long tentacles. Wash the stung area with sea water and seek medical help if the pain becomes intense or you have difficulty breathing. Theft of unguarded shoes, sunglasses and towels is routine along this beach.

EMERGENCY

Asistur (☑45-66-72-77; Av 1 No 4201, btwn Calles 42 & 43; ☻9am-4:30pm Mon-Fri) Tourist-oriented emergency assistance.

INTERNET ACCESS & TELEPHONE

Most hotels have internet access for CUC$6 to CUC$8 an hour. Buy a scratch card from the reception. If you're in a cheaper place, use the public **Etecsa Telepunto** (cnr Av 1 & Calle 30; ☻8:30am-7:30pm).

MEDICAL SERVICES

Many large hotels have infirmaries that can provide free basic first aid.

Clínica Internacional Servimed (☑45-66-77-11; cnr Av 1 & Calle 60; ☻24hr) Medical or dental consultations (CUC$25 to CUC$70) and hotel calls (CUC$50 to CUC$60). There's also a good pharmacy (open 24 hours) here with items in convertibles.

Farmacia Internacional Kawama (☑45-61-44-70; Av Kawama; ☻9am-9pm); Plaza América (☑45-66-80-42; Autopista Sur Km 7; ☻9am-9pm)

MONEY

In Varadero, European visitors can pay for hotels and meals in euros. If you change money at your hotel front desk, you'll sacrifice 1% more than at a bank.

Banco de Ahorro Popular (Calle 36, btwn Av 1 & Autopista Sur; ☻8:30am-4pm Mon-Fri) Probably the slowest option.

Banco Financiero Internacional Av 1 (cnr Av 1 & Calle 32; ☻9am-7pm Mon-Fri, to 5pm Sat & Sun); Plaza América (Autopista Sur Km 7; ☻9am-noon & 1-6pm Mon-Fri, 9am-6pm Sat & Sun) Traveler's checks and cash advances on Visa and MasterCard.

Cadeca (cnr Av de la Playa & Calle 41; ☻8:30am-6pm Mon-Sat, to noon Sun)

POST

Many of the larger hotels have branch post offices.

Post Office (Map p204; Calle 64, btwn Avs 1 & 2; ☻8am-noon & 1-5pm Mon-Fri, to noon Sat)

Post Office (Map p204; Av 1, btwn Calles 43 & 44; ☻8am-6pm Mon-Sat)

TOURIST INFORMATION

Infotur (Map p202; ☑45-66-29-61; cnr Av 1 & Calle 13) Main office is next to Hotel Acuazul, but it has a desk in most large resorts.

TRAVEL AGENCIES

Almost every hotel has a tourism desk where staff will book adventure tours, skydiving, scuba diving, whatever. It's almost always cheaper, however, to go directly to the tour agency.

Cubatur (☑45-66-72-16; cnr Av 1 & Calle 33; ☻8:30am-6pm) Reserves hotel rooms nationally; organizes bus transfers to Havana hotels and excursions to Península de Zapata and other destinations. Can act as general information point too.

ⓘ Getting There & Away

AIR

Juan Gualberto Gómez International Airport (☑45-61-30-16, 45-24-70-15) is 20km from central Varadero toward Matanzas and another 6km off the main highway. Airlines here include Thomas Cook from London and Manchester; Cubana from Buenos Aires and Toronto; Air Berlin from Düsseldorf and four other German cities; Arkefly from Amsterdam; and Air Transat and WestJet from various Canadian cities. The check-in time at Varadero is 90 minutes before flight time.

BUS

Terminal de Ómnibus (Map p204; cnr Calle 36 & Autopista Sur) has daily air-con **Víazul** (☑45-61-48-86; ☻7am-noon & 1-7pm) buses to a few destinations.

All four daily Havana buses (CUC$10, three hours) stop at Matanzas (CUC$6, one hour); all bar the second of these also call at Juan Gualberto Gómez International Airport (CUC$6, 25 minutes). Buses depart from Varadero at noon, 2:05pm, 4pm and 7:35pm.

Two buses run to Trinidad (CUC$20, six hours) via Cienfuegos (CUC$16, 4½ hours) at 7:30am and 2pm. The morning departure also stops at Santa Clara (CUC$11, 3¼ hours).

The Santiago bus (CUC$49, 12 hours) leaves nightly at 9:45pm stopping in Cárdenas (CUC$6, 20 minutes), Colón (CUC$6, 1½ hours), Santa Clara (CUC$11, 3¼ hours), Sancti Spíritus

(CUC$17, five hours), Ciego de Ávila (CUC$19, 6¼ hours), Camagüey (CUC$25), Las Tunas (CUC$33), Holguín (CUC$38) and Bayamo (CUC$41).

If you have the time, you can get to Havana by catching the Víazul bus to Matanzas and taking the Hershey Railway from there.

For Cárdenas, you can go on local bus 236 (CUC$1), which departs every hour or so from next to a small tunnel marked Ómnibus de Cárdenas outside the main bus station. You can also catch this bus at the corner of Av 1 and Calle 13. Don't rely on being able to buy tickets for non-Víazul buses from Varadero to destinations in Matanzas province and beyond: the official line is tourists can't take them, and tourists in Varadero are generally recognizable from Cubans. With decent Spanish you could get lucky.

Cubanacán's Conectando runs a handy bus service between hotels in Varadero and hotels in Havana (bookable through hotel receptions). There's also a daily service between Varadero and Trinidad via Cienfuegos. Prices are similar to Víazul. Book tickets at least a day in advance through Infotur.

CAR

You can hire a car from practically every hotel in town and prices are pretty generic between different makes and models. Once you've factored in fuel and insurance, a standard car will cost you approximately CUC$70 to CUC$80 a day.

Aside from the hotel reps, you can try **Havanautos** (☑ 45-66-73-32; cnr Av 1 & Calle 21) or **Cubacar** (☑ 45-66-81-96; cnr Av 1 & Calle 31).

Havanautos (☑ 45-25-36-30), **Vía** (☑ 45-61-47-83) and **Cubacar** (☑ 45-61-44-10, 45-25-36-21) all have car-rental offices in the airport car park. Expect to pay at least CUC$75 a day for the smallest car (or CUC$50 daily on a two-week basis).

Luxury cars are available at **Rex** (☑ 45-66-77-39, 45-66-75-39; cnr Av 1 & Calle 36). It rents Audi and automatic-transmission (rare in Cuba) cars starting from CUC$100 per day.

There's a **Servi-Cupet gas station** (☺ 24hr) on the Autopista Sur at Calle 17, and one at **Centro Todo En Uno** (Map p204; cnr Calle 54 & Autopista Sur).

If heading to Havana, you'll have to pay the CUC$2 toll at the booth on Vía Blanca upon leaving.

❶ Getting Around

TO/FROM THE AIRPORT

Varadero and Matanzas are each about 20km from the spur road to Juan Gualberto Gómez International Airport; it's another 6km from the highway to the airport terminal. A tourist taxi from the airport to Varadero/Matanzas costs

about CUC$35/30 respectively. Convince the driver to use the meter and it should work out cheaper. Buses bound for Havana call at the airport, leaving at noon, 2:05pm, 4pm and 7:35pm and arriving 25 minutes later. Tickets cost CUC$6.

BUS

Varadero Beach Tour (all-day ticket CUC$5; ☺ 9:30am-9pm) is a handy open-top double-decker tourist bus with 45 hop on/hop off stops linking all the resorts and shopping malls along the entire length of the peninsula. It passes every half-hour at well-marked stops with route and distance information. You can buy tickets on the bus itself.

There's an additional tour bus to Matanzas and all sights in between.

A gimmicky toy train connects the three large Meliá resorts.

Local buses 47 and 48 run from Calle 64 to Santa Marta, south of Varadero on the Autopista Sur; bus 220 runs from Santa Marta to the far eastern end of the peninsula. There are no fixed schedules. Fares are a giveaway at 20 centavos. You can also utilize bus 236 which runs the length of the peninsula to and from Cárdenas.

HORSE CART

A state-owned horse and cart around Varadero costs CUC$5 per person for a 45-minute tour or CUC$10 for a full two-hour tour – plenty of time to see the sights.

MOPED & BICYCLE

Mopeds and bikes are an excellent way of getting off the peninsula and discovering a little of the Cuba outside. Rentals are available at most of the all-inclusive resorts, and bikes are usually lent as part of the package. The generic price is CUC$9 per hour and CUC$25 per day, with gas included in hourly rates (though a levy of CUC$6 may be charged on a 24-hour basis, so ask). There's one **Palmares rental post** (cnr Av 1 & Calle 38) in the center of town with mopeds for those not staying at an all-inclusive. This guy might have a couple of rickety bikes with no gears and 'pedal-backwards' brakes: pay no more than CUC$2 per hour or CUC$15 per day.

TAXI

Metered tourist taxis charge a CUC$1 starting fee plus CUC$1 per kilometer (same tariff day and night). Coco-taxis (*coquitos* or *huevitos* in Spanish) charge less with no starting fee. A taxi to Cárdenas/Havana will be about CUC$20/85 one way. Taxis hang around all the main hotels or you can phone **Cuba Taxi** (☑ 45-61-05-55) or **Transgaviota** (☑ 45-61-97-62). The latter uses large cars if you're traveling with big luggage. Tourists are not supposed to use the older Lada taxis. It can be worth haggling.

Varadero to Matanzas

The wide, smooth sweep of the Vía Blanca highway southwest passes many of northern Matanzas' most magnificent sights: subterranean swimming holes, superb snorkeling and boat trips on hidden rivers.

◉ Sights & Activities

Playa Coral   BEACH
Your closest bet for shore snorkeling is Playa Coral, on the old coastal road (about 3km off the Vía Blanca) halfway between Matanzas and Varadero. You can snorkel solo from the beach, but it's far better (and safer) to enter via the Laguna de Maya (8am to 5pm). At the Flora and Fauna Reserve, 400m east of the beach, professional Ecotur guides rent snorkeling gear (CUC$2) and provide guides to take you out to the reef (CUC$5 one hour).

There are a reported 300 species of fish here and visibility is a decent 15m to 20m. Diving is on offer too. The Laguna de Maya also incorporates a snack-bar-restaurant by the eponymous lake nearby with boat rental and horseback-riding opportunities. A package including all the activities is offered for CUC$25 and can be organised through most Varadero hotels or the Barracuda Scuba Diving Center (p201). Most of the coast hereabouts is a gray-white coral shelf but there are beaches just west of Playa Coral.

Cueva Saturno   CAVE
(☑ 45-25-38-33, 45-25-32-72; admission incl snorkel gear CUC$5; ⊘ 8am-6pm) One kilometer south of the Vía Blanca, near the airport turnoff, is the freshwater Cueva Saturno, a highly popular (read: crowded) subterranean cave with a pool billed as a **snorkeling** and/or **swimming** spot. The water's about 20°C and the maximum depth is 22m, though there are shallower parts. There's a snack bar and equipment rental post on site.

Cuevas de Bellamar   CAVE
(☑ 45-26-16-83, 45-25-35-38; admission CUC$8, camera CUC$5; ⊘ 9am-5pm) Cuba's oldest tourist attraction, according to local propaganda, lies 5km southeast of Matanzas and is 300,000 years old. There are 2500m of caves here, discovered in 1861 by a Chinese workman in the employ of Don Manuel Santos Parga. A 45-minute Cuevas de Bellamar visit leaves almost hourly starting at 9:30am. The caves on show include a vast 12m stalagmite and an underground stream; cave walls glitter eerily with crystals.

Well-maintained, well-lit paths mean it's easy for kids to imbibe the stupendous geology, too. The entrance is through a small museum. Outside the Cuevas de Bellamar are two restaurants and a playground. To get there, take bus 12 from Plaza Libertad or use the Matanzas Bus Tour connecting to Varadero.

Cuevas de Santa Catalina   CAVE
(⊘ 9am-5pm) A less-visited cave system off the Matanzas–Varadero highway near Boca de Camarioca, where highlights include Amerindian cave paintings. Organize at the Cueva Saturno or ask at one of the Varadero all-inclusive accommodations about trips. It is not possible to go independently. One **local cave guide** (☑ 52-97-10-57), Cenén, offers trips here.

Río Canímar   RIVER
Boat trips on the Río Canímar, 8km east of Matanzas, are a truly magical experience. Gnarly mangroves dip their jungle-like branches into the ebbing water and a warm haze caresses the regal palm trees as your boat slides silently 12km upstream from an insalubrious start beneath the Vía Blanca bridge.

Cubatur (p213) in Varadero offers this wonderful excursion with lunch, horseback riding, fishing and snorkeling for CUC$25, or you can chance it by showing up at the landing below the bridge on the east side.

Alternatively, most Varadero hotels have tour agencies offering this trip (look for the Río Canímar 'Back to Nature' tour).

Rowboats (CUC$2 per hour) are also available for rent from the riverside Bar Cubamar, almost under the Vía Blanca bridge, though not to Cubans (on the pretext that they might use them to emigrate).

Castillo del Morrillo   CASTLE
(admission CUC$1; ⊘ 9am-5pm Tue-Sun) On the western side of the Río Canímar bridge, 8km east of Matanzas, a road runs 1km down to a cove presided over by the four guns of this yellow-painted castle (1720). The castle is now a museum dedicated to the student leader Antonio Guiteras Holmes (1906–35), who founded the revolutionary group Joven Cuba (Young Cuba) in 1934.

After serving briefly in the post-Machado government, Guiteras was forced out by army chief Fulgencio Batista and shot on May 8, 1935. A bronze bust marks the spot where he was executed.

VARADERO & MATANZAS PROVINCE VARADERO TO MATANZAS

🛏 Sleeping & Eating

Hotel Canimao HOTEL **$**
(☑45-26-10-14; Carretera Matanzas-Varadero Km 5; r incl breakfast CUC$23-30; P ❄ ⊠) Perched above the Río Canímar 8km east of Matanzas, the Canimao has 160 comfortable rooms with little balconies. It's handy for Río Canímar excursions, the Cuevas de Bellamar or to visit the Tropicana Matanzas, but otherwise you're isolated here. There are two restaurants. Matanzas Bus Tour stops on the main road.

El Ranchón Bellamar CARIBBEAN **$$**
(Cuevas de Bellamar; mains from CUC$10; ⊗noon-8:30pm) If you're visiting the Cuevas de Bellamar, you'd do well to grab a *comida criolla* lunch at this *ranchón*-style restaurant before heading back into town. Good pork or chicken meals with the trimmings are about CUC$10.

☆ Entertainment

Tropicana Matanzas CABARET
(☑45-26-53-80; Carretera Matanzas-Varadero Km 5; admission CUC$35; ⊗10pm-2am Tue-Sat) Capitalizing on its success in Havana and Santiago de Cuba, the famous Tropicana cabaret has a branch 8km east of Matanzas, next to the Hotel Canimao. You can mingle with the Varadero bus crowds and enjoy the same entertaining formula of lights, feathers, flesh and frivolity in the open air.

ℹ Getting There & Away

Most of the sights along this stretch of coast can be accessed by either the Varadero (p214) or Matanzas (p223) hop on/hop off bus tour, or with your own wheels.

Matanzas

POP 152,408

Much like a beloved but long-forgotten antique being polished back to its former glory, Matanzas is showing breathtaking signs of reclaiming its erstwhile place at the helm of Cuban culture. During the 18th and 19th centuries, it developed a gigantic literary and musical heritage, and was regularly touted as the 'Athens of Cuba.' Undeniably, its battle-scarred buildings and cars belching out asphyxiating diesel fumes now leave it a shadow of its former self and a long way from the vacation glitter of Varadero, but sample its revitalized plaza edifices and still-astounding cultural scene and the dignity soon emerges amid the dilapidation. If the city were a character it would be the fisherman, Santiago, in Hemingway's *The Old Man and the Sea:* 'thin and gaunt with deep wrinkles' yet, irrepressibly 'cheerful and undefeated.'

Two pivotal Cuban musical forms, *danzón* and rumba, were hatched here, along with various religions of African origin, including Arará, Regla de Ocha (Santería) and the secret Abakuá fraternity. Matanzas is also the home of Cuba's finest provincial theaters, the Sauto and Sala de Conciertos José White, and was the birthplace of some of its most eloquent poets and writers. Today, the city offers little in the way of standard sights, but plenty of under-the-radar pleasures. Hang with the artists in sophisticated ACAA or listen to some *bembe* drummers in the Marina neighborhood, and you'll quickly ascertain that Matanzas' greatest strength is its people, a proud, poetic populace infused with the spirit of stoic survivors. Welcome to the real Cuba, *asere.*

History

In 1508 Sebastián de Ocampo sighted a bay that the indigenous population called Guanima. Now known as the Bahía de Matanzas, it's said the name recalls the *matanza* (massacre) of a group of Spaniards during an early indigenous uprising. In 1628 the Dutch pirate Piet Heyn captured a Spanish treasure fleet carrying 12 million gold florins, ushering in a lengthy era of smuggling and piracy. Undeterred by the pirate threat, 30 families from the Canary Islands arrived in 1693, on the orders of King Carlos III of Spain, to found the town of San Carlos y Severino de Matanzas; the first fort went up in 1734. In 1898 the bay saw the first engagement of the Spanish-American War.

In the late 18th and 19th centuries, Matanzas flourished through the building of numerous sugar mills and coffee exporting. In 1843, with the laying of the first railway to Havana, the floodgates for prosperity were opened. The second half of the 19th century became a golden age: the city set new cultural benchmarks with the development of a newspaper, a public library, a high school, a theater and a philharmonic society. Due to the large number of writers and intellectuals living in the area, Matanzas became known as the 'Athens of Cuba' with a cultural scene that dwarfed even Havana.

It was then that African slaves, imported to meet burgeoning labor demands, began to foster another reputation for Matanzas as the spiritual home of rumba. In tandem, and from the same roots, spread a network of Santería *cabildos* (associations) – brotherhoods of those from slave descent who came together to celebrate the traditions and rituals of their African ancestors. Both rumba and *cabildos* flourish here to this day.

Other landmarks in Matanzas' history include staging Cuba's first *danzón* performance (1879); later the city produced nationally important poets Cintio Vitier and Carilda Oliver Labra.

⊙ Sights

⊙ Plaza de la Vigía

The original Plaza de Armas still remains as Plaza de la Vigía (literally 'lookout place'), a reference to the threat from piracy and smuggling that the first settlers faced. This diminutive square was where Matanzas was founded in the late 17th century and numerous iconic historical buildings still stand guard.

Teatro Sauto   THEATER
(☑45-24-27-21; Plaza de la Vigía) The defining symbol of the city according to Mexican painter (and admirer) Diego Rivera, the Teatro Sauto (1863) on Plaza de la Vigía's south side is one of Cuba's finest theaters and famous for its superb acoustics. The lobby is graced by marble Greek goddesses and the ceiling in the main hall bears paintings of the muses.

Three balconies enclose this 775-seat theater, which features a floor that can be raised to convert the auditorium into a ballroom. The original theater curtain is a painting of Matanzas' very own Puente de la Concordia, and notables like Soviet dancer Anna Pavlova have performed here. Much-needed restoration work was ongoing at the time of research.

Puente Calixto García   BRIDGE
If you've only got time to see *one* bridge (there are 21 in total) in Cuba's celebrated 'city of bridges,' gravitate toward this impressive steel structure built in 1899, spanning the Río San Juan with its kayaks floating lazily by. Just south is an eye-catching **Che Mural**, while the northern side leads directly into Plaza de la Vigía.

★Ediciones Vigía   WORKSHOP
(Plaza de la Vigía, cnr Calle 91; ☺9am-5pm Mon-Sat) To the southwest of Plaza de la Vigía is a unique book publisher, founded in 1985 ,that produces high-quality handmade paper and first-edition books on a variety of topics. The books are typed, stenciled and pasted in editions of 200 copies. Visitors are welcome in the Dickensian workshop where they can purchase beautiful numbered and signed copies (CUC$5 to CUC$40).

Palacio de Justicia   HISTORIC BUILDING
(cnr Plaza de la Vigía & Calle 85) This is another impressive construction on the Plaza de la Vigía opposite the Teatro Sauto, first erected in 1826 and rebuilt between 1908 and 1911.

Museo Histórico Provincial   MUSEUM
(cnr Calles 83 & 272; admission CUC$2; ☺10am-6pm Tue-Fri, 1-7pm Sat, 9am-noon Sun) Also known as Palacio del Junco (1840), this

VARADERO & MATANZAS PROVINCE MATANZAS

MATANZAS STREET NAMES

Matanzas residents ignore the numbering system of their streets and continue to use the old colonial street names. However, here we have used the numbers because that's what you'll see on street corners.

OLD NAME	NEW NAME
Contreras	Calle 79
Daoíz	Calle 75
Maceo	Calle 77
Medio/Independencia	Calle 85
Milanés	Calle 83
San Luis	Calle 298
Santa Teresa	Calle 290
Zaragoza	Calle 292

Matanzas

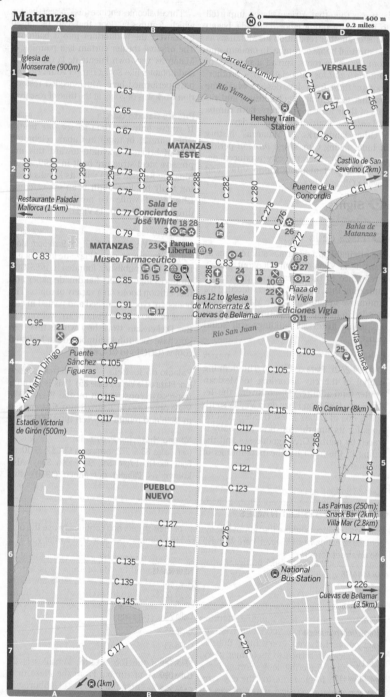

N
0 ————— 400 m
0 ————— 0.2 miles

Iglesia de
Monserrate (900m)

Carretera Yumurí

VERSALLES

Río Yumurí

C 278   7
C 57
C 266
C 270

Hershey Train
Station

C 63

C 65

C 67   C 71

C 67

MATANZAS
ESTE

Castillo de San
Severino (2km)

C 302   C 300   C 298   C 294   C 292   C 290   C 288   C 282   C 280

C 73

C 75

C 278

Puente de la
Concordia

C 61

Restaurante Paladar
Mallorca (1.5km)

C 77   Sala de
Conciertos
José White   18 28
3   ⊙   14

C 276

26

Bahía de
Matanzas

C 79

MATANZAS   23   ✕
Parque
Libertad   9

4

C 83

8
27

C 83

Museo Farmacéutico

C 85

16 15   2
C 286
5   24   13   19
10   12
22   1   Plaza de
la Vigía

C 91   20 ✕

C 93   17

Bus 12 to Iglesia
de Monserrate &
Cuevas de Bellamar

Ediciones Vigía
11

C 95   21

6

C 103

25

C 97

C 97
Puente
Sánchez
Figueras   C 105   C 105

Río San Juan

Vía Blanca

C 109

C 115

Río Canímar (8km)

C 117

C 115

Estadio Victoria
de Girón (500m)

C 117

C 298

C 119   C 272   C 268

C 121

C 264

PUEBLO
NUEVO

C 123

Las Palmas (250m);
Snack Bar (2km);
Villa Mar (2.8km)

C 127

C 276

C 171

C 131

C 135

National
Bus Station

C 139

C 226

C 145

Cuevas de Bellamar
(3.5km)

C 171

C 276

(1km)

Matanzas

◉ **Top Sights**
1 Ediciones Vigía C3
2 Museo Farmacéutico B3
3 Sala de Conciertos José White B3

◉ **Sights**
4 Archivo Histórico C3
5 Catedral de San Carlos
   Borromeo C3
6 Che Mural C4
7 Iglesia de San Pedro Apóstol D1
8 Museo Histórico Provincial D3
9 Palacio de Gobierno C3
10 Palacio de Justicia C3
11 Puente Calixto García D4
12 Teatro Sauto D3

◉ **Activities, Courses & Tours**
13 Casa del Danzón C3

◉ **Sleeping**
14 Evelio & Isel C3
15 Hostal Alma B3
16 Hostal Azul B3
17 Hostal Río B3

18 Hotel Velazco B3

◉ **Eating**
19 Café Atenas C3
20 Centro Variedades Commercial B3
21 Mercado la Plaza A4
22 Plaza la Vigía C3
23 Restaurante Romántico San
   Severino B3

◉ **Drinking & Nightlife**
24 ACAA C3
   Bistro Kuba .... (see 16)
25 Ruinas de Matasiete D4

◉ **Entertainment**
26 Centro Cultural Comunitario
   Nelson Barrera C3
27 Museo Histórico Provincial D3
   Sala de Conciertos José White ...... (see 3)
   Teatro Sauto .... (see 12)
28 Teatro Velazco B3

◉ **Shopping**
   Ediciones Vigía .... (see 1)

double-arched edifice on the Plaza de la Vigía showcases the full sweep of Matanzas' history from 1693 to the present. Cultural events are also held here.

◉ Parque Libertad & Around

The once-crumbling Parque Libertad is the focal point of Matanzas' current restoration drive, and looking grander by the day. A bronze statue (1909) of José Martí stands in its center.

★**Museo Farmacéutico**　　　MUSEUM
(Calle 83 No 4951; admission CUC$3; ☉10am-5pm Mon-Sat, to 4pm Sun) Museo Farmacéutico, on the park's south side, is one of the city's showcase sights. Founded in 1882 by the Triolett family, the antique pharmacy was the first of its type in Latin America. The fine displays include all the odd bottles, instruments and suchlike used in the trade.

★**Sala de Conciertos José White**　THEATER
(☏45-26-70-32; Calle 79, btwn Calles 290 & 288) Restoration of this 1876 building abutting Hotel Velazco began in 2003, and has now been completed with every inch, flourish and cornicing returned to its former glory; well worth a lingering look. Fitting for a building that formerly hosted the city symphony orchestra, classical music makes up

the majority of its performances, although there is also that made-in-Matanzas dance *danzón* performed here. A courtyard bar complements proceedings.

Palacio de Gobierno　　HISTORIC BUILDING
(Calle 288, btwn Calles 79 & 83) Dating from 1853, this muscular building dominates the east side of Parque Libertad; these days it's the seat of the Poder Popular (Popular Power), the local government.

Catedral de San Carlos Borromeo　CHURCH
(Calle 282, btwn Calles 83 & 85; donation welcome; ☉8am-noon & 3-5pm Mon-Sat, 9am-noon Sun) Standing back from the disorganized melee of Calle 83 behind shady Plaza de la Iglesia, this once-great, perennially shut, neoclassical cathedral was constructed in 1693 and contains some of Cuba's most famous frescoes, suffering terribly after years of neglect. Across the other side of Calle 83 is the **Archivo Histórico** (Calle 83 No 28013, btwn Calles 280 & 282), the city archives housed in the former residence of local poet José Jacinto Milanés (1814–63).

◉ Versalles & the North

North of the Río Yumurí, Versalles is the birthplace of rumba. From the Plaza de la Vigía you enter the *barrio* (neighborhood)

MATANZAS CIVIC PRIDE: THE NEXT STEPS

Aside from the painstakingly ponderous refurbishment of the Teatro Sauto, the next phase of the city's ambitious redevelopment will take place south of the two central plazas along the north bank of the Río San Juan. Every self-respecting Cuban capital needs a boulevard, so Matanzas is getting one. It's earmarked to stretch from the river bridge bearing Calle 298 seven blocks east to Puente Calixto García. When finished, it will be Cuba's third-best *malecón* (waterside promenade). Just east again, a Palacio de la Rumba is scheduled to be built in the city that gave this music genre to the world.

by taking Calle 272 across graceful **Puente de la Concordia**.

Castillo de San Severino   FORT
(Av del Muelle; ⏱10am-7pm Tue-Sat, 9am-noon Sun) Northeast of Versalles lies this formidable crenellation built by the Spanish in 1735 as part of Cuba's defensive ring. Slaves were offloaded here in the 18th century and, later, Cuban patriots were imprisoned within the walls – and sometimes executed. San Severino remained a prison until the 1970s and in more recent times has become the scantly populated slavery-themed **Museo de la Ruta de los Esclavos** (admission CUC$2; ⏱10am-6pm).

The castle itself, with its well-preserved central square, has great views of the Bahía de Matanzas. A taxi from the city center costs CUC$2.

Iglesia de Monserrate   CHURCH
For a mappable view of mildewed Matanzas and the broccoli green Valle de Yumurí, climb 1.5km northeast of the center up Calle 306 to this renovated church dating from 1875. The lofty bastion perched high above the city was built by colonists from Catalonia in Spain as a symbol of their regional power.

The **lookout** near here has a couple of *ranchón*-style restaurants good for skull-splitting music and basic refreshments.

Iglesia de San Pedro Apóstol   CHURCH
(cnr Calles 57 & 270) In the heart of Versalles, this neoclassical church is another Matanzas jewel that has benefited from a full renovation.

Courses

Casa del Danzón   DANCING
(Calle 85, btwn Calle 280 & Plaza de la Vigía) Weekend *danzón* classes.

Festivals & Events

Festival del Bailador Rumbero   MUSIC
(⏱Oct) During the 10 days following October 10, Matanzas rediscovers its rumba roots with talented local musicians at this festival. Until the Teatro Sauto is restored, this happens on a small park outside Museo Histórico Provincial. This coincides with the anniversary of the city's founding (October 12), a multiday party that includes celebrations of luminaries who have made the city what it is (or was).

Carnaval   CARNIVAL
(⏱Aug) Carnaval in Matanzas every August doesn't quite reach the dizzying heights of Santiago but it's still a lively affair.

Sleeping

Central Matanzas complements its one period hotel with a handful of equally retro *casas particulares*. Coast-hugging Playa – the name of the neighborhood stringing out along the Carrera Central southeast of the city center – has some super casas too.

★**Hostal Azul**   CASA PARTICULAR $
(☎45-24-24-49; hostalazul.cu@gmail.com; Calle 83 No 29012, btwn Calles 290 & 292; r CUC$25-30; ❄) With a front door large enough to ride an elephant through, this handsome blue house dating from the 1890s has original tiled floors, an antique wooden spiral staircase and four castle-sized rooms set around a spacious alfresco patio.

Even better, multilingual owner Joel is a true gent and happy to offer his sturdy 1984 Lada for taxi duty. And best? Possibly the spacious period bar that he has just opened at the front (10am to 10pm), with live music in the evenings, making this one extremely atmospheric address.

Hostal Alma   CASA PARTICULAR $
(☎45-29-08-57; hostalalma@gmail.com; Calle 83 No 29008, btwn Calles 290 & 292; r CUC$20-25; ❄) A house with *mucha alma* (soul), Mayra's place has Seville-invoking *azulejos* (tiles), relaxing rocking chairs, and rainbow *vitrales* (stained glass) that refract colored light across the tiled floors. You can enjoy a welcome cocktail on one of its two colossal

ABAKUÁ

A secret all-male society, a language understood only by initiates, a close-knit network of masonic-like lodges, and the symbolic use of the African leopard to denote power: the mysterious rites of Abakuá read like a Cuban *Da Vinci Code*.

In a country not short on foggy religious practices, Abakuá is perhaps the least understood. It's a complicated mixture of initiations, dances, chants and ceremonial drumming that testifies to the remarkable survival of African culture in Cuba since the slave era.

Not to be confused with Santería or other syncretized African religions, Abakuá's traditions were brought to Cuba by enslaved Efik people from the Calabar region of southeastern Nigeria in the 18th and 19th centuries. Organizing themselves into 'lodges' or *juegos*, the first of which was formed in the Havana suburb of Regla in 1836, Abakuá acted as a kind of African mutual aid society made up primarily of black dock workers whose main goal was to help buy their tribal brethren out of slavery.

In the early days, Abakuá lodges were necessarily anti-slavery and anti-colonialist and were suppressed by the Spanish. Nonetheless, by the 1860s, the lodges were increasingly admitting white members and finding that their strength lay in their secretiveness and invisibility.

Today, there are thought to be over 100 Abakuá lodges in Cuba, some up to 600-strong, based primarily in Havana, Matanzas and Cárdenas (the practice never penetrated central or eastern Cuba). Initiates are known as *ñáñigos* and their intensely secret ceremonies take place in a temple known as a *famba*. Although detailed information about the brotherhood is scant, Abakuá is well-known to the outside world for its masked dancers called *Ireme* (devils) who showcase their skills in various annual carnivals and were instrumental in the development of the *guaguancó* style of rumba. Cuba's great abstract artist, Wilfredo Lam, used Abakuá masks in his paintings, and composer, Amadeo Roldán, incorporated its rhythms into classical music.

While there is a strong spiritual and religious element to the brotherhood (forest deities and the leopard symbol are important), it differs from the more widespread Santería religion in that it does not hide its deities behind Catholic saints. Cuban anthropologist, Fernando Ortíz, once referred to Abakuá societies as a form of 'African masonry' while other researchers have suggested it acts like a separate state within a nation with its owns laws and language. The casual Cuban word *'asere'* meaning 'mate' is actually derived from the Abakuá term for 'ritual brother.'

VARADERO & MATANZAS PROVINCE MATANZAS

terraces while surveying Matanzas' semi-ruined rooftops. There are three spiffy rooms.

★ Villa Mar CASA PARTICULAR $
(☎45-28-81-32; http://villamar.info; Calle 127 No 20809, Playa; r CUC$35; P❄) This perfect green-and-yellow-painted house has three rooms and a large garden with a gazebo for dining, perched right on the bay.

Hostal Río CASA PARTICULAR $
(☎45-24-30-41; hostalrio.cu@gmail.com; Calle 91 No 29018, btwn Calles 290 & 292; r CUC$20-25; ❄) This house is owned by the parents of Joel, star of nearby Hostal Azul, so it comes with good recommendations. There are two comfortable rooms in a good location. Meals are served at Hostal Azul.

Evelio & Isel CASA PARTICULAR $
(☎45-24-30-90; evelioisel@yahoo.es; Calle 79 No 28201, btwn Calles 282 & 288; r CUC$20-25; P❄) Rooms at this 2nd-floor apartment have TV, security boxes, balconies and underground parking. The owner is a font of knowledge about the Matanzas music scene.

Hotel Velazco HOTEL $$
(☎45-25-38-80; Calle 79, btwn Calles 290 & 288; s/d/ste CUC$41/58/80; ❄@☎) After years of desolation, the city has got back a hotel it deserves restored in its original 1902 fin-de-siècle style and blending seamlessly with the horses, carts and antediluvian autos in the square outside. A beautiful mahogany bar lures you in; 17 elegant rooms (with flat-screen TVs and wi-fi) practically force you to stay.

If this is a taste of things to come in Matanzas, bring it on!

222

DON'T MISS

STREET RUMBA

'Without rumba there is no Cuba and without Cuba there is no rumba,' goes a wise old Cuban saying. To see the music in its gritty authenticity, come to Matanzas where the highly spiritual drumming and chanting was born. The best place for live alfresco rumba performances is in Plaza de la Vigía outside the Museo Histórico Provincial at 4pm on the third Friday of every month (check the museum's noticeboard for more details).

Eating

Matanzas' once scant dining scene has improved.

Plaza la Vigía CAFE $
(cnr Plaza de la Vigía & Calle 85; snacks CUC$2-3; ☺10am-midnight) Burgers and draft beer rule the menu, while young student types dominate the clientele in this throwback bar that looks like a scene from a Parisian art nouveau poster, circa 1909. The ultimate anti-Varadero escape!

Restaurante Romántico San Severino INTERNATIONAL $
(Calle 290, btwn Calles 279 & 283; mains CUC$4.50-6.50; ☺6-11pm) Parque Libertad now has a standout restaurant up a steep flight of steps on the west side. Colonial interior, good service and excellent shrimp-stuffed fish fillets.

Café Atenas CARIBBEAN $
(Calle 83 No 8301; CUC$2-5; ☺10am-11pm) Settle down on the *terraza* (terrace) with the local students, taxi drivers and hotel workers on a day off, and contemplate everyday life on Plaza de la Vigía. Decent sandwiches; grilled meats.

Snack Bar CUBAN, INTERNATIONAL $
(Via Blanca No 22014, Playa; mains CUC$5-8; ☺noon-2am) Bringing tongue-in-cheek creativity to standard Cuban 'international' food through flashy presentation (here chicken fajitas become delicious *trapos do viejas,* or old lady's rags; shrimps are *cuerpos revisitados* – unearthed corpses), Snack Bar then serves the concept in a neat open-air patio doubling as a lively bar.

★Restaurante Paladar Mallorca INTERNATIONAL $$
(☎45-28-32-82; Calle 334, btwn Calles 77 & 79; mains CUC$8-14; ☺11am-11pm; ⊞) The Mallorca out in Los Mangos neighborhood northwest of the center impresses with adventurous dishes such as fish in balsamic cream glaze, and some of Cuba's best piña coladas. Presentation is very nouveau and there are surprise touches such as a kids' menu, handwash brought to your table and live minstrel music.

Self-Catering

Centro Variedades Commercial SUPERMARKET
(Calle 85, btwn Calles 288 & 290; ☺9am-6pm) Groceries.

Mercado la Plaza MARKET
(cnr Calles 97 & 298) Near the Puente Sánchez Figueras; for produce/peso stalls.

Drinking & Nightlife

★ACAA BAR
(Association Cubana de Artistas y Artesanos; Calle 85, btwn Calles 282 & 284; ☺10am-late) What begins as a glam-looking arts supplies shop and exhibition venue leads back into a courtyard reminiscent of bohemian Paris where artsy culture-vulture types sit around slurping strong coffee and conversing animatedly. A rooftop bar gets going after dark, often with live music as an accompaniment.

Bistro Kuba BAR
(Calle 83, btwn Calles 292 & 290; ☺11am-2am) The tables in this cool dinky bar light up to show old city landmarks. Cocktails are incredible but we also love the espresso (practically the city's only coffee machine is here) and the ham and cheese tasting platters. Live music several nights per week.

Ruinas de Matasiete BAR
(cnr Vía Blanca & Calle 101; ☺10am-10pm, club 10pm-2am) The city's famed drinking hole is a frenetic (too frenetic for some) place housed in the ruins of a 19th-century, bay-facing warehouse. Drinks and grilled meats are served on an open-air terrace, but a better reason to come here is to hear live music (9pm Friday to Sunday; cover charge CUC$3).

Entertainment

Teatro Sauto THEATER
(☎45-24-27-21; Plaza de la Vigía) Across Plaza de la Vigía, Teatro Sauto is a national landmark and one of Cuba's premier theaters. Perfor-

VARADERO & MATANZAS PROVINCE MATANZAS

mances have been held here since 1863. You might catch the Ballet Nacional de Cuba or the Conjunto Folklórico Nacional de Cuba if the theater has recovered from its lengthy renovation.

Centro Cultural Comunitario
Nelson Barrera   CULTURAL CENTER
(cnr Calles 276 & 77; ☺9am-5pm Tue-Sun) A good starting point for anyone interested in Matanzas' Afro-Cuban history lies in this Marina neighborhood cultural center. Inquire about upcoming events and you could get lucky with religious processions, drum sessions, or just shooting the breeze with some *hombres* from the *barrio*.

Sala de Conciertos
José White   CLASSICAL MUSIC
(Calle 79, btwn Calles 290 & 288) Check this wonderful new venue for orchestra and *danzón* performances (listed on the board outside) or – at the least – sup a drink in its pleasant courtyard.

Museo Histórico Provincial   CULTURAL CENTER
(cnr Calles 83 & 272; admission CUC$2; ☺10am-6pm Tue-Fri, 1-7pm Sat, 9am-noon Sun) Check the board outside this building (also known as Palacio del Junco) for events ranging from theater to *danzón* performances to rumba, with listings for the month ahead.

Teatro Velazco   CINEMA
(cnr Calles 79 & 288) Movie house on Parque Libertad.

Las Palmas   LIVE MUSIC
(cnr Calles 254 & 127; admission CUC$1; ☺noon-midnight Mon-Wed, to 2am Fri-Sun) A good starlit night out for a fraction of the price of the Tropicana shindig can be had at this ARTex place.

Estadio Victoria de Girón   SPORTS
(Av Martín Dihigo) From October to April, baseball games take place at this stadium 1km southwest of the market.

🛍 Shopping
Bad luck, shopaholics: checking out the stores (what stores?) in Matanzas makes a car boot sale look like Hollywood Boulevard.

Ediciones Vigía   BOOKS
(Plaza de la Vigía; ☺9am-5pm Mon-Sat) Unique handmade books.

ℹ Information
Banco Financiero Internacional (cnr Calles 85 & 298) ATM.
Cadeca (Calle 286, btwn Calles 83 & 85; ☺8am-6pm Mon-Sat, to noon Sun)
Etecsa Telepunto (cnr Calles 83 & 282; per hour CUC$4.50; ☺8:30am-7:30pm) Internet terminals.
Post Office (cnr Calles 85 & 290)
Servimed (☑45-25-31-70; Hospital Faustino Pérez, Carretera Central Km 101) Clinic just southwest of town.

ℹ Getting There & Away
AIR
Matanzas is connected to the outside world through Juan Gualberto Gómez International Airport (p213), aka Varadero airport, 20km east of town.

CAR
The nearest car rental to the center is **Cubacar** (☑45-25-32-46; cnr Calles 127 & 204), in Playa neighborhood.

BICYCLE
Matanzas is reachable by bike from Varadero. The 32km road is well-paved and completely flat, bar the last 3km into the city starting at the Río Canímar bridge. Bike hire is available at some Varadero all-inclusive hotels.

BUS
All buses, long distance and provincial, use the National Bus Station in the old train station on the corner of Calles 131 and 272 in Pueblo Nuevo south of the Río San Juan.

Matanzas has decent connections, although for destinations like Cienfuegos and Trinidad you need to change at Varadero, taking the first Varadero bus of the day then waiting for the afternoon Varadero–Trinidad bus.

Víazul (www.viazul.com) has four daily departures to Havana (CUC$7, two hours, 1:15pm, 5:15pm, 7pm and 8:50pm) and Varadero (CUC$6, one hour, 8:30am, 10:20am, 3:05pm and 7:50pm), also calling at the airport (CUC$6, 25 minutes).

Matanzas Bus Tour
Matanzas Bus Tour is a hop on/hop off tourist bus linking Varadero with Matanzas and its various outlying sights. It stops at all the main hotels in Varadero frequented by the similar Varadero Bus Tour as well as Río Canímar, Cuevas de Bellamar, Iglesia de Monserrate and Hotel Velazco on Parque Libertad in Matanzas. It runs four times daily (with some low-season hiccups). All-day tickets cost CUC$10. Schedules are sometimes cancelled in low season.

TRAIN

The **train station** (📞 45-29-16-45; Calle 181) is in Miret, at the southern edge of the city. Foreigners usually pay the peso price in convertibles to the *jefe de turno* (shift manager). Most trains between Havana and Santiago de Cuba stop here. In theory, there are eight daily trains to Havana (CUC$3, 1½ hours). The daily Santiago de Cuba train (CUC$27) should leave in the evening (check well in advance as Cuban trains are notoriously fickle) stopping at Santa Clara, Ciego de Ávila, Camagüey and Las Tunas.

Latest train information is plastered on pieces of paper stuck to a billboard on the far wall of the waiting room. Get here well in advance to beat the bedlam.

The **Hershey Train Station** (📞 45-24-48-05; cnr Calles 55 & 67) is in Versalles, an easy 10-minute walk from Parque Libertad. There are three trains a day to Casablanca station in Havana (CUC$2.80, four hours) via Canasí (CUC$0.85), Jibacoa (CUC$1.10, 1½ hours; for Playa Jibacoa), Hershey (CUC$1.40, two hours; for Jardines de Hershey) and Guanabo (CUC$2). Departure times from Matanzas are 4:39am, 12:09pm (an express service that should take three hours) and 4:25pm.

Ticket sales begin an hour before the scheduled departure time and, except on weekends and holidays, there's no problem getting aboard. Bicycles may not be allowed (ask). The train usually leaves on time, but often arrives in Havana's Casablanca station (just below La Cabaña fort on the east side of the harbor) one hour late. This is the only electric railway in Cuba. It's a scenic trip if you're not in a hurry, and a great way of reaching the little-visited attractions of Mayabeque province.

❶ Getting Around

Bus 12 links Plaza Libertad with the Cuevas de Bellamar and the Iglesia de Monserrate. You can also use the handy hop on/hop off Matanzas Bus Tour (p223) to get to Cuevas de Bellamar and Canímar.

The Oro Negro gas station is on the corner of Calles 129 and 210, 4km outside central Matanzas on the Varadero road. If you're driving to Varadero, you'll pay a CUC$2 highway toll between Boca de Camarioca and Santa Marta (no toll between Matanzas and the airport).

Bici-taxis congregate next to the Mercado la Plaza and can take you to most of the city's destinations for one to two Cuban pesos. A taxi to Juan Gualberto Gómez International Airport should cost CUC$25 to CUC$30, with Varadero fares a bit more again.

Cárdenas

POP 109,552

Without the bright lights of Varadero or the rejuvenated historic and cultural legacy of Matanzas, Cárdenas can appear downright shabby. Looking like a sepia-toned photo from another era, this dilapidated town is home to countless resort-based waiters, front-desk clerks and taxi drivers, but with barely a restaurant, hotel or motorized cab to serve it.

Cárdenas has nevertheless played an episodic role in Cuban history. In 1850 Venezuelan adventurer Narciso López and a ragtag army of American mercenaries raised the Cuban flag here for the first time in a vain attempt to free the colony from its Spanish colonizers. Other history-making inhabitants followed, including revolutionary student leader José Antonio Echeverría, who was shot during an abortive raid to assassinate President Batista in 1957. This rich past is showcased in three fabulous museums stationed around Parque Echeverría, the city's main plaza, which today constitute the key reason to visit. Museums aside, the once-illustrious, now-dilapidated facades of Cárdenas can be a shock to travelers coming from Varadero. If you want to see a picture of real Cuban life, it doesn't get more eye-opening; if it's minty mojitos and all-day volleyball you're after, stick to the tourist beaches.

When asking for directions, beware that Cárdenas residents often use the old street names rather than the new street-naming system (numbers). Double-check if uncertain.

◉ Sights

In among the battered buildings and dingy peso restaurants of central Cárdenas, three excellent museums, all situated on pretty Parque Echeverría, stand out as city highlights.

★**Museo de Batalla de Ideas**   MUSEUM
(Av 6, btwn Calles 11 & 12; admission CUC$2, camera CUC$5; ⊙9am-5pm Tue-Sat, to 1pm Sun) The newest of Cárdenas' three museums offers a well-designed and organized overview of the history of US–Cuban relations, replete with sophisticated graphics. Inspired by the case of Elián González, a boy from Cárdenas whose mother, stepfather and 11 others drowned attempting to enter the US by boat in 1999, the museum is the solid form of

Castro's resulting *batalla de ideas* (battle of ideas) with the US government.

The displays' themes naturally center round the eight months during which Cuba and the US debated the custody of Elián – but it extends also to displays on the quality of the Cuban education system and a courtyard containing busts of anti-imperialists who died for the revolutionary cause. The exhibit that most epitomizes the purpose of the museum, however, is possibly the sculpture of a child in the act of disparagingly throwing away a Superman toy.

Museo Casa Natal de José Antonio Echeverría
MUSEUM

(Av 4 Este No 560; admission incl guide CUC$5; ⊙10am-5pm Tue-Sat, 9am-1pm Sun) This museum has a macabre historical collection including the original garrote used to execute Narciso López by strangulation in 1851. Objects relating to the 19th-century independence wars are downstairs, while the 20th-century Revolution is covered upstairs, reached via a beautiful spiral staircase.

In 1932 José Antonio Echeverría was born here, a student leader slain by Batista's police in 1957 after a botched assassination attempt in Havana's Presidential Palace. There's a statue of him in the eponymous square outside.

Museo Oscar María de Rojas
MUSEUM

(cnr Av 4 & Calle 13; admission CUC$5; ⊙9am-6pm Tue-Sat, to 1pm Sun) Cuba's second-oldest museum (after the Museo Bacardí in Santiago) offers a selection of weird artifacts, including a strangulation chair from 1830, a face mask of Napoleon, the tail of Antonio Maceo's horse, Cuba's largest collection of snails and, last but by no means least, some preserved fleas – yes fleas – from 1912.

The museum is set in a lovely colonial building and staffed with knowledgeable official guides.

Catedral de la Inmaculada Concepción
CHURCH

(Av Céspedes, btwn Calles 8 & 9) Parque Colón is the city's other interesting square, five blocks north of Parque Echeverría. Here stands the main ecclesiastical building of Cárdenas. Built in 1846, it's noted for its stained glass and purportedly the oldest statue of Christopher Columbus in the western hemisphere.

Dating from 1862, Colón, as he's known in Cuba, stands rather authoritatively with his face fixed in a thoughtful frown and a globe resting at his feet. It's Cárdenas' best photo op.

Flagpole Monument
MONUMENT

(cnr Av Céspedes & Calle 2) No, not just any old flagpole. Follow Av Céspedes past Catedral de la Inmaculada Concepción to its northern end and you will see *this* flagpole is attached to a monument and commemorates the first raising of the Cuban flag on May 19, 1850.

Arechabala Rum Factory
FACTORY

(cnr Calle 2 & Av 13) To the northwest of the city center in the industrial zone is where Varadero rum is distilled; the Havana Club rum company was founded here in 1878. The company (and its international partner Bacardí) has recently been entangled in a trademark dispute with the Cuban government and partner Pernod Ricard over the rights to sell Havana Club in the US. The victors? The Cuban government/Pernod Ricard. No tours are available.

🍴 Sleeping & Eating

Down the road Varadero flaunts more than 50 hotels. Here in humble Cárdenas there are precisely zero. Fortunately, Cárdenas sports a couple of good (if notoriously hard-to-find) casas particulares and to boot, two exceptional new restaurants on Parque Echeverría. There are many convertible supermarkets and stores near the cast-iron 19th-century market hall Plaza Molocoff (cnr Av 3 Oeste & Calle 12), where you can get cheap peso snacks.

★ Ricardo Domínguez
CASA PARTICULAR $

(☑52-89-44-31; cnr Av 31 & Calle 12; r CUC$35; [P][❋]) Ricardo's place is 1.5km northwest of Parque Echeverría and worth tracking down. The spick-and-span white terracotta-roofed house is cocooned within a large, leafy garden and seemingly just plucked from one of Miami's more tasteful suburbs. Three rooms available.

Hostal Ida
CASA PARTICULAR $

(☑45-52-15-59; Calle 13, btwn Avs 13 & 15; r CUC$35; [P][❋]) Don't let the tatty street setting put you off here. Inside this plush apartment (with private entrance and garage) you'll find a stunning living room/kitchenette, and a decadently furnished bedroom/bathroom that might have floated over from a decent Varadero hotel. Ample breakfasts (CUC$5).

★ Studio 55
CAFE, BAR $

(Calle 12, btwn Avs 4 & 6; light mains CUC$3-5; ⊙noon-midnight Mon-Thu, to 2am Fri & Sat) Heard of New York's Studio 54? This is the Cárdenas version. Name and logo aside, there's no other real similarities, other than a touch of class. Soak up the industrial-chic vibe and order great burgers or other well-executed fast food from menus designed like DVD cases. And appreciate the fact that just a couple of years ago Cárdenas was a culinary wasteland.

Restaurant Don Ramón INTERNATIONAL $
(Av 4, btwn Calles 12 & 13; mains CUC$3-8; ⊙ 11am-10pm) Overlooking Parque Echeverría, the lovely Don Ramón woos you with its old-style colonial charm. For a varied sit-down meal, there's nowhere better in Cárdenas. The steak gets good reports.

☆ Entertainment

Casa de la Cultura CULTURAL CENTER
(Av Céspedes No 706, btwn Calles 15 & 16) Housed in a beautiful but faded colonial building with stained glass and an interior patio with rockers. Search the handwritten advertising posters for rap *peñas* (performances), theater and literature events.

Cine Cárdenas CINEMA
(cnr Av Céspedes & Calle 14) Has daily movie screenings.

❶ Information

Banco de Crédito y Comercio (cnr Calle 9 & Av 3)

Cadeca (cnr Av 1 Oeste & Calle 12)

Centro Médico Sub Acuática (☑ 45-52-21-14; Carretera a Varadero Km 2; per hour CUC$80; ⊙ 8am-4pm Mon-Sat, doctors on-call 24hr) Two kilometers northwest on the road to Varadero at Hospital Julio M Aristegui; has a Soviet recompression chamber dating from 1981.

Etecsa Telepunto (cnr Av Céspedes & Calle 12; per hour CUC$4.50; ⊙ 8:30am-7:30pm) Telephone and internet access.

Pharmacy (Calle 12 No 60; ⊙ 24hr)

Post Office (cnr Av Céspedes & Calle 8; ⊙ 8am-6pm Mon-Sat)

❶ Getting There & Away

It's simplest to go to Varadero to get onward bus connections because whilst the Varadero–Santiago de Cuba Víazul bus does pass through, it doesn't officially stop here. Varadero also has many more bus services.

Bus 236 to/from Varadero leaves hourly from the corner of Av 13 Oeste and Calle 13 (50 centavos, but tourists are usually charged CUC$1). A taxi for the same journey costs CUC$15 to CUC$20.

Local buses leave from the **bus station** (cnr Av Céspedes & Calle 22) (a ten-block walk southwest from Parque Echeverría) to Havana and Santa Clara daily, but they're often full upon reaching Cárdenas. There are also trucks to Jovellanos/Perico, which puts you 12km from Colón and onto possible onward transport to the east. The ticket office is at the rear of the station.

❶ Getting Around

The main horse-carriage (1 peso) route through Cárdenas is northeast on Av Céspedes from the bus station and then northwest on Calle 13 to the hospital, passing the stop of bus 236 (to Varadero) on the way.

The **Servi-Cupet gas station** (cnr Calle 13 & Av 31 Oeste) is opposite an old Spanish fort on the northwest side of town, on the road to Varadero.

San Miguel de los Baños & Around

Nestled in the interior of Matanzas province amid rolling hills punctuated by vivid splashes of bougainvillea, San Miguel de los Baños is an atmospheric old spa town that once rivaled Havana for elegant opulence. Once, that is. Flourishing briefly as a destination for wealthy folk seeking the soothing medicinal waters that were 'discovered' here in the early 20th century, San Miguel saw a smattering of lavish neoclassical villas shoot up that still line the town's arterial Av de Abril today. But the boom times didn't last. Just prior to the Revolution, pollution from a local sugar mill infiltrated the water supply and the resort quickly faded from prominence. Now, it's a curious mix between an architectural time capsule from a bygone era and something out of a post-apocalyptic John Wyndham novel.

◉ Sights & Activities

Passing visitors will be shocked at the architectural contrasts here: the smaller houses of the current population juxtaposed with the surreally ostentatious ruined buildings of the glory days, such as the ornate multi-domed **Gran Hotel y Balneario**, on the north side of town, a replica of the Grand Casino at Monte Carlo. You can meander the eerie grounds down to the still-standing red-brick Romanesque bath houses. It's probably best to give bathing a miss, though.

Looming above town are the steep slopes of **Loma de Jacán**, a glowering hill with

COLÓN

Colón, tucked away in the east of the province 40km east of Jovellanos, makes an interesting journey-breaker on Cuba's Carretera Central. With its striking colonnaded buildings and one of Cuba's prettiest, greenest central plazas, this town is more about ambience than attractions. What you will be seeing in Colón is an example (and there are many across the country) of what Cuba is like for Cubans untouched by the tourism industry and the money it generates.

Stroll up the main thoroughfare Calle Martí and soak up local life on leafy **Parque de la Libertad** (aka Parque de Colón) with its statue of Christopher Columbus amongst numerous other busts. Nearby you can blow the cobwebs off the **Iglesia Catholica** (Catholic church), **Escuela de Artes y Oficios** (School of Arts and Works) with its striking colonial revivalist architecture and the optimistically named **Hotel Nuevo Continental** dating from 1937. There is also a museum, the **Museo José R Zuleta**, and an old fort to see.

448 steps embellished by faded murals of the Stations of the Cross. When you reach the small chapel on top you can drink in the town's best views with the added satisfaction that you are standing at the highest point in the province.

Sleeping & Eating

Finca Coincidencia CASA PARTICULAR $
(☎45-81-39-23; Carretera Central, btwn Coliseo & Jovellanos; r CUC$20; P) ◢ Enhance your taste for bucolic provincial life away from the razzmatazz of the province's north coast at this idyllic farm 14km northeast of San Miguel de los Baños and 6km east of Colesio on the Carretera Central. Chill in the grounds replete with mango and guava trees, participate in ceramics classes and help out on a farm where 83 types of plants are cultivated.

❶ Getting There & Away

To get to San Miguel de los Baños, follow Rte 101 from Cárdenas to Colesio where you cross the Carretera Central; the town is situated a further 8km to the southwest of Colesio. A taxi from Cárdenas should cost CUC$20 to CUC$25 – bargain hard. You may be able to catch a ride on a truck/local bus from Cárdenas bus station.

PENÍNSULA DE ZAPATA

A vast, virtually uninhabited swampy wilderness spanning the entirety of southern Matanzas, the 4520-sq-km Península de Zapata quickens the pulses of wildlife-watchers and divers alike with the country's most important bird species and some of the most magical offshore reef diving secreted in its humid embrace. Most of the peninsula, a protected zone now part of Gran Parque Natural Montemar, was formerly known as Parque Nacional Ciénaga de Zapata: in 2001, it was declared a Unesco Biosphere Reserve.

The sugar-mill town of Australia in the northeast of the peninsula marks the main access point to the park. Just south of here is one of the region's big tourist money-spinners, the cheesy yet oddly compelling Boca de Guamá, a reconstructed Taíno village.

The road hits the coast at Playa Larga, home to the peninsula's best beaches, at the head of the Bahía de Cochinos where propaganda billboards still laud Cuba's historic victory over the *Yanqui* imperialists in 1961.

Ornithologists and nature lovers will want to veer southwest from here, where the sugarcane plantations fade fast into sticky swamp. This is one of the remotest regions of Cuba, rarely penetrated by tourists. Yet intrepid visitors will reap the benefits: an incredible diversity of birds, as well as endemic reptile and plant species, can be glimpsed on the mangrove-flecked waterways here.

Aside from its reputation as a proverbial banana-skin for US imperialism, the east coast of Bahía de Cochinos also claims some of the best cave diving in the Caribbean and southeast of Playa Larga the dive sites fan out temptingly, accompanied by a couple of less-riveting resort hotels.

Accommodations outside of the resorts, however, are thankfully abundant. You can check out excellent options in Central Australia, Playa Larga and Playa Girón.

Decent Víazul bus connections run through the peninsula. There's also a handy shuttle service between Boca de Guamá and Caleta Buena.

ℹ️ Information

La Finquita (📱 45-91-32-24; Autopista Nacional Km 142; ⏰ 9am-5pm Mon-Sat, 8am-noon Sun), a highly useful information center-cum-snack bar run by Cubanacán, arranges trips into the Península de Zapata and books rooms at the Villa Guamá. It's just by the Península de Zapata turn-off from the Autopista Nacional at Jagüey Grande, 1.5km north of Australia. The **National Park Office** (📱 45-98-72-49; ⏰ 8am-5pm) is on the northern edge of Playa Larga on the road from Boca de Guamá.

Etecsa, the post office and convertible stores are across the Autopista in Jagüey Grande. Insect repellent is absolutely essential on the peninsula and while Cuban repellent is available locally, it's like wasabi on sushi for the ravenous buggers here.

Central Australia & Around

No, you haven't just arrived Down Under. About 1.5km south of the Autopista Nacional on the way to Boca de Guamá, is the large disused Central Australia sugar mill, built in 1904, now home to the Museo de la Comandancia.

◉ Sights

Museo de la Comandancia   MUSEUM (admission CUC$1; ⏰ 9am-5pm Tue-Sat, 8am-noon Sun) During the 1961 Bay of Pigs invasion, Fidel Castro had his headquarters in the former office of the sugar mill, but today the building is devoted to this revolutionary museum (closed for refurbishment at the time of research.) You can see the desk from which Fidel commanded his forces, along with other associated memorabilia. Outside is the wreck of an invading aircraft shot down by Fidel's troops.

The concrete memorials lining the road to the Bahía de Cochinos mark the spots where defenders were killed in 1961. A more moving testimony to the Bay of Pigs episode is the Museo de Playa Girón.

Finca Fiesta Campesina   WILDLIFE PARK (admission CUC$1; ⏰ 9am-6pm) Approximately 400m on your right after the Central Australia exit is a kind of wildlife-park-meets-country fair with labeled examples of Cuba's typical flora and fauna. The highlights of this strangely engaging place are the coffee (some of the best in Cuba and served with a sweet wedge of sugarcane), the bull-riding and the hilarious if slightly infantile games

of guinea-pig roulette overseen with much pizzazz by the gentleman at the gate.

It's the only place in Cuba – outside the cockfighting – where you encounter any form of open gambling.

🛏️ Sleeping & Eating

There are more casas in Playa Larga (32km) and Playa Girón (48km).

Motel Batey Don Pedro   CABIN $ (📱 45-91-28-25; Carretera a Península de Zapata; s/d CUC$26/34; 🅿️) The best bet for accommodations in the area, this sleepy motel has 12 rooms in thatched blue-and-white double units with ceiling fans, crackling TVs and patios – and a random frog or two in the bathroom. It's further down the Finca Fiesta Campesina track, just south of the Península de Zapata turnoff from Km 142 on the Autopista Nacional at Jagüey Grande.

The motel is designed to resemble a peasant settlement. For food, the best option is the Finca Fiesta Campesina at the beginning of the track, where English is spoken and energy-boosting *guarapo* (sugarcane juice) along with some of Zapata's best coffee is served.

Pío Cuá   CARIBBEAN $$ (Carretera de Playa Larga Km 8; meals CUC$8-20; ⏰ 11am-5pm) A favorite with Guamá-bound tour buses, this huge place is set up for big groups, but retains fancy decor with lots of stained glass. Shrimp, lobster or chicken meals are pretty good. It's 8km from the Autopista Nacional turnoff, heading south from Australia.

ℹ️ Getting There & Away

Your options are the thrice-daily Víazul bus between Havana and Cienfuegos/Trinidad and the erratic twice-daily Peninsula shuttle. With an engaging smile, Víazul drivers running the Autopista Nacional route between Havana and the east will stop at the La Finquita information center, plonking you around 2km from Jagüey Grande (north) and Australia (south). Get here earlier in the day to guarantee onward transportation.

Boca de Guamá

Boca de Guamá may be a tourist creation, but as resorts around here go it's among the more imaginative. Situated about halfway between the Autopista Nacional at Jagüey Grande and the famous Bahía de Cochinos, it takes its name from native Taíno chief Gua-

VARADERO & MATANZAS PROVINCE CENTRAL AUSTRALIA & AROUND

má, who made a last stand against the Spanish in 1532 (in Baracoa). The big attraction here is the boat trip through mangrove-lined waterways and across Laguna del Tesoro (Treasure Lake) to a 'recreation' of a Taíno village. Fidel once holidayed here and had a hand in developing the Taíno theme.

You'll soon be struggling to draw parallels with pre-Columbian Cuba, however: raucous tour groups and even louder rap music welcome your voyage back in time. Arranged around the dock the boats depart from a cluster of restaurants, expensive snack bars, knickknack shops and a crocodile farm. Palm-dotted grounds here make a pleasant break from the surrounding swampy heat.

◉ Sights

Laguna del Tesoro   LAKE
This lake is 5km east of Boca de Guamá via the Canal de la Laguna, accessible only by boat. On the far (east) side of the 92-sq-km body of water is a tourist resort named **Villa Guamá**, built to resemble a Taíno village, on a dozen small islands.

A sculpture park next to the mock village has 32 life-size figures of Taíno villagers in a variety of idealized poses. The lake is called 'Treasure Lake' due to a legend about some treasure the Taíno supposedly threw into the water just prior to the Spanish conquest (not dissimilar to South American El Dorado legends). The lake is stocked with large-mouth bass, so fishers frequently convene.

Criadero de Cocodrilos   CROCODILE FARM
(adult/child incl drink CUC$5/3; ☻9:30am-5pm)
🖉 On your right as you come from the Autopista, the Criadero de Cocodrilos is a highly successful crocodile breeding facility run by the Ministerio de Industrias Pesqueras. Two species of crocodiles are raised here: the native *Crocodylus rhombifer* (*cocodrilo* in Spanish), and the *Crocodylus acutus* (*caimán* in Spanish), which is found throughout the tropical Americas.

Rock up here and you could get a guided tour (in Spanish), taking you through each stage of the breeding program. Prior to the establishment of this program in 1962 (considered the first environmental protection act undertaken by the revolutionary government), these two species of marsh-dwelling crocodiles were almost extinct.

The breeding has been so successful that across the road in the Boca de Guamá complex you can buy stuffed baby crocodiles or dine, legally, on crocodile steak.

If you buy anything made from crocodile leather at Boca de Guamá, be sure to ask for an invoice (for the customs authorities) proving that the material came from a crocodile farm and not wild crocodiles. A less controversial purchase would be one of the attractive ceramic bracelets sold at the site's **Taller de Cerámica** (☻9am-6pm Mon-Sat), where you can see five kilns in operation.

🛏 Sleeping & Eating

At the boat dock you'll find **Bar la Rionda** (☻9:30am-5pm) and **Restaurante la Boca** (set meals CUC$12).

Villa Guamá   CABIN **$$**
(📱45-91-55-51; s/d CUC$51/62) This place was built in 1963 on the east side of the Laguna del Tesoro, about 8km from Boca de Guamá by boat (cars can be left at the crocodile farm; CUC$1). The 50 thatched *cabañas* (cabins) with bath and TV are on piles over the shallow waters.

The six small islands bearing the units are connected by wooden footbridges to other islands with a bar, cafetería, overpriced restaurant and a swimming pool containing chlorinated lake water. Rowboats are available for rent, and the bird-watching at sunrise is reputedly fantastic. You'll need insect repellent if you decide to stay. The ferry transfer (CUC$11) is not included in the room price.

❶ Getting There & Away

The thrice-daily Havana–Cienfuegos–Trinidad Vía-zul bus runs through the Zapata peninsula; ask the driver if they will leave you at the Boca de Guamá ferry dock. You can also travel on the hop on/hop off shuttle bus (CUC$3) between Boca de Guamá and Caleta Buena. Otherwise, it's your own wheels.

❶ Getting Around

A passenger ferry (adult/child CUC$12/6, 20 minutes) departs Boca de Guamá for Villa Guamá across Laguna del Tesoro four times a day. Speedboats depart more frequently and whisk you across to the pseudo-Indian village in just 10 minutes any time during the day for CUC$12 per person round-trip (with 40 minutes waiting time at Villa Guamá, two-person minimum). In the morning you can allow yourself more time on the island by going one way by launch and returning by ferry.

Gran Parque Natural Montemar

The largest *ciénaga* (swamp) in the Caribbean, **Ciénaga de Zapata** is also one of Cuba's most diverse ecosystems. Crowded into this vast wetland (essentially two swamps divided by a rocky central tract) are 14 different vegetation formations including mangroves, wood, dry wood, cactus, savannah, selva and semideciduous. There are also extensive salt pans. The marshes support more than 190 bird species, 31 types of reptiles, 12 species of mammals, plus countless amphibians, fish and insects (including the insatiable mosquito). There are more than 900 plant species here, some 115 of them endemic. It is also an important habitat for the endangered *manatí* (manatee), the Cuban *cocodrilo* (crocodile; *Crocodylus rhombifer*) and the *manjuarí* (alligator gar; *Atractosteus tristoechus*), Cuba's most primitive fish with an alligator's head but a fishlike body. The almost-extinct dwarf hutia (a kind of wild guinea pig) has the swamp as its only refuge.

The Zapata is the best bird-watching spot in Cuba, the place to come to see *zunzuncitos* (bee hummingbirds; the world's smallest bird), cormorants, cranes, ducks, flamingos, hawks, herons, ibis, owls, parrots, partridges and *tocororos* (Cuba's national bird). There are 18 birds endemic to the region. Numerous migratory birds from North America winter here, making November to April prime bird-watching season. It's also the nation's number-one nexus for catch-and-release sportfishing and fly-fishing, where the palometa, *sábalo* and *robalo*, as well as bonefish, thrive.

Communications in Zapata, unsuitable for agriculture, were almost nonexistent before the Revolution when poverty was the rule. Charcoal makers burn wood from the region's semideciduous forests, and *turba* (peat) dug from the swamps is an important source of fuel. The main industry today is tourism and ecotourists are arriving in increasing numbers. Public transport only runs as far as Playa Larga: to see anything of the *ciénaga* proper you'll need to come here as part of a tour, or with your own wheels.

☞ Tours

There are four main excursions into the park, with an understandable focus on bird-watching. Itineraries are flexible. Transport is not usually laid on; it's best to arrange beforehand. Cars (including chauffeur-driven jeeps) can be rented from Havanautos (p234) in Playa Girón; bank on CUC$40 for car and driver. Get more information on any of these activities at Playa Larga's National Park Office (p228) or La Finquita (p228) at the Playa Larga turn-off on the Autopista Nacional.

Aspiring fishers can arrange **fly-fishing** from canoes or (due to the shallowness of the water) on foot at either Las Salinas or Río Hatiguanico. Ask at La Finquita or just turn up if you have your own gear. Between them the two locations offer Cuba's best angling: Las Salinas has excellent fishing; Río Hatiguanico is great for tarpon.

Laguna de las Salinas   BIRD-WATCHING
(4hr-tour per person CUC$10) One of the most popular excursions is to this *laguna* where large numbers of migratory waterfowl can be seen from November to April: we're talking 10,000 pink flamingos at a time, plus 190 other feathered species. The road to Las Salinas passes through forest, swamps and lagoons (where aquatic birds can be observed). Guides (and vehicle) are mandatory to explore the refuge.

The 22km visit lasts over four hours but you may be able to negotiate for a longer visit.

Observación de Aves   BIRD-WATCHING
(per person CUC$19) This trip offers an extremely flexible itinerary and the right to roam (with a qualified park ornithologist)

around different sites, including the **Reserva de Bermejas**. Among 18 species of endemic bird found here you can see prized *ferminins*, *cabreritos* and *gallinuelas de Santo Tomás*. Inquire at the National Park Office (p228) or ask around Playa Larga for a private guide.

Río Hatiguanico   BIRD-WATCHING

(per person CUC$15) Switching from land to boat, this three-hour 12km river-trip runs through the densely forested northwestern part of the peninsula. You'll have to dodge branches at some points, while at others the river opens out into a wide delta-like estuary. Birdlife is abundant and you may also see turtles and crocodiles. Independent transport is needed to cover the 90km to the start point.

Señor Orestes Martínez
Garcías   BIRD-WATCHING

(☑52-53-90-04, 45-98-75-45; chino.zapata@gmail.com; excursions per person CUC$10-20) Garnering a reputation as the area's most knowledgeable resident bird-watcher, 'El Chino', as he is otherwise known, can take you on more personalized, and reportedly highly rewarding ornithological forays into the *ciénaga*. He runs a casa particular in the village Caletón near Playa Larga.

Santo Tomás   OUTDOORS

(per person CUC$10) It's also worth asking about this trip, available December through April, beginning 30km west of Playa Larga in the park's only real settlement (Santo Tomás) and proceeding along a tributary of the Hatiguanico – walking or boating, depending on water levels. It's another good option for bird-watchers.

ⓘ Information

Cubanacán's La Finquita (p228) on the Autopista near Central Australia is the park information point, and a good place to book your chosen excursion. The National Park Office (p228) is on the northern edge of Playa Larga and can arrange guided trips, but not vehicles to do them in: Playa Girón has the nearest car rental (p234). The Playa Larga or Girón hotels can also arrange tours, as can Hostal Enrique in the village of Caletón by Playa Larga.

Playa Larga

Continuing south from Boca de Guamá you reach Playa Larga, on the Bahía de Cochinos, after 13km. Larga was one of two beaches invaded by US-backed exiles on April 17, 1961 (although Playa Girón, 35km further south, saw far bigger landings). It's now a diver's paradise. There's a cheapish resort here, a scuba-diving center, and a smattering of casas particulares in the adjacent beachside village of Caletón. With the nearest accommodations for access to Gran Parque Natural Montemar, it is a good base for environmental excursions around the area.

🛏 Sleeping & Eating

★El Caribeño   CASA PARTICULAR $

(☑45-98-73-59; fidelscaribe@gmail.com; Al Final de Caletón, Caletón; r CUC$25-30; ❄) A Caribbean beach fantasy awaits you in this fine house whose rustic front terrace is practically diving distance from the sea. The sinuous beach here, backed by crooked palms, is gorgeous and the food (crab and lobster) is fantastically fresh. Friendly owner Fidel Fuentes has three nice sea-view rooms.

Hostal Enrique   CASA PARTICULAR $

(☑45-98-74-25; Caletón; r CUC$20-25; ❄) Five hundred meters down the road to Las Salinas is one of the area's better casas with five rooms, all with private bathrooms, a dining area (serving large portions of food), a rooftop terrace and a path from the back garden leading to the often-deserted Caletón beach. Enrique can help arrange diving and bird-watching at distinctly cheaper prices than the hotels hereabouts.

Villa Playa Larga   HOTEL $$

(☑45-98-72-94; s/d high season incl breakfast CUC$51/72; 🅿❄❄) On a small scimitar of white-sand beach by the road, just east of the village of Caletón, this hotel has huge rooms in detached bungalows with bathroom, sitting room, fridge and TV. There are also eight two-bedroom family bungalows and a rather forlorn on-site restaurant.

ⓘ Getting There & Away

The thrice-daily Havana–Trinidad Víazul bus runs through the Zapata peninsula and will stop on request outside Villa Playa Larga.

The twice-daily hop on/hop off shuttle bus (CUC$3) links Boca de Guamá with Playa Girón and Caleta Buena.

ⓘ Getting Around

Taxi, car/moped hire at Playa Girón or the peninsula shuttle service: your choice.

DIVING & SNORKELING IN THE BAHÍA DE COCHINOS

While the Isla de la Juventud and María la Gorda head most Cuban divers' wish lists, the Bahía de Cochinos has some equally impressive underwater treats. There's a huge drop-off running 30m to 40m offshore for over 30km from Playa Larga down to Playa Girón, a fantastic natural feature that has created a 300m-high coral-encrusted wall with amazing swim-throughs, caves, gorgonians and marine life. Even better, the proximity of this wall to the coastline means that the region's 30-plus dive sites can be easily accessed without a boat – you just glide out from the shore. Good south-coast visibility stretches from 30m to 40m and there is a handful of wrecks scattered around.

Organizationally, Playa Girón is well set up with highly professional instructors bivouacked at five different locations along the coast. Generic dive prices (CUC$25 per immersion, CUC$35 per night dive, CUC$100 for five or CUC$365 for an open-water course) are some of the cheapest in Cuba. Snorkeling is CUC$5 per hour.

The **International Scuba Center** (☎ 45-98-41-10, 45-98-41-18), at Villa Playa Girón, is the main diving headquarters here. Casa Julio y Lidia in Playa Girón is a great source of information on diving here.

La Guarandinga, a colorfully painted 'divers bus' picks up tourists at locations in Playa Girón and heads to **Playa el Tanque**, the best nearby dive spot, on the Playa Larga road; it's particularly good for learners because you start off in shallow water.

Eight kilometers southeast of Playa Girón is **Caleta Buena** (☉10am-6pm), a lovely sheltered cove perfect for snorkeling and kitted out with another diving office. Black coral ridges protect several sinkholes and underwater caves teeming with the oddly shaped sponges for which the area is renowned; this is a great opportunity for speleo-scuba diving! Because saltwater meets freshwater, fish here are different to other sites. Admission to the beach is CUC$15 and includes an all-you-can-eat lunch buffet and open bar. Beach chairs and thatched umbrellas are spread along the rocky shoreline. Snorkel gear is CUC$3.

More underwater treasures can be seen at the **Cueva de los Peces** (☉9am-6pm), a flooded tectonic fault (or cenote), about 70m deep on the inland side of the road, almost exactly midway between Playa Larga and Playa Girón. There are lots of bright, tropical fish, plus you can explore back into the darker, spookier parts of the cenote with snorkel/dive gear (bring torches). There's a handy restaurant and an on-site dive outfit.

Just beyond the Cueva de los Peces is **Punta Perdiz**, another phenomenal snorkeling/scuba-diving spot with the wreck of a US landing craft scuppered during the Bay of Pigs invasion to explore. The shallow water is gemstone-blue here and there's good snorkeling right from the shore. There's a smaller on-site diving concession. Nonwater-based activities include volleyball and chances to play the amiable custodians at dominoes. Beware the swarms of mosquitoes and *libélulas* (enormous dragonflies).

Playa Girón

The sandy arc of Playa Girón nestles peacefully on the eastern side of the infamous Bahía de Cochinos, 48km south of Boca de Guamá. Notorious as the place where the Cold War almost got hot, the beach is actually named for a French pirate, Gilbert Girón, who met his end here by decapitation in the early 1600s at the hands of embittered locals. In April 1961 it was the scene of another botched raid, the ill-fated, CIA-sponsored invasion that tried to land on these remote sandy beaches in one of modern history's classic David and Goliath struggles. Lest we forget, there are still plenty of propaganda-spouting billboards dotted around rehashing past glories, though these days Girón, with its clear Caribbean waters and precipitous offshore drop-off, is a favorite destination for scuba divers and snorkelers.

Besides some decent private houses, Playa Girón's one and only resort is the modest Villa Playa Girón, a low-key all-inclusive popular among the diving fraternity. Long, shady **Playa los Cocos**, where the snorkeling is good, is just a five-minute walk south along the shore, although be warned there's more *diente de perro* (dog's tooth) than soft white sand.

On the main entry road to the hotel there's a pharmacy, a post office and a Caracol shop selling groceries. The settlement of Playa Girón is a tiny one-horse town, so the hotel is the best pit stop if you need any goods or services.

Sights

Museo de Playa Girón MUSEUM

(admission CUC$2, camera CUC$1; ⊙8am-5pm) This museum with its gleaming glass display cases evokes a tangible sense of the history of the famous Cold War episode that unfolded within rifle-firing distance of this spot in 1961. Across the street from Villa Playa Girón, it offers two rooms of artifacts from the Bay of Pigs skirmish plus numerous photos with (some) bilingual captions.

The mural of victims and their personal items is harrowing and the tactical genius of the Cuban forces comes through in the graphic depictions of how the battle unfolded. The 15-minute film about the 'first defeat of US imperialism in the Americas' is CUC$1 extra. A British Hawker Sea Fury aircraft used by the Cuban Air Force is parked outside the museum; round the back are other vessels used in the battle.

Sleeping & Eating

Aside from Villa Playa Girón, the small settlement of Playa Girón has some good private houses, with most serving food.

★Hostal Luis CASA PARTICULAR $

(☑45-98-42-58; r incl breakfast CUC$30-35; P ❀) The first house on the road to Cienfuegos is also the village's premier casa. Instantly recognizable by the blue facade and the two stone lions guarding the gate, youthful Luis and his wife offer seven spotless rooms both here and in another just-renovated house opposite.

KS Abella CASA PARTICULAR $

(☑45-98-43-83; r CUC$20-25; ❀) The *señor* is a former chef at Villa Playa Girón now trying out his seafood specialties on his casa guests. The casa is the red-and-cream bungalow a few houses up the Cienfuegos road from Hostal Luis.

Casa Julio y Lidia CASA PARTICULAR $

(☑45-98-41-35, 52-52-77-06; r CUC$25; P ❀) Owner Julio is the most experienced dive instructor hereabouts, meaning his modern house with two huge rooms is a useful option

Bahía de Cochinos

for divers. The second house on the left as you're entering Playa Girón from the west.

Ivette & Ronel CASA PARTICULAR $

(☑45-98-41-29; r CUC$25; P ❀) The first house on the left (if entering Playa Girón from the west), Ivette and Ronel's benefits from having a casa-owner-cum-dive-master at the helm. Two rooms and a *jutía* (tree rat) farm.

Villa Playa Girón RESORT $$

(☑45-98-41-10; s/d all-incl CUC$43/65; P ❀ ☒) On a beach imbued with historical significance lies this very ordinary hotel. Always busy with divers, the villa has clean, basic rooms that are often a long walk from the main block. The beach is a 50m dash away, though its allure has been spoiled somewhat by the construction of a giant wave-breaking wall.

THE BAY OF PIGS

What the Cubans call Playa Girón, the rest of the world has come to know as the Bay of Pigs, a disastrous attempt by the Kennedy administration to invade Cuba and overthrow Fidel Castro.

Conceived in 1959 by the Eisenhower administration and headed up by deputy director of the CIA, Richard Bissell, the plan to initiate a program of covert action against the Castro regime was given official sanction on March 17, 1960. There was but one proviso: no US troops were to be used in combat.

The CIA modeled its operation on the 1954 overthrow of the left-leaning government of Jacobo Arbenz in Guatemala. However, by the time President Kennedy was briefed on the proceedings in November 1960, the project had mushroomed into a full-scale invasion backed by a 1400-strong force of CIA-trained Cuban exiles and financed with a military budget of US$13 million.

Activated on April 15, 1961, the invasion was a disaster from start to finish. Intending to wipe out the Cuban Air Force on the ground, US planes painted in Cuban Air Force colors (and flown by Cuban exile pilots) missed most of their intended targets. Castro, who had been forewarned of the plans, had scrambled his air force the previous week. Hence, when the invaders landed at Playa Girón two days later, Cuban sea furies were able to promptly sink two of their supply ships and leave a force of 1400 men stranded on the beach.

To add insult to injury, a countrywide Cuban rebellion that had been much touted by the CIA never materialized. Meanwhile a vacillating Kennedy told Bissell he would not provide the marooned exile soldiers with US air cover.

Abandoned on the beaches, without supplies or military back-up, the invaders were doomed. There were 114 killed in skirmishes and a further 1189 captured. The prisoners were returned to the US a year later in return for US$53 million worth of food and medicine.

The Bay of Pigs failed due to a multitude of factors. First, the CIA had overestimated the depth of Kennedy's personal commitment and had made similarly inaccurate assumptions about the strength of the fragmented anti-Castro movement inside Cuba. Second, Kennedy himself, adamant all along that a low-key landing should be made, had chosen a site on an exposed strip of beach close to the Zapata swamps. Third, no one had given enough credit to the political and military know-how of Fidel Castro or to the extent to which the Cuban Intelligence Service had infiltrated the CIA's supposedly covert operation.

The consequences for the US were far-reaching. 'Socialism or death!' a defiant Castro proclaimed at a funeral service for seven Cuban 'martyrs' on April 16, 1961. The Revolution had swung irrevocably toward the Soviet Union.

❶ Getting There & Away

The thrice-daily Havana–Trinidad Víazul bus runs through the Zapata peninsula and stops outside Villa Playa Girón.

The hop on/hop off shuttle bus (CUC$3) links with Caleta Buena, Playa Larga and Guamá.

❶ Getting Around

Havanautos (☏ 45-98-41-23) has a car-rental office at Villa Playa Girón or you can hire a moto for CUC$25 per day.

Servi-Cupet gas stations are located on the Carretera Central at Jovellanos and at Colón, and on the Autopista Nacional at Jagüey Grande and Aguada de Pasajeros (the latter in Cienfuegos province).

East of Caleta Buena the coastal road toward Cienfuegos is not passable in a normal car; backtrack and take the inland road via Rodas.

Cienfuegos Province

♪ 43 / POP 408,825

Includes ➔
Cienfuegos 236
Rancho Luna. 248
Castillo de Jagua . . . 249
Laguna Guanaroca. . . 250
Jardín Botánico
de Cienfuegos. 250
El Nicho 250
Caribbean Coast. 251

Best Places to Eat

➔ Restaurante Villa Lagarto
(p245)

➔ Finca del Mar (p245)

➔ Paladar Aché (p245)

Best Architectural Icons

➔ Palacio de Valle (p240)

➔ Casa de la Cultura
Benjamin Duarte (p238)

➔ Teatro Tomás Terry (p237)

➔ Club Cienfuegos (p245)

Why Go?

Bienvenue (welcome) to Cienfuegos, Cuba's Gallic heart, which sits in the shadow of the crinkled Sierra del Escambray like a displaced piece of Paris on Cuba's untamed southern coastline. French rather than Spanish colonizers were the pioneers in this region, arriving in 1819 and bringing with them the ideas of the European Enlightenment which they industriously incorporated into their fledgling neoclassical city: the result today is a dazzling treasure box of 19th-century architectural glitz.

Outside of the city, the coast is surprisingly underdeveloped, a mini-rainbow of emerald greens and iridescent blues, flecked with coves, caves and coral reefs. The province's apex is just inland at El Nicho, arguably the most magical spot in the Parque Natural Topes de Collantes.

Though ostensibly Francophile and white, Cienfuegos' once-muted African 'soul' gained a mouthpiece in the 1940s in Cuba's most versatile musician, Benny Moré. He wasn't the only Afro-Cuban improviser. Nearby, Palmira is famous for its Catholic-Yoruba Santería brotherhoods, which still preserve their powerful slave-era traditions.

When to Go

➔ Cienfuegos' high season doesn't really get going until January and runs through to April, when beach lovers and divers hit the Caribbean coast.

➔ Party-goers will prefer August and September when, despite the imminent hurricane season, the Cienfuegos carnival and the biannual Benny Moré festival, respectively, can be enjoyed.

➔ Up at El Nicho in the Sierra del Escambray, travel is tougher in the wet season (August to October) due to difficult road conditions.

History

The first settlers in the Cienfuegos area were Taínos, who called their fledgling principality Cacicazgo de Jagua – a native term for 'beauty'. In 1494 Columbus 'discovered' the Bahía de Cienfuegos (Cuba's third-largest bay, with a surface area of 88 sq km) on his second voyage to the New World, and 14 years later Sebastián de Ocampo stopped by during his pioneering circumnavigation of the island. He liked the bay so much he built a house there.

The pirates followed the explorers: during the 16th and 17th centuries buccaneering raids got so bad the Spanish built a bayside fort, the imposing Castillo de Jagua – one of the most important military structures in Cuba.

CIENFUEGOS

POP 165,113

La ciudad que más me gusta a mí (the city I like the best) singer Benny Moré once said of his home city in the song 'Cienfuegos.' He wasn't the settlement's only cheerleader. Cuba's so-called Perla del Sur (Pearl of the South) has long seduced travelers from around the island with its elegance, enlightened French spirit and feisty Caribbean panache. If Cuba has a Paris, this is most definitely it.

Arranged around the country's most spectacular natural bay, Cienfuegos is a nautical city with an enviable waterside setting. Founded in 1819, it's one of Cuba's newest settlements, but also one of its most architecturally interesting, a factor that earned it a Unesco World Heritage Site listing in 2005. Geographically, the city is split into two distinct parts: the colonnaded central zone with its elegant Paseo del Prado (commonly shortened to Prado) and Parque Martí; and Punta Gorda, a thin knife of land slicing into the bay with a clutch of eclectic early-20th-century palaces, including some of Cuba's prettiest buildings.

While much of Cuba is visibly reeling from the country's economic woes, Cienfuegos seems to positively glitter. It's not just Unesco money filtering through. The industry ringing the far side of the Bahía de Cienfuegos – a shipyard, the bastion of Cuba's shrimp-fishing fleet, a thermoelectric plant and a petrochemical hub – constitutes some of the country's most important. This, together with a pervading sense of tranquility resonating through

spruced-up colonial streets refreshingly free of *jineteros* (touts) and a revitalizing seaside vibe make the city as alluring today as Moré found it 60 years ago.

History

Cienfuegos was founded in 1819 by a pioneering French émigré from Louisiana named Don Louis D'Clouet. Sponsoring a scheme to increase the population of whites on the island, D'Clouet invited 40 families from New Orleans and Philadelphia, and Bordeaux in France to establish a fledgling settlement known initially as Fernandina de Jagua. Despite having their initial camp destroyed by a hurricane in 1821, the unperturbed French settlers rebuilt their homes and – suspicious, perhaps, that their first name had brought them bad luck – rechristened the city Cienfuegos after the then governor of Cuba.

With the arrival of the railway in 1850 and the drift west of Cuban sugar growers after the War of Independence (1868–78), Cienfuegos' fortunes blossomed, and local merchants pumped their wealth into a dazzling array of eclectic architecture that harked back to the neoclassicism of their French forefathers.

D-day in Cienfuegos' history came on 5 September 1957 when officers at the local naval base staged a revolt against the Batista dictatorship. The uprising was brutally crushed but it sealed the city's place in revolutionary history.

Modern-day Cienfuegos retains a plusher look than many of its urban counterparts. And now with some much-needed Unesco money on board, as well as the city's growing industrial clout, the future for Cienfuegos and its fine array of 19th-century architecture looks bright.

Sights

Parque José Martí

Arco de Triunfo   LANDMARK
(Map p238; Calle 25, btwn Avs 56 & 54) The Arch of Triumph on the western edge of Cienfuegos' serene central park catapults the plaza into the unique category: there is no other building of its kind in Cuba. Dedicated to Cuban independence, the Francophile monument ushers you through its gilded gateway toward a marble statue of revolutionary and philosopher José Martí.

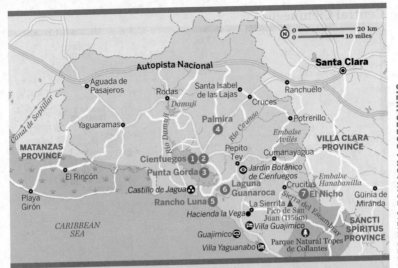

Cienfuegos Province Highlights

1 Strolling amid eclectic 19th-century architecture in gorgeous **Parque José Martí** (p244) in the capital.

2 Capitalizing on one of the country's best provincial dining scenes in **Cienfuegos** (p244) – and feasting!

3 Staying in an amazing casa particular in Cienfuegos' classic neighborhood of **Punta Gorda** (p240).

4 Tracking the legends of the Santería religion in **Palmira** (p251).

5 Basking at, or diving off, the beach in **Rancho Luna** (p248).

6 Spotting pink flamingos and pelicans at little-visited **Laguna Guanaroca** (p250).

7 Hiking to bracing **El Nicho** (p250) and cooling down underneath an invigorating waterfall.

Catedral de la Purísima Concepción Church CHURCH

(Map p238; Av 56 No 2902; ⏱7am-noon Mon-Fri) Opposite the park, the cathedral dates from 1869 and is distinguished by its wonderful French stained-glass windows. Chinese writing discovered on columns during the on-going restoration is thought to date from the 1870s. The cathedral is nearly always open; you can also join the faithful for a service (7:30am weekdays, 10am Sundays).

★Teatro Tomás Terry THEATER

(Map p238; ☎43-51-33-61, 43-55-17-72; Av 56 No 270, btwn Calles 27 & 29; tours CUC$2; ⏱9am-6pm) Sharing French and Italian influences, this theater on the northern side of Parque José Martí is grand from the outside (look for the gold-leafed mosaics on the front facade), but even grander within. Built between 1887 and 1889 to honor Venezuelan industrialist Tomás Terry, the 950-seat auditorium is embellished with Carrara marble, hand-carved Cuban hardwoods and whimsical ceiling frescoes.

In 1895 the theater opened with a performance of Verdi's *Aida* and it has witnessed numerous landmarks in Cuban music, as well as performances by the likes of Enrico Caruso and Anna Pavlova, and pulsates with plays and concerts still.

Colegio San Lorenzo HISTORIC BUILDING

(Map p238; cnr Av 56 & Calle 29) On the east side of Teatro Café Tomás, this building with its striking colonnaded facade was constructed during the 1920s with funds left by wealthy city patron Nicolás Salvador Acea whose name also graces one of the city's cemeteries. Admire from the outside only.

★Museo Provincial MUSEUM

(Map p238; cnr Av 54 & Calle 27; admission CUC$2; ⏱10am-6pm Tue-Sat, 9am-1pm Sun) The main

Central Cienfuegos

attraction on the south side of Parque José Martí, this dignified museum proffers a microcosm of Cienfuegos' history. The frilly furnishings of refined 19th-century French-Cuban society form the majority of displays, but there's also a rare insight into the province's prehistory. Go upstairs for the highlight: the mirrored work *Como ven los hombres de la guerra,* via which you get a close-up on the room's incredible ceiling murals.

Palacio de Gobierno   HISTORIC BUILDING
(Map p238; Av 54, btwn Calles 27 & 29) Most of Parque Martí's south side is dominated by this grandiose building where the provincial government (Poder Popular Provincial) holds forth. The Palacio de Gobierno doesn't allow visitors, but you can steal a look at the palatial main staircase through the front door.

Casa de la Cultura Benjamin Duarte   HISTORIC BUILDING
(Map p238; Calle 25 No 5401; ⊙ 8:30am-midnight) FREE On the western side of Parque Martí, this is the former Palacio de Ferrer (1918), a riveting neoclassical building with Italian marble floors and – most noticeably – a rooftop cupola equipped with a wrought-iron staircase. The downside? The stairs up are invariably closed – and otherwise there's only dingy art within.

Casa del Fundador   HISTORIC BUILDING
(Map p238; cnr Calle 29 & Av 54) On the park's southeastern corner stands the city's oldest building, once the residence of city founder Louis D'Clouet and now a souvenir store. **El Bulevar** (Map p238; Av 54), Cienfuegos' quintessential shopping street, heads east from here to link up with the Paseo del Prado.

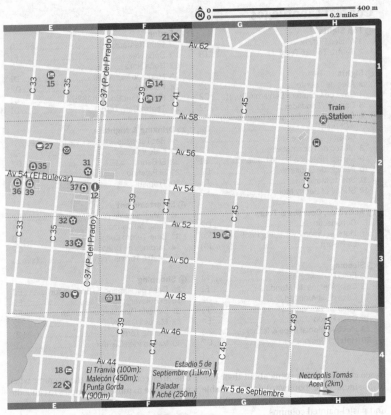

West of Parque José Martí

Museo Histórico Naval Nacional   MUSEUM
(Map p238; cnr Av 60 & Calle 21; admission CUC$2; ⊗8am-5pm Tue-Sun) Across the railway tracks five blocks northwest of Parque Martí is the eye-catching location of this rose-pink museum, dating from 1933. It's housed in the former headquarters of the Distrito Naval del Sur, and approached by a wide drive flanked with armaments dating from different eras. It was here in September 1957 that a group of sailors and civilians staged an unsuccessful uprising against the Batista government. The revolt is the central theme of the museum. The ramparts offer great bay views.

★**Cementerio la Reina**   CEMETERY
(☏43-52-15-89; cnr Av 50 & Calle 7; ⊗8am-5pm) A listed national monument, the city's oldest cemetery was founded in 1837, and is lined with the graves of Spanish soldiers who died in the Wars of Independence. La Reina is the only cemetery in Cuba where bodies are interred above ground (in the walls) due to the high groundwater levels. It's an evocative place if you're into graveyards (tours are available). Look for the marble statue called Bella Durmiente: a tribute to a 24-year-old woman who died in 1907 of a broken heart.

Approach is via Av 50: a long, hot walk or horse-cart ride via the sorry-looking collection of trains passing as the **Museo de Locomotivas** (Map p238; Calle 19).

Paseo del Prado & the Malecón

Stately Paseo del Prado (Calle 37), stretching from the Río el Inglés in the north to Punta Gorda in the south, is the longest street of its kind in Cuba and a great place

Central Cienfuegos

◎ Top Sights
1 Museo Provincial.................................D2
2 Teatro Tomás Terry D1

◎ Sights
3 Arco de Triunfo C2
4 Casa de la Cultura Benjamin Duarte....C2
5 Casa del Fundador.............................D2
6 Catedral de la Purísima Concepción
   Church..D2
7 Colegio San Lorenzo D2
8 Museo de Locomotivas.......................B2
9 Museo Histórico Naval Nacional...........B1
10 Palacio de Gobierno D2
11 Sports Museum F3
12 Statue of Benny Moré.........................E2

◎ Activities, Courses & Tours
13 Cubanacán..D2
   Hotel la Unión Swimming Pool....(see 20)
   La Bolera ....(see 30)

◎ Sleeping
14 Bella Perla Marina..............................F1
15 Casa Amigos del Mundo......................E1
16 Casa de la Amistad.............................D2
17 Casa las Golondrinas..........................F1
18 Casa Prado..E4
19 Hostal Colonial Pepe & Isabel..............G3
20 Hotel la Unión....................................D2

◎ Eating
   1869 Restaurant......................(see 20)
21 Doña Neli..F1
22 Doña Nora E4
23 Mercado Municipal..............................D1
24 Polinesio..D2
25 Restaurant Bouyón 1825......................C1
26 Teatro Café Terry D1

◎ Drinking & Nightlife
   Bar Terrazas ....(see 20)
27 Café Ven...E2
28 El Benny..D2
29 El Palatino...D2
30 Tropisur...E3

◎ Entertainment
31 Café Cantante Benny Moré....................E2
32 Casa del Danzón.................................E3
33 Cine-Teatro Luisa................................E3
34 Jardines de Uneac...............................C2
   Teatro Tomás Terry.......................(see 2)

◎ Shopping
35 Casa del Habano 'El Embajador' E2
36 El Bulevar...E2
37 Librería Dionisio San Román E2
38 Maroya Gallery....................................C2
   Tienda Terry................................(see 2)
39 Variedades Cienfuegos E2

to see *cienfuegueños* going about their daily business. The boulevard is a veritable smorgasbord of fine neoclassical buildings and pastel-painted columns.

Statue of Benny Moré   MONUMENT
(Map p238; cnr Av 54 & Calle 37) Before you hit the Malecón, at the intersection of Av 54 and the Paseo del Prado you can pay your respects to this life-size likeness of the musician with his trademark cane.

Sports Museum   MUSEUM
(Map p238; cnr Calle 39 & Av 48) FREE South of the Benny Moré statue, this little museum (undergoing renovation, but due to reopen), bizarrely sequestered at the back of a gym, is largely devoted to local boxing hero Julio González Valladores, who brought back a gold medal from the 1996 Atlanta Olympics.

Malecón   STREET
(Map p242) Keep heading south on Paseo del Prado and the street becomes the Malecón as it cuts alongside one of the world's finest natural bays, offering exquisite vistas. Like all sea drives (Havana's being the archetype),

this area comes alive in the evening when poets come to muse and couples to canoodle.

◎ Punta Gorda

When the Malecón sea wall runs out, you will know you have landed in Punta Gorda, Cienfuegos' old upper-class neighborhood, characterized by its bright clapboard homes and turreted palaces. Highlighting a 1920s penchant for grandiosity are the cupola-topped **Palacio Azul** (now the Hostal Palacio Azul) and the **Club Cienfuegos**, once an exclusive yacht club and still offering nautical excursions aplenty. Nearby, an inventive **Parque de Esculturas** (Map p242) throws some innovative modern sculpture into the mix.

Palacio de Valle   HISTORIC BUILDING
(Map p242; Calle 37, btwn Avs 0 & 2; ◎9:30am-11pm) The ultimate in kitsch comes near the end of Calle 37 when, with a sharp intake of breath, you'll stumble upon the *Arabian Nights*–like Palacio de Valle. Built in 1917 by Acisclo del Valle Blanco, a Spaniard from Asturias, the structure resembles an outrageously ornate Moroccan casbah.

Batista planned to convert this colorful riot of tiles, turrets and stucco into a casino, but today it's an (aspiring) upscale restaurant with an inviting terrace bar.

Centro Recreativo la Punta   PARK
(Map p242; ⊙9am-10pm Sun-Fri, to midnight Sat) Lovers come to watch the sunset amid sea-framed greenery at the gazebo on the extreme southern tip of this park. The bar is also oddly popular with local police officers.

⊙ East of City Center

Necrópolis Tomás Acea   CEMETERY
(☑43-52-52-57; Carretera de Rancho Luna Km 2; admission CUC$1; ⊙8am-5pm) One of two national monument–listed resting places in Cienfuegos, the Acea is classed as a 'garden cemetery' and is entered through a huge neoclassical pavilion (1926) flanked by 64 Doric columns modeled on the Parthenon in Greece. This cemetery contains a monument to the marine martyrs who died during the abortive 1957 Cienfuegos naval uprising. It's 2km east of the city center along Av 5 de Septiembre.

🏃 Activities

Marlin Marina Cienfuegos   FISHING, SAILING
(Map p242; ☑43-55-12-41; www.nauticamarlin. com; Calle 35, btwn Avs 6 & 8; ⊙11am-8:45pm) Hook up with this 36-berth marina a few blocks north of Hotel Jagua to arrange deep-sea fishing trips. Prices start at CUC$200 for four people for four hours. Multiday trips start at CUC$400/3900 for one night/week (gear and crew included), depending on the boat. Local bay excursions are also available (CUC$12 to CUC$16), including a Castillo de Jagua one. Book through Cubatur (p248)/Cubanacán (p241).

Base Náutica Club Cienfuegos   WATER SPORTS
(Map p242; ☑43-52-65-10; Calle 35, btwn Avs 10 & 12; ⊙10am-6pm) At this nautical base at the Club Cienfuegos you can organize all manner of aquatic activities from boat trips to kayaking and windsurfing, starting from CUC$12 per person. It also has a tennis court (there is no fence so get used to lots of ball retrieving) and an amusement center with bumper cars and video games. The swimming pool costs CUC$8 per person.

La Bolera   BOWLING
(Map p238; Calle 37, btwn Avs 46 & 48; per hr CUC$1-2; ⊙11am-2am) If you're into gimmick-free billiards or bowling, this is your hangout. It also has an ice-cream parlor and occasional live music.

Hotel la Unión Swimming Pool   SWIMMING
(Map p238; cnr Calle 31 & Av 54; nonguest pool access CUC$10) Even if you're a nonguest, you can use the beautiful Italianate pool at Hotel la Unión.

🎓 Courses

Universidad de Cienfuegos   LANGUAGE COURSE
(☑43-52-15-21; www.ucf.edu.cu; Carretera las Rodas Km 4, Cuatro Caminos) Offers Spanish courses ranging from beginner to advanced. The courses last one month and incorporate 64 hours of study (CUC$300). A new course starts each month. Check the website for details.

☞ Tours

Cubanacán   TOUR
(Map p238; ☑43-55-16-80; Av 54, btwn Calles 29 & 31) Cubanacán's helpful Cienfuegos office organizes interesting local tours, including bay boat trips (CUC$12), the ever-popular El Nicho excursion (CUC$35), plus other hard-to-reach places such as Jardín Botánico de Cienfuegos (from CUC$10) and the local cigar factory (CUC$5). Other possible excursions include diving at Rancho Luna, Península de Zapata and the new 'El Purial' trip to some little-known waterfalls and hikes at El Güije.

🎊 Festivals & Events

Alongside the big celebrations of Carnaval and Benny Moré music festival, in April Cienfuegos celebrates the foundation of the city on April 22, 1819 with various cultural events.

**Benny Moré International
Music Festival**   MUSIC
(⊙Aug) This festival remembers the province's biggest all-time hero, singer Benny Moré. Held in August on odd-numbered years, both in town and in nearby Santa Isabel de las Lajas.

Carnaval   CULTURAL
Cienfuegos' big street party, held in August.

🛏 Sleeping

Cienfuegos has some quality private rooms – your best bet for budget accommodations. Those at Punta Gorda are more removed, generally more atmospheric and pricier. There are excellent hotels in Cienfuegos proper and in Punta Gorda.

Punta Gorda

Central Cienfuegos

★ Bella Perla Marina
CASA PARTICULAR **$**

(Map p238; ☑43-51-89-91; bellaperlamarina@
yahoo.es; Calle 39 No 5818, cnr Av 60; r/ste
CUC$30/50; P❄@) Long popular for its city
center location and warm hospitality, Bella
Perla might well be Cuba's first 'boutique'
casa particular. The house, with two standard
rooms and a stunning rooftop suite, has taken
on fortress-like dimensions since a gorgeous
two-level, plant-filled terrace has crowned
everything off. Now you can round off your
evening meal with a game of billiards, too.

Hostal Colonial Pepe
& Isabel
CASA PARTICULAR **$**

(Map p238; ☑43-51-82-76; hostalcolonialisapepe@
gmail.com; Av 52 No 4318, btwn Calles 43 & 45; r
CUC$25; ❄) Ex-teacher Pepe greets you with
a smile as wide as the Bahía de Cienfuegos at
his deceptively large colonial house, which in-

corporates five modern rooms set around two
long, narrow upstairs and downstairs terraces. Each room has a queen bed and an extra
pull-down single Murphy bed, and two come
with additional living room or kitchen space.

Casa las Golondrinas
CASA PARTICULAR **$**

(Map p238; ☑43-51-57-88; Calle 39, btwn Avs 58
& 60; r CUC$25; ❄) Run by a doctor and his
wife, this is a gorgeous renovated colonial
house with two ample rooms. There's a lot of
TLC in the restoration, from the colonnaded
front room to the long, plant-bedecked roof
terrace.

Casa Prado
CASA PARTICULAR **$**

(Map p238; ☑43-52-89-66-13, 55-54-84; Calle 37
No 4235, btwn Avs 42 & 44; r CUC$25; ❄) This
has established itself as one of the very
best casas in the city center. The two high-
ceilinged rooms are replete with period furniture and a twisting staircase ascends to a
terrace with phenomenal city views. The lo-

Punta Gorda

◎ **Sights**
1 Centro Recreativo la Punta B4
2 Malecón B2
3 Palacio de Valle B3
  Parque de Esculturas .... (see 4)

◎ **Activities, Courses & Tours**
  Base Náutica Club Cienfuegos ..... (see 11)
4 Marlin Marina Cienfuegos B2

◎ **Sleeping**
5 Angel y Isabel B4
6 Hostal Palacio Azul B2
7 Hotel Jagua B3
8 Perla del Mar B3
9 Villa Lagarto – Maylin & Tony B4

10 Vista Al Mar B3

◎ **Eating**
  Bar Terraza .... (see 11)
11 Club Cienfuegos B2
  El Marinero .... (see 11)
12 Finca del Mar B1
  Palacio de Valle .... (see 3)
  Restaurante Café
    Cienfuegos .... (see 11)
  Restaurante Villa Lagarto .... (see 9)

◎ **Entertainment**
  Cabaret Guanaroca .... (see 7)
13 Estadio 5 de Septiembre D1
14 Patio de ARTex B1

cation is great too: poised on Prado halfway between the city center and the Malecón.

Summon forth your visions of haughty colonial elegance and you'll arrive prepared.

Casa de la Amistad CASA PARTICULAR $
(Map p238; 43-51-61-43; casaamistad@correocuba.cu; Av 56 No 2927, btwn Calles 29 & 31; r CUC$25; P✳) Friendship's the word in this venerable colonial house stuffed full of family heirlooms just off Parque Martí. Legendary food includes the exotic Cola chicken (yes, *pollo* cooked in the 'real thing'). Chatty hosts Armando and Leonor offer two wonderful, well-kept rooms and a lovely roof terrace.

Casa Amigos del Mundo CASA PARTICULAR $
(Map p238; 43-55-55-34; Av 60, btwn Calles 33 & 35; r CUC$25) The two ground-floor rooms are set a long way back from the road here, making them some of the quietest in central Cienfuegos, and are complemented by an inviting, newly completed roof terrace.

Hotel la Unión BOUTIQUE HOTEL $$$
(Map p238; 43-55-10-20; www.hotellaunion-cuba.com; cnr Calle 31 & Av 54; s/d CUC$88/143; ✳@≋) Barcelona, Naples, Paris? There are echoes of all these cities in this plush, colonial-style hotel with its European aspirations and splendid Italianate pool, fit for a Roman emperor. Tucked away in a maze of marble pillars, antique furnishings and two tranquil inner courtyards are 46 well-furnished rooms with balconies either overlooking the street or a mosaic-lined patio.

You'll also find a gym, Jacuzzi and local art gallery. Service is refreshingly efficient: there's an airy roof terrace that showcases live salsa and a well-regarded restaurant.

🏠 Punta Gorda

Villa Lagarto – Maylin & Tony CASA PARTICULAR $
(Map p242; 43-51-99-66; Calle 35 No 4B, btwn Avs 0 & Litoral; r CUC$35-45; ✳≋) Long a leading player in Cuba's casa particular scene, the Lagarto rents out three rooms cocooned on a delightful terrace, all with king-size beds, hammocks and glinting views of the bay. Welcome cocktails greet new guests. If it's full, they'll recommend Casa Los Delfines or Casa Amarilla, both next door. It's also home to the excellent Restaurante Villa Lagarto.

Angel y Isabel CASA PARTICULAR $
(Map p242; 43-51-15-19; Calle 35 No 24, btwn Av s0 & Litoral; r CUC$35) One of many vast abodes on that coveted mansion-studded final stretch of Punta Gorda. At the back of the turreted main house are three rooms facing on to a patio that leads down to the sea. Good for watching sunrises.

Vista Al Mar CASA PARTICULAR $
(Map p242; 43-51-83-78; www.vistaalmarcuba.com; Calle 37 No 210, btwn Avs 2 & 4; r CUC$25-30; P✳) It really is a *vista al mar* (sea view) – in fact, this highly professional casa has even got its own private scoop of beach out back with hammocks.

Hostal Palacio Azul HOTEL $$
(Map p242; 43-58-28-28; Calle 37 No 201, btwn Avs 12 & 14; s CUC$63-105, d CUC$83-145; P✳@) A palace posing as a hotel rather than a hotel posing as a palace, the Palacio Azul was one of the first big buildings to grace Punta Gorda on its construction in 1921. Its seven

CIENFUEGOS' FRENCH-INSPIRED ARCHITECTURE

C'est vrai, the elegant bay-side city of Cienfuegos is Cuba's most Gallic corner. Its innate Frenchness is best exemplified not in its cuisine, where rice and beans still hold sway over *bœuf à la Bourguignonne*, but in its harmonious neoclassical architecture. With its wide, paved streets laid out in an almost perfect grid, Cienfuegos' enlightened 19th-century settlers sought to quash slums, promote hygiene and maximize public space using a system of urban planning later adopted by Baron Haussmann in Paris in the 1850s and '60s. Porches, pillars and columns are the city's most arresting architectural features, with its broad Parisian-style main avenue (Prado) which runs north–south for over 3km embellished with neat lines of well-proportioned colonnaded facades painted in an array of pastel colors.

Although founded by French émigrés in 1819, most of Cienfuegos' surviving neoclassical buildings date from between 1850 and 1910. By the early 20th century, eclectic features had begun to seep into the architecture. One of the first to break the mold was the Palacio Ferrer (now Casa de la Cultura Benjamin Duarte) in Parque José Martí, built in 1917, whose uncharacteristically decorative cupola started a craze for eye-catching rooftop lookouts.

The flamboyance continued in the 1920s and '30s in the upscale Punta Gorda peninsula, where filthy-rich sugar merchants invested their profits in ever more ostentatious mansions, turning the neighborhood into a mini-Miami. You can track the evolution as you head south on Calle 37 past the regal Palacio Azul and the wedding-cake Club Cienfuegos to the baroque-meets-Moorish Palacio de Valle, possibly Cuba's most riotously eclectic building.

Cienfuegos' city center was declared a World Heritage Site by Unesco in 2005 for being 'an outstanding example of an architectural ensemble representing the new ideas of modernity, hygiene and order in urban planning' in Latin America. Money has since gone into livening up the main square, Parque José Martí, and its environs where various interpretive signboards pinpoint the most important buildings.

renovated rooms are named after flowers and sparkle with plenty of prerevolutionary character.

You'll find an intimate on-site restaurant called El Chelo and an eye-catching rooftop cupola with splendid views.

Perla del Mar
BOUTIQUE HOTEL **$$$**

(Map p242; ☑ 43-55-10-03; Calle 37, btwn Avs 0 & 2; s/d/tr CUC$90/150/210; ❄ @) Opened in September 2012, Perla del Mar takes the 'historical boutique' hotel theme of the nearby Palacio Azul and updates it to the 1950s. The nine rooms have a sleek modernist feel, and two alfresco Jacuzzis are invitingly positioned overlooking the bay. Stairs lead up to a made-for-sunbathing terrace.

Next door the equally boutique-y **Casa Verde** offers eight fin-de-siècle rooms for the same prices.

Hotel Jagua
HOTEL **$$$**

(Map p242; ☑ 43-55-10-03; Calle 37 No 1; s/d CUC$80/130; 🅿 ❄ @ ☎) It's not clear what Batista's brother had in mind when he erected this modern concrete giant on Punta Gorda in the 1950s, though making money was probably the prime motivation. Still, the Jagua is a jolly good hotel – airy and surprisingly plush. Upper rooms (there are seven floors) are best.

Eating

Cienfuegos has some truly memorable dining options, particularly on Punta Gorda.

Central Cienfuegos

Teatro Café Terry
CAFE **$**

(Map p238; Av 56 No 2703, btwn Calles 27 & 29; snacks CUC$1-5; ⊙9am-10pm) Cafe, souvenir stall and nightly music venue, this small space wedged between the Teatro Tomás Terry and the neoclassical Colegio San Lorenzo is the most atmospheric place to flop down and observe the morning exercisers in Parque José Martí. The flower canopy-covered patio to the side reveals its true personality in the evenings with great live music ranging from *trova* (traditional music) to jazz.

Polinesio SANDWICHES **$**
(Map p238; Calle 29, btwn Calles 54 & 56; mains CUC$5-12; ⊙11am-10pm) Right under the portals in Parque Jose Martí, this is a salubrious setting for a cold beer or snack.

★ **Paladar Aché** SEAFOOD, INTERNATIONAL **$$**
(☑43-52-61-73; Av 38, btwn Calles 41 & 43; mains CUC$10-15; ⊙noon-10.30pm Mon-Sat) One of only two surviving private restaurants from the austere 1990s, Aché has taken on the young new opposition and is still abreast of the pack. Interesting decor includes caged birds, the seven dwarfs re-created as garden gnomes and a wall relief map of Cienfuegos' cultural icons. Local prawns headline the comprehensive menu.

Restaurant Bouyón 1825 PARRILLA **$$**
(Map p238; ☑43-51-73-76; Calle 25 No 5605; mains around CUC$10; ⊙11am-11pm) Handily situated just off the main square, this private restaurant specializes in meat cooked *a la parrillada* (on the barbecue). Avowed carnivores will revel in the hearty mixed grill which includes four different meats and is complemented by some robust Chilean reds.

El Tranvia INTERNATIONAL **$$**
(cnr Calle 37 & Av 40; mains CUC$10-12; ⊙noon-11pm) Eight Cuban cities, including Cienfuegos, once had tram systems. The ambitious Tranvia has taken this almost forgotten segment of Cienfueguero history and bottled it in a restaurant. The theme extends to the waiters (dressed as station guards), grainy historical photos and vintage bar (incorporating part of an old carriage). Service, however, is barely chugging along at all and food is only station standard.

Doña Nora INTERNATIONAL **$$**
(Map p238; ☑43-52-33-31; Calle 37, btwn Avs 42 & 44; mains around CUC$10; ⊙8am-3pm & 6-11pm) One floor up is a long way in these chunky, colonial Paseo del Prado houses, so the views from this busy little place, should you be lucky enough to bag a table by the balcony, are great for people-watching. Food is outstanding here (mmm, rabbit in wine sauce) and the joint fills up fast.

1869 Restaurant INTERNATIONAL **$$**
(Map p238; cnr Av 54 & Calle 31; mains CUC$10; ⊙7:30-9am, noon-2pm & 6-10pm) One of Cienfuegos' most upmarket city-center dining experiences can be found in this elegant restaurant in La Unión hotel. Although the food doesn't quite match the lush furnishings, a varied international menu makes a welcome change from rice/beans/pork staples elsewhere.

Self-Catering
Mercado Municipal MARKET
(Map p238; Calle 31 No 5805, btwn Avs 58 & 60) Groceries in pesos for picnickers and self-caterers.

Doña Neli BAKERY
(Map p238; cnr Calle 41 & Av 62; ⊙10am-10pm) Provides breakfast goodies (pastries, bread, cakes) in convertibles.

✖ Punta Gorda

Club Cienfuegos SEAFOOD, INTERNATIONAL **$$**
(Map p242; ☑43-51-28-91; Calle 37, btwn Avs 10 & 12; ⊙noon-10:30pm) With a setting as good as this grand old sports-club-cum-restaurant, it's easy for the food to fall short, which it often does. But there are plenty of options here: **Bar Terraza** (Map p242; ⊙noon-11pm) for cocktails and beer, **El Marinero** (Map p242; ⊙noon-4pm), a smart sea-level establishment for snacks and light lunches; and the top-floor **Restaurante Café Cienfuegos** (Map p242; meals CUC$10-15; ⊙3-11pm), a more refined, adventurous place for a steak or fine paella.

The yacht-club vibe and wraparound dining terraces make for a memorable experience here.

Palacio de Valle SEAFOOD, CARIBBEAN **$$**
(Map p242; cnr Calle 37 & Av 2; mains CUC$7-12; ⊙10am-10pm) The food doesn't have as many decorative flourishes as the eclectic architecture but the setting is so unique it would be a shame to miss it. Seafood dominates the menu downstairs; if you aren't enthralled, use the rooftop bar here for a pre-dinner cocktail or post-dinner cigar.

★ **Finca del Mar** SEAFOOD **$$$**
(Map p242; Calle 35, btwn Avs 16 & 18; mains CUC$9-18; ⊙noon-midnight) Any coastal city in the world would wish for a beautiful seafood restaurant like this, where a review can't cover nearly enough of the things it excels at. But let's try: setting, service, generosity, lobster, wine, desserts, espresso.

Restaurante Villa Lagarto INTERNATIONAL **$$$**
(Map p242; ☑43-51-99-66; Calle 35 No 4B, btwn Av 0 & Litoral; mains CUC$10-18) The truly wondrous bayside setting is emulated by the food and made even more memorable by

some of the fastest yet most discreet service you'll see in Cuba. With its excellent prawns, lobster and roast pork, Lagarto is at the vanguard of Cuba's emerging private dining sector and could hold its own in Miami – easily!

 Drinking & Nightlife

Excellent drinking perches (especially at sunset) can be found at Club Cienfuegos and the upstairs bar of the Palacio de Valle.

Bar Terrazas
BAR

(Map p238; cnr Av 54 & Calle 31; ⏱10am-midnight) Re-create the dignified days of old with a mojito upstairs at the Hotel la Unión; live music starts at 10pm.

Café Ven
CAFE

(Map p238; Av 56, btwn Calles 33 & 35; ⏱8am-8pm) Strong, thick coffee for trained Cuban palates, or weak lattes for those reared on Starbucks, plus some ultra-sweet cakes.

El Benny
CLUB

(Map p238; Av 54 No 2907, btwn Calles 29 & 31; admission per couple CUC$8; ⏱10pm-3am Tue-Sun) It's difficult to say what the Barbarian of Rhythm, Benny Moré, would have made of this disco-club named in his honor. Bring your dancing shoes, stock up on the rum and Cokes, and come prepared for music that's more techno than mambo.

El Palatino
BAR

(Map p238; Av 54 No 2514; ⏱noon-midnight) Liquid lunches were invented with El Palatino in mind – a dark-wood bar set in one of the city's oldest buildings on the southern side of Parque Martí. Impromptu jazz sets sometimes erupt, but prepare to be hit up for payment at the end of song number three.

Tropisur
CLUB

(Map p238; cnr Calle 37 & Av 48; admission CUC$2; ⏱from 9:30pm Thu-Sun) A fiesty open-air venue on the Prado with a traditional Cuban vibe. Renowned for its cabaret.

 Entertainment

★Patio de ARTex
LIVE MUSIC

(Map p242; cnr Calle 35 & Av 16; ⏱6pm-2am) A highly recommendable and positively heaving patio in Punta Gorda where you can catch *son* (Cuba's popular music), salsa, *trova* and a touch of Benny Moré nostalgia live in the evenings as you mingle with true *cienfuegueños*. Do El Benny on Thursday and this on Friday night.

Teatro Tomás Terry
LIVE MUSIC, THEATER

(Map p238; ☑43-51-33-61, 43-55-17-72; Av 56 No 270, btwn Calles 27 & 29; ⏱10pm-late) Best theater in Cuba? The Tomás Terry is certainly a contender. The building is worth a visit in its own right, but you'll really get to appreciate this architectural showpiece if you come for a concert or play; the box office is open 11am to 3pm daily and 90 minutes before show time.

Jardines de Uneac
LIVE MUSIC

(Map p238; Calle 25 No 5413, btwn Avs 54 & 56; admission CUC$2; ⏱10am-2am) Uneac's a good bet in any Cuban city for live music in laid-back environs. Here it's quite possibly Cienfuegos' best venue, with an outdoor patio hosting Afro-Cuban *peñas* (musical performances), *trova* and top local bands such as the perennially popular Los Novos.

Café Cantante Benny Moré
LIVE MUSIC

(Map p238; cnr Av 54 & Calle 37; ⏱6pm-2am) This is where you might get some suave Benny tunes, especially after hours. A tatty restaurant by day, this place blacks out the blemishes in the evenings when it mixes up mean cocktails and tunes into live traditional music.

Cabaret Guanaroca
CABARET

(Map p242; Calle 37 No 1; admission CUC$5; ⏱9:30pm till late Tue-Fri, from 10pm Sat) In Hotel Jagua, the Guanaroca offers a professional tourist-orientated cabaret extravaganza.

Casa del Danzón
TRADITIONAL DANCE

(Map p238; Av 52, btwn Calles 35 & 37; ⏱from 9pm Fri & Sat, 2-7pm Sun) FREE *Danzón* (traditional Cuban ballroom dance) and boleras: good fun!

Estadio 5 de Septiembre
SPORTS

(Map p242; ☑43-51-36-44; Av 20, btwn Calles 45 & 55) From October to April, the provincial baseball team – nicknamed Los Elefantes – plays matches here. Its best-ever national series finish was fourth in 1979.

Cine-Teatro Luisa
CINEMA

(Map p238; Calle 37 No 5001) The most modern of the city's three cinemas.

 Shopping

Cienfuegos' main drag – known officially as Av 54, but colloquially as **El Bulevar** – is an archetypal Cuban shopping street with not a chain store in sight. The best traffic-free stretch runs from Calle 37 (Paseo del Prado) to Parque José Martí, full of shops of all shapes and sizes.

BENNY MORÉ

No one singer encapsulates the gamut of Cuban music more eloquently than Bartolomé 'Benny' Moré. A great-great-grandson of a king of the Congo, Moré was born in the small village of Santa Isabel de las Lajas in Cienfuegos province in 1919. He gravitated to Havana in 1936 where he earned a precarious living selling damaged fruit on the streets. He then played and sang in the smoky bars and restaurants of Habana Vieja's tough dockside neighborhood, where he made just enough money to get by.

His first big break came in 1943 when his velvety voice and pitch-perfect delivery won him first prize in a local radio singing competition and landed him a regular job as lead vocalist for a Havana-based mariachi band called the Cauto Quartet.

His meteoric rise was confirmed two years later when, while singing at a regular gig in Havana's El Temple bar, he was spotted by Siro Rodríguez of the famed Trío Matamoros, then Cuba's biggest son-bolero band. Rodríguez was so impressed that he asked Moré to join the band as lead vocalist for an imminent tour of Mexico. In the late 1940s, Mexico City was a proverbial Hollywood for young Spanish-speaking Cuban performers. Moré was signed up by RCA records and his fame spread rapidly.

Moré returned to Cuba in 1950 a star, and was quickly baptized the Prince of Mambo and the Barbarian of Rhythm. In the ensuing years, he invented a brand-new hybrid sound called batanga and put together his own 40-piece backing orchestra, the Banda Gigante. With the Banda, Moré toured Venezuela, Jamaica, Mexico and the US, culminating in a performance at the 1957 Oscars ceremony. But the singer's real passion was always Cuba. Legend has it that whenever Benny performed in Havana's Centro Gallego hundreds of people would fill the parks and streets to hear him sing.

With his multitextured voice and signature scale-sliding glissando, Moré's real talent lay in his ability to adapt and seemingly switch genres at will. As comfortable with a tear-jerking bolero as he was with a hip-gyrating rumba, Moré could convey tenderness, exuberance, emotion and soul, all in the space of five tantalizing minutes. Although he couldn't read music, Moré composed many of his most famous numbers, including 'Bonito y sabroso' and the big hit 'Que bueno baila usted.' When he died in 1963, more than 100,000 people attended his funeral. No one in Cuba has yet been able to fill his shoes.

Moré fans can follow his legend in the settlement of **Santa Isabel de las Lajas**, a few kilometers west of Cruces on the Cienfuegos–Santa Clara road, where there's a small **museum**. Regular buses (local, not Víazul) run to Santa Isabel de las Lajas from Cienfuegos Bus Station.

Check out the **Maroya Gallery** (Map p238; Av 54, btwn Calles 25 & 27; ☺9am-5:30pm Mon-Sat) for folk art, **Variedades Cienfuegos** (Map p238; cnr Av 54 & Calle 33; ☺10am-6pm Mon-Sat) for peso paraphernalia or **Casa del Habano 'El Embajador'** (Map p238; cnr Av 54 & Calle 33; ☺9am-5:30pm Mon-Sat) for cigars.

Tienda Terry (Map p238; Av 56 No 270, btwn Calles 27 & 29; ☺9am-6pm) in Teatro Tomás Terry is a good bet for books and souvenirs; another well-stocked bookstore is **Librería Dionisio San Román** (Map p238; Av 54 No 3526, cnr Calle 37; ☺9am-5:30pm Mon-Sat).

ℹ Information

INTERNET ACCESS & TELEPHONE

Etecsa Telepunto (Calle 31 No 5402, btwn Avs 54 & 56; per hr CUC$4.50; ☺8:30am-7:30pm)

MEDIA

5 de Septiembre The local newspaper comes out on Fridays.

Radio Ciudad del Mar 1350AM and 98.9FM.

MEDICAL SERVICES

Clínica Internacional (☎43-55-16-22; Av 10, btwn Calles 37 & 39, Punta Gorda) Excellent new-ish center catering to foreigners and handling medical (including dental) emergencies, with a 24-hour pharmacy.

Hotel la Unión Pharmacy (☎43-55-10-20; cnr Calle 31 & Av 54; ☺24hr) The pharmacy here is aimed at international tourists.

MONEY

Banco de Crédito y Comercio (Bandec) (cnr Av 56 & Calle 31; ☺9am-5pm Mon-Fri)

Cadeca (Av 56 No 3316, btwn Calles 33 & 35; ☺9am-5pm Mon-Fri) Change cash for convertibles or Cuban pesos.

POST

Post Office (Map p238; Av 56 No 3514, btwn Calles 35 & 37; ☺9am-5pm Mon-Fri)

TRAVEL AGENCIES

Cubatur (☑43-55-12-42; Calle 37 No 5399, btwn Avs 54 & 56; ☺9am-6pm Mon-Sat) Organizes excursions.

Paradiso (☑43-51-18-79; Av 54 No 3301, btwn Calles 33 & 35; ☺9am-6pm Mon-Sat) Most of the local city and surrounds tours for CUC$5 to CUC$16.

❶ Getting There & Away

AIR

Jaime González Airport, 5km northeast of Cienfuegos, receives weekly international flights from Miami and Canada (November to March only). There are no connections to Havana.

BUS

From the **bus station** (Map p238; ☑43-51-57-20, 43-51-81-14; Calle 49, btwn Avs 56 & 58) there are Víazul buses to Havana three times daily (CUC$20, four hours) at 9:30am, 12:25pm and 5:35pm; all call at Playa Girón (CUC$7, 1¼ hours) and Playa Larga (CUC$7, 1¾ hours) en route. Trinidad buses depart five times a day (CUC$6, 1½ hours) at 12:20pm, 1:30pm, 2:45pm, 3:20pm and 5:30pm.

There are also three daily buses to Varadero (CUC$17, 4½ hours) at 10:30am, 4:30pm and 4:40pm, with the afternoon departures also calling at Santa Clara (CUC$6, 1½ hours). The one Viñales (CUC$32, 7¾ hours) departure of the day is at 9:40am and calls at Havana and Pinar del Río (CUC$31, seven hours).

To reach other destinations, you have to connect in Trinidad or Havana. Note that when heading to Trinidad from Cienfuegos, buses originating further west may be full.

Cienfuegos' bus station is clean and well organized. A Víazul office on the lower level (down the stairs and left) issues tickets; for local buses to Rancho Luna, Santa Isabel de las Lajas and Palmira for CUC$1-ish, plus other destinations, check the blackboard on the lower level (down the stairs to the right, where the ticket counters have more queue-ban style waits for service).

TRAIN

The **train station** (☑43-52-54-95; cnr Av 58 & Calle 49; ☺ticket window 8am-3:30pm Mon-Fri, 8-11:30am Sat) is across from the bus station but, with a traveling time to Havana of 10 hours (versus three by bus), you have to be a serious rail geek to want to enter or exit Cienfuegos by the comically slow *ferrocarril*. Trains also trundle to Santa Clara and Sancti Spíritus: check departure times well in advance.

❶ Getting Around

BOAT

A 120-passenger ferry runs to the Castillo de Jagua (CUC$0.50, 40 minutes) from the **Muelle Real** (Map p238; cnr Av 46 & Calle 25). Take note – this is a Cuban commuter boat, not a sunset cruise. Check at the port for current schedules. It's supposed to run at 8am and 1pm. A smaller ferry (CUC$0.50, 15 minutes) also makes frequent runs between the Castillo and Rancho Luna's Hotel Pasacaballo. Last departure from the Castillo is 8pm.

CAR & MOPED

The Servi-Cupet gas station is on Calle 37 at the corner of Av 16 in Punta Gorda. There's another station 5km northeast of Hotel Rancho Luna.

Cubacar rents mostly manual transmission cars and has several branches: **Hotel Rancho Luna** (☑43-54-80-26; Hotel Rancho Luna, Carretera de Rancho Luna Km 16); **Hotel la Unión** (☑43-55-16-45; Hotel la Unión, cnr Av 54 & Calle 31); **Casa Verde** (☑43-55-20-14; Casa Verde, cnr Calle 37 & Av 2).

Club Cienfuegos (☑43-52-65-10; Calle 37, btwn Avs 10 & 12) Hires mopeds for CUC$25 per day.

HORSE CART

Horse carts and bici-taxis ply Calle 37 charging Cubans one peso a ride and foreigners CUC$1 (Spanish speakers might be able to 'pass' and pay a peso). It's a pleasant way to travel between town, Punta Gorda and the cemeteries.

TAXI

There are plenty of cabs in Cienfuegos. Most hang around outside Hotel Jagua and Hotel la Unión or linger around the bus station. Bici-taxis patrol the Malecón and will ferry you to/from Punta Gorda for about CUC$3. If you have no luck at these spots, phone **Cubacar** (☑43-51-84-54). A taxi to the airport from downtown should cost CUC$6.

AROUND CIENFUEGOS

Rancho Luna

Rancho Luna is a diminutive, picturesque beach resort 18km south of Cienfuegos close to the jaws of Bahía de Cienfuegos. It has two midrange, low-key hotel complexes, but it's also possible to stay in a scattering of casas particulares on the approach road to Hotel Club Amigo Faro Luna. Protected by a coral reef, the coast has good snorkeling. The beach isn't Varadero-standard sand; then again it isn't Varadero-standard noise or incessant development, either.

Activities

Dive Center
DIVING

(☑43-54-80-40; commercial@marlin.cfg.tur.cu; Carretera Pasacaballos Km 18; dives from CUC$35, open-water certification CUC$365) Besides sun-bathing or viewing the *faro* (lighthouse), the main activity here is diving organized through the dive center at Hotel Club Amigo Rancho Luna, which visits 30 sites within a 20-minute boat ride. There are caves, profuse marine life and dazzling coral gardens (dubbed Notre Dame by divers for its sheer, vast beauty). From November to February harmless whale sharks frequent these waters.

Other underwater sights include six sunken ships and remnants of a transmission cable once linking Cuba with Spain and laid by the Brits in 1895.

Sleeping

Villa Sol
CASA PARTICULAR **$**

(☑52-27-24-48; Carretera Faro Luna; r CUC$20-30; ❋) On the approach road to Hotel Club Amigo Faro Luna, this is the first house on the left. It's in a beautiful spot overlooking the ocean, with bougainvillea in the garden. There are four rooms, but other houses further on this road also rent rooms.

Hotel Pasacaballo
HOTEL **$**

(☑43-59-28-22; Carretera Pasacaballos Km 22; s CUC$24-30, d CUC$34-40; P❋☒) Once popular with Venezuelan medical students (those were the days), the Pasacaballo is architecturally repulsive but offers clean, perfectly decent accommodations at rock-bottom prices in a cracking location. Downstairs you'll find a spacious bar, a restaurant, a pool and pool tables – although given that there's nothing else around for kilometers, even this dazzling array of entertainment may prove insufficient.

The best strip of beach is a 4km hike away.

Hotel Club Amigo Faro Luna-Rancho Luna
RESORT **$$**

(☑43-54-80-30; Carretera Pasacaballos Km 18; s CUC$52-65, d CUC$74-90; P❋@☒) The dark horse of Cuba's south coast, Faro Luna is a refreshingly unpretentious place and one of only two hotels to grace what is possibly Cuba's most un-resort-like resort area. Unlike its neighbor, **Club Amigo Rancho Luna**, the Faro doesn't offer all-inclusive packages, but with a couple of new private restaurants in the vicinity there are options to eat out.

It is popular with language course groups from Canada. All-inclusive Hotel Rancho Luna next door is home to the local dive school.

Eating

Restaurante Vista al Mar
CARIBBEAN **$$**

(Carretera Pasacaballos Km 18; mains CUC$10; ⊙6-11pm) At the top of a steep slope not far from the approach road to Hotel Club Amigo Faro Luna, this private restaurant offers some rather unusual Cuban menu items, such as venison and whole roast turkey (CUC$30).

ⓘ Getting There & Away

Theoretically, there are half-a-dozen local buses from Cienfuegos daily, but this is Cuba – prepare for waits and chalked-up schedules. The Jagua ferry runs from the dock directly below Hotel Pasacaballo several times daily; more sporadic is the boat from Castillo de Jagua back to Cienfuegos (which runs between all three points, departing from the dock here at 10am and 3pm only at the time of research). Most reliable is a taxi; a one-way fare to Cienfuegos should cost around CUC$10 – bargain hard.

An even better way to get here is zipping along from Cienfuegos on a rented moped.

Castillo de Jagua

Predating the city of Cienfuegos by nearly a century, the **Castillo de Nuestra Señora de los Ángeles de Jagua** (admission CUC$3; ⊙8am-6pm), to the west of the mouth of Bahía de Cienfuegos, was designed by José Tantete in 1738 and completed in 1745. Built to keep pirates (and the British) out, it was at the time the third most important fortress in Cuba, after those of Havana and Santiago de Cuba.

Extensive renovation in 2010 gave the castle the makeover it sorely needed. In addition to a cracking view of the bay and a basic museum outlining the history of nuclear energy in Cienfuegos (!!), the castle also has a reasonably atmospheric restaurant down below.

Passenger ferries from the castle ply the waters to Cienfuegos (CUC$1, 40 minutes) twice daily, leaving Cienfuegos at 8am and 1pm and returning at 10am and 3pm. Another ferry leaves frequently to a landing just below the Hotel Pasacaballo in Rancho Luna (CUC$0.50, 15 minutes). Cubans pay the equivalent in pesos.

LANGUAGE IMMERSION IN CIENFUEGOS

Obviously, the best way to learn a language is to immerse yourself in its culture – preferably while staying in a paradisiacal beach resort. **Academia Cienfuegos** (www.formationcuba.com) is a Cuban-Canadian conceived Spanish-language program set up with the cooperation of the Cuban cultural agency Paradiso, which mixes 30 hours of language classes with 25 hours of cultural activities over a two-week period. Qualified Cuban teachers, when not in the classroom (which is set enticingly close to Rancho Luna beach in Hotel Club Amigo Faro Luna), take students on various sojourns to Cienfuegos and its environs incorporating film, poetry, dance, Santería, culture and the natural world. There are five teaching levels and a maximum of 10 students per class. The two-week package costs US$775 (without flight). Check the website for upcoming start dates.

Some distance away on this side of the bay, you might glimpse the infamous **Juragua nuclear power plant**, a planned joint venture between Cuba and the Soviet Union that was conceived in 1976 and incorporated the ominous disused apartment blocks of the adjacent Ciudad Nuclear. Only 288km from Florida Keys, construction met with strong opposition from the US and was abandoned following the collapse of communism. Foreigners can't visit.

Laguna Guanaroca

The representation of the moon on earth according to local Siboney legend, the shimmering **Laguna Guanaroca** (☑43-54-81-17; admission incl tour CUC$10; ⊗8am-3pm) 🏖 is a mangrove-rimmed saline lake southeast of Cienfuegos. It's second only to Las Salinas on the Zapata Peninsula as a bird magnet, and is the province's only *area protegida* (natural protected area). Trails lead to a viewing platform where flamingos, pelicans and *tocororos* (trogons; Cuba's national bird) are regular visitors. Plant life includes pear, lemon and avocado trees, as well as the *güira,* the fruit used to make maracas. Tours take two to three hours and include a boat

trip to the far side of the lake. Arrive early to maximize your chances of seeing a variety of birds.

The reserve entrance (accessible only by hire car or taxi) is 12km from Cienfuegos, off the Rancho Luna road on the cut-through to Pepito Tey. Cubanacán (p241) in Cienfuegos runs excursions here for a bargain CUC$10.

Jardín Botánico de Cienfuegos

The 94-hectare **botanic garden** (admission CUC$2.50; ⊗8am-5pm) 🏖, near the Pepito Tey sugar mill, 17km east of Cienfuegos, is one of Cuba's biggest gardens. It houses 2000 species of plants, including 23 types of bamboo, 65 types of fig and 280 different palms (purportedly the greatest variety in one place anywhere in the world). The botanic garden was founded in 1901 by US sugar baron Edwin F Atkins, who initially intended to use it to study different varieties of sugarcane, but instead began planting exotic tropical trees from around the globe.

To reach the gardens you'll need your own wheels. The cheapest method is to go with an organized excursion; Cubanacán (p241) in Cienfuegos runs trips for CUC$10. Drivers coming from Cienfuegos should turn right (south) at the junction to Pepito Tey.

El Nicho

While Cienfuegos province's share of the verdant Sierra del Escambray is extensive (and includes the range's highest summit, 1156m Pico de San Juan), access is limited to a small protected area around **El Nicho** (admission CUC$5; ⊗8:30am-6:30pm), an outlying segment of the Parque Natural Topes de Collantes.

El Nicho is the name of a beautiful waterfall on the Río Hanabanilla, but the area also offers a 1.5km nature trail (Reino de las Aguas), swimming in two natural pools, caves, excellent bird-watching opportunities and a number of *ranchón*-style (farm-style) restaurants.

The beautiful road to El Nicho via Cumanayagua is legendary for its twists and turns: *tienes mas curvas de la carretera por Cumanayagua* (you have more curves than the road to Cumanayagua) is reportedly a compliment to *chicas* (girls) hereabouts. That said, recent improvements mean the trip from Cienfuegos to El Nicho now takes two hours. The daily truck that serves the small local community leaves at very inconvenient times; hiring a car or a taxi (about CUC\$70) is far better. Half-day tours can be organized through the excellent Cubanacán (p241) in Cienfuegos, which also offers an El Nicho trip with onward transportation to Trinidad.

Caribbean Coast

Heading east toward Trinidad in Sancti Spíritus province, postcard views of the Sierra del Escambray loom ever closer until their ruffled foothills almost engulf the coast road, while offshore hidden coral reefs offer excellent diving.

◉ Sights & Activities

Hacienda la Vega HORSEBACK RIDING
(Carretera de Trinidad Km 52; per hr CUC\$6) On the main road, approximately 9km east of Villa Guajimico, this bucolic cattle farm is surrounded by fruit trees and has an attached restaurant serving Cuban staples (CUC\$5 to CUC\$10) – a good place to relax over a shady lunch. Unhurried travelers can hire horses and canter down to the nearby beach Caleta de Castro, where the snorkeling is excellent (BYO gear).

Villa Guajimico DIVING
(☑ 43-42-06-46; Carretera de Trinidad Km 42) Unusually for a campismo, Villa Guajimico has its own dive center situated atop an offshore coral ridge. The center serves 16 dive sites. Guajimico meant 'place of the fishes' in the language of the indigenous tribes that once lived here, and the dive sites harbor some stunning marine life – in a serene forest-rimmed inlet. Ask for latest prices and deals at reception.

⛏ Sleeping & Eating

Villa Yaguanabo CABINS $
(☑ 43-54-19-05; Carretera de Trinidad Km 55; s/d CUC\$24/32; ℗ ❄) Something of an unsung diamond located too close to Trinidad

OFF THE BEATEN TRACK

PALMIRA

If you're interested in Santería and its affiliated mysteries, stop by the amiable town of Palmira, 8km north of Cienfuegos, a town famous for its Santería brotherhoods, including the societies of Cristo, San Roque and Santa Barbara. A brief exposé of their raison d'être can be found at the **Museo Municipal de Palmira** (☑ 43-54-45-33; admission CUC\$1; ◷ 10am-6pm Tue-Sat, to 1pm Sun) on the main plaza. Cubanacán (p241) in Cienfuegos sometimes runs tours here. The main religious festivals are held in early December.

(26km) to delay most of the drive-by traffic, Villa Yaguanabo sits on a sublime stretch of coast at the mouth of the Yaguanabo River. Basic but clean motel rooms look out on a quiet swath of tan-colored beach.

Using the surprisingly salubrious hotel as a base, you can catch a boat (CUC\$3) for a 2km ride upriver to the Valle de Iguanas, where you'll find thermal waters, horseback riding and a small trail network in the foothills of the verdant Escambray. There's a private restaurant (Casa Verde) on the main road opposite the hotel offering alright lunch and dinner options.

Villa Guajimico CABINS $
(☑ 43-42-06-46; Carretera de Trinidad Km 42; s CUC\$22-25, d CUC\$38-44; ℗ ❄ ⛵) This is one of Cubamar's most luxurious campismos. The 51 attractive cabins with their idyllic seaside setting have facilities matching most three-star hotels, acting as a nexus for scuba divers. Also offered are bike hire, car rental, various catamaran or kayaking options and short hiking trails. It's a fully equipped Campertour site too. Cienfuegos–Trinidad buses pass by.

Villa Clara Province

Includes ➡

Santa Clara 253
Remedios. 264
Caibarién 267
Cayerías del Norte . . 269

Best Restaurants

➡ Restaurante 'El Bergantin' (p271)

➡ El Benyamino (p260)

➡ Restaurant Florida Center (p260)

Best Local Life

➡ Parque Vidal (p253), Santa Clara

➡ La Marquesina (p262), Santa Clara

➡ Parrandas (p268), Remedios

➡ Caibarién (p267)

Why Go?

What is that word hanging in the air over Villa Clara, one of the nation's most diverse provinces? 'Revolution', perhaps? And not just because Che Guevara liberated its capital, Santa Clara, from Batista's corrupt gambling party to kick-start the Castro brothers' 55-year (and counting) stint in power. Oh, no. Ultra-cultural Santa Clara is guardian of the Cuban avant-garde (having the nation's only drag show and its main rock festival). Meanwhile, the picturesque colonial town of Remedios and the beach-rimmed Cayerias del Norte beyond are experiencing Cuba's most drastic contemporary tourist development, a gargantuan undertaking which will over the next two years earn it position *numero dos* in the lengthy list of top Cuban holiday hot spots.

This region is indelibly stamped with Che's legacy and associated sights. Yet it should also win your heart for hosting the nation's most frenzied street party (Remedios), for its highs amongst the glimmering Escambray peaks and their adventure possibilities (around Embalse de Hanabanilla) and for its lows along the lolling white-sand strands off its northern coast (Cayo Santa María).

When to Go

➡ There's no better time to visit Villa Clara than December. Specifically, Christmas Eve. Swap your cold Christmas for the Caribbean's hottest street party in Remedios.

➡ Head over to the Cayerías del Norte for the start of the high season (December through March), when the chances of the skies raining on your beach parade are as low as they get.

History

The Taíno people were the first known inhabitants of the region, but a re-creation of a settlement at a hotel outside Santa Clara is their only surviving legacy. Strategically located in the island's geographical center, Villa Clara has historically been a focal point for corsairs, colonizers and revolutionaries vying for material gains.

Pirates were a perennial headache in the early colonial years, with the province's first town, Remedios, being moved twice and then abandoned altogether in the late 1600s by a group of families who escaped inland to what is now Santa Clara. Later, the area's demographics were shaken up further by Canary Islanders, who brought their agricultural know-how and distinctive lilting Spanish accents to the tobacco fields of the picturesque Vuelta Arriba region. In December 1958 Ernesto 'Che' Guevara – aided by a motley crew of scruffy *barbudas* (bearded ones) – orchestrated the fall of the city of Santa Clara by derailing an armored train carrying more than 350 government troops and weaponry to the east. The victory rang the death knell for Fulgencio Batista's dictatorship and signaled the triumph of the Cuban Revolution.

Things have calmed down since then, but provincial goings-on continue to keep everyone on the edge of their seats: resort development in the province's north has continued unabated since the 1990s and will have clocked up an astonishing 17,000 new rooms by 2017, potentially morphing tourist capacity to Varadero-like levels. Naysayers cite the adjacent Unesco Buenavista Biosphere Reserve and the damage this could wreak on this internationally important marine habitat.

Santa Clara

POP 239,000

While Varadero courts beach-lovers and Trinidad pulls in history geeks, gritty Santa Clara doesn't stand on ceremony for anyone. Smack bang in the geographic center of Cuba, this is a city of new trends and insatiable creativity, where an edgy youth culture has been testing the boundaries of Cuba's censorship police for years. Unique Santa Clara offerings include Cuba's only official drag show, a beauty pageant for transvestites and the best rock festival in the country, Ciudad Metal. The city's fiery personality has been shaped over time by the presence of the nation's most prestigious university outside Havana, and a long association with Che Guevara, whose liberating of Santa Clara in December 1958 marked the end of the Batista regime.

History

A good 10,000 miles out in his calculations, Christopher Columbus believed that Cubanacán (or Cubana Khan, an Indian name that meant 'the middle of Cuba'), an Indian village once located near Santa Clara, was the seat of the khans of Mongolia; hence his misguided notion that he was exploring the Asian coast. Santa Clara proper was founded in 1689 by 13 families from Remedios, who were tired of the unwanted attention of passing pirates. The town grew quickly after a fire emptied Remedios in 1692, and in 1867 it became the capital of Las Villas province. A notable industrial center, Santa Clara was famous for its prerevolutionary Coca-Cola factory and its pivotal role in Cuba's island-wide communications network. Santa Clara was the first major city to be liberated from Batista's army in December 1958. Today, industries include a textile mill, a marble quarry and the Constantino Pérez Carrodegua tobacco factory.

◎ Sights

Santa Clara's sights are liberally distributed to the north, east and west of Parque Vidal. All are within walking distance, with the big Che sight, Conjunto Escultórico Comandante Ernesto Che Guevara, 2km from the center.

◎ Parque Vidal

Parque Vidal SQUARE

A veritable alfresco theater named for Colonel Leoncio Vidal y Caro, who was killed here on March 23, 1896, Parque Vidal was encircled by twin sidewalks during the colonial era, with a fence separating blacks and whites. Scars of more recent division are evident on the facade of mint green **Hotel Santa Clara Libre** on the park's west side: it's pockmarked by bullet holes from the 1958 battle for the city between Guevara and Batista's government troops.

Today all the colors of Cuba's cultural rainbow mix in one of the nation's busiest and most vibrant urban spaces, with old men in *guayabera* shirts gossiping on the

Villa Clara Province Highlights

1 Trace the legend at Santa Clara's **monument to Ernesto Che Guevara** (p257) and **Monumento a la Toma del Tren Blindado** (p255).

2 Get your tobacco and caffeine fix at Santa Clara's cigar factory, **Fábrica de Tabacos Constantino Pérez Carrodegua** (p255), and the neighboring, coffee-concocting **La Veguita** (p262).

3 Plug into the electric nightlife in Santa Clara's **Club Mejunje** (p262).

4 Hike the trails, bathe in the pools and soak up the solitude of **Embalse Hanabanilla** (p264).

5 People-watch from the plaza's cafes in the unspoiled colonial pocket of **Remedios** (p264).

6 See the Villa Clara the tourist board forgot to mention

at ramshackle yet heart-warming **Caibarién** (p267).

7 Bask on the balmy beaches of **Cayo Santa María** (p269).

---

40 km
20 miles

ATLANTIC OCEAN

Cayo Guillermo
Cayo Santa María 7
Cayo Francés
Cayo Fragoso
Cavernas del Norte
Cayo las Picúas

Morón
El Salado
Laguna de la Leche
Máximo Gómez
CIEGO DE ÁVILA PROVINCE
Tamarindo
Chambas
Florencia
Marroquí
Ciego de
Punta de Judas
Bahía de Perros

Las Brujas
Airport
El Pedraplén 6
Caibarién
Remedios 5
Dolores
Boca del Río
El Estero
El Estero Real
Mayagua
Iguará
Yaguajay
Buena Vista
Jarahueca
SANCTI SPÍRITUS PROVINCE
Río Zaza

Bahía Buena Vista
Zulueta
Camajuaní
Placetas
Cabaiguán
Guayos
Fomento
Guinía de Miranda
Manicaragua
San Antón
Sierra del Escambray

Autopista Nacional
Santa Clara 1 2 3
Santamaría Airport
Ranchuelo
Esperanza
Potrerillo
Cumanayagua
El Salto del Hanabanilla
Embalse Hanabanilla 4
Embalse Minerva

Encrucijada
Cifuentes
Abel
Santo Domingo
Quemado de Güines
Sagua la Grande
Embalse Aloctunes

Cruces
Palmira
Rodas
Aguada de Pasajeros
Yaguaramas
CIENFUEGOS PROVINCE
Cienfuegos

CARIBBEAN SEA

Baños de Elguea
Hotel & Spa Elguea
Corralillo
Río La Palma
MATANZAS PROVINCE
Los Arabos
Colón
Martí

Cárdenas (26km)
Jovellanos (20km)
Playa Girón (60km); Havana (165km)
El Rincón
Caleta Buena
Playa Girón (8km)

shaded benches and young kids getting pulled around in carriages led by goats. Find time to contemplate the **statues** of local philanthropist Marta Abreu and the emblematic *El Niño de la Bota* (Boy with a Boot), a long-standing city symbol. Since 1902, the municipal orchestra has played rousingly in the park bandstand at 8pm every Thursday and Sunday, while classical music is played within the neoclassical **Palacio Provincial**, flanking the east side of the park.

Museo de Artes Decorativas   MUSEUM
(Parque Vidal No 27; admission CUC$2, photos CUC$5; ⊙9am-6pm Sun-Thu, 1-10pm Fri & Sat) Reserve an hour for this 18th-century mansion turned museum packed with period furniture from a whole gamut of styles that seem to ape Cuba's architectural heritage. Look for baroque desks, art nouveau mirrors and art deco furniture. Live chamber music adds to the romanticism in the evenings. Check the noticeboard.

Teatro la Caridad   THEATER, HISTORIC BUILDING
(cnr Marta Abreu & Máximo Gómez) Many are deceived by the relatively austere neoclassical facade. But toss CUC$1 to whoever is manning the door and you'll serendipitously discover why the 1885 Teatro La Caridad is one of the three great provincial theaters of the colonial era.

The ornate interior is almost identical to the Tomás Terry in Cienfuegos and the Sauto in Matanzas: three tiers, a U-shaped auditorium and decadent marble statues. The rich ceiling fresco by Camilo Zalaya provides the pièce de résistance.

◎ North of Parque Vidal

★Fábrica de Tabacos Constantino Pérez Carrodegua   CIGAR FACTORY
(Maceo No 181, btwn Julio Jover & Berenguer; admission CUC$4; ⊙9-11am & 1-3pm) Santa Clara's tobacco factory, one of Cuba's best, makes a quality range of Montecristos, Partagás and Romeo y Julieta cigars. Tours here are low-key compared to those in Havana, and so the experience is a lot more interesting and less rushed. Book tickets through Cubatur (p263).

Across the street is La Veguita (p262), the factory's diminutive but comprehensively stocked sales outlet, staffed by a friendly, ultra-professional team of cigar experts. You can buy cheap rum here, and the bar brews exquisite coffee.

La Casa de la Ciudad   CULTURAL CENTER
(☑20-55-93; cnr Independencia & JB Zayas; admission CUC$1; ⊙8am-5pm) Before closing for a lengthy refurbishment in 2014, this was the pulse of the city's progressive cultural life, hosting art expositions (including an original Wifredo Lam sketch), Noches del Danzón, a film museum and impromptu music events. Reopening is 'scheduled' for late 2015.

Iglesia de Nuestra Señora del Carmen   CHURCH
(Carolina Rodríguez) The city's oldest church is five blocks north of Parque Vidal. It was built in 1748, with a tower added in 1846. During the War of Independence, it stood in as a jail for Cuban patriots. A modern cylindrical monument facing the church commemorates the spot where Santa Clara was founded in 1689 by 13 refugee families from Remedios.

Museo Provincial Abel Santamaría   MUSEUM
(☑20-30-41; admission CUC$1, camera CUC$1; ⊙8:30am-4pm Mon-Fri, to 1pm Sat) Not actually a memorial to Señor Santamaría (Fidel's right-hand man at Moncada), but rather a small provincial museum quartered in former military barracks where Batista's troops surrendered to Che Guevara on January 1, 1959. Main displays are on natural history and on Cuban women throughout history.

The museum is on a hilltop at the north end of Esquerra across the Río Bélico. Look for the large cream-colored building behind the horse field.

◎ East of Parque Vidal

★Monumento a la Toma del Tren Blindado   MONUMENT
(boxcar museum admission CUC$1; ⊙boxcar museum 9am-5:30pm Mon-Sat) History was made at the site of this small **boxcar museum** on December 29, 1958, when Ernesto 'Che' Guevara and a band of 18 rifle-wielding revolutionaries barely out of their teens derailed an armored train using a borrowed bulldozer and homemade Molotov cocktails.

The battle lasted 90 minutes and improbably pulled the rug out from under the Batista dictatorship, ushering in 50 years of Fidel Castro. The museum – east on Independencia, just over the river – marks the spot where the train derailed and ejected its 350 heavily armed government troops. The celebrated bulldozer is mounted on its own plinth at the entrance.

Santa Clara

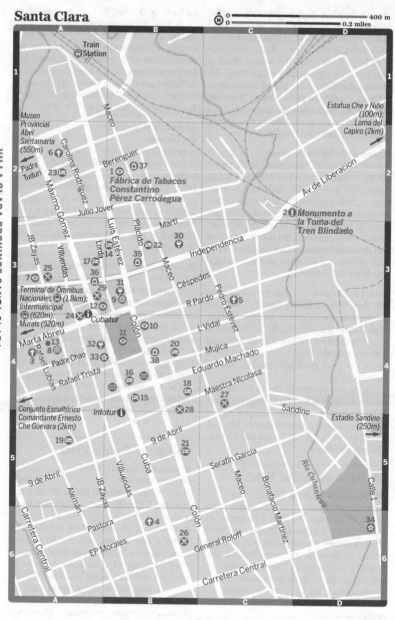

Estatua Che y Niño MONUMENT

Far more intimate and intricate a monument than its big brother on the other side of town, this statue in front of the Officina de la Provincia (PCC) four blocks east of Tren Blindado shows El Che with a baby (symbolizing the next generation) on his shoulder. Looking closer you'll see smaller sculptures incorporated into the revolutionary's uniform depicting junctures in his life, including likenesses of the 38 men killed with Guevara in Bolivia concealed within the belt buckle.

Santa Clara

⊙ Top Sights
1 Fábrica de Tabacos Constantino
   Pérez Carrodegua...............................B2
2 Monumento a la Toma del Tren
   Blindado..C2

⊙ Sights
3 Catedral de las Santas Hermanas de
   Santa Clara de Asís A4
4 Iglesia de la Santísima Madre del
   Buen Pastor...B6
5 Iglesia de Nuestra Señora del Buen
   Viaje...C3
6 Iglesia de Nuestra Señora del
   Carmen..A2
7 La Casa de la Ciudad.............................A3
8 Marta Abreu Residence A4
9 Museo de Artes Decorativas................B3
10 Palacio Provincial...................................B4
11 Parque Vidal..B4
12 Teatro la Caridad...................................A3

⊙ Activities, Courses & Tours
13 Club Mejunje..A4

⊙ Sleeping
14 Authentica Pérgola.................................B3
15 Casa de Mercy...B4
16 Hostal Alba B4
17 Hostal Familia Sarmiento A3
18 Hostal Florida Terrace B4
19 Hostal Marilin & Familia........................A5

20 Hotel América B4
21 La Casona Jover B5
22 Mary & Raicort...B3
23 Olga Rivera Gómez..................................A2

⊗ Eating
24 Dinos Pizza...A4
25 El Gobernador..A3
26 Mercado Agropecuario...........................B6
27 Panadería Doña Neli C4
28 Restaurant Florida Center B4
29 Restaurante Colonial 1878....................A3

⊙ Drinking & Nightlife
30 El Bar Club Boulevard............................B3
31 Europa...B3
32 Hotel Santa Clara Libre A4
   La Marquesina ....(see 12)

⊙ Entertainment
   Biblioteca José Martí ....(see 10)
33 Cine Camilo Cienfuegos.........................A4
   Club Mejunje ....(see 13)
34 El Bosque...D6
   Museo de Artes
   Decorativas ....(see 9)

⊙ Shopping
35 ARTex...B3
36 Boulevard A3
37 La Veguita..B2
38 Proyecto Atena Pepe Medina..............B4

Loma del Capiro LANDMARK
Continuing two blocks further east from the *Estatua Che y Niño*, a road to the right leads to Santa Clara's best lookout, the distinctive Loma del Capiro. The crest is marked by a flag and a series of stakes supporting the metallic but recognizable face of, you've guessed it, Che Guevara.

The hill was a crucial vantage point for his forces during the 1958 liberation of Santa Clara.

Iglesia de Nuestra Señora del Buen Viaje CHURCH
(cnr Pedro Estévez & R Pardo) East of the center is this riotous mix of Gothic, Romanesque and neoclassical architecture.

Iglesia de la Santísima Madre del Buen Pastor CHURCH
(EP Morales No 4, btwn Cuba & Villuendas) A singular colonial-style church south of the center.

⊙ West of Parque Vidal

★**Conjunto Escultórico Comandante Ernesto Che Guevara** MONUMENT
(Plaza de la Revolución) FREE The end point of many a Che pilgrimage, this monument, mausoleum and museum complex is 2km west of Parque Vidal (via Rafael Tristá on Av de los Desfiles), near the Víazul bus station. Even if you can't stand the Argentine guerrilla for whom many reserve an almost religious reverence, there's poignancy in the vast square that spans both sides of the *carretera*, guarded by a bronze statue of El Che.

The statue was erected in 1987 to mark the 20th anniversary of Guevara's murder in Bolivia, and can be viewed any time. Accessed from the statue's rear, the respectful **mausoleum** (Av de los Desfiles; ⊙9.30am-4:30pm Tue-Sun) contains 38 stone-carved niches dedicated to the other guerrillas killed in the failed Bolivian revolution. In 1997 the

MARTA ABREU

You won't find many places in Cuba without a street dedicated to Marta Abreu, the country's most famed philanthropist, but in her home city of Santa Clara her legacy is everywhere, including at the university (Cuba's second-most important). Before Che exploded onto the scene, Abreu had already established herself as the city's best-loved figure, and no wonder: the woman was responsible for the construction of most of Santa Clara's significant buildings, and was an important contributor to the demise of Spanish colonialism in the 1890s. At one time the city was known as the Ciudad de Marta and was renowned for its social services, instituted by Abreu.

Born into a wealthy family, Abreu soon came to realize the contrasts in living standards between Cuba and comparatively luxurious Europe, and brought about many changes to help Santa Clara rise to greater heights. Her most outstanding contribution remains the Teatro la Caridad, the building of which she oversaw, but the Biblioteca José Martí (within Palacio Provincial), Santa Clara's train station, four schools, a weather station, an old people's home and the provincial gas factory also exist because of her funding.

It isn't just her public works for which she is remembered. A humanitarian who stood for causes small and large, Abreu championed a campaign against homelessness in Santa Clara, funded construction of the power station that gave the city street lighting, and improved sanitation with the creation of public laundry stations. Perhaps most significantly, she raised a vast 240,000 pesos (equivalent to millions of dollars today) toward the liberation of Cuba from the Spanish in the 1890s.

Abreu's statue stands in Parque Vidal. You can see her former residences at **JB Zayas** (JB Zayas No 10) and **Restaurant Colonial 1878** (p260).

remains of 17 of them, including Guevara, were recovered from a secret mass grave in Bolivia and reburied in this memorial. Fidel Castro lit the eternal flame on October 17, 1997. The adjacent museum houses the details and ephemera of Che's life and death.

The best way to get to the monument is a 30-minute walk, or by hopping on a horse carriage in Calle Marta Abreu outside the cathedral for a couple of pesos. A standard taxi costs CUC$3.

Catedral de las Santas Hermanas de Santa Clara de Asís   CATHEDRAL
(Marta Abreu) Three blocks west of Parque Vidal, Santa Clara's cathedral was constructed amid huge controversy in 1923 after the demolition of the city's original church in Parque Vidal. It contains a collection of stained-glass windows and a mythical white statue of Mother Mary known (unofficially) as La Virgen de la Charca (Virgin of the Pond).

The statue was discovered in a ditch in the 1980s, having mysteriously disappeared shortly after the cathedral's consecration in 1954. It returned to grace the cathedral in 1995.

Murals   LANDMARK
(Carretera Central, btwn Vidaurreta & Carlos Pichado) Heading west on Carretera Central (the extension of Marta Abreu), you'll reach a series of comic-book-style murals with a tongue-in-cheek look at Cuban-American relations as the predominant theme. Glimpse such scenes as the *Statue of Liberty* being made off with by Cuban helicopters and an unsavory-looking man draped in the stars and stripes shouting *'terroristas!'* at Cuban guerillas while himself concealing a bomb. Even in this era of improved relations between the nations, they've not been wiped.

Easily incorporated into a walk to the Che monument, the pictures are just before the intermunicipal bus station.

Courses

Santa Clara has Cuba's second-most prestigious university, **Universidad Central Marta Abreu de las Villas** (28-14-10; www.uclv.edu.cu; Carretera de Camajuaní Km 5.5). Many international students study here, although most arrange everything through universities back home. Non-Cubans have, however, been able to turn up and study Spanish almost impromptu on occasion. Check the website for current details.

You might be able to pick up dancing and percussion lessons at **Club Mejunje** (Marta Abreu No 107; 4pm-1am Tue-Sun).

⭐ Festivals

Santa Clara's renegade annual offerings include **Miss Trasvesti**, a Miss World–type event with transvestite contestants in March, and November's **Ciudad Metal**, when headbanging to the country's leading rock acts happens at various venues citywide.

🛏 Sleeping

★ Hostal Familia Sarmiento   CASA PARTICULAR $

(☑ 52-83-47-21, 20-35-10; Lorda No 56, btwn Martí & Independencia; r CUC$25-30; ❋ 🛜) Santa Clara goes modern boutique rather than colonial in this bold, new, centrally located four-room house. The other unique selling point is that the family do not, unlike most casa particular owners, live at the property (they live across the road, where three more ground-floor rooms are available).

Hostess Geydis is a fantastic cook offering some of Cuba's most innovative food, while host Carlos is a driver, keen photographer and mine of information on all things Cuban. So expect an award-winning combination of personal service but private space. English spoken.

★ Hostal Florida Terrace   CASA PARTICULAR $

(☑ 22-15-80; Maestra Nicolasa, btwn Maceo & Pedro Estévez; CUC$25-30; ❋) Another new offering, this time served up by the owner of Restaurant Florida Center (and located across the street from there), this place has more floors (four) than most casas particulares have rooms. The smart colonial style from the restaurant is carried across, the rooms are top drawer and the upstairs bar has a *mirador* (viewpoint) with some of Santa Clara's best views. English, French and Italian spoken.

Hostal Alba   CASA PARTICULAR $

(☑ 29-41-08; Eduardo Machado No 7, btwn Cuba & Colón; r CUC$25-30; ❋) This architectural stunner – lovely antique beds, original tilework and a patio – serves amazing breakfasts and is just one block from the main square. The congenial owner Wilfredo is chef at Restaurante Florida Center – enough said!

Casa de Mercy   CASA PARTICULAR $

(☑ 21-69-41; casamecy@gmail.com; Eduardo Machado No 4, btwn Cuba & Colón; r CUC$25; ❋) There are two rooms with private bathrooms available in this beautiful family house which has two terraces, a dining room, a book exchange and a tempting cocktail menu. English, French and Italian are spoken by the engaging hosts.

Hostal Marilin & Familia   CASA PARTICULAR $

(☑ 20-76-55; 116 Maestra Nícolasa; CUC$20-25; ❋) A charming addition to the accommodation scene with two tasteful rooms, a back courtyard with a sunlounger and a beautiful cigar bar with an amazing array of cigars.

Authentica Pérgola   CASA PARTICULAR $

(☑ 20-86-86; www.hostalautenticapergola.blogspot.ca; Luis Estévez No 61, btwn Independencia & Martí; r CUC$25-30; ❋) The Pérgola is set around an Alhambra-esque patio draped in greenery and crowned by a fountain, from where several large rooms lead off. There's a beautiful roof-terrace restaurant.

Mary & Raicort   CASA PARTICULAR $

(☑ 20-70-69; Placído No 54, btwn Independencia & Martí; r CUC$20-25; ❋) A charming 1st-floor house with two rooms (one with balcony) for rent and possibly Santa Clara's fruitiest *desayuno* (breakfast); steep stairs ascend to a gorgeously done roof terrace. Bubbly hostess Mary is the other main reason to stay!

SANTA CLARA STREET NAMES

As in most Cuban cities, the streets have two names. The old names are used colloquially by the people who live there. The new ones are printed on street signs.

OLD NAME	NEW NAME
Candelaria	Maestra Nicolasa
Caridad	General Roloff
Nazareno	Serafín García
San Miguel	Calle 9 de Abril
Sindico	Morales
Union	Pedro Estevez

VILLA CLARA PROVINCE SANTA CLARA

La Casona Jover
CASA PARTICULAR $

(☑ 20-44-58; Colón No 167, btwn Calle 9 de Abril & Serafin García; r CUC$25; ✻) Four large rooms set well back from the road and a small terrace for contemplation. Chicken with honey is a tasty supper special.

Olga Rivera Gómez
CASA PARTICULAR $

(☑ 21-17-11; Evangelista Yanes No 20, btwn Máximo Gómez & Carolina Rodríguez; CUC$20-25; ✻) From the fabulous roof terrace, guests are spoiled with vistas of Santa Clara's prettiest church; below, the two rooms are large and clean.

Hotel América
HOTEL $$

(☑ 20-15-85; Mujica, btwn Colón & Maceo; s/d CUC$56/81; ✻ @ ✻) The first hotel in the city center that you'd recommend to your friends rather than your enemies, the 27-room América, which opened in 2012, can't quite claim a 'boutique' moniker. But it's new and keen to please with some interesting details (check out the metal staircase balustrades). There's an easygoing restaurant and a new outdoor pool.

Villa Los Caneyes
HOTEL $$

(☑ 20-45-13; cnr Av de los Eucaliptos & Circunvalación de Santa Clara; s/d CUC$43/68; P ✻ @ ✻) Recently spruced up, this out-of-town option should now be a serious consideration, particularly if you like peace and quiet. A mock-indigenous village, Los Caneyes has 95 thatched *bohios* (bungalows) in suitably verdant grounds replete with abundant birdlife, a good on-site restaurant, pool, well-stocked bar and souvenir shop. It's 3km from Santa Clara and a favorite with organized coach tours.

To get here, follow the continuation of Martha Abreu over the Carretera Central.

✗ Eating

For a city of Santa Clara's clout, dining options are not great, though there are exceptions. Roam the pedestrianized sections of Independencia (the Boulevard) for peso cafeterias. Self-caterers are well served by the small but centrally located and amply stocked **Mercado Agropecuario** (Cuba No 269, btwn EP Morales & General Roloff).

Panadería Doña Neli
BAKERY $

(cnr Maceo Sur & Calle 9 de Abril; bread/snacks around CUC$1; ☺ 7am-6pm) This joyous bakery amid the austere shopfronts on Calle Maceo will have your stomach rumbling with its aromatic fruit cakes, bread and pastries. Arrive early and celebrate breakfast.

El Gobernador
CUBAN $

(cnr Independencia & JB Zayas; mains CUC$3-8; ☺ noon-11pm) In this new era of competition from independents, state-run eateries have to perform better, and this one does. In a glamorous former state office, furnished in somber colonial splendor and hung with original artwork, El Gobernador's food was never going to *quite* live up to the ambience in which it is served, but hey: decent meat and fish dishes nevertheless.

Dinos Pizza
CAFETERIA $

(Marta Abreu No 10, btwn Villuendas & Cuba; pizzas CUC$3-6; ☺ 9am-11pm) The Santa Clara branch of this Cuban minichain has a pleasant bar, air-conditioning and friendly, helpful staff. It's generally packed with young students and serves OK pizza by Cuban standards.

Restaurante Colonial 1878
INTERNATIONAL $

(Máximo Gómez, btwn Marta Abreu & Independencia; mains CUC$4-8; ☺ noon-2pm & 7-10:30pm) Hold on to the table when you cut your steak here, or you might lose it on the floor. Tough meat aside, 1878 is amiable enough, though the food struggles to live up to the pleasant colonial setting.

★ Restaurant Florida Center
CUBAN, FUSION $$

(☑ 20-81-61; Maestra Nicolasa No 56, btwn Colón & Maceo; mains CUC$10-12; ☺ 6-8:30pm) The town's most famous restaurant – and justifiably so. Eating here in this colonial, plant-festooned, candlelit courtyard is a pleasure. It's presided over by owner Ángel and skilled chef Wilfredo (owner of nearby Hostal Alba). There are a profusion of dishes and wines, though the highlight is the lobster with prawns in a tangy tomato sauce. Two rooms for rent too.

★ El Benyamino
CUBAN, FUSION $$

(Carretera Central 605; mains CUC$4-10) The fountain-splashed waiting area, the sublime interior patio centered around a pool, the marble tables, the meat so tender it falls apart at the merest touch...El Benyamino might be 2km out of the center but it'll be worth getting here any which way you can. A taxi from the center costs CUC$3.

CHE COMANDANTE, AMIGO

Few 20th-century figures have successfully divided public opinion as deeply as Ernesto Guevara de la Serna, whose remains are now interred in a mausoleum (p257) in Santa Clara. Better known to his friends (and enemies) as El Che, he has been revered as an enduring symbol of Third World freedom and celebrated as the hero of the Sierra Maestra – and yet he was also the most wanted man on the CIA hit list. The image of this handsome and often misunderstood Argentine physician-turned-*guerrillero* is still plastered over posters and tourist merchandise across Cuba. But what would the man himself have made of such rampant commercialization?

Born in Rosario, Argentina, in June 1928 to a bourgeois family of Irish-Spanish descent, Guevara was a delicate and sickly child who developed asthma at the age of two. It was an early desire to overcome this debilitating illness that instilled in the young Ernesto a willpower that would dramatically set him apart from other men.

A pugnacious competitor in his youth, Ernesto earned the name 'Fuser' at school for his combative nature on the rugby field. Graduating from the University of Buenos Aires in 1953 with a medical degree, he shunned a conventional medical career in favor of a cross-continental motorcycling odyssey, accompanied by his old friend and colleague Alberto Granado. Their nomadic wanderings – well documented in a series of posthumously published diaries – would open Ernesto's eyes to the grinding poverty and stark political injustices all too common in 1950s Latin America.

By the time Guevara arrived in Guatemala in 1954 on the eve of a US-backed coup against Jacobo Arbenz' leftist government, he was enthusiastically devouring the works of Marx and nurturing a deep-rooted hatred of the US. Deported to Mexico for his pro-Arbenz activities in 1955, Guevara fell in with a group of Cubans that included Moncada veteran Raúl Castro. Impressed by the Argentine's sharp intellect and never-failing political convictions, Raúl – a long-standing Communist Party member himself – decided to introduce Che to his charismatic brother, Fidel.

The meeting between the two men at Maria Antonia's house in Mexico City in June 1955 lasted 10 hours and ultimately changed the course of history. Rarely had two characters needed each other as much as the hot-headed Castro and the calmer, more ideologically polished Che. Both were favored children from large families, and both shunned the quiet life to fight courageously for a revolutionary cause. Similarly, both men had little to gain and much to throw away by abandoning professional careers for what most would have regarded as narrow-minded folly. 'In a revolution one either wins or dies,' wrote Guevara prophetically years later, 'if it is a *real* one.'

In December 1956 Che left for Cuba on the *Granma* yacht, joining the rebels as the group medic. One of only 12 or so of the original 82 rebel soldiers to survive the catastrophic landing at Las Coloradas, he proved himself to be a brave and intrepid fighter who led by example and quickly won the trust of his less reckless Cuban comrades. As a result Castro rewarded him with the rank of Comandante in July 1957, and in December 1958 Che repaid Fidel's faith when he masterminded the battle of Santa Clara, an action that effectively sealed a historic revolutionary victory.

Guevara was granted Cuban citizenship in February 1959 and soon assumed a leading role in Cuba's economic reforms as president of the National Bank and minister of industry. His insatiable work ethic and regular appearance at enthusiastically organized volunteer worker weekends quickly saw him cast as the living embodiment of Cuba's New Man.

But the honeymoon wasn't to last. Disappearing from the Cuban political scene in 1965 amid many rumors and myths, Guevara eventually materialized again in Bolivia in late 1966 at the head of a small band of Cuban *guerrilleros*. After the successful ambush of a Bolivian detachment in March 1967, he issued a call for 'two, three, many Vietnams in the Americas.' Such bold proclamations could only prove his undoing. On October 8, 1967, Guevara was captured by the Bolivian army. Following consultations between the army and military leaders in La Paz and Washington, DC, he was shot the next day in front of US advisors. His remains were eventually returned to Cuba in 1997.

Drinking & Nightlife

La Veguita serves Santa Clara's best coffee, while peso bars along the Boulevard on Independencia might not look glam, but can rustle up good cocktails. Casas particulares also make for atmospheric evening drinks.

★ La Marquesina   BAR
(Parque Vidal, bwtn Máximo Gómez & Lorda; ⊙9am-1am) You can chin-wag and neck a cold bottled beer with locals of all types in this legendary dive bar under the porches of the equally legendary Caridad theater on the corner of Parque Vidal. The clientele is a potpourri of Santa Clara life – students, bohos, cigar-factory workers and the odd off-duty bici-taxi rider.

Europa   BAR
(cnr Independencia & Luis Estévez; ⊙noon-midnight) Everyone likes to drink at the Europa: it's in prime people-watching territory on the Boulevard, and locals and tourists alike feel welcomed on its laid-back street-facing terrace.

El Bar Club Boulevard   CLUB
(Independencia No 2, btwn Maceo & Pedro Estévez; admission CUC$2; ⊙10pm-2am Mon-Sat) This much-talked-about cocktail lounge has live bands and dancing, plus the odd comedy show. It generally gets swinging about 11pm.

Hotel Santa Clara Libre   BAR
(Parque Vidal No 6; ⊙6pm-midnight) The rooftop bar here is as high as you can get in the city center – thankfully, after the climb, the gentleman at the bar knows how to mix a mean mojito.

☆ Entertainment

Aside from the places listed here, don't discount the **Biblioteca José Martí** (Colón on Parque Vidal), inside the Palacio Provincial, for refined classical music; La Casa de la Ciudad (p255) for boleros (love songs) and *trova* (traditional poetic singing); and vibrant Parque Vidal (p253), which presents everything from mime artists to full-scale orchestras.

★ Club Mejunje   LIVE MUSIC, NIGHTCLUB
(Marta Abreu No 107; ⊙4pm-1am Tue-Sun; 🎦) Urban graffiti, children's theater, transvestites, old crooners belting out boleros, tourists dancing salsa. You've heard about 'something for everyone', but this is ridiculous. Welcome to Club Mejunje, set in the ruins of an old roofless building given over to sprouting greenery, a local – nay, national – institution, famous for many things, not least Cuba's only official drag show (every Saturday night).

Roll in any day of the week and enjoy an unforgettable 'only in Santa Clara' moment.

Museo de Artes Decorativas   LIVE MUSIC
(Parque Vidal No 27) In the museum's courtyard there is live music (mostly sit-down concerts) several times weekly. Expect everything from rock to *chachachá*.

Estadio Sandino   SPORTS
(Calle 9 de Abril Final) From October to April, you can catch baseball games in this stadium east of the center via Calle 9 de Abril. Villa Clara, nicknamed Las Naranjas (the Oranges) for their team strip, are Cuba's third-biggest baseball team, after the Havana and Santiago heavyweights, and were 2013 national-series champions.

El Bosque   CABARET, NIGHTCLUB
(cnr Carretera Central & Calle 1; ⊙9pm-1am Wed-Sun) Santa Clara's cabaret hot spot. It's best to get a taxi here.

Cine Camilo Cienfuegos   CINEMA
(Parque Vidal) This is below Hotel Santa Clara Libre; large-screen English-language films are shown.

🛍 Shopping

Independencia, between Maceo and JB Zayas, is the pedestrian shopping street called the Boulevard by locals. It's littered with all kinds of shops and restaurants and is the bustling hub of city life. An outlet of **ARTex** (Independencia, btwn Luis Estévez & Plácido; ⊙9am-5pm Mon-Sat, to midday Sun) sells handicrafts here. For a good bookshop, try **Proyecto Atena Pepe Medina** (Parque Vidal, cnr Colón & L Vidal; ⊙9am-6pm).

La Veguita   CIGARS, RUM
(📱20-89-52; Calle Maceo No 176A, btwn Julio Jover & Berenguer; ⊙9am-7pm Mon-Sat, 11am-4pm Sun) Sales outlet for Fábrica de Tabacos Constantino Pérez Carrodegua that is staffed by a friendly team of cigar experts. You can also buy cheap rum here and the bar out the back sells good coffee. It's across the street from the tobacco factory.

ℹ Information

INTERNET ACCESS & TELEPHONE

Etecsa Telepunto (Marta Abreu No 55, btwn Máximo Gómez & Villuendas; internet per hour CUC$4.50; ⊗ 8:30am-7pm) Eight internet terminals and three phone cabins.

MEDIA

Radio CMHW broadcasts on 840AM and 93.5FM. The *Vanguardia Santa Clara* newspaper is published on Saturday.

MEDICAL SERVICES

Farmacia Internacional (Colón No 106, btwn Maestra Nicolasa & Calle 9 de Abril; ⊗ 9am-6pm) In Hotel Santa Clara Libre.

Hospital Arnaldo Milián Castro (☎ 27-01-26; btwn Circumvalacion & Av 26 de Julio) Often called just Hospital Nuevo, it's southeast of the city center, just northwest of the intersection with Calle 3. It's the best all-round option for foreigners.

MONEY

Banco Financiero Internacional (Cuba No 6, cnr Rafael Tristá)

Cadeca (cnr Rafael Tristá & Cuba; ⊗ 8:30am-7:30pm Mon-Sat, to 11:30am Sun) Money-change service.

POST

DHL (Cuba No 7, btwn Rafael Tristá & Eduardo Machado; ⊗ 8am-6pm Mon-Sat, to noon Sun)

Post office (Colón No 10; ⊗ 8am-6pm Mon-Sat, to noon Sun)

TOURIST INFORMATION

Infotur (☎ 20-13-52; Cuba No 68, btwn Machado & Maestra Nicolasa; ⊗ 9am-5pm) Handy maps and brochures in multiple languages.

TRAVEL AGENCIES

Cubanacán (☎ 20-51-89; cnr Maestra Nicolasa & Colón; ⊗ 8am-8pm Mon-Sat)

Cubatur (☎ 20-89-80; Marta Abreu No 10; ⊗ 9am-noon & 1-8pm) Book tobacco-factory tours here.

ℹ Getting There & Away

Santa Clara's **Abel Santamaría Airport** (☎ 22-75-25; off Tte 311) receives several weekly flights from Montreal, Toronto and Calgary, plus there's a Copa Airlines flight to Panama City on Tuesday/Sunday, and is now the country's second-most important airport. There are no flights to Havana. Located in the center of the island, Santa Clara has excellent transport connections heading east or west.

BUS

The **Terminal de Ómnibus Nacionales** (☎ 20-34-70), which is also the Víazul bus station, is 2.5km west of the center out on the Carretera Central toward Matanzas, or 500m north of the Che monument. Tickets for air-conditioned **Víazul** (www.viazul.com) buses are sold at a special 'foreigners' ticket window at the station entrance.

Three buses leave for Havana (CUC$18, 3¾ hours) at 4:45am, 11:20am and 4:20pm. Buses to Varadero (CUC$11, three hours 20 minutes) leave at 7:45am, 6pm and 6.25pm.

The Santiago de Cuba (CUC$33) bus departs four times daily at 1:30am, 1:55am, 10:30am and 7:40pm, travelling via Sancti Spíritus (CUC$6, 1¼ hours), Ciego de Ávila (CUC$9, two hours 35 minutes), Camagüey (CUC$15, four hours 25 minutes), Holguín (CUC$26, seven hours 50 minutes) and Bayamo (CUC$26, nine hours 10 minutes).

The handy Víazul route north to Remedios, Caibarién, Morón and Ciego de Ávila, and south to Cienfuegos and Trinidad, was cancelled at the time of writing.

The **intermunicipal bus station** (Carretera Central), west of the center via Calle Marta Abreu, has cheap local buses to Remedios, Caibarién and Manicaragua (for Embalse Hanabanilla). Transport could be by bus or truck, gets overcrowded and isn't 100% reliable.

Casa owners usually know schedules, or will find them out on your behalf.

TRAIN

The **train station** (☎ 20-08-53) is straight up Luis Estévez from Parque Vidal on the north side of town. The **ticket office** (Luis Estévez Norte No 323) is across the park from the train station.

Notoriously erratic trains pass by en route to Santiago de Cuba (CUC$41, 12¾ hours) via Camagüey (CUC$19, 4¼ hours). In the other direction, they run to Havana (CUC$21, four hours), usually via Matanzas.

In the fickle world of Cuban trains, information can change weekly: double-check all this information at the station a day or two before departing.

ℹ Getting Around

Horse carriages congregate outside the cathedral on Marta Abreu and will angle for CUC$1 per ride. Bici-taxis (from the northwest of the park) cost the same. Taxis from the center to the Víazul bus station/airport cost CUC$3/15.

CAR & MOPED

Cubacar (☎ 21-81-77; Pedro Estévez, btwn 9 de Abril & Serafín García)

Rex (☎ 22-22-44; ⊘ 9am-6pm) Located at the airport. Rents mopeds/luxury cars for around CUC$25/80 per day.

Servicentro Oro Negro (cnr Carretera Central & Calle 9 de Abril) Southwest of the center.

TAXI

Private cabs loiter in front of the national bus station and will offer you lifts to Remedios and Caibarién. A state taxi to these same destinations will cost approximately CUC$30/35 respectively. You can get a *colectivo* (shared) taxi to Havana for as little as CUC$15 from here. To get to Cayo Santa María, bank on CUC$70-80 one way. Negotiate prices for return rides with waiting time. Drivers generally congregate in Parque Vidal outside Hotel Santa Clara Libre.

Around Santa Clara

Embalse Hanabanilla

In Santa Clara, greenery is never far away. Embalse Hanabanilla, Villa Clara's main gateway to the Sierra del Escambray, is a 36-sq-km reservoir nestled picturesquely amid traditional farms and broccoli-toned hills. The glittering lake is fjord-like and comes stocked with a famed supply of record-breaking bass. Fishers, boaters and nature-lovers are well catered for, with several excursions and some rewarding seldom-trodden hikes available. The area is best accessed by boat from the Hotel Hanabanilla on the reservoir's northwestern shore, some 80km by road south of Santa Clara. Cuba's largest hydroelectric generating station is also headquartered here.

🏃 Activities

Whopping 9kg largemouth bass have been caught on the lake, and **fishing trips** can be organized at the hotel: prices start at CUC$50 for four hours for two people with a guide.

Boats also ferry passengers over to **Casa del Campesino** offering coffee, fresh fruit and a taste of bucolic Cuban life. A trail from the hotel heads here too. Another popular boat trip is to the **Río Negro Restaurant** perched atop a steep stone staircase overlooking the lakeshore, 7km away. You can enjoy *comida criolla* (Creole food) surrounded by nature, and hike up to a **mirador**. Another 2km by boat from Río Negro Restaurant is a tiny quay; disembark for the 1km hike to the **Arroyo Trinitario waterfall**, where you can swim. A couple of other

trails lead off from here. Depending on duration and passenger numbers, return trips will be CUC$10 to CUC$20 per person.

A lesser-known boat trip runs to the spectacular El Nicho waterfall (p250), in Cienfuegos province, via the southwestern arm of the lake. Bank on CUC$35 return.

You can organize these activities at Hotel Hanabanilla or book a day excursion (CUC$33 from Santa Clara; CUC$69 from Cayo Santa María). Outside the hotel gates, locals offer all the above trips for cheaper prices.

🛏 Sleeping & Eating

Hotel Hanabanilla   HOTEL $
(☎ 20-84-61; Salto de Hanabanilla; s/d CUC$28/37; P ❄ ≋) Another page from the utilitarian school of Cuban architecture that blemished many a beauty spot in the 1970s, the 125-room Hanabanilla has attempted regular refurbs in the years since, though none have fully eradicated its incongruous ugliness. However, closer inspection reveals well-kept facilities inside, including an à la carte restaurant, swimming pool, vista-laden bar and lake-facing rooms with small balconies.

Peaceful during the week but packed with mainly Cuban guests at weekends, it's your only accommodation for kilometers and the best base for lakeside activities. To get here from Manicaragua, proceed west on Rte 152 for 13km. Turn left at a junction (the hotel is signposted) and follow the road 10km to the hotel.

❶ Getting There & Away

The chalked-up bus schedule in Santa Clara advertises daily buses to Manicaragua at 7:40am and 1:30pm (but check ahead). Theoretically, there are buses from Manicaragua on to Embalse Hanabanilla, but the only practical access is by car, bike or moped. Taxi drivers will energetically offer the trip (about CUC$50 one way). Negotiate hard if you want the driver to wait over while you participate in excursions.

Remedios

POP 45,836

A small, tranquil town that goes berserk every Christmas Eve in a cacophonous firework festival known as Las Parrandas, Remedios is one of Cuba's lesser-glimpsed colonial jewels. Some historical sources claim it is Cuba's second-oldest settlement (founded in 1513), although it is officially listed at number eight after Havana. Lack of

THE ESCAMBRAY'S LESSER-KNOWN TRAILS

The Sierra del Escambray is riddled with walking trails. The most accessible and well-publicized routes emanate out of Topes de Collantes in Sancti Spíritus province and are well traipsed by tourists based in nearby Trinidad. Far less crowded are the trails that surround Embalse Hanabanilla in Villa Clara province, most of which require a boat transfer from the Hotel Hanabanilla. The hotel has more information on the trails.

Ruta Natural por la Rivera A 3.4km trail that follows the contours of the lake, passing coffee plantations and humid foliage replete with butterflies.

Montaña por Dentro A 13km hike connecting Embalse Hanabanilla to the El Nicho waterfall on the Cienfuegos side of the Sierra del Escambray.

Un Reto a Loma Atahalaya A 12km all-encompassing walk that incorporates a climb up the 700m-high Loma Atahalaya with broad views north and south, a waterfall and local *campesino* house. It finishes at a cave, La Cueva de Brollo.

a Unesco listing or any Trinidad-style marketing means it's left off most standard tourist itineraries, a factor that lends its streets a charming, if slightly shabby authenticity. However, Remedios' lazy days look numbered. It has been chosen by Cuban tourism authorities as an unlikely focus for hotel development: boutique hotels are springing up and there's a vanguard of delightful colonial casas particulares too.

⊙ Sights

Remedios is the only city in Cuba with two churches in its main square, Plaza Martí. On our last visit it seemed almost the entire town was out facade polishing: some serious restoration of once-tatty central buildings is well underway.

Parroquia de San Juan Bautista de Remedios　CHURCH
(Camilo Cienfuegos No 20; ☉9am-noon & 2-5pm Mon-Thu) One of the island's finest ecclesiastical buildings, this church dates from the late 18th century, although a church was founded on this site as early as 1545. The campanile was erected between 1848 and 1858, and its famous gilded high altar and mahogany ceiling are thanks to a restoration project (1944–46) financed by millionaire philanthropist Eutimio Falla Bonet.

The pregnant *Inmaculada Concepción* to the left of the entrance is said to be the only sculpture of its kind (ie expectant) in Cuba. If the front doors are closed, go around to the rear or attend 7:30pm Mass.

Also on Parque Martí is the 18th-century **Iglesia de Nuestra Señora del Buen Viaje** (Alejandro del Río No 66), which is awaiting an overdue restoration and is currently closed.

Museo de Música Alejandro García Caturla　MUSEUM
(Parque Martí No 5; admission CUC$1; ☉9am-noon & 1-6pm Mon-Sat, 9am-1pm Sun) Between the churches is a museum commemorating García Caturla, a Cuban composer and musician who lived here from 1920 until his murder in 1940. Caturla was a pioneer who integrated Afro-Cuban rhythms into classical music and also served as a lawyer and judge. Look for occasional impromptu concerts.

Museo de las Parrandas Remedianas　MUSEUM
(Máximo Gómez No 71; admission CUC$1; ☉9am-6pm) Visiting this lively museum (and you don't often hear those two words together in provincial Cuba) two blocks off Parque Martí is no substitute for the real-life revelry on December 24, but what the hell. The downstairs photo gallery usually recaps the previous year's *parrandas*, while the upstairs rooms outline the history of this tradition, including scale models of floats and depictions of how the fireworks are made.

Galería del Arte Carlos Enríquez　ART GALLERY
(Parque Martí No 2; ☉9am-noon & 1-5pm) FREE
Overlooking the main plaza, this small gallery is named for the gifted painter who hailed from the small Villa Clara town of Zulueta. It displays absorbing works by artists from the province and includes some of the dramatic dance photography by Gabriel Davalos. There are occasional exhibitions by touring artists.

Remedios

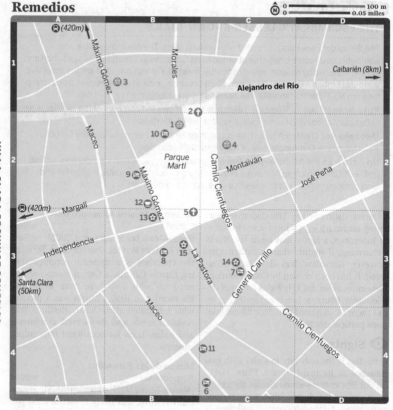

🛏 Sleeping & Eating

By the end of 2016 there should be six hotels in Remedios. The best eating options currently are at Hotels Barcelona and Mascotte, and the Villa Colonial and La Paloma casas.

★ 'Villa Colonial' –
Frank & Arelys   CASA PARTICULAR $
(☎ 39-62-74; Maceo No 43 cnr Av General Carrillo; r CUC$20-25; ❋ @) Frank & Arelys' wonderful colonial house is their pride and joy – and it shows. The three independent rooms have their own entrance, private bathroom, dining area (with stocked fridge), and living room where massive windows give onto the quiet but atmospheric street.

Internet is offered for CUC$3 for 30 minutes, and fine wines and food can be rustled up at short notice. A rooftop terrace has recently been added.

La Paloma   CASA PARTICULAR $
(☎ 39-54-90; Parque Martí No 4; r CUC$20-25; P ❋) Another grand Remedios casa with tilework and furnishings that would be worth zillions anywhere else, La Paloma dates from 1875 and is right on the main square. The three rooms have massive shower units, art deco beds, and doors big enough to ride a horse through.

Hostal La Estancia   CASA PARTICULAR $
(☎ 39-55-82; www.laestanciahostal.com; Camilo Cienfuegos 34, btwn Av General Carillo & José A Peña; r CUC$25; ❋ ☀) This house dating from 1849 has myriad museum-worthy furnishings, attractive beamed ceilings, a fancy drawing room with a piano, and four rooms surrounding the town's only swimming pool. Not bad!

Remedios

◉ Sights

1 Galería del Arte Carlos Enríquez.........B2
2 Iglesia de Nuestra Señora del
   Buen Viaje...B1
3 Museo de las Parrandas
   Remedianas......................................B1
4 Museo de Música Alejandro García
   Caturla...C2
5 Parroquia de San Juan Bautista de
   Remedios...B3

⊜ Sleeping

6 Hostal Casa Richard.......................... C4
7 Hostal La Estancia C3
8 Hotel Barcelona.................................B3
9 Hotel Mascotte..................................B2
10 La Paloma...B2
11 'Villa Colonial' – Frank & Arelys C4

◉ Drinking & Nightlife

12 El Louvre B2

◉ Entertainment

13 Centro Cultural las Leyendas.............B3
14 Teatro Rubén M Villena......................C3
15 Uneac B3

Hostal Casa Richard   CASA PARTICULAR **$**
(☑ 39-66-49;   r.richard.rondon@gmail.com;
Maceo No 68, btwn Fe del Valle & Cupertino Garcia;
r CUC$20-25) The friendly owners rent two
rooms, the second a veritable mezzanine,
abutting a courtyard that could use some
shade. Two more rooms are available down
the street.

Hotel Barcelona   BOUTIQUE HOTEL **$$**
(José Peña No 67; s/d CUC$55/70; ❇) The Bar-
celona must be one of Cuba's best boutique
hotels. Thirty-four rooms wrap around three
floors of a glorious vine-draped internal
courtyard. With no expense spared through-
out in achieving the elegance of yore, there
is also an atmospheric restaurant. Book
through its sister hotel, the Mascotte.

Hotel Mascotte   BOUTIQUE HOTEL **$$**
(☑ 39-53-41; Parque Martí; s/d CUC$55/70; ❇ @)
Take an eloquent colonial Remedios theme
and stick it inside a small 'Encanto' hotel (the
boutique branch of the Cubanacán chain) and
the results are breathtaking, as this 10-
room gem on the main plaza demonstrates.

🍷 Drinking & Entertainment

Additional cultural activities can be found
in **Uneac** (Maceo No 25), and outside in the
parks and squares.

★ **El Louvre**   CAFE
(Máximo Gómez No 122; ⊙ 7:30am-midnight) With
a gravitational pull on Remedios' scattering of
tourists, El Louvre is, so locals proclaim, the
oldest bar in the country in continuous service (since 1866) – and who are *you* to argue?
The bar was good enough for Spanish poet
Federico García Lorca, who heads the list of
famous former patrons. It does basic food too.

If you're looking for a room/private res-
taurant/taxi, park yourself here and wait for
offers.

**Centro Cultural las
Leyendas**   CULTURAL CENTER
(Máximo Gómez, btwn Margalí & Independencia)
Next door to El Louvre is an ARTex cultur-
al center with music till 1am Wednesday to
Saturday.

Teatro Rubén M Villena   THEATER
(Cienfuegos No 30) A block east of the park is
an elegant old theater with dance performances, plays and Theater Guiñol for kids.
The schedule is posted in the window and
tickets are in pesos.

❶ Getting There & Around

The **bus station** (Av Cespedes, btwn Margall &
Fragua y Pi) is on the southern side of town at the
beginning of the 45km road to Santa Clara. Half
a dozen daily buses chug through to Santa Clara
(one hour) and three go to Caibarién (20 minutes). Fares are negligible. Remedios had a happy
two-year stint on a Víazul route that wound southeast to Morón/Ciego de Ávila and southwest to
Santa Clara, but this was recently suspended.

A state taxi from the bus station to Caibarién
will cost roughly CUC$5; to Santa Clara or Cayo
Santa María the fare is CUC$30 to CUC$35.
A bici-taxi from the bus station to Parque Martí
costs 2 pesos.

Caibarién

POP 37,902

After metropolitan Santa Clara and the colonial splendor of Remedios, this once-busy,
now-bypassed shipping port on Cuba's Atlantic coast will come as a shock with its crumbling old buildings. Since the piers slumped
into the sea and the provincial sugar mills
closed down, Caibarién's economic foundations have been whipped out from under
it, and it's never really recovered. Just talking too loudly here seems enough to bring
whole houses tumbling down, so fragile
do they look.

PARRANDAS

Sometime during the 18th century, the priest at Remedios cathedral, Francisco Vigil de Quiñones, had the bright idea of providing local children with cutlery and crockery and getting them to run about the city making noise in a bid to increase Mass attendance in the lead-up to Christmas. He could not have imagined what he was starting. Three centuries later and *parrandas*, as these cacophonous rituals became known, have developed into some of the best-known Caribbean street parties. Peculiar to the former Las Villas region of Cuba, *parrandas* take place only in towns in Villa Clara, Ciego de Ávila and Sancti Spíritus provinces, and the biggest party erupts annually in Remedios on December 24.

Festivities kick off at 10pm, with the city's two traditional neighborhoods (El Carmen and El Salvador) grouping together to outdo each other with displays of fireworks and dance, from rumba to polka. The second part of the party is a parade of vast floats, elaborate carnival-like structures only with the fancifully dressed people in the displays standing stock-still as the tractor-towed artworks traverse the streets. Further fireworks round off the revelry.

The *parrandas* aren't confined to Remedios. Other towns in former Las Villas province (now Ciego de Ávila, Sancti Spíritus and Villa Clara) stage their own seasonal shenanigans. Though each is different, there are some generic party tricks, such as fireworks, decorative floats and opposing neighborhoods competing for the loudest, brightest and wildest stunts. Camajuani, Caibarién, Mayajigua and Chambas all have (almost) equivalently raucous *parrandas* celebrations.

But the town has a definite charm. Intrepid travelers report that some of their best Cuban experiences come at ultrafriendly Caibarién, which is colorfully framed by its restored *malecón* sea wall and weather-lashed fishing fleet. Nine kilometers east of Remedios and 40km from the alluring Cayerías del Norte, it's a 'real' corner of Cuba that the authorities forgot to dress up for tourists. The town is famous for its *cangrejo* (crab), the best in Cuba, and has a cracking museum and crackling December *parrandas* allegedly second only to Remedios in explosiveness.

The town makes a cheap base for those keen to catch a glimpse of the pristine *cayos* without shelling out the expensive all-inclusive prices. **Havanatur** (☑ 35-11-71; Av 9, btwn Calles 8 & 10) can arrange accommodation on Cayo Santa María. There's a **Cadeca** (Calle 10 No 907, btwn Avs 9 & 11) nearby.

🔴 Sights

Crab Statue   MONUMENT

The entrance to Caibarién is guarded by a giant crustacean designed by Florencio Gelabert Pérez and erected in 1983.

**Museo de Agroindustria Azucarero
Marcelo Salado**   MUSEUM

(☑ 35-38-64; admission CUC$3; ☺ 9am-4pm Mon-Sat) **FREE** Three kilometers past the crab statue on the Remedios road you'll find one of the nation's best potted histories of slave culture, the sugar industry and pre-diesel locomotives. There's a video of Cuba's sugar industry, models of figures toiling to harvest the product and lots of original machinery, which, while appearing Industrial Revolution-esque to most Western eyes, was imperative in Cuba right up until Castro's clampdown on the industry in the 1990s.

An added bonus is the extensive collection of locomotives (the place is also known as the Museo de Vapor, or Museum of Steam), featuring Latin America's largest steam engine, and there are steam-train rides daily.

**Proyecto Comunitario
'Por la Costa'**   ARTS CENTER

(☑ 35-35-99; Avenida 39, btwn Calles 10 & 12; ☺ 9am-5pm daily) 🌿 **FREE** A breath of fresh air in decrepit central Caibarién, this garishly decorated arts venue raises money for town restoration through offering arts classes, selling local art and serving coffee on its cute terrace. The colorfully clad *campesino* (agricultural worker) points the merry way in.

**Museo Municipal María Escobar
Laredo**   MUSEUM

(cnr Av 9 & Calle 10) Even humble Caibarién had a heyday (although it was a while ago): find out more about it here.

🛏 Sleeping & Eating

Caibarién is the most economical launchpad for the resort-strewn, casa particular–free zone of the Cayerías del Norte; many indie travelers alight here for this very reason.

Virginia's Pension   CASA PARTICULAR **$**
(📞 36-33-03; Ciudad Pesquera No 73; r CUC$20-25; 🅿️❄️) Among Caibarién's handful of sleeping options, this reputable professional place run by Virginia Rodríguez is the most popular. Food here is delicious and of course the star of the show is the obligatory *cangrejo*.

Complejo Brisas del Mar   HOTEL **$**
(📞 35-16-99; Reparto Mar Azul; s/d CUC$22/29; 🅿️❄️🏊) Bargain prices, and a strip of sand on Caibarién's seafront, but the rooms cry for refurbishment and Brisas struggles to pull in even the budget-minded punters. Still, it's a hotel on a beach for a tenth of what you'd pay across the causeway.

Restaurante La Vicaria   SEAFOOD **$**
(Calle 10 & Av 9; ⊙ 10am-10:30pm) Whooshing in at number one for eating choices (by default) is this establishment on the main square, specializing in fish.

🍷 Drinking & Nightlife

Piste de Baile   CLUB
(Calle 4; admission 2 pesos) Caibarién has a hot, happening disco near the train station.

ℹ️ Getting There & Away

Four local buses a day go to Remedios; two soldier on to Santa Clara and three go to Yaguajay from Caibarién's old blue-and-white **bus & train station** (Calle 6) on the western side of town. No trains run to Caibarién. The Servi-Cupet gas station is at the entrance to town from Remedios, behind the crab statue. **Cubacar** (📞 35-19-60; Av 11, btwn Calles 6 & 8) rents cars at the standard rates and mopeds for CUC$25. A one-way taxi to Villa los Brujas on Cayo Santa María costs about CUC$25; it's a shade more to the Cayo Santa María hotel strip or Santa Clara.

Cayerías del Norte

Cuba's next big tourist project is unfolding on a scattered group of pancake-flat keys off the north coast of Villa Clara province. While avoiding some of the erstwhile architectural hideousness of other Cuban resorts, development here is wide reaching and rapid, and sits a little awkwardly alongside the Buenavista Unesco Biosphere Reserve which it abuts. The keys were still a mosquito-infested wilderness until 1998 when the first hotel – Villa las Brujas – went up. These days there's several thousand hotel rooms supporting a demographic that is 85% Canadian, with an emphasis on the luxury end of the tourist market. Located on three different keys – **Cayo las Brujas**, **Cayo Ensenachos** and **Cayo Santa María** – linked by an impressive 48km causeway called **El Pedraplén**, the enclave now lists 11 hotels, two mini tourist 'towns' and one of Cuba's few nudist beaches.

But bulldozers haven't finished yet. There are now a dozen resorts here, with more scheduled to spring up, plus plans for an 18-hole golf course. The Cayerías' longest beach stretches for 13km along the north coast of Cayo Santa María where most hotels lie. Though different sections of beach go by different names, it is usually communally known as **Playa Santa María** and is perfect for a relaxed beachcombing stroll.

👁 Sights & Activities

Marina Gaviota   WATER SPORTS
(📞 35-00-13; Cayo las Brujas) Most water-based activities can be arranged at this marina by Villa las Brujas. Highlights include a day-long catamaran cruise with snorkeling (CUC$85), a sunset cruise (CUC$57) and deep-sea fishing (CUC$260 for four people). Diving to one of 24 offshore sites is also offered (CUC$65 for two immersions). Most water activities are cancelled if there is a cold weather front.

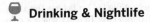

> ### WHERE FLAMINGOS RULE THE ROOST!
>
> The Cuban government might have paid little heed to the opposition over hotel development here but it did listen to a dozen pairs of breeding flamingos. When it was discovered the graceful pink birds had settled on a lagoon behind **Playa las Salinas** beach, scheduled resort construction was shelved. Visitors can reap the benefits. Turn left after the airfield on Cayo las Brujas to take the track to the lagoon where you can watch the flamingos and then continue to what is consequently a rare hotel-free stretch of sand. Bring food and water: there's no restaurant.

VILLA CLARA PROVINCE CAYERÍAS DEL NORTE

Cayo Santa María Area

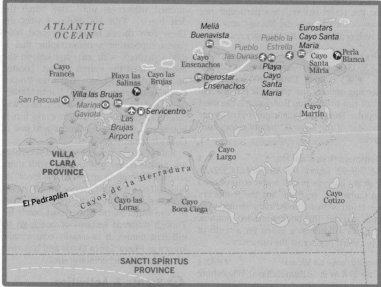

San Pascual HISTORIC SITE

FREE One of the area's oldest and oddest curiosities is the *San Pascual*, a San Diego tanker built in 1920 that got wrecked in 1933 on the opposite side of nearby Cayo Francés. Later the ship was used to store molasses, and later still it was opened up as a rather surreal hotel-restaurant (now closed).

The journey out to see the ship is included in snorkeling excursions and sunset cruises.

Pueblo la Estrella SPA, BOWLING

(⊙ 9am-7:30pm) Welcome to a Cuban town full of...Canadians. It's hard to know what to make of this mock colonial village with its imitation Manaca Iznaga tower and phony plaza surrounded by shops, a bowling alley, spa-gymnasium, and restaurants designed for the resort crowds. Think of it as a curious anomaly that's easier on the eye than your average North American shopping mall.

Opened in 2009, it has recently been followed by another faux town, **Pueblo Las Dunas**, 2km to the west. Come back in 300 years and see if they're still there.

🛏 Sleeping

★ **Villa las Brujas** HOTEL, RESORT $$

(☑ 35-01-99; Cayo las Brujas; all-incl s CUC$64-68, d CUC$79-84; P ❄) Atop a small, relatively untamed headland crowned by a statue of a *bruja* (witch), Villa las Brujas has the air of a tropical *Wuthering Heights* when a cold front blows in. It's a comfortable but affordable small resort, situated among mangroves on one of Cuba's prettiest northern keys.

The 24 spacious *cabañas* (cabins) are equipped with coffee machines, cable TV and massive beds (higher tarriffs for sea views), while the Farallón restaurant overlooks a magnificent scoop of Playa las Salinas. The nearest resort to the mainland, Villa las Brujas lies by the marina, 3km from the airport.

Playa Cayo Santa María RESORT $$

(☑ 35-08-00; Cayo Santa María; all-incl s/d from CUC$109/177; P ❄ ❄) The only Cuban-run resort on the *cayos*, this pleasant surprise, rimmed by its own minimoat, impresses from the start, with four pools, Chinese and Italian restaurants, a games room and theater, a spa and a cigar bar. It trumps many of the other resort newcomers by being well laid-out, by its courteous service and by the outstanding value.

Meliá Buenavista RESORT $$$

(☑ 35-07-00; Punta Madruguilla; all-incl s/d CUC$360/450; P ❄ @ ❄) Small really is beautiful at the Buenavista, where 105 rooms

MEDICINAL MECCA

Out-of-the-way, out-of-the-ordinary Baños de Elguea, 136km northwest of Santa Clara near the Matanzas provincial border, is a well-established health resort with among the most rejuvenating powers in Latin America (so say regulars). The tradition of coming here to be cleansed of ills dates back to 1860. According to local legend, a slave who had contracted a serious skin disease was banished by his master, sugar-mill owner Don Francisco Elguea, so that he wouldn't infect others. Sometime later, the man returned completely cured. He explained that he had relieved his affliction merely by bathing in the region's natural mineral spring. Somewhat surprisingly, his master believed him. A bathhouse was built and the first hotel opened in 1917. Today these sulfur springs and mud are used by medical professionals to treat skin irritations, arthritis and rheumatism. The waters here reach a temperature of 50°C and are rich in bromide, chlorine, radon, sodium and sulfur.

Situated north of Coralillo, **Hotel & Spa Elguea** (☑68-62-90; s/d incl breakfast CUC$21/28; Ⓟ❉❅) has 139 rooms with numerous spa treatments such as mud therapy, hydrotherapy and massages available at the nearby thermal pools. Treatments are in the CUC$5 to CUC$15 range. Fancy country spa, this is not – think more Soviet utilitarianism.

The hotel is all but inaccessible by public transport, which gets no further than Coralillo, 9km away. Those seeking cures had better have their own wheels or their best walking legs.

(a child by cayo standards) are located apart from the other hotels at the western end of Cayo Santa María. On its sunset-facing beach, where wine is brought to you by obliging butlers, this is a veritable romantic heaven (no kids allowed) where you feel guilty even raising your voice.

Iberostar Ensenachos RESORT $$$
(☑35-03-00; Cayo Ensenachos; all-incl r CUC$300-600; Ⓟ❉@❅❅) A top-end paradise reminiscent of a Maldives private island getaway, this is the only hotel on tiny Cayo Ensenachos and greedily bags two of Cuba's best beaches (Playas Ensenachos and Mégano). One portion of the hotel is adults only. The decor is refined, with Alhambra-esque fountains and attractive natural foliage. Guests are accommodated in pretty 20-unit blocks, each with their own private concierge.

Eurostars Cayo Santa María RESORT $$$
(☑53-42-35; Cayo Santa María; all-incl r from CUC$320; Ⓟ❉❅❅) Of all the latest arrivals on Cayo Santa María's ever-changing hotel strip this is biggest, at 846 rooms. The Fuego y Hielo restaurant is one of the sleekest resort eateries hereabouts, and the romantically inclined may appreciate the private dining in the middle of the three-level pool.

Earthy-toned rooms are big and bright but can't shake off the straight-out-of-the-catalog feel and, overall, it's hard to see how the Eurostars offers the archipelago anything different.

🍴 Eating

Pueblo la Estrella and Pueblo las Dunas on Cayo Santa María have several restaurants each.

★Restaurante 'El Bergantín' SEAFOOD $$$
(Acuario-Delfinario, Cayo Santa María; mains CUC$15) The lobster in the Gaviota-run restaurant might not be the cheapest in Cuba, but it's undoubtedly the freshest, courtesy of the on-site lobster nursery; yes, the clawed creatures are literally living within fishing-line distance of your table and they're divine.

Trattoria ITALIAN $
(Pueblo La Estrella; pizzas CUC$3-5; ⊙10am-5pm) Santa Clara or Remedios would love a restaurant like this; the all-inclusive crowd have to pay extra for the pleasure of eating here, so generally don't. That's a mistake, as the pizza here sure beats the majority of what's offered in the resorts.

Farallón Restaurant INTERNATIONAL $$$
(Cayo las Brujas; lunch CUC$20) A good bet for a decent meal is the Farallón at Villa las Brujas, perched like a bird's nest overlooking blissful Las Salinas beach. Nonhotel guests can enjoy lunch with use of beach, bathrooms and parking for CUC$20.

🍷 Drinking & Entertainment

If you get bored of drinking beer out of plastic cups in your all-inclusive, the two 'pueblos' – Las Dunas and Estrella – both have various bars (where you'll pay) and a disco. For a CUC$10 cover charge you can dance with bevies of Torontonians from 11pm till 2am.

❶ Getting There & Away

A typical all-inclusive zone, Cayo Santa María was not developed with public transport in mind. **Las Brujas airport** (☎ 35-00-09) has mainly charter flights to Havana. There's a Servicentro gas station opposite. For those not on package tours with airport pick-ups, access is by rental car or moped, or by taxi. From Cayo Santa María it is 56km to Caibarién, 65km to

Remedios and 110km to Santa Clara. The one-way fares from Caibarién/Remedios/ Santa Clara by taxi cost approximately CUC$30/35/70 to Cayo Santa María (depending on which hotel you're aiming for). Bargain hard – particularly if you want to get a return fare with waiting time. Cyclists: headwinds on the causeway make pedaling problematic. The causeway is accessed from Caibarién and there's a toll booth (CUC$2 each way), where you'll need to show your passport/visa.

❶ Getting Around

Panoramic Bus Tour is a double-decker open-topped shuttle bus that links Villa las Brujas and all the Cayo Santa María hotels several times daily. Fares are CUC$1.

Trinidad & Sancti Spíritus Province

🎣 41 / POP 466,106

Includes ➜

Trinidad 275

Playa Ancón
& Around 286

Valle de los
Ingenios 288

Topes de Collantes. . 289

Sancti Spíritus 291

Northern Sancti
Spíritus Province . . . 298

Best Hikes

➜ Sendero 'Centinelas del Río Melodioso' (p290)

➜ La Sabina trail (p297)

➜ Huellas de la História (p278)

➜ Sendero La Batata (p290)

Best Natural Swimming Pools

➜ La Poza del Venado (p290)

➜ Salto del Caburní (p290)

➜ La Solapa de Genaro (p298)

➜ Cascada Bella (p297)

Why Go?

The year 2014 was a big one for Sancti Spíritus province. Its two main colonial towns both celebrated their 500th anniversaries amid much publicity, partying and cleaning up of important public buildings. It was proof that this small but well-endowed province guards what is arguably Cuba's most precious historical legacy. Trinidad, thanks to careful preservation efforts, is considered one of the most intact colonial towns in the Americas, while Sancti Spíritus (the city) has a more intangible, crumbling allure.

Complementing its historical depth, Sancti Spíritus province boasts beaches – Playa Ancón is a stunner, easily the best on Cuba's underwhelming south coast – and mountains. Within mirror-glinting distance of Trinidad lies the haunting Escambray, which, with a network of decent trails, is Cuba's best hiking area. The rest of the province hides a surprisingly varied cache of oft-overlooked curiosities, including lightly trodden ecoparks, a seminal museum to guerrilla icon Camilo Cienfuegos, and the Unesco-protected Bahía de Buenavista.

When to Go

➜ Trinidadians don't wait long after Christmas to rediscover their celebratory style. The Semana de la Cultura Trinitaria (Trinidad Culture Week) takes place during the second week of January and coincides with the city's anniversary.

➜ The quiet month of May is a good time to visit this province, as you can avoid both crowds and bad weather during the off-season.

➜ Stick around until June and you'll witness Trinidad's second big annual shindig, the Fiestas Sanjuaneras, a local carnival where rum-fueled horsemen gallop through the streets. Take cover!

Trinidad & Sancti Spíritus Province Highlights

1 Visit museums and recline in colonial comfort in one of 90+ new restaurants in time-warped **Trinidad** (p282).

2 Climb the tower at the Manaca Iznaga for a killer view

3 Stroll without an itinerary around the recently beautified streets of **Sancti Spíritus city** (p291).

4 Explore woodland, waterfalls and war history in the **Jobo Rosado Reserve** (p298).

5 Rent a house in La Boca and stroll the sands of **Playa Ancón** (p286).

of the Unesco-listed **Valle de los Ingenios** (p288).

6 Hike down to the **Salto del Caburní** (p290) and jump into a frigid natural bathing pool.

7 Go **horseback riding** (p280) in the cowboy-inhabited countryside around Trinidad.

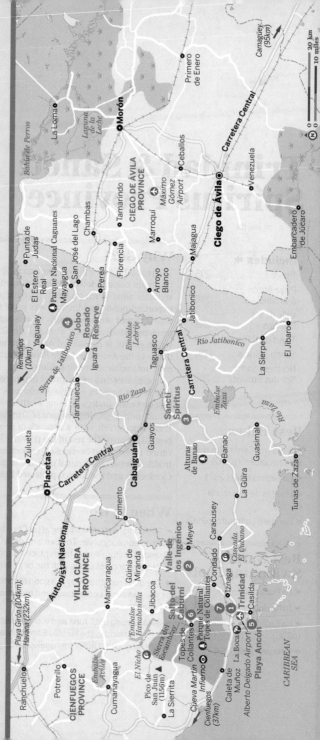

Trinidad

POP 52,896

The first sound in the morning is the clip-clop of horses' hooves on the cobbled streets followed by the cries of old men selling bread from bicycles (*El pan! El pan!*). Open your eyes, gaze up at the high wooden louvers of your 200-year-old colonial room, and try to convince yourself you're in the 21st century.

Trinidad is one-of-a-kind, a perfectly preserved Spanish colonial settlement where the clocks stopped ticking in 1850 and – apart from the tourists – have yet to restart. Built on huge sugar fortunes amassed in the adjacent Valle de los Ingenios during the early 19th century, the riches of the town's pre-War of Independence heyday are still very much in evidence in illustrious colonial-style mansions bedecked with Italian frescoes, Wedgwood china and French chandeliers.

Declared a World Heritage Site by Unesco in 1988, Trinidad's secrets quickly became public property, and it wasn't long before busloads of visitors started arriving to sample the beauty of Cuba's oldest and most enchanting 'outdoor museum.' Yet tourism has done little to deaden Trinidad's gentle southern sheen. The town retains a quiet, almost soporific air in its rambling cobbled streets replete with leather-faced *guajiros* (country folk), snorting donkeys and melodic, guitar-wielding troubadours.

Ringed by sparkling natural attractions, Trinidad is more than just a potential PhD thesis for history buffs. Twelve kilometers to the south lies platinum-blond Playa Ancón, the south coast's best beach, while looming 18km to the north the purple-hued shadows of the Sierra del Escambray (Escambray Mountains) offer a lush adventure playground.

With its Unesco tag and a steady stream of overseas visitors, Trinidad, not surprisingly, has an above-average quota of prowling *jineteros* (hustlers), though mostly they're more annoying than aggressive.

History

In 1514 pioneering conquistador Diego Velázquez de Cuéllar founded La Villa de la Santísima Trinidad on Cuba's south coast, the island's third settlement after Baracoa and Bayamo. In 1518 Velázquez' former secretary, Hernán Cortés, passed through the town recruiting mercenaries for his all-conquering expedition to Mexico, and the settlement was all but emptied of its original inhabitants. Over the ensuing 60 years it was left to a smattering of the local Taíno people to keep the ailing economy alive through a mixture of farming, cattle-rearing and a little outside trade.

Reduced to a small rural backwater by the 17th century and cut off from the colonial authorities in Havana by dire communications, Trinidad became a haven for pirates and smugglers who conducted a lucrative illegal slave trade with British-controlled Jamaica.

Things began to change in the early 19th century when the town became the capital of the Departamento Central, and hundreds of French refugees fleeing a slave rebellion in Haiti arrived, setting up more than 50 small sugar mills in the nearby Valle de los Ingenios. Sugar soon replaced leather and salted beef as the region's most important product; by the mid-19th century the area around Trinidad was producing a third of Cuba's sugar.

The boom ended rather abruptly during the Independence Wars, when the surrounding sugar plantations were devastated by fire and fighting. The industry never fully recovered. By the late 19th century the focus of the sugar trade had shifted to Cienfuegos and Matanzas provinces, and Trinidad slipped into an economic coma. The tourist renaissance began in the 1950s, when President Batista passed a preservation law that recognized the town's historical value. In 1965 the town was declared a national monument, and in 1988 it became a Unesco World Heritage Site.

◉ Sights

In Trinidad, all roads lead to **Plaza Mayor**, the town's remarkably peaceful main square, located at the heart of the *casco histórico* (old town) and ringed by a quartet of impressive buildings.

★**Museo Histórico Municipal**   MUSEUM
(Simón Bolívar No 423; admission CUC$2; ⊙9am-5pm Sat-Thu) For Trinidad's showpiece museum look no further than this grandiose structure just off Plaza Mayor, a mansion that belonged to the Borrell family from 1827 to 1830. Later the building passed to a German planter named Kanter, or Cantero, and it's still called Casa Cantero.

Trinidad

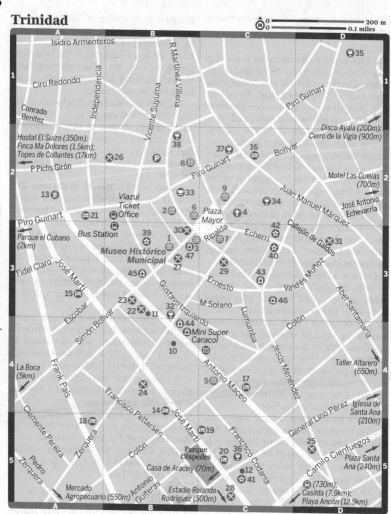

Reputedly, Dr Justo Cantero acquired vast sugar estates by poisoning an old slave trader and marrying his widow, who also suffered an untimely death. Cantero's ill-gotten wealth is well displayed in the stylish neoclassical decoration of the rooms. The view of Trinidad from the top of the tower alone is worth the price of admission. Visit before 11am, when the tour buses start rolling in.

Maqueta de Trinidad
MUSEUM

(Colón, cnr Maceo; admission CUC$1; ⊙9am-5pm Mon-Sat) Opened in 2014 and encased in the beautifully restored Casa Frias, this scale model of Trinidad's *casco histórico* displays amazing attention to detail (try to pick out your casa particiuar). A resident guide will fill you in on what's what with a conductor-like stick. Plans are afoot to turn Casa Frias into a full-on cultural center.

Iglesia Parroquial de la Santísima Trinidad
CHURCH

(⊙11am-12:30pm Mon-Sat) Despite its rather unremarkable outer facade, this church on the northeastern side of Plaza Mayor graces countless Trinidad postcard views. Rebuilt in 1892 on the site of an earlier church destroyed in a storm, the church mixes 20th-century touch-ups with artifacts from

Trinidad

◎ Top Sights
1 Museo Histórico Municipal................B3

◎ Sights
2 Casa Templo de Santería Yemayá....... B2
3 Galería de Arte................................B3
4 Iglesia Parroquial de la Santísima
   Trinidad.......................................C2
5 Maqueta de Trinidad........................C4
6 Museo de Arqueología Guamuhaya.....B2
7 Museo de Arquitectura Trinitaria........C3
8 Museo Nacional de la Lucha Contra
   Bandidos.......................................B2
9 Museo Romántico............................C2

◑ Activities, Courses & Tours
10 Cubatur...B4
11 Las Ruinas del Teatro Brunet.............B3
12 Paradiso..C5
13 Trinidad Travels..............................A2

◔ Sleeping
   Casa de Victor........................(see 13)
14 Casa Gil Lemes...............................B4
15 Casa Muñoz – Julio & Rosa................A3
16 El Rústico......................................C2
17 Hostal Colina.................................C4
18 Hostal José & Fatima.......................A5
19 Hotel La Ronda...............................C5
20 Iberostar Grand Hotel......................C5
21 Nelson Fernández Rodríguez.............A2

◕ Eating
22 Cubita Restaurant...........................B3

23 Dulcinea.......................................B3
24 Galería Comercial Universo...............B4
25 Guitarra Mia..................................D5
26 La Ceiba.......................................B2
27 Mesón del Regidor..........................B3
28 Paraito...C5
   Restaurant El Dorado..............(see 21)
29 Restaurante Plaza Mayor..................C3
30 Sol Ananda...................................B3
31 Vista Gourmet................................D3

◷ Drinking & Nightlife
32 Bodeguita Fando Brothers.................B3
33 Café Don Pepe...............................B2
34 Casa de la Música...........................C2
35 Disco Ayala...................................D1
   La Casa de la Cerveza.............(see 11)
36 La Floridita....................................C5
37 Taberna La Botija............................C2
38 Taberna la Canchánchara.................B2

◉ Entertainment
39 Bar Yesterday................................B3
40 Casa de la Trova.............................C3
41 Casa Fischer..................................C5
42 Palenque de los Congos
   Reales..C3

◎ Shopping
43 Arts & Crafts Market........................C3
44 Casa del Habano.............................B4
45 Galería La Paulet.............................B3
46 Taller Instrumentos Musicales............C3
47 Tienda Amelia Peláez.......................B3

as far back as the 18th century, such as the venerated Christ of the True Cross (1713), which occupies the second altar from the front to the left.

Museo Romántico MUSEUM
(Echerri No 52; admission CUC$2; ⊙9am-5pm Tue-Sun) Across Calle Simón Bolívar is the glittering Palacio Brunet. The ground floor was built in 1740, and the upstairs was added in 1808. In 1974 the mansion was converted into a museum with 19th-century furnishings, a fine collection of china and various other period pieces. Pushy museum staff may materialize out of the shadows for a tip.

The shop adjacent has a good selection of photos and books in English.

Museo de Arquitectura Trinitaria MUSEUM
(Ripalda No 83; admission CUC$1; ⊙9am-5pm Sat-Thu) Another public display of wealth sits on the southeastern side of Plaza Mayor in a museum showcasing upper-class domestic architecture of the 18th and 19th centuries.

The museum is housed in buildings that were erected in 1738 and 1785 and joined in 1819. It was once the residence of the wealthy Iznaga family.

Museo de Arqueología Guamuhaya MUSEUM
(Simón Bolívar No 457; admission CUC$1; ⊙9am-5pm Tue-Sun) On the northwestern side of Plaza Mayor is this odd mix of stuffed animals, native bones and vaguely incongruous 19th-century kitchen furniture. Given a radical rethink for the 2014 anniversary, it's now in far better shape.

Galería de Arte ART GALLERY
(cnr Rubén Martínez Villena & Simón Bolívar; ⊙9am-4:30pm Mon-Sat) FREE Admission is completely free at the 19th-century Palacio Ortiz, which today houses an art gallery on the southeastern side of Plaza Mayor. Worth a look for its quality local art, particularly the embroidery, pottery and jewelry. There's also a pleasant courtyard.

Casa Templo de Santería Yemayá

MUSEUM, LANDMARK

(R Martínez Villena No 59, btwn Simón Bolívar & Piro Guinart; ⊙hours vary) **FREE** No Santería museum can replicate the ethereal spiritual experience of Regla de Ocha (also known as Santería, Cuba's main religion of African origin), though this house has a try with a Santería altar to Yemayá, Goddess of the Sea, laden with myriad offerings of fruit, water and stones.

The house is presided over by *santeros* (priests of Santería), who'll emerge from the back patio and surprise you with some well-rehearsed tourist spiel. On the goddess' anniversary, March 19, ceremonies are performed day and night.

Museo Nacional de la Lucha Contra Bandidos

MUSEUM

(Echerri No 59; admission CUC$1; ⊙9am-5pm Tue-Sun) Perhaps the most recognizable building in Trinidad is the dilapidated pastel-yellow bell tower of the former convent of San Francisco de Asís. Since 1986 the building has housed a museum with photos, maps, weapons and other objects relating to the struggle against the various counter-revolutionary bands that took a leaf out of Fidel's book and operated illicitly out of the Sierra del Escambray between 1960 and 1965.

The fuselage of a US U-2 spy plane shot down over Cuba is also on display. You can climb the bell tower for good views.

Iglesia de Santa Ana

CHURCH

(Plaza Santa Ana, Camilo Cienfuegos) Grass grows around the domed bell tower, and the arched doorways were bricked up long ago, but the shell of this ruined church (1812) defiantly remains. Looming like a time-worn ecclesiastical stencil, it looks ghostly after dark.

Plaza Santa Ana

PLAZA

(Camilo Cienfuegos; ⊙11am-10pm) Located on the eponymous square, which delineates Trinidad's northeastern reaches, is a former Spanish prison (1844) that has been converted into the Plaza Santa Ana tourist center. The complex includes an art gallery, handicraft market, ceramics shop, bar and restaurant.

Taller Alfarero

POTTERY

(Andrés Berro No 51, btwn Pepito Tey & Abel Santamaría; ⊙8am-noon & 2-5pm Mon-Fri) **FREE** Trinidad is known for its pottery. In this large factory, teams of workers make trademark Trinidad ceramics from local clay using a traditional potter's wheel. You can watch them at work and buy the finished product.

Activities

Ride a bike to one of Cuba's outstanding beaches, work up a sweat on a couple of DIY hikes, or get a different perspective astride a horse.

Trinidad to Playa Ancón

CYCLING

The bicycle ride to Playa Ancón is a great outdoor adventure, and once there you can snorkel, catch some rays or use the swimming pool or Ping-Pong table. The best route by far is via the small seaside village of La Boca (18km one way).

Cerro de la Vigía

HIKING

For views and a workout, walk straight up Calle Simón Bolívar between the Iglesia Parroquial and the Museo Romántico to the destroyed 18th-century **Ermita de Nuestra Señora de la Candelaria de la Popa**, part of a former Spanish military hospital now occupied by a new luxury hotel.

From here it's a 30-minute hike further up the hill to the radio transmitter atop 180m-high Cerro de la Vigía, which delivers broad vistas of Trinidad, the Valle de los Ingenios and the Caribbean littoral.

Parque el Cubano

HIKING

(admission CUC$9) This pleasant spot within a protected park consists of a *ranchón* (farm)-style restaurant that specializes in *pez gato* (catfish), a fish farm and a 3.6km trail, the **Huellas de la História**, to the refreshing **Javira Waterfall**. There are also stables and opportunities for horseback riding. If you hike to El Cubano from Trinidad, you'll clock up a total of approximately 16km.

With a stop for lunch in the *ranchón*, it can make an excellent day trip. Alternatively, for CUC$17 you can organize an excursion with Cubatur (p285), including motor transport. To get to the park, hike west out of town on the Cienfuegos road. Pass the 'Welcome to Trinidad' sign and cross a bridge over the Río Guaurabo. A track on your left now leads back under the bridge and up a narrow, poorly paved road for 5km to Parque el Cubano.

Closer to town is the **Finca Ma Dolores** (✆41-99-64-81; Carretera de Cienfuegos, Km 1.5), a rustic Cubanacán hotel that hosts sporadic *fiestas campesinas* (country fairs).

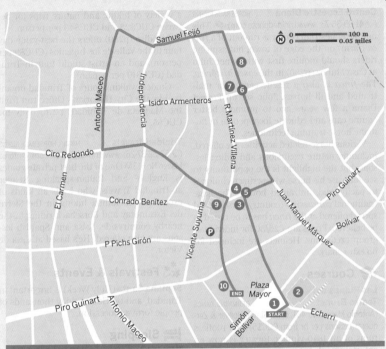

Samuel Feijó

Independencia

Antonio Maceo

Isidro Armenteros

Ciro Redondo

El Carmen

R Martínez Villena

Conrado Benítez

Juan Manuel Márquez

Piro Guinart

Bolívar

Vicente Suyuma

P Pichs Girón

Plaza Mayor

Simón Bolívar

Piro Guinart

Antonio Maceo

Echerri

🏃 City Walk
Photogenic Trinidad

START PLAZA MAYOR
END CASA TEMPLO DE SANTERÍA YEMAYÁ
LENGTH 2KM

In Trinidad, soft evening sunlight, striking colonial architecture and street scenes that have more in common with the 1850s than the 2010s conspire to create an ideal prowling ground for photographers.

Early evening, when the sunlight is less intense and the shadows longer, is a good time to undertake this walk. Start in **1** **Plaza Mayor** (p275), the colonial square that features in a thousand different postcards. With local life continuing at a lazy pace around you, there's always a new way of snapping it with the **2** **Iglesia Parroquial de la Santísima Trinidad** (p276) as backdrop.

The classic shot is looking northwest along cobbled Calle Echerri past colonial edifices to the tower of the **3** **Convento de San Francisco de Asís**. Walk a block northwest and try to capture the small sunlit **4** **park** opposite the convent. At the end of Echerri, stand back from the **5** **T-junction** with Calle Ciro

Redondo and wait...and wait. Something interesting will pass at the end of the street – a horse, a 1951 Plymouth, a bicycle.

Turn right on Ciro Redondo, left on Calle Juan Manuel Márquez and wander toward the shabbier, no less photogenic **6** **Barrio Los Tres Cruces**. Look out for ladies in curlers, old men sitting in doorways, cowboys, people dragging pigs and kids playing stickball in the neighborhood's **7** **plaza**. A row of rainbow-colored, single-story houses in **8** **Calle Juan Manuel Márquez** are given extra luminescence by the slanting evening sun. On Calle Samuel Feijó, horses and riders often congregate with the shadowy Sierra del Escambray looming behind them. More street life awaits back on Calle Ciro Redondo. Outside the iconic **9** **Taberna la Canchánchara** (p284) there's nearly always a 1958 Chevy being used as a communal seat, or perhaps a baseball backstop. Pass the **10** **Casa Templo de Santería Yemayá** (p278) dedicated to the *orisha* (Yoruba god) of the sea. With dusk falling you're back in Plaza Mayor.

Centro Ecuestre Diana
HORSEBACK RIDING

(☑41-99-36-73; www.trinidadphoto.com) 🏇 This unique equestrian center is run out of a *finca* (farm) on the edge of town, but aspiring riders should inquire first with owner Julio at Casa Muñoz (p280) in the *casco histórico*. The *finca* is also a rescue center for maltreated and ill horses. Julio set up Project Diana a few years ago to promote better equine care and educate local people in humane horse-training techniques.

Various horse-related activities are offered, including nature excursions and riding lessons, but the highlight is the opportunity to see Julio use his horse-whispering techniques to pacify wild, untrained horses. The huge traditional *campesino* (country person) food spread offered at the *finca* has to be tasted to be believed. Prices are €26/30 for individual/group excursions. Helmets are included for no extra charge.

🎓 Courses

Las Ruinas del Teatro Brunet
DRUMMING, DANCE

(Antonio Maceo No 461, btwn Simón Bolívar & Zerquera; lessons per hr from CUC$5) The roofless ruins of an 1840-vintage theater is now an entertainment space where you can take drumming and dance lessons (inquire within for times).

Paradiso
CULTURAL

(www.paradiso.cu; General Lino Pérez No 306, Casa ARTex) Paradiso in Casa Fischer has incorporated a number of interesting courses into its cultural program, including Cuban architecture (CUC$20), Afro-Cuban culture (CUC$20), *artes plásticas* (visual arts; CUC$20) and popular music (CUC$20). These courses last four hours and are taught by cultural specialists.

The courses require a minimum number of six to 10 people, but you can always negotiate. There are also percussion lessons for CUC$5 an hour and courses in Spanish language or Cuban culture for CUC$5 an hour.

👉 Tours

With its sketchy public transport and steep road gradients making cycling arduous, it's easiest to visit the extensive natural park of Topes de Collantes on a day tour. A tour to Topes by state taxi shouldn't cost more than CUC$35 including wait time; bargain hard. **Cubatur** (Antonio Maceo No 447; ⏰9am-8pm), just outside the *casco histórico*, organizes

a variety of hiking and nature trips for between CUC$23 and CUC$43 per person.

Paradiso (p280) offers the best-value day tour to the Valle de los Ingenios (CUC$9 per person), and an artist-studio tour in Trinidad (CUC$10 per person).

Guided walking tours of Trinidad organized by the City Historian's Office run from the Maqueta de Trinidad (p276) daily for CUC$5.

Trinidad Travels
HIKING, HORSEBACK RIDING

(☑52-82-37-26; www.trinidadtravels.com; Antonio Maceo No 613A) One of the best private guides is English- and Italian-speaking Reinier at Trinidad Travels, who leads all kinds of excursions, including hiking in the Sierra del Escambray and horseback riding in the nearby countryside. Salsa and Spanish lessons are also offered. He's based at Casa de Victor.

✨ Festivals & Events

Semana Santa (Holy Week) is important in Trinidad, and on Good Friday thousands of people form a procession.

🛏 Sleeping

Trinidad has, at a guesstimate, 500 casas particulares, meaning competition is hot. Arriving by bus or walking the streets with luggage, you'll be besieged by *jineteros* (hustlers) working for commissions, or by the casa owners themselves. With so many beautiful homes and hospitable families renting, there's no reason to be rushed. Take your time and shop around.

A boutique five-star hotel, **Pansea Trinidad**, run by the French Accor group was due to open in 2015. The much stalled project will integrate part of the Ermita de Nuestra Señora de la Candelaria de la Popa, the ruins of a church dating from the mid-18th century, into the hotel building.

★ Casa Muñoz – Julio & Rosa
CASA PARTICULAR $

(☑41-99-36-73; www.trinidadphoto.com; José Martí No 401, cnr Escobar; d/tr/q CUC$35/40/45; 🅿❄) Julio is an accomplished published photographer who runs workshops and courses out of his stunning colonial home on documentary photography, religion and life in Cuba's new economic reality (see the website for details). He's also a horse whisperer – his beautiful mare lives out back along with his three dogs and Russian Moskvich.

There are three huge rooms here and a separate duplex apartment (CUC$45 to CUC$65). Delicious food is served on a ground-floor patio or 1st-floor terrace. All the family speak English. Book early – it's insanely popular (licensed US people-to-people groups often come here).

Nelson Fernández Rodríguez
CASA PARTICULAR $

(☑41-99-38-49; Piro Guinart No 226, btwn Maceo & Gustavo Izquierdo; r CUC$25-30; ☀) Nelson's place above the lovely El Dorado restaurant bears all the hallmarks of a fine Trinidadian homestay – lush patio, romantic terrace and Unesco-standard colonial splendor. Four rooms are available.

Hostal Colina
CASA PARTICULAR $

(☑41-99-23-19; Antonio Maceo No 374, btwn General Lino Pérez & Colón; r CUC$25-35; ☀) Another place that leaves you struggling for superlatives. Although the house dates from the 1830s, it's got a definitive modern touch, giving you the feeling of being in a plush Mexican hacienda. Three pastel-yellow rooms give out onto a patio where you can sit at the plush wooden bar and catch mangoes and avocados as they fall from the trees.

Casa Gil Lemes
CASA PARTICULAR $

(☑41-99-31-42; José Martí No 263, btwn Colón & Zerquera; r CUC$25; ☀) This casa was one of Trinidad's first (and was listed in Lonely Planet's first edition Cuba guidebook in 1997). Cast an eye over the noble arches in the front room and the religious statues, and save some breath (yes, you'll gasp) for the patio and fountain, a unique array of pots and sea serpents. Get in early for this one – there's only one room.

Hostal José & Fatima
CASA PARTICULAR $

(☑41-99-66-82; Zerquera No 159, btwn Frank País & Pettersen; CUC$30-35; ☀) Highly popular casa with all the colonial trimmings including a terrace. The helpful hosts can hook you up with many local activities.

El Rústico
CASA PARTICULAR $

(☑41-99-30-24; Juan Manuel Márquez No 54A, btwn Piro Guinart & Simón Bolívar; ☀) Five rooms available in two adjacent houses below the popular El Criollo restaurant. Fittings are clean and modern and there's plenty of communal space. It's one cobbled block from Plaza Mayor.

Casa de Victor
CASA PARTICULAR $

(☑41-99-64-44; Maceo, btwn Piro Guinart & P Pichs Girón; r CUC$20-30; ☀) Handy to the bus station, Victor's place has three self-contained rooms that share a couple of spacious salas (living rooms), a balcony overlooking the street, and a fine rear terraza decorated rather ingeniously with the recycled ceramic pots for which Trinidad is famous.

Hostal El Suizo
CASA PARTICULAR $

(☑53-77-28-12; P Pichs Girón No 22; CUC$25-30; ☐☀) Away from the hustle of the center and handily located for a quick entry or exit on the Trinidad–Cienfuegos road, this pink reader-recommended room-terrace with independent entry is run by an expat Swiss hombre and his Cuban wife. It is clean, tranquil and known for its adventurous cooking – Thai curry anyone?

Casa de Aracely
CASA PARTICULAR $

(☑41-99-35-58; General Lino Pérez No 207, btwn Frank País & Miguel Calzada; r CUC$20-25; ☀) Had enough of the colonial splendor? Head away from the tourist frenzy to General Lino Pérez, where Aracely rents two upstairs rooms with a private entrance, a very quiet flower-bedecked patio and a splendid roof terrace.

Finca Ma Dolores
HOTEL $$

(☑41-99-64-10; Carretera de Cienfuegos, Km 1.5; s/d CUC$36/60; P❄️🔳) Trinidad goes rustic with the out-of-town Finca Ma Dolores, 1.5km west on the road to Cienfuegos and Topes de Collantes. It's equipped with hotel-style rooms and cabins – the latter are the better option (try for one with a porch overlooking the Río Guaurabo).

On nights when groups are present, there's a *fiesta campesina* with country-style Cuban folk dancing at 9:30pm (guests/nonguests free/CUC$5, including one drink). It also has a swimming pool, a *ranchón* restaurant, and boat and horseback-riding tours.

★ Iberostar Grand Hotel
BOUTIQUE HOTEL $$$

(☑41-99-60-70; www.iberostar.com; cnr José Martí & General Lino Pérez; s/d/ste CUC$165/220/313; ❄️@📶) Look out, Habaguanex! One of a handful of Spanish-run Iberostar's Cuban hotels, the five-star Grand oozes luxury the moment you arrive in its fern-filled, and tile-embellished lobby. Maintaining 36 classy rooms in a remodeled 19th-century building, the Grand shies away from the standard all-inclusive tourist formula, preferring to press privacy, refinement and an appreciation of history (you are, after all, in Trinidad). The wi-fi is free to guests – almost unheard of in Cuba.

Motel Las Cuevas
HOTEL $$$

(☑41-99-61-33; s/d incl breakfast CUC$88/126; P❄️🔳) Perched on a hill above town, Las Cuevas is more hotel than motel, with bus tours providing the main drive-by clientele. While the setting is lush, the rooms – which are arranged in scattered two-storied units – are a little less memorable, as is the breakfast.

Value is added with a swimming pool, gardens, panoramic views and the murky Cueva la Maravillosa, accessible down a stairway, where you'll see a huge tree growing out of a cavern (entry CUC$1). The hotel is accessed via a steep road that climbs northeast from the Iglesia de Santa Ana.

Hotel La Ronda
BOUTIQUE HOTEL $$$

(☑41-99-61-33; José Martí No 238; s/d CUC$123/138; ❄️@) Renovated in 2012, the Ronda's second incarnation is far better than its first. A modernist fountain, sharp color accents, old blown-up art nouveau photos and bolero (romantic love song) lyrics inscribed outside every room add individualistic touches to an impressive colonial whole, easily justifying the 'boutique' label.

🍴 Eating

Call it a tidal wave. In January 2011 there were three private restaurants in Trinidad, the same three that had been here for over a decade. Now there are over 90! Suddenly your problem is not finding one, but sifting through the raft of options.

Paraíto
FAST FOOD $

(☑41-99-23-47; José Martí No 181B, btwn Lino Pérez & Camilo Cienfuegos; snacks CUC$1-3; ⏱11am-9pm) Wave goodbye to weighty antiques and poorly coordinated foreign dancers and dive into this local 'dive' for cheap snacks (the fried rice is good), stand-up tables and quick-fire Spanish gossip. Welcome to the other, nontouristy side of Trinidad.

Dulcinea
CAFE $

(cnr Antonio Maceo & Simón Bolívar; snacks CUC$1-4; ⏱7:30am-10pm) The former Begonias cafe has long been a daytime nexus for Trinidad's transient backpacker crowd, meaning it's a good place to swap tips, books and *jinetero* stories. Reborn as a bakery and cake shop, it retains its busy street corner atmosphere, cleanish toilets, and five or six cheap – but always crowded – internet terminals (CUC$3 for 20 minutes).

Cubita Restaurant
INTERNATIONAL $$

(Antonio Maceo No 471; mains CUC$8-15; ⏱11am-midnight) When great food and fine service conspire, it can be a highly pleasurable experience – and one which, until recently, had been hard to find in Trinidad. Fighting hard in a highly competitive field, La Cubita has set a fast pace with its inventive starters, complimentary salads, some wonderfully marinated brochettes and highly discreet service. It's run by Trinidad's famous ceramic-makers.

Restaurant El Dorado
INTERNATIONAL $$

(☑41-99-38-49; Piro Guinart No 226, btwn Maceo & Gustavo Izquierdo; meals CUC$7-18; ⏱noon-midnight) An exquisite colonial house, meticulously polished period furniture, and highly courteous wait staff; Trinidad is full of such historic easy-on-the-eye eating establishments. But at El Dorado, the food effortlessly emulates the decor. Look forward to beef strips, well seasoned fish and grilled turkey, rounded off with some professional touches (complimentary bread basket and – if you're lucky – a comp house cocktail too).

Guitarra Mia
CUBAN $$

([☑]41-99-34-52; Jésus Menéndez No 19, btwn Camilo Cienfuegos & Lino Pérez; mains CUC$6-8; ⊘noon-midnight) Drift a few blocks from the Centro Histórico and the prices magically get cheaper without any measurable drop in food quality. Music is the theme in this interesting nook that is never short of a quintet or passing troubadour. From the menu, the *tostones* (plantain pan-fried in oil) stuffed with minced crab linger longest in the memory. Write your comments on the door (literally) on the way out.

Sol Ananda
INTERNATIONAL $$

([☑]41-99-82-81; Rubén Martínez Villena No 45, cnr Simón Bolívar; mains CUC$8-15; ⊘11am-11pm) Fine 18th-century china, grandfather clocks, even an antique bed: Sol Ananda in Trinidad's Plaza Mayor is, on first impressions, more museum than restaurant. Situated in one of the town's oldest houses (dating from 1750) it tackles an ambitious cross-section of global food from traditional Cuban (excellent lamb *ropa vieja*) to South Asian (fish kofta and samosas).

La Ceiba
CUBAN $$

(P Pichs Girón No 263; mains CUC$12; ⊘noon-11pm) Set in a back patio under the boughs of a giant ceiba tree, this fledgling paladar (private restaurant) specializes in chicken in honey and lemon sauce, and serves up Trinidad's favorite cocktail, the *canchánchara* (rum, honey, lemon and water) in ceramic cups. In good old-fashioned paladar style you must walk right through the middle of the owner's house to reach it.

Restaurante Plaza Mayor
CARIBBEAN $$

(cnr Rubén Martínez Villena & Zerquera; dishes from CUC$4, buffet CUC$10; ⊘noon-11pm) Trinidad's best government-run restaurant courtesy of its on-again/off-again lunchtime buffet, which ought to fill you up until dinnertime.

★ Vista Gourmet
CUBAN, INTERNATIONAL $$$

([☑]41-99-67-00; Callejón de Galdos; mains CUC$12-18; ⊘noon-midnight) The slickest of the town's private restaurants is perched on a lovely terrace above Trinidad's red-tiled rooftops and run by the charismatic sommelier Bolo. Among many novelties are the free cocktails on the 'Atardecer Forever' roof terrace.

Equally innovative is the appetizer and dessert buffet spread out invitingly on side tables – both are included in the price of your main dish (which you choose from an à la carte menu). The *lechón asado* (roast pork) and lobster are both recommended. Not surprisingly, the wine list is the best in town.

Self-Catering

Mercado Agropecuario
MARKET $

(cnr Pedro Zerquera & Manuel Fajardo; ⊘8am-6pm Mon-Sat, to noon Sun) Trinidad's *agropecuario* (vegetable market) isn't London's Covent Garden, but you should still be able to get basic fruits and vegetables.

Galería Comercial Universo
SUPERMARKET $

(José Martí, cnr Zerquera) Mini shopping center that includes a variety of shops for most of your immediate needs including Trinidad's best (and most expensive) grocery store. Head here for yogurt, lifesaving biscuits and pharmacy goods.

🍷 Drinking & Nightlife

★ Taberna La Botija
BAR, INTERNATIONAL

(Juan Manuel Márquez, cnr Piro Guinart; ⊘24hr) While other restaurants send their wait staff out into the street to fish for customers, La Botija crams half the town into its lively corner bar without even trying. The key: a warm talk-to-your-neighbor atmosphere, cold beer served in ceramic mugs and the best house band in Trinidad (think jazz meets soul over a violin). The food ain't bad either.

Café Don Pepe
CAFE

([☑]41-99-35-73; Piro Guinart, cnr Martínez Villena; ⊘8am-11pm) Best coffee in Trinidad served in ceramic mugs with a square of Baracoan chocolate on the side. Imbibe in a colonial courtyard decorated with modern graffiti.

Casa de la Música
CLUB

(Calle Cristo) One of Trinidad's (and Cuba's) classic venues, this casa is an alfresco affair that congregates on the sweeping staircase beside the Iglesia Parroquial off Plaza Mayor. A good mix of tourists and locals take in the 10pm salsa show here. Alternatively, full-on salsa concerts are held in the casa's rear courtyard (also accessible from Juan Manuel Márquez; cover CUC$2).

La Floridita
BAR

(General Lino Pérez No 313; ⊘24hr) Where the feistily local Bar Daiquiri once stood, the Trinidadian authorities have unveiled a cheap copy of Havana's much-hyped Hemingway bar, although this one – thankfully – peddles its daiquiris for a more reasonable CUC$3. A life-sized statue of the revered writer props up the bar.

La Casa de la Cerveza
BAR, LIVE MUSIC

(Antonio Maceo No 461, btwn Simón Bolívar & Zerquera; admission CUC$1; ⊙noon-midnight) The 1840-vintage Brunet theater has been a ruin since its roof collapsed in 1901. Today it serves as a beer hall and live music venue. Don't get too excited; there are no microbrews, just Cristal on tap.

Disco Ayala
CLUB

(admission CUC$10; ⊙10pm-3am) A slightly tacky cabaret with an indigenous theme that takes place in a cave up on the hill behind the Ermita Popa church. A frenetic disco, usually thick with *jineteras*, kicks off afterwards. Entry includes as many mojitos as you care to sink.

To get there follow Calle Simón Bolívar from Plaza Mayor up to the Ermita de Nuestra Señora de la Candelaria de la Popa. The disco is 100m further along on your left.

Bodeguita Fando Brothers
BAR, RESTAURANT

(Antonio Maceo No 162B, cnr Zerquera; ⊙24hr) Functioning both as a snack bar and a drinking hole, Fando's is best enjoyed in the early evening, while nursing a beer or cocktail. Unlike other private places, it's open 24/7.

Taberna la Canchánchara
BAR

(cnr Rubén Martínez Villena & Ciro Redondo; ⊙10am-6pm) This place is famous for its eponymous house cocktail made from rum, honey, lemon and water. Local musicians regularly drop by for off-the-cuff jam sessions, and it's certainly not unusual for the *canchánchara*-inebriated crowd to break into spontaneous dancing.

☆ Entertainment

Get ready for the best Cuban nightlife outside Havana.

Bar Yesterday
LIVE MUSIC

(Gustavo Izquierdo, btwn Piro Guinart & Simón Bolívar; ⊙4pm-midnight) They've changed the beat to 4/4 time in the old Casa de la Rumba where the decor is dedicated exclusively to The Beatles, including four life-sized statues. But there's nothing 'yesterday' about the audience, most of whom are barely out of their teens. Beatlemania redux?

Palenque de los Congos Reales
RUMBA

(cnr Echerri & Av Jesús Menéndez) A must for rumba fans, this open patio on Trinidad's music alley has an eclectic menu incorporating salsa, *son* (Cuban popular music) and *trova* (traditional poetic singing). The highlight, however, is the 10pm rumba drums with soulful African rhythms and energetic fire-eating dancers.

Casa Fischer
CULTURAL CENTER

(General Lino Pérez No 312, btwn José Martí & Francisco Codania; admission CUC$1) The local ARTex patio cranks up at 10pm with a salsa orchestra (on Tuesday, Wednesday, Thursday, Saturday and Sunday) or a folklore show (Friday). If you're early, kill time at the art gallery (free) and chat to the staff at the on-site Paradiso office about salsa lessons and other courses.

Casa de la Trova
LIVE MUSIC

(Echerri No 29; admission CUC$1; ⊙9pm-2am) Trinidad's spirited casa retains its earthy essence despite the high package-tourist-to-Cuban ratio. Local musicians to look out for here are Semillas del Son, Santa Palabra and the town's best *trovador* (traditional singer/songwriter), Israel Moreno.

Estadio Rolando Rodríguez
SPORTS

(Eliope Paz; ⊙Oct-Apr) This stadium, at the southeastern end of Frank País, hosts baseball games.

🛍 Shopping

You can shop until you drop from heat exhaustion in Trinidad, at least at the open-air markets, which are set up all over town. See local painters at work – and buy their paintings too. The town is full of picture-crammed, open-windowed workshops.

Arts & Crafts Market
CRAFTS, SOUVENIRS

(Av Jesús Menéndez; ⊙9am-6pm) This excellent open-air market in front of the Casa de la Trova is the place to buy souvenirs, especially textiles and crochet work. Note: should you see any black coral or turtle-shell items, don't buy them. They're made from endangered species and are forbidden entry into many countries.

Tienda Amelia Peláez
CRAFTS, SOUVENIRS

(Simón Bolívar No 418; ⊙9am-6pm Mon-Sat, 9am-noon Sun) Just down from Plaza Mayor, this government store has a good selection of Cuban handicrafts.

Taller Instrumentos Musicales
MUSICAL INSTRUMENTS

(cnr Av Jesús Menéndez & Valdés Muñoz) Musical instruments are made here and sold in the adjacent shop.

Casa del Habano
CIGARS

(cnr Antonio Maceo & Zerquera; ⊙9am-7pm)
Dodge the street hustlers and satisfy your
alcoholic (rum) and tobacco vices here.

Galería La Paulet
ART

(Simón Bolívar No 411) Interesting selection of
probing, mainly abstract art by local artists.

ℹ️ Information

INTERNET ACCESS

Dulcinea (Antonio Maceo No 473; internet per
20min CUC$3; ⊙9am-8:30pm) Half a dozen
terminals on the corner of Simón Bolívar.
Crowded.

Etecsa Telepunto (cnr General Lino Pérez &
Francisco Pettersen; internet per hr CUC$4.50;
⊙8:30am-7pm) Telepunto office with modern,
if slow, computer terminals. Not too crowded.

MEDICAL SERVICES

General Hospital (☎41-99-32-01; Antonio
Maceo No 6) Southeast of the city center.

Servimed Clínica Internacional Cubanacán
(☎41-99-62-40; General Lino Pérez No 103, cnr
Anastasio Cárdenas; ⊙24hr) There is an on-
site pharmacy selling products in convertibles.

MONEY

Banco de Crédito y Comercio (José Martí No
264; ⊙9am-3pm Mon-Fri) Has an ATM.

Cadeca (José Martí No 164, btwn Parque Céspedes & Camilo Cienfuegos; ⊙8:30am-8pm
Mon-Sat, 9am-6pm Sun)

POST

Post Office (Antonio Maceo No 418, btwn
Colón & Zerquera; ⊙9am-6pm Mon-Sat)

TRAVEL AGENCIES

Cubatur (Antonio Maceo No 447; ⊙9am-8pm)
Good for general tourist information, plus hotel
bookings, car rentals, excursions etc. State
taxis congregate outside.

Infotur (Gustavo Izquierdo, btwn Piro Guinart &
Camilo Cienfuegos; ⊙9am-5pm) Useful for general information on the town and its surroundings.

Ecotur (Simón Bolívar No 424; ⊙10am-10pm)
Has a desk in Mesón del Regidor restaurant.

Paradiso (General Lino Pérez No 306) Excellent selection of cultural tours in English,
Spanish and French.

ℹ️ Getting There & Away

BUS

The centrally located **bus station** (Piro Guinart
No 224) runs provincial buses to Sancti Spíritus
and Cienfuegos, though most foreigners use the
more reliable Víazul service. Tickets are sold at
a small window marked Taquilla Campo near the
station entrance. Check the blackboard for the
current schedule.

The **Víazul ticket office** (⊙8-11:30am &
1-5pm) is further back in the station. This office
is well organized and you can usually book tickets a couple of days in advance.

The Varadero departures can deposit you in
Jagüey Grande (CUC$15, three hours) with stops
on request in Jovellanos, Colesio and Cárdenas.
The Santiago de Cuba departure goes through
Sancti Spíritus (CUC$6, 1½ hours), Ciego de
Ávila (CUC$9, two hours 40 minutes), Camagüey
(CUC$15, five hours 20 minutes), Las Tunas
(CUC$22, 7½ hours), Holguín (CUC$26, eight
hours) and Bayamo (CUC$26, 10 hours).

The new Cubanacán Conectando bus service
has direct links daily with Havana, Varadero and
Viñales for similar prices as Víazul. Inquire at
Infotur (Antonio Maceo No 461).

TRAIN

Train transport out of Trinidad is awful even by
Cuban standards. The town hasn't been connected to the main rail network since a hurricane
downed a bridge in the early 1990s, meaning
the only functioning line runs up the Valle de los
Ingenios, stopping in Iznaga and terminating
at Meyer. The local train leaves at around 5am;
the more reliable tourist train leaves at 9:30am.
Always check ahead at the **terminal** (Lino Pérez
final), in a pink house across the train tracks on
the western side of the station.

VÍAZUL BUS DEPARTURES FROM TRINIDAD

DESTINATION	COST (CUC$)	DURATION	DEPARTURE
Cienfuegos	6	1½hr	7:40am, 9am, 10:30am, 3pm, 3:05pm, 3:45pm
Havana	25	6hr 20min	7:40am, 10:30am, 3:45pm
Santa Clara	8	3hr	3:05pm
Santiago de Cuba	33	12hr	8am
Varadero	20	6hr	9am, 3pm, 3:05pm

ℹ Getting Around

BICYCLE

There weren't any official bike rentals at last visit, but with 500+ casas particulares, it's inconceivable to think that you couldn't organize some kind of bike hire with a local. Just don't expect the latest Shimano gears. Trinidad to Playa Ancón is a pleasant and flat 30-minute ride; Trinidad to Topes de Collantes is akin to a tough stage in the Tour de France.

CAR & MOTORBIKE

The rental agencies at the Playa Ancón hotels rent mopeds (CUC$25 per day).

Cubacar (cnr Antonio Maceo & Zerquera) rents cars. Prices vary wildly depending on season, car type and length of hire; CUC$70 per day is a good general yardstick. They also have an office in Hotel Club Amigo Ancón.

The **Servi-Cupet gas station** (⊘24hr), 500m south of town on the road to Casilda, has an El Rápido snack bar attached. The Oro Negro gas station is at the entrance to Trinidad from Sancti Spíritus, 1km east of Plaza Santa Ana.

Guarded parking is available in certain areas around the *casco histórico*. Ask at your hotel or casa particular, where staff can arrange it.

TAXI

Trinidad has Havana-style coco-taxis; they cost approximately CUC$5 to Playa Ancón. A car costs from CUC$6 to CUC$8 one way. State-owned taxis tend to congregate outside the Cubatur office on Antonio Maceo. A cab to Sancti Spíritus (70km) should cost approximately CUC$35.

Playa Ancón & Around

Playa Ancón, a precious ribbon of white beach on Sancti Spíritus' iridescent Caribbean shoreline, is usually touted – with good reason – as the finest arc of sand on Cuba's south coast.

TRINIDAD TOUR BUS

Trinidad has a handy hop-on/hop-off tourist-oriented **minibus** (all-day ticket CUC$2), similar to Havana's and Viñales', linking its outlying sights. It plies a route from outside the Cubatur office on Antonio Maceo to Finca Ma Dolores, Playa la Boca, Bar las Caletas, and the three Playa Ancón hotels. It runs approximately four times a day in both directions starting at 9am and terminating at 6pm.

While not comparable in all-round quality to the north-coast giants of Varadero, Cayo Coco and Guardalavaca, Ancón has one important trump card: Trinidad, Latin America's sparkling colonial diamond, shimmering just 12km to the north. You can get here in less than 15 minutes by car or a leisurely 40 minutes on a bike. Alternatively, Ancón has three all-inclusive hotels and a well-equipped marina that runs catamaran trips to a couple of nearby coral keys.

Beach bums who want to be near the water but don't have the money or inclination to stay at one of the resorts, might consider a homestay in the seaside village of La Boca.

There's no doubting Ancón's beauty, but what gushing tourist brochures fail to mention are the sand fleas: they're famously ferocious at sunrise and sunset. Be warned.

The old fishing port of Casilda, 6km due south of Trinidad, is a friendly village with one paved road. On August 17 the Fiesta de Santa Elena engulfs little Casilda, with feasting, competitions, horse races and loads of rum. The road from Ancón to Casilda crosses a tidal flat, meaning abundant birdlife is visible in the early morning.

🏃 Activities

From Hotel Club Amigo Ancón it's 18km to Trinidad via Casilda, or 16km on the much nicer coastal road via La Boca. The hotel pool is also open to nonguests and you can usually nab the Ping-Pong table undetected.

Marina Trinidad   FISHING, SNORKELING

(☎41-99-62-05; www.nauticamarlin.com) The marina is a few hundred meters north of Hotel Club Amigo Ancón. Four hours of deep-sea fishing, including transport, gear and guide, costs CUC$280 for up to six people. Fly-fishing is also possible around the rich mangrove forests of Península de Ancón (CUC$250 for six hours, maximum two people).

Romantic types might want to check out the sunset cruise from CUC$20, which has been enthusiastically recommended by readers. The marina also runs an all-day snorkeling-and-beach tour to Cayo de Las Iguanas for CUC$50 per person with lunch.

Cayo Blanco International Dive Center   DIVING

(Marina Trinidad; single dive/open-water course CUC$35/320) The Cayo Blanco International Dive Center is located at the marina, and offers single/multiple dive packages as well as open-water courses. Cayo Blanco, a reef

Trinidad Area

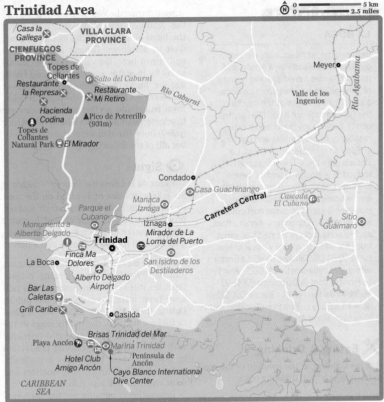

islet 25km southeast of Playa Ancón, has 22 marked scuba sites where you'll see black coral and bountiful marine life.

Windward Islands Cruising Company BOAT TRIPS
(www.caribbean-adventure.com; Marina Trinidad) This company charters crewed and bareboat monohulls and catamarans out of the Marina Trinidad to the Jardines de la Reina and the Archipiélago de los Canarreos. You can sail with or without guides, on a partial package or an all-inclusive tour. Interested parties should inquire using the contact details on the website.

Sleeping

Hotel Club Amigo Ancón RESORT $$
(☎41-99-61-23, 41-99-61-27; Playa Ancón; all-incl s/d CUC$54/86; P❋@☎) Built during Cuba's 30-year flirtation with Soviet architectonics, the Ancón wouldn't win any beauty contests. Indeed, this steamship-shaped

seven-story concrete pile looks more than a little incongruous next to the natural beauty of Ancón beach. But if it's beach proximity you're after, this deal could cut ice.

Some like the hotel's lack of pretension and low prices; others are apt to quote Groucho Marx and say that they'd rather not belong to a club (Amigo) that would have them as a member.

Brisas Trinidad del Mar RESORT $$
(☎41-99-65-00; Playa Ancón; all-incl s/d CUC$60/100; P❋@☎) Although a kitschy attempt to recreate Trinidad in a resort environment, Brisas wins kudos for rejecting monolithic architecture in favor of low-rise colonial-style villas. The swath of beach is stunning and the massage, sauna, gym and tennis courts handy for the sports-minded. However, after barely a decade in operation, the quality of this place has begun to suffer from poor maintenance and decidedly iffy service.

LA BOCA

Between the architecturally incongruous beach hotels of Playa Ancón and the sometimes frenetic tourist scene of Trinidad lies half-forgotten La Boca, a small fishing village at the mouth of the Guaurabo River. If you like lazy tranquility, fresh-from-the-ocean lobster, raspberry-ripple sunsets and bantering in Spanish with the local fishers, La Boca is pure bliss. The village has no reputable restaurants and its 'beach' is a little pebbly though splashed with ample scarlet-flowered acacia trees. However, it excels in casas particulares with wraparound porches, dinner offers, and relaxing rockers located just yards from the waterfront. Try **Villa Rio Mar** (☑41-99-31-08; San José No 65, La Boca; r with shared bathroom CUC$20-25; ▣✳) or **Hostal Idel & Domingo** (☑41-99-86-34; Av del Mar No 9, La Boca; r CUC$25; ▣✳). La Boca is 5km from Trinidad and 8km from Playa Ancón.

✖ Eating & Drinking

Bar las Caletas, at the junction of the road to Casilda, is a local drinking place.

Grill Caribe   CARIBBEAN **$$**
(meals CUC$10; ☉24hr) Other than the hotel restaurants, there's this place on a quiet beach, which specializes in seafood, such as fish and shrimp or lobster, and charges a pretty price. Strict vegetarians will be disappointed here. It's a great sunset spot.

❶ Getting There & Away

A shuttle bus run by Transtur links Ancón to Trinidad four times daily (CUC$2). Otherwise, it's a pleasant bike ride or a cheap taxi (CUC$6 to CUC$8).

Valle de los Ingenios

Trinidad's immense wealth was garnered not in the town itself, but in a verdant valley 8km to the east. The Valle de los Ingenios (or Valle de San Luis) still contains the ruins of dozens of 19th-century sugar mills, including warehouses, milling machinery, slave quarters, manor houses and a fully functioning steam train. Most of the mills were destroyed during the War of Independence and the Spanish-Cuban-American War, when the focus of sugar-growing in Cuba shifted west to Matanzas. Though some sugar is still grown here, the valley is more famous today for its status as a Unesco World Heritage Site. Backed by the shadowy sentinels of the Sierra del Escambray, the pastoral fields, royal palms and peeling colonial ruins are timelessly beautiful. A horseback-riding tour (p280) from Trinidad should take in most (if not all) of the following sights.

◉ Sights

Mirador de la Loma del Puerto   VIEWPOINT
Six kilometers east of Trinidad on the road to Sancti Spíritus, this 192m-high lookout provides the best eagle-eye view of the valley with – if you're lucky – a steam train chugging through its midst. There's also a bar.

San Isidro de los Destiladeros   HISTORIC SITE
(CUC$1; ☉9am-5pm) After lengthy excavations, the ruins of this once grand sugar mill have been made accessible to the public. Dating from the early 1830s and sophisticated for its time, the mill belongs to the pre-industrial age and functioned primarily with slave labor. After ceasing production in 1890, the main buildings – a hacienda, a three-story bell tower, slave quarters and some cisterns – fell into ruin.

Renovation is ongoing and has been criticized by some who think the ruins should have been left as, well, ruins. San Isidro is accessed by branching right off the Trinidad–Sancti Spíritus road, 10km east of Trinidad. It's a further 2km from there.

Manaca Iznaga   MUSEUM, LANDMARK
(admission to tower CUC$1; ☉9am-4pm) The valley's main focal point is 16km northeast of Trinidad. Founded in 1750, the estate was purchased in 1795 by the dastardly Pedro Iznaga, who became one of the wealthiest men in Cuba through the unscrupulous business of slave trafficking. The 44m-high tower next to the hacienda was used to watch the slaves, and the bell in front of the house served to summon them.

Today you can climb to the top of the tower for pretty views, followed by a reasonable lunch (from noon to 2:30pm) in the restaurant-bar in Iznaga's former colonial mansion. Don't miss the huge sugar press out back.

Casa Guachinango
LANDMARK

(⊙9am-5pm) Three kilometers beyond the Manaca Iznaga, on the valley's inland road, is an old hacienda built by Don Mariano Borrell toward the end of the 18th century. The building now houses a restaurant. The Río Ay is just below, and the surrounding landscape is truly wonderful. Horseback riding can be arranged.

To get to Casa Guachinango, take the paved road to the right, just beyond the second bridge you pass as you come from Manaca Iznaga.

The train stops right beside the house every morning, and you can walk back to Iznaga from Guachinango along the railway line in less than an hour.

Sitio Guáimaro
LANDMARK

(⊙7am-7pm) Seven kilometers east of the Manaca Iznaga turnoff, travel for another 2km south and you'll find the former estate of Don Mariano Borrell, a wealthy early-19th-century sugar merchant. The seven stone arches on the facade lead to frescoed rooms, now a restaurant.

❶ Getting There & Away

Trinidad's much revered but frustratingly unreliable steam train was out of action at last visit. A less loveable diesel train was plying the Valle de los Ingenios instead, leaving Trinidad at 9:30am and calling first at Manaca Iznaga and then Guachinango. The return train departs Guachinango at 2:35pm and Manaca Iznaga at 2:50pm, leaving sufficient time for seeing the sights. Cubatur (p285) in Trinidad will know when the next tourist-train trip is scheduled and if it's working. Train tickets are CUC$10. It's a beautiful ride. Tour desks at the Ancón hotels sell the same train tour for CUC$17, including bus transfers to Trinidad.

Horseback-riding tours can be arranged at the travel agencies in Trinidad or Playa Ancón. Alternatively, you can contract a horse and guide privately in Trinidad for CUC$15 per six hours.

Topes de Collantes
ELEV 771M

The crenellated, 90km-long Sierra del Escambray is Cuba's second-largest mountain range, and it straddles the borders of three provinces: Sancti Spíritus, Cienfuegos and Villa Clara. Though not particularly high (the loftiest point, Pico de San Juan, measures just 1156m), the mountain slopes are rich in flora and surprisingly isolated. In late 1958 Che Guevara set up camp in these hills on his way

to Santa Clara and, less than three years later, CIA-sponsored counterrevolutionary groups operated their own cat-and-mouse guerrilla campaign from the same vantage point.

Though not strictly a national park, Topes is, nonetheless, a heavily protected area. The umbrella park, comprising 200 sq km, overlays four smaller parks – Parque Altiplano, Parque Codina, Parque Guanayara and Parque el Cubano – while a fifth enclave, El Nicho in Cienfuegos province, is also administered by park authority Gaviota.

The park takes its name from its largest settlement, an ugly health resort founded in 1937 by dictator Fulgencio Batista to placate his sick wife, for whom he built a quaint rural cottage. The architecture went downhill thereafter with the construction of an architecturally grotesque tuberculosis sanatorium (now a health 'resort') begun in the late '30s but not opened until 1954.

Topes de Collantes has two basic hotels open to foreigners, plus the best network of hiking trails in Cuba. Its jungle-like forests, harboring vines, lichens, mosses, ferns and eye-catching epiphytes, are akin to a giant outdoor biology classroom.

The Centro de Visitantes (⊙8am-5pm), near the sundial at the entrance to the hotel complexes, is the best place to procure maps, guides and trail info.

◉ Sights

Museo de Arte Cubano Contemporáneo
MUSEUM

(admission CUC$2; ⊙8am-8pm) Believe it or not, Topes de Collantes' monstrous sanatorium once harbored a veritable Louvre of Cuban art, containing works by Cuban masters such as Tomás Sánchez and Rubén Torres Llorca. Raiding the old collection in 2008 inspired provincial officials to open this infinitely more attractive museum, which displays over 70 works in six *salas* spread over three floors. The museum is on the main approach road from Trinidad just before you get to the hotels.

Casa Museo del Café
MUSEUM

(⊙7am-7pm) ✐ Coffee has been grown in the Escambray mountains for over two centuries, and in this small rustic cafe you can fill in the gaps on its boom-bust history while sipping the aromatic local brew (called Cristal Mountain). Just up the road there is the Jardín de Variedades del Café, a short stroll around 25 different varieties of coffee plant.

Plaza de las Memorias   MUSEUM

(⊗8am-5pm) **FREE** Topes' token museum is this quaint little display housed in three small wooden abodes just down from the Casa Museo del Café. It tells the history of the settlement and its resident hotels.

Activities

Topes has the best network of hiking trails in Cuba. A recent relaxation in park rules means you can now tackle most of them solo, although you'll need wheels to reach some of the trailheads.

★ Salto del Caburní   HIKING, SWIMMING

(entry CUC$9) The classic Topes hike, and the one most easily accessed on foot from the hotels, is to this 62m waterfall that cascades over rocks into cool swimming holes before plunging into a chasm where macho locals dare each other to jump. At the height of the dry season (March to May) you may be disappointed by these falls.

The entry fee is collected at the toll gate to Villa Caburní, just down the hill from the Kurhotel near the Centro de Visitantes (it's a long approach on foot). Allow an hour down and 1½ hours back up for this 5km (round trip) hike. Some slopes are steep and can be slippery after rain.

Sendero Jardín del Gigante   HIKING, SWIMMING

(entry CUC$4) For those pressed for time who still want to get a small taste of Topes' ecosystems, this 1.2km ramble is ideal. It starts at the Plaza de las Memorias and finishes just downhill in the Parque la Represa on the Río Vega Grande. En route you can count 300 species of trees and ferns, including the largest *caoba* (mahogany) tree in Cuba.

The small restaurant at the entrance to the garden is in a villa built by Fulgencio Batista's wife, whose love for the area inspired her husband to build the Topes resort.

Sendero la Batata   HIKING, SWIMMING

(entry CUC$4) This 6km out-and-back trail to a small cave containing an underground river starts at a parking sign just downhill from Casa Museo del Café. When you reach another highway, go around the right side of the concrete embankment and down the hill. Keep straight or right after this point (avoid trails to the left). Allow an hour each way.

Vegas Grandes   HIKING, SWIMMING

(entry CUC$9) The Vegas Grandes trail begins at the apartment blocks known as Reparto

el Chorrito on the southern side of Topes de Collantes, near the entrance to the resort as you arrive from Trinidad. Allow a bit less than an hour to cover the 2km to the waterfall (and a refreshing dip), and the same for the return journey.

It's possible to continue to the Salto del Caburní, but consider hiring a guide as the paths are poorly signposted.

Hacienda Codina   HIKING

(entry CUC$6) The hacienda is 8km from Topes by a rough road (the 4km 4WD track begins on a hilltop 3km down the road toward Cienfuegos and Manicaragua). Alternatively you can hike there by taking La Batata trail and continuing 1.5km past the cave. Ask for directions at the Centro de Visitantes first and hire a guide if you're unsure.

At the hacienda itself there's an additional trail, the 1.2km circular **Sendero de Alfombra Mágica** through orchid and bamboo gardens and past the Cueva del Altar. Also here are mud baths, a restaurant and a scenic viewpoint.

Gruta Nengoa   HIKING, SWIMMING

(entry CUC$6) A newly developed 2.6km trail centered on a grotto and 12m-high waterfall with some good opportunities for bird-watching and swimming. The trailhead is located 16km from Topes, just south of the village of Cuatro Vientos.

Sendero 'Centinelas del Río Melodioso'   HIKING, SWIMMING

(entry CUC$9) The least accessible but by far the most rewarding hike from Topes de Collantes is the 3km (6km return) hike in the Parque Guanayara, 15km from the Centro de Visitantes along a series of steep and heavily rutted tracks. For logistical reasons you may want to organize this excursion with a guide from the Centro de Visitantes, or as part of an organized tour from Trinidad with Cubatur (CUC$45 with lunch).

The trail itself begins in cool, moist coffee plantations and descends steeply to El Rocío waterfall, where you can strip off and have a bracing shower. Following the course of the Río Melodioso (Melodic River), you pass another inviting waterfall and swimming pool, the Poza del Venado, before emerging into the salubrious gardens of the riverside Casa la Gallega, a traditional rural hacienda where a light lunch can be organized and camping is sometimes permitted in the lush grounds.

TRINIDAD & SANCTI SPÍRITUS PROVINCE TOPES DE COLLANTES

🛏 Sleeping

Hotel los Helechos   HOTEL $
(☎41-54-02-31; s/d CUC$36/49; 🅿❄🏊) Never 100% at home in its verdant natural surroundings, this clumsy chocolate-box building with its wicker furnishings and holiday-camp-style villas still looks a bit awkward. Not helping matters is the unattractive indoor pool, poky steam baths (if they're working), journeyman restaurant and kitschy local disco (in a natural park of all places!).

The saving grace is the restaurant's delicious homebaked bread – surely the best in Cuba.

Villa Caburní   CABINS $
(☎41-54-01-80; s/d CUC$31/44; 🅿❄) This place in a small park next to the Kurhotel has one- or two-story Swiss-style chalets with kitchenettes and private bathrooms. It is located just behind the Information Office.

🍴 Eating & Drinking

As well as the restaurants in Topas, three eating options exist on the trails (mains CUC$6 to CUC$9): the **Hacienda Codina**, **Restaurante la Represa** and **Casa la Gallega** (in Parque Guanayara). **El Mirador** (Carretera de Trinidad) is a simple bar with a stunning view halfway up the ascent road from Trinidad.

Restaurante Mi Retiro   CARIBBEAN $$
(Carretera de Trinidad; meals CUC$6-9) Situated 3km back down the road to Trinidad, Restaurante Mi Retiro does fair-to-middling *comida criolla* (Creole food) to the sound of the occasional traveling minstrel.

Bar-Restaurante Gran Nena   CUBAN $$$
(☎41-54-03-38; Carretera Principal; meals CUC$12-18; ☉24hr) A little garden of Eden in the village of Topes, this new private restaurant is about as farm-to-table as you can get. Bananas, papaya, avocado, oranges and peaches all grow abundantly in the adjacent sloping garden and you can follow a trail through them to a hidden cave.

Food is served under a traditional open-sided sitting area by the mega-friendly owner (his family has lived here for eons) and glows with the true taste of the countryside.

The restaurant is next door to the Museo de Arte Cubano Contemporáneo.

ℹ Getting There & Away

Without a car, it's very difficult to get to Topes de Collantes and harder still to get around to the various trailheads. Your best bet is a taxi (CUC$35 return with a two- to three-hour wait), an excursion from Trinidad (CUC$29) or a hire car.

The road between Trinidad and Topes de Collantes is paved, but it's very steep. When wet, it becomes slippery and should be driven with caution. There's also a spectacular 44km road that continues right over the mountains from Topes de Collantes to Manicaragua via Jibacoa (occasionally closed, so check in Trinidad before setting out). It's also possible to drive to/from Cienfuegos via Sierrita on a partly paved, partly gravel road (4WD only).

Sancti Spíritus

POP 114,360

Don't underestimate Sancti Spíritus. In any other country this attractive colonial city would be a cultural tour de force. But cocooned inside illustrious Sancti Spíritus province and destined to always play second fiddle to Trinidad, it barely gets a look-in. Of course, for many visitors therein lies the attraction. Sancti Spíritus is Trinidad without the tourist hassle. You can get served in a restaurant here and search for a casa particular without an uninvited assemblage of pushy 'guides' telling you that the owner is deceased, on vacation or living in Miami. You can also get decidedly comfortable sitting in Parque Serafín Sánchez watching talented kids play stickball while plaintive boleros infiltrate streets that never quite earned a Unesco listing.

Founded in 1514 as one of Diego Velázquez' seven original villas, Sancti Spíritus was moved to its present site on the Río Yayabo in 1522. But the relocation didn't stop audacious corsairs, who continued to loot the town until well into the 1660s.

While Trinidad gave the world Playa Ancón, filthy-rich sugar barons and *jineteros* on bicycles, Sancti Spíritus concocted the dapper *guayabera* (pleated, buttoned) shirt, the *guayaba* (guava) fruit and a rather quaint humpbacked bridge that wouldn't look out of place in Yorkshire, England.

Sancti Spíritus was impressively beautified in 2014 to celebrate its 500th anniversary. Visually, at least, it's not far off rivaling Trinidad.

Sancti Spíritus

0   200 m
0   0.1 miles

Rafael Río Entero

Parque Maceo

Silvestre Alonso

Julio A Mella

Frank País

Adolfo del Castillo

Máximo Gómez Norte Sur

Luz Caballero

Céspedes Norte

Martí

Tirso Marín

Independencia Norte

Maceo

Cándido Calderón

Laborni

Estadio José A Huelga (1.7km)

(1.5km);

Juan Gómez

Plácido

Parque Serafín Sánchez

Av de los Mártires

Maceo

M Solano

A Rodríguez

Máximo Gómez Norte Sur

Céspedes Sur

Martí

Independencia Sur

San Miguel

Máximo Gómez Norte Sur

Plaza Honorato

Agramonte

Honorato

Guairo

Plácido Sur

Agramonte Oeste

Río Yayabo

Panco Jiménez

20 de Julio

Av Jesús Menéndez

Llano

(50m)

Trinidad

Sancti Spíritus

Sights
1 Boulevard	D5
2 Casa de la Guayabera	C7
3 Colonia Española Building	D6
4 Fundación de la Naturaleza y El Hombre	B1
5 Iglesia de Nuestra Señora de la Caridad	B1
6 Iglesia Parroquial Mayor del Espíritu Santo	C6
7 Museo Casa Natal de Serafín Sánchez	C2
8 Museo de Arte Colonial	C6
9 Museo de Ciencias Naturales	C4
10 Museo Provincial	C4
11 Parque Serafín Sánchez	C4
12 Plaza Honorato	C5
13 Puente Yayabo	B7
14 Teatro Principal	B6

Sleeping
15 Estrella González Obregón	C4
16 Hostal del Rijo	C5
17 Hostal Don Florencio	D5
18 Hostal Paraíso	C5
19 Hotel Plaza	C4
20 'Los Richards' – Ricardo Rodríguez	C4

Eating
21 Dulce Crema	C4
22 El 19	C5
23 La Época	C3
24 Mercado Agropecuario	D5
25 Mesón de la Plaza	C5
26 Papo's Boulevard	C5
Restaurante Hostal del Rijo	(see 16)
27 Taberna Yayabo	B7

Drinking & Nightlife
28 Café ARTex	C5

Entertainment
29 Casa de la Cultura	C5
30 Casa de la Trova Miguel Companioni	C5
31 Cine Conrado Benítez	C4
Teatro Principal	(see 14)
32 Uneac	C5

Shopping
33 Colonia	D6
34 La Perla	C4
35 Librería Julio Antonio Mella	C5

Sights

The main streets north and south of the Av de los Mártires and Calle M Solano axis get an appropriate north/south suffix.

Puente Yayabo LANDMARK

Looking like something out of an English country village, this quadruple-arched bridge is Sancti Spíritus' signature sight. Built by the Spanish in 1815, it carries traffic across the Río Yayabo and is now a national monument. For the best view (and a mirror-like reflection) hit the outdoor terrace at the Taberna Yayabo.

The **Teatro Principal**, alongside the bridge, dates from 1876, and the sun-bleached cobbled streets that lead uphill toward the city center are some of the settlement's oldest. The most arresting is narrow **Calle Llano**, where old ladies peddle live chickens door to door, and feisty neighbors gossip noisily in front of their sky-blue or lemon-yellow houses. Also worth a wander are recently rehabilitated **Calle Guairo** and **Calle San Miguel**.

Parque Serafín Sánchez SQUARE

While not Cuba's shadiest or most atmospheric square, pretty Serafín Sánchez is full of understated Sancti Spíritus elegance.

Metal chairs laid out inside the pedestrianized central domain are usually commandeered by cigar-smoking grandpas and flirty young couples with their sights set on some ebullient local nightlife.

There's plenty to whet the appetite on the square's south side, where the stately Casa de la Cultura often exports its music onto the street. Next door the columned Hellenic beauty that today serves as the **Biblioteca Provincial Rubén Martínez Villena** (41-32-77-17; Máximo Gómez Norte No 1) was built originally in 1929 by the Progress Society.

The magnolia-colored grand dame on the square's northern side is the former **La Perla** hotel, which lay rotting and unused for years before being turned into a three-level government-run shopping center.

Casa de la Guayabera MUSEUM, BAR

(San Miguel No 60; 10am-5pm) The favored uniform of South American strongman presidents and blushing grooms at Mexican beach weddings, the *guayabera* shirt was purportedly 'invented' in Sancti Spíritus by the wives of agricultural workers who sewed the trademark pockets into the garments so that their men could safely store their tools and packed lunches. This new museum honors the iconic shirts displaying *guayaberas* worn by international icons such as Hugo Chávez, Gabriel Márquez and – yes – Fidel.

The complex, set on a charming riverside patio in front of the city's famous packhorse bridge, also has a bar, garden and workshop where you can watch *guayaberas* being made.

Fundación de la Naturaleza y El Hombre
MUSEUM

(Cruz Pérez No 1; recommended donation CUC$2; ☺10am-5pm Mon-Fri, to noon Sat) Replicating its equally diminutive namesake in Miramar, Havana, this museum on Parque Maceo chronicles the 17,422km canoe odyssey from the Amazon to the Caribbean in 1987 led by Cuban writer and Renaissance man Antonio Nuñez Jiménez (1923–98). Some 432 explorers made the journey through 20 countries, from Ecuador to the Bahamas, in the twin dugout canoes *Simón Bolívar* and *Hatuey*. The latter measures over 13m and is the collection's central, prized piece.

Beware of sporadic opening hours.

Museo de Arte Colonial
MUSEUM

(Plácido Sur No 74; admission CUC$2; ☺9am-5pm Tue-Sat, 8am-noon Sun) This small museum got a 2012 refurb and displays 19th-century furniture and decorations in an imposing 17th-century building that once belonged to the sugar-rich Iznaga family.

Iglesia Parroquial Mayor del Espíritu Santo
CHURCH

(Agramonte Oeste No 58; ☺9-11am & 2-5pm Tue-Sat) Overlooking Plaza Honorato is this beautiful blue church that underwent a Lazarus-like renovation for the 2014 anniversary. Originally constructed of wood in 1522 and rebuilt in stone in 1680, it's said to be the oldest church in Cuba still standing on its original foundations.

The best time to take a peek at the simple but soulful interior is during Sunday morning Mass (10am). A small donation will go a long way.

Plaza Honorato
SQUARE

Formerly known as Plaza de Jesús, this tiny square was where the Spanish authorities once conducted grisly public hangings. Later on, it hosted a produce market, and scruffy peso stalls still line the small connecting lane to the east. The north side of the square is now occupied by a boutique hotel, Hostal del Rijo.

Boulevard
STREET

The city's revived shopping street, Calle Independencia Sur, is traffic-free and lined with statues, sculptures and myriad curiosity shops. Check out the opulent Colonia Española Building, once a whites-only gentlemen's club, now a mini–department store. The *agropecuario* is unusually located right in the city center.

A flea market inhabits Calle Honorato just off Independencia and all around are *vendutas* (small private shops or stalls), illustrating the recent economic relaxation.

Museo de Ciencias Naturales
MUSEUM

(Máximo Gómez Sur No 2; admission CUC$1; ☺8:30am-5pm Mon-Sat, to noon Sun) Not much of a natural history museum, this colonial house just off Parque Serafín Sánchez has a stuffed crocodile (which will scare the wits out of your kids) and some shiny rock collections.

Museo Provincial
MUSEUM

(Máximo Gómez Norte No 3; admission CUC$1; ☺9am-5pm Tue-Thu, 2-10pm Fri, 9am-noon & 8-10pm Sat, 8am-noon Sun) This is one of those vaguely comical Cuban museums where guides follow you from room to room as if you're about to make off with the crown jewels. In reality the collection is less distinguished, logging the history of Sancti Spíritus with a dusty stash of ephemera that includes English china, cruel slave artifacts and the inevitable revolutionary M-26/7 paraphernalia.

Museo Casa Natal de Serafín Sánchez
MUSEUM

(Céspedes Norte No 112; admission CUC$1; ☺8am-5pm Mon-Sat) Serafín Sánchez was a local patriot who took part in both Wars of Independence and went down fighting in November 1896. The museum cataloguing his heroics will delay you for 20 minutes max.

Iglesia de Nuestra Señora de la Caridad
CHURCH

(Céspedes Norte No 207) Across from the Fundación de la Naturaleza y El Hombre is the city's second church, the recipient of a handsome 2014 paint job. Its internal arches are a favored nesting spot for Cuban sparrows, who seem unfazed by the church interior's continuing state of disrepair.

🛏 Sleeping

🛏 In Town

Sancti Spíritus is blessed with a trio of gracious boutique sleeping establishments, branded as Encanto hotels, belonging to the Cubanacán chain. Each occupies an attractive restored colonial building and is a blissful nook to spend a night or two. They are complemented by a handful of pleasant casas particulares.

Hostal Paraíso   CASA PARTICULAR **$**
(☑41-33-46-58; Máximo Gómez Sur No 11, btwn Honorato & M Solano; r CUC$25; ❄) Hang out amid the hanging plants in these centrally located colonial digs. The house itself dates from 1838, and the original two-bedroom capacity has recently been doubled. The bathrooms are huge and the surrounding greenery is spirit-lifting.

**'Los Richards' –
Ricardo Rodríguez**   CASA PARTICULAR **$**
(☑41-32-30-29; Independencia Norte No 28 Altos; r CUC$25; ❄) The dark unkempt stairway off the main square belies the size of this place. The two front rooms are enormous, dwarfing the numerous beds, indoor bar, private dining area and fridge. Best part – the wrought-iron protected balconies overlooking the theatrics of the main square.

Estrella González Obregón   CASA PARTICULAR **$**
(☑41-32-79-27; Máximo Gómez Norte No 26; r CUC$25; ❄) Two rooms wit=h plenty of space and some cooking facilities make this place ideal for families. There's a roof terrace with good views of the Escambray Mountains.

★Hostal del Rijo   BOUTIQUE HOTEL **$$**
(☑41-32-85-88; Honorato del Castillo No 12; s/d CUC$75/100; ❄@❅) Even committed casa particular fans will have trouble resisting this meticulously restored 1818 mansion situated on quiet (until the Casa de la Trova opens) Plaza Honorato. Sixteen huge, plush rooms – many with plaza-facing balconies – are equipped with everything a romance-seeking Cuba-phile could wish for, including satellite TV, complimentary shampoos and chunky colonial furnishings.

Downstairs in the elegant courtyard restaurant you'll be served the kind of sumptuous, unhurried breakfast that'll have you lingering until 11am. Oh, what the hell, might as well stay another night.

Hotel Plaza   BOUTIQUE HOTEL **$$**
(☑41-32-71-02; Independencia Norte No 1; s/d CUC$52/70; ❄@) The Plaza sits on the edge of the Parque Serafín Sánchez. Spreading 28 rooms over two stories, the recently refurbished hotel has pulled itself up to boutique standard with fluffy bathrobes, chunky furnishings, a romantic patio bar and prime viewing windows overlooking the ever-busy square.

Hostal Don Florencio   BOUTIQUE HOTEL **$$$**
(Independencia Sur; s/d CUC$75/120; ❄@) Sancti Spíritus doesn't often get one over on Trinidad, but it does have a better collection of hotels, especially with the addition of Don Florencio in 2014. Bright red antique furnishings draw you in. Two inviting Jacuzzis in the cool central patio force you to stay.

🛏 North of Town

There are two very agreeable hotels along Carretera Central as you head north; either one is a good choice if the city center is full or you're merely passing through. Zaza, 5km to the east, attracts fishers.

Villa los Laureles   HOTEL **$**
(☑41-32-73-45; Carretera Central, Km 383; s/d CUC$33/44; ᴘ❄@❅) Not content to rest on them, Los Laureles lines its laurel trees up along a shady entrance drive that beckons visitors into a surprisingly classy Islazul (Cuban hotel chain) out-of-towner.

Supplementing big, bright rooms (with fridge, satellite TV and patio/balcony) are an attractive pool, leafy flower-studded gardens and a colorful in-house cabaret, the Tropi, with a nightly show at 9pm.

Hotel Zaza   HOTEL **$**
(☑41-32-85-12; s/d incl breakfast CUC$25/33; ᴘ❄❅) Perched above expansive Embalse Zaza 5km east of Sancti Spíritus, this scruffy rural retreat looks more like a utilitarian apartment block transplanted from Moscow than a hotel – not that this discourages the armies of bass fishermen who descend on the lake in their droves (four-hour fishing trips go for CUC$30).

For nonfishermen there's a swimming pool and boat trips on the lake (one-hour cruise CUC$20 for two people).

Villa Rancho Hatuey   HOTEL **$$**
(☑41-32-83-15; Carretera Central, Km 384; s/d CUC$45/60; ᴘ❄@❅) This veritable Islazul gem is accessible from the southbound

lane of Carretera Central. Rancho Hatuey spreads 76 rooms in two-story cabins across expansive landscaped grounds set back a good 500m from the road. Catch some rays around the swimming pool or grab a bite in the serviceable on-site restaurant while observing Canadian bus groups and Communist Party officials from Havana mingling in awkward juxtaposition.

Eating

Never rated highly for its private restaurants, Sancti Spíritus has acquired a couple of good 'uns since the privatization laws were relaxed. The state sector has some equally strong contenders.

★**Papo's Boulevard** CUBAN **$**
(☑41-32-72-77; Independencia Sur No 124; meals CUC$2-4; ☺11am-11pm) The secret of Papo's – aside from its excellent boulevard location – is its *congrí*. Word on the street suggests that Sancti Spíritus mixes the best rice and beans in Cuba, and Papo's backs up the legend with subtly spicy *congrí* – good enough to outshine the fish and meat to which its serves as accompaniment.

Dulce Crema ICE CREAM **$**
(cnr Independencia Norte & Laborni; ice creams CUC$1-2; ☺8am-10pm) What, no Coppelia? Dulce Crema is Sancti Spíritus' long-standing provincial stand-in and is actually – ahem – better. Alternatively, hang around long enough in Parque Serafín Sánchez and a DIY ice-cream man will turn up with his ice-cream maker powered by a washing-machine motor.

Taberna Yayabo CUBAN, SPANISH **$$**
(☑41-83-75-52; Jesús Menéndez No 106; meals CUC$9; ☺9am-10:45pm) New state-run restaurant that combines an excellent location (next to the Puente Yayabo) and fine service with one of the best wine cellars in Cuba. There's a resident sommelier and a chef who does cooking demos in front of the assembled clientele.

Restaurante Hostal del Rijo INTERNATIONAL **$$**
(Honorato No 12; meals CUC$6-10; ☺7am-11pm) Quiet colonial ambience in the impressive central courtyard of the Rijp or on the lovely terrace. Service is equally good, and there is a notable selection of desserts and coffee.

El 19 INTERNATIONAL **$$**
(Máximo Gómez 9, btwn Manolo Solano & Honorato del Castillo; meals CUC$8-12; ☺6:30am-10pm)

One of the newer strings to Sancti Spíritus' formerly disheveled bow, El 19 is located in a central nook and specializes in sirloin steak, a dish largely unavailable in Cuba until recently. It is delivered to your table by eager-to-please servers.

Mesón de la Plaza CARIBBEAN, SPANISH **$$**
(Máximo Gómez Sur No 34; mains CUC$6-9; ☺noon-2:30pm & 6-10pm) Long a solid option, this state-run restaurant is encased in a 19th-century mansion that once belonged to a rich Spanish tycoon. You can tuck into classic Spanish staples such as *potaje de garbanzos* (chickpeas with pork) and some chewable beef while appetizing music drifts in from the Casa de la Trova next door.

Self-Catering

Mercado Agropecuario MARKET **$**
(cnr Independencia Sur & Honorato; ☺7am-5:30pm Mon-Sat, 7am-noon Sun) This centrally located *agropecuario* is just off the main shopping boulevard. Stick your head in and see how Cubans shop.

La Época SUPERMARKET **$**
(Independencia Norte No 50C; ☺9am-5pm Mon-Sat, 9am-noon Sun) Good for groceries and assorted knickknacks.

Drinking & Entertainment

Sancti Spíritus has a wonderful evening ambience: cool, inclusive and unpretentious.

★**Uneac** LIVE MUSIC
(Independencia Sur No 10) There are friendly nods as you enter, handshakes offered by people you've never met, and a starry-eyed crooner on stage blowing kisses to his girlfriend(s) in the audience. Uneac concerts always feel more like family gatherings than organized cultural events, and Sancti Spíritus' is one of the nicest 'families' you'll meet.

Casa de la Trova Miguel Companioni LIVE MUSIC
(Máximo Gómez Sur No 26) Another of Cuba's famous *trova* (traditional poetic singing) houses, this kicking folk-music venue in a colonial building off Plaza Honorato is on a par with anything in Trinidad. But here the crowds are 90% local and 10% tourist.

Café ARTex CLUB
(M Solano; admission CUC$1; ☺10pm-2am Tue-Sun) On an upper floor on Parque Serafín Sánchez, this place has more of a nightclub feel than the usual ARTex patio. It offers

ALTURAS DE BANAO

Still well off the antennae of most guidebooks, which push tourists toward Topes de Collantes, this ecological reserve, situated off the main road between Sancti Spíritus and Trinidad, hides a little-explored stash of mountains, waterfalls, forest and steep limestone cliffs. The reserve's highest peak – part of the Guamuhaya mountain range – is 842m, while its foothills are replete with rivers, abundant plant life, including epiphyte cacti, and the ruins of a handful of pioneering 19th-century farmhouses. The park HQ is at **Jarico** 3.5km up a beaten track leading off the Sancti Spíritus–Trinidad road. It incorporates a *ranchón*-style restaurant, visitors center and chalet with eight double rooms (CUC$25). Within shouting distance is the **Cascada Bella** waterfall and a natural swimming pool. From Jarico the 6km **La Sabina trail** leads to an eponymous biostation, where **La Sabina Chalet** (r CUC$56) offers overnight accommodations and food in four double rooms. Alternatively, you can do the hike in a single day with a guide (CUC$3). Entry to the Banao reserve will cost you an extra CUC$3. Ecotur (p285) in Trinidad can organize overnight trips.

dancing, live music and karaoke nightly, and a Sunday matinee at 2pm (admission CUC$3). Thursday is reggaetón night, and the cafe also hosts comedy. Clientele is mainly under 25.

Casa de la Cultura LIVE MUSIC
(41-32-37-72; M Solano No 11) Numerous cultural events that at weekends spill out into the street and render the pavement impassable. It's situated on the southwest corner of Parque Serafín Sánchez.

Teatro Principal THEATER
(232-5755; Av Jesús Menéndez No 102) This landmark architectural icon next to the Puente Yayabo has recently given a comprehensive clean-up. It has weekend matinees (at 10am) with kids' theater.

Cine Conrado Benítez CINEMA
(32-53-27; Máximo Gómez Norte No 13) Of the city's two main cinemas, this is your best bet for a decent movie (some in English with Spanish subtitles).

Estadio José A Huelga SPORTS
(Circunvalación) From October to April, baseball games are held at this stadium, 1km north of the bus station. The provincial team Los Gallos (the Roosters) last tasted glory in 1979.

Shopping

Anything you might need – from batteries to frying pans – is sold at stalls along the pedestrianized Independencia Sur (known colloquially as the 'boulevard'), which benefited from a very handsome refurbishment to tie in with the city's 500th anniversary in 2014.

Colonia ACCESSORIES
(cnr Independencia Sur & Agramonte; 9am-4pm) Mini–department store housed in one of the city's finest colonial buildings.

La Perla SHOPPING CENTER
(Parque Serafín Sánchez; 9am-4pm) Three levels of austerity-busting shopping behind a beautifully restored magnolia colonial edifice on Parque Serafín Sánchez.

Librería Julio Antonio Mella BOOKS
(Independencia Sur No 29; 8am-5pm Mon-Sat) Revolutionary (mainly in Spanish) reading material for erudite travelers in a store opposite the post office.

ℹ Information

INTERNET ACCESS & TELEPHONE
Etecsa Telepunto (Independencia Sur No 14; internet per hr CUC$4.50; 8:30am-7:30pm) Two rarely busy computer terminals.

MEDICAL SERVICES
Farmacia Especial (Independencia Norte No 123; 24hr) Pharmacy on Parque Maceo.
Hospital Provincial Camilo Cienfuegos (41-32-40-17; Bartolomé Masó No 128) Five hundred meters north of Plaza de la Revolución.
Policlínico Los Olivos (41-32-63-62; Circunvalación Olivos No 1) Near the bus station. Will treat foreigners in an emergency.

MONEY
Banco Financiero Internacional (Independencia Sur No 2; 9am-3pm Mon-Fri) On Parque Serafín Sánchez.
Cadeca (Independencia Sur No 31) Lose your youth in this line.

OFF THE BEATEN TRACK

JOBO ROSADO RESERVE

This region, protected as an area of 'managed resources,' is still little explored by independent travelers, although organized groups are sometimes brought here. Measuring just over 40 sq km, the reserve includes the Sierra de Meneses-Cueto, a range of hills that runs across the north of the province and acts as a buffer zone for the heavily protected Bahía de Buenavista. As in the Sierra Maestra, history is intertwined with the ecology here: General Máximo Gómez battled through these hills during the Spanish-Cuban-American War and in 1958 Camilo Cienfuegos' rebel army (Column No 2) pitched their final command post here. An imaginative **monument** by sculptor José Delarra marks the spot.

The nexus for the reserve is **Rancho Querete** (⊙9am-4pm Tue-Sun) just off the main road a few kilometers east of Yaguajay, which is equipped with a bar-restaurant, natural swimming hole, biological station and small 'zoo' (roosters mainly). Guided hikes from here can be organized to **La Solapa de Genaro** (1km) through tropical savannah to a gorgeous set of waterfalls and more swimming holes, and the **Cueva de Valdés** (800m) through semi-deciduous woodland to a cave. A longer hike heads 8km to **Chalet Los Álamos**, the house of an erstwhile sugar plantation near the village of Meneses.

You'll need a taxi or your own wheels to get to Jobo Rosado.

POST

Post Office (Independencia Sur No 8; ⊙9am-6pm Mon-Sat) There are two branches: the other (Bartolomé Masó No 167; ⊙9am-6pm Mon-Sat) is located at the Etecsa building.

TRAVEL AGENCIES

Cubatur (Máximo Gómez Norte No 7; ⊙9am-5pm Mon-Sat) On Parque Serafín Sánchez.

❶ Getting There & Away

BUS

The provincial **bus station** (Carretera Central) is 2km east of town. Punctual and air-conditioned **Víazul** (www.viazul.com) buses serve numerous destinations.

Five daily departures for Santiago de Cuba (CUC$28, eight hours) also stop in Ciego de Ávila (CUC$6, 1¼ hours), Camagüey (CUC$10, three hours), Las Tunas (CUC$17, five hours 40 minutes) and Bayamo (CUC$21, seven hours). Five daily Havana (CUC$23, five hours) buses stop at Santa Clara (CUC$6, 1½ hours). The link to Trinidad (CUC$6, one hour 20 minutes) leaves at a sleep-reducing 5:40am.

TRAIN

There are two train stations serving Sancti Spíritus. For Havana (eight hours, alternate days) via Santa Clara (two hours), and to Cienfuegos (five hours, once a week), use the main **train station** (Av Jesús Menéndez al final; ⊙ tickets 7am-2pm Mon-Sat), southwest of the Puente Yayabo, an easy 10-minute walk from the city center.

Points east are served out of Guayos, 15km north of Sancti Spíritus, including Holguín (8½ hours), Santiago de Cuba (10¼ hours) and Bayamo (8¼ hours). If you're on the Havana–Santiago de Cuba cross-country express and going to Sancti Spíritus or Trinidad, get off at Guayos.

The ticket office at the Sancti Spíritus train station can sell you tickets for trains departing Guayos, but you must find your own way to the Guayos train station (CUC$8 to CUC$10 in a taxi).

TRUCK & TAXI

Trucks to Trinidad, Jatibonico and elsewhere depart from the bus station. A state taxi to Trinidad will cost you around CUC$35.

❶ Getting Around

Horse carts on Carretera Central, opposite the bus station, run to Parque Serafín Sánchez when full (1 peso). Bici-taxis gather at the corner of Laborni and Céspedes Norte. There is a **Cubacar** (☑41-32-85-33) booth on the northeast corner of Parque Serafín Sánchez; prices for daily car hire start at around CUC$70. The **Servi-Cupet gas station** (Carretera Central) is 1.5km north of Villa los Laureles, on the Carretera Central, toward Santa Clara. Parking in Parque Serafín Sánchez is relatively safe. Ask in hotels Rijo and Plaza, and they will often find a man to stand guard overnight for CUC$1.

Northern Sancti Spíritus Province

For every 1000 tourists that visit Trinidad, a small handful gets to see the province's narrow northern corridor, which runs between Remedios, in Villa Clara, and Morón, in Ciego de Ávila.

The landscape is comprised of karstic uplands characterized by caves and covered in semi-deciduous woodland, juxtaposed with a flat, ecologically valuable coastal plain protected in the hard-to-visit (but worth it if you can) Parque Nacional Caguanes.

Sights & Activities

★Museo Nacional Camilo Cienfuegos   MUSEUM
(admission CUC$1; ⊙8am-4pm Tue-Sat, 9am-1pm Sun) This excellent museum at Yaguajay, 36km southeast of Caibarién, was opened in 1989 and is eerily reminiscent of the Che Guevara monument in Santa Clara. Camilo fought a crucial battle in this town on the eve of the Revolution's triumph, taking control of a local military barracks (now the Hospital Docente General, opposite the museum).

The museum is directly below a modernist plaza embellished with a 5m-high statue of *El Señor de la Vanguardia* (Man at the Vanguard). It contains an extremely well-curated display of Cienfuegos' life intermingled with facts and mementos from the revolutionary struggle. A replica of the small tank 'Dragon I,' converted from a tractor for use in the battle, stands in front of the hospital. Out back the **Mausoleo de los Mártires del Frente Norte de las Villas** is dedicated to the soldiers who died in the skirmish.

Parque Nacional Caguanes   HIKING, BOAT TRIP
Strict conservation measures mean public access to Parque Nacional Caguanes with its caves, aboriginal remains and flamingos is limited but not impossible. There is a basic biological station on the coast accessible by a rough road due north of Mayajigua but, rather than just turn up, your best bet is to check details first at the Villa San José del Lago or with Ecotur, which has a handy public office in Trinidad.

The one advertised excursion is **Las Maravillas que Atesora Caguanes** (2½ hours), which incorporates a path to the Humboldt, Ramos and Los Chivos caves and a boat trip around the Cayos de Piedra.

Sleeping

Villa San José del Lago   HOTEL $
(☑41-55-61-08; Antonio Guiteras, Mayajigua; s/d CUC$25/36; P✳❄) This novel spa, once popular with vacationing Americans, is just outside Mayajigua in northern Sancti Spíritus province. The tiny rooms set in a variety of two-story villas nestle beside a small palm-fringed lake (with pedal boats and two resident flamingos).

The complex is famous for its thermal waters (32°C), which were first used by injured slaves in the 19th century but are now mainly the preserve of holidaying Cubans. The 67 rooms are no-frills, but the setting, wedged between the Sierra de Jatibonico and Parque Nacional Caguanes, is magnificent and makes a good base for some of Cuba's lesser-known excursions. There's a restaurant and snack bar on-site.

Information

Ecotur (☑41-55-49-30; Pedro Díaz No 54, Yaguajay) The best information portal for the region, one block north of the Caibarién–Morón road in Yaguajay.

Getting There & Away

A Víazul bus used to ply this northern route, but it wasn't running at last visit, meaning you're on your own with a bike, hire car or taxi.

Ciego de Ávila Province

◪ 33 / POP 424,400

Includes ➔

Ciego de Ávila	302
Morón	307
Florencia	310
Cayo Coco	310
Cayo Guillermo	313

Best Water Sports

➜ Laguna de la Leche (p309)

➜ Jardines de la Reina (p306)

➜ Kiteboarding on Cayo Guillermo (p314)

➜ Cayo Media Luna (p314)

Best Places to Stay

➜ Meliá Cayo Coco (p311)

➜ Alojamiento Maité (p307)

➜ Iberostar Daiquirí (p314)

Why Go?

Diminutive Ciego de Ávila's finger-in-the-dyke moment came during the late-19th-century Cuban Wars of Independence: it became the site of an impressive fortified wall, the Trocha, built to keep out rebellious armies of the east from the prosperous west. Today, the province continues to be the cultural divide between the Oriente and Occidente. The main reason to stop off is the ambitious post–Special Period resort development of Cayo Coco and Cayo Guillermo. The brilliant tropical pearls that once seduced Ernest Hemingway have had their glorious beaches spruced up and daubed with over a dozen exclusive tourist resorts.

Ciego de Ávila has in reality been harboring intriguing secrets for over a century. Various non-Spanish immigrants first arrived here in the 19th century from Haiti, Jamaica, the Dominican Republic and Barbados, bringing with them myriad cultural quirks, exemplified by cricket in Baraguá, voodoo in Venezuela, country dancing in Majagua and explosive fireworks in Chambas.

When to Go

➜ Beach-goers should descend on the *cayos* (keys) between November and March for drier weather that, while cool by Cuban standards, is still pleasantly warm.

➜ Take to the field on August 1 in Baraguá, where people celebrate Slave Emancipation Day with music, dancing and cricket.

➜ Morón's Aquatic Carnival kicks off in September, in the channel leading to the Laguna de Leche.

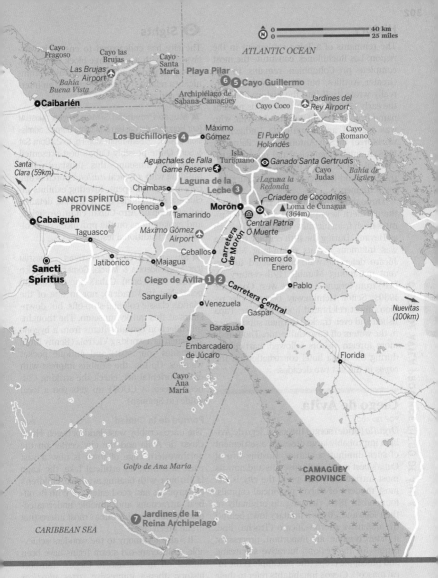

Ciego de Ávila Province Highlights

1 Browse through Ciego de Ávila's double act of delightful municipal museums, **Museo Provincial Simón Reyes** (p302) and **Museo de Artes Decorativas** (p302).

2 Marvel at how waste ground got transformed into one of Cuba's most interesting city parks at Ciego de Ávila's **Parque de la Ciudad** (p302).

3 Steer a boat across mangrove-fringed **Laguna de la Leche** (p309).

4 Roam the remains of the Caribbean's most extensive indigenous settlement, **Los Buchillones**.

5 Follow in the wake of 'Papa' Hemingway and take to the waters off **Cayo Guillermo** (p313).

6 Bask in the beach paradise of **Playa Pilar** (p314).

7 Explore the almost-virgin waters of the secluded **Jardines de la Reina** (p306) archipelago.

History

The remnants of a Taíno settlement in the region, Los Buchillones, constitute the most complete pre-Columbian remains in the Greater Antilles, but Ciego de Ávila only really wrote itself into the history books in the early 1500s. The province got its present name from merchant Jacomé de Ávila, who was granted an *encomienda* (indigenous workforce) in San Antonio de la Palma in 1538. A small *ciego* (clearing) on Ávila's estate was put aside as a resting place for tired travelers, and it quickly became a burgeoning settlement.

Throughout the 16th and 17th centuries the northern keys provided a refuge for pirates fresh from lucrative raids on cities such as Havana. During the 19th century, the area was infamous for its 68km-long Morón–Júcaro defensive wall: constructed to prevent marauding Mambís (19th-century rebels) from forging a passage west. Come the 1930s, Señor Hemingway became the region's most celebrated holiday-maker: Papa fished and even tracked German submarines in the waters off Cayo Guillermo. Thousands more foreign visitors followed, particularly during the mega hotel construction on the *cayos* in the last two decades.

Ciego de Ávila

POP 110,400

Orgullo (pride) surges through Ciego de Ávila in improbably large doses for a settlement of such diminutive stature. Hosting two of Cuba's best municipal museums and now its most intriguing urban park, the city is the most modern of Cuba's provincial capitals, founded in 1840. Growing up originally in the 1860s and '70s as a military town behind the defensive Morón–Júcaro (Trocha) line, it later became an important processing center for the region's lucrative sugarcane and pineapple crops (the pineapple is the local mascot). Ciego's inhabitants refer to their city as 'the city of porches' – a reference to the ornate colonnaded housefronts which characterize the center.

Famous *avileñas* (people from Ciego de Ávila) include Cuban pop-art exponent Raúl Martínez and local socialite Ángela Hernández Viuda de Jiménez, a rich widow who helped finance many of the city's early-20th-century neoclassical buildings, including the 500-seat Teatro Principal.

◉ Sights

The city has endeavored to ensure it waylays you, with a new three-block boulevard, appealing parks and museums which promulgate a relatively low-key history in an interesting and relevant way.

★ **Museo Provincial Simón Reyes**　MUSEUM
(cnr Honorato del Castillo & Máximo Gómez; admission CUC$1; ☺8am-10pm Mon-Fri, to 2:30pm Sat & Sun) Quite possibly Cuba's best-presented municipal museum, this mustard-yellow building with a typical *avileña* porch is one convertible well spent. Riveting exhibits include a scale model of La Trocha, detailed information on Afro-Cuban culture/religion, and explanations on the province's rich collection of traditional festivals.

★ **Museo de Artes Decorativas**　MUSEUM
(cnr Independencia & Marcial Gómez; admission CUC$1; ☺9am-5pm) Cuba's most beautiful beds? Not in Varadero, nor in one of the island's classic colonial stop-offs, but downstairs at this quirky museum. The thoughtful collection contains items from a bygone age, such as a working Victrola (Benny Moré serenades your visit) and antique pocket watches. Up top, the exhibits impress with ornate oriental art: check the striking Chinese screen. A CUC$1 tip gets you a local guide (in Spanish).

Parque de la Ciudad　PARK
The once-scrubby wasteland between Hotel Ciego de Ávila and the city center on the northwestern edge of town is now a vast park (featuring an artificial lake, the Lago la Turbina, with boating available, children's playgrounds and good eateries). With its offbeat attractions and amiable understatedness, it's just possibly Cuba's most interesting urban green space.

It's also testimony to the wonders achievable with scrap: old steam trains have been dusted off in homage to Ciego's transport history; there's impressive *artes plasticos* (modern art) including an elephant statue fashioned from old car parts; and, best among the eating possibilities, an old Aerocaribbean aircraft converted into a restaurant.

Parque Martí　SQUARE
All Ciego roads lead to this textbook colonial park laid out in 1877 in honor of the then king of Spain, Alfonso XII, but renamed in the early 20th century for newly martyred Cuban national hero, José Martí: here you'll

Ciego de Ávila

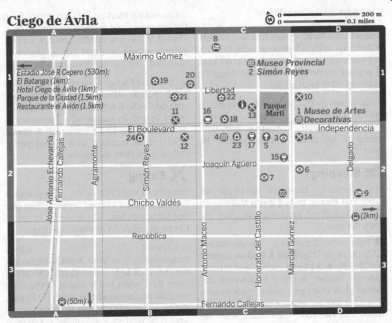

Máximo Gómez

Estadio José R Cepero (530m);
El Batanga (1km);
Hotel Ciego de Ávila (1km);
Parque de la Ciudad (1.5km);
Restaurante el Avión (1.5km)

Libertad

Museo Provincial
Simón Reyes

Museo de Artes
Decorativas

El Boulevard

Independencia

Joaquín Agüero

Chicho Valdés

República

Fernando Callejas

Ciego de Ávila

◉ Top Sights
1 Museo de Artes Decorativas...............D1
2 Museo Provincial Simón Reyes..........C1

◉ Sights
3 Ayuntamiento......................................C2
4 Centro Raúl Martínez Galería
   de Arte Provincial..............................C2
5 Iglesia Católico..................................C2
6 Plano-Mural de Ciego de Ávila...........D2
7 Teatro Principal.................................C2

⊟ Sleeping
8 María Luisa Muñoz Álvarez.................C1
9 Villa Jabon Candado..........................D2

⊗ Eating
10 Don Ávila..D1
11 El Colonial..B1
12 Restaurante Don Pepe......................B2

13 Solaris..C1
14 Supermercado Cruz Verde................D2

◉ Drinking & Nightlife
15 La Confronta.....................................C2
16 La Fontana..C1
17 Piña Colada.......................................C2

◈ Entertainment
18 Casa de la Cultura............................C1
19 Casa de la Trova Miguel Angel
   Luna...B1
20 Cine Carmen.....................................B1
21 Club de los Escritores......................B1
22 Patio de ARTex.................................C1

◉ Shopping
23 La Época...C2
24 Libreria Juan A Márquez...................B2

find a 1947 church, the **Iglesia Católico** (Independencia, btwn Marcial Gómez & Honorato del Castillo), and a 1911 **Ayuntamiento** (City Hall; no visitors).

The Iglesia Católico is notably emblazoned with the city's patron saint, San Eugenio de la Palma.

Teatro Principal THEATER
(cnr Joaquín Agüero & Honorato del Castillo) One block south of Parque Martí, the grand Teatro Principal more than compensates for the park's lack of illustrious edifices. Built in 1927 with help from local financier Ángela Jiménez, it purportedly has the island's best (theatrical) acoustics.

Centro Raúl Martínez Galería de Arte Provincial
GALLERY

(Independencia No 65; ☉8am-9pm Tue-Fri & Sun, to 11pm Sat) On Calle Independencia, this gallery has works by Raúl Martínez, Cuba's king of pop art, on permanent display, alongside works by other local artists.

Plano-Mural de Ciego de Ávila
HISTORIC SITE

(cnr Marcial Gómez & Joaquín de Agüero) A bronze map of the city in the late 19th century here marks the site of its founding on June 26, 1840.

🛏 Sleeping

Most tourists are bound for the beach-rich *cayos* and choose to bed down there or in Morón, but there are some adequate in-town options.

★ Villa Jabon Candado
CASA PARTICULAR $

(☎22-58-54; cnr Chico Valdés & Abraham Delgado; r CUC$15-20; P❄) Tired cyclists and drivers, look no further: here's a bright-pink detached place that's easy to find with owners who have accrued years of experience in the trade. The two rooms are clean, with the upstairs (balcony included) being best, and there's a carport.

Hotel Ciego de Ávila
HOTEL $

(☎22-80-13; Carretera a de Ceballos Km 1.5; s CUC$24-32, d CUC$32-42; P❄❄) Where have all the tourists gone? Cayo Coco probably, leaving this Islazul staple the domain of Cuban sports teams and workers on government-sponsored vacation time. Located 2km from the city center and overlooking Parque de la Ciudad, it has bog-standard rooms, a noisy swimming-pool area and boring breakfasts (included), but the staff seem friendly.

María Luisa Muñoz Álvarez
CASA PARTICULAR $

(☎52-39-39-95; Máximo Gómez No 74, btwn Honorato del Castillo & Antonio Maceo; r CUC$20-25; P❄) Two clean rooms off a looong corridor culminating in a patio equals textbook private-rental standard, with no real quirks. Only a block from the center.

🍴 Eating

Supermercado Cruz Verde
SUPERMARKET $

(cnr Independencia & Marcial Gómez; ☉9am-6pm Mon-Sat, to noon Sun) Sells groceries in one of Ciego's grandest fin de siècle buildings.

El Colonial
CUBAN $

(Independencia, btwn Simón Reyes & Antonio Maceo; meals CUC$2-6; ☉noon-11pm) Who needs fancy food when you're eating in the city's most atmospheric colonial building? Finally, dining in Ciego is an affair to linger over. A neat Wild West–style saloon bar opens onto a colonnaded patio behind. Cool chunky crockery, hot hearty portions. Pay in pesos.

Restaurante el Avión
CUBAN $

(Parque de la Ciudad; CUC$1-5; ☉noon-10pm) Touch down in Parque de la Ciudad for restaurant innovation. El Avión might not offer much extraordinary food on its menu (although the *ropa vieja* – shredded beef – is

---

TROCHA DE JÚCARO A MORÓN

Many of Ciego de Ávila's provincial towns grew up in the mid-19th century around the formidable **La Trocha**, a line of fortifications that stretched 68km from Morón in the north to Júcaro in the south, splitting the island in two.

Constructed by the Spanish in the early 1870s using black slaves and poorly-paid Chinese laborers, the gargantuan Trocha was designed to contain the rebellious armies of the Oriente and stop the seeds of anarchy from spreading west during the First War of Independence.

By the time it was completed in 1872, La Trocha was the most sophisticated military defense system in the colonies, a seemingly unbreakable bastion that included 17 forts, 5000 full-time military guards and a parallel railway line.

Armed to the hilt, it held firm during the First War of Independence, preventing the rebel armies of Antonio Maceo and Máximo Gómez from causing widespread destruction in the richer western provinces, where more conservative sugar planters held sway.

Despite renovations that doubled the number of forts and tripled the number of armed guards by 1895, La Trocha proved to be more porous during the Spanish-Cuban-American War, enabling the audacious Maceo to break through and march his army as far west as Pinar del Río.

A handful of old military towers that once acted as lookouts and guardhouses on La Trocha are still scattered throughout the countryside between Ciego de Ávila and Morón, standing as timeworn testaments to a more divisive and violent era.

great) but your repast will be in a novel venue: inside an old Aerocaribbean plane. It's just back from the lake near the scrap metal sculptures. Pay in pesos.

Restaurante Don Pepe
CARIBBEAN $

(Independencia No 103, btwn Antonio Maceo & Simón Reyes; mains CUC$1-5; ☺8am-11:45pm Wed-Mon) A bartender named Eladio invented the Coctel Don Pepe here (two shots of orange juice, 1.5 shots of white rum and half a shot of crème de menthe, stirred) back in the day. The restaurant, housed in a pleasant colonial building, still serves it, along with good old pork and chicken dishes.

Solaris
FUSION $

(Doce Plantas Bldg, cnr Honorato del Castillo & Libertad; mains CUC$1-5; ☺11am-11pm) City-center joint on the 12th floor of the rather ugly Doce Plantas building. Excellent city views, a *cordon bleu* (chicken stuffed with ham and cheese) special and its very own Solaris cocktail.

★Don Ávila
CARIBBEAN $$

(Marcial Gómez, cnr Libertad; CUC$1-5; ☺11am-11pm) *Numero uno* in Ciego's culinary greatest all-time hits. Plaza-abutting Don Ávila impresses with its regal ambience, on-site cigar outlet, old-gents-style bar, typically friendly *avileña* service and generous portions of *comida criolla* (Creole food).

🍷 Drinking & Nightlife

La Confronta
BAR

(cnr Marcial Gómez & Joaquín Agüero) Amid the well-worn bar stools and Benny Moré paraphernalia you can sample a range of 25 different cocktails. Prices are in Cuban pesos, a tempting (and potentially dangerous) proposition for a convertible-loaded traveler.

La Fontana
CAFE

(cnr Independencia & Antonio Maceo; ☺6am-2pm & 3-11pm) Ciego's famous coffee institution: long queues outside, a fog of cigarette smoke inside.

Piña Colada
BAR

(cnr Independencia & Honorato del Castillo; ☺3pm-midnight) Proudly mixing Caribbean cocktails with Antarctic air-con since 2011.

El Batanga
CLUB

(Carretera a de Ceballos Km 1.5; admission per couple CUC$3; ☺10pm-2am) Hotel Ciego de Ávila's rowdy disco.

☆ Entertainment

For total spontaneity hit the streets on a Saturday night for the wonderful Noches Avileñas, when music and temporary food stands set up in the streets around various venues, including the main park.

Cine Carmen
CINEMA

(Antonio Maceo No 51, cnr Libertad) provides big-screen and video offerings daily (in Spanish). Don't miss the big movie projector spilling film on the Libertad side of the building.

Casa de la Trova Miguel Angel Luna
LIVE MUSIC

(Libertad No 130) In the dice-roll of traditional musical entertainment, Ciego's *trova* (song) house scores a magic six with polished Thursday night regional *trovadores* in a pleasant colonial setting.

Club de los Escritores
LIVE MUSIC

(Libertad No 105) There are occasional concerts on the courtyard stage of this graceful colonial building, and a bar decked out in tribal art out back.

Casa de la Cultura
CULTURAL CENTER

(Independencia No 76, btwn Antonio Maceo & Honorato del Castillo) Dodge the slumbering receptionist, and all sorts of capers take place here, including a Wednesday *danzón* (ballroom dance) club and weekly *folklórico* (traditional Latin American dance).

Patio de ARTex
LIVE MUSIC

(Libertad, btwn Antonio Maceo & Honorato del Castillo; admission MN$5) This trusty alfresco patio has a bit of everything; check the *cartelera* (culture calendar) out front.

Estadio José R Cepero
SPORT

(Máximo Gómez) October to April, baseball games take place to the northwest of the center. Ciego's Tigres have experienced a dramatic turnaround in fortune of late: 2011 runners up and 2012 champions, following a thrilling, against-the-odds victory over Havana's Los Industriales.

🛍 Shopping

Stroll El Boulevard for typical Cuban fodder. Places that may have you reaching inside your money belt include ARTex souvenir store La Época (Independencia, btwn Antonio Maceo & Honorato del Castillo) and bookstore Libreria Juan A Márquez (Independencia Oeste No 153, cnr Simón Reyes; ☺9am-5pm Mon-Fri, 9am-noon Sat).

JARDINES DE LA REINA

Jardines de la Reina is a 120km-long mangrove-forest and coral-island system situated 80km off the south coast of Ciego de Ávila province and 120km north of the Cayman Islands. The local marine park measures 3800 sq km, with virgin territory left more or less untouched since the time of Columbus.

Commercial fishing in the area has been banned, and with a permanent local population of precisely zero inhabitants, visitors must stay on board a two-story, seven-bedroom houseboat called *Hotel Flotante Tortuga*, or venture in from the port of Embarcadero de Júcaro on the mainland aboard the yachts *Halcon* (six cabins) or *La Reina* (four cabins). Guests can also use *Caballones* (sleeping six to eight and suited to all kinds of fishing from fly to spin) or the luxury eight-cabin *Avalon Fleet 1*.

Below the waves the main attraction is sharks (whale and hammerhead) and this, along with the pristine coral and the unequaled clarity of the water, is what draws divers from all over the world.

Getting to the Jardines is not easy – or cheap. The main company currently offering excursions is the Italian-run **Avalon** (www.cubanfishingcenters.com). One-week dive packages, which include equipment, six nights of accommodation, guide, park license, 12 dives and transfer from Embarcadero de Júcaro, cost the better part of CUC$2000. Ask for a quote via the website. Another option is to sail with the **Windward Islands Cruising Company** (www.windward-islands.net), departing from Cienfuegos.

ℹ Information

Banco Financiero Internacional (cnr Honorato del Castillo & Joaquín Agüero Oeste)

Cadeca (Independencia Oeste No 118, btwn Antonio Maceo & Simón Reyes)

Etecsa Telepunto (Joaquín Agüero No 62; internet per hr CUC$4.50; ⊗8:30am-7pm)

General Hospital (☑22-40-15; Máximo Gómez No 257) Near the bus station.

Infotur (☑20-91-09; Doce Plantas Bldg, cnr Honorato del Castillo & Libertad; ⊗9am-noon & 1-6pm) Possibly Cuba's friendliest, most informative Infotur office. Good info on the city and Cayos Coco and Guillermo.

Post Office (cnr Chicho Valdés & Marcial Gómez)

ℹ Getting There & Away

AIR

Ciego de Ávila's **Máximo Gómez Airport** (AVI; Carretera a Virginia) is 10km northwest of Ceballos, 23km north of Ciego de Ávila and 23km south of Morón.

International flights arrive daily from Canada, Argentina, France, the UK and Italy, and visitors are bussed off to Cayo Coco (which also has its own far-busier airport, Aeropuerto Internacional Jardines del Rey, p313).

BUS

The **bus station** (Carretera Central), situated about 1.5km east of the center, has multiple daily Víazul services. The five daily Santiago de

Cuba (CUC$24, 8½ hours) departures are at 4:30am, 4:35am, 11am, 2:05pm and 10:25pm. These also stop at Camagüey (CUC$6, 1½ hours), Las Tunas (CUC$12, 4½ hours), Holguín (CUC$17, 5¼ hours) and Bayamo (CUC$17, six hours). Four of the five daily Havana (CUC$27, six to seven hours) buses also stop at Sancti Spíritus (CUC$6, 1½ hours) and Santa Clara (CUC$9, 2½ hours). There is also a daily bus to Trinidad (CUC$9, 2¾ hours) at 4:20am and one to Varadero (CUC$19, 6¼ hours) at 4:40am.

The *circuito norte* (north circuit) Víazul connection heading to Morón (40 minutes), Caibarién (for Cayo Santa María), Santa Clara, Cienfuegos and Trinidad (6¼ hours) was suspended at the time of research.

TRAIN

The **train station** (☑22-33-13) is six blocks southwest of the center. Ciego de Ávila is on the main Havana–Santiago railway line. There are nightly trains to Havana (CUC$15.50, 7½ hours), Bayamo (CUC$10.50, seven hours), Camagüey (CUC$3.50, 2¼ hours), Holguín (CUC$11, seven hours), Guantánamo (CUC$17, 9½ hours) and Santiago de Cuba (CUC$14, 9¼ hours). Check the latest timetable at least a day before you want to leave. There are also four trains daily to Morón (CUC$1, one hour).

TRUCK

Private passenger trucks leave from the Ferro Ómnibus bus station adjacent to the train station heading towards Morón and Camagüey. Check the blackboards for current details.

❶ Getting Around

CAR & MOPED

The **Carretera a Morón gas station** (Carretera de Morón) is just before the bypass road, northeast of the town center. The **Oro Negro gas station** (Carretera Central) is near the bus station.

Cubacar (Hotel Ciego de Ávila, Carretera a Ceballos) can help with vehicle rental for around CUC$70 per day. It also rents out mopeds for CUC$24 a day.

TAXI

A taxi ride to the airport will cost around CUC$12; bargain if they're asking more. Book a cab at Hotel Ciego de Ávila or find one in Parque Martí. A one-way ride to Morón is CUC$15-20, to Cayo Coco/Cayo Guillermo it's CUC$60/80.

Morón

POP 59,200

Despite its slightly removed position 35km north of Cuba's arterial Carretera Central, Morón remains an important travel nexus (thanks to its railway) and acts as a viable base camp for people not enamored with the resort-heavy Cayo Coco.

Founded in 1543, three centuries before provincial capital Ciego de Ávila, Morón is known island-wide as the Ciudad del Gallo (City of the Cockerel), for a notorious bullying official in the early days who eventually got his comeuppance. Morón has architecture to match its years, with more, better-preserved examples of those Ciego de Ávila column-flanked facades.

Compact and easygoing, Morón has some excellent casas particulares and offers a surprisingly varied list of things to do in the surrounding countryside.

◉ Sights

Morón is famous for its emblematic **cockerel**, which stands guard on a roundabout opposite the Hotel Morón on the southern edge of town. It's named after a 'cocky' and abusive 16th-century official who got his just deserts at the hands of locals and was driven out of town. The cock crows (electronically) at 6am every morning.

Terminal de Ferrocarriles NOTABLE BUILDING
(Train Station; Vanhorne, btwn Av de Tarafa & Narciso López) Morón has long been central Cuba's main railway crossroads and exhibits the most elegant railway station outside Havana. Built in 1923, the building's edifice is neocolonial, though inside the busy ticket hall hides a more streamlined art deco look. It's all remarkably well kept. Equally eye-catching is the stained glass skylight.

Museo Caonabo MUSEUM
(Martí; admission CUC$1; ⊙9am-5pm Mon-Sat, 8am-noon Sun) In among the teeming sidewalks and peeling colonnades, this well-laid-out museum of history and archaeology is housed in the city's former bank, an impressive neoclassical building dating from 1919. There is a rooftop *mirador* (lookout) with a good view out over town.

🛏 Sleeping

⭐ **Alojamiento Maité** CASA PARTICULAR $
(☏50-41-81; maite68@enet.cu; Luz Caballero No 40B, btwn Libertad & Agramonte; r CUC$25; P❋@🐾) The tireless Maité has added a swimming pool and a flash, fully-appointed suite to her already very well-appointed abode (current count: four rooms) and extended her famous restaurant alongside. This must be one of Cuba's most professionally run casas particulares. Cast your eye over the wall-mounted TVs, starched white sheets (changed daily), complimentary bottles of shampoo, and wine in the fridge.

Guests can lounge on the substantial roof terrace with a mojito.

Alojamiento Vista al Parque CASA PARTICULAR $
(☏50-41-81; yio@hgm.cav.sld.cu; Luz Caballero No 49D Altos, btwn Libertad & Agramonte; r CUC$20-25; P❋@) There's comfort and slick service in this lovely pale-blue house with two shimmering upstairs rooms and a terrace with views across a well-tended park, run by Idolka (who speaks some English).

Casa Belky CASA PARTICULAR $
(☏50-57-63; Cristobal Colón No 37; r CUC$20-25) Just one haughty colonial room but it's a whopper, and with a view onto Parque los Ferrocarriles it's possibly the most idyllic location in town. Just northeast of the train station.

Centro de Caza y Pesca
La Casona HISTORIC HOTEL $
(☏50-22-36; Colón No 41; s/d CUC$34/45; P❋) The yellow-and-white La Casona, near the train station, is a welcome break for those seeking relative luxury for low price tags, and trumps other hotels in many respects with its colonial features and cheery ambience. There are eight rooms and a small on-site restaurant-bar.

🍴 Eating

In Morón, going out at night is about drinking and dancing, not so much dining.

Doña Neli Dulcería (Serafín Sánchez No 86, btwn Narciso López & Martí) will sort self-caterers out with bread and pastries; likewise **Supermercado los Balcones** (Martí) with groceries.

Restaurante Maité la Qbana   PALADAR $$
(☑ 50-41-81; Luz Caballero No 40, btwn Libertad & Agramonte; mains CUC$10-15; ☺ breakfast, lunch & dinner; ☑) Maité is a highly creative cook whose international dishes, prepared with *mucho amor*, will leave you wondering how insipid all-inclusive buffets ever got so popular. Prepare for al dente pasta, fine wine, homemade cakes and paella that has visiting *valencianos* reminiscing about their homeland. It's a good idea to reserve early.

Don Pio Restaurante   CUBAN $$
(Cristobal Colón No 39; CUC$6.50-8.50; ☺ 10am-10pm) In the sumptuous back garden of a colonial house is this *ranchón*-style, plant-lined, covered patio restaurant. Chicken cordon bleu and the like offer diversion from standard restaurant offerings; occasional live piano music serenades.

🍷 Drinking & Entertainment

Arguably the best option for entertainment is Cabaret Cueva, 6km outside town on the shores of Laguna de la Leche.

Discoteca Morón   CLUB
(Hotel Morón, Av de Tarafa; ☺ 10pm-late) Young, raucous entertainment-seekers test the patience of sleep-deprived paying guests at the Hotel Morón.

Casa de la Trova Pablo Bernal   LIVE MUSIC
(Libertad No 74, btwn Martí & Narciso López) Vibrant alfresco music house; popular Wednesday comedy night.

Patio el Gallo   CLUB, CABARET
(Libertad, btwn Narciso López & Martí; Admission CUC$3; ☺ 6pm-midnight) A two-floor bit-of-everything bar-club, but it's focused on the stage where all manner of entertainment from live music to cabaret-esque *espectáculos* (shows) take place. Morón's most popular venue.

Buena Vista Social Club   BAR
(Martí 382; ☺ 6pm-2am) Smart air-conditioned bar-club.

ℹ️ Information

You'll find internet at **Etecsa** (El Centro Multiservicio de Morón; Martí, cnr Céspedes; per hour CUC$4.50; ☺ 8:30am-7:30pm); money-changing facilities are at **Cadeca** (Martí, cnr Gonzalo Arena) on the same street. Information on Lagunas de la Leche and la Redonda can be procured at **Cubatur** (Martí 169; ☺ 9am-5pm). Centrally located **Hospital Multiclinica Roberto Rodriguez** (☑ 50-50-11; Zayas, btwn Libertad & Sergio Antuñas) is three blocks east of Martí.

ℹ️ Getting There & Away

The **bus station** (Martí 12) is a block back towards the center (north) from the train station. A Víazul bus route formerly incorporated Morón in the *circuito norte* (north circuit) linking Ciego de Ávila, Caibarién (on Villa Clara's northern coast), Santa Clara, Cienfuegos and Trinidad. However, at the time of research this route had been suspended, although local buses still leave daily for Ciego de Ávila.

Never was there a better excuse, therefore, to take a Cuban train. From the **train station** (Vanhorne, btwn Av de Tarafa & Narciso López), four daily trains link with Ciego de Ávila (CUC$1), plus one to Júcaro and one to Camagüey (CUC$4).

Airports? Maximo Gómez Airport (p306) is 23km south (taxi CUC$12) and Aeropuerto Internacional Jardines del Rey (p313) is 60km north (taxi CUC$40). Loads of choice!

ℹ️ Getting Around

The roads from Morón northwest to Caibarién (112km) and southeast to Nuevitas (168km) are good. Rental cars are in short supply and it pays to reserve a vehicle several days ahead of when you need it: try **Havanautos** (☑ 50-21-15; Av Tarafa, btwn Calles 4 & 6). The **Servi-Cupet gas station** (☺ 24hr) is near Hotel Morón.

Around Morón

Laguna de la Leche & Laguna la Redonda

These two large natural lakes lie north of Morón. Redonda is best accessed via the road to Cayo Coco. The 5km entry road for Laguna de la Leche (the lake is accessed from the south) starts just north of Morón's Parque Agramonte. Your own wheels are required to visit either.

◉ Sights & Activities

★ Laguna de la Leche   LAKE

Laguna de la Leche (Milk Lake), named for its reflective underwater lime deposits, is Cuba's largest natural lake (66 sq km). Its water content is a mixture of fresh and salt water, and anglers flock here to hook the abundant stocks of carp, tarpon, snook and tilapia. Guided fishing trips (CUC$70 for four hours) can be arranged at the main southern-shore entrance.

For a little more you can keep your catch and cook it on a mobile barbecue aboard a ship. Nonfishing boat excursions (CUC$20 for 45 minutes) are also available.

The lake is also the venue for the annual **Morón Aquatic Carnival**.

Laguna la Redonda   LAKE

(◷9am-5pm) Anglers, listen up: 18km north of Morón, off the Cayo Coco road, this mangrove-rimmed, 4-sq-km lake has the island's best square-kilometer density of bass and trout. Four hours of fishing costs CUC$70. Boat trips are available too, and take in narrow, foliage-covered tributaries – as close to the Amazon as the province comes. You'll even be allowed to take the wheel if you want!

Not a fishing fanatic? Rock up at the decent, rustic **bar-restaurant** (mains CUC$4-8) just for a drink with a lake view. Try the house specialty, a fillet of fish called *calentico* – great with ketchup and Tabasco.

✖ Eating

★ La Atarraya   SEAFOOD $

(mains CUC$2-7; ◷noon-6pm) Raised on stilts in a clapboard building off the southern shoreline of Laguna de la Leche, you'll find one of Cuba's best natural fish restaurants. The insanely cheap menu is headlined by *paella valenciana* and *pescado monteroro* (fish fillet with ham and cheese), while the ambience is ebulliently local.

☆ Entertainment

Cabaret Cueva   CABARET, NIGHTCLUB

(Laguna de la Leche; ◷10pm-late Thu-Sun) Locals willingly hitch, walk or carpool to make the 6km trip from Morón to this cabaret in a cave on the southern shores of the Laguna de la Leche.

Loma de Cunagua

Rising like a huge termite mound above the surrounding flatlands, the **Loma de** Cunagua (admission CUC$5; ◷9am-4pm), 18km east of Morón, is a protected flora and fauna reserve harboring a *ranchón*-style restaurant, a small network of trails, and excellent bird-watching opportunities. At 364m above sea level, it's the province's highest point and views over land and ocean are excellent.

Navigate around the reserve via strolls along short bushy trails (in search of *tocororos*, *zunzúns* and the like), or by horseback riding. Turn left off the main road at the sign, pay your fee at the gate, and proceed up the steep unpaved road to the summit. The Loma is on the Carretera de Bolivia; visits are normally arranged through Cayo Coco hotel tourist information desks.

Central Patria O Muerte

Cuba's sugar industry is being preserved at this huge rusting ex-sugar mill (c 1914) in the village of Patria, 3km south of Morón. A 1920 Philadelphia-made Baldwin steam train takes prebooked tour groups on a 5km jaunt through cane fields to **Rancho Palma** (Carretera a Bolivia, Km 7), a bucolic *finca* (farmhouse) with a bar-restaurant where you can sample *guarapo* (pressed cane juice).

The mill and its 263-strong workforce were passed over to the Americans in 1919, and it remained in *Yanqui* hands until nationalization in 1960. Independent visitors can ask for a tour here, but to get the full train-and-sugar-cane treatment you'll need to tag onto a group. Check schedules with Cubatur in Morón.

Isla Turiguanó

Hold your horses (and cows). You're not in the keys quite yet; Turiguanó isn't a real island but a drained swamp that plays host to a cattle-breeding ranch, a model revolutionary community and one of Cuba's three pioneering wind farms. You'll need your own wheels to get here, though Cayo Coco and Cayo Guillermo hotels sometimes arrange tours.

◉ Sights

Ganado Santa Gertrudis   RANCH, RODEO

Santa Gertrudis cattle are bred at this large Isla Turiguanó farm on the main road just before you enter the causeway to Cayo Coco. The adjoining stadium is evidence that in rodeo-land, Cuba is right up there with the

LOS BUCHILLONES

Tucked away on the province's northwest coastline, **Los Buchillones archaeological site** was originally excavated during the 1980s after fishermen began discovering implements such as axe handles and needles in the surrounding swamps.

What became apparent was that Los Buchillones was the location of a sizeable Taíno settlement of between 40 and 50 houses predating European arrival in the region. Everything from *cemíes* (Taíno deities to various Gods of rain, cassava and the like) to canoes to house structures have been subsequently recovered from the excavation site, most of which remains a waterlogged work in progress. The mud at the bottom of the shallow lagoon here was what preserved the artifacts so well and yielded the most significant stash of pre-Columbian relics anywhere in the Greater Antilles.

Many of the artifacts can be seen in either the **Museo Municipal** (Agramonte 80, btwn Calixto García & Martí) in Chambas or Ciego de Ávila's Museo Provincial Simón Reyes. However anyone with a passing interest in pre-Columbian Cuba should make the trip to the poignant site, complete with a small museum displaying finds, halfway between the fishing villages of Punta Alegre and Punta San Juan. A handful of trains pass Chambas, from where Los Buchillones is a 35km drive (public transport is scarce) through Parque Nacional Caguanes.

Calgary Stampede. Cowboys, bulls, horses and lassos are out most weekends around 2pm for exciting 90-minute *espectáculos*.

El Pueblo Holandés   VILLAGE
A small community with 49 red-roofed, Dutch-style dwellings, El Pueblo Holandés is on a hill next to the highway, 4km north of Laguna la Redonda. It was built by Celia Sánchez in 1960 as a home for cattle workers. It's an interesting blip on the landscape and worth a short detour.

Florencia

Ringed by gentle hills, the town of Florencia, 40km west of Morón, was named after Florence in Italy by early settlers who claimed the surrounding countryside reminded them of Tuscany. In the early 1990s the Cuban government constructed a hydroelectric dam, the **Liberación de Florencia**, on the Río Chambas and the resulting lake has become a recreational magnet for nature lovers. Activities include horseback riding through the Florencia hills, kayaking, aqua biking, and a boat ride on the lake to a tiny key called La Presa with a restaurant and small zoo. The area's focal point is a ranch called **La Presa de Florencia** (⊘9am-5pm) by the side of the lake in Florencia. Get more details at Infotur (p306) in Ciego de Ávila or Cubatur (p308) in Morón. For a place to stay you may get lucky in the lovely **Campismo Boquerón**, 5km west of Florencia. Enquire at La Presa de Florencia.

Cayo Coco

Situated in the Archipiélago de Sabana-Camagüey, or the Jardines del Rey as travel brochures prefer to call it, Cayo Coco is Cuba's fourth-largest island and the main tourist destination after Varadero. The area north of the Bahía de Perros (Bay of Dogs) was uninhabited before 1992, when the first hotel – the Cojímar – went up on adjoining Cayo Guillermo. The bulldozers haven't stopped buzzing since.

While the beauty of the beaches on these islands is world famous, Cayo Coco pre-1990 was little more than a mosquito-infested mangrove swamp. Between 1927 and 1955 a community of 600 people scraped a living by producing charcoal for use as domestic fuel on the island but, with the rise of electrical power after the Revolution, this too died.

Since 1988 Cayo Coco has been connected to the mainland by a 27km causeway slicing across the Bahía de Perros. There are also causeways from Cayo Coco to Cayo Guillermo in the west and to Cayo Romano in the east.

◉ Sights

Parque Natural el Bagá   NATURE RESERVE
(⊘9:30am-5:30pm) Bagá was a commendable eco-project sited on what was Cayo Coco's original airport, a 769-hectare natural park sublimely mixing dense mangroves, lakes, idyllic coastline, trails and an incredible 130 species of bird. Unfortunately, fallen into

slight disrepair, it's now deemed 'unsafe' for tender tourists and visits are discouraged.

On the bright side, our last visit gleaned the information that reopening is scheduled for the future. In the meantime, try your luck with the guard or stick to safer terrain.

Cayo Paredón Grande ISLAND

East of Cayo Coco, a road crosses Cayo Romano and turns north to Cayo Paredón Grande and **Faro Diego Velázquez**, a 52m lighthouse dating from 1859. This area has a couple of beaches, including much-lauded Playa los Pinos, and is good for fishing.

🏃 Activities

The **Marina Marlin Aguas Tranquilas** (www.nauticamarlin.com), near the Meliá Cayo Coco, offers deep-sea fishing outings (CUC$270 per four hours).

The **Centro Internacional de Buceo Coco Diving** (www.nauticamarlin.com), between Hotel Tryp Cayo Coco and Hotel Colonial, is accessible via a dirt road to the beach. Scuba diving costs CUC$40, plus CUC$10 for gear. The open-water certification course costs CUC$365, less in low season. The diving area stretches for over 10km mainly to the east, and there are six certified instructors with the capacity for 30 divers per day. The same group offers similar services out of Hotel Meliá Cayo Coco. Dive masters are multilingual, and there are liveaboard options.

👉 Tours

There's no lack of day excursions available from the main hotel information desks, which are usually staffed by Cubatur (p308) or Cubanacán representatives. Highlights include Por la Ruta de Hemingway, a journey through the keys mentioned in Hemingway's novel *Islands in the Stream*; a motorboat cruise around Cayo Paredón Grande; a flamingo-spotting tour; or a jaunt out to Cayo Mortero via the fabulous snorkelling spot of Grunt Hole for downtime with cold beer and fresh fish. Prices are in the CUC$30 range.

🛏 Sleeping

Cayo Coco's resorts are policed diligently. Unless you're wearing the 'access all areas' plastic wristband, think twice about sneaking in to use the toilets.

Sitio la Güira CABINS $

(📞30-12-08; cabaña CUC$25; ❄) 🍃 A simple abode situated on a small farm 8km west of the Servi-Cupet gas station, La Güira rents four pseudo-rustic *bohíos* (thatched huts) with private bathrooms and air-con (to dissuade the mosquitoes apparently). There's a *ranchón*-style restaurant and bar here.

⭐Meliá Cayo Coco RESORT $$$

(📞30-11-80; s/d all-incl from CUC$165/230; P❄@☎) This intimate resort on Playa las Coloradas, at the hotel strip's eastern end, is everything you'd expect from Spain's Meliá chain. For a luxury twist try staying in one of the elegant white bungalows perched on stilts in a lagoon. Prices are high, but the Meliá is unashamedly classy and a 'no kids' policy enhances the tranquility.

Hotel Colonial RESORT $$$

(📞30-13-11; s/d all-incl CUC$125/210; P❄@☎) The Spanish colonial villas with attractively tiled public areas lend the Colonial a cloistered, refined air – a pleasant break from the notoriously appalling design of the usual Cuban all-inclusives. This was the island's first hotel when it opened in 1993 (ancient history by Cayo Coco standards). It gained notoriety in 1994 when, according to Cuban media, gunmen from right-wing Cuban exile movement Alpha 66 opened fire on the building. Fortunately no one was hurt.

Hotel Memories Flamenco HOTEL $$$

(📞30-41-00; www.memoriesresorts.com; s all-inc CUC$128-190, d all-incl CUC$257-380; P❄☎) One of the newest Cayo Coco offerings, with 624 decent-sized rooms (recently done up, they're pretty clean) in villa-style, three-floor buildings around two pools (one with a swim-up bar). There's an attractive Asian restaurant, although overall service will leave you wondering which planet those five stars descended from.

CIEGO DE ÁVILA PROVINCE CAYO COCO

CAYO OF CONSTRUCTION

The manic development which has marred the magnificent setting of Cayo for some years has finally taken on the form of several new megaresorts: **Pestana Cayo Coco Beach Resort**, near Hotel Memories Flamenco; on the same stretch of beach, **Memories Jardines del Rey**; and, on Playa las Coloradas, **Pullman Cayo Coco**. Construction is also raging on Cayo Guillermo rather close to Playa Pilar (p314).

Cayo Coco & Cayo Guillermo

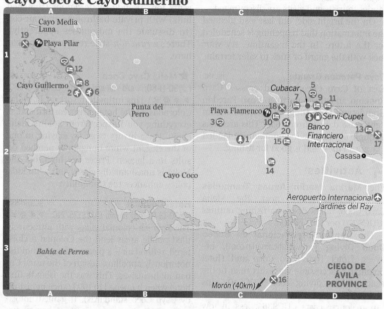

Cayo Coco & Cayo Guillermo

Sights
1 Parque Natural el Bagá......................... C2

Activities, Courses & Tours
2 Boat Adventure A1
3 El Penion C2
4 Green Moray Dive Center A1
5 La Jaula 1, 2, 3 & 4 .... D1
6 Marina Marlin Cayo Guillermo A1

Sleeping
7 Clinica Internacional Cayo
   Coco... D1
8 Hotel Club Cayo Guillermo A1
9 Hotel Colonial....................................... D1

10 Hotel Memories Flamenco.................... C2
11 Hotel Tryp Cayo Coco........................... D1
12 Iberostar Daiquirí A1
13 Meliá Cayo Coco................................... D2
14 Sitio la Güira.. C2
15 Villa Azul.. C2

Eating
16 Parador la Silla..................................... C3
17 Ranchón las Coloradas......................... D2
18 Ranchón Playa Flamenco...................... C2
19 Ranchón Playa Pilar A1

Entertainment
20 La Cueva del Jabalí................................ C2

Hotel Tryp Cayo Coco   RESORT $$$
(☑ 30-13-00; s/d/tr all-incl CUC$119/181/257;
🅿❄@☎🐾) The family choice. Tryp is a
quintessential all-inclusive with a pool, bars
and nightly tourist show. Facilities are good,
although overzealous poolside 'entertainers'
lend the place a holiday-camp feel at times.
The 500-plus rooms – in sunny three-story
apartment blocks – are big, with balconies
and huge beds, although finishes are a little
worn considering room prices.

Eating

Amid the ubiquitous as-much-as-you-can-eat
hotel buffets, the occasional *ranchón*-style
independent restaurant stands out.

Restaurant Sitio la Güira   CARIBBEAN $$
(dishes CUC$2-12; ☉ 8am-11pm) Set in the old
reconstructed charcoal burners' camp, La
Güira's food is plentiful and not too char-
coaly. Try the big, fresh sandwiches (CUC$2)
or the shrimp plates (CUC$12).

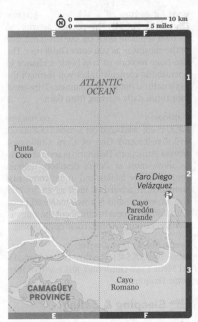

Banco Financiero Internacional At the Servi-Cupet gas station.

Clínica Internacional Cayo Coco (30-21-58; Av de los Hoteles al final) Provides medical treatment. West of Hotel Colonial.

Infotur (www.infotur.cu) Has a helpful office at the Jardines del Rey airport. There are also desks at the main hotels. Ciego de Ávila's Infotur (p306) office has bundles of information on Cayo Coco too.

ⓘ Getting There & Around

Cayo Coco's **Aeropuerto Internacional Jardines del Rey** (30-91-65) can process 1.2 million visitors annually. Weekly flights arrive here from Canada and the UK. There's a daily service to and from Havana (about CUC$110) with Aerogaviota.

Although getting to Cayo Coco is nigh on impossible without a car or taxi (or bike), getting around has become infinitely easier since the introduction of a **Transtur** (30-11-75) hop-on/hop-off minibus. The service varies according to season, but expect a minimum service of two buses per day in either direction, with six scheduled for peak times. The bus runs east–west between Meliá Cayo Coco and Playa Pilar, stopping at all Cayo Coco and Cayo Guillermo hotels. An all-day pass costs CUC$5.

A taxi to Cayo Coco from Morón will cost about CUC$40; from Ciego de Ávila, CUC$60. You pay a CUC$2 fee to enter the causeway.

You can rent a car or moped at **Cubacar** (30-12-75) on the second roundabout between the Meliá and Tryp complexes. Cubacar also has a desk at all the major hotels. Bicycles are in short supply at Cayo Coco's hotels. Ask around.

Parador la Silla CARIBBEAN **$$**
(mains CUC$7-12; ☺9am-5pm) A thatched-roof snack bar halfway along the causeway into Cayo Coco. After that coffee/beer/sandwich you could climb the adjacent lookout tower and try spotting distant specks of pink (flamingos).

Ranchón Playa Flamenco CARIBBEAN **$$**
(mains CUC$7-12; ☺9am-4pm) Eat exquisite seafood, drink cold beer, swim, sunbathe, drink more beer...you get the picture.

Ranchón las Coloradas CARIBBEAN **$$**
(mains CUC$7-12; ☺9am-4pm) Seafood in a paradisiacal beachside setting...but construction nearby might void the paradisiacal tag.

🍷 Drinking & Nightlife

The all-inclusive hotels have full nightly entertainment programs (usually only available to hotel guests) and a clutch of bars each.

La Cueva del Jabalí CLUB
(admission CUC$5; ☺10:30pm-2am Tue-Thu) This natural cave is the only non-all-inclusive entertainment venue. Features a cabaret show.

ⓘ Information

Euros are accepted in all the Cayo Coco resorts.

Cayo Guillermo

Ah, Cayo Guillermo: haunt of pink flamingos, stunning blond beaches and Cuba's second-most famous Ernesto after Mr Guevara – Señor Hemingway. It was Hemingway who initiated Guillermo's early publicity drive, describing it radiantly in his posthumously published Cuban novel *Islands in the Stream* (1970). Development of the northern *cayos* took off here in 1993 when the first land-based all-inclusive resort on the *cayos*, Villa Cojímar, received its formative guests. Long a prized deep-sea fishing spot, 13-sq-km Guillermo retains a more exotic feel than its larger eastern cousin to which it is connected by a causeway. The mangroves off the south coast are home to pink flamingos and pelicans, and there's a tremendous diversity of tropical fish and crustaceans on the Atlantic reef.

◎ Sights

★ Playa Pilar
BEACH

A sublime strip of sand regularly touted as Cuba's (and the Caribbean's) best beach, Playa Pilar earns its reputation courtesy of its diamond-dust white sand and the rugged 15m-high sand dunes (the largest of their kind in the Caribbean) strafed by trails that incite piratical exploration.

The sea here is warm, shallow and loaded with snorkeling possibilities. One kilometer away across a calm channel lies the shimmering sands of **Cayo Media Luna**, a one-time beach escape of Fulgencio Batista. There are excursions to the key (CUC$25), plus kayaks and aquatic bikes for rent, all arranged at the small office (open 9am to 3pm) along the sand from the excellent beach restaurant, Ranchón Playa Pilar.

The hop-on/hop-off bus from Cayo Coco stops at Playa Pilar six times daily in either direction during peak season (two to four times otherwise). And yes, the beach is named after Hemingway's fishing boat, *El Pilar*.

🏃 Activities

Marina Marlin Cayo Guillermo FISHING
(📞30-15-15) On the right of the causeway as you arrive from Cayo Coco, this 36-berth marina is one of Cuba's certified international entry ports. You can organize deep-sea fishing for mackerel, pike, barracuda, red snapper and marlin here on large boats that troll 5km to 13km offshore. Prices start at CUC$290 per half day (four persons).

KITEBOARDING

You'll glimpse the many multicoloured sails as you approach Cayo Guillermo before anything else comes into focus. The latest craze, kiteboarding, is currently possible in just three locations (Varadero and Guardalavaca being the other two) in Cuba. A kiteboarding course costs CUC$250, with schools based at three different hotels: Iberostar Daiquirí for English/French classes, Sol Cayo Guillermo (German) and Allegro Cayo Guillermo (Russian). Equipment hire costs CUC$50 per session. The main launch point is Hotel Club Cayo Guillermo. The lap of shallow, mangrove-festooned waters, the odd flash of flamingo...and you're away.

Boat Adventure BOAT TOUR
(2hr boat trip CUC$41) This popular activity has its own separate dock on the left-hand side of the causeway as you enter Guillermo. The two-hour motorboat trip (with a chance to operate the controls) takes you through the key's natural mangrove channels. Trips leave four times daily starting from 9am.

Delfinario DOLPHIN SWIM
(📞30-15-29; adult/child per session CUC$110/60; ⊗9:30am-3:30pm) One of Cayo Guillermo's newest attractions Delfinario is several notches above most of Cuba's desultory dolphin centers: in the facility and in environmental standards. It advertises itself as an 'interactive' experience and is a well-managed place, with staff who seem to care about the animals' welfare. Flamingos often congregate nearby.

Green Moray Dive Center DIVING
(single dive CUC$45) The dive center is in Hotel Meliá Cayo Guillermo, just north of Iberostar Daiquirí.

🛏 Sleeping & Eating

★ Iberostar Daiquirí
HOTEL **$$$**
(📞30-16-50; s CUC$175-345, all-incl d CUC$230-400; 🅿❄@🏊) Plenty of shade, a lily pond, and a curtain of water cascading in front of the pool bar add up to make the Daiquirí the pick of the bunch in Guillermo right now. The 312 rooms are encased in attractive colonial-style apartment blocks, and the thin slice of paradisiacal beach is straight out of the brochure.

Hotel Club Cayo Guillermo HOTEL **$$$**
(📞30-17-12; s/d CUC$102/163; 🅿❄@🏊) The oldest hotel on the Sabana-Camagüey archipelago (opened in 1993), it comprises a collection of bungalows in a quiet beachside location. The waterslides in the pool are fun; the kiteboarding off the hotel beach more fun.

★ Ranchón Playa Pilar
CARIBBEAN **$$**
(mains CUC$7-12; ⊗9am-4pm) Not staying here? Worry not – Cuba's greatest beach also has an excellent bar-restaurant with fresh lobster and chicken fillets as spectacular as the view.

❶ Getting There & Around

Access information is the same as for Cayo Coco. The twice-daily hop-on, hop-off bus (p313) carries people to and from Cayo Coco, stopping at all four Cayo Guillermo hotels and terminating at Playa Pilar. All-day tickets costs CUC$5.

Cars can be hired from **Cubacar** (📞30-17-43; Hotel Club Cayo Guillermo).

Camagüey Province

Includes ➡

Camagüey 317
Florida 328
Sierra del Chorrillo . . . 328
Guáimaro 329
Nuevitas 329
Brasil & Around 330
Cayo Sabinal 330
Playa Santa Lucía . . . 331

Best Places to Eat

➡ Casa Austria (p324)

➡ El Paso (p324)

➡ Mesón del Príncipe (p324)

➡ El Bucanero (p333)

Best Places for Bird-Watching

➡ Sierra del Chorrillo (p328)

➡ Reserva Ecológica Limones Tuabaquey (p331)

➡ Refugio de Fauna Silvestre Río Máximo (p333)

➡ Playa los Cocos (p332)

Why Go?

Neither Occidente nor Oriente, Camagüey is Cuba's provincial contrarian, a region that likes to go its own way in political and cultural matters – and usually does – much to the chagrin of folks in Havana and Santiago.

Seeds were sown in the colonial era, when Camagüey's preference for cattle ranching over sugarcane meant less reliance on slave labor and more enthusiasm to get rid of a system that bred misery.

Today Cuba's largest province is a mostly pancake-flat pastoral mix of grazing cattle, lazy old sugar-mill towns and, in the south, a few low-but-lovely hill ranges. It's flanked by Cuba's two largest archipelagos: the Sabana-Camagüey in the north and the Jardines de la Reina in the south, both underdeveloped and almost virgin in places.

Staunchly Catholic capital Camagüey, with its alluring architecture and cosmopolitan charm surpassed only by Havana, is the province's pin-up – a fiercely independent city that nurtured revolutionary poet Nicolás Guillén, groundbreaking scientist Carlos J Finlay and an internationally famous ballet company.

When to Go

➡ In February Camagüeyans celebrate Jornada de la Cultura Camagüeyana (Days of Camagüeyan Culture) to mark the city's founding in 1514.

➡ For outdoor enthusiasts, March is prime time for viewing migratory birds on the northern keys.

➡ In Playa Santa Lucía, the amazing underwater shark-feeding show is held when sharks are in the area between June and January.

➡ In September Camagüey showcases some more of its cultural prowess with the Festival Nacional de Teatro (National Theater Festival).

Map scale: 0 — 40 km / 0 — 20 miles (N)

ATLANTIC OCEAN

Cayo Guillermo · Cayo Coco · Faro Diego Velázquez · Cayo Paredón Grande · Cayo Romano · Cayo Judas · Jardines del Rey Airport · Archipiélago de Sabana-Camagüey · **Cayo Cruz** ⑥

Laguna de la Leche · Máximo Gómez Airport · **Morón** ▲

Ciego de Ávila · Caonao · Esmeralda · Brasil · Río Máximo · Cubitas · Cayo Guajaba · **Refugio de Fauna Silvestre Río Máximo** · Río Caoiley · Playa los Pinos · Morteva, Escalón Poseidon 2, El Canyon 2, Valentina

Sancti Spíritus (40km) ← Carretera Central · Embalse Porvenir · La Gloria · Sola · Checkpoint · Cayo Sabinal · Playa Bonita · **Nuevitas** ③

CIEGO DE ÁVILA PROVINCE · Reserva Ecológica Limones Tuabaquey · Lugareño · Playa Santa Lucía ②

Carlos Manuel de Céspedes · Florida · Altagracia · Senado · Playa Cuatro Vientos · Bahía de Nuevitas

Cayo Ana María · Embalse Muñoz · Cromo · Minas · San Miguel de Bagá · King Ranch

Camagüey ④ ⑦ · Ignacio Agramonte International Airport

La Tomatera · **Vertientes** · Sibanicú · Cascorro · Palo Seco · Hermanos Ameijeiras Airport

Golfo de Ana María · Contramaestre · **Guáimaro** ⑤ · **Las Tunas**

Najasa · La Hacienda la Belén · **Sierra del Chorrillo** ① · La Jagua · Jobabo · **LAS TUNAS PROVINCE** · Holgu (68km)

Archipiélago de los Jardines de la Reina · Laberinto de las Doce Leguas · Cabeza de Coral Negro, La Cueva del Pulpo, Faisy, Meseta de los Meros, Avalon, Pipin, Farallón · Santa Cruz del Sur · Golfo de Guacanayabo

CARIBBEAN SEA

Camagüey Province Highlights

① Retreat into the verdant hills of **Sierra del Chorrillo** (p328), harboring rare birdlife and petrified forests.

② Watch dive instructors fearlessly feed sharks off **Playa Santa Lucía** (p331).

③ Discover huge flamingo nesting sites on the **Refugio de Fauna Silvestre Río Máximo** (p333).

④ Say your penance in Camagüey and sally forth to find Cuba's Catholic soul in a stash of **colonial churches** (p323).

⑤ Stop in **Guáimaro** (p329), where Cuba's first constitution was signed.

⑥ Go fly-fishing for tarpon and bonefish in the shallow flats off **Cayo Cruz** (p330).

⑦ Tuck into one of the most sophisticated restaurant scenes outside Havana in a colonial **Camagüey eatery** (p324).

Camagüey

POP 306,400

Welcome to the maze. Camagüey's odd, labyrinthine layout is the by-product of two centuries spent fighting off musket-toting pirates like Henry Morgan: tumultuous times led the fledgling settlement to develop a peculiar street pattern designed to confuse pillaging invaders and provide cover for its long-suffering residents (or so legend has it). As a result, Camagüey's sinuous streets and narrow winding alleys are more reminiscent of a Moroccan medina than the geometric grids of Lima or Mexico City.

Sandwiched on Carretera Central halfway between Ciego de Ávila and Las Tunas is Cuba's third-largest city, easily the suavest and most sophisticated after Havana, and the bastion of the Catholic Church on the island. Well known for going their own way in times of crisis, the resilient citizens are popularly called *'agramontinos'* by other Cubans, after local First War of Independence hero Ignacio Agramonte, coauthor of the Guáimaro constitution and courageous leader of Cuba's finest cavalry brigade. In 2008 its well-preserved historical center was made Cuba's ninth Unesco World Heritage Site and in 2014 the city celebrated its quincentennial.

Camagüey's warren-like streets generally inspire travelers with their hidden plazas, rearing baroque churches, riveting galleries and congenial bars/restaurants. The flip side is the higher-than-average number of *jineteros* (touts) who can dog you as you stroll. Get lost for a day or two and discover it for yourself.

History

Founded in February 1514 as one of Diego Velázquez' hallowed seven 'villas,' Santa María del Puerto Príncipe was originally established on the coast near present-day Nuevitas. Due to a series of bloody rebellions by the local Taíno people, the site of the city was moved twice in the early 16th century, finally taking up its present location in 1528. Its name was changed to Camagüey in 1903, in honor of the camagua tree, which, so runs an indigenous legend, all life is descended from.

Camagüey developed quickly in the 1600s – despite continued attacks by corsairs – with an economy based on sugar production and cattle-rearing. Due to acute water shortages in the area, the townsfolk were forced to make *tinajones* (clay pots) in order to collect rainwater and even today Camagüey is known as the city of *tinajones* – with the pots now serving a strictly ornamental purpose.

Besides swashbuckling independence hero Ignacio Agramonte, Camagüey has produced several personalities of note, including poet and patriot Nicolás Guillén and eminent doctor Carlos J Finlay, the man who was largely responsible for discovering the causes of yellow fever. In 1959 the prosperous citizens quickly fell foul of the Castro revolutionaries when local military commander Huber Matos (Fidel's one-time ally) accused Castro of burying the Revolution. He was duly arrested and later thrown in prison for his pains.

Loyally Catholic, Camagüey welcomed Pope John Paul II in 1998 and in 2008 hosted the beatification of Cuba's first saint, 'Father of the Poor' Fray José Olallo, who aided the wounded of both sides in the 1868–78 War of Independence. In 2014 the city was comprehensively renovated (and given four new hotels) in honor of its quincentennial.

◉ Sights

◉ City Center

★ Plaza San Juan de Dios   SQUARE

(cnr Hurtado & Paco Recio) Looking more Mexican than Cuban (Mexico was capital of New Spain so the colonial architecture was often superior), Plaza San Juan de Dios is Camagüey's most picturesque and beautifully preserved corner. Its eastern aspect is dominated by the Museo de San Juan de Dios, formerly a hospital. Behind the square's arresting blue, yellow and pink building facades lurk several great restaurants.

Museo de San Juan de Dios   MUSEUM

(Plaza San Juan de Dios; admission CUC$1; ⊙9am-5pm Tue-Sat, to 1pm Sun) The Museo de San Juan de Dios is housed in what was once a hospital administered by Father José Olallo, the friar who became Cuba's first saint. It has a front cloister dating from 1728 and a unique triangular rear patio with Moorish touches, built in 1840. Since ceasing to function as a hospital in 1902, the building has served as a teachers college, a refuge during the 1932 cyclone, and the Centro Provincial de Patrimonio directing the restoration of Camagüey's monuments. The museum chronicles Camagüey's history and exhibits some local paintings.

Camagüey

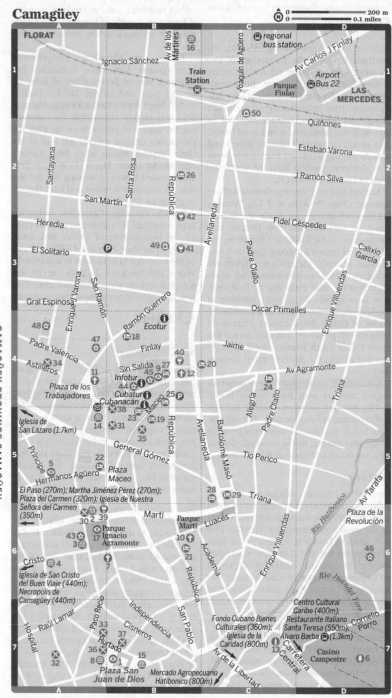

FLORAT

Ignacio Sánchez

Av de los Mártires

16

Joaquín de Agüero

regional bus station

Av Carlos J Finlay

Train Station

Airport
Bus 22

Parque
Finlay

LAS
MERCEDES

50

Quiñones

Santayana

Santa Rosa

San Martín

República

26

Esteban Varona

J Ramón Silva

Avellaneda

Fidel Céspedes

Heredia

El Solitario

42

Padre Olallo

Calixio
García

49   41

Gral Espinosa

San Ramón

Enrique Varona

Ramón Guerrero

Ecotur

Oscar Primelles

Enrique Villuendas

48

47

Padre Valencia

Astilleros

34

11

18

Finlay

45 9 27

Jaime

40

20

Av Agramonte

Triana

Sin Salida

Infotur

12

Plaza de los
Trabajadores

Cubatur

44

Cubanacán

14   31

38

23

25

Maceo

24

Alegría

Padre Olallo

35

19

República

Avellaneda

Bartolomé Masó

Iglesia de
San Lázaro (1.7km)

General Gómez

22

Plaza
Maceo

Tío Perico

El Paso (270m); Martha Jiménez Pérez (270m);
Plaza del Carmen (320m); Iglesia de Nuestra
Señora del Carmen (350m)

Príncipe

Hermanos Agüero

5

28   29

Triana

Av Tarafa

Río Hatibónico

Plaza de la
Revolución

30   39

43   3

Cristo   4

Iglesia de San Cristo
del Buen Viaje (440m);
Necropolis de
Camagüey (440m)

32

36

8

33

37

15

Plaza San
Juan de Dios

Hospital

Raúl Lamar

Paco Recio

Hurtado

Cisneros

Independencia

San Pablo

Martí

Parque
Ignacio
Agramonte

17

7

10

21

Academia

República

Parque
Martí

Luaces

Enrique Villuendas

Fondo Cubano Bienes
Culturales (360m);
Iglesia de la
Caridad (800m)

Av de la Libertad

Mercado Agropecuario
Hatibonico (800m)

Centro Cultural
Caribe (400m);
Restaurante Italiano
Santa Teresa (550m);
Álvaro Barba (1.3km)

13

Carretera
Central

Cornelio
Porro

Río Juan del Toro

Plaza de la
Revolución

46

Casino
Campestre

6

Camagüey

◎ **Top Sights**
1 Plaza San Juan de Dios..........................B7

◎ **Sights**
2 Casa de Arte Jover A6
3 Casa de la Diversidad............................A6
4 Casa Finlay..A6
5 Casa Natal de Nicolás Guillén..............A5
6 Casino Campestre..................................D7
7 Catedral de Nuestra Señora de la
   Candelaria...B6
8 Estudio-Galería Jover.............................A7
9 Galería el Colonial B4
10 Iglesia de Nuestra Corazón de
   Sagrado Jesús....................................B6
11 Iglesia de Nuestra Señora de la
   Merced...A4
12 Iglesia de Nuestra Señora de la
   Soledad...B4
13 Monument to Mariano Baberán &
   Joaquín Collar......................................C7
14 Museo Casa Natal de Ignacio
   Agramonte...A5
15 Museo de San Juan de Dios.................B7
16 Museo Provincial Ignacio
   Agramonte...B1
17 Parque Ignacio Agramonte..................A6

◎ **Sleeping**
18 Alba Ferraz..B4
19 Casa Angelito B5
20 Casa Láncara..C4
21 Casa los Helechos.................................B6
22 Dalgis Fernández Hernández................A5
23 Gran Hotel...B5
24 Hostal de Carmencita C4
25 Hotel Camino de Hierro B4

26 Hotel Colón..B2
27 Hotel Santa María.................................B4
28 'Los Vitrales' – Emma Barreto &
   Rafael Requejo.....................................C5
29 Natural Caribe.......................................C5

◎ **Eating**
30 Café Ciudad..A6
31 Café Cubanitas......................................B5
32 Casa Austria..A7
   Gran Hotel ....(see 23)
   Gran Hotel Snack Bar ....(see 23)
33 La Campana de Toledo..........................A7
34 Mesón del Príncipe...............................A4
35 Panadería Doña Neli.............................B5
36 Restaurante 1800..................................A7
37 Restaurante de los Tres Reyes.............B7
38 Restaurante la Isabella.........................B5

◎ **Drinking & Nightlife**
39 Bar El Cambio.......................................A6
40 Bodegón Don Cayetano B4
   Gran Hotel Bar Terraza ....(see 23)
41 La Bigornia...B3
42 Taberna Bucanero B3

◎ **Entertainment**
43 Casa de la Trova Patricio Ballagas.......A6
44 Cine Casablanca...................................B4
45 Cine Encanto...B4
46 Estadio Cándido González...................D6
47 Sala Teatro José Luis Tasende.............A4
48 Teatro Principal.....................................A4

◎ **Shopping**
49 ARTex Souvenir B3
50 Mercado Francisquito............................C1

Casa de Arte Jover   GALLERY
(Martí No 154, btwn Independencia & Cisneros; ⊙9am-noon & 3-5pm Mon-Sat) FREE Camagüey is home to two of Cuba's most creative and prodigious contemporary painters, Joel Jover and his wife Ileana Sánchez. Their magnificent home in Plaza Agramonte functions both as a gallery and a piece of art in its own right, with a slew of original art and delightfully kitschy antiques on show.

You're welcome to browse and, if you like high-quality original art, buy a painting. The artists also keep a studio and showroom, the **Estudio-Galería Jover** (Paco Recio; ⊙ 9am-noon & 3-5pm Mon-Sat) FREE, in Plaza San Juan de Dios.

**Museo Casa Natal de Ignacio
Agramonte**   MUSEUM
(Av Agramonte No 459; admission CUC$2; ⊙9am-4:45pm Mon-Sat, to 2:30pm Sun) This is the birthplace of the independence hero Ignacio Agramonte (1841–73), the cattle rancher who led the Camagüey area's revolt against Spain. The house – an elegant colonial building in its own right – tells of the oft-overlooked role of Camagüey and Agramonte in the First War of Independence.

In July 1869 rebel forces under Agramonte bombarded Camagüey, and four years later Agramonte was killed in action, aged only 32. You can hear Cuban folk singer Silvio Rodríguez' anthem to this hero, who was nicknamed 'El Mayor' (Major), on his album *Días y flores*. The hero's gun is one of his few personal possessions displayed. The museums is opposite Iglesia de Nuestra Señora de la Merced, on the corner of Independencia.

Parque Ignacio Agramonte   SQUARE
(cnr Martí & Independencia) Camagüey's most dazzling square in the heart of the city invites

relaxation with rings of marble benches and an equestrian statue (c 1950) of Camagüey's precocious War of Independence hero, Snr Agramonte.

Casa Finlay
MUSEUM

(Cristo, btwn Cisneros & Lugareño; admission CUC$1; ⏲9am-5pm Mon-Fri, 8am-noon Sat) Camagüey's other hero, Dr Carlos J Finlay (1833–1915), was more concerned with saving lives than taking them. Calling this place – his birth house – a museum is a stretch, but on a good day one of the attendents might be able to enlighten you on his life story and scientific feats, most notably his medical breakthrough in discovering how mosquitoes transmit yellow fever. There's a splendidly grizzled indoor patio.

Casa Natal de Nicolás Guillén
CULTURAL CENTER

(Hermanos Agüero No 58; ⏲9am-5pm) FREE This modest house gives visitors a small insight into Cuba's late national poet and his books, and today doubles as the Instituto Superior de Arte, where local students come to study music.

Casa de la Diversidad
MUSEUM

(Cisneros No 150; CUC$1; ⏲10am-6pm Mon-Fri, 9am-9pm Sat, 8am-noon Sun) Impossible to miss due to its exuberantly diverse facade (a mix of Moorish and neoclassical elements), this new museum's best exhibit is the building itself. You can go around the four exhibition rooms dedicated to slavery, costumes, art and architecture relatively quickly, but you'll want to dawdle in the ornate lobby with its soaring pillars. Pride of place, however, goes to the toilets (yes, *toilets*!) where intricate frescoes have been uncovered. The ladies is the most ornate.

◉ West of the City Center

Plaza del Carmen
SQUARE

(Hermanos Agüero, btwn Honda & Carmen) Around 600m west of the frenzy of República sits another sublimely beautiful square, one less visited than the central plazas. It's backed on the eastern side by the masterful Iglesia de Nuestra Señora del Carmen (p323), one of the prettiest city churches.

Little more than a decade ago Plaza del Carmen was a ruin, but it's now restored to a state better than the original. The cobbled central space has been infused with giant *tinajones*, atmospheric street lamps and unique life-sized sculptures of *camagüeyanos* people from Camagüey) going about

their daily business (reading newspapers and gossiping, mostly).

Martha Jiménez Pérez
GALLERY

(Martí No 282, btwn Carmen & Onda; ⏲8am-8pm) FREE You're in Cuba's ceramics capital so why not gravitate to the studio-gallery of Martha Jiménez Pérez, one of its best living artists, to see everything from pots to paintings being produced? The studio overlooks Pérez' magnum opus, Plaza del Carmen''s alfresco statue of three gossiping women entitled *Chismosas* (Gossipers). The *chismosas* also feature in many of her paintings inside.

Necropolis de Camagüey
CEMETERY

(Plaza del Cristo; ⏲7am-6pm) FREE This sea of elaborate, lopsided, bleached-white Gothic tombs makes up Cuba's most underrated cemetery, secreting the resting place of Camagüey-born independence hero Ignacio Agramonte, among others. It might not quite have the clout of Havana's Cementerio Colón but isn't too far behind in its roll call of famous incumbents.

Agramonte lies halfway down the second avenue on the left after the entrance (the blue-painted tomb). Harder to find are tombs such as those of Camagüey freedom-fighters Tomás Betancourt or Salvador Cisneros Betancourt (one-time President of Cuba); show up for tours which depart from the entrance behind Iglesia de San Cristo de Buen Viaje (early to mid-morning is best).

◉ North of the City Center

North of the train station, Avenida de los Mártires opens up in a kilometer-long symphony of noble colonnaded 19th-century buildings, the most complete such example in Cuba.

Museo Provincial Ignacio Agramonte
MUSEUM

(Av de los Mártires No 2; admission CUC$2; ⏲10am-1pm & 2-6pm Tue-Sat, 9am-1pm Sun) Named (like half of Camagüey) after the exalted local War of Independence hero, this cavernous museum, just north of the train station, is in a building erected in 1848 as a Spanish cavalry barracks. It now contains some impressive artwork as well as antique furniture and old family heirlooms.

The upstairs art collection features many Camagüey artists: there is both 19th- and early-20th-century art, such as the haunting work of *camagüeyano* Fidelio Ponce, and *artes plasticos* (modern art) by nationally renowned figures like Alfredo Sosabravo.

South & East of the City Center

Casino Campestre   PARK
(Carretera Central) Over the Río Hatibonico from the old town is Cuba's largest urban park, laid out in 1860. There are shaded benches, a baseball stadium, concerts and activities. On a traffic island near the park entrance is a **monument** dedicated to Mariano Barberán and Joaquín Collar, Spaniards who made the first nonstop flight between Spain (Seville) and Cuba (Camagüey) in 1933.

The pair made the crossing in their plane *Cuatro Vientos*, but tragically the plane disappeared when flying to Mexico a week later. Ubiquitous bici-taxis are on hand to pedal you around.

Mercado Agropecuario Hatibonico   MARKET
(Carretera Central; ⊙ 7am-6pm) If you visit just one market in Cuba, make it this one. Glued (by mud) beside the murky Río Hatibonico just off the Carretera Central, and characterized by its *pregones* (singsong, often comic, offering of wares) ringing through the stalls, this is a classic example of Cuban-style free enterprise juxtaposed with cheaper but lower-quality government stalls.

The best section to visit is the *herberos* (purveyors of herbs, potions and secret elixirs); also visit the plant nursery where Cubans can buy dwarf mango trees and various ornamental plants. Keep a tight hold on your money belt.

El Lago de los Sueños   PARK
The so-called 'Lake of Dreams' has been recently developed as an out-of-town escape from Camagüey's urban maze. It uses the same inventive if slightly kitschy methodology employed by a similar venture in Ciego de Ávila. Prize for the oddest installation is the **Cremería 1514** (ice cream CUC$0.25; ⊙ 10am-10pm) an ice-cream parlor encased in the fuselage of an old Soviet plane – a 1960s Antonov A26. Runner-up is the antediluvian train carriage-cum-restaurant.

Elsewhere, you can enjoy the lake, go for a boat ride (CUC$1), or even stroll along a specially constructed *malecón*. There are copious places to eat.

✷ Festivals & Events

The **Jornada de la Cultura Camagüeyana** celebrates the anniversary of the city's founding in February. The annual carnival, known as the **San Juan Camagüeyano** (⊙ Jun 24-29), runs from June 24 to 29 and includes dancers, floats and African roots music. On September 8, there's also a religious festival, the **Nuestra Señora de la Caridad** (⊙ Sep 8), to honor the city's – and Cuba's – patron saint.

⌂ Sleeping

★ **'Los Vitrales' – Emma Barreto & Rafael Requejo**   CASA PARTICULAR **$**
(☎ 29-58-66, 52-942-522; requejobarreto@gmail.com; Avellaneda No 3, btwn General Gómez & Martí; r CUC$20-25; P ❋) This enormous, painstakingly restored colonial house was once a convent. It sports broad arches, high ceilings and dozens of antiques. Four rooms are arranged around a shady patio embellished with over 50 different types of plants and a fantastic tile mural. Owner Rafael is an architect and it shows. The food (vegetarians catered for) is great too.

CAMAGÜEY PROVINCE CAMAGÜEY

CAMAGÜEY STREET NAMES

Asking for directions? To make things even more confusing, locals doggedly stick to using the old names of streets, even though signs and maps carry the new names.

OLD NAME	NEW NAME
Estrada Palma	Agramonte
Francisquito	Quiñones
Pobre	Padre Olallo
Rosario	Enrique Villuendas
San Estéban	Oscar Primelles
San Fernando	Bartolomé Masó
San José	José Ramón Silva
Santa Rita	El Solitario

Natural Caribe
CASA PARTICULAR **$**

(☑29-58-66; requejoarias@nauta.cu; Avellaneda 8; r CUC$25; ❀) ✎ If you haven't heard of an architectural style known as 'Tropical Mini-malism', you soon will, especially if you visit this exquisite new casa, cleverly designed by a local architect, that mixes elements of Ca-magüey's rich colonial heritage with furnish-ings that wouldn't look out of place in a New York loft apartment.

Two rooms and a terrace cleverly inter-grate light, space, water and sustainable building materials.

Casa Láncara
CASA PARTICULAR **$**

(☑28-31-87; Avellaneda No 160; r CUC$25; ❀) Feeling like a little bit of Seville in Camagüey on account of its beautiful blue and yellow *azulejos* (tiles) and location within earshot of the city's best flamenco club, the Láncara is overseen by Andalucian fanatic Alejan-dro and his wife, Dinorah. The two rooms are hung with original local art and there's a roof terrace all within spitting distance of the Soledad church.

Casa los Helechos
CASA PARTICULAR **$**

(☑52-31-18-97, 29-48-68; Republica No 68; r CUC$20-25; ❀) *Helechos* means 'ferns' and there are plenty in the long, thin courtyard of this pleasant colonial house, at the back of which is one sizable room with a private kitchen.

Hotel Colón
HOTEL **$**

(☑25-48-78; República No 472, btwn José Ramón Silva & San Martín; s/d incl breakfast CUC$33/48; ❀) A classic long mahogany bar, colorful tile-flanked walls and a stained-glass por-trait of Christopher Columbus over the lobby door give this place a mixed colonial/fin-de-siècle feel, although rooms are mostly tiny. But the Colón is a good base for both exploring and relaxing in the rear coloni-al patio; the bar is a favorite of European/Canadian men and their younger Cuban dates.

Casa Angelito
CASA PARTICULAR **$**

(☑29-82-71; Maceo No 62 (Altos); CUC$20-25; ℗❀) Angelito likes to position himself as a more economical and homely alternative to the Gran Hotel which sits directly oppo-site his 2nd-floor accommodations. Simple but clean rooms lead off a giant plant-filled terrace where you can imbibe cocktails or digest breakfast. It's an affable family home and very central.

Dalgis Fernández Hernández
CASA PARTICULAR **$**

(☑28-57-32; Independencía 251 (Altos), btwn Her-manos Agüeros & General Gómez; ❀) Prize for the largest rooftop terrace; you'll be spend-ing a lot of time sun-basking up here. Two lovely 2nd-floor rooms and an antique-filled common area are just below.

Hostal de Carmencita
CASA PARTICULAR **$**

(☑29-69-30; Av Agramonte No 259, btwn Padre Olallo & Alegría; r CUC$20-25; ℗❀) A well-equipped, self-contained room on the top floor with its own terrace and fridge. The common room below features a computer with internet access exclusively for guest use (rare in Cuba). There's a garage too (tight fitting but nonetheless another rarity in cen-tral Camagüey).

Alba Ferraz
CASA PARTICULAR **$**

(☑28-30-81; Ramón Guerrero No 106, btwn San Ramón & Oscar Primelles; r CUC$20-25; ❀) Two rooms sharing a bath open onto a grand colo-nial courtyard bedecked with plants. There's a roof terrace and your host, Alba, can ar-range dance and guitar lessons for guests.

Gran Hotel
HOTEL **$$**

(☑29-20-93; Maceo No 67, btwn Av Agramonte & General Gómez; s/d incl breakfast CUC$49/78; ❀@≋) This time-warped city-center hotel classic dates from 1939. A haughty pre-revolutionary atmosphere stalks the 72 clean rooms reached by a marble staircase or an-cient lift replete with cap-doffing attendants. There are bird's-eye citywide views from the 5th-floor restaurant or gorgeous rooftop bar. A piano bar is accessed through the lobby and an elegant renaissance-style swimming pool shimmers out back.

Hotel Santa María
BOUTIQUE HOTEL **$$**

(cnr República & Av Agramonte; s/d CUC$75/109; ❀@) One of a quartet of beautifully curated boutique hotels opened to tie in with Cama-güey quincentenial, the Santa María was only partially open at last visit, but displays promise with its elegant common areas dec-orated with classy local art.

★ Hotel Camino de Hierro
BOUTIQUE HOTEL **$$$**

(☑28-42-64; Plaza de la Solidaridad; s/d CUC$90/120; ❀@) This is the best of Cama-güey's boutique hotels, opened in 2014 and decorated with a railway theme and encased in an attractive city-center building that was once an office for the Cuban *ferrocarril* (railway).

CAMAGÜEY'S ECCLESIAL ARCHITECTURE

If Cuba has a Catholic soul, it undoubtedly resides in Camagüey, where ecclesial spires rise like minarets above the narrow tangle of streets.

Holiest

Any exploration of Camagüey's religious history should begin at the **Catedral de Nuestra Señora de la Candelaria** (Cisneros No 168), rebuilt in the 19th century on the site of an earlier chapel dating from 1530. The cathedral, which is named for the city's patron saint, was fully restored with funds raised from Pope John Paul II's 1998 visit. While not Camagüey's most eye-catching church, it is noted for its noble Christ statue that sits atop a craning bell tower. You can climb the tower for CUC$1.

Eclectic

The **Iglesia de Nuestra Señora de la Merced** (Plaza de los Trabajadores), dating from 1748, is arguably Camagüey's most impressive colonial church. Local myth tells of a miraculous figure that floated from the watery depths here in 1601; it's been a place of worship ever since. The active convent in the attached cloister is distinguished by its two-level arched interior, spooky catacombs and the dazzling Santo Sepulcro, a solid-silver coffin.

Baroque

Gleaming after a much-lauded 2007 renovation, **Iglesia de Nuestra Señora de la Soledad** (cnr República & Av Agramonte) is a massive baroque structure dating from 1779. Its picturesque cream-and-terracotta tower predates the rest of the church and is an attention-grabbing landmark on the city skyline. Inside there are ornate baroque frescoes and the hallowed font where Ignacio Agramonte was baptized in 1841.

Neo-Gothic

One of Cuba's rare neo-Gothic churches beautifies Parque Martí, a few blocks east of Parque Ignacio Agramonte. The triple-spired **Iglesia de Nuestra Corazón de Sagrado Jesús** (cnr República & Luaces) is technically from an architectural subgenre called Catalan Gothic and dazzles with its ornate stained glass, decorative ironwork and pointed arches.

The Twin-Towered

The **Iglesia de Nuestra Señora del Carmen** (Plaza del Carmen), a twin-towered baroque beauty dating from 1825, shares digs with a former convent. The Monasterio de las Ursalinas is a sturdy arched colonial building with a pretty, cloistered courtyard that once provided shelter for victims of the furious 1932 hurricane. Today it is the City Historian's offices.

Out-of-Town

The **Iglesia de San Lazaro** (cnr Carretera Central Oeste & Calle Cupey) is a beautiful (if diminutive), cream-coloured church dating from 1700, although as interesting is the nearby cloistered hospital constructed a century later by virtuous Franciscan monk Padre Valencia to nurse leprosy victims. It's 2km west of the center.

Unheralded

The **Iglesia de San Cristo del Buen Viaje** (Plaza del Cristo), next door to the Necropolis de Camagüey and overlooking a quiet square, is one of the least visited of Camagüey's ecclesial octet, but it is worth a peek if you're exploring the necropolis. An original chapel was raised here in 1723, but the current structure is of mainly 19th-century vintage.

Diminutive

Iglesia de la Caridad (cnr Av de la Libertad & Sociedad Patriotica) stands sentinel on the southeastern edge of the city. Constructed originally as a chapel in the 18th century, it got a couple of 20th-century renovations (1930 and 1945) and has a fine silver altar (c 1730) and image of the Virgin de la Caridad del Cobre with Cuba's national flower, *la mariposa* (white jasmine).

✕ Eating

Camagüey, Cuba's third-largest city, is threatening to usurp Santiago (its second largest) with the quality and elegance of its private restaurants.

Café Ciudad   CAFE $

(Plaza Agramonte, cnr Martí & Cisneros; snacks CUC$2-5; ⊙10am-10pm) Camagüey has made Agramonte efforts to carve culinary quality into its historical inheritance. This lovely plaza-hugging colonial cafe melds grandiosity with great service, emulating anything in Havana Vieja. Try the *jamón serrano* (cured ham) or savour a superb *café con leche* (coffee with milk) under the louvers. The picture occupying one wall shows the exact continuation of the old street.

Café Cubanitas   CAFE $

(cnr Independencia & Av Agramonte; snacks CUC$1-3; ⊙24hr) A cafe just off Plaza de los Trabajadores, Cubanitas is alfresco and lively, and really does stay open all hours (unlike many Cuban places that state the fact then close early). Most importantly it sells decent snacks and beer. So if you're craving that 3am *ropa vieja* (shredded beef and vegetables in a tomato salsa)...

★ Casa Austria   EUROPEAN $$

(☑28-55-80; Lugareño No 121, btwn San Rafael & San Clemente; meals CUC$5-14; ⊙7:30am-11:30pm) The name's teutonic and the menu's international, but the decor and ambience of this dashing new cafe/restaurant suggest that, in the year of its quincentennial (2014), Camagüey finally rediscovered its mojo. Admire the house's ponds, fountains, ferns and heavy colonial furniture and don't leave without trying one of the Austrian cakes served in a cafe out front.

Restaurante 1800   INTERNATIONAL $$

(☑28-36-19; Plaza San Juan de Dios; meals CUC$12-15; ⊙10am-midnight) There aren't many things this sensational colonial locale lacks. There is the grandiose front-of-house, plaza-facing part, which, once you've ordered your *camarones enchiladas* (shrimps in feisty tomato salsa) or, perhaps, *ensalada de pulpo* (octopus salad), you realize is merely the trailer to the eating experience.

Included with any meal you order is gratis access to a lavish buffet that usually contains European cheeses, meats and crisp salads. Right alongside is the Oriente's most impressive wine cellar and, at the back, there's the barbecue; sit alfresco and load up on succulent grilled meat.

Mesón del Príncipe   CUBAN $$

(☑52-40-45-98; Astilleros No 7; meals CUC$4-12; ⊙noon-midnight) Elegant restaurant that offers an affordable fine-dining experience in a typically refined Camagüeyan residence. It is places like this that have placed Camagüey at the cutting edge of Cuba's new culinary revolution – a notch above Santiago.

El Paso   INTERNATIONAL $$

(☑52-39-09-39; www.complejoelpaso.com; Hermanos Agüero, btwn Carmen & Honda; meals CUC$5-10; ⊙8am-midnight) Breakfast, lunch, dinner! It's rare for a private restaurant to chime in with all three in Cuba but, true to its name, El Paso is staying *un paso adelante* (one step ahead) with all-day opening hours, a funky interior and an enviable location overlooking the tranquil Plaza del Carmen. Good for breakfast, snack sandwiches and cocktails at the bar.

Restaurante Italiano Santa Teresa   ITALIAN $$

(☑29-71-08; Av de la Victoria No 12 , btwn Padre Carmelo & Freyre; meals CUC$3-7; ⊙noon-midnight) A block behind Centro Cultural Caribe, the idyllic, part-covered back patio at Santa Teresa is an Italian feast-in-waiting. Divine pizza, great ice cream and more-than-passable espresso in such environs definitely makes this a spot to savor. The same owners run another restaurant, **El Eden de Santa Teresa** (☑27-48-04; Callejón Villa Lola, & Monaco Sur; mains CUC$3-7; ⊙noon-midnight) nearby with Cuban-style food and Saturday night cabaret (8pm to 10pm).

Restaurante la Isabella   ITALIAN $$

(cnr Av Agramonte & Independencia; pizzas CUC$5-8; ⊙11am-4pm & 6:30-10pm) Camagüey's coolest restaurant was opened during a visit by delegates from Gibara's iconic film festival, Festival Internacional del Cine Pobre, in 2008. Blending Italian food (pizza, lasagna, fettuccine) with a maverick movie-themed decor and director-style seats, the restaurant occupies the site of Camagüey's first ever cinema.

Gran Hotel   INTERNATIONAL $$

(Maceo No 67, btwn Av Agramonte & General Gómez; dinner buffet CUC$12; ⊙6-11pm) The 5th-floor restaurant here has superb city views and a rather nice buffet; get here early to watch the sun set over the church towers. Way below on street level, cheaper **Gran Hotel**

Snack Bar (Maceo No 67, btwn Av Agramonte & General Gómez; snacks CUC$1-4; ☺9am-11pm) has coffee, sandwiches, chicken and ice cream. The hamburgers (when available) are good and the atmosphere is 1950s retro.

Restaurante de los Tres Reyes CARIBBEAN **$$** (Plaza San Juan de Dios No 18; meals CUC$7; ☺10am-10pm) A handsome state-run place that sells mainly chicken dishes, set in beautiful colonial digs on Plaza San Juan de Dios. Ruminate on Camagüey life by one of the giant iron-grilled windows out front or enjoy greater privacy on a plant-bedecked patio behind. Equally romantic, **La Campana de Toledo** (Plaza San Juan de Dios No 18; meals CUC$7; ☺10am-10pm) is next door.

Self-Catering

Mercado Agropecuario Hatibonico MARKET **$** (Carretera Central; ☺7am-6pm) 🖉 Located alongside the fetid Río Hatibonico, this is a classic example of a Cuban market where government (lower quality, but cheaper price) and private (vice versa) produce is sold side by side. Chew on peso sandwiches and fresh *batidos* (fruit shakes, sold in jam jars) and buy fruit and vegetables grown within 500m of where you stand.

There's a good herb section and the market also sells an excellent selection of fruit and vegetables. Watch out for pickpockets.

Panadería Doña Neli BAKERY **$** (Maceo; ☺7am-7pm) For bread and delicate cakes, try this particularly well-stocked bakery, opposite the Gran Hotel. Follow the aroma.

 Drinking

Maybe it's the pirate past, but Camagüey has great tavern-style drinking houses.

Bar El Cambio BAR (cnr Independencia & Martí; ☺7am-late) The Hunter S Thompson choice. A dive bar with graffiti-splattered walls and interestingly named cocktails, this place consists of one room, four tables and bags of atmosphere.

Bodegón Don Cayetano BAR (☎26-19-61; República No 79) This Spanish-style taverna, nestled beneath Iglesia de Nuestra Señora de la Soledad, is best used as a drinking option (there's better food elsewhere). Tables spill into the adjacent alley, there's a large (for Cuba) wine collection and flamenco shows take off at 10pm on Saturday night.

Gran Hotel Bar Terraza BAR (Maceo No 67, btwn Av Agramonte & General Gómez; ☺1pm-2am) The aesthete's choice. Up top of the Gran Hotel its cocktail maestro will prepare you impeccably concocted mojitos and daiquiris while you gaze at the city's premier vista – all Camagüey is laid out before you. Duck below to the swimming pool for the bizarrely addictive aquatic dance shows, happening several times weekly at 9pm.

Taberna Bucanero BAR (cnr República & Fidel Céspedes; ☺2-11pm) The beer-drinker's choice. Fake pirate figures and Bucanero beer on tap characterize this swashbuckling tavern, which is faintly reminiscent of a British pub.

La Bigornia BAR (República, btwn El Solitario & Oscar Primelles; ☺9am-midnight) The young person's choice. This lurid-purple boutique bar-restaurant, with a sports store on its mezzanine level, is where the city's well- (read scantily) dressed 18- to 25-year-olds come for date nights and Noche Camagüeyana warm-ups.

☆ Entertainment

Every Saturday night, the raucous **Noche Camagüeyana** (República from La Soledad) spreads up República from La Soledad to the train station, with food and alcohol stalls, music and crowds. Often a rock or reggaetón concert takes place in the square next to La Soledad.

★**Teatro Principal** THEATER (☎29-30-48; Padre Valencia No 64; tickets CUC$5-10; ☺shows 8:30pm Fri & Sat, 5pm Sun) If a show's on, go! Second only to Havana in its ballet credentials, the Camagüey Ballet Company, founded in 1971 by Fernando Alonso (ex-husband of number-one Cuban dancing diva Alicia Alonso), is internationally renowned and performances are the talk of the town. Also of interest is the wonderful theater building of 1850 vintage, bedizened with majestic chandeliers and stained glass.

Casa de la Trova Patricio Ballagas LIVE MUSIC (Cisneros No 171, btwn Martí & Cristo; cover CUC$3; ☺7pm-1am) An ornate entrance hall gives way to an atmospheric patio where old crooners sing and young couples *chachachá*. One of Cuba's best *trova* houses, where regular tourist traffic doesn't detract from the old-world authenticity. Tuesday's a good night for traditional music.

CINEMA STREET

Cinema Street, aka *La Calle de los Cines*, is one of the most inspired and creative of Camagüey's renovation projects organized to tie in with the 500th anniversary (in 2014) of the city's founding. The idea – to turn a short stretch of Calle Agramonte between the Iglesia de la Soledad and the Plaza de los Trabajadores into a homage to the big screen – makes perfect historical sense. The street has long been known for its cinemas and *sala*-videos (video rooms). The Cine Casablanca and the Cine Encanto opened in the 1940s and '50s, while the Sala-Video Nuevo Mundo dates from 1985. The latter was the first video room of its type in Cuba, a country where few families could afford home video-recorders in the '80s.

By the 2000s, the cinemas and *salas*, like much of Camagüey's once glittering cityscape, had fallen into a serious state of disrepair. Enter Camagüey's City Historian's Office with a bold artistic plan. In common with most restoration projects in Cuba, progress on Cinema Street has been slow but concise, paying meticulous attention to detail. By the end of 2014, the **Cine Casablanca** (Ignacio Agramonte No 428) had reopened as a three-screen multiplex; the **Cine Encanto** (Av Agramonte) had become a fount of video-art (the o-nsite Galería Pixel shows revolving documentary films); while the former Sala-Video Nuevo Mundo had become a film studies center offering expos, courses, documentaries and information.

Almost all of the other businesses in the street carry film themes. A local women's hairdresser is called 'La Ciudad de las Mujeres' after a 1980 Fellini movie. The great Italian director is also honored in the nearby Cafetería La Dolce Vita. Next door, Coffee Arábiga has a more daring moniker. It is named after a controversial 1968 documentary film by Nicolás Guillén Landrián, nephew of the famed Camagüeyan poet Nicolás Guillen. The flim *Coffee Arábiga* gained notoriety in the '60s for its subtle artistic protest. In it, Guillen played the intro to The Beatles' song, 'The Fool on the Hill', over news footage of Fidel Castro. The film was censored and Guillén was later imprisoned before fleeing Cuba in 1989.

The nexus of Calle Agramonte and Plaza de los Trabajadores is the site of Camagüey's first cinema, now a salubrious restaurant called La Isabella (p324) where diners recline in director's chairs beneath iconic film posters and enjoy mainly Italian food. Arrive early and you might be able to bag Fellini's or Tomas Gutiérrez Alea's much-sought-after pews.

Centro Cultural Caribe CABARET

(cnr Narciso Montreal (Calle 1) & Freyre; tickets CUC\$3-6; ⊘10pm-2am, to 4am Fri & Sat) Some say it's the best cabaret outside Havana and, at this price, who's arguing? Book your seat (from the box office on the same day) and pull up a pew *sin* (without) tourists for an eyeful of feathers and a few frocks. There's a trousers-and-shirt dress code.

Sala Teatro José Luis Tasende THEATER

(✆29-21-64; Ramón Guerrero No 51; ⊘shows 8:30pm Sat & Sun) For serious live theater, head to this venue, which has quality Spanish-language performances.

Estadio Cándido González SPORTS

(Av Tarafa) From October to April, baseball games are held here alongside Casino Campestre. Team Camagüey, known as the Alfareros (the Ceramicists), have an empty trophy cabinet despite representing Cuba's largest province.

Shopping

Calle Maceo is Camagüey's top shopping street, with a number of souvenir shops, bookstores and department stores, and an attractive pedestrian boulevard. At **Galería el Colonial** (cnr Av Agramonte & República; ⊘9am-5pm) you can check everything from cigars to rum off your to-get list.

ARTex Souvenir SOUVENIRS

(República No 381; ⊘9am-5pm) Che T-shirts, mini-*tinajones*, Che key rings, CDs, Che mugs. Get the picture?

Fondo Cubano Bienes Culturales CRAFTS

(Av de la Libertad No 112; ⊘8am-6pm Mon-Sat) Sells all kinds of artifacts in a pleasantly non-touristy setting, just north of the train station.

Mercado Francisquito MARKET

(Quiñones; ⊘9am-5pm) Shoes, nuts, bolts, watch parts...join the fray and purchase away.

ⓘ Information

DANGERS & ANNOYANCES

Camagüey invites more hassle than other cities. Thefts have been reported in its narrow, winding streets, mainly from bag-snatchers who then jump onto a waiting bicycle for a quick getaway. Keep your money belt tied firmly around your waist and don't invite attention. Then there's the *jineteros* (touts) who will try to squeeze money out of you any which way – maybe 'offering' to take you to the casa you've been searching for (it will transpire to be another one with almost certainly less-desirable facilities). Try to book your accommodation in advance, ideally arranging with the owners to meet you at the bus station/train station/airport. And, particularly at these places, be wary of strangers approaching and soliciting 'services' (eg to be your guide, find you a room).

INTERNET ACCESS

Etecsa Telepunto (República, btwn San Martín & José Ramón Silva; internet per hour CUC$4.50; ⊗8:30am-7pm) Camagüey is light on wi-fi, so grab one of the dozen terminals here.

MEDIA

The local newspaper *Adelante* is published every Saturday. Radio Cadena Agramonte broadcasts in the city over frequencies 910AM and 93.5FM; south of the city tune in to 1340AM and north of the city, 1380AM.

MEDICAL SERVICES

Farmacia Internacional (Av Agramonte No 449, btwn Independencia & República)

Policlínico Integral Rodolfo Ramirez Esquival (☑28-14-81; cnr Ignacio Sánchez & Joaquín de Agüero) North of the level crossing from the Hotel Plaza; it will treat foreigners in an emergency.

MONEY

Banco de Crédito y Comercio (cnr Av Agramonte & Cisneros; ⊗9am-3pm Mon-Fri)

Banco Financiero Internacional (Independencia, btwn Hermanos Agüero & Martí; ⊗9am-3pm Mon-Fri)

Cadeca (República No 353, btwn Oscar Primelles & El Solitario; ⊗8:30am-7pm Mon-Sat)

POST

Post Office (Av Agramonte No 461, btwn Independencia & Cisneros; ⊗9am-6pm Mon-Sat)

TOURIST INFORMATION

Infotur (☑25-67-94; Ignacio Agramonte; ⊗9am-5pm) Office in a gallery between Encanto and Casablanca cinemas.

TRAVEL AGENCIES

Cubanacán (Maceo No 67, Gran Hotel) The best place for information on Playa Santa Lucía.

Ecotur (☑24-49-57; República No 278; ⊗8am-noon & 1-4:30pm Mon-Sat) Can arrange excursions to the Hacienda la Belén and Reserva Ecológica Limones Tuabaquey. Office is inside the Complejo Turístico Bambú.

ⓘ Getting There & Away

AIR

Ignacio Agramonte International Airport (☑26-72-02; Carretera Nuevitas Km 7) is 9km northeast of town on the road to Nuevitas and Playa Santa Lucía.

Air Transat (www.airtransat.com) and **Sunwing** (www.sunwing.ca) fly in the all-inclusive crowd from Toronto, who are hastily bussed off to Playa Santa Lucía.

There are three flights weekly to/from Havana with **Aerocaribbean** (www.fly-aerocaribbean.com; cnr Republica & Callejon de Correa).

BUS & TRUCK

The regional bus station, near the train station, has trucks to Nuevitas (87km, twice daily) and Santa Cruz del Sur (82km, three daily). You pay in Cuban pesos. Trucks for Playa Santa Lucía (109km, three daily) leave from here as well: ask for *el último* (last in the queue) inside the station and you'll be given a paper with a number; line up at the appropriate door and wait for your number to come up.

Long-distance **Víazul** (www.viazul.com) buses depart **Álvaro Barba Bus Station** (Carretera Central), 3km southeast of the center.

The Santiago de Cuba departure also stops at Las Tunas (CUC$7, two hours), Holguín (CUC$11, 3¼ hours) and Bayamo (CUC$11, 4¼ hours). The Havana bus stops at Ciego de Ávila (CUC$6, 1¾ hours), Sancti Spíritus (CUC$10, four hours), Santa Clara (CUC$15, 4½ hours) and Entronque de Jagüey (CUC$25, 6¼ hours). For Víazul tickets, see the *jefe de turno* (shift manager).

Passenger trucks to nearby towns, including Las Tunas and Ciego de Ávila, also leave from this station. Arriving before 9am will greatly increase your chances of getting on one of these trucks.

Public transport to Playa Santa Lucía is scant unless you're on a prearranged package tour. Expect to pay CUC$70 for a one-way taxi from Camagüey.

TAXI

A taxi to Playa Santa Lucía should cost around CUC$70 one way: bargain hard.

TRAIN

The **train station** (cnr Avellaneda & Av Carlos J Finlay) is more conveniently located than the bus station – though its service isn't as convenient. Foreigners buy tickets in convertible/pesos (CUC$) from an unmarked office across the

CAMAGÜEY PROVINCE CAMAGÜEY

VÍAZUL BUS DEPARTURES FROM CAMAGÜEY

DESTINATION	COST (CUC$)	DURATION (HR)	DAILY DEPARTURES
Havana	33	9	12:35am, 6:30am, 11:05am, 2:25pm, 11:45pm
Holguín	11	3	12:30am, 4:30am, 6:25am, 1:20pm, 6:40pm
Santiago de Cuba	18	6	12:30am, 6:25am, 9:30am, 1:20pm, 4pm
Trinidad	15	4½	2:45am
Varadero	24	8¼	3:10am

street from the entrance to Hotel Plaza. The *Tren Francés* leaves for Santiago at around 3:19am every third day and for Havana (stopping in Santa Clara) at around 1:47am, also every third day. A 1st-class ticket is around CUC$23. Schedules change frequently: check at the station a couple of days before you intend to travel. Slower *coche motor* (cross-island) trains also serve the Havana–Santiago route, stopping at places such as Matanzas and Ciego de Ávila. Going east there are daily services to Las Tunas, Manzanillo and Bayamo. Heading north there are (theoretically) four daily trains to Nuevitas and four to Morón.

❶ Getting Around

TO/FROM THE AIRPORT

A taxi to the airport should cost around CUC$10 from town, but you can bargain. Or you can hang around for the local bus (No 22) from Parque Finlay (opposite the regional bus station) that runs every 30 minutes on weekdays and hourly on weekends.

BICI-TAXIS

Bici-taxis are found around most of the city's squares, with the main contingent in Plaza de los Trabajadores. They should cost five pesos, but drivers will probably ask for payment in convertibles.

CAR

Car-rental prices start around CUC$70 a day plus gas, depending on the make of car and hire duration. Companies include **Cubacar** (www.transturcarrental.com; Van Horne No 1, btwn República & Avellaneda).

Guarded parking (CUC$2 for 24 hours) is available for those brave enough to attempt Camagüey's maze in a car. Ask at your hotel or casa particular for details.

There are two **Servi-Cupet gas stations** (Carretera Central; ◷ 24hr) near Av de la Libertad. Driving in Camagüey's narrow one-way streets is a sport akin to base-jumping. Experts only!

HORSE CARTS

Horse carts shuttle along a fixed route (CUC$1) between the regional bus station and the train station. You may have to change carts at Casino Campestre, near the river.

Florida

POP 56,000

A million metaphoric miles from Miami, the hard-working sugar-mill town of Florida, 46km northwest of Camagüey on the Ciego de Ávila road, is a viable overnighter if you're driving around central Cuba and are too tired to negotiate the labyrinthine streets of Camagüey after dark (a bad idea, whatever your physical or mental state). There's a working rodeo and an Etecsa telephone office.

Two-story **Hotel Florida** (☑ 51-30-11; Carretera Central, Km 534; s/d CUC$18/28; P ❄ ☀) is located 2km west of the town center and has 74 adequate rooms. Next door is Cafetería Caney, a thatched restaurant that's better value than the flyblown hotel restaurant.

Passenger trucks run from Florida to Camagüey, where you can connect with Víazul long-distance buses. If you're driving, there's a Servi-Cupet gas station in the center of town on Carretera Central.

Sierra del Chorrillo

This protected area 36km southeast of Camagüey contains three low hill ranges: the Sierra del Chorrillo, the Sierra del Najasa and the Guaicanámar (highest point: 324m).

Nestled in their grassy uplands is **La Hacienda la Belén** (admission CUC$4), a handsome country ranch run as a nature reserve: contact the Camagüey branch of travel agency Ecotur (p327). As well as boasting many nonindigenous animals, such as zebras, antelopes, cattle and horses (it breeds among Cuba's best), the park functions as a **bird** reserve. It's one of the best places in Cuba to view rare species, such as the Cuban parakeet, the giant kingbird and the Antillean palm swift. Another curiosity is a three-million-year-old **petrified forest** of fossilized tree stumps spread over a hectare. To find the stumps, drive a few clicks past the hacienda entrance to the road junction and bear right to reach a dead end at a factory. There's also a far-larger fossilized tree nearby. Treks can be arranged around the reserve by 4WD or on horseback and there are two guided walks. Most popular is Sendero de las Aves (CUC$7, 1.8km), which reveals a cornucopia of birdlife; there's also Sendero Santa Gertrudis (4.5km), covering flora, fauna and a cave.

Simple and countrified in that spartan, semi-abandoned Cuban way, **Motel la Belén** (☑52-19-57-44; s/d CUC$28/40, full board CUC$42/66; ❄️🏊) reclines within the hacienda grounds and is equipped with a swimming pool, restaurant, TV room and 10 clean, air-conditioned rooms that can accommodate up to 16 people. Glorious landscapes are within stone-chucking distance.

You'll need your own wheels to get to Sierra del Chorrillo. Drive 24km east of Camagüey on Carretera Central, then 30km southeast following signs to Najasa. If approaching from Las Tunas, another potholed road to Najasa branches south off the Carretera Central in Sibanicú. The hacienda is 8km beyond Najasa along a rutted road. Alternatively, negotiate a rate with a taxi in Camagüey.

Guáimaro

POP 29,800

Guáimaro would be just another nameless Cuban town if it wasn't for the famous Guáimaro Assembly of April 1869, which approved the first Cuban constitution and called for the emancipation of slaves. The assembly elected Carlos Manuel de Céspedes as president.

Sights

Parque Constitución   PARK
The events of 1869 are commemorated by a large **monument** erected in 1940 in this central park. Around the base of the monument are bronze plaques with likenesses of José Martí, Máximo Gómez, Carlos Manuel de Céspedes, Ignacio Agramonte, Calixto García and Antonio Maceo, the stars of Cuban independence.

The park also contains the mausoleum of Cuba's first – and possibly greatest – hero-

ine, Ana Betancourt (1832–1901) from Camagüey, who fought for women's emancipation alongside the abolition of slavery during the First War of Independence.

Museo Histórico   MUSEUM
(Constitución No 85, btwn Libertad & Máximo Gómez; admission CUC$1; ⊘9am-5pm Mon-Fri) If you're making a pit stop, this small museum has a couple of rooms given over to art and history.

🛏️ Sleeping & Eating

There is a Servi-Cupet gas station on your entry into town from Camagüey with an El Rápido snack bar attached.

Casa de Magalis   CASA PARTICULAR $
(☑81-28-91; Olimpo No 5, btwn Benito Morell & Carretera Central; r CUC$20-25; 🅿️❄️) Here's a surprise: it's almost worth the stopover in Guáimaro just to stay at this salmon pink colonial villa just off the Carretera Central. There are two rooms, one of which has surely Cuba's largest private-rental bathroom, and a terrace to drink in the bucolic views.

ℹ️ Getting There & Away

Guáimaro is on the Carretera Central between Camagüey and Las Tunas. A number of Víazul buses pass through daily. Speak to the driver if you want to get off.

Nuevitas

POP 46,200

Nuevitas, 87km northeast of Camagüey, is a 27km jaunt north off the Camagüey–Playa Santa Lucía road. It's a small, amiable industrial town and sugar-exporting port with easy shore access, but not worth a major detour. In 1978 Cuban movie director Manual Octavio Gómez filmed his revolutionary classic *Una mujer, un hombre, una ciudad* (Woman, Man, City) here, giving the city its first, and to date only, brush with fame. It's also the terminus of Cuba's second-oldest railway.

Sights

Museo Histórico Municipal   MUSEUM
(Máximo Gómez No 66; admission CUC$1; ⊘9am-4pm Tue-Sun) The only specific sight in Nuevitas, near Parque del Cañón, is this museum. It has the standard, semi-interesting mix of stuffed animals and sepia-toned photographs; you could also hike up the steps in the town center for sweeping views of the bay and industry in ironic juxtaposition.

King Ranch

RANCH

(Carretera de Santa Lucía Km 35; ☺10am-10pm) Texans will be flummoxed by such a familiar-sounding name in the wilds of northern Camagüey, but this Wild West apparition is no phony. King Ranch, en route to Playa Santa Lucía, was once an off-shoot of its legendary Texan namesake (the largest ranch in the US). There's a restaurant, rodeo show and horses for rent.

The ranch was expropriated after the Revolution, kept much the same function and mostly caters for tour groups from Playa Santa Lucía, but you can turn up unannounced. It's 4km beyond the crossroads where you join the main highway from Camagüey.

Beaches

Below Hotel Caonaba there's a shaggy **amusement park**, and a bit further along the coast, a local beach, usually called **Playa Colonia**, from where you can see two of the three small islands, Los Tres Ballenatos, in Bahía de Nuevitas. Another 2km down the coast, you'll reach **Playa Santa Rita** at the end of the road – with a pier jutting into the bay.

🛏 Sleeping & Eating

Hotel Caonaba

HOTEL $

(☑24-48-03; cnr Martí & Albisa; s/d CUC$21/26; 🅿❄) A bog-standard Cuban one-star hotel on a rise overlooking the sea at the entrance to town. Rooms have fridges and the ones at the front have bay views but don't expect the Ritz. The terrace bar is good for a beer.

Casa Osvaldo

CASA PARTICULAR $

(☑41-20-78; Calle Martí 162; r CUC$25; ❄) These two tiled rooms in a private house on Nuevitas' main drag are, frankly, a lot better than the dusty digs in the town hotel.

Restaurante Toscana

CUBAN $

(☑41-55-66; Calle Enrique Vázquez 3; mains CUC$2-4; ☺Tue-Sun 6-11pm) The town's best private restaurant is aimed mainly at Cubans (prices in *moneda nacional*), but will happily welcome non-Cubans. It's not well-signposted, but is only a block or so from the hotel. Seafood dominates.

ℹ Getting There & Away

Your own wheels are best. A **Servi-Cupet gas station** is at the entrance to town. There's a **Cubacar** office on the main drag Calle Martí.

Nuevitas was once a pioneering railway town and is still the terminus of railway lines from Camagüey via Minas and Santa Clara via Chambas

and Morón. The station is near the waterfront on the northern side of town. There *should* be daily trains to Camagüey, and an alternate-day service to Santa Clara, but, when asked for a timetable, the locals just roll their eyes. Trucks, more reliable than buses, leave for Camagüey early in the morning.

Brasil & Around

A once active, now soporific, former sugar town situated halfway between Morón and Nuevitas, Brasil is the gateway to the still-virgin **Cayo Romano**, the archipelago's third-largest island. The area has recently been rediscovered by in-the-know fishers who ply the waters out as far as **Cayo Cruz**. The flats, lagoons and estuaries off Camagüey's north coast are fly-fishing heaven (bonefish, permit and tarpon concentrated in a designated fishing area of just under 350 sq km that's invariably deserted). The fishing season runs from November to August and no commercial fishing is allowed. **Ecotur** (☑Camaguey 24-36-93, Havana 27-49-95) runs trips.

For something completely different, you can stay at **Hotel Casona de Romano** (Calle 6, btwn Calles B & C; r from CUC$50; ❄), a beautiful, quasi-stately home with eight rooms, an on-site restaurant and bar. The place caters mainly for fishers in organized groups. Contact Ecotur for more details.

Cayo Sabinal

Cayo Sabinal, 22km to the north of Nuevitas, is virgin territory, a 30km-long coral key with marshes favored by flamingos and iguanas. The land cover is mainly flat and characterized by marshland and lagoons. The fauna consists of tree rats, wild boar and a large variety of butterflies. It's astoundingly beautiful.

◉ Sights & Activities

Fuerte San Hilario

FORT

Cayo Sabinal has quite some history for a wilderness area. Following repeated pirate attacks in the 17th and 18th centuries, the Spanish built a fort here (1831) to keep marauding corsairs at bay. The fort later became a prison and, in 1875, witnessed the only Carlist uprising (a counterrevolutionary movement in Spain that opposed the reigning monarchy) in Cuba – ever.

RESERVA ECOLÓGICA LIMONES TUABAQUEY

One of Cuba's newest protected reserves, Reserva Ecológica Limones Tuabaquey is best known for its pre-Columbian cave paintings, etched on the walls of the **Cueva Pichardo** and the **Cueva María Teresa** – considered to be the most important indigenous art in Cuba. The other great attraction is the unique **Hoyo de Bonet**, a 300m-wide, 90m-deep natural karstic depression covered in vegetation that retains its own cool, humid microclimate and is replete with trippy giant ferns. The reserve also hosts rich birdlife; indeed the abundance of toccoros and *cartacubas* is known to produce what local experts call a 'symphony of birdsong.' Paths fan out to caves, craters and a narrow natural gorge called the **Paso de los Paredones**, with sheer 40m-high walls. Historical infamy is recalled nearby: a post marks the spot where, in February 1869, a group of *mambises* (19th-century Cuban independence fighters) successfully saw off a Spanish attack.

Guided tours of the reserve can be arranged at Ecotur (p327) in Camagüey or you can turn up in person. Entrance is CUC$6. There is a visitor center on-site and accommodation in cabins is in the offing. Walking on the trails is permitted with a guide only.

The reserve lies approximately 35km north of the city of Camagüey on the main (bumpy) road between Morón and Nuevitas. The turnoff is near the village of Cubitas.

Faro Colón
LIGHTHOUSE

(Punta Maternillo) Erected in 1848, Faro Colón is one of the oldest lighthouses still operating on the Cuban archipelago. As a result of various naval battles fought in the area during the colonial era, a couple of Spanish shipwrecks – *Nuestra Señora de Alta Gracia* and the *Pizarro* – rest in shallow waters nearby, providing great fodder for divers.

Playas Bonita & Los Pinos
BEACH

Of Cayo Sabinal's 30km of beaches, these two compete for top billing. The former has been commandeered for use by daily boat excursions from Playa Santa Lucía and has a rustic *ranchón* serving food. Activities on the latter, since its five rustic cabins blew away in a hurricane, are more of the do-it-yourself variety (hiking, swimming, philosophizing etc).

❶ Getting There & Away

Choose from private car, taxi or boat. The dirt road to Cayo Sabinal begins 6km south of Nuevitas, off the Camagüey road. It's best to check ahead (in Nuevitas) if you are planning on using it as it's prone to impromtu closures – and bring your passport to show at the security checkpoint. The 2km causeway linking the key to the mainland was the first of its kind constructed in Cuba and the most environmentally destructive.

The vast majority of people access Cayo Sabinal on boat trips from Playa Santa Lucía. Trips run most days and cost from around CUC$69 including transfers and lunch. You'll be dropped off and picked up on Playa Bonita. Book through the Playa Santa Lucía hotels.

Playa Santa Lucía

Playa Santa Lucía is an isolated resort strip that's seen better days, situated 112km northeast of Camagüey on an unbroken 20km-long stretch of pale-yellow beach that competes with Varadero as Cuba's longest. Travelers generally come here to scuba dive on the north coast's best and most accessible coral reef, lying just a few kilometers offshore. Another highlight is the beach itself – a tropical idyll, most of it still deserted. The area around Playa Santa Lucía is flat and featureless, the preserve of flamingos, scrubby bushes and the odd grazing cow. Aside from the microvillage of Santa Lucía that serves as lodging for itinerant hotel workers, and the ramshackle hamlet of La Boca near the area's best beach (Playa los Cocos), there are no Cuban settlements of note. The swimming, snorkeling and diving are exceptional, however, and the four all-inclusive resorts lay on activities aplenty for those with time and inclination to explore. Packages to Playa Santa Lucía are usually cheaper than other resort areas, although the resorts themselves are less luxuriant and have a cheaper holiday-camp feel. In fact, the whole strip, which predates Cayo Coco and Cayo Santa María, is overdue for an extensive refurb. In peak season the clientele is primarily Canadian.

CAMAGÜEY PROVINCE PLAYA SANTA LUCÍA

Playa Santa Lucía

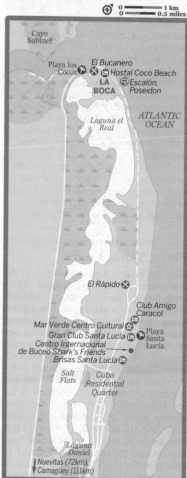

0 ___ 1 km
0 ___ 0.5 miles

Cayo Sabinel

El Bucanero
Playa los Cocos
Hostal Coco Beach
LA BOCA
Escalón, Poseidon

Laguna el Real

ATLANTIC OCEAN

El Rápido

Club Amigo Caracol
Mar Verde Centro Cultural
Gran Club Santa Lucía
Playa Santa Lucía
Centro Internacional de Buceo Shark's Friends
Brisas Santa Lucía

Salt Flats
Cuba Residential Quarter

Laguna Daniel

Nuevitas (72km);
Camagüey (111km)

◉ Sights

Playa los Cocos BEACH

This comma of beach at the end of 20km-long Playa Santa Lucía, 7km from the hotels at the mouth of the Bahía de Nuevitas, is a stunner, with yellow-white sand and iridescent jade water. Sometimes flocks of pink flamingos are visible in Laguna el Real, behind this beach. The great El Bucanero restaurant is located here.

A horse and carriage from the Santa Lucía hotels to Playa los Cocos is CUC$20 return plus the wait, or you can walk it, jog it, bike

it (free gearless-but-adequate bikes are available at all the resorts) or jump in a taxi. This is a fine swimming spot, with views of the Faro Colón (lighthouse) on Cayo Sabinal, but beware of tidal currents further out.

The small Cuban settlement here is known as **La Boca**. There's a good restaurant (in the pink, smart-looking house) where the fisher's just-landed catch is cooked up. Sometimes the locals roast a pig on a spit and will invite you across.

🏃 Activities

Playa Santa Lucía is a diving destination extraordinaire that sits alongside what is, purportedly, the world's second-longest coral reef (after Australia's Great Barrier Reef). The 35 scuba sites take in six Poseidon ridges, the Cueva Honda dive site, shipwrecks, and the abundant marine life, including several types of rays at the entrance to the Bahía de Nuevitas. A much-promoted highlight is the hand-feeding of 3m-long bull sharks (June to January). The hotels can organize other water activities, including a full-day catamaran cruise along the shoreline (CUC$57 with lunch and snorkeling), a flamingo tour (CUC$59) and deep-sea fishing (CUC$200 for the boat for 3½ hours).

Centro Internacional de
Buceo Shark's Friends DIVING

(www.nauticamarlin.com; Av Tararaco; shark feeds CUC$69) On the beach between Brisas Santa Lucía and Gran Club Santa Lucía, the center offers dives (from CUC$30) and the famous shark feeds (CUC$69), where cool-as-a-cucumber dive guides chuck food into the mouths of 3m-long bull sharks. November through January is the best time for the shark-feeding, or dive boats go out every two hours between 9am and 3pm daily (though the last dive is contingent on demand). The open-water course costs CUC$315; a resort course is CUC$74. It also has snorkeling excursions for CUC$25.

🛏 Sleeping

The small hotel strip begins 6km northwest of the roundabout at the entrance to Santa Lucía. The four big ones are Cubanacán resorts, the star ratings and quality of which decrease as you head northwest.

Hostal Coco Beach CASA PARTICULAR $

(☏ 52-48-83-59; La Boca; r CUC$20-25; ❄) For a bit of seclusion away from the all-inclusive strip, try this homestay right on the beach in the village of La Boca with its two well-equipped rooms and wraparound porch.

Club Amigo Mayanabo
RESORT $$

(☑ 36-51-68; s/d/tr all-incl CUC$35/58/79; P ✳ @ ✸ 🔥) Doing a good impersonation of a tacky postwar British holiday camp, the Mayanabo has seen better days – a long time ago. But if budget's your prime consideration, it's cheap and right on the beach.

Club Amigo Caracol
RESORT $$

(☑ 36-51-58; s/d all-incl CUC$47/72; P ✳ @ ✸ 🔥) With a large kids program this is usually promoted as the beach's family favorite.

Gran Club Santa Lucía
RESORT $$

(☑ 33-61-09; s/d all-incl CUC$75/100; P ✳ @ ✸ 🔥) Gran Club comes out top on the strip for its 249 colorfully painted rooms (in well-maintained two-story blocks), prettily landscaped grounds and poolside action.

Brisas Santa Lucía
RESORT $$

(☑ 33-63-17; s/d all-incl CUC$80/120; P ✳ @ ✸ 🔥) This resort has 412 rooms in several three-story buildings. Covering a monstrous 11 hectares, it has the strip's top rating – a hugely flattering four stars, though with its over-jaunty holiday-camp atmosphere, it rarely justifies the billing.

🍴 Eating

Aside from the hotel buffets, your choices are limited. There's an El Rápido on the roundabout at the western end of the hotel strip that serves cheap (for a reason) fast food.

★ El Bucanero
SEAFOOD $$

(Playa los Cocos; meals around CUC$12; ⊘ 10am-10pm) This place is in a different class, serving seafood – lobster and prawns (CUC$12) is the house special – which is enhanced immeasurably by the setting.

Restaurante Luna Mar
SEAFOOD $$

(Playa Santa Lucía; fish dishes CUC$7-20; ⊘ noon-9pm) This place, flush up against the beach and wedged between Gran Club Santa Lucía and Club Amigo Caracol, offers a seafood menu in an easy-to-reach setting.

☆ Entertainment

Outside of the resort entertainment, nothing much happens on the hotel strip although the Mar Verde Centro Cultural (admission CUC$1; ⊘ 10pm-3am) has a pleasant patio bar and a cabaret with live music nightly.

OFF THE BEATEN TRACK

REFUGIO DE FAUNA SILVESTRE RÍO MÁXIMO

Few know about it, and still fewer come here. The wetlands between the Ríos Máximo and Cagüey on the northern coast of Camagüey province are the largest flamingo nesting ground in the world. Add in migratory water fowl, American crocodiles and a healthy population of West Indian manatees and you're talking special, very special. Protected since 1998 as a Refugio de Fauna Silvestre (Wild Fauna Refuge) and, more recently, as a Ramsar Convention Site, the Río Máximo delta faces a precarious future due to human and agricultural contamination coupled with occasional droughts. The area is roadless and hard to reach, but trips in can sometimes be organized courtesy of Ecotur (p330).

ℹ Information

There's a Cadeca (⊘ 9am-4pm) in the Mar Verde shopping center where you can change money. In the Cuban residential quarter east of the hotels is the Clínica Internacional de Santa Lucía (☑ 33-62-03; Ignacio Residencial 14), a well-equipped Cubanacán clinic for emergencies and medical issues. The best pharmacy is in Brisas Santa Lucía. Etecsa, 1.5km further east along near the entrance to the hotel zone, has internet access for CUC$4.50 per hour and international phone capabilities. For tour agencies, Cubanacán, which owns four of the five hotels here, is well represented with a desk in each hotel. There's a good Cubatur office just outside Gran Club Santa Lucía.

ℹ Getting There & Around

The only regular bus heads out from Camagüey every Friday at noon, arriving at Playa Santa Lucía at 1:30pm (it's for workers but they'll normally let you on). A return bus leaves the resorts at 2pm on Sunday and arrives in Camagüey at 3:30pm. Check in advance at Cubatur (Av Agramonte No 421, btwn República & Independencia). Another option for independent travelers is to jump on one of the charter bus links with spare seats. Ask at your hotel desk. You shouldn't have to pay more than CUC$20 to Camagüey Airport. A taxi from Camagüey to Playa Santa Lucía will cost you CUC$70 one way. The extremely patient can get a train to Nuevitas from Morón or Camagüey and taxi it from there.

You can rent cars or mopeds (CUC$25 per day, including a tank of gas). Cubacar has desks in all the hotels.

Las Tunas Province

Includes ➡

Las Tunas.......... 335
Monte Cabaniguan...341
Puerto Padre........341
Punta Covarrubias...342
Playas La Herradura,
La Llanita &
Las Bocas 343

Best Bucolic Escapes

➡ Monte Cabaniguan (p341)

➡ El Cornito (p337)

➡ Playa La Herradura (p343)

Best Places to Stay

➡ Hotel Cadillac (p337)

➡ Mayra Busto Méndez (p337)

➡ Roberto Lío Montes de Oca (p342)

➡ Brisas Covarrubias (p343)

Why Go?

Most travelers say hello and goodbye to Las Tunas province in the time that it takes to drive across it on the Carretera Central (one hour on a good day). But, hang on a sec! This so-laid-back-it's-nearly-falling-over collection of leather-skinned cowboys and poetry-spouting country singers is known for its daredevil rodeos and Saturday night street parties where barnstorming entertainment is served up at the drop of a sombrero.

Although historically associated with the Oriente, Las Tunas province shares many attributes with Camagüey in the west. The flat grassy fields of the interior are punctuated with sugar mills and cattle ranches, while the eco beaches on the north coast remain wild and lightly touristed, at least by Varadero standards.

In this low-key land of the understated and underrated, accidental visitors can enjoy the small-town charms of the provincial capital, or head north to the old mill town Puerto Padre where serenity rules.

When to Go

➡ The wettest months are June and October, with over 160mm of average precipitation. July and August are the hottest months.

➡ Las Tunas has many festivals for a small city; the best is the Jornada Cucalambeana in June.

➡ Festival Internacional de Magia (Magic Festival), held in the provincial capital in November, is another highlight.

➡ The National Sculpture Exhibition, an event befitting the so-called 'City of Sculptures,' happens in February.

Las Tunas Province Highlights

① Hunt for the imaginative sculptures embellishing the sleepy cityscape of **Las Tunas** (below).

② Check out the dudes with lassos in **Parque 26 de Julio** (p340), Las Tunas' celebrated twice-annual rodeo.

③ Enjoy the unkempt beaches of **Playa la Herradura** (343), before resort developers shatter the tranquility.

④ Linger awhile in friendly, out-on-a-limb seaside town **Puerto Padre** (p341).

⑤ Roll into El Cornito in June to experience some country crooning at the **Jornada Cucalambeana** (p337) music festival.

⑥ Enjoy some slick private enterprise in **Las Tunas'** new Italian restaurants (p337).

⑦ Go diving in the largely undiscovered reefs off **Punta Covarrubias** (p342).

History

The settlement of Las Tunas was founded in 1759 but wasn't given the title of 'city' until 1853. In 1876 Cuban General Vicente García briefly captured the city during the War of Independence, but repeated Spanish successes in the area soon led the colonizers to rename it La Victória de Las Tunas. During the Spanish-Cuban-American War the Spanish burned Las Tunas to the ground, but the Mambís fought back, and in 1897 General Calixto García forced the local Spanish garrison to surrender in a pivotal Cuban victory.

Las Tunas became a provincial capital in 1976 during Cuba's post-revolutionary geographic reorganization.

Las Tunas

POP 154,000

If it was down to sights and historical attractions alone, it's doubtful many people would bother with La Victória de Las Tunas (as it's officially known), a sleepy agricultural town that seems like it hasn't woken up to the fact it's been a provincial capital almost 40 years. Its sleazy reputation for being the Oriente's capital of sex tourism hardly helps. But, thanks to a handy location on Cuba's arterial Carretera Central, handfuls of road-weary travelers drop by.

Referred to as the 'city of sculptures,' Las Tunas is certainly no Florence. But what it lacks in grandiosity it makes up for in small-town quirks. You can see a thigh-slapping rodeo here, admire a statue of a two-headed Taíno chief, go wild at one of the city's riotous Saturday-night street parties or wax lyrical at the weird and witty Jornada Cucalambeana, Cuba's leading country-music festival. Go on, give it a whirl!

⊙ Sights

Memorial a los Mártires de Barbados   MUSEUM

(Lucas Ortíz No 344; ⊙10am-6pm Mon-Sat) FREE
Las Tunas' most evocative sight is in the former home of Carlos Leyva González, an Olympic fencer killed in the nation's worst terrorist atrocity: the bombing of a Cubana airliner in 1976. Individual photos of victims of the attack line the museum walls, providing poignant reminders of the fated airplane.

On October 6, 1976, Cubana de Aviación Flight 455, on its way back to Havana from Guyana, took off after a stopover in Barbados' Seawell airport. Nine minutes after clearing the runway, two bombs went off in the cabin's rear toilet causing the plane to crash into the Atlantic Ocean. All 73 people on board – 57 of whom were Cuban – were killed. The toll included the entire Cuban fencing team fresh from a clean sweep of gold medals at the Central American Championships. At the time, the tragedy of Flight 455 was the worst-ever terrorist attack in the Western hemisphere.

Museo Provincial General Vicente García   MUSEUM

(cnr Francisco Varona & Ángel de la Guardia; admission CUC$1; ⊙9am-5pm Tue-Sat) Housed in the royal-blue town hall with a clock mounted on the front facade, the provincial museum documents local *tunero* history. A member of staff will happily lead you through the exhibits.

Memorial Vicente García   MUSEUM

(Vicente García No 7; admission CUC$1; ⊙3-7pm Mon, 11am-7pm Tue-Sat) A colonial-era structure near the eponymous park that commemorates Las Tunas' great War of Independence hero who captured the town from the Spanish in 1876, and torched it 21 years later when the colonizers sought to reclaim it. The building was once García's house, but only a small exposed section of floor tiles remains from the original structure. The museum's four rooms are best navigated with a guide who'll fill in the many historical gaps.

Plaza de la Revolución   SQUARE

Las Tunas' Revolution Square is huge and bombastic, particularly for such a small city. Photo opps abound. Check out the huge

---

SCULPTURE IN LAS TUNAS

It might not be Florence, but Las Tunas has an eclectic, sometimes eccentric collection of urban sculptures, over 150 of them in fact, dating back to a pioneering sculpture expo that was held in the city in 1974. For a small but precocious précis of the town's new young talent, check out the Galería Taller Escultura Rita Longa (p341), while true sculpture vultures should aim to visit in February (even-numbered years) for the Bienal de Escultura Rita Longa (p337) – a celebration of all things sculpted.

Las Tunas' most important and emblematic statue is Rita Longa's **La Fuente de Las Antilles**. First unveiled in 1977, it was elemental in reviving Cuba's sculpturing traditions and making Las Tunas its HQ. The sculpture comprises a huge fountain filled with elaborate interwoven figures symbolizing the emergence of the Greater Antilles' indigenous peoples from the Caribbean Sea. Cuba is represented by an *India dormida* (sleeping Taíno woman). The work reawakened interest in indigenous-themed art in Cuba and has spawned other complex sculptures, such as **Mestizaje**, a multifaced representation of Cuba's mixed races in the Parque de la India near the bus station.

In the central hub of Plaza Martí is another Longa work, an inventive **bronze statue** of the 'apostle of Cuban independence', José Martí, which doubles as a solar clock. It was opened in 1995 to commemorate the 100th anniversary of Martí's death.

Elsewhere in town you'll find sculptures with revolutionary themes. The 8m-high abstract **Monumento al Trabajo** (cnr Carretera Central & Martí), by José Peláez, pays cubist homage to Cuban workers, while the pencil-like **Monumento a Alfabetización** (Lucas Ortíz) marks the 1961 act passed in Las Tunas to stamp out illiteracy.

Further afield, the Janus-inspired **Cacique Maniabo y Jibacoa** is a two-headed Taíno chief looking in opposite directions, which dominates the surroundings at the rustic Motel Cornito 6km west of town. Also at Cornito is the **Columna Taina**, a kind of native totem pole, along with Las Tunas' newest sculpture, the **Cornito al Toro** (2013), a legendary bull made out of metal and cement that guards the approach road to the complex looking down from a giant pedestal.

Lenin-esque sculpture of Vicente García, sword raised, and the giant Che Guevara billboard.

El Cornito
OUTDOORS

(Carretera Central Km 8; ⊙9am-5pm) The grounds around Motel El Cornito (about 6km outside town) are bamboo woods which offer a welcome, shady diversion from the scorching city bustle. You'll find *ranchón*-style restaurants (favoring the usual booming reggaetón music), the site of the old farmhouse of great Las Tunas poet Juan Cristóbal Nápoles Fajardo (aka El Cucalambé) and a reservoir where you can swim.

Back toward the main road, there's a zoo, a fun park and a motocross circuit. A taxi here costs CUC$5 to CUC$7 return.

🎭 Festivals & Events

Bienal de Escultura Rita Longa SCULPTURE
(⊙Feb) Held in February in even-numbered years in this so-called 'City of Sculptures.'

Jornada Cucalambeana MUSIC
(⊙Jun) Jornada Cucalambeana is Cuba's biggest celebration of country music, where local lyricists impress each other with their 10-line *décima* verses. It happens in June, just outside Las Tunas, by Motel El Cornito.

Festival Internacional de Magia MAGIC
(⊙Nov) Magic festival held in the provincial capital each November.

🛏 Sleeping

After years in the doldrums, Las Tunas has at least one decent hotel (the Cadillac). Several private houses rent clean, affordable rooms along Calle Martí and Calle Frank País near the center.

★Mayra Busto Méndez CASA PARTICULAR $
(☎31-34-42-05; Hirán Durañona No 16, btwn Frank País & Lucas Ortíz; r CUC$25; P❖) Blink. The sheen coming off the furnishings in this immaculate bungalow might otherwise dazzle you. It's Tardis-like inside, too. The size of the room on the left could encompass a couple of most all-inclusive hotel rooms.

Caballo Blanco – Pepe CASA PARTICULAR $
(☎31-37-36-58; Frank País No 85 Altos; r CUC$20-25; ❖) Dazzling tiled floors, hotel-standard bathrooms, wall-mounted TVs and operating-room-level cleanliness (no surprise that Pepe is a doctor). There's a new privately run restaurant out back.

Hotel Las Tunas HOTEL $
(☎31-34-50-14; Av 2 de Diciembre; s/d CUC$27/43; P❖🛜❄) A last-gasp option: out-of-the-way location, austere rooms, dodgy restaurant and a wake-you-up-at-2am disco. Room TVs pick up HBO and there's wi-fi – small consolations.

★Hotel Cadillac HOTEL $$
(☎31-37-27-91; cnr Ángel de la Guardia & Francisco Vega; s/d CUC$45/70; ❖) A Las Tunas hotel that doesn't give you flashbacks to the Khrushchev and Brezhnev years. Opened in 2009, this rehabilitated, centrally located 1940s beauty is verging on boutique standard with just eight rooms including a lovely corner suite. There are flat-screen TVs, up-to-the-minute bathrooms and a dash of old-fashioned prerevolutionary class. Out front is the lively Cadillac Snack Bar.

🍴 Eating

Las Tunas has an abundance of Italian restaurants for a city of its size. The local culinary claim to fame around these parts is *caldosa kike y mariana,* a stew of meat and root vegetables with banana: it's even been sung about. Ask around.

Caché INTERNATIONAL $
(☎31-99-55-57; Francisco Varona, btwn Nicolás Heredia & Joaquin Agüera; sandwiches & burgers CUC$2-5; ⊙noon-2am) Proof that things could really be changing in Cuba is the presence of this new swanky cocktail bar/cafe/restaurant that attempts to bring the taste of

Las Tunas

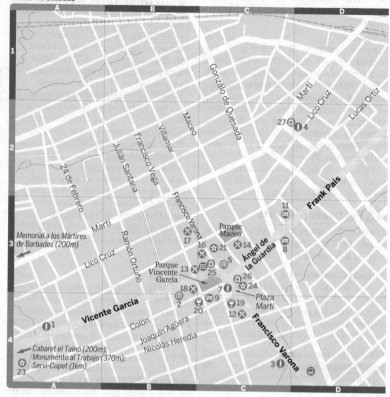

Miami to Las Tunas of all places. The dimly lit, air-conditioned interior is dressed to impress with leather seats, dexterous cocktail waiters and a menu heavy with deluxe burgers and club sandwiches.

La Patrona
CUBAN $

(☑31-34-05-11; Custodio Orive No 94; meals CUC$3-4; ☺11am-11pm) A new, largely local place with highly reasonable prices and equally reasonable food. The mains are primarily *comida criollla*, but they also do eggs and pasta for as little as CUC$0.75.

Cremería las Copas
ICE CREAM $

(cnr Francisco Vega & Vicente García; ice creams CUC$0.50-1; ☺9am-3:30pm & 4:45-11pm) Las Tunas' substitute Coppelia; queue up with your pesos for sundaes or *tres gracias* (three scoops) in flavors such as coconut, and *café con leche* (espresso with milk). Not surprisingly, it's insanely popular. If only they didn't

rush you, it would be one hugely enjoyable experience.

Restaurante la Bodeguita
CARIBBEAN $

(Francisco Varona No 293; meals CUC$5; ☺11am-11pm) A Palmares state-run joint, meaning that it's a better bet than the usual peso parlors. You'll get checkered tablecloths, a limited wine list and what the Cuban government calls 'international cuisine' – read spaghetti and pizza. Try the chicken breast with mushroom sauce.

★Ristorante La Romana
ITALIAN $$

(☑31-34-77-55; Francisco Varona No 331; meals CUC$6-8; ☺12:30-11pm) Spotted any Italians yet? No? Then drop by this new Roman abode on the main boulevard where the olive oil's extra virgin, the pasta's homemade and the coffee's Lavazza. The food – including the starter bruschettas – is *molta ottima*, according to Las Tunas' bevy of Italian visitors.

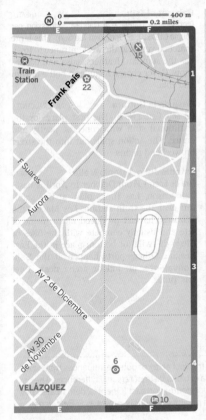

Las Tunas

◎ Sights
1	La Fuente de Las Antilles	A4
2	Memorial Vicente García	B4
3	Mestizaje	C4
4	Monumento a Alfabetización	D2
5	Museo Provincial General Vicente García	C3
6	Plaza de la Revolución	F4
7	Statue of José Martí	C3

◎ Sleeping
8	Caballo Blanco – Pepe	C3
9	Hotel Cadillac	C4
10	Hotel Las Tunas	F4
11	Mayra Busto Méndez	C3

◎ Eating
12	Caché	C4
13	Cremería las Copas	B3
14	La Patrona	C3
15	Mercado Agropecuario	F1
16	Restaurante la Bodeguita	C3
17	Ristorante La Romana	B3
18	Supermercado Casa Azul	B3

◎ Drinking & Nightlife
	Cadillac Snack Bar	(see 9)
19	Casa del Vino Don Juan	C4
20	Piano Bar	C4

◎ Entertainment
21	Cabildo San Pedro Lucumí	C3
	Casa de la Cultura	(see 25)
22	Estadio Julio Antonio Mella	E1
23	Parque 26 de Julio	A4
24	Teatro Tunas	C3

◎ Shopping
25	Biblioteca Provincial José Martí	C3
26	Fondo Cubano de Bienes Culturales	C3
27	Galería Taller Escultura Rita Longa	C2

Self-Catering

To stock up on groceries (or to break bigger bills), try **Supermercado Casa Azul** (cnr Vicente García & Francisco Vega; ◎9am-6pm Mon-Sat, to noon Sun). **Mercado Agropecuario** (Av Camilo Cienfuegos) is a small market not far from the train station.

Drinking & Nightlife

Casa del Vino Don Juan BAR
(cnr Francisco Varona & Joaquín Agüera; ◎9am-midnight) Wine-tasting in Las Tunas probably sounds about as credible as food rationing in Beverly Hills, yet here it is; only 7 pesos for a shot of the local poison, a sickly sweet red called Puerto Príncipe. Go just to say you've been there.

Cadillac Snack Bar CAFE
(cnr Ángel de la Guardia & Francisco Vega; ◎9am-11pm) This offshoot of the Hotel Cadillac has tables on a terrace overlooking the Plaza Martí action and serves decent cappuccinos thanks to its high quota of mature Italian guests who come here with their much (much!) younger Cuban escorts.

Piano Bar BAR
(cnr Colón & Francisco Vega; ◎9pm-2am) A little more suave than the blazing hotel discos, this place is where you go to hear local Oscar Petersons tinkle on the ivories while you knock back CUC$1 mojitos.

☆ Entertainment

Las Tunas comes alive on Saturday night when packed streets and fun-seeking locals defy the city's 'boring' image. The main hubs are: Parque Vicente García, where alfresco *son* music competes with modern reggaetón; and Parque 26 de Julio.

★ **Parque 26 de Julio** FAIRGROUND
(Av Vicente García; ⊙ 9am-6pm Sat & Sun) FREE Located in Parque Julio 26 where Vicente García bends into Av 1 de Mayo, it kicks off every weekend with a market, music, food stalls and kids' activities.

Cabildo San Pedro Lucumí CULTURAL CENTER
(Francisco Varona, btwn Vicente García & Lucas Ortíz; ⊙ from 9pm Sun) FREE Cultural activities happen at this friendly Afro-Caribbean association, HQ of the Compañía Folklórica Onilé. Drop in on Sunday for some dancing and drumming.

Teatro Tunas THEATER
(cnr Francisco Varona & Joaquín Agüera) This is a recently revitalized theater that shows quality movies and some of Cuba's best touring entertainment including flamenco, ballet and plays.

Cabaret el Taíno THEATER
(cnr Vicente García & A Cabrera; admission per couple CUC$10; ⊙ 9pm-2am Tue-Sun) This large thatched venue at the west entrance to town has the standard feathers, salsa and pasties show. Cover charge includes a bottle of rum and cola.

Casa de la Cultura CULTURAL CENTER
(Vicente García No 8) The best place for the traditional stuff with concerts, poetry and dance. The action spills out into the street on weekend nights.

Estadio Julio Antonio Mella SPORTS
(1ra de Enero) From October to April is baseball season. Las Tunas plays at this stadium near the train station. Los Magos (the Wizards) haven't produced much magic of late and usually compete with the likes of Ciego de Ávila for bottom place in the East League. Other sports happen at the **Sala Polivalente**, an indoor arena near Hotel Las Tunas.

THE BALCONY OF THE ORIENTE

Thanks to the nature of its colonization and the vast array of outside influences that have washed up intermittently on its shores, Cuba exhibits distinct regional differences. The most marked are those between the west (Occidente) and east (Oriente), demarcated by a line that runs roughly through Las Tunas, a province popularly known as *El Balcón del Oriente* (The Balcony of the Oriente).

Prior to 1976, Las Tunas and the four provinces to the east (Guantánamo, Santiago de Cuba, Granma and Holguín) were encased in a single culturally distinct province known simply as 'Oriente.' Although the political barriers were removed in the 1976 provincial shake-up, regional identity remains strong, especially among the traditional 'underdogs' from the east.

Geographically closer to Haiti than Havana, Cuba's Oriente has often looked east rather than west in its bid to cement an alternative Cuban identity, absorbing myriad influences from Jamaica, the Lesser Antilles and, in particular, French Haiti. It is this soul-searching, in part, which accounts for the region's rich ethnic diversity and long-standing penchant for rebellion.

It's no accident that all of Cuba's revolutionary movements have been ignited in the Oriente, inspired by such fiery easterners as Carlos Manuel de Céspedes (from Bayamo), Antonio Maceo (from Santiago) and Fidel Castro (from Birán near Holguín). The region has also been a standard-bearer for the lion's share of Cuba's hybrid musical genres, from *son* and *changüí* to *nueva trova*. Cuban hip hop might have had its genesis in Alamar, a suburb of Havana, but most of its instigators were eastern migrants from Santiago de Cuba.

Today, Cuba's east–west rivals continue to trade humorous insults on all number of topics. Listen carefully and you'll notice that people from the Oriente have a strong 'singsong' accent. They are also generally less well-off economically, resulting in the long-standing trend for easterners to migrate west for work. More subtle are the musical and religious nuances. The Oriente hides copious Afro-Haitian traditions left over from the era of slavery. These are most clearly manifested in Santiago's folkloric dance troupes and its manic July carnival.

Shopping

The 'city of sculptures' has some interesting local art.

Galería Taller Escultura Rita Longa GALLERY (cnr Av 2 de Diciembre & Lucas Ortíz; ☺9am-5pm Mon-Sat) The small gallery pulls together some fine local work for perusal or purchase.

Fondo Cubano de Bienes Culturales ARTS & CRAFTS (cnr Ángel de la Guardia & Francisco Varona; ☺9am-noon & 1:30-5pm Mon-Fri, 8:30am-noon Sat) This store sells fine artwork, ceramics and embroidered items opposite the main square.

Biblioteca Provincial José Martí BOOKS (Vicente García No 4; ☺9am-6pm Mon-Sat) Books galore.

❶ Information

Banco Financiero Internacional (cnr Vicente García & 24 de Febrero; ☺9am-3pm Mon-Fri)

Cadeca (Colón No 41) Money changing.

Etecsa Telepunto (Francisco Vega, btwn Vicente García & Lucas Ortíz; ☺8:30am-7pm) Spanking modern air-conditioned haven on the shopping boulevard.

Hospital Che Guevara (☎31-34-50-12; cnr Avs CJ Finlay & 2 de Diciembre) One kilometer from the highway exit toward Holguín.

Infotur (cnr Ángel de la Guardia & Francisco Varona; ☺8:15am-4:15pm Mon-Fri & alternate Sat) Possibly the friendliest information office in Cuba.

Post Office (Vicente García No 6; ☺8am-8pm)

❶ Getting There & Away

BUS

The main **bus station** (Francisco Varona) is 1km southeast of the main square. **Víazul** (www. viazul.com) buses have daily departures; tickets are sold by the *jefe de turno* (shift manager).

There are five daily buses to Havana (CUC$39, 11 hours) leaving at 4:30am, 9:10am, 12:25pm, 9:45pm and 10:40pm; four to Holguín (CUC$6, 70 minutes) at 2:40am, 6:35am, 8:30am and 3:30pm; one to Varadero (CUC$33, 10½ to 11 hours) at 12:55am; one to Trinidad (CUC$21, 6½ hours) at 12:25am; and four to Santiago (CUC$11, 4¾ hours) at 2:40am, 8:30am, 3:30pm and 6:10pm.

Most of these buses make stops at Camagüey (CUC$7, 2½ hours), Ciego de Ávila (CUC$13, 4¼ hours), Sancti Spíritus (CUC$17, 5½ to six hours), Santa Clara (CUC$22, seven hours) and Entronque de Jagüey (CUC$26, 9¼ hours). Santiago buses stop at Bayamo (CUC$6, 1¼ hours). To get to Guantánamo or Baracoa, you have to connect through Santiago de Cuba.

TRAIN

The **train station** (Terry Alomá, btwn Lucas Ortíz & Ángel de la Guardia) is near Estadio Julio Antonio Mella on the northeast side of town. See the *jefe de turno* for tickets. The fast Havana–Santiago Tren Francés doesn't stop in Las Tunas so you're left with slower, less reliable services. Trains to Havana and Santiago (via Camagüey and Santa Clara) leave two days out of three (check ahead). There are daily services to Camagüey and Holguín.

TRUCK

Passenger trucks to other parts of the province, including Puerto Padre, pick up passengers on the main street near the train station, with the last departure before 2pm.

❶ Getting Around

Taxis hang around outside the bus station, Hotel Las Tunas and the main square. Horse carts run along Frank País near the baseball stadium to the town center; they cost 10 pesos.

Cubacar (Av 2 de Diciembre) is at Hotel Las Tunas. An **Oro Negro gas station** (cnr Francisco Varona & Lora) is a block west of the bus station. The **Servi-Cupet gas station** (Carretera Central; ☺24hr) is at the exit from Las Tunas toward Camagüey.

Monte Cabaniguan

This fauna refuge just south of the municipality of Jobabo on the alluvial plains of the Río Cauto is a vital nesting ground for aquatic birds such as flamingos, the endangered Cuban parakeet and the Cuban tree-duck. The swamps are also the largest nesting ground for the American crocodile *(cocodrilo acutus)* in Latin America. The area is protected internationally as a Ramsar wetlands zone. Ecotur runs short boat trips here for aspiring twitchers.

Puerto Padre

Languishing in a half-forgotten corner of Cuba's least spectacular province, it's hard to believe that Puerto Padre – or the 'city of mills' as it is locally known – was once the largest sugar port on the planet. But for diehard travelers the wanton abandonment inspires a wistful sense of curiosity. Blessed with a Las Ramblas–style boulevard, a miniature Malecón, and a scrawny statue of Don Quixote standing rather forlornly beneath a weathered windmill that has registered one too many hurricanes, the town is the sort of place where you stop to ask the way at lunchtime and end up, a couple of hours later, tucking into fresh lobster at a bayside eating joint.

⊙ Sights

Museo Fernando García Grave de Peralta
MUSEUM

(Yara No 45, btwn Av Libertad & Maceo; admission CUC$1; ⊙9am-4pm Tue-Sat) Lashed regularly by hurricanes, the municipal museum – when it's not being renovated – contains the usual round of fallen revolutionaries, stuffed animals and antiques. Look out for the antique record players.

Fuerte de la Loma
FORT

(Av Libertad; admission CUC$1; ⊙9am-4pm Tue-Sat) This fort at the top of the sloping Av Libertad, also known as the Salcedo Castle, is testimony to Puerto Padre's former strategic importance. There's a small military museum with temperamental opening hours.

🛏 Sleeping & Eating

★ Roberto Lío Montes de Oca
CASA PARTICULAR $

(☑31-51-57-22; Francisco V Aguilera No 2, btwn Jesús Menéndez & Conrrado Benítez; r CUC$20-25; ※) The freshly painted pink facade of this house shines out amid Puerto Padre's ubiquitous dilapidation and acts as a portent for what's inside. The one prettily decorated bedroom smells, looks and is clean. Breakfast and dinner are available from the young hosts for CUC$3 and CUC$5 respectively.

El Bodegón de Polo
CUBAN $

(☑31-51-23-57; Calle Lenin 54; meals CUC$2-5; ⊙11am-11pm) Keen-to-please local restaurant serving delicacies such as crab, octopus and swordfish on an upstairs terrace. Best deal in town and friendly with it.

☆ Entertainment

There is a Casa de la Cultura (Parque de la Independencia) for nighttime activities or you can just surf the streets in search of friends, conversation or overnight accommodations in a casa particular. The town also has Cuba's newest branch of Uneac (Unión de Escritores y Artistas de Cuba; Union of Cuban Writers and Artists), which puts on shows, dancing and art expos.

❶ Getting There & Away

Puerto Padre is best accessed by truck, leaving from Las Tunas train station, or with your own wheels. A taxi from the provincial capital should cost approximately CUC$30.

Punta Covarrubias

Las Tunas province's only all-inclusive resort is also one of the island's most isolated, situated 41 rutted kilometers northwest of Puerto Padre on a spotless sandy beach at Punta

---

RODEOS

Cattle-herding has a long history in Cuba. Before the Revolution, Cuban cows produced some of the best beef in the Western hemisphere and, although the succulence of the steaks might have suffered since Castro nationalized the ranches, the skill and dexterity of the *vaqueros* (cowboys) has gone from strength to strength.

The cathedral of Cuban rodeo is the Rodeo Nacional in Parque Lenin in Havana – the host, since 1996, of the annual Boyeros Cattleman's Fair. But for a more authentic look at cowboy culture in the island's untrammeled hinterland, head to the prime cattle-rearing provinces of Camagüey and Las Tunas, where the cowboy spirit is particularly strong thanks to famous local son Jorge Barrameda.

Cuban rodeos exhibit all of the standard equestrian attractions with a few quirky Caribbean extras thrown in. Expect myriad horseback-riding events, obnoxious clowns, dexterous *vaqueros* lassoing steers, and rugged Benicio del Toro look-a-likes bolting out of rusty paddocks atop ill-tempered 680kg bulls to rapturous cheers from a noisy audience.

The Las Tunas rodeo is reason alone to visit this small city: main events take place twice annually in April and September, in Parque 26 de Julio (p340), but there are other, more impromptu rodeos: ask at the Infotur office.

Rodeos in Cuba operate along much the same lines as they do in other countries, and various organizations worldwide oppose them for being cruel to animals. For more information check the website of the Humane Society of the United States (www.humanesociety.org).

Covarrubias. Sitting aside the blue-green Atlantic, the **Brisas Covarrubias** (☎ 31-51-55-30; s/d CUC$88/132; [P] [✱] [@] [⊠]) has 122 comfortable rooms in cabin blocks (one room is designed for disabled guests). **Scuba diving** at the coral reef 1.5km offshore is the highlight. Packages of two dives per day start at CUC$45 at the Marina Covarrubias. There are 12 dive sites here. Almost all guests arrive on all-inclusive tours and are bussed in from Frank País Airport in Holguín, 115km to the southeast. It's very secluded.

Self-sufficient travelers can turn in to the beach at the **mirador** (a tower with fantastic panoramic views), 200m before the hotel, or procure a hotel day-pass for CUC$25.

ⓘ Getting There & Away

The road from Puerto Padre to Playa Covarrubias is what Cuban taxi drivers call *mas o menos* (more or less) due to regular hotel traffic. West to Manatí and Playa Santa Lucía is an African-style hole-fest. Drive slowly and carefully!

Playas La Herradura, La Llanita & Las Bocas

Congratulations! You've made it to the end of the road. A captivating alternative to the comforts of Covarrubias can be found at this string of northern beaches hugging the Atlantic coast 30km north of Puerto Padre and 55km from Holguín. There's not much to do here apart from read, relax, ruminate and get lost in the vivid colors of traditional Cuban life.

From Puerto Padre it's 30km around the eastern shore of Bahía de Chaparra to **Playa la Herradura**. The beach is a scoop of golden sand that will one day undoubtedly host an all-inclusive resort. Enjoy it by yourself while you can. There are a handful of houses legally renting rooms (look for the blue-and-white Arrendador Divisa sign). A long-standing choice is **Villa Rocio** (☎ 31-52-77-39-21; Casa No 185; CUC$20), close to the beach with a rustic interior and good food. Ask around. The place isn't big and everybody knows everybody else.

Continue west on this road for 11km to **Playa la Llanita**. The sand here is softer and whiter than in La Herradura, but the beach lies on an unprotected bend and there's sometimes a vicious chop.

Just 1km beyond, you come to the very end of the road at **Playa las Bocas** where there are several more houses for rent along with a small snack store and an open-air bar at the entrance to town. Wedged between the coast and Bahía de Chaparra, you can usually catch a local ferry to El Socucho and continue to Puerto Padre or rent a room in a casa particular.

ⓘ Getting There & Away

There are trucks that can take you as far as Puerto Padre from Las Tunas, from where you'll have to connect with another ride to the junction at Lora before heading north to the beaches. It's much easier to get up this way from Holguín, changing at the town of Velasco.

Driving is the best shot. The 52km between Las Tunas and Puerto Padre are well paved; after that it gets decidedly iffy. Taxis will often ask for more payment due to the bad driving conditions.

Holguín Province

Includes ➡

Holguín. 345
Gibara. 357
Guardalavaca
& Around 360
Banes 366
Birán. 367
Sierra del Cristal 367
Cayo Saetía 369

Best Beaches

➡ Playa Esmeralda (p360)

➡ Playa de Morales (p366)

➡ Playa Caletones (p358)

➡ Playa Pesquero (p360)

Best Rural Accommodations

➡ Villa Pinares del Mayarí (p369)

➡ Villa Cayo Saetia (p369)

➡ Villa Don Lino (p364)

➡ Campismo Silla de Gibara (p364)

Why Go?

Cuba's contradictions are magnified in Holguín. Perhaps something in the undeniable beauty of the province's hill-studded hinterland breeds extremes. Fulgencio Batista, and his ideological opposite, Fidel Castro, were both reared here, as were Reinaldo Arenas and Guillermo Infante, dissident writers who didn't have a lot in common with either leader. Then there are the dichotomies in the landscape. The environmental degradation around Moa's nickel mines jars rather awkwardly with the pine-scented mountains of the Sierra Cristal, while the inherent Cuban-ness of Gibara contrasts sharply with the tourist swank of resort-complex Guardalavaca.

Christopher Columbus was the first European to spy Holguín's beauty. By most accounts, he docked near Gibara in October 1492 where he was met by a group of curious Taíno. The Taínos didn't survive the ensuing Spanish colonization, though fragments of their legacy can be reconstructed in Holguín province, which contains more pre-Columbian archaeological sites than anywhere else in Cuba.

When to Go

➡ In April movie aficionados convene in Gibara for the Festival Internacional del Cine Pobre.

➡ May sees the city of Holguín show its religious spirit during the Romerías de Mayo.

➡ Avoid the hurricane season: July to mid-November.

➡ You can enjoy the Guardalavaca and Playa Pesquero resorts in prime tourist season from December until early March.

History

Most historians agree that Christopher Columbus first made landfall in Cuba on October 28, 1492, at Cayo Bariay near Playa Blanca, just west of Playa Don Lino (now in Holguín province). The gold-seeking Spaniards were welcomed ashore by *seborucos* and they captured 13 of them to take back to Europe as scientific 'specimens'. Bariay was boycotted in favor of Guantánamo 20 years later when a new colonial capital was set up in Baracoa, and the hilly terrain north of Bayamo was gifted to Captain García Holguín, a Mexican conquistador. The province became an important sugar-growing area at the end of the 19th century when much of the land was bought up and cleared of forest by the US-owned United Fruit Company. Formerly part of the Oriente territory, Holguín became a province in its own right after 1975.

Holguín

POP 277,000

Neither one of Cuba's seven founding villas nor a megaresort of carefully packaged Caribbean dreamscapes, the city of San Isidoro de Holguín barely features in Cuba's tourist master plan (which prefers to promote all-inclusive resorts over Cuba's hardworking cities). But, for a certain type of traveller, this is part of its magic – and mystery. Sit down in one of the city's central squares for an hour or two (Holguín is euphemistically coined the 'city of parks') and something interesting will undoubtedly distract you. It might be the religious solemnity of the annual procession to the hilltop Loma de la Cruz, or – more spontaneously – the exuberant cheers from the crowd in the oversized baseball stadium.

The nation's fourth-largest city serves up a slice of Cuba without the wrapping paper. What you won't find here is four-star hotels, revitalized colonial buildings or tour guides with shiny name badges talking to you in English. What you *will* find is eager-to-please casas particulares, cheap food in pioneering new restaurants and a city that loves (and brews) its own beer.

History

In 1515 Diego Velázquez de Cuéllar, Cuba's first governor, conferred the lands north of Bayamo to Captain García Holguín, one of the island's original colonizers. Setting up a cattle ranch in the province's verdant and fertile hinterland, Holguín and his descendants presided over a burgeoning agricultural

settlement that by 1720 had sprouted a small wooden church and more than 450 inhabitants. In 1752 San Isidoro de Holguín (the settlement was renamed after the church) was granted the title of city and by 1790 the population had expanded to 12,000.

Holguín was the setting of much fighting during the two wars of independence when ferocious Mambí warriors laid siege to the heavily fortified Spanish barracks at La Periquera (now the Museo de Historia Provincial). Captured and lost by Julio Grave de Peralta (after whom one of the squares is named), the city was taken for a second time on December 19, 1872, by Cuban general and native son Calixto García, Holguín's posthumous local hero.

With the division of Oriente into five separate provinces in 1976, the city of Holguín became a provincial capital. Besides beer, the key industries are agriculture and nickel. The city has also cultivated an international reputation for drug rehabilitation: Argentine soccer star Diego Maradona came here for rehab in 2000 (it was to be the start of a long-running friendship between the footballer and Fidel Castro). More recently, Holguín suffered a severe mauling from Hurricane Ike in 2008.

◉ Sights

Base yourself around the city's four central squares and you'll see most of what's on offer. However, no walk is complete without a climb up the emblematic Loma de la Cruz – a little off the grid, but well worth the detour.

★ **Museo de Historia Provincial**   MUSEUM
(Map p352; Frexes No 198; admission CUC$1; ⊗ 8am-4:30pm Tue-Sat, to noon Sun) Now a national monument, the building on the northern side of Parque Calixto García was constructed between 1860 and 1868 and used as a Spanish army barracks during the independence wars. It was nicknamed La Periquera (Parrot Cage) for the red, yellow and green uniforms of the Spanish soldiers who stood guard.

The prize exhibit is an old axe head carved in the likeness of a man, known as the Hacha de Holguín (Holguín Axe), thought to have been made by indigenous inhabitants in the early 1400s and discovered in 1860. Looking even sharper in its polished0glass case is a sword that once belonged to national hero and poet José Martí.

Parque Peralta   SQUARE
(Parque de las Flores; Map p352) This square is named for General Julio Grave de Peralta

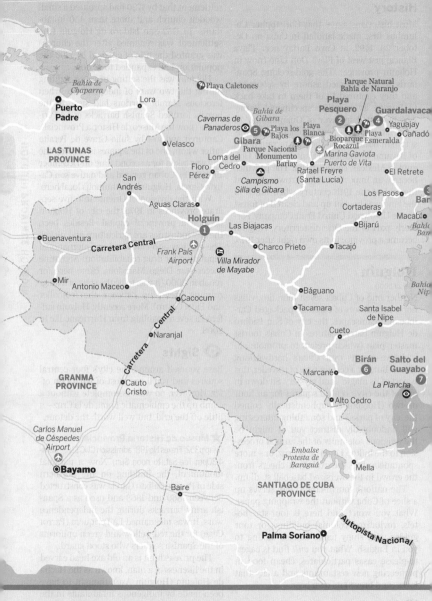

Holguín Province Highlights

1 See Holguín spread out like a map beneath you from the **Loma de la Cruz** (p350).

2 Fork out for some beach time at one of the plush resorts on **Playa Pesquero** (p360).

3 Take a bicycle ride through bucolic villages to the quintessential *holguiñero* town of **Banes** (p366).

4 Discover Taíno treasures in one of Cuba's most important archaeological sites at **Museo Chorro de Maita** (p360) in Guardalavaca.

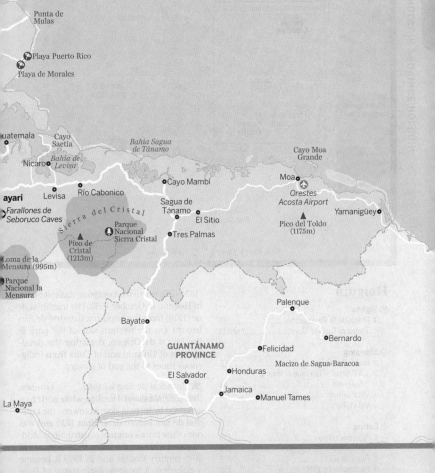

ATLANTIC OCEAN

0 ——— 40 km
0 ——— 20 miles

Punta de Mulas

Playa Puerto Rico
Playa de Morales

uatemala
Cayo Saetía
Nicaro
Bahía de Levisa
Bahía Sagua de Tánamo
Cayo Moa Grande
Moa
Orestes Acosta Airport
ayarí
Levisa
Río Cabonico
Cayo Mambí
Sagua de Tánamo
Yamanigüey
Farallones de Seboruco Caves
S i e r r a   d e l   C r i s t a l
El Sitio
Pico del Toldo (1175m)
Parque Nacional Sierra Cristal
Tres Palmas
Pico de Cristal (1213m)
Loma de la Mensura (995m)
Parque Nacional la Mensura

Palenque
Bayate
GUANTÁNAMO PROVINCE
Bernardo
Felicidad
Macizo de Sagua-Baracoa
El Salvador
Honduras
Jamaica
Manuel Tames
La Maya

5 Stay in arguably Cuba's best colonial accommodation, **Hotel Ordoño** (p358) in the mysterious yet romantic seaside town of Gibara.

6 Peep behind the mask and find out about the Castro family at Fidel's childhood home, **Museo Conjunto Histórico de Birán** (p368).

7 Splash out on a trip to the **Salto del Guayabo** (p369) from its spectacularly perched overlook.

Holguín

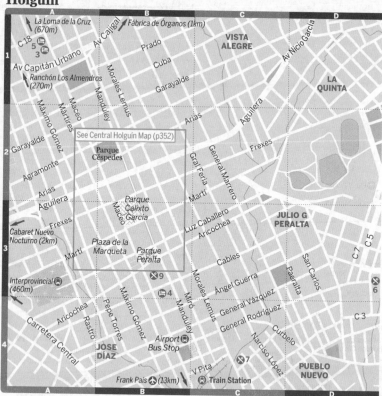

Holguín

◎ Sights
1 Plaza de la Revolución..........................F1
  Tomb of Calixto García ....(see 1)

◎ Sleeping
2 Hotel Pernik..F2
3 'La Palma' – Enrique R Interián
  Salermo...A1
4 Villa Janeth B3
5 Villa Liba A1

◎ Eating
6 Agropecuario...D3
7 Agropecuario.. C4
8 Peso Stalls E3
9 Restaurante 1910......................................B3
10 Taberna Pancho......................................F2

◎ Drinking & Nightlife
  Disco Havana Club........................(see 2)

◎ Entertainment
11 Estadio General Calixto García E2

(1834–72), who led an uprising against Spain in Holguín in October 1868. His marble statue (1916) faces the imposing Catedral de San Isidoro. On the western side of the park is the **Mural de Origen**, depicting the development of Holguín and of Cuba from indigenous times to the end of slavery.

★ **Catedral de San Isidoro**   CATHEDRAL
(Map p352; Manduley) Dazzling white and characterized by its twin domed towers, the Catedral de San Isidoro dates from 1720 and was one of the town's original constructions. Added piecemeal over the years, the towers are of 20th-century vintage and in 1979 it became a cathedral. A hyper-realistic statue of Pope John Paul II stands to the right of the main doors. If it's open you can take a peak inside, though the interior is relatively austere.

Parque Calixto García   SQUARE
(Map p352) This wide, expansive square is more about atmosphere than architecture.

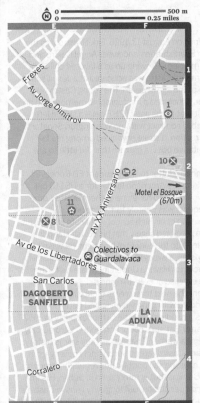

0 ——— 500 m
0 ——— 0.25 miles

Frexes
Av Jorge Dimitrov
Av XX Aniversario
Motel el Bosque
(670m)
Av de los Libertadores
Colectivos to
Guardalavaca
San Carlos
DAGOBERTO SANFIELD
LA ADUANA
Corralero

It was laid out in 1719 as the original Plaza de Armas and served for many years as the town's meeting point and marketplace. The centerpiece today is a 1912 statue of General Calixto García, around which congregate a multifarious mixture of old sages, baseball naysayers and teenagers on the prowl.

In the southwestern corner of Parque Calixto García is the **Centro de Arte** (Map p352; Maceo No 180; ⊕9am-4pm Mon-Sat) **FREE**, a gallery for temporary exhibitions that shares space with **Biblioteca Alex Urquiola** (Map p352; Maceo No 178), named after a local revolutionary and housing Holguín's biggest book collection.

Parque Céspedes   PARK

(Parque San José; Map p352) Holguín's youngest park is also its shadiest. Named for 'Father of the Motherland' Carlos Manuel de Céspedes (his statue stands center stage next to a monument honoring the heroes of the War of Independence) the cobbled central

square is dominated by the **Iglesia de San José** (Map p352; Manduley No 116).

The church, with its distinctive mezzanine floor, dome and bell tower, was once used by the Independistas as a lookout tower. Locals still refer to the park by its old name, San José.

Casa Natal de Calixto García   MUSEUM

(Map p352; Miró No 147; admission CUC$1; ⊕9am-5pm Mon-Sat) To learn more about the militaristic deeds of Holguín's local hero, head to this house situated two blocks east of the namesake park. The hugely underestimated García – who stole the cities of Las Tunas, Holguín and Bayamo from Spanish control between 1896 and 1898 – was born here in 1839.

This small collection gives a reasonable overview of his life: military maps, old uniforms and even a spoon he ate with on the campaign trail in 1885.

Museo de Historia Natural   MUSEUM

(Map p352; Maceo No 129, btwn Parques Calixto García & Peralta; admission CUC$1; ⊕9am-noon & 12:30-5pm Tue-Sat, 9am-noon Sun) You'll find more stuffed animals here than in a New York toy store – everything from the world's smallest frog to the world's smallest hummingbird. There's also a big collection of the unique yellow polymita seashells found on Cuba's far-east coastline but, to be frank, the building, guarded by two stone lions, is more impressive than what's inside.

Plaza de la Marqueta   SQUARE

(Map p352) Long earmarked for a major renovation, hopelessly ruined Plaza de la Marqueta is a plaza of possibilities that remains unfulfilled. Laid out in 1848 and rebuilt in 1918, the square is dominated by an impressive covered marketplace supposedly undergoing a transformation into a top-notch concert hall (after a decade of rumors, however, the work has yet to start).

Running along the north and south sides of the plaza are myriad shops that are meant to provide quality shopping but, to date, number only a couple of music and cigar outlets.

Plaza de la Revolución   SQUARE

Holguín is a city most *fiel* (faithful), and its bombastic revolutionary plaza, east of the center, is a huge monument to the heroes of Cuban independence, bearing quotations from José Martí and Fidel Castro. Massive rallies are held here every May 1 (Labor Day). The **tomb of Calixto García**, containing his ashes, is also here, as well as a smaller monument to García's mother.

FIDEL'S ROOTS

Born near the village of Birán in Holguín province on August 13, 1926, Fidel Castro was the illegitimate product of a relationship between Spanish-born landowner Ángel Castro and his cook and housemaid Lina Ruz (they later married). Growing up as a favored child in a large and relatively wealthy family of sugar farmers, Castro was educated at a Jesuit school and sent away to study in the city of Santiago at the age of seven. The young Castro was an exceptional student whose prodigious talents included a photographic memory and an extraordinary aptitude for sport. Legend has it that at the age of 21, Fidel – a skilled left-arm pitcher – was offered a professional baseball contract with the Washington Senators.

At the age of 13 Fidel staged his first insurrection, a strike organized among his father's sugarcane workers against their exploitative boss, a gesture that did little to endear him to the fraternal fold.

One year later the still-teenage Castro penned a letter to US President FD Roosevelt congratulating him on his re-election and asking the American leader for a US$10 bill 'because I have not seen a US$10 bill and I would like to have one of them.' Rather ominously for future US–Cuban relations, the request was politely turned down.

Undeterred, Fidel marched on. Upon completion of his high school certificate in 1945, his teacher and mentor Father Francisco Barbeito predicted sagely that his bullish star pupil would 'fill with brilliant pages the book of his life.' With the benefit of hindsight, he wasn't far wrong. Armed with tremendous personal charisma, a wrought-iron will and a natural ability to pontificate for hours on end, Fidel made tracks for Havana University where his forthright and unyielding personality quickly ensured he excelled at everything he did.

Training ostensibly as a lawyer, Castro spent the next three years embroiled in political activity amid an academic forum that was riddled with gang violence and petty corruption. Never one to follow the lead, he stood as a candidate for the Orthodox party in 1952 in an election that was ultimately cancelled after Batista's coup. Enraged, Castro quickly changed his tactics and was reborn as a guerrilla warrior. The rest, as they say, is history.

After ruling Cuba single-handed for 47 years, Castro retired surprisingly quietly from public life in 2006 after a brief illness. These days, he still pontificates regularly through self-penned articles in state-run newspaper *Granma*, but is rarely seen in public. His impending death has long been a topic of heated speculation, but longevity runs in Castro's genes (89 years old in 2015). Five of his six siblings are still alive, including older brother Ramón, aged 90 and younger brother Raúl, a relatively spritely 83 (in 2015).

★ **La Loma de la Cruz** LANDMARK
At the northern end of Maceo you'll find a stairway built in 1950, with 465 steps ascending a 275m-high hill with panoramic views, a restaurant and a 24-hour bar. A cross was raised here in 1790 in hope of relieving a drought, and every May 3 during Romerías de Mayo devotees climb to the summit where a special Mass is held.

It's a 20-minute walk from town or you can flag a bici-taxi to the foot of the hill for around 10 Cuban pesos. This walk is best tackled early in the morning when the light is pristine and the heat not too debilitating.

Fábrica de Órganos ORGAN FACTORY
(Carretera de Gibara No 301; ⊗ 8am-4pm Mon-Fri) This is the only mechanical music-organ factory in Cuba. The small factory produces about six organs a year, as well as guitars and other instruments. A good organ costs between the equivalent of US$10,000 and US$25,000. Eight professional organ groups exist in Holguín (including the Familia Cuayo, based at the factory): if you're lucky, you can hear one playing on Parque Céspedes on Thursday afternoon or Sunday morning.

Mirador de Mayabe LOOKOUT
The Mirador de Mayabe is a motel-cum-restaurant high on a hill 10km from Holguín city. It gained fame for a beer-drinking donkey named Pancho, who hung out near the bar in the 1980s. The original Pancho died in 1992 and they're now onto Pancho IV who also drinks beer. Traditional country shows occur here most weeks.

A bus runs to Holguín from the bottom of the hill, 1.5km from the motel, three times a day.

✦✧ Festivals & Events

Romerías de Mayo
RELIGIOUS

(☉May 3) Romerías de Mayo is Holguín's big annual pilgrimage, held on May 3: devotees climb Loma de la Cruz for a special Mass. The whole city turns out to follow the procession from the Catedral de San Isidro, a custom that dates back to the 1790s. In recent times the parade has become livelier with arty contributions from the Hermanos Saíz youth organization.

Carnaval
CARNIVAL

(☉Aug) Holguín's annual shindig happens in the third week of August with outdoor concerts and copious amounts of dancing, roast pork and potent drinks.

🛏 Sleeping

There's nothing exciting hotel-wise in Holguín, but some of the local casas particulares aren't bad.

'La Palma' – Enrique R Interián Salermo
CASA PARTICULAR $

(☑42-46-83; Maceo No 52A, btwn Calles 16 & 18, El Llano; r CUC$25; ❄) Enrique's detached neocolonial house dates from 1945 and is situated in the shadow of the Loma de la Cruz. The slightly removed location is worth the minor inconvenience. Enrique is a fantastic host and his spacious house has a pleasant garden – with table tennis and a baseball practice net!

Furthermore, Enrique's son is a talented painter and sculptor. Check out the terracotta bust of Che Guevara in the living room next to an unusual 3m-long canvas copy of Da Vinci's *The Last Supper* (with St John as a woman).

Casa Don Diego
CASA PARTICULAR $

(Map p352; ☑52-26-90-47; Arias No 167, btwn Mauduley & Maceo; r CUC$25; ❄) Wonderful spiral staircases characterize this colonial house, which is prettier inside than out. Two rooms with high ceilings, a pleasant rooftop terrace, and prime city-center location (right in Parque Céspedes) make it a jolly good deal.

Villa Liba
CASA PARTICULAR $

(☑42-38-23; Maceo No 46 , cnr Calle 18; CUC$20-25; ❄) At Jorge's smart, sizable bungalow, which looks like something out of a 1950s North American suburb, the *alma* (soul) fairly bubbles over. Jorge is a modern-day Pablo Neruda with whimsical anecdotes aplenty on Holguín life, while his wife is an accomplished masseuse and reiki specialist (treatments CUC$20), and his daughter gives violin recitals over dinner. The food has a Lebanese flair.

Villa Janeth
CASA PARTICULAR $

(☑42-93-31; Cables No 105; CUC$20-25; ❄) Janeth has a very clean, very spacious house with two upstairs rooms far above the average Holguín standard. Follow the passageway back and you'll get to a self-contained kitchen and terrace. There's another amenable house a few doors down on the corner with Manduley if these guys are full.

Motel El Bosque
HOTEL $$

(☑48-11-40; Av Jorge Dimitrov; s/d incl breakfast CUC$35/50; ❄❄) 🏊 At least one notch up the quality ratings over other midrange options, the 69 solar-powered duplex bungalows here are set among extensive green grounds. There's a relaxing bar beside the swimming pool (nonguests can use it for a small fee) and the late-night music decibels aren't as ear-shattering as some.

Villa Mirador de Mayabe
HOTEL $$

(☑42-54-98; Alturas de Mayabe; bungalows CUC$50; P❄❄) This motel, high up on the Loma de Mayabe, 10km southeast of Holguín, has 24 rooms tucked into lush grounds. The views, taking in vast mango plantations, are especially good from the pool.

Hotel Pernik
HOTEL $$

(☑48-10-11; cnr Avs Jorge Dimitrov & XX Aniversario; s/d incl breakfast CUC$40/55; P❄@❄) The nearest decent hotel to the city center is a dose of Soviet-inspired '70s nostalgia. It has attempted to counter its dour reputation in recent years by letting local artists decorate the rooms in edgy art. The breakfast buffet is plentiful and there's an information office, Cadeca (for changing money) and internet cafe; however, the hotel suffers from the usual foibles of interminable renovations and blaring late-night music.

🍴 Eating

The 2011 relaxing of restrictions on private restaurants benefited Holguín more than most cities: there's a stash of reasonable private restaurants here more frequented by locals than tourists.

Snack Bar La Begonia
SNACKS $

(Map p352; ☑46-85-86; Maceo No 176; snacks CUC$1-4; ☉9am-10pm) Sells drinks and snacks beneath flowering trellises on Parque Calixto García, and is a relaxed place to meet

Central Holguín

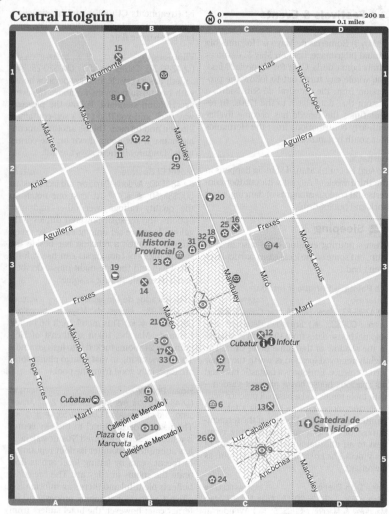

other travelers. If you don't like rubbery cheese sandwiches, stick to the beer and enjoy the cultural interchange.

Cafetería Cristal FAST FOOD $
(Map p352; Edificio Pico de Cristal, cnr Manduley & Martí; snacks CUC$1-3; ⏱24hr) Nothing wrong with this plaza-fronting joint, which is typical of such 'cafes' across Latin America: reliable and affordable chicken meals dished up by formal waiters whose elegance prepares you for cuisine far superior to what you end up getting. The air-con does its best to replicate a frigid day in Vancouver; perch on the

outside terrace with the surprisingly great house coffee and soak up Holguín life.

Taberna Pancho CARIBBEAN $
(Av Jorge Dimitrov; meals CUC$3-5; ⏱noon-10pm) This bar-restaurant inspired by the Mirador de Mayabe's famous beer-drinking donkey has echoes of a Spanish *taberna* (tavern), done up in dark wood. The menu includes actual chorizo (unusual in Cuba), and draft Mayabe beer comes in proper frosted glasses. It's located between Hotel Pernik (p351) and Motel El Bosque (p351).

Central Holguín

◎ Top Sights
1 Catedral de San Isidoro	D5
2 Museo de Historia Provincial	B3

◎ Sights
3 Biblioteca Alex Urquiola	B4
4 Casa Natal de Calixto García	C3
Centro de Arte	(see 3)
5 Iglesia de San José	B1
6 Museo de Historia Natural	C4
7 Parque Calixto García	C3
8 Parque Céspedes	B1
9 Parque Peralta	C5
10 Plaza de la Marqueta	B5

⬤ Sleeping
11 Casa Don Diego	B2

⬤ Eating
12 Cafetería Cristal	C4
13 Cremería Guamá	C4
14 La Luz de Yara	B3
15 Restaurante-Bar San José	B1
16 Salón 1720	C3
17 Snack Bar La Begonia	B4

◎ Drinking & Nightlife
Bar Terraza	(see 16)
18 Casa de la Música	C3
Disco Cristal	(see 12)
19 Las 3 Lucías	B3
20 Taberna Mayabe	C2

◎ Entertainment
Biblioteca Alex Urquiola	(see 3)
21 Casa de la Trova	B4
22 Casa Iberoamericana	B2
23 Cine Martí	B3
24 Cominado Deportivo Henry García Suárez	C5
25 Jazz Club	C3
26 Salón Benny Moré	C5
27 Teatro Comandante Eddy Suñol	C4
28 Uneac	C4

◎ Shopping
29 Bazar – Proyecto de Desarollo Local	B2
30 El Jigue	B4
31 Fondo de Bienes Culturales	B3
32 La Epoca	C3
33 Pentagrama	B4

Cremería Guamá ICE CREAM **$**

(Map p352; cnr Luz Caballero & Manduley; ice cream CUC$0.50; ⊙10am-10:45pm) A Coppelia in all but name. Lose an hour underneath the striped red-and-white awning overlooking pedestrianized Calle Manduley and enjoy peso ice cream alfresco.

★**Restaurante 1910** RESTAURANT **$$**

(☑42-39-94; www.1910restaurantebar.com; Mártires No 143, btwn Aricochea & Cables; meals CUC$8-11; ⊙noon-midnight) Holguín has too many restaurants named after dates but 1910 is red-letter day as far as innovative food goes in this city. Neither the eating area (a colonial house hung with chandeliers) nor the courteous service can be faulted, and that's before you've started on the specialty steak (CUC$11) with dried spaghetti latticework.

Wash it down with any one of a fine selection of South American wines (poured into specially embossed 1910 wineglasses) and enjoy an attention to detail you rarely get eating out in Cuba.

Ranchón Los Almendros PARRILLA **$$**

(☑42-96-52; José A Cardet No 68, btwn Calles 12 & 14; meals CUC$10; ⊙10am-11pm) So clean and professionally run is the Almendros kitchen that they've decided to make it open, meaning the aromas visit your table. The smoked meats are all excellent and come with copious trimmings. It's located near the Loma de la Cruz and doesn't look much from the outside. Rest assured – inside is a different story.

Restaurante-Bar San José CUBAN **$$**

(Map p352; ☑42-48-77; www.restaurantesanjose. com; Agramonte No 188; meals CUC$4-10; ⊙noon-11pm) The favored local eating choice sits slap-bang in the central square (Parque Céspedes) and stays faithful to its local name (San José). There's nothing fancy on the menu, but this is where you come for *comida criolla* not *duck á l'orange*.

Salón 1720 CARIBBEAN **$$**

(Map p352; Frexes No 190 cnr Miró; meals CUC$7-9; ⊙noon-10:30pm) This is a painstakingly restored wedding-cake mansion where you can tuck into paella (CUC$6) or chicken stuffed with vegetables and cheese (CUC$8); there's even complimentary crackers. In the same colonial-style complex there's a cigar shop, bar, boutique, car rental and a terrace with nighttime music. Check out the wall plaques that give interesting insights into Holguín's history.

Self-Catering

There is an *agropecuario* (vegetable market) off Calle 19, the continuation of Morales Lemus near the train station, and another *agropecuario* on Calle 3 in Dagoberto Sanfield. There are plenty of peso stalls beside the baseball stadium.

La Luz de Yara   SUPERMARKET **$**
(Map p352; cnr Frexes & Maceo; ☺ 8:30am-7:30pm Mon-Sat, to :30pm Sun) Relatively well-stocked Cuban department store and supermarket with a bakery section on Parque Calixto García.

Drinking & Nightlife

Welcome to beer city. The local bars aren't too flash, but you can cobble together a decent pub crawl here.

Taberna Mayabe   BAR
(Map p352; Manduley, btwn Aguilera & Frexes; ☺ noon-6pm & 8-11pm Tue-Sun) Pancho the beer-drinking donkey would have a field day at this tavern on pedestrian-only Manduley, where wooden tables and ceramic mugs create a hearty pub atmosphere. The eponymous local brew is served.

Las 3 Lucías   CAFE
(Map p352; cnr Mártires & Frexes; ☺ 7am-11pm) *Lucía* was a 1968 classic Cuban film about the lives of three women, each named Lucía, in different periods: the War of Independence, the 1930s and the 1960s. Such is the premise for this fancy bar, decorated in Cuban film memorabilia and evoking a classy atmosphere of yesteryear (save for the big wall-mounted TV). The cocktails are good, the coffee's alright and the atmosphere is pretty unique.

Bar Terraza   BAR
(Map p352; Frexes, btwn Manduley & Miró; ☺ 8pm-1am) Perched above Salón 1720, this is the city's poshest spot. Cocktails are in order as you drink in the views over Parque Calixto García amid regular musical interludes.

Casa de la Música   CLUB
(Map p352; cnr Frexes & Manduley; ☺ Tue-Sun) There's a young, trendy vibe at this place on Parque Calixto García. If you can't dance, stay static sinking beers on the adjacent Terraza Bucanero (entry via Calle Manduley).

Disco Cristal   CLUB
(Map p352; Manduley No 199, 3rd fl, Edificio Pico de Cristal; admission CUC$2; ☺ 9pm-2am Tue-Thu) A nexus for Holguín's dexterous dancers (most of whom are young, cool and determined to have a good time), this place is insanely popular at weekends when you'll find lots of inspiration for the salsa/rap/reggaetón repertoire.

Cabaret Nuevo Nocturno   CLUB
(admission CUC$8; ☺ 10pm-2am) This is a Tropicana-style cabaret club beyond the Servi-Cupet gas station 3km out on the road to Las Tunas.

Disco Havana Club   CLUB
(Hotel Pernik, cnr Avs Jorge Dimitrov & XX Aniversario; guest/nonguest CUC$2/4; ☺ 10pm-2am Tue-Sun) Holguín's premier disco at Hotel Pernik. If you're staying there, the music will visit you – in your room – like it or not, until 1am.

☆ Entertainment

★Uneac   CULTURAL
(Map p352; Manduley, btwn Luz Caballero & Martí) If you only visit one Uneac (Unión Nacional de Escritores y Artistas de Cuba; National Union of Cuban Writers and Artists) in Cuba (there are 14 in total, at least one per province) make it this one. Situated in the lovingly restored Casa de las Moyúas (1845) on car-free Calle Manduley, this friendly establishment offers literary evenings with famous authors, music nights, patio theater (including Lorca) and cultural reviews.

There's an intermittent bar on a gorgeous central patio, and an on-site art gallery/studio called La Cochera.

Teatro Comandante Eddy Suñol   THEATER
(Map p352; 🖂 42-79-94; Martí No 111; ♿) Holguín's premier theater is an art deco treat from 1939 on Parque Calixto García. It hosts both the Teatro Lírico Rodrigo Prats and the Ballet Nacional de Cuba and is renowned both nationally and internationally for its operettas, dance performances and Spanish musicals.

Check here for details of performances by the famous children's theater Alas Buenas and the Orquesta Sinfónica de Holguín (Holguín Symphony Orchestra).

Casa de la Trova   LIVE MUSIC
(Map p352; Maceo No 174; ☺ Tue-Sun) Old guys in Panama hats croon under the rafters, musicians in *guayaberas* (pleated, buttoned shirts) blast on trumpets, while ancient couples in their Sunday best map out a perfect *danzón* (traditional Cuban ballroom dance colored with African influences). So timeless, so Holguín.

Salón Benny Moré — LIVE MUSIC
(Map p352; cnr Luz Caballero & Maceo; ☺show 10:30pm) Holguín's impressive new outdoor music venue is the best place to round off a bar crawl with some live music and dancing.

Biblioteca Alex Urquiola — THEATER
(Map p352; ☎42-44-63; Maceo No 180) Culture vultures steam the creases out of their evening dresses to see live theater and performances by the Orquesta Sinfónica de Holguín here.

Casa Iberoamericana — CULTURAL
(Map p352; www.casadeiberoamerica.cult.cu; Arias No 161) Situated on quieter Parque Céspedes, this paint-peeled place frequently hosts *peñas* (musical performances) and cultural activities.

Jazz Club — JAZZ
(Map p352; cnr Frexes & Manduley; ☺2pm-2am) The jazz jams get moving around 8pm and continue weaving magic until 11pm. Then there's piped music until 2am. There's a sporadically functioning daytime cafe downstairs.

Cine Martí — CINEMA
(Map p352; Frexes No 204; tickets CUC$2) The best of a quintet of city-center cinemas, head here for big-screen movies (occasional English-language films with Spanish subtitles). It's on Parque Calixto García.

Estadio General Calixto García — SPORT
(off Av de los Libertadores; admission CUC$1-2) Mosey on down to this stadium to see Holguín's baseball team, former giant-killers the Perros (dogs) who snatched the national championship from under the noses of the 'big two' in 2002, but haven't barked much since. The stadium also houses a small but interesting sport museum.

Cominado Deportivo Henry García Suárez — SPORT
(Map p352; Maceo; admission MN$1; ☺boxing matches 8pm Wed, 2pm Sat) You can catch boxing matches at this spit-and-sawdust gym on the western side of Parque Peralta, where three Olympic medalists have trained. If you can pluck up the courage, ask about some (noncontact) training sessions.

🛍 Shopping

Bazar – Proyecto de Desarollo Local — SOUVENIRS
(Map p352; Manduley, btwn Aguilera & Áresas; ☺8am-6pm Mon-Sat) The local private market

LOCAL KNOWLEDGE

BEER CITY

Stand down all other claimants: Holguín brews the best beer in Cuba. The large Fábrica de la Cervezería Bucanero on the outskirts of the city produces the nation's three most popular beers. Cuba's most ubiquitous brand is Cristal (4.9% alcohol by volume), a light unexciting brew perennially popular with tourists looking to extinguish the heat of a long afternoon in the sunlounger. Regular visitors to the isles, or Cubans with enough *dinero*, usually opt for the stronger, darker Bucanero, the 'fuerte' variety of which rings in at 5.4%. Stronger and maltier is Bucanero 'Max,' an eye-widening 6.5%. Rarely seen in tourist resorts is Mayabe, a clear, light golden pilsner that registers at a weakish 4% and is generally sold in Cubans peso.

as opposed to the nearby government-run affair. This Bazar sells a similar stash of trinkets, Afro-Cuban masks and clothing, but the money goes directly into the pockets of the vendors. *Capitalismo* or *socialismo* – take your pick.

Fondo de Bienes Culturales — ARTS & CRAFTS
(Map p352; Frexes No 196; ☺10am-3pm Mon-Fri, 9am-noon Sat) This state-run shop on Parque Calixto García sells similar handicrafts to the private vendor market a few blocks away.

La Epoca — ACCESSORIES
(Map p352; Frexes No 194; ☺9am-5pm Mon-Sat, to noon Sun) Department store on Parque Calixto García with increasingly sophisticated wares.

Pentagrama — MUSIC
(Map p352; cnr Maceo & Martí; ☺8am-noon & 12:30-4:30pm) Official outlet of the Cuban state-record company Egrem, selling a small but decent stash of CDs.

El Jigue — BOOKS, SOUVENIRS
(Map p352; cnr Martí & Mártires; ☺9am-5pm) Well-stocked bookstore and souvenir outlet adjacent to Plaza de la Maqueta.

ℹ Information
The local newspaper *Ahora* is published on Saturday. Radio Ángulo CMKO can be heard on 1110AM and 97.9FM.

Etecsa Telepunto (Calle Martí, btwn Martires & Máximo Gómez; internet CUC$4.50 per hour; ⊙8:30am-7:30pm) There are telephones – no internet – at the Parque Calixto García (cnr Martí & Maceo, Parque Calixto García) branch, while this one has three (usually busy) computer terminals.

Post Office (Map p352; Manduley No 183; ⊙10am-noon & 1-6pm Mon-Fri) You'll find another post office at Parque Céspedes (Map p352; Maceo No 114; ⊙8am-6pm Mon-Sat).

Banco de Crédito y Comercio (Arias; ⊙9am-3pm Mon-Fri) Bank on Parque Céspedes with ATM.

Banco Financiero Internacional (Manduley No 167, btwn Frexes & Aguilera; ⊙9am-3pm Mon-Fri)

Cadeca (Manduley No 205, btwn Martí & Luz Caballero) Money-changing.

Cubatur (Map p352; Edificio Pico de Cristal, cnr Manduley & Martí) Travel agent bivouacked inside the Cafetería Begonias.

Farmacia Turno Especial (Maceo No 170; ⊙8am-10pm Mon-Sat) Pharmacy on Parque Calixto García.

Hospital Lenin (☑42-53-02; Av VI Lenin) Will treat foreigners in an emergency.

Infotur (Map p352; 1st fl, Edificio Pico de Cristal, cnr Manduley & Martí) Tourist information.

❶ Getting There & Away

AIR

There are up to 16 international flights a week into Holguín's well-organized **Frank País Airport** (HOG; ☑42-52-71), 13km south of the city, including from Amsterdam, Düsseldorf, London, Montreal and Toronto. Almost all arrivals get bussed directly off to Guardalavaca and see little of Holguín city.

Domestic destinations are served by **Cubana** (Edificio Pico de Cristal, cnr Manduley & Martí), which flies daily to Havana (about CUC$120 one way, 1¼ hours).

BUS

The **Interprovincial Bus Station** (cnr Carretera Central & Independencia), west of the center near Hospital Lenin, has air-conditioned **Víazul** (www.viazul.com) buses leaving daily.

The Havana bus (CUC$44, 12 hours, four times daily) stops in Las Tunas, Camagüey, Ciego de Ávila, Sancti Spíritus and Santa Clara. The Santiago bus (CUC$11, 3½ hours, thrice daily) also stops in Bayamo. There are also daily buses to Trinidad (CUC$26, 7¾ hours) and Varadero (CUC$38, 11¼ hours).

There's a daily bus that connects to the Guardalavaca resorts run by Transtur. It leaves from outside the Museo de Historia Provincial daily at 1pm and costs CUC$15 return.

CAR

Colectivos (shared cars) run to Gibara (CUC$4) and Puerto Padre in Las Tunas province from Av Cajigal. Colectivos to Guardalavaca (CUC$5) leave from Av XX Aniversario near Terminal Dagoberto Sanfield Guillén.

TRAIN

The **train station** (Calle V Pita) is on the southern side of town. Foreigners must purchase tickets in convertible/pesos (CUC$) at the special **Ladis ticket office** (⊙7:30am-3pm). The ticket office is marked 'U/B Ferrocuba Provincial Holguín' on the corner of Manduley, opposite the train station.

You will have to change trains at the Santiago–Havana mainline junction in Cacocum, 17km south of Holguín. Theoretically, there's one daily morning train to Las Tunas (CUC$3, two hours), an 8am train every three days to Guantánamo, three daily trains to Santiago de Cuba (CUC$5, 3½ hours), and two daily trains (10:19pm and 5:28am) to Havana (CUC$26, 15 hours). This train stops in Camagüey (CUC$6.50), Ciego de Ávila (CUC$10.50), Santa Clara (CUC$15.50) and Matanzas (CUC$22.50).

The only service that operates with any regularity is the train to Havana. The service to Santiago de Cuba is rather irregular. Research beforehand.

TRUCK

The **Terminal Dagoberto Sanfield Guillén** (Av de los Libertadores), opposite Estadio General Calixto García, has at least two daily trucks to Banes and Moa.

❶ Getting Around

TO/FROM THE AIRPORT

The public bus to the airport leaves daily around 2pm from the **airport bus stop** (General Rodríguez No 84) on Parque Martí near the train station. A tourist taxi to the airport costs from CUC$15 to CUC$20. It's also possible to spend your last night in Bayamo, then catch a taxi (CUC$20 to CUC$25) to Holguín airport.

BICI-TAXI

Holguín's bici-taxis are ubiquitous. They charge MN$5 for a short trip, MN$10 for a long one.

CAR

You can rent or return a car at **Cubacar**, with branches at **Hotel Pernik** (Av Jorge Dimitrov), **Aeropuerto Frank País** (☑46-84-14) and **Cafetería Cristal** (cnr Manduley & Martí).

A **Servi-Cupet gas station** (Carretera Central; ⊙24hr) is 3km out of town toward Las Tunas; another station is just outside town on the road to Gibara. An **Oro Negro gas station** (Carretera Central) is on the southern edge of town. The road to Gibara is north on Av Cajigal; also take this road and fork left after 5km to reach Playa la Herradura.

TAXI

A **Cubataxi** (Map p352; Máximo Gómez No 302 cnr Martí) to Guardalavaca (54km) costs around CUC$35. To Gibara one way should cost no more than CUC$20.

Gibara

POP 36,000

Matched only by Baracoa for its wild coastal setting, Gibara is one of those special places where geography, meteorology and culture have conspired to create something tempestuous and unique. Though your first impression might not be open-mouthed incredulity (Hurricane Ike almost wiped the town off the map in 2008), suspend your judgment; Gibara casts a more subtle spell.

Situated 33km from Holguín via a scenic road that undulates through friendly, eye-catching villages, Gibara is a small, intimate place that is currently benefiting from much-needed government investment. Unlike nearby Guardalavaca, development here is low-key and focused on renovating the town's beautiful but dilapidated architecture. The saddle-shaped Silla de Gibara that so captivated Columbus creates a wild, scenic backdrop. Nearby is the site of one of Cuba's first wind farms.

Each year in April Gibara hosts the Festival Internacional de Cine Pobre (p359), which draws films and filmmakers from all over the world.

History

Columbus first arrived in the area in 1492 and called it Río de Mares (River of Seas) for the Ríos Cacoyugüín and Yabazón that drain into the Bahía de Gibara. The current name comes from *jiba*, the indigenous word for a bush that still grows along the shore.

Refounded in 1817, Gibara prospered in the 19th century as the sugar industry expanded and the trade rolled in. To protect the settlement from pirates, barracks and a 2km wall were constructed around the town in the early 1800s, making Gibara Cuba's second walled city (after Havana). The once sparkling-white facades earned Gibara its nickname, La Villa Blanca.

Holguín's outlet to the sea was once an important sugar-export town that was linked to the provincial capital via a railway. With the construction of the Carretera Central in the 1920s, Gibara lost its mercantile importance and, after the last train service was axed in 1958, the town fell into a sleepy slumber from which it has yet to fully awaken.

◉ Sights & Activities

Gibara is undergoing a small renaissance with government investment aimed at restoring and renovating the city's architecture. Though the specific sights are few, rather like Baracoa, this is more a town to stroll the streets and absorb the local flavor.

Parque Calixto García   SQUARE
The centerpiece of this park lined with weird *robles africanos* – African oaks with large penis-shaped pods – is **Iglesia de San Fulgencio** (◷ 8am-noon & 2-4:30pm Tue-Sun), built in 1850 but recently the recipient of a gleaming renovation. The *Statue of Liberty* in front commemorates the Spanish-Cuban-American War. On the western side of the square, in a beautiful colonial palace (more interesting than the stuffed stuff it collects), is the **Museo de Historia Natural** (Luz Caballero No 23; admission CUC$1; ◷ 8am-noon & 1-5pm Tue-Sat, 1-4pm Mon). Through barred windows you can watch women rolling cheroots in the **cigar factory** across the square.

Caverna de Panaderos   CAVE
(excursion CUC$5) This complex cave system with 19 galleries and a lengthy underground trail is close to town at the top end of Calle Independencia. There are no official tourist facilities, so it's best to hire a local guide. **Alexis Silva García** (☎ 84-44-58) can be contacted by phone or by asking at the Museo de Historia Natural. The walk to the cave is 1km and there is a lake inside for swimming. Reserve two hours for the excursion.

Forts
At the top of Calle Cabada is **El Cuartelón**, a crumbling brick Spanish fort with graceful arches that provides stunning town and bay views. Continue on this street for 200m to Restaurante el Mirador (p359) for an even better vantage point. You'll see remnants of the old fortresses here and at the **Fuerte Fernando VII**, on the point beyond Parque de las Madres, a block over from Parque Calixto García. There's also a sentinel tower at the entrance to the town, coming in from Holguín.

Beaches
There are a couple of decent beaches within striking distance of Gibara.

Playa los Bajos   BEACH

(Map p361) Los Bajos, to the east of Gibara, is accessible by a local *lancha* (ferry; CUC$1 each way) that leaves at least twice daily from the fishing pier on La Enramada, the waterfront road leading out of town. These boats cross the Bahía de Gibara to Playa los Bajos, from where it's 3km east to Playa Blanca. Both beaches are sandy, with swimming.

Should the ferry be out of action, Los Bajos is a rough 30km drive via Floro Pérez and Fray Benito.

Playa Caletones   BEACH

You'll need some sort of transport (bike, taxi, rental car) to get to this lovely little beach, 17km west of Gibara. The apostrophe-shaped stretch of white sand and azure sea here is a favorite of Holguín vacationers. The town is ramshackle, with no services except rustic **Restaurante La Esparanza** (mains CUC$4-6) on the beachfront road, serving up some of Cuba's most delectable fresh seafood on an upstairs terrace overlooking the water.

Ask here about freshwater *pozas* (pools) where you can go swimming. DIY divers can part with CUC$10 to be guided to some caves 5km further along, which purportedly contain some of Cuba's best cave diving. You'll need your own equipment. The cave system goes back some 3000m, with water depth about 15m.

Climbing

Viñales might be Cuba's climbing capital, but word is spreading about the smaller, no-less attractive routes on the **Silla de Gibara**, the saddle-shaped limestone crag 35km southeast of Gibara. The Silla has around 20 'mapped' climbing routes on its shadowy north face, best tackled in the cooler months between November and February. With little government support, climbing here is similar to Viñales. Bring your own gear and use a guide. Alexis Silva García (p357) should be able to sort you out with information and guide services. Find him at the Museo de Historia Natural.

🛏 Sleeping

Gibara has some of the province's best options for bedding down. A new colonial hotel, the Arsenita, should be open by the time you read this.

★ Hostal los Hermanos   CASA PARTICULAR $

(☑84-45-42; Céspedes No 13, btwn Luz Caballero & J Peralta; r CUC$20-25; ❄) Bedizened with co-lonial splendor, here you can relax in one of four big bedrooms with hand-painted murals, decorative cherubs and trompe l'oeil. Signature Gibara stained glass and delicious meals add further flourishes. The house also doubles up as a private restaurant for nonguests.

Hostal Sol y Mar   CASA PARTICULAR $

(☑52-40-21-64; J Peralta No 59; CUC$20-25; ❄) In a blue-and-yellow house right on the waterfront, this house is filled with wonderful sea breezes and romantic views – especially if you take advantage of the ample roof terrace. At the time of writing there were two rooms with a third being built, and the young host, who can speak French, English, Dutch and German, will make your stay a pleasant one. There's a self-catering kitchen.

Villa Caney   CASA PARTICULAR $

(☑84-45-52; Sartorio No 36, btwn J Peralta & Luz Caballero; r CUC$20-25; ❄) There's more stunning Gibara beauty in Villa Caney, captured in a sturdy stone colonial house that withstood the category-4 force of Hurricane Ike. Two rooms off an impressive courtyard are large and have private baths.

Hostal El Patio   CASA PARTICULAR $

(☑84-42-69; J Mora No 19, btwn Cuba & J Agüe-ro; CUC$20-25; ❄) Tucked away behind this high-walled patio are Gibara's cosiest digs: a lovely part-covered patio leading to two rooms (the back one is best). Mealtimes are magical in this little getaway and the coffee, pretty much all the time, is great.

★ Hotel Ordoño   HOTEL $$

(☑84-44-48; J Peralta, cnr Donato Mármol & Independencia; s/d/ste CUC$65/82/112; ❄ @) Cuba has some plush five-star resorts on its north coast, but it's debatable if any of them can match the majestic colonial beauty of the Ordoño. Opened in 2013, the attention to architectural detail in this renovated 27-room palace is almost Michelangelo worthy – and all achieved by young *local* architects.

Throw in exemplary service and an ethereal Gibara setting and you'll feel like Louis XIV kicking back in Versailles (without the guilty conscience). Best hotel in Cuba? Definitely a contender.

🍴 Eating

Slowly, at the speed of a Cadillac on a potholed track, things are modernizing. Some enterprising casas particulares operate as private restaurants. Both Villa Caney and Hostal Los Hermanos are excellent.

> ### POOR MAN'S FILM FESTIVAL
>
> There's no red carpet, no paparazzi and no Brangelina, but what the **Festival Internacional de Cine Pobre** (International Low-Budget Film Festival; www.cinepobre.com) lacks in glitz it makes up for in raw, undiscovered talent. Then there's the setting – ethereal Gibara, Cuba's crumbling Villa Blanca, a perfect antidote to the opulence of Hollywood and Cannes.
>
> Inaugurated in 2003, the Cine Pobre was the brainchild of late Cuban director Humberto Solás, who fell in love with this quintessential fishing town after shooting his seminal movie *Lucía* here in 1968.
>
> Open to independent filmmakers of limited means, the festival takes place in April and, despite limited advertising, attracts up to US$100,000 in prize money. Lasting for seven days, proceedings kick off with a gala in the Cine Jiba followed by film showings, art expositions and nightly music concerts. The competition is friendly but hotly contested, with prizes used to reward and recognize an eclectic cache of digital-movie guerrillas drawn from countries as varied as Iran and the US.

La Cueva PARRILLA **$**
(Calle 2da, cnr Carretera a Playa Caletones; dishes CUC$4; ⊙noon-midnight) Finally, Gibara's eating scene starts to get imaginative with this private place which grows its own herbs to garnish those grills and even has a small farm. There's a *ranchón*-style part and a more formal restaurant area above. It's at the northern end of town.

Restaurante el Mirador FAST FOOD **$**
(snacks CUC$1-2; ⊙24hr) Perched high above town near El Cuartelón, this place has a view to die for but not much in the way of good food.

La Casa de Los Amigos SEAFOOD **$$**
(✆84-41-15; Céspedes No 15 btwn J Peralta & Luz Caballero; meals CUC$5-10) Both casa and private restaurant, this place has one of the most amazing interior patios in Cuba, with frescoes, a gazebo and hand-painted Gibara doors. It rents rooms, but we're recommending it for its fantastic food – a profusion of local fish dishes with ample trimmings.

🍸 Drinking & Entertainment

As in most Cuban seaside towns, the local 'yoof' hang around in the vicinity of the Malecón on weekend evenings. Spontaneous outbreaks of music are likely at any time in and around Parque Calixto García and Parque Colón.

Bar La Loge BAR
Another quiver in Gibara's freshly renovated bow, this mainly outdoor bar next to the Casa de la Cultura hosts live music on Friday and Sunday nights, but is always a good place to hang with the locals.

Siglo XX CULTURAL CENTER
(⊙8am-5pm Mon-Tue, to 11pm Wed-Sun) A fine new cultural center in the main square that hosts live traditional music on a Saturday night and provides the taped stuff at other times. The courtyard is a good place to chill with an icy *refresco* on a hot afternoon.

Cine Jiba CINEMA
(Parque Calixto García) Cuba's improbable poor man's film festival hosts most of its cutting-edge movies (some in English) in this small but quirky cinema covered with distinctive art-house movie posters. If you're going to go to the cinema anywhere in Cuba, it should be in Gibara – it's a local rite of passage.

Centro Cultural Batería Fernando VII CULTURAL CENTER
(Plaza del Fuerte) The diminutive Spanish fort hovering above the choppy ocean is today an atmospheric cultural center run by ARTex that puts on weekend shows and serves food and drink from a sinuous bar-restaurant.

ℹ️ Information

Most services line Calle Independencia.

Bandec (cnr Independencia & J Peralta; ⊙9am-3pm Mon-Fri) Also changes traveler's checks.

Post Office (Independencia No 15; ⊙8am-8pm Mon-Sat)

ℹ️ Getting There & Away

Annoyingly, there are no Víazul buses to Gibara. Travelers can tackle the route with Cuban transport on a truck or shared *colectivo* taxi (CUC$4) from Holguín. The bus station is 1km out on the road to Holguín. There are two daily buses in each direction. A regular taxi (to Holguín) should cost CUC$20.

For drivers heading toward Guardalavaca, the link road from the junction at Floro Pérez is hell at first, but improves just outside Rafael Freyre. There's an Oro Negro gas station at the entrance to town.

Guardalavaca & Around

Guardalavaca is a string of megaresorts draped along a succession of idyllic beaches 54km northeast of Holguín. But glimmering in the background, the landscape of rough green fields and haystack-shaped hills reminds you that rural Cuba is never far away.

In the days before towel-covered sunloungers and poolside bingo, Columbus described this stretch of coast as the most beautiful place he had ever laid eyes on. Few modern-day visitors would disagree. Love it or hate it, Guardalavaca's enduring popularity has its raison d'être: enviable tropical beaches, verdant green hills and sheltered turquoise coral reefs that teem with aquatic action. More spread out than Varadero and less isolated than Cayo Coco, Guardalavaca, for many discerning travelers, gets the R & R balance just right – relaxation and realism.

In the early 20th century this region was an important cattle-rearing area and the site of a small rural village (Guardalavaca means, quite literally, 'guard the cow'). The tourism boom moved into first gear in the late 1970s when local *holguiñero* Fidel Castro inaugurated Guardalavaca's first resort – the sprawling Atlántico – by going for a quick dip in the hotel pool. The local economy hasn't looked back since.

The resort area is split into three separate enclaves: **Playa Pesquero**, **Playa Esmeralda** and, 4km to the east, **Guardalavaca** proper, the original hotel strip that is already starting to peel around the edges. Of the three, Playa Pesquero (Fisher's Beach) is the most high end. There are four tourist colossi here, and the strip has a luxury Caribbean sheen missing elsewhere on the island. Not surprisingly, the adjacent beach is sublime, with golden sand, shallow, warm water and great opportunities for snorkeling.

The four resorts of Playa Pesquero are accessible from the main Holguín–Guardalavaca road via a spur road 12km west of Guardalavaca proper. Playa Esmeralda and its two resorts lie at the end of a short spur road 4km west of Guardalavaca.

Guardalavaca has long allowed beach access to Cubans, meaning it is less snooty and flecked with a dash of local color.

◎ Sights

Museo Chorro de Maita   MUSEUM
(Map p361; admission CUC$2; ☺9am-5pm Tue-Sat, 9am-1pm Sun) ✐ This archaeological-site-based museum protects the remains of an excavated Indian village and cemetery, including the well-preserved remains of 62 human skeletons and the bones of a barkless dog. The village dates from the early 16th century and is one of nearly 100 archaeological sites in the area. New evidence suggests indigenous peoples were living here many decades after Columbus' arrival.

Across from the museum is a reconstructed Aldea Taína (p368) that features life-sized models of native dwellings in a replicated indigenous village. Shows of native dance rituals are staged here and there's also a restaurant.

Parque Nacional Monumento
Bariay   HISTORIC SITE
(Map p361; admission CUC$8; ☺9am-5pm) Ten kilometers west of Playa Pesquero and 3km west of Villa Don Lino is **Playa Blanca**; Columbus is thought to have landed somewhere near here in 1492, and this great meeting of two cultures is commemorated in a varied mix of sights, the centerpiece of which is an impressive Hellenic-style monument designed by Holguín artist Caridad Ramos for the 500th anniversary of the landing in 1992.

Other points of interest include an **information center**, the remains of a 19th-century **Spanish fort**, three reconstructed **Taíno huts** and an **archaeological museum**. It makes a pleasant afternoon's sojourn.

⚲ Activities

You can arrange **horseback riding** at the Rancho Naranjo in Playa Esmeralda or privately. Try the Paladar Compay Carlos next to Villa Bely. CUC$10 per hour is the going rate.

You can rent **mopeds** at all the hotels for up to CUC$25 per day. Some all-inclusive resorts include bicycle use, but the bikes are fairly basic (no gears). The road between Guardalavaca and Playa Esmeralda, and on to Playa Pesquero, is flat and quiet and makes an excellent day excursion. For a bit more sweat you can make it to Banes and back (66km round-trip).

Guardalavaca Area

Boat Trips

Many water-based excursions leave from the **Marina Gaviota Puerto de Vita** (Map p361; ☑ 43-04-45) and can be booked through the hotels. There's another newer, but smaller marina at **Boca de Samá** (Map p361) 9km east of Guardalavaca, run by Cubanacán. Aside from the ubiquitous sunset cruise possibilities (CUC$52), you can organize deepsea fishing (CUC$300 for up to six people), and occasional catamaran trips across Bahía de Vita with snorkeling and open bar.

Parque Natural Bahía de Naranjo

NATURE RESERVE

(Map p362; ☑ 43-00-06; excursions from CUC$50) The Parque Natural Bahía de Naranjo, 4km southwest of Playa Esmeralda and about 8km from the main Guardalavaca strip, is an island complex designed to keep the resort crowds entertained. An **aquarium** (☉ 9am-9pm; 🛪) is on a tiny island in the bay and your entry fee includes a zippy boat tour of the islands included in the complex.

There are various packages starting at around CUC$50, depending on what you want to do – yacht trips, seafaris etc – so check around before you embark. Boats to the aquarium leave from the Marina Bahía de Naranjo.

Diving

Guardalavaca has some excellent diving (better than Varadero and up there with Cayo Coco). The reef is 200m out and there are 32 dive sites, most of which are accessed by boat. Highlights include caves, wrecks, walls and La Corona, a giant coral formation said to resemble a crown.

Guardalavaca Area

◉ Sights
1 Aldea Taína	D1
2 Museo Chorro de Maita	D1
3 Parque Nacional Monumento Bariay	B1
4 Playa los Bajos	B1

◉ Activities, Courses & Tours
5 Bioparque Rocazul	C1

◉ Sleeping
6 Campismo Silla de Gibara	B2
7 Hotel Playa Costa Verde	C1
8 Hotel Playa Pesquero	C1
9 Memories Holguín	C1
10 Villa Don Lino	B1

Eagle Ray Marlin Dive Center

DIVING

(Cubanacán Náutica; Map p362; ☑ 43-01-85; dives from CUC$45) Guardalavaca beach's one dive center abuts the sand about 300m west of the Club Amigo Atlántico-Guardalavaca. There are open-water certification courses for CUC$365 and two-hour Discover courses for CUC$70. Immersions start at CUC$45, with discounts for multiple dives.

Hiking

★ **Bioparque Rocazul** NATURE RESERVE
(Map p361; ☉ 9am-5:30pm) Located just off the link road that joins Playa Turquesa with the other Pesquero resorts, this protected bio-park (part of the Parque Natural Cristóbal Colón) offers the usual hand-holding array of outdoor activities under the supervision of a nonnegotiable government guide. It's a commendable environmental

Guardalavaca

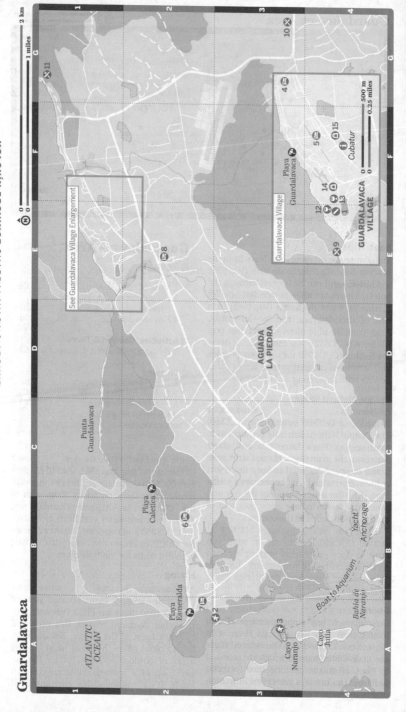

Guardalavaca

Activities, Courses & Tours
1 Eagle Ray Marlin Dive Center...............E4
2 Las Guanas Eco-Archaeological
   Trail...A3
3 Parque Natural Bahía de Naranjo.......A3

Sleeping
4 Brisas Guardalavaca G3
5 Club Amigo Atlántico –
   Guardalavaca F4
6 Paradisus Río de Oro...........................B2
7 Sol Río Luna Mares Resort A2
8 Villa Bely..E2

Eating
9 El Ancla...E4
10 El Uvero...G3
11 Restaurante Lagomar.........................G1

Drinking & Nightlife
12 Bar Pirata...E4
13 La Rueda...F4

Shopping
14 Boulevard...F4
15 Centro Comercial Los
   Flamboyanes......................................F4

effort in a major resort area, but the limitations on your right to roam can be a little stifling (and costly).

Leisurely walking excursions go for CUC$8/10/12 for one/two/three hours. You can go horseback riding for CUC$16 an hour or fishing for CUC$29. All-inclusive packages cost CUC$40. The park is extensive with hills, trails, ocean access and the **Casa de Compay Kike**, a working farm where you can sample Cuban food and coffee. There's a friendly bar at the entrance to the park where you weigh can up the financial pros and cons.

Las Guanas Eco-Archaeological Trail   NATURE RESERVE
(Map p362; admission CUC$3; ☺8am-4:30pm) At the end of the Playa Esmeralda road is this self-guided hike, which at CUC$3 for 1km, is quite possibly Cuba's (and one of the world's) most expensive trails. Walk slowly to get your money's worth! The marked route (with several more kilometers of bushwhacking on fire trails leading to a picturesque bluff with a lighthouse) apparently boasts 14 endemic plant species. Inauthentic sculptures of indigenous Taínos guard the route.

The bluff was originally touted for hotel development, but was saved from the bulldozers by government intervention.

Kiteboarding

Luís Riveron   WATER SPORTS
(☑53-78-48-57; luiskitesurf@nauta.cu) Cuba's newest sport has sprouted a private Guardalavaca operator who offers lessons for CUC$25 an hour, or board rental for CUC$7 per hour. His perch is on the beach next to Bar Pirata.

☞ Tours

The Cubanacán travel desk in the lobby of the Club Amigo Atlántico – Guardalavaca (p363) offers an interesting 'beer tour' of Holguín city, leaving at 6:30pm every Sunday (CUC$20).

🛏 Sleeping

Guardalavaca now offers private rooms, so you are not obliged to shell out for the all-inclusives if you don't want to. There are dozens of apartments to rent in Guardalavaca village opposite the entrance to the all-inclusive zone. A new five-star hotel – the Albatros – is in the process of being built.

🛏 Guardalavaca

★**Villa Bely**   CASA PARTICULAR $
(Map p362; ☑52-61-41-92; www.villabely.org-free.com; CUC$25-30; ▣✳) A resort-hater's dream. The top-floor apartment at this rose pink house is bigger and better than your average hotel room, coming with a kitchen-diner and a lovely sleeping area raised on a dais. There's a second room below. It's just opposite the last highway exit from the all-inclusive zone.

Brisas Guardalavaca   RESORT $$$
(Map p362; ☑43-02-18; all-incl s/d CUC$154/228; ▣✳@☏♦) This uber-resort made up of the Villa las Brisas and Hotel las Brisas at the eastern end of the beach is a package-tour paradise that stirs memories of 1970s British holiday camps. Bonuses are the huge comfortable rooms, floodlit tennis courts and general lack of pretension. The kitsch is never far from the surface, but it's quieter and more upmarket than Club Amigo's offerings.

Club Amigo Atlántico – Guardalavaca   RESORT $$$
(Map p362; ☑43-01-21; all-incl s/d CUC$81/122; ▣✳@☏♦) This hard-to-fathom resort is a fusion of the former Guardalavaca and Atlántico hotels, the latter of which is the resort's oldest, completed in 1976 and christened by Fidel Castro with a swim in the

pool. The architecture in this small 'village' (there are an astounding 600 rooms here) is a bog-standard mishmash of villas, bungalows and standard rooms.

It's ever-popular with families for its extensive kids activities program. The hotel has two locations. The rooms associated with the former Hotel Guardalavaca are further from the beach but also less noisy.

Playa Pesquero

Campismo Silla de Gibara CABIN $

(Map p361; ☑ 42-15-86; s/d CUC$14/22; P ≋) This rustic campismo (camping installation) sits on sloping ground beneath Gibara's signature saddle-shaped hill. Reached via a rough road between Floro Pérez and Rafael Freyre, it's 35km southeast of Gibara itself and 1.5km off the main road. There are 42 rooms sleeping two, four or six people, but come for the views, not the comfort.

There's also a cave you can hike to, 1.5km up the hill, and horses for rent. It's best to make reservations with Cubamar (p501) in Havana rather than just turn up.

Villa Don Lino CABIN $$

(Map p361; ☑ 43-03-08; s/d from CUC$49/78; P ✽ ≋) The cheap alternative to Playa Pesquero's 'big four', Don Lino's 36 single-story cabañas are planted right on its own diminutive white beach, and make for a romantic retreat. There's a small pool, nighttime entertainment and an element of Cuban-ness missing in the bigger resorts. It's 8.5km north of Rafael Freyre along a spur road.

★ Hotel Playa Pesquero RESORT $$$

(Map p361; ☑ 43-35-30; all-incl s/d CUC$175/280; P ✽ @ ⟨ ≋ ⛵) Once Cuba's biggest hotel, Playa Pesquero had its mantle stolen in recent years, but who cares? With 933 rooms, the Pesquero is no slouch and no ugly duckling either. Beautifully landscaped grounds over 30 hectares include Italianate fountains, fancy shops, seven restaurants, spa, floodlit tennis courts, and acres of swimming-pool space.

And then there's the beach...in a word, beautiful. Opened in 2003 by Fidel Castro, the loquacious leader's speech is reprinted on a wall in the reception area. Fortunately, it was one of his shorter efforts.

Memories Holguín RESORT $$$

(Map p361; ☑ 43-35-40; all-incl s/d CUC$150/200; P ✽ @ ≋) Slightly apart from the other resorts on its own clean scoop of beach (known as Playa Yuraguanal), the recently rebranded

Memories writes the word 'privacy' into its four stars. Otherwise you're looking at all the usual high-end, all-inclusive givens – meaning most guests are happy to never leave the complex.

Hotel Playa Costa Verde RESORT $$$

(Map p361; ☑ 43-35-20; all-incl s/d CUC$130/210; P ✽ @ ≋ ⛵) Stuck somewhere between elegance and simplicity, the Costa Verde feels a bit faux – not that top-notch facilities are lacking. There's a Japanese restaurant, a gym, colorful gardens and a lagoon you cross to get to the beach. Good diving trips are run out of the confusingly named Blau Costa Verde next door.

Playa Esmeralda

Two megaresorts line this superior stretch of beach, 6km to the west of Guardalavaca and accessed by a spur just east of the Cayo Naranjo boat launch. Esmeralda occupies the middle ground between Guardalavaca's economy and Playa Pesquero's opulence.

★ Paradisus Río de Oro RESORT $$$

(Map p362; ☑ 43-00-90; all-incl s/d CUC$455/510; P ✽ @ ⟨ ≋) ⚓ Elegant and environmentally conscious (a tough combination), this 292-room place has five-star resort written all over it, and is often touted as the best resort in Cuba. There's massage available in a cliffside hut, a Japanese restaurant floating on a koi pond, and garden villas with private pools. Paradise is the word. It's adults only.

Sol Río Luna Mares Resort RESORT $$$

(Map p362; ☑ 43-00-30; all-incl s/d CUC$182/280; P ✽ @ ⟨ ≋ ⛵) This two-in-one hotel is an amalgamation of the former Sol Club Río de Luna and the Meliá Río de Mares. Rooms are large and come with a few extras (such as coffee machines), but the main advantages for luxury seekers over Guardalavaca are the superior food (French and Italian restaurants) and the truly sublime beach (beach toys are included in the price).

✕ Eating

There are a handful of options outside of the all-inclusive resorts, mainly in Guardalavaca itself.

Restaurante Lagomar PALADAR $

(Map p362; meals CUC$3-5; ☺ noon-midnight) You can get some esoteric magic in Guardalavaca if you walk for 10 minutes along the coast beyond Las Brisas hotel to the tiny village of El Cayuelo. The last house still standing is Lagomar which serves up classic Cuban dishes in its atmospheric little restaurant. Only the odd all-inclusive-guest-in-the-know stops by, but El Cayuelo is earmarked for more hotel development: enjoy it while you can.

El Uvero
CUBAN $$

(Map p362; ☎52-39-35-71; Carretera Guardalavaca-Banes; meals $10-18; ☻noon-11pm) Four kilometers and a short taxi ride east of Guardalavaca's main resort strip, this modest-looking local house in the village of Cuatro Caminos is well worth the small effort to get here. Pride of the menu is the *tres hermanos* (three brothers) consisting of prawns, lobster and white fish. The place is guarded by an *Uvero* (sea grape tree), as the name implies.

El Ancla
SEAFOOD $$$

(Map p362; meals CUC$12-25; ☻noon-9:30pm) Somehow El Ancla, situated on a rocky promontory of land at the far western end of Guardalavaca beach, didn't get blown away by Hurricane Ike in 2008. Come here for excellent lobster in front of magnificent sea views.

Drinking & Entertainment

Bar Pirata
BAR

(Map p362; ☻9am-9pm) At the epicenter of Guardalavaca's liveliest strip of beach (accessed via the flea market just west of Club Amigo Atlántico), Pirata is a bog-standard beach shack with beer, music and enough ingredients to muster up a sand-free sandwich lunch.

La Rueda
BAR

(Map p362; ☻7am-11pm) An alfresco bar in the Boulevard flea market that provides a welcome haven from the resorts. Small snacks and ice cream are also available.

Shopping

Boulevard
SOUVENIRS

(Map p362) This touristy handicraft market caters to resort clients from the surrounding area. It sells crafts, postcards, cheap clothing and Che Guevara – there's nothing much outside the knickknack box.

Centro Comerical los Flamboyanes
SHOPPING CENTER

Guardalavaca's small, slightly grotty shopping mall has a limited cache of stores, including a handy Casa del Habano which has all the smoke you need and then some.

ℹ Information

Euros are accepted in all the Guardalavaca, Playa Esmeralda and Playa Pesquero resorts. Additionally, all the big hotels have money-changing facilities. The Clinica Internacional is a 24-hour pharmacy but the major hotels here all have drugstores.

Banco Financiero Internacional (Centro Comercial los Flamboyanes; ☻9am-3pm Mon-Fri) In the shopping complex just west of Club Amigo Atlántico – Guardalavaca.

Canadian Consulate (☎43-03-20; Club Amigo Atlántico – Guardalavaca, ste 1; ☻9am-1pm Mon-Fri)

Cubatur (Map p362; ☻24hrs) Travel agent just behind the Centro Comercial los Flamboyanes.

ℹ Getting There & Away

Transtur runs a tourist bus from Guardalavaca to Holguín via Playa Esmeralda and Playa Pesquero once a day leaving from outside Brisas at 8:45am, Sol Rio Luna Mares Resort at 9am and Playa Pesquero at 9:30am. It arrives at Holguín's Parque Calixto García at 10pm. A return bus leaves Holguín at 1pm. Cost is CUC$15 return.

A taxi from Guardalavaca to Holguín will cost a heftier CUC$35 one way for the car. For radio taxis, call **Cubataxi** (☎43-01-39) or **Transgaviota** (☎43-49-66). *Colectivos* run from Guardalavaca village to Holguín for CUC$5.

Marina Gaviota Puerto de Vita (p361) is an international entry port for yachts and boats and has 38 berths. There's a hardware store, restaurant, electricity and customs authorities on-site.

ℹ Getting Around

A hop-on/hop-off double-decker bus in Guardalavaca links the three beach areas and the Aldea Taína. The red-and-blue bus is operated by Transtur. Theoretically it runs three times a day in either direction, but check at your hotel to see if there are any glitches. Drop-offs include Parque Rocazul, Playa Pesquero, Playa Costa Verde, Playa Esmeralda hotels, Club Amigo Atlántico – Guardalavaca and the Aldea Taína. Tickets cost CUC$5 for an all-day pass.

Coches de caballo (horse carriages) run between Playas Esmeralda and Guardalavaca, or you can rent a moped (CUC$25 per day) or bicycle (free if you're staying at an all-inclusive) at any of the resort hotels.

For car rental, try **Cubacar** (Club Amigo Atlántico – Guardalavaca). A **Servi-Cupet gas station** (☻24hr) is situated between Guardalavaca and Playa Esmeralda.

Banes

POP 44,500

The former sugar town of Banes, just north of the Bahía de Banes, is the site of one of Cuba's biggest oxymorons. Cuban president Fulgencio Batista was born here in 1901. Then, 47 years later, in the local clapboard church of Nuestra Señora de la Caridad, another fiery leader-in-waiting, Fidel Castro, tied the knot with the blushing Birta Díaz Balart. A generous Batista gave them a US$500 gift for their honeymoon. Ah, how history could have been so different.

Founded in 1887, this effervescent company town was a virtual fiefdom of the US-run United Fruit Company until the 1950s, and many of the old American company houses still remain. These days in the sun-streaked streets and squares you're more likely to encounter cigar-smoking cronies slamming dominoes and moms carrying meter-long loaves of bread; in short, everything Cuban that is missing from the all-inclusive resorts.

Thanks its Taíno museum and the various indigenous sites that nestle in the surrounding countryside, Banes is known as the archaeological capital of Cuba.

◎ Sights

If you're coming from the resorts, Banes' biggest attraction may be enjoying the street life provided by a stroll through town. Don't miss the fine old company houses that once provided homes for the fat cats of United Fruit. If you're fit and adventurous, getting here from Guardalavaca by bicycle is a rare treat through undulating bucolic terrain.

★ Museo Indocubano Bani   MUSEUM

(General Marrero No 305; admission CUC$1; ⊙9am-5pm Tue-Sat, 8am-noon Sun) This museum's small but rich collection of indigenous artifacts is one of the best on the island. Don't miss the tiny golden fertility idol unearthed near Banes (one of only 20 gold artifacts ever found in Cuba). Excellent guides will enthusiastically show you round. La Plaza Aborigen outside has replicas of local cave paintings.

The museum's resident expert, Luis Quiñones García (☑80-26-91; votico@gmail.com), will fill you in on every facet of indigenous culture and local archaeology. He also offers tours of the town.

Iglesia de Nuestra Señora de la Caridad   CHURCH

On October 12, 1948, Fidel Castro and Birta Díaz Balart were married in this unusual art deco church on Parque Martí in the center of Banes. After their divorce in 1954, Birta remarried and moved to Spain. Through their only child, Fidelito, Fidel has several grandchildren.

Steam Locomotive 964   TRAIN

(Calle Tráfico, El Panchito) Railway enthusiasts shouldn't miss this old steamer built at the HK Porter Locomotive Works in Pittsburgh, Pennsylvania, in 1888, now on display 400m east of the bus station.

Playa de Morales   BEACH

One day in the not-too-distant future (after its been Cancun-ized), we'll all wax nostalgic about this precious strip of sand situated 13km east of Banes along the paved continuation of Tráfico. For the time being enjoy this fishing village while you can, whiling away an afternoon dining with locals and watching the men mend their nets. A seafood restaurant, El Banquete (Playa Morales; mains CUC$2-4; ⊙24hr), sits on poles above the water. A few kilometers to the north is the even quieter Playa Puerto Rico.

🛏 Sleeping

There are no hotels in the town proper, but Banes has some superfriendly private renters.

Villa Lao   CASA PARTICULAR $

(☑80-30-49; Bayamo No 78, btwn José M Heredia & Augusto Blanco; CUC$20-25; ✳) Shimmering clean, professionally run house with two rooms; grab the upstairs one with its kitchen and plant-laden terrace if possible. It's got the front-porch rocker thing going on too, overlooking the central park.

Casa 'Las Delicias'   CASA PARTICULAR $

(☑80-29-05; Augusto Blanca No 1107, btwn Bruno Merino & Bayamo; r CUC$20-25; ✳) One spick-and-span room, a private entrance, friendly owners and decent food in the downstairs private restaurant; what more could you ask from tranquil Banes?

Villa Gilma   CASA PARTICULAR $

(☑80-22-04; Calle H No 15266, btwn Veguitas & Francisco Franco; r CUC$20-25; ✳) This classic colonial abode stands guard at the entrance to the town center and has one huge room (those ceilings must be 7m high) with private bath and fridge.

✗ Eating

DIYers can find groceries in a couple of supermarkets, La Epoca and Isla de Cuba, on the main nexus of General Marrero.

Restaurante Don Carlos   CUBAN $
(☑ 80-21-76; Veguitas No 1702 cnr Calle H; meals CUC$2.50-5; ☺ noon-10pm) Salt-of-the-earth, meet-the-locals private restaurant where you can discover the other side of Cuba over some pretty decent seafood. Not 30 minutes from Guardalavaca's gigantic resorts.

Restaurant el Latino   CARIBBEAN $
(General Marrero No 710; meals around CUC$5; ☺ 11am-11pm) A long-standing Banes favorite, this state-run place has all the usual Creole dishes delivered with a little extra flair and charm. Service is good, and the accompanying musicians unusually talented and discreet.

Casa del Chef   CUBAN $
(☑ 80-44-49; General Marrero No 721; meals CUC$1.50-3; ☺ noon-11pm) This Cuban chain acts as a training ground for young chefs hoping to gravitate to the resort kitchens but isn't as bad as it sounds. It's also great value for money in Banes, with most dishes going for $35 Cuban pesos (CUC$1.60). Prawns are the specialty.

☆ Entertainment

Cafe Cantante   LIVE MUSIC
(General Marrero No 320) This gregarious, music-filled patio is the top spot in Banes, with honking municipal-band rehearsals, discos, *son* (Cuba's popular music) septets and zen-inducing jazz jams. It's colloquially known as the Casa de la Trova.

Casa de Cultura   CULTURAL CENTER
(General Marrero No 320) This venue, housed in the former Casino Español (1926), has a regular Sunday *trova* (traditional poetic song) matinee at 3pm and Saturday *peña del rap* (rap-music session) at 9pm.

ⓘ Information

Banes is one of those towns with no street signs and locals who don't know street names, so prepare to get lost.

ⓘ Getting There & Away

From the **bus station** (cnr Tráfico & Los Ángeles), there are two daily buses to Holguín (72km). There are no timetables; check the chalkboards. Trucks leave Banes for Holguín more frequently. A taxi from Guardalavaca (33km) will cost around CUC$20 one way, or you can tackle it with a moped (easy) or bicycle (not so easy) in a fantastic DIY day trip.

Birán

Fidel Castro Ruz was born on August 13, 1926, at the **Finca las Manacas** (aka Casa de Fidel) near the village of Birán, south of Cueto. The farm, which was bought by Fidel's father Ángel in 1915, is huge, and includes its own workers village (a cluster of small thatched huts for the mainly Haitian laborers), a cockfighting ring, a post office, a store and a telegraph. The several large yellow wooden houses that can be glimpsed through the cedar trees are where the Castro family lived.

◉ Sights

★ Museo Conjunto Histórico de Birán   MUSEUM
(admission/camera/video CUC$10/20/40; ☺ 9am-3:30pm Tue-Sat, 9am-noon Sun) Finca las Manacas opened as a museum in 2002 under this unassuming name, supposedly to downplay any Castro 'personality cult.' This gaggle of attractive wooden buildings on an expanse of lush grounds constitutes a *pueblito* (small town) and makes a fascinating excursion. The complex includes Castro's schoolhouse, family home and everything from a post office to a butcher's. It appears as a backwater today, but once sat on the *camino real*, Cuba's main east–west road in colonial times.

Around the various houses, you can see more than a hundred photos, assorted clothes, Fidel's childhood bed and his father's 1918 Ford motorcar. Perhaps most interesting is the schoolhouse (Fidel sat in the middle of the front row, apparently), with pictures of young Fidel and Raúl, and Fidel's birth certificate, made out in the name of Fidel Casano Castro Ruz. A cemetery contains the grave of Fidel and Raúl's father, Ángel. The site illustrates, if nothing else, the extent of the inheritance that this hot-headed ex-lawyer gave up when he lived in the Sierra Maestra for two years, surviving on a diet of crushed crabs and raw horse meat.

Sierra del Cristal

Cuba's own 'Little Switzerland' is a rugged amalgam of the Sierra del Cristal and the Altiplanicie de Nipe that contains two

HOLGUÍN PROVINCE BIRÁN

CUBA'S ARCHAEOLOGICAL CAPITAL

The pre-Columbian history of Cuba can be traced back over 8000 years, yet it rarely receives more than a passing mention in contemporary history books. Those interested in padding out the details should come to Holguín province, where the region around Banes has the highest concentration of pre-Columbian archaeological sites in the country.

The bulk of archaeological remains unearthed so far in Cuba are from the Taíno era, dating from around 1050 to the early 1500s. The Taínos were the third wave of immigrants to reach the isles in the footsteps of the less sophisticated Guanahatabeys and Siboneys with whom they ultimately coexisted. Primarily peace-loving, they were skilful farmers, weavers, ceramicists and boatbuilders, and their complex society exhibited an organized system of participatory government that was overseen by a series of local *caciques* (chiefs). Sixty percent of the crops still grown in Cuba today were pioneered by Taíno farmers, who even planted cotton for use in hammocks, fishing nets and bags. Adults practiced a form of artificial cranial deformation by flattening the soft skulls of their young children, and groups lived together in villages characterized by their thatched *bohíos* (living huts) and *bateys* (communal 'plazas'). A reconstructed Taíno village can be seen at the **Aldea Taína** (Taíno village; Map p361; admission CUC$5; 🖵) near Guardalavaca. Next door in Chorro de Maita (p360), Cuba's most extensive archaeological site, some of the exhumed skeletons exhibit cranial deformation.

Columbus described the Taíno with terms such as 'gentle,' 'sweet,' 'always laughing' and 'without knowledge of what is evil,' which makes the genocide that he inadvertently unleashed even harder to comprehend. Estimates vary wildly as to how many indigenous people populated Cuba pre-Columbus, though 100,000 is a good consensus figure. Within 30 years 90% of the Taínos had been wiped out.

As Taíno villages were built of wood and mud they left no great towns or temples. Instead, the most important and emblematic artifacts unearthed are of *cemís* (idols), small figurines depicting Taíno deities. *Cemís* were cult objects that represented social status, political power or fertility. The *hacha del Holguín*, a 600-year-old god-like figure made of peridotite rock, is on display in Holguín's Museo de Historia Provincial (p345). The *ídolo del oro*, a rare 10-carat gold fertility symbol from the 13th century or earlier, is in Banes' Museo Indocubano Bani (p366). The oldest *cemí* found to date in Cuba was discovered near Maisí in Guantánamo province in the 1910s. Called the *ídolo de tabaco*, it dates from the 10th century and is made of Cuban hardwood. It is currently on display at the Museo Antropológico Montané (p87) in Havana University.

important national parks. Parque Nacional Sierra Cristal, Cuba's oldest, was founded in 1930 and harbors 1213m Pico de Cristal, the province's highest summit. Of more interest to travelers is the 5300-hectare Parque Nacional la Mensura, 30km south of Mayarí, which protects the island's highest waterfall, yields copious Caribbean pines and hosts a mountain research center run by the Academia de Ciencias de Cuba (Cuban Academy of Sciences). Notable for its cool alpine microclimate and 100 or more species of endemic plants, La Mensura offers hiking and horseback riding and accommodation in a Gaviota-run ecolodge.

There should be no forgetting, either, those lines to the song you've certainly heard more than any other in Cuba since your plane touched down: '*De alto cedro voy para Macarné, llego a Cueto, voy para*

Mayarí' – the opener, in other words, to the Buena Vista Social Club album's hit song 'Chan Chan.' The towns of Macarné, Cueto and Mayarí flank the Sierra del Cristal and the road between them is often dubbed **Ruta de Chan Chan** (Chan Chan Route), frequently traversed by aficionados of lead singer Compay Segundo and co.

◉ Sights & Activities

Most activities can be organized at Villa Pinares del Mayarí or via excursions from Guardalavaca's or Santiago de Cuba's hotels (CUC$92 by 4WD).

Salto del Guayabo   WATERFALL
At just over 100m in height, Guayabo (15km from the Villa Pinares de Mayarí) is considered the highest waterfall in Cuba. There's a spectacular overlook and the guided 1.2km

hike to its base through fecund tropical forest costs CUC$5 and includes swimming in a natural pool.

Salto de Capiro   WATERFALL
A short 2km trail from Villa Pinares del Mayarí brings you to this hidden waterfall in lush forest.

Sendero la Sabina   TRAIL
(admission CUC$3) More flora can be observed on the Sendero la Sabina, a short interpretive trail at the Centro Investigaciones para la Montaña (1km from the hotel), which exhibits the vegetation of eight different ecosystems, a 150-year-old tree – the 'Ocuje Colorado' – and some rare orchids.

Farallones de Seboruco   CAVES
Speleologists may want to ask about trips to these ghostly caves, designated a national monument, which contain aboriginal cave paintings.

Hacienda la Mensura   FARM
Eight kilometers from Villa Pinares del Mayari is this breeding center for exotic animals such as antelope and *guapeti*. Horseback riding can be arranged here.

🛏 Sleeping

★ Villa Pinares del Mayarí   HOTEL $
(☑45-56-28; s/d CUC$25/35; P❄☸) 🖊
One in a duo of classic Gaviota Holguín hideaways (Villa Cayo Saetía is the other) Pinares del Mayarí stands at 600m elevation between the Altiplanicie de Nipe and Sierra del Cristal, 30km south of Mayarí on a rough dirt road. Part chalet resort, part mountain retreat, this isolated rural hideaway is situated in one of Cuba's largest pine forests and the two- and three-bedroom cabins, with hot showers and comfortable beds, make it seem almost alpine-esque.

There's also a large restaurant, bar, sports court, gym, sublime pool and a small natural lake (El Cupey) 300m away, which is great for an early-morning dip.

ℹ Getting There & Away
The only way to get to Villa Pinares del Mayarí and Parque Nacional la Mensura outside an organized tour is via car, taxi or bicycle (if you're adventurous and it's not a Cuban one). The access road is mostly a rough collection of holes with the odd bit of asphalt thrown in, but it's passable in a hire car if driven with care. You'll need at least 1½ hours to cover the 30km from Mayarí.

Cayo Saetía

East of Mayarí the road becomes increasingly potholed and the surroundings, while never losing their dusty rural charm, progressively more remote. The culmination of this rustic drive is lovely Cayo Saetía, a small, flat, wooded island in the Bahía de Nipe that's connected to the mainland by a small bridge. During the 1970s and '80s this was a favored hunting ground for communist apparatchiks who enjoyed spraying lead into the local wildlife. Fortunately those days are now gone. Indeed, Cayo Saetía is now a protected wildlife park with 19 species of exotic animals, including camels, zebras, antelopes, ostriches and deer. Bisected by grassy meadows and adorned by hidden coves and beaches, it's the closet Cuba gets to an African wildlife reserve. There is also a gorgeous beach often commandeered by organized catamaran groups from Guardalavaca.

🛏 Sleeping

Villa Cayo Saetía   CABINS $$
(☑42-53-20; d CUC$60-70, ste CUC$85-100; ❄) This wonderfully rustic but comfortable resort, on a 42-sq-km island at the entrance to the Bahía de Nipe, is small, remote and more upmarket than the price suggests. The 12 rooms are split into rustic and standard *cabañas* with a minimal price differential. You'll feel as if you're a thousand miles from anywhere.

The in-house restaurant, La Güira – decked out Hemingway-style with hunting trophies mounted on the wall like gory art – serves exotic meats such as antelope.

ℹ Getting There & Around
There are three ways to explore Cayo Saetía, aside from the obvious two-legged sorties from the villa itself. A one-hour 4WD safari costs CUC$9, while there are also excursions by horse and boat. Though Cayo Saetía is isolated, you can secure passage on a bus-boat combo from Guardalavaca via the town of Antilles (CUC$98). If arriving by car, the control post is 15km off the main road. Then it's another 8km along a rough, unpaved road to the resort. A hire car will make it – with care.

Granma Province

Includes ➡
Bayamo 372
Gran Parque Nacional
Sierra Maestra 381
Manzanillo 384
Media Luna 386
Niquero 386
Parque Nacional
Desembarco del
Granma 386
Pilón 388

Best Hikes

➡ Comandancia de la Plata (p382)

➡ El Salto (p389)

➡ Pico Turquino (p383)

➡ Morlotte-Fustete (p388)

Best Revolutionary Sites

➡ Alegria del Pio (p388)

➡ Comandancia de la Plata (p382)

➡ Casa Natal de Carlos Manuel de Céspedes (p373)

➡ Museo las Colorados (p387)

➡ Museo Histórico la Demajagua (p384)

Why Go?

Few parts of the world get named after yachts, which helps explain why in Granma (christened for the boat in which Fidel Castro and his bedraggled revolutionaries clambered ashore to kick-start a guerrilla war in 1956), Cuba's *viva la Revolución* spirit burns most fiercely. This is the land where José Martí died and where Granma native Carlos Manuel de Céspedes freed his slaves and formally declared Cuban independence for the first time in 1868.

The alluringly isolated countryside helped the revolutionary cause. Road-scarce Granma is one of Cuba's remotest regions, with lofty tropical mountains dense enough to have harbored a fugitive Fidel Castro for over two years in the 1950s.

Its isolation has bred a special brand of Cuban identity. Granma's settlements are esoteric places enlivened with weekly street parties (with outdoor barbecues and archaic hand-operated street organs), and provincial capital Bayamo is among the most tranquil and clean places in the archipelago.

When to Go

➡ Pockets of Granma have a balmy climate and during January and February Marea del Portillo is the warmest place in Cuba.

➡ Bayamo's biggest celebration is the Incendio de Bayamo on January 12.

➡ In the far wetter Sierra Maestra mountains, March and April are the driest times for hiking, with bearable nighttime temperatures.

➡ December 2 is the anniversary of the Granma landing, which is celebrated with a ceremony at Los Coloradas.

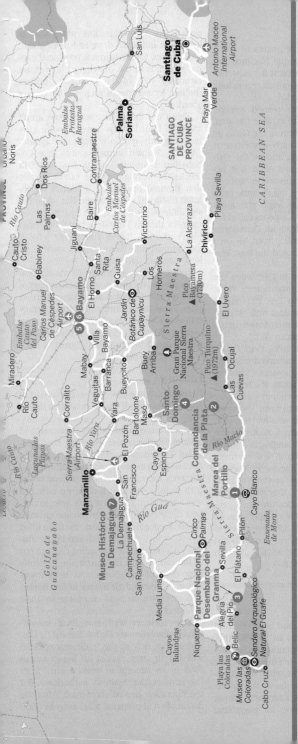

Granma Province Highlights

1 Enjoy one of Cuba's balmiest microclimates in secluded **Marea del Portillo** (p389).

2 Trek up to Fidel's wartime headquarters at **Comandancia de la Plata** (p382) in Gran Parque Nacional Sierra Maestra.

3 Investigate marine terraces and archaeological remains in **Parque Nacional Desembarco del Granma** (p386).

4 Get a dose of mountain air and customs in **Santo Domingo** (p382) in Gran Parque Nacional Sierra Maestra's bucolic entrance.

5 Immerse yourself in the unique Bayamo party spirit with pork roast, street organs, and a chess game in the **Fiesta de la Cubanía** (p379).

6 Relax by the river with the *bayameses* (people from Bayamo) in **Parque Chapuzón** (p375).

7 Visit the site where the Cubans uttered their first cry of independence in **Museo Histórico la Demajagua** (p384).

History

Stone petroglyphs and remnants of Taíno pottery unearthed in Parque Nacional Desembarco del Granma suggest the existence of native cultures in the Granma region long before the Spanish arrived.

Columbus, during his second voyage, was the first European to explore the area, taking shelter from a storm in the Golfo de Guacanayabo. All other early development schemes came to nothing and by the 17th century Granma's untamed coast had become the preserve of pirates and corsairs.

Granma's real nemesis didn't come until October 10, 1868, when sugar-plantation owner Carlos Manuel de Céspedes called for the abolition of slavery from his Demajagua sugar mill near Manzanillo, freed his own slaves by example and incited the First War of Independence.

Drama unfolded again in 1895 when the founder of the Cuban Revolutionary Party, José Martí, was killed in Dos Ríos just a month and a half after landing with Máximo Gómez off the coast of Guantánamo to ignite the Spanish-Cuban-American War.

Then on December 2, 1956, Fidel Castro and 81 rebel soldiers disembarked from the yacht *Granma* off the province's coast at Playa las Coloradas (ironically, the boat that literally launched the Revolution – and later gave the province its present name – was purchased from an American, who had named it in honor of his grandmother). Routed by Batista's troops shortly after landing in a sugarcane field at Alegría del Pío, 15 or so survivors managed to escape into the Sierra Maestra, establishing headquarters at Comandancia de la Plata. From there they coordinated the armed struggle, broadcasting their progress and consolidating their support among sympathizers nationwide. After two years of harsh conditions and unprecedented beard growth, the forces of the M-26-7 (July 26 Movement) triumphed in 1959.

Bayamo

POP 166,200

Predating both Havana and Santiago, and cast for time immemorial as the city that kick-started Cuban independence, Bayamo has every right to feel self-important. Yet somehow it doesn't. The city's affectionate name-tag, *ciudad de los coches* (*coches* means horse carts) is a far more telling appraisal of its ambience: an easygoing, slow-paced, trapped-in-time place that is less about industrial drive and more about, well, horses. Cuba's balmiest provincial capital resounds to the clip-clop of hooves; an estimated 40% of the population utilizes the four-legged friends each day for getting about.

That's not to say that *bayameses* aren't aware of their history. '*Como España quemó a Sagunto, así Cuba quemó a Bayamo*,' ('As the Spanish burnt Sagunto, the Cubans burnt Bayamo') wrote José Martí in the 1890s, highlighting the sacrificial role that Bayamo has played in Cuba's convoluted historical development. But while the self-inflicted 1869 fire might have destroyed many of the city's classic colonial buildings (don't worry – there's still plenty left), it didn't undermine its underlying spirit or its long-standing traditions.

Today, Bayamo is known for its cerebral chess players (Céspedes was the Kasparov of his day) and Saturday night street parties, often to the tune of antiquated street organs (imported via Manzanillo). All three are on show at the weekly Fiesta de la Cubanía, one of the island's most authentic street shows – *bayamés* to its core.

History

Founded in November 1513 as the second of Diego Velázquez de Cuéllar's seven original villas (after Baracoa), Bayamo's early history was marred by Indian uprisings and bristling native unrest. But with the indigenous Taíno decimated by deadly European diseases such as smallpox, the short-lived insurgency soon fizzled out. By the end of the 16th century, Bayamo had grown rich and was established as the region's most important cattle-ranching and sugarcane-growing center. Frequented by pirates, the town filled its coffers further in the 17th and 18th centuries via a clandestine smuggling ring run out of the nearby port of Manzanillo. Bayamo's new class of merchants and landowners lavishly invested their money in fine houses and expensive overseas education for their offspring.

One such protégé was local lawyer-turned-revolutionary Carlos Manuel de Céspedes, who, defying the traditional colonial will, led an army against his hometown in 1868 in an attempt to wrest control from the conservative Spanish authorities. But the liberation proved short-lived. After the defeat of an ill-prepared rebel army by 3000 regular Spanish troops near the Río Cauto on January 12, 1869, the townspeople – sensing an imminent Spanish reoccupation – set their town on fire rather than see it fall into enemy hands.

Bayamo was also the birthplace of Perucho Figueredo, composer of the Cuban national anthem, which begins, rather patriotically, with the words *Al combate corred, bayameses* (Run to battle, people of Bayamo).

In 2006, Fidel Castro gave his last (to-date) large-scale public oration in Bayamo's Plaza de la Patria; there to give his annual commemorative 'Triumphs of the Revolution' speech, he was taken ill shortly after and within days handed power over to his brother Raúl.

⊙ Sights

★ Casa Natal de Carlos Manuel de Céspedes
MUSEUM

(Maceo No 57; admission CUC$1; ⊙9am-5pm Tue-Fri, 9am-2pm & 8-10pm Sat, 10am-1:30pm Sun) Birthplace of the 'father of the motherland,' this museum is where Céspedes was born (on April 18, 1819) and spent his first 12 years. Céspedes memorabilia inside is complemented by a collection of period furniture. It's notable architecturally as Bayamo's only remaining two-storey colonial house, one of the few buildings to survive the 1869 fire.

★ Parque Céspedes
SQUARE

(Plaza de la Revolución) One of Cuba's leafiest and friendliest squares, Bayamo's central meeting point is officially known as Plaza de la Revolución. Despite its easygoing airs and secondary role as the city's best outdoor music venue (orchestras regularly play here), the square is loaded with historical significance.

In 1868 Céspedes proclaimed Cuba's independence for the first time in front of the columned **Ayuntamiento** (City Hall). The square is surrounded by a smorgasbord of grand monuments and beautified further by big, shady trees. Facing each other in the center are a bronze statue of Carlos Manuel de Céspedes, hero of the First War of Independence, and a marble bust of Perucho Figueredo, with the words of the Cuban national anthem, which Figueredo scribed, carved upon it.

Iglesia Parroquial Mayor de San Salvador
CHURCH

There's been a church on this site since 1514. The current edifice dates from 1740 but got devastated in the 1869 fire, so much of what you see results from building work in 1919. One original section surviving the fire is the **Capilla de la Dolorosa** (donations accepted; ⊙9am-noon & 3-5pm Mon-Fri, 9am-noon Sat) with its gilded wooden altar.

A highlight of the main church is the central arch, which exhibits a mural depicting the blessing of the Cuban flag in front of the revolutionary army on October 20, 1868. Outside, Plaza del Himno Nacional is where the Cuban national anthem, 'La Bayamesa,' was sung for the first time in 1868.

Museo Provincial
MUSEUM

(Maceo No 55; admission CUC$1; ⊙10am-6pm Mon-Fri, 9am-1pm Sat & Sun) Directly next door to Céspedes' ex-home, the provincial museum completes Bayamo's historical trajectory with a yellowing city document dating from 1567 and a rare photo of Bayamo immediately after the fire.

Paseo Bayamés
NEIGHBORHOOD

(Calle General García) Bayamo's main shopping street (officially known as Calle General García) was pedestrianized in the 1990s and reconfigured with funky artwork. Here you'll find wax museum Museo de Cera, various public utilities and plenty of Cuban-style commerce.

Casa de Estrada Palma
CULTURAL CENTER

(Céspedes No 158) Welcome to where Cuba's first post-independence president, Tomás Estrada Palma, was born in 1835. Onetime friend of José Martí, Estrada Palma was disgraced post-Revolution for his perceived complicity with the US over the Platt Amendment. His birth house is now the seat of Uneac (Unión Nacional de Escritores y Artistas de Cuba; National Union of Cuban Writers and Artists).

You'll find little about the famous former occupant inside, but the courtyard contains a palm (dating from 1837) that would (probably) have come into contact with Palma.

Ventana de Luz Vázquez
LANDMARK

(Céspedes, btwn Figueredo & Luz Vázquez) A forerunner of the national anthem, co-written by Céspedes (and, confusingly, also called 'La Bayamesa') was first sung from here on March 27, 1851. A memorial plaque has been emblazoned onto the wall next to the wood-barred colonial window.

Museo de Cera
MUSEUM

(☑42-65-25; General García No 261; admission CUC$1; ⊙9am-noon & 1-5pm Mon-Fri, 2-9pm Sat,

Bayamo

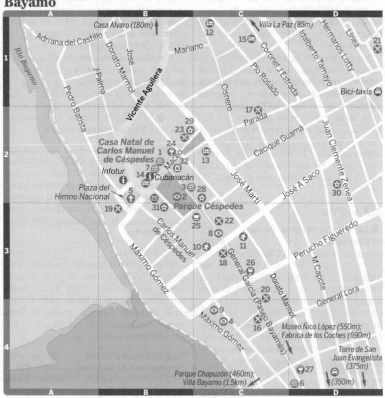

9am-noon Sun) The tiny Museo de Cera, Bayamo's diminutive version of Madame Tussaud's, has convincing waxworks of Cuban personalities such as Polo Montañez, Benny Moré and local hero Carlos Puebla. On a more internationalist note, there's Gabriel García Márquez and Hugo Chávez.

Torre de San Juan Evangelista　LANDMARK
(cnr José Martí & Amado Estévez) A church dating from Bayamo's earliest years stood at this busy intersection until it was destroyed in the great fire of 1869. Later, the church's tower served as the entrance to the first cemetery in Cuba, closed in 1919. The cemetery was demolished in 1940 but the tower survived.

A **monument** to local poet José Joaquín Palma (1844–1911) stands in the park diagonally across the street from the tower, and beside the tower is a bronze **statue of Francisco Vicente Aguilera** (1821–77), who led the independence struggle in Bayamo.

Plaza de la Patria　PLAZA
(Av Felino Figueredo) This square is where Fidel Castro gave his final, rousing public speech in July 2006 before being taken ill and stepping down as president. The monument to the Cuban greats here features Manuel de Céspedes, Antonio Maceo, Máximo Gomez, Perucho Figueredo and, subtly placed left of center, Fidel: it's the only monument he appears on in Cuba. It's six blocks northeast of the bus station.

Museo Ñico López　MUSEUM
(Abihail González; ⊗ 8am-noon & 2-5:30pm Tue-Sat, 9am-noon Sun) **FREE** This museum is in the former officers' club of the Carlos Manuel de Céspedes military barracks, 1km southeast of Parque Céspedes. On July 26, 1953, this garrison was attacked by 25 revolutionaries led by Ñico López in tandem with the assault on Moncada Barracks in Santiago de Cuba in order to prevent reinforcements from being sent.

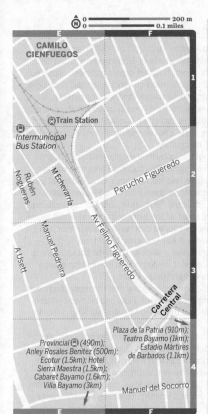

Bayamo

◎ Top Sights
1 Casa Natal de Carlos Manuel de Céspedes	B2
2 Parque Céspedes	B2

◎ Sights
3 Ayuntamiento	B2
4 Casa de Estrada Palma	C4
5 Iglesia Parroquial Mayor de San Salvador	B2
6 Museo de Cera	D4
7 Museo Provincial	B2
8 Paseo Bayamés	C3
9 Ventana de Luz Vázquez	C4

⚙ Activities, Courses & Tours
10 Academia de Ajedrez	C3
11 Cubanacán Desk	C3

🛏 Sleeping
12 Casa de la Amistad	C1
13 Casa Olga	C2
14 Hotel Royalton	B2
15 Villa Pupi & Villa América	C1

✖ Eating
16 Cuadro Gastronómica de Luz Vázquez	C4
17 El Polinesio	C2
18 El Siglo	C3
19 La Bodega	B3
20 La Sevillana	C3
21 Mercado Agropecuario	D1
22 Mercado Cabalgata	C3
Restaurante Plaza	(see 14)
23 Restaurante San Salvador de Bayamo	B2

◎ Drinking & Nightlife
24 Bar la Esquina	B2
25 Café Literario Ventana Sur	C3
26 La Taberna	C3
27 Piano Bar	D4

◎ Entertainment
28 Casa de la Cultura	C2
29 Casa de la Trova la Bayamesa	B2
30 Centro Cultural Los Beatles	D2
31 Cine Céspedes	B3
Uneac	(see 4)

🛍 Shopping
32 ARTex	B2

López escaped to Guatemala, and was the first Cuban to befriend Ernesto 'Che' Guevara, but was killed shortly after the *Granma* landed in 1956.

Fabrica de los Coches FACTORY
(Prolongacion General García No 530; donation CUC$1; ⊙7am-3pm) It's worth the jaunt to observe the goings-on at Cuba's only handcrafted *coche* (horse cart) production line. Most horse carts you'll see in Cuba are metal, but these are fashioned in wood and take far longer (up to three months per cart) to produce.

You'll see horse carts in various stages of completion, meet the workers and be able to buy Bayamo's best souvenir: miniature model horse carts with incredible attention to detail. The big ones cost about 8000 pesos (CUC$325) and don't fit quite so well into a suitcase.

Parque Chapuzón PARK
(Av Amado Éstevez; 🚼) Greenery beckons not a kilometer from Bayamo's center where the Bayamo River has carved a lush belt through the urban grid. Locals come to this blissful spot to water their horses, have a family

CASTRO IN THE SIERRA MAESTRA

It seemed like an ignominious defeat. Three days after landing in a crippled leisure yacht on Cuba's southeastern coast, Castro's expeditionary force of 82 soldiers had been decimated by Batista's superior army. Some of the rebels had fled, others had been captured and killed. Escaping from the ambush, Castro found himself cowering in a sugarcane field along with two ragged companions: his 'bodyguard,' Universo Sánchez, and diminutive Havana doctor, Faustino Pérez. 'There was a moment when I was commander-in-chief of myself and two others,' said the man who would one day go on to overthrow the Cuban government, thwart a US-sponsored invasion, incite a nuclear standoff and become one of the most enduring political figures of the 20th century.

Hunted by ground troops and bombed from the air by military planes, the trio lay trapped in the cane field for four days and three nights. The hapless Pérez had inadvertently discarded his weapon; Sánchez, meanwhile, had lost his shoes. Wracked by fatigue and plagued by hunger, Fidel continued to do what he always did best. He whispered incessantly to his beleaguered colleagues – about the Revolution, about the philosophies of José Martí. Buoyantly he pontificated about how 'all the glory of the world would fit inside a grain of maize.' Sánchez, not unwisely, concluded that his delirious leader had gone crazy and that their grisly fate was sealed – it was just a matter of time.

At night, Fidel – determined not to be caught alive – slept with his rifle cocked against his throat, the safety catch released. One squeeze of the finger and it would have been over. No Cuban Revolution, no Bay of Pigs, no Cuban Missile Crisis.

Fatefully, the moment didn't arrive. With the army concluding that the rebels had been wiped out, the search was called off. Choosing their moment, Fidel and his two companions crept stealthily northeast toward the safety of the Sierra Maestra, sucking on stalks of sugarcane for nutrition.

It was a desperate fight for survival. For a further eight days the rebel army remained a bedraggled trio as the fugitive soldiers dodged army patrols, crawled through sewers and drank their own urine. It wasn't until December 13 that they met up with Guillermo García, a *campesino* sympathetic to the rebel cause, and a corner was turned.

On December 15 at a safe meeting house, Fidel's brother, Raúl, materialized out of the jungle with three men and four weapons. Castro was ecstatic. Three days later a third exhausted band of eight soldiers – including Che Guevara and Camilo Cienfuegos – turned up, swelling the rebel army to an abject 15.

'We can win this war,' proclaimed an ebullient Fidel to his small band of not-so-merry men. 'We have just begun the fight.'

barbecue or swim (as can you). Footpaths and gazebo-shaped stalls selling food and drink embellish the banks, but never detract from the all-pervading mood of tranquillity.

Activities

The Cubans love chess, and nowhere more so than in Bayamo. Check out the streetside chess aficionados who set up on Saturday night during the Fiesta de la Cubanía. The **Academia de Ajedrez** (José A Saco No 63, btwn General García & Céspedes) is the place to go to improve your pawn-king-four technique.

Forty-five-minute **horse-and-cart tours** can be arranged at the **Cubanacán desk** (José A Saco, cnr Donato Marmol, Hotel Telégrafo) for CUC\$4 per person.

Tours

There are good private guided tours operating in Bayamo, for the city and, further afield, for Gran Parque Nacional Sierra Maestra.

Anley Rosales Benitez GUIDED TOUR
(☑ 52-92-22-09; www.bayamotravelagent.com; Carretera Central No 478) Anley specializes in trips to the Sierra Maestra, which can be difficult to access without your own transport. The highlight tour (two people CUC\$40) takes in the Revolutionary sites of the 1956–58 years when the rebels were holed up hereabouts, like the village where Fidel famously played baseball with locals. But these guys will arrange everything from day trips to the Jardín Botánico Cupaynicu (CUC\$40) to Bayamo airport pick-up. All-inclusive Comandancia de la Plata excursions are CUC\$115 for two people.

Festivals

Incendio de Bayamo CULTURAL

(☉ Jan 12) The biggest annual event is the Incendio de Bayamo, on January 12, remembering the city's 1869 burning with live music and theatrical performances in Parque Céspedes, and culminating in fireworks launched from nearby buildings.

Sleeping

Casa de la Amistad CASA PARTICULAR $

(☑ 42-57-69; gabytellez2003@yahoo.es; Pío Rosado No 60, btwn Ramíriez & N López; r CUC$25; P ❄ @) Gabriel and Rosa let out most of the upper floor of their pastel-shaded house as a separate apartment with its own entrance, kitchen, sitting area, bedroom and bathroom. They are fine hosts who speak excellent English, and there's even an internet connection.

Villa Pupi & Villa América CASA PARTICULAR $

(☑ 42-30-29; yuri21504@gmail.com; Coronel J Estrada No 76-78; r CUC$20-25; ❄) Three rooms in this family run enterprise (two upstairs in América, one next door and downstairs in Pupi). All three have use of Villa Pupi's vast roof terrace, where you can dine on superb local cooking.

Villa La Paz CASA PARTICULAR $

(☑ 42-39-49; Coronel J Estrada No 32, btwn William Soler & Av Milanés; r CUC$20-25; ❄ @) There's nothing antiquated about this house boasting mod cons such as broadband internet and downstairs guest room with flat-screen TV. The Russian-Cuban English-speaking hosts are good fun, too. Try scoring the upstairs room: it looks right onto the expansive wraparound terrace.

Casa Olga CASA PARTICULAR $

(☑ 42-38-59; Parada 16 Altos, cnr Martí; r CUC$20-25; ❄) Two 1st-floor rooms in the city center with a shared rocking chair terrace above Parque Marti. Olga is a welcoming host who prepares substantial breakfasts. Open your window and suave sounds from the Casa de la Trova (situated opposite) waft in.

Casa Alvaro CASA PARTICULAR $

(☑ 42-48-61; Av Vincente Aguilera No 240; r CUC$20-25; ❄) Three sizeable, modern rooms here, and breakfasts among Bayamo's best, with divine *bocadillos* (toasted ham-and-cheese sandwiches) and Spanish tortilla on a terrace that exudes tranquillity despite the busy location.

Villa Bayamo HOTEL $

(☑ 42-31-02; s/d/cabin CUC$15/24/32; P ❄ ⚏) Out-of-town option (it's 3km southwest of the center on the road to Manzanillo) with a definitive rural feel and a rather pleasant swimming pool overlooking fields at the back. Well-appointed rooms and a reasonable restaurant.

★**Hotel Royalton** HOTEL $$

(☑ 42-22-90; Maceo No 53; s/d CUC$57/76; ❄ ⛛) The Royalton is Bayamo's best hotel. The 33 rooms have been upgraded to boutique standard with power showers and flat-screen TVs; there's also a roof terrace. Downstairs an attractive bar complements the reception area with seats spilling out onto a sidewalk terrace overlooking Parque Céspedes. The on-site Restaurante Plaza is a good eating option.

Hotel Sierra Maestra HOTEL $$

(☑ 42-79-70; Carretera Central; s/d CUC$38/50; P ❄ ⛛ ⚏) With a ring of the Soviet '70s about it, the Sierra Maestra hardly merits its three stars, although rooms have had some much-needed attention in the last three years, and public areas have acquired wi-fi. Three kilometers from the town center, it's OK for an overnighter.

Eating

There's some unique street food in Bayamo, sold from the stores along Calle Saco and in Parque Céspedes. Otherwise you're dealing with mainly local restaurants with prices in Cuban pesos. Aside from the places reviewed here, you'll find decent *comida criolla* (Creole food) in the Royalton's atmospheric **Restaurante Plaza** (☑ 42-22-90; Maceo No 53, Hotel Royalton; mains CUC$6-10; ☉ 7:30am-10:30pm).

★**Restaurante San Salvador de Bayamo** CARIBBEAN $

(☑ 42-69-42; Maceo 107; meals CUC$3-10; ☉ noon-11pm) This splendid colonial place has been a candidate for Bayamo's best restaurant since opening in 2012. Get serenaded by violinists as you taste food that, thanks to the knowledgeable owner, plumbs way deeper than the obvious and taps into indigenous/bucaneer influences on regional cuisine. Try tortilla with cassava and local cheese, for example. Oh, and those shrimps come with a very special garlic sauce.

GRANMA PROVINCE BAYAMO

El Polinesio
CUBAN $

(☑42-24-49; Parada No 125, btwn Pío Rosado & Cisnero; meals CUC$6-8; ☺noon-11pm) The Polinesio has been around for years, ever since the days when private restaurants could only seat 12 people and serve pork and chicken. These days the menu's expanded to include more adventurous seafood and a specialty *mar y tierra* (fish and meat) dish.

What hasn't changed is the venue – upstairs in an open-fronted family dining room with five or six tables – and the service. Big smiles all round.

La Sevillana
SPANISH $

(☑42-14-95; General García, btwn General Lora & Perucho Figueredo; meals CUC$1-2; ☺noon-2pm & 6-10pm) Come and see Cuban chefs attempt Spanish cuisine – paella and *garbanzos* (chickpeas). This is a new kind of peso restaurant, with a dress code (no shorts), a doorman in a suit, and a reservations policy. Press your trousers, brush up on your Spanish, but don't expect *sevillano* creativity.

Cuadro Gastronómica de Luz Vázquez
FAST FOOD $

(off General García, btwn Figueredo & General Lora; dishes from MN$10; ☺hours vary) Along this short lane are parked at least a dozen clean-looking food carts selling *bayamés* street snacks in Cuban pesos. Bank on hot dogs, croquettes, ice cream, sardines and empanadas.

La Bodega
CARIBBEAN $$

(Plaza del Himno Nacional No 34; meals CUC$5-15, cover after 9pm CUC$3; ☺11am-1am) The front opens out onto Bayamo's main square; the rear terrace overlooks Río Bayamo and is fringed by a bucolic backdrop that will leave you wondering if you've been transported to an isolated country villa. Try the beef and taste the coffee, or relax on the open terrace before the tour groups arrive.

Self-Catering

El Siglo
BAKERY

(cnr General García & Saco; ☺9am-8pm) Fresh warm cakes sold in pesos.

Mercado Agropecuario
MARKET

(Línea) The vegetable market is in front of the train station. There are many peso food stalls along here also.

Mercado Cabalgata
SUPERMARKET

(General García No 65; ☺9am-9pm Mon-Sat, to noon Sun) This store on the main pedestrian street sells basic groceries.

 Drinking

Café Literario Ventana Sur
CAFE, BAR

(Figueredo No 62; ☺10am-midnight) At last, Bayamo's gorgeous main square gets the bohemian bar-cafe it needed. This is where the town's poets, artists and musicians come to imbibe strong coffee, read magazines and swap ideas. You'll see them at the alfresco tables strumming their guitars before launching into spontaneous outbreaks of music – Silvio Rodríguez meets Radiohead.

Bar la Esquina
BAR

(cnr Donato Marmol & Maceo; ☺11am-1am) International cocktails are served in this tiny corner bar replete with plenty of local atmosphere.

La Taberna
BAR

(General García, btwn Saco & Figueredo; ☺10am-10pm) This busy local place on the main shopping street has beer on tap in ceramic mugs and a constant buzz of conversation. Pay in Cuban pesos.

Piano Bar
BAR

(cnr General García & Bartholomé Masó; ☺2pm-2am) Ice-cold air-con, starched tablecloths, stern waiters, good live music from piano recitals to *trovadores* (folk singers) and crooners of *musica romantica*. So plush it's sometimes invite-only.

☆ **Entertainment**

The two main hotels, the Royalton (p377) and the Sierra Maestra (p377), have decent bars; the latter also has a loud-but-popular disco. Café Literario Ventana Sur hosts numerous cultural activities. Pick up its bulletin paper, *La Palma de Auriga*.

Cine Céspedes
CINEMA

(admission CUC$2) This cinema is on the western side of Parque Céspedes, by the post office. It offers everything from Gutiérrez Alea to the latest Hollywood blockbuster (occasional English-language films with Spanish subtitles).

Teatro Bayamo
THEATER

(☑42-51-06; Reparto Jesús Menéndez) Six blocks northeast of the bus station, opposite Plaza de la Patria, lies one of the Oriente's most impressive theaters, converted into its current function only in 2007, and constructed originally in 1982. The *vitrales* (stained-glass windows) in the lobby are sensational. Performances are usually Wednesday, Saturday or Sunday.

Centro Cultural Los Beatles
LIVE MUSIC

(Zenea, btwn Figueredo & Saco; admission MN$10; ☺6am–midnight) Just as the rest of the world fell for the exoticism of the Buena Vista Social Club, Cubans fell for the downright brilliance of the Fab Four. This quirky place hosts Beatles tribute bands (in Spanish) every weekend. Unmissable!

Uneac
CULTURAL CENTER

(Céspedes No 158; ☺4pm) **FREE** You can catch heartfelt boleros on the flowery patio here in the former home of disgraced first president Tomás Estrada Palma, the man invariably blamed for handing Guantánamo to the *Yanquis.*

Cabaret Bayam
CABARET

(Carretera Central Km 2; ☺9pm Fri-Sun) Bayamo's glittery nightclub/cabaret opposite the Hotel Sierra Maestra draws out the locals on weekends in their equally glittery attire. It's the largest indoor cabaret in Cuba.

Casa de la Trova la Bayamesa
TRADITIONAL MUSIC

(cnr Maceo & Martí; admission CUC$1; ☺10am-1am) One of Cuba's best *trova* houses, in a lovely colonial building on Maceo. Pictures on the wall display the famous '70s afro of Bayamo-born *trova* king Pablo Milanés. There's an ARTex gift shop on-site.

Casa de la Cultura
CULTURAL CENTER

(General García No 15) Wide-ranging cultural events, including art expos, on the east side of Parque Céspedes.

Estadio Mártires de Barbados
SPORTS

(Av Granma) From October to April, there are baseball games at this stadium, approximately 2km east of the center.

🔒 Shopping

Paseo Bayamés is the main pedestrian shopping street but, with few tourists, stores are mainly aimed at Cubans.

ARTex
SOUVENIRS

(General García No 7; ☺9am-4:30pm Mon-Sat) The usual mix of Che Guevara T-shirts and bogus Santería dolls in Parque Céspedes.

ℹ Information

Banco de Crédito y Comercio (cnr General García & Saco; ☺9am-3pm Mon-Fri)

Cadeca (Saco No 101) Money changing.

Campismo Popular (☎42-24-25; General García No 112) Make bookings for La Sierrita and Las Coloradas campismos here.

Cubanacán (Maceo No 53, Hotel Telegrafo) Arranges hikes to Pico Turquino (two days per person CUC$68, transport included) and Parque Nacional Desembarco del Granma (CUC$45 per person, transport included), among other places.

Ecotur (☎48-70-06 ext 639; Hotel Sierra Maestra) Excellent helpful office. Good for booking excursions to Pico Turquino and Parque Nacional Desembarco del Granma. Ask about the Ruta de la Revolución hike.

Etecsa Telepunto (General García, btwn Saco & Figueredo; per hr CUC$4.50; ☺8:30am-7pm) Three internet terminals; rarely busy.

Farmacia Internacional (☎42-95-96; General García, btwn Figueredo & Lora; ☺8am-noon & 1-5pm Mon-Fri, 8am-noon Sat & Sun) Pharmacy.

Hospital Carlos Manuel de Céspedes (☎42-50-12; Carretera Central, Km 1)

Infotur (☎42-34-68; Plaza del Himno Nacional, cnr Joaquín Palma; ☺8am-noon & 1-4pm) One of those really courteous, helpful information offices: often a rare breed in Cuba.

Post Office (cnr Maceo & Parque Céspedes; ☺8am-8pm Mon-Sat)

ℹ Getting There & Away

AIR

Bayamo's **Carlos Manuel de Céspedes Airport** (airport code BYM) is about 4km northeast of town, on the road to Holguín. **Cubana** (Martí No 52) flies to Bayamo from Havana twice a week (about CUC$100, two hours). There are no international flights to or from Bayamo.

RETRACING REVOLUTIONARY HISTORY

Movie-script-worthy history and rare unspoiled ecosystems are just two of the attractions for potential hikers in mountainous Granma province. Although travelers have long been able to summit Pico Turquino and visit Castro's ridgetop wartime HQ at La Plata, most of the region has remained an unknown quantity to outsiders. But, in an attempt to boost green tourism, government agency Ecotur is starting to open the area up. Ascents of **Pico La Bayamesa** (1730m), Cuba's fourth-highest mountain encased in a recently created national park, could soon be possible. A path already exists to the peak's summit – indeed, in 2008, a Cuban environmental group placed a bust of Carlos Manuel de Céspedes there.

Another hike on the cards is the so-called **Ruta de la Revolución** that follows in the footsteps of the *Granma* yacht survivors from Los Coloradas, via Alegría de Pío and Cinco Palmas, to La Plata. Paths already link these sites, and are used by some in-the-know travelers. Enquire at the Ecotur (p379) office in Bayamo as to their current status and accessibility before setting out. Due to poor signposting, it is sensible to employ a guide. The distance between Los Coloradas and La Plata is huge, but smaller segments of the route (eg the 18km between Los Coloradas and Alegría de Pío) can be done in a day.

BUS & TRUCK

The **provincial bus station** (cnr Carretera Central & Av Jesús Rabí) has **Víazul** (www.viazul. com) buses to several destinations.

There are three buses a day to Havana (CUC$44, 13½ hours); one to Varadero at 10:20pm (CUC$42, 12½ hours); one to Trinidad at 9:50pm (CUC$26, nine hours); and five to Santiago (CUC$7, two hours). Buses heading west also stop at Holguín, Las Tunas, Camagüey, Ciego de Ávila, Sancti Spíritus and Santa Clara.

Passenger trucks leave from an adjacent terminal for Santiago de Cuba, Holguín, Manzanillo, Pilón and Niquero. You can truck it to Bartolomé Masó, as close as you can get on public transport to the Sierra Maestra trailhead. Trucks leave when full and you pay as you board.

The **intermunicipal bus station** (cnr Saco & Línea), opposite the train station, receives mostly local buses of little use to travelers, although trucks to Guisa leave from here.

TAXIS

State taxis can be procured for hard-to-reach destinations such as Manzanillo (CUC$30), Pilón (CUC$75) and Niquero (CUC$80). Prices are estimates and will depend on the current price of petrol. Nonetheless, at the time of writing it was cheaper to reach all these places by taxi than by hired car.

TRAIN

The **train station** (cnr Saco & Línea) is 1km east of the center. There are three local trains a day to Manzanillo (via Yara). Other daily trains serve Santiago and Camagüey. The long-distance Havana–Manzanillo train passes through Bayamo every third day (CUC$25).

ⓘ Getting Around

Cubataxi (☐ 42-43-13) can supply a taxi to Bayamo airport for CUC$5, or to Aeropuerto Frank País in Holguín for CUC$35. A taxi to Villa Santo Domingo (setting-off point for the Alto del Naranjo trailhead for Sierra Maestra hikes) or Comandancia la Plata will cost approximately CUC$35 one way. There's a taxi stand in the south of town near Museo Ñico López.

Cubacar (Carretera Central) rents cars at the Hotel Sierra Maestra.

The **Servi-Cupet gas station** (Carretera Central) is between Hotel Sierra Maestra and the bus terminal as you arrive fresh from Santiago de Cuba.

The main horse-cart route (MN$1) runs between the train station and the hospital, via the bus station. Bici-taxis (a few pesos a ride) are also useful for getting around town. There's a stand near the train station.

Around Bayamo

Most visitors are lured towards the so-close-you-can-almost-touch-them mountains, but Bayamo's hinterland hides some less-obvious haunts.

◉ Sights & Activities

Jardín Botánico de Cupaynicu GARDENS (Carretera de Guisa Km 10; admission CUC$2; ⊙8am-4:30pm Tue-Sun) For a floral appreciation of Bayamo's evergreen hinterland, head to this botanic garden about 16km outside the city off the Guisa road. It's on very few itineraries, so you can have the serene, serendipitous 104 hectares more or less to yourself. There are 74 types of palms, scores

Gran Parque Nacional Sierra Maestra

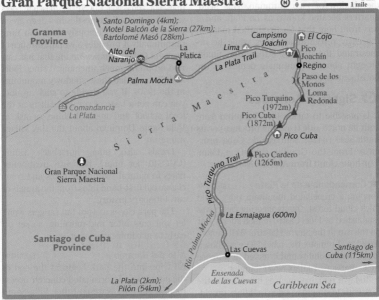

of cacti, blooming orchids and sections for endangered and medicinal plants.

The guided tour (Spanish only) gains you access to greenhouses, notable for the showy ornamentals. To get here, take the road to Santiago de Cuba for 6km and turn left at the signposted junction for Guisa. After 10km you'll see the botanic garden sign on the right. Trucks in this direction leave from the intermunicipal bus station in front of the train station.

Laguna de Leonero   LAKE
This algae-filled natural lake in the Cauto River delta, 40km northwest of Bayamo, is loaded with memorable fly-fishing possibilities. Black bass are the prized catch here: fishing season is November to March. Ecotur (p379) runs yacht excursions from CUC$250 for a maximum of six people. For more details contact its office in Bayamo.

Dos Ríos Obelisk   MONUMENT
At Dos Ríos, 52km northeast of Bayamo and almost in Holguín, a white obelisk overlooking the Río Cauto marks the spot where José Martí was shot and killed on May 19, 1895. Go 22km northeast of Jiguaní on the road to San Germán and take the unmarked road to the right after crossing the Cauto.

Gran Parque Nacional Sierra Maestra

Comprising a sublime mountainscape of broccoli-green peaks and humid cloud forest, and home to honest, hardworking *campesinos* (country folk), the Gran Parque Nacional Sierra Maestra is an alluring natural sanctuary that still echoes with the gunshots of Castro's guerrilla campaign of the late 1950s. Situated 40km south of Yara, up a very steep 24km concrete road from Bartolomé Masó, this precipitous, little-trammeled region contains the country's highest peak, Pico Turquino (1972m; just over the border in Santiago de Cuba province), unlimited birdlife and flora, and the rebels' onetime wartime headquarters, Comandancia la Plata.

History

History resonates throughout these mountains, the bulk of it linked indelibly to the guerrilla war that raged between December 1956 and December 1958. For the first year of the conflict Fidel and his growing band of supporters remained on the move, never staying in one place for more than a few days. It was only in early 1958 that the rebels established a permanent base on a ridge in the shadow of Pico Turquino. This headquarters became known as La Plata and it was from here that Castro drafted many of the early revolutionary laws while he orchestrated the military strikes that finally brought about the ultimate demise of the Batista government.

◉ Sights & Activities

It is possible to tackle Pico Turquino from both its north side (Granma province) or its south side (p426; Santiago de Cuba province). From the Granma side it's a 13km, four-hour climb from Alto del Naranjo.

★ Comandancia de la Plata   LANDMARK

Topping a crenellated mountain ridge amid thick cloud forest, this pioneering camp was established by Fidel Castro in 1958 after a year on the run in the Sierra Maestra. Well camouflaged and remote, the rebel HQ was chosen for its inaccessibility and it served its purpose well – Batista's soldiers never found it.

Today it remains much as it was left in the '50s, with 16 simple wooden buildings providing an evocative reminder of one of the most successful guerrilla campaigns in history. It's easy to appreciate the site's strategic location. The main site, culminating in the Casa de Fidel (Fidel's House) is approached via an open space, then a climb through thick trees.

Highlights include the small museum, near the beginning of the complex, the masterfully designed Casa de Fidel with its seven concealed escape routes in case the Revolution's leaders got discovered, and the steep climb up Radio Rebelde to the radio-communications buildings where the rebel's early broadcasts were aired. The hospital buildings, a wake-up call to the brutality of guerrilla medical care, lie far below along a separate path (positioned here so the injured wouldn't give the camp location away in their agony).

Comandancia de la Plata is controlled by the Centro de Información de Flora y Fauna in Santo Domingo. Aspiring guerrilla-watchers must first hire a guide at the park headquarters, then get transport (or walk) 5km up to Alto del Naranjo, and then proceed on foot along a muddy track for the final 4km. The guided excursion costs CUC$33 including transport, water and a snack (CUC$5 extra if you want to use a camera). You can organize it at the Ecotur office in Villa Santo Domingo.

★ Santo Domingo   VILLAGE

(museum admission CUC$1; ⊘ museum hours vary) This tiny village nestles in a deep green valley beside the deliciously clean Río Yara. Communally it provides a wonderful slice of peaceful Cuban *campesino* life that has carried on pretty much unchanged since Fidel and Che prowled these shadowy mountains in the 1950s. If you decide to stick around, you can get a taste of rural socialism at the local school and medical clinic, or ask at Villa Santo Domingo about the tiny village museum.

Locals also offer horseback riding (CUC$10 per hour), pedicure treatments, hikes to natural swimming pools and some classic old first-hand tales from the annals of revolutionary history.

The park closes at 4pm but rangers won't let you pass after mid-morning, so set off early to maximize your visit.

Alto del Naranjo   LANDMARK

All trips into the park begin at the end of the near-vertical, corrugated-concrete access road at Alto del Naranjo (after Villa Santo Domingo the road gains 750 vertical meters in less than 5km). To get there, it's an arduous two-hour walk, or zippy ride in a 4WD. There's a wondrous view of the plains of Granma from this 950m-high lookout, otherwise it's a launching pad for La Plata (3km) and Pico Turquino (13km).

🛏 Sleeping & Eating

★ Villa Santo Domingo   HOTEL $

(☑ 56-55-68, 56-58-34; s/d CUC$38/50, bungalow CUC$63; P ❄) This villa, 24km south of Bartolomé Masó, flanks the gateway to Gran Parque Nacional Sierra Maestra. There are 40 cabins (20 cheaper concrete ones and 20 newer ones in smart wooden buildings) next to the Río Yara. The setting, among cascading mountains and *campesino* huts, is idyllic, and the best jumping-off point for Comandancia de la Plata and Pico Turquino.

You can also test your lungs going for a challenging early morning hike up a painfully steep road to Alto del Naranjo. Other attractions include horseback riding, river swimming and traditional music in the villa's restaurant. Fidel stayed here on various occasions (in hut 6) and Raúl dropped by in 2001 after scaling Pico Turquino at the ripe old age of 70. Breakfast is included.

CLIMBING PICO TURQUINO

Towering 1972m above the calm Caribbean, Pico Turquino – so named for the turquoise hue that colors its steep upper slopes – is Cuba's highest and most regularly climbed mountain.

Carpeted in lush cloud forest and protected in a 140-sq-km national park, the peak's lofty summit is embellished by a bronze bust of national hero José Martí. In a patriotic test of endurance, the statue was dragged to the top in 1953 by a young Celia Sánchez and her father, Manuel Sánchez Silveira, to mark the centennial of the apostle's birth.

Four years later, Sánchez visited the summit again, this time with a rifle-wielding Fidel Castro in tow to record an interview with American news network CBS. Not long afterwards, the rebel army pitched their permanent headquarters in the mountain's imposing shadow, atop a tree-protected ridge near La Plata.

Best tackled as a through trek from the Santo Domingo side, the rugged, two- to three-day grind up Turquino starts from Alto del Naranjo above Santo Domingo and ends at Las Cuevas on the Caribbean coast (an out-and-back Alto del Naranjo–Pico Turquino hike is also possible). Guides are mandatory and can be arranged through Flora y Fauna employees at Villa Santo Domingo or at the small hut at Las Cuevas. The cost varies, depending on how many days you take. If you organize it through Ecotur/Cubanacán in Bayamo, bank on CUC$68 per person for two days. You'll also need to stock up on food, warm clothing, candles and some kind of sleeping roll or sheet (dinner/breakfast at the overnight shelters are included but nothing in-between). Even in August it gets cold at the shelters, so be prepared. Water is available along the trail, but is scarce: carry reserves.

The trail through the mountains from Alto del Naranjo passes the village of La Platica (water), Palma Mocha (campsite), Lima (campsite), Campismo Joachín (shelter and water), El Cojo (shelter), Pico Joachín, Paso de los Monos, Loma Redonda, Pico Turquino (1972m), Pico Cuba (1872m; with shelter/water at 1650m), Pico Cardero (1265m) and La Esmajagua (600m; with basic refreshments) before dropping down to Las Cuevas on the coast. The first two days are spent on the 13km section to Pico Turquino (normally overnighting at the Campismo Joachín and/or Pico Cuba shelters), where a prearranged guide takes over and leads you down to Las Cuevas. As with all guide services, tips are in order. Prearranging the second leg from Pico Cuba to Las Cuevas is straightforward and handled by park staff.

These hikes are well coordinated and the guides efficient. The sanest way to begin is by overnighting at Villa Santo Domingo and setting out in the morning (you should enter the park gate by 10am). Transport from Las Cuevas along the coast is sparse with one scheduled truck on alternate days. Arrange onward transport from Las Cuevas in advance. Approaching from Santo Domingo, you will not (officially) be able to do the Comandancia de la Plata and Pico Turquino hikes the same day, but must stay overnight in the village then begin the Pico Turquino hike the following day.

Casa Sierra Maestra CASA PARTICULAR $
(Santo Domingo; r CUC$20-25) Rustic heaven! Across the river from the park entrance in Santo Domingo (cross on the stepping stones), this place has four perfectly decent rooms (two in separate cabins) and an atmospheric *ranchón*-style bar-restaurant. Chickens cluck, and rural bliss descends. Reservations are difficult as there are no phone lines, so contact Anley Rosales Benitez (p376) in Bayamo.

Motel Balcón de la Sierra HOTEL $
(☑59-51-80; s/d CUC$35/48; P✱☀) One kilometer south of Bartolomé Masó and 16km north of Santo Domingo, this simple hotel is nestled in the mountain foothills but a little distant for easy access to the park. A swimming pool and restaurant are perched on a small hill with killer mountain views, while 20 air-conditioned cabins are scattered below. Lovely natural ambience juxtaposed with the usual basic-but-functional Islazul furnishings.

ℹ Information

Ecotur (☑56-58-34; ⊗8am-noon & 2-5pm) maintains a very handy desk at Villa Santo Domingo. If you want to book in advance try the always helpful Ecotur office (p379) in Bayamo.

ℹ️ Getting There & Around

There's no public transport from Bartolomé Masó to Alto del Naranjo (and trucks to Bartolomé Masó from Bayamo are infrequent and uncomfortable). A taxi from Bayamo to Villa Santo Domingo should cost around CUC$35 one way. Ensure it can take you all the way; the last 7km before Villa Santo Domingo is extremely steep but passable in a (decent) normal car. Returning, the hotel should be able to arrange onward transport for you to Bartolomé Masó, Bayamo or Manzanillo.

A 4WD vehicle with good brakes is necessary to drive the last 5km from Santo Domingo to Alto del Naranjo; it's the steepest road in Cuba with 45-degree gradients near the top. Powerful 4WDs pass regularly, usually for adventurous tour groups, and you may be able to find a space on board for approximately CUC$5 (ask at Villa Santo Domingo). Alternatively, it's a tough but rewarding 5km hike (or a gut-wrenching morning run!).

Manzanillo

POP 105,800

Bayside Manzanillo might not be pretty but, like most low-key Granma towns, it has an infectious feel. Hang out in the semi-ruined central park with its old-fashioned street organs and distinctive neo-Moorish architecture and you'll quickly make a friend or three. With bare-bones transport links and only one grim state-run hotel, few travelers make it here. As a result, Manzanillo is a good place to get off the standard guidebook trail and see how Cubans have learned to live with 50 years of austerity.

Founded in 1784 as a small fishing port, Manzanillo's early history was dominated by smugglers and pirates trading in contraband goods. The subterfuge continued into the late 1950s, when the city's proximity to the Sierra Maestra made it an important supply center for arms and men heading up to Castro's revolutionaries in their secret mountaintop headquarters.

Manzanillo is famous for its hand-operated street organs, which were first imported into Cuba from France in the early 20th century (and are still widely in use). The city's musical legacy was solidified further in 1972 when it hosted a government-sponsored *nueva trova* festival that culminated in a solidarity march to Playa las Coloradas.

👁️ Sights

Manzanillo is well known for its striking architecture, a psychedelic mélange of wooden beach shacks, Andalusian-style townhouses and intricate neo-Moorish facades. Check out the old **City Bank of NY building** (cnr Merchán & Dr Codina), dating from 1913, or the ramshackle wooden abodes around Perucho Figueredo, between Merchán and JM Gómez.

Parque Céspedes PARK

Manzanillo's central square is notable for its priceless **glorieta** (gazebo/bandstand), an imitation of the Patio de los Leones in Spain's Alhambra, where Moorish mosaics, a scalloped cupola and arabesque columns set off a theme that's replicated elsewhere. Nearby, a permanent **statue of Carlos Puebla**, Manzanillo's famous homegrown troubadour, sits contemplatively on a bench.

On the eastern side of Parque Céspedes, Manzanillo's **Museo Histórico Municipal** (Martí No 226; ☉8am-noon & 2-6pm Tue-Fri, 8am-noon & 6-10pm Sat & Sun) **FREE** gives the usual local history lesson with a revolutionary twist, while the **Iglesia de la Purisma Concepción** is a neoclassical beauty from 1805, with an impressive gilded altarpiece.

Celia Sánchez Monument MONUMENT

About eight blocks southwest of the park lies Manzanillo's most evocative sight. Built in 1990, this terracotta tiled staircase embellished with colorful ceramic murals runs up Calle Caridad between Martí and Luz Caballero. The birds and flowers on the reliefs represent Sánchez, linchpin of the M-26-7 (July 26 Movement) and longtime aid to Castro, whose visage appears on the central mural near the top of the stairs. It's a moving memorial with excellent views out over the city and bay.

⭐ **Museo Histórico la Demajagua** MUSEUM (admission CUC$1; ☉8am-5pm Mon-Sat, 8am-1pm Sun) It started with a cry. Ten kilometers south of Manzanillo is the moving sight of the sugar estate of Carlos Manuel de Céspedes, whose *Grito de Yara* and subsequent freeing of his slaves on October 10, 1868, marked the opening of Cuba's independence wars. There's a small museum and the Demajagua bell that Céspedes tolled to announce Cuba's (then unofficial) independence.

In 1947 an as yet unknown Fidel Castro 'kidnapped' the bell and took it to Havana in a publicity stunt to protest against the corrupt Cuban government. Also awaiting at La Demajagua are the remains of Céspedes' *ingenio* (sugar mill), and a poignant monument (with a quote from Castro). To get here, travel south 10km from the Servi-Cupet gas station in Manzanillo, in the direction of Media Luna, and then another 2.5km off the main road, toward the sea.

Criadero de Cocodrilos CROCODILE FARM
(admission CUC$5; ⊙7am-6pm Mon-Fri, 7-11am Sat) The nearby Cauto River delta is home to a growing number of wild crocodiles, so it's no surprise to encounter one of Cuba's half dozen or so crocodile farms here. There are close to 1000 crocs at this breeding farm, although they're all of the less-endangered 'American' variety. The farm is 5km south of Manzanillo on the road to Media Luna.

Sleeping & Eating

Manzanillo – thank heavens – has a smattering of private rooms, as there's not much happening on the hotel scene. The city's renowned for its fish, including the delicious liseta, but overall restaurant choices are dire: if in doubt eat at your casa particular, or drop in on the weekend Sábado en la Calle when the locals cook up traditional whole roast pig.

★ Adrián & Tonia CASA PARTICULAR $
(⌨57-30-28; Mártires de Vietnam No 49; r CUC$20-25; P❀) This attractive casa would stand out in any city, let alone Manzanillo. The position, on the terracotta staircase to the Celia Sánchez monument, obviously helps. But Adrián and Tonia have gone beyond the call of duty with a vista-laden terrace, plunge pool and separate apartment with private entrance and kitchen facilities.

Casa Peña de Juan Manuel CASA PARTICULAR $
(⌨57-26-28; Maceo No 189 cnr Loma; r CUC$20-25) The public areas resemble a refined museum and the one ample room and quiet plant-filled terrace don't disappoint.

Hotel Guacanayabo HOTEL $
(⌨57-40-12; Circunvalación Camilo Cienfuegos; s/d CUC$25/40; P❀❀) The austere Islazul-run Guacanayabo resembles a tropical reincarnation of a Gulag camp. Stay if you must.

Paladar Rancho Luna CUBAN $
(⌨57-38-58; José Miguel Gómez No 169; meals CUC$3-5; ⊙noon-11pm) No, you haven't missed anything. This is the best restaurant in Manzanillo. The decorative, typically Manzanillan facade sets the tone. The food, though never legendary, is perfectly OK as long as you stick to the local specialty – prawns.

Complejo Costa Azul PARRILLA $
(⊙food noon-9:30pm daily, cabaret 8pm-midnight Tue-Sun) Down by the bay is this grillhouse and cabaret thrown into one. It's highly likely neither amenity will blow your mind but, nevertheless, the eating/entertainment are nigh-on as good as it gets here. Pay in pesos.

Drinking & Entertainment

Manzanillo's best 'gig' takes place on Saturday evening in the famed **Sábado en la Calle**, a riot of piping organs, roasted pigs, throat-burning rum and, of course, dancing locals. Don't miss it! The local 'yoof' prefer the Malecón.

Teatro Manzanillo THEATER
(Villuendas, btwn Maceo & Saco; admission MN$5; ⊙shows 8pm Fri-Sun) Touring companies such as the Ballet de Camagüey and Danza Contemporánea de Cuba perform at this lovingly restored venue. Built in 1856 and restored in 1926 and again in 2002, this 430-seat beauty is packed with oil paintings, stained glass and original detail.

Casa de la Trova TRADITIONAL MUSIC
(Merchán No 213; admission MN$1) In the spiritual home of *nueva trova,* a renovation of the local *trova* house was long overdue. Pay a visit to this hallowed and freshly painted musical shrine where Carlos Puebla once plucked his strings.

Uneac CULTURAL CENTER
(cnr Merchán & Concession) FREE For traditional music you can head to this dependable option, which has Saturday and Sunday night *peñas* (musical performances) and painting expos.

Bodegón Pinilla BAR
(Martí 212; ⊙9am-8pm Mon-Thu, to 2am Fri & Sat) A new two-level place on the *peatonal* (pedestrianized section) and a good bet for a beer.

ℹ Information

Banco de Crédito y Comercio (cnr Merchán & Saco; ⊙9am-3pm Mon-Fri)
Cadeca (Martí No 188) Two blocks from the main square. With few places accepting convertibles here, you'll need some Cuban pesos.
Etecsa (cnr Martí & Codina; internet per hour CUC$4.50; ⊙8:30am-7pm) Internet terminals.
Post Office (cnr Martí & Codina; ⊙8am-8pm Mon-Sat) One block from Parque Céspedes.

❶ Getting There & Away

AIR
Manzanillo's **Sierra Maestra Airport** (airport code MZO) is on the road to Cayo Espino, 8km south of the Servi-Cupet gas station in Manzanillo. **Sunwing** (www.sunwing.ca) flies direct from Toronto and Montreal in winter and transfers people to the Marea del Portillo hotels.

A taxi between the airport and the center of town should cost approximately CUC$6.

BUS & TRUCK
The **bus station** (Av Rosales) is 2km northeast of the city center. There are no Víazul services. This narrows your options down to *guaguas* (local Cuban buses) or trucks (no reliable schedules and long queues). Services run several times a day to Yara and Bayamo in the east and Pilón and Niquero in the south. For the latter destinations you can also board at the crossroads near the Servi-Cupet gas station and the hospital, which is also where you'll find the *amarillos* (transport officials).

CAR
Cubacar (☑ 57-77-36) has an office at the Hotel Guacanayabo (p385). There's a sturdy road running through Corralito up into Holguín, making this the quickest exit from Manzanillo toward points north and east.

TRAIN
All services from the train station on the north side of town are via Yara and Bayamo. All are painfully slow. Every third day there's a link to Havana.

❶ Getting Around
Horse carts (MN$1) to the bus station leave from Dr Codina between Plácido and Luz Caballero. Horse carts along the Malecón to the shipyard leave from the bottom of Saco.

Media Luna
POP 15,493
One of a handful of small towns punctuating the swaying sugar fields between Manzanillo and Cabo Cruz, Media Luna is worth a pit stop on the basis of its Celia Sánchez connections. The Revolution's 'first lady' was born here in 1920 in a small clapboard house that is now the fastidiously curated **Celia Sánchez Museum** (Paúl Podio No 111; admission CUC$1; ⊙9am-5pm Mon-Sat, 8am-noon Sun).

If you have time, take a stroll around this quintessential Cuban sugar town dominated by a tall soot-stained mill (now disused) and characteristic clapboard houses decorated with gingerbread embellishments. There is also a lovely **glorieta**, almost as outlandish as Manzanillo's. The main **park** is the place to get a take on the local street theater while supping on quick-melting ice cream.

A signposted road from Media Luna leads 28km to Cinco Palmas.

Niquero
POP 21,600
Niquero, a small fishing port and sugar town in the isolated southwest corner of Granma, is dominated by the Roberto Ramírez Delgado sugar mill, built in 1905 and nationalized in 1960. It is one of the few mills in the area still in operation after the 2002 closedowns. Like many Granma settlements, Niquero is characterized by its distinctive clapboard houses and has a lively **Noche de Cubanilla**, when the streets are closed off and dining is at sidewalk tables. Live bands replete with organ grinders entertain the locals.

Ostensibly, there isn't much to do in Niquero, but you can explore the **park**, where there's a **cinema**, and visit the town's small **museum**. Look out for a **monument** commemorating the oft-forgotten victims of the *Granma* landing, who were hunted down and killed by Batista's troops in December 1956.

Niquero makes a good base from which to visit the Parque Nacional Desembarco del Granma. There are two Servi-Cupet petrol stations, a bank, a nightclub and plenty of spontaneous streetside action.

🛏 Sleeping

Hotel Niquero HOTEL **$**
(☑59-23-68; Esquina Martí; s/d CUC$18/28; ❚❚❋)
Here's a surprise, and a far-from-unpleasant one. Nestled in Niquero's center, this low-key, out-on-a-limb hotel situated opposite the local sugar factory actually has substantially sized, amenable rooms with little balconies overlooking the street. The affordable on-site restaurant can rustle up a reasonable beef steak with sauce. Better hunker down because it's the only accommodation in town.

Parque Nacional Desembarco del Granma

Mixing unique environmental diversity with heavy historical significance, the **Parque Nacional Desembarco del Granma** (admission CUC$5) consists of 275 sq km of teeming

CINCO PALMAS

At Cinco Palmas hamlet, as in much of western Granma, pristine natural landscapes are doused in poignant revolutionary history. This is where Castro's rebels regrouped on December 18, 1956, after their baptism of fire at Alegría de Pío 28km away. A bronze **monument** of three *campesinos* who helped the beleaguered rebel army, then down to a dozen men, was erected in 2008. The monument guards the finca of Ramón 'Mongo' Pérez where Castro and others sought shelter. Nearby, accommodations are available in **Ecologica Alojamiento UCTC**, which has several cabins (CUC$25) with on-site bathrooms and eating facilities – all very rustic. There's also a small, free **museum** with a 3D map of the hilly terrain.

Cinco Palmas lies 28km southeast of the town of Media Luna along a rough but passable road. Trails from the site lead west to Alegría de Pío and east to Comandancia de la Plata. Ask about guided hikes at Ecotur (p379) in Bayamo.

forests, peculiar karst topography and uplifted marine terraces. It is also a spiritual shrine to the Cuban Revolution – the spot where Castro's stricken leisure yacht *Granma* limped ashore in December 1956.

Named a Unesco World Heritage Site in 1999, the park protects some of the most pristine coastal cliffs in the Americas. Of the 512 plant species identified thus far, about 60% are endemic and a dozen of them are found only here. The fauna is equally rich, with 25 species of mollusk, seven species of amphibian, 44 types of reptile, 110 bird species and 13 types of mammal.

In El Guafe, archaeologists have uncovered the second-most important community of ancient agriculturists and ceramic-makers discovered in Cuba. Approximately 1000 years old, the artifacts discovered include altars, carved stones and earthen vessels along with six idols guarding a water goddess inside a ceremonial cave. As far as archaeologists are concerned, it's probably just the tip of the iceberg.

The park has two main access points: Las Colorados and the village of Alegría de Pío.

Las Colorados & Around

◉ Sights & Activities

Museo las Colorados   MUSEUM
(admission CUC$5; ◷8am-6pm) A large monument just beyond the park gate marks the *Granma's* landing spot. A small museum outlines the routes taken by Castro, Guevara and the others into the Sierra Maestra, and there's a full-scale replica of the *Granma*, which – if you're lucky – a machete-wielding

guard will let you climb inside to wonder how 82 men ever made it.

The entry ticket includes a visit to the simple reconstructed hut of the first *campesino* (a poor charcoal-burner) to help Fidel after the landing. An enthusiastic guide will also accompany you along a 1.3km path through dense mangroves to the ocean and the spot where the *Granma* ran aground, 70m offshore.

**Sendero Arqueológico
Natural el Guafe**   TRAIL
(admission CUC$3) About 8km southwest of Las Colorados is this well-signposted 2km-long trail, the park's headline nature/archaeological hike. An underground river here has created 20 large caverns, one of which contains the famous **Ídolo del Agua**, carved from stalagmites by pre-Columbian Indians; there's also a 500-year-old cactus, butterflies, 170 different species of birds (including the tiny colibrí), and multiple orchids.

You should allow two hours for the stroll in order to take everything in. A park guide can show you the more interesting features for an extra CUC$2. There are hundreds of flies here. Bring repellent.

The park is flecked with other trails, the best of which is the 30km **trek to Alegría de Pío** replicating the journey of the 82 rebels who landed here in 1956. Due to its length and lack of suitable signage, this rarely tackled trail is best done with a guide (the trail actually runs on a further 70km into the Sierra Maestra, if you're feeling energetic). Inquire at Ecotur (p379) in Bayamo beforehand. You'll need to arrange for transport to meet you at Alegría de Pío.

Comunidad Cabo Cruz VILLAGE

Three kilometers beyond the El Guafe trailhead is a tiny fishing community with skiffs bobbing offshore and sinewy men gutting their catch on the golden beach. The 33m-tall **Vargas lighthouse** here (erected 1871) now belongs to the Cuban military. In its shadow lies Restaurante el Cabo, source of the cheapest fresh seafood you'll find anywhere.

There's good swimming and shore snorkeling east of the lighthouse; bring your own gear as there are no facilities.

Sleeping & Eating

Campismo las Colorados CAMPISMO $

(Carretera de Niquero Km 17; s/d CUC$8/12; ❀) A Category 3 campismo with 28 duplex cabins standing on 500m of murky beach, 5km southwest of Belic, just outside the park. All cabins have air-con and baths and there's a restaurant, a games hall and water-sport rental on site. You can book through Cubamar (p95) in Havana.

Restaurante el Cabo SEAFOOD $

(meals CUC$2; ⊙7am-9pm Tue-Sun) The cheapest seafood in Cuba comes straight out of the Caribbean behind this restaurant that lies in the shadow of the Vargas lighthouse. Expect fresh fillets of snapper and swordfish, and prices in Cuban pesos.

Ranchón las Colorados CARIBBEAN $

(meals CUC$1-3; ⊙noon-7pm) A traditional thatched-roof restaurant selling fairly basic *comida criolla* just before the park gates, this place does the business if you're hungry after a long drive.

Alegría de Pío

Pause for a moment. You're on hallowed revolutionary ground. Accessed via 28km of potholed purgatory from a turnoff in Niquero, this is the spot where Castro's shipwrecked rebels were intercepted by Bastista's army in 1956 and forced to split up and flee. A monument went up in 2009 in the sugar cane field where the rebels were suprised. It is emblazoned with the names of the fallen and the words '*Nadie se rinde aquí cojone!*' (No one surrenders here, bollocks!), supposedly shouted by Camilo Cienfuegos and repeated by Juan Almeida as all hell broke loose. A guide will show you around the site, which includes various graves, billboards and a **cave** in which Che Guevara and Juan Almeida hid for two days.

Alegría de Pío is a tiny village with a school and a park lodge offering very basic accommodations in dorms with shared bathrooms. Food is available but, to ensure decent supplies, you might want to reserve ahead with Ecotur (p379) in Bayamo.

The site lies inside the Parque Nacional Desembarco del Granma and guides can take you on various park trails. **Morlotte-Fustete** is a 2km trail that traverses spectacular marine terraces (sometimes using wooden ladders) and takes in the **Cueva del Fustete** – a 5km-long cavern replete with stalagmites and stalactites – and the **Hoyo de Morlotte**, a 77m deep dolina caused by water corrosion. **El Samuel** is a 1.3km trail to the **Cueva Espelunca**, another cave thought to have been used by indigenous people for religious ceremonies. The **Boca de Toro** is a 6km trail to high cliffs overlooking a river valley and takes in the **Farallón de Blanquizal**, a beautiful natural lookout.

Alegría de Pío is also the official finish point for the 18km hike from Las Colorados that replicates the path of the shipwrecked *Granma* rebels in December 1956. From here the trail continues east to Cinco Palmas and, ultimately, Comandancia de la Plata. Bring plenty of drinking water.

❶ Getting There & Away

Ten kilometers southwest of Media Luna the road divides, with Pilón 30km to the southeast and Niquero 10km to the southwest. Belic is 16km southwest of Niquero. It's another 6km from Belic to the national park entry gate. The turn off for Alegría de Pío is just after the Servicentro in Niquero.

If you don't have your own transport, getting here is tough. Irregular buses go as far as the Campismo las Colorados daily and there are equally infrequent trucks from Belic. As a last resort, you can try the *amarillos* in Niquero. The closest gas station is in Niquero.

Pilón

POP 12,700

Pilón is a small, isolated settlement wedged between the Marea del Portillo resorts and the Parque Nacional Desembarco del Granma. It is the last coastal town of any note before Chivirico over 150km to the east. Since its sugar mill shut down nearly a decade ago, Pilón has lost much of its raison d'être, though the people still eke out a living despite almost nonexistent transport links and merciless bludgeonings from assorted hurricanes. The **Casa Museo Celia Sánchez Manduley** (admission CUC$1; ☉9am-5pm Mon-Sat) is a museum in honour of the Revolution's 'first lady' who briefly lived at this address in Pilón. Pilón does host a weekly street party – similar to those in Manzanillo and Bayamo – with whole roast pig, shots of rum and plenty of live music. This is the **Sábado de Rumba** (☉8pm Sat), and is your best chance of seeing the popular Cuban dance called the *pilón* (named after the town), which imitates the rhythms of pounding sugar.

Pilón has sprouted a couple of casas particulares in recent years. Look for the blue 'Arrendador Divisa' sign by the main highway.

The hotels at Marea del Portillo 11km away run a weekly Saturday evening transfer bus to Pilón for CUC$5 return. Getting here otherwise will involve a car, long-distance bike or winging it with the *amarillos*. The Servi-Cupet gas station is by the highway at the entrance to Pilón and sells snacks and drinks. Drivers should be sure to fill up here; the next gas station is in Santiago de Cuba nearly 200km away.

Marea del Portillo

There's something infectious about Marea del Portillo, a tiny south-coast village bordered by two low-key all-inclusive resorts. Wedged into a narrow strip of dry land between the glistening Caribbean and the cascading Sierra Maestra, it occupies a spot of great natural beauty – and great history.

The problem for independent travelers is getting here. There is no regular public transport, which means that you may, for the first time, have to go local and travel with the *amarillos*. Another issue for beach lovers is the sand, which is of a light gray color and may disappoint those more attuned to the brilliant whites of Cayo Coco.

The resorts themselves are affordable and well-maintained places but they are isolated; the nearest town of any size is lackluster Manzanillo 100km to the north. Real rustic Cuba, however, is a gunshot outside the hotel gates.

Activities

There's plenty to do here, despite the area's apparent isolation. Horseback riding can be arranged for CUC$35 (usually to El Salto) or a rustic 'Three Villages' tour to Sevilla, Pilón and Mota for CUC$20. A jeep tour to El Macio River is CUC$32 and trips to Parque Nacional Desembarco del Granma are around CUC$60. Trips can be booked at Cubanacán desks in Hotel Marea del Portillo (p390) and Hotel Farallón del Caribe (p390).

Centro Internacional de Buceo Marea del Portillo   DIVING, FISHING

Adjacent to Hotel Marea del Portillo, this Cubanacán-run dive center offers scuba diving for a giveaway CUC$30/59 per one/two immersions. A more exciting dive to the *Cristóbal Colón* wreck (sunk in the 1898 Spanish-Cuban-American War) costs CUC$70 for two immersions. Open-sea fishing starts at a highly reasonable CUC$45 with bar and lunch.

Other water excursions include a seafari (with snorkeling) for CUC$35, a sunset cruise for CUC$15 and a trip to uninhabited Cayo Blanco for CUC$25.

El Salto   HIKING

This wondrous DIY 20km out-and-back hike takes you through fields and valleys, a small village, past a lake, across a river and, finally, to El Salto, where there's a small waterfall, a shady thatched shelter and an inviting swimming hole.

Starting right outside the hotel complex, turn right onto the coast road and then, after approximately 400m, hang left onto an unpaved track just before a bridge. The track eventually joins a road and traverses a dusty, scattered settlement. On the far side of the village a dam rises above you. Rather than take the paved road up the embankment to the left, branch right and, after 200m, pick up a clear path that rises steeply up above the dam and into view of the lake behind. This beautiful path tracks alongside the lake before crossing one of its river feeds on a wooden bridge. Go straight on and uphill here and, when the path forks on the crest, bear right. Heading down into a verdant tranquil valley, pass a *casa de campesino* (the friendly owners keep bees and will give you honey, coffee and a geographical reorientation), cross the river (Río Cilantro) and then follow it upstream to El Salto.

Salto de Guayabito
HIKING

Starting in the village of **Mata Dos** about 20km east of Marea, this hike is normally done as part of an organized trip from the hotels. Groups – who often embark on horseback – follow the Río Motas 7km upstream to an enchanting waterfall surrounded by rocky cliffs, ferns, cacti and orchids.

🛏 Sleeping

★ Hotel Marea del Portillo
HOTEL $$

(🕿 59-70-08; all-incl s/d/tr CUC$37/59/80; P ❄ @ ☎) It's not Cayo Coco, but it barely seems to matter here. In fact, Marea's all-round functionalism and lack of big-resort pretension seem to work well in this traditional corner of Cuba. The 74 rooms are perfectly adequate, the food buffet does a good job, and the dark sandy arc of beach is within baseball-pitching distance of your balcony/patio.

Servicing loyal repeat-visit Canadians and some Cuban families means there is a mix of people here, plus plenty of interesting excursions to some of the island's lesser heralded sights.

Villa Turística Punta Piedra
HOTEL $$

(🕿 59-44-21; s/d CUC$55/80; P ❄ ☎) On the main road 5km west of Marea del Portillo and 11km east of Pilón, this small low-key resort, comprising 13 rooms in two single-story blocks, makes an interesting alternative to the larger hotels. There's a restaurant, and an intermittent disco located on a secluded stretch of sandy beach. Staff will be delighted (if not absolutely gobsmacked) with your custom!

Hotel Farallón del Caribe
HOTEL $$$

(🕿 59-70-82; all-incl s/d CUC$95/120; P ❄ @ ☎) Perched on a low hill with the Caribbean on one side and the Sierra Maestra on the other, the Farallón is the bigger, richer option here. Three-star all-inclusive facilities are complemented by five-star surroundings and truly magical views.

The resort is popular with snow-fleeing Canadians bussed in from Manzanillo and is only open seasonally (November to April).

❶ Getting There & Away

The journey east to Santiago is one of Cuba's most spectacular, but the road quality is awful and regularly affected by the weather. Options are your own car (check ahead regarding road conditions); a taxi (bank on at least CUC$160 for Marea to Santiago de Cuba); bicycle (a two- to three-day view-loaded roller coaster); or winging it with 'public transport' (possibly one of Cuba's greatest adventures, but only for the hardy who are not averse to long waits and some hitchhiking). Warning – the road sees very little traffic and has virtually no facilities and no gas stations (the nearest is in Pilón). Travel with supplies.

❶ Getting Around

The hotels rent out scooters for approximately CUC$25 a day. **Cubacar** (🕿 59-70-05; ☎) has a desk at Hotel Marea del Portillo, or you can join in an excursion with Cubanacán. The route to El Salto can be covered on foot.

Santiago de Cuba Province

🎵 22 / POP 1,048,000

Includes ➡

Santiago de Cuba... 393
Siboney 418
La Gran Piedra 419
Parque Baconao.... 420
El Cobre 423
El Saltón........... 424
Chivirico........... 425
El Uvero 425
Pico Turquino Area . . . 426

Best Battle Sites

➡ Cuartel Moncada (p402)

➡ Loma de San Juan (p403)

➡ El Uvero (p425)

➡ Museo de la Lucha Clandestina (p400)

Best Natural Sites

➡ La Gran Piedra (p419)

➡ Pico Turquino (p426)

➡ El Saltón (p424)

➡ Laguna Baconao (p421)

Why Go?

Stuck out in Cuba's mountainous 'Oriente' region and long a hotbed of rebellion and sedition, Santiago's cultural influences have often come from the east, imported via Haiti, Jamaica, Barbados and Africa. For this reason the province is often cited as being Cuba's most 'Caribbean' enclave, with a raucous West Indian–style carnival and a cache of *folklórico* dance groups that owe as much to French-Haitian culture as they do to Spanish.

As the focus of Spain's new colony in the 16th and early 17th centuries, Santiago de Cuba enjoyed a brief spell as Cuba's capital until it was usurped by Havana in 1607. The subsequent slower pace of development has some distinct advantages. Drive 20km or so along the coast in either direction from the provincial capital and you're on a different planet, a land full of rugged coves, crashing surf, historical coffee plantations and hills replete with riotous endemism.

When to Go

➡ July is the key month in Santiago de Cuba's cultural calendar, when the city is *caliente* (hot) in more ways than one. The month begins with the vibrant Festival del Caribe and ends with the justifiably famous Carnaval.

➡ More music is on offer in March at the Festival Internacional de Trova, when the city rediscovers its musical roots.

➡ The period between these two events (March through June) is renowned for its high water clarity, ensuring excellent diving conditions off the south coast.

Santiago de Cuba Province Highlights

1 Stroll around Santiago de Cuba's **Cementerio Santa Ifigenia** (p404).

2 Visit the **Cuartel Moncada** (p402) in Santiago de Cuba and evaluate the audacity (or folly) of Castro's 1953 insurrection.

3 Escape to luscious mountain getaway **El Saltón** (p424).

4 Explore Cuba's numerous Afro-Cuban dance genres at a **folklórico show** (p412) in Santiago de Cuba.

5 Trace the history of Cuba's French-inspired coffee culture at **Cafetal la Isabelica** (p419) in Gran Piedra.

6 Undertake a pilgrimage to **El Cobre** (p423) to visit the shrine of Cuba's patron saint, La Virgen de la Caridad.

7 Stand atop Cuba's highest mountain, **Pico Turquino** (p426), next to the bust of José Martí, and admire the view.

8 Dive to the wreck of Spanish warship **Cristóbal Colón** (p426) off the wild coast near Chivirico.

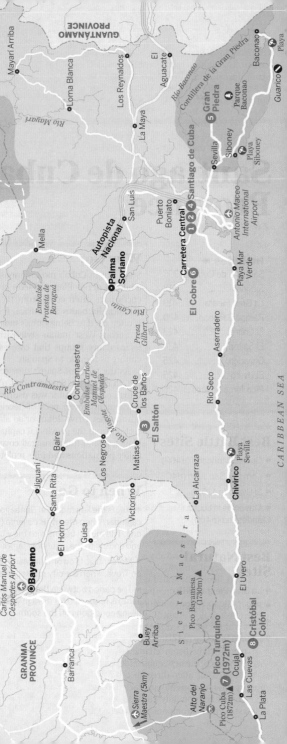

History

Founded in 1514 by Diego Velázquez de Cuéllar (his bones purportedly lie underneath the cathedral), the city of Santiago de Cuba moved to its present site, on a sharp horseshoe of harbor in the lee of the Sierra Maestra, in 1522. Its first mayor was Hernán Cortés – Velázquez' wayward secretary – who departed to explore Mexico in 1518.

Installed as the colony's new capital after the abandonment of Baracoa in 1515, Santiago enjoyed a brief renaissance as a center for copper-mining, and a disembarkation point for slaves arriving from West Africa via Hispaniola. But the glory wasn't to last. In 1556 the Spanish captains-general departed for Havana and in 1607 the capital was transferred permanently to the west. Raided by pirates and reduced at one point to a small village of only several hundred people, embattled Santiago barely survived the ignominy.

The tide turned in 1655 when Spanish settlers arrived from the nearby colony of Jamaica; this influx was augmented further in the 1790s as French plantation owners on the run from a slave revolt in Haiti settled in the city's Tivolí district. Always one step ahead of the capital in the cultural sphere, Santiago founded the Seminario de San Basilio Magno as an educational establishment in 1722 (six years before the founding of the Universidad de La Habana) and in 1804 the city's top cleric was promoted to the post of archbishop.

In 1898, just as Cuba seemed about to triumph in its long struggle for independence, the US intervened in the Spanish-Cuban-American War, landing a flotilla of troops on nearby Daiquirí beach. Subsequently, decisive land and sea battles of both Wars of Independence were fought in and around Santiago. The first was played out on July 1 when a victorious cavalry charge led by Teddy Roosevelt on outlying Loma de San Juan (San Juan Hill) sealed a famous victory. The second ended in a highly one-sided naval battle in Santiago harbor between US (under Admiral William T Sampson) and Spanish ships which led to the almost total destruction of the Spanish fleet.

A construction boom characterized the first few years of the new, quasi-independent Cuban state, but after three successive US military interventions, things started to turn sour. It was here on July 26, 1953, that Fidel Castro and his companions launched an assault on the Cuartel Moncada (Moncada Barracks). This was the start of a number of events that changed the course of Cuban history. At his trial in Santiago, Castro made his famous *History Will Absolve Me* speech, which became the basic platform of the Cuban Revolution.

On November 30, 1956, the people of Santiago de Cuba rose in rebellion against Batista's troops in a futile attempt to distract attention from the landing of Castro's guerrillas on the western shores of Oriente. Although not initially successful, an underground movement led by Frank and Josué País quickly established a secret supply line that ran vital armaments up to the fighters in the Oriente's Sierra Maestra. Despite the murder of the País brothers and many others in 1957-58, the struggle continued unabated, and it was in Santiago de Cuba, on the evening of January 1, 1959, that Castro first appeared publicly to declare the success of the Revolution. All these events have earned Santiago the title 'Hero City of the Republic of Cuba.'

Santiago continued to grow rapidly in the years that followed the Revolution, enjoying a construction boom in the 1990s. The city was tarted up again in 2015 to celebrate its quincentennial.

Santiago de Cuba

POP 444,800

You can take Santiago de Cuba in one of two ways: a hot, aggravating city full of hustlers and hassle that'll have you rushing to get on the first bus back to Havana; or a glittering cultural capital that has played an instrumental part in the evolution of Cuban literature, music, architecture, politics and ethnology. Yes, Santiago divides opinions among Cubans and foreigners almost as much as one of its most famous former scholars, Fidel Castro. Some love it; others hate it; few are indifferent.

Enlivened by a cosmopolitan mix of Afro-Caribbean culture and situated closer to Haiti and the Dominican Republic than to Havana, Santiago's influences tend to come as much from the east as from the west, a factor that has been crucial in shaping the city's distinct identity. Nowhere else in Cuba will you find such an inexorably addictive colorful combination of people or such a resounding sense of historical destiny. Diego Velázquez de Cuéllar made the city his second capital,

Santiago de Cuba

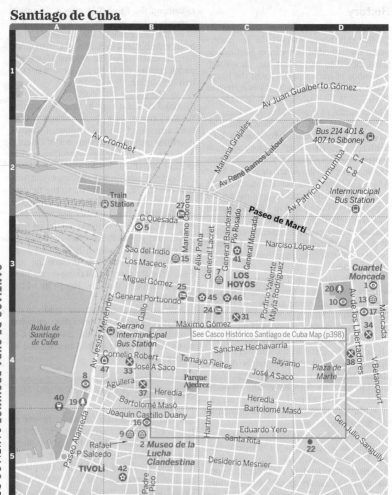

See Casco Histórico Santiago de Cuba Map (p398)

Fidel Castro used it to launch his embryonic nationalist Revolution, Don Facundo Bacardí based his first-ever rum factory here, and just about every Cuban music genre from salsa to *son* first emanated from somewhere in these dusty, rhythmic and sensuous streets.

Setting-wise, Santiago could rival any of the world's great urban centers. Caught dramatically between the indomitable Sierra Maestra and the azure Caribbean, the city's *casco histórico* (historical center) retains a time-worn and slightly neglected air that's vaguely reminiscent of Salvador in Brazil, or the seedier parts of New Orleans.

Santiago is also hot, in more ways than one. While the temperature rises into the 30s out on the street, *jineteros* (touts) go about their business in the shadows with a level of ferocity unmatched elsewhere in Cuba. Then there's the pollution, particularly bad in the central district, where cacophonous motorcycles swarm up and down narrow streets better designed for horses or pedestrians. Travelers should beware. While never particularly unsafe, everything in Santiago feels a little madder, more frenetic, a tad more desperate, and visitors should be prepared to adjust their pace accordingly.

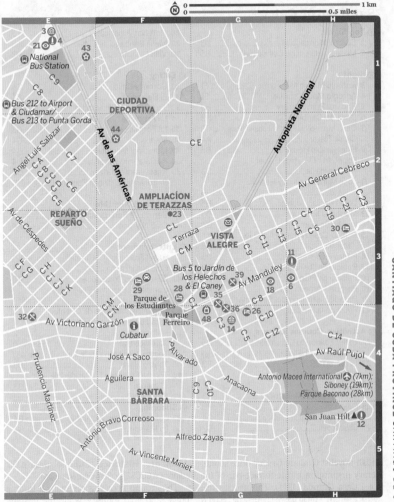

◎ Sights

◎ Casco Histórico

Parque Céspedes PARK
(Map p398) If there's an archetype for romantic Cuban street life, Parque Céspedes is it. A throbbing kaleidoscope of walking, talking, hustling, flirting, guitar-strumming humanity, this most ebullient of city squares, with the bronze bust of **Carlos Manuel de Céspedes**, the man who kick-started Cuban independence in 1868, at its heart, is a sight to behold any time of day or night.

Old ladies gossip on shady park benches, a guy in a panama hat drags his scarred double bass over toward the Casa de la Trova, while sultry señoritas in skin-tight lycra flutter their eyelashes at the male tourists on the terrace of the Hotel Casa Granda. Parque Céspedes is also, aside from a jarring modernist bank on its west side, a treasure trove of colonial architecture.

The **Casa de la Cultura Miguel Matamoros** (Map p398; General Lacret 651), on the square's eastern aspect, is the former San Carlos Club, a social center for wealthy *santiagüeros* until the Revolution. Next door

Santiago de Cuba

⊙ **Top Sights**

1 Cuartel Moncada	D3
2 Museo de la Lucha Clandestina	B5

⊙ **Sights**

3 Antonio Maceo Museum	E1
4 Antonio Maceo statue	E1
5 Bacardí Rum Factory	B3
6 Casa del Caribe	H3
7 Casa Museo de Frank y Josué País	C3
8 Clock Tower	A4
9 Fidel Castro House	B5
10 Fountain of Martí and Abel Santamaría	D3
11 José María Heredia y Heredia Statue	H3
12 Loma de San Juan	H5
13 Moncada Museum	D3
14 Museo de la Imagen	G4
15 Museo-Casa Natal de Antonio Maceo	B3
16 Padre Pico steps	B5
17 Palacio de Justicia	D3
18 Palacio de Pioneros	G3
19 Parque Alameda	A4
20 Parque Histórico Abel Santamaría	D3
21 Plaza de la Revolución	E1

⊙ **Activities, Courses & Tours**

22 Ballet Folklórico Cutumba	D5
Casa del Caribe	(see 6)
23 UniversiTUR	F3

⊙ **Sleeping**

24 Casa Colonial 'Maruchi'	C3
25 Casa Lola	B3
26 Casa Mili	G4
27 Casa Yoyi	B2

28 Hotel las Américas	F3
29 Meliá Santiago de Cuba	F3
30 Villa Gaviota	H3

⊙ **Eating**

31 Compay Gallo	C4
32 El Barracón	E4
33 Jardín de los Enramadas	B4
34 La Arboleda	D4
35 La Fortaleza	G3
36 Madrileño	G4
37 Municipal Market	B4
38 Restaurante España	D4
39 Restaurante Zunzún	G3
Ristorante Italiano la Fontana	(see 29)

⊙ **Drinking & Nightlife**

Barrita de Ron Havana Club	(see 5)
40 Club Nautico	A4

⊙ **Entertainment**

Ballet Folklórico Cutumba	(see 22)
41 Carabalí Izuama	C3
42 Casa de las Tradiciones	B5
Compañia Danzaría Folklórica Kokoyé	(see 6)
43 Conjunto Folklórico de Oriente	E1
44 Estadio de Béisbol Guillermón Moncada	F2
Santiago Café	(see 29)
Teatro José María Heredia	(see 43)
45 Teatro Martí	C3
46 Tumba Francesa La Caridad de Oriente	C3

⊙ **Shopping**

47 Centro de Negocios Alameda	B4
48 La Maison	G4

British novelist Graham Greene once sought literary inspiration in the terrace-bar of the Hotel Casa Granda (1914). The neoclassical **Ayuntamiento** (Map p398; cnr General Lacret & Aguilera), on the northern side of the square, was erected in the 1950s using a design from 1783 and was once the site of Hernán Cortés' mayoral office. Fidel Castro appeared on the balcony of the present building on the night of January 2, 1959, trumpeting the Revolution's triumph.

★**Casa de Diego Velázquez**   MUSEUM
(Map p398; Felix Peña No 602) The oldest house still standing in Cuba, this arresting early colonial abode dating from 1522 was the official residence of the island's first governor. Restored in the late 1960s, the Andalusian-style facade with fine, wooden lattice windows was inaugurated in 1970 as the **Museo de**

Ambiente Histórico Cubano (Map p398; admission CUC$2; ⊙9am-5pm Mon-Sun).

The ground floor was originally a trading house and gold foundry, while the upstairs was where Velázquez lived. Today, rooms display period furnishings and decoration from the 16th to 19th centuries. Check the two-way screens, where you could look out without being observed: a Turkish influence (Turkey had a big influence on European style at this time). Visitors are also taken through an adjacent 19th-century neoclassical house.

★**Catedral de Nuestra Señora de la Asunción**   CHURCH
(Map p398; ⊙Mass 6:30pm Mon & Wed-Fri, 5pm Sat, 9am & 6:30pm Sun) Santiago's most important church is stunning both inside and out. There has been a cathedral on this site since the city's inception in the 1520s,

though a series of pirate raids, earthquakes and dodgy architects put paid to at least three previous incarnations. The present cathedral, characterized by its two neo-classical towers, was completed in 1922; the remains of first colonial governor, Diego Velázquez, are still buried underneath.

The church was being comprehensively restored both inside and out at last visit in time for Santiago's quincentennial in 2015. Expect a thorough upgrade of the intricate ceiling frescoes, the hand-carved choir stalls and the altar that honors the venerated Virgen de la Caridad. The adjacent **Museo Arquidiocesano** (Map p398; ⊗9am-5pm Mon-Fri, 9am-2pm Sat, 9am-noon Sun) is rather a disappointment by comparison, housing a dullish collection of furniture, liturgical objects and paintings including the *Ecce homo*, believed to be Cuba's oldest painting.

Balcón de Velázquez   VIEWPOINT
(Map p398; cnr Bartolomé Masó & Mariano Corona) The alfresco Balcón de Velázquez is the site of an old Spanish fort which offers ethereal views over the terracotta-tiled roofs of the Tivolí neighborhood toward the harbor.

Calle Heredia   STREET
(Map p398) The music never stops on Calle Heredia, Santiago's most sensuous street and also one of its oldest. The melodies start in the paint-peeled Casa de Cultura Josue País García (p414), where *danzón*-strutting pensioners mix with svelte rap artists barely out of their teens. One door up is Cuba's original Casa de la Trova (p414), a beautiful balconied townhouse redolent of New Orleans' French Quarter.

The Casa is dedicated to pioneering Cuban *trovador*, José 'Pepe' Sánchez (1856–1928) and first opened as Cuba's orginal *trova* (traditional poetic singing/songwriting) house in March 1968.

★ **Museo Municipal Emilio Bacardí Moreau**   MUSEUM
(Map p398; admission CUC$2; ⊗1-5pm Mon, 9am-5pm Tue-Fri, 9am-1pm Sat) Narrow Pío Rosado links Calle Heredia to Calle Aguilera and the fabulous Grecian facade of the Bacardí Museum. Founded in 1899 by the rum magnate war hero and city mayor, Emilio Bacardí y Moreau (the palatial building was built to spec), the museum is one of Cuba's oldest and most eclectic, with some absorbing artifacts amassed from Bacardí's travels.

These include an extensive weapons collection, paintings from the Spanish *costumbrismo* (19th-century artistic movement that predates Romanticism) school and the only Egyptian mummy on the island.

Casa Natal de José María Heredia y Heredia   MUSEUM
(Map p398; Heredia No 260; admission CUC$1; ⊗9am-7pm Tue-Sat, 9am-2pm Sun) A miniscule museum illustrating the life of one of Cuba's greatest Romantic poets and the man after whom the street is named, José María Heredia y Heredia (1803–39). Heredia's most notable work, 'Ode to Niagara,' is inscribed outside; it attempts to parallel the beauty of Canada's Niagara Falls with his personal feelings of loss about his homeland. Like many Cuban independence advocates, Heredia was forced into exile, dying in Mexico in 1839.

Museo del Carnaval   MUSEUM
(Map p398; Heredia No 303; admission CUC$1; ⊗2-5pm Mon, 9am-5pm Tue-Fri & Sun, 2-10pm Sat) A worthwhile museum displaying the history of Santiago's biggest shindig, the oldest and biggest carnival between Río and Mardi Gras. Drop in to see floats, effigies and the occasional *folklórico* dance show on the patio.

Maqueta de la Ciudad   MUSEUM
(Map p398; Mariano Corona No 704; admission CUC$1; ⊗9am-5pm Mon-Sat) Aping Havana's two impressive scale models of the city, Santiago has come up with its own incredibly detailed *maqueta*. Interesting historical and architectural information is displayed on illustrated wall panels and you can climb up to a mezzanine gallery for a true vulture's-eye view. For more views, gravitate to the cafe/terrace at the back.

Museo del Ron   MUSEUM
(Map p398; Bartolomé Masó No 358; admission CUC$2; ⊗9am-5pm Mon-Sat) While not as impressive as its Havana equivalent, this museum is also refreshingly devoid of the Havana Club sales bias. It offers an insightful outline of the history of Cuban rum (old machinery, examples of bottlings throughout the last century) along with a potent shot of the hard stuff (*añejo*).

Encased in a handsome townhouse, it has a bar below (same hours as museum) so hidden away it's reminiscent of a speakeasy, but with a knowledgeable bartender on hand to serve you up their 'recommendations.'

Casco Histórico Santiago de Cuba

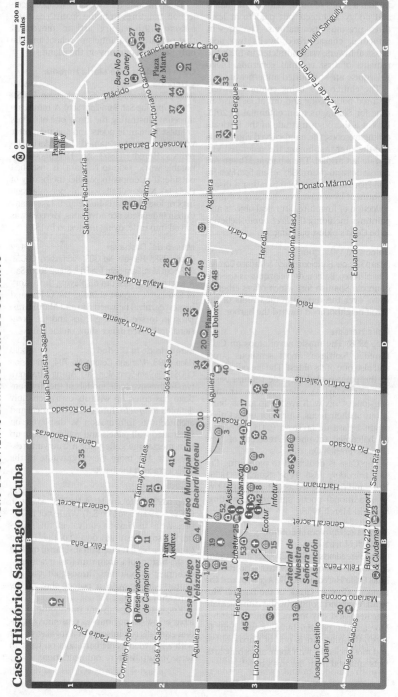

Casco Histórico Santiago de Cuba

◎ Top Sights
1 Casa de Diego Velázquez B2
2 Catedral de Nuestra Señora de la
   Asunción B3
3 Museo Municipal Emilio Bacardí
   Moreau C3

◎ Sights
4 Ayuntamiento B2
5 Balcón de Velázquez A3
6 Calle Heredia C3
7 Casa de la Cultura Miguel
   Matamoros B3
8 Casa de la Trova C3
9 Casa Natal de José María Heredia y
   Heredia C3
10 Gobierno Provincial C2
   Iglesia de Nuestra Señora de
   los Dolores .... (see 48)
11 Iglesia de Nuestra Señora del
   Carmen B2
12 Iglesia de San Francisco A1
13 Maqueta de la Ciudad A3
14 Memorial de Vilma Espín Guillois D1
15 Museo Arquidiocesano B3
16 Museo de Ambiente Histórico
   Cubano B3
17 Museo del Carnaval C3
18 Museo del Ron C3
19 Parque Céspedes B3
20 Plaza de Dolores D2
21 Plaza de Marte G2

◎ Sleeping
22 Aichel & Corrado E2
23 Casa Terraza Pavo Real B4
24 Hostal San Basilio C3
25 Hotel Casa Granda B3
26 Hotel Libertad G3
27 Hotel Rex G2

28 Nelson Aguilar Ferreiro & Deysi
   Ruíz Chaveco E2
29 Reydel Aguilar Ruiz E2
30 Roy's Terrace Inn A4

✪ Eating
31 Bendita Farándula F3
   Hotel Casa Granda .... (see 25)
32 La Teresina D2
33 Panadería Doña Neli G3
34 Restaurante Matamoros D2
35 Rumba Café C1
36 Santiago 1900 .... C3
37 St Pauli F2
38 Supermercado Plaza de Marte G2

◯ Drinking & Nightlife
39 Bar Sindo Garay B2
40 Café la Isabelica D3
41 Café Ven C2

✪ Entertainment
42 Casa de Cultura Josue País García B3
   Casa de la Trova .... (see 8)
43 Cine Rialto B3
44 Iris Jazz Club G2
45 Orfeón Santiago A3
46 Patio ARTex D3
47 Patio los Dos Abuelos G2
48 Sala de Conciertos Dolores E3
49 Subway Club E2
50 Uneac C3

◯ Shopping
   ARTex .... (see 8)
   ARTex .... (see 25)
51 Discoteca Egrem C2
52 Galería de Arte de Oriente B3
53 Librería Internacional B3
54 Librería la Escalera C3

SANTIAGO DE CUBA PROVINCE SANTIAGO DE CUBA

Plaza de Dolores   SQUARE
(Map p398; cnr Aguilera & Porfirio Valiente) East of Parque Céspedes is the pleasant and shady Plaza de Dolores, a former marketplace now dominated by the 18th-century Iglesia de Nuestra Señora de los Dolores (Map p398; cnr Aguilera & Porfirio Valiente). After a fire in the 1970s, the church was rebuilt as a concert hall (Sala de Conciertos Dolores). Many restaurants and cafes flank this square. It's also Santiago's most popular gay cruising spot.

Plaza de Marte   SQUARE
(Map p398) Guarding the entrance to the casco histórico, motorcycle-infested Plaza de Marte was formerly a macabre 19th-century Spanish parade ground, where prisoners were executed publicly for revolutionary ac-

tivities. Today, the plaza is Santiago de Cuba's esquina caliente (hot corner), where local baseball fans plot the imminent downfall of Havana's Industriales. The tall column with a red cap perched on top symbolizes liberty.

Memorial de Vilma Espín Guillois   MUSEUM
(Map p398; Sánchez Hechavarría No 473; admission CUC$2; ⊙ 9am-12:30pm Mon-Sat, 1-5pm Sun) This erstwhile home of Cuba's former 'first lady,' Vilma Espín, the wife of Raúl Castro, and instrumental force in the success of the Cuban Revolution, opened in 2010, three years after her death. This house, where she lived from 1939 to 1959, is packed with lucid snippets of her life.

The daughter of a lawyer to the Bacardí clan, Vilma was first radicalized after a meeting with Frank País in Santiago in 1956. Joining the rebels in the mountains, she went on to found the influential Federation of Cuban Women in 1960.

Iglesia de Nuestra Señora del Carmen
CHURCH

(Map p398; Félix Peña No 505) You can dig deeper into Santiago's ecclesiastical history in this tumbledown construction, a hall church dating from the 1700s that is the final resting place of Christmas-carol composer Esteban Salas (1725–1803), one-time choir master of Santiago de Cuba's cathedral.

Iglesia de San Francisco
CHURCH

(Map p398; Juan Bautista Sagarra No 121) This three-nave, 18th-century ecclesiastical gem is situated three blocks north of Parque Céspedes.

Gobierno Provincial
NOTABLE BUILDING

(Poder Popular; Map p398; cnr Pío Rosado & Aguilera) Situated opposite the Bacardí Museum, the equally Hellenic provincial government seat is another building from Cuba's 20th-century neoclassical revival. No public entry is permitted.

◎ South of the Casco Histórico

Tivolí
NEIGHBORHOOD

Santiago's old French quarter was first settled by colonists from Haiti in the late 18th and early 19th centuries. Set on a south-facing hillside overlooking the shimmering harbor, its red-tiled roofs and hidden patios are a tranquil haven these days, with old men pushing around dominoes and ebullient kids playing stickball amid pink splashes of bougainvillea.

The century-old **Padre Pico steps** (Map p394; cnr Padre Pico & Diego Palacios), cut into the steepest part of Calle Padre Pico, stand at the neighborhood's gateway.

★ Museo de la Lucha Clandestina
MUSEUM

(Map p394; General Jesús Rabí No 1; admission CUC$1; ⊙9am-5pm Tue-Sun) This gorgeous yellow colonial-style building now houses a museum detailing the underground struggle against Batista in the 1950s. It's a fascinating, if bloody, story enhanced by far-reaching views from the balcony. Across the street is the **house** (Map p394; General Jesús Rabí No 6) where Fidel Castro lived from 1931 to 1933, while a student in Santiago de Cuba (not open for visits).

🏃 City Walk
A Walk Through History

START PARQUE ALAMEDA
END CUARTEL MONCADA
LENGTH 2KM; THREE TO FOUR HOURS

Against a backdrop of spinach-green mountains and a steely blue bay, a walking tour of Santiago's *casco histórico* (old town) is an obligatory rite of passage for first-time visitors keen to uncover the steamy tropical sensations that make this city tick.

Start beside the bay with your sights set uphill. Parque Alameda inhabits the run-down thoroughfare facing Santiago's not-so-busy port. Most of the excitement lies to the east in a hilly neighborhood colonized by French-Haitians in the early 1800s and baptized ❶ **El Tivolí** (p400). Tivolí is one of Santiago's most picturesque and traffic-lite quarters where red-roofed houses and steep streets retain a time-warped Cuban atmosphere. The neighborhood's only real 'sight' is the ❷ **Museo de la Lucha Clandestina** (p400) reached by following Calle Diego Palacios uphill from the port. From the museum take the famous ❸ **Padre Pico steps** (p400) – a terracotta staircase built into the hillside – downhill to Calle Bartolomé Masó where a right turn will deposit you on the breeze-lapped ❹ **Balcón de Velázquez** (p397), site of an ancient fort. This stupendous view once inspired less calming contemplations; early Spanish colonists used it to look out for meddlesome pirates.

Head east next, avoiding the angry roar of the motorbikes, until you resurface in ❺ **Parque Céspedes** (p395). The ❻ **Casa de Diego Velázquez** (p396), with its Moorish fringes and intricate wooden arcades, is believed to be the oldest house still standing in Cuba and anchors the square on its west side. Contrasting impressively on the south side is the mighty, mustard facade of the ❼ **Catedral de Nuestra Señora de la Asunción** (p396). This building has been ransacked, burned, rocked by earthquakes and rebuilt, then remodeled and restored and ransacked again. Statues of Christopher Columbus and Fray Bartolomé de las Casas flank the entrance in ironic juxtaposition.

If you're tired already, step out onto the lazy terrace bar at ⑧ **Hotel Casa Granda** (p410) on the southeastern corner of the park, for mojitos and Montecristo cigars. Graham Greene came here in the 1950s on a clandestine mission to interview Fidel Castro. The interview never came off, but he managed instead to smuggle a suitcase of clothes up to the rebels in the mountains.

Follow the music as you exit and plunge into the paint-peeled romance of Calle Heredia, Santiago's – and one of Cuba's – most atmospheric streets, which rocks like New Orleans at the height of the jazz era. Its centerpiece is the infamous ⑨ **Casa de la Trova** (p414).

Heading upstream on Heredia, you'll pass street stalls, cigar peddlers, a guy dragging a double bass, and countless motorbikes. That yellowish house on the right with the poem emblazoned on the wall is ⑩ **Casa Natal de José María Heredia y Heredia** (p397), birthplace of one of Cuba's greatest poets. You might find a living scribe in ⑪ **Uneac** (p415), the famous national writers' union a few doors down. Stick your head inside and check out the *cartelera* (culture calendar) advertising the coming week's offerings. Plenty more dead legends are offered up in

print in funky ⑫ **Librería la Escalera** (p416), an unkempt but roguish bookstore across the street where busking musicians often crowd the stairway. Cross the street next (mind that motorbike) and stick your nose into the ⑬ **Museo del Carnaval** (p397).

Divert along Pío Rosado one block to Aguilera where you'll be confronted by the sturdy Grecian columns of the ⑭ **Museo Municipal Emilio Bacardí Moreau** (p397). Back outside, narrow Aguilera winds uphill to the shady ⑮ **Plaza de Dolores** (p399), which remains amazingly tranquil, considering the ongoing motorcycle mania.

Stalwarts should continue east to ⑯ **Plaza de Marte** (p399), the third of the *casco histórico's* pivotal squares and far more manic than the other two.

The walk ends in what is perhaps Santiago's most politically significant site, the art deco ⑰ **Cuartel Moncada** (p402), a one-time military barracks where the first shots of Cuba's Castro-led Revolution were fired in 1953. Today it functions more innocuously as a school, but a preserved section at the rear where the short skirmishes between the soldiers and the rebels took place is now one of Cuba's most interesting and poignant museums.

The museum was a former police station attacked by M-26-7 activists on November 30, 1956, to divert attention from the arrival of the tardy yacht *Granma*, carrying Fidel Castro and 81 others. It's up the slope from the western end of Diego Palacios.

Parque Alameda PARK

(Map p394; Av Jesús Menéndez) Below the Tivolí quarter, this narrow park embellishes a little-visited dockside promenade that opened in 1840 and was redesigned in 1893. At the north end you'll see the old **clock tower** (Map p394), *aduana* (customs house) and cigar factory. A curious mix of smart architecture and port-side sketchiness, its fresh(er) sea air makes it good for a stroll.

To tie in with the 2015 quincentennial, plans are afoot to improve the harbor area with an elegant 'Malecón' beautified with palm trees, restaurants, a playground and a new park.

⊙ North of Casco Histórico

North of the historic center, Santiago de Cuba turns residential in the Los Hoyos and Sueño neighborhoods.

★ Cuartel Moncada BARRACKS

(Moncada Barracks; Map p394; Av Moncada) Santiago's famous Moncada Barracks, a crenellated art deco building completed in 1938, is now synonymous with one of history's greatest failed putsches. Moncada earned immortality on July 26, 1953, when more than 100 revolutionaries led by then little-known Fidel Castro stormed Batista's troops at what was then Cuba's second-most important military garrison.

After the Revolution, the barracks, like all others in Cuba, was converted into a school called Ciudad Escolar 26 de Julio, and in 1967 a **museum** (Map p394; admission CUC$2; ☉9am-5pm Mon-Sat, 9am-1pm Sun) was installed near gate 3, where the main attack took place. As Batista's soldiers had cemented over the original bullet holes from the attack, the Castro government remade them (this time without guns) years later as a poignant reminder. The museum (one of Cuba's best) contains a scale model of the barracks plus interesting and sometimes grisly artifacts, diagrams and models of the attack, its planning and its aftermath. Most moving, perhaps, are the photographs of the 61 fallen at the end.

The first barracks on this site was constructed by the Spanish in 1859, and actually takes its name after Guillermón Moncada, a War of Independence fighter who was held prisoner here in 1874.

Museo-Casa Natal de Antonio Maceo MUSEUM

(Map p394; Los Maceos No 207; admission CUC$1; ☉9am-5pm Mon-Sat) This important museum is where the *mulato* general and hero of both Wars of Independence was born, on

....

SANTIAGO DE CUBA STREET NAMES

Welcome to another city where the streets have two names.

OLD NAME	NEW NAME
Calvario	Porfirio Valiente
Carniceria	Pío Rosado
Enramada	José A Saco
José Miguel Gómez	Havana
Paraíso	Plácido
Reloj	Mayía Rodríguez
Rey Pelayo	Joaquín Castillo Duany
San Félix	Hartmann
San Francisco	Sagarra
San Gerónimo	Sánchez Hechavarría
San Mateo	Sao del Indio
Santa Rita	Diego Palacios
Santo Tómas	Félix Peña
Trinidad	General Portuondo

June 14, 1845, and exhibits highlights of Maceo's life with photos, letters and a tattered flag that was flown in battle. Known as the Bronze Titan in Cuba for his bravery in battle, Maceo was the definitive 'man of action.'

In his 1878 Protest of Baraguá, he rejected any compromise with the colonial authorities and went into exile rather than sell out to the Spanish. Landing at Playa Duaba in 1895, he marched his army as far west as Pinar del Río before being killed in action in 1896.

Casa Museo de Frank y Josué País MUSEUM
(Map p394; General Banderas No 226; admission CUC$1; ☺9am-5pm Mon-Sat) Integral to the success of the Revolution, the young País brothers organized the underground section of the M-26-7 in Santiago de Cuba until Frank's murder by the police on July 30, 1957. The exhibits in this home-turned-museum tell the story. It's located about five blocks southeast of Museo-Casa Natal de Antonio Maceo.

Plaza de la Revolución SQUARE
(Map p394) As with all Cuban cities, Santiago has its bombastic Revolution square. This one's placed strategically at the junction of two sweeping avenues and anchored by an eye-catching **statue** (Map p394; Plaza de la Revolución) of dedicated city hero (and native son), Antonio Maceo, atop his horse and surrounded by 23 raised machetes. Underneath the giant mound/plinth a small reverential **museum** (Map p394; ☺8am-4pm Mon-Sat) FREE contains info on his life. Other notable buildings bordering the square include modern Teatro Heredia and the National Bus Station.

Bacardí Rum Factory LANDMARK
(Fábrica de Ron; Map p394; Av Jesús Menéndez, opposite train station) While it's not as swanky as its modern Bermuda HQ, the original Bacardí factory, which opened in 1868, oozes history. Spanish-born founder Don Facundo dreamt up the world-famous Bacardí bat symbol after finding a colony of the winged mammals living in the factory's rafters. The Cuban government continues to make traditional rum here – the signature Ron Caney brand as well as Ron Santiago and Ron Varadero.

The Bacardí family, however, fled the island post-Revolution. In total, the factory knocks out nine million liters of rum a year, 70% of which is exported. There are currently no factory tours, but the **Barrita**

de Ron Havana Club (Map p394; Av Jesús Menéndez No 703; ☺9am-6pm), a tourist bar attached to the factory, offers rum sales and tastings. A great billboard opposite the station announces Santiago's modern battle cry: *Rebelde ayer, hospitalaria hoy, heroica siempre* (Rebellious yesterday, hospitable today, heroic always).

Parque Histórico Abel Santamaría PARK
(Map p394; cnr General Portuondo & Av de los Libertadores) This is the site of the former Saturnino Lora Civil Hospital, stormed by Abel Santamaría and 60 others on that fateful July day (they were later tortured and killed). On October 16, 1953, Fidel Castro was tried in the Escuela de Enfermeras for leading the Moncada attack. It was here that he made his famous *History Will Absolve Me* speech.

The park contains a giant Cubist **fountain** (Map p394) engraved with the countenances of Abel Santamaría and José Martí that gushes out a veritable Niagara Falls of water.

Palacio de Justicia LANDMARK
(Map p394; cnr Av de los Libertadores & General Portuondo) On the opposite side of the street to the park, this court building was taken by fighters led by Raúl Castro during the Moncada attack. They were supposed to provide cover fire to Fidel's group from the rooftop but were never needed. Many of them came back two months later to be tried and sentenced in the court.

⊙ Vista Alegre

In any other city, Vista Alegre would be a leafy upper-middle-class neighborhood (indeed, it once was); but in revolutionary Cuba the dappled avenues and whimsical early-20th-century architecture are the domain of clinics, cultural centers, government offices, state-run restaurants and a handful of esoteric points of interest.

Loma de San Juan MONUMENT
(Map p394; San Juan Hill) Future American president Teddy Roosevelt forged his reputation on this small hillock where, flanked by the immortal rough riders, he supposedly led a fearless cavalry charge against the Spanish to seal a famous US victory. Protected on pleasantly manicured grounds adjacent to the modern-day Motel San Juan, Loma de San Juan marks the spot of the Spanish-Cuban-American War's only land battle (on July 1, 1898).

In reality, it is doubtful Roosevelt even mounted his horse in Santiago, while the purportedly clueless Spanish garrison – outnumbered 10 to one – managed to hold off more than 6000 American troops for 24 hours. Cannons, trenches and numerous US monuments, including a bronze rough rider, enhance the classy gardening, while the only acknowledgement of a Cuban presence is the rather understated monument to the unknown Mambí soldier.

Casa del Caribe BUILDING
(Map p394; Calle 13 No 154; ☺9am-5pm Mon-Fri) **FREE** Founded in 1982 to study Caribbean life, this cultural institution organizes the Festival del Caribe and the Fiesta del Fuego every July and also hosts various concert nights. Interested parties can organize percussion courses or studies in Afro-Cuban culture.

Museo de la Imagen MUSEUM
(Map p394; Calle 8 No 106; admission CUC$1; ☺9am-5pm Mon-Sat) A short but fascinating journey through the history of Cuban photography from Kodak to Korda, with little CIA spy cameras and lots of old and contemporary photos. The museum also guards a library of rare films and documentaries.

Palacio de Pioneros LANDMARK
(Map p394; cnr Av Manduley & Calle 11) This eclectic mansion (built between 1906 and 1910) was once the largest and most opulent in Santiago. Since 1974 it has been a developmental center for kids (pioneros). In the garden is an old MiG fighter plane on which the younger pioneers play. The traffic circle at the corner of Av Manduley and Calle 13 contains an impressive marble **statue** (Map p394) of poet José María Heredia y Heredia.

◉ Greater Santiago de Cuba

Cementerio Santa Ifigenia CEMETERY
(Av Crombet; admission CUC$1; ☺8am-6pm) Nestled peacefully on the city's western extremity, the Cementerio Santa Ifigenia is second only to Havana's Necrópolis Cristóbal Colón in its importance and grandiosity. Created in 1868 to accommodate the victims of the War of Independence and a simultaneous yellow-fever outbreak, the Santa Ifigenia includes many great historical figures among its 8000-plus tombs, notably the mausoleum of José Martí.

Names to look out for include Tomás Estrada Palma (1835–1908), Cuba's now disgraced

first president; Emilio Bacardí y Moreau (1844–1922) of the famous rum dynasty; María Grajales, the widow of independence hero Antonio Maceo, and Mariana Grajales, Maceo's mother; 11 of the 31 generals of the independence struggles; the Spanish soldiers who died in the battles of San Juan Hill and Caney; the 'martyrs' of the 1953 Moncada Barracks attack; M-26-7 activists Frank and Josué País; father of Cuban independence, Carlos Manuel de Céspedes (1819–74); and international celebrity-cum-popular-musical-rake, Compay Segundo (1907–2003) of Buena Vista Social Club fame.

The highlight of the cemetery, for most, is the quasi-religious mausoleum to national hero José Martí (1853–95). Erected in 1951 during the Batista era, the imposing hexagonal structure is positioned so that Martí's wooden casket (draped solemnly in a Cuban flag) receives daily shafts of sunlight. This is in response to a comment Martí made in one of his poems that he would like to die not as a traitor in darkness, but with his visage facing the sun. A round-the-clock guard of the mausoleum is changed, amid much pomp and ceremony, every 30 minutes.

Horse carts go along Av Jesús Menéndez, from Parque Alameda to Cementerio Santa Ifigenia (1 peso); otherwise it's a good leg-stretching walk.

★Castillo de San Pedro de la Roca del Morro FORT, MUSEUM
(El Morro; admission CUC$4; ☺8am-7:30pm; ⊞) A Unesco World Heritage Site since 1997, the San Pedro fort sits impregnably atop a 60m-high promontory at the entrance to Santiago harbor, 10km southwest of the city. The stupendous views from the upper terrace take in the wild western ribbon of Santiago's coastline backed by the velvety Sierra Maestra.

The fort was designed in 1587 by famous Italian military engineer Juan Bautista Antonelli (who also designed La Punta and El Morro forts in Havana) to protect Santiago from pillaging pirates who had successfully sacked the city in 1554. Due to financial constraints, the building work didn't start until 1633 (17 years after Antonelli's death) and it was carried on sporadically for the next 60 years. In the interim British privateer Henry Morgan sacked and partially destroyed it. Finally finished in the early 1700s, El Morro's massive batteries, bastions, magazines and walls got little opportunity to serve their true purpose. With the era of piracy in decline, the fort was converted into a prison in the 1800s

Greater Santiago de Cuba

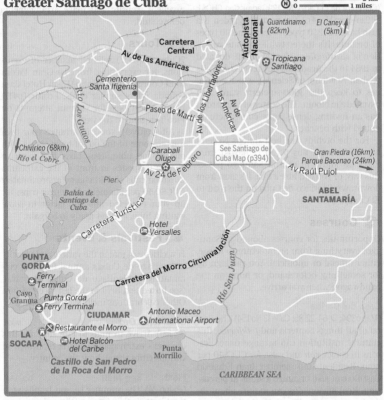

and it stayed that way – bar a brief interlude during the 1898 Spanish-Cuban-American War – until Cuban architect Francisco Prat Puig mustered up a restoration plan in the late 1960s.

Today, the fort hosts the swashbuckling Museo de Piratería, with another room given over to the US-Spanish naval battle that took place in the bay in 1898.

The fort, like Havana, has a **cañonzao ceremony** (firing of the cannon) each day at sunset when actors dress up in Mambises regalia.

To get to El Morro from the city center, you can take bus 212 to Ciudamar and cover the final 20 minutes on foot. Alternatively, a round-trip taxi ride from Parque Céspedes with wait should cost no more than CUC$15.

Cayo Granma   ISLAND
A small, populated key near the jaws of the bay, Cayo Granma is a little fantasy island of

red-roofed wooden houses – many of them on stilts above the water – that guard a traditional fishing community. You can hike up to the small whitewashed **Iglesia de San Rafael** at the key's highest point, or walk around the whole island in 15 minutes.

The best thing about this place, however, is just hanging out and soaking up a bit of the real Cuba. The only official eating establishment is the seafood-biased Restaurante el Cayo, although the just-refurbished blue-and-white clapboard Palmares restaurant, jutting out over the water on the Cayo's far side, should expand options.

To get to the key, take the regular ferry (leaving every one to 1½ hours) from Punta Gorda just below El Morro fort. The boat stops en route at La Socapa (actually still the mainland; the western jaw of the Bahía de Santiago) where there are decent swimming beaches.

Jardín de los Helechos GARDENS

(Carretera de El Caney No 129; admission CUC$1; 9am-5pm Mon-Fri) The peaceful garden is a lush haven of 350 types of ferns and 90 types of orchids. It's the erstwhile private collection of *santiagüero* Manuel Caluff, donated in 1984 to the Academia de Ciencias de Cuba (Cuban Academy of Science), which continues to keep the 3000-sq-eterm garden in psychedelic bloom. The center of the garden has an inviting dense copse-cum-sanctuary dotted with benches.

For the orchids, the best time is November to January. Bus 5 (20 centavos) from Plaza de Marte in central Santiago passes this way, or you can hire a taxi. It's 2km from downtown Santiago de Cuba on the road to El Caney.

Courses

Opportunities for courses abound in Santiago; everything from architecture to music, either official or unofficial. You can sign up for something beforehand, or jump on the bandwagon when you arrive.

Casa del Caribe MUSIC, DANCE

(Map p394; 64-22-85; Calle 13 No 154) The portal of all things Santería and *folklórico*, this cultural institution can arrange dance lessons in conga, *son* and salsa for CUC$10 per hour. Resident staff member Juan Eduardo Castillo can also organize lessons in percussion. Real aficionados can inquire about in-depth courses on Afro-Cuban religions and culture. These guys are experts and they're very flexible.

UniversiTUR LANGUAGE

(Map p394; 64-31-86; www.uo.edu.cu; Universidad de Oriente, cnr Calle L & Ampliación de Terrazas) Arranges Spanish courses. Monthly rates for 60-hour courses (three hours a day, five days a week) start at CUC$250.

Ballet Folklórico Cutumba MUSIC, DANCE

(Map p394; Teatro Galaxia, cnr Avs 24 de Febrero & Valeriano Hierrezuelo) Santiago's *folklórico* groups are highly inclusive and can organize dance and percussion lessons either in groups or individually. Start with the Cutumba who often perform at Hotel las Américas. Also helpful are Conjunto Folklórico de Oriente.

Cuban Rhythm MUSIC, DANCE

(www.cubanrhythm.com) This organization offers dance lessons and percussion les-

sons for CUC$10 an hour. Take a look at its excellent website and make arrangements beforehand.

Tours

7Cubatur (p417) sells all manner of excursions, for everything from La Gran Piedra to El Cobre. Cubanacán (p417) in Hotel Casa Granda offers similar deals. Ecotur (p417) has the best bets for summit attempts on Pico Turquino to the west.

Alternatively, you can arrange your own tour to some of the out-of-town sights with one of the ubiquitous taxis that park in Parque Céspedes in front of the cathedral. Cubataxi cabs should charge approximately CUC$0.50 per kilometer for longer trips. Tot up your expected mileage, factor in some waiting time, and get ready to bargain.

Festivals & Events

Few cities can match the variety and vivacity of Santiago de Cuba's annual festivals, culminating in Santiago de Cuba's Carnaval, (see boxed text held in the last week of July. Other celebrations include the following:

Boleros de Oro MUSIC

(Jun) Arrive in mid- to late June for this crooner's extravaganza that is replicated in various cities throughout the country.

Fiesta de San Juan CULTURAL

(Jun 24) The summer season begins with the Fiesta de San Juan, celebrated with processions and conga dancing by cultural associations called *focos culturales*.

Fiesta del Fuego CULTURE

(early Jul) Fire celebration.

Festival del Caribe CULTURE

(Jul) Festival of Caribbean culture.

Festival Internacional Matamoros Son MUSIC

(Oct) A tribute to one of Santiago de Cuba's musical greats, Miguel Matamoros, this festival kicks off in late October with dances, lectures, concerts and workshops. Main venues include the Casa de la Trova and the Teatro Heredia.

Festival Internacional de Coros MUSIC

(Nov) The international choir festival in late November brings in some strong international singing groups for some cultural cross-fertilization and spirit-lifting music.

CARNAVAL CRAZINESS: A VERY VIVID HISTORY

Santiago's cultural complexity ensures its raucous July **Carnaval** is one of the largest and most authentic in the Caribbean with a kaleidoscope of costumes, copious food stalls, and enough music and noise to summon up the dead. If you can brave the heat of the summer and don't mind a bit of neck-craning and jostling, this is the real deal.

Unlike most Latin American carnivals, Santiago's annual knees-up did not develop around a Lent-based celebration of deep religious significance. Instead, it was an amalgam of several separate days of fun and diversion called *mamarrachos* which fell around the time of saintss days such as San Juan on June 24 or Santa Ana on July 26 (but lacked any further religious significance). Their primary purpose was to give laborers downtime after the January to May period of sugar cane harvesting. At one time, they were even dubbed '*festivales de las clases bajas*' (festivals of the lower classes). Spanish authorities tolerated the festivities as a means of distracting the poor from other more serious forms of rebellion and quickly Carnaval became synonymous with debauchery and scandal. In a delicious touch of modern-day irony, Carnaval now culminates in the Día de la Rebeldía Nacional (July 26), held in honour of Cuba's most famous rebellion (albeit failed): the assault on the Moncada Barracks.

Santiago's carnivals were probably at their zenith in the late 19th century, although people back then knew them only as *mamarrachos*: a byword for parties in which more or less anything could happen: horse races, large-scale bonfires, food fights, copious alcohol consumption, *cantos de pullas* (mocking, satirical songs) and what the Spanish authorities considered overly sensual dancing.

These days, Santiago's carnival isn't quite so *loco* (crazy) although it hasn't toned down too much. The horse races and food fights have gone, but alcohol and music remain key elements. A distinguishing theme are the *comparasas* (parades) which are satirical or even anti-establishment in origin. *Comparasas* subdivide again into the *congas*, traditionally simpler but feistier performances by poorer people in large groups with somewhat manic percussion accompaniment. Also on show are more-elaborate *paseos*, usually horse-drawn parades, more lavish in scale and similar to European-style carnival floats. Av Victoriano Garzón is the hub of parade action.

Santiago's Museo del Carnaval (p397) offers some background on the carnival's culture and history.

Sleeping

★**Casa Terraza Pavo Real**   CASA PARTICULAR **$**
(Map p398; ☑65-85-89; juanmarti13@yahoo.es; Santa Rita No 362, cnr San Félix; r CUC$25; ❄) Casa? The meticulously maintained family home of Juan Martí is more like a palace, a riot of antique furniture, light-filtering vitrales and coiled spiral staircases. The crowning glory is a huge Alhambra-esque patio with a sleep-invoking fountain and an expansive roof terrace that's home to two elegant peacocks.

Throw in photo-worthy breakfast spreads, elegantly painted ceilings, and vital little details such as fresh flowers in your room, and this could be one of the best casas particulares in Cuba.

Roy's Terrace Inn   CASA PARTICULAR **$**
(Map p398; ☑62-05-22; roysterraceinn@gmail. com; Diego Palacios No 177, btwn Padre Pico & Mariano Corona; r CUC$25; P❄) Already an established casa when it was bought by Roy Pérez in 2014, the Terrace Inn continues to rule the Santiago accommodations scene with its stunning hand-painted mural of the city on its 1st-floor terrace. Roy's experience working in the cruise industry has instilled in him the spirit of a true perfectionist.

The three rooms are decorated in themes (Afro-Cuban culture, mysteries and maritime) and have plenty of free extras including tea and coffee, dominoes and alarm clocks.

Casa Colonial 'Maruchi'   CASA PARTICULAR **$**
(Map p394; ☑62-07-67; maruchib@yahoo.es; Hartmann No 357, btwn General Portuondo & Máximo Gómez; r CUC$25; ❄) Maruchi's colonial pile is a temple to all things Santería and the hostess herself an encyclopedia of Cuban religions of African origin. You'll meet all types here: *santeros* (priests of Santería), backpackers, and foreign students

MONCADA – THE 26TH OF JULY MOVEMENT

Glorious call to arms or poorly enacted putsch – the 1953 attack on Santiago's Moncada Barracks, while big on bravado, came to within a hair's breadth of destroying Fidel Castro's nascent revolutionary movement before the ink was even dry on the manifesto.

With his political ambitions decimated by Batista's 1952 coup, Castro – who had been due to represent the Orthodox Party in the canceled elections – quickly decided to pursue a more direct path to power by swapping the ballot box for a rifle.

Handpicking and training 116 men and two women from Havana and its environs, the combative Fidel, along with his trusty lieutenant, Abel Santamaría, began to put together a plan so secret that even his younger brother Raúl was initially kept in the dark.

The aim was to storm the Cuartel Moncada, a sprawling military barracks in Santiago (in Cuba's seditious Oriente region) with a shabby history as a Spanish prison. Rather than make an immediate grab for power, Castro's more savvy plan was to capture enough ammunition to escape up into the Sierra Maestra from where he and Santamaría planned to spearhead a wider popular uprising against Batista's malignant Mafia-backed government.

Castro chose Moncada because it was the second-biggest army barracks in the country, yet distant enough from Havana to ensure it was poorly defended. With equal sagacity, the date was set for July 26, the day after Santiago's annual carnival when both police and soldiers would be tired and hungover from the boisterous revelries.

But as the day of attack dawned, things quickly started to go wrong. The plan's underlying secrecy didn't help. Meeting in a quiet rural farmhouse near the village of Siboney, many recruits arrived with no idea that they were expected to fire guns at armed soldiers and they nervously baulked. Secondly, with all but one of the Moncadistas drawn from the Havana region (the only native *santiagüero* was an 18-year-old local fixer named Renato Guitart), few were familiar with Santiago's complex street layout and after setting out at 5am in convoy from the Siboney farm, at least two cars became temporarily lost.

The attack, when it finally began, lasted approximately 10 minutes from start to finish and was little short of a debacle. Splitting into three groups, a small contingent led by Raúl Castro took the adjacent Palacio de Justicia, another headed up by Abel Santamaría stormed a nearby military hospital, while the largest group led by Fidel attempted to enter the barracks itself.

Though the first two groups were initially successful, Fidel's convoy, poorly disguised in stolen military uniforms, was spotted by an outlying guard patrol and only one of the cars made it into the compound before the alarm was raised.

In the ensuing chaos, five rebels were killed in an exchange of gunfire before Castro, seeing the attack was futile, beat a disorganized retreat. Raúl's group also managed to escape, but the group in the hospital (including Abel Santamaría) were captured and later tortured and executed.

Fidel escaped into the surrounding mountains and was captured a few days later; but, due to public revulsion surrounding the other brutal executions, his life was spared and the path of history radically altered.

Had it not been for the Revolution's ultimate success, this shambolic attempt at an insurrection would have gone down in history as a military nonevent. But viewed through the prism of the 1959 Revolution, it has been depicted as the first glorious shot on the road to power.

It also provided Fidel with the political pulpit he so badly needed. 'History will absolve me,' he trumpeted confidently at his subsequent trial. Within six years it effectively had.

studying for PhDs on the Regla de Ocha. Furthermore, the food's legendary and the fecund courtyard equally sublime.

There are three guestrooms, one upstairs and two courtyard-facing beauties with bare-brick walls below.

Hotel Libertad　　　　　　　　　HOTEL $

(Map p398; ☑ 62-77-10; Aguilera No 658; s/d CUC$31/42; ✳ @) Cheap Cuban hotel chain Islazul breaks out of its ugly Soviet-themed concrete block obsession and goes colonial in this venerable sky-blue beauty on Plaza de Marte. Eighteen clean (if sometimes dark) high-ceilinged rooms and a pleasant street-side restaurant are a bonus. The belting (until 1am) rooftop disco isn't.

Nelson Aguilar Ferreiro & Deysi Ruíz Chaveco
CASA PARTICULAR $

(Map p398; ☑65-63-72; José A Saco No 513; r CUC$20-25; ❄) Slap-bang in the center but with a quieter, more suburban feel, this is one of Santiago's better casas with a secluded plant-filled patio guarding two spick-and-span double rooms. The dinner menu is huge, and the hosts specialize in vegetarian dishes.

Reydel Aguilar Ruiz
CASA PARTICULAR $

(Map p398; Donato Marmol; CUC$20-25; ❄) New casa in a completely renovated building in the colonial core with three smart modern rooms and a private terrace.

Casa Yoyi
CASA PARTICULAR $

(Map p394; ☑62-31-66; Mariano Corona No 54; CUC$25-30; ❄) Ten minutes' walk from the center in the Los Hoyos neighborhood, Casa Yoyi offers modernity and tranquility in its large 1st-floor rooms decked out with flat-screen TVs, bright flower prints and various bed configurations. English and Russian are spoken.

Casa Lola
CASA PARTICULAR $

(Map p394; ☑65-41-20; Mariano Corona No 309, btwn General Portuondo & Miguel Gómez; r CUC$15-20; ❄) With a large back garden crowned by a gazebo, you'll hardly be needing plaza chill-out time (there's your own central square, right outside your room). The room itself is attractively done up, with a large balcony overlooking the street.

Casa Mili
CASA PARTICULAR $

(Map p394; ☑66-74-56; Calle 6 No 156, btwn Av 5 & 7; CUC$12-15; ❄) If you can't bear the motorcycle madness of the city center, escape to the residential quarter of Vista Alegre and this spacious casa with its fine frontal columns and shiny floors.

Aichel & Corrado
CASA PARTICULAR $

(Map p398; ☑62-27-47; José A Saco No 516, btwn Mayía Rodríguez & Donato Mármol; r CUC$20-25; ❄) A thick-in-the-action house on José A Saco (Enramadas) with two rooms perched on a terrace high above the street. The one at the front is the spiffiest. New rooms and an Italian restaurant were in the offing at last visit.

Hotel Balcón del Caribe
HOTEL $

(☑69-15-06, 69-10-11; Carretera del Morro Km 7.5; s/d incl breakfast CUC$24/38; P❄❄) The tremendous setting next to El Morro castle is counterbalanced by the usual humdrum Islazul hotel-chain foibles: flowery curtains, ancient mattresses and furnishings salvaged from a 1970s garage sale. But there's a pool and the view is stunning. Get a room inside the complex; not a grottier external cabin. It's located 10km from the city center, making transport a headache.

Villa Gaviota
HOTEL $

(Map p394; ☑64-13-70; Av Manduley No 502, btwn Calles 19 & 21, Vista Alegre; s/d CUC$29/40; P❄❄) Sitting pretty in an oasis of calm in Santiago's salubrious Vista Alegre district, Villa Gaviota has been upgraded from the tacky holiday camp of yore to embrace a sharper, edgier look. Features include a swimming pool, restaurant, three bars, a billiards room and laundry.

★Hostal San Basilio
BOUTIQUE HOTEL $$

(Map p398; ☑65-17-02; Bartolomé Masó No 403, btwn Pío Rosado & Porfirio Valiente; s/d CUC$65/90; ❄@) The lovely eight-room San Basilio (named for the original name of the street on which it lies) is cozy, comfortable and refreshingly contemporary – with a romantic colonial setting. Rooms come with clever little frills such as DVD players, umbrellas, bathroom scales and mini bottles of rum, and the communal patio drips with ferns. A small restaurant serves breakfast and lunch.

Hotel Rex
HOTEL $$

(Map p398; Victoriano Garzón; s/d CUC$50/80; ❄🖥) Back in business after decades as a moth-eaten wreck, the Rex is no longer just a rusty signpost on the corner of Plaza de Marte. The hotel that once served as a pre-raid base for the Moncadistas in 1953 has been reborn as a modest but comfortable midrange accommodations option that hangs suspended above the motorcycle madness and musical backbeat of central Santiago. Tranquil it isn't; unmistakably Cuba, it most definitely is.

Hotel Versalles
HOTEL $$

(☑69-10-16; Alturas de Versalles; s/d incl breakfast CUC$43/62; P❄❄) Not to be confused with the namesake rumba district of Matanzas, or the resplendent home of Louis XIV, this modest hotel is on the outskirts of town off the road to El Morro. A recent upgrade has injected some style into its inviting pool and its comfortable rooms with small terraces.

Hotel Casa Granda · HOTEL $$

(Map p398; ☑ 65-30-24; Heredia No 201; s/d CUC$72/106; ☺ Roof Garden Bar 11am-1am; ❋ @) This elegant hotel (1914), artfully described by Graham Greene in his book *Our Man in Havana,* has 58 rooms and a classic red-and-white-striped front awning. Greene used to stay here in the late 1950s where he enjoyed relaxing on the streetside terrace while his famous pen captured the nocturnal essence of the city as it wafted up from the bustling square below. Half a century or so later, the atmosphere remains potent.

Aside from Che Guevara posters and some seriously erratic service on reception, not much has changed. The hotel's 5th-floor Roof Garden Bar is well worth the CUC$2 minimum consumption charge, and the terrace just above Parque Céspedes is an obligatory photo stop for tourists on the lookout for bird's-eye city views. There's music here most nights and an occasional buffet on the roof.

Hotel las Américas · HOTEL $$

(Map p394; ☑ 64-20-11; cnr Avs de las Américas & General Cebreco; s/d CUC$44/70; P ❋ @ ≋) The 70 rooms here offer the usual Islazul interiors, though the general facilities – restaurant, 24-hour cafetería, small pool, nightly entertainment, and car rental – are comprehensive for the price.

Meliá Santiago de Cuba · HOTEL $$$

(Map p394; ☑ 68-70-70; cnr Av de las Américas & Calle M; s/d CUC$120/160; P ❋ @ ⊜ ≋) A blue-mirrored monster (or marvel, depending on your taste) dreamed up by respected Cuban architect José A Choy in the early '90s, the Meliá is Santiago's only 'international' hotel. There are real bathtubs in every room, three pools, four restaurants, various shopping facilities and a fancy bar on the 15th floor. The downsides are its out-of-center location and lack of genuine Cuban charm.

🍴 Eating

How is it possible? More than one million inhabitants and a medley of culture to intimidate most similarly sized cities around the globe, but a restaurant scene that's so lean it's laughable. The outlook is generally mediocre though the situation has improved slightly in the last couple of years.

In the heart of the *casco histórico*, Calle José A Saco is designated traffic-free daily until at least 9pm. It offers all manner of mobile food units selling *comida ligera* (light food).

★ Rumba Café · CAFE, SNACKS $

(Map p398; ☑ 58-02-21-53; Hartmann No 466; sandwiches CUC$2-5; ☺ 9:30am-9pm Mon-Thu, 9:30am-10pm Fri-Sat) Imagine. It's a typical Santiago afternoon. Boiling hot and on the run from your new posse of 'fren's' trying to offer you cigars, chicas or a bike tour, you duck into the cool confines of Rumba Café. Appearing like a dreamy escape from the hot, agitated streets of Cuba's second-largest city, the Rumba resonates with elegance, discretion and jolly good management.

Pros: great snacks, fantastic small cakes and damn fine lattes. Cons: none.

Bendita Farándula · CARIBBEAN $

(Map p398; Monseñor Barranda s/n, btwn Aguilera & Heredia; meals CUC$5-9; ☺ noon-11pm) Of the city's emerging private restaurants, try this one. You would probably never wander in here unbidden, but with an ambience somehow reminiscent of a bistro in a provincial French town, this cozy two-floored place with guests' musings on the walls does Santiago's only *pescado con leche de coco* (fish with coconut sauce; a Barracoan specialty) and a really nice *bistek de cerdo con jamon y queso* (pork steak with ham and cheese).

El Barracón · CARIBBEAN $

(Map p394; ☑ 66-18-77; Av Victoriano Garzón; meals CUC$3-6.50; ☺ noon-11pm) El Barracón tries to reignite the roots of Afro-Cuban culture and cuisine with mixed results. The state-run restaurant's interior, a mix of atmospheric Santería shrine and *cimarrón* (runaway slave) is intriguing, but the food can't match its private competition. Stick to the delicious *tostones* (fried plantain patties) filled with chorizo and cheese, or opt for the lamb special.

Hotel Casa Granda · CAFE $

(Map p398; Heredia No 201, Casa Granda; snacks CUC$2-6; ☺ 9am-midnight) Positioned like a whitewashed theater box overlooking the unscripted cabaret of Parque Céspedes, the Casa Granda's Parisian-style terrace cafe has to be one of the best people-watching locations in Cuba. Food-wise, you're talking snacks (burgers, hot dogs, sandwiches etc) and service-wise you're talking impassive, verging on grumpy; but with this setting, who cares?

Jardín de los Enramadas · ICE CREAM $

(Map p394; cnr José A Saco & Gallo; ice cream CUC$1-2; ☺ 9:45am-11:45pm) Occupying a block just down from the *casco histórico* en route

TUMBA FRANCESA: VOODOO MEETS VERSAILLES

The specter of Haiti, Cuba's Gallic eastern neighbor loomed large over the isles throughout the late colonial period, especially in the Oriente. The reason? Revolution! Haiti's 1791 slave rebellion sent thousands of terrified French-Haitian landowners scurrying west to the safer climes of Cuba's eastern mountains, bringing their black slaves with them. As the displaced entrepreneurs set about building sugar mills and coffee plantations in their new home, their indentured slaves were put to work on nascent rural estates where they continued to celebrate the music and cultural practices of the land they had left behind. Descended from slaves originally brought to Haiti from the French colony of Dahomey (now Benin) in Africa, the centerpiece of Cuban-Haitian culture is a hybrid music and dance style known as *tumba francesa*. An unusual marriage between 18th-century French ballroom dancing and the frenetic drum rhythms of West Africa, *tumba francesa* is perhaps best described as a kind of voodoo meets Versailles. Picture a trio of drummers accompanied by a chorus of female singers chanting words in a barely decipherable French-African patois. The music provides accompaniment to two key dances: the *masón*, a stately couples' dance that parodies the high society balls of the erstwhile slave owners and wouldn't have looked out of the place in the corridors of Louis XIV-era Paris; and the *yuba*, a more improvised and athletic dance also partaken in couples. Both are performed by dancers dressed in elegant 19th-century garb: white shirts and colored shawls for men, and wide ankle-length dresses and fans for ladies.

When freed slaves started migrating to Cuba's cities from the countryside in the late 1800s, they took their music with them and *tumba francesa* societies quickly sprang up all over the Oriente. At one time there were over 100 of them. Today, just three remain: the Santa Catalina de Ricci Pompadour founded in 1902 in the city of Guantánamo, La Caridad de Oriente dating from the 1870s in Santiago de Cuba, and the Bejuco de Sagua de Tánamo in Holguín province. Witnessing a performance is a unique insight into an increasingly rare art. In 2008 the endangered *tumba francesa* was declared an intangible cultural heritage by Unesco.

to the port, this garden is devoted to ornamental plants and great ice cream (which comes with marshmallows and biscuits). Service is exemplary.

La Arboleda
ICE CREAM $

(Map p394; cnr Avs de los Libertadores & Victoriano Garzón; ice cream under CUC$1; ⊙10am-11:40pm Tue-Sun) Santiago's ice-cream cathedral is a little out of the center, not that this lessens the queue length. Yell out *¿Quién es último?* (who is last?) and take your place on the Av de los Libertadores side of the parlor. Milkshakes are sometimes sold from the outside window.

Santiago 1900
CARIBBEAN $

(Map p398; Bartolomé Masó No 354; meals CUC$2-6; ⊙noon-midnight) In the former Bacardí residence you can dine on the standard chicken, fish or pork for Cuban pesos in a plush dining room that recently recovered its fin de siècle colonial airs. Beware the draconian dress code: no shorts or T-shirts.

La Fortaleza
CUBAN $

(Map p394; cnr Av Manduley & Calle 3; meals CUC$3-7; ⊙noon-11:30pm) What a shame. A conducive setting amid Vista Alegre's mansions, a spacious, inviting shady patio and above-average food (pay in pesos) made infinitely more palatable by the lunchtime live music. But? A big fat zero for the quality of service.

Restaurante España
SEAFOOD $

(Map p394; Av Victoriano Garzón; meals CUC$3-7; ⊙noon-10pm) Get ready for the Arctic blast of air-con and readjust your Cuban food preconceptions before you walk into España. It specializes in seafood cooked with panache and – on occasion – fresh herbs. Try the lobster or tangy prawns, but bypass the Cuban wine which is almost undrinkable.

★ St Pauli
INTERNATIONAL $$

(Map p398; ☑65-22-92; José A Saco 605; meals CUC$4-11; ⊙noon-11pm) In a city of no great culinary tradition, St Pauli has arrived like a hurricane in a stagnant gastronomic desert. Creep up its mural decorated corridor off pedestrianized Calle Saco and you'll find a restaurant that offers a big *bienvenido* and a wide menu of reasonably priced food inscribed on a blackboard.

Try the *pulpo al ajillo* (octopus with garlic) or grilled chicken topped with ham and cheese – both fine enough to make even the most snobby Habanero jealous. Ambitious owner, Alfredo, has also opened a cocktail bar cum nightclub next door.

Compay Gallo   INTERNATIONAL $$
(Map p394; ☑ 65-83-95; Máximo Gómez No 503 (altos); meals CUC$4-10; ☺ noon-11pm) Upstairs in a typical narrow Santiago street on the cusp of the city center, Compay Gallo is a leading light in the local grapevine and is not afraid to truss up traditional dishes in a way that makes the economic meltdown of the 1990s seem like a distant memory. Try the prawn cocktail starter, and the *ragout de codero* (lamb ragu) with ample vegetables.

Ristorante Italiano la Fontana   ITALIAN $$
(Map p394; cnr Av de las Américas & Calle M, Meliá Santiago de Cuba; pizzas CUC$5-8; ☺ noon-11pm) Pizza *deliciosa* and lasagna *formidable*, ravioli and garlic bread; *mamma mía,* this

has to be the number-one option for breaking away from all that chicken and pork!

Restaurante Matamoros   CARIBBEAN $$
(Map p398; cnr Aguilera & Porfirio Valiente; meals CUC$5-10) Some interesting wall art, a couple of bolero-singing *muchachas* and a decent menu (if you're happy with chicken and pork) have breathed a bit of life into this once-dingy joint on Plaza Dolores that celebrates the life and career of Cuba's greatest *son* exponents, the Trio Matamoros.

Restaurante el Morro   CARIBBEAN $$
(☑ 69-15-76; Castillo del Morro; meals CUC$12; ☺ 10am-4:30pm) The spectacular cliffside, castle-hugging location helps buff up the flavors, but years of dealing with big tour groups has made El Morro's staff jaded, and the eating experience, crammed amid the busloads of European/North American 50-somethings, not particularly authentic. Not that this put off Paul McCartney, who once ate here during a whistle-stop 2000 visit (his plate is proudly mounted on the wall).

According to the waiters, the world's most famous vegetarian made do with an omelette. For meat-eaters, the complete *comida criolla* (Creole food) lunch (CUC$12)

FOLKLÓRICO DANCE IN SANTIAGO DE CUBA

Seeing a *folklórico* dance group is a definitive Santiago de Cuba cultural experience. The city is home to a dozen such groups (more than anywhere else in Cuba), which exist to teach and perform traditional Afro-Cuban *bailes* (dances) and pass their traditions on to future generations. Most of the groups date from the early 1960s and all enjoy strong patronage from the Cuban government.

A good place to find out about upcoming *folklórico* events is at the Casa del Caribe (p406) in Vista Alegre where many of the groups hang out and perform.

Santiago's oldest *folklórico* group is the **Conjunto Folklórico de Oriente** (Map p394; Teatro Heredia) formed in 1959; they are currently bivouacked at the Teatro Heredia. They perform a huge range of Afro-Cuban dance genres from *gagá* and *bembé* to *tumba francesa*. The **Ballet Folklórico Cutumba** (Map p394; Teatro Galaxia, cnr Avs 24 de Febrero & Valeriano Hierrezuelo; admission CUC$2) is an offshoot of the Oriente group formed in 1976. You can usually see them rehearsing at their HQ, the Teatro Galaxia, from 9am to 1pm Tuesday to Friday.

For pure *tumba francesa* dancing check out the **Tumba Francesa La Caridad de Oriente** (Map p394; Pío Rosado No 268), one of only three of these French-Haitian groups left in Cuba. They can be seen in their rehearsal rooms on Tuesday and Thursday at 9pm.

The **Carabalí Olugo** (Carretera del Morro, cnr Av 24 de Febrero) and the **Carabalí Izuama** (Map p394; Pío Rosado No 107) are *comparsas* (carnival music and dance groups) who represent the Tivolí and Los Hoyos neighborhoods in Santiago's July carnival. They are both descendants of 19th-century *cabildos* or mutual aid societies formed along ethnic lines, a factor still reflected in their music.

Compañia Danzaría Folklórica Kokoyé (Map p394) is a more modern group, formed in 1989 to promote Afro-Cuban dance to tourists. They can be seen performing on Saturday evening and Sunday afternoon in the Casa del Caribe.

is a better bet, a filling spread that includes soup, roast pork, a small dessert and one drink. Take bus 212 to Ciudamar and walk the last 20 minutes, or take a taxi.

La Teresina   CARIBBEAN **$$**
(Map p398; Aguilera, btwn Porfirio Valiente & Mayía Rodríguez; meals CUC$5-12; ⊘11am-11pm) One in a triumvirate of inviting-looking restaurants along the north side of Plaza de Dolores, La Teresina doesn't quite live up to its splendid colonial setting. But the terrace is shady, the beers affordable and the food – a familiar mix of spaghetti, pizza and chicken – enough to take the edge off a hungry appetite.

Madrileño   INTERNATIONAL **$$$**
(Map p394; ☑64-41-38; meals CUC$7-18; ⊘noon-11pm) A brave, respectful effort to breathe a bit of life into Santiago's restaurant scene, the Madrileño occupies a classy colonial abode in Vista Alegre with dining on a back patio enlivened with chirping caged birds.

There's dependable Italian fare like pasta, or Caribbean flavors that have been marinated on the barbecue and glazed and trussed to spicy perfection. The succulent smoked steaks or seafood *brochetas* are both good. No harm in booking early: it's popular.

Restaurante Zunzún   CARIBBEAN **$$$**
(Map p394; Av Manduley No 159; meals CUC$12-18; ⊘noon-10pm) Dine in bygone bourgeois style in this mansion-turned-restaurant. Zunzún, in the once upscale Vista Alegre neighborhood, has always been one of Santiago's best restaurants, if a little overpriced. Exotic dishes include chicken curry, paella or a formidable cheese plate and cognac. Expect professional, attentive service and entertaining troubadours.

Self-Catering

**Supermercado Plaza
de Marte**   SUPERMARKET **$**
(Map p398; Av Victoriano Garzón; ⊘9am-6pm Mon-Sat, to noon Sun) One of the better-stocked supermarkets in town, with a great ice-cream selection and cheap bottled water. It's in the northeastern corner of Plaza de Marte.

Panadería Doña Neli   BAKERY **$**
(Map p398; cnr Aguilera & Gen Serafín Sánchez; breads/snacks CUC$0.50-1; ⊘7am-7pm) Hard-currency bakery on Plaza de Marte, vending divine-smelling bread and cakes with a scowl.

Municipal Market   MARKET **$**
(Map p394; cnr Aguilera & Padre Pico) The main market, two blocks west of Parque Céspedes, has a poor selection considering the size of the city.

🍷 Drinking & Nightlife

For drinks with a view the roof terrace of Hotel Casa Granda (p410) is recommended, as is the surprise back terrace of Maqueta de la Ciudad (p397) (in daytime). The Museo del Ron (p397) has a divey but decent bar down below (also daytime only).

★ Bar Sindo Garay   BAR
(Map p398; cnr Tamayo Fleites & General Lacret; ⊘11am-11pm) As much a museum to one of Cuba's most famous *trova* musicians (Sindo Garay, most renowned for his composition 'Perla marina') as a bar, this is a smart, usually packed place with two levels, serving great cocktails on pedestrianized Tamayo Fleites.

Café Ven   CAFE
(Map p398; José A Saco, btwn Hartmann & Pío Rosado; ⊘9am-9pm) Small cafe tucked into busy Saco (Enramadas) with lung-enriching aircon, interesting coffee *cafetal* (plantation) paraphernalia and enough male Italian clientele to keep the cappuccino-making staff on their toes.

Café la Isabelica   CAFE
(Map p398; cnr Aguilera & Porfirio Valiente; ⊘9am-9pm) Smoky, dark cantina-type cafe selling coffee with the prices in pesos. Forget lattes – this is straight-up Cuban java only.

Club Nautico   BAR
(Map p394; off Paseo Alameda; ⊘noon-midnight) Enlivening Paseo Alameda with its lively *ranchón*-style bar suspended over the water with a great view across the bay, is a breezy locale to escape the sizzling Santiago heat. It does cheap food too, including lobster and other seafood. Pay in pesos or CUC$.

☆ Entertainment

'Spoilt for choice' would be an understatement in Santiago. For what's happening, look for the bi-weekly *Cartelera Cultural*. The reception desk at Hotel Casa Granda (p410) usually has copies. Every Saturday night Calle José A Saco becomes a happening place called **Noche Santiagüera**, where street food, music and crowds make an all-night outdoor party. Calle Heredia, meanwhile, is

Santiago's Bourbon Street, a musical cacophony of stabbing trumpets, multilayered bongos and lilting guitars. For the more secretive corners, prowl the streets with your ears open and let the sounds lure you in.

★ **Casa de las Tradiciones** LIVE MUSIC
(Map p394; General J Rabí No 154; admission CUC$1; ⊙ from 8:30pm) The most discovered 'undiscovered' spot in Santiago still retains its smoke-filled, foot-stomping, front-room feel. Hidden in the genteel Tivolí district, some of Santiago de Cuba's most exciting ensembles, singers and soloists take turns improvising. Friday nights are reserved for straight-up classic *trova*, à la Ñico Saquito and the like. There's a gritty bar, and some colorful artwork.

Casa de la Trova LIVE MUSIC
(Map p398; Heredia No 208) Santiago's shrine to the power of traditional music is still going strong five decades on, continuing to attract big names such as Buena Vista Social Club singer Eliades Ochoa. Warming up on the ground floor in the late afternoon, the action slowly gravitates upstairs where, come 10pm, everything starts to get a shade more *caliente*.

Tropicana Santiago CABARET
(entry from CUC$35; ⊙ from 10pm Wed-Sun) Anything Havana can do, Santiago can do better – or at least cheaper. Styled on the Tropicana original, this 'feathers and baubles' Las Vegas–style floor show is heavily hyped by all the city's tour agencies who offer it for CUC$35 plus transport (Havana's show is twice the price, but no way twice as good).

It's located out of town, 3km north of the Hotel las Américas, so a taxi or rental car is the only independent transport option, making the tour-agency deals a good bet. The Saturday night show is superior.

Casa de Cultura Josue País García LIVE MUSIC
(Map p398; ☑ 62-78-04; Heredia No 204; admission CUC$1; ⊙ from 9pm Wed, Fri & Sat, 1pm Sun) Grab a seat (or stand in the street) and settle down for whatever this spontaneous place can throw at you: orchestral *danzón*, folkloric rumba, lovelorn *trovadores* (traditional singers) or rhythmic reggaetón.

Patio ARTex LIVE MUSIC
(Map p398; Heredia No 304; ⊙ 11am-11pm) FREE Art lines the walls of this shop-and-club combo that hosts live music both day and night in a quaint inner courtyard; a good bet if the Casa de la Trova is full, or too frenetic. It was being renovated at last visit.

Patio los Dos Abuelos LIVE MUSIC
(Map p398; Francisco Pérez Carbo No 5; admission CUC$2; ⊙ 9:30pm-2am Mon-Sat) The old-timers label (*abuelos* means grandparents) carries a certain amount of truth. This relaxed live-music house is a bastion for traditional *son* sung the old-fashioned way. The musicians are seasoned pros and most of the patrons are perfect ladies and gentlemen.

★ **Iris Jazz Club** JAZZ
(Map p398; General Serafín Sánchez, btwn José A Saco & Bayamo; admission CUC$5; ⊙ shows 10:30pm) When Santiago get too hot, noisy and agitated, you need a dose of Iris, one of Cuba's suavest and best jazz clubs where you can sit in a comfy booth surrounded by pictures of puffing jazz greats and watch some incredibly intuitive exponents of Santiago's small but significant jazz scene.

Teatro José María Heredia THEATER
(Map p394; ☑ 64-31-90; cnr Avs de las Américas & de los Desfiles; ⊙ box office 9am-noon & 1-4:30pm) Santiago's huge, modern theater and convention center went up during the city refurbishment in the early 1990s. Rock and folk concerts often take place in the 2459-seat Sala Principal, while the 120-seat Café Cantante Niagara hosts more esoteric events. The Conjunto Folklórico de Oriente is based here.

Santiago Café CABARET
(Map p394; cnr Av de las Américas & Calle M; admission CUC$5; ⊙ 10pm-2am Sat) This is the Hotel Meliá Santiago de Cuba's slightly less spectacular version of the Tropicana. Cabarets take place on Saturday with a disco afterwards. It's on the hotel's 1st floor. Head up to the 15th floor for the exciting Bello Bar.

Teatro Martí THEATER
(Map p394; Félix Peña No 313; ☎) Children's shows are staged at 5pm on Saturday and Sunday at this theater near General Portuondo, opposite the Iglesia de Santo Tomás.

Sala de Conciertos Dolores LIVE MUSIC
(Map p398; cnr Aguilera & Mayía Rodríguez; ⊙ from 8:30pm) You can catch the Sinfónica del Oriente at this former church on Plaza de Dolores, plus the impressive children's choir (at 5pm). The *cartelera* (culture calendar) is posted outside.

MYSTERIES OF PALO MONTE

Understanding Cuban religions of African origin can be complicated. The most widely practiced and well-known Afro-Cuban religion is Santería. Less studied and infinitely more mysterious is Palo Monte, also known as Regla de Congo or Palo Mayombe.

Like Santería, Palo Monte is a syncretized religion with antecedents in the slave era. Indentured workers brought over from Africa via the Middle Passage hid their animist beliefs behind a Catholic smokescreen, pretending to venerate Christian saints while worshipping their own pantheon of religious deities in secret.

However, while Santería originated in the Yoruba-speaking regions of present-day Nigeria, Palo Monte is Bantu in origin. Its rites and belief system were introduced by slaves imported to Cuba from the Congo Basin in Central Africa.

Another key difference between Palo Monte and Santería is in its essence. Santería emphasizes its deities; Palo Monte revolves around ancestor worship and a belief in natural earthly powers, such as water, mountains and particularly sticks, which are said to yield spiritual powers. Special sticks (palos) are used to decorate altars adorned with sacred religious vessels called nkisi (human-like dolls or figurines) believed to be inhabited by spirits. You'll know you're in a Palo Monte temple when you see an 'altar' consisting of a cauldron (called a nganga) filled with sticks, stones and bones of the dead, often with a crucifix hanging above it.

The Palo Monte has its own deities called Kimpungulu and a creator god known as Nzambi. Though less important and less widely known than Santería orishas, Palo Monte deities are similarly associated with Catholic saints. Kimbabula, god of the wind, relates to St Francis, while Nsasi, god of thunder, is represented by Santa Barbara (Changó in Santería).

Due to its secretive nature, Palo Monte is often misunderstood and tales of black magic and grave-robbing abound, most of them false. The strongholds of the religion are Santiago de Cuba; Regla and Guanabacoa in Havana; Matanzas; Bahía Honda in Artemisa Province; and Palmira in Cienfuegos province.

Orfeón Santiago LIVE MUSIC
(Map p398; Heredia No 68) This classical choir sometimes allows visitors to attend its practice sessions from 9am to 11:30am Monday to Friday.

Subway Club LIVE MUSIC
(Map p398; cnr Aguilera & Mayía Rodríguez; CUC$5; ⏰8pm-2am) Stylish new venue with interesting solo acts singing their hearts out to great piano music come nightfall. Good fun.

Cine Rialto CINEMA
(Map p398; Félix Peña No 654) This cinema, next to the cathedral, is one of only a few currently operating in Santiago de Cuba. Occasional English-language films.

Uneac CULTURAL CENTER
(Unión Nacional de Escritores y Artistas de Cuba | Union of Cuban Writers & Artists; Map p398; Heredia No 266) First stop for art fiends seeking intellectual solace in talks, workshops, encounters and performances – all in a gorgeous colonial courtyard.

Estadio de Béisbol Guillermón Moncada SPORT
(Map p394; Av de las Américas) This stadium is on the northeastern side of town. During the baseball season, from October to April, there are games at 7:30pm Tuesday, Wednesday, Thursday and Saturday, and 1:30pm Sunday (1 peso). The Avispas (Wasps) are the main rivals of Havana's Industriales, with National Series victories in 2005, 2007, 2008 and 2010.

Cubanacán runs trips to Avispa games with a visit to the dressing room afterwards to meet the players.

🛍 Shopping

Innovative creativity is inscribed into the louvers in colonial Santiago, and a brief sortie around the casco histórico will reveal exciting snippets of eye-catching art. Decent craft stalls are set up in Calle Heredia most days.

ARTex SOUVENIRS
From mouse pads to Che trinkets, the branch (Map p398; General Lacret, btwn Aguilera & Heredia; ⏰9am-4:30pm Mon-Sat) below Hotel Casa Granda collects any type of Cuban

souvenir imaginable. The other branch (Map p398; Heredia No 208, Patio ARTex; ⊙11am-7pm Tue-Sun) at the Casa de la Trova focuses more on music, with a respectable selection of CDs and cassettes.

Discoteca Egrem   MUSIC
(Map p398; José A Saco No 309; ⊙9am-6pm Mon-Sat, to 2pm Sun) The definitive Cuban specialist music store; this retail outlet of Egrem Studios has a good selection from local musicians.

La Maison   CLOTHING
(Map p394; Av Manduley No 52; ⊙10am-6pm Mon-Sat) The Santiago version of the famous Havana fashion house is located in an appropriately grand Vista Alegre *maison* (house).

Galería de Arte de Oriente   ARTS & CRAFTS
(Map p398; General Lacret No 656) Probably the best gallery in Santiago de Cuba, the art here is consistently good.

Centro de Negocios Alameda   SHOPPING CENTER
(Map p394; Av Jesús Menéndez, cnr José A Saco; ⊙8:30am-4:30pm) The port's latest regeneration project is opening this shopping center in a colonial building: internet, a pharmacy, the immigration office and a Cubanacán desk besides shops.

Librería Internacional   BOOKS
(Map p398; ☎68-71-47; Heredia, btwn General Lacret & Félix Peña) On the southern side of Parque Céspedes. Decent selection of political titles in English; sells postcards and stamps.

Librería la Escalera   BOOKS
(Map p398; Heredia No 265; ⊙10am-11pm) A veritable museum of old and rare books stacked ceiling high. Sombrero-clad *trovadores* often sit on the stairway and strum.

ℹ Information

DANGERS & ANNOYANCES
Santiago is well known, even among Cubans, for its overzealous *jineteros* (hustlers), all working their particular angle – be it cigars, private restaurants, *chicas* (girls) or unofficial 'tours.' Sometimes it can seem impossible to shake off the money-with-legs feeling, but a firm 'no' coupled with a little light humor ought to keep the worst of the touts at bay.

Santiago's traffic is second only to Havana's in its environmental fallout. Making things worse for pedestrians is the plethora of noisy motorcyclists weaving for position along the city's sinuous 1950s streets. Narrow or nonexistent sidewalks throw further obstacles into an already hazardous brew.

EMERGENCY
Asistur (Map p398; ☎68-61-28; www.asistur.cu; Heredia No 201) Situated under the Casa Granda Hotel, this office specializes in offering assistance to foreigners, mainly in the insurance and financial fields.

Police (☎116; cnr Mariano Corona & Sánchez Hechavarría)

INTERNET & TELEPHONE
There's wi-fi in Hotel Rex (p409) and the Meliá Santiago de Cuba (p410). For the Meliá buy a two-hour pass at reception for CUC$12. For the Rex use an Etecsa CUC$4.50 card (one hour).

Etecsa Multiservicios (cnr Heredia & Félix Peña; per hr CUC$4.50; ⊙8:30am-7:30pm) Three internet terminals in a small office on Plaza Céspedes.

Etecsa Telepunto (cnr Hartmann & Tamayo Fleites; per hr CUC$4.50; ⊙8:30am-7:30pm)

MEDICAL SERVICES
Clínica Internacional Cubanacán Servimed (☎64-25-89; cnr Av Raúl Pujol & Calle 10, Vista Alegre; ⊙24hr) Capable staff speak some English. A dentist is also present.

Farmacia Clínica Internacional (☎64-25-89; cnr Av Raúl Pujol & Calle 10; ⊙24hr) Best pharmacy in town, selling products in convertibles.

Farmacia Internacional (☎68-70-70; Meliá Santiago de Cuba, cnr Av de las Américas & Calle M; ⊙8am-6pm) In the lobby of the Meliá Santiago de Cuba, it sells products in convertibles.

MONEY
Banco de Crédito y Comercio (Félix Peña No 614; ⊙9am-3pm Mon-Fri) Housed in the jarring modern building in Plaza Céspedes.

Banco Financiero Internacional (cnr Av de las Américas & Calle I; ⊙9am-3pm Mon-Fri)

Bandec (cnr Félix Peña & Aguilera; ⊙9am-3pm) Another branch at José A Saco (cnr José A Saco & Mariano Corona).

Cadeca Branches at Hotel las Américas (cnr Avs de las Américas & General Cebreco; ⊙7:30am-7:30pm); José A Saco (José A Saco No 409; ⊙8:30am-4pm Mon-Fri, 8:30-11:30am Sat) and Meliá Santiago de Cuba (cnr Av de las Américas & Calle M; ⊙7:30am-7:30pm).

POST
Post Office (⊙8am-8pm Mon-Sat) You can find a post office on Aguilera (Map p398; Aguilera No 519) and Calle 9 (Map p394; Calle 9, Ampliación de Terrazas), near Av General Cebreco; telephones are here too.

TOURIST INFORMATION

Cubanacán (Map p398; Heredia No 201) This very helpful desk is in the Hotel Casa Granda.

Cubatur (Map p394; Av Victoriano Garzón No 364, cnr Calle 4) Another branch at Heredia. (Map p398; Heredia No 701; ☺8am-8pm)

Ecotur (Map p398; ☑68-72-79; General Lacret No 701, cnr Hartmann) In the same building as Infotur. The best bet for guided summit attempts on Pico Turquino.

Infotur (Map p398; ☑66-94-01; General Lacret No 701, cnr Heredia) Helpful location and staff. There's also a branch in Antonio Maceo International Airport.

Oficina Reservaciones de Campismo (Map p398; Cornelio Robert No 163; ☺8:30am-noon & 1-4:30pm Mon-Fri, 8am-1pm Sat) For information on the Caletón Blanco and La Mula campismos.

ⓘ Getting There & Away

AIR

Antonio Maceo International Airport (SCU; ☑69-10-14) is 7km south of Santiago de Cuba, off the Carretera del Morro. International flights arrive from Santo Domingo (Dominican Republic), Toronto and Montreal on **Cubana** (cnr José A Saco & General Lacret). Toronto and Montreal are also served by **Sunwing** (www.sunwing.ca); **AeroCaribbean** (www.fly-aerocaribbean.com) flies weekly between here and Port Au Prince, Haiti. **American Eagle** (www.aa.com) runs regular charters to and from Miami serving the Cuban-American community.

Internally, Cubana flies nonstop from Havana to Santiago de Cuba two or three times a day (about CUC$136 one-way, 1½ hours). There are also services to Holguín with Aerogaviota.

BUS

The **National Bus Station** (Map p394; cnr Av de los Libertadores & Calle 9), opposite the Heredia Monument, is 3km northeast of Parque Céspedes. **Víazul** (www.viazul.cu) buses leave from the same station.

The Havana bus stops at Bayamo (CUC$7, two hours), Holguín (CUC$11, 3½ to four hours), Las Tunas (CUC$11, five hours), Camagüey (CUC$18, 7½ hours), Ciego de Ávila (CUC$24, 9½ hours), Sancti Spíritus (CUC$28, 10 to 10½ hours)

and Santa Clara (CUC$33, 11 to 12 hours). The Trinidad bus can drop you at Bayamo, Las Tunas, Camagüey, Ciego de Ávila and Sancti Spíritus. The Baracoa bus stops in Guantánamo.

TRAIN

The modern French-style **train station** (cnr Av Jesús Menéndez & Martí) is situated near the rum factory northwest of the center. The *Tren Francés* leaves every third day for Havana (CUC$50 'especial' or CUC$62 'first class', 16 hours) stopping at Camagüey (CUC$11) and Santa Clara (CUC$20) en route. It was suspended at last visit while carriages were being overhauled, but should be back in business by 2015. Check ahead regarding departure times.

Another slower *coche motor* (cross-island) train (CUC$30) also plies the route to Havana every third day when a *Tren Francés* isn't running, additionally stopping at Las Tunas, Ciego de Ávila, Guayos and Matanzas.

Cuban train schedules are fickle, so you should always verify beforehand what train leaves when and get your ticket as soon as possible thereafter.

TRUCK

Intermittent passenger trucks leave **Serrano Intermunicipal Bus Station** (Map p394; cnr Av Jesús Menéndez & Sánchez Hechavarría) near the train station to Guantánamo and Bayamo throughout the day. Prices are a few pesos and early morning is the best time to board. For these destinations, don't fuss with the ticket window; just find the truck parked out front going your way. Trucks for Caletón Blanco and Chivirico also leave from here.

The **Intermunicipal Bus Station** (Map p394; Terminal Cuatro, cnr Av de los Libertadores & Calle 4), 2km northeast of Parque Céspedes, has two buses a day to El Cobre. Two daily buses also leave for Baconao from here.

ⓘ Getting Around

TO/FROM THE AIRPORT

A taxi to or from the airport should cost CUC$10, but drivers will often try to charge you more. Haggle hard before you get in. You can also get to the airport on bus 212, which leaves from Av de los Libertadores opposite the Hospital de Maternidad. Bus 213 also goes to the airport

SANTIAGO DE CUBA PROVINCE SANTIAGO DE CUBA

VÍAZUL BUS DEPARTURES FROM SANTIAGO DE CUBA

DESTINATION	COST (CUCS)	DURATION (HR)	DAILY DEPARTURES
Baracoa	15	4¾	1:50am, 8am
Havana	51	13-14½	12:30am, 6:30am, 4pm
Trinidad	33	11½	7:30pm
Varadero	49	15	8pm

from the same stop, but visits Punta Gorda first. Both buses stop just beyond the west end of the airport car park to the left of the entrances.

TO/FROM THE TRAIN/BUS STATIONS

To get into town from the train station, catch a southbound horse cart (1 peso) to the clock tower at the north end of Parque Alameda, from which Aguilera (to the left) climbs straight up to Parque Céspedes. Horse carts between the National Bus Station (they'll shout 'Alameda') and train station (1 peso) run along Av Juan Gualberto Gómez and Av Jesús Menéndez. A taxi to the Víazul bus station costs CUC$4-ish.

BUS & TRUCK

Useful city buses include bus 212 to the airport and Ciudamar, **bus 213** (Map p394) to Punta Gorda (both of these buses start from Av de los Libertadores, opposite Hospital de Materni-dad, and head south on Félix Peña in the *casco histórico*), and **bus 214 or 407** (Map p394) to Siboney (from near Av de los Libertadores No 425). **Bus 5** (Map p394) to El Caney stops on the northwestern corner of Plaza de Marte and at General Cebreco and Calle 3 in Vista Alegre. These buses (20 centavos) run every hour or so; more frequent trucks (1 peso) serve the same routes.

Trucks to El Cobre and points north leave from Av de las Américas near Calle M. On trucks and buses you should be aware of pickpockets and wear your backpack in front.

CAR & MOPED

Santiago de Cuba suffers from a chronic short-age of rental cars (especially in peak season) and you might find there are none available; though the locals have an indefatigable Cuban ability to *conseguir* (to manage or get) and *re-solver* (to resolve or work out). The airport offic-es usually have better availability than those in town. If you're completely stuck, you can usually rent one at the Hotel Guantánamo (p433), two hours to the east.

Cubacar (Hotel las Américas, cnr Avs de las Américas & General Cebreco; ☺8am-10pm) rents out mopeds for CUC$25 per day. There is also an office at Antonio Maceo International Airport.

Guarded parking is available in Parque Cés-pedes, directly below the Hotel Casa Granda (p410). Official attendants, complete with small badges, charge CUC$1 a day and CUC$1 a night.

The **Servi-Cupet gas station** (cnr Avs de los Libertadores & de Céspedes) is open 24 hours. There's an **Oro Negro gas station** (cnr Av 24 de Febrero & Carretera del Morro) on the Carretera del Morro and another **Oro Negro** (Carretera Central) on the Carretera Central at the north-ern entrance to Santiago de Cuba.

TAXI

There's a **Turistaxi** (Map p394) stand in front of Meliá Santiago de Cuba. Taxis also wait on Parque Céspedes near the cathedral and hiss at you expectantly as you pass. Always insist the driver uses the *taxímetro* (meter) or hammer out a price beforehand. To the airport, it will be between CUC$5 and CUC$7 depending on the state of the car.

Bici-taxis charge about 5 pesos per person per ride.

Siboney

Playa Siboney is Santiago's answer to Ha-vana's Playas del Este, a low-key seaside town 19km east that's more rustic village than deluxe resort. Guarded by precipitous cliffs and dotted with a mixture of craning palms and weather-beaten clapboard hous-es, the setting here is laid-back and charm-ing, with a beach scene that mixes fun-seeking Cuban families and young, nubile *santiagüeras* with their older, balder for-eign partners.

In terms of quality, Siboney's small cres-cent of grayish sand is none too inspiring. But Siboney compensates for this in price (cheap), location (it's on the doorstep of Parque Baconao) and all-embracing Cuban atmosphere. There are a few legal casas particulares here and a decent sit-down res-taurant on a hill overlooking the beach. For those craving a break from hustler-heavy, sweltering Santiago, it makes a good little hideaway.

◉ Sights

Granjita Siboney   MUSEUM
(admission CUC$1; ☺9am-5pm Tue-Sun, 9am-1pm Mon) Had the Revolution been unsuccessful, this unassuming red-and-white farmhouse 2km inland from Playa Siboney on the road to Santiago de Cuba would be the forgotten site of a rather futile putsch. As it is, it's an-other shrine to the glorious national episode that is Moncada. It was from this place, at 5:15am on July 26, 1953, that 26 cars under the command of Fidel Castro left to attack the military barracks in Santiago de Cuba.

The house retains many of its original de-tails, including the dainty room used by the two *compañeras* (female revolutionaries) who saw action, Haydee Santamaría and Melba Hernández. There are also displays of weapons, interesting documents, photos and personal effects related to the attack.

Notice the well beside the building, where weapons were hidden prior to the attack.

Overlooking the stony shoreline nearby is an American war memorial dated 1907, recalling the US landing here on June 24, 1898.

🛏 Sleeping & Eating

There are a good dozen casas particulares in this small seaside settlement. Cheap peso food stalls hog the beachfront.

María González   CASA PARTICULAR **$**
(📞39-92-00; Obelisco No 10; CUC$20-25; **P ☀ ≋**) The three slightly gnarled rooms here are outshone by the terrace (with rocking chairs) that hangs over the adjacent beach and ocean, and – guess what? – a swimming pool. The owner can use his 1968 Peugeot as a taxi – handy in these parts.

Ovidio González Salgado   CASA PARTICULAR **$**
(📞39-93-40; Av Serrano; r CUC$20-25; ☀) A spacious if slightly dated place with three rooms above the local pharmacy, serving great meals. Only open November to April.

Sitio del Compay   CARIBBEAN **$**
(Av Serrano s/n; meals CUC$5-10; ⊙11am-7pm) Take note, dear diner, you're in the former house of musical-sage-turned-international-icon, Francisco Repilado, the man responsible for writing the immortal song 'Chan Chan,' which you've probably already heard a dozen times since your plane landed.

Born in a small shack by this site in 1907, Compay Segundo, as he was more commonly known, shot to superstardom aged 90 as the guitarist/winking joker in Ry Cooder's Buena Vista Social Club. Sitio del Compay (formerly Restaurante La Rueda) is Siboney's only real dining option and would have kept old Francisco happy with its no-frills *comida criolla*, friendly service and good beach views.

ℹ Getting There & Away

Bus 214 runs from Santiago de Cuba to Siboney from near Av de los Libertadores 425, opposite Empresa Universal, with a second stop at Av de Céspedes 110. It leaves about once hourly between 4am and 8:45am (hit-and-miss thereafter), and bus 407 carries on to Juraguá three times a day. Passenger trucks also shuttle between Santiago de Cuba and Siboney.

A taxi to Playa Siboney will cost CUC$20 to CUC$25, depending on whether it's state or private.

La Gran Piedra

Crowned by a 63,000-tonne boulder that perches like a grounded asteroid high above the Caribbean, the Cordillera de la Gran Piedra forms part of Cuba's greenest and most biodiverse mountain range. Not only do the mountains have a refreshingly cool microclimate, they also exhibit a unique historical heritage based on the legacy of some 60 or more coffee plantations set up by French farmers in the latter part of the 18th century. On the run from a bloody slave rebellion in Haiti in 1791, enterprising Gallic immigrants overcame arduous living conditions and terrain to turn Cuba into the world's number-one coffee producer in the early 19th century. Their craft and ingenuity have been preserved for posterity in a Unesco World Heritage Site that is centered on the Cafetal la Isabelica. The area is also included in the Baconao Unesco Biosphere Reserve, instituted in 1987.

⊙ Sights

The steep 12km road up the mountain range becomes increasingly beautiful as the foliage closes in and the valley opens up below. Mango trees are ubiquitous here.

La Gran Piedra   MOUNTAIN
(admission CUC$1) You don't need to be Tenzing Norgay to climb the 459 stone steps to the summit of La Gran Piedra at 1234m. The huge rock on top measures 51m in length and 25m in height and weighs...a lot. On a clear day there are excellent views out across the Caribbean and on a dark night you are supposedly able to see the lights of Jamaica.

Cafetal la Isabelica   MUSEUM
(admission CUC$2; ⊙8am-4pm) The hub of the Unesco World Heritage Site bestowed in 2000 upon the First Coffee Plantations in the Southeast of Cuba is this impressive two-story stone mansion, with its three large coffee-drying platforms, built in the early 19th century by French émigrés from Haiti. It's a 2km hike beyond La Gran Piedra on a rough road.

The complex includes a workshop and numerous metal artifacts. You can also stroll around the pine-covered plantation grounds at will. It's worth using a guide (for a tip) to show you round as there are no explanatory notices. There were once more than 60 such coffee *cafetales* in the area.

La Gran Piedra & Parque Baconao

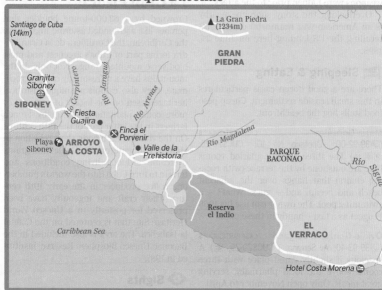

SANTIAGO DE CUBA PROVINCE PARQUE BACONAO

🏃 Activities

You can visit the ruins of many of the 100-plus coffee plantations on foot. Trails lead out from Cafetal la Isabelica, but there are no signs. Inquire at La Isabelica about the possibility of hiring a local farmer to show you around for a prearranged fee.

🛏 Sleeping & Eating

Villa la Gran Piedra   HOTEL **$$**
(📞65-12-05; s/d CUC$35/50; 🅿❄) Villa la Gran Piedra, Cuba's highest hotel at 1225m, had its cabins destroyed in the 2012 hurricane so now it's more a restaurant with rooms, right by the entrance to the La Gran Piedra viewpoint. The restaurant is good enough, the rooms are plain and various short hiking trips are available.

ℹ Getting There & Away

A steep, winding paved road climbs 1.2 vertical kilometers from the junction with the coast road near Siboney (on the 214 bus route) through *muchos* potholes. A taxi from Santiago de Cuba will cost approximately CUC$50 to CUC$65 (bargain hard) for the round trip. Sturdy Cubans and the odd ambitious foreigner hike up 12km from the bus stop at the road junction in Las Guásimas.

Parque Baconao

Parque Baconao, covering 800 sq km between Santiago de Cuba and the Río Baconao, is as wondrous as it is weird. A Unesco Biosphere Reserve that is also home to an outdoor car museum and a rather odd collection of 240 life-sized dinosaur sculptures, it looks like an historically displaced Jurassic Park, yet in reality acts as an important haven for a whole ecosystem of flora and fauna.

Not surprisingly, the Unesco tag wasn't earned for a museum full of old cars (or for a field full of concrete dinosaurs, for that matter). According to biological experts, Baconao hosts more than 1800 endemic species of flora and numerous types of endangered bats and spiders. Encased in a shallow chasm with the imposing Sierra Maestra on one side and the placid Caribbean on the other, the biodiversity of the area (which includes everything from craning royal palms to prickly cliffside cacti) is nothing short of remarkable.

The beaches are smaller here than those on the northern coast, but there's fishing and some 70 scuba-diving sites nearby, including the *Guarico*, a small steel wreck just south of Playa Sigua. Baconao is also famous for its crabs. From mid-March to early May,

tens of thousands of large land crabs congregate along the coast beyond Playa Verraco.

Sights & Activities

There are several beaches along the coast, of which the best is probably **Playa Cazonal**, by Club Amigo Carisol – Los Corales.

Fiesta Guajira   RANCH
(admission CUC$5; ⊙ 9am & 2pm Wed & Sun) Situated in the El Oasis artists' community, opposite the turnoff to the old Club Bucanero, this Ecotur-run *finca* (farm) formerly ran rodeos with *vaqueros* (Cuban cowboys) but post-hurricane is focused round a rustic restaurant, and a cockpit.

Valle de la Prehistoria   AMUSEMENT PARK
(admission CUC$1; ⊙ 8am-6pm) One of the oddest in a plethora of odd attractions in Parque Baconao is this Cuban Jurassic Park cast in stone that serendipitously materializes beside the meandering coastal road. Giant Apatosauruses mix with concrete cavemen and women, seemingly oblivious to the fact that 57 million years separated the two species' colonization of planet Earth.

You can take in the full 11 hectares of this surreal kitsch park with its 200 life-size concrete dinosaurs built by inmates from a nearby prison. The **Museo de Historia Nat-**

ural (admission CUC$1; ⊙ 8am-4pm Tue-Sun) is also here, but something of an anticlimax after the surrealism of the prehistoric beasts.

There's a basic Freddie Flinstone–style cafe on-site.

**Museo Nacional de Transporte
Terrestre**   MUSEUM
(admission CUC$1; ⊙ 8am-5pm) What's the point? you might well ask, when you stumble upon this alfresco museum 2km east of Valle de la Prehistoria. It's all very impressive that they've nabbed Benny Moré's 1958 Cadillac, the Chevrolet Raúl Castro got lost in on the way to Moncada Barracks and Cuban singer Rosita Fornes' lovely Ford T Bird. But in Cuba where '50s car relics are as common as cheap cigars, it's the equivalent of a Toyota Yaris museum in Kyoto.

Playa Daiquirí   BEACH
The main US landings during the Spanish-Cuban-American War took place on June 24, 1898, at this beach, 2km down a side road from the Museo Nacional de Transportes. They might have named a cocktail after it, but the area is now a holiday camp for military personnel and entry is prohibited.

Comunidad Artística Verraco   GALLERY
(⊙ 9am-6pm) Ten kilometers past the Playa Daiquirí turnoff lies another village of painters, ceramicists and sculptors who maintain open studios (turnoff unsigned). Here you can visit the artists and buy original works of art. All it lacks is a good organic cafe.

Exposición Mesoamericana   PARK
(admission CUC$1) Every Cuban resort area seems to have an attraction replicating indigenous scenes. Here it's the Exposición Mesoamericana, just east of Club Amigo Carisol – Los Corales. Indigenous cave art from Central and South America is arranged in caves along the coastal cliffs.

Laguna Baconao   LAKE
At the Laguna Baconao, 2km northeast of Los Corales, you'll find a restaurant, rowboats for hire and several short lakeside hikes, plus a folorn-looking zoo with crocodiles and the like. The lake supposedly contains five resident 'wild' dolphins. Various trails ply the lakeshore including one that circumnavigates it completely (8km). As it's a flora and fauna reserve you must first hire a guide for CUC$2. Multilingual Norge Ramos Barroso is your main man. Horse riding is also available for CUC$10.

SANTIAGO DE CUBA PROVINCE PARQUE BACONAO

COFFEE TALES & CAFETALES

The Cubans have always been enthusiastic coffee drinkers. But, while the shade-loving national coffee crop thrives in the cool tree-covered glades of the Sierra del Escambray and Sierra Maestra, it's not indigenous to the island.

Coffee was first introduced to Cuba in 1748 from the neighboring colony of Santo Domingo, yet it wasn't until the arrival of French planters from Haiti in the early 1800s that the crop was grown commercially.

On the run from Toussaint Louverture's slave revolution, the displaced French found solace in the mountains of Pinar del Río and the Sierra Maestra, where they switched from sugarcane production to the more profitable and durable coffee plant.

Constructed in 1801 in what is now the Sierra del Rosario Reserve in Artemisa province, the Cafetal Buenavista was the first major coffee plantation in the New World. Not long afterward, planters living in the heavily forested hills around La Gran Piedra began constructing a network of more than 60 *cafetales* (coffee farms) using pioneering agricultural techniques to overcome the difficult terrain. Their stoic efforts paid off and, by the second decade of the 19th century, Cuba's nascent coffee industry was thriving.

Buoyed by high world coffee prices and aided by sophisticated new growing techniques, the coffee boom lasted from 1800 to about 1820, when the crop consumed more land than sugarcane. At its peak, there were more than 2000 *cafetales* in Cuba, concentrated primarily in the Sierra del Rosario region and the Sierra Maestra to the east of Santiago de Cuba.

Production began to slump in the 1840s with competition from vigorous new economies (most notably Brazil) and a string of devastating hurricanes. The industry took another hit during the War of Independence, though the crop survived and is still harvested today on a smaller scale using mainly traditional methods.

The legacy of Cuba's pioneering coffee industry is best evidenced in the Archaeological Landscape of the First Coffee Plantations in the Southeast of Cuba, a Unesco World Heritage Site dedicated in 2000 that sits in the foothills of the Sierra Maestra close to La Gran Piedra.

A road from the hamlet of Baconao follows the lake's north shore to the decent **Restaurante Casa Rolando** (Carretera Baconao Km 53; mains CUC$5-8; ☉ 10:30am-5pm), decorated bizarrely with native totems.

From **Playa Baconao** at the eastern corner of the lake, the paved road continues 3.5km up beautiful **Valle de Río Baconao** before turning into a dirt track. Soldiers at a checkpoint at the village turn back people trying to use the direct coastal road to Guantánamo because it passes alongside the US Naval Base. To continue east, you must backtrack 50km to Santiago de Cuba and take the inland road.

Centro Internacional de Buceo Carisol los Corales DIVING
(www.nauticamarlin.com; Club Amgio Carisol – Los Corales) Situated in the hotel of the same name 45km east of Santiago, this center nevertheless picks up divers at the other hotels around-about daily. Scuba diving costs CUC$30/59 per one/two dives with gear, and two boats can take up to 20 people to

any of the 24 local dive sites. The open-water certification course is CUC$365. There are shipwrecks close to shore here and you can feed black groupers by hand.

The water off this bit of coast is some of Cuba's warmest (25°C to 28°C); best visibility is between February and June.

🛏 Sleeping

Beware; the following all-inclusives usually close in low season (May to October). Check ahead.

Club Amigo Carisol – Los Corales RESORT $$
(☑ 35-61-21; all-incl s/d/tr CUC$91/130/178; P ✳ @ 🏊) There's the swim-up bar, umbrellas in the piña coladas, and the government-sponsored band knocking out 'Guantanamera' as you tuck into your lukewarm buffet dinner: you must be back in all-inclusive land. This two-piece Cubanacán resort is situated 44km east of Santiago on the coast's best section of beach (although it's been damaged by successive hurricanes).

Bonuses are a tennis court, a disco, multiple day trips on offer and bright spacious clean rooms. Nonguests can purchase a day pass for CUC$15 including lunch.

Hotel Costa Morena
HOTEL $$
(☑ 35-61-35; all-incl s/d CUC$44/70; P ✴ ☎) This place is at Sigua, 44km southeast of Santiago de Cuba. It has attractive architecture, a large terrace right on the cliffs, but no direct beach access. There is nevertheless good sea swimming, with protection afforded by a reef. A shuttle will bus you to the beach at Club Amigo Carisol – Los Corales.

Eating

If you're stuck you can try the restaurant at Club Amigo Carisol – Los Corales (p422) or the restaurant at **Aquario Baconao** (Carretera Baconao, btwn Costa Morena and Club Amigo Carisol – Los Corales; admission CUC$7; ☉ 9am-5pm).

Finca el Porvenir
CARIBBEAN $$
(☑ 68-64-94; Carretera de Baconao Km 18; meals CUC$8-12; ☉ 9am-5pm) Situated on the left of the main Carretera about 4km east of El Oasis, this Palmares-run *finca* knocks out no-frills *comida criolla* with a great swimming pool and horseback riding available on-site. The only obstacle to chillaxing is the blaring poolside music: sound familiar?

Fiesta Guajira
CARIBBEAN $$
(☑ 39-95-86; Carretera Baconao, El Oasis; meals CUC$7-10; ☉ 9am-5pm) Once a rodeo; now mainly just a restaurant.

ⓘ Getting There & Away

Most people access Baconao's spread-out sights by private car, taxi or as part of an organized trip from Santiago de Cuba. Cubataxi usually charges approximately CUC$0.50 per kilometer out this way or you can hire a moped from **Cubacar** (Club Bucanero) for CUC$25 per day.

Bus 415 from the municipal bus terminal in Santiago's Av de la Libertad plies this route three times a day, but the bus timetables are not set in stone. Check ahead.

When planning your visit, remember the coastal road from Baconao to Guantánamo is closed to nonresidents.

ⓘ Getting Around

Cubacar in Club Amigo Carisol – Los Corales has cars and mopeds.

The **Servi-Cupet gas station** (Complejo la Punta; ☉ 24hr) is 28km southeast of Santiago de Cuba.

El Cobre

The Basílica de Nuestra Señora del Cobre, high on a hill 20km northwest of Santiago de Cuba on the old road to Bayamo, is Cuba's most sacred pilgrimage site and shrine of the nation's patron saint: La Virgen de la Caridad (Our Lady of Charity), or Cachita, as she is also known. In Santería, the Virgin is syncretized with the beautiful *orisha* Ochún, Yoruba goddess of love and dancing, and a religious icon to almost all Cuban women. Ochún is represented by the color yellow, mirrors, honey, peacock feathers and the number five. In the minds of many worshippers, devotion to the two religious figures is intertwined.

Legend dictates that the Virgin figurine was first discovered floating on a board in the Bay of Nipe in 1612 by three fishermen called the 'three Juans' caught up in a violent storm. With their lives in danger they pulled the figurine from the water and found the words 'I am the Virgin of Charity' inscribed on the board. As the storm subsided and their lives were spared, they assumed a miracle had been granted and a legend was born.

The copper mine at El Cobre has been active since pre-Columbian times and was once the oldest European-operated mine in the Western hemisphere (by 1530 the Spanish had a mine here). However, it was shut in 2000. Many young villagers, who previously worked in the mine, now work over tourists hereabouts, offering to 'give' you shiny but worthless chalcopyrite stones from the mine. You'll find a firm but polite '*No, gracias!*' usually does the trick. The road to the basilica is lined with sellers of elaborate flower wreaths, intended as offerings to La Virgen, and hawkers of miniature 'Cachitas'.

◉ Sights

Basílica de Nuestra Señora del Cobre
CHURCH
(☉ 6am-6pm) Stunning as it materializes above the village of El Cobre, Cuba's most revered religious site shimmers against the verdant hills behind. Having been recently renovated – along with many other of Cuba's churches – the church's interior is impressive; light, but unostentatious with some vivid stained glass. The existing basilica was built in 1927, though a sanctuary has existed on this site since 1648.

FAMOUS GIFTS TO CACHITA

Many have offered gifts and keepsakes to the Virgin of El Cobre – some of them famous. The most celebrated donor was Ernest Hemingway, who elected to leave the 23-karat gold medal he won for the Nobel Prize for Literature in 1954 to the 'Cuban people.' Rather than hand it over to the Batista regime, Hemingway donated the medal to the Catholic Church who subsequently placed it in the *sanctuario*. The medal was stolen temporarily in the 1980s and, despite being retrieved a few days later, it has since been kept locked away from public view.

In 1957 Lina Ruz left a small guerilla figurine at the feet of the Virgin to pray for the safety of her two sons, Fidel and Raúl Castro, who were then fighting in the Sierra Maestra. Fate – or was it the spirit of Cachita? – shone brightly. Both sons are now into their 80s and still going!

More recently, dissident Cuban blogger Yoani Sánchez visited the Virgin and left her Ortega and Gasset journalistic award in the sanctuary, out of reach of the arm of censorship.

Despite an almost unending line of pilgrims, many of whom will have traveled from as far as the US, the church maintains a respectful silence and is overlooked by La Virgen who resides in a glass case high above the altar. For such a powerful entity, she's amazingly diminutive, some 40cm from crown to the hem of her golden robe. Check out the fine Cuban coat of arms in the center; it's a wondrous work of embroidery.

In a small chapel at the side of the basilica you'll see a small collection drawn from thousands of offerings giving thanks for favors bestowed by the virgin. Clumps of hair, a TV, a thesis, a tangle of stethoscopes, a raft inner-tube sculpture (suggesting they made it across the Florida Straits safely) and floor-to-ceiling clusters of teeny metal body parts crowd the room.

Follow the signs through the town of El Cobre to the **Monumento al Cimarrón**. A 10-minute hike up a stone staircase brings you to this anthropomorphic sculpture commemorating the 17th-century copper-mine slave revolt and now the location of one of Cuba's most important Santería gatherings in July, **Ceremonia a las Cimarrones** (part of the Fiesta del Caribe). Views are superb from up here; walk to the far side of the sculpture for a vista of copper-colored cliffs hanging over the aqua-green reservoir.

🛌 Sleeping & Eating

Hospedaría el Cobre　　　　　HOSTEL **$**

(☑ 34-62-46; r MN$20) This large building behind the basilica has 15 basic rooms with one, two or three beds, all with bath. Meals are served punctually at 7am, 11am and 6pm, and there's a large, pleasant sitting room. The nuns here are very hospitable.

House rules include no drinking and no unmarried couples. A convertible donation to the sanctuary is appreciated. Foreigners should reserve up to 15 days in advance.

The downstairs lobby of the *hospedaría* serves as a small **museum** with a dozen large instructive boards detailing the history of the Virgin and the church from the 1600s through to the visit of Pope Benedict XVI in 2012.

❶ Getting There & Away

Bus 2 goes to El Cobre twice a day from the **Intermunicipal Bus Station** (cnr Av de los Libertadores & Calle 4), in Santiago de Cuba. Trucks are more frequent on this route.

A Cubataxi from Santiago de Cuba costs around CUC$25 for a round-trip.

If you're driving toward Santiago de Cuba from the west, you can join the Autopista Nacional near Palma Soriano but, unless you're in a hurry, it's better to continue on the Carretera Central via El Cobre, which winds through picturesque hilly countryside.

El Saltón

Basking in its well-earned eco-credentials, El Saltón is a tranquil mountain escape in the Tercer Frente municipality, where hills that once echoed with the sound of crackling rifle fire now reverberate to the twitter of tropical birds. Secluded and hard to reach (that's the point), it consists of a lodge, a hilltop *mirador* (viewpoint) and a 30m cascading waterfall with an adjacent natural pool ideal for swimming. Eco-guides can offer horseback riding or hiking to thermal baths or into the nearby cocoa plantations at Delicias del Saltón. Alternatively, you can just wander off on your own through myriad mountain villages with alluring names like Filé and Cruce de los Baños.

🛏 Sleeping

Hotel Horizontes el Saltón HOTEL **$$**
(☑ 56-64-95; Carretera Puerto Rico a Filé; s/d with breakfast CUC$45/65; P ❄ 🏊) ✎ The 22-room lodge is spread over three separate blocks that nestle like hidden tree houses amid thick foliage. Spirit-lifting extras include a sauna, hot tub, massage facilities and the hotel's defining feature, a refreshing natural waterfall and pool. The hotel has an OK restaurant/bar with a popular pool table, adjacent to a gushing mountain river. All this compensates for the rooms themselves (which are nothing special).

❶ Getting There & Away

To get to El Saltón, continue west from El Cobre to Cruce de los Baños, 4km east of Filé village. El Saltón is 3km south of Filé. With some tough negotiating in Santiago de Cuba, a sturdy taxi will take you here for CUC$40. Money well spent.

Chivirico

POP 5800

Chivirico, 75km southwest of Santiago de Cuba and 106km east of Marea del Portillo, is the only town of any significance on the enticing south-coast highway, itself a roller-coaster of plummeting mountains, crinkled bays and crashing surf that makes up one of Cuba's loveliest road trips. Transport links are relatively good up until Chivirico but, heading west, they quickly deteriorate.

Chivirico itself has little to offer, although there's a challenging trek that begins at Calentura, 4km west. It crosses the Sierra Maestra to Los Horneros (20km), from where truck transport to Guisa is usually available. Whether skittish local authorities will let you loose in the area is another matter. Don't just turn up – ask around at somewhere like Cubatur (p417) in Santiago or the Brisas Sierra Mar (p425) hotel.

🛏 Sleeping

Campismo Caletón Blanco CABINS **$**
(☑ 62-57-97; Caletón Blanco Km 30, Guamá; r CUC$26.60; P ❄) One of two handy campismos situated along this route (the other is La Mula), this is one of Cubamar's top campismos, the closest to Santiago (30km) and the newest. Twenty-two bungalows sleep two to four people. There's also a restaurant, snack bar, bike rental and facilities for campervans. Make your reservations with Cubamar's Havana office (p95) before arrival.

Brisas Sierra Mar RESORT **$$**
(☑ 32-91-10; all-incl s/d CUC$75/105; P ❄ @ 🏊 🚣) This isolated but inviting place is at Playa Sevilla, 63km west of Santiago de Cuba and a two-hour drive from the airport. The big, pyramid-shaped hotel is built into a terraced hillside and has a novel elevator to take you down to a brown-sand beach famous for its sand fleas. A remarkable coral wall great for snorkeling is just 50m offshore (dolphins sometimes frequent these waters too).

Horseback riding is available here, there's a **Marlin Dive Center** on the premises, and plenty of special kids' programs (kids under 13 stay free). The hotel gets a lot of repeat visits. Nonguests can buy a CUC$35 day pass that includes lunch, drinks and sport until 5pm. If you're doing the south coast by bike, it's a nice indulgence.

❶ Getting There & Away

Trucks run to Chivirico throughout the day from the Serrano Intermunicipal Bus Station opposite the train station in Santiago de Cuba. There are also three local buses a day.

Theoretically, one daily truck trundles along to Campismo la Mula and the Pico Turquino trailhead but, since Hurricane Sandy in 2012, transport on to Marea del Portillo is almost unheard of and road conditions vary from bad to downright impassable.

El Uvero

A major turning point in the revolutionary war took place in this nondescript settlement 23km west of Chivirico, on May 28, 1957, when Castro's rebel army – still numbering less than 50 after six months on the run – audaciously took out a government position guarded by 53 of Batista's soldiers. By the main road are two red trucks taken by the rebels and nearby a double row of royal palms leads to a large **monument** commemorating the brief but incisive battle. It's a poignant, little-visited spot.

Pico Turquino Area

Near the border of Granma and Santiago de Cuba provinces is the pinprick settlement of Las Cuevas, embarkation point for quick ascents of Cuba's highest mountain.

◉ Sights

Museo de la Plata   MUSEUM

(admission CUC$1; ☉ Tue-Sat) Five kilometres west of Las Cuevas (which is 40km west of El Uvero) is this small museum at La Plata, just below the highway. The first successful skirmish of the Cuban Revolution happened here on January 17, 1957. Museum exhibits include the piece of paper signed by the 15 *Granma* survivors who met up at Cinco Palmas in late 1956.

Marea del Portillo is 46km to the west. Don't confuse this La Plata with Comandancia La Plata, Fidel Castro's Sierra Maestra Revolutionary headquarters.

🏃 Activities

Cristóbal Colón   DIVING

The well-preserved wreck of Spanish cruiser *Cristóbal Colón* lies where it sank in 1898, about 15m down and only 30m offshore near La Mula. This is Cuba's greatest wreck dive; a genuine remnant of the Spanish-Cuban-American War. Dive centers from Sierra Mar and Club Amigo Carisol – Los Corales (in Parque Baconao) come here. No scuba gear is available, but you can see the wreck with a mask and snorkel.

Hiking

You can hike up the Río Turquino to Las Posas de los Morones, which has a few nice swimming pools (allow four hours round-trip). You must wade across the river at least three times unless it's dry.

The **Pico Turquino** (shelter 2 days/1 night CUC$30) hike (p383) is often tackled from Las Cuevas on the remote coast road 130km west of Santiago de Cuba (along with the other trailhead, Santo Domingo in Granma province). If summiting the mountain is your main aim, this is probably the quickest, easiest route. If you want to immerse yourself in the area's history and hike to Comandancia la Plata, set out from Santo Domingo. Both options can be linked in a spectacularly thorough trek with Ecotur (p417; onward transport is better from the Santo Domingo side).

The hike from Las Cuevas can be organized at relatively short notice at the trailhead. A good option is to book through Ecotur in Santiago de Cuba. Cost for a two-day/one-night trip is CUC$68 without transport; CUC$171 for through hike to Santo Domingo with transport at both ends; CUC$187 including trip to La Plata.

CAMPS & SHELTERS

The trail from Las Cuevas begins on the south-coast highway, 7km west of Ocujal and 51km east of Marea del Portillo. This trek also passes Cuba's second-highest peak, Pico Cuba (1872m). Allow at least six hours to go up and four hours to come down, more if it has been raining, as the trail floods and becomes a mud slick in parts. Be sure you're on the trail by 6:30am at the latest to do the out-and-back day hike. You can sleep at Campismo la Mula, 12km east; self-sufficient hikers can also pitch camp or take the basic beds at Las Cuevas visitors center. The CUC$15 per person fee (camera CUC$5 extra) that you pay at the visitors center/trailhead includes a compulsory Cuban guide. You can stay overnight at the shelter on Pico Cuba (an additional CUC$30) if you don't want to descend the same day. Alternatively, you can do the entire Las Cuevas–Santo Domingo two-day hike by arranging to be met by a new team of guides at Pico Turquino, including a side trip to Castro's former headquarters at Comandancia la Plata, for CUC$68.

THE ROUTE

This hike is grueling: you're gaining almost 2km in elevation across only 9.6km of trail. But shade and peek-a-boo views provide plenty of respite. Fill up on water before setting out. The well-marked route leads from Las Cuevas to La Esmajagua (600m; 3km; there's water here), Pico Cardero (1265m; quickly followed by a series of nearly vertical steps called Saca la Lengua, literally 'flops your tongue out'), Pico Cuba (1872m; 2km; water and shelter here) and Pico Turquino (1972m; 1.7km). When the fog parts and you catch your breath, you'll behold a bronze bust of José Martí standing on the summit of Cuba's highest mountain. You can overnight at the rudimentary **Pico Cuba shelter** on the ascent or descent. There's a basic kitchen, wood-fired stove and plank beds (no mattresses) or, if those are taken, floor space.

CUBA'S BEST & WORST ROAD

The 180km-long coastal road that connects Santiago de Cuba with the small isolated village of Pilón in Granma province is the best in Cuba for raw natural beauty, but the absolute *worst* for drivers who prefer smooth asphalt to endless gaping potholes.

Not surprisingly, traffic on the road is extremely light, and no regular buses operate west of Chivorico. Good taxis and rental cars can ply the route if road conditions are agreeable, but make sure the car is well-maintained and check ahead to see if the road is blocked, closed or washed away. Taxi drivers were asking approximately CUC$160 for the one-way trip between Santiago and the Marea del Portillo hotels at last visit.

Another option is to use a bicycle. Caught between escarpment and sea, the road makes for a truly epic ride, but beware: there are very few facilities, scant places to eat and drink along the way and, should you have bike problems in the remoter areas, only occasional vehicles passing by, at half-hour intervals or less. Additionally, although the route generally hugs the coast, it periodically ascends and descends steep headlands requiring proper gears and good levels of fitness. Stock up on food and water in Santiago, and spread the ride over three days with stops in Brisas Sierra Mar (p425), Campismo La Mula (p427; check availability in Santiago) and Hotel Marea del Portillo (p390).

Fortunately, the magnificence of the scenery makes slow travel highly desirable. This remote segment of southeast Cuba has remained completely and utterly unspoiled, a glorious ribbon of hidden bays and crashing surf backed by precipitous cloud-enshrouded mountains. Such settlements that exist are bucolic and etched in revolutionary folklore. El Uvero and La Plata were the sites of guerrilla attacks in the 1950s by Castro's nascent army, while just off the coast lie the wrecks of two Spanish destroyers sunk in the Cuban-Spanish-American War. On the land side the road skirts the foothills of Cuba's two highest mountain massifs topped by Pico Turquino and Pico Bayamesa. The mountains create a rain shadow effect, rendering their southern slopes dry and speckled with dwarf foliage.

WHAT TO BRING

Trekkers should bring sufficient food, warm clothing, a sleeping bag and a poncho – precipitation is common up here (some 2200mm annually), from a soft drizzle to pelting hail. Except for water, you'll have to carry everything you need, including extra food to share if you can carry it and a little something for the *compañeros* (comrades) who take 15-day shifts up on Pico Cuba.

Ask ahead if you would like an English-speaking guide (there are several, but most are based on the Santo Domingo side). Also ask about food provision at Pico Cuba. Drinks are available for purchase at the Las Cuevas trailhead. Tipping the guides is mandatory – CUC$3 to CUC$5 is sufficient. For competitive types, the (unofficial) summit record by a guide is two hours, 45 minutes. So if you're feeling energetic...

🛏 Sleeping

Campismo la Mula   CABINS **$**
(☏ 32-62-62; Carretera Granma Km 120; r CUC$10.80) On a remote pebble beach, 12km east of the Pico Turquino trailhead, La Mula has 50 small cabins popular with holidaying Cubans, hikers destined for Turquino and the odd hitchhiking south-coast adventurer. It's pretty much the only option on this isolated stretch of coast. Check with Cubamar or the Oficina Reservaciones de Campismo (p417) in Santiago de Cuba before turning up.

There's a rustic cafe and restaurant on-site.

❶ Getting There & Away

Private trucks and the odd rickety bus connect La Mula to Chivirico, but they are sporadic; don't bank on more than one per day. A taxi from Santiago should cost CUC$50 to CUC$60. Traffic is almost nonexistent in this neck of the woods, but the views are fabulous.

Guantánamo Province

♪ 21 / POP 511,100

Includes →

Guantánamo 430

Around Guantánamo
US Naval Base 435

South Coast 436

Punta de Maisí 436

Boca de Yumurí
& Around 436

Baracoa 437

Northwest of
Baracoa 444

Parque Nacional
Alejandro de
Humboldt.......... 445

Best Off-the-Beaten-Track

→ Güirito (p440)

→ Punta de Maisí (p436)

→ Zoológico de Piedras (p434)

Best Places to Eat

→ Bar-Restaurant La Terraza – Casa Nilson (p442)

→ El Buen Sabor (p442)

→ La Rosa Nautica (p443)

→ Restaurante La Punta (p443)

Why Go?

Banish those grainy news images of prisoners in orange jumpsuits from your consciousness; the Cuban version of Guantánamo (on the *other* side of the security fence) is a fantasy land of crinkled mountains and exuberant foliage that seems as far away from modern America as a star in another galaxy. In the region's isolated valleys and wild coastal microclimates (arid in the south, lush in the north), you'll encounter Cuba at its most mysterious and esoteric. Herein lie primitive musical sub-genres, little-known Afro-Cuban religious rites, and echoes of an indigenous Taíno culture supposedly wiped out by the Spanish centuries ago – or so you thought. The town of Baracoa and its rural surroundings is the regional highlight, closely followed by the vibrant endemism of the semi-virgin Parque Nacional Alejandro de Humboldt. Further west, the city of Guantánamo, perennially bypassed by most travelers, hides another saucerful of secrets.

When to Go

→ Baracoa's biggest festival, the Semana de la Cultura Baracoesa, is in late March/early April.

→ The city of Guantánamo gets animated in mid-December for the Festival Nacional de Changüí.

→ Avoid the worst of Baracoa's heavy storms by staying away in September and October. Guantánamo's climate varies hugely, but it's dependent more on geography than season.

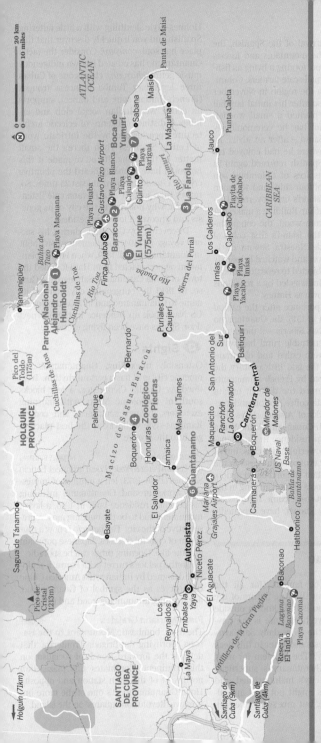

0 km — 20 km
0 — 10 miles

ATLANTIC OCEAN

Punta de Maisí

HOLGUÍN PROVINCE

Holguín (71km)

Pico de Cristal (1213m)

Pico del Toldo (1175m)

SANTIAGO DE CUBA PROVINCE

Santiago de Cuba (9km)
Santiago de Cuba (4km)

Yamaniguey
Bahía de Taco
Playa Maguana
Playa Duaba
Baracoa ②
Gustavo Rizo Airport
Finca Duaba ⑤
Playa Blanca
Cajuajo
Güirito
Playa Barigua
Playa Cajuajo
Río Yumurí
La Máquina
Sabana
Maisí
Punta Caleta
Jauco

Parque Nacional Alejandro de Humboldt ①
Cuchillas de Moa
Cuchillas de Toa
Río Toa
El Yunque (575m)
Boca de Yumurí ⑦
La Farola ③

Río Duaba
Sierra del Purial
Puriales de Caujerí
Los Calderos
Imías
Playa Imías
Playa de Cajobabo
Cajobabo

CARIBBEAN SEA

Macizo de Sagua-Baracoa
Bernardo
Palenque
Boquerón ④
Zoológico de Piedras
Honduras
Jamaica
Manuel Tames
San Antonio del Sur
Baitiquirí
Playa Yacabo

Sagua de Tánamo
Bayate
El Salvador
Maqueicito
Ranchón La Gobernador
Carretera Central
Boquerón
Mirador de Malones

Guantánamo ⑥
Mariana Grajales Airport
Caimanera
US Naval Base
Bahía de Guantánamo
Hatibonico

Los Reynaldos
La Maya
Niceto Pérez
El Aguacate
Autopista
Embalse la Yaya
El Indio
Baconao
Reserva El Indio
Laguna Baconao
Cordillera de la Gran Piedra
Playa Cazonal

Guantánamo Province Highlights

① Search for the world's smallest frog in **Parque Nacional Alejandro de Humboldt** (p445), the most diverse national park in the Caribbean.

② Sample the culinary smorgasbord of exotic **Baracoa** (p442).

③ Cycle **La Farola** (p436), the lighthouse road from Cajobabo to Baracoa.

④ Get an eyeful of the stony statues at the **Zoológico de Piedras** (p434).

⑤ Hike through the tropical jungle up to Baracoa's mysterious flat-topped mountain, **El Yunque** (p444).

⑥ Uncover multiple music genres in the city of **Guantánamo** (p430).

⑦ Jump on board a local boat upstream from the **Boca de Yumurí** (p436) and navigate through the jaws of a narrow river gorge.

History

Long before the arrival of the Spanish, the Taíno populated the mountains and forests around Guantánamo, forging a living as fishers, hunters and small-scale farmers. Columbus first arrived in the region in November 1492, a month or so after his initial landfall near Gibara, and planted a small wooden cross in a beautiful bay he christened Porto Santo – after an idyllic island off Portugal where he had enjoyed his honeymoon. The Spanish returned again in 1511 under the auspices of Columbus' son Diego in a flotilla of four ships and 400 men that included the island's first governor, Diego Velázquez de Cuéllar. Building a makeshift fort constructed from wood, the conquistadors consecrated the island's first colonial settlement, Villa de Nuestra Señora de la Asunción de Baracoa, and watched helplessly as the town was subjected to repeated attacks from hostile local Indians led by a rebellious *cacique* (chief) known as Hatuey.

Declining in importance after the capital moved to Santiago in 1515, the Guantánamo region became Cuba's Siberia – a mountainous and barely penetrable rural backwater where prisoners were exiled and old traditions survived. In the late 18th century the area was recolonized by French immigrants from Haiti who tamed the difficult terrain in order to cultivate coffee, cotton and sugarcane on the backs of African slaves. Following the Spanish-Cuban-American War, a new power took up residence in Guantánamo Bay – the all-powerful Americans, intent on protecting their economic interests in the strategically important Panama Canal region. Despite repeated bouts of mudslinging in the years since, the not-so-welcome *Yanquis,* as they are popularly known, have repeatedly refused to budge.

Guantánamo

POP 216,700

Its name might be famous (for all the wrong reasons), but the true nature of the city of Guantánamo is little known outside the people who live here. Rare is the traveler who gets off the twice-daily Santiago–Baracoa bus and tests the water in this neck of the woods. Why? The problem for most travelers lies in Guantánamo's superficial dilapidation. The city's malnourished grid of crusty buildings might not look appealing on the surface, but mix some Sherlock Holmes-style sleuthing with a little faltering Spanish and you'll quickly discover that this place has soul, *compay*! Consider the facts: Guantánamo has created its own indigenous music genre *(changüi)*, claims one of Cuba's three legendary Tumba Francesa troupes (French-Haitian song and dance), supports an active West Indian social club and exhibits a distinct subgenre of eclectic architecture spearheaded by the intricate work of Leticio Salcines. Then there's the small matter of that song. If you've made it this far you'll have probably heard the plaintive cries of *Guantanamera* at least 25 times. So, rather than just sit in a Havana café listening to it, why not visit to the city of its genesis and uncover a lot more besides?

'Discovered' by Columbus during his second voyage in 1494, a settlement wasn't built in Guantánamo until 1819, when French plantation owners evicted from Haiti founded the town of Santa Catalina del Saltadero del Guaso. In 1843 the burgeoning city changed its name to Guantánamo and in 1903 the bullish US Navy took up residence in the bay next door. Sparks have been flying ever since.

◉ Sights

Ostensibly unexciting, Guantánamo's geometric city grid has a certain rhythm. Tree-lined Av Camilo Cienfuegos, a few blocks south of Bartolomé Masó, with morning exercisers, bizarre sculptures and central Ramblas-style walkway, is the best place to get into the groove.

Palacio Salcines   NOTABLE BUILDING
(cnr Pedro A Pérez & Prado) Local architect Leticio Salcines (1888–1973) left a number of impressive works around Guantánamo including his personal residence built in 1916, a lavish monument said to be the building most representative of the city. The *palacio* is now a **museum** of colorful frescoes, Japanese porcelain and the like. Opening times can be sporadic

On the palace's turret is **La Fama**, a sculpture designed by Italian artist Americo Chine that serves as the symbol of Guantánamo, her trumpet announcing good and evil.

Plaza Mariana Grajales   SQUARE
The huge, bombastic **Monument to the Heroes**, glorifying the Brigada Fronteriza 'that defends the forward trench of socialism on this continent,' dominates this plaza, 1km northwest of the train station and opposite Hotel Guantánamo. It's one of the more impressive 'Revolution squares' on the island.

Guantánamo

Guantánamo

◎ Sights
1 Biblioteca Policarpo Pineda Rustán.....	C4
2 Museo Provincial.................................	A3
3 Palacio Salcines..................................	B3
4 Parque Martí......................................	B3
5 Parroquia de Santa Catalina de Riccis...	B3

✦ Activities, Courses & Tours
6 Oficina de Monumentos y Sitios Históricos......................................	C4

🛏 Sleeping
7 Elsye Castillo Osoria...........................	B2
8 Hotel Martlí......................................	B3
9 Lissett Foster Lara.............................	B2

✖ Eating
10 Bar-Restaurante Olimpia.....................	B3
11 Restaurante 1870................................	B3

🍷 Drinking & Nightlife
12 Casa de las Promociones Musicales 'La Guantanamera'...............................	B4
13 La Ruina...	B4

★ Entertainment
14 Casa de Changüí................................	D2
15 Casa de la Trova (Parque Martí)...........	B3
16 Casa del Son....................................	D2
17 Cine Huambo....................................	B3
18 Tumba Francesa Pompadour................	D2

Museo Provincial   MUSEUM
(cnr José Martí & Prado; admission CUC$1; ☉8am-
noon & 12:30-4:30pm Mon-Fri, 8am-noon Sat)
Housed in an old jail guarded by two canons,

the city museum has *salas* (rooms) dedicated
to aboriginal culture, local nature, weapons
(lots of Mambí swords) and decorative arts.

GITMO – THE STORY SO FAR...

Procured via the infamous Platt Amendment in 1903 in the aftermath of the Spanish-Cuban-American War, the US' naval base in Guantánamo Bay (or Gitmo, as generations of homesick US marines have unsentimentally dubbed it) was initially established primarily to protect the eastern approach to the strategically important Panama Canal.

In 1934 an upgrade of the original treaty reaffirmed the lease terms and agreed to honor them indefinitely unless both governments accorded otherwise. It also set an annual rent of US$4085, a sum that the US continues to cough up, but which the Cubans won't bank on the grounds that the occupation is illegal (Fidel Castro allegedly stored the checks in the top drawer of his office desk).

The US Naval Base sits at the jaws of Guantánamo Bay with military installations on both sides and the interior of the bay actually lying inside Cuban territory. Facilities include a dozen beaches, a water-desalination plant, two airstrips and Cuba's only McDonald's, KFC and Starbucks. Approximately 9500 military personal are based here.

The recent history of the facility has been notorious. In January 1992, 11,000 Haitian migrants were temporarily held here, and in August 1994 the base was used to house 32,000 Cuban *balseros* (rafters) picked up by the US Coast Guard while trying to reach Florida.

Since 2002 the US has held more than 770 prisoners with suspected Al-Qaeda or Taliban links at Camp Delta in Guantánamo Bay without pressing criminal charges. Denied legal counsel and family contact while facing rigorous interrogations, the detainees mounted hunger strikes and at least four are known to have committed suicide. Following calls from Amnesty International and the UN in 2004 to close the base down and reports from the Red Cross that certain aspects of the camp regime were tantamount to torture, the US released 420 prisoners and charged just three of them.

In January 2009, President Barack Obama promised to shut down Guantánamo's detention camps and thus end what he termed 'a sad chapter in US history.' However, due to bipartisan opposition in Congress, Obama's one-year deadline was never met. The saga continued. The force-feeding of some 100 inmates on hunger strike in May 2013 was widely condemned by the international community, putting pressure on the president to renew his efforts to close the camp. Notwithstanding, Congress has successively blocked any further attempts to move prisoners to the US for trial.

As of early 2015, 136 prisoners remain in Guantánamo. At least half of them are cleared to leave but, so far, the authorities have struggled to find a country that will take them. They remain stuck in limbo, trapped by legal and political red tape.

Parque Martí
SQUARE

Anchored by the tiny **Parroquia de Santa Catalina de Riccis** (1863), Parque Martí has benefited from a substantial facelift of late: a lick of paint, information boards and a clutch of interesting new shops, restaurants and entertainment nooks, strung along vibrant boulevards. Sitting timelessly amid the action is a seated **statue** of 'El Maestro' from whom the square takes its name.

Biblioteca Policarpo Pineda Rustán
LIBRARY

(cnr Los Maceos & Emilio Giro) Another architectural gift from Leticio Salcines is this beautiful provincial library which was once the city hall (1934–51). Trials of Fulgencio Batista's thugs were held here in 1959, and a number were killed when they snatched a rifle and tried to escape.

Tours

Oficina de Monumentos y Sitios Históricos
WALKING TOUR

(Los Maceos, btwn Emilio Giro & Flor Crombet) For a fuller exposé of Guantánamo's interesting architectural heritage, ask here about walking tours. There were five offered at last visit including 'In the Footsteps of José Lecticio Salcines' (the architect).

🎊 Festivals & Events

Festival Nacional de Changüí
MUSIC

(☺ mid-Dec) Celebration of *changüí* music.

Noches Guantanameras
STREET PARTY

(☺ 8pm Sat) Saturday night is reserved for this local coming together, when Calle Pedro A Pérez closes to traffic and stalls are set up in the street: come and enjoy whole roast pig, belting music and copious amounts of rum.

🛏 Sleeping

Lissett Foster Lara
CASA PARTICULAR $

(☑32-59-70; Pedro A Pérez No 761, btwn Prado & Jesús del Sol; r CUC$20-25; ❄) Like many *guantanameras*, Lissett speaks perfect English and her house is polished, comfortable and decked out with the kind of plush fittings that wouldn't look amiss in a North American suburb. There are three rooms, including a delightful one on the substantial roof terrace.

Elsye Castillo Osoria
CASA PARTICULAR $

(☑35-45-12; Calixto García No 766, btwn Prado & Jesús del Sol; CUC$20-25; ❄ ▨) You'll struggle to remember what side of the heavily guarded frontier you're on in this super-modern house with two massive rooms sharing polished communal areas including a kitchen. There's an ample terrace and – we kid you not – a swimming pool.

Hotel Guantánamo
HOTEL $

(☑38-10-15; Calle 13 Norte, btwn Ahogados & 2 de Octubre; s/d CUC$25/40; P❄▨) Hotel Guantánamo is something approaching comfortable. The generic rooms are clean, the pool has water in it, and there's a good reception bar-cafe mixing up tempting mojitos and serving coffee. It's 1km northwest of the train station.

★ Hotel Martlí
HOTEL $$

(☑32-95-00; cnr Aguilera & Calixto García; s/d CUC$35/56; ❄🛜) A relatively recent hotel refurb overlooking Parque Martí, this pleasant little box sits in a revamped colonial building with, by Guantánamo standards, what could be described as sumptuous rooms. Entertainment-wise, there's the rooftop terrace restaurant with deafening music and the street-level bar circled by *jineteras* (female touts).

🍴 Eating

At weekends Parque Martí is an outdoor 'buffet' of mobile food stalls selling cheap fried *comida ligera* (light food).

★ Sabor Melián
CARIBBEAN $

(☑32-44-22; Camilo Cienfuegos No 407; meals CUC$3-6; ⏰noon-midnight) Pictures of Venice adorn the walls of this new private restaurant which, despite the in-house art, tends to focus on good old-fashioned Caribbean chow. Judging by our unofficial street poll, it's the most popular eating place in town among locals.

Restaurante 1870
CUBAN $

(Flor Crombet; meals CUC$2-5; ⏰noon-11pm) Before this place opened opposite Parque Martí, you would be forgiven for thinking Guantánamo never had a colonial heyday. But here we go. The sweeping marble staircase takes you up to the plushly ornamented balcony-bar from where you can gaze down on the main eating area. The *ropa vieja* (shredded beef in a tangy sauce) is not bad.

Restaurante Girasoles
CARIBBEAN $

(Calle 15 Norte, cnr Ahogados; meals CUC$1-5; ⏰noon-9.30pm) A nude statue rather than a *girasol* (sunflower) marks the entrance to what is, by process of elimination, one of Guantánamo's best restaurants. Behind the Hotel Guantánamo, Girasoles serves up (albeit at a snail's pace) chicken and fish, occasionally in interesting sauces. The terrace is popular for an afternoon drink.

Bar-Restaurante Olimpia
BURGERS $

(cnr Calixto García & Aguilera; meals CUC$1-4; ⏰9am-midnight) A celebration of Guantánamo's remarkable Olympic Games performances, this bar-restaurant displays baseball shirts, athletics memorabilia and the boxing vest of three-time Olympic gold medalist Félix Savón (a local boy). Inside there's a small open patio and a mezzanine bar where you can enjoy beers and Cuban-style burgers, all with a vista of adjacent Parque Martí.

🍸 Drinking & Nightlife

Two pedestrianized streets – Aguilera and Flor Crombet – leading a block east of Parque Martí are embellished by lively bars where preened *guantanameros* like to flaunt their fake designer clothing.

La Ruina
BAR

(cnr Calixto García & Emilio Giro; ⏰10am-1am) This shell of a ruined colonial building has 9m ceilings; there are plenty of benches to prop you up after you've downed your nth beer and there's a popular karaoke scene for those with reality-TV ambitions. The bar menu's good for a snack lunch.

Casa de las Promociones Musicales 'La Guantanamera'
CLUB

(Calixto García, btwn Flor Crombet & Emilio Giro) Another well-maintained concert-orientated venue, with Thursday rap *peñas* (performances) and Sunday *trova* (verse, song) matinees.

ZOOLÓGICO DE PIEDRAS

A surreal spectacle even by Cuban standards, the **Zoológico de Piedras** (admission CUC$1; ⊙ 9am-6pm Mon-Sat) is an animal sculpture park set amid thick foliage in the grounds of a mountain coffee farm, 20km northeast of Guantánamo. Carved out of the existing rock by sculptor Angel Iñigo Blanco, starting in the late 1970s, the sculptures now number more than 300 and range from hippos to giant serpents. Señor Blanco passed away in 2014, but the stone zoo looks set to continue in his memory. To get here you'll need your own wheels or a taxi (CUC$10 one way from Guantánamo). Head east out of town and fork left toward Jamaica and Honduras. The 'zoo' is in the settlement of Boquerón.

⭐ Entertainment

Guantánamo bleeds music. The city even has its own distinctive musical culture, enshrined in a subgenre of *son* (Cuba's popular music) known as *changüí*. You can get a taste of this and other sounds at some of the following venues.

⭐ Tumba Francesa Pompadour LIVE MUSIC
(Serafín Sánchez No 715) One of only three Tumba Francesa societies left in Cuba, this house, situated four blocks east of the train station, specializes in a unique form of Haitian-style dancing. Programs include *mi tumba baile* (*tumba* dance), *encuentro tradicional* (traditional get-together) and *peña campesina* (country music). Opening times vary. Ask at the Casa de Changüí opposite.

Casa de Changüí LIVE MUSIC
(Serafín Sánchez No 710, btwn N López & Jesús del Sol; ⊙ 5pm-midnight) As primary pulpit for Guantánamo's indigenous music, this is *the* place to experience *changüí* and a shrine to its main exponent, local *timbalero* (percussionist) Elio Revé. There's a small **Sala de Historia** museum on-site.

Casa de la Trova (Parque Martí) LIVE MUSIC
(cnr Pedro Pérez & Flor Crombet; admission CUC$1; ⊙ 8pm-1am) The only Cuban city with two *trova* houses, Guantánamo offers options galore. This one is the more traditional

haunt, with *viejos* (old men) in Panama hats casting aside their arthritis to dance athletically.

Casa de la Trova (ARTex) LIVE MUSIC
(Máximo Gómez No 1062; admission CUC$1; ⊙ 8pm-1am Tue-Sun) Housed in a royal blue building on a quiet street, Casa de la Trova Mark 2 is openly referred to as 'the place.' It attracts a younger demographic and music to reflect their tastes, eg rap and fusion.

Casa del Son LIVE MUSIC
(cnr Serafín Sánchez & Prado; ⊙ 5pm-midnight) A new venue for old music, this casa shares lovingly restored digs with the Casa de Changüí in Calle Serafín Sánchez, the city's boisterous 'music street.'

Cine Huambo CINEMA
(Parque Martí) Revamped cinema in the heart of the Parque Martí action. Mainly in Spanish; a few films in English with Spanish subtitles.

Estadio Van Troi SPORTS
Baseball games are played from October to April at this stadium in Reparto San Justo, 1.5km south of the Servi-Cupet gas station. Despite a strong sporting tradition, Guantánamo – nicknamed Los Indios – are perennial underachievers who seldom make the play-offs.

ⓘ Information

Banco de Crédito y Comercio (Calixto García, btwn Emilio Giro & Bartolomé Masó; ⊙ 9am-3pm Mon-Fri) One of two branches on this block.

Cadeca (cnr Calixto García & Prado) Money changing.

Clínica Internacional (Flor Crombet No 305, btwn Calixto García & Los Maceos; ⊙ 9am-5pm) On the northeast corner of Parque Martí.

Etecsa Telepunto (cnr Aguilera & Los Maceos; per hour CUC$4.50; ⊙ 8:30am-7:30pm) Four computers plus hardly any tourists equals no queues.

Havanatur (Aguilera, btwn Calixto García & Los Maceos; ⊙ 8am-noon & 1:30-4:30pm Mon-Fri, 8:30-11:30am Sat) Travel agency.

Hospital Agostinho Neto (📞 35-54-50; Carretera de El Salvador Km 1; ⊙ 24hr) At the west end of Plaza Mariana Grajales near Hotel Guantánamo. It will help foreigners in emergencies.

Post Office (Pedro A Pérez; ⊙ 8am-1pm & 2-6pm Mon-Sat) On the west side of Parque Martí. There's also a DHL office here.

❶ Getting There & Away

AIR

Cubana (Calixto García No 817) flies four times a week (CUC$159 one way, 2½ hours) from Havana to Mariana Grajales Airport (also known as Los Canos Airport). There are no international flights.

BUS

The rather inconveniently placed Terminal de Ómnibus (bus station) is 5km west of the center on the old road to Guantánamo (a continuation of Av Camilo Cienfuegos). A taxi from the Hotel Guantánamo should cost CUC$3 to CUC$4.

There are two daily **Víazul** (www.viazul.com) buses to Baracoa (CUC$10, three hours, 9:30am and 3:30pm) and one to Santiago de Cuba (CUC$6, 1¾ hours, 11:30pm).

CAR

The Autopista Nacional to Santiago de Cuba ends near Embalse la Yaya, 25km west of Guantánamo, where the road joins the Carretera Central (work to extend this road continues). To drive to Guantánamo from Santiago de Cuba, follow the Autopista Nacional north about 12km to the top of the grade, then take the first turn to the right. Signposts are sporadic and vague, so take a good map and keep alert.

Cubacar (Hotel Guantánamo) has an office in Hotel Guantánamo.

The **Oro Negro gas station** (cnr Los Maceos & Jesús del Sol) is a place to fill up on gas before the 150km trek east to Baracoa.

TRAIN

The **train station** (Pedro A Pérez), several blocks north of Parque Martí, has one departure for Havana (CUC$32, 19 hours) every third day via Camagüey, Ciego de Ávila, Santa Clara and Matanzas. Purchase tickets in the morning of the day the train departs at the office on Pedro A Pérez.

TRUCK

Trucks to Santiago de Cuba and Baracoa leave from the Terminal de Ómnibus and allow you to disembark in the smaller towns in between.

Trucks for Moa park on the road to El Salvador north of town near the entrance to the Autopista.

❶ Getting Around

Bus 48 (20 centavos) runs between the center and the Hotel Guantánamo every 40 minutes or so. There are also plenty of bici-taxis. Taxis hang out around Parque Martí.

Around Guantánamo US Naval Base

Ranchón La Gobernador

Back in the old days you could get a decent view of the US Naval Base from the 320m-high Mirador de Malones 20km to the east of Guantánamo City, but visits were curtailed in the late 2000s. Now, just off the main road to Baracoa, close to the where the entrance to the old Mirador used to be, is the new **Ranchón La Gobernador** (⊘9am-9pm) **FREE**, a simple rustic bar-restaurant with a lookout tower equipped with strong binoculars. An on-site multilingual guide is on hand to help you pick out the admittedly distant US installations. And no, you can't see Cuba's only McDonald's.

Caimanera

Contrary to popular belief, Caimanera (not Guantánamo) is the nearest Cuban town to the US Naval Base. Situated on the west shore of Guantánamo Bay just north of the US military checkpoint, this fishing settlement of 10,000 people (many of them first- or second-generation Jamaicans) was a boomtown before the Revolution when local workers were employed in the naval station. According to old-timers, the most popular profession was prostitution. Since 1959, Caimanera has struggled economically. A sole hotel acts as a lookout spot for curious 'Bay-watchers.'

To the west of Caimanera the dry cacti-covered hills are characterized by *moni-tongos* (rocky, wind-eroded plateaus). The region has a high level of endemism and is protected as a fauna reserve. There are trails here, but you'll need to be on an organized trip to access them.

🛏 Sleeping

Hotel Caimanera HOTEL $
(☎49-94-14; s/d incl breakfast from CUC$16/25, 2-person bungalows CUC$42; P❄✸) This oddly attractive (considering its position) hotel is on a hilltop at Caimanera, near the perimeter of the US Naval Base, 21km south of Guantánamo. It has peculiar rules which permit only groups of seven or more on prearranged tours with an official Cuban guide to stay and enjoy the lookout. Ask at the Havanatur office in Guantánamo about joining a trip.

ⓘ Getting There & Away

Caimanera is the eastern terminus of the Cuban railway network (which doesn't extend to Baracoa). There are supposedly four trains a day to Guantánamo City.

South Coast

The long, dry coastal road from Guantánamo to the island's eastern extremity, Punta de Maisí, is Cuba's spectacular semi-desert region, where cacti nestle on rocky ocean terraces and prickly aloe vera poke out from the scrub. Several little stone beaches between Playa Yacabo and Cajobabo make refreshing pit stops for those with time to linger, while the diverse roadside scenery – punctuated at intervals by rugged purple mountains and impossibly verdant riverside oases – impresses throughout.

◉ Sights

Playita de Cajobabo BEACH

Cajababo's main beach is stony and flanked by dramatic cliffs, but nonetheless makes a good snorkeling spot. Follow the road at its far end over a headland and the asphalt dead-ends at another beach. Walk east along this beach for 400m and you'll come to a boat-shaped monument commemorating the spot where José Martí landed in 1895 to launch the Second War of Independence.

Martí and Máximo Gómez arrived in a rowing boat with four others at 10pm on the night of April 11. The disembarkation served as inspiration for Fidel Castro's subsequent landing in *Granma* 61 years later.

Museo de 11 Abril MUSEUM

(⊙8am-noon & 1:30-5:30pm) **FREE** Set in a tiny casa on the approach road to Cajababo beach is the former home of Salustiano Leyva who, at the age of 11 in 1895, helped the freshly landed Martí and Gómez to rest and plan their subsequent march west. The museum charts the events with maps and mementos. Leyva lived into the 1970s and was one of the few people to have met both Martí and Castro.

La Farola ROAD

One of the seven modern engineering marvels of modern Cuba, the so-called 'Lighthouse road' runs 55km from Cajobabo all the way to Baracoa, connecting cacti-sprinkled semi-desert with lush rainforest. There are soaring pines and a lookout at its highest point, Alto de Cotilla.

Punta de Maisí

From Cajobabo, the coastal road continues 51km northeast to La Máquina. As far as Jauco, the road is good; thereafter less so. Coming from Baracoa to La Máquina (55km) it's a good road as far as Sabana, then rough in places from Sabana to La Máquina. Either way, La Máquina is the starting point of the very rough 13km track down to Punta de Maisí – best covered in a 4WD.

This is Cuba's easternmost point and there's a lighthouse (1862) and a small fine white-sand beach. You can see Haiti 70km away on a clear day.

After a long time as an off-limits military zone, the Maisí region is being opened up to travelers. At the time of writing, Gaviota was starting a day tour to the area including entry to the lighthouse. Enquire in Hostal la Habanera (p440) in Baracoa.

Boca de Yumurí & Around

Five kilometers south of Baracoa a road branches east off La Farola and travels 28km along the coast to Boca de Yumurí at the mouth of Río Yumurí. Near the bridge over the river is the Túnel de los Alemanes (German Tunnel), an amazing natural arch of trees and foliage. Though lovely, the dark-sand beach here has become *the* day trip from Baracoa. Hustlers hard-sell fried-fish meals, while other people peddle colorful land snails called *polymitas*. They have become rare as a result of being harvested wholesale for tourists, so refuse all offers. From beneath the bridge at the mouth of the river, boat taxis (CUC$2) head 400m upstream to where the steep riverbanks narrow into a haunting natural gorge. You can arrange to be dropped off here for a picnic on an island in the river delta.

Boca de Yumurí makes a superb bike jaunt from Baracoa (56km round-trip): hot but smooth and flat with great views and many potential stopovers (try Playa Bariguá at Km 25). You can arrange bikes in Baracoa; ask at your casa particular. Taxis will also take you here from Baracoa, or you can organize an excursion either privately or with Cubatur (CUC$22). Tours generally stop off at Guirito to visit a cocoa plantation on the way.

Between Boca de Yumurí and Baracoa there are some beautiful beaches. Heading west, first up is Playa Cajuajo, a little-visited sandy expanse accessible via a 5km trail from the Río Mata through biologically diverse woodland. Ecotur in Baracoa runs trips here. There's also delightful little **Playa Mangalito**, where the beach-abutting **Restaurant Tato** (mains CUC$5-7; ⊙8am-midnight) will prepare you fresh octopus caught in the shallows just meters from your plate.

Baracoa

POP 40,800

Magic, weird, beguiling, outlandish, unorthodox, mysterious, surreal, psychedelic and hallucinogenic; you can throw a thousand words at Baracoa, but still not come close to nailing its essence. Located over the hills and far away on the wet and windy side of the Cuchillos del Toa Mountains, Cuba's oldest and most isolated town is a thing to behold, less for the beauty of its architecture (which is scruffy and unimpressive), but more for its atmosphere, people and je ne sais quoi. Not surprisingly, epiphanies are rife in these parts. Feast your eyes upon the foliage (deep green, fast-growing and wonderfully abundant after the stark aridity of Guantánamo's south coast), delve into the fantastical legends, and acquaint yourself with a Tolkienesque cast of local characters both alive and dead. There's Cayamba, the self-styled 'Guerrilla troubadour' who once claimed he was 'the man with the ugliest voice in the world'; La Rusa, the aristocratic Russian émigré who swapped one form of *socialismo* for another and became the inspiration for a novel by magic-realist author Alejo Carpentier; and Enriqueta Faber, a French woman who passed herself off as a man so that she could practice as a doctor and somehow managed to dupe a local heiress into marrying her in Baracoa's cathedral in – ahem – 1819! (Cuba's first same-sex marriage?)

History

Founded in 1511 by Diego Velázquez de Cuéllar, and semi-abandoned in the mid-16th century, the town became a Cuban Siberia where rebellious revolutionaries were sent as prisoners. In the early 19th century French planters crossed the 70km-wide Windward Passage from Haiti and began farming the local staples of coconut, cocoa and coffee in the mountains; the economic wheels finally began to turn. Baracoa developed in relative isolation from the rest of Cuba until the opening of La Farola in 1964, a factor that has strongly influenced its singular culture.

◉ Sights & Activities

◉ In Town

★ **Museo Arqueológico 'La Cueva del Paraíso'** MUSEUM
(Moncada; admission CUC$3; ⊙8am-5pm) Baracoa's most impressive museum is exhibited in a series of caves, Las Cuevas del Paraíso, that were once Taíno burial chambers. Among nearly 2000 authentic Taíno pieces are unearthed skeletons, ceramics, 3000-year-old petroglyphs and a replica of the *Ídolo de Tabaco*, a sculpture found in Maisí in 1903 and considered to be one of the most important Taíno finds in the Caribbean.

One of the staff will enthusiastically show you around. The museum is 800m southeast of Hotel El Castillo.

Fuerte Matachín FORT
(cnr José Martí & Malecón; admission CUC$1; ⊙8am-noon & 2-6pm) Baracoa is protected by a trio of muscular Spanish forts. This one, built in 1802 at the southern entrance to town, houses the **Museo Municipal**. The small but beautiful building showcases an engaging chronology of Cuba's oldest settlement including *polymita* snail shells, the story of Che Guevara and the chocolate factory, and the particular strand of music Baracoa gave birth to: *kiribá*, a forefather of *son*.

There are also exhibits relating to Magdalena Menasse (née Rovieskuya, 'La Rusa'), after whom Alejo Carpentier based his famous book, *La Consagración de la Primavera* (The Rite of Spring).

Catedral de Nuestra Señora de la Asunción CHURCH
(Antonio Maceo No 152) After years of neglect in which it was nearly felled by one hurricane too many, Baracoa's historic cathedral has been lovingly restored using primarily Italian money. There's been a building on this site since the 16th century, though this present, much-altered incarnation, dates from 1833.

The church's most famous artifact is the priceless **Cruz de la Parra**, the only survivor of 29 wooden crosses erected by Columbus in Cuba on his first voyage in 1492. Carbon dating has authenticated the age of the cross (it dates from the late 1400s), but has indicated it was originally made out of indigenous Cuban wood, thus disproving the legend that Columbus brought the cross from Europe.

GUANTÁNAMO PROVINCE BARACOA

Baracoa

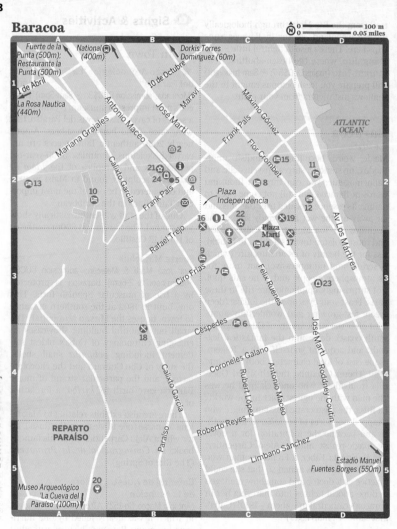

Facing the cathedral is the **Bust of Hatuey**, a rebellious Indian *cacique* who was burned at the stake near Baracoa in 1512 after refusing to convert to Catholicism. Also on triangular Plaza Independencia (this being Baracoa, they couldn't have a square plaza) is the neoclassical **Poder Popular** (Antonio Maceo No 137), a municipal government building which you can admire from the outside.

Casa del Cacao
MUSEUM

(Antonio Maceo, btwn Maraví & Frank País; ⏰ 7am-11pm) **FREE** Baracoa, you will quickly ascertain (via your nose), is the center of Cuba's

chocolate industry; cocoa is grown hereabouts and subsequently chocolate-ized in a local factory. Thus this cafe-cum-museum chronicles the history of cacao and its importance in eastern Cuba as well as offering cups full of the pure, thick stuff (hot or cold) in a pleasant indoor cafe. It also sells bars of dark, agreeably bitter Baracoan chocolate.

El Castillo de Seboruco
FORT

Baracoa's highest fort was begun by the Spanish in 1739 and finished by the Americans in 1900. Barely recognizable as a fort these days, it serves as Hotel El Castillo.

Baracoa

⊙ **Sights**
1 Bust of Hatuey C2
2 Casa del Cacao........................... B2
3 Catedral de Nuestra Señora
   de la Asunción.................................... C3
   El Castillo de Seboruco................(see 10)
4 Poder Popular B2

🏃 **Activities, Courses & Tours**
5 Gaviota... B2

🛏 **Sleeping**
6 Casa Colonial Lucy C3
7 Casa Colonial Ykira
   Mahiquez C3
8 Casa Yamicel.................................... C2
9 Hostal 1511...................................... C3
   Hostal la Habanera......................(see 5)
10 Hotel El Castillo A2
11 Hotel la Rusa.................................... D2
12 Hotel Río Miel D2
13 Isabel Castro Vilato A2

14 La Casona.. C3
15 Nilson Abad Guilaré C2

🍴 **Eating**
   Bar-Restaurant La Terraza –
   Casa Nilson ....(see 15)
16 Cafetería el Parque C2
17 Dorado Café..C3
18 El Buen Sabor B4
19 Tienda la Primada C2

🍷 **Drinking & Nightlife**
20 El Ranchón A5

🎭 **Entertainment**
21 Casa de la Cultura B2
22 Casa de la Trova Victorino
   Rodríguez C2

🛍 **Shopping**
23 ARTex...D3
24 Taller Mirate B2

There's an excellent view of El Yunque's flat top over the shimmering swimming pool. A steep stairway at the southwest end of Calle Frank País climbs directly up.

Fuerte de la Punta   FORT
This Spanish fort has watched over the harbor entrance at the northwestern end of town since 1803. The super-thick, hurricane-resistant walls now hide a rather pleasant restaurant (p443).

⊙ Southeast of Town

Parque Natural Majayara   PARK
🡒 Southeast of town in the Parque Natural Majayara are a couple of magical **hikes** and **swimming** opportunities plus an archaeological trail in the grounds of a lush family farm. It's a very low-key, DIY diversion.

Passing the Fuerte Matachín, hike southeast past the baseball stadium and along the dark-sand beach for 20 minutes to the Río Miel, where a long low bridge crosses the river.

On the other side, bear left following a track up through a cluster of rustic houses to another junction. A guard post here is sometimes staffed by a park official who will collect CUC$2. Turn left again and continue along the vehicle track until the houses clear and you see a signposted single-track path leading off left to an idyllic spot for a picnic.

Staying straight on the track, you'll come to a trio of wooden homesteads. The third of these houses belongs to the Fuentes family. For a donation, Señor Fuentes will lead you on a hike to his family **finca**, where you can stop for coffee and tropical fruit. Further on he'll show you the **Cueva de Aguas**, a cave with a sparkling, freshwater swimming hole inside. Tracking back up the hillside you'll come to an **archaeological trail** with more caves and marvelous ocean views.

Alternatively, you can organize a 'Ruta Taína' excursion with Ecotur (p443) for around CUC$14.

⊙ Northwest of Town

Follow the aroma of chocolate on the road out of town toward Moa.

Playa Duaba   BEACH
Heading north on the Moa road, take the Hotel Porto Santo/airport turnoff and continue for 2km past the airport runway to a black-sand beach at the river mouth where Antonio Maceo, Flor Crombet and others landed in 1895 to start the Second War of Independence. There's a memorial **monument** here and close-up views of El Yunque, though the beach itself isn't sunbathing territory.

Fábrica de Chocolate   FACTORY
The delicious sweet smells filling the air in this neck of the woods are concocted in the famous chocolate factory 1km past the airport

GUANTÁNAMO PROVINCE BARACOA

turnoff, opened, not by Willy Wonka, but by Che Guevara in 1963. It's not currently accepting visits (or golden tickets!).

Fábrica de Cucuruchu FACTORY
Undoubtedly the only factory in the world that makes *cucurucho,* Baracoa's sweetest treat, wrapped in an environmentally friendly palm frond. You can buy it on-site, although most people procure from the local farmers who sell it from the roadside on La Farola. It's 500m beyond the Fábrica de Chocolate on the road to Moa.

Tours

Organized tours are a good way to view Baracoa's hard-to-reach outlying sights, and the Cubatur and Ecotur offices on Plaza Independencia can book excursions including El Yunque (CUC$16 to CUC$20), Parque Nacional Alejandro de Humboldt (CUC$22 to CUC$25), Río Toa (CUC$18 to CUC$20) and Boca de Yumurí (CUC$22).

★ **José Ángel Delfino Pérez** GUIDED TOUR
(☑ 64-13-67; joseguia@nauta.cu) Walking plant encyclopedia and enthusiastic geological expert José has to be Baracoa's best private guide. His professional tours visit El Yunque

(CUC$20), Punta de Maisi (CUC$27), Humboldt (CUC$25) and – best of all – Boca de Yumurí (CUC$25), a trip that takes in cacao plantations, chocolate tastings and visits to isolated beaches. Prices drop the more people participate.

Ask to see José's ID, as he has some unwelcome local impersonators You can contact him by phone, email or at the casa particular of Nilson Abad Guilaré.

Gaviota TOURS
(☑ 64-41-15; cnr Frank País & Calle Maceo; ☉ 8am-6pm Sun-Fri) Has a very useful desk in the Hotel Habanera which can organize tours, flights and bus tickets.

Festivals & Events

Semana de la Cultura Baracoesa FESTIVAL
(☉ late Mar/early Apr) Locals hit the streets to celebrate the 1895 landing of Antonio Maceo.

Sleeping

Hostal la Habanera HOTEL $
(☑ 64-52-73; Antonio Maceo No 126; s/d CUC$40/45; ❈ ☎) Atmospheric and inviting in a way only Baracoa can muster, La Habanera sits in a restored and regularly repainted

KIRIBÁ & NENGÓN: THE ROOTS OF SON

If you're on a mission to unravel the complex family tree of Cuban music (a jolly good holiday plan if you've got time), the tiny village of **Güirito**, 18km southeast of Baracoa, should be one of your first stops. Herein lie two of the primitive precursors to Cuba's national music, *son.* Except that while *son* and its rhythmic cousin, salsa, got exported around the world, the orphic genres of *kiribá* and *nengón* never got much further than – well – Güirito.

So what exactly are these rugged and rootsy musical forms? Both *kiribá* and *nengón* are rustic antecedents of *son* (rather than variants of it) that have been passed down orally from generation to generation since the First Independence War in the mid-19th century. *Kiribá*'s fast beat and relatively free choreography incorporates a couples' dance in which partners move together in broad circular steps. *Nengón* is a slower dance with a distinctive foot-dragging motion said to imitate erstwhile farmworkers who stamped their feet on dried coffee and cacao beans to grind them. The accompanying music is invariably played by a septet consisting of *tres* (Cuban-style guitar), guiro, claves, marimbula, bongos, maracas and voice. *Nengón* has 22 registered songs; in *kiribá*, there are no songs as such – singers make up the words as they go along. The costumes worn at musical gatherings are equally distinctive. Women wear white blouses and long flower-patterned skirts. Men wear *guayabera* shirts, *Yarey* hats and carry handkerchiefs.

Thanks to a local revival in 1982, *kiribá* and *nengón* are still widely practiced in Güirito by a 21-person music and dance group who have meticulously safeguarded the old traditions. On most (but not all) Saturday afternoons the group gets together in Güirito for a traditional fiesta, an informal affair with a wide interchange of Baracoan food. There's *bacán* (crab and plantain tamales), *frangollo* (dried banana mixed with sugar and wrapped in a banana leaf) and rice cooked inside the stomach of a whole roasted pig. Fuelled by rum drawn from oak barrels, the dancing can go on until the small hours. Anyone is welcome.

colonial mansion. The four front bedrooms share a street-facing balcony replete with tiled floor and rocking chairs: perfect for imbibing that quintessential Baracoa ambience (street-hawkers, hip-gyrating music, and seafood a-frying in the restaurants).

The downstairs lobby has a bar, a restaurant and a handy Gaviota tour desk.

Nilson Abad Guilaré CASA PARTICULAR $
(☑64-31-23; abadcub@gmail.com; Flor Crombet No 143, btwn Ciro Frías & Pelayo Cuervo; r CUC$25-30; ✴) Nilson's a real gent who keeps one of the cleanest houses in Cuba. His fantastic self-contained apartment has a huge bathroom, kitchen access and roof terrace with sea views. Dinner is available at his acclaimed on-site private restaurant, La Terraza. Two brand-new rooms were being built at last visit.

Hotel Río Miel HOTEL $
(cnr Ciro Frias & Ave Malecón; s/d CUC$40/45; ✴🖥) The newest of government-run Gaviota's sextet of Baracoa hotels, this one sits bravely on the Malecón where it embraces some of the most inclement weather in Cuba. It's ruggedly romantic if nothing else.

Isabel Castro Vilato CASA PARTICULAR $
(☑64-22-67; Mariana Granjales No 35; r CUC$25; P✴) This elegant green clapboard-and-stone house secretes three massive rooms and a beautiful garden where they grow half of your breakfast provisions. Unusually for Baracoa there's a secure garage/car-parking space.

Hostal 1511 HOTEL $
(☑64-57-00; Ciro Frías, btwn Rubert López & Maceo; s/d CUC$40/45; ✴🖥) The year 1511 is Baracoa's foundation date, and this diminutive place is a landmark too for offering dead-central accommodations with abundant colonial vibe. The model ship in reception sets the tone for an overtly nautical decor (blues, whites) that works best in the more-charming upstairs rooms.

Casa Colonial Ykira Mahiquez CASA PARTICULAR $
(☑64-38-81; ykiram@nauta.cu; Antonio Maceo No 168A, btwn Ciro Frías & Céspedes; r CUC$20; ✴) Welcoming and hospitable, Ykira is Baracoa's hostess with the mostess and serves a mean dinner made with homegrown herbs. Her cozy two-bedroom house is one block from the cathedral, with a full terrace and *mirador* (viewpoint) with sea views.

Casa Yamicel CASA PARTICULAR $
(☑64-11-18; Martí No 145A, btwn Pelayo & Ciro Frias; CUC$20-25; ✴) Doctor-proprietors that make killer mojitos? You'd better believe it at this three-room colonial house with gorgeous wooden window bars (two rooms up, one down). The roof terrace catches reviving sea breezes.

La Casona CASA PARTICULAR $
(☑64-21-33; Félix Ruenes No 1 Altos; r CUC$20-25; ✴) Rarely is a city's most central casa among its best, but thus have the young hosts made this place: two 2nd-floor rooms and a knockout terrace. And it's all spotless.

Dorkis Torres Dominguez CASA PARTICULAR $
(☑64-34-51; Flor Crombet No 58 Altos; r CUC$20-25; ✴) Upstairs at Dorkis' place you'll find two clean, nicely furnished rooms flooded with natural light. There's an azulejo-tiled terrace with Atlantic views – ideal for a couple of days of lazy relaxation. Dorkis has recently opened up the very handy **Dorado Café** (☑52-38-53-16; Martí No 171; snacks CUC$3; ⊙10am-2pm & 6-10pm) in town serving snacks and coffee.

Casa Colonial Lucy CASA PARTICULAR $
(☑64-35-48; astralsol36@gmail.com; Céspedes No 29, btwn Rubert López & Antonio Maceo; r CUC$20; ✴) A perennial favorite, Casa Lucy – which dates from 1840 – has a lovely local character with patios, porches and flowering begonias. There are two rooms as well as terraces here on different levels and the atmosphere is quiet and secluded. Lucy's son can speak four languages and offers salsa lessons and massage.

Hotel la Rusa HOTEL $
(☑64-30-11; Máximo Gómez No 161; s/d CUC$26/35; ✴🖥) Russian émigré Magdalena Rovieskuya (aka 'La Rusa') once posted aid to Castro's rebels up in the Sierra Maestra and first came to Baracoa in the 1930s, built a 12-room hotel and became a local celebrity receiving esteemed guests like Errol Flynn, Che Guevara and Fidel Castro. After her death in 1978, La Rusa became a more-modest government-run joint right on the seafront.

★Hotel El Castillo HOTEL $$
(☑64-51-65; Loma del Paraíso; s/d CUC$44/65; P✴🖥🏊) You could recline like a colonial-era conquistador in this historic fort turned hotel in the hilltop Castillo de Seboruco, except that conquistadors didn't have access to

GUANTÁNAMO PROVINCE BARACOA

swimming pools, wi-fi or a room maid who folds towels into ships, swans and other advanced forms of origami. Plump for one of the 28 newer rooms in a separate block with jaw-dropping El Yunque views.

Hotel Porto Santo
HOTEL **$$**

(☑64-51-06; Carretera del Aeropuerto; s/d CUC$44/65; 🅿❄🛜🏊) On the bay where Columbus allegedly planted his first cross is this peaceful, well-integrated low-rise hotel. Situated 4km from the town center and 200m from the airport, there are 36 more-than-adequate rooms all within earshot of the sea. A steep stairway leads down to a tiny, wave-lashed beach.

Eating

After the dull monotony of just about everywhere else, eating in Baracoa is a full-on sensory experience. Cooking here is creative, tasty and – above all – different. To experience the real deal, eat in your casa particular. Self-caterers will find a limited selection of groceries at **Tienda la Primada** (cnr Ciro Frías & Plaza Martí; ⊙8:30am-8:30pm).

Cafetería el Parque
FAST FOOD **$**

(Antonio Maceo No 142; snacks CUC$1-3; ⊙24hr; 🛜) The favored meeting place of just about everyone in town, so you're bound to end up at this open terrace at some point, if only to crack open a Bucanero beer and log in to the wi-fi.

★Bar-Restaurant La Terraza – Casa Nilson
BARACOAN **$$**

(Flor Crombet No 143, btwn Ciro Frías & Pelayo Cuervo; meals CUC$6-8; ⊙noon-3pm & 6:30-11pm) Up above his house on a quirky spectacular two-level terrace decorated in quirky Afro-Caribbean style, owner Nilson serves some of the best authentic Baracoan food in town (and hence Cuba). The wonderfully rich *pescado con leche de coco* (fish fillet with coconut sauce) is just the start.

There's also octopus, massive freshwater prawns, *bacán* (stuffed savory tamales) and – my word – chocolate confections for dessert. Unforgettable!

El Buen Sabor
BARACOAN **$$**

(☑64-14-00; Calixto García No 134 Altos; meals CUC$9-18; ⊙noon-midnight) Flavors abound on the upstairs terrace at Buen Sabor, especially ones permeated by coconut. You can expect the best of Baracoan cuisine at this private restaurant, including swordfish in a coconut sauce, *bacán* and chocolate-y desserts. Service is attentive.

BARACOAN CUISINE

Unlike more complex cuisines, Cuban cooking doesn't really have a strong *regional* identity, at least not until you arrive in Baracoa where everything – including the food – is different. Home to the country's most fickle weather, Baracoa has used its wet microclimate and geographic isolation to jazz up notoriously unambitious Cuban cuisine with spices, sugar, exotic fruits and coconuts. Fish anchors most menus yet even the seafood can pull some surprises. Count on tasting freshwater prawns the size of mini-lobsters or tiny tadpole-like *teti* fish drawn from the Río Toa between July to January during a waning moon.

The biggest taste explosion is a locally concocted coconut sauce known as *lechita*, a mixture of coconut milk, tomato sauce, garlic and a medley of spices best served over prawns, *aguja* (swordfish) or dorado. Other main-course accompaniments include *bacán* (raw green plantain melded with crabmeat and wrapped in a banana leaf) or *frangollo* (a similar concoction where the ground bananas are mixed with sugar).

Sweets are another Baracoa tour de force thanks largely to the ubiquity of the cocoa plant and the presence of the famous Fábrica de Chocolate factory. Baracoan chocolate is sold all over the island, but the local Casa del Cacao (p438) is an obvious sampling point. You're likely to get it for breakfast in your casa particular, stirred into a local hot-chocolate drink made with banana powder known as *chorote*. Baracoa's most unique culinary invention is undoubtedly *cucurucho*, a delicate mix of dried coconut, sugar, honey, papaya, *guayaba* (guava) , mandarin and nuts (no concoction is ever quite alike) that is wrapped in an ecologically friendly palm frond. There's a *cucurucho* factory on the coast road to Moa just past the chocolate factory but, by popular consensus, the best stuff is sold by the *campesinos* (country people) on La Farola coming into town from Guantánamo.

La Rosa Nautica
CARIBBEAN **$$**

(1 de Abril No 185 Altos; meals CUC$4-16; ☺noon-midnight) Out on the airport road, this nautically themed 2nd-floor restaurant is now Baracoa's upmarket option, particularly if you can nab the cozy private eating area up above the main deck. Some of the city's best waiters preside over proceedings, and you could go for chicken, pizza or pasta besides the standout seafood options.

Restaurante la Punta
CARIBBEAN **$$**

(Fuerte de la Punta; meals CUC$6-12; ☺10am-11pm) Cooled by Atlantic breezes (and the occasional full-on gale), the Gaviota-run La Punta aims to impress with well-prepared, garnished food in the lovely historical surrounds of the La Punta fort. Go on a Saturday night when there's accompanying music.

Drinking & Entertainment

⭐**Casa de la Trova Victorino Rodríguez**
TRADITIONAL MUSIC

(Antonio Maceo No 149A) Cuba's smallest, zaniest, wildest and most atmospheric *casa de la trova* (*trova* house) rocks nightly to the voodoo-like rhythms of *changüí-son*. One night the average age of the band is 85, the next it's 22. The common denominator? It's all good. Order a mojito in a jam jar and join in the show.

Casa de la Cultura
CULTURAL CENTER

(Antonio Maceo No 124, btwn Frank País & Maraví) This venue does a wide variety of shows including some good rumba incorporating the textbook Cuban styles of *guaguancó*, *yambú* and *columbia* (subgenres of rumba). Go prepared for *mucho* audience participation. There's a good *spectaculo* (show) on the terrace, La Terraza, every Saturday at 11pm: expect rumba, Benny Moré, and the local hairdresser singing songs by Omara Portuondo.

El Ranchón
CLUB

(admission CUC$1; ☺from 9pm) Atop a long flight of stairs at the western end of Coroneles Galano, El Ranchón mixes an exhilarating hilltop setting with taped disco and salsa music and legions of resident *jineteras*. Maybe that's why it's so insanely popular. Watch your step on the way down – it's a scary 146-step drunken tumble.

Estadio Manuel Fuentes Borges
SPORTS

From October to April, baseball games are held at this stadium situated literally on the beach. It's possibly the only ground in Cuba where players come in to bat with the taste of fresh sea spray on their lips. It's just southeast of the Museo Municipal. Boxers spar on the beach in the mornings.

Shopping

Good art is easy to find in Baracoa and, like most things in this whimsical seaside town, it has its own distinctive flavor.

Taller Mirate
ART

(Antonio Maceo; ☺10am-8pm) An artists' co-op where you'll always find one of the young creative painters sitting at a palette in the window. The very local painting style is best described as Gauguin meets Van Gogh in the pages of a Gabriel García Márquez novel.

ARTex
SOUVENIRS

(José Martí, btwn Céspedes & Coroneles Galano; ☺9am-4:30pm Mon-Sat) For the usual tourist trinkets check out this place.

❶ Information

Banco de Crédito y Comercio (Antonio Maceo No 99; ☺8am-2:30pm Mon-Fri)

Banco Popular de Ahorro (José Martí No 166; ☺8-11:30am & 2-4:30pm Mon-Fri)

Cadeca (José Martí No 241; ☺8:15am-4pm Mon-Fri, to 11:30 Sat & Sun) Shortest queues.

Clínica Internacional (☑64-10-37; cnr José Martí & Roberto Reyes; ☺24hr) A newish place that treats foreigners; there's also a hospital 2km out of town on the road to Guantánamo.

Cubatur (Antonio Maceo No 181; ☺8am-noon & 2-5pm Mon-Fri) Helpful office that organizes tours to El Yunque and Parque Nacional Alejandro de Humboldt.

Ecotur (☑64-24-78; ☺8:30am-noon & 1-5:30pm Mon-Sat) Office is in Hotel 1511.

Etecsa Telepunto (cnr Antonio Maceo & Rafael Trejo; per hour CUC$4.50; ☺8:30am-7:30pm) Buy your wi-fi internet cards here for use in any of the six Gaviota hotels.

Infotur (Antonio Maceo, btwn Frank País & Maraví; ☺8:30am-noon & 2-6pm Mon-Fri, 8:30am-noon Sat) Very helpful.

Post Office (Antonio Maceo No 136; ☺8am-8pm)

❶ Getting There & Away

The closest train station is in Guantánamo, 150km southwest.

AIR

Gustavo Rizo Airport (airport code BCA) is 4km northwest of the town, just behind the Hotel Porto Santo. The five weekly flights from Havana to Baracoa are with Aerocaribbean (CUC$164, Tuesday, Thursday and Sunday) and Aerogaviota (CUC$126, Wednesday and Sunday at 2:20pm). Book with Gaviota (p440).

The planes (and occasionally buses) out of Baracoa can be fully booked, so don't come here on a tight schedule without outbound reservations.

BUS

The **National Bus Station** (cnr Av Los Mártires & José Martí) has two **Víazul** (www.viazul.com) buses to Guantánamo (CUC$10, three hours) at 8:15am and 2pm; the first one continues to Santiago de Cuba (CUC$15, five hours). Bus tickets can be reserved in advance through Gaviota for a CUC$5 commission, or you can usually stick your name on the list a day or so beforehand. Trucks to Moa (departures from 6am) also leave from here along the very bumpy road northwest.

Conectando buses run to Santiago leaving from Baracoa's Hotel La Rusa (p441) on Monday, Wednesday and Friday at noon in high season only (November to April). Same prices as Víazul.

Transgaviota has a Saturday service from the main hotels via Moa to Holguín (CUC$30). Ask at Hostal la Habanera (p440).

ⓘ Getting Around

The best way to get to and from the airport is by taxi (CUC$5), or bici-taxi (CUC$2) if you're traveling light.

There's a helpful **Via Gaviota** (⏰ 64-16-71) car-rental office at the airport and also at Cafetería el Parque (p442). The **Servi-Cupet gas station** (José Martí; ⏰24hr) is at the entrance to town and also 4km from the center, on the road to Guantánamo. If you're driving to Havana, note that the northern route through Moa and Holguín is the most direct but the road disintegrates rapidly after Playa Maguana. Most locals prefer the La Farola route.

Bici-taxis around Baracoa should charge 5 pesos a ride, but they often ask 10 to 15 pesos from foreigners.

Most casas particulares will be able to procure you a bicycle for CUC$3 per day. The ultimate bike ride is the 20km ramble down to Playa Maguana, one of the most scenic roads in Cuba. Lazy daisies can rent mopeds for CUC$24 either at Cafetería el Parque or Hotel El Castillo (p441).

Northwest of Baracoa

The rutted road heading out of town toward Moa is a green paradise flecked with palm groves, rustic farmsteads and serendipitous glimpses of the ocean.

⦿ Sights & Activities

Finca Duaba   FARM
(⏰8am-7pm) **FREE** Five kilometers out of Baracoa on the road to Moa and then 1km inland, Finca Duaba offers a fleeting taste of the Baracoan countryside. It's a verdant farm surrounded with profuse tropical plants and embellished with a short cacao (cocoa) trail that explains the history and characteristics of the plant. There's also a good *ranchón*-style restaurant and the opportunity to swim in the Río Duaba. A bici-taxi can drop you at the road junction.

Río Toa   RIVER
Ten kilometers northwest of Baracoa is the third-longest river on the north coast of Cuba and the country's most voluminous. The Toa is also an important bird-and-plant habitat. Cocoa trees and the ubiquitous coconut palms are grown in the Valle de Toa. A vast hydroelectric project on the Río Toa was abandoned after a persuasive campaign led by the Fundación de la Naturaleza y El Hombre convinced authorities it would do irreparable ecological damage; engineering and economic reasons also played a part.

The **Rancho Toa** (meals CUC$10-12) is a Palmares restaurant reached via a right-hand turnoff just before the Toa bridge. You can organize boat or kayak trips here for CUC$5 to CUC$10 and watch acrobatic Baracoans scale *cocoteros* (coconut palms). A traditional Cuban feast of whole roast pig is available if you can rustle up enough people (eight usually).

Most of this region lies within the **Cuchillas Toa Unesco Biosphere Reserve**, an area of 2083 sq km that incorporates the Alejandro de Humboldt World Heritage Site. This region contains Cuba's largest rainforest, with trees exhibiting many precious woods, and has a high number of endemic species.

El Yunque   MOUNTAIN
Baracoa's rite of passage is the 8km (up and down) hike to the top of this moody, mysterious mountain. At 575m, El Yunque (Anvil) isn't Kilimanjaro, but the views from the summit and the flora and birdlife along the way are stupendous. Cubatur offers this tour almost daily (CUC$16 per person, minimum four people). The fee covers admission, guide, transport and a sandwich. The hike is hot (bring up to 2L of water) and usually muddy. It starts from the campismo 3km past the Finca Duaba (4km from the Baracoa–Moa

LOCAL KNOWLEDGE

CUBA'S TALLEST WATERFALL

Little known, even to most Cubans, Salto Fino is the Caribbean's tallest insular waterfall and the 20th tallest in the world. It sits surrounded by thick rainforest inside Parque Nacional Alejandro de Humboldt, inaccessible by road and rarely visited on foot. The 305ft-high cascade, which is split into eight smaller falls, drops the Arroyo El Infierno (Stream of Hell) off a steep platform in the Cuchillas del Toa Mountains. Amazingly, it wasn't properly measured and mapped until 1966, and the first scientific expedition, under the tutelage of prominent Cuban explorer Antonio Núñez Jiménez, bushwhacked a rough path through in 1996.

road). Bank on seeing *tocororo* (Cuba's national bird), *zunzún* (the world's smallest bird), butterflies and *polymitas*.

If you're not up to bagging the peak itself, ask about the 7km Sendero Juncal-Rencontra that bisects fruit plantations and rainforest between the Duaba and Toa rivers. Ecotur (p443) in Baracoa runs trips from CUC$19 per person.

Playa Maguana   BEACH
Not quite the tranquil getaway it once was, Maguana is still nonetheless magical, a relatively undone Caribbean beach with a rustic food shack that is populated primarily by fun-seeking Cubans who roll up in their vintage American cars and haul their prized music boxes out of the boot. Aside from the fenced-off Villa Maguana and a couple of basic food concessions (snacks CUC$2-5; ⊗9am-5pm), there's no infrastructure here – all part of the attraction. Watch your valuables!

🛏 Sleeping

Campismo el Yunque   CABIN $
(☑64-52-62; r CUC$10) Simple Cuban-style campismo offering very basic cabins at the end of the Finca Duaba road, 9km outside of Baracoa. The El Yunque hike starts here.

★**Villa Maguana**   HOTEL $$
(☑64-53-72; Carretera a Moa Km 20; s/d CUC$66/83; P❄) Knocking the socks off any Cuban all-inclusive resort is this delightful place 22km north of Baracoa, and consisting of four rustic wooden villas housing 16 rooms in total. Environmental foresight sees it cling precariously to Maguana's famously dreamy setting above a bite-sized scoop of sand guarded by two rocky promontories. There's a restaurant and some less rustic luxuries in the rooms such as satellite TV, fridge and air-con.

Parque Nacional Alejandro de Humboldt

'Unmatched in the Caribbean' is a phrase often used to describe this most dramatic and diverse of Cuban national parks, named after German naturalist-explorer Alexander von Humboldt who first came here in 1801. The accolade is largely true. Designated a Unesco World Heritage Site in 2001, Humboldt's steep pine-clad mountains and creeping morning mists protect an unmatched ecosystem that is, according to Unesco, 'one of the most biologically diverse tropical island sites on earth.' Perched above the Bahía de Taco, 40km northwest of Baracoa, lies 600-odd sq km of pristine forest and 26.41 sq km of lagoon and mangroves. With 1000 flowering plant species and 145 types of fern, it is far and away the most diverse plant habitat in the entire Caribbean. Due to the toxic nature of the underlying rocks in the area, plants have been forced to adapt in order to survive. As a result, endemism here is high – 70% of the plants found here are endemic, as are nearly all 20 species of amphibians, 45% of the reptiles and many of the birds. Endangered bird species protected here include Cuban Amazon parrots, hook-billed kites and ivory-billed woodpeckers.

🦅 Activities

The park contains a small visitors center (Carretera a Moa) where you pay the CUC$10 park entrance fee. It's staffed with biologists and has a network of trails leading to waterfalls, a *mirador* and a massive karst system with caves around the Farallones de Moa. Four trails are currently open to the public, taking in only a tiny segment of the park's 594 sq km. Typically, you can't just wander around on your own. The available hikes are: **Balcón de Iberia**, at 7km the park's most challenging loop which bisects both agricultural land and pristine rainforest and includes a swim in a natural pool near the Salto de Agua Maya waterfall; **El Recreo**, a 2km stroll around the bay; and the **Bahía de Taco** circuit, which incorporates a boat trip (with a manatee-friendly motor developed by scientists here) through the mangroves and the idyllic horseshoe-shaped bay, plus a 2km hike. A newer hike encompasses an eight-hour reconnoiter deeper into the forest, featuring bird and orchid observation. Each option is accompanied by a highly professional guide (if you're showing up independently get to the visitor center

before 10am to secure one). Prices range from CUC$5 to CUC$10, depending on the hike, but most people organize an excursion through Cubatur (p443) or Gaviota (p440) in Baracoa which includes transport and a pit stop on Playa Maguana on the way back (CUC$24).

ℹ Getting There & Away

The park visitors center is approximately halfway between Baracoa and Moa. You can arrange a tour through an agency in Baracoa or get here independently. The gorgeously scenic road is a collection of holes but passable in a hire car if driven with care. This road continues into Holguín province, improving just before Moa.

Understand Cuba

CUBA TODAY 448

After years of isolation, Cuba is opening up. How far it will go is anyone's guess.

HISTORY 450

Cuban history is an edge-of-your-seat tale of a nation's long search for freedom.

FOOD & DRINK 463

The Cuban culinary revolution is in full swing.

THE CUBAN WAY OF LIFE 467

Multicultural, gregarious and masters of survival, Cubans live their lives with an infectious joie de vivre.

LITERATURE & THE ARTS 473

Cuban artists have created some of the best literature, art and cinema in Latin America.

ARCHITECTURE 478

With its eclectic array of buildings, Cuba's architecture is unashamedly unique.

MUSIC & DANCE 486

Nothing can match the richness, diversity and sheer ebullience of Cuba's music and dance.

LANDSCAPE & WILDLIFE 492

Fifty years of political isolation have preserved some of the most spectacular landscapes in the Caribbean.

Cuba Today

Since 2011, the Cuban government has gradually relaxed its tightly clenched fist, dispensing piecemeal reforms that have allowed long-suffering citizens to experiment with business start-ups, travel abroad, and buy and sell houses for the first time in 50 years. It's not democratic socialism quite yet, but word on the street is that Raúl Castro has done more to improve the economy in the last five years than his brother Fidel did in the previous 50.

Best on Film

Che: The Argentine (Steven Soderbergh; 2008) First part of the classic biopic focuses on Che's Cuban years.
Before Night Falls (Julian Schnabel; 2000) The life and struggles of Cuban writer Reinaldo Arenas.
Fresa y Chocolate (Tomás Gutiérrez Alea; 1993) Marries the improbable themes of homosexuality and communism.
El Ojo del Canario (Fernando Pérez; 2010) Pérez' atmospheric biopic of José Martí picked up numerous Latin film awards.

Best in Print

Our Man in Havana (Graham Greene; 1958) Greene pokes fun at both the British Secret Service and Batista's corrupt regime.
Cuba and the Night (Pico Iyer; 1995) Perhaps the most evocative book about Cuba ever written by a foreigner.
Dirty Havana Trilogy (Pedro Juan Gutiérrez; 2002) Dirty, itchy study of life and sex in Havana during the Special Period.
Che Guevara: A Revolutionary Life (Jon Lee Anderson; 1997) Anderson's meticulous research led to the unearthing of Che's remains in Bolivia.

New Chapter in US–Cuba Relations

By far the biggest eyebrow-raiser in the last couple of years has been Cuba's tentative rapprochement with the United States, a process that gained traction in December 2014 when the two countries brokered a prisoner swap involving US international development contractor, Alan Gross. On December 17, 2014, Barack Obama appeared on television to announce the most significant thaw in US–Cuba relations in 54 years, measures that included US telecommunications aid to Cuba, the authorization of American credit and debit cards, a gentle easing of US travel restrictions, and – most important of all – the reestablishment of diplomatic relations between the two countries for the first time since 1961.

Whether this defrosting will confine the embargo to the history books is hard to predict. In making his announcement, President Obama unequivocally opened up a new chapter in US–Cuba relations and made it clear that he wants to try to end the embargo before his presidency expires in 2017. For this, he requires Congressional approval. Despite strong pockets of resistance in the Senate and House of Representatives, polls suggest that a majority of Americans and an increasing number of Cuban-Americans want the embargo to end. However, with a solid block of long-established Cuban exiles still determined not to negotiate with the Castros, it could be a tough political fight.

New Class of Entrepreneurs

The 2011–15 reforms have helped unleash the creativity and entrepreneurship of a generation of economically stifled Cubans. Private business has rocketed in numerous trades, especially for people with ready access to hard currency. With fewer bureaucratic regulations, some casas particulares (Cuban homestays) have morphed into mini-hotels employing dozens of staff, and advertising via websites and street signage (unheard of under Fidel). Restaurants have improved exponentially, not just in their food, but in their edgy, imaginative decor. The recent trend is for voguish cafes, hip bars and swanky nightclubs, particularly in Havana. The Fábrica de Arte Cubano, an avant-garde art co-op that opened in Havana in 2014 to promote the interchange of artistic ideas with impromptu concerts and 'happenings', can be seen as the mark of a trend. Equally creative are budding vintage magazine shops, retro barbers, private hiking guides and genre-bending artists – private businesses that were just pipe-dreams five years ago.

Testing the Limits

While most discussion about Cuba's reforms focuses on economic matters, there's reason for hope in the political sphere too. Subtle shifts in the country's culture are starting to question the unwavering authoritarianism of yore. In 2014, Havana quietly opened its first recognizably gay-friendly bar. The LGBT community has also benefited from an annual pride parade and its first openly transgender elected official, Adela Hernández in Villa Clara province, both championed by head of the National Center for Sex Education, Mariela Castro, daughter of Raúl. Freedom to travel has also opened doors for those who can afford it. While some people have sold up and left the isles permanently there has been no mass exodus, although plenty of Cubans have returned home from trips abroad loaded with ideas, inspiration and boxes of fancy consumer goods.

For every opening in Cuba, there is always a niggling back-shuffle, a notion that breeds cynicism among the majority of Cubans and keeps them constantly on their toes. Raúl Castro answered Obama's speech in December 2014 by stressing that Cuba would neither stray from its socialist economic path nor yield to US pressure to change its political system. True to form, the Cuban government has shown no real appetite for extending political liberties beyond their current limits and given no indication as to what might happen when Raúl relinquishes the presidency in 2018. The future, as ever, is uncertain.

POPULATION: **11.05 MILLION**

PERCENTAGE OVER 65 YEARS: **12.3%**

LIFE EXPECTANCY: **78.2 YEARS**

INFANT MORTALITY: **4.7 PER 1000**

DOCTOR/PATIENT RATIO: **1:149**

LITERACY RATE: **99.8%**

if Cuba were 100 people

65 would be White
25 would be Mixed
10 would be Black

belief systems
(% of population)

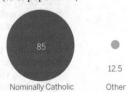

85
Nominally Catholic

12.5
Other

2.5
Protestant

population per sq km

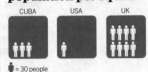

CUBA   USA   UK

≈ 30 people

History

Embellished by extraordinary feats of revolutionary derring-do, and plagued routinely by the meddling armies of foreign invaders, Cuba has achieved a historical importance far greater than its size would suggest. The underlying and – until the 1960s – ongoing historical themes have been outside interference and internal rebellion, and the results of both have often been bloody.

A Turbulent Historical Trajectory

Since the arrival of Columbus in 1492, Cuba has witnessed a turbulent historical trajectory that has included genocide, slavery, two bitter independence wars, a period of corrupt and violent quasi-independence, and, finally, a populist revolution that, despite early promise, hit a metaphoric pause button. The fallout has led to the emigration of almost one-fifth of the Cuban population, mostly to the US.

For the sake of simplicity, the country's historical eras can be divided into three broad categories: pre-colonial, colonial and post-colonial. Before 1492 Cuba was inhabited by a trio of migratory civilizations that originated in the Orinoco Basin of South America before island-hopping north. Their cultures have been only partially evaluated to date, primarily because they left very little behind in the way of documentary evidence.

Cuba's colonial period was dominated by the Spanish and the divisive issue of slavery, which spanned the whole era from the 1520s until abolition in 1886. Slavery left deep wounds on Cuba's collective psyche, but its existence and final quashing was integral to the evolution of the country's highly distinctive culture, music, dance and religion. Understand this and you're halfway to understanding the complexities of the contemporary culture.

Post-colonial Cuba has had two distinctive sub-eras, the second of which can be further subdivided in two. The period from the defeat of Spain in 1898 to the Castro coup of 1959 is usually seen as an age of quasi-independence with a strong American influence. It was also a time characterized by violence, corruption and frequent insurrection on the part of opposition groups intent on toppling the government.

TIMELINE	2000 BC	AD 1100	1492
	The Guanahatabeys, Cuba's earliest known Stone Age civilization, is known to be living in the caves along the coast of present-day Pinar del Río province.	Taíno people start arriving in Cuba after leapfrogging their way across the islands of the Lesser Antilles from the Orinoco Basin in present-day Venezuela.	Christopher Columbus lands in Cuba in modern-day Holguín province. He sails for a month along the coast, as far as Baracoa, planting religious crosses and meeting with the indigenous Taínos.

The post-1959 Castro epoch breaks conveniently into two stages: the age of Soviet domination from 1961 to 1991, and the modern era that stretches from the Special Period till the present day, when Cuba, despite its devastating economic difficulties, became a truly independent power for the first time.

Pre-Colonial Cuba

The first known civilization in Cuba was that of the Guanahatabeys, a primitive Stone Age people who lived in caves and eked out a meager existence as hunter-gatherers. At some point over a 2000-year period, the Guanahatabeys were gradually pushed west into what is now Pinar del Río province, displaced by the arrival of another pre-ceramic culture known as the Siboneys. The Siboneys were a slightly more developed group of fishers and small-scale farmers who settled down comparatively peacefully on the archipelago's sheltered southern coast. By the second millennium AD, they were similarly displaced by the more sophisticated Taíno, who liked to use Siboneys as domestic servants.

The Taínos first started arriving in Cuba around 1050 AD in a series of waves, concluding a migration process that had begun on mainland South America several centuries earlier. Related to the Greater Antilles Arawaks, the new peace-loving natives were escaping the barbarism of the cannibalistic Caribs who had colonized the Lesser Antibes, pushing the Taínos northwest into Puerto Rico, Hispaniola and Cuba.

Taíno culture was more developed and sophisticated than that of its predecessors. Unlike the Guanahatabeys and Siboneys, they were capable ceramicists and subsisted by farming crops. Their villages were made from mud and thatch meaning little has survived, though they have left their imprint in other areas, particularly the language. Words such as hurricane, hammock, *guajiro* (country folk) and tobacco are all derived from the Taíno vernacular. The Taínos were also the first of the world's pre-Columbian cultures to nurture the delicate tobacco plant into a form that could easily be processed for smoking.

Colonial Cuba

Columbus & Colonization

When Columbus neared Cuba on October 27, 1492, he described it as 'the most beautiful land human eyes had ever seen,' naming it 'Juana' in honor of a Spanish heiress. But deluded in his search for the kingdom of the Great Khan, and finding little gold in Cuba's lush and heavily forested interior, Columbus quickly abandoned the territory in favor of Hispaniola (modern-day Haiti and the Dominican Republic).

Best Historical Sites

Museo de la Revolución (p83), Havana

Cuartel Moncada (p402), Santiago de Cuba

Comandancia de la Plata (p382), Granma

Fortaleza de San Carlos de la Cabaña (p77), Havana

HISTORY PRE-COLONIAL CUBA

1494	1508	1511	1519
Columbus returns to Cuba on his second voyage docking briefly at various points along Cuba's south coast and 'discovering' La Isla de la Juventud.	Spanish navigator, Sebastián de Ocampo circumnavigates Cuba, establishing that it's an island and disproving Columbus' long-held idea that it might be a peninsula of the Asian continent.	Diego Velázquez lands at Baracoa with 400 colonizers, including Hernán Cortés (the future colonizer of Mexico). The new arrivals construct a fort and quickly make enemies of the local Taínos.	Havana, the last of Cuba's seven founding 'villas' is moved to its present site at the mouth of a fine natural harbor. It is inaugurated with a solemn mass under a ceiba tree in what is now Plaza de Armas.

'DISCOVERERS' OF CUBA

Cuba wasn't discovered by Europeans; people had lived on the archipelago for millennia before 1492. Nonetheless, Cubans popularly like to claim that their country has had three nominal 'discoverers.' The role of the first, Christopher Columbus, is well documented, but the contributions of the second and third deserve more explanation.

Alexander von Humboldt (1769–1859)

Arriving in Cuba in 1800, German naturalist and geographer Humboldt was one of the first outsiders to recognize Cuba's special cultural, ecological and historical heritage. For him, the archipelago belonged neither to North nor South America, but to an independent domain of its own. Its uniqueness was embedded in its ecology. Humboldt was amazed by Cuba's striking endemism and vast array of unique species, describing it as a kind of Caribbean Galapagos where conflicting natural processes appeared to exist in contradiction. He also noted marked differences between Cuba and the other countries in South America. Though colonially backward, Cuba was, nonetheless, highly metropolitan; it had a strong national identity but still relied heavily on its Spanish overlords; and, while ostensibly civilized, it maintained a highly uncivilized slave system (which ultimately lingered longer than any other country in Latin America, bar Brazil). Above all, Humboldt concluded, Cuba was fascinatingly complex.

Fernando Ortíz (1881–1969)

Ortíz was an anthropologist and Renaissance man from Havana who, building on Humboldt's themes, concentrated his studies on the archipelago's unique cultural synthesis made up of a mix of African slaves, colonizing Spaniards, French exiles, immigrant Chinese and watered-down remnants of pre-Columbian Taíno culture. Ortíz called what had happened in Cuba 'transculturation,' the melding of old imported cultures into a new one that was unique and original in its own right. His specialty was black culture (he invented the term 'afrocuban') and his studies in this area led to a far better understanding and appreciation of African art, music, religion and language in Cuban culture. In 1955 Ortíz was nominated for the Nobel Peace Prize for his vast anthropological work and his 'love for culture and humankind.'

The colonization of Cuba didn't begin until nearly 20 years later in 1511, when Diego Velázquez de Cuéllar led a flotilla of four ships and 400 men from Hispaniola to conquer the island for the Spanish Crown. Docking near present-day Baracoa, the conquistadors promptly set about establishing seven *villas* (towns) on the main island – Havana, Trinidad, Baracoa, Bayamo, Camagüey, Santiago de Cuba and Sancti Spíritus – in a bid to bring their new colony under strong central rule. Watching nervously from the safety of their *bohíos* (thatched huts), a scattered population of Taínos looked on with a mixture of fascination and fear.

1522	1555	1607	1741
The first slaves arrive in Cuba from Africa, ushering in an era that was to last for 350 years and have a profound effect on the development of Cuban culture.	The age of piracy is inaugurated. French buccaneer Jacques de Sores attacks Havana and burns it to the ground. In response, the Spanish start building a huge network of forts.	Havana is declared capital of Cuba and becomes the annual congregation point for Spain's Caribbean treasure fleet, loaded up with silver from Peru and gold from Mexico.	A British Navy contingent under the command of Admiral Edward Vernon briefly captures Guantánamo Bay during the War of Jenkins' Ear, but is sent packing after a yellow fever epidemic.

Despite Velázquez' attempts to protect the local Taínos from the gross excesses of the Spanish swordsmen, things quickly got out of hand and the invaders soon found that they had a full-scale rebellion on their hands. Leader of the embittered and short-lived Taíno insurgency was the feisty Hatuey, an influential *cacique* (chief) and archetype of the Cuban resistance, who was eventually captured and burned at the stake, Inquisition-style, for daring to challenge the iron fist of Spanish rule.

With the resistance decapitated, the Spaniards set about emptying Cuba of its relatively meager gold and mineral reserves, using the beleaguered natives as forced labor. As slavery was nominally banned under a papal edict, the Spanish got around the various legal loopholes by introducing a ruthless *encomienda* system, whereby thousands of natives were rounded up and forced to work for Spanish landowners on the pretext that they were receiving free 'lessons' in Christianity. The brutal system lasted 20 years before the 'Apostle of the Indians', Fray Bartolomé de Las Casas, appealed to the Spanish Crown for more humane treatment, and in 1542 the *encomiendas* were abolished for the indigenous people. For the unfortunate Taínos, the call came too late. Those who had not already been worked to death in the gold mines quickly succumbed to fatal European diseases such as smallpox, and by 1550 only about 5000 scattered survivors remained.

The Independence Wars

With its brutal slave system established, the Spanish ruled their largest Caribbean colony with an iron fist for the next 200 years despite a brief occupation by the British in 1762. Cuba's creole landowners, worried about a repetition of Haiti's brutal 1791 slave rebellion, held back when the rest of Latin America took up arms against the Spanish in the 1810s and 1820s. As a result, the nation's independence wars came more than half a century after the rest of Latin America had broken away from Spain. But when they arrived, they were no less impassioned – or bloody.

The First War of Independence

Fed up with Spain's reactionary colonial policies and enviously eyeing Lincoln's new American dream to the north, *criollo* (Spaniards born in the Americas) landowners around Bayamo began plotting rebellion in the late 1860s. The spark was auspiciously lit on October 10, 1868, when Carlos Manuel de Céspedes, a budding poet, lawyer and sugar-plantation owner, launched an uprising from his Demajagua sugar mill near Manzanillo in the Oriente. Calling for the abolition of slavery and freeing his own slaves as an example, Céspedes proclaimed the famous *Grito de Yara,* a cry of liberty for an independent Cuba, encouraging other disillusioned separatists to join him. For the colonial administrators in Havana, such

In the 17th century the Spanish forced the remaining indigenous population into towns known as *pueblos indios*. Old and New World cultures cross-fertilized, allowing Indian practices and words to seep into everyday Cuban life.

1762	1791	1808	1850
Spain joins France in the Seven Years' War, provoking the British to attack and take Havana for 11 months before exchanging it for Florida in 1763.	A bloody slave rebellion in Haiti causes thousands of white French planters to flee west to Cuba, where they set up the earliest coffee plantations in the New World.	Pre-empting the Monroe Doctrine, US president Thomas Jefferson proclaims Cuba 'the most interesting addition which could be made to our system of states,' thus beginning a 200-year US fixation.	Venezuelan filibuster Narciso López raises the Cuban flag for the first time in Cárdenas during an abortive attempt to 'liberate' the colony from Spain.

an audacious bid to wrest control was an act tantamount to treason. The furious Spanish reacted accordingly.

Fortunately for the loosely organized rebels, the cagey Céspedes had done his military homework. Within weeks of the historic *Grito de Yara,* the diminutive lawyer-turned-general had raised an army of more than 1500 men and marched defiantly on Bayamo, taking the city in a matter of days. But initial successes soon turned to lengthy deadlock. A tactical decision not to invade western Cuba, along with an alliance between *peninsulares* (Spaniards born in Spain but living in Cuba) and the Spanish, soon put Céspedes on the back foot. Temporary help arrived in the shape of *mulato* (mixed race) general Antonio Maceo, a tough and uncompromising Santiagüero, nicknamed the 'Bronze Titan' for his ability to defy death on countless occasions, and the equally formidable Dominican Máximo Gómez. But despite economic disruption and the periodic destruction of the sugar crop, the rebels lacked a dynamic political leader capable of uniting them behind a singular ideological cause.

With the loss of Céspedes in battle in 1874, the war dragged on for another four years, reducing the Cuban economy to tatters and leaving an astronomical 200,000 Cubans and 80,000 Spanish dead. Finally, in February 1878 a lackluster pact was signed at El Zanjón between the uncompromising Spanish and the exhausted separatists, a rambling and largely worthless agreement that solved nothing and acceded little to the rebel cause. Maceo, disgusted and disillusioned, made his feelings known in the antidotal 'Protest of Baraguá,' but after an abortive attempt to restart the war in 1879, both he and Gómez disappeared into a prolonged exile.

The Spanish-Cuban-American War (Second War of Independence)

Cometh the hour, cometh the man. José Martí – poet, patriot, visionary and intellectual – had grown rapidly into a patriotic figure of Bolívarian proportions in the years following his ignominious exile in 1871 in the US, not just in Cuba but in the whole of Latin America. After his arrest at the age of 16 during the First War of Independence for a minor indiscretion, Martí had spent 20 years formulating his revolutionary ideas abroad in places as diverse as Guatemala, Mexico and the US. Although impressed by American business savvy and industriousness, he was equally repelled by the country's all-consuming materialism and was determined to present a workable Cuban alternative.

Dedicating himself passionately to the cause of the resistance, Martí wrote, spoke, petitioned and organized tirelessly for independence for well over a decade and by 1892 had enough momentum to coax Maceo and Gómez out of exile under the umbrella of the Partido Revolucionario

Che Guevara – whose father's family name was Guevara Lynch – can trace his Celtic roots back to a Patrick Lynch, born in Galway in Ireland in 1715, who emigrated to Buenos Aires via Bilbao in 1749.

1868	1878	1886	1892
Céspedes frees his slaves in Manzanillo and proclaims the *Grito de Yara,* Cuba's first independence cry and the beginning of a 10-year war against the Spanish.	The Pact of El Zanjón ends the First War of Independence. Cuban general Antonio Maceo issues the Protest of Baraguá and resumes hostilities the following year before disappearing into exile.	After more than 350 years of exploitation and cross-Atlantic transportation, Cuba becomes the second-last country in the Americas to abolish slavery.	From exile in the US, José Martí galvanizes popular support and forms the Cuban Revolutionary Party, starting to lay the groundwork for the resumption of hostilities against Spain.

Cubano (PRC; Cuban Revolutionary Party). At last, Cuba had found its spiritual leader.

Predicting that the time was right for another revolution, Martí and his compatriots set sail for Cuba in April 1895, landing near Baracoa two months after PRC-sponsored insurrections had tied down Spanish forces in Havana. Raising an army of 40,000 men, the rebels promptly regrouped and headed west, engaging the Spanish for the first time on May 19 in a place called Dos Ríos. It was on this bullet-strafed and strangely anonymous battlefield that Martí, conspicuous on his white horse and dressed in his trademark black suit, was shot and killed as he charged suicidally toward the Spanish lines. Had he lived he would certainly have become Cuba's first president; instead, he became a hero and a martyr whose life and legacy would inspire generations of Cubans in years to come.

Conscious of mistakes made during the First War of Independence, Gómez and Maceo stormed west with a scorched-earth policy that left everything from the Oriente to Matanzas in flames. Early victories quickly led to a sustained offensive and, by January 1896, Maceo had broken through to Pinar del Río, while Gómez was tying down Spanish forces near Havana. The Spaniards responded with an equally ruthless general named Valeriano Weyler, who built countrywide north–south fortifications to restrict the rebels' movements. In order to break the underground resistance, *guajiros* (country people) were forced into camps in a process called *reconcentración,* and anyone supporting the rebellion became liable for execution. The brutal tactics started to show results, and on December 7, 1896, the Mambís (the name for the 19th-century rebels fighting Spain) suffered a major military blow when Antonio Maceo was killed south of Havana trying to break out to the east.

Enter the Americans

By this time Cuba was a mess: thousands were dead, the country was in flames, and William Randolph Hearst and the US tabloid press were leading a hysterical war campaign characterized by sensationalized, often inaccurate reports about Spanish atrocities.

Preparing perhaps for the worst, the US battleship *Maine* was sent to Havana in January 1898, on the pretext of 'protecting US citizens.' Its touted task never saw fruition. On February 15, 1898, the *Maine* exploded out of the blue in Havana Harbor, killing 266 US sailors. The Spanish claimed it was an accident, the Americans blamed the Spanish, and some Cubans accused the US, saying it provided a convenient pretext for intervention. Despite several investigations conducted over the following years, the real cause of the explosion may remain one of history's great mysteries, as the hulk of the ship was scuttled in deep waters in 1911.

HISTORY COLONIAL CUBA

In the 1880s there were over 100,000 Chinese people living in Cuba, mainly as cheap labor on sugar plantations in and around the Havana region.

Independence War Heroes

Carlos Manuel de Céspedes (1819–74)

Máximo Gómez (1836–1905)

Calixto García (1839–98)

Ignacio Agramonte (1841–73)

Antonio Maceo (1845–96)

1895	1896	1898	1902
José Martí and Antonio Maceo arrive in Cuba to ignite the Second Independence War. Martí is killed at Dos Ríos in May and is quickly elevated to a martyr.	After sustaining more than 20 injuries in a four-decade military career, Antonio Maceo meets his end at Cacahual, Havana, where he is killed in an ambush.	Following the loss of the battleship USS *Maine,* the US declares war on Spain and defeats its forces near Santiago. A four-year US occupation begins.	Cuba gains nominal independence from the US and elects Tomás Estrada Palma as its president. US troops are called back three times within the first 15 years of the republic.

José Martí Sites

Museo-Casa Natal de José Martí (p76), Havana

Memorial a José Martí (p92), Havana

Cementerio Santa Ifigenia (p404), Santiago de Cuba

Dos Ríos (p381), Granma

After the *Maine* debacle, the US scrambled to take control. They offered Spain US$300 million for Cuba and, when this deal was rejected, demanded a full withdrawal of the Spanish from the island. The long-awaited US–Spanish showdown that had been simmering imperceptibly beneath the surface for decades had finally resulted in war.

The only important land battle of the conflict was on July 1, 1898, when the US Army attacked Spanish positions on San Juan Hill just east of Santiago de Cuba. Despite vastly inferior numbers and limited, antiquated weaponry, the under-siege Spanish held out bravely for over 24 hours before future US President Theodore Roosevelt broke the deadlock by leading a celebrated cavalry charge of the Rough Riders up San Juan Hill. It was the beginning of the end for the Spaniards, and an unconditional surrender was offered to the Americans on July 17, 1898.

Post-Colonial Cuba

Independence or Dependence?

On May 20, 1902, Cuba became an independent republic – or did it? Despite three years of blood, sweat and sacrifice during the Spanish–Cuban–American War, no Cuban representatives were invited to the historic peace treaty held in Paris in 1898 that had promised Cuban independence *with conditions*. The conditions were contained in the infamous Platt Amendment, a sly addition to the US 1901 Army Appropriations Bill that gave the US the right to intervene militarily in Cuba whenever it saw fit. The US also used its significant leverage to secure itself a naval base in Guantánamo Bay in order to protect its strategic interests in the Panama Canal region. Despite some opposition in the US and a great deal more in Cuba, the Platt Amendment was passed by Congress and was written into Cuba's 1902 constitution. For Cuban patriots, the US had merely replaced Spain as the new colonizer and enemy. The repercussions have been causing bitter feuds for over a century and still continue today.

The Batista Era

Fulgencio Batista, a *holguiñero* (person from Holguín) of mixed race from the town of Banes, was a wily and shrewd negotiator who presided over Cuba's best and worst attempts to establish an embryonic democracy in the 1940s and '50s. After an army officers' coup in 1933, he had taken power almost by default, gradually worming his way into the political vacuum it left amid the corrupt factions of a dying government. From 1934 onwards Batista served as the army's chief of staff and, in 1940 in a relatively free and fair election, he was duly elected president. Given an official mandate, Batista began to enact a wide variety of social reforms and set about drafting Cuba's most liberal and democratic constitution to date. But neither the liberal honeymoon nor Batista's good humor were

1920	1925	1933	1940
Sharp increases in world sugar prices after WWI spearhead the so-called 'Dance of the Millions' in Cuba. Huge fortunes are made overnight. A heavy economic crash quickly follows.	Gerardo Machado is elected president and institutes a massive program of public works, but his eight-year reign turns increasingly despotic as his declining popularity leads to resentful unrest.	The 1933 revolution is sparked by an army officers' coup that deposes the Machado dictatorship and installs Fulgencio Batista in power.	Cuba adopts the '1940 Constitution', considered one of the most progressive documents of its era, guaranteeing rights to employment, property, minimum wage, education and social security.

to last. Stepping down after the 1944 election, the former army sergeant handed power over to the politically inept President Ramón Grau San Martín, and corruption and inefficiency soon reigned like never before.

The Revolutionary Spark is Lit

Aware of his erstwhile popularity and sensing an easy opportunity to line his pockets with one last big paycheck, Batista cut a deal with the American Mafia, promising to give them carte blanche in Cuba in return for a cut of their gambling profits, and positioned himself for a comeback. On March 10, 1952, three months before scheduled elections that he looked like losing, Batista staged a military coup. Wildly condemned by opposition politicians inside Cuba, but recognized by the US government two weeks later, Batista quickly let it be known, when he suspended various constitutional guarantees including the right to strike, that his second incarnation wouldn't be as enlightened as his first.

After Batista's coup, a revolutionary circle formed in Havana around the charismatic figure of Fidel Castro, a lawyer by profession and a gifted orator who had been due to stand in the canceled 1952 elections. Supported by his younger brother Raúl and aided intellectually by his trusty lieutenant Abel Santamaría (later tortured to death by Batista's thugs), Castro saw no alternative to the use of force in ridding Cuba of its detestable dictator. Low on numbers but determined to make a political statement, Castro led 119 rebels in an attack on the strategically important Moncada army barracks in Santiago de Cuba on July 26, 1953. The audacious and poorly planned assault failed dramatically when the rebels' driver (who was from Havana) took the wrong turning in Santiago's badly signposted streets and the alarm was raised.

Fooled, flailing and hopelessly outnumbered, 64 of the Moncada conspirators were rounded up by Batista's army and brutally tortured and executed. Castro and a handful of others managed to escape into the nearby mountains, where they were found a few days later by a sympathetic army lieutenant named Sarría, who had been given instructions to kill them. 'Don't shoot, you can't kill ideas!' Sarría is alleged to have shouted on finding Castro and his exhausted colleagues. By taking Castro to jail instead of murdering him, Sarría ruined his military career, but saved Fidel's life. (One of Fidel's first acts after the Revolution triumphed was to release Sarría from prison and give him a commission in the revolutionary army.) Castro's capture soon became national news, and he was put on trial in the full glare of the media spotlight. Fidel defended himself in court, writing an eloquent and masterfully executed speech that he later transcribed into a comprehensive political manifesto entitled *History Will Absolve Me.* Basking in his newfound legitimacy and backed by a growing sense of dissatisfaction with the old regime in the

US Presidents Who Tried to Buy Cuba

··················

1808 –
Thomas Jefferson
(undisclosed sum)

··················

1848 – James Polk
(US$100 million)

··················

1854 –
Franklin Pierce
(US$130 million)

··················

1898 –
William McKinley
(US$300 million)

1952	1953	1956	1958
Batista stages a blood-less military coup, canceling the upcoming Cuban elections in which an ambitious young lawyer named Fidel Castro was due to stand.	Castro leads a band of rebels in a disastrous attack on the Moncada army barracks in Santiago. He uses his subsequent trial as a platform to expound his political plans.	The *Granma* yacht lands in eastern Cuba with Castro and 81 rebels aboard. Decimated by the Cuban Army, only about a dozen survive to regroup in the Sierra Maestra.	Che Guevara masterminds an attack against an armored train in Santa Clara, a military victory that finally forces Batista to concede power. The rebels march triumphantly on Havana.

country at large, Castro was sentenced to 15 years imprisonment on Isla de Pinos (a former name for Isla de la Juventud). Cuba was well on the way to gaining a new national hero.

In February 1955 Batista won the presidency in what were widely considered to be fraudulent elections and, in an attempt to curry favor with growing internal opposition, agreed to an amnesty for all political prisoners, including Castro. Believing that Batista's real intention was to assassinate him once out of jail, Castro fled to Mexico, leaving Baptist schoolteacher Frank País in charge of a fledgling underground resistance campaign that the vengeful Moncada veterans had christened the 26th of July Movement (M-26-7).

The Revolution

In Mexico City, Castro and his compatriots plotted and planned afresh, drawing in key new figures such as Camilo Cienfuegos and the Argentine doctor Ernesto 'Che' Guevara, both of whom added strength and panache to the nascent army of disaffected rebel soldiers. On the run from the Mexican police and determined to arrive in Cuba in time for an uprising that Frank País had planned for late November 1956 in Santiago de Cuba, Castro and 81 companions set sail for the island on November 25 in an old and overcrowded leisure yacht named *Granma*. After seven dire days at sea they arrived at Playa Las Coloradas near Niquero in Oriente on December 2 (two days late). Following a catastrophic landing – 'It wasn't a disembarkation; it was a shipwreck,' a wry Guevara later commented – they were spotted and routed by Batista's soldiers in a sugarcane field at Alegría de Pío three days later.

Of the 82 rebel soldiers who had left Mexico, little more than a dozen managed to escape. Splitting into three tiny groups, the survivors wandered around hopelessly for days half-starved, wounded and assuming that the rest of their compatriots had been killed in the initial skirmish. 'At one point I was Commander in Chief of myself and two other people,' Fidel commented sagely years later. However, with the help of the local peasantry, the dozen or so hapless soldiers finally managed to reassemble two weeks later in Cinco Palmas, a clearing in the shadows of the Sierra Maestra, where a half-delirious Fidel gave a rousing and premature victory speech. 'We will win this war,' he proclaimed confidently. 'We are just beginning the fight!'

The comeback began on January 17, 1957, when the guerrillas scored an important victory by sacking a small army outpost on the south coast in Granma province called La Plata. This was followed in February by a devastating propaganda coup when Fidel persuaded *New York Times* journalist Herbert Matthews to come up into the Sierra Maestra to interview him. The resulting article made Castro internationally famous and gained him much sympathy among liberal Americans. Suffice to say, by this point he wasn't the only anti-Batista agitator. On March 13, 1957, university

In December 1946 the Mafia convened the biggest ever get-together of North American mobsters in Havana's Hotel Nacional, under the pretense that they were going to see a Frank Sinatra concert.

1959	1960	1961	1962
Castro is welcomed ecstatically in Havana. The new government passes the historic First Agrarian Reform Act. Camilo Cienfuegos' plane goes missing over the Cuban coast off Camagüey.	Castro nationalizes US assets on the island, provoking the US to cancel its Cuban sugar quota. Castro immediately sells the sugar to the Soviet Union.	US-backed Cuban mercenaries stage an unsuccessful invasion at the Bay of Pigs. The US declares a full trade embargo. Cuba embarks on a highly successful literacy campaign.	The discovery of medium-range nuclear missiles in Cuba, installed by the Soviet Union, brings the world to the brink of nuclear war in the so-called Cuban Missile Crisis.

students led by José Antonio Echeverría attacked the Presidential Palace in Havana in an unsuccessful attempt to assassinate Batista. Thirty-two of the 35 attackers were shot dead as they fled, and reprisals were meted out on the streets of Havana with a new vengeance. Cuba was rapidly disintegrating into a police state run by military-trained thugs.

Elsewhere passions were running equally high. In September 1957 naval officers in the normally tranquil city of Cienfuegos staged an armed revolt and set about distributing weapons among the disaffected populace. After some bitter door-to-door fighting, the insurrection was brutally crushed and the ringleaders rounded up and killed, but for the revolutionaries the point had been made. Batista's days were numbered.

Back in the Sierra Maestra, Fidel's rebels overwhelmed 53 Batista soldiers at an army post in El Uvero in May and captured more badly needed supplies. The movement seemed to be gaining momentum and despite losing Frank País to a government assassination squad in Santiago de Cuba in July, support and sympathy around the country was starting to mushroom. By the beginning of 1958 Castro had established a fixed headquarters in a cloud forest high up in the Sierra Maestra he christened 'La Plata', and was broadcasting propaganda messages from Radio Rebelde (710AM and 96.7FM) all across Cuba. The tide was starting to turn.

Sensing his popularity waning, Batista sent an army of 10,000 men into the Sierra Maestra in May 1958, on a mission known as Plan FF (*Fin de Fidel* or End of Fidel). The intention was to liquidate Castro and his merry band of loyal guerrillas who had now burgeoned into a solid fighting force of 300 men. The offensive became something of a turning point as the rebels – with the help of the local *campesinos* (country people) – gradually halted the onslaught of Batista's young and ill-disciplined conscript army. With the Americans increasingly embarrassed by the no-holds-barred terror tactics of their one-time Cuban ally, Castro sensed an opportunity to turn defense into offense and signed the groundbreaking Caracas Pact with eight leading opposition groups calling on the US to stop all aid to Batista. Che Guevara and Camilo Cienfuegos were promptly dispatched to the Escambray Mountains to open up new fronts in the west, and by December, with Cienfuegos holding down troops in Yaguajay (the garrison finally surrendered after an 11-day siege) and Guevara closing in on Santa Clara, the end was in sight. It was left to Che Guevara to seal the final victory, employing classic guerrilla tactics to derail an armored train in Santa Clara and split the country's battered communications system in two. By New Year's Eve 1958, the game was up: a sense of jubilation filled the country, and Che and Camilo were on their way to Havana unopposed.

In the small hours of January 1, 1959, Batista fled by private plane to the Dominican Republic. Meanwhile, materializing in Santiago de Cuba the same day, Fidel made a rousing victory speech from the town hall in

Cuba's First Three Presidents

Tomás Estrada Palma (1902–06)

José Miguel Gómez (1909–13)

Mario García Menocal (1913–21)

1967	1968	1970	1976
Che Guevara is hunted down and executed in Bolivia in front of CIA observers after a 10-month abortive guerrilla war in the mountains.	The Cuban government nationalizes 58,000 small businesses in a sweeping socialist reform package. Everything falls under strict government control.	Castro attempts to achieve a 10-million-ton sugar harvest. The plan fails and Cuba begins to wean itself off its unhealthy dependence on its mono-crop.	Terrorists bomb a Cuban jet in Barbados, killing all 73 people aboard. A line is traced back to anti-Castro activists with histories as CIA operatives working out of Venezuela.

Parque Céspedes before jumping into a 4WD and traveling across the breadth of the country to Havana in a Caesar-like cavalcade. The triumph of the Revolution was seemingly complete.

Post-Revolutionary Realities

Cuba's history since the Revolution has been a David and Goliath tale of confrontation, rhetoric, Cold War stand-offs and an omnipresent US trade embargo that has featured 11 US presidents and two infamous Cuban leaders – both called Castro. For the first 30 years, Cuba allied itself with the Soviet Union as the US used various retaliatory tactics (all unsuccessful) to bring Fidel Castro to heel, including a botched invasion, 600-plus assassination attempts and one of the longest economic blockades in modern history. When the Soviet bloc fell in 1989–91, Cuba stood alone behind an increasingly defiant and stubborn leader surviving, against all odds, through a decade of severe economic austerity known as the Special Period. GDP fell by more than half, luxuries went out the window, and a wartime spirit of rationing and sacrifice took hold among a populace that, ironically, had prized itself free from foreign (neo)colonial influences for the first time in its history.

THE SPECIAL PERIOD

Following the demise of the Soviet Union in 1991, the Cuban economy – reliant since the 1960s on Soviet subsidies – went into freefall. Almost overnight half of the country's industrial factories closed, the transport sector ground to a halt, and the national economy shrunk by as much as 60%.

Determined to defend the Revolution at all costs, Fidel Castro stubbornly battened down the hatches and announced that Cuba was entering a 'Special Period in a Time of Peace' (período especial), a package of extreme austerity measures that reinforced widespread rationing and made acute shortages an integral part of everyday life. It was an unprecedented turnaround that quickly resonated throughout all levels of society. Suddenly Cubans, who had been relatively well-off a year or so earlier, faced a massive battle just to survive.

The stories of how ordinary Cubans got through the darkest days of the Special Period are as remarkable as they are shocking. In three fearsome years the average Cuban lost over a third of their body weight and saw meat pretty much eradicated from their diet. In the social forum, the Special Period invented a whole new culture of conservation and innovation, and elements of this communal belt-tightening still characterize the Cuban way of life today.

The worst years of the Special Period were 1991–94, though the recovery was slow with proper progress only possible after Cuba forged closer ties with Venezuela (and its oil) in the early 2000s.

1980	1988	1991	1993
Following an incident at the Peruvian embassy, Castro opens the Cuban port of Mariel. Within six months 125,000 have fled the island for the US in the so-called Mariel Boatlift.	Cuban forces play a crucial role in the Battle of Cuito Cuanavale in Angola, a serious defeat for the white South African army and its system of apartheid.	The Soviet Union collapses and Cuba heads toward its worst economic collapse of modern times, entering what Castro calls a 'Special Period in a Time of Peace.'	Attempting to revive itself from its economic coma, Cuba legalizes the US dollar, opens up the country to tourism and allows limited forms of private enterprise.

HUMAN RIGHTS

'Human rights' in Cuba has long been the Revolution's Achilles heel. To speak out against the government in this tightly controlled, politically paranoid society is a serious and heavily punishable crime that – if it doesn't first land you in jail – is likely to lead to job stagnation, petty harassment and social ostracism.

The Castro era got off to a bad start in January 1959 when the revolutionary government – under the auspices of Che Guevara – rounded up Batista's top henchmen and summarily executed them inside Havana's La Cabaña fort with barely a lawyer in sight. Within a matter of months the Cuban press had been silenced and worried onlookers in the US were vociferously calling 'foul.'

In the years since, Cuba has scored badly on most global human rights indices with the world's two most respected human rights bodies, Amnesty International and Human Rights Watch, regularly berating the government for its refusal to respect the rights of assembly, association and expression, and other basic civil liberties.

Cuba's international image took another hit during 2003's 'Black Spring' when the government rounded up 75 dissidents who they claimed were agents of the US and handed them all lengthy jail terms. After an international outcry, all of the dissidents were eventually released, the last in 2011. Notwithstanding, harassment and intimidation of dissidents, including peaceful protesters such as the 'Ladies in White,' continues.

Cuba's supporters often justify the alleged human rights violations with tit-for-tat arguments. When the US questioned the 2011 jailing of American development contractor Alan Gross, they pointed to the incarceration of the 'Cuban Five' (five Cubans imprisoned in the US on equally flimsy spying charges). Gross and the Cuban Five were finally released in a prisoner swap in December 2014.

There have been other improvements in recent years. Gay persecution, once rife at all levels of Cuban society, is largely a thing of the past. Religious persecution is similarly rare. Freedom of expression and the press, however, remain frustratingly stifled, although, in the internet age, some high-profile bloggers, most notably Yoani Sánchez, have managed to reach an international audience.

Enter Raúl

In July 2006, the unimaginable happened. Fidel Castro, rather than dying in office and paving the way for an American-led capitalistic reopening (as had long been predicted), retired from day-to-day governing due to poor health and passed power quietly onto his younger brother, Raúl. Inheriting the country's highest office on the cusp of a major worldwide recession, Raúl began a slow package of reforms. It kicked off modestly in 2008 when Cubans were permitted access to tourist hotels, and allowed to purchase mobile phones and myriad electronic goods; rights taken for granted in most democratic countries, but long out of reach to the average Cuban.

1996	2002	2003	2006
Miami 'Brothers to the Rescue' planes are shot down by Cuban jets, provoking Bill Clinton to sign the Helms-Burton Act, further tightening the terms of the US embargo.	Half of Cuba's sugar refineries are closed, signaling the end of a three-century-long addiction to the boom-bust mono-crop. Laid-off sugar workers continue to draw salaries and are offered free education.	The Bush administration tightens the noose for US citizens traveling to Cuba. Many political dissidents are arrested by Cuban authorities in an island-wide crackdown.	Castro is taken ill just before his 80th birthday with diverticulitis disease and steps down from the day-to-day running of the country. He is replaced by his brother Raúl.

FREEZE & THAW: CUBA'S RELATIONSHIP WITH THE US

Whether the thaw between Cuba and the US is permanent remains to be seen. In the past, sporadic rapprochements between the Cuban and US governments have been limited and ephemeral. President Jimmy Carter loosened the regulations for licensed travel to Cuba for religious, educational and cultural groups in the late 1970s but, following the Mariel Boatlift and the accession of Ronald Reagan in 1980–81, the doors quickly shut. The Clinton administration attempted a second relaxation in 1995 and by the early 2000s an estimated 150,000 licensed US travelers were visiting Cuba annually (along with another 50,000 illegal 'tourists'). However, following Castro's crackdown on Cuban dissidents in 2003's 'Black Spring' and the ensuing diplomatic finger-wagging, the George W Bush administration closed the doors to all but the most determined American travelers.

The Obama administration first started widening the goalposts in 2009 allowing Cuban-Americans to visit their families in Cuba as often as they liked (under Bush II they had been restricted to one visit every three years). The process took a significant leap forward in December 2014 when, using his powers of presidential decree, Obama initiated the biggest changes in US–Cuba relations since the early 1960s making it clear that he wanted to end the embargo before his presidency expired in 2017.

These moves were followed in January 2011 by the biggest economic and ideological shake-up since the country waved *adiós* to Batista. Radical new laws laid off half a million government workers and tried to stimulate the private sector by granting business licenses to 178 state-recognized professions – everything from hairdressers to disposable-lighter refillers.

In October 2011, car sales were legalized and Cubans were allowed to buy and sell their homes for the first time in half a century. Even bolder was a decree announced in late 2012 that allowed Cubans to travel freely abroad, a basic right that had been barred to all but the favored few since 1961.

By 2013, Cuba had witnessed its most dramatic economic shift in decades with nearly 400,000 people working in the private sector, 250,000 more than in 2010, though it was still far from anything like Western-style capitalism.

Of the 12 or so men that survived the disastrous *Granma* landing in December 1956, only three were still alive in 2015: Fidel Castro, Raúl Castro and Ramiro Valdés.

2008	2009	2011	2014
Raúl Castro is officially inaugurated as Cuban president and embarks on his first set of reforms, permitting Cubans access to tourist hotels and allowing them to purchase mobile phones and electronic goods.	The inauguration of Barack Obama signifies a long-awaited thaw in Cuba–US relations. In an early act of rapprochement, Obama loosens restrictions for Cuban-Americans returning to the island to visit relatives.	Raúl Castro signals an economic thaw by announcing that the government plans to cut half a million jobs from the state sector and open up private enterprise to over 175 licensed businesses.	Following a prisoner swap, Barack Obama announces the reestablishment of diplomatic ties with Cuba and a raft of measures including telecommunications aid and the easing of financial restrictions.

Above Rum-based cocktail, mojito

Food & Drink

Until recently, Cuba was a country where veterans of WWII rationing were known to get nasty flashbacks. Then something epiphanic happened. Inspired and enabled by the on-going political and economic reform of the post-Fidel years, the nation's long-suppressed chefs have woken up and smelt the coffee. A bold culinary revolution is in full swing.

The Culinary Revolution

Señores and señoras, we are pleased to announce that Cuba – despite what you may have read in previous editions of this and other guide-books – is no longer the proverbial 'leftover' plate of the culinary world. The turnaround has been astronomical and unprecedented. The eco-nomic reforms of 2011, when the Cuban government allowed private restaurants (until then limited to 12 people) to expand and diversify, has been a massive game-changer. Taste-deprived travelers who once wisely elected to skip Cuban appetizers and main dishes and proceed directly to the 'rum and cigars' course, now ogle over honey-glazed chicken, lovingly prepared béchamel sauces, and rejigged renditions of old Cuban favorites such as *ropa vieja* (spicy shredded beef). Feeding the trend, Havana and other cities are awash with creative new private restaurants experimenting with previously unheard of cooking methods and ingredients. Free from the shackles of austere 1990s rationing, Cuban chefs bandy around words such as 'fusion' and 'medium-rare', and inscribe their menus with dishes such as eggplant caviar.

For first-time visitors accustomed to French-style creativity or American abundance, the food might not seem so remarkable. But, if you last visited Cuba in the early 2000s in the days when all chickens were fried to smithereens and soggy cheese-and-ham sandwiches served as the only viable lunch option, you're in for a big, and rather pleasant, surprise.

Five Hundred Years of Marination

The pain and shortages of the 1990s didn't do Cuban cuisine any favors, starving it of all but the most basic of ingredients and obscuring what, beneath the surface, has always been a rich and surprisingly diverse food culture.

In common with its music and architecture, Cuba's cuisine is a creative stew of selective morsels, recipes and cooking techniques left behind by successive travelers since the epoch of Columbus and Velázquez. Imagine a bubbling cauldron filled with ingredients plucked from Spain, Africa, France, pre-colonial Taínos, and cultures from various other islands in the Caribbean that has been left to intermingle and marinate for 500 years. From the original Taínos came indigenous root vegetables such as yucca and sweet potato, and native fruits such as guava; from the Spanish came pork, rice, flavor-enhancing spices and different frying techniques; African slave culture brought plantains in their various guises along with *congrí* (rice and beans cooked together with spices in the same pot); while, along with its island neighbors, Cuba shares the unmistakable taste of the Caribbean enshrined in the *sofrito*, a base sauce of tomatoes seasoned with onions, peppers, garlic, bay leaf and cumin.

Mix it all together and you get what the world now knows as 'Cuban' cuisine: simple, hearty, but healthy food that's light on spice (cumin and oregano predominate), but has no shortage of flavor. Whole roast pork is the meat of choice, closely followed by chicken, fried or roasted and often

Best Eating Cities

Havana: Cuba's most creative food

Baracoa: spiciest and sweetest cuisine

Trinidad: over 90 new private restaurants

Viñales: best whole roast pork

REGIONAL SPECIALTIES

Caibarién This small town in Villa Clara province is Cuba's crab capital.

Baracoa A completely different food universe to the rest of Cuba. Specialties include *cucurucho* (sweet blend of honey, coconut, guava and nuts), *bacán* (tamale with mashed banana, crab and coconut), *teti* (tiny fish indigenous to Río Toa), and *lechita* (spicy coconut sauce).

Playa Larga & Zapata Peninsula Crocodiles are farmed and consumed in stews in hotels and casas particulares in southern Matanzas province.

Bayamo *Ostiones* (oysters usually served in a tomato sauce) are a staple street-food in Granma's main city.

Oriente *Congrí* (rice and red beans seasoned with cumin, peppers and pork chunks) has its roots in the African-influenced culture of eastern Cuba. In the west, you're more likely to get *moros y cristianos* (with black beans but no pork).

Las Tunas Birthplace of *la caldosa*, a soup-like stew made with root vegetables, chicken and spices.

Congrí, a traditional dish of red beans, rice and pork

flavored with citrus sauces or honey. Never far from the sea, the Cubans love fish; lobster, crab, prawns, *aguja* (swordfish) and *pargo* (snapper) are all common. The key starch is rice usually mixed with beans as either *moros y cristianos* (made with black beans) or *congrí* (made with red beans). Root vegetables are another mainstay and are complemented by plantains, cooked any number of ways.

In season, Cuban avocados are sublime and tropical fruit is abundant. Most set-you-up-for-the-day breakfasts in your local casa particular start with an ambrosial plate of tropical fruit, which can vary according to season and location, but typically consists of a juicy quintet of banana, papaya, mango, pineapple and guava. Of the five fruits, only two – guava and pineapple – pre-date the arrival of the Spanish on the isles. Bananas and mangoes were brought to Cuba from Asia during the colonial period, while the papaya is indigenous to South America.

Dishes you shouldn't leave Cuba without trying are the national dish, *ropa vieja* (spicy shredded beef), whole roast pork with all the trimmings, *picadillo* (ground beef with olives and capers), *tostones* (twice-fried plantains) and *moros y cristianos*.

Rum Tales

Pioneers in the field of rum manufacture in the mid-19th century, the Cubans successfully transformed *aguardiente,* the coarse and unrefined 'fire water' imbibed by sailors and pirates on the Spanish Main into the smooth, clear 'Ron Superior' used today in sophisticated cocktails such as mojitos and daiquiris. The man behind the metamorphosis was a Spanish immigrant from Catalonia called Don Facundo Bacardí Massó (1814–86). Don Facundo's Santiago de Cuba rum factory was inaugurated in a bat-infested dockside warehouse in 1862 where he experimented

A woman drinking sugarcane juice

Guarapo is pure sugarcane juice mixed with ice and lemon that is served from quaint little roadside stalls called *guaraperos* all over rural Cuba.

with the region's high-quality sugarcane to create a new kind of aged rum that was delicate, crisp and fruity on the palate. Winning instant popularity, Bacardí's name quickly became a byword for rum and the family emerged as powerful and influential voices in Cuban politics. It wasn't to last. The Bacardís ultimately fell out with the Castro regime in the early 1960s and fled abroad, moving their headquarters to Bermuda. Although you won't find any Bacardí drinks on sale in Cuba today, the company's old factory in Santiago still produces the domestically popular, Ron Caney (the so-called 'rum of the revolution') that's stored in the same barrels once used by Don Facundo.

The other famous Cuban rum dynasty is Havana Club, founded by José Arechabala in the town of Cárdenas in 1878. In common with Bacardí, the Arechabala family fled Cuba after the Revolution although they were less successful in maintaining their company trademark, which was seized by the Cuban government in 1973. Today, Havana Club accounts for 40% of Cuba's alcohol market.

Aside from the Ron Caney factory in Santiago and the Havana Club operation now based in Santa Cruz del Norte near Havana, Cuba supports over 100 rum factories. Tap a local and they'll probably wax poetically about Ron Santiago de Cuba, Ron Mulata (made in Villa Clara) or Ron Varadero.

Rum is made from molasses, a by-product of sugarcane. Its fabrication in Cuba has been overseen by generations of skillful *maestros romeros*, or 'rum masters' who must have a minimum of 15 years of rum-tasting experience. The drink is classified by both color (dark, golden or clear) and age *(añejo)*. Good rums can range from anything from three years to 14 years in age. As a rule, rum cocktails (always made with clear rum) are more popular with tourists than Cubans. Cubans, on the other hand, usually prefer to drink their rum dark and neat (without ice) in order to enjoy the full flavor.

The Cuban Way of Life

Slipping through the outskirts of a provincial Cuban city on a tour bus, the country, on first impression, can seem austere, poor, and devoid of color. But what you see in this perennially contradictory archipelago isn't always what you get. Cuba requires patience, clandestine sleuthing, and plenty of scratching beneath the surface. Decipher the local way of life – warts and all – and you will quickly uncover its irrepressible musical energy, a non-stop dance that carries on in spite of everything.

A Recipe for Being Cuban

Take a dose of WWII rationing, and a pinch of Soviet-era austerity, add in the family values of South America, the educational virtues of the US, and the loquaciousness of the Irish. Mix with the tropical pace of Jamaica and innate musicality of pastoral Africa before dispersing liberally around the sultry streets of Havana, Santiago de Cuba, Camagüey and Pinar del Río.

Life in Cuba is an open and interactive brew. Spend time in a local home and you'll quickly start to piece together an archetype. There's the pot of coffee brewing on the stove, and the rusty Chinese bike leaning languidly against the wall of the front room, the faded photo of José Martí above the TV, and the statue of the venerated Virgin of El Cobre lurking in the shadows. Aside from the house-owner and their mother, brother, sister and niece, every Cuban home has a seemingly endless queue of 'visitors' traipsing through. A shirtless neighbor who's come over to borrow a wrench, the local busybody from the CDR (Committee for the Defense of the Revolution), a priest popping by for a glass of rum *sin hielo* (no ice); plus the cousin, the second cousin, the long-lost friend, the third cousin twice removed... you get the picture. Then there are the sounds: a cock crowing, a saxophonist practicing his scales, dogs barking, car engines exploding, a salsa beat far off, and those all-too-familiar shouts from the street. *Dime, hermano! Que pasa, mi amor? Ah, mi vida – no es fácil!*

Yes. *No es fácil* – it ain't easy. Life in Cuba is anything but easy but, defying all logic, it's perennially colorful and rarely dull.

> Cuba has 70,000 qualified doctors. The whole of Africa has only 50,000.

Lifestyle

Survivors by nature and necessity, Cubans have long displayed an almost inexhaustible ability to bend the rules and 'work things out' when it matters. The two most overused verbs in the national phrasebook are *conseguir* (to get, manage) and *resolver* (to resolve, work out), and Cubans are experts at doing both. Their intuitive ability to bend the rules and make something out of nothing is borne out of economic necessity. In a small nation bucking modern sociopolitical realities, where monthly salaries top out at around the equivalent of US$25, survival can often mean getting innovative as a means of supplementing personal income. Cruise the crumbling streets of Centro Habana and you'll see people *conseguir*-ing and *resolver*-ing wherever you go. There's the off-duty doctor using his car as a taxi, or the street cartoonist scribbling sketches of unsuspecting tourists in the hope of earning a tip. Other schemes may be ill-gotten or garnered through trickery, such as the *compañero* (comrade) who pockets the odd blemished cigar from the day job to sell to unsuspecting Canadians. Old Cuba hands know one of the most popular ways to make extra cash is working with (or over) tourists.

In Cuba, hard currency (ie convertible pesos) rules, primarily because it is the only way of procuring the modest luxuries that make living in this austere socialist republic more comfortable. Paradoxically, the post-1993 double economy has reinvigorated the class system the Revolution worked so hard to neutralize, and it's no longer rare to see Cubans with access to convertibles touting designer clothing while others hassle tourists for bars of soap. This stark re-emergence of 'haves' and 'have-nots' is among the most irksome issues facing Cuba today.

Other social traits that have emerged since the Revolution are more altruistic and less divisive. In Cuba sharing is second nature and helping out your *compañero* with a lift, a square meal or a few convertibles when they're in trouble is considered a national duty. Check the way that strangers interact in queues or at transport intersections and log how in Cuban houses neighbors share everything from tools, to food, to babysitting time without a second thought.

Cubans are informal. The *tú* form of Spanish address is much more common than the formal *usted,* and people greet each other with a variety of friendly addresses. Don't be surprised if a complete stranger calls you *mi amor* (my love) or *mi vida* (my life), and expect casa particular owners to regularly open the front door shirtless (men), or with their hair in rollers (women). To confuse matters further, Cuban Spanish is rich in colloquialisms, irony, sarcasm and swear words.

> Havana City Historian Eusebio Leal Spengler was born in the city in 1942. He has a degree in history and archaeological sciences, and a masters in Latin American, Caribbean and Cuban studies.

The Home Front

While Cuban homes sport the basics (fridges, cookers, microwaves), they still lack the expensive trappings of 21st-century consumerism. Car ownership is approximately 38 per 1000, compared to 800 per 1000 in the US; few households sport tumble dryers (spot the flailing lines of drying clothes); and that impressive breakfast laid out by your casa particular owner at 8am probably took three hours of searching and queuing to procure (Cuban supermarkets have nothing like the variety and abundance of goods as their counterparts in the US or Europe). Not that this dents home pride; gathered ornaments and mementos, however old and kitschy, are displayed with love and kept ruthlessly clean. Nonetheless, to most outsiders, the local lifestyle seems old-fashioned and austere. What makes Cuba different from somewhere like Mexico City or Philadelphia though, is the government's heavy subsidies of every facet of life, meaning there are few mortgages, no health-care bills, no college fees and fewer taxes. Expensive nights out cost next to nothing in Cuba where tickets for the theater, the cinema, the ballpark or a music concert are state-subsidized and considered a right of the people.

The Winds of Change

> In June 2008 the Cuban government legalized sex-change operations and agreed to provide them free to qualifying parties.

Fueled by cautious reform, the Cuban way of life has been changing slowly and subtly since Raúl Castro took the reins from his sick brother Fidel in 2008. Though the progress may seem sluggish to insiders, a returning exile who has spent the last six years in Miami or Madrid would have some illuminating epiphanies.

Barely anyone had a cell phone in Cuba in the mid-2000s; today, the devices are almost as ubiquitous as they are in the rest of the world, although lack of decent wi-fi coverage still makes internet connections nigh-on impossible. Other electronic goods legalized in 2008 have also found their way into Cuban households where, these days, it is not unusual to see a DVD-player and a modern flat-screen TV beneath a yellowing picture of José Martí. The ability of Cubans to travel abroad since

READ ALL ABOUT IT – THE BLOGGING REVOLUTION

With a literacy rate of 99.8% and a long-standing love of books, it is not surprising that Cuba is producing a growing number of eloquent bloggers, despite the difficulties in gaining internet access. Here are a few of the higher profile sites representing views right across the political spectrum.

Generación Y (Yoani Sánchez; www.desdecuba.org/generaciony) Sánchez is Cuba's most famous blogger (and dissident) and her gritty blog 'Generación Y' has been testing the mettle of Cuba's censorship police since April 2007. An unapologetic critic of the Cuban government she has attracted a huge international audience (US President Barack Obama once replied to one of her posts) and won numerous awards, including the Ortega & Gasset prize for digital journalism.

Havana Times (www.havanatimes.org) A website and 'blog cooperative' started by American writer, Circles Robinson, in 2008 that positions itself as anti-Castro and anti-embargo.

Along the Malecon (Tracy Eaton; www.alongthemalecon.blogspot.com) Former bureau chief for the *Dallas Morning News* in Havana (2000–05), Eaton is still a regular in-depth reporter in Cuba.

Café Fuerte (www.cafefuerte.com; Spanish only) Blog spot set up by four Cuban writers and journalists with international experience in 2010. It reports independently on Cuban-related news matters both inside and outside Cuba.

Yasmin Portales (http://yasminsilvia.blogspot.ca; Spanish only) Yasmin, who describes herself as a Marxist-feminist, is a strong voice in the Rainbow Project, an initiative for LGBT rights.

Babalú Blog (www.babalublog.com) Based in Miami and unyieldingly pro-US embargo, this blog is edited by Alberto de la Cruz. Carlos Eire, professor of History and Religious Studies at Yale University and author of the celebrated memoir *Waiting for Snow in Havana*, is a contributor.

La Joven Cuba (www.jovencuba.com; Spanish only) Blog set up and maintained by three professors from Matanzas University who style themselves as followers of Antonio Guíteras, a socialist Cuban politician from the 1930s.

January 2013 has enabled the lucky few who can afford it to shop overseas. Consequently, some of the more successful casas particulares are now equipped with shiny new consumer goods brought back from other countries such as sandwich-makers and coffee machines.

Cuba's improved culinary scene (p463) is one of the most visible changes for people who remember the hungry 1990s. Notwithstanding, the dilemma of any new private restaurant owner is how to pitch their pricing – at foreigners or Cubans, or a mix of both? Top restaurants in Havana are still generally the preserve of tourists and diplomats, while private restaurants in the smaller provincial towns are patronized primarily by locals and are thus more reasonably priced, often charging in *moneda nacional*.

Until 2008, Cubans were inexplicably barred from staying in tourist hotels. High prices still keep out many but, these days, some of the more economical resorts (eg Playa Santa Lucía) welcome plenty of Cuban guests during the long hot summer holiday.

A quick drive around the Cuban countryside will induce further surprises. While it's hardly LA yet, there are noticeably more cars on the road than there were in the early 2000s. That said, the new law permitting Cubans to buy and sell their own vehicles is little more than a political gesture. Precious few people can afford Toyotas and Audis, meaning 'yank tanks' and Ladas remain the cars of necessity. Agriculture has also registered significant improvements. Pre-2008, Cuba's notoriously emaciated and unproductive cows wandered around pathetically in twos or threes.

Main Cuban Crops

Bananas

Citrus fruit

Coffee

Mangoes

Pineapples

Rice

Sugarcane

Tobacco

Now whole fields full of plump healthy-looking livestock populate the farms of Las Tunas and Camagüey provinces.

Markets and shops, though still far from lavish, have fewer empty shelves these days and there has been a surge in shops selling large household items such as fridges and washing machines. In urban centers, private business resonates everywhere, from street-side barbers to sophisticated tour guides with their own business cards and websites. You'll even see professional street-signs advertising casas particulares or restaurants – something that was unheard of (and prohibited) until recently.

Inevitably these changes, while almost universally welcomed, have accentuated income divisions in a country long accustomed to socialism. People with ready access to convertibles – primarily those working in the tourist sector – have prospered; indeed, some casas particulares in Havana (who were limited to renting just two rooms until 2011) have morphed into mini-hotels in all but name. Meanwhile, the lives of people in the more isolated parts of rural Cuba have changed little. In small towns in the Oriente, the foibles that have haunted Cuba since the Special Period – shortages of bottled water, crumbling public buildings and awful roads – continue to bite.

Sport

Considered a right of the masses, professional sport was abolished by the government after the Revolution. Performance-wise it was the best thing the new administration could have done. Since 1959 Cuba's Olympic medal haul has rocketed into the stratosphere. The crowning moment came in 1992 when Cuba – a country of 11 million people languishing low on the world's rich list – brought home 14 gold medals and ended fifth on the overall medals table. It's a testament to Cuba's high sporting standards that their 11th-place finish in Athens in 2004 was considered something of a national failure.

Characteristically, the sporting obsession starts at the top. Fidel Castro was once renowned for his baseball-hitting prowess, but what is lesser known was his personal commitment to the establishment of a widely accessible national sporting curriculum at all levels. In 1961 the National Institute of Sport, Physical Education and Recreation (INDER) founded a system of sport for the masses that eradicated discrimination and integrated children from a young age. By offering paid leisure time to workers and dropping entrance fees to major sports events, the organization caused participation in popular sports to multiply tenfold by the 1970s and the knock-on effect to performance was tangible.

Cuban *pelota* (baseball) is legendary and the country is riveted during the October–March season, turning rabid for the play-offs in April. You'll see passions running high in the main square of provincial capitals, where fans debate minute details of the game with lots of finger-wagging in what is known as a *peña deportiva* (fan club) or *esquina caliente* (hot corner).

Cuba is also a giant in amateur boxing, as indicated by champions Teófilo Stevenson, who brought home Olympic gold in 1972, 1976 and 1980, and Félix Savón, another triple medal winner, most recently in 2000. Every sizeable town has an arena called *sala polivalente,* where big boxing events take place, while training and smaller matches happen at gyms, many of which train Olympic athletes.

Multiculturalism

A convergence of three different races and numerous nationalities, Cuba is a multicultural society that, despite difficult challenges, has been relatively successful in forging racial equality.

Cuba high-jumper, Javier Sotomayor, has held the world record (2.45m) for the event since 1993, and has recorded 17 of the 24 highest jumps ever.

The annihilation of the indigenous Taíno by the Spanish and the brutality of the slave system left a bloody mark in the early years of colonization, but the situation had improved significantly by the second half of the 20th century. The Revolution guaranteed racial freedom by law, though black Cubans are still far more likely to be stopped by the police for questioning, and over 90% of Cuban exiles in the US are of white descent. Black people are also under-represented in politics; of the victorious rebel army officers that took control of the government in 1959 only a handful (Juan Almeida being the most obvious example) were black or mixed race.

According to the most recent census, Cuba's racial breakdown is 24% *mulato* (mixed race), 65% white, 10% black and 1% Chinese. Aside from the obvious Spanish legacy, many of the so-called 'white' population are the descendants of French immigrants who arrived on the island in various waves during the early part of the 19th century. Indeed, the cities of Guantánamo, Cienfuegos and Santiago de Cuba were all either pioneered or heavily influenced by French *émigrés,* and much of Cuba's coffee and sugar industries owe their development to French entrepreneurship.

Elements of French culture imported via Haiti in the 1790s are still visible in Cuba today, particularly in the French-founded settlements of Guantánamo and Cienfuegos.

The black population is also an eclectic mix. Numerous Haitians and Jamaicans came to Cuba to work in the sugar fields in the 1920s and they brought many of their customs and traditions with them. Their descendants can be found in Guantánamo and Santiago in the Oriente or places such as Venezuela in Ciego de Ávila province, where Haitian voodoo rituals are still practiced.

Religion

Religion is among the most misunderstood and complex aspects of Cuban culture. Before the Revolution, 85% of Cubans were nominal Roman Catholics, though only 10% attended church regularly. Protestants made up most of the remaining church-going public, though a smattering of Jews and Muslims have always practiced in Cuba and still do. When the Revolution triumphed, 140 Catholic priests were expelled for reactionary political activities and another 400 left voluntarily, while the majority of Protestants, who represented society's poorer sector, had less to lose and stayed.

When the government declared itself Marxist-Leninist and therefore atheist, life for *creyentes* (literally 'believers') took on new difficulties. Though church services were never banned and freedom of religion never revoked, Christians were sent to Unidades Militares de Ayuda a la Producción (UMAPs; Military Production Aid Units), where it was hoped hard labor might reform their religious ways; homosexuals and vagrants were also sent to the fields to work. This was a short-lived experiment, however. More trying for believers were the hard-line Soviet days of the '70s and '80s, when they were prohibited from joining the Communist Party and few, if any, believers held political posts. Certain university careers, notably in the humanities, were off-limits as well.

Things have changed dramatically since then, particularly in 1992 when the constitution was revised, removing all references to the Cuban state as Marxist-Leninist and recapturing the laical nature of the government. This led to an aperture in civil and political spheres of society for religious adherents, and to other reforms (eg believers are now eligible for party membership). Since Cuban Catholicism gained the papal seal of approval with Pope John Paul II's visit in 1998, church attendance has surged and was rewarded further with the arrival of his successor Pope Benedict XVI in 2012. It's worth noting that church services have a strong youth presence. There are currently 400,000 Catholics regularly attending Mass and 300,000 Protestants from 54 denominations. Other denominations such as the Seventh Day Adventists and Pentecostals are rapidly growing in popularity.

CUBAN CIGARS

From the sombrero-clad *guajiros* in the tobacco fields of Pinar del Río to the high-end smoking rooms and cigar-pushing hustlers of Havana, cigars are deeply embedded in Cuban culture. Here are some local favorites:

Cohiba The cigar championed by Fidel Castro. Made with Cuba's finest Pinar del Río province tobacco; production allegedly comes from a coveted 10 fields from the princedom of the nation's plantations, the Vuelta Abajo region around San Juan y Martínez.

Vegas Robaina Hard to come by outside Cuba, the brand is named after tobacco-growing legend Alejandro Robaina, famous for the outstanding quality of the tobacco used, which heralds from the Alejandro Robaina Tobacco Plantation outside Pinar del Río.

Partagás One of the best-loved cuban cigars since before the Revolution, known now for its annual *ediciones limitada* (limited editions).

Puro Cubano An unbranded cigar that Cubans prefer because of its vastly cheaper price, but nevertheless is rolled with some of Pinar del Río province's best leaves.

Santería

A syncretistic religion that hides African roots beneath a symbolic Catholic veneer, Santería is a product of the slave era, but remains deeply embedded in contemporary Cuban culture where it has had a major impact on the evolution of the country's music, dance and rituals. Today, over three million Cubans identify as believers, including numerous writers, artists and politicians.

Santería's misrepresentations start with its name; the word is a historical misnomer first coined by Spanish colonizers to describe the 'saint worship' practiced by 19th-century African slaves. A more accurate moniker is Regla de Ocha (way of the *orishas*), or Lucumí, named for the original adherents who hailed from the Yoruba ethno-linguistic group in southwestern Nigeria, a prime looting ground for brutal slave traders.

Fully initiated adherents of Santería (called *santeros*) believe in one God known as Oludomare, the creator of the universe and the source of Ashe (all life forces on earth). Rather than interact with the world directly, Oludomare communicates through a pantheon of *orishas,* various imperfect deities similar to Catholic saints or Greek gods, who are blessed with different natural (water, weather, metals) and human (love, intellect, virility) qualities. *Orishas* have their own feast days, demand their own food offerings, and are given numbers and colors to represent their personalities.

Santería has no equivalent to the Bible or Koran. Instead, religious rites are transmitted orally and, over time, have evolved to fit the realities of modern Cuba. Another departure from popular world religions is the abiding focus on 'life on earth' as opposed to the afterlife, although Santería adherents believe strongly in the powers of dead ancestors, known as *egun,* whose spirits are invoked during initiation ceremonies.

Santería's syncretism with Catholicism occurred surreptitiously during the colonial era when African animist traditions were banned. In order to hide their faith from the Spanish authorities, African slaves secretly twinned their *orishas* with Catholic saints. Thus, Changó the male *orisha* of thunder and lightning was hidden somewhat bizarrely behind the feminine form of Santa Bárbara, while Elegguá, the *orisha* of travel and roads became St Anthony de Padua. In this way an erstwhile slave praying before a statue of Santa Bárbara was clandestinely offering his/her respects to Changó, while Afro-Cubans ostensibly celebrating the feast day of Our Lady of Regla (September 7) were, in reality, honoring Yemayá. This syncretization, though no longer strictly necessary, is still followed today.

The Committees for the Defense of the Revolution, or CDRs, are Cuba's controversial local political committees. On the one hand, CDRs act as prime government tools in quashing dissent and maintaining a compliant population; on the other, they organize important community festivals, blood banks and vaccination campaigns.

Literature & the Arts

Leave your preconceptions about 'art in a totalitarian state' at home. The breadth of Cuban cinema, painting and literature could put many far more politically libertarian nations to shame. The Cubans seem to have a habit of taking almost any artistic genre and reinventing it for the better. You'll pick up everything here, from first-class flamenco and ballet through to classical music and alternative cinema to Shakespearean theater and Lorca plays.

Literary Cuba

Spend an evening conversing with the Cubans and you'll quickly realize that they *love* talking. This loquaciousness extends to books. Maybe it's something they put in the rum, but since time immemorial, writers in this highly literate Caribbean archipelago have barely paused for breath, telling and retelling their stories with zeal and, in the process, producing some of Latin America's most groundbreaking, influential literature.

The Classicists

Any literary journey should begin in Havana in the 1830s. Cuban literature found its earliest voice in *Cecilia valdés*, a novel by Cirilo Villaverde (1812–94), published in 1882 but set 50 years earlier in a Havana divided by class, slavery and prejudice. It's widely considered to be the greatest 19th-century Cuban novel.

Preceding Villaverde, in publication if not historical setting, was romantic poet and novelist Gertrudis Gómez Avellaneda. Born to a rich Camagüeyan family of privileged Spanish gentry in 1814, Avellaneda was a rare female writer in a rigidly masculine domain. Eleven years before *Uncle Tom's Cabin* woke up America to the same themes, her novel *Sab,* published in 1841, tackled the prickly issues of race and slavery. It was banned in Cuba until 1914 due to its abolitionist rhetoric. What contemporary critics chose not to see was Avellaneda's subtle feminism, which depicted marriage as another form of slavery.

Further east, neoclassical poet and native *santiagüero* (person from Santiago de Cuba), José María de Heredia lived and wrote mainly from exile in Mexico, after being banished for allegedly conspiring against the Spanish authorities. His poetry, including the seminal *Himno del desterrado*, is tinged with a nostalgic romanticism for his homeland.

The Experimentalists

Cuban literature grew up in the early 1900s. Inspired by a mixture of José Martí's modernism and new surrealistic influences wafting over from Europe, the first half of the 20th century was an age of experimentation for Cuban writers. The era's literary legacy rests on three giant pillars: Alejo Carpentier, a baroque wordsmith who invented the much-copied style of *lo real maravilloso* (magic realism); Guillermo Cabrera Infante, a Joycean master of colloquial language who pushed the parameters of Spanish to barely comprehensible boundaries; and José Lezama Lima, a gay poet of Proustian ambition, whose weighty novels were rich in layers, themes and

Best Cuban Books

Cecelia Valdés (Cirilo Villaverde; 1882)

El siglo de las luces (Explosion in a Cathedal; Alejo Carpentier; 1962)

Infante: Tres tristes tigres (Three Trapped Tigers; Guillermo Cabrera; 1967)

Antes que anochezca (Before Night Falls; Reinaldo Arenas; 1992)

MARTÍ – A CATEGORY OF HIS OWN

Rarely does an author step out of normal categorization and stand alone, but José Julián Martí Pérez (1853–95) was no ordinary human being. A pioneering philosopher, revolutionary and modernist writer, Martí broadened the political debate in Cuba beyond slavery (which was abolished in 1886) to issues such as independence and – above all – freedom. His instantly quotable prose remains a rare unifying force among Cubans around the world, whatever their political affiliations, and he is similarly revered by Spanish-speakers globally for his internationalism, which has put him on a par with Simón Bolívar.

Martí's writing covered a huge range of genres: essays, novels, poetry, political commentaries, letters and even a hugely popular children's magazine called *La edad de oro* (Golden Age). He was an accomplished master of aphorisms, and his powerful one-liners still crop up in everyday Cuban speech. His two most famous works, published in 1891, are the political essay *Nuestra América* (Our America) and his collected poems, *Versos sencillos* (Simple Verses), both of which laid bare his hopes and dreams for Cuba and Latin America.

anecdotes. None were easy to read, but all broke new ground inspiring erudite writers far beyond Cuban shores (Gabriel García Márquez and Salman Rushdie among them). Swiss-born Carpentier's magnum opus was *El siglo de las luces* (Explosion in a Cathedral), which explores the impact of the French revolution in Cuba through a veiled love story. Many consider it to be the finest novel ever written by a Cuban author. Infante, from Gibara, rewrote the rules of language in *Tres tristes tigres* (Three Trapped Tigers), a complex study of street life in pre-Castro Havana. Lezama, meanwhile, took an anecdotal approach to novel writing in *Paradiso* (Paradise), a multilayered, widely interpreted evocation of Havana in the 1950s with homoerotic undertones.

Grasping at the coattails of this verbose trio was Miguel Barnet, an anthropologist from Havana, whose *Biografía de un cimarrón* (Biography of a Runaway Slave), published in 1963, gathered testimonies from 103-year-old former slave Esteban Montejo and crafted them into a fascinating written documentary of the brutal slave system nearly 80 years after its demise.

Contemporary writer Leonardo Padura Fuentes is well known for his quartet of Havana-based detective novels, *Los cuatro estaciones* (Four Seasons).

Enter Guillén

Born in Camagüey in 1902, *mulato* (mixed race) poet Nicolás Guillén was far more than just a writer: he was a passionate and lifelong champion of Afro-Cuban rights. Rocked by the assassination of his father in his youth, and inspired by the drum-influenced music of former black slaves, Guillén set about articulating the hopes and fears of dispossessed black laborers with the rhythmic Afro-Cuban verses that would ultimately become his trademark. Famous poems in a prolific career included the evocative 'Tengo' (I Have) and the patriotic 'Che comandante, amigo' (Commander Che, Friend).

Working in self-imposed exile during the Batista era, Guillén returned to Cuba after the Revolution whereupon he was given the task of formulating a new cultural policy and setting up the writer's union, Unión de Escritores y Artistas de Cuba (Uneac).

The Dirty Realists

In the 1990s and 2000s, baby boomers that had come of age in the era of censorship and Soviet domination began to respond in their writing to radically different influences in their writing. Some fled the country, others remained; all tested the boundaries of artistic expression in a system weighed down by censorship and creative asphyxiation.

Stepping out from the shadow of Lezama Lima was Reinaldo Arenas, a gay writer from Holguín province, who, like Guillermo Cabrera Infante, fell out with the Revolution in the late '60s and was imprisoned for his efforts. Arenas finally escaped to the US in 1980 during the Mariel boatlift. He went on to write his hyperbolic memoir, *Antes que anochezca* (Before Night Falls), about his imprisonment and homosexuality. Published in the US in 1993, it met with huge critical acclaim.

The so-called 'dirty realist' authors of the late '90s and early 2000s took a more subtle approach to challenging contemporary mores. Pedro Juan Gutiérrez earned his moniker, 'tropical Bukowski', for the *Dirty Havana Trilogy*, a sexy, sultry study of Centro Habana during the Special Period. The trilogy held a mirror up to the desperate economic situation but steered clear of direct political polemics.

Zoé Valdés, born the year Castro took power, has been more direct in her criticism of the regime, particularly since leaving Cuba for Paris in 1995. Her most readily available novels (translated into English) are *I Gave You All I Had* and *Dear First Love*.

The Fascinated Foreigners

Several foreign writers have also been inspired by Cuba to pen fiction, most notably Ernest Hemingway and Graham Greene. Hemingway first visited Cuba in the late 1930s on his boat *El Pilar*, partly as a break from his soon-to-be ex-wife. His love affair with the country continued until his death. His novels *The Old Man and the Sea* (1952; a portrayal of an old man's quest to bag a giant fish) and *Islands in the Stream* (1970; a harrowing trilogy following the fortunes of writer Thomas Hudson) were based on his experiences fishing – and, during WWII, hunting for German submarines – off Cuba's coast.

Greene visited the island several times in the 1950s and it became the setting for his book *Our Man in Havana* (1958), a tongue-in-cheek look at espionage that casts an interesting light on pre-Cuban Missile Crisis Havana.

Whilst none of his novels take place in Cuba, Colombian author Gabriel García Márquez developed a long-standing friendship with Fidel Castro during the 1960s, and wrote several articles on Cuba including *Memories of a Journalist* (1981) which recalls the Bay of Pigs invasion.

Heberto Padilla (1932–2000) was a Cuban poet whose dissident writings in the 1960s led to his imprisonment, inspiring the 'Padilla Affair'.

Graham Greene originally set his comic take on British espionage in Soviet-occupied Tallinn, Estonia. But a chance visit to Havana changed his mind. The novel ultimately became Our Man in Havana.

Cinema

Cuban cinema has always been closer to European art-house traditions than to the formula movies of Hollywood, especially since the Revolution, when cultural life veered away from American influences. Few notable movies were made until 1959, when the new government formed the Instituto Cubano del Arte e Industria Cinematográficos (Icaic), headed up by longtime film sage and former Havana University student Alfredo Guevara, who held the position on and off until 2000. The 1960s were Icaic's *Década de oro* (golden decade) when, behind an artistic veneer, successive directors were able to test the boundaries of state-imposed censorship and, in some cases, gain greater creative license. Innovative movies of this era poked fun at bureaucracy, made pertinent comments

PRIZE-WINNING PAZ

Senel Paz, author of *El Lobo, El Bosque y El Hombre nuevo* (The Wolf, the Forest and the New Man), the book that inspired famed movie *Fresa y Chocolat*, returned to international attention in 2008 with the publication of his novel *En el cielo con diamantes* (In the Sky with Diamonds) – a poignant tale of friendship in 1960s Havana. This garnered him literary prizes and status as Cuba's most widely read contemporary writer.

CASAS DE LA CULTURA

Every provincial town in Cuba, no matter how small, has a Casa de la Cultura acting as a nexus for the country's bubbling cultural life. Casas de la Cultura stage everything from traditional salsa music to innovative comedy nights, with upcoming events penned onto a *cartelera* (culture caldendar) outside. On top of this, countless other theaters, organizations and institutions bring highbrow art to the masses completely free – yes, *free* – of charge.

on economic matters, questioned the role of intellectualism in a socialist state and, later on, tackled previously taboo gay issues. The giants behind the camera were Humberto Solás, Tomás Gutiérrez Alea, and Juan Carlos Tabío, who, working under Guevara's guidance, put cutting-edge Cuban cinema on the international map.

Cuba's first notable post-revolutionary movie, the joint Cuban-Soviet *Soy Cuba* (I am Cuba; 1964), was directed by a Russian, Mikhail Kalatozov, who dramatized the events leading up to the 1959 Revolution in four interconnecting stories. Largely forgotten by the early '70s, the movie was resurrected in the mid-1990s by American director Martin Scorsese, who, upon seeing the film for the first time, was astounded by its cinematography, atmospheric camera work and, above all, technically amazing tracking shots. The film gets a rare 100% rating on the Rotten Tomatoes website and has been described by one American film critic as 'a unique, insane, exhilarating spectacle.'

Serving his apprenticeship in the 1960s, Cuba's most celebrated director, Tomás Gutiérrez Alea, cut his teeth directing art-house movies such as *La muerte de un burócrata* (Death of a Bureaucrat; 1966), a satire on excessive socialist bureaucratization; and *Memorias de subdesarrollo* (Memories of Underdevelopment; 1968), the story of a Cuban intellectual too idealistic for Miami, yet too decadent for the austere life of Havana. Teaming up with fellow director Juan Carlos Tabío in 1993, Gutiérrez went on to make another movie classic, the Oscar-nominated *Fresa y chocolate* (Strawberry and Chocolate) – the tale of Diego, a skeptical homosexual who falls in love with a heterosexual communist militant. It remains Cuba's cinematic pinnacle. Humberto Solás, a master of *cine pobre* (low budget) movies first made his mark in 1968 with the seminal *Lucía*. It explored the lives of three Cuban women at key moments in the country's history: 1895, 1932 and the early 1960s. Solás made his late-career masterpiece, *Barrio Cuba,* the tale of a family torn apart by the Revolution, in 2005.

Since the death of Gutiérrez Alea in 1996 and Solás in 2008, Cuban cinema has passed the baton to a new and equally talented stash of movie guerrillas. Their uncrowned king is Fernando Pérez, who leapt onto the scene in 1994 with the Special Period classic *Madagascar,* focusing on an intergenerational struggle between a mother and daughter, and followed it up with 2003's *Suite Habana*, a moody documentary about a day in the life of 13 real people in the capital that uses zero dialogue. Pérez'

In 2010, Cuban film director Fernando Pérez brought the early life of José Martí to the screen in a film called *El ojo del canario* (Eye of the Canary).

RAÚL MARTÍNEZ & THE GRUPO DE LOS ONCE

Ciego de Ávila, born Raúl Martinez (1927–1995), spearheaded the Cuban pop-art movement during the 1950's and '60's with iconic depictions of José Martí, Camilo Cienfuegos and Che Guevara, although much of his work was inspired by Soviet socialism as much as by the American pop-art movement. Martinez was a member of the Grupo de los Once, a group of groundbreaking abstract painters and sculptors who exhibited together between 1953 and 1955 and left a lasting impression on Cuban art. You can see much of the work of Martínez in Ciego de Ávila's Centro Raúl Martínez Galería de Arte Provincial (p304).

LITERATURE & THE ARTS PAINTING & SCULPTURE

closest 'rival' is Juan Carlos Cremata, whose 2005 road movie *Viva Cuba*, a study of class and ideology as seen through the eyes of two children, garnered much international praise.

The last few years have seen few classics of the same clout, but 2011's *Juan of the Dead*, Cuba's version of UK horror-comedy *Shaun of the Dead* broke ground as Cuba's first zombie movie. In a thinly veiled critique on the regime, an idler-turned-slayer-of-the-undead fights for survival in a Havana overrun by zombies.

Havana's significant influence in the film culture of the American hemisphere is highlighted each year in the Festival Internacional del Nuevo Cine Latinoamericano, held every December in Havana. Described as the ultimate word in Latin American cinema, this annual get-together of critics, sages and filmmakers has been fundamental in showcasing recent Cuban classics to the world.

Painting & Sculpture

Thought-provoking and visceral, modern Cuban art combines lurid Afro-Latin American colors with the harsh reality of the 52-year-old Revolution. For foreign art-lovers visiting Cuba, it's a unique and intoxicating brew. Forced into a corner by the constrictions of the culture-redefining Cuban Revolution, modern artists have invariably found that, by co-opting (as opposed to confronting) the socialist regime, opportunities for academic training and artistic encouragement are almost unlimited. Encased in such a volatile, creative climate, abstract art in Cuba – well established in its own right before the Revolution – has flourished.

The first flowering of Cuban art took place in the 1920s, when painters belonging to the so-called Vanguardia movement relocated temporarily to Paris to learn the ropes from the avant-garde European school then dominated by the likes of Pablo Picasso. One of the Vanguardia's earliest exponents was Victor Manuel García (1897–1969), the genius behind one of Cuba's most famous paintings, *La gitana tropical* (Tropical Gypsy; 1929), a portrait of an archetypal Cuban woman with her luminous gaze staring into the middle distance. The canvas, displayed in Havana's Museo Nacional de Bellas Artes, is often referred to as the Latin *Mona Lisa*. Amelia Peláez (1896–1968), Victor Manuel's contemporary, was another Francophile who studied in Paris, where she melded avant-gardism with more primitive Cuban themes. Though Peláez worked with many different materials, her most celebrated work was in murals, including the 670-sq-meter tile mural on the side of the Hotel Habana Libre.

After the high-water mark of Wifredo Lam, Cuban pop art was a major influence during the 1950s and 1960s. Art has enjoyed strong government patronage since the Revolution (albeit within the confines of strict censorship), exemplified with the opening of the Instituto Superior de Arte in the Havana neighborhood of Cubanacán in 1976.

Best Uneac Cultural Venues

El Hurón Azul (p115), Havana

Holguín (p354)

Santiago de Cuba (p415)

Cienfuegos (p246)

Puerto Padre (p341)

Top Modern Artists

José Villa

Joel Jover

Flora Fong

José Rodríguez Fúster

Tomás Sánchez

Architecture

There is nothing pure about Cuban architecture. Rather like its music, the nation's eclectic assemblage of buildings exhibits an unashamed hybrid of styles, ideas and background influences. The result is a kind of architectural 'theme and variations', that has absorbed a variety of imported genres and shaped them into something that is uniquely Cuban.

Styles & Trends

Emerging relatively unscathed from the turmoil of three revolutionary wars and buffered from modern globalization by Cuba's peculiar economic situation, the nation's well-preserved cities have survived into the 21st century with the bulk of their colonial architectural features intact. The preservation has been helped by the nomination of Habana Vieja, Trinidad, Cienfuegos and Camagüey as Unesco World Heritage Sites, and aided further by foresighted local historians who have created a model

Above Art deco-style windows, Havana

for self-sustaining historical preservation that might well go down as one of the revolutionary government's greatest achievements.

Cuba's classic and most prevalent architectural styles are baroque and neoclassicism. Baroque designers began sharpening their quills in the 1750s; neoclassicism gained the ascendency in the 1820s and continued, amid numerous revivals, until the 1920s. Trademark buildings of the American era (1902–59) exhibited art deco and, later on, modernist styles. Art nouveau played a cameo role during this period influenced by Catalan *modernisme;* recognizable art nouveau curves and embellishments can be seen on pivotal east–west axis streets in Centro Habana. Ostentatious eclecticism, courtesy of the Americans, characterized Havana's rich and growing suburbs from the 1910s onwards.

Building styles weren't all pretty, though. Cuba's brief flirtation with Soviet architectonics in the 1960s and '70s threw up plenty of breeze-block apartments and ugly utilitarian hotels that sit rather jarringly alongside the beautiful relics of the colonial era. Havana's Vedado neighborhood maintains a small but significant cluster of modernist 'skyscrapers' constructed during a 10-year pre-revolutionary building boom in the 1950s.

Coastal Fortifications

While European kings were hiding from the hoi polloi in muscular medieval castles, their Latin American cousins were building up their colonial defenses in a series of equally colossal Renaissance forts.

The protective ring of fortifications that punctuates Cuba's coastline stretching from Havana in the west to Baracoa in the east forms one of the finest ensembles of military architecture in the Americas. The construction of these sturdy stone behemoths by the Spanish in the 16th, 17th and 18th centuries reflected the colony's strategic importance on the Atlantic trade routes and its vulnerability to attacks by daring pirates and competing colonial powers.

As Cuban capital and the primary Spanish port in the Caribbean, Havana was the grand prize to ambitious would-be raiders. The sacking of the city by French pirate Jacques de Sores in 1555 exposed the weaknesses of the city's meager defenses and provoked the first wave of fort building. Havana's authorities called in Italian Military architect Bautista Antonelli to do the job and he responded with aplomb, reinforcing the harbor mouth with two magnificent forts, El Morro and San Salvador de la Punta. The work, which started in the 1580s, was slow but meticulous; the forts weren't actually finished until after Antonelli's death in the 1620s. Antonelli also designed the Castillo de San Pedro de la Roca del Morro in Santiago, started around the same time but, thanks to ongoing attacks, most notoriously by British buccaneer Henry Morgan in 1662, not finished until 1700.

More forts were added in the 18th century, most notably at Jagua (near present-day Cienfuegos) on the south coast and Matanzas in the north. Baracoa in the far east was encircled with a bulwark of three small fortifications, all of which survive.

With their thick walls, and polygon layout designed to fit in with the coastal topography, Cuba's forts were built to last (all still survive) and largely served their purpose at deterring successive invaders until 1762. In that year the British arrived during the Seven Years' War, blasting a hole in San Severino in Matanzas and capturing Havana after a 44-day siege of El Morro. Spain's response when it got back Havana from the British in 1763 was to build the humungous La Cabaña, the largest fort in the Americas. Not surprisingly, its heavy battlements were never breached.

In the 1980s and 90s, Havana's and Santiago's forts were named Unesco World Heritage Sites.

Best Colonial Plazas

Plaza de la Catedral (p64), Havana

Plaza Mayor (p275), Trinidad

Parque José Martí, Cienfuegos

Parque Ignacio Agramonte (p319), Camagüey

Plaza Martí (p265), Remedios

Castillo de San Pedro de la Roca del Morro (p404)

Trinidad's remarkably homogenous architecture features large one-story houses with terracotta-tiled roofs, wooden beams, wall frescos, barred windows, *aljibes* (storage wells), Mudéjar-style courtyards and balconies with wooden balustrades raised above the street.

Theatrical Architecture

Attend a dance or play in a provincial Cuban theater and you might find your eyes flicking intermittently between the artists on the stage and the equally captivating artistry of the building.

As strong patrons of music and dance, the Cubans have a tradition of building iconic provincial theaters and most cities have a historic venue where you can view the latest performances. By popular consensus, the most architecturally accomplished Cuban theaters are the Teatro Sauto (p217) in Matanzas, the Teatro la Caridad (p255) in Santa Clara, and the Teatro Tomás Terry (p237) in Cienfuegos. All three gilded buildings were constructed in the 19th century (in 1863, 1885 and 1890 respectively) with sober French neoclassical facades overlaying more lavish Italianate interiors. A generic defining feature is the U-shaped three-tiered auditoriums which display a profusion of carved wood-paneling and wrought iron, and are crowned by striking ceiling frescos. The frescos of angelic cherubs in the Caridad and Tomás Terry were painted by the same Filipino artist, Camilo Salaya, while the Sauto's was the work of the theater's Italian architect, Daniele Dell'Aglio. Other features include ornate chandeliers, gold-leafed mosaics and striking marble statues: the Sauto's statues are of Greek goddesses, while the Tomás Terry sports a marble re-creation of its eponymous financier, a Venezuelan-born sugar baron.

Philanthropy played a major part in many Cuban theaters in the 19th century, none more so than Santa Clara's Caridad (the name means 'charity') which was paid for by local benefactor, Marta Abreu. In an early show of altruism, Abreu, who donated to many social and artistic causes, ensured that a percentage of the theater's ongoing profits went to charity.

Lack of funds in recent times has left many Cuban theaters in dire need of repair. Some buildings haven't survived. The Colesio, Cuba's earliest

BRENT WINEBRENNER / GETTY IMAGES ©

Museo de la Revolución (p83), Havana

modern theater built in 1823 in Santiago de Cuba was destroyed by fire in 1846. The Teatro Brunet in Trinidad built in 1840 is now a ruin used as an atmospheric social center. Havana's oldest theater, the Tacón, survives, but was overlaid by a Spanish social center (the Centro Gallego) in the 1910s. Pinar del Río's recently refurbished Teatro Milanés (1838) has a lovely Sevillan patio, while the neoclassical Teatro Principal (1850) in Camagüey is home of Cuba's most prestigious ballet company.

Cuban Baroque

Baroque architecture arrived in Cuba in the mid 1700s, via Spain, a good 50 years after its European high-water mark. Fueled by the rapid growth of the island's nascent sugar industry, nouveau riche slave-owners and sugar merchants plowed their juicy profits into grandiose urban buildings. The finest examples of baroque in Cuba adorn the homes and public buildings of Habana Vieja, although the style didn't reach its zenith until the late 1700s with the construction of the Catedral de San Cristóbal de la Habana and the surrounding Plaza de la Catedral.

Due to climatic and cultural peculiarities, traditional baroque (the word is taken from the Portuguese noun *barroco,* which means an 'elaborately shaped pearl') was quickly 'tropicalized' in Cuba, with local architects adding their own personal flourishes to the new municipal structures that were springing up in various provincial cities. Indigenous features included: *rejas,* metal bars secured over windows to protect against burglaries and to allow for a freer circulation of air; *vitrales,* multicolored glass panes fitted above doorways to pleasantly diffuse the tropical sun rays; *entresuelos,* mezzanine floors built to accommodate live-in slave families; and *portales,* galleried exterior walkways that provided pedestrians with shelter from the sun and the rain. Signature baroque buildings, such as the Palacio de los Capitanes Generales in Plaza de Armas in Havana were made from hard local limestone dug from the nearby San Lázaro quarries and constructed using slave labor. As a result, the intricate exterior decoration that characterized baroque architecture in Italy and Spain was noticeably toned down in Cuba, where local workers lacked the advanced stonemasonry skills of their more accomplished European cousins.

Some of the most exquisite baroque buildings in Cuba are found in Trinidad and date from the early decades of the 19th century when designs and furnishings were heavily influenced by the haute couture fashions of Italy, France and Georgian England.

Neoclassicism

Neoclassicism first evolved in the mid-18th century in Europe as a reaction to the lavish ornamentation and gaudy ostentation of baroque. Conceived in the progressive academies of London and Paris, the movement's early adherents advocated sharp primary colors and bold symmetrical lines, coupled with a desire to return to the perceived architectural 'purity' of ancient Greece and Rome. The style eventually reached Cuba at the beginning of the 19th century, spearheaded by groups of French émigrés who had fled west from Haiti following a violent slave rebellion in 1791. Within a couple of decades, neoclassicism had established itself as the nation's dominant architectural style.

By the mid-19th century sturdy neoclassical buildings were the norm among Cuba's bourgeoisie in cities such as Cienfuegos and Matanzas, with striking symmetry, grandiose frontages and rows of imposing columns replacing the decorative baroque flourishes of the early colonial period.

Havana's first true neoclassical building was El Templete, a diminutive Doric temple constructed in Habana Vieja in 1828 next to the spot where Father Bartolomé de las Casas is said to have conducted the city's first Mass. As the city gradually spread westward in the mid-1800s, outgrowing its 17th-century walls, the style was adopted in the construction of more ambitious buildings, such as the famous Hotel Inglaterra overlooking Parque Central. Havana grew in both size and beauty during this period, bringing into vogue new residential design features such as spacious classical courtyards and rows of imposing street-facing colonnades, leading seminal Cuban novelist Alejo Carpentier to christen it the 'city of columns.'

A second neoclassical revival swept Cuba at the beginning of the 20th century, spearheaded by the growing influence of the US on the island. Prompted by the ideas and design ethics of the American Renaissance (1876–1914), Havana underwent a full-on building explosion, sponsoring such gigantic municipal buildings as the Capitolio Nacional and the Universidad de la Habana. In the provinces, the style reached its high-water mark in a series of glittering theaters.

Most Attractive Hotels

Hotel Ordoño
(p358), Gibara

Hotel Raquel (p97),
Havana

Hostal del Rijo
(p295), Sancti
Spíritus

Hotel Camino de
Hierro (p322),
Camagüey

HAVANA'S PARISIAN INFLUENCE

French landscape architect, Jean-Claude Forestier added a Parisian flavor to Havana's modern urban layout in the 1920s. Fresh from high-profile commissions in the French capital, Forestier arrived in Havana in 1925 where he was invited to draw up a master-plan to link the city's disparate urban grid. He spent the next five years sketching broad tree-lined boulevards, Parisian-style squares and a harmonious city landscape designed to accentuate Havana's iconic monuments and lush tropical setting. Forestier's plans were unhinged by the Great Depression, but his Parisian vision was ultimately realized 30 years later with the vast construction projects enacted in the 1950s. The focal point was Plaza de la Revolución with its grand Martí Memorial which sits atop a small hill with broad avenues radiating on all sides. Best for strolling along are Paseo and Avenida de los Presidentes (Calle G) both adorned with tree-lined central walkways and punctuated with heroic statues.

Above Capitolio Nacional (p79), Havana

Right Colonial-era building

Cuartel Moncada (p402), Santiago de Cuba

Notable Art Deco Buildings

Edificio Bacardí (p77), Havana

Teatro América (p116), Havana

Iglesia de Nuestra Señora de la Caridad (p366), Banes

Cuartel Moncada (p402), Santiago de Cuba

Art Deco

Art deco was an elegant, functional and modern architectural movement that originated in France at the beginning of the 20th century and reached its apex in America in the 1920s and '30s. Drawing from a vibrant mix of Cubism, futurism and primitive African art, the genre promoted lavish yet streamlined buildings with sweeping curves and exuberant sun-burst motifs such as the Chrysler building in New York and the architecture of the South Beach neighborhood in Miami.

Brought to Cuba via the United States, the nation quickly acquired its own clutch of 'tropical' art-deco buildings with the lion's share residing in Havana. One of Latin America's finest examples of early art deco is the Edifico Bacardí in Habana Vieja, built in 1930 to provide a Havana headquarters for Santiago de Cuba's world-famous rum-making family. Another striking creation was the 14-story Edificio López Serrano in Vedado, constructed as the city's first real *rascacielo* (skyscraper) in 1932, using New York's Rockefeller Center as its inspiration. Other more functional art-deco skyscrapers followed in Havana, including the Teatro América on Av de la Italia, the Teatro Fausto on Paseo de Martí and the Casa de las Américas on Calle G. A more diluted and eclectic interpretation of the genre can be seen in the famous Hotel Nacional in Havana, whose sharp symmetrical lines and decorative twin Moorish turrets dominate the view over the Malecón.

Hotel Raquel (p97), Havana

Eclecticism

Eclecticism is the term often applied to the non-conformist and highly experimental architectural zeitgeist that grew up in the United States during the 1880s. Rejecting 19th-century ideas of 'style' and categorization, the architects behind this revolutionary new genre promoted flexibility and an open-minded 'anything goes' ethos, drawing their inspiration from a wide range of historical precedents.

Thanks to the strong US presence in the decades before 1959, Cuba quickly became a riot of modern eclecticism, with rich American and Cuban landowners constructing huge Xanadu-like mansions in burgeoning upper-class residential districts. Expansive, ostentatious and, at times, outlandishly kitschy, these fancy new homes were garnished with crenellated walls, oddly shaped lookout towers, rooftop cupolas and leering gargoyles. For a wild tour of Cuban eclecticism, head to the neighborhoods of Miramar in Havana, Vista Alegre in Santiago de Cuba and Punta Gorda in Cienfuegos.

Music & Dance

Juxtapose two ancient cultures from two very different continents (Africa and Europe). Relocate them to a slave society in a far-off tropical land. Give them some drums, a maraca and a couple of improvised guitars. See what happens.

Into the Mix

Rich, vibrant, layered and soulful, Cuban music has long acted as a standard-bearer for the sounds and rhythms emanating out of Latin America. This is the land where salsa has its roots, where elegant white dances adopted edgy black rhythms, and where the African drum first fell in love with the Spanish guitar. From the down-at-heel docks of Matanzas to the bucolic villages of the Sierra Maestra, the amorous musical fusion went on to fuel everything from *son*, rumba, mambo, *chachachá, charanga, changüí, danzón* and more.

Aside from the obvious Spanish and African roots, Cuban music has drawn upon a number of other influences. Mixed into an already exotic melting pot are genres from France, the US, Haiti and Jamaica. Conversely, Cuban music has also played a key role in developing various melodic styles and movements in other parts of the world. In Spain they called this process *ida y vuelta* (return trip) and it is most clearly evident in a style of flamenco called *guajira*. Elsewhere the 'Cuban effect' can be traced back to forms as diverse as New Orleans jazz, New York salsa and West African Afrobeat.

Described by aficionados as 'a vertical representation of a horizontal act,' Cuban dancing is famous for its libidinous rhythms and sensuous close-ups. Inheriting a love for dancing from birth and able to replicate perfect salsa steps by the age of two or three, most Cubans are natural performers who approach dance with a complete lack of self-consciousness – a notion that can leave visitors from Europe or North America feeling as if they've got two left feet.

Cuba's first hybrid musical genre was the *habanera*, a traditional European-style dance with a syncopated drumbeat, that rose to the fore in the mid-19th century and lasted until the 1870s.

Danzón Days

The invention of the *danzón* is usually credited to innovative Matanzas band leader Miguel Faílde, who first showcased it with his catchy dance composition 'Las Alturas de Simpson' in Matanzas in 1879. Elegant and purely instrumental in its early days, the *danzón* was slower in pace than the *habanera*, and its intricate dance patterns required dancers to circulate in couples rather than groups, a move that scandalized polite society at the time. From the 1880s onward, the genre exploded, expanding its peculiar syncopated rhythm, and adding such improbable extras as conga drums and vocalists. By the early 20th century, the *danzón* had evolved from a stately ballroom dance played by an *orchestra típica* into a more jazzed-up free-for-all known alternatively as *charanga, danzonete* or *danzón-chá*. Not surprisingly, it became Cuba's national dance, though since it was primarily a bastion of moneyed white society, it was never considered a true hybrid.

Africa Calling

While drumming in the North American colonies was ostensibly prohibited, Cuban slaves were able to preserve and pass on many of their musical traditions via influential Santería *cabildos,* religious brotherhoods that re-enacted ancient African percussive music on simple *batá* drums or *chequeré* rattles. Performed at annual festivals or on special Catholic saints' days, this rhythmic yet highly textured dance music was offered up as a form of religious worship to the *orishas* (deities).

Over time the ritualistic drumming of Santería evolved into a more complex genre known as rumba. Rumba was first concocted in the docks of Havana and Matanzas during the 1890s when ex-slaves, exposed to a revolving series of outside influences, began to knock out soulful rhythms on old packing cases in imitation of various African religious rites. As the drumming patterns grew more complex, vocals were added, dances emerged and, before long, the music had grown into a collective form of social expression for all black Cubans.

Spreading in popularity throughout the 1920s and '30s, rumba gradually spawned three different but interrelated dance formats: *guaguancó,* an overtly sexual dance; *yambú,* a slow dance; and *columbia,* a fast, aggressive dance often involving fire torches and machetes. The latter originated as a devil dance of the Náñigo rite, and today it's performed only by solo males.

Pitched into Cuba's cultural melting pot, these rootsy yet highly addictive musical variants slowly gained acceptance among a new audience of middle-class whites, and by the 1940s the music had fused with *son* in a new subgenre called *son montuno,* which, in turn, provided the building blocks for salsa.

Indeed, so influential was Cuban rumba by the end of WWII that it was transposed back to Africa with experimental Congolese artists, such as Sam Mangwana and Franco Luambo (of OK Jazz fame), using ebullient Cuban influences to pioneer *soukous,* their own variation on the rumba theme.

Raw, expressive and exciting to watch, Cuban rumba is a spontaneous and often informal affair performed by groups of up to a dozen musicians. Conga drums, claves, *palitos* (sticks), *marugas* (iron shakers) and *cajones* (packing cases) lay out the interlocking rhythms, while the vocals alternate between a wildly improvising lead singer and an answering *coro* (chorus).

The *danzón* was originally an instrumental piece. Words were added in the late 1920s and the new form became known as the *danzonete.*

Charangas were Cuban musical ensembles that showcased popular *danzón*-influenced pieces.

DANCE FUSION

Cuban dance is as hybridized as the country's music; indeed many dance genres evolved from popular strands of Cuban music.

Early dance forms mimicked the European-style ballroom dances practiced by the colonizers, but added African elements. This unorthodox amalgamation of styles can be seen in esoteric genres such as the French-Haitian tumba francesa (p411), a marriage between 18th-century French court dances and imported African rhythms: dancers wearing elegant dresses wave fans and handkerchiefs while shimmying to the drum patterns of Nigeria and Benin. Other dances reflected the working lives of Cuban slaves. The *pilón* in Granma province copies the motion of pounding sugarcane. *Nengón* and *kiribá* in Baracoa mimic the crushing of cocoa and coffee beans beneath the feet.

The first truly popular dance hybrid was the *danzón*, a sequence dance involving couples its origins lay in the French and English *contradanza*, but its rhythm contained a distinctive African syncopation. The mambo and *chachachá* evolved the *danzón* further, creating dances that were more improvised and complicated. Mambo's creator, Pérez Prado, specifically pioneered mambo dancing to fit his new music in the 1940s while the *chachachá* was codified as a ballroom dance in the early 1950s by a Frenchman named Monsieur Pierre.

Rising Son

Cuba's two most celebrated 19th-century sounds, rumba and *danzón*, came from the west – specifically the cities of Havana and Matanzas. But as the genres remained largely compartmentalized between separate black and white societies, neither can be considered true hybrids. The country's first real musical fusion came from the next great sound revolution, *son*.

Son emerged from the mountains of the Oriente region in the second half of the 19th century, though the earliest-known testimonies go back as far as 1570. It was one of two genres to arise at around the same time (the other was *changüí*), both of which blended the melodies and lyricism of Spanish folk music with the drum patterns of recently freed African slaves. *Son's* precursor was *nengón*, an invention of black sugar-plantation workers who had evolved their percussive religious chants into a form of music and song. The leap from *nengón* to *son* is unclear and poorly documented, but at some point in the 1880s or '90s the *guajiros* (country folk) in the mountains of present-day Santiago de Cuba and Guantánamo provinces began blending *nengón* drums with the Cuban *tres* (guitar with three sets of double strings) while over the top a singer improvised words from a traditional 10-line Spanish poem known as a *décima*.

In its pure form, *son* was played by a sextet consisting of guitar, *tres*, double bass, bongo and two singers who played maracas and claves (sticks that tap out the beat). Coming down from the mountains and into the cities, the genre's earliest exponents were the legendary Trio Oriental, who stabilized the sextet format in 1912 when they were reborn as the Sexteto Habanero. Another early *sonero* was singer Miguel Matamoros, whose self-penned *son* classics such as 'Son de la Loma' and 'Lágrimas Negras' are de rigueur among Cuba's ubiquitous musical entertainers, even today.

In the early 1910s *son* arrived in Havana, where it adopted its distinctive rumba clave (rhythmic pattern), which later went on to form the basis of salsa. Within a decade it had become Cuba's signature music, gaining wide acceptance among white society and destroying the myth that black music was vulgar, unsophisticated and subversive.

By the 1930s the sextet had become a septet with the addition of a trumpet, and exciting new musicians such as blind *tres* player Arsenio Rodríguez – a songwriter who Harry Belafonte once called the 'father of salsa' – were paving the way for mambo and *chachachá*.

Barbarians of Rhythm

In the 1940s and '50s the *son* bands grew from seven pieces to eight and beyond, until they became big bands boasting full horn and percussion sections that played rumba, *chachachá* and mambo. The reigning mambo king was Benny Moré, who with his sumptuous voice and rocking 40-piece all-black band was known as El Bárbaro del Ritmo (The Barbarian of Rhythm).

Mambo grew out of *charanga* music, which itself was a derivative of *danzón*. Bolder, brassier and more exciting than its two earlier incarnations, the music was characterized by exuberant trumpet riffs, belting saxophones and regular enthusiastic interjections by the singer (usually in the form of the word *dilo!* or 'say it!'). The style's origins are mired in controversy. Some argue that it was invented by *habanero* (person from Havana) Orestes López after he penned the new rhythmically dextrous 'Mambo' in 1938. Others give the credit to Matanzas band leader Pérez Prado, the first musician to market his songs under the increasingly lucrative mambo umbrella in the early '40s. Whatever the case, mambo soon spawned the world's first universal dance craze, and from New York to Buenos Aires, people couldn't get enough of its infectious rhythms.

'Guajira Guantanamera' means 'country girl from Guantánamo.' Written by *trovador* Joseito Fernández, most of the original lyrics have been replaced with words from José Martí's *Versos sencillos*.

Best Casas de la Trova

Baracoa (p443)

Santiago de Cuba (p414)

Trinidad (p284)

Camagüey (p325)

Sancti Spíritus (p296)

A variation on the mambo theme, the *chachachá* was first showcased by Havana-based composer and violinist Enrique Jorrín in 1951 while playing with the Orquesta América. Originally known as 'mambo-rumba,' the music was intended to promote a more basic kind of Cuban dance that less-coordinated North Americans would be able to master, but it was quickly mambo-ized by overenthusiastic dance competitors, who kept adding complicated new steps.

Salsa & Its Off-Shoots

Salsa is an umbrella term used to describe a variety of musical genres that emerged out of the fertile Latin New York scene in the 1960s and '70s, when jazz, *son* and rumba blended to create a new, brassier sound. While not strictly a product of Cubans living in Cuba, salsa's roots and key influences are descended directly from *son montuno* and indebted to innovators such as Pérez Prado, Benny Moré and Miguel Matamoros.

The self-styled Queen of Salsa was Grammy-winning singer and performer Celia Cruz. Born in Havana in 1925, Cruz served the bulk of her musical apprenticeship in Cuba before leaving for self-imposed exile in the US in 1960. But due to her long-standing opposition to the Castro regime, Cruz' records and music have remained largely unknown on the island despite her enduring legacy elsewhere. Far more influential on their home turf are the legendary salsa outfit Los Van Van, a band formed by Juan Formell in 1969 and one that still performs regularly at venues across Cuba. With Formell at the helm as the group's great improviser, poet, lyricist and social commentator, Los Van Van were one of the few modern Cuban groups to create their own unique musical genre – that of songo-salsa. The band also won top honors in 2000 when they memorably took home a

Types of Cuban Dance

Chachachá

Guaguancó

Mambo

Danzón

Columbia

Yambú

MUSIC & DANCE SALSA & ITS OFF-SHOOTS

CUBA'S BEATLEMANIA

Pop trivia question: who is the only member of The Beatles to have visited Cuba? Answer: Paul McCartney, who briefly helicoptered into Santiago de Cuba for less than 24 hours in 2000. Despite the brevity of Sir Paul's visit, you'll meet an inconceivably large number of people who claim to have met the ex-Beatle that day as he breezed by the Casa de la Trova. Then there's the appearance of his oddly clean dinner plate mounted on the wall of Restaurante El Morro where he apparently enjoyed a vegetarian omelet.

But Cuba's obsession with The Beatles doesn't end with Paul McCartney's dinner plate. The band once banned for being too Western and decadent, but later endorsed by Fidel Castro, have become icons in Cuba in recent years. At last count there were at least half-a-dozen Beatles-inspired bars and clubs across the country, most of them relatively new, from Havana's Submarino Amarillo to Trinidad's Bar Yesterday.

So what's with the delayed Beatlemania? Jolly good music, is the obvious reason. But, in Cuba, where the excitement of hearing *The White Album* will be forever associated with the thrill of indulging in what was once a subversive act, the band has an edgier appeal. Listening to The Beatles was a clandestine affair in the '60s when the music could only be picked up on fuzzy American radio stations by Cubans lying under their bed covers in Havana. The Fab Four got people into trouble in other ways too. In 1968 film director Nicolás Guillén Landrián played the song 'The Fool on the Hill' over footage of Fidel Castro in an edgy documentary called *Coffea Arábiga*. El Comandante was not amused and Guillén was later imprisoned for his 'cheek.'

Castro was more generous in 2000 when, unveiling a statue of John Lennon in Havana, he hailed The Beatles as 'revolutionaries' in one of his more outrageous U-turns.

Today, Beatles-themed clubs are a haven for Cuba's once underground *roquero* (rock music) community (most of whom are surprisingly young), and showcase tribute bands who play storming versions of Beatles hits along with songs from the canon of Pink Floyd, The Kinks, Led Zeppelin and AC/DC.

Grammy for their classic album *Llego Van Van*. Despite the death of Formell in 2014, the band continues to play, record and tour.

Modern salsa mixed and merged further in the '80s and '90s, allying itself with new cutting-edge musical genres such as hip-hop, reggaetón and rap, before coming up with some hot new alternatives, most notably *timba* and songo-salsa.

Timba is, in many ways, Cuba's own experimental and fiery take on traditional salsa. Mixing New York sounds with Latin jazz, *nueva trova*, American funk, disco, hip-hop and even some classical influences, the music is more flexible and aggressive than standard salsa, incorporating greater elements of the island's potent Afro-Cuban culture. Many *timba* bands such as Bamboleo and La Charanga Habanera use funk riffs and rely on less-conventional Cuban instruments such as synthesizers and kick drums. Others – such as NG La Banda, formed in 1988 – have infused their music with a more jazzy dynamic.

Filin' is a term derived from the English word 'feeling'. It was a style of music showcased by jazz crooners in the 1940s and '50s. In Cuba *filin'* grew out of bolero and *trova* (verse, song).

Traditional jazz, considered the music of the enemy in the Revolution's most dogmatic days, has always seeped into Cuban sounds. Jesús 'Chucho' Valdés' band Irakere, formed in 1973, broke the Cuban music scene wide open with its heavy Afro-Cuban drumming laced with jazz and *son*, and the Cuban capital boasts a number of decent jazz clubs. Other musicians associated with Cuban jazz include pianist Gonzalo Rubalcaba, Isaac Delgado and Adalberto Álvarez y Su Son.

Nueva Trova – the Soundtrack of a Revolution

The 1960s were heady days for radical new forms of musical expression. In the US, Dylan released *Highway 61 Revisited*, in Britain the Beatles concocted *Sgt Pepper's Lonely Hearts Club Band* while, in the Spanish-speaking world, musical activists such as Chilean Víctor Jara and Catalan Joan Manuel Serrat were turning their politically charged poems into passionate protest songs.

Determined to develop their own revolutionary music apart from the capitalist West, the innovative Cubans – under the stewardship of Haydee Santamaría, director at the influential Casa de las Américas – came up with *nueva trova*.

A caustic mix of probing philosophical lyrics and folksy melodic tunes, *nueva trova* was a direct descendent of pure *trova*, a bohemian form of

---

CONTEMPORARY SOUNDS

Interactivo An artists' collective that has showcased countless individual talent since its formation in 2001, including hip-hop artist Kumar, jazzy poet and instrumentalist Yusa, and founder, the jazz pianist Roberto Carcassés. Cuban fusion personified.

Buena Fe Creative rock duo from Guantánamo whose penetrating lyrics appeal to Cuba's awakening youth movement.

Haydée Milanés Jazzy singer and daughter of *trova* (verse, song) great Pablo Milanés.

X-Alfonso The man behind Havana's exciting new Fábrica de Arte Cubano is a king of many genres, from Hendrix-style rock to Latin hip-hop. Listen out also for his sister M-Alfonso, another great fusion singer.

Diana Fuentes Singer with a R & B and funk bent who has worked with everyone who's anyone in the Cuban music scene including X-Alfonso.

Yissy Probably Cuba's most talented drummer, Yissy García lays down her beat with a strong nod to Yoruba tradition.

Doble Filo Pioneering Cuban hip-hop artists with outspoken lyrics. They once rapped with Fidel Castro.

guitar music that had originated in the Oriente (the eastern part of the island) in the late 19th century. Post-1959, *trova* became increasingly politicized and was taken up by more sophisticated artists such as Carlos Puebla, who provided an important bridge between old and new styles with his politically tinged ode to Che Guevara, 'Hasta Siempre Comandante' (1965).

Nueva trova came of age in February 1968 at the Primer Encuentro de la Canción Protesta, a concert organized at the Casa de las Américas in Havana and headlined by such rising stars as Silvio Rodríguez and Pablo Milanés. In a cultural context, it was Cuba's mini-Woodstock, an event that resounded forcefully among leftists worldwide as a revolutionary alternative to American rock 'n' roll.

In December 1972 the nascent *nueva trova* movement gained official sanction from the Cuban government during a festival held in Manzanillo city commemorating the 16th anniversary of the *Granma* landing. Highly influential throughout the Spanish-speaking world during the '60s and '70s, *nueva trova* has often acted as an inspirational source of protest music for the impoverished and downtrodden populations of Latin America, many of whom looked to Cuba for spiritual leadership in an era of corrupt dictatorships and US cultural hegemony. This solidarity was reciprocated by the likes of Rodríguez, who penned numerous internationally lauded classics such as 'Canción Urgente para Nicaragua' (in support of the Sandinistas), 'La Maza' and 'Canción para mi Soldado' (about the Angolan War).

Rap, Reggaetón & Beyond

The contemporary Cuban music scene is an interesting mix of enduring traditions, modern sounds, old hands and new blood. With low production costs, solid urban themes and lots of US-inspired crossover styles, hip-hop and rap are taking the younger generation by storm.

Born in the ugly concrete housing projects of Alamar, Havana, Cuban hip-hop, rather like its US counterpart, has gritty and impoverished roots. First beamed across the nation in the early 1980s when American rap was picked up on homemade rooftop antennae from Miami-based radio stations, the new music quickly gained ground among a young urban black population who were culturally redefining themselves during the inquietude of the Special Period. By the '90s groups such as Public Enemy and NWA were de rigueur on the streets of Alamar and by 1995 there was enough hip-hop to throw a festival.

Tempered by Latin influences and censored by the parameters of strict revolutionary thought, Cuban hip-hop has shied away from US stereotypes, instead taking on a progressive flavor all its own. Instrumentally the music uses *batá* drums, congas and electric bass, while lyrically the songs tackle important national issues such as sex tourism and the difficulties of the stagnant Cuban economy.

Despite being viewed early on as subversive and anti-revolutionary, Cuban hip-hop has gained unlikely support from inside the Cuban government, whose art-conscious legislators consider the music to have played a constructive social role in shaping the future of Cuban youth. Fidel Castro went one step further, describing hip-hop as 'the vanguard of the Revolution' and – allegedly – trying his hand at rapping at a Havana baseball game.

The same cannot be said for reggaetón, a melding of hip hop, Spanish reggae and Jamaican dance hall that emerged out of Panama in the 1990s and gained mainstream popularity in Puerto Rico in the mid-2000s. The Cuban government banned explicit reggaetón songs from TV and radio in 2012, and many hip hop artists have expressed their discomfort with the genre's overtly sexist and narcissistic lyrics. Nonetheless, reggaetón remains popular among certain sections of Cuba's youth who idolize homegrown artists such as Osmani Garcia.

Landscape & Wildlife

Measuring 1250km from east to west and between 31km and 193km from north to south, Cuba is the Caribbean's largest island with a total land area of 110,860 sq km. Shaped like one of its signature crocodiles and situated just south of the Tropic of Cancer, the country is actually an archipelago made up of 4195 smaller islets and coral reefs. Its unique set of ecosystems have been fascinating and perplexing scientists and naturalists ever since Alexander von Humboldt frst mapped them in the early 1800s.

The Cuban Landscape

Formed by a volatile mixture of volcanic activity, plate tectonics and erosion, Cuba's landscape is a lush, varied concoction of mountains, caves, plains and *mogotes* (strange flat-topped hills). The highest point, Pico Turquino (1972m), is situated in the east among the Sierra Maestra's lofty triangular peaks. Further west, in the no less majestic Sierra del Escambray, ruffled hilltops and gushing waterfalls straddle the borders of Cienfuegos, Villa Clara and Sancti Spíritus provinces. Rising like purple shadows in the far west, the 175km-long Cordillera de Guanguanico is a more diminutive range that includes the protected Sierra del Rosario Biosphere Reserve and the distinctive pincushion hills of the Valle de Viñales.

Lapped by the warm turquoise waters of the Caribbean Sea in the south, and the foamy white chop of the Atlantic Ocean in the north, Cuba's 5746km of coastline shelters more than 300 natural beaches and features one of the world's largest tracts of coral reef. Home to approximately 900 reported species of fish and more than 410 varieties of sponge and coral, the country's unspoiled coastline is a marine wonderland and a major reason why Cuba has become renowned as a diving destination extraordinaire.

The 7200m-deep Cayman Trench between Cuba and Jamaica forms the boundary of the North American and Caribbean plates. Tectonic movements have tilted the island over time, creating uplifted limestone cliffs along parts of the north coast and low mangrove swamps on the south. Over millions of years Cuba's limestone bedrock has been eroded by underground rivers, creating interesting geological features including the 'haystack' hills of Viñales and more than 20,000 caves countrywide.

As a sprawling archipelago, Cuba contains thousands of islands and keys (most uninhabited) in four major offshore groups: the Archipiélago de los Colorados, off northern Pinar del Río; the Archipiélago de Sabana-Camagüey (or Jardines del Rey), off northern Villa Clara and Ciego de Ávila; the Archipiélago de los Jardines de la Reina, off southern Ciego de Ávila; and the Archipiélago de los Canarreos, around Isla de la Juventud. Most visitors will experience one or more of these island idylls, as the majority of resorts, scuba diving and virgin beaches are found in these regions.

Being a narrow island, never measuring more than 200km north to south, Cuba's capacity for large lakes and rivers is limited (preventing hydroelectricity). Cuba's longest river, the 343km-long Río Cauto that flows from the Sierra Maestra in a rough loop north of Bayamo, is only navigable by small boats for 110km. To compensate, 632 *embalses* (reservoirs) or *presas* (dams), covering an area of more than 500 sq km altogether,

Cuba's Highest Mountains

....

Pico Turquino
1972m, Santiago de Cuba province

....

Pico Cuba
1872m, Santiago de Cuba province

....

Pico Bayamesa
1730m, Granma province

have been created for irrigation and water supply; these supplement the almost unlimited groundwater held in Cuba's limestone bedrock.

Lying in the Caribbean's main hurricane region, Cuba has been hit by some blinders in recent years, notably 2012's Sandy, which wrought over US$2 billion in damage.

Protected Areas

Cuba protects its land in multiple ways: at a local level it has set up fauna reserves, bio-parks and areas of managed resources; at a national level it sponsors national and natural parks; and international protection is provided in Unesco Biosphere Reserves, Unesco World Heritage Sites and Ramsar Convention Sites. The most ecologically important and vulnerable zones are protected at more than one level. For example, Parque Nacional Alejandro de Humboldt is a national park, a Unesco World Heritage Site *and* part of the Cuchillas del Toa Unesco Biosphere Reserve. Lower down the pecking order, the smaller parks suffer from less watertight restrictions and are more open to rule-bending.

Unesco & Ramsar Sites

The highest level of environmental protection in Cuba is provided by Unesco, which has created six biosphere reserves over the last 25 years. Biosphere reserves are areas of high biodiversity that rigorously promote conservation and sustainable practices. After a decade and a half of successful reforestation the Sierra del Rosario became Cuba's first Unesco Biosphere Reserve in 1985. It was followed by Cuchillas del Toa (1987), Península de Guanahacabibes (1987), Baconao (1987), Ciénaga de Zapata (2000) and the Bahía de Buenavista (2000). Additionally, two of Cuba's nine Unesco World Heritage Sites are considered 'natural' sites, ie nominated primarily for their ecological attributes. They are Parque Nacional Desembarco del Granma (1999), hailed for its uplifted marine terraces, and Parque Nacional Alejandro de Humboldt (2001), well known for its extraordinary endemism. Complementing the Unesco sites are half a dozen Ramsar Convention Sites earmarked in 2001–02 to conserve Cuba's vulnerable wetlands. These lend added protection to the Ciénaga de Zapata and Bahía de Buenavista, and throw a lifeline to previously unprotected regions such as Isla de la Juventud's Lanier Swamp (prime crocodile territory), the expansive Río Cauto delta in Granma/Las Tunas, and the vital flamingo nesting sites on the north coasts of Camagüey and Ciego de Ávila provinces.

National Parks

The definition of a national park is fluid in Cuba (some are often referred to as natural parks or flora reserves) and there's no umbrella organization as in Canada or the USA. A handful of the 14 listed parks – most notably Ciénaga de Zapata – now lie within Unesco Biosphere Reserves or Ramsar Convention Sites, meaning their conservation policies are better monitored. The country's first national park was Sierra del Cristal, established in 1930 (home to Cuba's largest pine forest), though it was 50 years before the authorities created another, Gran Parque Nacional Sierra Maestra (also known as Turquino), which safeguards Cuba's highest mountain. Other important parks include Viñales, with its *mogotes*, caves and tobacco plantations and Gran Piedra, near Santiago de Cuba, which is overlaid by the Baconao Unesco Biosphere Reserve. Two important offshore national parks off the south coast are the Jardines de la Reina, an archipelago diving haven off Ciego de Ávila province's coast; and the rarely visited Cayos de San Felipe off the coast of Pinar del Río province.

LANDSCAPE & WILDLIFE THE CUBAN LANDSCAPE

Cuba's Longest River
....
Name *Río Cauto*
....
Length *343km*
....
Navigable length
110km
....
Basin area
8928 sq km
....
Source
Sierra Maestra Mountains
....
Mouth
Caribbean Sea

Cuba's Isla Grande (main island) is the 17th-largest island in the world by area; slightly smaller than Newfoundland, but marginally bigger than Iceland.

Agriculture

Agricultural land accounts for some 30% of the Cuban landmass and one in every five Cubans is engaged in some form of agricultural work.

Tobacco, grown primarily in prosperous Pinar del Río province, is Cuba's third-most important industry in the embattled Cuban economy. Like most farming in Cuba, it's still carried out in a way that's changed little in centuries, with fields plowed by yoked oxen, and is as photogenic to watch as it is gut-busting to do.

Sugar was an economic powerhouse before the US embargo and, despite the many closed sugar mills, is becoming more important again, with China the major importer. The other big crop grown is rice, while coffee is cultivated on the Cordillera de la Gran Piedra near Santiago de Cuba.

Parque Nacional Alejandro de Humboldt is named for the German naturalist Alexander von Humboldt (1769–1859) who visited the island between 1801 and 1804.

Wildlife

While it isn't exactly the Serengeti, Cuba has an unusual share of indigenous fauna and serious animal-watchers won't be disappointed. Birds are probably the biggest draw and Cuba is home to more than 350 different varieties, two dozen of them endemic. Head to the mangroves of Ciénaga de Zapata in Matanzas province or to the Península de Guanahacabibes in Pinar del Río for the best sightings of the blink-and-you'll-miss-it *zunzuncito* (bee hummingbird), the world's smallest bird and, at 6.5cm, not much longer than a toothpick. These areas are also home to the *tocororo* (Cuban trogon), Cuba's national bird, which sports the red, white and blue colors of the Cuban flag. Other popular bird species include *cartacubas* (a type of bird indigenous to Cuba), herons, spoonbills, parakeets and rarely seen Cuban pygmy owls.

Flamingos are abundant in Cuba's northern keys where they have established the largest nesting ground in the Western hemisphere in the Camagüey province's Río Máximo delta.

Land mammals have been hunted almost to extinction with the largest indigenous survivor the friendly *jutía* (tree rat), a 4kg edible rodent that

CUBA'S PROTECTED AREAS

AREA NAME	YEAR DESIGNATED	OUTSTANDING FEATURES
Unesco Biosphere Reserves		
Sierra del Rosario (p494)	1985	eco practices
Cuchillas del Toa (p494)	1987	primary rainforest
Península de Guanahacabibes (p494)	1987	turtle nesting site
Baconao (p494)	1987	coffee culture
Ciénaga de Zapata (p494)	2000	largest wetlands in Caribbean
Buenavista	2000	karst formations
Ramsar Convention Sites		
Ciénaga de Zapata (p230)	2001	largest wetlands in Caribbean
Buenavista	2002	karst formations
Ciénaga de Lanier	2002	unusual mosaic of ecosystems
Humedal del Norte de Ciego de Ávila	2002	unique coastal lakes
Humedal Delta del Cauto	2002	large population of aquatic birds
Humedal Río Máximo-Cagüey (p494)	2002	significant flamingo nesting site
'Natural' Unesco World Heritage Sites		
Parque Nacional Desembarco del Granma (p494)	1999	pristine marine terraces
Parque Nacional Alejandro de Humboldt (p445)	2001	high endemism

scavenges on isolated keys and lives in relative harmony with iguanas. The vast majority of Cuba's other 38 species of mammal are from the bat family.

Cuba harbors a species of frog so small and elusive that it wasn't discovered until 1996 in what is now Parque Nacional Alejandro de Humboldt near Baracoa. Still lacking a common name the endemic amphibian is known as *Eleutherodactylus iberia*; it measures less than 1cm in length, and has a range of only 100 sq km.

Other odd species include the *mariposa de cristal* (Cuban clear-winged butterfly), one of only two clear-winged butterflies in the world; the rare *manjuarí* (Cuban alligator gar), an ancient fish considered a living fossil; the *polimita*, a unique land snail distinguished by its festive yellow, red and brown bands; and, discovered only in 2011, the endemic *Lucifuga*, a blind troglodyte fish.

Reptiles are well represented in Cuba. Aside from iguanas and lizards, there are 15 species of snake, none of them poisonous. Cuba's largest snake is the *majá*, a constrictor related to the anaconda that grows up to 4m in length; it's nocturnal and doesn't usually mess with humans. The endemic Cuban crocodile *(Crocodylus rhombifer)* is relatively small but agile on land and in water. Its 68 sharp teeth are specially adapted for crushing turtle shells. Crocs have suffered from major habitat loss in the last century though greater protection since the 1990s has seen numbers increase. Cuba has established a number of successful crocodile breeding farms *(criaderos)*, the largest of which is at Guamá near the Bay of Pigs. Living in tandem with the Cuban croc is the larger American crocodile *(Crocodylus acutus)* found in the Zapata Swamps and in various marshy territories on Cuba's southern coast.

Cuba's marine life compensates for what the island lacks in land fauna. The manatee, the world's only herbivorous aquatic mammal, is found in the Bahía de Taco and the Península de Zapata, and whale sharks frequent the María la Gorda area at Cuba's eastern tip from November to February. Four turtle species (leatherback, loggerhead, green and hawksbill) are found in Cuban waters and they nest annually in isolated keys or on protected beaches in Península de Guanahacabibes.

Endangered Species

Due to habitat loss and persistent hunting by humans, many of Cuba's animals and birds are listed as endangered species. These include the critically endangered Cuban crocodile, which has the smallest habitat range of any crocodile, existing only in 300 sq km of the Ciénaga de Zapata (Zapata Swamp) and in the Lanier Swamp on Isla de la Juventud. Protected since 1996, wild numbers now hover at around 6000. Other vulnerable species include the *jutía*, which was hunted mercilessly during the Special Period, when hungry Cubans tracked them for their meat (they still do – in fact, it is considered something of a delicacy); the tree boa, a native snake that lives in rapidly diminishing woodland areas; and the elusive *carpintero real* (ivory-billed woodpecker) spotted after a 40-year gap in the Parque Nacional Alejandro de Humboldt near Baracoa in the late 1980s, but not seen since.

The seriously endangered West Indian manatee, while protected from illegal hunting, continues to suffer from a variety of human threats, most notably from contact with boat propellers, suffocation caused by fishing nets and poisoning from residues pumped into rivers from sugar factories.

Cuba has an ambiguous attitude toward turtle hunting. Hawksbill turtles are protected under the law, though a clause allows for up to 500 of them to be captured per year in certain areas (Camagüey and Isla de la Juventud). Travelers will occasionally encounter *tortuga* (turtle) on the menu in places such as Baracoa. You are advised not to partake as these turtles may have been caught illegally.

LANDSCAPE & WILDLIFE WILDLIFE

Agri-cultural Highlights

Valle de Viñales (p183)

Alejandro Robaina Tobacco Plantation (p194)

Cafetal la Isabelica (p419)

Finca Raúl Reyes (p178)

It is estimated that Cuba harbors between 6500 and 7000 different species of plant, almost half of which are endemic.

BIRD-WATCHING

Cuba offers a bird-watching bonanza year-round and no serious ornithologist should enter the country without their binoculars. Your experience will be enhanced by the level of expertise shown by many of Cuba's naturalists and guides in the key bird-watching zones. Areas with specialist bird-watching trails or trips include the Cueva las Perlas (p196) trail in Parque Nacional Península de Guanahacabibes, the Maravillas de Viñales (p184) trail in Parque Nacional Viñales, the Sendero la Serafina (p152) in the Reserva Sierra del Rosario, the Observación de Aves (p230) tour in Gran Parque Natural Montemar, Parque Natural el Bagá (p310) on Cayo Coco, and the Sendero de las Aves in Hacienda la Belén (p328) in Camagüey province.

Must-sees include the *tocororo* (Cuban trogon), the *zunzuncito* (bee hummingbird), the Cuban parakeet, the Antillean palm swift, the *cartacuba* (Cuban tody; an indigenous Cuban bird) and, of course, the flamingo – preferably in a flock. Good spots for some DIY bird-watching are on Cayo Romano and adjacent Cayo Sabinal, although you'll need a car to get there. Specialists and ivory-billed-woodpecker seekers will enjoy Parque Nacional Alejandro de Humboldt.

Plants

Cuba is synonymous with the palm tree; through songs, symbols, landscapes and legends the two are inextricably linked. The national tree is the *palma real* (royal palm), and it's central to the country's coat of arms and the Cristal beer logo. It's believed there are 20 million royal palms in Cuba and locals will tell you that wherever you stand on the island, you'll always be within sight of one of them. These majestic trees reach up to 40m in height and are easily identified by their lithe trunk and green stalk at the top. There are also *cocotero* (coconut palm); *palma barrigona* (big-belly palm) with its characteristic bulge; and the extremely rare *palma corcho* (cork palm). The latter is a link with the Cretaceous period (between 65 and 135 million years ago) and is cherished as a living fossil. You can see examples of it on the grounds of the Museo de Ciencias Naturales Sandalio de Noda in Pinar del Río. Cienfuegos' Jardín Botánico also boasts some 280 different palm varieties. Cuba itself has 90 palm-tree types.

Other important trees include mangroves, in particular the spiderlike mangroves that protect the Cuban shoreline from erosion and provide an important habitat for small fish and birds. Mangroves account for 26% of Cuban forests and cover almost 5% of the island's coast; Cuba ranks ninth in the world in terms of mangrove density, and the most extensive swamps are situated in the Ciénaga de Zapata.

The largest native pine forests grow on Isla de la Juventud (the former Isle of Pines), in western Pinar del Río, in eastern Holguín's Sierra Cristal and in central Guantánamo. These forests are especially susceptible to fire damage, and pine reforestation has been a particular headache for Cuba's environmentalists.

Rainforests exist at higher altitudes – between approximately 500m and 1500m – in the Sierra del Escambray, Sierra Maestra and Macizo de Sagua-Baracoa mountains. Original rainforest species include ebony and mahogany, but today most reforestation is in eucalyptus, which is graceful and fragrant, but invasive.

Dotted liberally across the island, ferns, cacti and orchids contribute hundreds of species, many endemic, to Cuba's cornucopia of plant life. For the best concentrations check out the botanical gardens in Santiago de Cuba for ferns and cacti and Pinar del Río for orchids. Most orchids bloom from November to January, and one of the best places to see them is in the Reserva Sierra del Rosario. The national flower is the graceful

Endemic Fauna

Cuban crocodile

Bee hummingbird

Tocororo (bird)

Jutía (tree rat)

Cuban gar (fish)

Eleutherodactylus iberia (frog)

Cuban boa (snake)

Cuban red bat

mariposa (butterfly jasmine); you'll know it by its white floppy petals and strong perfume.

Medicinal plants are widespread in Cuba due largely to a chronic shortage of prescription medicines (banned under the US embargo). Pharmacies are well stocked with effective tinctures such as aloe (for cough and congestion) and a bee by-product called *propólio*, used for everything from stomach amoebas to respiratory infections. On the home front, every Cuban patio has a pot of *orégano de la tierra* (Cuban oregano) growing and if you start getting a cold you'll be whipped up a wonder elixir made from the fat, flat leaves mixed with lime juice, honey and hot water.

Environmental Issues

Most of Cuba's environmental threats are of human origin and relate either to pollution or habitat loss, often through deforestation. Efforts to conserve the archipelago's diverse ecology were almost nonexistent until 1978, when Cuba established the National Committee for the Protection and Conservation of Natural Resources and the Environment (Comarna). Attempting to reverse 400 years of deforestation and habitat destruction, the body set about designating green belts and initiating ambitious reforestation campaigns. The conservation policies are directed by Comarna, which acts as a coordinating body, overseeing 15 ministries and ensuring that current national and international environmental legislation is being carried out efficiently. This includes adherence to the important international treaties that govern Cuba's six Unesco Biosphere Reserves and nine Unesco World Heritage Sites.

Cuba's greatest environmental problems are aggravated by an economy struggling to survive. As the country pins its hopes on tourism to save the financial day, a contradictory environmental policy has evolved. Therein lies the dilemma: how can a developing nation provide for its people *and* maintain high (or at least minimal) ecological standards?

Deforestation

It is estimated that at the time of Columbus' arrival in 1492, 95% of Cuba was covered in virgin forest. By 1959, thanks to unregulated land-clearing for sugarcane and citrus plantations, this area had been reduced to a paltry 16%. The implementation of large-scale tree-planting and the organization of significant tracts of land into protected parks has seen this figure creep back up to 24% (making it the leader in Latin America), but there is still a lot of work to be done. Las Terrazas in Pinar del Río province provided a blueprint for reforestation efforts in the late 1960s, when it saved hectares of denuded woodland from ecological disaster. More recent efforts have focused on safeguarding the Caribbean's last virgin rainforest in Parque Nacional Alejandro de Humboldt and adding protective forest fringes to wetlands in the Río Cauto delta.

Causeways

An early blip in Cuba's economy-versus-ecology struggle was the 2km-long stone *pedraplén* (causeway) constructed to link offshore Cayo Sabinal with mainland Camagüey in the late 1980s. This massive project, which involved piling boulders in the sea and laying a road on top (without any bridges), interrupted water currents and caused irreparable damage to bird and marine habitats. And to what end; no resorts, as yet, inhabit deserted Cayo Sabinel. Other longer causeways were later built connecting Jardines del Rey to Ciego de Ávila (27km long) and Cayo Santa María to Villa Clara (a 48km-long monster). This time more eco-friendly bridges have enabled a healthier water flow, though the full extent of the ecological damage won't be known for another decade at least.

The Caribbean manatee can grow 4.5m long and weigh up to 600kg. It can consume up to 50kg of plant life a day.

On top of its national parks and Unesco sites, Cuba protects land in flora and fauna reserves, eco-reserves and areas of managed resources, including the Sierra del Chorrillo in Camagüey and the Reserva Ecológica Varahicacos in Varadero.

Wildlife & Habitat Loss

Maintaining healthy animal habitats is crucial in Cuba, a country with high levels of endemism and hence a higher threat of species extinction. The problem is exacerbated by the narrow range of endemic animals, such as the Cuban crocodile that lives almost exclusively in the Ciénaga de Zapata, or the equally rare *Eleutherodactylus iberia* (the world's smallest frog). The latter has a range of just 100 sq km and exists only in the Parque Nacional Alejandro de Humboldt, whose formation in 2001 undoubtedly saved it from extinction. Other areas under threat include the giant flamingo nesting sites on the Archipiélago de Sabana-Camagüey, and Moa, where contaminated water runoff has played havoc with the coastal mangrove ecosystems favored by manatees.

Building new roads and airports, and the frenzied construction of resorts on virgin beaches, exacerbate the clash between human activity and environmental protection. The grossly shrunken extent of the Reserva Ecológica Varahicacos in Varadero due to encroaching resorts is one example. Cayo Coco – part of an important Ramsar-listed wetland that sits adjacent to a fast-developing hotel strip – is another.

Overfishing (including turtles and lobster for tourist consumption), agricultural runoff, pollution and inadequate sewage treatment have contributed to the decay of coral reefs. Diseases such as yellow band, black band and nuisance algae have begun to appear. The rounding up of wild dolphins as entertainers in tourist-oriented *delfinarios* has also rankled many activists).

> Approximately 2% of Cuba's arable land is given over to coffee production and the industry supports a workforce of 265,000.

Pollution

As soon as you arrive in Havana or Santiago de Cuba, the air pollution hits you like a sharp slap on the face. Airborne particles, old trucks belching black smoke and by-products from burning garbage are just some of the culprits. Cement factories, sugar refineries and other heavy industries have also made their (dirty) mark. The nickel mines engulfing Moa serve as stark examples of industrial concerns taking precedence: this is some of the prettiest landscape in Cuba, turned into a barren wasteland of lunar proportions. Unfortunately there are no easy solutions; nickel is one of Cuba's largest exports, a raw material the economy couldn't do without. And while old American cars in Havana might paint a romantic picture to tourists, they're hardly fuel efficient. Then there's the public transport – even Fidel has gone on the record to lament the adverse health effects of Cuba's filthy buses.

Environmental Successes

On the bright side of the environmental equation is the enthusiasm the Cuban government has shown for reforestation and protecting natural areas – especially since the mid-1980s – along with its willingness to confront mistakes from the past. Havana Harbor, once Latin America's most polluted, has been undergoing a massive cleanup, as has the Río Almendares, which cuts through the heart of the city. Both programs are beginning to show positive results. Sulfur emissions from oil wells near Varadero have been reduced, and environmental regulations for developments are now enforced by the Ministry of Science, Technology and the Environment. Fishing regulations, as local fishers will tell you, have become increasingly strict. Striking the balance between Cuba's immediate needs and the future of its environment is one of the Revolution's increasingly pressing challenges.

> **Cuba's Top Eco-Resorts**
> ....
> *Hotel Moka (p153)*
> ....
> *Hotel Horizontes el Saltón (p425)*
> ....
> *Villa Pinares del Mayarí (p369)*

Las Terrazas is the nation's most obvious eco-success, though there have been others, including the implementation of three windfarm sites (in La Isla de la Juventud, Isla Turiguanó in Ciego de Ávila province and Gibara in Holguín province). Cuba's first solar farm opened in August 2014 in Cienfuegos province. In terms of fauna, the nation can point to major crocodile reintroduction programs in the Ciénaga de Zapata and on Isla de la Juventud.

Survival Guide

DIRECTORY A–Z... 500

Accommodations....... 500

Climate............... 502

Customs
Regulations............ 502

Electricity 503

Embassies & Consulates... 503

Food 503

Gay & Lesbian Travelers ...504

Health................ 504

Internet Access......... 505

Language Courses...... 505

Legal Matters 505

Maps................. 506

Money................ 506

Post................. 507

Public Holidays........ 507

Safe Travel............ 507

Telephone 507

Tourist Information 508

Travelers with
Disabilities............ 508

Visas & Tourist Cards ... 508

Volunteering 509

Women Travelers 510

TRANSPORTATION...511

GETTING THERE & AWAY... 511

Entering the Country..... 511

Air 511

Sea 513

Tours...................513

GETTING AROUND....... 513

Air 513

Bicycle 514

Bus 515

Car 516

Ferry 518

Hitchhiking 518

Local Transportation 518

Tours...................519

Train 519

Truck.................. 520

LANGUAGE 521

Glossary................. 526

Directory A–Z

Accommodations

Cuban accommodations run the gamut from CUC$10 beach cabins to five-star resorts. Solo travelers are penalized price-wise, paying 75% of the price of a double room.

Budget

In this price range, casas particulares are almost always better value than a hotel. Only the most deluxe casas particulares in Havana will be over CUC$50, and in these places you're assured quality amenities and attention. In cheaper casas particulares (CUC$15 to CUC$20) you may have to share a bathroom and will have a fan instead of air-con. In the rock-bottom places (campismos mostly), you'll be lucky if there are sheets and running water, though there are usually private bathrooms. If you're staying in a place

intended for Cubans, you'll compromise materially, but the memories are guaranteed to be platinum.

Midrange

Cuba's scant midrange category is a lottery, with some boutique colonial hotels and some awful places with spooky Soviet-like architecture and atmosphere to match. In midrange hotels you can usually expect air-con, private hot-water bathrooms, clean linens, satellite TV, a swimming pool and a restaurant, although the food won't exactly be gourmet.

Top End

The most comfortable top-end hotels are usually partly foreign-owned and maintain international standards (although service can sometimes be a bit lax). Rooms have everything that a midrange hotel has, plus big, quality beds and linens, a minibar, international phone service, and perhaps a terrace or view. Also falling into this category are the main all-inclusive resorts.

Price Differentials

Factors influencing rates are time of year, location and hotel chain. Low season is generally mid-September to early December and February to May (except for Easter week). Christmas and New Year is what's called extreme high season, when rates are 25% more than high-season

rates. Bargaining is sometimes possible in casas particulares – though as far as foreigners go, it's not really the done thing. The casa owners in any given area pay generic taxes, and the prices you will be quoted reflect this. You'll find very few casas in Cuba that aren't priced between CUC$15 and CUC$50, unless you're up for a long stay. Prearranging Cuban accommodation has become easier now that more Cubans (unofficially) have access to the internet.

Types of Accommodations

CAMPISMOS

Campismos are where Cubans go on vacation (an estimated one million use them annually). Hardly camping, most of these installations are simple concrete cabins with bunk beds, foam mattresses and cold showers. There are over 80 of them sprinkled around the country in rural areas. Campismos are ranked either *nacional* or *internacional*. The former are (technically) only for Cubans, while the latter host both Cubans and foreigners and are more upscale, with air-con and/or pools. There are currently a dozen international campismos in Cuba ranging from the hotel-standard Villa Aguas Claras (Pinar del Río) to the more basic Puerto Rico Libre (Holguín).

For advance bookings, contact the excellent **Cubamar** (☏7-833-2523, 7-833-2524; www.cubamarviajes.cu; Calle 3, btwn Calle 12 & Malecón, Vedado; ☺8:30am-5pm Mon-Sat) in Havana for reservations. Cabin accommodation in international campismos costs from CUC\$10 to CUC\$60 per bed.

CASAS PARTICULARES

Private rooms are the best option for independent travelers in Cuba and a great way of meeting the locals on their home turf. Furthermore, staying in these venerable, family-oriented establishments will give you a far more open and less censored view of the country, and your understanding and appreciation of Cuba will grow far richer as a result. Casa owners also often make excellent tour guides.

You'll know houses renting rooms by the blue insignia on the door marked 'Arrendador Divisa.' There are thousands of casas particulares all over Cuba; well over 1000 in Havana alone and over 500 in Trinidad. From penthouses to historical homes, all manner of rooms are available from CUC\$15 to CUC\$50. Although some houses will treat you like a business paycheck, the vast majority of casa owners are warm, open and impeccable hosts.

Government regulation has eased since 2011, and renters can now let out multiple rooms if they have space. Owners pay a monthly tax per room depending on location

(plus extra for off-street parking) to post a sign advertising their rooms and to serve meals. These taxes must be paid whether the rooms are rented or not. Owners must keep a register of all guests and report each new arrival within 24 hours. For this reason, you will also be requested to produce your passport (not a photocopy). Regular government inspections ensure that conditions inside casas remain clean, safe and secure. Most proprietors offer breakfast and dinner for an extra rate. Hot showers are a prerequisite. In general, rooms these days provide at least two beds (one is usually a double), fridge, air-con, fan and private bathroom. Bonuses could include a terrace or patio, private entrance, TV, security box, kitchenette and parking space.

BOOKINGS & FURTHER INFORMATION

Due to the plethora of casas particulares in Cuba, it is impossible to include even a fraction of the total. The ones chosen are a combination of reader recommendations and local research. If one casa is full, they'll almost always be able to recommend to you someone else down the road.

The following websites list a large number of casas across the country and allow online booking.

Cubacasas (www.cubacasas.net) The best online source for casa particular information and booking; up to date, accurate and with colorful links to hundreds of private rooms across the island (in English and French).

Casa Particular Organization (www.casaparticularcuba.org) Reader-recommended website for prebooking private rooms.

HOTELS

All tourist hotels and resorts are at least 51% owned by the Cuban government and are administered by one of five main organizations. Islazul is the cheapest and most popular with Cubans (who pay in Cuban pesos). Although the facilities can be variable at these establishments and the architecture a tad Soviet-esque, Islazul hotels are invariably clean, cheap, friendly and, above all, Cuban. They're also more likely to be situated in the island's smaller provincial towns. One downside is the blaring on-site discos that often keep guests awake until the small hours.

Cubanacán is a step up and

PRACTICALITIES

Newspapers Three state-controlled, national newspapers: *Granma*, *Juventud Rebelde* and *Trabajadores*.

Smoking Technically banned in enclosed spaces but only sporadically enforced.

TV Five national television channels with some imported foreign shows on the newer *Multivisión* channel.

Weights & Measures Metric system except in some fruit and vegetable markets where imperial is used.

offers a nice mix of budget and midrange options in cities and resort areas. The company has recently developed a new clutch of affordable boutique-style hotels (the Encanto brand) in attractive city centers such as Sancti Spíritus, Baracoa, Remedios and Santiago. Gaviota manages higher-end resorts including glittering 933-room Playa Pesquero, though the chain also has a smattering of cheaper 'villas' in places such as Santiago and Cayo Coco. Gran Caribe does midrange to top-end hotels, including many of the all-inclusive resorts in Havana and Varadero. Lastly, Habaguanex is based solely in Havana and manages most of the fastidiously restored historic hotels in Habana Vieja. The profits from these ventures go toward restoring Habana Vieja, which is a Unesco World Heritage Site. Except for Islazul properties, tourist hotels are for guests paying in convertible pesos only. Since May 2008 Cubans have been allowed to stay in any tourist hotels, although financially most of them are still out of reach.

At the top end of the hotel chain you'll often find foreign chains such as Sol Meliá and Iberostar running hotels in tandem with Cubanacán, Gaviota or Gran Caribe – mainly in the resort areas. The standards and service at these types of places are not unlike resorts in Mexico and the rest of the Caribbean.

Climate

Havana

Sancti Spíritus

Santiago De Cuba

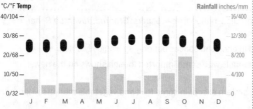

Customs Regulations

Cuban customs regulations are complicated. For the full up-to-date scoop see www.aduana.co.cu.

Entering Cuba

Travelers are allowed to bring in personal belongings including photography equipment, binoculars, a musical instrument, radio, personal computer, tent, fishing rod, bicycle, canoe and other sporting gear, and up to 10kg of medicines. Canned, processed and dried food are no problem, nor are pets (as long as they have veterinary certification and proof of rabies vaccination).

Items that do not fit into the categories mentioned above are subject to a 100% customs duty to a maximum of CUC$1000.

Items prohibited from entry into Cuba include narcotics, explosives, pornography, electrical appliances broadly defined, light motor vehicles, car engines and products of animal origin.

Leaving Cuba

You are allowed to export 50 boxed cigars duty free (or 23 singles), US$5000 (or equivalent) in cash and only CUC$200.

Exporting undocumented art and items of cultural patrimony is restricted and involves fees. Normally, when you buy art you will be given an official 'seal' at point of sale. Check this before you buy. If you don't get one, you'll need to obtain one from the **Registro Nacional de Bienes Culturales** (Calle 17 No 1009, btwn Calles 10 & 12, Vedado, Havana; ⊙9am-noon Mon-Fri) in Havana. Bring the objects here for inspection; fill in a form; pay a fee of between CUC$10 and CUC$30, which covers from one to five pieces of artwork; and return 24 hours later to pick up the certificate.

Travelers should check local import laws in their home country regarding Cuban cigars. Some countries, including Australia, charge duty on imported Cuban cigars

Electricity

The electrical current in Cuba is 110V with 220V in many tourist hotels and resorts.

110V/220V/60Hz

Embassies & Consulates

All embassies are in Havana, and most are open from 8am to noon on weekdays. Australia is represented in the Canadian Embassy. New Zealand is represented in the UK Embassy. The US is represented by a 'US Interests Section.' Canada has additional consulates in Varadero and Guardalavaca.

Austrian Embassy (☑7-204-2825; Av 5A No 6617 cnr Calle 70, Miramar)

Canadian Embassy (☑7-204-2516; Calle 30 No 518, Playa) Also represents Australia.

Danish Consulate (☑8-66-81-28; Paseo de Martí No 20, 4th fl, Centro Habana)

Dutch Embassy (☑7-204-2511; Calle 8 No 307, btwn Avs 3 & 5, Miramar)

French Embassy (☑7-201-3131; Calle 14 No 312, btwn Avs 3 & 5, Miramar)

German Embassy (☑7-833-2539; Calle 13 No 652, Vedado)

Italian Embassy (☑7-204-5615; Av 5 No 402, Miramar)

Japanese Embassy (☑7-204-3508; Miramar Trade Center, cnr Av 3 & Calle 80, Playa)

Mexican Embassy (☑7-204-7722; Calle 12 No 518, Miramar)

Spanish Embassy (☑7-866-8025; Cárcel No 51, Habana Vieja)

Swedish Embassy (☑7-204-2831; Calle 34 No 510, Miramar)

Swiss Consulate (☑7-204-2611; Av 5 No 2005, btwn Avs 20 & 22, Miramar)

UK Embassy (☑7-214-2200; Calle 34 No 702, Miramar) Also represents New Zealand.

US Interests Section (☑7-839-4100; Calzada, US Interests Section, btwn Calles L & M, Vedado) Due to become a full-blown embassy when US–Cuba diplomatic ties are restored.

Food

Cuban cuisine – popularly known as *comida criolla* – has improved immensely since new privatization laws, passed in 2011, inspired a plethora of pioneering restaurants to take root, particularly in Havana. Travel outside the bigger cities, however, and Cuban food can still be limited and insipid. See also p463 for more on food and drink in Cuba.

Where to Eat & Drink
GOVERNMENT-RUN RESTAURANTS

Government-run restaurants operate in either *moneda nacional* or convertibles. *Moneda nacional* restaurants are nearly always grim and are notorious for handing you a nine-page menu (in Spanish) when the only thing available is fried chicken. There are, however, a few newer exceptions to this rule. *Moneda nacional* restaurants will normally accept payment in CUC$, though sometimes at an inferior exchange rate to the standard 25 to one.

Restaurants that sell food in convertibles are generally more reliable, but this isn't capitalism: just because you're paying more doesn't necessarily mean better service. Food is often limp and unappetizing and discourse with bored waiters can be worthy of a *Monty Python* sketch. Things have got progressively better in the last five years. The Palmares group runs a wide variety of excellent restaurants countrywide, from bog-standard beach shacks to the *New York Times*–lauded El Aljibe in Miramar, Havana. The government-run company Habaguanex operates some of the best restaurants in Cuba in Havana, and Gaviota has recently tarted up some old staples. Employees of state-run restaurants will not earn more than CUC$20 a month (the average Cuban salary), so tips are highly appreciated.

PRIVATE RESTAURANTS

First established in 1995 during the economic chaos of the Special Period, private restaurants – formerly known as paladares – owe much of their success to the sharp increase in tourist traffic on the island, coupled with the bold experimentation of local chefs who, despite a paucity of decent ingredients, have heroically managed to keep the age-old traditions of Cuban cooking alive. They have proliferated since new business laws were passed in 2011, especially in Havana. Private-restaurant meals are generally more expensive than their state-run equivalents, costing anything between CUC$8 and CUC$30.

Vegetarians

In a land of rationing and food shortages, strict vegetarians (ie no lard, no meat bouillon, no fish) will have a hard time. Cubans don't really understand vegetarianism, and when they do (or when they *say* they do), it can be summarized rather adroitly with one key word: omelet – or, at a stretch, scrambled eggs. Cooks in casas particulares, who may already have had experience cooking meatless dishes for other travelers, are usually much better at accommodating vegetarians; just ask.

Gay & Lesbian Travelers

While Cuba can't be called a queer destination (yet), it's more tolerant than many other Latin American countries. The hit movie *Fresa y Chocolate* (Strawberry and Chocolate, 1994) sparked a national dialogue about homosexuality, and Cuba is pretty tolerant, all things considered. People from more accepting societies may find this tolerance too 'don't ask, don't tell' or tokenistic (everybody has a gay friend/relative/coworker, whom they'll mention when the topic arises) but what the hell, you have to start somewhere and Cuba is moving in the right direction.

Lesbianism is less tolerated and seldom discussed and you'll see very little open displays of gay pride between female lovers. There are occasional *fiestas para chicas* (not necessarily all-girl parties but close); ask around at the Cine Yara in Havana's gay cruising zone.

Cubans are physical with each other and you'll see men hugging, women holding hands and lots of friendly caressing. This type of casual touching shouldn't be a problem, but take care when that hug among friends turns overtly sensual in public.

Health

From a medical point of view, Cuba is generally safe as long as you're reasonably careful about what you eat and drink. The most common travel-related diseases, such as dysentery and hepatitis, are acquired by the consumption of contaminated food and water. Mosquito-borne illnesses are not a significant concern on most of the islands within the Cuban archipelago.

Prevention is the key to staying healthy while traveling around Cuba. Travelers who receive the recommended vaccines and follow commonsense precautions usually come away with nothing more than a little diarrhea.

Insurance

Since May 2010, Cuba has made it obligatory for all foreign visitors to have medical insurance. Random checks are made at the airport, so ensure you bring a printed copy of your policy.

Should you end up in hospital, call **Asistur** (☎7-866-4499, emergency 7-866-8527; www.asistur.cu; Paseo de Martí No 208, Centro Habana; ⊗8:30am-5:30pm Mon-Fri, 8am-2pm Sat) for help with insurance and medical assistance. The company has regional offices in Havana, Varadero, Cayo Coco, Guardalavaca and Santiago de Cuba.

Outpatient treatment at international clinics is reasonably priced, but emergency and prolonged hospitalization gets expensive (the free medical system for Cubans should only be used when there is no other option).

Should you have to purchase medical insurance on arrival, you will pay between CUC$2.50 and CUC$3 per day for coverage of up to CUC$25,000 in medical expenses (for illness) and CUC$10,000 for repatriation of a sick person.

Health Care for Foreigners

The Cuban government has established a for-profit health system for foreigners called **Servimed** (☑7-24-01-41; www. servimedcuba.com), which is entirely separate from the free, not-for-profit system that takes care of Cuban citizens. There are more than 40 Servimed health centers across the island, offering primary care as well as a variety of specialty and high-tech services. If you're staying in a hotel, the usual way to access the system is to ask the manager for a physician referral. Servimed centers accept walk-ins. While Cuban hospitals provide some free emergency treatment for foreigners, this should only be used when there is no other option. Remember that in Cuba medical resources are scarce and the local populace should be given priority in free health-care facilities.

Almost all doctors and hospitals expect payment in cash, regardless of whether you have travel health insurance or not. If you develop a life-threatening medical problem, you'll probably want to be evacuated to a country with state-of-the-art medical care. Since this may cost tens of thousands of dollars, be sure you have insurance to cover this before you depart.

There are special pharmacies for foreigners also run by the Servimed system, but all Cuban pharmacies are notoriously short on supplies, including pharmaceuticals. Be sure to bring along adequate quantities of all medications you might need, both prescription and over the counter. Also, be sure to bring along a fully stocked medical kit. Pharmacies marked *turno permanente* or *pilotos* are open 24 hours.

Water

Tap water in Cuba is not reliably safe to drink and outbreaks of cholera have been recorded in the past few years. Bottled water called Ciego Montero rarely costs more than CUC$1, but is sometimes not available in small towns. Stock up in the cities when going on long bus or car journeys.

Internet Access

State-run telecommunications company Etecsa has a monopoly as Cuba's internet service provider. For public internet access, you'll have to decamp to one of their Etecsa *telepuntos* available in almost every provincial town. The drill is to buy a one-hour user card (CUC$4.50) with scratch-off *usuario* (code) and *contraseña* (password) and help yourself to an available computer. These cards are interchangeable in any *telepunto* across the country, so you don't have to use up your whole hour in one go. The downside of the Etecsa monopoly is that there are few, if any, independent internet cafes outside the *telepuntos*. As a general rule, most three- to five-star hotels (and all resort hotels) will have their own internet terminals. Usually the terminals in these places are less busy and more reliable than Etecsa, although the fees are often higher (sometimes as much as CUC$12 per hour).

As internet access for Cubans is ostensibly limited, you may be asked to show your passport when using a *telepunto* (although if you look obviously foreign, they won't bother). On the plus side, the Etecsa places are open long hours and are seldom crowded.

Wi-fi is slowly catching on in Cuba's better hotels. Towns with reasonable wi-fi coverage include Baracoa, Havana and Trinidad. You can use your CUC$4.50 Etecsa card for wi-fi when it is available. Warning: connections are often slow and temperamental.

Language Courses

Cuba's rich cultural tradition and the abundance of highly talented, trained professionals make it a great place to study Spanish. Technological and linguistic glitches, plus general unresponsiveness, make it hard to set up courses before arriving, but you can arrange everything once you get here. In Cuba, things are always better done face to face.

The best official Spanish-language courses are available at Cuba's two leading universities: the **Universidad de La Habana** (Map p88; ☑7-831-3751, 7-832-4245; www. uh.cu; Calle J No 556, Edificio Varona, 2nd fl, Vedado) and the **Universidad Central Marta Abreu de las Villas** (☑28-14-10; www.uclv.edu.cu; Carretera de Camajuaní Km 5.5) in Santa Clara. It's useful, though not imperative, to book in advance.

Students heading to Cuba should bring a good bilingual dictionary and a basic 'learn Spanish' textbook, as such books are scarce or expensive in Cuba. You might sign up for a two-week course at a university to get your feet wet and then jump into private classes once you've made some contacts.

Legal Matters

Cuban police are everywhere and they're usually very friendly – more likely to ask you for a date than a bribe. Corruption is a serious offense in Cuba, and typically no one wants to get mixed up in it. Getting caught out without identification is never good; carry some around just in case (a driver's license, a copy of your passport or a student ID card should be sufficient).

Drugs are prohibited in Cuba, though you may still get offered marijuana and cocaine on the streets of Havana. Penalties for buying, selling, holding or taking drugs are serious, and Cuba is making a concerted effort to treat demand and curtail supply; it is only the foolish traveler who partakes while on a Cuban vacation.

Maps

Signage is awful in Cuba, so a good map is essential for drivers and cyclists alike. The comprehensive *Guía de Carreteras*, published in Italy, includes the best maps available in Cuba. It usually comes free when you hire a car, though some travelers have been asked to pay between CUC$5 and CUC$10. It has a complete index, a detailed Havana map and useful information in English, Spanish, Italian and French. Handier is the all-purpose *Automapa Nacional*, available at hotel shops and car-rental offices.

The best map published outside Cuba is the Freytag & Berndt 1:1.25 million *Cuba* map. The island map is good, and it has indexed town plans of Havana, Playas del Este, Varadero, Cienfuegos, Camagüey and Santiago de Cuba.

For good basic maps, pick up one of the provincial *Guías* available in Infotur offices.

Money

This is a tricky part of any Cuban trip, as the double economy takes some getting used to. As of early 2015, two currencies were still circulating in Cuba: convertible pesos (CUC$) and Cuban

pesos (referred to as *moneda nacional*, abbreviated MN$). Most things tourists pay for are in convertibles (eg accommodation, rental cars, bus tickets, museum admission and internet access). At the time of writing, Cuban pesos were selling at 25 to one convertible, and while there are many things you can't buy with *moneda nacional*, using them on certain occasions means you'll see a bigger slice of authentic Cuba. The prices we list are in convertibles unless otherwise stated.

Making everything a little more confusing, euros are also accepted at the Varadero, Guardalavaca, Cayo Largo del Sur, Cayo Coco and Cayo Guillermo resorts, but once you leave the resort grounds, you'll still need convertibles.

The best currencies to bring to Cuba are euros, Canadian dollars or pounds sterling. The worst is US dollars, for which you will be penalized with a 10% fee (on top of the normal commission) when you buy convertibles (CUC$). Since 2011, the Cuban convertible has been pegged 1:1 to the US dollar, meaning its rate will fluctuate depending on the strength/weakness of the US dollar. Australian dollars are not accepted anywhere in Cuba.

Cadeca branches in every city and town sell Cuban pesos. You won't need more than CUC$10 worth of pesos a week. There is almost always a branch at the local *agropecuario* (vegetable market). If you get caught

without Cuban pesos and are drooling for that ice-cream cone, you can always use convertibles; in street transactions such as these, CUC$1 is equal to 25 pesos and you'll receive change in pesos. There is no black market in Cuba, only hustlers trying to fleece you with money-changing scams.

ATMs & Credit Cards

The acceptance of credit cards has become more widespread in Cuba in recent years and was aided by the legalization of US and US-linked credit and debit cards in early 2015. When weighing up whether to use a credit card or cash, bear in mind that the charges levied by Cuban banks are similar for both (around 3%). However, your home bank may charge additional fees for ATM/credit-card transactions. Ideally, it is best to arrive in the Cuba with a stash of cash and a credit card and debit card as backup. (An increasing number of debit cards work in Cuba, but it's best to check with both your home bank and the local Cuban bank before using them.)

Almost all private business in Cuba (ie casas particulares and private restaurants) is still conducted in cash.

Cash advances can be drawn from credit cards, but the commission is the same. Check with your home bank before you leave, as many banks won't authorize large withdrawals in foreign countries unless you notify them of your travel plans first.

ATMs are becoming more common. They are the equivalent to obtaining a cash advance over the counter. This being Cuba, it is wise to only use ATMs when the bank is open, in case any problems occur.

Cash

Cuba is a cash economy and credit cards don't have the importance or ubiquity that they do elsewhere in the western hemisphere.

CURRENCY UNIFICATION

In October 2013, Raul Castro announced that Cuba would gradually unify its dual currencies (convertibles and *moneda nacional*). As a result, prices are liable to change. At the time of writing, the unification process had yet to begin and no further details had emerged as to when or how the government will go about implementing the complex changes. Check www.lonelyplanet.com for updates.

Although carrying just cash is far riskier than the usual cash/credit card/debit card mix, it's infinitely more convenient. As long as you use a concealed money belt and keep the cash on you or in your hotel's safety deposit box at all times, you should be OK.

It's better to ask for CUC$20/10/5/3/1 bills when you're changing money, as many smaller Cuban businesses (taxis, restaurants etc) can't change anything bigger (ie CUC$50 or CUC$100 bills) and the words *no hay cambio* (no change) echo everywhere. If desperate, you can always break big bills at hotels.

DENOMINATIONS & LINGO

One of the most confusing parts of a double economy is terminology. Cuban pesos are called *moneda nacional* (abbreviated MN) or *pesos Cubanos* or simply pesos, while convertible pesos are called *pesos convertibles* (abbreviated CUC), or simply pesos (again!). More recently people have been referring to them as *cucs*. Sometimes you'll be negotiating in *pesos Cubanos* and your counterpart will be negotiating in *pesos convertibles*. It doesn't help that the notes look similar as well. Worse, the symbol for both convertibles and Cuban pesos is $. You can imagine the potential scams just working these combinations.

The Cuban peso comes in notes of one, five, 10, 20, 50 and 100 pesos; and coins of one (rare), five and 20 centavos, and one and three pesos. The five-centavo coin is called a *medio,* the 20-centavo coin a *peseta*. Centavos are also called *kilos*.

The convertible peso comes in multicolored notes of one, three, five, 10, 20, 50 and 100 pesos; and coins of five, 10, 25 and 50 centavos, and one peso.

Post

Letters and postcards sent to Europe and the US take about a month to arrive. While *sellos* (stamps) are sold in Cuban pesos and convertibles, correspondence bearing the latter has a better chance of arriving. Postcards cost CUC$0.65 to all countries. Letters cost CUC$0.65 to the Americas, CUC$0.75 to Europe and CUC$0.85 to all other countries. Prepaid postcards, including international postage, are available at most hotel shops and post offices and are the surest bet for successful delivery. For important mail, you're better off using DHL, which is located in all the major cities; it costs CUC$55 for a 900g letter pack to Australia, or CUC$50 to Europe.

Public Holidays

Officially Cuba has nine public holidays. Other important national days to look out for include: January 28 (anniversary of the birth of José Martí); April 19 (Bay of Pigs victory); October 8 (anniversary of the death of Che Guevara); October 28 (anniversary of the death of Camilo Cienfuegos); and December 7 (anniversary of the death of Antonio Maceo).

January 1 Triunfo de la Revolución (Liberation Day)

January 2 Día de la Victoria (Victory of the Armed Forces)

May 1 Día de los Trabajadores (International Worker's Day)

July 25 Commemoration of Moncada Attack

July 26 Día de la Rebeldía Nacional – Commemoration of Moncada Attack

July 27 Commemoration of Moncada Attack

October 10 Día de la Indepedencia (Independence Day)

December 25 Navidad (Christmas Day)

December 31 New Year's Eve

Safe Travel

Cuba is generally safer than most countries, and violent attacks are extremely rare. Petty theft (eg rifled luggage in hotel rooms or unattended shoes disappearing from the beach) is common, but preventative measures work wonders. Pickpocketing is preventable: wear your bag in front of you on crowded buses and at busy markets, and only take what money you'll need when you head out at night.

Begging is more widespread and is exacerbated by tourists who hand out money, soap, pens, chewing gum and other things to people on the street. If you truly want to do something to help, pharmacies and hospitals will accept medicine donations, schools happily take pens, paper, crayons etc, and libraries will gratefully accept books. Alternatively, pass stuff onto your casa particular owner or leave it at a local church. Hustlers are called *jineteros/jineteras* (male/female touts), and can be a real nuisance.

Telephone

The Cuban phone system is still undergoing upgrades, so beware of phone-number changes. Normally a recorded message will inform you of recent upgrades. Most of the country's Etecsa *telepuntos* have now been completely refurbished, which means there will be a spick-and-span (as well as air-conditioned) phone and internet office in almost every provincial town.

Cell-phone usage has become much more widespread in Cuba in the last few years.

Cell Phones

Cuba's cell-phone company is called **Cubacel** (www.cubacel.com). You can use your own GSM or TDMA phones in Cuba, though you'll have to pay an activation fee (approximately CUC$30). Cubacel has numerous offices around the country (including at the Havana airport) where you can do this. After this you're looking at between CUC$0.30 to CUC$0.45 per minute for calls within Cuba and CUC$2.45 to CUC$5.85 for international calls. To rent a phone in Cuba costs CUC$6 plus CUC$3 per day activation fee. You'll also need to pay a CUC$100 deposit. Charges after this amount to around CUC$0.35 per minute. For up-to-date costs and information see www.etecsa.cu.

Phone Codes

➜ To call Cuba from abroad, dial your international access code, Cuba's country code (53), the city or area code (minus the '0,' which is used when dialing domestically between provinces) and the local number.

➜ To call internationally from Cuba, dial Cuba's international access code (✆119), the country code, the area code and the number. To the US, you just dial ✆119, then 1, the area code and the number.

➜ To call cell phone to cell phone just dial the eight-digit number (which always starts with a '5').

➜ To call cell phone to landline dial the provincial code plus the local number.

➜ To call landline to cell phone dial '✆01' (or '0' if in Havana) followed by the eight-digit cell-phone number.

➜ To call landline to landline dial '✆0' plus the provincial code plus the local number.

Phone Cards

Etecsa is where you buy phone cards, use the internet and make international calls. Blue public Etecsa phones accepting magnetized or computer-chip cards are everywhere. The cards are sold in convertibles (CUC$5, CUC$10 and CUC$20), and in *moneda nacional* (five and 10 pesos). You can call nationally with either, but you can call internationally only with convertible cards.

You will also see coin-operated phone booths good for Cuban pesos *(moneda nacional)* only.

Phone Rates

Local calls cost from five centavos per minute and will vary with time of day and distance, while interprovincial calls cost from around CUC$1.40 per minute (note that only the peso coins with the star work in pay phones). Since most coin phones don't return change, common courtesy means that you should push the 'R' button so that the next person in line can make their call with your remaining money.

International calls made with a card cost from CUC$2 per minute to the US and Canada and CUC$5 to Europe and Oceania. Calls placed through an operator cost slightly more.

Hotels with three stars and up usually offer slightly pricier international phone rates.

Tourist Information

Cuba's official tourist-information bureau is called **Infotur** (www.infotur.cu). It has offices in all the main provincial towns and desks in most of the bigger hotels and airports. Travel agencies, such as Cubanacán, Cubatur, Gaviota and Ecotur, can usually supply some general information.

Travelers with Disabilities

Cuba's inclusive culture extends to disabled travelers, and while facilities may be lacking, the generous nature of Cubans generally compensates. Sight-impaired travelers will be helped across streets and given priority in lines. The same holds true for travelers in wheelchairs, who will find the few ramps ridiculously steep and will have trouble in colonial parts of town where sidewalks are narrow and streets are cobblestone. Elevators are often out of order. Etecsa phone centers have telephone equipment for the hearing-impaired, and TV programs are broadcast with closed captioning.

Visas & Tourist Cards

Regular tourists who plan to spend up to two months in Cuba do not need visas. Instead, you get a *tarjeta de turista* (tourist card) valid for 30 days, which can be extended once you're in Cuba (Canadians get 90 days plus the option of a 90-day extension). Package tourists receive their card with their other travel documents. Those going 'air only' usually buy the tourist card from the travel agency or airline office that sells them the plane ticket, but policies vary (eg Canadian airlines give out tourist cards on their airplanes), so you'll need to check ahead with the airline office via phone or email. In some cases, you may be required to buy and/or pick up the card at your departure airport. Some independent travelers have been denied access to Cuba flights because they inadvertently haven't obtained a tourist card.

Once in Havana, tourist-card extensions or replacements cost another CUC$25. You cannot leave Cuba without presenting your tourist card. If you lose it, you can expect to face at least a day of frustrating Cuba-style bureaucracy to get it replaced.

You are not permitted entry to Cuba without an onward ticket.

Fill the tourist card out clearly and carefully, as Cuban customs are particularly fussy about crossings out and illegibility.

Business travelers and journalists need visas. Applications should be made through a consulate at least three weeks in advance (longer if you apply through a consulate in a country other than your own).

Visitors with visas or anyone who has stayed in Cuba longer than 90 days must apply for an exit permit from an immigration office. The Cuban consulate in London issues official visas (£32 plus two photos). They take two weeks to process, and the name of an official contact in Cuba is necessary.

Licenses for US Visitors

The US government issues two sorts of licenses for travel to Cuba: 'specific' and 'general.' Specific licenses require a lengthy and sometimes complicated application process and are considered on a case-by-case basis; it is recommended that you apply at least 45 days before your intended date of departure. General licenses are self-qualifying.

Supporting documentation to back up your claim must be sent to an authorized travel-service provider when you book your flight ticket. The nature of this documentation will vary depending on which category you fall into. To minimise bogus claims, travel-service providers require all US travelers to sign a 'travel affidavit' (a sworn statement) which may be viewed by US immigration officials when returning from Cuba. Check with the **US Department of the Treasury** (www.treasury. gov/resource-center/sanctions/Programs/pages/cuba. aspx) to see if you qualify for a license.

Extensions

For most travelers, obtaining an extension once in Cuba is easy: you just go to the *inmigración* (immigration office) and present your documents and CUC$25 in stamps. Obtain these stamps from a branch of Bandec or Banco Financiero Internacional beforehand. You'll only receive an additional 30 days after your original 30 days (apart from Canadians who get an additional 90 days after their original 90), but you can exit and re-enter the country for 24 hours and start over again (some travel agencies in Havana have special deals for this type of trip). Attend to extensions at least a few business days before your visa is due to expire and never attempt travel around Cuba with an expired visa.

Cuban Immigration Offices

Nearly all provincial towns have an immigration office (where you can extend your visa), though the staff rarely speak English and aren't always overly helpful. Try to avoid Havana's office if you can, as it gets ridiculously crowded. Hours are normally 8am to 7pm Monday, Wednesday and Friday, 8am to 5pm Tuesday, 8am to noon Thursday and Saturday.

Immigration Office (Antonio Maceo No 48, Baracoa)

Immigration Office (Carretera Central, Km 2, Bayamo) In a big complex 200m south of the Hotel Sierra Maestra.

Immigration Office (Calle 3 No 156, btwn Calles 8 & 10, Reparto Vista Hermosa, Camagüey)

Immigration Office (cnr Delgado & Independencia, Ciego de Ávila)

Immigration Office (☑43-52-10-17; Av 46, btwn Calles 29 & 31, Cienfuegos)

Immigration Office (Calle 1 Oeste, btwn Calles 14 & 15 Norte, Guantánamo) Directly behind Hotel Guantánamo.

Immigration Office (Calle 17 No 203, btwn J&K, Vedado, Havana)

Immigration Office (Calle Fomento No 256 cnr Peralejo, Holguín) Arrive early – it gets crowded here.

Immigration Office (Av Camilo Cienfuegos, Reparto Buenavista, Las Tunas) Northeast of the train station.

Immigration Office (☑41-32-47-29; Independencia Norte No 107, Sancti Spíritus)

Immigration Office (cnr Av Sandino & Sexta, Santa Clara) Three blocks east of Estadio Sandino.

Immigration Office (☑22-65-75-07; Av Pujol No 10, btwn Calle 10 & Anacaona) Stamps for visa extensions are sold at the Banco de Crédito y Comercio at Felix Peña No 614 on Parque Céspedes.

Immigration Office (Julio Cueva Díaz, Trinidad) Off Paseo Agramonte.

Immigration Office (cnr Av 1 & Calle 39, Varadero)

Volunteering

There are a number of bodies offering volunteer work in Cuba, though it is always best to organize things in your home country first. Just turning up in Havana and volunteering can be difficult, if not impossible.

Canada-Cuba Farmer to Farmer Project (www.farmertofarmer.ca) Vancouver-based sustainable agriculture organization.

Cuban Solidarity Campaign (www.cuba-solidarity. org) Head office in London, UK.

Pastors for Peace (www. ifconews.org) Collects donations across the US to take to Cuba.

Witness for Peace (www. witnessforpeace.org) Looking for Spanish-speakers with a two-year commitment.

Women Travelers

In terms of physical safety, Cuba is a dream destination for women travelers. Most streets can be walked alone at night, violent crime is rare and the chivalrous part of machismo means you'll never step into oncoming traffic. But machismo cuts both ways, protecting on one side and pursuing – relentlessly – on the other. Cuban women are used to *piropos* (the whistles, kissing sounds and compliments constantly ringing in their ears), and might even reply with their own if they're feeling frisky. For foreign women, however, it can feel like an invasion.

Ignoring *piropos* is the first step. But sometimes ignoring isn't enough. Learn some rejoinders in Spanish so you can shut men up. *No me moleste* (don't bother me), *está bueno ya* (all right already) or *que falta respeto* (how disrespectful) are good ones, as is the withering 'don't you dare' stare that is also part of the Cuban woman's arsenal. Wearing plain, modest clothes might help lessen unwanted attention; topless sunbathing is out. An absent husband, invented or not, seldom has any effect. If you go to a disco, be very clear with Cuban dance partners what you are and are not interested in.

Transportation

GETTING THERE & AWAY

Entering the Country

Whether it's your first or 50th time, descending low into José Martí International Airport, over rust-red tobacco fields, is an exciting and unforgettable experience. Fortunately, entry procedures are relatively straightforward, and with approximately three million visitors a year, immigration officials are used to dealing with foreign arrivals.

Outside Cuba, the capital city is called Havana, and this is how travel agents, airlines and other professionals will refer to it. Within Cuba, it's almost always called La Habana. For the sake of consistency, we use the former spelling.

Flights, tours and rail tickets can be booked online at lonelyplanet.com/bookings.

Air

Airports

Cuba has 10 international airports. The largest by far is José Martí in Havana. The only other sizeable airport is Juan Gualberto Gómez in Varadero.

'Special Authority Charter flights' for legally sanctioned Cuban-Americans currently fly into four Cuban airports from Miami, Tampa, Atlanta, Fort Lauderdale and New York.

Airlines

In Havana most airline offices are situated in one of two clusters: the **Airline Building** (Calle 23 No 64) in Vedado, or in the **Miramar Trade Center** (Map p128; Av 3, btwn Calles 76 & 80, Miramar) in Playa.

Cubana (www.cubana.cu), the national carrier, operates regular flights to Bogotá, Buenos Aires, Mexico City, Cancún, Caracas, Madrid, Paris, Toronto, Montreal, São Paulo, San José (Costa Rica) and Santo Domingo (Dominican Republic). Its modern fleet flies major routes and its airfares are usually among the cheapest. However, overbooking and delays are nagging problems. The airline has a zero-tolerance attitude toward overweight luggage, charging stiffly for every kilogram above the 20kg baggage allowance. In terms of safety, Cubana had back-to-back crashes in December 1999, with 39 fatalities, but it hasn't had any major incidents since. You might want to check the latest at www.airsafe.com.

AFRICA

Direct flights from Africa originate in Luanda, Angola. From all other African countries you'll need to connect in London, Paris, Madrid, Amsterdam or Rome.

TAAG (www.taag.com) Weekly flights from Luanda to Havana.

ASIA & AUSTRALIA

There are no direct flights to Cuba from Australia. Travelers can connect through Europe, Canada, the US or Mexico.

Air China (www.airchina.com) Thrice weekly flights between Beijing and Havana starting in September 2015.

CANADA

Flights from Canada serve 10 Cuban airports from 22 Canadian cities. Toronto and Montreal are the main hubs. Other cities are served by direct charter flights. **A Nash Travel** (www.anashtravel.com), based in Toronto, can sort out any flight/holiday queries.

Air Canada (www.aircanada. com) Flies to Havana, Cayo Coco, Cayo Largo del Sur, Holguín, Santa Clara and Varadero.

Air Transat (www.airtransat. com) Flies to Camagüey, Cayo Coco, Holguín, Santa Clara and Varadero.

CanJet (www.canjet.com) Flies to Camagüey, Cayo Coco, Cayo Largo del Sur, Holguín, Santa Clara, Santiago de Cuba, Varadero.

Sunwing (www.flysunwing. com) Flies to Cayo Coco, Camagüey, Cienfuegos, Manzanillo, Holguín, Santiago de Cuba, Varadero and Havana.

Westjet (www.westjet.com) Calgary-based low-cost carrier serving destinations throughout Canada, flying to Varadero, Cayo Coco, Santa Clara and Holguín.

CARIBBEAN

Cubana and subsidiary **Aerocaribbean** (www.fly-aerocaribbean.com) are the main airlines. The other three are listed below.

Air Caraibes Airlines (www. aircaraibes.com) Direct flights from Pointe-a-Pitre on the French island of Guadeloupe to Havana.

Bahamasair (www.bahamasair.com) Nassau, in the Bahamas, to Havana.

Cayman Airways (www. caymanairways.com) Grand Cayman to Havana.

EUROPE & UK

Regular flights to Cuba depart from Belgium, France, Germany, the Netherlands, Italy, Russia, Spain, Switzerland and the UK.

Aeroflot (www.aeroflot.ru) Moscow to Havana, twice weekly.

Air Europa (www.aireuropa. com) Twice weekly flights from Madrid to Havana.

Air France (www.airfrance. com) Daily flights from Paris-Charles de Gaulle to Havana.

Arkefly (www.arkefly.nl) Amsterdam to Varadero.

Blue Panorama (www. blue-panorama.com) Milan and Rome to Cayo Largo del Sur, Santa Clara, Santiago, Varadero and Havana.

Condor (www.condor.com) Frankfurt to Holguín, Varadero and Havana.

Edelwiess (www.edelweissair. ch) From Zurich to Holguín and Varadero.

Jetairfly (www.jetairfly.com) Charter flights from Brussels to Varadero.

KLM (www.klm.com) Amsterdam to Havana on Sunday, Monday, Wednesday and Thursday.

Neos (www.neosair.it) Charter linking Milan with Cayo Largo del Sur, Holguín, Havana and Varadero.

Thomas Cook (www.thomascook.com) Charter flights from London and Manchester to Holguín, Cayo Coco, Santa Clara and Varadero.

Transaero (www.transaero. com) Seasonal charter from Moscow to Havana Varadero.

Virgin Atlantic (www.virgin-atlantic.com) Twice weekly flights from London Gatwick to Havana.

MEXICO

Mexico City and Cancún are good places to connect with a wide number of US cities.

Interjet (www.interjet.com. mx) Flights from Mexico City to Havana.

SOUTH & CENTRAL AMERICA

Avianca (www.avianca.com) Flies from Bogotá, Colombia into Havana and Varadero.

Conviasa (www.conviasa. aero) Weekly flights from Caracas, Venezuela, to Havana.

Copa Airlines (www.copaair. com) Regular flights linking Panama City with Havana and Santa Clara.

Lan Peru (www.lan.com) Weekly flights from Lima to Havana.

UNITED STATES

Since the moves by the Obama administration to ease travel restrictions to Cuba in early 2015, charter flights between the US and Cuba have proliferated. The US Department of the Treasury issues a regularly updated list of 'Authorized Travel Service Providers' who can make charter bookings. Top companies include **Cuba Travel Services** (www. cubatravelservices.com), **ABC Charters** (www.abc-charters. com) and **Marazul** (www. marazulcharters.com). You will be required to furnish the service provider with your license details along with a signed travel affidavit when booking tickets.

At the time of writing, regular charters were flying on routes between New York, Miami and Tampa, and at least six Cuban airports including Havana, Santa Clara and Santiago de Cuba. With new flights being added all the time, it is advisable to check ahead with your travel service provider before booking.

In April 2015 **Cheap Air** (www.cheapair.com) became the first company to offer online flight bookings between the US and Cuba.

Tickets

Since unlicensed Americans can't buy tickets to Cuba and can't use US-based travel agents, a host of businesses in Mexico, Canada and the Caribbean specialize in air-only deals. They sometimes won't sell you the first leg of your trip to the 'gateway' country for fear of embargo-related repercussions. When booking online, or if an agency requires financial acrobatics to steer clear of US embargo laws (which sometimes happens), be sure to confirm details, take contact names and clarify the procedure. You will need a Cuban tourist card and these agencies should arrange that. Except during peak holiday seasons, you can usually just arrive in Mexico, Bahamas or whatever gateway country and buy your round-trip ticket to Cuba there.

Sea

Cruises

Thanks to the US embargo, which prohibits vessels calling at Cuban ports from visiting the US for six months, few cruise ships include Cuba on their itineraries. Canadian company **Cuba Cruise** (www.yourcubacruise.com) runs an interesting circumnavigation of Cuba calling in at Havana, Holguín, Santiago, Montego Bay (Jamaica), Cienfuegos and La Isla de la Juventud. Trips run weekly December to March. Prices start at approximately US$780. Another option is with British-based **Thomson** (www.thomson.co.uk) whose seven-night *Cuban Fusion* trip runs out of Montego Bay, Jamaica, and costs around £700.

Ferry

At the time of writing. there were no scheduled ferry services to Cuba. It is expected that ferry and catamaran services between Florida and Cuba will begin in the latter part of 2015 sailing between Miami/Fort Lauderdale and Havana. High-speed boats will make the crossing in around four hours and likely charge cheaper fares than the airlines.

Private Yacht

If you have your own private yacht or cruiser, Cuba has seven international entry ports equipped with customs facilities:

➡ Marina Hemingway (Havana)

➡ Marina Dásena (Varadero)

➡ Marina Cienfuegos

➡ Marina Cayo Guillermo

➡ Marina Santiago de Cuba

➡ Puerto de Vita (near Guardalavaca in Holguín province)

➡ Cayo Largo del Sur

➡ Cabo San Antonio (far western tip of Pinar del Río province)

Boat owners should communicate with the Cuban coast guard on VHF 16 and 68 or the tourist network 19A.

Tours

Cuba is popular on the organized-tour circuit, especially in the realm of soft adventure. There are also specialist tours focusing on culture, the environment, adventure, cycling, bird-watching, architecture, hiking, you name it.

Cuban Adventures (www.cubagrouptour.com) Australian-based company specializing in Cuba travel, running small tours with mainly local guides.

Exodus (www.exodus.co.uk) British-based adventure-travel company offering over half a dozen regular Cuba trips, including family travel and a two-week cycling excursion.

Explore (www.explore.co.uk) Eleven different trips including a hiking-focused 'revolutionary trails' excursion that ascends Pico Turquino.

GETTING AROUND

Air

Cubana de Aviación (www.cubana.cu) and its regional carrier Aerocaribbean have flights between Havana and 11 regional airports. There are no internal connections

TOURS FROM THE US

Since January 2011, Americans have been able to travel legally to Cuba on government-sanctioned people-to-people trips (cultural trips with licensed providers). The people-to-people program reflects efforts by the US government to engage US citizens in 'purposeful travel' to Cuba by bringing them into contact with ordinary Cubans in the hope of bolstering trust and mutual understanding between the two countries. On these trips, authorized agents handle the license paperwork, leaving participants with fewer legal worries and more downtime to enjoy organized excursions in a similar way to other vacationers. The **US Treasury department** (www.treasury.gov/resource-center/sanctions/Programs/pages/cuba.aspx) has issued licenses to approximately 140 registered people-to-people travel companies since 2011, including travel pioneers **Insight Cuba** (www.insightcuba.com), who first ran excursions to the country during the Clinton era, along with **Moto Discovery** (www.motodiscovery.com), **Friendly Planet** (www.friendlyplanet.com), **Grand Circle Foundation** (www.grandcirclefoundation.org) and **Geographic Expeditions** (www.geoex.com).

Marazul Charters Inc (www.marazulcharters.com) Has been facilitating travel to Cuba for over 30 years and can help place you on legal sponsored trips. The company can also book tickets on their own charter flights direct from Miami to Havana or Camagüey.

Cuba Travel Services (www.cubatravelservices.com) Can arrange and book flights between the US and Cuba.

Insight Cuba (www.insightcuba.com) A well-established registered people-to-people operator. Tours include a one-week jazz-themed excursion and a trip to run the Havana marathon in November.

Air Routes

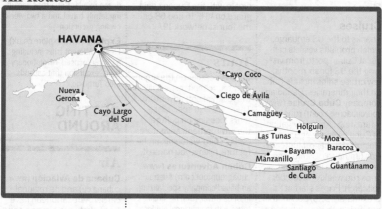

DOMESTIC FLIGHTS FROM HAVANA

DESTINATION	FREQUENCY	DURATION
Baracoa	1 weekly	2½hr
Bayamo	2 weekly	2hr
Camagüey	daily	1½hr
Cayo Coco	daily	1¼hr
Cayo Largo del Sur	daily	40min
Ciego de Ávila	1 weekly	1¼hr
Guantánamo	5 weekly	2½hr
Holguín	2-3 daily	1½hr
Isla de la Juventud	2 daily	40min
Manzanillo	1 weekly	2hr
Moa	1 weekly	3hr
Santiago de Cuba	2-3 daily	2¼hr

between the airports except via Havana.

One-way flights are half the price of round-trip flights and weight restrictions are strict (especially on Aerocaribbean's smaller planes). You can purchase tickets at most hotel tour desks and travel agencies for the same price as at the airline offices, which are often chaotic.

Aerogaviota (www. aerogaviota.com; Av 47 No 2814, btwn Calles 28 & 34, Playa, Havana) runs more expensive charter flights to La Coloma and Cayo Levisa (Pinar del Río province), Nueva Gerona, Cayo Largo del Sur, Varadero, Cayo Las Brujas, Cayo Coco,

Playa Santa Lucía and Santiago de Cuba.

Bicycle

Cuba is a cyclist's paradise, with bike lanes, bike workshops and drivers accustomed to sharing the road countrywide. Spare parts are difficult to find – you should bring important spares with you. Still, Cubans are grand masters at improvised repair and, though specific parts may not be available, something can surely be juryrigged. *Poncheros* (puncture repair stalls) fix flat tires and provide air; every small town has one.

Helmets are unheard of in Cuba except at upscale resorts, so you should bring your own. A lock is imperative, as bicycle theft is rampant. *Parqueos* are bicycle parking lots located wherever crowds congregate (eg markets, bus terminals, downtown etc); they cost one peso.

Throughout the country, the 1m-wide strip of road to the extreme right is reserved for bicycles, even on highways. It's illegal to ride on sidewalks and against traffic on one-way streets and you'll be ticketed if caught. Road lighting is deplorable, so avoid riding after dark (over onethird of vehicle accidents in

Cuba involve bicycles); carry lights with you just in case.

Trains with *coches de equipaje* or *bagones* (baggage carriages) should take bikes for around CUC$10 per trip. These compartments are guarded, but take your panniers with you and check over the bike when you arrive at your destination. Víazul buses also take bikes.

Purchase

Limited selection and high prices make buying a bike in Cuba through official channels unattractive. Better to ask around and strike a deal with an individual to buy their *chivo* (Cuban slang for bike) and trade it or resell it when you leave. With some earnest bargaining, you can get one for around CUC$30 – although the more you pay, the less your bones are likely to shake. Despite the obvious cost savings, bringing your own bike is still the best bet by far.

Rental

Official bike rental places are scant in Cuba, though, with the private economy taking off so rapidly, this could change. You can usually pro-

cure something roadworthy for between CUC$3 per hour or CUC$15 per day. Bikes are usually included as a perk in all-inclusive resort packages, but beware of bad brakes and zero gears.

Bus

Bus travel is a dependable way of getting around Cuba, at least in the more popular areas. **Víazul** (www.viazul.com) is the main long-distance bus company available to non-Cubans, with fairly punctual, air-conditioned coaches going to destinations of interest to travelers. Víazul charges for tickets in convertibles, and you can be confident you'll get where you're going on these buses – usually on time. Buses schedule regular stops for lunch/dinner and always carry two drivers. They have daily departures, but are becoming increasingly busy. Reserve ahead on the more popular routes.

Conectando run by Cubanacán is a newer option set up to relieve some of Víazul's overcrowding. The

pros are that they run between city center hotels and can be booked head of time at Infotur and Cubanacán offices. The cons are that the schedules aren't as reliable or extensive as Víazul. Check ahead that your bus is running.

Many of the popular tourist areas now have 'bus tours,' hop-on/hop-off buses that link all the main sights in a given area and charge CUC$5 for an all-day ticket. The services are run by government transport agency **Transtur** (☏7-831-7333). Havana and Varadero both have open-topped double-decker buses. Smaller minibuses are used in Viñales, Trinidad, Cayo Coco, Guardalavaca, Cayo Santa María and Baracoa (seasonal).

Cubans travel over shorter distances in provincial buses. These buses sell tickets in *moneda nacional* and are a lot less comfortable and reliable than Víazul. They leave from the provincial bus stations in each province. Schedules and prices are usually chalked up on a board inside the terminal.

VÍAZUL ROUTES

ROUTE	DURATION (HR)	PRICE (CUC$)	STOPPING AT...
Havana–Santiago de Cuba	15½	51	Entronque de Jagüey, Santa Clara, Sancti Spíritus, Ciego de Ávila, Camagüey, Las Tunas, Holguín, Bayamo
Trinidad–Santiago de Cuba	12	33	Sancti Spíritus, Ciego de Ávila, Camagüey, Las Tunas, Holguín, Bayamo
Havana–Viñales	3¼	12	Pinar del Río
Havana–Holguín	10½	44	Santa Clara, Sancti Spíritus, Ciego de Ávila, Camagüey, Las Tunas
Havana–Trinidad	6	25	Entronque de Jagüey, Cienfuegos
Havana–Varadero	3	10	Matanzas, Varadero Airport
Santiago de Cuba–Baracoa	4¾	15	Guantánamo
Varadero–Santiago de Cuba	16	49	Cárdenas, Colón, Santa Clara, Sancti Spíritus, Ciego de Ávila, Camagüey, Las Tunas, Holguín, Bayamo
Trinidad–Varadero	6	20	Cárdenas, Colón, Entronque de Jagüey, Cienfuegos

CLIMATE CHANGE & TRAVEL

Every form of transport that relies on carbon-based fuel generates CO_2, the main cause of human-induced climate change. Modern travel is dependent on airplanes, which might use less fuel per kilometer per person than most cars but travel much greater distances. The altitude at which aircraft emit gases (including CO_2) and particles also contributes to their climate change impact. Many websites offer 'carbon calculators' that allow people to estimate the carbon emissions generated by their journey and, for those who wish to do so, to offset the impact of the greenhouse gases emitted with contributions to portfolios of climate-friendly initiatives throughout the world. Lonely Planet offsets the carbon footprint of all staff and author travel.

Reservations

Reservations with Víazul are advisable during peak travel periods (June to August, Christmas and Easter) and on popular routes (Havana–Trinidad, Trinidad–Santa Clara, and Santiago de Cuba–Baracoa). You can usually prebook a day or two beforehand.

The Víazul bus out of Baracoa is almost always booked, so reserve a seat on this service when you arrive. It is now possible to make reservations online at www. viazul.com. However, like all Cuban websites it is prone to 'crashing.'

Car

Renting a car in Cuba is easy, but once you've factored in gas, insurance, hire fees etc, it isn't cheap. Prices vary with car size, season and length of rental. Bank on paying an average of CUC$70 per day for a medium-sized car. It's actually cheaper to hire a taxi for distances of under 150km (at the time of writing taxis were charging CUC$0.50 per kilometer for intercity routes).

Driver's License

Your home license is sufficient to rent and drive a car in Cuba.

Gas

Gas sold in convertibles (as opposed to peso gas) is widely available in stations all over the country (the north coast west of Havana being the notable exception). Gas stations are often open 24 hours and may have a small parts store on-site. Gas is sold by the liter and comes in *regular* (CUC$0.90 per liter) and *especial* (CUC$1.10 per liter) varieties. Rental cars are advised to use *especial*. All gas stations have efficient pump attendants, usually in the form of *trabajadores sociales* (students in the process of studying for a degree).

Spare Parts

While you cannot count on spare parts per se to be available, Cubans have decades of experience keeping old wrecks on the road without factory parts and you'll see them do amazing things with cardboard, string, rubber and clothes hangers to keep a car mobile.

If you need air in your tires or you have a puncture, use a gas station or visit the local *ponchero*. They often don't have measures, so make sure they don't overinflate them.

Insurance

Rental cars come with a recommended CUC$15 to CUC$30 per day insurance, which covers everything but theft of the radio (which you'll need to put in the trunk of the car at night). You can choose to decline the insurance, but then the refundable deposit you must leave upon renting the car soars from CUC$250 to CUC$500. If you do have an accident, you must get a copy of the *denuncia* (police report) to be eligible for the insurance coverage, a process which can take all day. If the police determine that you are the party responsible for the accident, say *adiós* to your deposit.

Rental

Renting a car in Cuba is straightforward. You'll need your passport, driver's license and a refundable deposit of between CUC$250 and CUC$800 (cash or credit card). You can rent a car in one city and drop it off in another for a reasonable fee, which is handy. If you're on a tight budget, ask about diesel cars – some agencies stock a few and you'll save bundles in gas money considering a liter of non-diesel is CUC$0.90 while a liter of *petróleo* (diesel) is CUC$0.65. Note that there are very few rental cars with automatic transmission.

If you want to rent a car for three days or fewer, it will come with limited kilometers, while contracts for three days or more come with unlimited kilometers. In Cuba, you pay for the first tank of gas when you rent the car (CUC$1.10 per liter) and return it empty (a suicidal policy that sees many tight-fisted tourists running out of gas a kilometer or so from the drop-off point). Just to make it worse, you will not be refunded for any gas left in the tank. Petty theft of mirrors, antennas, taillights etc is common, so it's worth it to pay someone a convertible or two to watch your car for the night. If you lose your rental contract or keys you'll pay a CUC$50 penalty. Drivers under 25 pay a CUC$5 fee, while additional drivers on the same contract pay a CUC$3 per day surcharge.

Check over the car carefully with the rental agent before driving into the sunset, as you'll be responsible for any damage or missing parts. Make sure there is a spare tire of the correct size, a jack and a lug wrench. Check that there are seatbelts and that all the doors lock properly.

We have received many letters about poor or non-existent customer service, bogus spare tires, forgotten reservations and other car-rental problems. Reservations are only accepted 15 days in advance and are still not guaranteed. While agents are usually accommodating, you might end up paying more than you planned or have to wait for hours until someone returns a car. The more Spanish you speak and the friendlier you are, the more likely problems will be resolved to everyone's satisfaction (tips to the agent might help). As with most Cuban travel, always have a Plan B.

Road Conditions

Driving here isn't just a different ballpark, it's a different sport. The first problem is that there are no signs – almost anywhere. Major junctions and turnoffs to important resorts or cities are often not indicated at all. Not only is this distracting, it's also incredibly time-consuming. The lack of signage also extends to highway instructions. Often a one-way street is not clearly indicated or a speed limit not highlighted, which can cause problems with the police (who won't understand your inability to telepathically absorb the road rules), and road markings are nonexistent everywhere.

The Autopista, Vía Blanca and Carretera Central are generally in a good state, but be prepared for roads suddenly deteriorating into chunks of asphalt and unexpected railroad crossings everywhere else (especially in the Oriente). Rail crossings are particularly problematic, as there are hundreds of them and there are never any safety gates. Beware: however overgrown the rails may look, you can pretty much assume that the line is still in use. Cuban trains, rather like its cars, defy all normal logic when it comes to mechanics.

While motorized traffic is refreshingly light, bicycles, pedestrians, oxcarts, horse carriages and livestock are a different matter. Many old cars and trucks lack rearview mirrors and traffic-unaware children run out of all kinds of nooks and crannies. Stay alert, drive with caution and use your horn when passing or on blind curves.

Driving at night is not recommended due to variable roads, drunk drivers, crossing cows and poor lighting. Drunk-driving remains a troublesome problem despite a government educational campaign. Late night in Havana is particularly dangerous, as it seems there's a passing lane, cruising lane and drunk lane.

Traffic lights are often busted or hard to pick out and right-of-way rules thrown to the wind. Take extra care.

Road Rules

Cubans drive how they want, where they want. It seems chaotic at first, but it has its rhythm. Seatbelts are supposedly required and maximum speed limits are technically 50km/h in the city, 90km/h on highways and 100km/h on the Autopista, but some cars can't even go that fast and those that can go faster still.

With so few cars on the road, it's hard not to put the pedal to the floor and just fly. Unexpected potholes are a hazard, however, and watch out for police. There are some clever speed traps, particularly along the Autopista. Speeding tickets start at CUC$30 and are noted on your car contract; the fine is deducted from your deposit when you return the car. When pulled over by the police, you're expected to get out of the car and walk over to them with your paperwork. An oncoming car flashing its lights means a hazard up ahead (and usually the police).

The Cuban transport crisis means there are a lot

of people waiting for rides by the side of the road. Giving a *botella* (a lift) to local hitchhikers has advantages aside from altruism. With a Cuban passenger you'll never get lost, you'll learn about secret spots, and you'll meet some great people. There are always risks associated with picking up hitchhikers; giving lifts to older people or families may reduce the risk factor. In the provinces, people waiting for rides are systematically queued by the *amarillos* (official state-paid traffic supervisors; so-named for their mustard yellow uniforms), and they'll hustle the most needy folks into your car, usually an elderly couple or a pregnant woman.

Ferry

The most important ferry services for travelers are the catamaran from Surgidero de Batabanó to Nueva Gerona, **Isla de la Juventud** (☑7-878-1841), and the passenger ferry from Havana to Regla and **Casablanca** (☑7-867-3726). These ferries are generally safe, though in 1997 two hydrofoils crashed en route to Isla de la Juventud. In both 1994 and 2003, the Regla/Casablanca ferry was hijacked by Cubans trying to make their way to Florida. The 2003 incident involved tourists, so you can expect tight security.

Hitchhiking

The transport crisis, culture of solidarity and low crime levels make Cuba a popular hitchhiking destination. Here, hitchhiking is more like ride-sharing, and it's legally enforced. Traffic lights, railroad crossings and country crossroads are regular stops for people seeking rides. In the provinces and on the outskirts of Havana, the *amarillos* organize and prioritize ride seekers, and you're welcome to jump in line.

Rides cost five to 20 pesos depending on distance. Travelers hitching rides will want a good map and some Spanish skills. Expect to wait two or three hours for rides in some cases. Hitchhiking is never entirely safe in any country in the world, and we don't recommend it. Travelers who decide to hitchhike should understand that they are taking a small but potentially serious risk. People who do choose to hitchhike will be safer if they travel in pairs and let someone know where they are planning to go.

Local Transportation
Bici-Taxi

Bici-taxis are big pedal-powered tricycles with a double seat behind the driver and are common in Havana, Camagüey, Holguín and a few other cities. In Havana they'll insist on a CUC$1 minimum fare (Cubans pay five or 10 pesos). Some bici-taxistas ask ridiculous amounts. The fare should be clearly understood before you hop aboard. By law, bici-taxis aren't allowed to take tourists (who are expected to use regular taxis), and they're taking a risk by carrying foreigners. Bici-taxi rules are more lax in the provinces and you should be able to get one for five pesos.

Boat

Some towns, such as Havana, Cienfuegos, Gibara and Santiago de Cuba, have local ferry services that charge in moneda nacional.

Bus

Very crowded, very steamy, very challenging, very Cuban – *guaguas* (local buses) are useful in bigger cities. Buses work fixed routes, stopping at *paradas* (bus stops) that always have a line, even if it doesn't look like it. You have to shout out *¿el último?* to find out who was the last in

line when you showed up as Cuban queues aren't lines in the normal sense of the word. Instead, people just hang around in a disorganized fashion in the vicinity of the bus stop.

Buses cost a flat MN$0.40 or five centavos if you're using CUC$. Havana and Santiago de Cuba have recently been kitted out with brand-new fleets of Chinese-made metro buses. You must always walk as far back in the bus as you can and exit through the rear. Make room to pass by saying *permiso*, always wear your pack in front and watch your wallet.

Colectivo & Taxi

Colectivos are taxis running on fixed, long-distance routes, leaving when full. They are generally pre-1959 American cars that belch diesel fumes and can squash in at least three people across the front seat. State-owned taxis that charge in convertibles hang about bus stations and are faster and usually cheaper than the bus.

Horse Carriage

Many provincial cities have *coches de caballo* (horse carriages) that trot on fixed routes, often between train/bus stations and city centers. Prices in *moneda nacional* cost around one peso.

Taxi

Car taxis are metered and cost CUC$1 to start and CUC$1 per kilometer in cities. Taxi drivers are in the habit of offering foreigners a flat, off-meter rate that usually works out very close to what you'll pay with the meter. The difference is that with the meter, the money goes to the state to be divided up; without the meter it goes into the driver's pocket.

Tours

Of the many tourist agencies in Cuba, the following are the most useful:

Cubamar Viajes (📞7-833-2524, 7-833-2523; www.cubamarviajes.cu) Rents campismo cabins and mobile homes (caravans).

Cubanacán (📞7-873-2686; www.cubanacan.cu) General tour agency that also has divisions called Cubanacán Náutica (scuba diving, boating and fishing) and Turismo Y Salud (surgery, spas and rehabilitation).

Cubatur (📞7-835-4155; www.cubtur.cu)

Ecotur (📞7 273 1542; www.ecoturcuba.tur.cu)

Gaviota (📞7-204-4411; www.gaviota-grupo.com) Represented in all Gaviota hotels including the H10 Habana Panorama.

Havanatur (📞7-835-3720; www.havanatur.cu) Works with Marazul Tours in the US.

Paradiso (📞7-832-9538/9; www.paradiso.es) Multiday cultural and art tours.

San Cristóbal Agencia de Viajes (📞7-861-9171; www.viajessancristobal.cu)

Train

Public railways operated by Ferrocarriles de Cuba serve all of the provincial capitals and are a unique way to experience Cuba, as long as you have the patience of a saint (ie they're *slow*). While train travel is safe, the departure information provided is purely theoretical. Getting a ticket is usually no problem, as there's a quota for tourists paying in convertibles.

Foreigners must pay for their tickets in cash, but prices are reasonable and the carriages, though old and worn, are fairly comfortable. The toilets are foul – bring toilet paper. Watch your luggage on overnight trips and bring some of your own food. Only the Tren Francés has snack facilities, although vendors often come through the train selling coffee (you supply the cup).

THE TREN FRANCÉS

Cuba's best and fastest train is the Tren Francés, which runs between Havana and Santiago de Cuba in both directions every third day (1st/2nd class CUC$62/50, 15½ hours, 861km). Train No 1 leaves Havana at 6.27pm, passing Santa Clara and Camagüey, before reaching Santiago de Cuba at 9am-ish. Train 2 leaves Santiago de Cuba at 8:17pm and reaches Havana at 11am-ish. The trains use secondhand French carriages (hence the name), which formerly operated on the Paris–Brussels–Amsterdam European route. They were bought by the Cubans in 2001. The carriages are relatively comfortable, if a little worn, with frigid air-conditioning, a limited cafe, a purser (one per carriage) and decidedly dingy toilets. As with many things in Cuba, it's not so much the quality of the carriages that's the problem, but their upkeep – or lack thereof. The Tren Francés has two classes, *primera* and *primera especial*. The latter is worth the extra CUC$12 investment.

The Tren Francés was being overhauled at the time of research and was scheduled to re-hit the rails soon.

A regularly updated précis of Cuban train times, types and nuances is available on the website **The Man in Seat Sixty-one** (www.seat61.com), run by Mark Smith in the UK. The website covers train travel across the globe, but has a decent printed rundown on Cuba's main train services.

Train Stations

Cuban train stations, despite their occasionally grandiose facades, are invariably dingy, chaotic places with little visible train information. Departure times are displayed on black chalkboards or handwritten notices; there are no electronic or printed timetables. Always check train info two to three days before your intended travel.

Classes

Trains are either *especial* (air-conditioned, faster trains with fewer departures), *regular* (slowish trains with daily departures) or *lecheros* (milk trains that stop at every little town on the line). Trains on major routes such as Havana–Santiago de Cuba will be *especial* or *regular* trains.

Costs

Regular trains cost under CUC$3 per 100km, while *especial* trains cost closer to CUC$5.50 per 100km. The Hershey Train is priced like the *regular* trains.

Reservations

In most train stations, you just go to the ticket window and buy a ticket. In Havana, there's a separate waiting room and ticket window for passengers paying in convertibles in La Coubre train station. Be prepared to show your passport when purchasing tickets. It's always wise to check beforehand at the station for current departures because things change.

Rail Network

Cuba's train network is comprehensive, running almost the full length of the main island from Guane in Pinar del Río province to Caimanera, just south of the city of Guantánamo. There are also several branch lines heading out north and south and linking up places such as Manzanillo, Nuevitas, Morón and Cienfuegos. Baracoa is one of the few cities without

CUBA'S TRAIN SERVICES FROM HAVANA

The following information is liable to change or cancellation. Always check ahead.

DESTINATION	TRAIN NO	FREQUENCY
Pinar del Río	71	every other day
Bayamo	5	every 3rd day
Guantánamo	15	every 3rd day
Santiago de Cuba	1, 5	2 days out of 3
Matanzas	3, 5, 7, 15	daily
Morón	29	daily
Manzanillo	28	every 3rd day
Cienfuegos	73	every other day
Santa Clara	1, 3, 5, 7, 9, 15	daily
Camagüey	1, 3, 5, 15	daily
Sancti Spíritus	7	every other day

a train connection. Other trainless enclaves are the Isla de la Juventud, the far west of Pinar del Río province and the northern keys. Trinidad has been detached from the main rail network since a storm brought down a bridge in 1992, though it has a small branch line that runs along the Valle del los Ingenios.

Services

Many additional local trains operate at least daily and some more frequently. There are also smaller trains linking Las Tunas and Holguín, Holguín and Santiago de Cuba, Santa Clara and Nuevitas, Cienfuegos and Sancti Spíritus, and Santa Clara and Caibarién.

The Hershey Train is the only electric railway in Cuba and was built by the Hershey Chocolate Company in the early years of the 20th century; it's a fun way to get between Havana and Matanzas.

Truck

Camiones (trucks) are a cheap, fast way to travel within or between provinces. Every city has a provincial and municipal bus stop with camiones departures. They run on a (loose) schedule and you'll need to take your place in line by asking for el último to your destination; you pay as you board. A truck from Santiago de Cuba to

Guantánamo costs five pesos (CUC$0.20), while the same trip on a Víazul bus costs CUC$6.

Camion traveling is hot, crowded and uncomfortable, but is a great way to meet local people, fast; a little Spanish will go a long way.

Sometimes terminal staff tell foreigners they're prohibited from traveling on trucks. As with anything in Cuba, never take 'no' as your final answer. Crying poor, striking up a conversation with the driver, appealing to other passengers for aid etc usually helps.

Language

Spanish pronunciation is pretty straightforward – Spanish spelling is phonetically consistent, meaning that there's a clear and consistent relationship between what you see in writing and how it's pronounced. Also, most Latin American Spanish sounds are pronounced the same as their English counterparts. Note though that the kh in our pronunciation guides is a throaty sound (like the 'ch' in the Scottish *loch*), v and b are similar to the English 'b' (but softer, between a 'v' and a 'b'), and r is strongly rolled. If you read our colored pronunciation guides as if they were English, you'll be understood just fine. The stressed syllables are in italics.

Spanish nouns are marked for gender (masculine or feminine). Endings for adjectives also change to agree with the gender of the noun they modify. Where necessary, both forms are given for the phrases in this chapter, separated by a slash and with the masculine form first, eg *perdido/a* (m/f).

Spanish has two words for the English 'you': an informal (*tú*) and polite form (*Usted*) which are accompanied by a different form of the verb. When talking to people familiar to you or younger than you, use the informal form of 'you', *tú*, rather than the polite form *Usted*. In all other cases use the polite form. The polite form is used in the phrases provided in this chapter; where both options are given, they are indicated by the abbreviations 'pol' and 'inf'.

WANT MORE?

For in-depth language information and handy phrases, check out Lonely Planet's *Latin American Spanish Phrasebook*. You'll find it at **shop.lonelyplanet.com**, or you can buy Lonely Planet's iPhone phrasebooks at the Apple App Store.

BASICS

Hello.	Hola.	o·la
Goodbye.	Adiós.	a·dyos
How are you?	¿Qué tal?	ke tal
Fine, thanks.	Bien, gracias.	byen gra·syas
Excuse me.	Perdón.	per·don
Sorry.	Lo siento.	lo syen·to
Yes./No.	Sí./No.	see/no
Please.	Por favor.	por fa·vor
Thank you.	Gracias.	gra·syas
You're welcome.	De nada.	de na·da

My name is ...
Me llamo ...   me ya·mo ...

What's your name?
¿Cómo se llama Usted? ko·mo se ya·ma oo·ste (pol)
¿Cómo te llamas?   ko·mo te ya·mas (inf)

Do you speak English?
¿Habla inglés?   a·bla een·gles (pol)
¿Hablas inglés?   a·blas een·gles (inf)

I don't understand.
Yo no entiendo.   yo no en·tyen·do

ACCOMMODATIONS

I'd like to book a room.
Quisiera reservar una   kee·sye·ra re·ser·var oo·na
habitación.   a·bee·ta·syon

How much is it per night/person?
¿Cuánto cuesta por   kwan·to kwes·ta por
noche/persona?   no·che/per·so·na

Does it include breakfast?
¿Incluye el desayuno?   een·kloo·ye el de·sa·yoo·no

campsite	terreno de cámping	te·re·no de kam·peeng
hotel	hotel	o·tel
guesthouse	pensión	pen·syon
youth hostel	albergue juvenil	al·ber·ge khoo·ve·neel

I'd like a ... room.	Quisiera una habitación ...	kee·sye·ra oo·na a·bee·ta·syon ...
single	individual	een·dee·vee·dwal
double	doble	do·ble

air-con	aire acondicionado	ai·re a·kon·dee·syo·na·do
bathroom	baño	ba·nyo
bed	cama	ka·ma
window	ventana	ven·ta·na

DIRECTIONS

Where's ...?
¿Dónde está ...?   don·de es·ta ...

What's the address?
¿Cuál es la dirección?   kwal es la dee·rek·syon

Could you please write it down?
¿Puede escribirlo, por favor?   pwe·de es·kree·beer·lo por fa·vor

Can you show me (on the map)?
¿Me lo puede indicar (en el mapa)?   me lo pwe·de een·dee·kar (en el ma·pa)

at the corner	en la esquina	en la es·kee·na
at the traffic lights	en el semáforo	en el se·ma·fo·ro
behind ...	detrás de ...	de·tras de ...
far	lejos	le·khos
in front of ...	enfrente de ...	en·fren·te de ...
left	izquierda	ees·kyer·da
near	cerca	ser·ka
next to ...	al lado de ...	al la·do de ...
opposite ...	frente a ...	fren·te a ...
right	derecha	de·re·cha
straight ahead	todo recto	to·do rek·to

EATING & DRINKING

What would you recommend?
¿Qué recomienda?   ke re·ko·myen·da

What's in that dish?
¿Que lleva ese plato?   ke ye·va e·se pla·to

I don't eat ...
No como ...   no ko·mo ...

That was delicious!
¡Estaba buenísimo!   es·ta·ba bwe·nee·see·mo

Please bring the bill.
Por favor nos trae la cuenta.   por fa·vor nos tra·e la kwen·ta

Cheers!
¡Salud!   sa·loo

KEY PATTERNS

To get by in Spanish, mix and match these simple patterns with words of your choice:

When's (the next flight)?
¿Cuándo sale (el próximo vuelo)?   kwan·do sa·le (el prok·see·mo vwe·lo)

Where's (the station)?
¿Dónde está (la estación)?   don·de es·ta (la es·ta·syon)

Where can I (buy a ticket)?
¿Dónde puedo (comprar un billete)?   don·de pwe·do (kom·prar oon bee·ye·te)

Do you have (a map)?
¿Tiene (un mapa)?   tye·ne (oon ma·pa)

Is there (a toilet)?
¿Hay (servicios)?   ai (ser·vee·syos)

I'd like (a coffee).
Quisiera (un café).   kee·sye·ra (oon ka·fe)

I'd like (to hire a car).
Quisiera (alquilar un coche).   kee·sye·ra (al·kee·lar oon ko·che)

Can I (enter)?
¿Se puede (entrar)?   se pwe·de (en·trar)

Could you please (help me)?
¿Puede (ayudarme), por favor?   pwe·de (a·yoo·dar·me) por fa·vor

Do I have to (get a visa)?
¿Necesito (obtener un visado)?   ne·se·see·to (ob·te·ner oon vee·sa·do)

I'd like to book a table for ...	Quisiera reservar una mesa para ...	kee·sye·ra re·ser·var oo·na me·sa pa·ra ...
(eight) o'clock	las (ocho)	las (o·cho)
(two) people	(dos) personas	(dos) per·so·nas

Key Words

appetisers	aperitivos	a·pe·ree·tee·vos
bottle	botella	bo·te·ya
bowl	bol	bol
breakfast	desayuno	de·sa·yoo·no
children's menu	menú infantil	me·noo een·fan·teel
(too) cold	(muy) frío	(mooy) free·o
dinner	cena	se·na
food	comida	ko·mee·da
fork	tenedor	te·ne·dor
glass	vaso	va·so

highchair	trona	tro·na
hot (warm)	caliente	kal·yen·te
knife	cuchillo	koo·chee·yo
lunch	comida	ko·mee·da
main course	segundo plato	se·goon·do pla·to
market	mercado	mer·ka·do
menu (in English)	menú (en inglés)	me·noo (en een·gles)
plate	plato	pla·to
restaurant	restaurante	res·tow·ran·te
spoon	cuchara	koo·cha·ra
vegetarian food	comida vegetariana	ko·mee·da ve·khe·ta·rya·na
with/without	con/sin	kon/seen

Meat & Fish

beef	carne de vaca	kar·ne de va·ka
chicken	pollo	po·yo
duck	pato	pa·to
fish	pescado	pes·ka·do
lamb	cordero	kor·de·ro
pork	cerdo	ser·do
turkey	pavo	pa·vo
veal	ternera	ter·ne·ra

Fruit & Vegetables

apple	manzana	man·sa·na
apricot	albaricoque	al·ba·ree·ko·ke
artichoke	alcachofa	al·ka·cho·fa
asparagus	espárragos	es·pa·ra·gos
banana	plátano	pla·ta·no
beans	judías	khoo·dee·as
beetroot	remolacha	re·mo·la·cha
cabbage	col	kol
carrot	zanahoria	sa·na·o·rya
celery	apio	a·pyo
cherry	cereza	se·re·sa
corn	maíz	ma·ees
cucumber	pepino	pe·pee·no
fruit	fruta	froo·ta
grape	uvas	oo·vas
lemon	limón	lee·mon
lentils	lentejas	len·te·khas
lettuce	lechuga	le·choo·ga
mushroom	champiñón	cham·pee·nyon
nuts	nueces	nwe·ses
onion	cebolla	se·bo·ya

orange	naranja	na·ran·kha
peach	melocotón	me·lo·ko·ton
peas	guisantes	gee·san·tes
(red/green) pepper	pimiento (rojo/verde)	pee·myen·to (ro·kho/ver·de)
pineapple	piña	pee·nya
plum	ciruela	seer·we·la
potato	patata	pa·ta·ta
pumpkin	calabaza	ka·la·ba·sa
spinach	espinacas	es·pee·na·kas
strawberry	fresa	fre·sa
tomato	tomate	to·ma·te
vegetable	verdura	ver·doo·ra
watermelon	sandía	san·dee·a

Other

bread	pan	pan
butter	mantequilla	man·te·kee·ya
cheese	queso	ke·so
egg	huevo	we·vo
honey	miel	myel
jam	mermelada	mer·me·la·da
oil	aceite	a·sey·te
pasta	pasta	pas·ta
pepper	pimienta	pee·myen·ta
rice	arroz	a·ros
salt	sal	sal
sugar	azúcar	a·soo·kar
vinegar	vinagre	vee·na·gre

Drinks

beer	cerveza	ser·ve·sa
coffee	café	ka·fe
(orange) juice	zumo (de naranja)	soo·mo (de na·ran·kha)
milk	leche	le·che
tea	té	te

Signs	
Abierto	Open
Cerrado	Closed
Entrada	Entrance
Hombres/Varones	Men
Mujeres/Damas	Women
Prohibido	Prohibited
Salida	Exit
Servicios/Baños	Toilets

| (mineral) water | agua (mineral) | a·gwa (mee·ne·ral) |
| (red/white) wine | vino (tinto/ blanco) | vee·no (teen·to/ blan·ko) |

EMERGENCIES

| Help! | ¡Socorro! | so·ko·ro |
| Go away! | ¡Vete! | ve·te |

Call ...!	¡Llame a ...!	ya·me a ...
a doctor	un médico	oon me·dee·ko
the police	la policía	la po·lee·see·a

I'm lost.
Estoy perdido/a. es·toy per·dee·do/a (m/f)

I'm ill.
Estoy enfermo/a. es·toy en·fer·mo/a (m/f)

I'm allergic to (antibiotics).
Soy alérgico/a a soy a·ler·khee·ko/a a
(los antibióticos). (los an·tee·byo·tee·kos) (m/f)

Where are the toilets?
¿Dónde están don·de es·tan
los servicios? los ser·vee·syos

SHOPPING & SERVICES

I'd like to buy ...
Quisiera comprar ... kee·sye·ra kom·prar ...

I'm just looking.
Sólo estoy mirando. so·lo es·toy mee·ran·do

May I look at it?
¿Puedo verlo? pwe·do ver·lo

I don't like it.
No me gusta. no me goos·ta

How much is it?
¿Cuánto cuesta? kwan·to kwes·ta

That's too expensive.
Es muy caro. es mooy ka·ro

Can you lower the price?
¿Podría bajar un po·dree·a ba·khar oon
poco el precio? po·ko el pre·syo

There's a mistake in the bill.
Hay un error ai oon e·ror
en la cuenta. en la kwen·ta

Question Words		
How?	¿Cómo?	ko·mo
What?	¿Qué?	ke
When?	¿Cuándo?	kwan·do
Where?	¿Dónde?	don·de
Who?	¿Quién?	kyen
Why?	¿Por qué?	por ke

ATM	cajero automático	ka·khe·ro ow·to·ma·tee·ko
credit card	tarjeta de crédito	tar·khe·ta de kre·dee·to
internet cafe	cibercafé	see·ber·ka·fe
post office	correos	ko·re·os
tourist office	oficina de turismo	o·fee·see·na de too·rees·mo

TIME & DATES

What time is it?	¿Qué hora es?	ke o·ra es
It's (10) o'clock.	Son (las diez).	son (las dyes)
It's half past (one).	Es (la una) y media.	es (la oo·na) ee me·dya

morning	mañana	ma·nya·na
afternoon	tarde	tar·de
evening	noche	no·che
yesterday	ayer	a·yer
today	hoy	oy
tomorrow	mañana	ma·nya·na

Monday	lunes	loo·nes
Tuesday	martes	mar·tes
Wednesday	miércoles	myer·ko·les
Thursday	jueves	khwe·ves
Friday	viernes	vyer·nes
Saturday	sábado	sa·ba·do
Sunday	domingo	do·meen·go

January	enero	e·ne·ro
February	febrero	fe·bre·ro
March	marzo	mar·so
April	abril	a·breel
May	mayo	ma·yo
June	junio	khoon·yo
July	julio	khool·yo
August	agosto	a·gos·to
September	septiembre	sep·tyem·bre
October	octubre	ok·too·bre
November	noviembre	no·vyem·bre
December	diciembre	dee·syem·bre

TRANSPORTATION

Public Transportation

boat	barco	bar·ko
bus	autobús	ow·to·boos
plane	avión	a·vyon
train	tren	tren

Numbers		
1	uno	oo·no
2	dos	dos
3	tres	tres
4	cuatro	kwa·tro
5	cinco	seen·ko
6	seis	seys
7	siete	sye·te
8	ocho	o·cho
9	nueve	nwe·ve
10	diez	dyes
20	veinte	veyn·te
30	treinta	treyn·ta
40	cuarenta	kwa·ren·ta
50	cincuenta	seen·kwen·ta
60	sesenta	se·sen·ta
70	setenta	se·ten·ta
80	ochenta	o·chen·ta
90	noventa	no·ven·ta
100	cien	syen
1000	mil	meel

first	primero	pree·me·ro
last	último	ool·tee·mo
next	próximo	prok·see·mo

I want to go to ...
Quisiera ir a ... — kee·sye·ra eer a ...

Does it stop at ...?
¿Para en ...? — pa·ra en ...

What stop is this?
¿Cuál es esta parada? — kwal es es·ta pa·ra·da

What time does it arrive/leave?
¿A qué hora llega/sale? — a ke o·ra ye·ga/sa·le

Please tell me when we get to ...
¿Puede avisarme cuando lleguemos a ...? — pwe·de a·vee·sar·me kwan·do ye·ge·mos a ...

I want to get off here.
Quiero bajarme aquí. — kye·ro ba·khar·me a·kee

a ... ticket	un billete de ...	oon bee·ye·te de ...
1st-class	primera clase	pree·me·ra kla·se
2nd-class	segunda clase	se·goon·da kla·se
one-way	ida	ee·da
return	ida y vuelta	ee·da ee vwel·ta

airport	aeropuerto	a·e·ro·pwer·to
aisle seat	asiento de pasillo	a·syen·to de pa·see·yo
bus stop	parada de autobuses	pa·ra·da de ow·to·boo·ses
cancelled	cancelado	kan·se·la·do
delayed	retrasado	re·tra·sa·do
platform	plataforma	pla·ta·for·ma
ticket office	taquilla	ta·kee·ya
timetable	horario	o·ra·ryo
train station	estación de trenes	es·ta·syon de tre·nes
window seat	asiento junto a la ventana	a·syen·to khoon·to a la ven·ta·na

Driving & Cycling

I'd like to hire a ...	Quisiera alquilar ...	kee·sye·ra al·kee·lar ...
4WD	un todo-terreno	oon to·do·te·re·no
bicycle	una bicicleta	oo·na bee·see·kle·ta
car	un coche	oon ko·che
motorcycle	una moto	oo·na mo·to
child seat	asiento de seguridad para niños	a·syen·to de se·goo·ree·da pa·ra nee·nyos
diesel	petróleo	pet·ro·le·o
helmet	casco	kas·ko
hitchhike	hacer botella	a·ser bo·te·ya
mechanic	mecánico	me·ka·nee·ko
petrol/gas	gasolina	ga·so·lee·na
service station	gasolinera	ga·so·lee·ne·ra
truck	camion	ka·myon

Is this the road to ...?
¿Se va a ... por esta carretera? — se va a ... por es·ta ka·re·te·ra

(How long) Can I park here?
¿(Por cuánto tiempo) Puedo aparcar aquí? — (por kwan·to tyem·po) pwe·do a·par·kar a·kee

The car has broken down (at ...).
El coche se ha averiado (en ...). — el ko·che se a a·ve·rya·do (en ...)

I have a flat tyre.
Tengo un pinchazo. — ten·go oon peen·cha·so

I've run out of petrol.
Me he quedado sin gasolina. — me e ke·da·do seen ga·so·lee·na

GLOSSARY

altos – upstairs apartment; caps when in an address

agropecuario – vegetable market; also sells rice, fruit

amarillo – a roadside traffic organizer in a yellow uniform

americano/a – in Cuba this means a citizen of any Western hemisphere country (from Canada to Argentina); a citizen of the US is called a *norteamericano/a* or *estado-unidense*; also gringo/a and yuma

Arawak – linguistically related Indian tribes that inhabited most of the Caribbean islands and northern South America

Autopista – the national highway that has four, six or eight lanes depending on the region

babalawo – a *Santería* priest; also *babalao*; see also *santero*

bahía – bay

bailes – dances

barbuda – name given to Castro's rebel army; literally 'bearded one'

barrio – neighborhood

bici-taxi – bicycle taxi

bodega – stores distributing ration-card products

bohío – thatched hut

bolero – a romantic love song

botella – hitchhiking; literally 'bottle'

cabaña – cabin, hut

cabildo – a town council during the colonial era; also an association of tribes in Cuban religions of African origin

cacique – chief; originally used to describe an Indian chief and today used to designate a petty tyrant

Cadeca – exchange booth

cafetal – coffee plantation

caliente – hot

calle – street

camión – truck

campesinos – people who live in the *campo*

campismo – national network of 82 camping installations, not all of which are open to foreigners

casa particular – private house

that lets out rooms to foreigners (and sometimes Cubans); all legal casas must display a green triangle on the door

casco histórico – historic center of a city (eg Trinidad, Santiago de Cuba)

CDR – Comités de Defensa de la Revolución; neighborhood-watch bodies originally formed in 1960 to consolidate grassroots support for the Revolution; they now play a decisive role in health, education, social, recycling and voluntary labor campaigns

chachachá – cha-cha; dance music in 4/4 meter derived from the rumba and mambo

Changó – the *Santería* deity signifying war and fire, twinned with Santa Barbara in Catholicism

chivo – Cuban slang for 'bike'

cimarrón – a runaway slave

claves – rhythm sticks used by musicians

coches de caballo – horse carriages

Cohiba – native Indian name for a smoking implement; one of Cuba's top brands of cigar

colectivo – collective taxi that takes on as many passengers as possible; usually a classic American car

comida criolla – Creole food

compañero/a – companion or partner, with revolutionary connotations (ie 'comrade')

congrí – (rice flecked with black beans)

conseguir – to get, obtain

convertibles – convertible pesos

coppelia – Cuban ice creamery

criollo – Creole; Spaniard born in the Americas

Cubanacán – soon after landing in Cuba, Christopher Columbus visited a Taíno village the Indians called Cubanacán (meaning 'in the center of the island'); a large Cuban tourism company uses the name

danzón – a traditional Cuban ballroom dance colored with African influences, pioneered in Matanzas during the late 19th century

décima – the rhyming, eight-

syllable verse that provides the lyrics for Cuban son

duende – spirit/charm; used in flamenco to describe the ultimate climax to the music

El Líder Máximo – Maximum Leader; title often used to describe Fidel Castro

el último – literally 'the last'; this term is key to mastering Cuban queues (you must 'take' *el último* when joining a line and 'give it up' when someone new arrives)

entronque – crossroads in rural areas

finca – farm

Gitmo – American slang for Guantánamo US Naval Base

Granma – the yacht that carried Fidel and his companions from Mexico to Cuba in 1956 to launch the Revolution; in 1975 the name was adopted for the province where the Granma arrived; also name of Cuba's leading daily newspaper

guajiros – country folk

guarapo – fresh sugarcane juice

habanero/a – someone from Havana

herbero – seller of herbs, natural medicines and concocter of remedies; typically a wealth of knowledge on natural cures

ingenio – an antiquated term for a sugar mill; see central

inmigración – immigration office

jardín – garden

jinetera – a female tout; a woman who attaches herself to male foreigners

jinetero – a male tout who hustles tourists; literally 'jockey'

M-26-7 – the '26th of July Movement,' Fidel Castro's revolutionary organization, was named for the abortive assault on the Moncada army barracks in Santiago de Cuba on July 26, 1953

maqueta – scale model

máquina – private peso taxi

mercado – market

mirador – lookout or viewpoint

mogote – a limestone monolith found at Viñales

Moncada – a former army barracks in Santiago de Cuba named for General Guillermo Moncada (1848-95), a hero of the Wars of Independence

moneda nacional – abbreviated to MN; Cuban pesos

mudéjar – Iberian Peninsula's Moorish-influenced style in architecture and decoration that lasted from the 12th to 16th centuries and combined elements of Islamic and Christian art

nueva trova – philosophical folk/guitar music popularized in the late '60s and early '70s by Silvio Rodríguez and Pablo Milanés

Operación Milagros – the unofficial name given to a pioneering medical program hatched between Cuba and Venezuela in 2004 that offers free eye treatment for impoverished Venezuelans in Cuban hospitals

Oriente – the region comprised of Las Tunas, Holguín, Granma, Santiago de Cuba and Guantánamo provinces; literally 'the east'

orisha – a Santería deity

paladar – a privately owned restaurant

parada – bus stop

parque – park

PCC – Partido Comunista de Cuba; Cuba's only political party, formed in October 1965 by merging cadres from the Partido Socialista Popular (the pre-1959 Communist Party) and veterans of the guerrilla campaign

peña – musical performance or get-together in any genre: son, rap, rock, poetry etc; see also esquina

período especial – the 'Special Period in Time of Peace' (Cuba's economic reality post-1991)

pregón – a singsong manner of selling fruits, vegetables, brooms, whatever; often comic, they are belted out by pregoneros/as

puente – bridge

quinceañera – Cuban rite of passage for girls turning 15 (quince), whereby they dress up like brides, have their photos taken in gorgeous natural or architectural settings and then have a big party with lots of food and dancing

ranchón – rural farm/restaurant

reggaetón – Cuban hip-hop

Regla de Ocha – set of related religious beliefs popularly known as Santería

resolver – to resolve or fix a problematic situation; along with el último, this is among the most indispensable words in Cuban vocabulary

río – river

salsa – Cuban music based on son

salsero – salsa singer

Santería – Afro-Cuban religion resulting from the syncretization of the Yoruba religion of West Africa and Spanish Catholicism

santero – a priest of Santería; see also babalawo

santiagüero – someone from Santiago de Cuba

s/n – sin número; indicates an address that has no street number

son – Cuba's basic form of popular music that jelled from African and Spanish elements in the late 19th century

Taíno – a settled, Arawak-speaking tribe that inhabited much of Cuba prior to the Spanish conquest; the word itself means 'we the good people'

tambores – Santería drumming ritual

telepunto – Etecsa (Cuban state-run telecommunications company) telephone and internet shop/call center

temporada alta/baja – high/low season

Behind the Scenes

SEND US YOUR FEEDBACK

We love to hear from travelers – your comments keep us on our toes and help make our books better. Our well-traveled team reads every word on what you loved or loathed about this book. Although we cannot reply individually to postal submissions, we always guarantee that your feedback goes straight to the appropriate authors, in time for the next edition. Each person who sends us information is thanked in the next edition – the most useful submissions are rewarded with a selection of digital PDF chapters.

Visit **lonelyplanet.com/contact** to submit your updates and suggestions or to ask for help. Our award-winning website also features inspirational travel stories, news and discussions.

Note: We may edit, reproduce and incorporate your comments in Lonely Planet products such as guidebooks, websites and digital products, so let us know if you don't want your comments reproduced or your name acknowledged. For a copy of our privacy policy visit lonelyplanet.com/privacy.

OUR READERS

Many thanks to the travelers who used the last edition and wrote to us with helpful hints, useful advice and interesting anecdotes: A Aimee Kok, Al Webb, Amanda Bresnan, Andreja Počkaj, Andrew Temperton, Angret Sinnige, Anita Geertsen, Anja Heinicke **B** Barb Johnston, Bastian Pauls, Benoit Lammens, Brit Myrvoll **C** Camille van Wessem, Cathalia Goodall, Colin & Robyn Mills **D** Dale Ashley, David Connor, David Olubuyide, David Searle, Denis Hoddinott **E** Edward Ellis, Eeke Riegen, Eline Franckaert, Emmanuel Massa **F** Francesca Braghetta, Frans Honselaar **G** Gord Smith **H** Heikki Valkama, Henri Kas, Herwig Temmerman **J** Jaap de Korver, Janet Armstrong, Jenni Houston, Jessica Gordon-Burroughs, Johanna Vos, John Stansfield, Jonathan Bradbury, Jonathan Kaplinsky, Jordi Romeu, Joseph Keach, Joycka Neirinck, Judith Raab, Juliane Schmidt, Julie Bay **K** Katharina Meyer, Kirsti Malterud **L** Laura Tyler, Lee Woodall, Lepretre Charlotte, Lesley Cranna, Lone Larsen, Lynda Goddard **M** Marcus Neal, Marea Rubins, Marlene Irwin , Marta Maggioni, Martin Erichsen, Martin Hämmerle, Matthieu Eichholtz, Melanie Ittmann, Mette Krarup, Michiel Hennus **N** Neil Croft, Niek Achten, Niklas Carlsson **O** Oliver Kraatz **P** Paul Booker, Pauline Benoit, Per Bråmå, Peter Fried, Peter Newby, Phil Vintin, Philipp Heltewig **R** Rachel Papworth, Raquel Lome, Rene Echevarria, Rob Currie, Rob Eikenaar, Rodolfo Perez, Rolf Siegel **S** Sander Warnas, Shayne Konar, Sue Yearley, Susanne Lanz **T** Thomas Kaller, Tommy Smidt **V** Viktor Pesek, Vincent Nadeau **W** Walther TjonPianGi, Willemijn Brouwer

AUTHOR THANKS

Brendan Sainsbury

Muchas gracias to all my Cuban *amigos*; in particular Carlos Sarmiento for his fantastic company and driving skills, Julio Muñoz for horse-riding and photo tips, Rafael Requejo for his architectural insights, and Julio and Elsa Roque for their indispensable help in Havana. Special mentions also to Maité and Idolka in Morón, Nilson and José in Baracoa, and Luis Miguel in Havana.

Luke Waterson

The list is headed by Carlos Sarmiento who drove me to all those hard-to-get-to spots and shared his incredible knowledge of Cuba with me. Silver medal is shared by ever-reliable Waldo in Cienfuegos, Maité and Idolka in Morón, Yoan and Yarelis in Viñales, Luis Miguel in Havana and Joel in Matanzas. I would also like to particularly thank the señorita in Varadero's Cubatur, Ramberto and Marco in Nueva Gerona and Julio in Playa Girón: I'll dive better next time!

ACKNOWLEDGMENTS

Climate map data adapted from Peel MC, Finlayson BL & McMahon TA (2007) 'Updated World Map of the Köppen-Geiger Climate Classification', *Hydrology and Earth System Sciences*, 11, 1633¬44.

Cover photograph: Bass player, Trinidad, Ray Hems/Alamy.

THIS BOOK

This 8th edition of Lonely Planet's *Cuba* guidebook was researched and written by Brendan Sainsbury and Luke Waterson. This guidebook was produced by the following:

Destination Editors
Lorna Parkes, Sarah Reid

Product Editors Anne Mason, Tracy Whitmey

Senior Cartographer Mark Griffiths

Book Designer Jennifer Mullins

Assisting Editors Michelle Bennett, Kate Evans, Kate Kiely, Anne Mulvaney, Rosie Nicholson, Charlotte Orr, Erin Richards

Assisting Cartographer Alison Lyall

Cover Researcher Naomi Parker

Thanks to Sasha Baskett, Andi Jones, Claire Naylor, Karyn Noble, Ellie Simpson, Tony Wheeler

Index

A

Abakuá 221
Abreu, Marta 258
accommodations 500-2, *see also individual locations*
activities 42-50, *see also individual activities*
Acuario Nacional 126
Acueducto de Albear 94
agriculture 494, 495
air travel
   to/from Cuba 511-12
   within Cuba 513-14, **514**
Aldea Taína 368
Alegría de Pío 388
Alto del Naranjo 382
Alturas de Banao 297
amusement parks 421
animals, *see* bird-watching, wildlife, *individual species*
Antiguo Cafetal Angerona 149
aquariums 126
archaeological sites 310, 360, 368
architecture 12, 27, 75, 478-85
   Camagüey 323
   Cienfuegos 244
   tours 96
Arco de Triunfo 236
area codes 508
Arechabala Rum Factory 225
Arenas, Reinaldo 448, 473, 475
Arroyo Trinitario waterfall 264
Artemisa 148-9
Artemisa province 54, 145-58, **146**
   accommodations 145
   climate 145

highlights 146
hiking 145
travel seasons 145
art galleries, *see* museums & galleries
arts 473-7
ATMs 506
Av de los Presidentes 93
Avellaneda, Gertudis 473

B

Bacardí Rum Factory 403
Bacuranao 143
Bahía de Buenavista 493
Bahía de Cochinos 232-4, **46**, **233**
Balcón de Velázquez 397
Banes 366-7
Baños de Elguea 271
Baracoa 18, 437-44, **438**, **18**
   accommodations 440-2
   activities 437-40
   drinking & entertainment 443
   festivals & events 440
   food 442-3
   history 437
   shopping 443
   sights 437-40
   tours 440
   travel to/from 443-4
   travel within 444
Bay of Pigs 234, *see also* Bahía de Cochinos
Bayamo 372-80, **374-5**
   accommodations 377
   activities 376
   drinking 378
   entertainment 378-9
   festivals 377
   food 377-8
   history 372
   shopping 379
   sights 373-6
   tours 376

travel to/from 379-80
travel within 380
beaches 13, 29
   Playa Ancón 278, 286, 287-8
   Playa Bailén 195
   Playa Baracoa 149
   Playa Bibijagua 167
   Playa Blanca 360, 439
   Playa Bonita 331
   Playa Cajuajo 436-7
   Playa Caletones 358
   Playa Cazonal 421
   Playa Colonia 330
   Playa Coral 215
   Playa Daiquirí 421
   Playa de Morales 366
   Playa Duaba 439
   Playa Esmeralda 360
   Playa Girón 232-4
   Playa la Herradura 343
   Playa la Llanita 343
   Playa Larga 169, 231, 464
   Playa las Bocas 343
   Playa las Salinas 269
   Playa los Bajos 358
   Playa los Cocos (Camagüey) 332
   Playa los Cocos (Isla de la Juventud) 170
   Playa los Pinos 331
   Playa Maguana 445
   Playa Mangalito 437
   Playa Paraíso 167
   Playa Pesquero 360
   Playa Pilar 314
   Playa Salado 149
   Playa Santa Lucía 331-3, **332**
   Playa Santa María 269
   Playa Santa Rita 330
   Playa Siboney 418-19
   Playa Sirena 169-70
   Playa Tortuga 170
   Playas del Este 141-4, **142-3**

Playita de Cajobabo 436
bee hummingbirds 230
beer 355
Bejucal 154
Biblioteca Policarpo Pineda Rustán 432
bici-taxis 518
bicycling 44-5, 514-15
   Las Terrazas 152
   Playa Ancón 278
   Valle de Viñales 16
   Viñales 178
Bienal Internacional del Humor 31
Birán 367
bird-watching 13, 31, 496, **13**
   Camagüey province 315
   Gran Parque Natural Montemar 230-1
   Península de Zapata 227
   Sierra la Güira 188
   Soroa 150
blogs 469
boat travel 513
boating 43
Boca Ciega 143
Boca de Guamá 228-30
Boca de Yumurí 436-7
bocadito 157
Bolívar, Simón 69
books 448, 473-5
boxing 94
Brasil 330
budget 21, 500
bus travel 515-16, 518
bushwalking, *see* hiking
business hours 21

C

cabaret 27, 117
cachita 424
cafetales 422
Cafetal la Isabelica 419
Caibarién 267-9
Caimanera 435-6
Calle Heredia 397

Calle Mercaderes 68-70
Camagüey 19, 317-28,
 318, 19
 accommodations 321-2
 architecture 323
 drinking 325
 entertainment 325-6
 festivals & events 321
 food 324-5
 history 317
 internet access 327
 medical services 327
 shopping 326
 sights 317-21
 street names 321
 tourist information 327
 travel to/from 327
 travel within 328
Camagüey province 56,
 315-33, **316**
 bird-watching 315
 climate 315
 food 315
 highlights 316
 travel seasons 315
camiones 520
campismos 22, 500-1
canopy tours 152
Capitolio Nacional 79
car travel 516-18
Cárdenas 224-6
Caribbean coast 251
Carnaval de la Habana 32
Carnaval de Santiago
 de Cuba 30, 32
Carnaval Isla de la
 Juventud 30
Carpentier, Alejo 473
Casablanca 140
Casa de Estrada Palma 373
Casa de la Cultura Benja-
 min Duarte 238, **15**
Casa de la Guayabera
 293-4
Casa del Caribe 404
Casa del Fundador 238-9
Casa Guachinango 289
Casa Templo de Santería
 Yemayá 278
casas particulares 12, 22,
 501, **12**
Castillo de Jagua 249-50
Castillo de las Nubes 150
Castillo de Nuestra Señora
 de los Ángeles de Jagua
 249-50
Castillo del Morrillo 215
Castro, Fidel 350
Castro, Raúl 461, 367, 372,

408, 457, 460
cathedrals, *see* churches &
 cathedrals
causeways *(pedraplén)* 497
caves
 Caverna de
 Panaderos 357
 Cueva de Aguas 439
 Cueva de Ambrosio 200
 Cueva de los Portales
 188-9
 Cueva de San Miguel 183
 Cueva Saturno 215
 Cueva del Indio 183
 Cuevas de Bellamar 215
 Cuevas de Santa
 Catalina 215
 Farallones de Seboruco
 369
 Gran Caverna de Santo
 Tomás 185
caving 43-4
Cayerías del Norte 269-72
Cayo Blanco 286
Cayo Coco 310-13, **312-13**
Cayo Cruz 330
Cayo del Rosario 170
Cayo Ensenachos 269
Cayo Granma 405
Cayo Guillermo 313-14,
 312-13
Cayo Iguana 170
Cayo Jutías 185, 186
Cayo Largo del Sur 169-73,
 170-1
Cayo las Brujas 269
Cayo Levisa 186-7
Cayo Media Luna 314
Cayo Paredón Grande 311
Cayo Piedras del Norte 201
Cayo Rico 170
Cayo Romano 330
Cayo Sabinal 330-1
Cayo Saetía 369
Cayo Santa María 269, **270**
Cayos de San Felipe 172
Celia Sánchez Monument
 384
cell phones 20, 507-8
cemeteries
 Cementerio Colombia 167
 Cementerio la Reina 239
 Cementerio Santa
 Ifigenia 404
 Necrópolis Cristóbal
 Colón 92
 Necrópolis de
 Camagüey 320
 Necrópolis Tomás

Acea 241
Central Australia 228
Central Camilo
 Cienfuegos 155
Central Patria O Muerte
 309
Céspedes, Carlos Manuel de
 453-4, 455
chachachá 487
Chalet Los Álamos 298
Chibás, Eduardo 92
children, travel with 51-2
Chivirico 425
churches & cathedrals
 Basílica de Nuestra
 Señora del Cobre
 423-4
 Catedral de la Inmacu-
 lada Concepción 225
 Catedral de la Purísima
 Concepción
 Church 237
 Catedral de las Santas
 Hermanas de Santa
 Clara de Asís 258
 Catedral de Nuestra
 Señora de la Asunción
 437-8 (Baracoa)
 Catedral de Nuestra
 Señora de la Asunción
 396-7 (Santiago de
 Cuba)
 Catedral de Nuestra
 Señora de la
 Candelaria 323
 Catedral de San Carlos
 Borromeo 219
 Catedral de San Cristóbal
 de la Habana 64
 Catedral de San
 Isidoro 348
 Catedral de San
 Rosendo 191
 Catedral Ortodoxa
 Nuestra Señora
 de Kazán 76
 Convento & Iglesia del
 Carmen 85
 Iglesia de
 Guanabacoa 138
 Iglesia de la Caridad 323
 Iglesia de la Santísima
 Madre del Buen Pastor
 257
 Iglesia de Monserrate
 220
 Iglesia de Nuestra
 Corazón de Sagrado
 Jesús 323
 Iglesia de Nuestra Señora
 de la Caridad 294
 Iglesia de Nuestra Señora
 de la Merced 323

Iglesia de Nuestra Señora
 de la Soledad 323
Iglesia de Nuestra
 Señora del Buen Viaje
 (Remedios) 265
Iglesia de Nuestra
 Señora del Buen Viaje
 (Santa Clara) 257
Iglesia de Nuestra Señora
 del Carmen (Santa
 Clara) 255
Iglesia de Nuestra Señora
 del Carmen
 (Camagüey) 323
Iglesia de Nuestra Señora
 del Carmen (Santiago
 de Cuba) 400
Iglesia de Nuestra Señora
 de los Dolores 399
Iglesia de Nuestra
 Señora de Regla 137
Iglesia de San Antonio
 de los Baños 147
Iglesia de San Cristo del
 Buen Viaje 323
Iglesia de San
 Francisco 400
Iglesia de San Francisco
 de Paula 76
Iglesia de San
 Fulgencio 357
Iglesia de San José 349
Iglesia de San Lazaro 323
Iglesia de San Pedro
 Apóstol 220
Iglesia de Santa Ana 278
Iglesia del Sagrado
 Corazón de Jesús 85
Iglesia del Santo Ángel
 Custodio 77
Iglesia Jesús de
 Miramar 126
Iglesia Parroquial de la
 Santísima Trinidad
 276-7
Iglesia Parroquial del
 Espíritu Santo 76
Iglesia Parroquial Mayor
 del Espíritu Santo 294
Iglesia Parroquial Mayor
 de San Salvador 373
Iglesia y Convento de
 Nuestra Señora de
 la Merced 76
Nuestra Señora de los
 Dolores 163
Parroquia de San Juan
 Bautista de Remedios
 265
Santuario de San
 Lázaro 137
Ciego de Ávila 302-7, **303**

Ciego de Ávila province 56, 300-14, **301**
accommodations 304
climate 300
food 300
highlights 301
travel seasons 300
watersports 300
Ciénaga de Zapata 15, 230, **15**
Cienfuegos 15, 236-48, **238-9**, **242**, **15**
accommodations 241-4
activities 241
architecture 244
courses 241, 250
drinking & nightlife 246
entertainment 246
festivals & events 241
food 244-6
history 236
internet access 247
Malecón 240
medical services 247
Parque José Martí 236-8
Paseo del Prado 239
Punta Gorda 240-1, 243-4, 245-6, **242**
shopping 246
sights 236-41
tours 241
travel to/from 248
travel within 248
Cienfuegos province 55, 235-51, **237**
architecture 235
climate 235
food 235
highlights 237
travel seasons 235
cigar factories
Fábrica de Tabacos Constantino Pérez Carrodegua 255
Fábrica de Tabacos Francisco Donatien 189
cigars 120, 472, **24**
Cinco Palmas 387
cinema 475-7
Cinema Street 26, 326
Ciudad Metal 33
climate 20, 502, see also individual regions
Club Habana 131
Cocodrilo 169

coffee 120, 153, 422
Cojímar 140
colectivos 518
Colegio San Lorenzo 237
Colón 227
Comandancia de la Plata 382
Comunidad Cabo Cruz 388
Conjunto Escultórico Comandante Ernesto Che Guevara 257-8
conservation 493, 497-8
consulates 503
convents
Iglesia y Convento de Nuestra Señora de Belén 76
Iglesia y Convento de Nuestra Señora de la Merced 76
Iglesia y Convento de Santa Clara 76
convertibles 20, 23, 506, 507
Coppelia 110
courses
art 95
cultural 280
dance 95, 203, 220, 258, 280, 406
drumming 280
language 95, 241, 258, 406, 505
music 95
credit cards 506
Cristóbal Colón 426
crocodiles 167, 229, 385
cruises 513
Cruz, Celia 489
Cruz de la Parra 437
Cuartel Moncada 402
Cubadisco 31
Cubanacán 127, 133
Cuban Campaign Against Homophobia 31
Cuban Missile Crisis 458
Cueva del Indio 183, **42**
Cueva de los Peces 232, **37**
Cueva de Punta del Este 169
Cueva de Valdés 298
culture 448-9, 467-72
currency 20, 506-7
customs regulations 502-3

mambo 487, 488-9
tumba francesa 411
rumba 222, 487-9
dangers, see safety
deep-sea fishing 47
deforestation 497
Día de la Liberación 30
Día de la Rebeldía Nacional 32
disabilities, travelers with 508
diving 16, 28, 45-7, **46**
Bahía de Cochinos 232, **46**
Caya Coco 311
Cayo Jutías 186
Cayo Levisa 186-7
Cayos de San Felipe 172
Cristóbal Colón 426
Guardalavaca 361
Isla de la Juventud 165
Jardines de la Reina 306, **46**
María la Gorda 196, **46**, **44**
Parque Baconao 421
Península de Guanahacabibes 196
Playa Ancón 286-7
Playa Santa Lucía 332, **46**
Rancho Luna 249
Varadero 201
Dos Hermanas 185
Dos Ríos Obelisk 381
drinks 463-6
driving, see car travel

D
dance 27, 486-91
courses 95, 203, 220, 258, 280, 406
danzón 486-7
folklórico 412

E
economics 448-9
eco-resorts 498
Las Terrazas 151
Ediciones Vigía 217
Edificio Bacardí 77
Edificio Focsa 86-7
El Balcón del Oriente (The Balcony of the Oriente) 340
El Barrio Chino 84-5
El Che 261
El Cobre 423-4
El Cornito 337
El Mégano 144
El Moncada 185
El Nicho 250-1
El Pedraplén 269
El Pueblo Holandés 310
El Saltón 424-5
El Uvero 425

El Yunque 444-5
electricity 503
Embalse Hanabanilla 264
Embalse Laguna Grande 194
embassies 503
emergencies 21
endangered species 495
environmental issues 492-8
Estatua Che y Niño 256
Estrada Palma, Tomás 455, 459
etiquette 23
events 30-3
exchange rates 21
ExpoCuba 136
Exposición Mesoamericana 421

F
Fábrica de Arte Cubano 26
Fábrica de Chocolate 439-40
Fábrica de Cucuruchu 440
Fabrica de los Coches 375
Faro Colón 331
fauna 494-5, 496
Feria Internacional del Libro 30
ferries 513, 518
festivals & events 18, 30-3
Bienal de Escultura Rita Longa 337
Boleros de Oro 406
Carnaval (Cienfuegos) 241
Carnaval (Holguín) 351
Carnaval (Matanzas) 220
Carnaval (Nueva Gerona) 164
Carnaval (Pinar del Río) 191
Carnaval (Santiago de Cuba) 407
Festival del Bailador Rumbero 220
Festival del Caribe, Fiesta del Fuego 32
Festival Internacional 'Boleros de Oro 31
Festival Internacional de Ballet de la Habana 30, 32-3
Festival Internacional de Cine Pobre 30, 31, 359
Festival Internacional de Coros 406
Festival Internacional de Magia 337

Festival Internacional de Música Benny Moré 32, 241
Festival Internacional de Jazz 30, 33
Festival Internacional de Trova 30
Festival Internacional del Nuevo Cine Latino-americano 33
Festival Internacional Matamoros Son 406
Festival Nacional de Changüí 31, 432
Fiesta de la Cubanía 379
Fiesta de los Bandas Rojo y Azul 33
Fiesta de Nuestra Señora de la Caridad 32
Fiesta del Fuego 406
Fiestas Sanjuaneras 32
Fiesta de San Juan 406
Fundación de la Ciudad 337
Habanos Festival 30
Incendio de Bayamo 377
Jornada Cucalambeana 337
Noches Guantanameras 432
Nuestra Señora de la Caridad 321
Romerías de Mayo 351
San Juan Camagüey-ano 321
Semana de la Cultura Baracoesa 440
Semana Santa (Holy Week) 280
films 448, 475-7
Festival Internacional de Cine Pobre 359
Festival Internacional del Nuevo Cine Latino-americano 33
Finca Duaba 444
Finca Fiesta Campesina 228
fishing 47-8, see also fly-fishing, deep-sea fishing, freshwater fishing
flamingos 269, 494
Florencia 310
Florida 328
fly-fishing 47
folklórico 15, 412, **15**
food 19, 463-6, 503-4, see also individual locations
Baracoan cuisine 442
regional specialties 464
forts 29, 479

Castillo de la Real Fuerza 67
Castillo de los Tres Santos Reyes Magnos del Morro 77
Castillo de Nuestra Señora de los Ángeles de Jagua 249-50
Castillo de San Pedro de la Roca del Morro 404-5
Castillo de San Salvador de la Punta 84
Castillo de San Severino 220
El Castillo de Seboruco 438-9
El Cuartelón 357
Fortaleza de San Carlos de la Cabaña 77-8
Fuerte de la Loma 342
Fuerte de la Punta 439
Fuerte Fernando VII 357
Fuerte Matachín 437
Fuerte San Hilario 330
Torreón de Cojímar 140
Fotosub International Underwater Photo-graphy competition 30
freshwater fishing 47-8
Fuentes, Leonard Padura 474
Fusterlandia 132

G
Ganado Santa Gertrudis 309
García, Calixto 349
gardens, see parks & gardens
gay travelers 114, 504
Gibara 357-60
Gitmo 432
Gobierno Provincial 400
Gran Parque Nacional Sierra Maestra 381-4, **381**
Gran Parque Natural Montemar 230-1
Gran Teatro de la Habana 83
Granma province 57, 370-90, **371**
climate 370
highlights 371
hiking 370
history 370
travel seasons 370
Guáimaro 329
Guanabacoa 138-9

Guanabo 141, 143
Guantánamo 430-5, **431**
Guantánamo Bay 432, 435-6
Guantánamo province 58, 428-46, **429**
climate 428
food 428
highlights 429
travel seasons 428
Guardalavaca 360-5, **361**, **362**
Guevara, Ernesto 'Che' 257, **14**
Guevara de la Serna, Ernesto 261
Guillén, Nicolás 474
Güirito 440
Gutiérrez Alea, Tomás 476
Gutiérrez, Pedro Juan 475

H
Hacienda Cortina 188
Havana 53, 60-144, **62-3**
accommodations 60, 96-104
activities 94
architecture 75
Centro Habana 78-85, 99-101, 107-8, 112-13, 120
climate 60
courses 95
drinking & nightlife 111-14
entertainment 114-18
festivals & events 94
food 60, 104-11
Habana Vieja 64-77, 96-8, 104-6, 111-12, 119-20, **66-7**, **12**, **24**
highlights 62-3
history 61, 75
internet access 121-2
itineraries 65
medical services 121
nightlife 114-18
Parque Histórico Militar Morro-Cabaña 77-8, 106-7, **78**
postal services 122
scams 121
shopping 118-26
sights 64-94
street names 70
tourist information 122
tours 95-6
travel agencies 122
travel seasons 60

travel to/from 123-4
travel within 124-6
Vedado 86-94, 102-4, 108-11, 113-19, 120-1, **88-9**
walking tour 72-3, **72-3**
health 504-5
Hemingway, Ernest 139
Hershey Electric Railway 156
hiking 48
El Salto 389
Las Terrazas 152
Parque Nacional Viñales 183
Península de Guanahacabibes 196
Pico Turquino 19, 426-7
Salto de Guayabito 390
Sendero Arqueológico Natural el Guafe 387
Sierra del Escambray 265
Topes de Collantes 290
Trinidad 278
history 29, 450-62
Batista Era 456-7
Bay of Pigs 234
colonial period 451
Cuban revolution 14
First War of Independence 453-4
human rights 461
post-colonial period 456-62
pre-colonial period 451
revolution 458-60
Spanish-Cuban-American War 454-5
Special Period 460
US-Cuba relations 462
hitchhiking 518
Holguín 345-57, **348-9**, **352**
accommodations 351
drinking & nightlife 354
entertainment 354-5
festivals & events 351
food 351-4
history 345
shopping 355
sights 345, 248-50
travel to/from 356
travel within 356-7
Holguín province 57, 344-69, **346-7**
accommodations 344
beaches 344
climate 344
highlights 346-7
travel seasons 344

holidays 507
horseback riding 48
Hotel Capri 26
Hotel Habana Libre 86
Hotel Inglaterra 83
Hotel Nacional 86
human rights 461

I
Ídolo del Agua 387
immigration 509, 511
Incendio de Bayamo 30
indigenous culture 29
insurance 504
internet access 505
internet resources 21
Isla de la Juventud 161-9
Isla de la Juventud
    (Special Municipality)
    54, 159-73, **160**
    accommodations 159
    beaches 159
    climate 159
    highlights 160
    travel seasons 159
    travel to/from 168
Isla de los Pinos 164
Isla Turiguanó 309-10
itineraries 34-41

J
Jardín Botánico de
    Cienfuegos 250
Jardines de la Reina 306
Jarico 297
Jaruco 157
jineteros 281
Jobo Rosado Reserve 298
Jornada Cucalambeana 31

K
kayaking 43
King Ranch 330
kiteboarding 26, 50, 314

L
La Boca 288
La Calle de los Cines 26
La Casa de la Ciudad 255
La Farola 436
La Gran Piedra 419-20,
    420-1
La Isla see Isla de la

Juventud (Special
    Municipality)
La Loma de la Cruz 350
Laguna Baconao 421-2
Laguna de la Leche 308-9
Laguna de Leonero 381
Laguna Guanaroca 250
Laguna la Redonda 308-9
Lam, Wifredo 477
landscape 492-8
language 23, 521-7
    courses 505
La Rosita 149-50
La Solapa de Genaro 298
La Trocha 304
Las Charangas de
    Bejucal 33
Las Colorado 387-8
Las Cuevas 426
Las Guanas Eco-
    Archaeological Trail 363
Las Parrandas 30, 33
Las Terrazas 16, 151-5, **16**
Las Tunas 335-41, **338-9**
Las Tunas province 57,
    334-43, **335**
    accommodations 334
    climate 334
    highlights 335
    outdoor escapes 334
    travel seasons 334
legal matters 505-6
lesbian travelers 114, 504
Lezama Lima, José 84
literature 448, 473-5
Loma de Cunagua 309
Loma de San Juan 403-4
Loma del Capiro 257
Los Aquáticos 183
Los Buchillones 310
Los Malagones 185

M
Malecón 11, 92-3, **11**
mambo 487, 488-9
Manaca Iznaga 288
Mansión Xanadú 199
Manzanillo 384-6
maps 506
Marabana 33
Marea del Portillo 389-90
María la Gorda 196, **44**
Marianao 126-35, 127,
    128-9
    accommodations 127-31
    activities 127
    drinking &
        entertainment 134

food 131-4
internet access 135
medical services 135
nightlife 140
postal services 135
shopping 134-5
sights 126-7
travel to/from 135
travel within 135
Marina Gaviota 201
Marina Hemingway 127,
    131, 134
Martí, José 87, 474
Martinez, Raúl 476
Mata Dos 390
Matanzas 17, 216-24,
    218, **17**
    accommodations 220-1
    courses 220
    drinking & nightlife 222
    entertainment 222-3
    festivals & events 220
    food 222
    history 216
    shopping 223
    sights 217, 219-20
    street names 217
    travel to/from 223
    travel within 223
Matanzas province 55,
    198-234, **200**
    accommodations 198
    climate 198
    highlights 200
    outdoor adventures 198
    travel seasons 198
Mayabeque province 54,
    145-58, **146**
    accommodations 145
    climate 145
    highlights 146
    hiking 145
    travel seasons 145
measures 501
Media Luna 386
medical services 505
Memorial a José Martí 92
Mercado Agropecuario
    Hatibonico 321
Minas de Matahambre 185
Mirador de la Loma del
    Puerto 288
Miramar 126-7, 128-31,
    131-3, 134-5
mobile phones 20, 507-8
Moncada Barracks 408
money 20, 21, 506-7
Monte Cabaniguan 341

Monumento a Antonio
    Maceo 85-6
Monumento a Julio Antonio
    Mella 87, 90
Monumento a la Toma del
    Tren Blindado 255
Moré, Benny 247
Morón 307-8
Mural de la Prehistoria 183
museums & galleries
    Armería 9 de Abril 68-9
    Asociación Cultural
        Yoruba de Cuba 79, 82
    Cafetal la Isabelica 419
    Casa de África 69
    Casa de Arte Jover 319
    Casa de Asia 68
    Casa de Diego
        Velázquez 396
    Casa de la Diversidad 320
    Casa de México Benito
        Juárez 69-70
    Casa del Cacao 438
    Casa Finlay 320
    Casa Museo Celia
        Sánchez Manduley 389
    Casa Museo de Frank y
        Josué País 403
    Casa Museo del Café 289
    Casa Natal de Calixto
        García 349
    Casa Natal de Carlos
        Manuel de Céspedes 373
    Casa Natal de José María
        Heredia y Heredia 397
    Casa Oswaldo
        Guayasamín 70
    Casa Taller 189
    Celia Sánchez
        Museum 386
    Centro Provincial de Artes
        Plásticas Galería 189
    Centro Raúl Martínez
        Galería de Arte
        Provincial 304
    Comunidad Artística
        Verraco 421
    Edificio Santo Domingo
        75-6
    Fototeca de Cuba 74
    Fundación de la Natu-
        raleza y El Hombre 294
    Fundación Naturaleza y
        El Hombre 126
    Gabinete de
        Arqueología 67
    Galería de Arte 277
    Galería del Arte Carlos
        Enríquez 265
    Galería Provincial
        Eduardo Abela 148

Galleria de Lester Campa 151
Granjita Siboney 418-19
Iglesia y Monasterio de San Francisco de Asís 71
Il Genio di Leonardo da Vinci 71
La Casona Centro de Arte 74
La Maqueta de la Capital 126-7
Maqueta de la Ciudad 397
Maqueta de La Habana Vieja 70
Maqueta de Trinidad 276
Martha Jiménez Pérez 320
Memorial a los Mártires de Barbados 336
Memorial de Vilma Espín Guillois 399-400
Memorial Vicente García 336
Museo 28 Septiembre de los CDR 74
Museo Alejandro Humboldt 71
Museo Arqueológico 'La Cueva del Paraíso' 437
Museo Arquidiocesano 397
Museo Caonabo 307
Museo-Casa Natal de Antonio Maceo 402-3
Museo Casa Natal de Ignacio Agramonte 319
Museo Casa Natal de José Antonio Echeverría 225
Museo-Casa Natal de José Martí 76
Museo Casa Natal de Serafín Sánchez 294
Museo Casa Natal Jesus Montané 161
Museo Chorro de Maita 360
Museo Conjunto Histórico de Birán 367
Museo de 11 Abril 436
Museo de Agroindustria Azucarero Marcelo Salado 268
Museo de Arqueología Guamuhaya 277
Museo de Arquitectura Trinitaria 277
Museo de Arte Colonial 294
Museo de Arte Cubano Contemporáneo 289
Museo de Arte Religioso 71

Museo de Artes Decorativas 90, 255, 302
Museo de Batalla de Ideas 224-5
Museo de Bomberos 69
Museo de Cera 373-4
Museo de Ciencias Naturales 294
Museo de Ciencias Naturales Sandalio de Noda 190
Museo de Danza 91
Museo de Historia Natural 163, 349, 357
Museo de Historia Provincial 345
Museo de la Alfabetización 127
Museo de la Ciudad 65, 67
Museo de la Comandancia 228
Museo de la Farmacia Habanera 76
Museo de la Imagen 404
Museo de la Lucha Clandestina 400, 402
Museo de la Plata 426
Museo de la Revolución 83-4
Museo de las Parrandas Remedianas 265
Museo del Carnaval 397
Museo del Ferrocarril 76
Museo del Humor 147-8
Museo del Ron 71, 397
Museo de Música Alejandro García Caturla 265
Museo de Naipes 74
Museo de Numismático 74
Museo de Pintura Mural 74
Museo de San Juan de Dios 317
Museo de Simón Bolívar 69
Museo de Transporte Automotor 68
Museo el Templete 65
Museo Farmacéutico 219
Museo Fernando García Grave de Peralta 342
Museo Finca el Abra 163
Museo Hemingway 139
Museo Histórico 329
Museo Histórico la Demajagua 384-5
Museo Histórico Municipal (Nuevitas) 329

Museo Histórico Municipal (Trinidad) 275-6
Museo Histórico Naval Nacional 239
Museo Histórico Provincial 217, 219
Museo las Colorados 387
Museo Lezama Lima 84
Museo Municipal 161, 175, 178
Museo Municipal de Guanabacoa 139
Museo Municipal de Regla 138
Museo Municipal de Varadero 199
Museo Municipal Emilio Bacardí Moreau 397
Museo Municipal María Escobar Laredo 268
Museo Nacional Camilo Cienfuegos 299
Museo Nacional de Bellas Artes 83
Museo Nacional de Bellas Artes (Arte Cubano) 83
Museo Nacional de Bellas Artes (Arte Universal) 83
Museo Nacional de la Lucha Contra Bandidos 278
Museo Nacional de Transporte Terrestre 421
Museo Napoleónico 90
Museo Ñico López 374-5
Museo Oscar María de Rojas 225
Museo Provincial 238, 294, 373, 431
Museo Provincial Abel Santamaría 255
Museo Provincial de Historia 191
Museo Provincial General Vicente García 336
Museo Provincial Ignacio Agramonte 320
Museo Provincial Simón Reyes 302
Museo Romántico 277
Peña de Polo Montañez 151
Plaza de las Memorias 290
music 11, 29, 486-91, 11
contemporary 490
danzón 486
hip-hop 491
mambo 488-9
nueva trova 490-1

reggaetón 491
salsa 489-90
son 488
tumba francesa 411

N

national parks & protected areas 493, 494, see also Unesco Biosphere Reserves
Alturas de Banao 297
Bioparque Rocazul 361, 363
Gran Parque Nacional Sierra Maestra 381-4
Jobo Rosado Reserve 298
La Hacienda la Belén 328-9
Monte Cabaniguan 341
Parque Nacional Alejandro de Humboldt 445-6
Parque Nacional Caguanes 299
Parque Nacional Desembarco del Granma 386-8
Parque Nacional Monumento Bariay 360
Parque Natural Bahía de Naranjo 361
Parque Natural Cristóbal Colón 361
Parque Natural el Bagá 310
Parque Natural Majaya 439
Refugio de Fauna Silvestre Río Máximo 333
Reserva Ecológica Limones Tuabaquey 331
newspapers 501
nightlife 27, see also individual locations
Niquero 386
Nueva Gerona 161-6, 162
Nuevitas 329-30

O

opening hours 21
Ortíz, Fernando 452

P

Padre Pico steps 400
painting 477
Palacio de Gobierno 219, 238
Palacio de Justicia 217, 403
Palacio de las Convenciones 127

Palacio de los
　Matrimonios 189
Palacio de Pioneros 404
Palacio Salcines 430
Palmira 251
Palo Monte 415
Pan de Guajaibón 187
parks & gardens
　Casino Campestre 321
　Centro Recreativo la
　　Punta 241
　El Jardín Botanico de las
　　Hermanas Caridad y
　　Carmen Miranda 178
　El Lago de los Sueños 321
　Jardín Botánico de
　　Cienfuegos 250
　Jardín Botánico de
　　Cupaynicu 380-1
　Jardín Botánico
　　Nacional 136-7
　Jardín de los
　　Helechos 406
　Jardines de Hershey 155
　La Jungla de Jones 167
　Orquideario Soroa 149
　Parque Alameda 402
　Parque Almendares 127
　Parque Baconao 420-3,
　　420-1
　Parque Calixto García
　　348-9, 357
　Parque Central 82-3
　Parque Céspedes
　　(Bayamo) 373
　Parque Céspedes
　　(Holguín) 349
　Parque Céspedes
　　(Manzanillo) 384
　Parque Céspedes
　　(Santiago de Cuba)
　　395-6, **38-9**
　Parque Chapuzón 375-6
　Parque Constitución 329
　Parque de la Ciudad 302
　Parque de la
　　Fraternidad 79
　Parque de los
　　Enamorados 84
　Parque Escaleras de
　　Jaruco 157
　Parque Histórico Abel
　　Santamaría 403
　Parque Ignacio
　　Agramonte 319-20
　Parque Josone 199
　Parque la Güira 26

Parque Lenin 135-7
Parque Maestranza 64
Parque Martí 302-3, 432
Parque Nacional
　Alejandro de
　Humboldt 445-6, 38
Parque Nacional
　Caguanes 299
Parque Nacional
　Desembarco del
　Granma 386-8
Parque Nacional
　Península de Guana-
　hacabibes 195-7
Parque Nacional
　Viñales 183-5
Parque Natural el
　Bagá 310
Parque Peralta 345, 348
Parque Serafín
　Sánchez 293
Parque Vidal 253
parrandas 268
Paseo Bayamés 373
Paseo de Martí (Prado) 84
passports 511
pedraplén (causeways) 497
Península de Guanahaca-
　bibes 195-7
Península de Zapata
　227-34
people 467-72
Pérez, Faustino 376
phone cards 508
phone rates 508
Pico La Bayamesa 380
Pico Turquino 19, 383,
　426-7, **19**
Pilón 388-9, 427
Pinar del Río 189-94, **190-1**
Pinar del Río province 54,
　174-97, **176-7**
　climate 174
　highlights 176-7
　tobacco tours 174
　travel seasons 174
　water sports 174
pirates 29
planning, see also
　individual regions
　budgeting 20-1
　calendar of events 30-3
　checklists 22
　children, travel with 51-2
　Cuba basics 20-1
　Cuba's regions 53-8
　internet resources 20-1
　itineraries 34-41
　repeat visitors 26
　travel seasons 20-1

Plano-Mural de Ciego de
　Ávila 304
plants 496-7
Playa 126-35, **128-9**
　accommodations 127-31
　drinking &
　　entertainment 134-5
　food 131-4
　medical services 135
　shopping 134
　tourist information 135
　travel to/from 135
　travel within 135
Playa Ancón 286-8, **13**
Playa Girón 232-4
Playa Jibacoa 155-7
Playa la Herradura 343
Playa la Llanita 343
Playa Larga 231
Playa las Bocas 343
Playa los Cocos
　(Camagüey) 332
Playa los Cocos (Isla de la
　Juventud) 170
Playa Mulata 187
Playa Santa Lucía 331-3,
　332
Playa Tortuga 170
Playas del Este 141-4,
　142-3
Plaza de Dolores 399
Plaza de la Catedral 64,
　36-7
Plaza de la Marqueta 349
Plaza de la Patria 374
Plaza de la Revolución
　(Havana) 91
Plaza de la Revolución
　(Holguín) 349
Plaza de la Revolución
　(Las Tunas) 336-7
Plaza de la Revolución
　(Santiago de Cuba) 403
Plaza de Marte 399
Plaza del Carmen 320
Plaza Honorato 294
Plaza Mariana Grajales 430
Plaza San Juan de Dios 317
Plaza Santa Ana 278
politics 448-9
pollution 498
population 449
postal services 507
Presidio Modelo 167
Procesión de San Lázaro 33
public holidays 507
Pueblo la Estrella 270
Puente Calixto García 217
Puente de Bacunayagua 155
Puente Yayabo 293

Puerto Esperanza 186
Puerto Padre 341-2
Punta Covarrubias 342-3
Punta de Maisí 436
Punta Francés 167, **46**

Q
Quinta de los Molinos 92

R
Ramsar Convention
　Sites 493, 494, see also
　national parks &
　protected areas,
　Unesco Biosphere
　Reserves
　Ciénaga de Zapata 230-1
　Monte Cabaniguan 341
　Refugio de Fauna
　　Silvestre Río
　　Máximo 333
Rancho la Guabina 195
Rancho Luna 248
Ranchón La
　Gobernador 435
Real Fábrica de Tabacos
　Partagás 79
reggaetón 491
Regla 137-8
religion 449, 471-2
　Palo Monte 415
Remedios 264-7, **266**
Reserva Ecológica Limones
　Tuabaquey 331
Reserva Ecológica
　Varahicacos 201
resorts 28-9
Río Canímar 215
Río Toa 444
Río Turquino 426
rock climbing 48, 50
　Pico Turquino 383
　Silla de Gibara 358
　Viñales 184
rodeos 342
Romerías de Mayo 31
ropa vieja 465, **19**
rum 120, 465-6
rumba 222, 487-9
Ruta de la Revolución 380

S
safety 507
Sala de Conciertos José
　White 219
Salto del Caburní 290
San Antonio de los Baño
　147-8
Sánchez, Universo 376

Sancti Spíritus 291-8, **292**
Sancti Spíritus province 56, 273-99, **274**
  climate 273
  highlights 274
  hiking 273
  natural swimming pools 273
  travel seasons 273
San Diego de los Baños 187-8
San Isidro de los Destiladeros 288
San Juan y Martínez 194
San Miguel de los Baños 226-7
San Pascual 270
Santa Clara 17, 253-64, **256**, 17
  accommodations 259-60
  courses 258
  drinking & nightlife 262
  entertainment 262
  festivals 259
  food 260
  history 253
  internet access 263
  medical services 263
  postal services 263
  shopping 262
  sights 253-8
  street names 259
  tourist information 263
  travel to/from 263
  travel within 263
Santa Cruz del Norte 155
Santa María del Mar 142-3
Santiago de Cuba 393-418, **394-5**, **398**, **405**
  accommodations 407-10
  courses 406
  drinking & nightlife 413
  entertainment 413-15
  festivals & events 406, 407
  food 410-13
  internet access 416
  medical services 416
  safe travel 416
  shopping 415-18
  sights 395-406
  street names 402
  tourist information 417
  tours 406
  travel to/from 417
  travel within 417
  walking tour 400-1, **401**
Santiago de Cuba province 58, 391-427, **392**, **420**
  climate 391

highlights 392
history 391
national parks & protected areas 391
travel seasons 391
Santiago de las Vegas 137
Santo Domingo 382
sculpture 336, 477
Semana de la Cultura 31
Seven Years' War 85
Siboney 418-19
Sierra del Chorrillo 328-9
Sierra del Cristal 367-9
Sierra del Escambray 265
Sierra la Güira 188-9
Silla de Gibara 358
Sitio Guáimaro 289
skydiving 201-2
smoking 501
snorkeling 16, 28, 45, 232
son 488
Soroa 149-51
Southern Military Zone 168-73
sports 118, 470
Surgidero de Batabanó 158
swimming 150, 152, 184, 241, 250, 273, 290, 439

T
Taíno people 368
Taller Alfarero 278
taxis 518, **7**
Teatro José Jacinto Milanés 190-1
Teatro la Caridad 255
Teatro Principal 303
Teatro Sauto 217
Teatro Tomás Terry 237
telephone services 20, 507-8
Terminal de Ferrocarriles 307
time 20
tipping 23
Tivolí 400
tobacco plantations 174, **24**
  Alejandro Robaina Tobacco Plantation 194-5
  La Casa del Veguero 178
Topes de Collantes 289-91, **49**
Torre de San Juan Evangelista 374
tourist cards 508-9
tourist information 508
tours 513, 518-19
train travel 519-20

travel to/from Cuba 511-13
travel within Cuba 513-20, **514**
trekking 48
Tren Francés 519
Trinidad 14, 273-86, **274**, **276**, **287**, 14
  accommodations 280-2
  activities 278-80
  climate 273
  courses 280
  drinking & nightlife 283-4
  entertainment 284
  festivals & events 280
  food 282-3
  highlights 274
  hiking 273
  internet access 285
  medical services 285
  natural swimming pools 273
  shopping 284-5
  sights 275-8
  tours 280
  touts 281
  travel seasons 273
  travel to/from 285
  travel within 286
  walking tour 279, **279**
Trocha de Júcaro a Morón 304
truck travel 520
tumba francesa 411
Túnel de los Alemanes 436
turtles 169, 170, 197
TV 501

U
Unesco Biosphere Reserves 493, 494
  Cuchillas Toa 444
  Las Terrazas 151-4
  Parque Baconao 420-3, **420**
  Parque Nacional Península de Guana-hacabibes 195-7
  Península de Zapata 227-34
Unesco World Heritage Sites 494
  Parque Nacional Desembarco del Granma 386-7
  Parque Nacional Alejandro de Humboldt 445-6
Universidad de la Habana 87

V
vacations 507
Valle de la Prehistoria 421
Valle de los Ingenios 288-9
Valle del Silencio 181
Valle de Viñales 174-97, **176-7**, **180**, 16, 35, 49
  climate 174
  highlights 176-7
  tobacco tours 174
  travel seasons 174
  water sports 174
Varadero 199-214, **202-3**, **204-5**, **206-7**
  accommodations 205-9
  activities 201-3
  courses 203
  drinking & nightlife 211
  entertainment 211-12
  festivals & events 205
  food 209-11
  hotel zone 208, **206-7**
  shopping 212
  sights 199-201
  tourist information 213
  tours 203-4
  travel to/from 213-14
  travel within 214
Varadero province 198-234, **200**
  accommodations 198
  climate 198
  highlights 200
  outdoor adventures 198
  travel seasons 198
vegetarians 504
Ventana de Luz Vázquez 373
Villa Clara province 55, 252-72, **254**
  climate 252
  food 252
  highlights 254
  local experiences 252
  travel seasons 252
Viñales 175-83, **179**
visas 20, 508-9
volunteering 509
von Humboldt, Alexander 71, 452

W
walking, *see* hiking
walking tours
  Havana 72-3, **72-3**
  Trinidad 279, **279**
  Santiago de Cuba 400-1, **401**
water 505

waterfalls
El Nicho 250
Salto de Capiro 369
Salto del Guayabo 368-9

weather 20, 502, *see also individual regions*
websites, *see internet resources*
weights 501

wildlife 27-8, 494-7, *see also individual species*
wind-boarding 50
women travelers 510

Z
ziplining 152
Zoológico de Piedras 434

NOTES

Map Legend

Sights

- Beach
- Bird Sanctuary
- Buddhist
- Castle/Palace
- Christian
- Confucian
- Hindu
- Islamic
- Jain
- Jewish
- Monument
- Museum/Gallery/Historic Building
- Ruin
- Shinto
- Sikh
- Taoist
- Winery/Vineyard
- Zoo/Wildlife Sanctuary
- Other Sight

Activities, Courses & Tours

- Bodysurfing
- Diving
- Canoeing/Kayaking
- Course/Tour
- Sento Hot Baths/Onsen
- Skiing
- Snorkelling
- Surfing
- Swimming/Pool
- Walking
- Windsurfing
- Other Activity

Sleeping

- Sleeping
- Camping

Eating

- Eating

Drinking & Nightlife

- Drinking & Nightlife
- Cafe

Entertainment

- Entertainment

Shopping

- Shopping

Information

- Bank
- Embassy/Consulate
- Hospital/Medical
- @ Internet
- Police
- Post Office
- Telephone
- Toilet
- Tourist Information
- Other Information

Geographic

- Beach
- Hut/Shelter
- Lighthouse
- Lookout
- ▲ Mountain/Volcano
- Oasis
- Park
-)(Pass
- Picnic Area
- Waterfall

Population

- Capital (National)
- Capital (State/Province)
- City/Large Town
- Town/Village

Transport

- Airport
- Border crossing
- Bus
- Cable car/Funicular
- Cycling
- Ferry
- Metro station
- Monorail
- Parking
- Petrol station
- Subway station
- Taxi
- Train station/Railway
- Tram
- Underground station
- Other Transport

Note: Not all symbols displayed above appear on the maps in this book

Routes

- Tollway
- Freeway
- Primary
- Secondary
- Tertiary
- Lane
- Unsealed road
- Road under construction
- Plaza/Mall
- Steps
- Tunnel
- Pedestrian overpass
- Walking Tour
- Walking Tour detour
- Path/Walking Trail

Boundaries

- International
- State/Province
- Disputed
- Regional/Suburb
- Marine Park
- Cliff
- Wall

Hydrography

- River, Creek
- Intermittent River
- Canal
- Water
- Dry/Salt/Intermittent Lake
- Reef

Areas

- Airport/Runway
- Beach/Desert
- Cemetery (Christian)
- Cemetery (Other)
- Glacier
- Mudflat
- Park/Forest
- Sight (Building)
- Sportsground
- Swamp/Mangrove

OUR STORY

A beat-up old car, a few dollars in the pocket and a sense of adventure. In 1972 that's all Tony and Maureen Wheeler needed for the trip of a lifetime – across Europe and Asia overland to Australia. It took several months, and at the end – broke but inspired – they sat at their kitchen table writing and stapling together their first travel guide, *Across Asia on the Cheap*. Within a week they'd sold 1500 copies. Lonely Planet was born.

Today, Lonely Planet has offices in Franklin, London, Melbourne, Oakland, Beijing and Delhi, with more than 600 staff and writers. We share Tony's belief that 'a great guidebook should do three things: inform, educate and amuse'.

OUR WRITERS

Brendan Sainsbury

Coordinating Author, Havana, Trinidad & Sancti Spíritus, Camagüey, Las Tunas, Holguín, Granma, Santiago de Cuba, Guantánamo Born and bred in Hampshire, England, Brendan first visited Cuba in 1997 as a curious traveler aided by the first edition of this guidebook. He has been back 18 times in the years since, both as a travel guide and a writer, but never again as a tourist. This is his sixth Cuba-related guidebook, though he has covered numerous other countries for Lonely Planet, including Angola, Italy and Jamaica. Cuba remains a favorite haunt and he lists Havana (along with London, and Granada in Spain) as one of his top world cities. When not writing or traveling, Brendan enjoys following the fortunes of Southampton football club, listening to old Clash records and running ridiculous distances across deserts.

Read more about Brendan at:
http://auth.lonelyplanet.com/profiles/brendansainsbury

Luke Waterson

Artemisa & Mayabeque, Isla de la Juventud, Valle de Viñales & Pinar del Río, Varadero & Matanzas, Cienfuegos, Villa Clara, Ciego de Ávila, Strong coffee, stronger rum, still-stronger cigars and the prospect of watching sunrise over his beloved Viñales mogotes: Luke was easily persuaded into returning for his third edition of Lonely Planet *Cuba* on the tenth anniversary of his initial visit. A writer specialising in Latin America for over a decade, Luke also writes for the BBC, the *Telegraph* and Insight Guides, and is author/contributor to 30 travel and fiction books. He lives in Bratislava, Slovakia, where he runs quirky travel/culture blog englishmaninslovakia.com. Luke also wrote the Literature & the Arts and Landscape & Wildlife chapters.

Read more about Luke at:
http://auth.lonelyplanet.com/profiles/lukewaterson

Published by Lonely Planet Publications Pty Ltd
ABN 36 005 607 983
8th edition – Oct 2015
ISBN 978 1 74321 678 1
© Lonely Planet 2015   Photographs © as indicated 2015
10 9 8 7 6 5 4 3 2
Printed in China